Acknowledgements

I should like to thank Stephen Cant for reading the text of this novel and offering his advice. I should also like to thank him for that conversation in the Sailors' Home, Kessingland in 1990. This was the one of our many conversations about books that inspired me to plan, and eventually write, the story.

I should like to thank Andrew Evans for his permission to use the photograph he took of me, as Abraham van Helsing in the Sewell Barn's production of *Dracula*, which appears on the cover of the book, and also on my website (www.jameswarden.co.uk).

I used many books as reference for the background material, and there are three, in particular, I should acknowledge. *The Victorian House* by John Marshall and Ian Willox provided me with the information I needed to describe Horst Brultzner's restoration, Peter Cherry's booklet *Kessingland and its Characters* gave me the historical background and helped with the local flavour of the story, and Michael Counsell's *A Basic Christian Dictionary* clarified many concepts I had only partly understood. Any deviations, fictionalisations and misunderstandings are mine.

I wish to acknowledge the use of verse 3 from the hymn *Lift up your heads, ye gates of brass* written by J Montgomery (1771-1854), the opening lines from *O come, all ye faithful* by J F Wade (c1711-86), lines from the poem *Death is nothing at all* by Henry Scott Holland (1847-1918) and lines from *Gone from my sight* by Henry Van Dyke (1852-1933).

I should, also, like to thank David Buck of Pakefield, Lowestoft for his painting which I have used for the cover of this book.

The Victorian House by John Marshall and Ian Willox: published by Sidgwick and Jackson in Association with Channel Four Television Company Limited in 1986
Kessingland and its Characters by Peter Cherry: published by Peter Cherry in 1971
A Basic Christian Dictionary by Michael Counsell: published by The Canterbury Press, Norwich in 2007

Content

Book One
Spring Arrivals

CONTENT

Book Two

Summer Blossoms

CONTENT

Book Three

Autumn Falls

CONTENT

Book Four

Winter Carol

Characters

Sarah Marjoram, a young mother
Shane Marjoram, her husband
Clive 'Froggy' Brown, her father and people's warden
Matthew Marjoram, her son

Corvin Unwood, the Anglican priest of Dunburgh-on-sea
Esther Unwood, his wife
Rebecca Unwood, his daughter

Sidney Close, a shopkeeper
Mavis Close, his wife
Wendy Close, their oldest daughter
Angela Close, their youngest daughter

Bishop Twiddle, Diocese of Norbridge
Mrs Cushion, his housekeeper

Tony Crewes, friend of Martin Billings
Beth Crewes, his wife

Martin Billings, village policeman
Amy Billings, his wife

The 'Inn Crowd', friends of several main characters, who act as Chorus:
Lianne Snooks
Barry Snooks
Boller Skeat
Pliny Skeat
Ample Bassett
Billy Bassett
Joney Chine
Ben Chine

Peter Vishnya, an Estonian who lives in Dunburgh
Yevgeny Vishnya, his son
Anton, their 'dog'

Horst Brultzner, the catalyst

Lord Wangford, local aristocrat

Crafty Catchpole, villager

Clara Gobley, church organist & choir mistress
Bert, her partner

Grise Culman, owner of the local Health Club
Owen Culman, her husband, also owner of the Health Club
Margaret Culman, their daughter
William Culman, their son

Penny Read, teacher and Junior Church leader
Alan Read, her husband & a doctor
Amos Read, their eldest son
Ann-Maria Read (known as Nell), their eldest daughter
George Read, their youngest son
Helen Read, their youngest daughter

Jim Maxwell, Alan's senior partner

Bernard Shaw, rector's warden
Liz Shaw, his wife

Plumptious Walters, landlady of the Jolly Sailors
Benny Walters, landlord of the Jolly Sailors
Kate Walters, daughter of Plumptious and Benny

Mark Chambers, local builder
Nin Chambers, his wife
Mark Junior, their son

Totto Briggs, village butcher

Superintendent Junket, Martin's senior officer

Necker Utting, Cub Scout helper and undertaker's assistant
Rollie Wiggs, a youth

Members of the Fishermen's Hut: villagers who also act as Chorus:

Deaf Charlie Utting)
Boiler Brown) close friends of Clive Brown
Dick Utting)
Butch Strowger
Daff Mallet
Boss Wigg
Jumbo Gooch, father to Mrs Turrel
John Barker, leader of bell ringers
Harry Bailey, works for Mark Chambers
Scrub Turrel, works for Mark Chambers
Yammer Utting, a local loudmouth

Simon 'Sly' Palmester, Bethel priest
Nadine Palmester, a journalist, daughter of Simon

Sandra Bint, everybody's friend
Ainsley Bint, her son
Milly Bint, his wife

John Stokes, herdsman to Lord Wangford
David Stokes, his son
Sam Cleat, retired gardener to Lord Wangford
Hewitt, butler to Lord Wangford

Miss Mealey, villager
Mrs Teale, her friend Mrs Netty Turrel
Sharon Turrel, her daughter
Luke Turrel, her son

Joanne Podd, a farmer's wife

Omar, an Estonian friend of Peter Vishnya
Vera, his wife
Valya, their daughter
Eva Schulz, housekeeper to Horst Brultzner in Leipzig
Katerina Schnell, housekeeper to Horst Brultzner in Prague
Maxine Fox, housekeeper to Horst Brultzner in York

Members of the Brotherhood:
The policeman
The man with the torch
The tremulous man

Book One

Spring Arrivals

CHAPTER 1

A loss out of time

On an evening in late March, just before the clocks were put forward, the graveyard of St George's Church at Dunburgh-on-Sea was in almost complete darkness. The tower lights, reflected greenly from flint walls, illuminated gravestones immediately round the church, but only served to intensify the blackness beyond. Two figures walked across the gravel pathway in front of the church, were lit momentarily from the walls, and then passed out of the light.

The man was short and stocky. His legs were bowed at the knees as though he carried a great weight on his shoulders, or was about to spring forward into unexpected action. His trousers, old and marked by the garden, slumped untidily over his shoes from below a beer gut that had long since decided his posture and gait. There was strength in his shoulders and hands, and the ruddiness of his complexion marked him as someone who worked long hours in the open air. The young woman with him was his daughter although, from their physical appearance, this would only have been noticeable to anyone who had watched children age into the likeness of their parents. The lightness of her step, the suppleness in her shoulders when she leaned to catch her father's words and the way her legs swung easily from the hips contrasted sharply with the movements of the man. What drew attention to their relationship was the closeness with which they walked and the similarity of expression as they leaned into the slight, but cold, easterly wind.

After they had passed into the darkness, the pale yellow light of a fisherman's lantern lit their place in the churchyard. It moved to and fro for a while, searching the ground, and was then raised so that the young woman's face sprang out of the night. She glanced behind her, and then quickly back towards her father whose hunched shape could just be seen crouched over something in the grass. He appeared to be untying a bundle, and there was the clatter of metal as his arms moved. After a while, he stood and leaned on a wooden handle. He paused for a moment, before raising the handle and shoving it hard into the ground. He then bent forward and pulled a sandy lump from the earth. This apparently pleased him for he suddenly stood up, tugged off his jacket, tossed it into the dark below the lamp and rolled up his sleeves. There was an unforgiving energy in him as he raised the spade again and plunged it downwards. He began to move about, and the girl followed him with the lantern, giving him light for his task, but she stood quite still. On her face was a look of intense horror. Only once did she move, and that was to lift his thrown jacket from the ground and fold it carefully over her arm.

3

"Nice and steady, Sarah, there's a good gal. I 'ont be that long an' then we'll be done."

His speech was made to reassure his daughter rather than to convey any truth. The task before them was a long one and she expected it to take many hours, but it was a comfort to her, at a time so full of anguish for him, that her father should show concern. She looked down at his back and watched the sweat trickle from beneath his cap. Sarah knew it was no good offering to help him dig: he was doing 'man's work' and, had he a son, she would not be there.

After a while, his frenzied digging subsided and he stood to survey his work, scratching his head and smiling grimly to himself.

"A drink, dad?"

"No, not 'til I've finished. Wouldn't be right."

The sweat was running freely from him even as he spoke and, after another back-breaking hour, he stood to rest, sucking on his own spit to moisten his throat. He was shoulder deep in the hole now, and the effort of lifting spadefuls of earth was beginning to tell – if one was to judge from his taut expression and slowing movements. There was a craftsman's pride in his face whenever he climbed from the hole to level off the soil around it, or check that the pit was descending smoothly downward. At these moments, he would gesture to Sarah, who would approach the hole with trepidation and lower the lantern so that he could inspect his work.

Sarah, eventually, seemed to accept that, to help her father effectively, she must move closer to the yawning pit and hold the lantern over it. She pulled her hood up around her head and, settling herself on the mound of soil he had made at one end, leaned over and hung her lantern above the point where he was digging. She was strongly built, and possessed an unaffected grace of movement. Her face was pretty, and the hood pushed forward a mass of honey-coloured hair that shone yellow in the light of the dull lantern. The dreamy look in her eyes was habitual. She had always given the impression that her inner fancies were her own, and not to be shared with others; the temptation drew men to her.

The lantern rocked in her hand – leaving the pit in darkness, lighting the gravestones and flittering their shadows across the grass. Her father looked up from the pit and, as the swinging light momentarily picked out his face from the blackness, Sarah saw tears in his eyes. With her free hand, she steadied the lantern.

"Sorry, dad."

" 's all right, gal. You don't much approve o' this do you?"

"No, dad, I don't."

"Oi can't hev strange hands on her, Sarah, and oi've heard 'em here laughin' and jokin'. Oi ent heving that. Not with yer mum."

"I can understand that, dad, but you're taking too much on. You don't have to do this all by yourself."

"It's family, Sarah. You can't hev outsiders involved in this. We do it for our own. Necker 'll lay her out. This is the least oi ken do. She were a good woman, Sarah. This didn't ought ter happen. The least we ken do is do right by her now."

He was clearly glad of the rest, and climbed from the pit to talk. He looked about them at the dark, ragged line of the hedges. He was used to the graveyard; it held no fears for him. As people's warden at the church, Clive Brown was responsible for keeping the grass cut, the hedges trimmed and the gravel pathways free from weeds. He would come, sometimes, at night, and sit in the quiet after a hard day's work, before going home to supper. He would light a small cigar – "his only vice" – and feel calmly guilty as he smoked behind the church. His love for his daughter was taken for granted between them. Whenever he had disapproved of her, Clive had said so – once – and then let the matter drop. He had not hesitated in asking her to come tonight. He had needed close family for his task and Sarah had accompanied him without question as he knew she would, but he had not liked asking. Graveyards were no place for women and he knew the fear that lurked within her, and the sadness and the anticipation of what was to come – what had to be faced. In the end she would face it better than he: what had happened would finish him, forever.

Sarah touched his arm and nodded towards the pit. The sadness within her was overwhelming. Watching the bereavement in her father's eyes brought back the knowledge of her own loss. She felt empty and, suddenly, very hungry. It had best be done quickly, and then they could get home. As father and daughter stood, sharing each other's misery, another person appeared from the darkness around the church and joined them in the enclosing light of her lantern.

"Good evening, Froggy. Hello, Sarah. Have you nearly finished?"

The voice – rich, resounding with education and carrying a West Country burr – was concerned but uncertain, as though the speaker had arrived unsure of his welcome at the graveside. Corvin Unwood, rector of St George's, was not comfortable with his Suffolk flock.

"Evenin' rector. Sarah and I are almost done - another hour, perhaps, to finish off and get things tidy."

The priest hesitated – clearly unwilling to pursue the reason he had come, but feeling obliged to do so; he was a kindly man at heart and he was concerned for Sarah.

"It's all right, rector," she said. "We know what we're doing."

"We've hed this out, rector, and oi int changing my moind now. We'll dig the grave and see ter the coffin, and she stays at home 'til it's time ter bury her, and oi int divertin' from that fer no one."

Corvin looked about him. He did not like churchyards; he lacked the natural stoicism of the Suffolk people. From where they stood, he could see the tombstones of the old graveyard silhouetted in a sheen of light that seemed to rise from the sea beyond: old gravestones, pitted by time and the salt winds that blew from the east, tumbling from generations of neglect. The long, rough coastal grass – bent dry by the winds – was taking over. Brambles invaded from the hedge that bordered Podd's field and the blown, twisted shapes of blackthorn trees rose up and leaned over with a display of almost human curiosity. Corvin could never shake the conviction that these were the familiars of demons.

"And where's Matthew?" he said, to shake the fear from him.

"With a neighbour, rector. People are good at a time like this. No problem looking after the baby."

"And who's sitting with … your wife?"

"She'll be OK, rector. Don't you worry. The wimen'll see ter Florrie."

Corvin could picture the scene: the corpse in the front room, and the family, dressed in black, sitting round in the living room watching each other. They would be saying little, and the silence would hang upon the chance visitor like a pall, and yet they would be comfortable, passing the odd pleasantry and speaking only good of the dead. The grief would be intense, but well borne.

Clive was back in his wife's grave now, digging out the last spadefuls – making a neat, "proper job" of her final resting place. Sarah moved the lantern forward again, leaving Corvin in darkness.

"Excuse us, rector," she said.

"Yes, of course."

From the darkness he began to speak words of comfort – talking quietly of Florrie Brown, of her busyness for the church, her goodness to neighbours, her love of the Lord and her qualities as a mother. Corvin was a good listener when his parishioners wanted to talk, and when – as now with Sarah and Clive Brown – they had no words to express themselves, he touched upon the right clichés to cultivate a sense of well-being, even in the face of irreparable grief. None in Dunburgh who knew him could fault his footwork. Corvin was good with his people. He knew those who wanted to be known, and reached those who didn't. Corvin did not spare the shoe leather.

When he had finished, Sarah and her father heard the crunch of his feet as the priest stepped back onto the gravel path. While Corvin spoke, Clive had paused in his work without actually moving from it – a kind of respectful stillness marked his attention to the words of the priest.

"I'll drop by tomorrow morning, Clive. You'll be in?"

"Oh yes, rector. Oi'll be there. Oi'll pay you more heed then."

Corvin smiled to himself, as he turned right at the lych-gate and walked down Church Hill towards the new rectory in Shore Lane. He had no more to do that night. He might take a slim glass of sherry, and let the day drain from him. He crossed himself, and quietly intoned the introductory sentence for the dead.

"Since we believe that Jesus died and rose again, so will it be for those who have died: God will bring them to life with Jesus."

He turned away and walked down the hill.

"I thought he'd never go," said Clive Brown, smoothing the mounds.

"Dad!"

"Well, if the truth be told I coulder done without that tonight, oi'll tell you, Sarah."

"He was only trying to help, dad."

"I know, I know, and he'll do her a nice service. I know that, too."

6

Father and daughter returned to their easy silence, and completed their task. When they had finished, Clive cleared around the grave and then bundled his tools – the metal pegs, ropes, pickaxe and spade – together. The chill wind from the east had risen slightly during the hours they worked, and dark clouds now drifted across the sky, brushing the floodlit tower. The howling of wolves could be heard from the Wildlife Park. Clive nodded towards the lych-gate, indicating that they were to leave that way rather than behind the church from where they had entered. The main path was lit by the street lamp shining through the lych-gate and Sarah, as a child, had always wanted to rush down the path towards the light, away from whatever might be in the darkness. She had the same feeling now as she lit her father's way through the graves. Yet she knew that the real terror would lie in returning to the church, behind her mother's coffin for the funeral, the day after tomorrow.

The figures of father and daughter were turned into shadows by the lamp, as they moved into the area of light cast through the arch of the gate. They were bent together in their sadness – she walking easily and light-limbed, he with the heavy frame and bowed legs which had earned him the nickname of Froggy.

CHAPTER 2

The social scene – first barbecue of the year

Mr and Mrs Snooks were holding the first barbecue of the year. This was not good. It was much better to hold the last: only then was it possible to outshine one's friends, only then could Mrs Snooks provide a fish course that nobody else had thought of and upstage their burgers, sausages and chicken portions with honeyed lamb, liver and kidney kebabs, and fruity pork chops. However, her September spot had been lost and she was now obliged to be first this year. Mrs Snooks was still unsure whether the double booking by the Conservative Club had been genuine or whether she had been out-manoeuvred by Amy Billings.

Mr Snooks had known better Saturday afternoons. Not only was he expected to help with the culinary preparations, but he also faced the problem of which punch to provide. He was torn between a red wine cup and a summer sparkle. He favoured the first because it was cheaper but, as Mrs Snooks pointed out, the latter contained gin and nobody had ever served spirits in a punch.

Bishop Twiddle had no such problems as he stood, with a "slim glass" of sherry, warming his backside on the radiator in Corvin Unwood's study. It was good sherry; Twiddle was renowned for offering his clergy sound advice on such matters. He was a man of bland passions, and half a lifetime serving the public had enabled him to subdue them even further than nature intended. His overall philosophy, borne out of years of consideration and scholarly endeavour, was that things were more or less all right and generally turned out as well as could be expected – given the complexity of the circumstances.

Twiddle has been instrumental in appointing Corvin as parish priest at Dunburgh-on-Sea. A few well-chosen, ecclesiastical words in the ear of the rector's warden, and the matter was settled satisfactorily before the Parochial Church Council had time to open their mouths in protest. Dunburgh had always been a fractious parish – with its uneasy mixture of farmers, fisherman, London overspill and what Mrs Snooks called the "county set" – and Twiddle needed someone who would toddle around the coop without ruffling any feathers. In Corvin Unwood, he felt that he had found such a man.

He had also been responsible for initiating the idea that the new rectory, in which he now sipped his pre-vesputinal sherry, was desperately needed if the church was to fulfil its obligations to the souls of the diocese. A "place of retreat" had been his line with the Diocesan Council – a place where harassed clergy could find refuge and emotional sanctuary in times of stress, and where Anglican dignitaries and other progressive thinkers might gather. He had personally supervised the furnishing of his own occasional room at the rectory and the design of the dining room, which had to be big enough to give those who might gather there a sense of community, and which he insisted upon calling the "refectory", much to Esther's annoyance. Besides, the old rectory – the Old Vicarage, as it was known – was damp and the walls crumbling in places. It would be a financial burden, forever.

These comforting thoughts passed quietly through the bishop's mind as, on one of his frequent visits to the new rectory, he sipped his sherry and awaited Esther Unwood's call to dinner.

Mrs Snooks's household preparations had been exhaustive and she was ready to receive her guests. In particular, she was keen to meet her first guests because, from the upstairs landing window where she had just finished adjusting her final arrangement of dried flowers, Mrs Snooks had seen Boller and Pliny Skeat arrive.

Half-a-dozen toilet rolls had been arranged elegantly in a basket of potpourri, and candles placed in water at strategic points about the house. She had carefully re-arranged the Tunbridge Ware writing slope on Mr Snooks's desk so that it looked as though he used it, although he had not actually written a letter to anybody – even when his children were at university, as his wife reminded him at choice moments – for years. A Messenger fountain pen – bought for her daughter Cassandra's eighteenth birthday, but never used by her – was laid casually to the side of the slope.

She was keen to greet Boller Skeat, provided his wife Pliny had gone on ahead, because Boller – a man of merry and vulgar disposition – could be relied upon to grab her from behind and give her breasts a squeeze or, if she was lucky, a good fondle. Mrs Snooks never acknowledged enjoying this, but she felt a surge of youthfulness when it happened. She never turned down a dance with him – especially a late dance when Mr Snooks was likely to be asleep on the settee, and Boller could be relied upon to steer her towards the corner of someone's lounge. Besides, the responsibility of providing the first barbecue was heavily upon her, and making sure that Boller was in a good humour would set things off with a swing.

He did not disappoint her, and Mrs Snooks was subjected to a friendly grope behind the corner of the house. Boller's wife, Pliny, received a chaste kiss from Mr Snooks, who poured her a glass of red wine with one hand, while turning the fruity pork chops with the other. Mr Snooks enjoyed being at the centre of entertaining guests; he relished the role of 'mine host'. Over the years his wife's brand of snobbery had rubbed off on him, and he had developed a kind of self-protective knowledge of wines and foods; nobody made Mr Snooks "look a fool" on matters of culinary etiquette.

Bishop Twiddle had enjoyed eating his dinner more than Esther Unwood had enjoyed cooking it: she resented the bishop's intrusion into their lives. Bishops were all very well, but a parish priest had a right to his private life; tomorrow was Sunday and a busy day for her husband. She had watched the bishop, devouring her chicken pie, with some anger. Had she been a young woman, Esther Unwood would have been called a "firebrand", and the object of lustful fantasies for those men of the parish who enjoyed a woman "with a bit of spirit". As it was, at seventy or so, she was simply a "crotchety old biddy who ought to keep her nose out of parish business". Esther knew the parish opinion of her, but was too old to care. Her father had been a priest, with all that meant to the marriage prospects of a young girl, and she had been relieved to meet Corvin when he came – late in life – to theological college. On a quiet day, Esther might have admitted her failings, but Esther did not have many quiet days; it was not in her nature. She had an overwhelming desire to change and influence events but, like many women of her generation, no means by which to do so – except through her husband. It did not make for an easy marriage.

Much to Mrs Snooks's gratification and relief, the barbecue was going well. Sitting by the waterfall Mr Snooks had built on the edge of the patio, laughing with Martin and Amy Billings, she was able to enjoy the fruits of her endeavours. Mr Snooks was busy serving recent arrivals his summer sparkle, and she had been able to help by occasionally reminding him to offer claret or Liebfraumilch as an alternative "in case people didn't like gin … there was gin in Mr Snooks's punch you see … expensive but you know Barray". (Mrs Snooks always extended the last syllable of her husband's name: she thought it sounded more "county set".)

The conversation wasn't yet crackling and sparkling across the patio, but small groups were enjoying themselves. Boller was listening to Joney Chine, who had just returned on a flying visit from her retirement home in France, and he was passing remarks to Ample and Billy Bassett – "French women like their baguettes big, don't they … haah, aah, aaah?" They all laughed. Well you had to, didn't you? Tony Crewes, collared early on by Joney and standing by the edge of the group, joined in. His wife, Beth, was deep in conversation with Pliny Skeat about next week's WI meeting.

Pliny was president for the year and determined to make it a successful one. A hard-working woman, good at delegation, she left early for the garden centre (where she was employed) each Saturday morning, after waking her husband with a cup of weak tea, one round of thin toast and marmalade (without butter), and a memo listing what he had to do that day.

It was Pliny in who Beth Crewes had confided a few years before when her husband had left her, briefly, for another woman, and provided the group's only piece of internal spice. Mrs Snooks, sensing a scandal, had invited the Skeats round for gratinee Lyonnaise, cote de boeuf a la moelle and oranges soufflees followed by tete-a-tete. For all her culinary efforts, however, she learned nothing. Her pique was augmented at the end of the evening when Mr Snooks, who had so carefully selected the Beaujolais to accompany the meal, insisted upon drinking beer because he knew what Boller preferred. Mr Snooks still had a touch of the vulgarian about him.

Tony Crewes was listening, with skilfully feigned interest, to what Ample Bassett had to say about the church selling the old rectory and what the village had to say about the buyer.

"We-ell, according to Necker Utting, it's a foreigner who's bought it. If you ask me, the church had no business selling it in the first place let alone selling it to a foreigner. I can't see what was wrong with the old rectory that a bit of paint wouldn't have put right. The church is always complaining about having no money, and then they go and build a new rectory."

"... build a new rectory."

It was rare that Ample Bassett paused for breath, but if she did her husband, Billy, took the chance to repeat her last phrase – possibly in case someone had dozed and missed it, but more likely simply out of habit. It was Tony Crewes's view that Billy was a master at switching-off from his wife's interminable chatter, while appearing to pay attention. Crewes pointed out, in support of his theory, that Ample had never been heard to accuse Billy of not having listened to her.

"... and if she doesn't know, I don't know who does," continued Ample, "It's somebody from Russia – a count or something. You'd wonder why a Russian count wanted to buy an old rectory in Dunburgh-on-Sea, wouldn't you?"

"... Dunburgh-on-Sea, wouldn't you," repeated Billy, dutifully.

"We could always get rid of him, Ample – invite him to a barbecue and sit him next to you for fifteen minutes," said Tony.

"Ooh you," she replied, with a laugh, "Here Beth, your husband's being rude to me."

"He's rude to everyone," responded Beth Crewes, without looking.

"Anyway," continued Ample, "I think it's a bit fishy, if you ask me. I mean how did a count from Russia come to know about an old rectory on the east coast of England?"

"He isn't Russian," cut in Martin Billings.

"Isn't Russian?" said Ample, "What do you mean he isn't Russian?"

".... isn't Russian?" repeated Billy Bassett.

"The man who has bought the old rectory isn't Russian," repeated Martin Billings, with relish. Billings had been seething for some while, listening to Ample's gossip. As village policeman, he was privy to most goings-on in the district, and he was a friend of Corvin Unwood. Like most coppers, he was cautious about what he said at parties, but he had a particular dislike for the soporific drone of Ample's voice and could not resist the chance to put her down. Besides, there was a tension within him – which he had yet to understand – that forced him from the sidelines to the limelight of such situations.

"And how are your flock, Corvin? Faithful and multiplying?" enquired Bishop Twiddle, as Esther stood to clear her dessert, which had been a particularly delicious home-made lemon meringue tart, from the table. She sat down again as her husband chose his words.

"Well, my lord ..."

"Peter, please, Corvin. No need for formalities after such a delicious meal," urged the bishop – pleased, nonetheless, to have been addressed in a manner befitting his title.

"The Junior Church is growing," said Corvin, "Our efforts to attract the younger people of the community are bearing fruit. We have a particularly good Junior Church leader in Penny Read."

"Ah, yes," interjected Twiddle, "the doctor's wife. What a charming person."

Corvin was slightly taken aback to find that the bishop knew Penny Read. Esther was annoyed with his favourable opinion. It wasn't that she had anything against Penny. On the contrary, they were the best of friends; but Penny, under her mild English manner, was stubborn.

"The elderly members of the congregation have a different perception of the morning service," said Corvin, who had caught the expression on his wife's face.

"You must continue to give them Matins, Corvin," said the bishop. "Tradition is important?" The comment was couched in a questioning manner. Corvin, uncertain of the bishop's stance and aware of his wife's orthodox views, was silent. Esther, finding herself apparently supported by the bishop, hesitated to intercede. Eventually, during which time the bishop smiled benevolently down upon them, Corvin said:

"Mrs Read is keen to involve the children in the morning service."

"Of course," said the bishop.

"This is not always compatible with the concept of Matins."

"Naturally."

"We are in the process of accommodating two opposing points of view."

"The role of the priest has always been such, Corvin."

"Mrs Read is not a traditionalist," Esther cut in, "She has views on the way in which the morning service might be re-shaped."

"Her approach is vibrant," said Corvin, "but does not always meet with the approval of the choir-mistress."

"Clara Gobley is a dyed-in-the-wool bigot," snapped Esther.

"But she has support within the congregation," replied Corvin, "There are many who do not wish for change. Indeed," he added with some feeling, "there are many who oppose any change whatsoever."

"And Mrs Gobley, as well as being the choir-mistress is also the organist – is she not?" asked the bishop, with a reassuring smile. He was beginning to feel a trifle uncomfortable, which was not to be tolerated after such a fine meal.

"It is the children singing that appears to pose the immediate problem."

"Indeed, Corvin?" 'Suffer little children'?"

"One or two of our more elderly ... eh, flock do not suffer them too gladly."

"I'm sure, Corvin, I'm sure."

Of what the bishop was sure, Corvin could not be certain, but he seemed, at least, to apprehend some of the problems. Emboldened, Corvin pursued his troubles.

"Mrs Read's choice of song does not always fit in with the organist's idea of what is suitable music for Matins."

"Or any other service for that matter," said Esther, "The woman is beyond the Pale."

The bishop himself was now in doubt as to who stood where on the matter. He could not determine whether Esther spoke of Clara Gobley or Penny Read. Either way, the matter was becoming, once more, contentious, and that would never do. He looked at the table. Had there been no cheese and biscuits, or had he forgotten? He picked up his empty wine glass and twirled it between slim, white fingers.

"An excellent meal, Esther – as always."

"I tried to keep it simple, Bishop. It is Lent."

"Quite … indeed. No, no. No more wine. Thank you, Corvin."

He spoke as though to restrain Corvin, who had not actually moved. When she made remarks like that, Esther terrified and exhilarated her husband; at moments like that he felt ashamed, but knew why he loved her.

Sidney and Mavis Close arrived late at the first barbecue of the year: this was usual. There was a reluctance in Sidney to arrive at all and he had, much to the annoyance of Mavis, been held up visiting his mother. Mrs Snooks had feared starting without them – this would never have done – and so she was delighted to see them enter the driveway and make their way towards the pergola. Sidney stood aside, held the gate for his wife to pass through to the patio, and caught Mrs Snooks in a two-handed grip on the buttocks under cover of the Russian vine, which shrouded the pergola. He did it with the same air of jollity and the same public bar expression of lust as Boller, but not to quite the same effect. It seemed to Mrs Snooks that every muscle in Sidney's body tensed as his fingers tightened in her backside. She saw the laughter of his mouth tighten, twitch and fade into a dull faraway expression in the eyes. As he let her go, Sidney ran his hands along her back and pressed her breasts hard against the muscles of his chest. He sighed, and laughed again. Mrs Snooks said "Ooh" and felt, momentarily, discomfited before laughing with him and allowing herself to be escorted, on his arm, to the patio.

Mrs Snooks had agonised over which salads her husband was to prepare, but had finally decided on water lily timbale, broccoli with avocado and red pepper, beetroot with yogurt, green pea salad with fresh ginger and olives, and Chinese leaf and bean sprout salad with oranges. She also served new potatoes, cheesy baked potatoes and simple jacket potatoes with an array of dips and sauces. Guests did not go hungry at a Snooks's barbecue – and neither did the pets and garden birds on the following day.

Sidney Close looked upon this with the same disdain as he looked upon his friends of many years who were now laughing, and red of face. 'Here, Lord, in flesh but not in spirit.'

"All right then Sid? Cor, come on, you nearly missed the best bit," called Boller, who was already being served with his honeyed lamb by Mr Snooks.

Plates stacked and overflowing, Mrs Snooks's friends turned their mouths and minds to eating. Their palates moistened with Mr Snooks's summer sparkle, they now quenched their thirsts with beer, lager, fruit juice, lemonade and various combinations of each. The tang of orange and rosemary, in which the kebabs had marinated, jostled with the fresh broccoli and red pepper of the avocado salad – the softness of the innards contrasting splendidly with the crunchy texture of the finely sliced peppers. The fruity sauce of the pork chops, served best with a simple baked potato, elbowed for precedence on the palate with the finely chopped root ginger and roughly chopped stuffed green olives.

"Cor, this lamb aint half juicy. I aint had as much juice as this for a long time," said Boller, with a vulgar laugh.

"Now, Boller," said Beth Crewes, "that's not a nice thing to say about Pliny's cooking."

"I wasn't talking about her cooking."

"Ooh," said Ample Bassett.

A roar went round the patio from the men, and mock reproaches from the women. Pliny gave her husband a look to indicate that he had drunk too much, and was in danger of breaching the agreement she had made with him about what he could and could not say at the barbecue.

"Nothin' like a bit of juice, is there?" he persisted.

"You'd find more juice these days in a pint at the pub," said Barry Snooks.

"I take it that you are finding the parish fractious, Corvin?"

"I wouldn't say that my ... er ... Peter. We are having ... some success with our Step Forward Together campaign."

"Ye-es ... good, good. You need to rally your troops, Corvin. You need to cultivate the ... er, substantial people – the farmers, doctors, vets, teachers. People like that. Build upon rock, Corvin. Nothing stands against the shifting sands of time like a solid foundation."

They were in Corvin's study with the bishop's backside against the radiator, and with Corvin hovering between the door and his desk. He didn't like to sit down while the bishop stood. Besides, he feared that Esther might walk in at any moment, and had no desire to face her comments should she find the bishop drinking port during Lent. Corvin was still unsure how he came to pour the drink. Somehow, without uttering a word, the bishop had made it clear that an after-dinner port was expected. Corvin had felt obliged to join him. He could hear Esther clattering the dishes between the 'refectory' and the kitchen.

"The parish has changed much in recent years ... er, Peter. A substantial number of the people living here are what are termed – often in an unnecessarily derisory manner – London overspill. These are the people who offer the church its challenge. Dunburgh is no longer a village of farmers and fishermen."

"True, true and well spoken, Corvin – but the base, the foundation – you must secure your foundations. The people of substance are those who will abide as we move towards the millennium ... Have you met the buyer of the Old Vicarage, yet, Corvin? ... an interesting buyer ... I think a man of substance in his own country. Czechoslovakia was it not?"

"East Germany, my lord – as was – Leipzig to be exact."

"Ah yes, they boast a fine opera house, do they not?"

"I wouldn't know, my lord."

"No ... Cultivate him, Corvin. The church cannot let opportunities slip by."

They stood for a while in silence during which Corvin found he was pouring a second glass of port for the bishop, who then excused himself and asked Corvin to wish Esther "good night". He, too, had no wish to be found drinking port.

Corvin watched his slim frame pass out of the study and make its way up the stairs to bed. He wondered why a working class priest like himself lacked the style. Did the bishop have an air of duplicity about him, or was this jealousy on Corvin's part? Esther came into the study and raised her eyebrows at the absence of the bishop.

"Compline?" she said, smiling.

"Compline", replied Corvin, arranging the wooden crucifix on his desk. They always enjoyed this moment together, and neither was disappointed that the bishop had retired. They knelt, and Corvin began to intone the last service of the day.

Mr and Mrs Snooks sat dissecting their guests of the evening. Mr Snooks had been able to corroborate his wife's impression that the first barbecue of the year had been a success, and that no one was likely to out-do their efforts. Mr Snooks had been in no hurry to go to bed, and had started the washing-up, hoping that his wife would be asleep before he felt obliged to retire. Mrs Snooks, though, was exhilarated by the flow of the evening, and wished to discuss it in detail. She had brewed herbal tea to "relax them". Eventually – and inevitably, after such a successful barbecue – the talk turned to diets, and Mr Snooks said he would be happy to support Mrs Snooks in her endeavours to "fight the flab". Was Mr Snooks "coming up now"? Well, why not? Most of their friends would now be in bed together. Boller and Pliny kept to a set time and routine: that was why they always left at eleven – so that she wouldn't oversleep in the morning. Mr Snooks put out the kitchen light and followed his wife upstairs. Less than ten minutes later, she was asleep and he was down, watching the video-recording of that afternoon's match, which his son had dropped off, quietly, during the first barbecue of the year.

CHAPTER 3

A funeral

Tony Crewes stood on the church path, with his wife Beth, grinding the toe of his right foot into the gravel. It was, he mused, the perfect day for a funeral – cold, clear and crisp. Looking up at the blue bowl of the sky, he could well believe that somewhere beyond was an eternity with your God. For that moment – as he viewed the spread of blue, bright and clear, stretching from marsh to rooftops – he had no doubts. He was tall, rather on the lean side, and looked his age, which was nearly fifty. He dressed with unconventional flair, having once had pretensions to be an artist, although he now worked for an insurance company in Norbridge. Like most men, he had been dragged somewhat reluctantly into any kind of involvement with village life, and stood now more as escort to his wife than in his own right.

Beth Crewes was well-known in village circles. She taught at the local school and sat on St George's Parochial Church Council. She was a small, dark, pinched woman who took an intense interest in whatever came her way and worried, incessantly, about what people thought of her and her family. She never refused a request for help from anyone – headteacher, vicar or friend. Indeed, more or less everyone came first for Beth: time was her great headache.

They had arrived early, but Beth did not want to be "first in" and so they stood waiting for someone they knew to arrive. Tony knew the Browns as members of the congregation; during his active time with the church he had worked with Clive clearing and maintaining the graveyard. The sudden death of Clive's wife had shocked them all, but Tony had not really known her; he felt the pain of her death only selfishly, realising how he would feel in Clive's place. Beth had anguished about asking for time off work, but she felt that attendance at the funeral was a duty. She felt the need to be seen supporting the family.

He listened, but could hear no sound from the road. He glanced across at the fresh grave. The story of Clive and Sarah digging it had circulated at the first barbecue of the year, although no one really believed it. Beyond the mounded soil loitered a youth who appeared to be gripping a headstone for support. As Tony watched, the youth lurched, fell and struggled to his feet. For a while, Tony thought that he was drunk, but dismissed the idea.

"Who's that?" he asked, leaning towards his wife's ear as he spoke. He assumed Beth would know – women tended to know such things.

"The son-in-law."

"What?"

"I said the son-in-law. Sarah's husband."

"But he looks drunk."

"He probably is."

"At his mother-in-laws funeral?"

Beth looked up at him, the contempt in her face suggesting that he knew nothing of the world. The contempt in her face reflected her view of Shane Marjoram, and all other Shane Marjorams who had ever existed; those "types" who had arrived at school abusing teachers and putting the world to rights, while their own despicable behaviour broke families and wrecked the lives of children.

"Perhaps you ought to take a look at him," she said.

"Yes, perhaps I ought."

"Be careful … get someone to help you."

Tony Crewes glanced quickly around, but could see no one who looked as though they might help. He crossed to the other side of the path. Shane caught his eye as Tony sauntered, with an air of measured casualness, through the gravestones. Given that they did not know each other, he refused to comprehend the look of sullen resentment with which Shane viewed him.

"OK?"

"Wha'? Why shouldn't I be?"

"Well – the glazed look in your eyes … the yellow tinge to your gills, the smell of beer on your breath, the pile of vomit behind that headstone, the fact that you can't actually stand up without the support of the dead. They all seem to suggest that you might be a little under the weather."

"Wha' yer mean? You tryin' be funny?"

"I can't say that I'm aware of any particular effort on my part – no."

He paused, quite deliberately, and gave Marjoram a hard, almost contemptuous, look.

"Do you want a hand?" he asked.

"You sayin' I'm drunk or somefun?"

"I think you're saying your drunk. I'm just offering to help you out of the churchyard. Shall we go and stick your head under the water tap?"

Had Crewes cast aspersions on the youth's football team or slept with his wife, he could not have provoked a more violent reaction. Marjoram reared up and lunged at him with a wide, curving swipe. Tony stepped back, sedately, and watched Marjoram fall on his face beside the grave. He lay for a while, grunting, and Tony, aware of his wife's agitation and the approaching funeral, decided he had to act swiftly.

"Are you going to lie there all day, looking like a complete arse, or do you want a hand?"

The face that turned to look up at him from the ground bore a quite murderous expression. Tony felt a sense of power in having provoked so immediate and so violent a reaction with so few words. What was it that struck home so deeply about being called a drunk? As he pondered this, a voice said quietly:

"Can I help? Clive phoned and said he might cause trouble. Here."

It was the rector's warden, Bernard Shaw – a large, overweight man with a chesty wheeze. He stooped and grasped Marjoram by his right arm and shoulder, lifting him to his knees. He looked sharply at Tony, who raised his eyebrows and stepped forward to assist. Marjoram struggled, but allowed himself to be steered through the gravestones towards the taps behind the church. Watching warily out of the corner of his eye, Tony filled one of the buckets used by relatives changing headstone flowers and poured it over the youth's head. Marjoram yelled and staggered to his feet, spluttering and cursing. Tony wasn't quite sure why he had acted as he did and neither, judging by the expression on his face, was Bernard Shaw, who kept a firm grip on the youth and forced him down to the bench seat.

"Calm down, now. Cool off. Water will do you no harm. It'll sober you up."

"Sober? I don't need no water to be sober. I can drink myself sober."

"You haven't exactly made a spectacular job of it so far," said Tony.

"I'll remember you, mate, I'll tell yer. No one pours water over my head and gets away wiv it."

"Now, now – none of that. Clive told us to look after you. He thought you might be the worse for wear."

"What's all this 'worse fer wear', 'under the weather'. I aint worse fer wear. I aint under no bleedin' weather. Om just pissed off. Would you like it if yer wife's old man wouldn't let yer carry his misses's coffin?"

"I can't say that I've ever found myself facing that particular dilemma ... but you're in no fit state to carry yourself, let alone a coffin," said Tony.

"'Carry meself?' 'Fit state'. Om all right, mate. You don't want to worry about me. I can handle myself."

As if to prove this he made a second lunge at Tony, tripped over the bucket and knocked himself out on the stand-pipe.

"You get back to your wife, Tony. I'll watch him for a while, and then one of the sidesmen can take over. What made you provoke him like that?"

"I don't know. Something about his manner annoyed me."

When Tony reached the door of the church, his wife had already gone inside. He found her gripping her hymn book in a pew half-way down the aisle, and looking frantically over her shoulder. The relief in her face, when he joined her, was manifest.

"Where have you been? What kept you so long?"

"A little business with a drunk: nothing to worry about."

"Is he all right, now?"

"If you call unconscious, sozzled and sodden wet 'all right', I suppose he is."

"Unconscious?"

"He knocked himself out on a stand-pipe."

"I don't know what to make of you these days. I just asked you to help."

"I'll tell you about it, afterwards."

Clive Brown had not realized how heavy the coffin would be, or considered why undertakers choose men of a similar height to do the carrying. He and his brother had the same build, but his friends were both on the tall side. The constant stooping by the taller men and stretching by the shorter ones had robbed the funeral cortege of the elegance and simplicity Clive intended.

A long time had passed in the four days since Sarah and he dug the grave. They arrived home to find their friends and relatives seated round the room watching the body in the coffin. Clive's wife looked older than he remembered. Her face was drawn, lined and haggard: features he had never noticed before. Looking at her body, he realised how rarely he must have watched her since they married. He had expected a younger woman in the coffin; this corpse did not look like his wife. After the family had gone, Clive sat with her throughout the night. In the days that followed, he grieved alone, his elbows resting upon the table on which the coffin stood.

No one disturbed him during the vigil of the first night. He had no wish to share his grief, and those who knew him respected that: such grief was, anyway, not shareable. They had been an old-fashioned couple, living their lives together and through each other. Evenings, weekends and holidays were spent in the company of the other, and the other's friends. He would accompany her to church socials, and she would accompany him to the Working Men's Club. It had been a good life, and now it was over. Clive did not suppose that he could pick up the pieces; he would have neither the desire nor the ability to do so. Most unbearable of all was the knowledge that he did not expect to see her again – never mind what the old vicar might say (the new one would not commit himself). He did not expect to see her again, nor touch her, nor feel the warmth of her, nor hear her voice – not in the way he had been used to, anyway. She'd never call to him again from the kitchen on a Sunday morning. Whatever Heaven was to be like, it wasn't going to include a Sunday roast dinner.

Clive looked at the body in the coffin, and knew that the wife he loved was no longer within it; he had realised that when he returned from digging the grave. He bent and kissed the cold forehead and ran his finger over the lips. The hardness in the face was not hers; her soul had departed. He had no wish to be maudlin, but he could not shake her off. He knew he must now live without her, but could not let her go.

He had always intended to bury her himself. He had seen undertakers laughing and joking as they handled corpses. You couldn't blame them – it was a difficult job – but Mary wasn't going out of this world in the hands of undertakers. It was just that he hadn't expected to bury her quite yet – not for many years. Sarah had been good as always: a phone call and she was there, seeming to expect it (with the wisdom of women), her child in her arms. He had felt useful holding the baby, while she cried over her mother. Sarah had sobbed her heart out, and held the warm body as though she could howl life back into it. Afterwards, she was calm and businesslike, while he stood there, numbed. It was Sarah who had called Jack to make the coffin, and Sarah who had negotiated with the vicar and seen to the bell-ringers, the choir, the newspaper announcements, the informing of friends and family and the funeral meal.

Clive wondered how he was to help his daughter through her grief. They had always been close, but he was no good with words. He wouldn't find the right things to say, and her husband, Shane, was no help. Shane Marjoram! Sarah's marriage to him had cast a blight over the entire family.

"You will let him help, won't you dad?" she asked, knowing the answer.

"Oi can't Sarah. Oi can't hev him touching your mother."

"Please, dad. It'll mean so much to him. He's never felt welcome in the family. Let him help out – if only to carry the coffin."

A lesser person would have added "for my sake", but Sarah had pride and no wish to bring emotional pressure to bear on her father at such a time. Clive had turned away, and a lifetime of acknowledging the man's final word on such matters was enough for Sarah. She turned to the sink and carried on with the dishes.

On the morning of the funeral, Clive stood in front of the dressing table mirror – where Mary had so often sat dolling herself up for a Saturday night at the "Working Men's" – straightening his black tie. The tie had been part of his father's uniform during the war, and one or other of them had worn it for funerals ever since.

Downstairs, he found Boiler Brown, Deaf Charlie and his brother Dick waiting in the front room where, last night, they had screwed down the coffin lid. All three were dressed in dark suits and black ties. Dick, as close family, also wore a black armband. Boiler had once worked on the deep sea fishing boats out of Lowestoft, and Deaf Charlie was still a long-shore fisherman at eighty – although more for the tradition than the money. Each wore a solemn face as befitted the occasion: hardened drinkers, none of them had touched a drop for twenty four hours.

"Froggy," said Dick, with a nod, when Clive entered the room.

"If you and I take the front on her, and Boiler and Deaf Charlie the rear, I think that'll be best."

"Aye."

Outside, the rest of the family waited. Clive looked along the street towards the sea and the boats. He noted Martin Billings, his eyes on the traffic, standing in the road ... and he saw the Reverend Unwood. He hadn't expected that: there was no need for the rector to have come down – he could have waited at the church. It was kind of him; people didn't always understand or appreciate rectors. Clive's misery overcame him again in the face of such kindness, and he looked out from his front door for something upon which he could depend – someone upon who he could grasp a hold; and there was Sarah, dressed completely in black, neat and trim and as lithe as a dancer. Clive stood down from his front step, as his brother and friends manipulated the coffin through the front door. His hands rested on the wrought iron railings which were his front fence. He glanced over his left shoulder towards the sea, caught a glimpse of the betting shop and the Jolly Sailors where he had sunk many a pint and, beyond that, the beach and the boats. Clive avoided the eyes of his friends. His mouth was tight and grim. He wanted to understand what life without Mary was to be like, but had no pictures in his mind – just a blankness where once there was comfort and home. To his right were the new houses that sat on the edge of the marsh; in wet weather they were damp and the drains flooded. He, and others in the trade, had told the council, but no one listened: now, it didn't seem to matter. He looked further on towards the flagpole outside the Bethel – the fishermen's church – and stepped down into the road to take his place at the front right-hand corner of his wife's coffin.

Corvin Unwood stepped ahead of the coffin to lead the way, and Mary Brown's funeral cortege moved along Beach Road towards the church of St George on the hill. It was the longest mile for Clive, coming from a generation of men who did not cry but took a deep breath and held hard on their emotions. They passed the Marsh Lane houses and the Bethel, whose flag the priest – Simon 'Sly' Palmester – had lowered to half mast. They passed Cod Piece – the fish restaurant, which charged double the local price to summer tourists – and The Paper Shop where Clive had cancelled his order of forty years when the new owner's husband suggested, one Saturday morning, that he had not paid a bill. Opposite the newsagents was Mona's, the cheap sweet shop, where the village school children spent their Friday night pocket money on junk sweets which Mona served, traditionally, in a white paper bag. The weight of the coffin pressed heavily as they passed the derelict Beach school, which had given way to a new building in the main village. Dunburgh-on-Sea was actually two villages – the Beach and the Street – and the Street had won when it came to deciding the site of the new school.

Both Clive and the rector cast their eyes along Shore Lane when the procession reached the foot of the hill which led to the church – Corvin wondering whether his wife was late at the gate of the rectory, Clive remembering the days when Sarah was in Junior Church and he and Mary would watch her follow the donkey up the hill on Easter Sunday. The cross used to go before them to the church – Clive rather embarrassed, Mary determined to support their only child.

The hill was bordered on the south by Podd's field and on the north by the "posh" houses where lived the chemist, the family of the man from the Department of Agriculture and Fisheries, the French family who kept their grandmother locked in an upstairs room and only allowed her into the back garden on summer days, the church organist – Clara Gobley – who lived with a man called Bert and the count from Russia, who lived in the Old Vicarage (if Ample Bassett was to be believed).

Ascending the hill had been the easier part of their walk – not on the calf muscles, which pulled hotly and painfully, but on the hands that gripped the coffin. With the taller men at the rear, it had been better for Clive and his brother than descending to the marsh houses or making their way along the flat by Mona's. At last, with the church in sight, they had kept Mary level and their backs as straight as possible. Quite a crowd had gathered to watch. There were many strangers, who had come not to pay their respects but simply from vulgar curiosity, wondering why anyone but a tight man would want to carry his wife to her grave.

Martin Billings had diverted the beach traffic along Shore Lane, with the judicious and illegal use of signs, and steered traffic from the main road through the new estate which linked the two original villages. They had processed quietly, led by the rector, the trail of black mourners walking in pairs, and with Sarah escorted by her mother's brother. Matthew was in her arms, sleeping quietly, and the family strung out behind her like a drift net.

They came, at last, to the lych-gate of St George's and passed through and along the gravel path to the main door of the church, with the freshly-dug grave to their right. Sarah breathed deeply, and gently kissed her child. Her mother was never, now this had happened, to know Matthew, never watch him through school, never see him grow into a man, never share her worries as only another woman can share them. It seemed to Sarah, as she entered the church, that she was burying her future with her mother. She had known times of desperate unhappiness, but never such deep sadness. She heard Corvin Unwood's voice – "Jesus said, I am the resurrection, and I am the life; he who believes in me, though he die, yet shall he live, and whoever lives and believes in me shall never die" – and realised her mother's funeral service had begun.

Tony Crewes turned in his pew when the cortege entered, and was first to stand as he heard the words intoned. He watched the coffin pass, saw Clive Brown and his friends lower it gently on to the rests that had been placed between the choir stalls, and then his eyes caught Sarah as she walked down the aisle to the front pews.

"Don't stare," hissed his wife, nudging him.

"We believe that Jesus died and rose again; and so it shall be for those who die as Christians ..."

Tony could think of nothing worse than rising again to live through all eternity. Why would anybody want to do that? Wasn't getting through this life enough? If God was going to take him at the end, then let Him do it – but let him rest, for heaven's sake.

"... you have given us a true faith and a sure hope."

'If only you had, Lord, if only you had.' Crewes had a burning desire to find spiritual fulfilment through the church, but could not relegate his reason. Nothing that he knew convinced him that man came from a spiritual inception, that the spirit of God had existed before all things and had made all things possible. The believer (never mind which faith) claimed too much for Him.

"... and the resurrection to eternal life ..."

Corvin was in his element. His humanity shone through and his love of ritual carried the day. "The good old C of E," he had once said to Tony, "as comfortable as an easy chair". Corvin lacked the pomposity of many traditional priests – those who had come from a clerical background, whose voices had the resonance of certainty, of knowing throughout all of their lives that what their forefathers had believed was right, the comfortable fruity vowel sounds that separated their workday voice from their Sunday voice. He seemed to have thought his way to faith, and to have brought himself to the altar.

Corvin walked up into the pulpit and looked down upon his flock. Always, at this moment, whatever the service, he felt a surge of power – and knew that he shouldn't. He looked down at his wife, sitting at the back of the church, and turned his gaze across the mourners. He had visited them all, and would again; he was a good priest. He cared for his parish and his people; he was able to bring comfort, and to lead them from the valley of the shadow to an acceptance of God's true light. What more could anyone ask of him? His words came sure and true for the comfort of the bereaved.

"Mary Florence Brown was a Dunburgh girl, born and bred: one of the Strowger family. Those who knew her at school remember a hard-working, helpful girl – always ready to be a classroom monitor, to give out the ink, to clean the blackboard, to look for another child's lost toy. When she left the village school at eleven, in 1955, she was Head Girl …"

It was comforting to hear the rector run over the outline of your life, putting in place those things you had never really thought about. It was re-assuring to know that someone out there was aware of these things, and could now say them for all to hear. Clive and Mary had waited a long time for Sarah, and resigned themselves to never having children. One night – after Mary had too much to drink at the Working Men's – they had walked home and stopped at his allotment. He could remember her cool lips turning to him, and dropping his coat for her to lie on and lifting her skirt and, afterwards, cradling her in his arms, lying on his back, watching the clear summer moon through the wigwam of his runner beans. Clive blushed.

"Sarah's birth was a turning point in their lives. Clive gave up the sea and found work with Chambers's Builders where he has been ever since. Sarah drew them into the life of the village as only children can …"

Corvin looked around and caught his wife's eye: even she was absorbed in his words. He noticed so many grey heads, so many elderly people who were the bulwark of the church – all of who had come to pay their last respects to a friend.

"When I came to the parish such a relatively short time ago to whom did I turn, but to Clive and Mary. He as my people's warden, and she – so supportive – as his wife … Their loss is our loss, their grief is our grief. Let us join together now in prayer."

Corvin stepped down from the pulpit and stood beside the coffin. "Lord, have mercy upon us." He led the congregation through the Lord's Prayer. Sarah felt her mother about to be taken from her, and she looked at her father whose head was bowed. She looked up at Corvin. "Grant us, Lord, the wisdom and the grace to use aright the time that is left to us here on earth." How was she to do that now, without her mother? A moment of panic overcame her, and she felt the tears run down her cheeks – not for her mother, now safe in the arms of the Lord, but for herself. Suddenly, they were standing and she heard her voice, somehow clear and bright as the day, leading them all in her mother's favourite hymn.

"Breathe on me, Breathe of God
Fill me with life anew,

That I may love what thou dost love,
And do what thou wouldst do."

As the congregation stood, all eyes upon the coffin for Mary's hymn, Tony Crewes, who had been watching Sarah intently throughout the sermon, caught a movement at the back of the church. Shane Marjoram was lolling against the wall by the rope of the communion bell, and reaching up towards it. His face was yellow with drink, his mouth gaping as though to vomit and his body bent forward from the waist. Fascinated, Crewes watched Shane's right arm groping blindly for the bell rope. It flopped backwards and forwards across the whitewashed wall, as he tried to grip the sally. As he appeared to tighten his grip, a figure stepped forward – seemingly from the church door – and grasped Marjoram's wrist. The cry Crewes expected to hear from the drunken mouth never came. Marjoram's body was jerked round by a tall figure, which Crewes seemed to remember from some party or other. It was the Russian – not the one who was supposed to have bought the old vicarage, but the one who had the child and had been married to the English girl.

Tony moved to help him, but Beth's arm was a restraint and – before he could step from the pew – Bernard Shaw was upon Marjoram. The rector's warden and the Russian, whose name was Peter Vishnya, removed Shane from the church, and from sight. When Tony turned back, he saw Sarah's eyes upon him, but whether she had been aware of what was happening with her husband he could not tell.

"Man born of a woman has but a short time to live. Like a flower he blossoms and then withers; like a shadow he flees and never stays. In the midst of life we are in death; to whom can we turn for help, but to you, Lord ..."

The coffin was lifted high upon the shoulders of Clive, his brother and friends. There was no struggle now, but a determination to get it done and done well. They came to the graveside, and Mary Brown was lowered into the earth, slowly and steadily. With all the care he had lavished upon her in life, Clive gave to his wife her last resting place, and he and Sarah dropped a handful of soil on to the coffin.

"We have entrusted our sister, Mary, to God's merciful keeping, and we now commit her body to the ground: earth to earth, ashes to ashes, dust to dust; in sure and certain hope ..."

Boiler Brown and Deaf Charlie Utting stepped forward in their funeral suits, ready to fill in the grave, as the funeral party stepped back on to the gravel path outside the main door of the church. Two fishermen from the Dunburgh Hut moved forward to help them. Clive nodded thanks and tightened his mouth as he took Sarah's arm. Now, would come the difficult part – the funeral meal, the condolences, comforting Sarah, learning to live without Mary.

Martin Billings had only just removed his uniform jacket, and turned to make himself a cup of coffee, when the telephone rang. It was Superintendent Junket, his superior officer from Lowestoft.

"Ah, Billings, how did the funeral go today?"

"Very well, sir. As smoothly as could be expected, I think."

"No hiccups?"

"No, sir."

"No hitches?"

"Not that I'm aware of, sir."

"Really?"

"Yes, sir."

"Only I'm picking up these vibes, Billings. Drunks in church, traffic jams?"

"Vibes, sir? From where, may I ask?"

"We have our sources, Martin. Any truth in them?"

"Excuse me, sir – the kettle's boiling," said Martin, placing the receiver on the mahogany table, and pretending to switch off the kettle.

"Sorry about that, sir."

"You don't have an automatic kettle there, Martin?"

"Not in the station office, sir – no we don't."

"We'll have to see what we can do about that, Martin. We can't have our community stations under-resourced."

"No, sir."

"Was that a wooden desk you placed the receiver down on, Martin?"

"Yes, sir."

"The old mahogany one?"

"Yes, sir."

"I thought we'd issued you with one of the updated metal ones, custom built."

"I don't think it quite made it, sir."

"We must look into this, Billings. All officers were issued with the new desks as part of our efficiency drive."

"The metal desk wouldn't have done the job any better, sir, and it doesn't have the beauty of this one. They'll never make them like this again, sir – except for millionaires and cabinet ministers. It would be a shame to let this one go."

"Regulations, Martin. Do everything by the book, stick to the regulations and they can find no fault with your work. We'll look into that desk. Now about these traffic jams ... and drunks."

"I'll have to look into it, sir."

She had said goodbye to the last of her relatives, done the washing-up, stacked her best crockery safely away, put the cutlery in her mother's velvet-lined case, walked her father home, put Matthew snugly to bed and sat down by a late fire with a quiet cup of tea when Sarah heard her husband's key in the lock. She knew he would have been drinking steadily all day, and was alert and ready to circumvent trouble. Sarah rose quickly and opened the door.

"Hello! Do you want something to drink?"

Nobody but Sarah could have used those words to Shane Marjoram at that moment, without flaring him up: from other lips they would have carried an edge. Sarah opened the door wide and helped him, unobtrusively, across the step. She had her child to care about. Before he knew it, Shane was in his armchair by the fire, and the warmth of his home and of the evening spread through him like the first haze of alcohol he knew so well. Sarah placed a mug of warm, milky coffee in his hands.

"Thanks," he said, surprising himself but not Sarah, "The babe in bed?"

"Yes. Sound asleep ... go and see him, if you like."

"No, no. I don't want to wake him. O'll see him later. Did he behave himself at ... at ..., the little beggar?"

The word 'funeral' wouldn't come, but Shane's interest was now on their child, and Sarah hoped she might ease herself through the rest of the day without mishap.

"Yes. He was a good boy."

"He always is. It's the way you bring him up. He ain't got much of a faver, but he's got a good muver."

"You're not a bad father, Shane. You mustn't think that. You work hard. You keep your family. We don't go cap in hand to anyone."

"No, I know that. I'm good at me job."

"It means a lot."

"Yeah."

Shane stretched his short legs before the fire and eased off his shoes. Sarah stooped to remove them, and he flexed his toes. The warm coffee and the heat from the fire were making him drowsy, and Sarah was so tired that she could think of nothing nicer than to doze off where they sat. It was a pleasant room in their little fisherman's cottage; both had worked hard, in the early days of their marriage, to make it so. It was warm and cosy, and Sarah liked nothing more than to sit in winter watching the frost glisten at night on the stretch of grass between them and the houses in Marsh Lane. She wondered whether things would have been different if she and Shane had courted each other before she became pregnant, and had come to marriage in the same way as her parents; but no, it was not something about which she could wonder.

"Things will be OK won't they Sarah? Between us I mean."

"Why shouldn't they be? Whatever made you ask that?"

"Well, wiv yer mum and everyfing. I wondered how you felt."

"We have Matthew. We have our whole future in front of us – everything to look forward to."

"Yeah ... and you do look forward to it, don't yer?"

"Yes, you know that."

"Not always. I'm a bit of rough compared to you. I know that. If I hadn't of got you pregnant there's no telling what you might have done. Wiv your education, I mean. You could have done better than me, if I hadn't got you in the club."

"There's no good talking about that now, Shane. What's done is done. You can't live with regrets."

"But you ain't got no regrets – marrying me, I mean."

"I said – you can't live with regrets. Mum always said that ... not that she had any really."

"Thanks for coming round."

Martin Billings opened his front door and nodded Tony Crewes into the living room. A bottle of Beaujolais was waiting. Tony slumped into the leather armchair and looked around the room he admired so much. It was predominantly wood – good quality wooden furniture and fittings made by craftsmen long ago, and acquired by Martin for next to nothing because people were stupid enough to want to throw it out.

The mantle-piece had come from a local school when they updated their furnishings, and threw mahogany desks and beech shelving out in favour of the more modern metal and plastic. Martin had persuaded a local cabinet maker to teach him the technique of French polishing, so that he could burnish it until winter fires glowed in the underside. On each end stood a pair of Victorian brass candlesticks tossed into the dustbin by a couple from London who thought they looked "old-fashioned" in their new Dunburgh house. The bookcase, stripped of years of dirty lacquer, was actually made of oak and reflected deeply the covers of the video tapes Martin collected. A 19th century copper coffee pot, complete with dovetail seam and with the wooden handle and lid hinge crudely riveted to the body, had pride of place in the hearth. This was accompanied by a French pewter coffee-maker rescued by Martin from an elderly widow making a fresh start. In the corner, stood Martin's pride and joy – the base of an 18th century tallboy which had been turned into a fashionable writing table; it was made of walnut, and he had spent uncountable hours restoring it with patience, love and lately-acquired skills.

"You like it?" asked Martin.

"Who wouldn't? Where do you find the time?"

"A village policeman's lot is a fairly happy one."

"You like the village, don't you?"

"What do you think? I've put in a lot of work here. They're funny people are Dunburgh people, but do you see any signs of vandalism about the village? Do we have spates of car theft? Know your community, and keep your ear to the ground. That's what policing is about. I'm on duty twenty four hours a day, every day, and I love it. No one ever phones Police House and gets a "no". Right?"

"True enough."

"Remember those yobbos who thought it might be fun to overturn the bus shelter? What did I do? Make out half-a-dozen reports in triplicate and send them to a boot camp? No, no. We needed a children's playground down the Beach. Who built it? Which local businessmen were only too pleased to put up the money? How long did it take to organise from start to finish? And who are the ones who keep an eye on it now they've finished building it? Hmm? Give people a stake in the community and they'll care about it."

Martin's physique matched his style of delivery. He was bullet-headed and wore his hair close-cropped, which emphasised the thick, red neck on the broad muscular shoulders. He was a strong man, and spoke with a glare of blue eyes and a thrust of fist. His eyes were constantly on the move. Tony had never ceased to be amazed at his powers of observation. He had once run marathons and cycled across mountains, but was now a little paunchy. His muscle was slowly being replaced by fat and his keen vegetarianism by a developing fascination for haute cuisine.

"Enjoying the Beaujolais?" asked Martin, "Wonderfully drinkable, even when young – very fruity yet never bitter or tannic, and characterised by an abundance of bubble-gum flavours"

"Undoubtedly", responded Tony.

The conversation drifted on through two bottles of the Beaujolais, some fine French Brie with a warmed baguette, and Martin's account of every piece of furniture in the room – the 18th century mahogany kettle stand, a chest of drawers sadly minus the drawers but beautifully adapted by Martin to house his television and video unit, and three George II walnut dining chairs rescued from the dusty back of a lonely suicide's garage.

Tony finally left, when Amy Billings returned from her WI meeting, and strolled down the hill towards home, passing St George's Church where Mary Brown had been buried that morning.

CHAPTER 4

The rectory family

Corvin Unwood was secure in his study, ostensibly and (at times) actually writing his sermon for the Family Communion Service on Easter Sunday. 'Everything that is done in the world is done by hope.' Why couldn't he have thought of a phrase like that, and sent it ringing round the church? He did not aspire to greatness, but wanted to make his mark. He needed someone to acknowledge that he had made his mark, and to pat him on the back and say "Well done, Corvin" as a schoolmaster might have done when he was a boy, as his mother had done, listening quietly while she baked and he sat in the kitchen, resting his head on the worktop, breathing in the warm scent of freshly-cooked pastry.

He looked up at the picture on the wall, and Martin Luther frowned down upon him. Luther was a priest consumed by his principles. Corvin had found that he could not live in that way. The endless jumble sales raising money to re-carpet the aisle, the marathon smile of Gift Day when he was expected to sit by the lych-gate and receive the beneficence of his parishioners in aid of the soft furnishings – these and more seemed far, far from the urgency of Luther. In a real life there had to be compromises. How else was he to remain open and approachable to his flock? Easter was a time of hope. After the misery of the crucifixion, Mary found her Master once again in the garden: risen, alive – the Light of the World, and worlds to come. That was the message of Easter – the rebirth of hope.

Sitting safely in his study, Corvin could acknowledge a certain amount of self doubt, but not about his faith. He wasn't what the public termed a 'modern priest'. He never doubted the possibility of Christ's resurrection on Easter Sunday, or questioned the wondrous mystery of the Virgin Birth – yet accepted that others, without loss of integrity, might do so; but he did question his ability to be a good priest, and anguished silently about his capacity as the Cure of Souls.

He glanced furtively towards the door – savouring his sanctuary, not wanting to be disturbed – although he knew he was secure from intrusion. One unwritten rule for the wife of a priest was that you did not disturb the writing of his sermons, or alter the position of his books. Corvin reached into the back of a wall cupboard and found a small kettle underneath a pile of vestments. He would make himself a cup of tea, secretly. Corvin opened his study door and peeped out. The kitchen door was ajar, but no one would notice as he crept quietly across the hall and filled his kettle from the cold tap in the toilet underneath the stairs. Back in his study, he took a one-ring gas burner from the bottom of a wardrobe, in which hung his robes, and struck a match.

The tea was good as was the chocolate biscuit he dunked. Corvin felt the drink flow through him and open up his mind, as the taste rose over his palate. He loved ritual. No one knew about the kettle; no one would ever need to know. Esther would only worry, and niggle over the fire risk and the weight he carried round his stomach. Corvin was corpulent; the fat hung round his belly and jowls. Parishioners always offered him tea and biscuits, sometimes tea and cake, sometimes a sherry; it would be discourteous to refuse. A parish priest, who cared for his parish, must expect to carry the weight.

Corvin stepped across to his vestment wardrobe and opened it. He looked into the long mirror, which hung inside the door, at his face with its five o'clock shadow and heavy cheeks, at the dark eyes that stared back at him, at the wide nostrils and fleshy upturn of his nose. Corvin sniffed. He smoothed forward his dark hair – still dark, but thinning. He had combed it forward since his late forties to cover the rising forehead.

He turned back to his sermon on the desk: the re-birth of hope, the re-birth of faith in the village. Secure within the womb of his study, Corvin composed. The room was small and crowded. The large desk was pushed up against one wall and covered with papers, set piles of books and a litter of pens and pencils. Above the desk, bookshelves hung from the wall, their contents balanced precariously. Corvin's own chair was of carved wood. It had been given to him by the local schoolmaster when the old Victorian school closed, and the new one was built. The other two were low easy chairs salvaged from a skip at his previous parish in Hereford. They were pushed away from his desk – one up against his vestment wardrobe, the other against the radiator under the window. The window sill, like every other surface in the study, had momentary things placed upon it: match boxes, pencil rubbers, unused tissues, a paschal candle, the baptism video he used with parents he had never seen at church and a palm cross.

As he wrote, he thought of Hereford and, particularly, of his mother who surrounded him with books. It was Corvin's mother who had first made him aware of the soul, and the spiritual fulfilment of Sunday at the Bethel. Even so, Corvin had not entered the church as a young man. Feeling the need to get a job, he had trained as a joiner and worked on building sites and in furniture factories. It was only after his father's death that Corvin had known his vocation. With his mother's support, he had begun the long process of education and training which brought him to the priesthood, the parish of Dunburgh-on-Sea and, on the way, Esther.

Esther was aware of their age difference, and that she had aged Corvin both in manner and dress. A younger wife entering middle-age with him would have cultivated another image; as it was, his baggy trousers and tweed jackets matched her cardigans and woollen skirts. Esther was white-haired and stooped; the onset of arthritis leant rigidity to her shoulders and slowness to her step. Her mind was sharp, however, and her cold grey eyes keen. The two loves of her life consumed all her energies. God must take his place in line. He would understand. She never questioned her faith or His love for her. She was the daughter of a priest, and the wife of a priest. Faith was always, and ever, second nature. Corvin, arriving in his late twenties when she was past forty and set for spinsterhood, had been her white knight. They married quickly – before his training was complete but while Esther was still able to bear children. When Rebecca was born, no child had ever been more welcome or more precious, and no mother more possessive of her good fortune.

"Is dinner ready, my love?" he asked, walking into the kitchen, later.

"Yes, yes. Don't pressure me, Corvin. You know very well it is. See if Rebecca is ready ... Is your sermon complete?"

"Oh yes – I think so. I may spend a little more time on it later."

Corvin added the proviso in case he should feel like a quiet hour or so after dinner, but it only added to his tone of vacillation and annoyed Esther.

"You must know whether it is finished, Corvin. Don't be so indecisive. You preach very good sermons. The parish is lucky to have a priest who works so hard ... There were no complaints about the absence of flowers in Lent, this year?"

"I wouldn't express it quite like that, my dear."

"In that case, the lesson is well-learned. It was a bad habit they got themselves into. Whoever heard of flowers in Lent?"

Noting the flower ladies desire to continue decorating the church throughout Lent, the previous rector had turned a blind eye. Corvin inherited the tradition – or lack of regard, as Esther saw it – and bore the blistering anger of his wife's tongue.

"The colours chosen were subdued, Esther."

"Subdued or not, flowers are inappropriate in church during Lent. I cannot imagine why you hesitated to stop it at once."

Corvin breathed heavily, recalling the scene when Esther had tackled the ladies on the flower rota; without a word from him, the issue was decided. He helped her carry the serving bowls through to the "bishop's refectory", and he placed the three sets of table mats and cutlery at one end of the long table: serviettes followed, each with its own named silver ring. Corvin bent to open another of the bishop's refinements – the refrigerator in the dining room which was reserved solely for wine. Corvin's palate could think of nothing nicer than a cool, crisp rosé from Coteaux d'Aix-en-Provence at that moment, and he uncorked a bottle. Esther's expression, as she entered, showed the pleasure she felt in seeing her husband asserting his right to open a bottle from the bishop's store.

"Did you sort out, with Penny Read, what the Junior Church is doing?"

"In part, my dear," replied Corvin, sensing Esther's antagonism towards Penny.

"She insists that the children perform at a critical moment in the service?"

"She is not convinced that Clara Gobley will play the right music," Corvin answered, evading the question.

"After the debacle at Christmas, you can hardly blame her. Penny chose well-known hymns for the crib service, and Clara played the wrong tunes," replied Esther, in defence of Penny.

"And insisted on including other hymns that none of the families knew," said Corvin.

"Her argument was that they should have known them – that many of the families only come to the services they choose," continued Esther, in defence of Clara.

"Clara Gobley isn't going to win either hearts or minds. Penny Read will."

It was Rebecca Unwood who spoke from the doorway, having listened to both of them riding two horses in opposite directions.

"You're both as bad as each other. Neither of you like Clara Gobley, but you both hanker after what she represents – tradition: unknown words to unknown tunes. That will show the young families what Christianity is all about – standing speechless in a cold church."

"It isn't as simple as that, Rebecca, and you know it. There is no reason why the church should forsake its traditions to attract bigger congregations. There is something to be said for tradition," said Esther.

Corvin's view of Rebecca was one of bewildered indulgence. His wife loved this, and rebuked him for it. Perhaps if Corvin had taken a firmer line with her, Rebecca would now have been less wilful? Quietly, she took delight in their closeness. Corvin found her his great ally. If the church took a new direction, Rebecca spoke on his behalf, smoothing the ground between himself and his wife. Those innovations that Esther considered "reaching down when we should be expecting people to reach up to the church" – such as open air services on the beach, children singing in church or meetings with the Methodists – Rebecca supported. She thought of them as ways forward to a brighter, more tolerant future "for the church in this place", as Corvin was fond of expressing his responsibilities.

Rebecca scooped the last mouthful of her cheese and lentil gratin onto the piece of crisp green lettuce she had saved for the purpose, and ate it; her mother was a good cook. Her dad had enjoyed the spring chicken. She watched him gnaw at the bones, and chomp mouthfuls of the citrus-flavoured flesh mixed with the purple sprouting broccoli which one of his parishioners dropped off, weekly, in season. It was good to be sitting together, in the evening, as the nights began to draw out.

There was a knock at the door. Each looked at the other, not wanting to move. Esther was irritated because she had made it clear to parishioners at what time they sat down to dinner, and Corvin was suddenly tired because he was comfortable with the food and did not want an emergency. Rebecca walked into the hallway and opened the door. Peter Vishnya stood smiling, apologetically, in the porch.

"If it is inconvenient, I will come back later."

"What makes you think it would be less inconvenient then?"

Rebecca regretted the sharpness of her words the moment they were spoken although nothing in his expression suggested that he was offended, let alone hurt, by her comment. Before she could speak again, her mother, having heard Vishnya's voice, came into the hallway.

"It is not at all inconvenient, Mr Vishnya. Come in, please. We are just finishing dinner."

"Thank you."

He smiled at Rebecca and stepped immediately across the threshold. Rebecca drew back. There was something about Peter Vishnya with which she had never quite felt at ease, although her mother liked him without reservation.

"Come in, come in, Peter. Do join us. Have you eaten? Would you like some dessert? ... How is your son?"

"He is well. Thank you."

Peter Vishnya found himself sitting at the table and another place being laid. He saw Rebecca's quizzical look and Esther's eagerness, as they brought out cutlery, an orange ice sorbet and a wine glass.

"Where is your son?" asked Rebecca.

"He is at home."

"Alone?"

"Oh yes. The children of single parents learn independence, quickly."

"Is he safe, Peter?"

"I think so, or I would not leave him. He is only eight. I know this. But he is a sensible boy – my Yevgeny. And he has Anton."

He spoke the last name with a quick smile and a flash of sound white teeth. Village gossip said that the Anton was a wolf brought over from Siberia; Peter Vishnya did nothing to dispel the rumour.

"If it really is not inconvenient, rector, I have come to ... flesh out? ... my report of the Easter activities in the village for next week's Journal. This is OK?"

There was something too good to be true about the man, for Rebecca. His directness, which bordered on bluntness, she could tolerate: English was, after all, his second language. The respect in which everyone seemed to hold him she could understand: his wife had died tragically and he had brought up their son on his own. His courtesy, which contrasted so sharply with almost all other men she knew, she could accept: foreigners were often like that away from their homeland. The attractiveness of his voice and demeanour she could not deny; it was the contrast which appealed. Each she could comprehend, but the whole seemed a blatant attempt to create an impression.

As they ate, they talked. Esther was pleased that someone listened, without interruption, to her husband as he detailed his plans for a Step Forward Together campaign of evangelism to develop from Easter. Every house in the village was to receive a visit, and all four thousand inhabitants were to be invited to contribute what they could to the church.

"...we need bell ringers as well as worshippers. We must offer a social dimension to the church, a gathering point. The Church Centre itself is an ideal place for a mother and toddler group. Caught not taught is the key, Peter."

Corvin's mind raced on: he felt safe with this man, somehow knew that his words would not be used against him, that a commitment made would be taken in the broadest sense, the detail left to time. Peter Vishnya's eye was kind, and his smile steady. He made notes and read them back when Corvin finished, and Rebecca gathered the plates.

"Coffee, Peter?"

"No. Thank you, Mrs Unwood. I really must go. I have interrupted your meal for long enough. The orange dessert was very good. Thank you."

They sat in silence after he had left, a light spring breeze blowing in through the french doors which Rebecca opened. His visit had lifted their already easy mood, and widened the family. Esther, listening to her husband's plans for summer beach services for the tourists, had not challenged the idea. Rebecca had seen her father open up and speak freely, spilling out ideas at which he had only hinted – the renewal of marriage vows, a Sunday creche, regular work parties caring for the church, going out to the holiday camps, Saturday night barbecues at the Church Centre with hymn singing. "No matter who comes, they will hear us giving witness. They will know we sing for the Lord and in joy." Corvin had barely realised that such ideas existed, brooding upon them in his study, or half suggesting them undercover in church; talking to Peter Vishnya made them all seem possible.

"How did Mr Vishnya's wife die?" asked Rebecca.

"It was before we came to the village. Liz Shaw told me that she was a local girl. She was driving home one night along London Road – at about forty five miles an hour – and the car turned over. It must have hit something – the kerb perhaps – and the car turned over. Peter's wife seemed all right and then, some months afterwards, she collapsed and died of a brain haemorrhage. It seemed too much of a coincidence."

"How did they meet?"

"She was a very able girl," said Corvin. "Studied languages at Camwich and, afterwards, went to Russia where she met Peter. She brought him back and they settled in the village. It was a love match made in heaven, as they say. Tragic."

"And the little boy without a mother," said Esther.

"Yes, my dear."

"How does he look after the child, and make a living?"

"I don't know exactly, Rebecca. He does some translation work for the UEA, I believe, and contributes to technical journals. Electronics?"

Their conversation drifted into the details of someone else's business, but most of their knowledge was based on village gossip. Perhaps he had left Russia for a reason? If he returned, would his son be denied an English passport? All were questions to which they could have no answers.

"How did he get the job with the Journal? I thought Nadine Palmester was the local reporter."

"Nadine is a professional reporter, my dear. Peter just sends in items of possible interest of a small, local nature."

"His wife was a Morling, Rebecca. Her father did the job, and when she died it somehow passed to Peter."

The light faded as they sat quietly building a picture of this man's life, and eventually Corvin left the table to finish his sermon. When they noticed that he had gone, Esther and Rebecca cleared the table and washed up before Rebecca went upstairs to bed.

Rebecca locked the bedroom door quietly; she wanted to be sure there was no chance of being disturbed by her parents. They were very considerate of her privacy, but Rebecca never felt able to be completely alone. She tried the handle, tugged gently on the door, sighed and then stretched her arms sideways and behind. Her back muscles tensed, she flexed her fingers a few times and then let her arms hang loosely.

She walked to the window and looked out at the Old Vicarage through the thin spread of trees. There was a light in one of the windows, and Rebecca watched for any movement across the curtains. The thought of past rectors living there with their families attracted her, but she had only ever wandered about the grounds, finding her way among overgrown shrubs and rank lawns, and looked up at the blank-faced windows; and now it was inhabited by a man who no one had yet seen.

She reached up and opened the small top window. A light breeze entered, cooling her hand. Rebecca drew the curtains, walked to the dressing table, unzipped her dress, placed it carefully on a hanger and slipped it into the wardrobe. She wriggled quickly out of the rest of her clothes, folded them neatly ready for the wash and stood naked in front of the long wardrobe mirror. Her figure was good: her muscles in fine condition. She ran and swam; she worked hard to keep her body lithe and supple. At university she had joined local sports clubs, playing netball, hockey and tennis. She enjoyed the feel of fitness, and of knowing her body was strong and attractive. She was aware that men watched her, and felt both annoyed and pleased.

Vicars' daughters fell into one of two types, she had been told by a boy in the sixth form when she refused his offer of a date. Rebecca had determined, from that insightful moment, to fall into neither category – the 'slut' or the 'professional virgin'. She was twenty-seven, however, and had never really known a man. She had been roused, but casual sex was not for her; she had a belief in its spiritual dimension, and felt that would only come with the right man, in time.

The right man, the right man – and who was he? None of the men at university, who fancied the vicar's daughter, had roused more than her passing interest; there had never been that click in the mind – that moment of certainty. Had her faith attracted, and then scared, them or was it really her unwillingness to yield?

The Russian had disturbed her; she admitted it to herself. Rebecca opened her eyes and looked at her blonde hair, cropped to neck length, which swayed and bobbed when she tossed her head. She looked at the large blue eyes and fresh, glistening cheeks. He had seemed not to notice her – not as a woman, anyway. Peter Vishnya had been married, of course. He had known a woman, loved her and with her brought a child into the world. How must it have been for him to have known a wife – to have gained such a love and then lost it? She liked the Russian but the liking, since he had once been married to another, seemed almost adulterous.

Rebecca stood for a moment more lost in thought, and then glanced over the reflection of her body in the mirror. She felt some shame, acknowledging her desire for this man – but only a little. Real shame was in the act, and not the thought. She had always considered the Lord intended that part of His sermon to be ironic. From the mirror, Rebecca realized that her room was darkening – night was drawing on.

She walked over to her bed and stretched out. It was warm enough, even this early in the year, to lie on the duvet, naked. She reached for a small bottle containing a mixture of the essential oils – clary sage and juniper berry. Placing her right palm flat on her chest, Rebecca began her evening massage. She had learned the art of self-massage at a weekend aromatherapy course, and practised it once or twice a week, after a taxing day at work or when she was … disturbed, ever since.

She moved the whole hand in large clockwise circles. As the oils spread, she brought her other hand into position and began circling with her finger-pads up into her neck and behind the ears. The sweet, sensuous, pervading aroma of the oil made her feel heady, as she brought her right hand down between her breasts and rested it on the solar plexus. With the palm of her left hand, she massaged in large clockwise circles round her navel, starting on the right side of the pubic bone and working up along the abdomen until she reached her other hand, and on down to the starting point. Rebecca repeated this movement many times. She found the aroma of the oils both relaxing and invigorating; they calmed, uplifted and led her into profound, dream-filled sleep.

As the hands moved and the room darkened, a strange and intense silence filled her. The dreams of her sleep opened up into wild mountains. Shadows passed across her eyes and watched her, expecting some movement on her part. Rebecca could not move, but only watch, as the shadows merged and faded. Somewhere, an animal cried in the night, and she heard herself call to it. Her eyes opened, and around her was the soft urgent movement of flesh, gently massaged until it tingled with an almost unbearable softness. She could do nothing but wait.

The room was filled with the sound of her moaning. There was urgency in her feelings now, and a sound she could not quite place, but a sound that was … attentive to her. She felt unnerved, and then frightened. The pale room was full of shadows that gathered about her bed and leaned towards her. A gentle touch flickered across her lips and passed to her throat; the sensitive skin of her neck fluttered. She struggled against the desire and the shadows dispersed – almost, she felt, in fear.

Rebecca sat bolt upright on the bed, running with sweat, and looked around her. She was breathing in rapid gasps, her heart racing, invigorated and yet sleepy. She swung her legs over the edge of the bed and sat looking around the room. It seemed as it had been, with the curtain flapping lightly in the chill March breeze, and yet she was filled with exhilaration and loathing. She touched her throat and let her hand slide through the perspiration that trickled between her breasts and into her navel. Her hot, damp thighs shivered and she ran over to shut the window. The light was still on in the Old Vicarage, but there was no movement in the night. The bare branches of the silver poplars were still and black. She wanted to shower, but felt she could not disturb her parents. She reached for her cotton nightdress and slipped it over her head. Rebecca then sat quietly at her dressing table until her heart stopped pounding and she was calm again.

CHAPTER 5

The Old Vicarage

Crafty Catchpole was the archetypal casual worker, and as well known a figure in the village as the local butcher or the rector. No one was quite sure what he did for a living, but the sight of him pedalling his bike along the village streets was a familiar one. Crafty appeared to work hard looking for work. It had been a butcher's bike, long ago, with a large metal frame at the front to hold the basket the delivery boy used on his rounds. Crafty had acquired it subtly, and without having to pay a penny: a strong-framed black bike with square-set handlebars and solid lever brakes. Astride it, the wind from the sea kept from whistling up his trouser legs by black cycle clips, Crafty toured Dunburgh with a nonchalance more appropriate to a country road in deepest Slovenia. On his face, however, was a fixed expression that gave him the appearance of a man with a mission.

Crafty was a member of the local pigeon club and on race days his bike once again held a basket – only now the meat was alive and eager to fly. It had been a hectic week for Crafty. His birds had begun their pre-flight routine. For four days they had been confined to the loft, except for a precisely timed fifteen minutes daily when Crafty stood outside the loft shaking grain in a tin to call them back. He had added salt to their drinking water, one teaspoon to every quart, and given each a bath outside the loft. On the fourth day, Crafty had placed them lovingly in their basket. Taking a firm hold of each bird's body – with his thumb across the middle of their backs, his fingers and palm around the folded wings and with the pigeon's feet slipped carefully between his first and second fingers – Crafty had held each pigeon close to his chest and whispered, caressingly, into its ear. He had then cycled to the A12 where a lorry driver friend waited in the lay-by on the village by-pass. Only a nod and a note passed between them, as Crafty handed over his birds. They were driven north of Norbridge along the A47 until they reached Honingham where the driver checked the time on his watch, waited until the second hand reached its zenith, held the basket aloft, released the birds, made a telephone call to Crafty and settled down for a swift pint at The Buck.

On what was to be an exceptionally busy day for him, Crafty now rode to the club to leave his precious load for collection and delivery to British Rail, who would take them to their destination, 250 miles away, and liberate the birds. He also took his time clock for it to be set precisely to GMT by the Club Secretary. In his mouth he chewed upon an unlit cigar that he rolled across his lips, occasionally. He had perfected the knack of this, after watching a Clint Eastwood film, by practising in front of his hall mirror until he could move the cigar without dropping it. Crafty was aware of the young teenage lads watching him as he pedalled about the village, and felt that the cigar gave him a certain authority they could not dispute. He wore a peaked cloth cap, which had a piece of braid along the base of the peak, and a dark-blue seaman's jacket. Both these had been inherited from his father who had died many years before; only time and the inevitability of wear would separate Crafty from them.

This, however, was to be only one of his intended errands that day. Having passed a few words with Clive Brown, who was the Club Secretary and responsible for the setting of clocks, Crafty now pedalled hurriedly to the turf accountants to fulfil another of his engagements. Like most of the spasmodically employed in the village, he bet on a regular basis, and much of his quality time was taken up in assessing the form. While his mother had been alive, Crafty's visits to Ladbrokes had been secret, since she did not approve of her only child gambling. Her death leant him a new freedom, however, and he now left his betting slips on the kitchen table with the *Daily Mail* open at the racing page. His system was simple: in each race, Crafty always placed money on the favourite and an outsider with a chance.

His bets placed, Crafty rode on down the hill and along the sea front where the fishing boats were moored. A group of darkly-dressed men, their skins burnt ruddy-brown by the sea winds over many years, stood watching his approach. Twenty-five years previously, Crafty (as a young lad of seventeen) had upset these men, and today's initiative was to be his "second chance" to redeem himself and "put matters right". Crafty had been entrusted with taking out, long-shore, a group of Dutch tourists who wanted to try their hand at fishing. It was to be his way into the closely guarded privileges of the Dunburgh Long-shore Fishermen – a sure way of making money during the summer season. Crafty could not refuse, despite having another job lined up. He had cast off with the tourists and taken them out to the fishing grounds, then stripped off to his underclothes, grabbed a parcel wrapped in oil-skins from under the engine housing and swam to the beach.

Crafty carried bricks and mixed mortar for the bricklayers all day, before returning to the beach and swimming out to the boat. The Dutchmen seemed unperturbed – Crafty had secured the boat and helped set up their lines before leaving – but, when news leaked out on their return, Crafty found no favour with the likes of Jumbo Gooch, Daff Mallet, Scrub Turrell or Boss Wigg. He was barred from their fraternity for the next quarter of a century. Memories hold fast in Dunburgh, and grudges last for a while.

Although disowning him, the long-shore fishermen afforded Crafty a certain respect, however. It was from that moment that his nickname originated. Some said it should have been 'Crazy' and others preferred 'Sly', but 'Crafty' stuck and conferred upon him a certain reputation for deviousness and craft that was not without its benefits. He leaned his bike against the fence of the Fishermen's Hut and, for the first time in twenty five years, walked passed the self-appointed doorman, Butch Strowger, and sat at the long table. A deal was struck. Crafty was again entrusted with looking after tourists and shared a privileged pint in hallowed walls.

In much that drove and bedevilled him, the hand of his dead mother was apparent. He had never married, but lived with her in a small cottage off Sea Row Lane. During her lifetime, it had been scrupulously clean; she had scrubbed everything in sight and, in the end, scrubbed herself to death. She had not considered it right that either Crafty or his father, who died from a lifetime's overdose of blended whisky when Crafty was in his mid-twenties, should be involved in any form of housework. Their job was to find a livelihood, while hers was to keep house. Several weeks after her death, Crafty was still placing his shoes outside her bedroom door each night for cleaning and dropping his clothes into the laundry basket. It was as though he thought the basket possessed some power to wash them, peg them on the line (strung between two flag poles across the garden), iron and fold them, air them and place them in the correct drawer in the little back bedroom, which overlooked the sea and was where he had slept since his birth. When this did not happen, Crafty had sat watching the basket for a long time "seeing his way clear" as to how the dirty clothes might make their way to his chest of drawers.

He was still, three years after her death, attempting to re-discover his mother's routines, and during this time the neat, little cottage had become shabby. Everything still had its place – her soup ladle (now dusty) hung from the Welsh dresser, her pickle jars (now empty) lined the shelves to the left of the deep earthenware sink, her baskets (still containing three year dead flowers) adorned the walls overlooking the lane, china and glassware (dulled by dirty tea-clothes) still lined up in the living room cabinet, the patchwork quilt (plucked in places) covered the armchair she had always used by the open fire in the living room – but disuse touched them all. Even her bedroom, although remaining exactly as she left it from the scrubbed stone floor to the tiny porcelain pig on the window sill, was dulled from lack of use. What the cottage missed was her constant, nagging reminders that doors needed painting or pelmets needed mending, and the relentless scrubbing of her brush.

His personal hygiene, however, remained immaculate. Floors, steps, window sills and fireplaces were not the only objects that Crafty's mother had cleaned scrupulously each week. Crafty himself was included as part of the cottage and habits, inculcated young, die hard. Until his death, Crafty would continue the rituals of nail cutting, hair combing, nit picking (just in case), navel clearing, nose scouring, ear de-waxing, eyeball washing, between-the-toe scraping, teeth gouging and neck scrubbing. Crafty shone, from head to toe, like a new pin; his cheeks, in particular, gleamed like headlamps as he rode through the village.

He now cycled up Church Hill, where a few weeks before Clive Brown had carried his wife's coffin, and stopped at the end of the Old Vicarage drive. It was a long time since Crafty had walked along the drive and even he, devoid of an excess of imagination, paused for a moment. The old house had always felt cut off – much to the old vicar's delight, but much to the unease of the villagers. Gloomy trees overhung the track that was unkempt. Brambles and scraggy grass grew in profusion and straggled their way across the path and, always, something tugged at your legs. It was a bright April morning, however, and the gloom of the walk was broken by sunshine spattering through the leaves on to the track. Crafty glanced briefly behind him and cycled across the road along the unmade pathway. Once on the track, he kept his head down and cycled for the light beyond the tunnel of beech trees, but when he reached it a cloud covered the sun and the Old Vicarage was shrouded in shade.

Crafty looked at the short flight of steps leading up to the terrace in front of the house; the remnants of last year's 'star-kissed' spread dryly over them. The stone urns on the buttresses were bare except for old, yellow moss. Crafty placed his cycle carefully against the wall and, stepping cautiously in case any of the paving slabs were loose, walked up the steps. The terrace had once been divided symmetrically by flower beds surrounded by low, neat privet hedges in the Italian style, but these were now overgrown or dying for lack of water and care. He looked around, and then up at the facade of the Old Vicarage. It was the uniform flatness which he noticed first – the four windows on either side of the porched doorway, each complete with sash windows set back from the wall face – and then the wood-panelled doorway with its plain pediment arching the stained glass skylight.

Crafty noticed that the front door was partly open and, having glanced quickly over his shoulder to check that he was not being observed, he walked between the beds of dying privets and up to the door. He reached out his hand to push it, cautiously. As he did so, Crafty noticed what appeared to be the figure of an old man at the end of the hallway. The figure was tall with rounded shoulders and was dressed in a dull grey tweed jacket and grey flannels. The face was arrogant and thoughtful; the raised eyebrows suggested an unassuming contempt. As he watched, the figure – which had shown no sign of noticing Crafty – turned and disappeared into the shadows. As it faded from view, a voice from behind Crafty spoke.

"Curiosity killed the cat. Is that not one of your country's colloquialisms?"

The speaker took Crafty by surprise; a few moments before he was sure that no one had been near him. He whirled round and fell backwards, hitting himself against the elegant column of the porch. For a time he dare not look up, but eventually forced his eyes open and lifted his head, half expecting to see the figure from the hall; but the man who stood over him was quite different. A hand stretched out and gripped his arm. Even through the thick blue wool of his seaman's jacket, Crafty felt a chill as the fingers tightened and lifted him from the ground.

"You need not be startled. Perhaps it is I who should wonder what you are doing almost in my hallway."

The single assurance that he was looking for work would have sufficed to remove the threat of the question, but Crafty had never sought work in so direct a manner for fear of an immediate refusal. The old habit of "warming his prospects up" would not desert him. He could find nothing to say, and stood staring at the speaker, feeling a terror he did not understand.

The man appeared to be in his late fifties or early sixties, and Crafty noticed that his eyes seemed to be yellow or light brown, and so faded that they had become sear as an autumn leaf. There were no lashes, and the lids were reddened like those of an albino rat. They were very steady eyes, and the mind behind them looked straight into Crafty and turned his thoughts over as he struggled to find the words to speak. The man's nose was rather long, but finely shaped; it was what Crafty's mother had called a Roman nose. The face was pale and tinged with a greyness that was emphasised by the silvery hair. When Crafty stood in silence, the man smiled and ran his fingers over lips almost as pale as the face. From the look of the tendons in the neck, Crafty judged that the rest of the man's body would be lean, with old muscles, to the point of gauntness.

"I'd heard from the pub that you'd come," he blurted.

"Gossip, like the dead, travels fast?"

He spoke slowly and chuckled at his reference, but Crafty (who was not a reader) saw no humour either in the comment or the laugh. He only wished to step beyond the man so that he could find space to explain, but he dare not without the man's permission. Crafty looked helplessly beyond the face and the yellow eyes. A large cloud was passing from over the sun. The man strode by Crafty into his hallway, and Crafty ran forward as far as the ruined flowerbeds.

"These need seeing to ... I can garden. This could look something, given the chance."

"You will be given your chance. Return tomorrow in the morning – early."

The door was closed, the sun shone down and Crafty breathed in deeply as it warmed his back.

"Catchpole – that's my name – Crafty Catchpole."

He turned from the door and hurried to the steps. Before him, he could see the copse of sycamore, elm and hawthorn on the slope that led down to the new rectory. The copse was overgrown with brambles, holly and nettles. It seemed to form an impenetrable barrier between the two houses – the rectories of yesterday and today. The new rectory was visible between the branches of the spring trees. If he worked fast, he could clear them before the summer leaves came. Already, rooks were busy nesting in the elms whose long branches, still black from winter, waved against the blue of the sky.

Crafty sat quietly at the long table in the Hut, his fingers clenched over a pint of beer, gnawing at his thumb.

"Why, you look as though you seed a ghost, Crafty."

"Ay, thas what it feels loike."

"Where you bin?"

"Up at the Old Vicarage."

"Why – what you bin doin' there?"

"Wouldn't you like to know!"

"Be like that then."

Scrub Turrel, who had questioned him, took a swig of his beer and sucked in as he licked the foam from his lips. Another regular, Harry Bailey, looked up and cast a thoughtful, narrowed eye in Crafty's direction. Harry worked full-time as a bricklayer for Mark Chambers. His right to membership of the Hut had been inherited through his father-in-law and his usefulness: Harry spent much of every weekend building walls and extensions for friends. Clive Brown, also sitting quietly at the table, caught Harry's look.

"You bin there, Harry?" he asked.

"Aye," replied Harry.

"I thought as much. I heard you'd bin there with Mark."

"Ah."

"What does Mark Chambers want with the Old Vicarage then?" asked Crafty.

"Ah, wouldn't you like to know, Crafty Catchpole."

"I only asked."

"And I only told yer," retorted Harry.

"The new owner – that foreign gent with the funny name – wants some work done. Mark were up there lookin' things over," said Clive Brown.

"He took Mark and me all over," cut in Harry, eager not to be upstaged by Clive Brown, "I int sin a house like that for years. They don't make 'em like that anymore. Mind you, it gave me the creeps goin' round the place with him, but he knew his houses did ... whatever his name is. Not that he were anything but polite. Met us at the front door with a smile of his white teeth, then stood aside and told us to enter freely. When yew go in through the front door, the stairway's right ahead – with a narrow hallway goin' by it to the kitchen. Lovely owd stairs – goin' ter be a joy doin' them up. Cut-string stair, see, with plain slender balusters and panelled spandrels."

"Lot o' work involved int there?" queried Scrub.

"Oh yeah. Mark weren't sure at first. Said it were a bit beyond the firm, like. Said we didn't go in for restoration. But this bloke, he seemed to know more 'an Mark. He said he'd heard Mark's son were up to the job. Knew he'd studied architecture at university and knew his architrave from his cornice, like ... We went in the front parlour. Lovely old open fireplace with a hob grate and a surround of dark, shiny marble and one of them deep mantle-pieces fer all the clocks and vases they had in them days ... and the winders, phew. I reckon there's nuthin' lovelier than a good old sash winder. They were a work of art them sash winders. Bordered sashes they call 'em. The shutters went up an' down like the windows ..."

"Vertical sliding shutters ..."

"Thas what I said, Froggy – they went up and down ... He showed Mark the winders. Said he wanted them restored jest as they were – no double glazing, nuthin' modern. He took us all round – dinin' room, back parlour, kitchen ... funny thing in the kitchen – he wouldn't talk about havin' a modern cooker. Said he wanted it jest as it were – built up to take the coal range, and with the bread oven restored. Said it wouldn't be an inconvenience to him, food wasn't one of his indulgences. He spoke like that all the time ...We went upstairs ter the bedrooms, then - four of 'em. Big place. The old vicar used ter use one of them fer his study. I remember goin' there once. Cold old place except where the fires were ... but this bloke don't seem to mind the cold. He didn't want no radiators, anywhere. Said he'd be takin' his guests back in time, and laughed."

"Was there any furniture, Harry? Where'd yew sit?" asked Scrub.

"We didn't. He kept us on the move. But there was furniture all covered with dust sheets in the middle of the rooms. No beds though. One room hadn't got no furniture, moind yer. The back parlour was full of pictures. It were funny that. Them pictures were all covered in dust sheets – only one bit were turned up, see, sort of caught over the top, and under it were a Monet."

"A Monet?" interrupted Froggy, "What a real one?"

"It were one of them he painted at La Grenouillere – only, as I say, I'd never seen it before."

"Well, why should yer?"

"'cause the missis went to evenin' classes, dint she? I sin her try to paint that, and she dint half get in a ross, I can tell yew, tryin' to get it roight. We went up to London, see, to hev a look at it – only this one, that this foreign bloke had got, were different. It were his *Bathing at La Grenouillere* only sort of more detailed, the surface smoother to look at. The brightly lit bit in the top part of the canvas hed a more varied range of colours than the one they've got in London. The distant sky had a far more luminous quality. Monet was obsessed with what he called his "envelope" – the idea that an object is surrounded by its own light. Well, in the picture in the Old Vicarage the river is filled with bathers each enveloped in their own light. I didn't see no more. The new bloke turned in the hallway and saw me looking at the painting through the door so I had to go. He aint the sort of bloke yew ignore ..."

"He's a wealthy bloke, then," said Crafty.

"He'd need to be to own a Monet no one else has ever seen. Yew'd need a long reach ter get somethun like that."

Crafty sat, head in hands, at his kitchen table. He had much to think about. Cycling to the Old Vicarage that morning, he had seen only the chance of some work; but now his new employer offered fresh prospects. The man was rich and strange and knew pictures. He struck terror into you without realising it. He had power. Crafty was convinced of that. Here was a man who lived his own way – as he wished. Here was a man who had the village talking about him, and doing for him. Here was a man who made others act, but there was a weakness here – a dependence, a need. To be powerful you needed others. Crafty saw himself going between the village and the newcomer – controlling: all of them needing him. His power lay in their need.

Anger grew within him towards Harry Bailey and the others who had already begun to move into the Old Vicarage – planning and changing without him. Their knowledge was their power. Mark Chambers and his men knew about Victorian houses, Harry and Froggy knew about Monet, Scrub Turrel knew nothing and kept quiet. Be circumspect (he wasn't sure where he'd come across that word, but it sounded cautious) – watch, listen, and wait. Your time will come. Crafty felt better within himself. He looked up at a flap of wings beyond the kitchen. A bell rang. His grille-trap had opened, and he rushed from the room. Every second counted: the ring had to be off the bird's leg and into the recording clock without delay.

Early next morning, Crafty – having scrubbed himself clean – arrived at the Old Vicarage, ready for work, only to find the house shut tight and apparently deserted. His knock brought no reply, and he seized the chance to make his way to the rear of the house. He found a wrought iron gate, in the garden wall, which was stuck partly open. He slipped through the gap. The wall of the house to his right faced south, and was covered with ivy and lichen. A neglected kitchen garden stretched towards the rear of the house. Crafty made his way along the footpath which edged this, and turned into a backyard overlooked by the kitchen windows. He peered through the dusty glass and was disappointed to see a common enough electric cooker, presumably used by the old rector.

Crafty's hands went instinctively to the sash window, and it slid easily upwards. He had not expected this; he had wanted to look all round the house, but without gaining access. He pulled down the window, tried the backdoor and was relieved to find it locked. He knocked loudly, but the house remained silent and he moved to the outhouses built across the yard from the kitchen. Here, he might legitimately expect to find gardening tools.

Inside the first was a brick-built copper heated by coal, smelling still of hard soap and washing. A drying rack was still pulled up to the ceiling. Inside the second, which he took to have been an outside toilet, were a few simple tools. Both outhouses had whitewashed inner walls, long since left to the spiders and the grime of the years. Crafty turned, walked across the yard and peered through the window of the back parlour. Just as Harry had said, stacks of something were covered with sheets. He made his way round the side of the house without trying the back parlour window. Crafty had the feeling that it would open. At the corner of the north wall he turned and looked back at the outhouses. It suddenly occurred to him that it would be a good thing to be seen to be doing something. Crafty selected a Dutch hoe from among the tools, and wandered on to the terrace.

As he did so, a Range Rover turned in from the shrouded driveway and parked untidily in front of the house. He recognised the driver as the old man in the tweed jacket who had disappeared into the shadows of the main hallway yesterday, and he recognised the old man – it was Lord Wangford. The baronet clambered out of the vehicle accompanied by two young Labradors, which immediately lolloped up the steps and made for Crafty. They barked noisily and inanely in the way that Labradors do, all sound and fury, and then crouched for their heads to be scratched between the ears. The baronet must have seen Crafty, but ignored him completely. He walked to the back of the Range Rover and opened the door.

"Har, you. Give me a hand, har."

The voice was aristocratic and dismissive – a voice used to being obeyed. It was a moment before Crafty realised it was him to whom Lord Wangford spoke.

He heard a frenzied yapping, and a Jack Russell rushed from the open doors and lunged at his feet – snarling and piping, its fur on end, its tail erect and its ears bristling. The little dog scattered the Labradors and proceeded to yap and dive at Crafty's feet. The old man ignored this, and continued to struggle with something in the back of the Range Rover.

"I come fer the job o' gard'ner. Spoke to the other gent yesdee. Said I was to come early. I'm Crafty Catchpole."

The old man pulled at some rope and threw a tarpaulin back. Apparently oblivious to what Crafty had said, he called again.

"I said over har. Take one end of this davenport."

As a casual worker Crafty was honed to obedience, but reluctant to heed such a summons. A man has his dignity, and is not on call to every posh voice that demands his help without first acknowledging his presence. Besides, the terrier had worked itself into a frenzy and was now courageous enough to be plucking away at the thick woollen socks hanging from the top of Crafty's half-length Wellington boots. The agitated Labradors had joined the melee – more from enjoyment of the noise than with any intent to harm or damage, but Crafty deemed his wisest move was to stand still.

"Crafty? More by name than by nature I trust, Mr Catchpole?"

The voice spoke from the doorway and the man's yellow eyes fixed themselves upon the terrier's back. The dog's tail dropped, its ears fell and a whine emanated from the throat. The Labradors flopped over and rolled on to their backs at his feet.

"Give Lord Wangford a hand with the davenport, Mr Catchpole."

Crafty placed the hoe against the wall and scurried over to the old man. As Crafty took one end of the writing desk, Lord Wangford looked down at him. His stoop was matched by tiredness in his eyes – a tiredness that indicated a desire to be done and be elsewhere.

"Be careful, Catchpole. It would be better to crush yourself against the wall than to damage Herr Brultzner's desk."

There was ruthlessness in his tone, and fear.

"You have done well, Wangford. I did not expect to find such a piece quite so readily. The legs are made in the solid from walnut, and they are shaped – not turned. Aahh – and the back is finished!"

As he spoke and ran his long fingers over the legs of the desk, Crafty and Lord Wangford struggled to carry it up the steps to the terrace. Crafty, though small in stature, was used to manual work. His muscles were hard and well-used and he knew the knack of lifting heavy weights, but Wangford puffed and sweated in the cold spring air. The weight of the desk on his stretched arms pulled his loosening fingers apart. He staggered as they reached the top, and his knees bent to catch the falling desk. Brultzner reached out and took the weight. Wangford sagged backwards, and Brultzner nodded at him to help Crafty who had placed himself at the upper end of the lift where the weight was less. In this way, they managed to carry the davenport into the Old Vicarage and up the stairs to a room on the first floor.

"You have not seen my house, Mr Catchpole? Come."

It was a tour of love. Brultzner had a passion for the house that kindled in Crafty a realisation of his own love for the cottage of his parents off Sea Row Lane.

"You will have noticed how the windows on the stairwell make the best use of the available light, Mr Catchpole. We now go below stairs, which is lit only by the light able to pass through the grid in the yard above."

Crafty found himself in a basement hallway, which ran between four rooms. One of these turned out to be the original kitchen complete with coal range and bread oven; another, judging from the cold slabs, had been a scullery and a third, which had no natural light at all, had been the coal cellar. Brultzner opened the fourth door, briefly, and Crafty saw rows of wine racks pushed to one side.

"Your last rector enjoyed his wine, Mr Catchpole. He kept a fine cellar."

On some of the racks Crafty could see rows of dusty bottles, their corks in place. After the Old Vicarage had been closed, not even the most reckless youth had approached the place.

"You are already under the spell of my house, Mr Catchpole. Good."

All idea of turning the situation to his advantage had – at least, momentarily – left Crafty. Standing with Brultzner in the basement of his home was a fearful ordeal. Crafty was rendered powerless by the man's enthusiasm, and the chill of standing next to him in such a confined space as the basement hallway. At one end, steps led to the yard above where the outside stairwell was surrounded by spiked railings. Cobwebs hung everywhere, covered with grit and coal dust. In the webs, old spiders lounged, waiting for Crafty knew not what; would any insect venture here, willingly?

"I shall transform the old house, Mr Catchpole. Renovations, I am told by Marshall and Willox, fall into three categories – the mausoleum, the mimic and the modernist. I have no time for the latter two. Dunburgh Old Vicarage shall become a mausoleum, restored to its rightful time. For you, Mr Catchpole, history is the past times of other people. For me, it is ever present. I remember each time as though it were yesterday. It is many years since I was here, but the memories for me are good."

It only increased Crafty's fear to be taken into this man's confidence in such a way. Brultzner had told him things that could not be repeated if only because he did not fully understand them. He did not fear for his life, but for his freedom.

When he had shown Crafty round the house, Brultzner led him to the back door of the house and out into the yard.

"You will find me a good master, Mr Catchpole. You are to retain your present lifestyle, seeking work where it is to be found. You will be my eyes in the village. I shall use your knowledge as I need it. At sunset each day, you will report to the house – here."

"I am not to garden, sir?"

"Indeed you are, Mr Catchpole, when it has been restored to what it once was. You yourself have already noticed the Italianate terrace. When I have finished there will be statuary, serpentine paths, a pond, beds for plants, a rockery, a herb garden, topiary … even a monkey tree, Mr Catchpole. Over this you will have dominion, but first it must be re-created. Long work left to one pair of hands."

"I know a landscape gardener, sir."

"In such knowledge lies your usefulness. Be sure Mr Dix reports to me tomorrow, and I will discuss with him what needs to be done."

Before leaving, Crafty replaced the hoe in the outhouse.

That evening he sat in his living room, brooding. He was to have dominion over the garden. Away from the power of Brultzner's presence, Crafty began to see his way still clearer towards further masteries. He had noticed the immediate fear of the dogs when Brultzner first spoke. He had been aware that the man knew things about the village outside his immediate experience. Brultzner had knowledge and power. Knowledge was power. Brultzner trusted him. He had shown him round the house – further round than even Harry Bailey. Crafty was to be his eyes in the village. Brultzner would come to depend on him as the transformation of the house progressed. Animals! Brultzner had power over animals. Crafty thought of his pigeons racing home against all odds. Where had Brultzner gained his strength and speed? Crafty had never seen a man lift such a heavy piece of furniture so easily or move so quickly about the house.

CHAPTER 6

The Jolly Sailors

The Jolly Sailors stood on a small rise at the southern end of the village, where the marsh met the sea. Between these two, the rough-edged Beach Road made its way towards the holiday camps before petering out amongst the dunes and, finally, disappearing amongst the small, saltwater lakes of Blacksands Ness. The public house still served the remnants of its traditional fishing community, but these men were now spliced with holidaymakers and young men from the upper village. The soft, steady trundling of Suffolk voices jostled for recognition amongst a know-it-all London twang and a Midland sing-song during the summer.

The public house was an unattractive, Victorian building that had been gutted in the 1980s. The inside now consisted of one large room, remarkable for its lack of cosiness, and a side room boasting a pool table and two one-armed bandits. Pushed into a corner, face to the wall, was an un-tuned piano that had once provided nightly entertainment under the hands of John Barker, leader of St George's bell-ringers, but was now deemed "old-fashioned".

The locals had secured a small back room – containing a dart-board and sets of cards and dominoes – with a side bar of its own. Technically, this room was open to all; in reality, no one ever entered except local people and, even then, no one under the age of thirty. A separate door gave access to this room, but holidaymakers, young locals and those new to the village (anyone who had not been known there for at least a generation) never made the mistake of using it twice. It took someone of amazing insensitivity to face-out the room of blank stares, which followed the opening of the door by a stranger. Those who had the temerity to enter were greeted with an harmonious chorus of "other door".

It is not to be supposed that local Dunburgh men are unfriendly. They used the Jolly Sailors all year round, and had a right to their comforts over those who used it for two weeks a year during an annual holiday. A traditional village pub had been invaded and gutted for commercial reasons and in the name of modernity; let them who wanted those things enjoy them where they might.

Standing, as it did, on a small rise, the Jolly Sailors was caught between the cold winds of the north and east (which blew furiously across the North Sea from Russia and Europe) and the warm, wet winds of the south, which rotted the woodwork during late summer and autumn. The views, however, were fine. The long line of the beach stretched south to the River Cassyn. Between the pub and the river, the beach was mainly pebbles. Long-shore fishing boats were scattered about, apparently at random; rusted and derelict winches lined the top of the beach by the sea wall, interspersed with dilapidated sheds. The river wound a twisting path across the marshes to a number of small salty lakes.

The Seaview Cafe, which successfully served homemade snacks and Sunday lunch to holidaymakers in season and to locals all year, stood just below the pub at the point that took Beach Road away from the village and out towards the marsh.

The marsh was accessible from both sides, but was impassable. Ditches of cold, brown water criss-crossed and looped it; thick stems of coarse, stagnant grasses sprouted from the soggy soil; mothers held their children tightly as they passed along the sides of the dykes. In winter, the winds swept low over the marsh to the church on the hill; in summer, a faint miasma (reminiscent of urine) rose from the marsh and permeated the village on those hot salty days when the wind blew from the south or south-west. Those young men of the village who had belonged to Ticker Tyler's scout group were said to possess knowledge of a secret route across but this information, if it existed at all, had never been put at the disposal of their families.

Dunburgh had once been the most important harbour on the East Anglian coast. The Romans used the estuary, and it had been one of the northern naval bases of the Count of the Saxon Shore. The Vikings had found – according to Peter Vishnya's researches – a 'snug winter harbour' in the area. At the time of the Conquest the fisherman of 'Portu de Dunburgh' paid an annual rent of 22,000 herrings a year to their Norman lords. Throughout its history, the village had attracted invaders; the Romans had been obliged to guard it against the marauding Saxons and, following the retreat of the legions, successive hordes of plunderers had ravished the coast. The 'richest village in England', its estuary now silted up, had once possessed a harbour, which offered a haven for sailing ships. The only reminder, now, of such a time was when winter seas broke over the shore, threatening to batter their way inland and bury the vast expanse of marsh twenty feet beneath them.

It must be said that none of these thoughts were crossing the mind of Plumptious Walters as she polished the glasses and gazed out of the kitchen window. Plumptious was all that a landlady should be; it was worth asking her to pull a pint – especially in summer when a little bead of sweat would run down into the deep valley of her breasts. Plumptious was attractive in a way not then fashionable in the magazines, but this hardly mattered since her attractions were perennial, and she was blessed with knowing this. Apart from the low-cut dresses and blouses – which revealed her full, firm cleavage to perfection – Plumptious had a ready smile and what men like to call "bedroom eyes". Her skin was fresh, and her dark hair was rich and full; any extra weight she carried, from time to time, was neither here nor there.

She and her husband, Benny, were the latest of several recent tenants placed in 'the Sailors' since the death of a long standing original who had run the local without profit for most of a lifetime. Plumptious and Benny came with experience, however. They had stamped their identity on the local brewery by creating a bustling one room pub based upon home-cooked food, log fires and bar-side banter to suit all customers from tired Friday night teachers to bristling weekend bikers. Plumptious rallied the kitchen and Benny smoothed the bar, moving with ease among customers he did not remember, assuring them all that it was "nice to see you again". Benny always presented the menu with an opening gesture of the hands and an interest and aplomb which left no doubt who was the landlord with the culinary credentials. Plumptious and he were a superb team and they both knew and appreciated the fact; she would appear when the last meals had been served, and make herself as pleasant with the customers as Benny – circulating easily, a ready smile for one and all.

The sound of raised voices attracted her attention, and Plumptious walked through from the kitchen to find Shane Marjoram, his face a mixture of anger and sexual smirking, leaning across the bar. Plumptious glanced at her daughter, who stood facing Marjoram with her right hand on the Adnams bitter pump, and smiled.

"All right, Kate. Leave this to me ... Out."

"Ah, come on Plumptious ..."

"Don't Plumptious me, Shane Marjoram. I'm not to be plumptioused by the likes of you. Out."

"You're a pub ... Mrs Walters. You're supposed ..."

"I'm neither Plumptious – to you – nor a pub."

"You're supposed ..."

"What I am, or am not, supposed to do is neither here nor there. I'm not doing it for you. You know the way to the door."

"You're supposed ..."

"You're still supposing are you? I thought you'd left."

"What's a pub for if it don't serve drinks to thirsty customers."

"You're neither thirsty nor a customer."

"You're glad enough of my custom through the winter."

"Don't confuse my serving you with my being glad of your custom."

"What you got against me?"

"Fortunately – nothing!"

Shane laughed at that; he was not used to being refused, and mistook her dismissal for provocation.

"Bet you wish you had though – hey?"

Plumptious feigned consideration for a moment and then said:

"No ... no, I can't say I do."

He laughed again: not believing her, in his self-assurance.

"Go home to that nice little wife of yours ... How is Sarah?"

"What? ... She's all right."

"Still grieving, I expect?"

"Well it's natural init. She's all right though. She'll get over it. She's a good un, my Sarah. Bit of all right."

"Well, you want to see that you look after her properly."

"No harm in a drink."

"You don't need a drink, Shane. You need to get home."

Plumptious lifted the bar and walked passed him to the door, which she opened. Her demeanour was quiet now; she wanted him on the road. It was a chill, April evening and a sharp breeze blew off the sea. Shane slouched passed her and out. He scowled, and then smirked over his shoulder; he needed to believe that all women wanted him. Having Plumptious on the run made up for her refusing him a drink; he'd make trouble when he was ready.

She watched him assume a swagger and strut off along the road in the direction of the church. Plumptious felt sorry for Sarah. She was a bright girl who could have made something of herself. One moment can change your whole life – in the club, and up the aisle with the likes of Shane Marjoram. Her thoughts turned to the evening. Benny was out, and soon she'd be behind the bar welcoming her Thursday night regulars.

Yammer Utting was the first, making his way towards some Dutch courage ready for the Parochial Church Council meeting. A short, stocky man bursting with leathery muscle, Yammer always wore the jacket of an old suit (the trousers having long since gone on the crotch) that was now far too tight, and a Norbridge supporter's bobble hat. His face was ruddy with drink and a generalised anger for which he needed a focus.

"Evening, Yammer."

Not feeling the need to answer, he turned through the private door and sat down at the plain, scrubbed table in the back room. Plumptious appeared in the bar and drew him off a double brandy, which she presented on a tray. She hovered about in case Yammer burst into a tirade of abuse – about the state of the allotments, or Lowestoft Council's plans to extend house building into the area of outstanding natural beauty, or anything that might occur to him – but tonight he was evidently saving himself. Yammer sat in silence, watching the brandy warm in the glass.   Scrub Turrel walked in and waited, while Plumptious poured him a pint of Adnams bitter, before he walked to the table, collecting a set of dominoes on the way, and sat opposite Yammer. The two men watched their drinks in silence, while Plumptious observed them. She wondered, idly, how they would react to the plans she and Benny had for turning 'the Sailors' into an out-of-town restaurant specialising in traditional local cuisine. They may have been brought up on duck and green peas, Suffolk dumplings and Suffolk raisin roly-poly, but they were going to be less than amused watching other people packing out the pub to eat it.

As Plumptious smiled to herself, Deaf Charlie and Boiler Brown entered through the private door, gave her a nod and sat opposite each other across the dominoes table. Yammer's hands automatically opened the box as she pulled two more pints, and the shuffling had begun before she reached the table with the beer.

"Froggy coming?" said Scrub, after the game had settled down.

"After the PCC meetun."

"He all right, now?"

"He's gettin' over it. He's still got Sarah and her boy."

"Aint quite like a wife, though, is it?"

"I s'pose not."

"He goes round there a lot, though, for Sunday lunch and so on."

"Froggy misses his wife – he aint likely to get over her in five minutes."

Deaf Charlie looked sharply at Boiler as he spoke, and marked up another three on the board. Boiler was a pot-bellied man who obviously enjoyed his food; winter or summer, Boiler seethed with steam, and his face and arms glowed red in the cold or the heat. He breathed heavily and snorted through his nostrils during moments of anxiety. He rapped the table and said "pass". Yammer laid his last domino.

John Barker entered the pub at that moment and gave Plumptious a quick, habitually nervous smile as he went to the bar for his pint.

"Evenin' John. Yew goin ter the meetun?" asked Yammer.

"No. I'm not on the PCC."

"Thought you'd be interested."

"Why's that, Yammer?"

"They're votin ter give Clara Gobley a stipend fer playin' the organ."

"That right, now?"

"What do you think o' that, then?"

"What should I think of it?"

"Well, did they pay yew when yew were organist?"

"I can't say as I noticed they did, no."

"Right then. Aint right is it?"

John Barker smiled his quick smile, refusing to be drawn. Gossip in the bell tower had told him that Clara Gobley was out to secure payment for playing the organ, which had always been considered a privilege – even a duty – but never looked upon as work. John could not consider any payment to be right, and relied upon Corvin Unwood to see that it did not happen. What he was not prepared to do was to have anything he might say in a public house reach the rector's ears by way of village tittle-tattle.

"You do what you think right, Yammer," he said, "but don't you do it for me."

Yammer Utting banged down his brandy glass and left the room. The door closed decisively behind him and John Barker, with another nod to check his welcome, took Yammer's place at the dominoes table.

Clive Brown walked, with Sidney Close, passed his wife's grave, through the lych-gate and on to Church Hill. Clive had no wish to linger in company at such a spot, but Sidney felt obliged to make a comment of conciliation.

"Mary's grave is looking nice, Clive."

"Aye, thanks, Sidney – we try and keep it looking something, me and Sarah."

Clive sniffed as he spoke the name, and his heart lingered in a moment of pride and pleasure. He and Sarah had been ever closer since Mary's death; his greater dependency upon her enhancing the tenderness he had always felt for his daughter. He watched her carefully now, attending to details that before had gone unnoticed: the way she stooped to lift the Sunday joint from the oven, the way she held young Matthew high, her hand on a door latch, the folding back of bed sheets. He saw Mary in her movements, of course – alive and well, and a force in the world.

"That son-in-law of yours is a good worker, Clive."

Sidney was not quite sure why he mentioned Shane's name at that moment – to gauge Clive's reaction, provoke some gossip, or because he wanted him to know that things were all right?

"So they tell me. We must be grateful for small mercies."

"It's no small thing to have a job, these days. Let alone do it well."

"No, you're right there. He's always been a worker ..."

The two men had reached the allotment gate next to the old Beach School, by this time. It was now dark, and the bells were ringing down their weekly practice peals. Both men had lived their lives in the village under the sound of the Thursday bells. They paused for a moment to listen.

"Oive never understood why people in the village grumble about them bells," said Clive. "If you cun tell me a nicer sound then that, oi'd loike ter know what it is."

"It's the newcomers. Londoners don't have any appreciation of village traditions. Some of them have actually complained, you know. They reckon it spoils their enjoyment of the television."

The new moon was still young, and the light from Froggy's old rubber torch – reflecting, greenly, the allotment gate – was all they had to see each other's faces.

"What did you think of the meeting, then, Clive?"

"Howd you mean?"

"Clara Gobley getting that payment."

"I s'pose the rector knows what he's doin'."

"You don't think he should have stood up to her?"

"I didn't notice anybody else standin' up to her, Sidney – no one."

"It doesn't strike you as right, though, does it?"

"It were our decision, Sidney – not the rectors. We must back it."

The two men walked on towards the Bethel. Sidney, as a local businessman, had taken the role of treasurer on the PCC, and it was a role he guarded jealously. As the annual re-election approached, he would begin to stress the difficulty of the work – how time-consuming it was and what responsibility there was in balancing the books – but he always, reluctantly, accepted the post "just once more".

"Mavis all right?"

"Yes thanks, Froggy."

They drew level with Sidney's house. He pictured Mavis in her brushed nylon dressing-gown, working at her embroidery, waiting for the front door to click before she rose to make him a cup of tea. Sidney's parents had come to Suffolk when he was a child, and lived in nearby Eastwold. His father had been a Methodist preacher, but when Sidney was drawn to Mavis he was drawn to Dunburgh and to St George's church. Within him, there was a conflict between the clear-cut doctrines of his father and the broader-based beliefs of Anglicanism. The teachings of the Bible left no shadow of doubt, but (at the same time, it seemed) were open to interpretation. Sidney's dilemmas usually assumed a moral perspective; his denunciations possessed a religious sheen.

"I'm jest goin fer a pint, Sid," said Clive, more out of politeness than from any expectation that Sidney would join him. Sidney's lips tightened and he sniffed down his nose. He enjoyed a beer himself but there was a time and place for drinking, and after a Church Council meeting did not fit the bill.

"I don't think so, Clive. I shall be glad to get to bed."

"As you like. Goodnight, Sid."

"Goodnight", said Sidney, as he crossed the road towards his front door and a cup of Mavis' tea. She would sit on one side of the old fire-place, now occupied by an electric heater, and he on the other. Sidney would listen politely to the happenings of her day, and she to the outcomes of Clara Gobley's bid for payment.

As he made his way to the Jolly Sailors, Clive looked across at Sarah's house. A light shone from the latticed window of the old fisherman's cottage she had turned into a home, and the curtains were drawn back. He thought that he would just pop in when he left the pub.

As Clive passed by, Sarah was enjoying a quiet moment. It had, in the end, been a good evening – salvaged from the defeat of Shane's arrival from the pub after Plumptious had sent him packing.

"Do you know what? That bitch-fuck wouldn't serve me a drink."

"Quiet, Shane. Not in front of the boy."

"He can't hear. He can't know."

"He will, though, Shane, he will, one day he will. Do you want him speaking like that? Do you want your son speaking like that?"

"She hadn't no right. No fucking …"

"Shane."

"Don't you start, Sarah. Don't you … start."

Sarah knew that he would have left Plumptious with a smile on his face. The landlady of the Jolly Sailors never had a problem ridding her pub of drunks. In less than a quarter of a mile, his mood had turned, and it was frightening. There would be doors to kick in, and bottles to smash. She would watch the body she had loved – his fit, lean, taut body, over whose muscles she had run and stroked her fingers – twisting and threatening as it uncoiled and unleashed its anger. She did not fear him. He had never touched her in anger. Sarah feared his temper unbridled in the world.

"You've had enough, Shane. You don't need any more. Plumptious was right. Settle by the fire. I'll bring you something nice."

Shane had not settled. He had roared from the house, slamming the door as he went. Sarah knew that he would return, chastened, with his anger spent. She had seen it all before. She was tired, and Matthew was ready for bed. It was a nice time to come – a time to indulge herself. She turned to her son, lifted him from the floor and took him up to his room.

Sarah loved her son's bedroom. Quickly pregnant and quickly married, she – and Shane – had bought the house, and renovated it together. In every sense, it had been a labour of love, and they had started with her child's room. Her initial worries about the cramped look of the low-sloping roof had gone, when Shane suggested the pretty printed border that had given the room definition and added a splash of pattern to the plain and uneven old walls. Together, they had chosen the soft pastel colours. Matthew's bedroom had a wonderfully warm, "cottagey" feel. Facing slightly south-west, it just caught the last rays of the dying sun which spilled across the floor each evening. Sarah relished that moment when she walked into the light and fondled her child on the Pooh Bear rug. Through the lace curtains, the sun dappled over them both, bathing each in the same warmth. She had washed him there, powdering him as her mother had powdered her, breathing in the smell of the talc and the soft freshness of his body. Her nose burrowed into his chest and he giggled, and the tiny hands reached up and pulled her hair gently.

She cuddled him into the cot, or rocked with him in the chair brought for her by Shane. Draped with her old-fashioned night dress, the chair looked perfect. The gentle curves of its frame had been lovingly restored by her husband. Sarah wriggled her feet into the carpet, rocking Matthew gently backwards and forwards on her lap until he dozed into sleep and she rested him for the night. Her eyes swept the room. She noted the picture of herself as a baby on the wall between the flowers and the cot, and almost closed the door. She would listen at the bottom of the stairs, leaving the door into the living room open.

Sarah was grateful that they had never been poor. The dark, rather pokey little cottage had been opened up by them – both learning the tricks of the trade as they went along. She passed briefly into the kitchen to make herself a cup of tea to hold by the fire. They had panelled the kitchen to cover the bumps on the walls and make the low ceiling appear higher. Shane and her father had polished the vertical panels of tongue-and-groove to show off the natural grain of the wood. It was the one moment when the two had come (grudgingly on her father's part) together, and given Sarah hope for her future. The panelling reached shoulder height, and was finished with a narrow shelf upon which Sarah displayed her collection of china plates that picked up the blue of the gingham table cloth. Sarah loved gingham – especially blue gingham. She had fond memories of herself at school, fresh and cool on hot summer days, running from her mother's hand across the playing field, the blue dress lifting and flapping against her thighs. The coolness of the kitchen did not, however, invite her tonight. She made for the living room and the fire.

Sarah sat by the fireplace on a low stool and curled her legs to one side. They had pulled out the old fifties tiled surround, and built one of arched rustic bricks. It was topped with a wooden mantle-piece on which she arranged a Napoleon clock of her mothers, a brass hotel bell, several large brass cartridge cases her grandfather had brought back from the war, photographs of her and Shane, and of Matthew and of all three. Within the fireplace, she had persuaded Shane to build two niches – for a small copper kettle, which belonged to her grandmother, and her father's glue pot. They had argued about the niches. She had taken him to the edge, knowing full well that he would give in to her wishes. They had enjoyed the cut and thrust of giving in, one to the other.

Sarah looked into the flames. A last fire to take them through the chill of spring on the east coast, and then she would put an arrangement of fresh flowers in the fireplace, just as her mother had always done in summer. It was only just over a month since they had dug the grave. In some ways it seemed to be of another time. Sarah had walked Matthew along the paths taken by her and her mother over the years. The white, drooping flowers of the snowdrops, which grew in the copses and thin woods bordering the marsh, had almost disappeared before her mother was cold in the earth. The bluebells were profuse along the shady banks of the higher paths leading to the church, and now the daffodils danced everywhere – in hedgerows and gardens, along the roadsides, clustered under trees – bringing a splash of colour to worn grass. That very afternoon she had walked passed the church and down to the marshland paths. In the damp meadows and beside the dykes, she saw marsh marigolds with their smooth shiny leaves and beautiful yellow-golden flowers.

Sarah looked into the fire and tried to read their futures in the red flickering flames, white ash and charred wood of the logs. She knew that her mother had not liked Shane, but possessed the wisdom to hold her tongue and support the marriage. Mary had always spoken up for Sarah's husband, and Shane had responded warmly. Now that Mary had gone, Sarah was without this support, alone in creating a place for Shane within the family in the face of her father's antagonism and Shane's temper. Marriage had quietened Shane, but only just: there had been his drunkenness at her mother's funeral, and numerous scuffles at various pubs. The police knew him, and Martin Billings had once indicated to her that he was only a phone call away if Shane became violent. "It's all right, PC Billings. My Shane wouldn't lay a hand on me."

It was always difficult standing up to him. She knew that if she once crossed him, if she once let a dislike set in between them, all was over. Shane would never pull himself round. He needed her, and he needed her trust; she must never let him lose that because, then, there would be no telling what he might do. Sarah heard the usual click of the latch as she pondered the flames, and looked up as Shane came, sideways, through the front door. He went into the kitchen, without speaking, and called out:

"Do you want a coffee, Sare?"

"Please. My tea's cold."

Sarah knew that he would bring in the coffees and a biscuit and sit by her feet, waiting for her to forgive him. It was his way, and nowhere near as submissive as the picture it painted. His body would be tense and the muscles ready for retaliation – not that she feared a blow, but Sarah hated his anger. Yet, one word from her – the right word – and his violence was spent. While he waited for the kettle to boil, Sarah heard him go up the stairs to look at Matthew.

"Is he all right?"

"Yeah. The little devil's sound asleep. He bin down long?"

"A while. He's no trouble."

They sat in silence for a while, and he slid his hand behind her calves and up between her thighs, easing them apart. His head, which had been resting on Sarah's knees, slid along her inner thigh where it lodged. Gently, Shane kissed her knee cap and ran his tongue around it, while his free hand stroked the shin of her right leg and eased its way along the smooth join of bone and muscle.

"You've got nice legs, Sarah."

"Thanks very much."

"Are we going to have another baby?"

"What made you ask that?"

"I just wondered."

"I want one, but not just yet. Not now mum's gone. It doesn't seem right. It's too soon. She was always wondering if we were thinking about it. She'd have liked a little granddaughter. Oh Shane, I'm so sad when I think of her. One minute you're laughing about something or other, and the next it overcomes you. I can't get used to it. I don't know quite where I'm going without her. It's like walking into the night not knowing what you're going to meet. I can't see my way clear sometimes."

"Come on, Sarah, cheer up. Your mum wouldn't have wanted you to mope. She wasn't like that."

"No, but I am. I need to grieve, Shane. I can't always be thinking of others."

They sat again in silence and Shane withdrew his hand from her thigh, but continued stroking her leg with his thumb.

"I could get on with your dad, Sarah, if only he'd let me."

"I know. I don't blame you for that, Shane. Dad's stubborn. He always has been. He used to drive mum mad sometimes ... You tired?"

"Yeah – a bit."

"Go up then, Shane. I'll be with you in a minute. I'll just lock up. Just give me a minute on my own."

"OK. All right then."

Suddenly perky, Shane leapt to his feet and made for the stairs door, while Sarah collected their cups together and took them to the kitchen. She reached for the key from the small herb cupboard, and locked the back door. She bolted it, and checked the windows. She positioned the fireguard, and went to the front door, opening it on to Beach Road. 'Living on a knife edge.' The phrase came to her, and she shook it off. 'No, not really.' Once she had control again – once she was over her mother's death – things would come together. Sarah glanced along the road and saw the figure of a man making his way home from the Jolly Sailors. He was short and stocky with his legs bowed at the knees. Sarah smiled to herself. There was a reassurance in the continuity of life – however the omens might look at the time.

"Dad?"

57

"Hello, Sarah. I weren't guner disturb you. Thought you might be in bed."

Clive Brown closed the gate behind him and clicked the lock. A game of dominoes had held him until Plumptious almost threw them out. The sky had now cleared of cloud, and they could see the new moon quite distinctly.

"St George's Day parade on Sunday. I always like to see the lads in their uniforms," he said.

"Dad ... I thought we might go out for a drive afterwards ... or even out to a pub for lunch."

"Where to? ... Why?"

"I thought it might make a change, that's all. We could go down to Eastwold and walk along the front. Sit Matthew on the guns. It would be nice. We could go after church. I'll book it up."

"Shane coming to church?"

"I hope so. He was in the scouts for a while."

" 'til they threw him out."

"Now, Dad, that's not helpful. It's in the past. We've got to go forward as a family, now – together – or we're going to break up. And you've got to help. I can't do it all. It's up to Shane and you as well."

Mary had spoken to him like that when he grumbled about his son-in-law. Clive was old enough to understand what his daughter was saying. The funeral had been a watershed, and he had behaved badly. Shane ought to have been allowed to help with the coffin, but he just couldn't bear the thought of that lout's hands near Mary. With his wife gone, though, they had lost their mediator. Sarah was right; she sounded like her mother. There was no one, now, to hide his anger behind. It was up to him.

"OK, Sarah, it sounds a good idea to me."

They kissed goodnight, and Clive squeezed the hand he loved most in the world. It must have been a good evening because things were beginning to turn. Sarah felt hope in her heart and power pass through her – the power of women down the generations: home and hearth, holding life together.

CHAPTER 7

Crafty Catchpole makes a proposal

Crafty Catchpole was nervous. Caught between his fear of the woman and his greed for what he supposed she could do for him, he had three times approached the house and three times turned away. Now, he stood once more on the pavement, opposite where she lived, and dithered, moving awkwardly from leg to leg. His expectations won, and he crossed the road onto Clara Gobley's driveway. Crafty had thought his way to this moment, ever since he began to see his way clear to dipping into the knowledge and power he fancied Herr Brultzner possessed.

The front door was slightly ajar, and Crafty pushed it open as he tapped. A flood of cats poured through the gap. They trampled his feet, shoved between his legs and spat in all directions, as they made their escape from the house. Crafty watched them disappear into the overgrown grass of the driveway banks, through the unkempt hedges on either side, out into the road and down to the beach, or scuttle through the neighbouring gardens towards the church. Some were lumpily fat, others old and decrepit: all were tangled and scruffy. They hissed and meowed their way from each other. As they departed the house, an odour followed them; it was a dense smell, deeply imbued with stale air, cats' urine, rancid food, faeces unplaceable and English breakfast tea. Crafty gagged and turned his head away from the house to catch a breath of fresher air from the passing cats.

Clara Gobley's bungalow stood alone in a road of mainly Victorian houses, which were bought only by those who could afford the cost of renovation. Alone among them, Clara's bungalow resembled a compost heap, 'half-hidden from the eye'. Whichever weed was prevalent in any particular year could be seen at her fence. The careless growth of shrub and tree shrouded her home from the road and the view of passers-by. Its southern outlook was lost on Clara, and the house crouched, gloomy and forsaken, like a toad sheltering from the sun on a summer's day.

Crafty waited a moment – wondering whether he had done wrong in releasing the cats, however inadvertently – and then turned to the door. Clara was watching him through the gap. When he saw her face, the witch stories of the village children filled his mind; in every community, one old woman becomes the local witch – the terror who inspires 'dares'. Staring into her eyes, Crafty knew why Clara was the witch of Dunburgh. Her eyes peered at him like those of a hawk – unblinking, piercing and making him feel like a field mouse, which glances up a moment too late.

"My cats don't seem to like you, Mr Catchpole. They have all run away."

"The door was ajar. They jest came out."

Clara continued to stare at him, making him feel like a little boy who was about to wet his trousers but deems it an inappropriate moment to ask for the toilet.

"Oi've cum ter make a proposal."

The unblinking stare did not flicker for a moment and the eyes remained expressionless. If Clara saw any humour in his bald statement her face betrayed none.

"Oi'm seein' moi way clear."

She shot a ferocious glance across his shoulder, and scanned the narrow span of Church Hill visible through her shrubs and weeds.

"Come in, Mr Catchpole, and find yourself a seat."

The invitation to take the weight off his legs could have been made in jest – or so it seemed to Crafty as he walked into Clara's living room. The first thing that caught his attention was the carrion crow on the television set, and the second was the pile of excrement the bird had deposited upon the table beneath. His gaze hung upon the bird. But for the stench rising from the faeces, Crafty might have been driven to believe that the whole thing – bird, television and droppings – was some form of modernist sculpture. So transfixed was he, Crafty could only nod when Clara said:

"Would you like a cup of tea? I don't keep coffee in the house."

Eventually, his gaze traversed the room. His own house was cluttered, but Crafty had never seen anything like Clara's lounge. He could not help noticing the piles of newspapers and magazines bulging from under chairs and settees, the trails of flex and leads across the floor and walls, calendars still hanging years out of date, the wartime Marconi radio standing in the corner (a faint murmur coming from its Home Service station), the hard-backed volumes sealed with dust littering the bookshelves, a jumble of copper saucepans, a cobblers last, three standard lamps pushed behind the door, the coal-box without a handle, a chest freezer humming against the far wall, the pile of 78s perched in the apple basket, the wrought-iron candlestick propped against the gramophone or the tub of grey washing on the 1950s slide-leaf table. These, and numerous other pieces, simply formed a backdrop to the activities of the livestock.

Two white rats ran up and down the sloping candlestick, making their way to the gramophone cupboard where they sniffed for a while before running down to the dark recesses of the settee. They were ignored by the several cats, still remaining in the house, who lounged with a detachment approaching boredom across chairs, rolls of carpet, bookcases and the laundry basket. In a large cage, which hung low from the ceiling in the far corner of the room, was a black bird Crafty took to be a jackdaw; it was clearly the worse for wear, and one wing seemed to have been splinted and bandaged. It watched Crafty, lop-sidedly. He clambered through an arrangement of chairs, all of which were home to a pile of some sort, and, not fancying the settee, made his way towards the table where one chair seemed clear of obstacles. Under the table, two hedgehogs lapped milk from a saucer and ran in and out of the assortment of legs.

When Clara emerged from the kitchen, she did not carry a tray of tea as he had expected. She had a bell in one hand, and a black-headed gull in the other. The bell was ringing, as she placed it on the table.

"I found him on the beach this morning, Mr Catchpole. Where does the oil come from, that's what I'd like to know? If the government has banned the swilling out of tanks at sea – and are enforcing their own laws – where is the oil coming from?"

"Oi can't say as I roightly know. It's a puzzle."

"It's no puzzle! These oil companies are just ignoring the regulations set up to control their nefarious activities. We have a government pumping out legislation, which they haven't got the backbone to enforce. That's what's happening! And the church does nothing about it."

She picked up the bell, paused, replaced the bell on the table and said:

"Mr Catchpole, would you pull the rope in the corner, please – behind that little door."

Crafty struggled across the room, making his way between two wartime arm chairs, and pushed at a door that opened on to a narrow, spiral, stone stairway. An old piece of hemp rope hung down through a hole in the ceiling. As he tugged upon the rope, a single dull clanging sounded across the garden.

"They were going to throw the bell away when they tore down the old school, but I wouldn't allow that. It had been in the village over a hundred years. The church showed not the slightest interest until they thought that there was money to be made, and then they had the audacity to ask how much I was prepared to pay for the privilege of saving it from the vandals. So we had the turret room built to house it."

Everyone in the village knew of Clara's turret room; there are not many bungalows with a circular turret adjoining their north western corner, particularly not with a single bell tower at the top. It was, in part, the turret room which had brought Crafty to her door. Rumour had it that Clara used her small room to keep an eye on the village.

As she spoke, Clara had been gently sponging detergent from the feathers of the gull. Her grip on the bird was irresistible, and it made no attempt to struggle. Her hands were soft, and the strength insidious rather than muscular. They were the hands of a musician.

"What is your proposal, Mr Catchpole? Are you offering to sing tenor in the choir? We are desperately short of good tenors. You read music, of course?"

"Oive never roightly seen my way clear to singing. It ain't something that comes natural loike. I int what you'd call moosical. I int never had toime fer that sort of thing. Oi might be able ter clean the organ, if that would be of any help."

Clara scarcely listened to his answer. Her mind, never still for a moment, drifted from his mention of the organ to her own problems in playing one.

"It's the feet, Mr Catchpole – they never touch the ground. If they are not in use, one tucks them back – otherwise they hover over the pedals. Can you imagine how that feels at my age? One must balance the body, so that it does not fall forward, with the legs swinging from side to side. Try that, Mr Catchpole, while at the same time allowing your arms to hang relaxed and vertical from your shoulders."

Crafty felt obliged to do so – under Clara's stare – and found himself rocking backwards and forwards on the dining chair; it was a pleasant enough sensation.

"Here, tuck these cushions under your seat, and sit up straight. Flex your right elbow at ninety degrees and place your hand, palm down, on the table. Now, reach forward without allowing your forearms to touch the table. Can you feel your body pivot? You need to focus on your navel, Mr Catchpole. Your navel, not your stomach, is the centre of your body."

Crafty sat transfixed, his limbs gradually tightening.

"Relax, Mr Catchpole, and drop the shoulders – we don't want those muscles tightening – and do not poke your head forward. Shrug a little, and relax the trapeziums. It's a dynamic muscle, Mr Catchpole. It cannot maintain a state of contraction for long periods without fatigue."

While Crafty sat in this position, a man entered from the kitchen. This was Bert, who was Clara's companion. Resting along his right forearm, he held a fox cub. In his left hand he held a baby's bottle, the teat dripping milk.

"You rang, Clara?"

An Anglican organist living unmarried with a man would normally have drawn unfavourable comment in Dunburbgh (even as the twentieth century neared its end), but such gossip had never plagued Clara and Bert. He stood with her in St George's as he stood now at the table – slightly stooped, apparently deferential, and waiting for her to speak. Bert was not conventionally attractive. His nose was pudgy and his face flat. He was as bald as a coot, and with the side hair greased against his head. The small, rather fleshy, mouth had a top lip which was always puckering against the bottom one. His shoulders were rounded. He wore an old short-sleeved pullover, and shoes of cracked leather.

"Would you make a pot of tea for Mr Catchpole, Bert?"

"Certainly, my love. What would you prefer, Crafty – Earl Grey, Lapsong Souchong, Chamomile or Mixed Herb? Our herb tea contains, mint, lavender, marigolds, rose petals and orange peal. Or would you prefer Assam, Orange Pekoe or English Breakfast?"

"Oi'm not rightly inter tea. Oi'll hev what you're hevin'."

Bert disappeared into the kitchen.

"Can you manage with that cub, Bert," asked Clara.

"Certainly, my love. You have enough to do holding the gull."

However, despite his assurance, Bert soon called from the kitchen and Crafty, relieved to be released from his position at the organ, went to offer his help. Bert, who had placed the feeding bottle on top of a vegetable slice balanced on a biscuit tin, was trying to extricate a cup and saucer from underneath a bread board. Secured by the steadiness of the board was a mixing bowl, an Agatha Christie novel, a half-empty beer mug containing an assortment of knives, a loaf of hard bread, a plastic cutting board balanced between the bowl and the edge of the knives, two unwashed dinner plates and a butter dish. Unfortunately, the fox was wriggling.

Eventually, after much searching for cups deemed suitable for a guest and some more thumb-cleaning by Bert under running water, a pot of tea was produced and brought to the table.

"You won't join us, Bert?"

"No, my love."

As Bert left with the fox, Clara turned again to Crafty.

"Perhaps you would care to share your proposal, Mr Catchpole?"

"Oi aint sure how to put this so you must listen. Oi aint one with the words and Oi'm seein' my way clear. Oi've come with a proposal and Oi don't see the end of it, but Oi reckon you might. It's about the new owner of the Old Vicarage. He's got a way with animals, and he needs watchun'."

Clara was an intelligent and educated woman, and she realised that Crafty must approach what he had to say in his own way. She remained silent, as he spoke.

"Oi'm the gardener at the Old Vicarage and Oi've seen things. The new owner – Oi haven't quite got his name yet – has a way with him. Oi've seen him quieten dogs at a glance, and Oi've seen him call birds to him. One night he was in the garden. It was after dark. Oi think he thought Oi'd gone hoom, but I was down in the copse. He began to howl, jest like a wolf. He came and sat in the middle of the lawn and howled. You ain't heard nothing loike it. And them timber wolves down on the wildlife park they answered. It set every dog in the village a-going. Oi daren't move, Oi can tell you.

But that aint nothin to what Oi hev sin. We hed rats in the old basement, and I got the traps from Totto Briggs. I hed them at the top of the back steps that lead down into the basement, and I was goin' ter bait them. They don't get out of them traps once they're in, I can tell yer. Anyhow, the guv'nor appears. He's like that – one minute you're alone and the next he's standin' behind yer. And he says "What are you doing, Mr Catchpole?" Always very polite he is. So I told him. "Ah, yes." he says, "I suppose they must go." He seemed reluctant to do anything about them. I couldn't understand that. I don't know no-one who loikes rats ... anyway, he stood there behind me and then he knelt down by the cage and began to whistle – not a toon. It's hard to describe what it sounded loike, more a sort of wailin' sound. It went up and down, on and on. I thought I was going crazy, and then the rats began to come out and he didn't budge, jest knelt there beside the cage and held open the door and they walked in, cage after cage of 'em. They crawled straight inter the traps, jest loike that. No bait, nuthin'. And when the cages were full he dropped the doors, one by one. I aint never sin so many rats. And then he stopped whistling, and they stopped comin' and he said "I think we have a full house, Mr Catchpole. We shall present our visiting card on another occasion." And then he walked away."

"And you got rid of the rats?"

"Oh no. He walks slowly when he's thinkin', and he walked jest loike a panther to the corner of the house and then turned his head – jest his head – and said

"Leave our friends where they are, Mr Catchpole. I shall find them other quarters tonight." I never see 'em again, and there were never any more rats in the cellar. No droppin's, nuthin'."

Clara watched Crafty after he had finished speaking, reading his face. She began to see what he had in mind and why he had approached her with a proposal that, at the best, could only be described as gauche and, at the worst, gormless. Nevertheless, she asked the question:

"I can see how that might help you, Mr Catchpole – knowing your hobby – but how would it help me?"

"Well, I don't rightly know, but I thought you might."

"And you want Bert and me to watch Herr Brultzner from the turret room to learn his secrets and pass them on?"

"I can see things in the day. It's at night he needs watching. I'll take my turn."

Clara was fascinated and appalled by Crafty's scheme and his treachery. She could not imagine anyone working for her, while betraying her at the same time. She was a verbally abusive and irascible woman, but she had her principles. She decided to float a few ideas of her own.

"I'll be in touch, Crafty. I'm not entirely happy with your idea. You have finished your tea? Good. I shall ask Bert's advice. Bert is good at these things. He will know best what to do."

Before he realised what had happened, Crafty found himself at the front door and outside amongst the bindweed and cats' urine. It was noon and 'the Sailors' was open. Feeling vaguely dissatisfied, he lit a cheroot and strutted away towards the beach. As he walked, Crafty heard Clara's bell ringing.

Clara hurriedly told Bert what had happened.

"Does it matter what I think, my angel?"

"I wouldn't ask if it didn't."

"Oh you would, you would. Testing out your ideas on me is one of your little idiosyncrasies, my love."

"But you will watch with me? … Crafty Catchpole is a sly, natural villager. He would turn anything to his own needs. If this man has powers we can tap, it will be to help animals, not make pigeons fly home faster."

CHAPTER 8

Horst Brultzner takes a walk

It was an overcast morning in early May when Horst Brultzner took his first walk round the village. He did not favour bright, sunny weather and April that year had been just that - bright and blustery and rattled by rain – but today the forecast was good with little possibility of showers, and no chance of the sun shining through the thick layer of stratus cloud that hung, like a shroud, over Dunburgh. He was in a good humour; the night before had been fulfilling and he felt refreshed and invigorated. Mark Chambers's men were on schedule and his house was beginning to take the shape he wanted. Crafty Catchpole had proved a shrewd investment: what he did not know about the village he found out and (despite an instinctive idleness which Brultzner had, anyway, expected from Englishmen) he could be persuaded to work hard, long and fast. After so many years in the East – though Leipzig had its attractions – he felt the breezes of freedom around him. There was a truth, anyway, in the English saying 'There's no place like home'. Dunburgh had its limitations, its drawbacks, its irritating small-mindedness, but here he had come into being so long, long ago and Brultzner felt a sense of belonging and of comfort.

He had dressed with care, for this first walk, in a light summer suit cut in the style known as French Colonial. It was a good suit, made for him many years before in Paris, and Brultzner was very fond of it. Over his left arm he carried a furled, black umbrella. His shoes were leather – soft brogues in a beautiful shade of cream; no one could have found such a pair these days. Brultzner looked after his clothes.

He strolled casually towards the church, and paused at the foot of the short flight of steps which led directly into the graveyard. He was tempted to cross the road, but resisted this and made his way gracefully up the rough, uneven pathway into the churchyard. Brultzner looked up at the east window of St George's. The stained-glass window above the altar carried the figures of notable European royals, the Blessed Virgin and Child, and St Francis of Assisi. Brultzner – who had, at times, lived among more wolves than any living man was ever likely to see – found the story of Francis and the wolf, fascinating. He shared none of the modern views of such Christian stories. He was not caught up in acts of interpretation, or wound round with symbolism. He saw clearly the saint's hand calming the crazed beast, and heard the unearthly voice speak soothingly into its ear.

He passed on, and was tempted to make his way into the old graveyard, which was unkempt and unloved. He sought among the dilapidated headstones and eventually found what he was looking for – the tombstone of a young man whose death was dated 1897; on it was the inscription 'Death is the path to life'. Brultzner cleared away the coarse grass and weeds. With a mighty effort, he straightened the large slab and heeled it firm. He knew he should not have come; when such memories were stirred, his mood would turn with a suddenness that he now found frightening. He had killed as necessary in his time; not all of them had been cowards.

The mood passed as quickly as it had come upon him; there would be time to find out those things he might wish to know. Brultzner walked round the church and paused by Mary Brown's grave. The fresh stone told him that it was a recent burial. He leaned forward, and saw that she had been a woman of only fifty four. Death – he had often relished the idea and yet restrained his hand; eternity had its attractions as long as the mind stayed active. Brultzner decided that he could not have known Mary Brown, and passed on through the lych-gate.

He made his way to the butcher's shop in the High Street. Totto Briggs was well-known for the quality of his fresh meat and home-made produce. Brultzner paused outside, noting for a few minutes the women who stood gossiping at the counter, and then pushed open the door and strode in. The bell rang and the women looked up. Brultzner bowed slightly and bid them "good morning" before saying:

"I have come to see Mr Briggs."

"Be with you in a moment, squire. Make yourself comfortable."

The sarcasm was intended – unless the butchery assistant (a young man from London who had recently joined the family firm) imagined that Brultzner could find a relaxing spot among the pig carcases hanging from hooks at the back of the shop – but Brultzner was beyond offence. Stepping across the saw-dusted floor, he moved quickly behind the butcher and into the slaughter-house. His speed was such that the man had no time to speak, and stood opened-mouthed in the act of wrapping some kidneys.

Totto Briggs looked up as he entered.

"We have business to conduct, Mr Briggs. I am holding a luncheon at the Old Vicarage in early June. You have been recommended to me. I understand that your hams have no equal in Suffolk, that your pork pies give new meaning to the word succulent, and your sausages boast spices unknown in other butchery circles ... These, however, I do not want."

Before Brultzner finished speaking, Totto's assistant burst in – wrapped kidneys in one hand and trussing string in the other. Totto gestured that he should say nothing, and nodded him out. He smelt business.

"Well ... if you don't like our succulent pork pies, our home-baked hams or our spicy beef sausages – how can we help you, Mr ...?"

"Brultzner, Horst Brultzner."

"Ah yes – Herr Brultzner. The Reverend Unwood spoke of you."

"I have not yet had the pleasure of meeting your rector."

"You will. He visits everyone. Corvin is a good man."

"He does not 'spare the leather'?"

"Right … how can I help you?"

"I wish for cold meats. Boeuf en daube – you will use dripping and only German wine for the casserole. Topside – not brisket. Yes?"

"You'll need a good-sized piece if it's to be really tender … and I always cook it in a light, French red."

"German white – a dry white. The cattle are local?"

"Oh yes … you can rely on the freshness of the beef."

"Good. We shall also have shoulder of lamb a la Turque … You smile, Mr Briggs? You have never eaten lamb a la Turque, cold? Garnished with chutney and, dare I say, prunes? Delicious. Pork Alsacienne – again with a dry German white, and the English Bramley. We shall serve hot, buttered potatoes with this. And then one of your specialities – glazed baked gammon."

"The juniper berries are not optional?" said Totto, anticipating that his new customer had done his homework.

"Indeed not," replied Horst Brultzner, with a smile. "Pressed tongue? Give it a full five hours, Mr Briggs, and test near the root with your skewer. Finally – game pie."

"With hot-water crust pastry, port wine and jellied beef stock?"

Both men smiled as Totto rattled off the ingredients; no stranger was going to advise him in his own slaughter house.

"I can see I am in excellent hands, Mr Briggs."

"Who told you about the juniper berries?"

"You are a family business and go back many generations. I had friends dining upon your grandfather's cold meats long before you were born, Mr Briggs … In those days your family provided the Harvest Supper."

"We still do. I remember my granddad well – even though I was a boy."

"Of course. The meats for my luncheon are in the very best of hands."

While they spoke, neither man had taken his eyes from the other. Both were oblivious to the work of the abattoir around them. Totto stretched his open hand towards Brultzner, once it was clear to both that their deal was agreed, and drew partly back at the touch of a thin, soft glove.

"You will excuse my not removing the glove, Mr Briggs. I suffer from the cold of your climate at this time of year."

His voice was assured, but his manner embarrassed; it was an awkwardness he had never overcome. Horst Brultzner held his own discourtesy in contempt, but he could not risk the cold of his hand against the butcher's flesh. He turned quickly to look around the room.

"It is many years since I was in a slaughter-house. What is it your man holds?"

"An humane killer, they call it. It drives a bolt into the animal. Death is instantaneous. We have used them for many years. It's not new."

A cow had been driven into the killing stall, its body harnessed ready for lifting and butchering. One of Brigg's men held the stun gun ready.

"But how is this better than the pole-axe? A single blow and the creature dies – as instantaneous as death can ever be."

"That's not the way the public sees it. They like their meat killed painlessly. Axes are messy things. You can miss with an axe."

"You have missed, Mr Briggs?"

"Not often," said Totto, and shrugged.

"You keep the one on the wall only decoratively?"

"Old times sake. The law forbids their use nowadays."

"Really."

Brultzner removed his thin, silk gloves and placed them carefully in his pocket. He removed his coat and handed it to Totto with a slight bow.

"If you would be so kind? Thank you."

He took the pole-axe from the hooks on the wall, and balanced it in his hands. The weight between head and shaft was well designed. He swung it gently through the air, and enjoyed the sensation of the smooth wood running across his right palm. He was aware of Totto's eyes upon him, and felt the sense of ancestry in his hands. Brultzner turned the head of the pole-axe, spun it through his fingers, felt the body-weight secure on his right leg and stepped neatly round and forwards with his left, so that the toes pointed towards the cow. He swung the axe up, over his head and down in a single sweep.

Talking about it afterwards, Totto and his men all commented upon the beauty of the movement: a smooth, single turn, full of grace, almost balletic in its controlled power. His right hand guided and his left provided the strength; at the height of the arc Brultzner's body was fully stretched. His muscles were superbly poised under the light summer clothes and, at the last moment, his hands and the muscles of both arms became taught. The spike caught the cow, superbly, in the spine; the wound was well placed, neat and perfect. The animal died as it stood. In a simple gesture, Brultzner handed the axe to Totto, took his jacket, bowed and left the slaughter-house. No-one spoke for some while after he had departed.

Brultzner turned right from the slaughter-house and made his way to the High Street. On the other side of the road, a man left the hairdressing salon. His curiosity aroused, Brultzner paused and watched. He had a problem with his own hair, which fluctuated between slight and full, and he could see – through the pseudo-Victorian windows – three young women moving between customers. He crossed the quiet High Street and walked in through the door. Another bell rang and the three women looked up, greeting him with a collective "hello". He enquired whether they cut men's hair and the girls laughed and said "oh many". Horst Brultzner made an appointment.

All three were blonde – one unnaturally so, which did not appeal to Brultzner – but the youngest, who must have been in her teens, had a head of the most beautiful hair he had seen for many years. It was thick and long, shining with health and youth and he desired, at least, to run his fingers through the lush blondeness and have the weight of it fall on his palms. The girl's skin was completely without make-up. She had what the English call 'a peaches and cream' complexion – unblemished, flawless, perfect. Brultzner smiled at her as she handed him the appointment card, and he noticed the soft fluttering of her neck where the pulse beat steadily. He would bring her gloves to wear when she touched his scalp, explaining that he had a "condition" that made his skin cold, and therefore unpleasant, to the touch. In a few years, the bloom would be gone. There was no way in which such beauty could be preserved: the semblance of it, yes, but not the essence.

He made his way along the High Street and turned into School Road. He saw that the old school had now gone, replaced by more houses, but noted with pleasure the village police station where Crafty had told him it would be. Brultzner made his way to the office attached to the side of the house and knocked with the handle of his umbrella. A woman in her late thirties or early forties opened the front door of the main house and called to him.

"Martin is out in the village. What can I do for you?"

"Mrs Billings? I am Horst Brultzner from the Old Vicarage. I hoped to seek your husband's advice upon security for the building."

"Right. I'll give him a call on the mobile. Go in. The door is open. I won't keep you a moment."

Martin Billing's office had a warmth about it – a comfort. Brultzner ran his fingers along the edge of the mahogany desk and glanced at the clock on the wall, as Amy Billings came in through the connecting door.

"Martin won't be long. He's down at the beach. Welcome to Dunburgh. How are you settling in?"

"I have been here little over a month only. I do not go out much in the daytime. The sun is not good for my skin. I am hoping the Old Vicarage will provide me with a retreat from the world."

"Don't retreat too far – you're still a young man. I'm sorry not to invite you into the house, but Martin insists that business is conducted in the office."

"Quite rightly so, Mr Billings. It is a comfortable room. Your husband has a flair for interior decoration."

Amy laughed, lifting her head back and tossing waves of tight, dark brown hair.

"Martin has a flair for being awkward. He doesn't like being told what to do. For a policeman that is not good news. They tried to change his desk for a metal one and he sent it back ... or rather he sent it on. Nobody knows where it ended up, but Martin couldn't see any point in throwing this one out ... Can I get you a coffee, while you're waiting?"

"No, no, I drink little."

"Well, at least take a seat."

Brultzner sat on the leather padded chair across from Martin's desk and Amy walked to the french windows which opened, behind the desk, into the garden. He allowed his eyes to wander round the room. Against the wall to his left stood a large cupboard and on the wall to his right a small pendulum clock of the sort seen in the classrooms of village schools. Over the mantle-piece was a picture of the Queen in Coronation regalia; the fireplace, itself, was black-leaded cast iron. When he looked up, Amy was watching him with a smile on her lightly tanned face; her white teeth gleamed, emphasising her dark eyes.

"You admire his taste?"

"It could be a Victorian police station."

"Yes ... Martin is still after a blue lamp for the door ... He'll be able to help you find the furnishings you require for the Old Vicarage."

She laughed again, and Horst Brultzner felt her infectious sense of fun.

"It's all rather a joke to Martin, Mr Brultzner – an up-yours, so to speak, a touch of the Harvey Smith's – as Martin would say. He thought the picture of the Queen a masterstroke. It is difficult for officialdom to object to a picture of the Queen – although they would like to. As Martin says, most public buildings have removed them without comment. Why? ... It certainly has an effect on the village ne'er-do-wells he brings in for questioning ... He is still after an original of Queen Victoria to go alongside it. You like the fireplace?"

"It is admirable."

"Martin knows everybody. He can get you as many of those as you like from a friend in Pakefield. Have you noticed the desk – behind you?"

Brultzner looked carefully at the high desk of solid wood with the seat linked to it as one piece of furniture. He had seen many such in East Germany; they stood imposingly at the front of classrooms.

"That is a genuine Victorian Station Sergeant's desk. When Martin found that he was on a high for a month. Big buzz time – as he would say. It still has the inkwell intact. Occasionally, he sits on it looking down on the lads he has to sort out ... however, enough of our joys. You're looking forward to turning your vicarage into a real home."

"Indeed, we are doing very nicely. People have been most obliging."

"I would have thought the Old Vicarage secure enough. Not many people dare go up the lane. It is rather spooky."

"You are right. Over the years, empty and derelict as it was, the old house has remained remarkably free from what you now call vandals."

"Still, you can't be too careful and you've come to the right man."

The still dull light shone in through the thin summer dress and Brultzner admired her figure. He had found that women worried, quite unnecessarily, about growing old. The beauty of a woman, like Mrs Billings, in mid-life, was different from that of a young girl, but it was a difference of kind rather than quality. Amy would never re-capture the bloom of young skin, but her body had a physical assurance a girl's could never have. There was an attraction in the wisdom of such women; they came to know that life was not forever, and lived accordingly. The child-bearing years were over; their bodies could be re-claimed. Modern diets and exercise gave women of Amy's age a muscle tone and a fitness that was alluring. She turned from looking into the garden and smiled. Her hair was tinged with russet, her dark eyes gleamed and the fresh lips drew back into a smile.

Amy looked across at Brultzner; he was so nicely and carefully dressed. She was drawn to the sear-yellow eyes and walked over to him, leaning back with her buttocks resting on the desk. He reminded her of BBC arts programmes of the classical kind. Horst Brultzner might have been a presenter; he had just the right touch of learned anxiety. Amy could see the admiration in his gaze. It would be easy to change her jogging route round the village; the idea of leaning over his gate, and chatting, was enticing. It was nice to be admired and she worked hard to keep her body in trim. There was no lust in this man's unequivocal stare, but simply unqualified appreciation. He seemed to want nothing from her. Brultzner stood and approached her gently. Later, Amy re-called his hand on her shoulder and a gentle squeeze on her arm.

When Martin Billings came through the door of his office, Horst Brultzner was standing at the window looking out upon the garden.

"Sorry to have kept you, Mr Brultzner. Has Amy been looking after you?"

"Yes indeed. She has made me feel quite at home."

"You've had a coffee?"

"No, no. Mrs Billings was kind enough to offer me a drink, but I explained that I rarely touch stimulants. We took a turn in your garden, but then Mrs Billings felt slightly faint and has gone to lie down. Please," he said, noticing a look of anxiety in Billing's eyes, "see to her first. I am happy to wait."

Martin found Amy sound asleep – her face paler than usual, her natural good colour faded beneath an early tan. She was curled up in bed with the duvet cuddled round her neck, breathing easily.

"I've never known Amy sleep during the day. She's so fit."

"A slight tiredness, perhaps, due to the weather? I am sure she will be well again this evening."

"Yes, I expect you're right. Now ... what can I do for you?"

"I seek your advice concerning the security of my house, Constable Billings. My improvements will attract attention. I do not fear burglars – they have more to fear from me – but I do not wish to be molested or even annoyed by them. I would rather that they did not get near the house, whether or not I am in residence. However, I do not want obtrusive measures taken. The ambience of the Old Vicarage must remain intact."

Martin Billings found himself warming both to the man and the subject. Here was someone with taste – unusual in the modern world – who also had no time for louts, thieves and vandals.

"There's a lot you can do. To start with, lay shingle along the driveway and round the house. No one can walk over shingle without making a noise and it will blend in nicely with the lawn, which runs down to the copse, and the Italianate terrace. The only approach to your house is along the driveway. Secure the boundaries and have gates put in place, and keep a dog loose at night. Not a vicious dog – just a noisy one. Have your mail delivered to a post box outside the gates. You're secure."

"The dog may not always prove convenient. There will be mornings when I shall wake late, and my servants will need safe access to the grounds."

"Crafty Catchpole could feed and kennel a dog – provided you train it to him. There's nothing like a dog to warn against villains. But if you don't fancy that then secure the house itself. Non-drying paint deters access via drainpipes and, used strategically, makes it very unpleasant to raise sash windows. Have the doorways lit with sensors that activate a green spray. As soon as the villains step into the light, they're covered. And the beauty of it is - the spray is DNA coded to your premises so there's no point in them claiming they weren't there because the paint – which they can't wash off – proves they were. Besides, it takes the buzz out of a burglary if you have to proceed covered in sticky paint. And it takes the value off any antiques they might have had it in mind to nick."

"And inside the house?"

"You don't want riff-raff walking around inside your house. It makes it feel unclean afterwards. They spoil everywhere they go. I always shower when I come off duty, just to wash away the smell. If you want to secure the inside, there's always the standard alarm. Movement sensors built into the light fittings and contact sensors built into the door jambs. They might get in, but they can't move round. And none of this will spoil the ambience of your restoration. We can have it all built into period fittings."

"Lord Wangford told me that you were an enthusiast."

"His lordship was sensible enough to take my advice after a few unnecessary break-ins. Antique thieves make occasional forays up from London and – unlike lightning – they always strike the same place twice. People can't believe it, see. It won't happen to them – again, will it? Only it does – until they get their security sorted out. All the advice is out there. You've paid for it in your taxes, and so why not take advantage of it? Makes sense? Of course it does."

"These devices would secure the house against any workman?"

"You wouldn't want them activated during the day. Crafty wouldn't take kindly to going home looking like the Green Man."

"But he could be trained to keep clear of the doorways."

Martin Billings found himself admiring Brultzner. He deduced him to be a decisive master, someone who knew exactly what he wanted and went for it; if he was aristocracy, it said something for foreigners. Charlie Wangford had muttered and mumbled even after the second burglary, but you can't play about with villains.

"You have no time for the criminal classes, Constable Billings?"

"None at all. I wouldn't give them room on the pavement."

"Dunburgh has always had its criminal element, Constable Billings. At one time a gallows stood down near the harbour. The annual fair always attracted its share of what you call riff-raff. Merchants came from far and near, even from across the sea, with goods of all kinds. They set up their stalls in the market-place and the church yard and all along the main streets. There were luxuries only to be had at such times. You can imagine the kind of people who were attracted. The villagers from all around, the farmers, the ship-owners, stewards from the local manors and the parasites – always the parasites."

Brultzner saw it as he spoke – the small dwelling houses with one living-room for the family and another partitioned off for the beasts, the houses packed closely together growing taller or deeper as the merchants and master-craftsmen grew prosperous and enlarged them, and the rubbish in the streets either washed down to the sea or scavenged by animals. He saw the deaths from frequent epidemics, and the fires sweeping through the thatch and wooden shingles. At times, it seemed as though the whole port would burn down, unless the wind decreased on the turn of the tide and the flames were brought under control.

Martin saw Brultzner's eyes glaze over and stood in awe. He had never heard anyone speak so passionately about the history of the village as this stranger.

"You must excuse me, Constable Billings. I, too, have my enthusiasms."

"Don't apologise. It's good to think that someone has bothered to look into these things. Perhaps you could give a talk to the WI?"

"The WI?"

"A group of women who meet once a month."

"Perhaps I could. Your wife is a member?"

"Oh yes. Amy wouldn't miss the monthly meeting."

Brultzner smiled to himself and – having arranged for Martin to visit the Old Vicarage at a suitable time, and trusted that Mrs Billings would soon feel better – he left to complete his walk. At the corner of School Road he glanced across the wide junction towards Mardles Lane. He noted, gratefully, that the sky was still dull and saw a man sitting on the hummock of grass which supported the footpath sign. Brultzner had unusually keen eyesight for someone of his apparent years, and observed every detail of the stranger's face. The man was watching him intently, and lowered his head slightly as Brultzner passed.

Brultzner decided to ignore him and strolled casually on down Church Hill towards St George's. Without looking back, he realised that the stranger had risen from the mound and was following him. He suddenly crossed the road, walked through the lych-gate and into the churchyard. His pursuer had only two options; to follow him or pass on along the road and – if he were desperate not to lose sight of his quarry – head him off at the steps on the eastern side of the church. Brultzner turned the corner of the bell tower, walked quickly under the overhang of the ruined wall and waited. As he had expected, the stranger suddenly appeared walking with forced casualness along the path trodden by Brultzner only an hour or so before. Brultzner smiled.

"Good morning. Is there any way in which I may help you?"

"I had hoped to ask you the same question, Herr Brultzner."

"You have the advantage."

"My name is Peter Vishnya. I have been intending to call upon you."

Brultzner raised only an eyebrow in reply.

"When I saw you pass, the opportunity was too good to miss."

Again, Brultzner was silent.

"I would welcome the chance to be of assistance to you. I am able to translate freely across the European languages."

"Why should I need such a service, Mr Vishnya?"

"You will excuse my presumption, Herr Brutzner. I took you for ... an entrepreneur. I had hoped to avail myself of the chance of work."

"You are correct in at least one thing, Mr Vishnya – you presume too much."

Peter Vishnya laughed and the sound, even to Horst Brultzner at that moment, was attractive. Vishnya extended his hand and said:

"We seem to have 'got off on the wrong foot', as they say. Perhaps I may call upon you at your house on another occasion. I would simply like to make your acquaintance."

Brultzner stared at Peter Vishnya for as long as good manners would allow.

"You are Russian, Mr Vishnya?" he asked.

"Estonian."

"A proud people, Mr Vishnya, who were forced to abandon their language under the Communist jackboot ... But you have a Russian face."

"My father was from Moscow. It is my mother who is Estonian."

Brultzner gestured to a wooden bench, which was placed with its back to the church in loving memory of a lady who now lay in the graveyard. They both sat down, and were silent for a moment. Eventually Brultzner spoke:

"I believe the local people talk of me as 'the Russian count'."

"Yes."

"Those, that is, who do not refer to me as 'the German'? I am neither. The nearest race to which I could be assigned in this age would be Italian, but I am a Roman by birth ... You are attracted to the English?"

"My wife was English."

Horst Brultzner was unable to pursue the "was" – he had no capacity for discussions of family and relatives, and no desire to value loss.

"We are both Europeans, then, Mr Vishnya, in a way that the English are not. Perhaps, after all, we have something in common."

"You have travelled widely in Europe?"

"Wider than you could ever imagine possible."

"My offer to translate freely across Europe was amusing to you?"

"I speak all the main European languages, Mr Vishnya."

Sitting close to Horst Brultzner on the bench, Peter Vishnya was frightened.

"You, too, have travelled widely, Mr Vishnya?"

"I experienced my freedom as you did – when the wall came down."

"There is only a small truth in that from my perspective. I was confined to East Germany for some years, but my freedom goes back many generations."

Peter Vishnya left the bench and stood at the edge of the path looking out over the graveyard. He wished now that he had not followed this man.

"Is this part of your love, Mr Vishnya – an English country churchyard?"

"Yes," said Peter Vishnya.

"Come, show me your church."

The two men strolled together along the shingled path towards the south porch. Peter Vishnya pushed open the door, and stepped back. Horst Brultzner trod carefully down the stone steps and stood facing the font.

"You value your faith, Mr Vishnya?"

"I grew into manhood with the beliefs of my parents under threat."

"But do your English have such a faith?"

Peter Vishnya stepped passed the font and along the aisle. Horst Brultzner followed. Vishnya had been married here amongst his wife's people; every time he entered the church, memories of that day flooded through him. He could recall looking round against the strict instructions of his best man – his wife's brother – and watching his fiancee walking towards him on her father's arm. His own people had not been able to come; such money was not within their reach, and his own pride forbad any offers from his wife's family. A love match, they had said, made in Heaven, and it was true. He remembered his wife's assumption that they should make love before the wedding and her amusement at his refusal. Such was the way with westerners, but it was not Vishnya's way. First, they had made their promises before God, and beyond that was the endless binding of man and woman. He was not a 'churchy' man; his faith went far deeper than the rectory garden party. Horst Brultzner caught his eye, and seemed to apprehend the depth and nature of his thoughts.

"You have been baptised into the Anglican church, Mr Vishnya?"

"No. My wife thought it would be a betrayal of my family. But they are happy for me to worship here. Corvin Unwood is a worldly man."

"And a priest of substance?"

"Why do you ask?" enquired Peter Vishnya, feeling a sickness within him.

"I sense a power in you, Mr Vishnya, but I do not sense it in this church."

He walked passed Peter Vishnya and strode to the altar rail. The figures in the east window could be seen more clearly from the inside of the church. He noted again the person of St Francis, and recognised Edmund Crouchback. He turned from the altar cross. The Virgin and Child stared down at him in coloured glass.

"I am from the old world, Herr Brultzner. My ancestors go back countless generations. My faith is undiluted by the considerations of the modern western mind – whether the Resurrection was real or symbolic, whether the Christ child was born in a stable, whether Christianity owes more to St Paul than to Jesus himself. These are wood whittling problems for the end of the day, when the real work is done. I do not lack imagination nor do I under-value its power."

"I, too, have no time for such things but – unlike you who can only wonder at the momentousness of belief – I have looked over the edge and I know."

He turned quickly upon Vishnya who recoiled. Brultzner smiled.

"Neither is my faith 'diluted'. I like the expression ... you use your English well. Thank you for showing me your church. Perhaps our paths will cross again? A good friend I have been to many, Mr Vishnya ..."

Horst Brultzner left the phrase unfinished, as he swept away down the aisle and out through the porch door. He left Peter Vishnya standing, as though lost, between the choir stalls.

CHAPTER 9

The Brotherhood

Horst Brultzner reclined almost absent-mindedly, cosseted in the warm leather of the Bentley. He had telephoned Lord Wangford upon his return to the Old Vicarage, and was savouring, with satisfaction, his visit to the estate now known as Wangford Park. The black car passed silently through the pillars of Cotswold stone, which were surmounted by a white bull in the act of hoofing the ground. The chauffeur shut the iron gates behind them, and returned to continue their drive. The informality, the very lack of security, reinforced Brultzner's sense of belonging and certainty. He watched the parkland, as the car cruised steadily towards the house. It was so traditionally English: carefully spaced oak and chestnut trees giving shade to the grazing sheep.

Wangford Hall had been built by the present incumbent's family early in the eighteenth century on the site of a castle believed to have dated from the time of the Conquest. During the reign of Henry VIII, Wangford Hall and the surrounding estates formed huge sheep runs, and the family built a vast fortune from the woollen industry. Most of the sons pursued a military career and one became Lieutenant General of Ordnance to Charles I. The king's defeat and Cromwell's accession to power proved only a temporary stumbling block. Wangford's private army was disbanded by the Parliamentarians, but their lands were never sequestrated. The family's wealth remained apparently inviolate until the present incumbent's father, Christopher Wangford, squandered it on the gaming tables of London and Paris. On his ignominious return home, faced with the prospect of selling the estates to meet his debts, he was met by a foreign doctor who handed him a note for the amount owed and a revolver. The following day the family debts were paid; and Christopher Wangford lay dead on the beach at Blacksands Ness where their lands met the sea. Horst Brultzner smiled with pleasurable remembrance.

The car passed the hall along a shingled path, which led towards a small hillock on the flat Suffolk farmland. At a curve in the track, the present Lord Wangford stood waiting for them. He nodded, with familiarity, to Brultzner. Both men waited patiently, while the chauffeur reversed the Bentley and the car passed from sight. Brultzner was in no hurry; indeed, he was luxuriating in his memories of this place.

"The many times I have stood here never diminish my feelings towards this place, Wangford. I was a man when I first came – a seasoned soldier. I still remember drawing my cloak about me to ward off the chill east wind which, even then, gusted up this slope. The night I took my oath, there were twenty five of us in this temple of the Brotherhood. The river below us flowed freely into the sea, and the estuary down there contained many ships of the Empire. It was a flourishing, bustling harbour. I stood here looking down, knowing that they watched our torches processing up the hill. I have never lost the sense of power I felt that night."

Charles Wangford listened politely to Brultzner, not wishing to interrupt the drift of his thoughts. The aristocrat seemed more relaxed in Brultzner's company than he had previously, when struggling with the davenport.

"The estate goes well, Wangford?"

"Indeed. Despite the heart falling out of the meat market we continue to thrive – without having to open our gates to the public. Our interests abroad tied us over these difficult times."

Charles Wangford resented Brultzner's right to make comments about his estates, and considered any questions to verge on the impertinent, but the Brotherhood was another matter and he knew what he owed to the man who stood on his hillside.

"You have good business acumen. You are not a waster like your father."

"He paid his debt and, before I die, I will have repaid the doctor's loan."

Brultzner ignored the sharpness of the retort. His brief acquaintance with Charles Wangford had already assured him that the tradition was safe. His amiability did not extend to those who served him, even when they did so as loyally as the baronet.

"And the Brotherhood?"

"Thirty strong ... This was so during my father's time."

"I am aware of that, Wangford. This is my temple. The tradition has always been strong – even among the servants. The line is still unbroken?"

"The present herdsman's stock has served my family for generations."

"And the future?"

"The son is being trained. The welfare of the herd is safe with us."

"Always your herdsmen produce sons, Wangford."

Brultzner laughed as he spoke, and Wangford joined him; part of the conspiracy between them involved a shared corruption. Securing the future of the Brotherhood was central to their lives; any young wives of past herdsmen, prone to girl children, had not resisted the attempts of past Wangfords to produce a male child in the stately bed. Charles Wangford, loved by his tenants and admired by the neighbourhood because he was perceived as "an eccentric old bastard", was fond of parodying himself as a grouse-hunting toff. He appeared at the parish church three times a year, sat on the Parochial Church Council and did his duty at summer fetes and carnivals: appearances were everything.

Charles Wangford shuffled aside, when Brultzner turned, and ushered him down the short flight of steps to the doorway of his temple. Wangford unlocked the heavy oak door and pushed; it opened silently on dark hinges. The stones from which it was built had been shipped from the north, and the moss of time had weathered them well into the Suffolk landscape. Inside the temple, which was sunk a little into the natural slope, the stones were burnished with care and use. The two men paused in the antechamber while Wangford lit two torches which spluttered, flared and then burned steadily, lighting their way into the inner sanctuary. To the left of the central aisle stood a short statue, holding a carved torch downwards towards darkness and twilight; to the right, a similar statue held his torch upwards to light and the dawn. Both wore a short Roman cloak and a Phrygian cap painted bright red.

The only light, apart from that given by the torches, came from several small windows set high in the roof. The silence held a splendour of its own, and Horst Brultzner stood gazing along the aisle as Wangford brushed passed him. At the far end, he could see the three altars of the Brotherhood. As the curtains were drawn back, the eyes of the god stared back at him. Brultzner inclined his head in a moment of prayer. '… a young god, fair of aspect … clad in … scarlet cloak and having a crown of fire.'

The words crossed fifteen centuries in his memory. He walked towards the altars, pausing to run his hands along the benches that flanked the aisle. The wood was oak – carefully seasoned, hard, polished, good for centuries to come. He touched the altar on the left, inclined his head to a small image of the god, and ran his fingers reverently along the surface of each of the others where, soon, members of the Brotherhood would place their offerings.

Brultzner raised his torch and lit the stone walls, which only just exceeded the height of a man. A raised platform, on which the benches stood, ran the length of the temple on each side of the aisle. He stooped to examine these, and then raised his head to the beamed, wooden ceiling. He stretched to run his fingers along each of the beams, and then stroked the supporting posts as a man might fondle the mane of his dog.

The temple gleamed in the light of the torches. He wandered back to the antechamber. Next to the fireplace was the grave – a stone pit six feet long. Brultzner remembered being directed to lie down in it for his first initiation; he recalled the cold of the pit and the heat of the fire. When the ordeal was over he had emerged as if from a tomb, re-born into the sanctuary of the god. The grave was clean and fresh to his touch, and not one speck of dust sullied the surface.

"The temple is a credit to the care of your family, Father."

"It is an honour to serve, Excellency."

Brultzner addressed Wangford by his title, but the Father of the temple replied only with courtesy. Brultzner's grade remained the unspoken word.

"I look forward to the celebration of our Lord's birth."

"Born on a rock at the time of the winter solstice."

"Armed with a sword and a torch at birth."

"He fought to deliver the world from evil."

"And achieved salvation for all men …."

Both men stood by the three altars, as they intoned their creed. They bowed and left the temple quietly, extinguishing the torches on a blackened hollow of stone and placing them carefully in iron brackets on the wall of the antechamber.

They followed the shingle path round the curve of the slight hillside in an unspoken walk until they reached a point from where they could look down across the meadows to the River Cassyn. A copse ran alongside the broad and to the west of this, in the shelter of the trees, grazed a herd of white cattle. This was the Wangford Herd, whose bloodstock could be traced back to Roman Britain. They were huge animals with long curved horns, and the bull who watched over them was massive. It raised a disdainful head when it became aware of the two men watching from the edge of the pasture, and then continued grazing, its dewlap brushing the ground. Admiration was evident in Brultzner's gaze, and Wangford was pleased. He signalled to a man and boy who were busying themselves with feeding troughs and water on the far side of the field. They made their way across, oblivious to the herd. Wangford introduced them as John Stokes and his son, David.

Brultzner inclined his head, and they both gave a slight bow, instinctively rather than by custom or training.

"The herd is magnificent, Mr Stokes. It is a credit to you and your son."

His tone suggested that he had expected no less. Horst Brultzner placed his hand on a fence post and leapt into the pasture from a standing jump. He walked slowly into the midst of the herd. The boy's eyes widened.

"They don't take to strangers, sir."

"You need have no fear for me, David Stokes."

Brultzner made for the great bull. As he approached, the animal watched and pawed the ground. The nostrils snorted and the head shook. Brultzner passed within a touch of the horns and slid his hands into the mane. He ran them along the beast's back and slapped under the chest and belly. There was love in his strokes; his fingers probed and teased every inch of the bull's body.

As he watched, John Stokes knew that this was the man of whom his great-grandfather had spoken. He was never named, yet remained vivid in the memory of the family over generations. He was mentioned only after drinks on dark evenings when the men sat and talked. The cowman could remember none who had actually met him, but the tales persisted down the years. A tall figure striding across a pasture was how John, listening from under the table to the talk of the men, had first imagined him. His presence had, as they say, "been spoken of in whispers". John knew that he came for the temple, and the slaying of the great white bull. The cowman looked down at his son.

"It's not in every lifetime we see this."

"No father, but why must it happen?"

"That's not for us to ask."

They spoke quietly and were scarcely audible to Charles Wangford, who stood by them, but Brultzner heard and walked over to the boy.

"Do you go to your church?"

"Yes sir."

"And what does your father drink from the silver chalice?"

"The blood of Christ, sir."

"To what purpose?"

"To take away his sins, sir"

"To take away the sins of the world, have mercy upon us. Long before your god there was another, who brought salvation to the world – but not by slaying his dearly beloved son. It was the blood of a bull which brought life to the Earth."

"That's a bit beyond us, sir," said John Stokes on his son's behalf.

Brultzner looked at the cowman and his son as though to speak, seemed to think better of it and laughed.

"Come," he said to Charles Wangford, "we have more to do before sunset."

John Stokes and his son watched as Lord Wangford and his guest strode towards the hall. David did not speak to his father; they stood quietly sharing the same thoughts. He had seen it once – or pretended he had – the slaying of the bull.

Brultzner had stood in the library of Wangford Hall only a few times since it had been built and furnished almost two hundred years before, but he felt immediately at home. He sat at the mahogany pedestal desk and passed his fingers along the reeding on the pilasters. This matched exactly that on the secretaire chiffonier which Wangford unlocked to remove several leather bound ledgers; he placed these carefully on the desk in front of Brultzner.

The baronet turned to the french windows, as Brultzner opened the first of the ledgers. Charles had inherited these with the baronetcy and kept them scrupulously up to date. His father's suicide had precipitated him into the business of the Brotherhood at eighteen when he had opened the sealed envelope. The three books, which Brultzner now studied so quietly and patiently, contained financial records, biographies of the local Temple members and details of the network of Temples across Britain.

Charles Wangford's initiation had been followed by a rapid learning. He had been surprised to converse with political leaders in France, merchants in Holland, bankers in Russia, faded but powerful aristocrats in what had been Eastern Germany, priests in Italy, architects in England, senior civil servants in Luxembourg, lawyers in Spain and – everywhere – high ranking members of other influential secret societies.

Brultzner was like none of these men. His name seemed woven inextricably throughout the movement, but he was beyond consultation. His presence in the Brotherhood gave credence, historical authenticity and a weave of fearfulness, but he was a spectre rather than an agent provocateur.

"Has the god of the Brotherhood any meaning for our members, Wangford? This is an atheistic age. You only have to observe the Christian church to know that. Ritual undergone lightly is meaningless. How often do you gobble down the bread and wine on your Sabbath without giving its significance one thought –hmm?"

"I ... eh ... never take Communion, sir – it doesn't seem appropriate – but I don't think one should undervalue ritual, even when its meaning is ... obscured."

"The Brotherhood has given succour to its initiates since before the rise of the Persian empire. It has always been held together by the Brothers' zeal for the struggle between good and evil, darkness and light. This is not an ardent age."

"We are a fraternity, sir. We intervene when the cause demands that we should – on behalf of a Brother or for the social good."

"There is no other secret society, Wangford, which has remained so. Exclusive they may be, but not secret. Their histories, rituals and activities are daubed over every newspaper in the world. You know why ours is different?"

"Yes, sir," replied Charles Wangford, recalling the body of his father sprawled on the beach at Blacksands Ness.

The two men were silent and motionless for a long time. Even after Brultzner had the car summoned, and could be seen passing out under the Jacobean arch, Wangford stood wondering on his front door step – wondering whether his own son would one day have dealings with Horst Brultzner.

The chauffeur took Brultzner to Shore Lane, and parked the Bentley outside the rectory gates. The new tenant of the Old Vicarage had come to make the acquaintance of the present incumbent of the new rectory. He arrived just as the rector's warden, Bernard Shaw, and his wife, Liz, were leaving the rectory after a meeting. Liz's jaw was moving in its usual incessant way, continuing a conversation which had started an hour or so before. Even as her chin wagged up and down, her eyes scanned the road. Her mind was coping quite adequately with talking about one thing, while thinking of another. She saw the Bentley draw away and Horst Brultzner standing on the opposite pavement, as her husband fiddled with the latch on the rectory gate.

"There's the man who has bought the Old Vicarage, if I'm not mistaken, and I don't think I am ...," said Liz, nudging her husband.

Bernard crossed the road, with the rapidity of a fat man, and stretched out his hand.

"Herr Brultzner? My name is Bernard Shaw. I'm the rector's warden. Pleased to meet you. If there is anything we can do to make you welcome in Dunburgh, don't hesitate to mention it ... eh, my wife, Liz."

"I am pleased to make your acquaintance, Mr Shaw. Madame, at your service."

"We were discussing the Summer Fete, Herr Brultzner. We hold it at the end of June. We were looking for someone interesting to open it ..." She paused as the idea suddenly occurred to her. "... but I don't suppose ... no, it's too much to ask."

"My dear, madame," replied Brultzner, "the idea of opening an English village fete entrances me. In all my centuries upon this earth, I have never been given a more enticing invitation. You have opened the door on this charming village."

They had no chance to wonder whether his "centuries" was an eccentricity or not because as they spoke, Corvin Unwood appeared from the rectory. He walked cautiously – even submissively – towards them; Corvin was never at ease with the "gentry". Despite his ideals regarding the equality of man, he could not shake off the shackles of his childhood – the doffing of his father's cap, the importance of the social order not being disrupted. Brultzner turned to him as he reached the gate. Liz Shaw was half-way across the road as she spoke.

"This is …." she spluttered.

"Horst Brultzner – at your service."

"Corvin Unwood – priest of this parish."

"…. and Cure of Four Thousand Souls. You have an unenviable task, rector."

"But a joyful one."

The two men watched each other as children fresh to a new playground might – each, apparently, unsure of where he stood with the other. Even Liz Shaw stopped speaking as she watched them, and Bernard drew her slowly away. She looked up at her husband who smiled, touched his hat to Corvin and led her off along Church Hill.

"Corvin?"

Esther Unwood's voice shook Corvin from his reverie, and he smiled at Brultzner. Their meeting, brief as it had been, unnerved him.

"Esther – this is our neighbour, Herr …."

"Mr …"

"Mr Brultzner – Esther, my wife."

"Madame – at your service. I am charmed."

"Pleased to meet you, Mr Brultzner. It doesn't go, you know!"

"I beg your pardon?"

"Mr doesn't go with Brultzner. You'll have to get used to Herr."

Corvin smiled with relief; his wife had taken charge. Horst Brultzner looked at her – this old woman with the silver-grey hair. He wasn't used to being put down, but he smiled and took her arm as she led him into the rectory.

Sitting in the lounge, sipping tea, Brultzner noticed how closely the old woman watched him while the husband talked.

"Another slice of cake, Herr Brultzner?" asked Esther.

He had already felt obliged to eat one slice with his cup of tea, and knew that it would trouble him all night. His stomach had long since grown used to a liquid diet, and the crumbs from Esther's date and walnut spice cake would keep him awake. Corvin had rhapsodised over his wife's cooking, but the thought of her cake – with its indigestible mixture of brown sugar, grated nutmeg, buttermilk, dates and walnuts – did not excite Brultzner. Living with the English again might have its drawbacks. He accepted another cup of the Earl Grey, which he found a particularly insipid, but easily digestible, tea.

"If it does not appear rude, Mrs Unwood, I must decline. At my age …"

He raised his hands in a gesture of helplessness. Esther smiled, but not with her eyes. Brultzner had run his eyes over the lounge as he entered, and Esther was conscious of what she laughingly called their "gentile poverty". The church had furnished much of the rectory in a modern style, straight from the catalogues, on the grounds that if it looked up-to-date the church must be forward thinking. Their private rooms, however, contained furniture handed down from her parents who bought it pre-war. It was sedate and might, one day, have antique value, but looked forever re-covered and vaguely shabby. Esther didn't mind, but objected when others did. Brultzner, she felt, had looked down his nose.

She could not have known that nothing was further from Brultzner's mind. He had several purposes in visiting the rectory, but none of them had anything to do with valuing the furniture. He had been hunted many times in the past by religious bigots and – like any old soldier – he wanted to reconnoitre the enemy. He shared, with Crafty Catchpole, the belief that knowledge was power.

"Have you been to England before?" Esther asked.

"Many times. I am, you might say, a student of history. I like to see things at first hand. I have stood in the kitchen at Steventon rectory, and seen cooking done on open fires with the meat and poultry roasting on rotating spits ..."

"Steventon rectory?" queried Corvin.

"Jane Austen's father was parson there," said Esther.

"Ah – you have a powerful imagination, Herr Brultzner," laughed Corvin.

"As you say. How much we owe the imagination!"

"And you read Jane Austen?" enquired Esther.

"In her own kitchen!"

Esther had read and re-read Jane Austen, but thought her books were not to the taste of most men. For a moment, Horst Brultzner went up in her estimation. During their laughter, the back door clicked and they heard Rebecca's voice call from the kitchen.

"Our daughter, Rebecca. She has just returned from work. She's a nurse."

"Ah – the world of medicine. How much we owe it."

When Rebecca entered the room, Brultzner stood. As they were introduced, he inclined his head. She blushed, and turned pale – as though the blood had gone suddenly from her. Brultzner caught her in his arms. Careful to avoid actually touching her flesh with his hands, he led her gently to a chair.

"I'm sorry. I think I almost fainted."

"You have returned from work. You will need to eat and rest. I am intruding ... Another time, perhaps?"

"No, please, do not leave on my account. I shall be fine. We have looked forward to meeting you."

Like Crafty Catchpole, Rebecca found herself overcome by the man's eyes; if ever a season resided in flesh, Brultzner was autumn. His eyes seemed to be yellow and so faded that they had become like autumn leaves. As she looked into them, Rebecca became conscious that the shape of his face changed, almost imperceptibly, into leaves so that the head seemed to be composed entirely of them, curled and crisp. It was astonishing how many moods passed across his face as she watched – menace, humour, fear, tranquillity – and then the face crumbled and began to disintegrate as brown leaves crunch in your hand.

"Rebecca!"

It was her mother's voice which called her round – her mother's voice, urgent and fearful. Esther stepped between her daughter and the stranger, and the mood was broken. She was herself again, and Brultzner stepped back into the light of the window.

"Perhaps I'd better lie down for a while."

"No, we'll take a stroll round the garden."

When Esther and Rebecca left the room for the fresh air, Corvin turned uncomfortably to Brultzner. He was quick to reassure him how unlike Rebecca it was to feel faint – how normally robust she was, how full of energy.

In the garden, Esther kept her daughter on the move: instinct drove her to do so – instinct borne of age and time. It seemed to her important that Rebecca should not drop off into sleep. She had felt at odds with herself ever since Brultzner entered the rectory. Without any reason, she sensed in him a pervading malice. She had never trusted charm; perhaps the man's very charm was simply off-putting? Esther, however, knew it was more than that; he reminded her of an animal – a vicious animal. If only he would go, and they could get back into the rectory, everything would be all right. In the meantime, she must keep Rebecca awake and on the move.

Corvin found himself standing in his study with Horst Brultzner, gazing at his picture of Martin Luther. He wasn't sure how he came to be there, but was sure that Brultzner knew all about his secret kettle.

"You are an admirer of Luther, rector?"

"Yes. He was, you might say, my inspiration."

"You are impressed by his belief that your sect are saved not through their own efforts, but by the gift of God's grace, which they accept in faith?"

"Yes."

"But sin destroys a man's relationship with God and leads to eternal damnation?"

"Sin is a state of estrangement from God. Christ is our redemption."

"It is only through faith that you are granted your God's presence in the afterlife?"

"Yes."

"When your soul is, at last, free from the sins of this world?"

"Yes – one has only to come to God ...."

"... through his Son?"

"Yes."

"And this grace is open to us all?"

"It is open to all believers."

For a moment, Corvin held Brultzner's respect. Sensing a deadly vacillation, he had dismissed him as a weakling, and yet he was sure in his faith. Sure – and steadfast?

Rebecca had, at last, persuaded her mother to let them both sit down when Peter Vishnya arrived at the rectory. Anton, his 'dog', was with him.

"Mr Vishnya, how nice to see you!" exclaimed Esther, "Rebecca was feeling faint so we took a turn in the garden."

"Nothing serious, I hope."

"No, Mr Vishnya, nothing serious. I'm quite all right now, thank you."

Rebecca wished that she could keep the exasperation out of her voice. If only he didn't sound so agreeable it would have been much easier.

"Herr Brultzner is here and ..."

"Brultzner!"

Without another word, Peter Vishnya walked rapidly across the lawn, knocked on the rectory door in a peremptory fashion and, without waiting for a reply, entered.

"What a strange man," said Esther, "So courteous and yet ..."

Corvin was taken aback when Peter Vishnya walked into his study.

"The rector and I have been discussing Martin Luther's contribution to the Protestant arm of the church," said Horst Brultzner, smiling at Peter Vishnya.

"Mr Brultzner is well-informed for one who does not share our views," said Corvin.

"He has, perhaps, had many years to study the subject."

"As you say, Mr Vishnya – many years."

The words passed between them in a fleeting exchange, but long enough for Anton to enter the study behind his master. When he saw the dog, Brultzner smiled and stared quietly at the animal. Anton's tail didn't droop, his ears didn't fall and no whine emanated from his throat – nor did he flop over and roll on his back at Brultzner's feet. He sat and stared calmly. Brultzner was taken aback.

"That's a remarkable dog you have there, Mr Vishnya. He is from your native Estonia?"

"Yes. As you say, he is a remarkable 'dog'. No anger, no barking and yet neither does he cower nor whimper. You find him unsettling, Herr Brultzner?"

"Unusually so – and I cannot place his breed."

"I believe Anton is a gentle animal, Peter," said Corvin in his best, priestly, tone.

"We must have a 'chat' about your Anton, one day, Mr Vishnya. I have had more to do with wolves myself. The other night, as I strolled in my garden, I thought I heard them howling."

"The wildlife park specialises in European species. They have a pack of timber wolves."

"Then I must make their acquaintance."

He looked at Anton once more, and the dog eyed him mildly.

"But now, rector, I must take my leave. I have taken too much of your time, already, and I am sure Mr Vishnya and yourself have much to discuss."

Brultzner took his leave, with a slight nod in Peter Vishnya's direction. Standing in the hallway outside Corvin's study, they saw him bid Rebecca and Esther goodbye as he passed across the lawn and through the front gate.

On the lawn, Peter Vishnya paused to speak with Rebecca. Esther took Corvin's arm and led him inside.

"Have you had much to do with Horst Brultzner?" Peter asked Rebecca.

"Why do you ask? Are you vetting my friends for me?"

"You look upon him – already – as a friend?"

"He seems a very courteous man to me, Mr Vishnya."

"Who invited him into your house?"

"I really don't know. Are we to ask you to vet who we might have to tea?"

Rebecca was smiling. Peter Vishnya's anxiety amused her and she was vain enough to take it, at that moment, for jealousy. She could not bring herself to believe that he actually admired her, but it seemed obvious that he was – at the very least – interested.

"This is not the moment for word games, Rebecca. Brultzner is from the Old World. Things are different there and you know nothing of them. Not all in Europe is as cosy as in these quiet, English villages."

CHAPTER 10

The social scene – the Health Club party

May had come in kindly, not wanting to disturb the equanimity of village life, and Grise and Owen Culman approached their al fresco event with a great degree of certainty. Grise had dispensed with any idea of a barbecue; above all she wanted a clean, healthy, tidy party with people leaving as smartly as they arrived. Barbecues – with their smoke, insects and the threat of rain – were not her idea of creating a good impression, and she was keen that Owen should become a Conservative councillor, whatever his reservations. Being on the council meant power and planning permission when you needed it.

The Beachlands Health Club had been a staggering success. They had created the club on a dilapidated caravan site owned by her mother. The club was conveniently sited next to their bungalow, which was on the cliff top near the edge of the village. It had started in a small way with little more than two squash courts and a changing room, but Grise had an eye for business and, being popular with the women in the village, was able to promote their venture. So 'The Squash Club', by which name many of the original clients still referred to it, had become 'The Health Club' when they built a small gym. This had been further extended to include a bar – people always seemed to want to drink after exercise – which served light snacks. Now, she and Owen had extended still further – adding a large terrace, two tennis courts and a swimming pool. It was this third extension that their party was to celebrate.

Grise also had a special flair for food, and planned to extend the bar to a restaurant while, at the same time, extending the gym still further. If you were going to be successful, you had to match the town gyms with their expensive machines and offer classes in aerobics, body combat and Pilates. She was a good advertisement for a health club – slim, fit and shining with energy. She turned the heads of all the men in the village.

Her preparations for the 'Health Club Party' were well underway. She supplemented her natural flair with some intensive research and came up with a range of food which would inspire all her potential clients – 'food optimising dishes to help you lose weight and feel great this summer' was to be the slogan. Her guests could look forward to, for starters, grilled vegetables with herb salsa, spiced koftes with minted yogurt dip, Thai prawn and lemongrass soup and Moroccan spiced fish kebabs. For the main courses, they could expect griddled scallops with a herb dressing, seared tuna with hot pepper sauce, coriander and mint grilled chicken skewers, chive and ginger pork stir-fry or – if you were a vegetarian – spinach, pea and mint frittata and vegetable balti. These were supported by spiced roasted new potatoes, fennel and wild rice salad, wholewheat Brazil salad, grape with watercress and Stilton salad and sauteed aubergines with mustard seeds and yogurts. The desserts were equally enticing, with no expense spared and barely a calorie in sight – pears poached in spiced red wine, raspberry and vanilla terrine and rum and chocolate pots. No one, but no one, in the village ever equalled Grise Culman's dos – and all of it put down to business expenses.

She had invited Mark and Nin Chambers, but doubted whether they would turn up. Her affair with Mark during the building of the small gym – his firm had the contract – was known only to a select few (and Nin knew nothing of it) but Mark always seemed embarrassed to meet Grise afterwards. Mark had ended the affair, prematurely, and she had not really forgiven him.

Owen Culman was a quiet man in everything he did – reserved, and rather nervous in public. Part of his wife's keenness to get him involved in local politics was the desire to bring him out of himself. Like her, he worked hard, but without the same vivacity. It was enough for him that they had two nice children and a nice home. If you had to work, the Health Club was as good a way of making a living as any other; but he could sell up tomorrow, square his accounts and get a less stressful job in a bank.

He loved Grise as any quiet man would – he was attracted to her energy and excitement. She was the driving force behind Beachlands, while he did the sums. Unknown to her – and thanks to a stray remark dropped by Martin Billings whose wife had told him in confidence – he knew about her brief affair with Mark Chambers, but didn't really give a damn. It took the pressure off at home for a while, and allowed him to get a full night's sleep. Mark Chambers was a decent enough bloke – hard-working and amiable – and Owen could well understand anyone being seduced by his wife. His role – in the launch of their new extension – was to be there, chat up the councillors and local businessmen, dress smartly in the latest style and promote, in his mumbling way, their new attractions.

He had met Grise at a cricket match; she had appeared with her current boyfriend and watched Owen play. Owen remembered, vividly, the wide-brimmed floral hat and matching dress. She wouldn't have been seen dead in it now, of course, but then it had bowled everybody over. By the end of tea in the pavilion, she had arranged to see him the following week, and he'd walked out to finish the match feeling like a giant of the game. He'd adored her ever since.

Bishop Twiddle was also calm as he waited for his housekeeper to serve the evening meal, but Peter Twiddle was always calm. Nothing had ever ruffled his feathers, and nothing ever would – he was determined that it should be so.

He sipped his sherry quietly. He wasn't sure about this Croft Original, which one of his young priests had given him, in a moment of rash appreciation, for his advice over a sermon on the problem of pain. It was from the reputable Gonsalez Byass, of course, but he really preferred an oloroso – with its dark, dry, mahogany flavour and full rich nose – to these rather pale wines. If only the young man had asked – but then the young always went at things hammer and tongs.

His advice had, of course, been much appreciated. This was to say as little as possible in as many words as possible, and to choose those words or phrases which everybody thought they should understand but nobody really did. Bishop Twiddle didn't actually say this to the young priest, of course; its very directness would have been offensive. He spoke at length using such phrases as "divine omnipotence", "laws of nature", "intrinsically possible", "neutral field", "material system", "frames of reference", "the presupposed doctrine", "the uniqueness of man's relationship with the Creator", "mortifying the usurped self" until he thought the young man had picked up the general idea. Above all, he stressed, it was vital (not that he used that word, which had too great a sense of urgency) to leave the congregation feeling relieved and happy. It was very important to round off with such comments as "not, perhaps, for us to question", "resolved in Heaven", "divine understanding" or "patient forbearance".

He was particularly looking forward to this evening's meal because Mrs Cushion was serving casserole of pigeons with apples and cider. This was to be preceded by prawn and mushroom cocktail, and followed by butterscotch pie.

As he stood warming himself by what would, regrettably, be one of the last fires of the season, Bishop Twiddle allowed his thoughts to stray to Dunburgh where, it seemed, things were progressing quietly enough. He had been a little uneasy after meeting Esther Unwood – dominant women were not something he greatly appreciated – but reports from one or two people of substance persuaded him that Corvin was doing a fine balancing act keeping both the traditional and modern elements in the air. "Never let them land, Corvin, they might go somewhere." Sometimes, but only when really necessary, his advice could be quite direct.

He had heard, too, that someone of moment had purchased the Old Vicarage and was having it restored to its proud Victorian state. Indeed, he had only a few days ago received an invitation, from one Horst Brultzner, to a luncheon which, according to Totto Briggs the local butcher, was to be a meal to remember! He had made a few enquiries regarding Brultzner, through his European contacts, but had discovered little about him. There had been some mumblings in Leipzig amongst the Lutheran church. A young priest had been found dead, killed by a cross driven through his heart, in 1993, and a 'Horst Brultzner', who was singing in the choir at the time, had found him – but that was all. Prior to arriving in Leipzig, he did not seem to exist at all. Experience had taught Twiddle that it didn't pay to delve too deeply into these things: one's discoveries could sometimes be unsettling.

Everybody was enjoying themselves at the Beachlands Health Club party. Nin Chambers – without Mark – had been the first to arrive, and Owen had felt sorry for her. How many other people, he wondered, knew about her husband and Grise? Clearly, she didn't – so, perhaps, the matter had been kept quiet.

"I'm sorry, Owen. I know it is Saturday night. I'm really angry with him."

"Never mind. Business?"

"Yes. He's sitting over his catalogues. That blasted man, Brultzner, has set him off on another wild trail."

"What's it, this time?"

"A study mantelpiece!"

"Has he tried that man in Pakefield?"

"Yes, but his were too plain."

"Plain?"

"Evidently, the Victorian study mantelpiece was very masculine – decorated with swords, guns, armour ...you name it!"

"Even in a rectory?"

"Especially in a rectory. Those old vicars spent most of the week out hunting with the nobs, according to Herr Brultzner."

"He certainly knows his stuff. Still, it's a good contract for Mark."

"Oh yes, I know that. It'll take years."

"And money no object?"

"They didn't even discuss it. Herr Brultzner said he'd know if Mark cheated him. It wasn't something that anyone ever did!"

"I'll look forward to meeting him at his 'Vicarage Luncheon' next month."

Nin passed on, with a rueful laugh, to speak to Grise. Owen noticed how thin she was; one of those women caught up in the desire not to put on weight, she'd gone the other way and was, not to mince words, scrawny. Owen hated it and thanked his lucky stars that Grise was not like that; still, better thin than fat at the Health Club Party – if you kept your clothes on!

Lianne and Barry Snooks stood by the edge of the new swimming pool. Lianne had never been athletically inclined. If she couldn't be the best, she didn't want to be anything. Coming last in school races, missing the netball hoop time after time and stumbling over someone else's hockey stick hadn't really appealed to her; she'd avoided sport, whenever possible, at the earliest opportunity. She had met Barry at a hospital social and watched him in the odd sporting event when this was unavoidable, but quickly dropped away from such distractions once the ring was on the finger.

She looked around and caught the eye of Ample Bassett, who was standing with a mixed plateful of grilled vegetables with herb salsa, spiced koftes with minted yogurt dip and Moroccan spiced fish kebabs.

"They looked so lovely! I just had to have a little of each."

"... little of each," repeated Billy, so that everyone was kept in touch with his wife's thoughts.

"Have you heard how things are going at the Old Vicarage?" asked Lianne.

"They're goin' well," said Billy, "I was talkin' ter Harry Bailey only yes'dee and he said ..."

"Where did you see Harry Bailey yesterday, Billy Bassett?" asked Ample.

"At the squash club," he replied.

"I didn't know Harry Bailey played squash."

"Well, you don't know everything."

"So it's a good thing that Billy keeps you in touch, Ample," said Barry, cutting into the husband and wife conversation with a laugh.

Lianne laughed with him, and Billy joined in. She liked to see anyone discomforted, and Billy relished his wife being put down.

"Just as long as I know where you are, that's all," was Ample's riposte.

"Amy's met the new owner," cut in Martin Billing's, as he came up to the group with his wife on his arm

"Met him?" blurted Ample, her voice agog with disbelief.

The question, which he had hoped she would ask, made Martin's day. It was always so good to out-manoeuvre, surprise, irritate or simply shut-up Ample, while she was in full, garrulous flight. If Billy repeated what she'd said, it would complete Martin's pleasure – but no, it was only two words, and too much to ask of him.

"He came to see Martin, and we had a little chat. Very nice – lovely manners," said Amy.

"Well – what's he like, this mystery man?" asked Ample.

"He's only a mystery to people who haven't met him, Ample. Amy had a long conversation with him. He asked her advice on furnishing his new home."

"Shut up, Martin," said Amy, nudging him in the ribs with her elbow, "We were in Martin's office and he was admiring the furniture."

"As well he might. There aren't many modern police stations that respect the wonder of wood, or have any sense of tradition," said Martin.

"But what's he like?" Ample persisted.

"Well, he was nicely dressed in an old fashioned sort of way. His face reminded me of that chap who used to be on TV a lot talking to Michael Parkinson about the theatre – what was his name?"

"Jonathan Miller," said Martin, who never forgot a face or a name.

"Yes – he's the one," agreed Amy.

"Ooh good looking then, but a big nose ...."

"... big nose," said Billy.

"Yes – and he had sort of yellow eyes. I could see he fancied me," Amy laughed, "You know in the way that older men do – with appreciation. He was nice to talk to. I thought I might change my jogging route round the village. I quite fancied leaning over his gate and having a chat."

"Enjoying yourselves?" Grise asked, as she came up to them. She liked Amy, and the way she kept her body in trim. Turning to her, she continued "Are you feeling better now?"

"Better?" asked Amy.

"Last month you said you'd been feeling a bit faint – tired."

"Oh yes – that passed off. We were talking about Mr Brultzner."

"Haven't met him yet," Grise responded, "They say he's very handsome."

"Amy says he's got yellow eyes," cut in Ample.

"... yellow eyes," said Billy, helpfully.

"I'd invited Alan Read and Penny," said Grise, "but he was called away, and she couldn't leave the children."

Alan Read was one of the village doctors, and had a reputation for being conscientious. The old woman who'd called him out to change a light bulb because she couldn't see her way across the hall only did it once; gossip had it that she'd been on the verge of changing doctors after what he said to her. All the patients "on his list", however, had his card, and none ever had to worry about being refused attention by the "sharp tongued harpy in reception".

"He's too soft," said one of the councillors who Grise was trying to impress.

"No, he's not," said Martin, "He's a professional. You know – or do you? It's someone trained to do a job, with the qualifications and experience to do the job, and who actually enjoys doing the job, and with the guts to give a Harvey Smith to the pen-pushers who peddle the paperwork because it's their only concept of what the job is about – and they need to look useful doing something, even if it's getting in the way of those of us trying to give a service to the public. There aren't too many of us left these days – you should be grateful."

"It's all public money."

"It's Alan's time – does he put in a claim for over-time?"

"It all has to be paid for …"

"… but not by you, or anyone else on the trust," Martin insisted, stubbornly. He didn't like his friends – or anyone who served the public – being put down.

"It's true," said Nin, who had been drawn to the conversation by Martin's sharp retort to the councillor, "and it sets the standard for the whole practice."

"What was he called away for, then?" asked Ample, as she came to the table for a plate of pears poached in spiced red wine. She'd enjoyed the raspberry and vanilla terrine and, after all, they were low calorie!

"Penny wouldn't tell me that, would she?" said Grise.

"I just wondered if it was that girl from the hairdressers."

"What girl, Ample?" asked Amy.

"Haven't you heard? She lives on St George's Crescent. Her mum found her in bed this morning. She was as white as a sheet and there were little drops of blood on her pillow."

"That was nuthin'. She was always up at the Duke's Head. They hed a heavy metal band there last night. She'd hed too much ter drink and a nose bleed, that's all."

Billy Bassett's comments on any sickness or illness were always scathing. He came from a line of butchers who were at work early whatever the weather, and "got on with it".

"You've got the wrong girl," explained Ample, pleased to be in full flow again, "She wasn't a drinker. She had a lovely skin. Never wore make-up. She had what you call a peaches and cream complexion and the most beautiful hair you can imagine."

"Oh, that one."

"Yes that one, Billy Bassett. I bet you didn't mind her doing your hair!" laughed his wife.

"No, I can't say I did. I wouldn't have moinded runnin' my fingers through her mane."

Bishop Twiddle was hard put to know whether to doze off in his easy chair or to take what his generation called a "constitutional" round the cathedral grounds. In the end, the call of duty prevailed over the soporific effects of the bottle of Medoc he had enjoyed with his meal. He shared Keith Floyd's view that the Bordeaux wines had a tendency to be over-rated, but this particular bottle had been mellow on the nose with hints of blackcurrant, peat and – inexplicably – cigar. The long, cherry finish had obliged him to return to it again and again, and he was left with the feeling that he would actually enjoy a cigar. The bishop had given up regular smoking some years before, but he did miss his evening cigar: three times a year – at Easter, Michaelmas and Christmas – just wasn't the same. If only life wasn't so complex – coping with the bouquet of the Medoc had been quite sufficient for one evening. Still, a little suffering was good for the soul.

The late evening air refreshed him enormously, however, as he set off across the green towards the west door of the cathedral. Standing in the nave, the bishop felt his composure return, and he walked calmly down the north aisle where he was reminded that the monks had been renowned for their singing.

He made his way towards the altar and knelt before it, looking up at the great Rood, the huge crucifix flanked by statues of Our Lady and St John. Here, after the Reformation, they had actually held markets! The Dean would have undoubtedly endorsed that – arguing that it was the business of the church to welcome travellers into an open, holy place. Peter Twiddle wasn't so sure; hadn't our Lord scourged the traders from the temple?

Peter Twiddle crossed himself, stood, and walked back down the nave. He looked up at the circular opening in the vaulted ceiling two thirds of the way towards the west window. Some said that an angel flew down through this opening carrying burning incense to purify the air and create clouds of smoke, which raised the prayers of the people to God, but the bishop was not an imaginative man. He had given that up – wisely he thought – long ago.

Outside in the night air he looked up again – not this time at his God, but noticing, for the first time, the full moon that had helped to light his way round the cathedral. The bishop had been a contemplative man in his younger days, but was now careful his musings should not stray too far down the alleyways of contention; contemplation served its purpose best when pragmatic.

He walked with some vigour through the Close towards the river. To his left was the Deanery where, he noted, a light still burned in an upstairs window; to his right, the cathedral herb garden (dating from the time of the monks) whose current produce often adorned Mrs Cushion's most notable meals.

He headed for Hook's Ferry – the former water gate for the cathedral – and stood under its arch looking out over the river. The lights of the town twinkled on its softly rippling water. By the edge of the river was the statue of Mother Catherine – a fourteenth century mystic. She had lived in or near the cathedral for fifty years, and had there – in her small cell – achieved a mystical union with her God; her sins purged, her soul illuminated she had become one with the Creator. Standing alone at the rivers edge, Bishop Twiddle was terrified by the very thought; it was both a peaceful and frightening spot.

The councillor who had questioned Dr Alan Read's right to visit his patients without authorisation from the state listened thoughtfully as Owen Culman outlined his plans to further extend the Beachlands Health Club. He was impressed. Here, clearly, was a man of vision – someone who could see the way forward and make some money at the same time. The nation was obsessed by its health – a recent report had highlighted the growing problem of obesity and, as he listened, he drew in his paunch. The councillor owned a building firm and prided himself on knowing the ropes when it came to getting planning permission for good causes.

"You need to be on the Council, Owen. You're the right colour, aren't you?"

"I've never really thought about it."

"Owen will make a good councillor," said Grise, choosing that moment to cut into the conversation. "He'll care about people."

"That's what it's all about. Why don't you stand?"

"Me?" queried Grise.

"Why not? We could do with a bit of glamour on the council. It'd brighten things up a bit."

Grise went into 'girlie-mode', laughing loudly and wondering why any man found her glamorous – although at least seventy five percent of her time was geared towards that end. Her laugh was infectious and drew more guests round them, including Amy Billings.

"Has Martin put the world to rights, then?" said the paunchy councillor, laughing.

"That's a copper's job, isn't it, councillor?" said Amy. "Besides, Martin has a well developed sense of fairness and doesn't like to hear people he respects criticised."

"Oh, I don't doubt he's a good man."

"Good – because he is."

"Nice to hear a wife standing up for her husband," laughed the councillor.

"No one criticises Martin when Amy's around," laughed Grise, wishing her friend would shut up.

"Quite right, too," said the councillor, joining in the laughter, "I'll go and make my peace with him."

When he'd gone, followed by Owen, Amy turned to Grise.

"Sorry about that but I couldn't ..."

"That's all right – I don't blame you. He's a fat slob, anyway, but he'll support Owen's nomination ... Are you better now?"

"Oh yes – really. It was funny. I've never suffered from faints, low blood pressure – anything like that – but I was just so listless. It was all over in forty eight hours, but it was a bit grim at the time. I had difficulty breathing and sleeping for a couple of days. When I did manage to nod off, I woke again, dreaming."

"What about – George Clooney?"

"No – stupid! ... Well, I'll tell you – Horst Brultzner!"

"Is he that attractive, then?"

"I said – in an old-fashioned kind of way. But these were horrible dreams. On the first night, I must have actually wandered off in my sleep because Martin found me at the gate."

"You ought to see Alan Read. You know, just to be sure."

"You make me feel like an invalid."

"You're a picture of health. Why do you think I invited you to the party?"

"To annoy the fat councillor?"

Grise slipped out of the bed, wrapped her silk dressing gown around her and walked out through the lounge on to the new terrace. She was so pleased with it, she could have screamed with joy into the night for all the world to hear; everything had gone so well. They had a thriving business, they could afford to send the children to private school, their home was out of this world, Owen was all set to join the council and (who knows?) might even, with a little help, go further still in politics. Their social circle was widening like the ripples on a pond.

The Beachlands Health Club Party had been a success. They'd felt pleased with themselves, and Grise had stripped Owen before he had time to blink or mumble. She'd undressed rapidly and pushed him down onto the bed. She'd straddled him, pressed herself down, held his arms firmly behind his head until she heard his shoulder muscles crack, felt the blood rise in her with such force that she wanted to possess him, and then ridden Owen as though she were on horseback. It was over for her, as all their love-making was, quickly. After she pulled herself off and flopped back on the bed, Grise leaned towards him, took his head between her hands and kissed him again, kissed him with such force that he almost lost consciousness for want of breath. After a while she turned to him but found that he was already asleep, mumbling to himself.

It was a pleasant night and Grise walked over to the edge of the swimming pool, feeling comfortable and relaxed. She crossed her arms over her breasts and hugged herself, looking up into the dark sky where clouds gathered, keeping the earth warm. She loved the night, and had always loved it. Even as a child, it had held no fears for her. The stars twinkled in the sky, jostling their way between the gathering clouds. The moon could still be seen between the clouds – full and pale, grey rather than yellow and pitted with marks that looked like veins.

She smiled into the water of the pool. It would be cold she knew, but somehow that didn't matter. Grise wanted to swim, so she slipped the robe from her shoulders and walked down into the water which closed around her body. Long, easy strokes took her through the water. She was the first to have swum here and it was glorious. It was weird, but in this cold water she felt alive and actually felt her skin glow as she passed, time and again, through the moon in the water. She wanted the moon, like the princess in the story, and now she had it – almost.

She was desperate that this moment should not pass; she wanted to hold on to whatever was happening, forever. The sensation of the water swilling around her was wonderful. It ran between her fingers, around her legs, swirling softly over her shoulders, neck and hair. It trembled on her throat. Grise gasped. She felt a quickening of her breath, and her body turned and yielded across the face of the moon reflected on the water. There was a shadow there – indistinct, diaphanous and hovering easily over the surface of the pool. She was raised up, and she stretched her neck so that her head was lifted high from the shoulders.

Grise's hair flopped back to the water. She opened her mouth, sighed and reached up with her arms. She felt diffused as though her body had become part of the moon reflected beneath her in the pool and gleamed down upon her from the dark sky. Soon she would disintegrate and become part of the power that held her in its grip. Her consciousness began to fade, and she let it happen. Grise leaned into the emptiness that surrounded her as though she might fill it, and become one with it.

She heard a drum beat. Slowly, rhythmically, incessantly the drum tapped a pulse. At first it was firm and loud in her ears. Then, frighteningly, it seemed to become softer and fainter, disappearing almost into some unknown distance. She realised that it was her own heart and, with the realisation, Grise knew fear. The yellow moon began to fade – its gleam started to die. She fought against believing this, wanting the moment of exultation when she would become one with the moon to last forever. Yet, somewhere deep within her, she knew that if that happened it would be the end.

A low, animal cry came from somewhere – not from her, but near – and it woke her from a dream that left her as tired as waking from a nightmare. Grise felt wan – drained. Her body splashed back into the pool, and she shivered. She felt a hand beneath her buttocks, and felt it rub against her. It slid down the back of her thigh and pressed into her soft flesh and lifted her. The body against hers was firm, and she turned into it with a mixture of desire and distaste. She was surrounded by darkness, but insisted on drawing herself into it. Fingers tightened across her shoulders, hurting her. She became impatient – eager to hurry on the end. Her body shook in convulsive spasms and, once again, the sensation of light-headedness and nausea swept over her.

Someone was shouting, faintly, in a muffled, mumbling voice. Her body slipped into the water, which closed over her head. As she surfaced – spluttering, fearful – the face of the moon broke around her. It shattered, splintered into nothing and was at one with the cold water of the pool. The shouting grew louder.

"Grise!" shouted Owen and, suddenly, he was standing beside her in the pool, his right arm round her shoulder.

"I'm bruised."

"Bruised?"

"My shoulders – look!"

"I'm sorry. You .... I thought you were drowning. I woke and you were gone. I heard the splashing, and just ran."

Owen lifted her from the water and carried her across their new terrace to the house. Grise curled into him, wrapping her arms round his shoulders.

"You never kissed me."

"What?" he said, realising she was dazed and confused.

"You never kissed me. All those promises and you never kissed me."

"Let's get you into a warm shower."

CHAPTER 11

The fall of the cards

Mark Chamber's affair with Grise Culman had occurred, briefly, a few years before. Mark was, as Owen Culman had mused, "a decent enough bloke – hard-working and amiable". They were, after all, the best of friends and met, once a month, with their wives, for a game of bridge.

Mark came from a large, traditional Suffolk family, one branch of which farmed near Dunburgh as had their parents before them. Mark's side of the family had gone into the building business and his father had brought the firm "into the twentieth century" during the years that followed the Second World War. When Mark left school he attended the city college in Norbridge and got his ticket in every area of his trade. His father had then, with enormous pride and tears in his eyes, added '& Son' to the 'Mark Chambers's above their workshops and yard. Mark was now just into his forties, well established and well-liked. His son was also going into the business and each day, as he drove into the yard, Mark looked up at his father's sign and realised it was still going to be true.

The firm's office was their house – a large one built on the outskirts of the village; everyone phoned them there and, as often as not, it was Nin Chambers who answered. Mark felt that keeping the office at home gave their customers a feeling of comfort and reassurance. "Phoning someone's home isn't the same as phoning a business. You know what voice you're going to hear when the phone is picked up". Mark was always on the end of the phone and this caused no resentment with his wife or children; they were all aware that this was what buttered the bread. Moreover, Mark never refused a call. Many a Dunburghite, hearing their slates or tiles rattling to the ground during a winter storm, had cause to remember that – and be grateful. One call to the phone in the hall, and Mark Chambers would be on their roof fixing a tarpaulin in place to keep their house dry until the storm subsided, and he – or his men – returned to fix the problem. He wasn't cheap – but he was there!

Mark was good looking in an old-fashioned way. He reminded the older women of an American actor – Richard Egan – who graced the screens when men looked like men and not something that had stepped out of a fashion ad. He was big, strong and muscular – with real muscles that came from hard work rather than a daily work-out at the gym. He had a well-fleshed face, permanently tanned and with a broad smile. He had no more interest in women than the average man and didn't measure his manhood by his success with them. Apart from the usual girl-friends he had as a younger man, there had only been Nin. They'd married, got to know each other as a couple (in that order) and then had children – a boy and two girls. The children had gone to the local primary school and then on to the local secondary school, which Mark decided "was good enough" having got to know the headteacher when he added an extension to his house.

He and Nin also met his brothers and their wives socially on numerous family occasions throughout the year – big occasions when, to steal Dickens phrase, "the tables would be groaning with food". Mark also went shooting and hunting with his brothers. He handled a gun and a horse with equal ease, and had taught his son and daughters to do so. He was fond of meat – red meat and game, in particular – and every Sunday, after church, the family all sat down to a traditional Sunday roast. This was the quintessential Sunday roast – a prime piece of English beef, crisply coated roast potatoes with a melt-in-the-mouth centre and a light-as-air Yorkshire pudding with richly flavoured gravy. The beef was popped in the oven just before church and Mark had sat through many a tedious sermon with the smell of it in his nostrils. "The rector's got seventy five minutes or the joint will be spoiled Fifteen minutes a pound, Nin. Anymore and it's only fit for heeling your shoes".

His other great favourites were venison, rabbit and pheasant. He wouldn't eat deer which had been hunted with hounds, having witnessed an horrendous hunt in Scotland on one occasion when a twenty stone man launched himself from a horse onto the neck and antlers of the deer as it crossed a stream. "The poor creature was forced down into the water with this great hulk on top of it. The hounds closed in and began ripping at it and then, while it was gasping for breath, the bastards gutted it. I've never seen anything so unsportsmanlike in my life".

Nin had come into the family as a young, married woman and learned to cope; there was no other way for the marriage to survive. She was from Norbridge, and had met Mark at the city college where she was on a secretarial course. His good looks had "bowled her over" and there had never been anyone else in her life. Nin was the antithesis of Mark – thin to the point of anorexia, and an ardent fan of fashion magazines and health clubs. She loved the indoor life – televisions, sofas, thick-pile carpets, neatly arranged flowers. She was, as are many women of her generation, obsessive about her weight. The liberating influences of feminism passed her by, and she was forever modelling herself on the Sunday papers' latest skinny piece.

She loved Mark, and she loved her children. She wanted to keep herself looking good and young for them. She cooked the meals Mark liked to eat and which the children had grown used to, but she hated them and would nibble round the edges of her plate, picking here and there in the modern fashion. She hated his family gatherings where everyone seemed so "hale and hearty". Her sisters-in-law annoyed her with their comments about her "slimness" – meaning "skinny-ness". Following such weekends, she consoled herself with a visit to Grise's club, and a good workout.

She and Grise were good friends. It had been their idea to meet once a month for bridge – the game being particularly fashionable in the village at the time. It was through them that Mark and Owen became acquainted.

Like most wives, she was the last to know and, anyway, hadn't believed it. Nin had decided that it was nonsense and, if it wasn't, nothing was to be gained and everything lost by bringing it out into the open. She would lose a friend and – possibly, though she didn't believe this for some reason – a husband. At the same time, she couldn't simply let it go. So Nin stewed on it and waited, asked Mark where he'd been whenever he came in, or where he was going whenever he went out, but couldn't bring herself to challenge him.

The bridge games continued and she had Grise at her table every second month, and sat at Grise's table on the alternate month. She found an ally in Grise as far as food was concerned, and the two of them conspired to serve healthy alternatives.

Whenever Grise and Owen came to theirs, Nin was obliged to show her round the house, while the men had a drink and got the table ready for the game. There wasn't a thing out of place in Nin's house. It was the source of admiration and aggravation to every other woman who visited. Grise was clean and tidy to a fault, but Nin out-sparkled everyone. Grise, looking round each time she went, stoked her jealousy. It wasn't simply that everything was perfect – it was more that it was always slightly ahead of everyone else; everything was absolutely straight from each season's glossy magazines. Nin scoured these avidly and immediately replaced anything that was not mentioned or pictured – down to the latest style of toothbrush holder.

While Grise and Nin continued to meet at the Health Club, Mark and Owen went shooting together on Mark's family farm: usually, it was wood pigeons or rabbits but, in season, pheasants and quail. It always horrified Nin when Mark arrived home with a brace of pheasants or a clutch of rabbits in his fist and dropped them on the kitchen table. After he'd skinned, plucked and gutted them she would cook him a meal, or freeze them for later. Mark enjoyed the shooting, and Owen got used to it after a while; it had seemed unmanly to refuse.

Although he rode well, Mark always refused to be involved in foxhunting. He was part of the "county set" so much admired by Lianne Snooks, but turned his back on the hunt. This annoyed Grise no end because she so much wanted to be invited to join. The thought of seeing herself dressed in red and mounted on a stallion was too enticing to be let go without a fight. The whole paraphernalia excited her – the Huntsman (or woman), the Whippers-in, the Master (or Mistress), the farmers and landowners you mixed with, the fact that it was a very expensive activity, the hunt supporters' club and being a private donor.

Last season, she had actually managed to ride with them for the first time. Mark had refused to be involved, but asked his brother to take her along. The meet had begun in the morning. They had all assembled at the village inn. Drinks had flowed, and then the hounds moved off, drawing for a fox. Through woodland, over fields and heathland they'd gone, the Huntsman keeping in touch with the hounds by voice or horn. As the hounds drew, the Huntsman had encouraged them by crying "leu". Grise gripped the flanks of her horse between her legs and loved it – the sweat of the chase, the smell of the horses, the yelling, the tight-lipped look of triumph on the faces of the men whenever the hounds picked up a lost scent, the closeness of the riders and the exhilaration of the wind on her face. It was the sheer animality which excited her; she felt part of a hunting pack – a living, sensuous organism.

The fox had been ingenious – with strength, speed and stamina which surprised the Huntsman. The scenting conditions had not been good; they'd hunted him for fifteen miles, and not once had he gone to ground. He'd been elusive, cunning as his reputation and swift. The fox had been wily – doubling back on his tracks to foil his own scent, going through water, leading them across manured fields, through fields where there were cattle, crossing roads and old railway lines or running along the tops of walls and along ditches. Every fox, she was told, had its own territory, which it knew in intimate detail. Foxes were capable of complete vanishing tricks – one minute there was a fox with a good scent, and the next minute there was no fox and no scent. When the scent became weak the hounds were checked. Then they fanned out – forwards, sideways and backwards to recover the line. The Huntsman lifted his head like an animal and cast about, his nostrils wide.

They'd got him, but Grise had been galled at having been so far behind in the line of riders that she missed the end. There was some blood. She saw the fox's bush tossed from hand to hand, but thirty hounds had surrounded the fox for the final kill, and she had seen nothing. Mark had met her when they returned to the village mid-afternoon, and the hunters had ribbed him – "Bloody socialist, that's what you are Mark" which was, of course, the highest insult.

"You won't get Mark to join the hunt, Grise," Nin had said, over coffee one morning. "I've heard him arguing with them enough times to know that. Mark has got nothing against killing foxes – they can be a nuisance – but he objects to making a ritual of it. He has ridden with the hunt. He said that, at the end, the fox was a piece of living string as the hounds tore it apart."

Grise said nothing, but was somehow determined that Mark should take her himself. She wanted him there at the kill.

Mark Chambers wasn't sure when his fascination with Grise Culman began. He felt that, somehow, it had crept up on him like a mugger on a dark road. Their bridge games were innocent enough (or so they seemed at the time) spiced as they were with politics of the urban kind – town halls, council meetings, working parties, minutes of meetings, agendas for meetings, applications for grants, site visits. There was nothing here that seemed particularly enticing, or maybe the smell of power was simply less apparent. They were all Conservatives – small business people and farmers invariably are – and there was an air of harmonious agreement as they played.

She was attractive – no doubt about that; more than attractive – Grise was exciting. He'd noticed the dark brown eyes across the table without realising it, and the black hair, cut short, and the way she had of looking down and then up under her lashes without lifting her head. When she smiled – and she had a smile that lit up her whole face and made those eyes seem bigger than ever – it felt that she was smiling just at you, as though you were the only person in the room. Looking back, Mark realised that Grise radiated affection; it seemed a strange word, but it was true. She also had this enormous energy. More than other woman in his social circle, she was a physical presence in the room. He hadn't noticed it at the time. He hadn't even been aware of the off-the-shoulder dresses she wore when they played through the winter.

When he'd got the contract for their extension, things had seemed relaxed enough. Nin had been pleased because their club was just across the road, and she thought Mark could come home for lunch. His thanks and refusal didn't surprise her because Nin knew he always ate with his men.

Owen hadn't always been about at the club, but Mark's workmen had and Mark had usually been with them or off supervising other sites. Grise had offered him a coffee occasionally, but he'd always refused, politely, because it didn't give the right impression to his men for them to be working while he was drinking coffee. She'd teased him about not taking her fox-hunting, but that was a standing joke between them. He remembered thinking how easy it was in her company.

Then, the day had come when he'd arranged to go pigeon shooting with Owen and Grise had turned up, Owen's shotgun under her arm, wrapped in scarves, wearing a wax coat and with a boyish cap on her head, pushed slightly back to reveal her hair.

"Owen had to take the children to their swimming class so I thought I'd come instead. He didn't mind."

They'd driven to his brother's farm in her Range Rover – Grise had insisted on that – and he'd found it strangely erotic, being driven by a woman. "You're not used to being driven by a woman, are you Mark?" She'd seemed manly at the wheel, steering the large vehicle along rocky, muddy farm tracks and through broken five-barred gates. The Range Rover had rocked to and fro, throwing them together, and they'd laughed. It had been a good feeling. She'd looked at him, once or twice, in that way of hers, and given him that smile – the affectionate smile. Mark had smiled back. He was going to enjoy the shoot. It was a rough shoot. There would be just the two of them. He remembered looking forward to it.

When the vehicle pulled up by the barn, he jumped down and went round to help her out. Their coats were open – it had been warm in the vehicle – and Grise slipped inside his as easily as you like. Her hips slid against his groin, and she had looked up and laughed. He'd thought, afterwards, that it was her smallness against the size of him – the way she so easily fitted inside his wax coat as though under a duvet – which excited him. Whatever it was, the next moment his arms were round her waist, down over her buttocks and he was lifting her to him. Grise reached up and clutched his mouth with hers, the difference in their heights stretching her neck to its fullest extent. The heavy coat held her arms down, so she shrugged it from her, and she was small and lithe in his arms.

He carried her to the barn and went in among the bales of straw stacked ready for the sheep. She was warm and inviting. He felt his juices flood into her, and it had been glorious – to be wanted like that. "You needed that," she'd said.

Grise had taken charge then. She'd gone back to the Range Rover, locked it and brought their shotguns and bags into the barn. She'd taken his arm and lifted him from the ground where he sat, his back against a straw bale, watching her.

"If anyone sees the car, they'll just think we've gone hunting."

She led him deeper into the barn and took her clothes off. There was a chill in the air and her body glowed.

"We've got all morning – and most of the afternoon, too, if we like," she laughed, "Well, are you going to get undressed or not? I can't do much on my own."

It had been intense. In all honesty, Mark had to admit to himself that he remembered it with pleasure. They'd met frequently – sometimes at his, sometimes at hers, often when both were out on other business. They'd met with one thing in mind – sex – and the acuteness of their desire had been almost virulent. It was Mark who had finished it. "I'm sorry Grise." "You use that word a lot." "It's true – but I can't go on." "Why not?" "Because it's wrong." "You haven't thought it wrong over the last three months." "Oh, I have." "Well you seemed to be enjoying yourself." "I have – but it's got to stop." "Why?" The word had been uttered with a long sigh of anguish that wrenched his heart. "What harm are we doing? I love it with you Mark. We're like animals and I love it. I feel so alive. I can't wait to see you again, and get my knickers off." "You know why." "Nin, Owen, the children!" "Yes." "But we're doing them no harm." "We are – even if we're never found out, we are." "How?" "Because they trust us, and we've broken that trust." "They'll never know!" "But we will."

Although he wasn't consciously a religious man – in that he never thought about God or the implications of his faith – Mark attended the Morning Service each Sunday because his family had always done so. When he was there the Sunday following his ending of the affair with Grise, Mark Chambers had got down on his knees and prayed for forgiveness.

"Lord, forgive me and please keep the harm I may have done from my family – not for my sake, because I don't deserve it, but for theirs. I don't want my sins to come back on my family. I don't want my children hurt by what I have done should they find out."

Nin wasn't used to seeing Mark on his knees for so long before the service. He wasn't the kind of man who did things for show. He'd been over-solicitous to her afterwards, and Nin guessed that there must have been something in Ample's gossip. She had said nothing, and neither had Mark. He wasn't that kind of man: to him a trouble shared was a trouble doubled.

CHAPTER 12

Hints and allegations

Tony Crewes was looking forward to his drink with Martin Billings. They met quite often to sample wine at each other's houses – always when their wives were out at some village meeting or other. The WI and Young Wives had many virtues, not least being their ability to relieve husbands from the company of their wives every now and then. They would talk what Martin Billings like to call "squit" for an hour or so, enjoy some good food and conclude the evening mildly drunk, and smiling. He opened the gate of the Police House and grinned at the blue lamp above the front door. Where the hell had Martin got that from?

"I'll probably get away with that," said Martin as he took Tony into his office, "Although they haven't the sense to put them on new stations, they haven't actually gone completely nuts and removed them from all the old ones – just those they're unimaginative enough to close down. I got that from one of the old village stations. They'll be no copper there anymore – let's give the yobbos a free rein, and have 'him and her' pass through in the squad car once in a while. Still, we'll let that rest for one night. What have you brought?"

"You said Alsace?"

"I've a cheese from there – they only make one of any note – Munster ..."

"... from the mountains of the Vosges ..."

"... semi-soft with a red orange crust and a distinctive smell."

"I'm afraid I brought a Reisling."

"The Gewurztraminer is better with cheese, but we'll suffer both. Let's enjoy."

They sat quietly at Martin's dining table with a selection of french bread spread before them. Martin had provided the Munster fermier veritable, and among the standard baguettes had placed a loaf of berawecka – a rich bread made from dried pears with prunes, figs, raisins, walnuts; it was spiced with cinnamon, cloves and lemon zest, and flavoured with kirsch. It had been a pleasant evening and there was still some Pinot Blanc to come.

They both liked the pretension of knowing a lot about French cuisine. It amused them to spout at gatherings of their wives' friends, and their wine trips to Calais added to their mystique. They realized that, for some inexplicable reason, the English felt they ought to know about French food and wine, and yet somehow didn't. So when Martin and Tony vented what little they did know, everybody else was embarrassed at their own lack of knowledge. It was a form of gamesmanship which Martin loved.

Unlike Martin, Tony disliked his job intensely. He'd left university with a desire to opt out and paint, but had got nowhere. It had been fun slopping around with his friends, and wearing the painter's gear. Days on the river bank, or pressed up against some factory wall, while the yoicks drifted by and wished they could paint too, were hard to beat for sheer wanton pleasure; but they didn't buy you a decent bottle of wine or a meal at a good restaurant. He'd spent some time in Thailand, but kipping out on the beach – under what amounted to a straw umbrella on legs – got on your nerves after a while, and his mate hadn't been the best of company.

When he got back to England, Beth had been waiting – well, not exactly waiting, but moving in the art exhibition circle – and she'd reminded him of Sally Field, although – now – he couldn't think why. She'd tidied up the flat he was sharing with a mate and cooked some great suppers, and eventually they'd got married. Tony liked his home comforts – although he was grossly untidy himself and couldn't be bothered to cook – and Beth seemed to provide these. He wanted to get married; it was a positive direction in which to go. Having done brilliantly well at university – a first class maths degree with honours – he turned his hand to the insurance business, which he mastered in under six months, and was now earning a very nice salary, thank you, with a locally-based international firm, but was bored out of his skull. He found Martin an amusing diversion, and enjoyed their times together.

His wife, Beth, disliked Martin deeply. "He's a bad influence, Tony. He's got a lot to answer for." The "lot to answer for" was Tony's affair (some years before) with a colleague – a divorced woman at the office who had an interest in art. It had been an unfortunate interest. A couple of quite innocent visits to exhibitions in London, including the Dali, had been misinterpreted and led to a row that grieved Tony and brought out a childish streak in his nature. "If she thinks I'm having an affair, I might as well. No point in being accused of something while you're not actually getting the pleasure of it". The divorcee had been only too keen and, before he really knew what was happening, Tony had moved out – splitting his family and friends. Despite his behaviour, he was a family man. He actually loved his children who were still young, and he moved back in quickly, hoping to stem the tide of the damage. This had been partially successful. The friends who knew accepted him, and his children were just glad to see him sitting at the table carving Sunday lunch; but, for Tony and Beth themselves, his betrayal had left deep scars that were still festering.

"Amy OK is she?"

"You're the second person to ask that in the past week."

Martin went on to relay the conversation at the Health Club party.

"You say you found Amy wandering in her sleep?"

"She was at the gate – in her nightdress."

"And the young hairdresser had bite marks on her throat?"

"There was blood on her pillow – a spot or two, I believe. Why?"

"Nothing – just curious … Beth bumped into Ample Bassett in the corner shop. Ample told her that Owen found Grise in their new pool – livid-white and freezing cold with what appeared to be a giant bat hovering over her, and Grise noticed a trickle of blood on her throat when she was exercising the next morning."

"Go on."

"Three women – all bloodless or, at least, pale and wan – as they used to say. What does that suggest to you, Martin?"

"What are you driving at, Tony?"

"Don't they teach you the skills of deduction, anymore – is it all down to technology, now? Three women lose enough blood to turn them white – we must have a vampire in the village."

For a moment, Martin – who had no sense of humour at all when his professional competence was concerned, and who perceived an immediate threat to the peace and contentment of his 'patch' – stared blankly at Tony, who laughed.

"You silly bastard – I thought you were serious for a moment."

"Trouble in the village – keep your ear to the phone – an inspector calls."

"Junket's a superintendent. Let's open that last bottle. We'll drink it in the study – I've got something to show you."

Tony smiled at the leather padded Windsor chair across the room from Martin's Victorian police sergeant's desk, the large walnut-veneered cupboard, the small pendulum clock with its Roman numerals, the Queen in coronation regalia and the black-leaded, cast iron fireplace. Martin took an inkwell from the cupboard.

"It's a pewter capstan inkwell. They had them on ships, but the base was wider – obviously. Then they were adapted and used in banks, post offices and …"

"… police stations?"

"You have it. Do you notice – the well is fairly shallow so that only the quill point could be inked. Brilliant, isn't it? That way, the officer taking down a statement didn't have to watch his pen – he could keep his eyes on the villain with whom he was having the cosy chat."

"You're as mad as a bloody hatter, Martin."

"There's no harm in a little eccentricity," replied Martin, laughing and delighted that his friend should recognise his oddness. "I was hoping for an actual inkstand – the likes of Junket would have had one of those, you can bet. There's a beautiful one in Tunbridge ware with two glass wells, a stamp box and a recess – with a lift-out lid – for the pens."

Tony loved enthusiasm, while acknowledging that he was the least enthused person in the office at work, and he rose to Martin's. At that moment, the door-bell rang.

"Expecting anyone?"

"No, but a village copper is on duty …"

"Twenty four hours a day, seven days a week …"

"Three hundred and sixty five days a year – and that's what it's all about. I'm always hoping for a call during Christmas lunch …"

"Just so you can ring Junket for advice?"

"I wouldn't miss the chance."

Martin walked across his office, and opened the side door that led directly into the station. Corvin Unwood stood on the threshold.

"Corvin – what a pleasant surprise. No problems, I hope?"

"Not insuperable ones, Martin, but I would welcome a small chat."

"Come in. You've met Tony."

"Uh ... yes. I didn't realise ..."

"No trouble, rector," said Tony Crewes – enjoying the priest's obvious discomfort, "I'll pop into Martin's dining room and keep this bottle of Pinot Blanc company."

Corvin's own hesitation in not urging Tony to stay embarrassed the priest. He'd never liked Tony Crewes, and felt that he was being less than generous. He sensed, too, that Tony had never liked him, and this was true – although not for the reasons Corvin supposed. Corvin was a courteous man, and realised he had interrupted Martin's evening. The matter on which he'd come was a small thing with which he needed Martin's support. Martin, out of kilter, coughed but said nothing.

"It's not confidential – only a small matter – I'll come back tomorrow."

"Not at all, rector – I wouldn't hear of it. As I say, a bottle of Pinot Blanc is very good company – I shall not be lonely," taunted Tony.

It was the man's dissolute manner which irritated Corvin. He felt sorry for his wife, Beth, who was on the PCC – the whole village had heard the gossip.

"No, please, I really wouldn't want to disrupt your evening."

"Well, if you won't impart your business to Martin – although he'll worry all night if you don't – why not join us for a glass or two?"

"Wonderful," said Martin, pleased the tension was relieved.

"No, I really ..."

"Really must, rector. Beth would never forgive me if I did not insist. She's always telling me how hard you work and how you need to relax more."

There was a sardonic note in the man's voice even as he extended the invitation. Corvin could cope with direct sarcasm, but veiled taunts left him speechless, usually because he was inclined to give the speaker the benefit of the doubt.

"Corvin, I've already put a third glass on the table," urged Martin, who took the bull by the horns, and led Corvin through from his office into the dining room.

"A pleasant evening," said Corvin by way of moving the conversation on, "I noticed that the bryony is already out as I walked up Church Hill."

"And the bluebells are in full blossom," answered Tony.

It amused him that Corvin felt the need to talk of flowers. Most men would have commented on the wine or the food so why did the priest feel he needed to be different? The man's girth was a sure indication that he enjoyed his food.

"Indeed, the little wood that leads from our garden to the old vicarage is always a profusion of colour at this time of year," replied Corvin.

Normally either Tony or Martin would have capped this, urging the conversation to slightly surreal levels of flower appreciation. 'I notice that the red campion is particularly vibrant this year' occurred to Tony, but he held his tongue – not wishing to embarrass Martin further, and feeling that the rector would not latch on to that particular style of humour. He followed with the rather flat – to his mind, but mildly sarcastic to Corvin's:

"You are renowned for your walking, rector. Two centuries ago, your secondary pre-occupation would have been as a naturalist. Those old rectors spent much of their time cataloguing the countryside."

"Indeed – and we owe much to them. Many were scientists in their own right."

"No time for that these days, hey Corvin – too many people sitting at their desks working out just how much more they can squeeze out of you?" said Martin.

"You're enjoying the wine, I see," said Tony, "drink up. Martin and I have a Pinot Gris to follow this – yellow gold on the appearance, deep and rich on the nose."

"Help yourself to bread, Corvin, please – it's to be eaten and enjoyed."

Corvin reached, almost self-consciously, for the loaf of berawecka, which had yet to be cut. Tony Crewes handed him the bread-knife.

"Good choice, rector – pears, prunes, figs, raisins, walnuts and flavoured with kirsch."

"Not to mention the cinnamon, cloves and lemon zest," added Martin.

"One feels glutted merely looking at it, Martin," said Corvin, quite jovially. He was easing, visibly – with a greedy smile on his fat face.

"The Pinot Gris?"

"Why not?

All three men laughed. Corvin, in particular, felt pleased and relieved to be free of the rectory for a while, and in the company of men. The humour was rough, but unquestioned. Tony Crewes sensed that Corvin was beginning to relax, and he thought how amusing it would be to tell Beth that he had "toddled down the hill with a drunken rector". Martin wished his friend would desist from baiting Corvin; first in making him feel uncomfortable that he'd come, and then in insisting that he stayed. There had been the skit about his fondness for walking and the comment that he was enjoying the wine. He had then offered the bread knife, as no-one else could have done, when Corvin reached for the uncut loaf.

Martin had his ear closer to the ground than anyone else in the village – the nosey-parkers, included – and he had allied himself to Corvin's cause when the priest arrived. Corvin was not overly popular. He was a little too high church for the likes of Dunburgh people, enjoying (as he did) the ritual of each service. His manner on these occasions did tend to verge on the pompous, with his flourishes embellishing the delivery of the body and blood of Christ. He had been foursquare behind his wife pushing for the re-introduction of liturgical colours and abandoning flowers during Lent. His sermons were pedantic, but Martin had challenged those in the Fishermen's Hut when they grumbled about this - "If he didn't give good value from the pulpit, you'd say he wasn't bothered". Similarly, he had taken to task the women who grumbled about the autumn bazaar – "What would you say if he didn't want one? The village is dead?" "He's never at home!" "How can he be if he's out visiting?" "He's too fond of the sound of his own voice." "Anyone else like that in the room, Yammer?" This had been met with uproarious laughter because Yammer Utting was known for expressing his own opinions vehemently.

"It was the Pinot Blanc which started our conversation about Grise Culman in her swimming pool," said Tony.

"And the giant bat," laughed Martin.

"Giant bat?" queried Corvin.

Martin relayed the conversation which had stemmed from Ample's gossip.

"That couldn't have been a vampire bat, you know," said Corvin, "whatever might have been said."

"I was only joking, rector, but why do you say that?"

"Vampire bats are small."

"How on earth do you know that?"

"I come across all sorts of information in my line of work, Tony. There are three sorts of bats which can be called true vampires. They live on a diet of fresh blood, which they lick from tiny wounds inflicted with their razor-sharp incisor teeth. There is an anti-clotting substance in their saliva, which allows them to feed continuously for up to eighteen minutes. They drink forty percent of their body weight in that time. A groove on either side of the tongue widens and narrows to draw blood from the wound. They prey on domestic animals and birds ..."

"And humans?"

"Rarely, but it has been known for them to settle on an exposed foot."

"Is that true? ... I'm sorry, rector, of course it is."

"Yes, Tony – but not just because I'm a priest: even priests have been known to lie."

"Never!"

Tony and Corvin laughed and, as they did so, Tony looked up at Martin who had been about to pour another glass of wine. He'd paused as Corvin began his explanation and was now quite sullen; there was a deep frown between his eyes and his lips tightened. He stared hard at Corvin, caught his friend's eye and looked away. Corvin looked uneasy, despite his laughter, and so Tony decided to twist the conversation along another controversial route (one he and Beth had pursued many times to no avail) – the question of the soul.

Tony's attendance at church was to please his wife and keep the household harmonious. He made no great claims to faith himself and, in the right company, would skit it with relish. Beth, however, had the faith of the desperate; she needed to know that this life had a meaning, and sought this meaning through religion, trying to take Tony with her. She became quite fearful sometimes that they would go their separate ways after death. Why this alarmed her, Tony could not quite make out, but then – to him – death would not be a conscious state.

"Do you mind talking shop, rector? For most of us there is seldom the chance – at least to talk your shop."

"Not at all – I've had my most useful conversations over a glass or two."

"Tell me, then, about the soul."

Martin moved away; abstract conversation held little appeal for him, and he still wore that frown, and glared occasionally at Corvin.

"The word soul comes from the Hebrew word – nefesh. It can be translated as 'soul', 'life' or even 'breath'. In that sense, the soul is not an aspect of the person, but the whole person as a living being. It is a poetic way of saying 'I'. As in Luke's gospel when Mary says ..."

"My soul doth magnify the Lord."

"You know your scriptures, Tony?"

"Beth and I talk about it a lot – anyway, I remember that verse from going to church as a child – the Magnificat, isn't it?"

"Mary's beautiful song to the Lord – indeed."

"So when she uses the word 'soul' she means her whole self?"

"Yes – the idea that the body and soul were separate is a Greek one."

"Forgive my materialistic question, rector, but it is the soul which goes to your Heaven – not the body?"

"That was a medieval idea – that the body and soul separated on death – the body to die and the soul to live on with God."

"And you believe that?"

"No – I believe that the eternal life, which I am living now, will continue into eternity. After death, I shall have a spiritual body."

"So eternity is ...?"

"Timelessness."

"And this spiritual body – how does it relate to your ... uh ...?"

"The fat priest you see before you?"

"If you say so."

"Our spiritual body, after death, grows out of our earthly life as a plant grows from a seed. Our spiritual body expresses the personality we have developed in our earthly bodies."

"And where does our spiritual body ... live?"

Martin, sitting with them but distracted, looked at his friend – drawn by what he took to be the sarcasm in his voice. He was surprised to see nothing of the sort in his face.

"Heaven – which is what you are after, isn't it Tony? – is the state of being with God. It is when we are with God all the time and consciously aware of his presence."

"How awful."

"You mean awesome."

Tony Crewes thought for a while, and there was silence in the room. They could all hear the ticking of the tavern clock on the dining room wall.

"So mystics and the like have already attained that state on earth – that consciousness of God's presence?" he asked.

"Yes – but they are not free of their earthly body."

"More cheese?" asked Martin, "Or bread – and I do have some smoked salmon."

"No, really ..."

"Open the Reisling I bought, Martin – if you're serious about the fish."

"Really ...," began Corvin, trying to keep the conversation on track, "... Tony, do you know Peter Vishnya?"

"Vaguely."

"You should talk to him. He has the full picture right across the three main movements – Catholic, Anglican and Orthodox. It really is a very wide subject, and I detect that your interest is academic rather than personal – at the moment?"

"Both, rector. Occasionally the state of my soul perturbs even me."

"And so it should – remember St Paul's image of the seed and the plant."

"I see the idea of being conscious of God – are we conscious of each other?"

"Our loved ones?"

"Yes."

"Yes – but remember, we can only come to the Father through the Son and, in accepting Him as our Saviour, our sins are taken from us."

"Quite mind boggling, isn't it?"

"Do you prefer the simple concepts of Heaven and Hell?"

"Perhaps not – the intellect goes beyond such things."

"There have been bishops who have pointed us further along the road."

"And you would follow their lead?"

"I know my own mind on these things, Tony. You must come to them for yourself."

"Yes ... Peter Vishnya is an academic, I take it?"

"To be honest, I am not sure – for all I know he could be an ordained priest – but he certainly knows his faiths."

Tony Crewes would never have thought that he could sit in silence with Corvin Unwood for whom he had always held a certain, mild, contempt. He wasn't quite sure why – perhaps it was the man's pomposity, his 'hedging-my-bets' sermons, his over-anxiety about the trivia of village religious life such as jumble sales, coffee mornings, flower rotas and churchyard grass cutting, or his reluctance to take a firm lead. Sitting in Martin's dining room, however, over a glass of Reisling the priest seemed almost human – much like other men. He was relaxed and easy company.

The smell of Martin's cooking wafted in from the kitchen and he soon appeared with a steaming bowl.

"Tagliatelle with smoked salmon – wonderful – chestnut mushrooms, fresh tagliatelle, a squeeze of lemon, a dash of parsley and some crème fraiche – all ready in twenty minutes!"

"I really ..."

"Come on, Corvin – you obviously enjoy your food – tuck in!"

"I was going to say, I really do admire your versatility, Martin. I would not have known where to start. Indeed, I doubt whether I could have cut the mushrooms correctly."

At that moment, the telephone in the office rang. Martin smiled.

"Twenty four hours a day, seven days a week ..."

"... three hundred and sixty five days a year!" cut in Tony, "You might just as well be a priest!"

Corvin laughed; he was pleased with the solidarity.

When Martin returned from his office, his face was grim, but happy. The call had come from Plumptious Walters at the Jolly Sailors. She was, unusually, having serious trouble with Shane Marjoram, who was drunk, abusive and, she felt, potentially violent. Would Martin stroll down?

"I'm afraid you will have to finish our late snack alone. Duty calls!"

"I must be going, anyway, Martin. It really is quite late. Esther will wonder where I am. You will excuse me, Tony. I enjoyed our talk."

"So did I, rector – perhaps we might pursue it again sometime?"

"If you're going, Corvin, I'll walk down the hill with you. I'm heading for the Jolly Sailors."

"Trouble?" asked Tony.

"Business," said Martin.

The little gathering came to its abrupt end, and the three men walked together down Church Hill until they came to the corner of Shore Lane and Beach Road where Martin indicated that Tony might like to leave them. When he had gone on his way, Martin turned to Corvin.

"You'll excuse me, Corvin, but I have to ask you this – our friendship depends upon it. Why did you lie about the vampire bat?"

"I'm glad you ask. I would have ..."

"I know – you looked uneasy when you made the excuse of 'coming across all sorts of information in your line of work' – but why did you lie?"

"Some months ago – in March, it was – Rebecca had a strange experience. She'd gone to bed early, as I remember, and locked her door, which is not usual with her – Esther and I would never dream of entering her room without knocking, whether she was there or not. When Esther called her in the morning, with a cup of tea, and Rebecca unlocked the door to let her mother in, she noticed a few drops of blood on her nightdress. Naturally she expressed her alarm at this – more so when she also found some on Rebecca's pillow. Rebecca was quite snappy, which is not in her nature. When she had calmed down, however, and we were able to speak, she acknowledged that she felt weak and, indeed, her face was white. She said that she remembered her curtains blowing in the night – "flapping" was her word for it – and feeling sick. There were two marks on her throat – she had clearly been bitten – and Esther, always ready to be alarmed where Rebecca is concerned, concluded that a bat must have bitten her."

"Why a bat?"

"What else could reach a first floor bedroom? Besides, Esther has always been convinced that there is a colony of them in the roof of the Old Vicarage."

"But why a vampire bat?"

"What other bat sucks blood?"

"But vampire bats are restricted to South America, aren't they? They couldn't live through an English winter."

"I know, I know, Martin – but women do not see things like that: certainly Esther doesn't. Her beloved daughter had been bitten by something larger than a gnat. Whatever it was appeared to have come in through the bedroom window, and there were bats in the Old Vicarage and a wildlife park up the road! Possibly a foreign species had escaped from there! You understand?"

"Yes."

Corvin had been driven by hysteria – not that Martin would have said so.

"To ease Esther's mind I looked up 'vampire bat' on Rebecca's laptop – hence my knowledge. I did not wish to go into all this in front of Tony – so, my little white lie."

"Yes – I understand ... And Rebecca recovered?"

"Yes – within a few days she had returned to normal."

They continued in each other's company until they reached the gate to the allotments where, years before, Clive and Mary Brown had stopped off on their way from the Working Men's Club and made love under the wigwam of his runner beans. Here they shook hands and said goodnight – Corvin going along Shore Lane to a wondering Esther, and Martin heading down Beach Road to a violent Shane Marjoram. He detested Marjoram with a silent loathing; but for the likes of Marjoram, the village would have been a decent place where families could raise their children in safety and peace. Plumptious had sounded anxious on the phone, and now that he had settled his mind over Corvin's lie the policeman was focussed on the task ahead.

He arrived at the Jolly Sailors to find Marjoram gone, but Plumptious relieved.

"Thanks for coming, Martin. He stormed out about five minutes ago ..."

"Don't worry, I'll find him. Give me the details."

"Well, as you know, I'm not normally bothered by him, but he was raging angry tonight. He must have been drinking before he got here because I keep my eye on him for Sarah's sake and I served him no more than four lagers – I swear it. He was playing pool with some of his mates – and losing – and raving on about his father-in-law, Froggy. How he showed him no respect, wouldn't let him carry his mother-in-law's coffin and made a fool of him in front of his wife. What he wasn't going to do to Froggy was nobody's business! I didn't like to kick him out in that state – I've always been worried that, one day, he'll do Sarah real harm. He'd have had a go at John Barker had John let him but, of course, he's got more sense ...."

"Why John?"

"He told him to calm down – nothing more than that. You should have seen his face! Anyway, when he eventually lost the match, he swore at his mates, swore at me, smashed the pool cue across the table and stormed out."

"Which way did he go?"

"Oh, I noticed that – towards the beach. Don't know why – there's nothing there. I thought he might go home to Sarah. That was my worry."

Their conversation had taken place, in muttered tones, at the hatch to the locals' back room. Martin now walked through to the main bar and spoke to the locals who sat waiting for something to happen.

"Anyone know where Clive might be?"

"He were at the Hut earlier – might still be there," said Dick Utting.

"I ent shure about that," said Scrub Turrell, "there weren't enuf sittin round for Froggy's loikin'."

"He loikes company these days," said Jumbo Gooch.

"Nat'ral enuf – with his woife garn," said Deaf Charlie.

"That's what I said," cut in Scrub, "there weren't enuf sittin' 'round."

Much as he normally liked what he called the local "squit", Martin was eager to trace both Clive and his son-in-law, and so he turned abruptly to Plumptious.

"I'll be back. If he returns, try to keep him here – even if it means giving him a pint. If he does turn up, call me on the mobile – you've got the number. OK, Plumptious?"

"You can rely on it."

After he'd gone, the locals looked at each other and grinned; they were expecting some trouble.

"He's OK – that PC Billings," said Deaf Charlie.

"For a copper," replied Scrub.

"We're lucky to have him," snapped Plumptious, "Would you turn out at this hour when you're supposed to be off-duty, to find Shane Marjoram?"

"I ent sayin' …" stuttered Scrub.

"Then don't."

Outside, Martin turned right along the sea wall. The clear evening had now grown dark, and the moon appeared to come and go behind the gathering clouds. A breeze had sprung up and blew in from the sea, shaking the water into little waves, which lapped and fell against the groynes. Pieces of loose net bounced gently across the pebbled beach, and the occasional thin rope stirred or a tarpaulin quivered. Martin normally loved the changing patterns of the beach, but tonight he was anxious and barely noticed. The breeze, though slight, came from the east and was cold; even with summer approaching, that wind continued to chill. The policeman peered along the beach hoping to see a stumbling figure, but there were only the long-shore fishing boats, silhouetted against the lights that shone over the water from Lowestoft.

He walked down onto the beach, skirting lobster pots, which were heaped against the sea wall, and looked behind the winch housings to see if Shane Marjoram was slumped against one, sleeping off his drunkenness. There was nothing except his sense of ill-ease – a professional feeling honed over the years. Something was wrong, or going to be wrong, but Martin Billings couldn't place his finger on what; he looked back over his shoulder and felt the wind on his right cheek. He hunched his shoulders. It would be blow over – there'd be no rain tonight. As he ran his eyes along the sea wall, he saw a figure saunter into view from Beach Road. It paused at the end of the road, just opposite the Seaview Café, as though deciding whether to turn left along the beach or continue its walk along the promenade. He stood still and waited. The figure came towards him. As it got nearer, he realized – from the casual swing of the legs – that it was Tony Crewes.

"What the hell are you doing here?" he asked.

CHAPTER 13

A death on the beach

It turned out that Tony Crewes had decided to take a stroll in the fresh evening air before returning to the bosom of his wife. Martin reserved his judgement on whether or not this was true. Despite his disinclination to mix business with pleasure, he was rather relieved to see Tony.

"You need to know that Shane Marjoram is on the loose – drunk and violent. So you're here at your own risk – not with me. Do you understand?"

This agreed, the two friends proceeded, in harmony, to explore the rest of the beach and sea wall between Dunburgh and Blacksands Ness. The breeze continued to blow from the sea, somewhat stiffened now, and the mood of their evening together changed from lightly reflective to reflectively sombre. The dunes opened up before them – a long stretch of undulating sand and shingle, held together by marram grass, which ran from the end of the sea wall to the River Cassyn.

"You think he'll be out there?"

"It's possible. I found a drunk out here a few winters back – frozen to death with his unfinished six-pack by his side."

"Rather you than me."

"You get used to it. The shock comes when it's someone you know – someone you've been drinking with only a few nights before. But we don't want that, do we – that's why we're here. We can do without bodies on the beach at Dunburgh."

"You really think he might do someone damage?"

"It's his wife, Sarah, we worry about. Lovely girl – born here – went through all the local schools. She deserves better than him."

The stiffened breeze cut a little now, making them wish – even on this spring night – for the warmth of their homes or, at least, the pub. It was hard walking on the sand, but Martin was determined to find Marjoram if he was here. They struggled into the dunes, their feet catching on the spiky grass, keeping their eyes open for rabbit scrapes. The wind was behind them so that the backs of their necks shivered and their faces glowed with sweat. As they reached the top of the dunes and rested on the grassy bank, the lighted tower of the church sprung up in the distance – far from them across the marsh.

The moon was out and the grubby dykes shone between the tall, straggling reeds. Tony thought how cold it all looked – not the kind of place in which to get lost. Beyond the marsh, in front of the church, a small copse of trees straggled along the edge of a slope, eventually surrounding an old house that had, as far as

Tony knew, been uninhabited forever. It was too remote to be vandalised, and attracted only the usual wildlife – gnats and house martins in summer, spiders and cockroaches all year, rats, possibly bats, an occasional owl and the odd tramp.

"Done up, it would make a fine place," said Martin, reading Tony's thoughts.

"Who owns it?"

"Well, that's part of the problem. It's not so much the house as the fact that the owners won't – for whatever reason – sell it."

They followed the grassy tracks down on the leeward side of the dunes, and made their way to the river. Martin scoured the banks with his eyes, searching beyond the sluice, but there was no sign of Shane Marjoram – dead or alive.

"I had hoped the bugger might have fallen in the river," he said.

"He's rather averse to water. He can't have cut back, can he?"

"That's what's worrying me," muttered Martin.

Beyond the river, three salt water lagoons stretched towards Blacksands. Rough, stony tracks crossed these lagoons; some threaded their way through gorse and broom, and one – wide enough to take a tractor and trailer – ran towards the Ness. Across the tracks they walked, Tony scrambling down to search the most seaward lake, Martin moving quickly inland. Searching was a difficult business in the half-light of that chill, May evening – the mud was dry but sticky, the reeds and grass clung to their heels, the gorse and broom pulled at their clothing, the brambles tugged at their legs – and, by the time both men reached the far end, they were sweating.

They stood for a while, watching the sea breaking gently along the line of the shore, its huge power broken and spread as it crashed onto the pebbles. The moonlight was reflected brightly from the waves, and long-shore boats could be seen far to sea. There would be a fresh catch on the beach in the morning, Tony thought; he wondered if there would be time to pick something up for dinner. When he suggested that they return by the water's edge, Martin seemed disinclined. He was agitated. In his heart, he had not expected to find Marjoram along the shore, once they had passed the boats where he might have fallen.

"We'll go back now, Tony, and wait at the Jolly Sailors. If he has skirted round or returned along the shore he might drop in there again."

"No, he's not been back here," said Plumptious, when they were once again seated in the back room at the Jolly Sailors. "Thanks for trying to find him, Martin. I didn't like the idea of him on the loose."

"Perhaps we should check his wife."

"I've already rung her. He's not there. I expect you boys could do with a drink, couldn't you?"

They could and did; a pint of Adnams Broadside chased down with a whisky suited both men very well, and Plumptious was pleased to offer them "on the house" so they bought themselves a second round, by way of courtesy. The locals were still sitting in the main bar lingering out a last game of dominoes, putting off the moment when Plumptious called 'time'. Welcoming as they were, neither she nor her husband, Benny, kept the pub open beyond the traditional closing time – The Jolly Sailors was one pub where "time gentlemen please" still meant what it said.

"Froggy been in?" asked Martin.

"He 'ont come now," cut in Scrub Turrel, "Froggy's reg'lar as clockwork. If he int here by ten, he int cumin'. He 'll have gone from the Hut hoom, and dropped awf ter see Sarah on the way."

"She never mentioned he was there when I rang," said Plumptious.

"She'd got no reason to, hed she?" said Scrub.

Tony began to feel drowsy in the pub – an evening of pleasant wine (and lots of it) supported by breads and cheeses, and followed up with beer and whisky was agreeable enough, but prepared you for bed rather than beach. He thought of 'souls' and 'eternities', as his head dropped onto his chest. He began to doze. He lived very much in his own world most of the time and the back room induced that feeling in him now; it was enclosed and womb-like. The wooden floors gave off a warmth, attenuated by the padded chairs and polished bar. Voices droned around him – the soft, seductive velvet of Plumptious, the self-satisfied knowing of the locals. Feeling his breath rise and fall, he understood how a man might walk along the shore until he was exhausted and then fall asleep permanently to the sound of the sighing sea. It wouldn't be such a bad way to go – peacefully, soothed by drink at the end of another tiresome week.

Martin moved into the main bar. He wanted the locals to talk. He thought they might have a clue of which they were unaware, but they were still sure that Marjoram had gone off towards the dunes. He was agitated, and wanted the matter done with; if he could find Marjoram and get him home to Sarah before the lout did any damage, he'd be satisfied. Sarah seemed able to handle him, and Martin guessed how she would take the steam out of him. The village had been pretty much free of violence of any serious sort since Martin had taken over, but it was only because he kept on top of the likes of Shane Marjoram. Returning to the back room, he saw Tony was dozing.

"I'm just taking another look. If Tony wakes, tell him to hang on – not to follow me. OK?" he said to Plumptious.

"Thanks Martin."

Outside, the night sky was still clear and the moon, in its last quarter, was bright. It would stay chilly, and tomorrow would come bright and crisp as a spring day should. Martin wondered about walking the shoreline; it would be the proper thing to do. He set off at an angle across the pebbles. If Marjoram was about, he'd hear Martin coming.

The breeze had dropped by the time he reached the shoreline, and he strolled southwards again towards the sluice, his eyes scanning every part of the beach. The detritus of the sea always fascinated him – tarred rope, broken lobster pots, egg cases of the dog whelk, old nets, bladder wrack, pieces of wood worn smooth by the sea, and bits of tree swept down from Coveacre. Occasionally, he stopped and listened. Away from the village it was intensely still, but all he heard was the swish of the sea and the rattle of pebbles on the beach.

When he reached the sluice he turned inland. Here, the detritus was heavier; great coils of rope had been thrown against the concrete wall, together with beams and clumps of tree that must have been battered in the waves for ages. It was then he heard a wolf howl. There was no mistaking the sound: he'd listened to those in the wildlife park many times. It seemed to come from along the beach. It was drawn out and, somehow, pitiful. His hair stood on end: there was always the irrational fear that one would escape. Martin stooped and picked up a large, heavy clump of root. The cry had seemed to come from further down the tide-line, northwards towards the far end of the village. He hurried by the sluice wall until he came to the dunes where he found a grassy track, and Martin kept to it. Slipping and sliding, he reached the promenade, now at beach level with all the long-shore drift, and slowed his pace. There had been the one howl, and then silence. Feeling foolish, he dropped the root behind one of the moored boats and then, having second thoughts, retrieved it.

As he turned the bend by the amusement arcade, he saw the lights of the village and felt comforted. In the morning he'd go up to the Wildlife Park and check; at the moment, he was just glad to be within running distance of the pub.

Tony was woken by the sound of a woman's voice – one he could vaguely remember hearing before, but belonging to someone who was more or less unknown to him. When he opened his eyes – discreetly, under his lids so as not to draw attention to himself – he saw that it was the young woman who had attracted his attention at Mary Brown's funeral. It was Marjoram's wife, Sarah. He was taken, once again, by her strength and the grace of her movements. She was pretty, with a mass of honey-coloured hair and that dreamy look in her eyes which he always found so fascinating in women.

"Thanks for calling me again, Plumptious."

"I was worried, that's all. Martin is out looking, but I didn't want Shane to turn up at your house in the state he was in when he left here. Where's Matthew?"

"It's all right. My next door neighbour is keeping an eye on him."

Tonight, that dreamy look was haunted; Tony saw anxiety and fear. She'd obviously come down to the Jolly Sailors hoping to find her husband, and take him home. He opened his eyes wide and stirred so that they could see he was awake, and wouldn't say anything they didn't want him to hear. The young woman turned as he did so and stared at him – almost, he thought, with a kind of loathing? He couldn't imagine why he thought that but, yes, that was her look.

"Have you met?" said Plumptious, "This is Sarah Marjoram – Tony Crewes. He's here with Martin."

"Hello," said Tony, receiving Sarah's smile as they shook hands.

He didn't know what else to say that wouldn't seem banal. There was something so appealing in the young woman's helplessness that he wanted to reach out, put his arms round her shoulders and assure her that everything would be all right. It seemed ridiculous now that he had actually poured water over her husband's head in a moment of amusement; how had Shane Marjoram behaved when he got home that night – the night of Mary Brown's funeral?

"Would you care for a drink?"

What had made him say that? The girl wouldn't want a drink – not at this moment. This was part of the pattern of her life. He went to the office, picked up a huge salary for doing very little and came home to Beth who'd be pre-occupied by her latest obsession – what someone at work thought of her or how on earth he expected her to get the baking done for Saturday's cake stall. He'd sigh, having heard it all before and absorbed all the flack that went with it, think himself hard done by and wander away. Living just down the road was this girl with real problems — dealing with a violent drunk, protecting her child and building her home. Tony felt small.

"Martin will find him," he said.

"Have that drink, Sarah. It'll do you good," said Plumptious.

"I think I will."

Tony paid and sat down at the table, looking closely at Sarah as she sipped her coke. She was a woman in age, but scarcely more than a girl in appearance; and yet she had lived through things he would never have to face. Her experience of life, young as she was, outstripped his by years. He guessed that there would be about ten years between them, maybe twelve; she in her early twenties, he in his late thirties. He could see that they came from different worlds and that, in the normal course of events, their paths would never have crossed. Yet here they were, sitting in their local, sharing a table and a drink. He smiled to himself.

"Thank you for helping to look for Shane."

"It was nothing. I'm just sorry that we didn't find him."

"My dad's missing, too. He normally calls in on the way home."

"Scrub Turrel said he'd been down at the Fishermen's Hut," said Plumptious.

"No I dint," shouted Scrub from the main bar, "I said he'd hev gone hoom from the Hut if he'd hev bin there. I never saw him down there."

"I'd forgotten you lot were still here," said Plumptious, leaving the back room, "Off you go. You've got wives waiting up for you. They'll be all excited. How can you bear to keep them hanging on?"

She laughed towards Sarah, who smiled back, and then she went through the little door to clear out the dominoes players. Afterwards – after hell had broken loose in the village and they were all involved in "clearing up the mess", "limiting the damage", "pulling souls back from the brink", "committing acts of perversion" as various people expressed it according to their lights – Tony was to remember that moment, when the two of them sat alone in the little back room of the Jolly Sailors, as the peaceful time before the storm. She sat silently, ignoring him politely, absorbed in her own thoughts, and he had time to study her closely. She was dressed inexpensively but nicely, and was neat and tidy – something Tony liked in women. He could imagine her little house with its view of the marsh – the washing-up done, her child safely in bed, Sarah sitting there waiting for her husband's lurching footstep or her father's tap on the door, the kettle warm in the kitchen. There was something homely about the girl; he kept thinking of her as a girl.

It was only a few months since she had lost her mother, and he remembered watching her in church as the rector had described Mary Brown. This girl would have seen out the rest of her life in the village – just like her mother – or would she? Sarah was clearly intelligent. He could imagine her having done well at school. How had she come to be involved with Marjoram and how could she love him – love such a lout? Maybe she didn't ask such questions, but just accepted them as part of the deal life had handed her? She also had courage: to live with someone like Marjoram, you would have to have courage. Women like her fought hard for their homes and families.

Sarah stirred slightly, as Plumptious locked the outer door to the main bar, thinking perhaps that it was her husband returning. When it was quiet again, she sank back in her chair, still oblivious to Tony, who watched the frown of sadness pucker her forehead. Yet the face itself was not sad; there was a smile that hovered there somewhere, behind the eyes, round the corners of the mouth. Tony was over-whelmed by the awesomeness of other people's lives. He always had been – the more you knew, the less you understood. He had to believe that a woman like this must bring out the best side in everybody – even a Shane Marjoram; perhaps, with her, he had a tender side.

Sarah looked up and caught his watchfulness. She was beyond caring at the moment, but she rather disliked the man. There was something supercilious about him – an unnecessary sneer about his mouth. Shane had told her about the bucket of water, but it wasn't that – he'd probably deserved the soaking. It was the feeling that this man felt himself to be in some way superior to those around him. Perhaps it was the fact that he was educated in a way that she and Shane were not. Sarah didn't begrudge him that, or even envy him his knowledge, but it wasn't for him to look down on those less fortunate. They looked at each other without speaking.

"Well, that's the last one gone. I think Martin will be back in a moment, Sarah. He can't be much longer. He must have searched the whole beach by now. No news is good news," said Plumptious, coming into the small bar.

"I'll go when he gets back. I don't want to leave Matthew much longer. If you hadn't phoned, I wouldn't have been so worried …"

"I didn't mean …. I just thought," mumbled Plumptious.

"It's all right – if Shane was that drunk. Thank you for the drink, Mr Crewes."

Tony only nodded, lost in the many-layered nature of women's conversation. He wondered whether he should offer to walk her back, but decided against it. It would be misinterpreted and, anyway, he and her husband were not exactly on speaking terms. His dilemma was solved by the arrival of Martin Billings, who stepped in through the side door quickly and with a look of anxiety on his face.

"Sarah," he said, his expression changing.

"Hello, PC Billings."

Martin hesitated for a moment, and then asked the same question as Plumptious.

"Where's Matth …?"

"Matthew," laughed Sarah, "A neighbour's looking after him."

"How long have you been here?"

Sarah looked at Plumptious, enquiringly, and she answered for her.

"No more than half an hour."

"Let's get you back. I've no idea where Shane is, and if he arrives home you need to be there."

"You haven't found him then?"

"No – he's nowhere between here and the sluice – not among the dunes or down on the shoreline. If he did go that way he must be beyond the Ness or has turned back, and I think it's more likely to be the latter. Have you seen your dad?"

"No."

Tony had never seen his friend in action before – at least not like this with a grim look on his face and anxiety in every word. Goodbyes were said, and then the policeman ushered Sarah out of the pub and down the road to her home. Before he left, he asked Tony to wait and asked Plumptious to keep the back room available.

"I'll have a drink while we wait, Mrs Walters – if you don't mind," said Tony.

Plumptious poured him another Broadside, and they waited. Tony listened while she ran through a list of Sarah's virtues and Shane's vices, and Tony learned what he'd already anticipated – that Sarah had her eye on university before she got herself "in the club" with Shane.

"You can't blame him. She was an attractive girl, and men are men. I'll say this for him – he did stick by her, and he works. They've a lovely house, you know. He's got everything to be proud of – except his drinking and his violent nature. He's never touched her, of course. In his own selfish way he thinks the world of her ... I just don't trust his temper. He was a bloody nuisance at school, by all accounts, and he'll be a bloody nuisance till he dies. We all pray he doesn't wear her down ..."

When Martin returned, Plumptious poured him a drink.

"He wasn't there," said Martin, "I went in with her and waited while she checked. Where the hell can he be – and why? Why hasn't the bugger gone home? Then we could all get some rest."

"You've done your best, Martin," said Plumptious.

"You called me out, Plumptious – and now it's my responsibility. Until I know where he is, I shan't sleep. And it puzzles me why Froggy isn't home either."

"Have you ..."

"Checked his house – yes, he isn't there."

"Why don't we search the other side of the beach – between here and Pakefield – at least as far as the Beachlands Health Club?"

"I was going to suggest that, Tony. Are you game?"

"Count me in."

"By the way, did either of you hear a wolf earlier on?"

They both stared at him, open-mouthed, and both wanted to laugh but realised from the expression on his face that Martin was not joking. He went on to tell them of the howl he had heard while searching the shoreline. Plumptious made a remark about keeping an eye on the chicken run, but saw no real threat. Tony, in the ignorant way of the "townie", thought – quietly to himself – that a wolf on the loose might be fun. Martin poured his drink down and nodded to his friend that he was ready to begin the third search of the night. As he did so, they heard a car pull up in the pub yard and, a few moments later, the side door opened and in walked Benny Walters. He eyed his wife casually and Plumptious nodded back, but without a smile.

"Trouble, Constable Billlings?" he asked, seeing Martin.

"Plumptious called me earlier. Shane Marjoram's on the loose."

"Why the hell do you let him in the pub in the first place?"

"He'd drink somewhere," said Plumptious, "It might as well be here where I can keep my eye on him."

"We don't run a Family Welfare Centre."

"That's where you're wrong, Benny. That's exactly what we run."

Martin laughed; he rather agreed.

"Anyway, you needn't worry about him. He's just arrived home," said Benny. He told them he'd seen a light in Sarah's doorway, and Shane and she in conversation. He'd fancied Sarah himself, and always glanced towards her house on the way home. He'd always rather envied Shane.

"False call – sorry!"

"Don't say that. I've told you – always give me a ring. I'd rather nip trouble in the bud than have to clean up the mess. Have you had any trouble here since I've been in the village? … Let's keep it that way."

He was suddenly off-duty – or, at least, relieved. He shook Benny's hand and leaned over and kissed Plumptious on the cheek. He then suggested that he and Tony should stroll back via Clive's place and see if he'd arrived home.

It was now well into the next day – the small hours – and the village was asleep. Martin led the way, and they turned left from the Jolly Sailors, making their way along Beach Road. Martin ran his eyes over the Victorian terraced houses to the left of the road, noting their small alleyways, which led to the back gardens of the houses. He didn't like them, and had advised that the householders should gate them off; trouble lurked in alleyways. On the right, raised slightly above the road on a natural slope, were the old fishermen's cottages where Clive Brown lived. Martin gave Tony a nod, and they made their way along one of the disputed alleyways to the back of Clive's house. There was one light on, but Martin ignored this; he'd advised everyone to leave a light shining always, and he clicked up the Suffolk latch on the gate and made his way to the back door. Under the water butt he found Clive's key, and knew that he wasn't in. Everything pointed to what he refused to believe. Tony Crewes read his friend's face and shrugged.

Martin gestured his friend to stay put, turned the key in the lock and entered through Clive's back door. His search of the house took less than two minutes. Clive definitely wasn't there – dead or alive. He replaced the key under the butt, and the two agreed to take up their search of the beach. They followed the little pathway to High Path and thence on to the cliffs. They walked in silence, hearing the waves breaking on the shore as the tide began to turn. It was a still night, but somewhere along the beach – from where they had come because no boats were moored this end – could be heard the slap of metal on wood as a sheet hit a mast. There was the flapping of loose canvas, and the occasional crack of cooling wood; a stone would be dislodged from somewhere by a passing rat. Behind them, the scrubby bushes that overhung High Path leaned over and tapped the top of the fences as a cat moved between them. The night was not so dark. The moon was in its last quarter, waning but lighting the sea beneath, so that they could see the odd long-shore boat dragging its nets and the momentary figure of a fisherman standing to pull them in. Watching these silhouettes, Martin had a sudden thought – had Clive gone out with a friend; it would be just like him. Why hadn't he thought of that before? Clive had last been seen at the Fishermen's Hut.

They reached the end of the path, glanced quickly along Sea Row Lane which led up into the village, and turned to make their way down the steps. Tony realised, suddenly, that he had not telephoned his wife; she would have no idea where he was – still, too late now. Beth would be asleep or sitting up in that chair waiting for him.

Several miles along the coast, the lights of Lowestoft provided a curve of yellow. They were about to make their way down the steps to the sea wall when Martin suddenly grabbed Tony's arm and gestured him in against the fence of Beach House. Here, no chance light from the village behind would show them up on the cliff top. He gestured down at the beach, and Tony saw a figure running southwards towards the dune area. The figure had appeared suddenly, but this wasn't surprising given the mounds of shingle, tossed up by the tide, which obscured the shoreline at this point. Martin thought that the figure would turn and head for the very steps on which they hid but it continued on its way, pressing towards the Jolly Sailors.

Tony could see it clearly now against the wet pebbles, left by the retreating tide, which were lit by the moon. The manner of its running suggested a man, and the ragged, desperate progress a man eager to reach the village. The figure looked back over its head many times as though fearing pursuit. Watching it, Martin came to a decision. He pulled Tony to him and whispered in his ear. He was to head back along High Path and Tony was to descend to the sea wall and follow the trail of the figure along the wall. Under no circumstances was he to approach it. In this way, Martin thought that they might head off whoever it was running so fearfully.

Tony Crewes did as his friend wanted, and scrambled down to the sea wall. He barely saw the figure as he ran, but continued in the same direction. He cast an occasional eye towards the cliff top, but Martin – if he was there at all – was no more than a shadow passing along the track which skirted the holiday camp. As Tony reached a curve in the wall, his path was lit by the street lights on Beach Road. Tony paused, not wanting to be seen but eager to keep the figure in sight. Time passed as he waited. The figure continued its frantic run for a while, and then halted, seemingly unsure what to do. Tony became uneasy. What the hell was he doing chasing an unknown man along a beach in the early hours of the morning?

The figure turned, looked about, and then ran straight for the iron steps. Tony still did not dare to move. If the man saw him, the game was up. He moved down onto the beach under the sea wall. Here, though hidden, he was on pebbles and could not move without attracting the man's attention. Bloody hell, thought Tony, I'm no good at this. He stumbled along, trying to keep his feet on the sloping curve of the wall. Every time he drifted towards the pebbles, Tony struggled upwards. In this way he came, at last, to the steps and waited. There was no sound from above, and yet he knew that Martin must have reached the road. What the hell was going on? Tony crouched for what seemed an age and then, cautiously, lifted his head above the level of the steps. There was nothing to be seen – no figure, no Martin, nothing. He ducked down. This was like one of those scouting games the boys played with Ticker Tyler, but just so ridiculous for middle-aged men.

He heard the sound of banging. Someone was thumping on a door. Lights appeared in the upper rooms of the Jolly Sailors, windows were thrown up and people were shouting. He heard what he thought was the voice of Plumptious Walters and then – minutes later – the sliding of bolts and the scratching of old doors. Voices questioned, argued and a door slammed. Tony peered over the top of the steps. The road was silent and empty, and then a hand grabbed his shoulder. The hand went over his mouth, and closed down any sound he might have made. The hand yanked his head upwards, and he was staring into the face of Martin Billings, who signalled that he should be silent. Martin helped him up the steps and then elbowed him towards the Jolly Sailors. With two stabs of his finger and thumb Martin indicated that the figure they had pursued was now in the public house.

"We wait. I don't know what the hell is going on, but we wait."

Suddenly, Martin's phone rang, and both men started. It was Amy Billings – where was he? Plumptious Walters was phoning from the Jolly Sailors and wanted him there as soon as he could make it. Martin mumbled something into the mobile, lead Tony across the road and knocked on the side door of the public house.

"Blimey, you were quick," said Benny, opening the door.

All Martin wanted was answers. They seemed a long way now from Shane Marjoram – tucked up in bed with his lovely young wife – and from Clive Brown, who was still missing. Overwhelmed by a bitter sense of déjà vu, Martin walked into the back room of the Jolly Sailors. Sitting at the table occupied so recently by Tony and Sarah was Peter Vishnya – ashen-faced.

"I was on the beach," he said, "I didn't know where else to come. It seemed a long way to the police station and it's here you need to be, Constable Billings."

Plumptious made them all a coffee and they sat looking at each other. Martin knew that this was to be the beginning of the end of an already long night.

"How can I be of assistance, Mr Vishnya?"

"I've found a body on the beach."

"Where?" asked Martin, looking up at Plumptious and Benny.

"Just to the north of those steps that go up to Sea Row Lane."

"Mr Walters – have you a tarpaulin or something like that?"

"Yes – out back."

"Right, please get it for me – in a moment. Now listen – neither of you are to make any phone calls while I'm gone. Do you understand? Not a word. I would seriously consider it as 'obstructing the police in the execution of their duty'. Do you follow me?

Plumptious and Benny nodded.

"Now, I'll have that tarpaulin. Tony, I'd like you to come with me and Mr Vishnya. I might need a hand."

Martin's official manner had an edginess to it because what he was about to do was unorthodox. He should have phoned the station, immediately, and brought in the big boys with their equipment, but he wanted to hear Peter Vishnya's story himself first – before the tapes, cautions and impedimenta of bullshit got in the way. Even before that he had to see to the body on the beach, and risk sullying the crime scene.

With the tarpaulin under his arm, he led Peter Vishnya out of the pub and – with Tony Crewes in tow – followed him along the sea wall to the beach. The night was still moon bright, which pleased him; there was nothing worse than dealing with bodies in the dark or by the light of torches. They hurried along the sea wall and, when they were level with the steps, turned sharply towards the sea, stumbling with difficulty across the shingle mounds. It seemed cold now, but the cold was emotional rather than real. They'd been up all night on what they'd hoped was a wild goose chase, and it had turned out anything but; the faces of all three men were drawn as they approached the spot where Peter Vishnya had found the body. The moonlight scudded across the water, glistening from the gentle waves and lighting the wet stones. Peter Vishnya led them along by the foot of one of the mounds, well above the tide line and, as they scrambled down the slope, hesitated and pointed so that Martin moved in front. The Estonian's finger was directed at the body of an elderly man, and the policeman's heart sank.

"Wait here."

Martin skirted what he now supposed to be a dead man, and approached from the sea so that nothing should be kicked down upon the body. There were footprints everywhere among the stones and sea wrack. The old man had been wearing a flat cap, which was now some feet from the body so that Martin could see the bald skull and the fine hair whipping gently across it. The body sprawled with its head huddled down into the shoulders as though protecting itself from rain, and he could see that the left hand side of the face and head were shattered and covered with blood. It looked as though the body had fallen, from the force of these blows, onto its face which was now sinking into the sand. He approached with caution, and distaste, to feel the pulse, knowing that this was a waste of time, but feeling he just had to be sure. Within sixty seconds he knew the body was, indisputably, a corpse.

Martin leaned over and saw enough of the face to know that the corpse was that of Clive Brown. Even in death, the man showed the stamp of his nickname:

the short, stocky legs were bowed out at the knees although the feet were now turned inwards. His left hand, which had been raised to protect his head and neck from what Martin supposed were blows, was covered with blood. Blood had also run from the neck, which showed what looked like a gaping wound, and the sand beneath it was soaked with blood. It would be up to the forensic boys to determine cause, but it seemed to Martin that the old man had bled to death. Had this been while they searched the other end of the beach?

He looked up and signalled the other two to stay where they were. He could see that Peter Vishnya was sitting down, and that Tony was also now ashen-faced. There was no comfort in sudden death, and violent death was always shocking. In all his years in the force, Martin had never come to terms with dealing with corpses. He looked down at Clive with whom he was never again to share a pint. His trousers, old and marked by the garden, still slumped untidily over his shoes, and Martin could discern the strength in his shoulders – the strength and determination which had dug his wife's grave not so many months before. There would be no comfort for Sarah now; it was too late for any reconciliation.

He took the tarpaulin and laid it gently over the corpse, weighting each corner with the heaviest stones he could find. It was over half-an-hour since Peter Vishnya had appeared at the pub, and he still wanted to speak with him before phoning headquarters. He told Tony so, and asked him to stay with the corpse.

"You don't mind do you? I want to listen to what Mr Vishnya has to say, and I do not want to leave the body alone. You understand, Tony – I'm relying on you."

Seated again in the little back room, Martin took out his notebook.

"Now, Mr Vishnya, just tell me what happened."

"We were out walking …"

"We?"

"My son and I."

"At three in the morning!?"

"I had been up all night working on a translation, having put Yevgeny to bed with a headache. When he couldn't sleep, rather than give him another tablet, I suggested that we went for a walk in the cool night air with Anton …"

"Ah yes – the dog everyone thinks is a wolf … And you were out walking?"

"Yes. We had come down Solomon's Lane and walked towards Pakefield for a while – along the cliffs? Anton likes to run around there – the rabbits are plentiful. Then we had come back – through the holiday chalet site and down onto the beach."

"What time was this?"

"I cannot be sure. It may have been two, two thirty."

"Where is Yevgeny now?"

"I sent him home before he had time to see the body – Anton was with him … I did look at the body, but saw no signs of life, and so I ran to the pub."

"Who found the body?"

"I have told you."

"Have you?"

"Ah, I see – Anton, of course. He was running ahead as dogs do."

"How long before you caught him up?"

"I cannot say – perhaps a minute – no more. Why, may I ask?"

"There is no chance that the dog touched the body is there?"

"I don't know."

"Is there any chance someone may have run when the dog arrived?"

"It is possible. The shingle is high there. Coming from the tide-line we would not have noticed."

"But you would have heard someone running over shingle. Think carefully. Can you remember any sound?"

"No, I am sure not. Besides, Anton would have given chase."

"Possibly – it would depend on where his interests were at that moment."

Tony Crewes sat by the corpse of Clive Brown, knowing he was only yards from his house, and wondering why he wasn't in bed. The tarpaulin rose occasionally, even on that still night, as though the body was trying to escape. However rationally you tried to subdue your imagination, a dead body was fearful. He remembered – as a child, having read a forbidden book from his father's bookshelf – sitting in the corner of his bedroom, back pressed into the wall so that no fiend could approach him from behind. The fiend had though; they come through walls, don't they, squeeze into them as you might? So he'd concentrated on just one spot on the rug – a magic circle. If he concentrated hard enough on that circle then nothing could harm him.

There were few clouds in the sky that night, but those few passed over the moon after the others had left, leaving him in temporary darkness. The light went from the pebbles, and shadows crossed the beach. Tony yawned and stretched, rubbed his hands together and looked about him. There was nothing: the tarpaulin quivered, but otherwise nothing. Along the beach, as shingle ran into sand, marram grass stirred on the dunes. He turned slightly so that he could keep an eye on both the cliffs and the sea. When does the soul leave the body, Corvin – at the moment of death or the moment of burial? He looked around him and thought he saw a movement on the cliff top – a furtive movement, not Martin returning – but dismissed it before it took hold. 'I have no prayers to guard me from the dead. I am an atheist. I have no torch to shine on the faces of those who watch me in the night.' As though impelled (he had always had a contrary nature) Tony did what he was clearly not supposed to do. He crept down the shingle bank to look under the tarpaulin. He only lifted it slightly – just to be sure the body hadn't moved. He dropped the tarpaulin down, and turned to move away, but something impelled him to look again. He couldn't resist it.

The wound, or wounds, on Clive Brown's neck and head were terrible. Tony had less idea than Martin about how they were inflicted. The skull was broken at its lower end near the jaw as though it has been struck by a piece of heavy stone or wood, but the wounds were also jagged as though left by giant teeth. It did not seem possible that only a few hours before this man's friends had spoken to him – had a joke or a grumble and expected to see each other tomorrow for the same kind of banter. Now, they'd never speak to each other again; a place at the fishermen's table would always be empty.

He thought of the young woman and her dreamy beauty. She and her father had possessed a similar expression behind their eyes. There had been close; he knew that, despite never having seen them together. What was she to do know – her mother and father both dead within a few months of each other, and she left in the world with a lout? Tony felt drawn to Sarah, and for two pins would have left the body to go to her; she needed protection. He'd put his arms round her and tell her that her parents were ... were where? There was no comfort in the world, anymore; none but the comfort we brought ourselves and each other. Who was to comfort Sarah?

The soft sound of the sea only emphasised the silence around him. The body was motionless, and the moonlight unchanging. Tony felt the cramp in his legs and stood to stretch them. Again, his eye thought it caught a movement – this time closer, somewhere just beyond the mounds along the sea wall. He felt frightened, and looked wildly about. It was as though something evil was coming towards him. Where the hell was Martin? He looked back at the body, and made an effort to control himself. He walked down to the retreating tide and kicked lone pebbles into the waves. Something was coming towards him out of the scattered shadows of the beach. He didn't believe in evil spirits but the sense of a presence was terrifying. There was anger in the air, and a violent wilfulness that would have its own way. Had the wilfulness possessed a face it would have been livid. Dead eyes would open and see him, teeth would grind in fury, and arms would flail about raining down blows while a face quivered in delight – in a kind of manic exultation. Tony tried to regain his self possession. Sweat poured from him, and he looked desperately about to see whatever it was – to see something! At least, then, he would know with what he was dealing.

Sarah sat bolt upright in bed, the sweat running from her, and looked wildly around. The little clock showed four in the morning. Shane stretched naked beside her, his beautiful body exposed to the night – joyful and shameless. She was scared, but didn't know why. She slipped quietly out of bed and went across the tiny landing to see that Matthew was all right. Her eyes swept around, noting from habit the picture of herself as a baby on the wall between the flowers and the cot. Matthew slept the sleep of the innocent. She kissed him lightly on the forehead, and tucked the little duvet closer to his neck before going quietly to the kitchen to make a cup of tea. She would drink this alone in the quiet hours just as her mother used to do.

She sat peacefully at the table sipping her tea, thinking of Shane's late arrival – "I was bit drunk, Sare. I didn't want to come in 'til I'd sobered up so I slept it off on the beach". He'd been exultant. She had never seen him so full of himself, and she still ached from the forcefulness of their love-making. He'd pulled the nightdress up and over her head, and taken her with relish; she'd come quickly but he'd waited, holding on before satisfying himself. When he'd finished, Shane cradled her in his arms until Sarah fell asleep.

Despite her contentment, Sarah had an air of unease which she could not shake off, and which the tea did nothing to assuage. Her dad hadn't called in on his way home from the Fishermen's Hut, and it was unlike him – the poor, lonely old man. Sarah felt the tear run from her eye. Shane didn't like to see her like this. Her grieving was best done alone – here, in the kitchen, in the quiet hours of the morning.

There was a sound outside; somewhere a latch had clicked. At this hour of the morning when you had the right to be alone with yourself? She heard the soft tap-tap on the front door; someone was trying to wake her quietly so as not to disturb the house. Sarah went from the kitchen through to the little front room and peeped through the curtains discreetly. PC Billings was at the door.

It was well over two hours later – perhaps five or after in the morning – before the police began to arrive and the manic circus of tents and tapes imposed itself on the quiet life of the village. Why did they think that dashing round, ordering people about and making as much noise as possible indicated that their activity was purposeful and efficient? Martin viewed the arriving vans with distaste. He had stayed with Sarah for about an hour, and then woken Corvin before walking along the route which Peter Vishnya had said he'd taken. He wanted to satisfy himself about one or two things before calling in the real policemen (and women) with their sirens, bustle, clipboards and over-bearing sense of self-importance. He relieved Tony Crewes who he'd found "shaken, my friend, but not unduly stirred" and telephoned headquarters. Tony looked both shaken and well stirred, and retired home, quickly.

Martin stood watching now as the "experts" – the Scene of Crime Team as they liked to call themselves – cordoned off the beach and strutted around in their spaceman costumes as though they were the first coppers in the world to mix some plaster of Paris and take a few foot casts. Martin had located the weapon – a long, heavy piece of driftwood, spiked with a rusty nail or two and slanted to a rough point at one end. An opportunist killing – a spur of the moment thing brought on by anger, jealousy or drink – you name it. Did the victim know his assailant? Definitely! Did they meet by chance? Probably – and walked home together. What was the motive? There wasn't one – unless jealousy fuelled by sheer ill-temper charged with too much drink counts as motive. Martin hoped the coppers below would obtain enough hard evidence to tie the investigation up quickly. It shouldn't be too difficult, should it? Footprints, possibly fingerprints, traces of clothing – from someone who shouldn't have been there or said he wasn't there. Then, you began asking the questions, and the agony for the relations would begin.

If only he hadn't taken notice of what the pub regulars had to say. If only he and Tony had walked both ways along the beach. If only ... Martin reckoned that the killing took place between eleven and twelve – probably nearer eleven so the body had lain there until Vishnya found it at about three o'clock. Marjoram must have been along the beach somewhere – holed up, shitting himself – because, according to Benny Walters, he'd arrived home about two o'clock. Sarah, without knowing it, had confirmed this. He'd ask the Scene of Crime Team to snout further along the beach. They'd probably know better than him, of course, and refuse – unless he could give them "solid reasons for extending the forensic examination". It was possible he was wrong and that someone else did the killing, but Martin didn't think so. He just wanted the whole thing tied up as quickly as possible for everyone's sake. If only … if only he'd known then what he was to discover later, would it have made any difference? Could he or anyone else have forestalled the horrendous chain of events of which the killing of Clive Brown was only the beginning?

Corvin Unwood was in his element. As always, he rose to such occasions with the vocation of the true priest. He'd been awake when Martin came knocking on his door, and had listened with genuine anguish in his heart to what the policeman had to tell him. He'd invited Martin in – even the professionals, especially the professionals, need helping through such times – but the policeman had refused, saying that he had one or two things to see to, and he wanted Corvin to attend to Sarah before "the circus comes to town".

Corvin had woken Esther who listened, without interruption, while her husband told her what had happened, and told her to get ready to receive Sarah should it be necessary. He'd then put on his cassock and made his way to Sarah's cottage. This wasn't simply a matter of duty to Corvin, nor was it that he knew the family. Corvin would have moved as quickly for any stranger to the village. His compassion was absolute and, in times of such crisis, he took charge, naturally and brooking no opposition. Not even Esther would have questioned him at such moments.

Sarah was relieved to see him. She had woken her husband, but the baby was still asleep. Corvin was used to grief, but he had seldom seen it as he saw it in Sarah that morning. The cliché phrase 'beside herself' expressed it, exactly. With her mother buried, her father dead and her husband useless, Sarah Marjoram stood utterly alone in the world. She knew, clearly at that moment, that it would always be so. If she faltered, the worlds of those she loved would collapse around her. If Corvin had ever seen anyone 'on the brink' he saw it in Sarah on that awful morning.

The priest went into her living room and, uncharacteristically, put his arms round her; Sarah collapsed into them, and he helped her to a chair by the fireside. Shane offered to make them both a cup of tea, and then left on the pretext of seeing to Matthew. Corvin did not speak for a while. Condolences at such moments were not only a waste of time – they were almost offensive. Sarah was glad that he was there, and pleased that he said nothing. Martin Billings had advised her to wait before seeing her father and she accepted that; her mind was racing along other paths. How would she see to the details? There sat Corvin. How would she explain to people? There sat Corvin. How would she get up tomorrow? There sat Corvin. He sipped his tea quietly, waiting. Sarah got up and began to tidy the room – quite unnecessarily; it was already, as always, perfectly clean and tidy. Somehow, though, if you saw to little things like that, the bigger ones took care of themselves.

Corvin knew that she was trying to accept – to actually believe – what had happened, although it wasn't until Clive no longer came tap-tapping on her cottage door that the dreadful truth would begin to sink in. It wasn't until she no longer saw him in the old familiar places that she would realise he had gone. In the meantime, she must keep the cottage nice and look after Matthew.

They sat for an hour or more, through to the end of that long night, waiting for something familiar to happen. They talked about Clive as though he would now be waking in bed. They talked about how much he still missed Mary. "Dad used to say that you didn't get a Sunday roast in Heaven." "I'm sure the good Lord would provide one if you asked him." It was nice to joke like that – along the line of familiar things. Familiar – that word again; how much we need it! Only those sure in its warmth will toss it away with such contempt. They heard cars being started, and then passing the window – the lattice window she and Shane loved so much. "Who would kill dad, rector? He had no enemies." "No. We must leave that to the police." The sounds of the waking village woke Matthew, and Sarah heard him stir. It was the spur she needed to move; the child's cry for his mother broke the unfamiliar silence of the morning. People were going to work. Sarah was waking her family, and getting breakfast. Corvin left her gently, making sure that she had the rectory number. Corvin closed the door quietly behind him. He knew it would be several days before the shock came – before realisation hit Sarah – and then the church would be ready.

Tiredness came at last to Martin Billings. He'd been at work the previous day, had supped heavily and then spent a long, long night looking after his village – and all to no avail. A death had occurred – on his patch – and it could, it should, have been avoided. Plumptious had called him at eleven; he'd had time to intervene. Clive Brown should still be alive. The memory of that night would haunt him forever.

Amy knew what he was thinking when he arrived home at what would normally have been coffee time. She had phoned work, and told them she would be late. She wanted to be there when he arrived home; she wanted to cook him breakfast.

Martin sat at their table in the kitchen while she busied herself on the ceramic hob. It was reassuring to watch and listen as she grilled the sausages and placed the bacon in a dry frying pan, then remove it to a warm place while the eggs fried in the bacon fat. Amy added a little oil, fried the bread and then placed the tomato halves with the sausages. She drizzled with a little oil and seasoned to taste before grilling them. She then added a little more oil to the frying pan and cooked the mushrooms. How wonderful, he thought, as Amy arranged it all on a warmed plate and placed it in front of him. They now sat together, while he ate his full English breakfast and she had a cup of tea with her low-fat marmalade and crispbread.

"You mustn't blame yourself, Martin."

"Then who is to blame?"

"No one – these things happen."

"No they don't – not in a well-ordered community."

"You know who did it, don't you?"

"I've a pretty shrewd idea. I'll have him."

While he ate, the telephone rang in his office. It was Junket – Superintendent Junket – but he could wait. Amy smiled to herself, as Martin continued to eat his breakfast. Calmed by the breakfast, by the welcome return to normality, he kissed Amy goodbye as she shot off to work, and then went into his office. He had a report to write – in triplicate – and he wanted it well on the way before Superintendent Junket phoned again. He ignored the phone twice more, but picked it up the third time, just over two hours later, when he had finished.

"Billings?"

"Yes, sir."

"What went wrong, Martin?"

"A man was murdered, sir. I assumed HQ would have told you that."

"I meant with procedures, Martin."

"Procedures, sir?"

"HQ was not informed until two hours after the body was found. Why?"

"There were one or two things to sort out, sir."

"Like what?"

"I wanted a chat with the man who found the body. I needed to see the murdered man's daughter."

"Not your role, Martin. We have experts for that kind of thing."

"I knew the girl, sir."

"Too close, Martin. Leave it to those with training."

"It doesn't need training, sir, to talk with the bereaved – just a touch of compassion."

"I'm not here to argue with you, Martin. This is a very serious matter. Do you mean you spoke with the daughter?"

"Yes, sir."

"And the man who found the body?"

"Yes, sir."

"You taped the interview?"

"I made notes, sir."

"Notes aren't modern, Martin. These days we tape."

"My notes are pretty good, sir."

"You left the crime scene unattended?"

"No, sir. It was watched closely."

"By who?"

"A friend, sir."

"Friend?"

"You know the procedures, Martin. The days of the maverick are over. Procedures mean efficiency ... I've had HQ on the line all morning over this. The Assistant Chief Constable isn't pleased. He wants some input ... He wants answers, Martin. He wants to know why procedures and policies were not followed ... He'll have the press on his back, Martin. He's a man under pressure."

"Can't he just tell them that we're busy solving a crime, sir?"

"Crime?"

"The murder, sir."

"We leave crime to the experts, Martin. You'll be receiving a visit over this. I want a report on my desk by mid-afternoon. We have targets to meet."

"Have you checked your e-mails, sir? You'll find my report already there."

Martin put the phone down. He'd nothing to lose, and everything to gain, if they retired him early.

CHAPTER 14

The slaying of the white bull

Horst Brultzner sat in his newly restored study and admired the handiwork of Mark Chambers and his men. It was good to see the traditional skills still alive; the insistent descent into cheap shoddiness had been stemmed, at least in Dunburgh.

The davenport, which had given Lord Wangford and Crafty Catchpole so much trouble when they had tried to carry it into the house, was now perfectly at home. Brultzner took a child-like delight in examining it – the hidden drawers, the fitted stationery compartments released by spring locks, the slope with its self-opening ratchet, the wooden knobs so favoured by the Victorians, the mother-of pearl escutcheon plates and the little touches such as 'VR Patent' on the lock.

A fire burned in the grate – not that Horst Brultzner ever felt the cold, but he was expecting a guest and the glow of a real coal fire always added to the ambience of a room. Indeed, it was essential to the whole look he was determined to achieve. Brultzner had insisted on a slate fireplace, much to Harry Bailey's indignation. Harry had argued that the study was a masculine preserve, should be more utilitarian in appearance and therefore needed a cast-iron fireplace. Brultzner took real pleasure in these arguments. It was a novelty for someone to argue with him, and he respected these craftsmen who knew their business and cared about their work.

The mass of the fireplace was balanced by large furniture on the opposite wall. This consisted of a superb walnut sofa with its deep-buttoned back, boldly carved arm terminals and sturdy cabriole legs, as well as a William IV armchair. Horst Brultzner did not like sharing a seat with anyone else and this chair, with its leather padded arms, was essential to his ease and comfort. At the davenport, he had a mahogany side-chair with a balloon back and french-style feet obtained for him by Martin Billings, who knew his nineteenth century cabriole leg from his eighteenth.

Opposite the window – again in the interests of balance – there should have been a mirror, but Horst Brultzner had never been comfortable with these. Instead, he had hung the Monet, painted in 1869, so much admired by Harry Bailey.

The restoration was moving on apace, and Brultzner loved the excitement. He also loved sharing this with the workmen around him. He saw them, not as servants but as fellow artists, collaborating in a work of genius – the Old Vicarage.

Living by day was not natural to his kind, but he was becoming acclimatised; it was the only way to share in the pleasure of his restoration. He naturally avoided sunlight, and the impending summer was a worry to him; but the spring days had been kind. He had been round to see the completion of the structural work on the roof, exterior walls and ground floor rooms. Mark Chambers had wanted to finish all the main structural work before the detailed interior work began, but Horst had wanted to show off his home and they had reached a compromise – so that the ground floor was nearing the point where it could be fully furnished.

He rubbed his hands joyfully, eager for his guest to arrive. He walked proudly round the study where he proposed to receive him with a mock apology for not doing so in the front parlour, which would have been the custom in Victorian times. His own cleverness and extensive, first-hand knowledge was a constant joy to Horst Brultzner. Just as joy is tempered with sadness, however, anticipation is tempered with anxiety. Horst Brultzner was concerned that his impending guest – Peter Vishnya – should pose him no threat. Since their clash in St George's Church, he had been mindful of Vishnya, unsure of what he actually knew as distinct from what he supposed. Despite his enormous powers, Brultzner was aware that he had inherent weaknesses. He had asked Crafty Catchpole to deliver an invitation for Vishnya to visit the vicarage in advance of the June luncheon; the invitation had been accepted three days ago.

When he heard Vishnya's step on the gravel path, Brultzner moved quickly across the hallway to open the door. He thought that a parlour-maid would have struck a more authentic note but, as yet, his household did not stretch to such a luxury.

"Mr Vishnya, how good of you to come. Welcome to my house. Enter freely," said Brultzner with a smile, and ushered Vishnya into the study, "Please – be seated. May I get you some coffee?"

"Thank you – that would be appreciated."

"Arabian or African?"

"I normally drink American, Herr Brultzner, but African would make a pleasant substitute."

Brultzner smiled to himself. Vishnya had obviously regained some of the composure he had lost in the church, and was determined to show it.

"When we met before, Mr Vishnya, I feel that we – as you say, 'got off on the wrong foot' – yes?"

"We made assumptions about each other that were ..."

"Yes ... that is why I asked you to call round today ... You offered to assist me with any translation I might need?"

"And you said that you spoke all the main European languages."

"That is correct," replied Brultzner, whose eyes had never left Vishnya's since he entered the room. He smiled, and added "But I do not speak Estonian."

"Few people, who are not native Estonians, do. It was a banned language under the Russians – not even taught in the schools. We all learned in Russian."

"But now the jackboot is on the other foot?" proposed Brultzner and smiled at his little joke, as Vishnya joined him.

"Any Russians living in the country are being required to speak Estonian – yes. It is no longer a secret language."

"Official papers are written in Estonian, and business carried on in Estonian?"

"Yes – we are re-claiming our inheritance."

"But not without difficulties, I believe?"

"The Russian Party has expressed concerns about the treatment of ethnic Russians in Estonia, and the Supreme Court ruled that amendments to the language law were unconstitutional."

"But the Riigikogu is keen that those working in the state service sector should be proficient in Estonian?"

"You are well-informed, Herr Brultzner."

"I have a passion for all things European, Mr Vishnya. Your lovely country is emerging from what the English would call 'its dark ages'. Much money has been poured into its continuing economic growth. It has a future in the European Community, but there is much to be done – yes?"

"Yes – the industries need modernising. The old plants are polluting our rivers. It is a major problem."

Peter Vishnya raised his hands in a gesture of resignation, and Brultzner closed in upon him.

"So why aren't you – a native Eesti speaker – returning to help?"

"Perhaps I am too comfortable here?" suggested Peter, with a smile.

"You must have considered returning, following the death of your wife?"

"My son speaks no Estonian and no Russian. He was born here. English is his only language, and England the only home he knows."

"Excuses, Mr Vishnya. Your son would learn Eesti in the playground. The question is – do you want to return?"

"In all honesty, I do not know."

"When we first met you wished to be of service to me – 'I would welcome the chance to be of assistance to you' were your exact words. 'I am able to translate freely across the European languages'."

"You have a good memory."

"I am a lonely man, Mr Vishnya. I lack the company of my intellectual equals. I have to explain so much before a conversation can begin that I am weary before views are exchanged. I am of a proud race. But – to continue – you wish to be of assistance to me?"

Peter Vishnya had no option but to answer in the affirmative.

"Yes – I would welcome the chance."

"Then prepare to return to Estonia, Mr Vishnya."

Brultzner rated Vishnya even less than previously, as he watched him sipping his coffee on the Victorian sofa. He was slightly built without muscle or weight. He had a soft, hesitant voice and manner: the English cricket mentality. Brultzner smiled.

"You look startled – are things moving too quickly for you? Let me explain. I have entrepreneurial interests across Europe – I am an explorer of nations. For many years I have been, if not exactly trapped then certainly incommoded, behind the Iron Curtain. To travel freely was not impossible, but extremely difficult even for one of my connections. One of the countries I never penetrated was Estonia. I now intend to change that. Since 1994 your various troubled governments have sought to attract the free market, proposals have been made for the construction of a natural-gas pipeline from Norway and considerable progress has been made in boosting your trade with the West. In 1994, about 31 per cent of your export trade was with the countries of the EU. Foreign investment has jumped to US$139 per capita – the third highest in Eastern Europe. These are exciting times, Mr Vishnya, for your country, and you can be part of it. It is quite clear to me that your officialdom would be obstructive to a foreigner. I have, for example, had difficulty in simply purchasing a property on one of your fifteen hundred islands. You will represent my interests – and your own – in the country of your birth. You speak the language, and you have the passport. Once there you will, also, find yourself indispensable to others – translating for your countrymen and your foreign investors across Europe! All I ask is that my interests come first. Agreed?"

"I need to ..."

"... think? No, Mr Vishnya – you need to act! In this country you will toddle along translating for others. In Estonia you will translate for your country, for yourself and for me."

"I have a son here. I should consult him ..."

"Consult a child? Tell him. You can come and go – keep your little English house. Take your son round the world – he is a citizen of the New Europe."

"And your interests would be? I have no knowledge of the business world."

"You would not need it – you are intelligent enough to learn as you go. Besides, my interests would be far wider – artistic, cultural, industrial. You will be my voice in Estonia."

"I ...."

"What is there to keep you here?"

"I have certain commitments here which I should need to resolve. If I accepted your offer when would you require me to leave?"

"Whenever you wished – given that it would not be in the too distant future."

"I have the habit of sleeping on things, Herr Brultzner. Might I return and give you my answer in three days?"

"In three days, Mr Vishnya, we will shake upon it. And now to another enterprise – let me show you my house, or as much as Mr Chambers and his men have completed."

Horst Brultzner became as a child again, leading Peter Vishnya, gleefully, round the Old Vicarage. Brultzner's enthusiasm was overwhelming. Whether it was the sheer excitement he felt or the intense charisma of his personality, Peter Vishnya had no chance to ponder. He was led with astonishing speed into the main hallway, and up the first flight of stairs. Three rooms led off the spacious landing. Brultzner put his hand on the door of one of these, changed his mind and ushered Vishnya into another.

"These rooms are yet to be finished. We move things about – we probe."

The room was bare except for the fireplace, and Peter Vishnya was shocked at the contrast with the study in which he had been received. The internals walls were in a bad state of repair. The lath and plaster had peeled off the timber frames in places, and wallpaper trailed in grubby sheets across the floor.

"The only thing keeping the plaster on the walls, Mr Vishnya, was the wall paper!" he laughed – a laugh picked up from Mark Chamber's men, a laugh in the face of adversity, "The English find these things amusing – yes? … And rightly so! I was impressed that Mr Chambers did not simply wall paper over the old."

Some of the floor boards, too, had been removed, exposing the floor joists.

"They are like the human skeleton, Mr Vishnya! They run from the front to the back of the house through here …"

He took Vishnya to an internal wall running parallel with the external wall.

"…the spine wall! This wall holds the house together – supporting the roof and pulling in the external walls! Tamper with the spine and your house will end up the cellar!" he laughed again, uproariously, "Mr Bailey found that most amusing. Come – one more thing, two more flights."

Peter Vishnya found himself sharing with Crafty Catchpole a sense of disbelief that anyone could move so fast. One moment, Horst Brultzner was at the foot of a flight of stairs and the next he was at the top, beckoning on his guest.

"… a living organism, Mr Vishnya!"

Seated once again in the study, Peter was exhausted. Horst Brultzner laughed.

"I am very old, Mr Vishnya, much older than I may appear, although I believe the air here has done me good. The east coast is very refreshing! Much of my life would have been spent in unimaginable boredom had I not developed my enthusiasms. Occasionally I find others to share them with me, and then the pleasure is increased tenfold. You can see we have much to do, but there is something to show for my luncheon – yes? Then you will see the other ground floor rooms in all their glory – the front parlour, the dining room, the morning room! How English!"

"You'll need servants to run such a house, Herr Brultzner."

"My very thoughts when I opened the door to you this morning – at least I thought that a parlour maid would be proper! Where should I find such a one, hmm?"

"Ask Corvin Unwood – his wife would know."

"Aah – the village priest. His wife would know! Very amusing! You have captured the English humour, Mr Vishnya."

"I try – it helps."

There was a moment's pause while one of them envied the 'Englishness' the other had captured, and then Brultzner completed his train of thought and brought the morning to a close.

"You will consider my offer and let me know within three days?"

"I will."

Watching Peter Vishnya's departing back as he disappeared along the avenue of beech trees, Horst Brultzner was unsure whether or not his guest would accept his offer. He had done his best to portray himself as a harmless crank, but the Estonian was a shrewd man. Whether he accepted or not would depend upon just how shrewd he was, and where he thought the advantage might lie. If Peter Vishnya remained in the village, Brultzner knew that he would sleep less easily by day.

The sound of Crafty Catchpole's hoe attracted his attention, and annoyed him. He was well aware of Catchpole's 'game' and what he saw as the man's inherent idleness, but he had his uses at the moment.

"Mr Catchpole! How is our garden?"

"Seeing our way clear, sir, seeing our way clear."

Crafty had seen his way clear – or done his best to do so – ever since Brultzner had taken him on as a gardener. He had, at first, been peeved that Brultzner brought in an expert to advise on the Italianate garden, but when he realised that the man was to come and go, while he remained a fixture, Crafty settled down to make the Old Vicarage grounds his own. Harry Bailey knew his bricks, Scrub Turrel knew his tiles, Clive Brown had known his sash windows, and Crafty was determined to know his gardens.

He bought a computer, assuming it would tell him something about Italianate gardens. After several weeks of switching the device on and off, after long cadging conversations in the pubs and the Hut and the help of Scrub Turrel's son, Click, Crafty had found his way through 'Encarta' to 'the Web', and the work of such luminaries as Sir Charles Barry. Crafty kept close notes of everything Click Turrel told him, plotting his route through the new technology as Victorian explorers had planned their routes across continents; as they sought the source of rivers, he sought the ultimate Italianate garden. The phrase haunted him. He muttered it in his sleep, whistled it as he cycled through the village with his pigeons, hummed it as he cleaned out his loft, trundled it as he sat in the pub and spat it out in gasps in the Hut.

"You are proud of the garden, Mr Catchpole?"

"Oh yes, sir. You can rely on me, sir."

"Oh, I know that Mr Catchpole – if it were not the case, you would not be standing there now ... I have a busy evening ahead of me. I am going to 'take a nap', 'get my head down', 'have forty winks'. Your language is so rich, Mr Catchpole – you should be proud of it."

When the front door closed behind Brultzner, Crafty heaved a sigh of relief. Although the new owner of the Old Vicarage had never been anything but pleasant, the man terrified him. The Old Vicarage was now Crafty's domain. He thought of it as such, and he spoke of it as such around the village. Looking up, he could see Clara Gobley's turret room where he had arranged that she should keep her eye on Brultzner's night-time activities. He imagined that Bert might now be at the telescope watching him striding along the little pathways of his Italianate garden.

Since the caging of the rats, nothing spectacular had happened – except for the incident of the grey wolf. Bert called Clara to the turret room one bright moonlit night, and urged her to look. A large grey wolf was running round the garden, as excited as a dog expecting a walk. The huge creature had raced around, in and out of the trees. It had run down to the garden of the new rectory, and vanished for a while before appearing on Church Hill, from where it made its way towards the Street village. Clara had followed – she didn't lack courage, and even if she had her curiosity would have got the better of her – while Bert watched through the telescope.

Clara pursued the wolf into the old graveyard of St George's Church, and watched as the animal nosed among the headstones. Eventually, the wolf must have found what it was looking for because it sat watching one headstone for a long time, raising its head occasionally and howling. The sound was awful – more the cry of a tortured soul than an animal. Clara crouched down and waited. As the wolf turned and looked in her direction, she felt her spine tingle. It couldn't have seen her – she was too well hidden – but she felt the creature look through her, and smile.

Clara had waylaid hunts, had pulled riders from their horses and taken foxes from the maw of the pack as they yelped around her. She was not easily scared, but was unnerved by the eyes of the wolf staring at her through the gravestone. She wet herself, and felt the urine soak into the ground around her knees. When the timber wolves from the Wildlife Park joined in, she filled her drawers. She thought they were coming for her. The big wolf took up the howling, and the others became quiet.

When she looked up, the grey wolf was sloping off towards the lych-gate. Ignoring the mess in her drawers, Clara followed, glancing at the headstone which had so absorbed the wolf's attention. She hurried down the path passed the south porch. The wolf moved from the shadow of the tower, and loped out of the churchyard. It skirted the estate known as Little London, passed the Cedars of Lebanon retirement home and turned right into School Road. A few hundred yards along the road the wolf half-turned. It gazed into the nearby field where, as always, several animals, including a donkey, roamed free, but the wolf showed no interest.

Clara was sweating freely, and knew that she – a fat, old lady out of condition in messed drawers – should never have come this far. Hugging the hedges and walls and their shadows, however, she followed. At the Duke's Head corner, the wolf hesitated, and then turned right into the main street. Clara reached the corner, peeped quickly round before emerging, and set off after it. The wolf turned and ran towards her. She dropped to her knees, and closed her eyes.

When she opened them again, the wolf had passed her, and was lingering outside Totto Brigg's butcher's shop. Panting ferociously, Clara reached the corner and saw the wolf disappearing down Market Place. Her lungs were afire, and every breath she took painful, while the wolf was clearly as fresh as ever. At times, if she slowed down to catch her breath, the wolf appeared to return for her; at others, she would come upon it round a corner, and it would disappear for a while into a garden as though giving her time to rest her lungs.

In this way, they passed the butcher's shop again and returned down School Road. At the bottom of the road the creature hesitated, and then bounded down

Mardles Lane, across the grassy hummock where Horst Brultzner had first seen Peter Vishnya. Clara reached the spot, and collapsed. Looking over her left shoulder towards the beach, she saw a man approaching, and supposed that it was he who had disturbed the wolf. The moon was behind him, but she knew from his stooped walk that it was Bert. He had come to find her, and the chase was over.

She had told Crafty a shortened version of this incident when he had turned up at her bungalow to check progress on their spying. She was keeping her "sly, natural villager" interested and frightened. He recalled the story now with the apprehension she intended. Crafty looked up at the facade of the old vicarage, and wondered where Horst Brultzner was taking his forty winks.

Brultzner was, indeed, resting. He had one of the most important nights of his long life ahead – a night which he had lived through many times, but which always remained unique; the time had come for one more slaying of the white bull. He rose at dusk and dressed with his usual care. Whether dining alone or with others, Horst Brultzner always dressed for the evening. He was in England now (he liked to think, in Victorian England) and he would normally dress as a gentleman of that time – in evening dress if he was dining out, or in a smoking jacket if staying in, alone.

Tonight, however, he opened an old carpet bag and took from it a red cap with a rounded point, a pair of baggy trousers, a green tunic and a red cloak. He placed these, reverently, across his chair and went into the adjoining bathroom. This was as the old priest had left it – still to be lovingly restored by Mark Chambers and his men – and Brultzner enjoyed using it. He was always a clean man, but tonight his washing was more an act of purification. He stripped naked. His body was lean, the muscles taut (he was not a man to gorge himself on unnecessary food) and lightly covered with fine, grey hair. At the sink, he washed his hands and then his face – being scrupulous about his ears, nostrils and mouth. He bathed, in order, his arms, chest, legs, buttocks and feet – prising apart each toe, and working his fingers between them.

He dressed himself slowly, fixing the cloak with a gold buckle across his right shoulder, and placing a pair of Roman sandals on his feet. Lastly, he took from the bag a short sword, which he tucked into the belt of the tunic. Overall, he threw a black cloak, long enough to reach his feet, with a hood that covered his costume completely. The whole ablution, lovingly performed with pauses for prayer and reflection, had taken him over two hours. He looked out of the first storey window at the sky – moon-bright, clear – as he heard Lord Wangford's Bentley on the gravel driveway.

When he arrived at the temple, others were waiting for him. The silence was now intensified by the presence of the Brotherhood, who sat on the oak benches awaiting the arrival of the Father and the one whose name was never spoken, and rarely known. The curtains were drawn back as they entered. The torch passed behind the screen, and the eyes of the god stared into the temple over the three altars. Brultzner went forward and inclined his head. He began to chant the creed.

"I look forward to the celebration of our Lord's birth.
Born on a rock at the time of the winter solstice,
Armed with a sword and a torch at birth,
He fought to deliver the world from evil
And achieved salvation for all men."

The Brotherhood repeated each line as he spoke. He touched the altar on the left, and inclined his head to a small image of the god. He ran his fingers, respectfully, along the surface of each of the altars – just as he had on that first day of his return.

The members of the Brotherhood came forward to place their offerings. When the last had given, Brultzner raised his torch, which lit the stone walls, and then moved down among them, passing along the central aisle. They followed him, row by row in order of their grade, and left the temple quietly. Brultzner extinguished his torch on the blackened hollow of stone and placed it carefully in the iron bracket on the wall of the antechamber, as they walked out into the night. The Father of the Temple was the last to leave. He extinguished his torch and then locked the heavy oak door that closed silently on dark hinges, before passing up the short flight of steps in the long procession which wound its way down to where the white bull grazed.

David Stokes had feared that this moment would come ever since the man Brultzner arrived. He'd known all day that something was afoot. The herd had been moved, leaving the white bull alone in the field, proud as ever, grazing quietly, its dewlap brushing the ground. His father had scurried about washing the beast, brushing buttermilk into its coat so that it shone, and working away with his strong hands all over the body until it was soft and glistening. As he watched from the shelter of the fence, David felt a cloud gathering.

His father had been quiet at tea time. When he took him to bed, and read the usual story before tucking him in, he had said – with that quiet insistence which always meant he was very serious – "You stay in tonight, David. Whatever you might hear, you ignore. Do not be tempted to leave the house". It was a strange thing for him to say; after all, he knew his son would not have thought of leaving the house at night for any reason. His father did not make him promise, however, and so, when he heard the sound of Lord Wangford's Bentley pass the cottage, David Stokes slid out of bed, pulled his clothes on quickly, went quietly downstairs and slipped outside, gesturing the dog to be silent. He wore his favourite body-warmer and carried the knife his father had given him – against his mother's wishes – in his pocket.

He reached the white bull's pasture before the Brotherhood and watched them walking slowly down the shingle path towards him. David had always steered clear of the temple in the hillside. He knew nothing of the Brotherhood, despite having lived so close to one of their most active temples all his life. Like the other locals, he knew that it was healthy to show no interest, and he had never spoken of even the white bull in the playground at school. So secret was the Brotherhood, pride went beyond gossip. For all he knew his own father might be one of them, but he didn't think so. They had a reputation for ruthlessness, deserved or otherwise, and that didn't square with how he thought of his father.

This strange procession was the first he had seen of them. He counted thirty-one figures silhouetted on the slope against the night sky. The man who led them he knew was Brultzner; his loping walk would have given him away, even if David had not seen his face under the dark cap. Behind him came nine with the head and wings of a large, evil bird – a raven, David thought; they carried a cup in their hands. The next seven wore veils, like a bride at a wedding, and short tunics; they carried a cloth over one arm and in the right hand carried a lamp. Following them were six more dressed also in short tunics with a quiver of arrows over one shoulder and a kit bag over the other. David could make out no colours in the moonlight. The next four in the line were lion-headed; in one hand they carried a spear shaped like a thunderbolt and in the other a rattle. Next, came three with ears of corn over their shoulders and a sickle in their right hands, followed by two in radiate crowns, carrying a flaming torch and an orb. Last in the procession came a figure David recognised, by his stooped shoulders, as Lord Wangford. He was dressed like Brultzner, but carrying a flat dish and a long staff.

When they arrived at the pasture, David crouched lower behind the bush that was hiding him and waited. He could not move now – whatever might happen, he was condemned to remain where he was until the Brotherhood returned to the temple.

They formed a large circle in the field, slowly and with no sign of fear, until the bull was enclosed within their number. The great creature continued to munch and showed no real interest in the strangers, but when Brultzner stepped into the centre of the circle and called "Viros servasti eternali sanguini fuso" it turned and faced him as a prisoner might face the firing squad. The beast pawed the ground, snorted and then charged. In that moment, David's heart gladdened – he felt that nothing could defeat the creature he had reared and admired. Perhaps no human could have done, but Brultzner waited until the last possible moment and side-stepped. One of the huge horns tore through his body, and then the bull was passed him, puzzled and angry.

Again and again, this pantomime took place and each time it was hard to know who remained the most unperturbed – the bull or Brultzner. The white bull was a strong animal and David lost count of the times it attempted to gore Brultzner, who had not moved from his position in the centre of the circle. Hours passed and the Brotherhood held their positions. During one of the charges, David felt a hand close over his mouth and turn his head round, gently. It was his father, who signalled that he should remain silent and then crouched down beside him to wait and watch. David knew that his dad was there only because he was; in his keenness to know, the boy realised that he had put his father's life at risk.

The night remained bright with not a cloud in the sky. Low in the south as it was, the moon cast shadows across the pasture so that the battle took place across the shapes of the Raven men on the grass. Each time the bull stopped and turned, it pawed the ground furiously; each time it ran at Brultzner, the field thundered under its hooves. At times the creature turned towards the circle of the Brotherhood – a solid ring more effective than the strongest fence against its escape – but each time it did so a gesture from one of them turned it, and all the while Brultzner held his position in the centre of the circle.

David had read about bulls and bullfighting – the grace of the fighter, his tranquillity in the face of danger, the natural savageness of the bulls, their instinct to charge anything that moves. Brultzner and the white bull possessed all these qualities, and yet there was no teasing of the bull, no attempt to increase yet control his personal danger on the part of the fighter, no internal struggle to maintain the balance between suicide and survival. Rather, the ritual of movement brought them closer together until bull and fighter became almost one being. All round the central pair, the eyes of the Brotherhood watched – un-flurried, ever silent, awaiting the moment of truth.

When it came, even David had to admire – for seconds – the courage and agility of Brultzner, who stood his ground in front of the bull, which after two hours of fighting was still vigorous and fierce. At the last moment, as it passed so close that the horns seemed to tear through the swirling cloak, Brultzner grabbed its left horn with his left hand and swung onto the beast's back. David had seen this in old Roman drawings – acrobats facing a rampant bull, grabbing its horns and vaulting over its back, but Brultzner stayed on the creature – his hands on both horns – and strained at the unruly bull in an attempt to lift its head up and round. It was a moment of relentless power in which the very strength of the bull seemed to surge upwards and into its slayer. The sheer brute force and vitality of the creature flowed into the hands and body of Brultzner as the bull's neck came round, stretched and exposed. David saw Brultzner release one of the horns and reach down into the belt of his tunic. The short, Roman sword glittered in the moonlight and he leaned forward over the right horn of the bull and drove the blade in and across the neck. Three times the blade passed across the great white neck of the bull and, as its blood vaulted from its torn throat, the creature sank to the ground, its knees buckling, its head flopping sideways on Brultzner's left arm.

David felt his father's hand close once again over his mouth to stop him crying out, and the boy closed his eyes against the horror he had witnessed.

The Brotherhood moved forward, closing their circle upon the dying bull until the sight of it was shielded from the boy. Within the circle, the torches of the two were held aloft, the cups of the raven-headed ones were filled, clothes were laid, lamps lit, the dish of the Father filled and passed round as the power of the white bull passed into the Brotherhood. Their backs were now to David and his father. The heads and wings of the evil bird, the veils, the tunics and the lion heads moved in a kind of exulted silence. John Stokes beckoned his son to follow him. It was a risk, but the father guessed at the carnage to follow and wanted his son away and safe. They moved slowly, sliding backwards across the grass away from the meadow, which would never be the same for them again, until they reached the grassy track that led down to their cottage. John Stokes, in dread fear of his son's life and his own, never took his eyes from the circle of men in the field of the white bull. He wanted to know their danger – not wake one night to find two of them standing by his bedside with swords in their hands.

It was a fearful retreat. They kept their eyes on the Brotherhood, as their feet moved backwards and side-wards along the track until they passed from the sight of the feasters. Neither spoke and, although the breath was hard and rough on their chests, neither breathed but lightly. The sweat was pouring from them – the sweat of scrambling as well as the sweat of fear – by the time they reached the kitchen door, lifted the latch, signalled for the dog to hold his excitement and closed their cottage against the world.

"Sorry, dad."

"It's done now. Hopefully, we were not seen and are safe. Are you all right?"

"Yes."

It wasn't true, of course. John Stokes knew that his son was anything but all right Even he – who had seen bulls killed for meat – couldn't rationalise away the ritual they had witnessed. It did not help that he knew they would never see it again – not in their lifetimes or even, perhaps, the lifetimes of David's grandchildren. It had happened before their eyes, and they knew.

John stayed with his son that night. They had returned famished from their ordeal and shared a cold, quiet meal of bread, cheese and water. John did want to risk the sound of even a boiling kettle – such was his fear of discovery. They hugged each other and, eventually, the boy fell into a fitful sleep while John watched the dark night passing and saw the sun rise over Blacksands Ness.

When his son woke, John cooked a large breakfast for both of them – porridge followed by a full English, and then they walked up to the pasture together. It was normal for them to do this, and John wanted the return of normality.

All that remained of the great white bull was a dark stain on the meadow. John could not explain it to himself let alone his son. David Stokes made himself a promise as he stood by the fence. Horst Brultzner may have re-created the central event of his Brotherhood that night – may, as they say, have made history – but he had also made himself an enemy.

CHAPTER 15

Peter Vishnya faces up to things

Horst Brultzner's proposal had thrown Peter Vishnya into turmoil. He had choices to make that he had hardly acknowledged to himself, or to those who they concerned. Since his wife's death he had drifted. He made a bare living doing translations for technical journals, through some work with the university at Norbridge and by a little journalism. He was still in his early thirties, with a child of eight, and he really needed (in the English idiom) "to buck his ideas up a bit".

He knew he owed the beginnings of a whole new life to his wife; she had given him everything, and he had been unable to make any return. They had enjoyed each other and their home. He had seen their love blossom – in their child, in their interests and in their togetherness. They had shared so much. Yevgeny was named after their favourite poet – Yevgeny Yevtushenko – who they both admired. They would sit and read his poetry together. A particular favourite was *Lies*, and the lines 'Who never knew the price of happiness will not be happy' were ones they quoted over and over again.

Anton had been one of the jokes they shared. The fun was in the fact that the rumour he was a wolf was actually true. Peter had been used to dealing with mindless authority in his home country. So, when they decided to return to England, and he had wanted to bring Anton with him, he suggested to his wife that they should say he was a wolf, which no one would believe – enabling them to get him licensed as a dog.

Peter still lived in the house they had shared and made into a home – the one she had owned before they met. Her family had been good to him. They were well-connected business people, and had put him in touch with others who could help him – mainly in the world of journalism and electronics. His wife's life insurance had paid off her mortgage, and so his actual financial needs were small. He and Yevgeny lived simply, and enjoyed each other's company. Peter knew, however, that he was living off something he had not earned, that his present life had been given him by his dead wife and that his contribution was derisible. He was not a sentimental man; he had a streak of the pragmatist about him. Should he fall in love again, he would court the woman with no disrespect to his wife who he would always love.

He was a religious man. His mother had brought him up so, and he had no doubts. He valued his faith – the Orthodox Church – as he had told Brultzner. He also respected the faith of others, and had been pleased to be married here among his wife's people in their church. He had seen his marriage as an "endless binding of man and woman". He had seen it this way, with joy. He would never have divorced his wife under any circumstances, but now she was taken from him.

Peter Vishnya sat in the long garden of the terraced house on London Road with these thoughts running through his mind. Yevgeny was at school, and Anton was at his feet. His garden was divided into two parts – the lawn and shrubbery for Yevgeny, and the vegetable plot that he tended with loving care. His spring planting was complete, and already he could see the fruits of his labours. He and Yevgeny depended on the garden's produce. It was a comfortable life, but it was time to move on, and Brultzner's proposal would enable him to do that; it was his duty.

"Come on, then," he said to the wolf, "Let's go and shake things up."

Anton followed him out of the side gate and along the road. He wore neither lead nor collar. Every now and then someone reported this, and Martin Billings dropped by, but there the matter rested; you don't harness a wolf.

As he passed the butchers, Necker Utting came out followed by a youth who should have been at school. She was short, stocky, bustling woman who went about the village in a manner which suggested that if she slowed down, or seemed less important, everything would go to pot. Necker had got her name because she helped out with the village Cub Scouts and was obsessed with their "neckers" being folded correctly, hung straight and with the woggle in place. When Yevgeny joined the group, Peter had been bewildered by all this; the language of electronics he understood, but not the jargon of the wolf pack. He and Necker had several confrontations over Yevgeny's 'necker' and 'woggle' until he'd grasped the technicalities. It was she – among others – who had reported the collarless Anton. For Yevgeny's sake, he had complied with regulations and they were now on speaking terms. He greeted her, warmly, nodding to the youth as he spoke.

Necker introduced the youth as Rollie, who muttered something under his breath in a tone of subdued aggression. Peter had heard from Corvin that Rollie was a bright lad, but with no idea about how to behave with other people. He lived in his world, with a mother who smothered him, muttering to himself until his temper finally broke and he exploded. Corvin told of how he pushed his mother into a holly bush opposite the primary school when her fussing had finally got on his nerves. In the past he would have been seen as the village idiot, but now he was "a freak" and the target of adolescent bully boys. Necker had taken him under her wing when he was in Cub Scouts, and he wandered round with her when he bunked off school.

"You goin' to Clive's funeral then?" asked Necker.

Peter had forgotten – quite forgotten – and realised his mission, his off-chance visit to the rectory, was doomed before it got started. Clive Brown's murder had shocked the village – shaken its natural acceptance of peace and order to the core.

"Are you on your way, Mr Vishnya?" asked Necker, sensing his discomfort.

"Yes, I think I should pay my last respects," he lied, diplomatically.

"You'll need a black tie. We wear black in this country at funerals."

"Yes," muttered Peter, noticing, for the first time, that Rollie was wearing a black tie and that Necker had a black shawl round her shoulders.

1 4 7

"And you can't take the dog."

"No."

"You'll have to be quick. It starts at noon. I did the laying out for him and his wife. It's a shame – one so soon after the other."

"I remember Mary Brown's funeral as though it were yesterday," he replied, knowing that this would please Necker.

"Well that's how it seems to all of us. It's a crying shame. He's going to be buried with her, of course ... What about your tie?" said Necker.

"I shall wear my collar high," said Peter.

"You can't do that. Here, have Rollie's – children don't matter," spluttered Necker before Rollie could protest, yanking his tie from the youth's neck and placing it in Peter Vishnya's hands.

Rollie looked offended and startled; anger replaced amusement in his eyes.

"No, no," said Peter, quickly, "He will feel awkward."

He handed Rollie back his tie, and helped him fix it so that it hung straight.

Corvin was once again in his element, but saddened beyond words. They had just listened to the quotation from Paul's letter to the Thessalonians – "We would not have you ignorant, brethren, concerning those who are asleep, that you may not grieve as others do who have no hope ... God will bring with him those who have fallen asleep." Would Sarah now see her father, once again, in the arms of his Mary? Everyone who loved Sarah could only hope so. As the coffin had processed down the aisle, carried this time by the undertaker's men, Sarah looked a broken figure. Shane walked by his wife's side, his face a picture of concern and commiseration.

The church was packed. It had been decorated for Clive's funeral, by the members of the Fishermen's Hut, with symbols of the sea – crossed oars bestrode the aisle, nets were draped from the rafters and ship's lamps swung from the pews. It wasn't the effect but the effort which was important. It was from this that Corvin took his sermon, using a quote from Henry Van Dyke's poem *Gone from my sight*.

"'I am standing upon the seashore ...' – as Clive did so often, sometimes with a pint in his hand, sometimes helping with a net, but always with a twinkle in his eye and a kindly word for those around him. Now we must watch him go, as he so often watched the ships pass on ... As our hearts go out to Sarah and Shane and Matthew, as we try to help them through this difficult time, we should remember Clive as he was – and is now – 'as large in mast and hull and spar as when he left our side ... His diminished size is in us, not in him'."

Corvin paused at that point, waiting for his congregation to grasp the image of the ship disappearing beyond the horizon, but actually remaining as it had always been. Sarah's eyes lifted to him as he spoke. She didn't know the poem, but the image gelled in her mind and she wondered what was coming that could give her comfort.

"'And just at the moment when someone at my side says, 'There, she is gone!' there are other eyes watching her coming, and other voices ready to take up the glad shout 'Here she comes!'"

Corvin paused again, waiting. It was better for people to grasp the truth for themselves rather than spell it out. Then he said, with intended slowness:

"And whose voice will cry for Clive – 'Here she comes!'"

"Mary" – the word passed round the church. Corvin and Esther had spent most of the time since Clive's murder with Sarah. They had done what was humanly possible to ease her suffering – suffering that came from the knowledge that she would never see, or be with, her dad again. Now it was time to let him pass over the horizon – not in despair, but in the hope that he and Mary were, once again, together.

It was that image which Sarah took with her as she left the church behind her father's coffin – the image of him sailing into the arms of Mary whose loneliness would now be over.

"'And that is dying.'"

The churchyard emptied slowly as Clive was laid to rest. Peter Vishnya found himself among the last to leave, and standing next to Rebecca Unwood.

"Miss Unwood."

The tone was respectful and enquiring, but she just wished Peter Vishnya had not spoken. As always she found him too good to be true, and it annoyed her.

"Mr Vishnya?"

"Might I, at some time over the next two days, have a word with you?"

"Is it sufficiently brief for it to be said on the way home?"

"I thought, perhaps, this moment might not be appropriate."

"We are used to funerals at the rectory, Mr Vishnya. I can commiserate with Sarah, and talk with you of other things within the same day."

"Then, it will be my pleasure to walk with you."

He led her from the churchyard and turned down a rough track by the lower steps. Rebecca hadn't expected this and frowned, but said nothing. They passed the field where the Scouts had their campfires, breasted a small rise in the lane and were in another world, away from the nearby road. Along the hedge-bank, she saw the rich green leaves and white flowers of the greater stitchwort and the final flowers of a few wood anemones on their long slender stalks. Towards Pedlers Lane and the river, there were the drooping, purplish flowers of the water avens and some early, very early, purple loosestrife. Rebecca loved wild flowers, and had tried to introduce them in the rectory garden. Here, in their natural habitat, they seemed so full of themselves.

Peter Vishnya had not spoken by the time they reached the river, but Rebecca found she did not mind his silence. It was just so wonderful, having turned that corner into the lane, to be away from the real world: the world of her work – nursing – and the world of the church. They paused by the bridge; it was old and only just usable, but really only led into the marsh beyond the river. Yellow flag grew prolifically along the bank under the bridge, and Rebecca stooped to pluck one of the brilliant yellow flowers. Her action seemed to break the silence between.

"I have the chance to return to my own country ..." said Peter.

"Estonia?"

"Yes ... and play my part in its future."

"Well, that's wonderful. There's nothing to stop you – yet you sound unsure."

"I am not unsure about this being the right thing to do, but – yes – there may be something stopping me."

"Yevgeny?"

"No – I have yet to discuss this with Yevgeny, but there is another – in a sense, more urgent – consideration."

"What is that?"

"You do not know? ... Then perhaps it is not a consideration at all."

It was at that moment, of course, that she did know and really, really couldn't cope with knowing. She could never quite get out of her head that he had 'known a woman' – how those old Biblical terms plagued her thoughts! Rebecca was acutely aware that he had loved another woman and that they had a child. Peter Vishnya irritated her, but she liked him and the liking seemed wrong. He would be another's in life and in death – wouldn't he? Peter ploughed on, a note of desperation in his voice.

"I would wish to make my meaning clear. It is important to me ... I have strong feelings for you ..."

She had to speak, then. She couldn't let him say more, uninterrupted.

"Please, Mr Vishnya ..."

"Let me finish ... I hesitate to use the words I should, for fear that they will separate us forever when they should bring us together. It was not my intention to ... accost ... you in this way. I have known what my feelings for you were for a long time – this is not something new to me. I did not express them for a multitude of reasons – my wife, my son – all those things – but I felt them in truth. And now I have this offer to which I must respond within three days. This forces my hand. This makes me rush when time would have resolved these things in its own way ... we would have come to know ... naturally ... without rush ... without ... forcing the issue ..."

His voice faded and died. Rebecca was left alone.

"Mr Vishnya ..."

She was aware that she had returned to the cold 'Mr' but couldn't help it. She couldn't be rushed.

"... I am honoured ..."

Oh dear! Rebecca knew in her heart that she was moving down another track – not where she wanted to go but where she felt she had to go, and didn't know why.

"... but this has come as a ... surprise to me ..."

A lie - she knew it, and knew that he did, also.

"... and I need ... I cannot be rushed as a matter of expediency."

What on earth was she talking about? What on earth was she saying? What did these words mean – "a matter of expediency"? In a moment she was going to get irritated with him and with the situation in which he had placed her. Here she was

150

– stifling her natural feelings, and telling lies about her real wishes; but what could she do – throw herself into this man's arms?

"I don't wish to rush you, Rebecca …"

"Oh really! That's nice – very considerate of you!"

"I need only to know whether there might be a possibility … such a possibility of … of such a relationship growing between us … before I leave these shores …"

"You're going forever?"

"No. I shall retain my home here. If Yevgeny is happy to go … then I cannot … let him down. He must have a settled place for his schooling …. I think this would be a … 'holiday home' …. Is that the phrase? There is so much to think about?"

She could see that, and she wanted to help him but couldn't without committing herself. Her silence forced him to speak.

"I need only know …"

"You've said that!"

"I need only know … what your feelings might be."

"Have I ever given you cause to wonder?"

"I have had a sense that there might be …"

"Oh, really!?"

"Just the sense ….just the possibility …"

For Rebecca, this was one of the watershed moments of her life, like the moment she decided to leave for university. On that occasion she knew – however painful it might have been for her mother – that she had made the right decision. On this occasion she knew that she was about to make the wrong one.

"I cannot think, Mr Vishnya, that I have ever given you reason to suppose that I might be … how shall I put it …?"

"There is no need. I understand."

She knew that he was hurt. He was hurt because he knew she was retreating, and did not understand why. He failed to understand that Rebecca, being who she was, could not commit herself with obvious abandon to such a proposal.

"I think it might be better if I go now."

"I will accompany …"

"No – there is no need. I have only to walk along Marsh Lane to the road, and it is a bright, sunny afternoon."

"Of course," Peter sighed, lamely, as he watched her back disappearing along the rough track, and realised how much he ached for her.

Rebecca reached the corner, turned and looked back at him.

"Thank you, Mr Vishnya … Peter," she said, her voice full of uncertainty.

For Peter Vishnya, it was a moment of hope, and he took that as her intention. He stood for a long while at the bridge – giving her time to reach home, and finalising his plans. Then he followed, slowly, the way she had gone. He would speak to Yevgeny, but felt he already knew the answer to his query. The boy would want to go – it was exciting. They had often talked of Estonia and Peter's life there with his parents. Now, at long last, he would see his grandparents and a new life would begin for them both – father and son with their wolf, Anton.

CHAPTER 16

Horst Brultzner hosts his luncheon

For Horst Brultzner the great day had arrived and a late, inspired, suggestion from Amy Billings had put the icing on his cake: everyone attending the luncheon was to go in Victorian costume. Amy had assured him that the women would rise to the occasion as they did for the twice-annual village musical, and that the costumes would be second to none – clothes of which a West End theatre company could be proud; she had proved to be right. The young women proudly displayed their breasts and waists by wearing off-the-shoulder dresses drawn in tightly above the hips, and accentuated their buttocks with a modern version of the bustle. The older women settled for layers of dress and petticoat either falling from the shoulder or laced high at the neck, depending upon how wrinkly they felt themselves to be. The men were resplendent and at ease in frock coats, waist coats, trousers without flies or zips and floppy top hats.

One or two, of course, had excelled themselves. Martin Billings, who had a replica Peeler's uniform hanging on the back of his office door – in order, as he said, "to give a sense of history to the oicks" – turned up in this, much to the gratification of Horst Brultzner, who was dressed in the style of Arthur Clennam from *Little Dorrit*. He wore a calf length frock coat with a wide collar and tight shoulders, beautifully tailored trousers strapped under his arches, a crossed waistcoat ending exactly on the waist, frilled cuffs and collar and a tall, shiny top hat; he looked most authentic. When asked, he assured Martin Billings that the clothes were, indeed, genuine Victorian articles which he had kept scrupulously clean for decades. Everybody laughed. Much to everyone's joy and pleasure, it was the priests who took the day. Both Corvin and Bishop Twiddle had acquired genuine Victorian cassocks – Corvin's being a true cassock which hid his corpulence most effectively, and Peter Twiddle's more of a frock coat, but with an ecclesiastical cut.

Even the servants had rallied to the spirit of the occasion. Totto Briggs had provided the catering staff from within his own family or business – not trusting his meats to anyone else – and his wife, Fanny, had seen to the costumes with bonnets, baskets, starched white aprons, blue or brown dresses and shawls in profusion. Crafty Catchpole, lingering on the edges of the garden, had spent fruitless hours on the computer trying to find out what Victorian gardeners wore, and had finally gone to ask Clara Gobley, who togged him out in sacking and leather; the trousers itched but the leather was smooth, and he felt that he looked the part.

They were blessed by the weather. Approaching the start of summer, England could have thrown anything at them, but Horst Brultzner had a fluffily-clouded sky, no wind and gentle warmth. He was careful to keep his eye on the clouds and tended to keep within the shadows of the trees or house, but this was simply a sensible precaution; in reality, he could roam freely about his garden as he wished.

The whole scene would have been a credit to a BBC quality drama production, and the players in Herr Brultzner's little pantomime felt this. People in costume cease to be themselves, and take on the persona of the clothes or extend their own personalities in hidden directions. Here, in an English vicarage garden, pretence was played out to the satisfaction of everyone – sunshine, smiles and the bonhomie of summer.

Horst Brultzner was fascinated by the women. His first meeting of any consequence with a woman in the village had been with Amy Billings, and he excused himself from Bishop Twiddle, who immediately approached Lord Wangford, to go and speak with her. He had found that 'his' women always remembered their encounters with pleasure and puzzlement. They longed for him again, but didn't quite know why; Amy was no exception and turned to him almost with a look of love.

She chatted volubly to him, and he listened with contentment to the sound of her voice. He felt sexual desire for her as he listened, and regretted that such a simple satisfaction was beyond him, now. The warmth of two bodies was a delightful thing, but any attempt at gratification would bring only terror to the woman. He took her arm gently in his gloved hand and led her over to Martin, who was talking to Mark Chambers and the fat councillor who had been at the Health Club party, and told him what a lovely wife he had; Martin smiled his appreciation.

Horst Brultzner hadn't quite weighed the policeman up. He was an English eccentric of the traditional sort, it was true, but there was also something else about him – an almost manic obsession with his place in the village. He quizzed him about the killing on the beach, and concluded that it was obvious from his reluctance to talk that Martin was nowhere near finding the killer. There had been talk from Crafty Catchpole of wolves and torn throats, and it puzzled Brultzner as to who could have been on the beach that night. When he had arrived – as nothing more than a shadow on the promenade – only the policeman's friend had been around, clearly guarding the body. He remembered the man from their first meeting in Martin Billing's office. He had an air of impertinence about him, but was clearly educated. He'd enjoyed watching Crewes, the sweat pouring from him as he looked desperately about to see whatever it was approaching, as he tried to regain his self possession.

Horst turned to Mark Chambers – who had been showing Brultzner's guests round the Old Vicarage, and displaying his work with pride – and ascertained how the luncheon was going. As far as he liked anyone (in the usual sense of that word) Brultzner 'liked' Mark Chambers. He admired the man's directness, care, craftsmanship and what the English call 'lack of side'. As far as he trusted anyone, Brultzner would trust Mark Chambers.

The work had gone well but there was still much to do, and Brultzner knew that they would be unlikely to see the renovation complete before the following spring. This pleased him; a year was nothing in his world and he would enjoy waiting. Sheer enjoyment was not something he usually experienced, but among Mark Chambers and his men Horst Brultzner felt happy (if that is the right word) to be part of the endeavour.

As he and the builder spoke, Grise Culman came up to them and he noticed the change in the man's expression. He realised that there was, or had been, something between them. Like any normal man, he realised that she was more than attractive – she had a smile that lit up her whole face and it felt as though she was smiling just at you. Grise was a physical presence. Brultzner remembered her desperation that night in the pool – her vivacious desire to hold on to whatever was happening to her, and how she had trembled in his arms as she yielded to him across the reflection of the moon.

Grise clung to his arm, insisting that he should meet Alan and Penny Read, who were talking to Lord Wangford. They were his guests, she said, and he ought to greet them. Horst thought she was playing a part, so wifely was her manner. He had never been married; it wasn't allowed in the Roman army until you were past military service and, by then, his fate had already been decided.

He respected Alan Read on sight – again, as far as 'respected' meant anything to Brultzner. His 'respect' for Alan Read was akin to his 'liking' for Mark Chambers. They were more thoughts than emotions. The man was clearly his own person. There was a fearlessness about him – a quiet, measured assertion. He was aware the doctor watched him closely throughout their brief conversation.

And watch him he might, for Brultzner was fascinated by his wife, Penny. She was what is thought of as the English rose type. At one level she was the epitome of feminine purity – even as a married woman with children she exuded an air of chaste innocence; at another, she appealed to the darker side of certain men – the kind of man who would want to break through that unsullied demeanour to see what might lie beneath. She spoke quietly with a gliding warmth; there wasn't a shrill note in her voice. Brultzner knew that she ran the Sunday school – at some time Corvin Unwood must have told him that – but this was their first meeting. She asked how he was settling in, how he was coping with having builders around him all the time and how delighted the village was that someone had taken an interest in that beautiful old house. If she could be of any help he wasn't to hesitate to call. He asked if she had seen round the ground floor, which was the only part renovated and, on her replying in the negative, insisted that he should take her round himself.

Everyone was delighted and so, leaving Alan Read to chat with Lord Wangford, Horst Brultzner found himself, with Penny Read on one arm and Grise Culman on the other, in the hallway of his vicarage. To their right was the front parlour and to their left the dining room. Further down the hallway, to the left, was the study, where he had welcomed Peter Vishnya, and to the right, the morning room. It was here towards which the ladies urged Horst Brultzner, first. This was the 'ladies study' but neither Grise nor Penny, who knew about Victorian antiques, had expected it to be furnished as such; they were wrong. The furniture here was light in style, contrasting with the heaviness of his study, and Penny noticed immediately a William Morris rush-seated chair and a Godwin occasional table, ebonized and with gilt decoration. The utter surprise on her face was most gratifying to Horst Brultzner.

Brultzner watched Grise watching Penny as she spoke. Here was power – two beautiful women, two completely different types of women, hanging on his every whim. One he had already enjoyed, and the other he intended to visit as soon as it was discreetly possible. They both admired him, he thought – an admiration that courted jealousy. The intense darkness of Grise contrasted superbly with the demure blondeness of Penny. He wondered how each of their husbands enjoyed them – the quiet, reserved, rather nervous Owen, and the quiet, assertive, confident Alan. Was it the women who decided?

As he mused, Penny Read went and sat at the Pembroke, which he'd had covered with a light, lace tablecloth and a Tunbridge ware writing slope. "May I?" Of course, she might. Penny opened the slope and, sharing Horst's child-like pleasure, looked into its compartments and examined the pens, pencils, seals and rulers within. Her long, blonde hair, flowing over her shoulders and half-way down her back, glistened in the pale afternoon light from the window, which shone, diffused by the lace curtains, across her. "Would he stand by her and have his picture taken?" wondered Grise; he would be delighted. Horst moved swiftly across the room, passed the pier mirror hurriedly without a glance, and stood in the shadow cast by Penny – slightly beyond the subdued light. His hand touched her shoulder, but only just, in the standard 'Victorian pose', and Grise – with her infectious laugh – pressed the shutter. Now it was her turn – perhaps in front of the mirror so that it caught their reflections behind? Horst felt not – perhaps by the Godwin, with Grise sitting on the Morris. They all laughed – do any other peoples have the English sense of humour? Horst thought not – it was a unique characteristic, and one he admired tremendously.

When they returned to the Italianate garden, Alan Read and Lord Wangford were still talking, having been joined by Corvin Unwood. It amused Brultzner that everyone referred to Lord Wangford as either Charles or Charlie – except the rector who always called him "My lord". Wangford did nothing to put the priest out of his misery. Did he have a cruel streak in him, or was it simply the bloody-mindedness of the English aristocracy?

It was several months now since Horst Brultzner had appeared at the butcher's shop, pole-axed the cow and placed his order. Totto Briggs and his family did not disappoint him. The meats and their accompaniments were being served in a marquee erected on the lawn below the Italianate garden, which stretched down from the house alongside the copse. The boeuf en daube – using dripping and only German wine for the casserole with topside, not brisket, from local cattle – was proving most popular. Several guests had taken a little on their plates in order to leave room for the shoulder of lamb a la Turque, eaten cold and garnished with chutney and prunes. "Delicious!" Bishop Twiddle, notably first among the guests to approach the marquee (mainly, of course, to re-new his acquaintance with Mr Briggs), preferred the pork Alsacienne – again cooked in dry German white with the English Bramley, and served with hot, buttered potatoes. Corvin, with Esther and Rebecca, followed closely in the bishop's footprints, and also selected the pork despite his wife's assurance that he would like the glazed baked gammon (with the juniper berries in the stock) much more.

Rebecca, enquired whether Mr Briggs was providing a "vegetarian alternative", which he was not. "Could he interest her in the additional fare he had cooked – succulent pork pies, home-baked hams or spicy beef sausages?" "No?" So, she was directed towards the other end of the marquee where Sandra Bint presided.

Sandra Bint had been commandeered to provide a selection of desserts. She and her son, Ainsley, who had helped out at the Beachlands Health Club party, were well-known for their quality catering, and had been recommended by Amy Billings when she paid Horst Brultzner a visit to suggest the Victorian dress.

Sandra had followed suit and, believing Horst to be Italian, had suggested "some dishes from his own country". Horst was flattered – although not charmed by Sandra – and readily agreed to such traditional delicacies as Neapolitan tart with ricotta and almonds, caramelized oranges (although she withdrew this idea when she discovered to her astonishment that Herr Brultzner had no fridge), almond peaches with amaretti filling and Sicilian cheesecake.

While at the Old Vicarage, she also suggested that one or two of the guests might not eat meat – something not anticipated by Horst – and would he like her to serve country risotto, provided there was some way of keeping it hot? Again, Horst was charmed by the idea, and readily agreed.

He had his reservation about Sandra. There was, to his mind, something coarse about her as though she'd "slept" (as the phrase goes) in a few too many beds. People pick up diseases that way, and diseases affect the blood; the quality of blood was important to Brultzner.

But today, as the sun shone on his luncheon, all was well with the world and Sandra Bint's open smile and ready laugh attracted many of his guests to her end of the marquee where the risotto steamed over one of Totto's open-air stoves and the aroma of gently cooking peas, asparagus tips, courgettes, tomatoes, onion and basil filled the air.

As he approached to thank Sandra, he noticed Rebecca Unwood receiving her plate of risotto and bowed his head. She blushed, looked angry with herself and smiled back, but there was reserve in her eyes. He remembered her intensity on the night he had come to her – how she had pulled back until the shadow faded and then regretted it. She had wanted only to sink into the stillness that surrounded her – the quiet place deep within her, which she could not seem to reach. She'd waited, and when the moment came her arms reached up and held him. Amy and Grise had looked at him almost with love; in Rebecca's eyes there was only fear.

He wandered with her into the garden. As yet, the work on this had barely begun. Mr Catchpole's enthusiasm for the Italianate Garden had moved that project on quickly, but there was still so much to be done. Rebecca, despite herself, found that she was caught up in the man's enthusiasm. "Didn't he find Victorian gardens fussy – all those statues, pathways, ponds, fiddly trees, rockeries sundials, vases?" Not in the least – giant gardens in miniature, another room to the house.

Rebecca laughed; it was difficult not to take Horst Brultzner seriously. As they chatted – she with her plate of risotto, he smiling with contentment – Lord Wangford joined them, nursing a plate of Totto's pork Alsacienne. "Did she know her father was eating his lunch in the dining room?" She had guessed as much – her mother liked to eat at a table.

Rebecca liked Charles Wangford – everyone did, it was difficult not to; he was inoffensive and did his bit round the village. She wondered, sometimes, what he thought of her father; it would be hurtful if there was any trace of contempt in his view. People like Charles Wangford had slipped into life; people like her father had struggled every inch of the way. She hated his servility and didn't understand it. Why did he insist on calling Charles Wangford "My lord"?

Charles Wangford ate the pork with relish. Rebecca knew that her father would be wondering whether or not "his lordship" could name the Riesling in which it was cooked or detect the presence of the English Bramley. Perhaps it was just that – her father felt humbled by these people. Their very knowledge, and the way they took for granted what he had strived to learn, daunted him. He wanted to be part of it, but never would.

As they ate, she noticed Nadine Palmester and beckoned her over. Nadine came at a lope and both men stood, without thinking about it, and greeted her. Nadine was tall, rather thin and angular. Like many tall women, she walked with a bit of a stoop – quite unnecessarily – and this gave her a cadaverous appearance. Brultzner and Wangford, however, were both tall, and she was able to look across at them without feeling self-conscious about her height. Like Rebecca, she was in her late twenties and unmarried – possibly for similar reasons. Coming from a background of religious certainties, it was difficult to meet a man who shared any of your beliefs. Nadine herself held liberal views about most things, but they were 'informed' by her upbringing. Her father was Simon 'Sly' Palmester, a fundamentalist preacher from the village Bethel. She was a professional journalist and Horst hoped she would "put a little piece in the paper" – he loved aping that style of conversation. Oh, more than a little – the renovation of the Old Vicarage was exciting debate in local heritage circles, and she hoped Mr Brultzner would welcome a double page spread?

Horst Brultzner was more expansive than ever when he eventually walked into his dining room to find Alan Read chatting with Corvin and Esther Unwood. He was aware that Esther Unwood was suspicious of him. In her steely grey eyes he had already detected an opponent, and he was feeling keen enough to exert some charm in her direction. Yes – they loved the dining room. It was certainly cosy – just the place for a family to gather to share food, said Corvin, but didn't (if he remembered correctly) the Victorians always hang their family portraits in the dining room? They did! And was Mr Brultzner going to follow suit? That might be difficult – he had no portraits of his ancestors, and no family as such for generations – but the essence of the dining room would remain the same, a place devoted to hospitality.

They all agreed that the food had been excellent, but then Totto Briggs always turned up trumps as Herr Brultzner would find if he attended the Harvest Supper next October. Brultzner noticed Esther's 'Herr', and smiled.

Talk turned to Alan's wife; Penny was a treasure – not, as Brultzner surmised, because of her golden, shoulder-length hair but because she held the Junior Church together. Alan and Penny had four children of their own – it was natural that she would want to be involved. She also sang and this was a distinct advantage. Certainly, the Melody Makers were a vital part of Sunday worship – an "outward and visible sign" of this "caring, spirit-filled community of love". This was one of Corvin's favourite phrases, and he used it every Sunday in his prayers and his sermons.

Perhaps Herr Brultzner would come and talk to the children some time? Penny ran a multi-cultural Junior Church. It would broaden the children's horizons to hear from someone who had travelled so widely across Europe, and lived among so many different people. Herr Brultzner wasn't absolutely sure that his experiences would necessarily be of benefit to the children, but if Mrs Read would like to "get in touch" with him …?

The amiability was in full swing when Penny arrived looking for her husband. The grandparents had somewhere to go that evening, and perhaps they ought to be "making a move"? Horst Brultzner smiled to himself; how discreet the English were – how unnecessarily civil! Alan Read thanked Horst and turned to his wife who took his arm in what Corvin felt was a most beguiling way. Brultzner stood and gave the little bow the English liked so much.

As Horst escorted them to the gate, Bishop Twiddle approached, sensing the time had come for the early leavers to make a move. He was moved by the invaluable work Penny was doing for the church "in this place", and overwhelmed by the contribution to English Heritage being made by Mr Brultzner. Horst said his farewells to Dr and Mrs Read, who were joined, hurriedly, by Martin and Amy Billings. "It would be nice to walk back together." Horst saw his luncheon disappearing before his eyes, but was charmed by his guests and deeply appreciative (he was learning the style of speech very quickly) of the efforts made by Martin in the hunt for Victorian furniture.

When he had given his final wave, Horst turned and saw the bishop – with Corvin and Esther – making his way down the driveway. The gravel recommended by Martin Billings crunched beneath their feet. "A few matters to discuss with the rural dean". Corvin flushed with pleasure. Esther's eyes saw only the bishop sitting in their lounge or garden sipping a glass of white wine from his fridge in the 'refectory'.

Totto Briggs and his family, and Sandra Bint, were delighted; there was little left of the food they had so lovingly prepared. "A hungry crowd – they devoured the lot", but Horst "hadn't touched a thing." He ate sparingly these days – a stomach condition, but he was most appreciative of the efforts Totto and Sandra had made. It was a luncheon the village would remember for a long time to come. Now, he must find Lord Wangford with whom he needed a few words.

Charles Wangford was chatting easily with Grise Culman, the fat councillor and a group of businessmen and women from Norbridge. Grise held centre stage, but it was Wangford who was making the conversation. There was more to him, thought Horst, than met the eye. He rubs shoulders so naturally with everyone. It was not a skill common to all aristocracies – especially the newer ones on the edge of Europe. As Horst approached, the group opened to welcome him.

It was late afternoon or early evening – what you will – and the sun had yet to set. Horst Brultzner was alone in his Victorian mausoleum. The last of his guests to leave – Totto's family, Grise and Owen Culman, Rebecca Unwood – had helped him put his house in order. It was as neat and tidy as when they began to arrive at noon.

He walked up the first flight of stairs to his bedroom, which went off the first landing. This was, as yet, untouched by workmen. Mark Chambers had offered to "just sort it out so as it's comfortable", but Horst had waved his concerns away with a smile. So the lath and plaster stood bare and old wallpaper hung in shreds; under his feet were bare boards and exposed floor joists.

When it was complete, it would be splendid – a four-poster bed, heavy hangings in rich colours to break up the straightness of the walls, a few chairs arranged casually, a delicate figure in Dresden china, photographs (such as he had) of those he had known, polished brass-work and soft pools of light from oil lamps or gas jets; but, more than anything, colour, deep colour in real sealing-wax reds, deep oranges and clear yellows. The bed would have to be blessed and the sheets spun from his native cloth, but neither of those requirements would be a problem.

For now, however, he had his "box" – in the words of the delivery man – and that would suffice as it had so often done on his travels. He removed his costume, and laid each item neatly across the back of the Sheraton chair.

A few hours 'sleep' and he would be strong again for the night. His guests had feasted well, and the light of morning would see him refreshed from the veins of Penny Read. He demanded little of life – his essential needs were small. She would be asleep beside her husband, and he would come to her and she would wake – in that warm, half-stupor of women in bed. She would know him then, but – come daylight – he would be nothing more than a shadowy dream. For a few days she would feel weak and tired, and then all would be well. When they met, the desire would show in her face, and she would wonder why it was she felt love for this stranger.

Book Two

Summer Blossoms

CHAPTER 1

Closing in

Sidney Close stood in the corner of his shop and watched Shame Marjoram opening a newly arrived box containing a television set. He watched the young man's lean, muscular figure with envy. Sidney knew that not only had Shane a good physique, but that he also made full use of it. The stray comment, the extravagant boast and the leering muscles told Sidney that Shane had a good sex life, a full sex life – a sex life that gave him the physical release every man needed. Sidney could see it in every move Shane made – the long stroke of his arm as he slit the tape that held the cardboard, the crouch as he stooped to remove the set, the lift as he swung it up and over onto the counter, the sheer confidence of his every move. After a hard day, the young man went home to his succulent Sarah – not a dry stick like Mavis. When he fancied a bit, he got it. He walked through the door of their little cottage, lifted her onto the kitchen table and took her where she stood; and she enjoyed it – after tea, she came back for more.

He shook himself and went to open up the back of the shop; it was a small space in which they worked. Sidney threw up the blinds, wrenched down the bolts and opened a few windows. June had proved to be hot; '…warm, young virgins stirring restlessly in their beds'. He'd read that somewhere; some dirty sod had written it. He couldn't get the image of Shane and Sarah writhing on their bed out of his mind. A slight, cool breeze drifted in through the windows and he shook himself, again.

It was Monday morning and he was looking forward to the week: he always did. Once he was into his work, Sidney was second to none. The small electrical goods business he ran in the village was thriving. He had the right touch for a village shop: nothing was too much trouble – or didn't appear to be – and he could butter-up the ladies. It was a prime site on the village main street, just down from the butcher's and next to the chemist's shop. Sidney had made it work. He had a smile for everybody as they entered. He cultivated a clean-cut image; he wore a sports jacket, with a collar and tie, in the shop. Shane had company overalls with their logo – as did Sidney when he went out to do a repair, or when he was on one of his "We'll set everything up so that all you have to do is turn it on" missions. That always did the trick – the big companies couldn't touch that kind of approach. The other ace up their sleeves was service; customers got 'service' from Sidney Close – "today, not tomorrow" was their slogan.

When he'd taken on Shane Marjoram, who Sidney knew had been a trouble-maker at school, he told him from the start – "The customer's needs come first. Nothing gets in the way of that. You understand me, son? You may have to work beyond half-past five some nights to keep everybody happy? They are our bread and butter. They put the food in your belly, the roof over your head and the warmth in your hearth." Sidney, to be fair, had to admit that the youth had come up trumps. He was clean, reliable and knew his trade; he was a hundred miles from the tearaway who'd driven teachers to despair, skipped off school and dominated every playground in which he'd ever set foot. Sarah had tamed him, they all said; she'd given him the security he'd wanted and never got from his family.

His own education hadn't been much better than Shane's – although he wouldn't have admitted that to anyone. Sidney had left school at fifteen with no particular qualifications and gone to the local technical college where he had learned his trade. An electrical qualification had taken him into the television business and he'd worked his way up from there. He'd been diligent, conscientious and loyal to the firm for whom he worked. He was also intelligent. What he didn't know he could appear to understand; keeping quiet at the right moments is an admirable strategy.

He'd met Mavis through the church. His father was an elder in the Baptist church in Eastwold, she was a Dunburgh girl who went to St George's with her parents, and they had come together over a Christian weekend in Bungay. Their courtship had simply happened from that weekend. Driven together by what seemed the right thing to do and the anxiety from both sets of parents that they should "settle down", Sidney had married Mavis in her own church and had two girls over the next few years.

Sidney had moved to Dunburgh when they married, putting a hard-saved deposit down on the house they now lived in, and had become a well-respected figure in the community. He attended Mavis's church (although he still felt the pull of the Baptist community and often attended the Dunburgh Bethel) and, through adopting the right attitudes and striking that note of integrity which was his hallmark, had once held the post of rector's warden at St George's. Sidney was very proud of that; it gave him status in his own eyes, in the eyes of the community and in the eyes of his family.

Sidney had a very definite notion of right and wrong. It wasn't something he'd thought about a great deal – it was simply something he had grown up with; shades of grey were excuses for fudging the issue. His parents had taught him this, and the church had re-enforced it. What might be right for non-Christians was one thing – Christians always had the Bible to which they could refer. It made life simple, it ironed out the creases, it gave you a basis on which to bring up your own children and it gave security to the community in which you lived.

He liked a tidy life and the shop reflected this; there were two main rooms – the shop itself and a workshop – and both were spick and span. There was a place for everything, and everything was in its place. His customers loved the clean feel of the shop, and even Shane respected the importance of "doing things right" and left the workshop "immaculate" (one of Sidney's favourite words) every night. He accepted that there could be worse places to work than Close Electrical.

They were chalk and cheese, but worked well together and Sidney was pleased to have been able to do something positive to help Froggy Brown's daughter when she had been unfortunate enough to have to marry one of the Marjorams. Mavis's line had been a trifle different – more along the lines of "if she'd kept her legs together it wouldn't have happened" – but Sidney, like most men of his generation, had a soft spot for women, and his view was more tolerant. Whatever the differences, Clive and Mary Brown had been grateful, and that had been enough for both Sidney and Mavis.

Sidney and Shane sat together in the workshop, over an early morning cup of coffee, running through the day's schedule. Sidney was to remain in the shop; Shane had various sets to install and modifications to carry out. 'Modifications' was another of Sidney's favourite words. It usually implied some alteration to an existing television or audio system that didn't actually need doing, but brought in a little more money and gave the customer the impression that they were one technological step ahead of the people next door. Sidney was good at that kind of thing; he kept up with the latest gadgets and smarmed his customers into believing that they couldn't live without them. The microwave oven had been a boon to his business and now the mobile phone was proving equally lucrative as 'improved' model pursued 'improved' model with amazing alacrity.

Shane glowed as he listened. Sidney's anguished surmises regarding the previous night had been completely on the mark. Shane had enjoyed Sarah as soon as Matthew had been put to bed. Moreover, he had woken early that morning, naked and still covered in sweat, and rolled his wife over again.

"It's lovely that, init Mr Close – havin' a little bit in the mornin' before you go to work. I mean – it's nice the night before, but yer jest roll over and go ter sleep, don't you? When yer have it in the mornin', yer can think about it all day, can't yer?"

Sidney had no answer to that, rhetorical though the question was; he had never had "a little bit in the mornin'" in all his married life, and there hadn't been a great deal "the night before" since the girls were born. He'd watched Sarah Marjoram looking at her husband; he'd seen the dreamy look in her eyes, and envied Shane with a deep and abiding envy. He almost couldn't bear the thought, and Sidney gripped the edge of the workbench and ground his knuckles into the metal fixings of the vice.

"You OK, Mr Close? Yer look a bit white."

"Fine. Late night."

"Hey, hey! Nufin' like it, is there?"

Sidney ran through the work schedule with a degree of venom which Shane could not understand. His boss was certainly a tense man – one minute he was laughing with you, and the next he was spitting bolts. Shane couldn't know that, as he ran through the list, Sidney's mind was on Sarah watching her husband's body.

"Are you OK with that?"

"Sure – no problem, Mr Close – jest leave it to Shane."

After Shane had gone, Sidney went into his shop and 'prepared a face to meet the faces that you meet'. He'd read that somewhere, or somebody had quoted it to him – Tony Crewes, probably. He was always coming out with things like that, things that meant nothing to anybody else, just to show that he had been to university.

He enjoyed his shop – it was his livelihood and his duty – but on some days it was boring, especially when his mind was on other things. The 'other things' were often sex; for a man who enjoyed so little of the real thing, sex occupied a large part of Sidney's life or – to be more exact – the repression of it occupied a large part of his life, and Sydney had to live within that repression. Sometimes the thought of Mavis in her brushed nylon dressing-gown, working at her embroidery and waiting for the front door to click before she rose to make him a cup of tea, was almost too much to bear.

He would go home on some nights and – having had the cup of tea, listened to the details of her day and eaten the meal she had prepared for him – Sidney would go to the back room. This was the room they kept for guests and rarely used, but it was perfect for Sidney. Here he kept his books – quite decent books to improve his mind – and his exercise equipment. Sidney was big and heavily muscled because each day, every day, without fail, he exercised. The equipment was old-fashioned by modern standards. It was the equipment currently fashionable at the time of his youth, and Sidney had stuck with it – chest expanders, hand grips, punch bags. While Mavis caught up with the lives of her soap friends, Sidney worked out hard; to him it was a physical release – from the tedium of the day and the knowledge of what he wasn't going to get that night.

It had been Ample Basset's barbecue the previous weekend, and they'd had a good time; Billy and Ample were easy company. The barbecues put Sidney on the horns of a dilemma. On the one hand he enjoyed the company, enjoyed greeting the women: on the other hand, there was the drink and the laughter of his friends which grew more lustful as the evening wore on. 'Here, Lord, in flesh but not in spirit' – as his father used to say.

His daughters were now growing up – they'd reached the sleep-over stage and Sidney felt uneasy about what would happen to them. It was a funny world out there – drink, drugs and sex; a young girl could easily be lured into ... into marriage with the likes of Shane Marjoram. Sidney shuddered. He didn't think he'd be able to bear that; he and Mavis would have to stop a relationship like that before it got started. He would have to tighten the coils around them – trawl them in.

Thoughts like these would run through Sidney's head as he exercised. Pushing his body to the limits, his mind was never at rest. He could still manage forty two real press-ups easily, and when he'd finished his shoulders ached and the sweat was pouring from him. As the television droned on next door he would force his way through squat thrusts (five sets of ten), knee lifts (five sets of ten) and abdominal crunches (up to twenty, rest, start again). He found a sense of release in this – the pressing, crunching, lifting and thrusting. He forced his body to its utmost until each muscle burned with its own fire.

The thoughts he pursued were vague. They flitted though his head like the images from a television set. Sidney never allowed them to crystallize. Some were memories, often second-hand, from his youth; others were images from books he'd read or plays he'd seen on the box. In unguarded moments, he found himself fixed on these, taking them on with himself as the main protagonist. He became the lover of half-known women – sometimes as a white knight in shining armour, at other times as a pirate or some other rogue. One image he had was of someone like Errol Flynn lifting someone like Maureen O'Hara in his arms – breasts straining at her off-the-shoulder dress, long hair dangling – and then taking her into his cabin.

Once in a while he glimpsed – only fleetingly and with the image at once extinguished – what it might be like to take a woman, and find satisfaction. 'There, Lord, but for the grace of God, go I.' He strapped his religion on like armour and could not forgive in others what he feared most in himself – that the beast within him would rise up and consume the better man. He was no Jekyll and Hyde – the two beings that were Sidney Close were there, alive and kicking, at one and the same time.

He loved Mavis, of course. They'd had two children together and created a nice home for them; they were a family and his daughters were delightful girls growing into fine young women. This was what life was about, but it lacked the great adventure – the journeying forth on some noble cause. He liked the tales of Arthur and his knights – the maidens they rescued, the rewards they reaped.

The shop door-bell rang and Sidney looked up. It was just after five o'clock and he'd planned to leave on time, but there stood Miss Mealey and Mrs Teale. His heart sank, as a smile rose to his face from somewhere deep within him.

"Ladies – lovely to see you, to see you …"

"… lovely!"

The two women chortled with joy at his take on Bruce Forsyth's famous catchphrase.

"Hello, Mr Close, what a lovely day it's been," said Mrs Teale.

"Lovely," said Miss Mealey, who always agreed with her friend.

"Ladies – I don't know when I've seen a lovelier day," rejoined Sidney, "and what can I do for you?"

"Miss Mealey's son worries that she hasn't got a mobile phone," said Mrs Teale.

"In case of emergencies," said Miss Mealey.

"Only we don't know anything about them," said Mrs Teale.

"Nothing at all," said Miss Mealey.

"You have two options, ladies – to buy one outright and pay as you go, or to pay a monthly line rental and get one free – or nearly free!"

He couldn't resist it – paying out the temptation as a fisherman pays out his line – although he knew full well that they could not face the concept of a monthly rental.

"Free?" said Mrs Teale.

"Free!" echoed Miss Mealey.

"Free!" repeated Sidney Close.

"Why would anyone give us …" commenced Mrs Teale.

"… a phone free?" finished Miss Mealey.

"A sprat to catch a mackerel," offered Sidney Close, in his wisdom.

"And we would be the sprats!" they said together.

"Indeed you would, ladies!"

"We'll buy one then," said Mrs Teale.

"We knew we'd do right to come to you, Mr Close," said Miss Mealey.

"You flatter me, ladies, you flatter me."

Sidney was pleased and felt expansive; he prided himself on his salesmanship. To his mind, selling an item without having explained anything about it to the customer was the highest achievement possible for any salesman: the second being to sell something without the customer understanding a thing about what they were buying. This was no con trick: the first kind of sale meant that his customers trusted him absolutely, the second that they didn't need to know anything to use the device. Customer satisfaction was the hallmark of both kinds of sale – no doubts, no worries, and no comeback! He glanced at his watch; it still wasn't a quarter past the hour so Sidney decided to sell the phone twice.

"Now what kind of 'pay-as-you-go' phone had you in mind, ladies?"

"There are different kinds?" queried Miss Mealey.

"There's a nice pink one in the window," said Mrs Teale.

"Do you want your phone to act as a camera, a database, an address book, an alarm clock or a text pad? Do you want it to link up with the internet and beam your photos round the world? Do you want to download your favourite CDs from the web? Do you want it to switch on your central heating so that your house is warm when you get home? Do you want it to top up your fridge by placing next week's order with the supermarket? Do you want it to book your holiday for you? …"

He paused. Their faces were a picture and he wanted to go on, but he also wanted to clinch the deal and close the shop by five-thirty. Miss Mealey said:

"I don't know why I want it. My son says I ought to have one."

"To phone him?"

"In emergencies."

"Then Mrs Teale is right – the pink one is the one for you!!"

Sidney always liked to finish on a double exclamation mark. It showed the class of the true salesman. Within ten minutes, he'd set up the pink phone, showed Miss Mealey how to charge it and what buttons to press when she wanted to speak to her son, taken her cheque and popped the pink phone into the little bag provided.

"Who do I pay as I go, Mr Close?"

"The phone will tell you when you need credit and then you come to see me. Play with it tonight – give your son a ring – and come back tomorrow if you have any problems."

Confidence was the thing – success bred success. Sidney had always believed he would make a good teacher. There was little to choose between a teacher, a salesman and a con-man – it was just a question of degree. The shop door rang as he held it open for the ladies – both immensely satisfied with Miss Mealey's purchase – to leave.

"You should never have resigned as rector's warden, Mr Close – the church needs men like you," said Mrs Teale.

"A matter of principle, ladies, cannot be ignored."

"It's a crying shame," said Miss Mealey.

"The rector was a fool to let you go," said Mrs Teale, in support of her friend.

Sidney's exodus from the post of rector's warden had, in fact, not been a simple matter – and he hadn't actually intended to resign. Like many people in such voluntary posts, he considered himself to be indispensable, and had tended his resignation expecting Corvin Unwood to beg him to stay. No one had been more surprised than Sidney when Corvin accepted with what he considered to be undue haste, and Sidney was still unsure as to how it had happened.

In the eyes of many, and Sidney was one of them, Corvin had proved to be a weak appointment. His wife chose to do nothing, but had much to say behind the scenes and it was she (rumour had it) who ran the parish. There had been trouble over the flowers in Lent, the organist had been awarded a stipend for what had always been a voluntary appointment, Penny Read had stepped in (without Sidney being consulted) to run the Junior Church when both Esther and Rebecca Unwood declined, wrangling over the cost of maintaining the churchyard had reached a fever pitch when Tony Crewes suggested grazing sheep to solve the problem and Penny Read had taken him to task about "wasting hours of our time talking about the parish quota when he knew perfectly well that there was sufficient funds in the Snoreton Trust to meet the bill".

Sidney hadn't liked any of that. As each dispute took hold of the village, Sidney did all he could to undermine Corvin's position in the parish, and also spread it about that he was "seriously considering handing in his resignation when the time came". Penny Read – unknown to everyone except her husband, Alan, who had listened patiently to her tales of the PCC – had laid her plans and approached Bernard Shaw about accepting the post of rector's warden. Penny approached him through his wife and was, therefore, successful very quickly. She then had a quiet word with Corvin Unwood, who had suffered several other setbacks at the hands of Sidney and Clara through the choir. No one was more surprised than Sidney, therefore – as he placed his resignation in Corvin's hands at the annual re-election meeting – when the rector accepted – with reluctance, of course, but appreciating all that Sidney had done over the years.

He still burned with the humiliation of that moment, when he waved cheerily goodbye to Miss Mealey and Mrs Teale as they toddled off with the pink mobile phone. As he locked the shop door, Shane arrived and parked the company van. He stuck his head out of the window.

"You haven't fergotten the satellite dish have yer, Mr Close?"

He had: he'd promised to take it round to Shane's that night and help him fix it. They went back into the shop, loaded the van and drove down to Shane's little cottage on Beach Road. Far from being irked, Sidney realized he was looking forward to seeing Sarah. It was, therefore, a disappointment for him – and an annoyance for Shane – when Nadine Palmester opened the door. Shane's immediate reaction was 'What the fuck's that cunt doing here?' but he didn't voice it; he just looked astonished and angry.

"Where's Sare?"

"She's just popped out. She asked me to keep an eye on Matthew."

Shane was immediately in turmoil. Here was a woman he hated, '*not* telling him where his fucking wife was. Who the fuck did she think she was?' His dislike of Nadine Palmester was based on fear – the fear that she might, in some way he couldn't quite place, stir things up, 'mess around with his life, piss him about.' He also knew that she disliked him, that she saw right through him, saw him for what he was – a lout. He wanted to say 'Where the fuck's she gone?' but couldn't, so he kept quiet – the words simply wouldn't come.

Nadine Palmester was a feminist of the decent sort – that is to say she saw the benefit and advantages of feminism for both sexes – rather than simply being a member of the have-your-cake-and-eat-it brigade. In Shane Marjoram she saw someone who would hold Sarah back, keep her down, put her in what he perceived to be 'the woman's place'. She was right. Unless someone like her intervened, Sarah's destiny as wife and mother was clearly mapped out. Yet Nadine knew Sarah was an intelligent woman – they had been at school together – and, by now, would have obtained her degree and been on the road to somewhere interesting and fulfilling, rather than being tied to Marjoram for the next sixty or seventy years.

This was the basis of their mutual antipathy. Unknown to Shane, Nadine and Sarah spent a lot of time together whenever Nadine was free from her journalist's work. Sarah had what Nadine wanted – a home and child; Nadine had what she thought Sarah would one day yearn for – a career.

Nadine also disliked Sidney Close although she wasn't quite sure why. Somewhere inside him lurked an hypocrite – she was sure of this although she would have been pushed to cite a convincing incident which would illustrate her feelings. He was very friendly with her father and seemed to share many of his religious views, which Nadine considered extreme, and she couldn't square this with his Anglicanism.

"Your dad OK?" Sidney asked.

"As always – and if he wasn't help would be at hand."

Nadine did not dispute with her father. She had learned a long time ago that this would be a waste of time. She attended the Bethel as she had been brought up to do. Indeed, she had no problems with religious belief at all; it was simply the novelty of her father's views which she found ludicrous. Her comment to Sidney was a laugh at the situation to keep her sane, and simply referred to the fact that Simon Palmester believed – and preached his belief – that you only had to ask God for something and it would be given. If he had been ill, therefore, Simon would have asked God to make him better, and the Lord would have obliged.

Sidney ignored the comment. He enjoyed Simon Palmester's preaching – more or less believed what he said – and had no wish to dispute with Nadine Palmester, who he knew was far more intelligent than him and would tie him in knots.

"Come in."

She said it deliberately. Nadine couldn't resist inviting Shane into his own house; it would amuse her all the way home and for days to come. It might even amuse Sarah, although she was fiercely loyal to her husband and wouldn't actually laugh at him.

"Thanks very much!" said Shane.

"We've come to fix the dish," said Sidney.

"Well, I'm sure the lady of the house won't mind me letting you in. Would you like me to make you a cup of tea while you're doing it?"

Sidney had to laugh, despite himself. Watching Shane, Nadine was glad that looks couldn't kill. 'Fuck off' he thought, but was stymied. He pushed through the doorway like an angry adolescent whose parents have refused to take into town.

Sidney followed with a smile for Nadine, as she closed the door behind them. He felt the love in the place and immediately resented it. Sarah and Shane had opened up the dark, rather pokey, little cottage and Sidney imagined her sitting by the fireplace on the low stool with her silken legs curled to one side. He saw Shane walk across and sit by her on the floor, running his hands along the back of her calves and up onto her thighs. He saw Sarah roused and take Shane's head in her hands to kiss him full on the lips. He saw Shane rise to her and slide his hands onto her buttocks.

"They've made a good job of this, haven't they Sidney?" said Nadine.

"Yeah – yes, it's lovely."

The fireplace drew him. Even in summer it looked warm – with the niches, the copper kettle, the glue pot, the wooden mantelpiece and the arrangement of fresh flowers (a mixture of dog rose, foxglove and white campion Sarah had picked from the hedgerows on her walks with Matthew). The hearthrug was thick, warm and inviting: the power of women, home and hearth. Sarah would wake him and they would make love, and she would hold him as she wanted. It would be her night. She would be eager ... her hands on him. She would draw him to her. 'It wasn't bloody fair!'

"Penny for them?" said Nadine, knowing full well what he was thinking.

"What! We'd better get on."

He walked quickly through the kitchen, noticing the polished wooden panels, the china plates and the blue gingham table cloth. Gingham! How many girls, in their gingham dresses, had he fancied at school? He saw Sarah running, fresh and cool on a hot summer's day, across a cornfield full of poppies and campion, the blue dress lifting and flapping against her thighs. The coolness invited him. He chased her, brought her down, down among the corn and the flowers and took her there, in the field, roughly, with immeasurable pleasure, and she came for him and cried for more until they were both spent and the flowers were crushed beneath their strewn clothes.

"Haven't they done wonders in here?"

'Fucking wonders. It's a wonder they've got any fucking time at all with all the fucking that goes on!' It was his voice, speaking to him; he couldn't find the words he wanted. Sidney knew, with a dreadful certainty, that he had to see the bedroom; the satellite dish would give him the chance – he'd suggest that he fed it through the loft and down. Outside, Shane was already poised at the top of the ladder with another in place for Sidney. He called down.

"Can you come and hold this for me, Mr Close. I checked the position and angle before so I know it's right."

Nadine watched them for a second or two – the fucker and the one who would fuck. She didn't often think like that, and would never have spoken the word, but it amused her to think how it would offend both men – Sidney because he didn't approve of swearing, and Shane because he thought only men should do it. She went into the kitchen to make them all a cup of tea. Sarah would be back soon; she'd only popped to the shops. Nadine was happy in her work but a part of her, somewhere, envied Sarah. It would be nice – just occasionally – to be at home, looking after your baby. There was something about domesticity which appalled her, but she enjoyed finding the tea-tray and setting out the cups and biscuits as Sarah would have done. She enjoyed taking it into the back garden and calling out:

"Tea's ready."

It annoyed them, of course, since both men were intent on fixing the dish, but it was nice – even momentarily fulfilling. Sidney came down his ladder, sipped at his tea and said:

"Where's the trapdoor to the loft?"

"On the landing."

He went up the stairs two at a time, peered down over the banister of the small landing and stepped quickly into the nearest bedroom. He saw Sarah on the Pooh Bear rug. His eyes swept the room. He reached down for her ... A slight, cool breeze drifted in through the windows and he shook himself.

"Nice room?" said Nadine, watching him from the doorway, "You can get into the loft easily. Shane has put a ladder in ... I think he's waiting."

"Yes."

"Are you all right, Sidney?"

"Yes."

"Do you need a hand? Your tea's getting cold."

"I can manage. I can handle it myself."

"I'm sure."

When he came downstairs, Sarah was standing in the kitchen, a basket of groceries over her arm. His awareness of her strong build, her grace of movement; her pretty face, her mass of honey-coloured hair and the dreamy look in her eyes only increased his desire.

"Hello, Mr Close. Nice of you to help Shane – we've been looking forward to getting satellite TV."

She moved across to the dresser to unpack her shopping basket. The lightness of her step, the suppleness in her shoulders and the way her legs swung easily from the hips seemed designed to taunt him.

"Pleased to help."

"Thanks, Mr Close."

Shane had stowed the ladders and come in through the back door.

"I'll be off now, then, Sarah," said Nadine.

"Oh yes. Thanks for keeping an eye on Matthew. I just needed to pop out for a few things, Shane, and the babe was asleep."

It was only then that Sidney realised the child had been in his cot when he stood in the bedroom transfixed by his fantasy. He felt sick and wanted to leave quickly.

"You OK now then, Shane?"

"Yeah – thanks. I can finish it off when we've had our tea."

"Well, I'll be going."

"We can walk part of the way together, Sidney," said Nadine.

"Yes, right, that'll be nice."

Sarah gave them a pretty wave as they left, and Sidney felt worse than ever. He felt sure that Nadine, when she found him in the bedroom, had read his thoughts. He was right, more or less, and she said:

"Are you sure you're all right, Sidney. You look sweaty."

"I'm OK."

"You don't want to succumb, you know. That would never do. See dad – he's probably got just the remedy for what ails you."

She left Sidney at his house and walked to where she lived with her father on Shore Lane. They got on all right. She'd been brought up in his church and outgrown it, but didn't like to tell him so she went through the motions – but gladly. Simon 'Sly' Palmester was waiting for her with the tea ready. Sometimes they talked at the table, sometimes not, but they were comfortable in each other's company.

"How's Sarah?" he asked.

"She's 'pulling through' – as they say. What a terrible thing for her – mother, and now father, gone, and all in a few months."

"It's the will of the Lord, tell her."

"No, dad – it isn't the will of the Lord that Clive was brutally murdered on the beach he loved."

"We may not understand, Naddie," said Simon, "but that doesn't mean we should question."

She didn't argue; Nadine had made her point. She was free now – university had seen to that – and no longer caught in her father's coils. Simon, too, accepted her attitude. He had no wish to upset his daughter. Since the death of his wife, she had been his greatest earthly comfort, and he enjoyed her company.

"Are they anywhere near catching who did it, yet?"

"Keep your eye on your local paper."

He smiled; Simon wasn't a man to laugh out loud, but he enjoyed a quiet joke.

"You think it was that son-in-law, don't you?" he said.

"So does everyone else, except Sarah."

"Well, there are other possibilities – torn throats and howling wolves."

"There's no evidence for that. Clive was killed by blows to the head."

"That other man was on the beach, wasn't he?"

"Peter Vishnya?"

"That's right – the Russian."

"He's Estonian, dad."

"Same thing – all godless people from behind the Iron Curtain."

"Peter Vishnya is a Christian, dad."

"But not like you and me – anyway, they say he's scarpered."

"He's gone back to Estonia, yes."

"Bit suspicious, isn't it?"

"He took a job with Horst Brultzner."

"The German?"

"Roman."

Simon was a local man and he was presenting local views to his daughter – views he had picked up on his religious rounds. He did not necessarily believe them (he could see their basis in rumour and gossip) but he found it helpful to test them on his daughter. When he spoke to his 'people', he often sounded like her.

Nadine cleared the table of their simple tea – bread and butter, tea and cake – and went to her room. She kept a journal; it was her friend – someone intelligent to whom she could talk. Working on the local paper was fine – it was something she could never have dreamed of doing as a child – but the views were often parochial even though the conversation was informed. The time would come when Nadine would have to make a move. She opened her laptop and wrote:

June 24:

I spent a little time with Sarah today. She is distraught and doesn't really know where to turn. Shane is no use to her at all. He really is not up to her mark. It's quite impossible for her to hold a conversation of any depth with him, and I think she's given up trying as far as her dad is concerned. I think she's on the edge of a nervous breakdown, and yet she seems so calm and peaceful on the surface. She is very upset by the rumours about Shane. I hope she's right and he isn't guilty. I can't think what Sarah would do if she found out that her husband had killed her father. She was so close to her mum and there is no one to fill the gap although I do try. Martin Billings has said very little, but I get the impression that real evidence is thin on the ground and that the police are having difficulty building a solid case, forensically.

While I was there Sidney Close came in. He's a strange man. I caught him in Matthew's little bedroom. He was sweating, and his eyes were glazed. He looked as though he'd just had sex. I don't trust him at all. There's a lot of hidden violence in men. Well, let's be fair, some men!

Dad was testing my views at tea-time. He's a crafty one; no wonder they call him 'Sly'. It's not nice, but I know what they mean. A better word would be 'Fly' meaning to be clever in using people to gain advantage. He sifts out your views and then looks at them from his religious point of view. He's not 'sly' in the underhand, crafty sense. He wouldn't try to gain advantage for himself in the usual way. His purpose is to make you see for yourself the error of your ways. Is there any difference? I'll pop and see Sarah whenever I can, now, to keep an eye on her.

Sidney and Mavis had finished their tea; for them, as with most of their friends, it was their main meal of the day – a time to catch up on the gossip. Sidney was not in a talkative mood tonight, however; his mind was on Sarah Marjoram and her husband. It didn't seem fair, somehow, that the likes of him should be married to her. Now that he'd seen the inside of their cottage, it was even worse – he could imagine where they were doing it.

Mavis had handed him his usual cup of tea when he came in. They didn't even kiss anymore; there didn't seem much point – it never led anywhere. Unspent vigour – what on earth was he going to do with it? He'd hate to end up like Tony Crewes – a feckless adulterer. He wouldn't – he had his faith.

"It's a Church Centre meeting tonight, Sid, but I won't be back late."

When Mavis closed the front door, Sidney went to his room for his work-out. It would be a rigorous one tonight – his testicles were like rocks; he had to work that off somehow. He counted thirty one as he pushed upwards, feeling the burn in his shoulders, and the breath panting from his mouth – eleven to go! Some men just seemed to get away with it – how did Tony Crewes have the brass neck to join the PCC – was it one of Corvin's nutty ideas to welcome sinners? 'Let he who is without sin among you cast the first stone.' That was all very well but ... The ache in his shoulders was feeling good; he was being punished. The sweat was pouring from him. Crewes had even appeared at one of their barbecues after he came back to his wife! Crunch – 'I want you to do five sets of ten crunches; grind your balls to powder!' And he never took communion – it wasn't as if he was a real member of the church. Squat, up, squat, up – increase the weights – squat, up, squat, up; his knees were on fire and each time he came down, his balls dangled between his legs. 'She reached under his buttocks and gave them a tweak with her silky smooth fingers.' Aah – if only she would! Crunch, lift, thrust, crunch, lift, thrust ... 'the language of the military is the language of rape – thrusting in, opening up, taking out!' Where had he read that – some silly feminist like Nadine Palmester? His anger rose with his endeavour – pressing, crunching, lifting and thrusting. Sidney burned with his own fire.

Shane Marjoram was having no such problems. He and Sarah were in each other's arms, their sweat running in little trickles down their chests and legs and across their stomachs. Shane had no idea of the turmoil in his wife's mind. He had long since forgotten about Froggy – closed it off and moved on. Their love-making, vigorous as always, cleared Sarah's mind for a while, but now it came trickling back like the sweat running between her breasts. She hoped Shane wouldn't want any more tonight; she had enough to think about.

"Sare – what was that Nadine Palmester doing here?"

"She was passing and just dropped in."

"Passin'? She lives on Shore Lane! … I don't trust her."

"We've always been friends. We were at school together."

"That don't make any difference – I don't trust her."

"She's nice, Shane. She's been kind to me. It gives me someone to talk to."

"You can talk to me."

"I mean another woman, Shane."

"Yeah – right."

"Women see things differently."

"Yeah … but I still don't like her."

Sarah knew what Shane didn't like about Nadine – she was educated, and education was a threat to the ignorant. Shane felt himself to be ignorant because he had skived off school; he had come out with no qualifications. She'd met him at the pub, soaked with booze and on the edge of drugs and turned him. She'd only been young herself – eighteen. What age is that? He'd listened to her, and phoned the college. It had been the making of him – a trade, a wife, a baby, a job – but Sarah paid the price; her own chances of an education and a career had vanished. It hadn't been his fault, though; he hadn't forced her to drop her knickers the night Matthew was conceived.

"I need a woman friend, Shane. I like Nadine. I feel comfortable with her."

"Well so long as she doesn't go putting ideas in yer head."

"What ideas?"

"I don't know – jest ideas."

It pleased Sarah that he had a fear of losing her. She was a good wife; she knew that she kept the house well, she cared for her baby and she was good in bed. If only her mum were here, if only her dad were round the corner – but she was alone now, and the head of the family. Another baby soon – was that the answer? Shane wanted one; she only had to stop taking the pill and she'd be pregnant in no time but what would the children grow up like – her or Shane? Did it matter? Shane had his good side, and she could see that the children were brought up properly. Shane's problem had been that no one in his family cared what he turned out like, whereas her mum and dad just lived for her.

Sarah knew her mind was rambling, groping to fill a gap. She wanted to scream sometimes and Nadine calmed her, put her thoughts into some kind of order. "You need to be driven by desire, not necessity"; that was one of Nadine's ideas. She didn't mean sexual desire, but more what you planned to do with your life.

She turned to look at Shane. He was sleeping beautifully as he always did; he looked like one of those Greek gods. She had seen them in books at school – white togas, blonde hair and flawless bodies – sprawling on those fancy sofas. Sarah got out of bed quietly and dressed quickly. She had to get away – just for a moment – and decided that she must leave Shane a note. She wrote this on the reminder pad in the kitchen and then crept back upstairs. She glanced first to see how Matthew was sleeping, and then left the note on her pillow. Shane would be furious but, after all, he was in the house if Matthew woke.

Downstairs she pulled on her light summer coat – on the east coast the evenings can be chill all through summer – and closed and locked the door behind her. The night was still warm and she suddenly realised that it was not yet ten o'clock. She wanted to take a walk – possibly to Nadine's house, possibly to her parent's grave. She could still feel where Shane had been inside her, but that would pass as she walked.

To her right were the new houses that sat on the edge of the marsh. She looked further on to the flagpole outside the Bethel – the fishermen's church – and Sidney Close's house which was next door. She walked passed Cod Piece, and The Paper Shop; opposite the newsagents was Mona's, the cheap sweet shop. Matthew loved going in there! She stopped by the allotment gate; her mum and dad always laughed and hugged each other when they passed there and, once, while they were in the kitchen together, Mary had hinted as to the reason. Sarah smiled at the memory and, instead of turning into Shore Lane towards Nadine's bungalow, carried on up Church Hill to the graveyard.

The moon was in its first quarter and the longest day had just passed so it was a clear night as she entered the churchyard, unlike the night when she and her father dug her mother's grave. What an ordeal that had been, and so full of sadness. She remembered looking down at her father's back and watching the sweat trickle from beneath his cap. Now, he was in there with her mother – his beloved Mary. Sarah had not attempted to do the digging this time; the undertakers had taken away the immediacy of that pain.

The gravestone was clean and bright. She made out the letters easily – her father's name and her mother's, barely three months apart, and the inscription which she had taken from the poem the rector had used at her mother's funeral – 'All is well' from Henry Scott Holland's reflection on death. She remembered the lines – 'I am waiting for you ... just round the corner', which completed the reading, and hoped that it was true.

Sarah knew, with a terrible certainty, that she needed to be strong. She was just twenty-one and responsible for so much – head of the family, mother of Matthew. She should have been far from here, enjoying herself at university, expecting to come home for the holidays, for Christmas, whatever, and be spoiled by her parents; both were now gone, never to return, never to be seen again ever – not in this world.

It was peaceful in the churchyard, by the light of that early summer moon. With her two responsibilities asleep she could come here and be quiet. She became aware, very slowly and with no apprehension, that she was being watched. The figure stood in the shadow of the church tower. It had stood there for a while before she acknowledged it – stood watching her, but without moving. Sarah turned and looked. The figure was that of a tallish man, rather on the lean side; it didn't move when she turned, but shrank back into the shadows. She turned back to her parents' gravestone and waited, watching slightly over her right shoulder. She saw the figure stir and move away.

"Good evening," she said.

Her own voice surprised her; she hadn't expected to hear herself speak.

"Good evening. I didn't want to disturb you."

Sarah looked up as the man approached. It was the one who had been with Constable Billings in the Jolly Sailors the night her dad had been killed – the one she'd rather disliked, the man with the supercilious sneer about his mouth, the one who had poured the bucket of water over Shane.

"I didn't mean to disturb you," he said.

"You didn't – it's all right."

"I expect you'd rather be alone."

"Why were you watching me?"

"I saw you come into the churchyard."

"And followed me?"

"Yes."

"Why?"

"I don't know."

"Have you ever lost anyone close to you?"

"No – not this close and not ..."

"... so suddenly?"

There was a long pause which neither of them seemed to mind as they stood quietly watching the gravestone.

"If I can be of any help ..." began Tony Crewes.

"How could you be?"

"I don't know ... There seems so little that anyone else can do."

"It's very kind of you ... Time heals all things, they tell me."

"I don't believe that – do you?" he replied.

"Not at this moment."

"Does your faith help?"

"I don't know."

Sarah realised that he had followed her into the churchyard to be of some comfort.

"You're very kind, Mr Crewes. It was good of you to follow me."

They both laughed. Sarah hadn't expected to be at ease with this man.

"How is your husband taking this?"

"The one you poured the bucket of water over?"

"I'm sorry – it seemed the only way to calm him down."

It was a lie and he knew it; that wasn't the reason at all.

"It did exactly the opposite. Did you really think it would calm him down?"

"No – I'm a capricious fellow. He annoyed me."

"Shane has always annoyed people. That's part of his problem."

"But you love him and he's helping you through this awful ordeal."

It wasn't a question; it was an assumption, and not an impertinent one. Most people expected Shane to be useless in the circumstances, but this man had given him the benefit of the doubt. She appreciated that: it made things easier to bear. It was late now – eleven or after – and the light had gone. Somehow, it seemed that she should not be standing here with a stranger. You can stand with a strange man in the light, but not in the dark; passers-by would be suspicious. Sarah laughed.

"What are you laughing at?"

"It seems strange that we should be standing here talking about my husband."

"Perhaps I'd better go, but my offer is open – however ... inappropriate."

"Your offer?"

"To be of help – but how could I be?"

"You already have. It's first time I've ever talked to anyone – except mum and dad – about Shane."

They turned from the graveside and walked to the lych-gate where they stopped and looked at each other. Perhaps this man did not feel himself to be superior to those around him; perhaps that was just a veneer – a reflection of themselves that others saw in him. He was, though, educated and he had spoken to her as an equal. More than that, he had made her think, and drawn from her thoughts she never knew she held.

"Thank you, Mr Crewes ... for talking to me and making me think."

"My name's Tony."

"I'm Sarah."

"I'm pleased to know you Sarah."

"And I, you."

They shook hands; it had been a strange meeting. Nadine said that her father believed that nothing ever happened by chance or by accident – that somewhere in everything, however small, there was the hand of the Lord. Each of us merely played a part in His Grand Plan.

"Sarah - are you all right?"

The voice came from across the road. A stiff, muscular man was passing by on the other side. He crossed towards them, and she saw Tony Crewes stiffen. It was Sidney Close. The two men eyed each other like protagonists in a prize fight. She didn't feel like explaining to this man that she had been visiting her parents' grave, but Tony Crewes said nothing by way of offering an explanation.

"I've been to mum and dad's grave," she said.

"At this time of night?"

"Graveside visits are not circumscribed by some arcane convention, Sidney," said Tony, "You may rest assured that my presence here is purely accidental – as, indeed, presumably is yours."

Sidney said nothing, which made Tony wonder where he might have been in that part of the village so late at night; he wasn't a man to frequent the pubs or the Working Men's Club – and there was no light in the Church Centre.

It was a strange trio that made its way down Church Hill. They passed under the arch of trees which formed a tunnel of green by the gateway to the old vicarage, a tunnel lit from the lamp post by the allotments. Sidney pressed ahead; there was anger in his walk. Tony Crewes watched him with a smile, but Sarah was concerned that he made no trouble. When they reached the newsagents she stopped.

"Thank you again. It's best I walk on alone from here."

"Goodnight."

He watched her all the way until she was just a small figure at the door of her cottage. As Sarah unlocked the door she turned and looked back along the road. He was still there and gave her a cheery wave. Sarah knew that she had made a friend that night; she had yet to find out how good a friend he would prove to be.

CHAPTER 2

Friends in Need

Her meeting with Tony Crewes had a strangely liberating influence on Sarah Marjoram; she said this to her friend, Nadine Palmester, when they next met.

"Be careful, Sarah. He's a dangerous man."

Nadine could imagine just how attractive a man like Tony Crewes might be to the likes of her friend.

"I don't mean like that …"

"It's natural for someone like you to be attracted to a man like Tony. He's intelligent and educated …. "

"And Shane isn't?"

"I'd be no friend if I lied to you, Sarah."

"You don't like Shane, do you?"

"You are an intelligent woman who needs more to satisfy you …"

"Than Shane?"

"At the moment, your life is full of other things – but, one day, certainly."

Nadine reached out and put her arms round Sarah, who did not resist. They were walking along the cliff top towards Pakefield, and the day was glorious. Summer had arrived with warmth, and had not since disappointed them: corn marigolds with their smooth, bluish-green leaves spread their stems in the cornfields, scentless mayweed grew by the sides of the track where it was protected from the salt winds, honeysuckle was everywhere – its sweetly scented flowers still powerful in the evenings. Matthew, walking with them, reached over and plucked at the mayweed.

"Is this a daisy?" he asked.

"Like a daisy," laughed Sarah, "I'll make you a chain."

"Keeping him in touch with his feminine side?"

"Shane hates me making him daisy chains."

"He would."

"Shane has his sensitive side – no one more so."

"I'm sure."

"You don't sound convinced."

"I'm not doing Shane down, Sarah ….."

"Oh no – not half!"

"I'm not. I'm just saying that one day he will not be enough for you. Know that – know yourself."

"I'd never betray Shane. I know what you're saying, Nadine, but I do love him, and he loves me."

Sarah looked at her friend who had now taken hold of the push chair, which she had insisted on bringing in case Matthew got tired, and wondered how close Nadine had got to a man. She scared Shane. Sarah knew that, but realised that her friend would be very attractive to some men – those with wit and education who loved a good wrangle with a woman of spirit. Sometimes she wondered whether Nadine was just a trifle too brittle, too acerbic in her wit. There had been one man, she knew, at university. Nadine had worshipped him. "I wanted to get rid of my virginity," she had said when they talked about it. He had left her for a "brainless hairdresser" and Nadine returned home, buoyed up only by her sense of humour, and sought fulfilment through her work.

"We're like two sides of the same coin – you and I," said Sarah.

"Are we both heading for stormy weather, or a safe haven?"

"You are funny, Nadine. You do have a quirky way of looking at things. Is there no one in your life at present?"

"I'm happy enough in my work ... I would like to meet the right man and have a family – but on my terms. I'm not prepared, Sarah, to just settle for being a housewife – and nor will you be as the years pass."

They walked on; it was mid afternoon and the sun had passed its meridian. It glowed for them both and for Sarah's child, warming their backs and their left sides, while a soft breeze from the sea cooled them on the right. They had passed beyond the parish line of Dunburgh. Below them the beach rattled down to the edge of the sea, which whooshed and sloshed on the pebbles. Lumps of the sandstone cliffs were scattered on the beach, as yet unbroken by their fall but soon to be washed along the coast to Lowestoft or to crumble among the dunes and be bound by marram grass.

The pathway became wider, giving way in places to fields. Rabbits dodged in and out of the sun, seeking shade under the gorse and broom that clung precariously to the sandy soil of the cliff-top. Matthew ran towards them and laughed when they sat upright, ears pricked in alarm, and then hopped away, white tails bobbing.

"It's a good place to bring up children – Dunburgh."

"Yes. You mustn't mind me, Sarah. Do your own thing, as they say."

"We both had a happy childhood here."

"Oh yes, we certainly did."

They sat on a bench by the fence and stretched their legs.

"How has Shane been since your dad was killed?" asked Nadine, surprised by her own question.

"Why do you ask?"

"I wondered whether he had been ... supportive."

"He doesn't talk about it much – unless he finds me crying."

"And then?"

"He's nice – says mum and dad are together, and that we have each other."

"They will catch whoever it was, you know, Sarah."

"That's what Shane says – and then we'll have closure."

"Shane said that?"

"Yes."

It was an odd word – 'closure': as though you could ever close down something as awful as a wanton killing. What was it about people today that they wanted this closure – this bringing to an end, and moving on as though the past could be filed away like unwanted papers? Couldn't they accept that you would live in anguish ever afterwards – that there was no escape from such pain, that the trick was learning to live with it? Nadine reached over and squeezed her friend's hand.

"Do you believe that?"

"No."

"Neither do I – whatever happens, Sarah, I'll be around for you."

That was the nature of their friendship – unconditional kindness – and both women valued it. As they sat, watching that Matthew didn't stray too close to the cliff edge, a figure approached from the north – lean, lolloping, disappearing from view as the gorse and broom obstructed the path, swaying through the hazy warmth of the afternoon. Nadine was reminded of the senses of summer as she watched it – dry grass, seeds bursting, leaves shining, branches stooping, magnolia blossoms falling. Both women recognised the shape of the man; both gasped quietly to themselves as he saw them.

"I'm playing hooky," said Tony Crewes.

Nadine and Sarah laughed together. It seemed so ridiculous – a grown man saying something like that; to them, and Sarah in particular, he was simply a respectable office worker.

"May I sit down?"

The women moved closer together so that he lounged on one end of the bench, one long leg stretched before him, the other curled over the arm of the seat, his briefcase tossed on the grass.

"Can you imagine what it is like – at a desk, facing a hot terminal in an insurance office on an afternoon like this? I really could bear it no longer."

"I thought you worked in Norbridge, Tony?"

"I do. I took the train to work this morning and took it back again after lunch. I couldn't face going to my nice, untidy, pristine metal desk again. The afternoon was so beautiful."

"And you decided to walk home along the cliff-top?"

"I did. When the train pulled into Lowestoft, I thought sod the bus, I'll walk. Don't tell Beth," he said, smiling at them both in their silence, "Would your little boy like a humbug?"

Without waiting for an answer, he reached into his pocket and brought out a white paper bag that he offered to Matthew, who was sliding the seeds from the dry grass by the fence.

"I get them from Mona's – only Mona still sells sweets in white, paper bags. Would you like one?"

They took one each, and the three of them sat on the bench sucking their humbugs, feeling vaguely ridiculous and childlike. Sarah laughed and Tony looked at her, but said nothing for a while until he turned to Nadine.

"What it is to be a woman!"

"We get a better deal than men, I suppose?" said Nadine, knowing what he was about, and rising to the occasion.

"Oh you do, you do."

"In what way," said Sarah, "Not that I'm complaining."

"You're not complaining because you know the truth of it."

"You envy Matthew and I having the freedom to walk along the cliff top?"

"Not envy – yes envy ... well, sort of envy."

"Sarah does have other calls on her time."

"Don't bore me with the details, Nadine – so do we all. Beth once said that "it was all right for you – you get out to the office each day". I immediately offered to stay at home and bring up the children, while she went out to work. What do you think she said?"

"That isn't the point," interrupted Nadine.

"It is the point – it is the very point. She had the choice – I didn't. Oh, what your feminism has done for women!"

"Would you really have done that ...Tony?"

There was just the slightest pause before Sarah used his Christian name; she didn't know him as well as Nadine, and had only spoken to him once, privately.

"Like a shot!"

"There aren't many men would say that."

"How do you know? Has anyone ever given us the chance?"

"Shane wouldn't. He'd be scared stiff and he wouldn't think it ..."

"...manly?" concluded Tony.

"Yes."

"There you go. Society has us in a strait jacket. Boys are conditioned from birth to be the hunters."

"You're twisting the argument, Tony Crewes – and you know it! The point is that women were never given the chance to pursue a career – and now they are, thanks to feminism."

"But are men given the chance to stay at home and bring up the children?"

"It is more natural for the women to do that," said Sarah.

"Don't tell Nadine that, Sarah!"

"Nadine would agree, but it is only right that women were given the choice."

Tony looked across at the journalist as she spoke and smiled at her; it was a complicit smile – they were both concerned for Sarah, in their own ways.

"Just be happy, Sarah, that on this glorious summer afternoon you have the chance to walk the golden cliff top with your little boy and your friend – without having to play truant from your place of work."

Sarah smiled. She wanted to pursue the argument, to see it from all sides but, like many educated people she had met, Tony Crewes seemed to have thrown it into conversation and then dismissed it.

"You've got a lovely little boy there, Sarah. Never mind the feminists – you just enjoy staying at home and bringing him up."

"I just think that ... if I were better educated Matthew might benefit more," said Sarah.

"Then why don't you go for it?" he replied.

Nadine listened, and then supported him, as he browbeat Sarah along the road she had already pointed out to her – a part-time degree at the local college.

"I'll think about it ... I'll talk to Shane."

"Bugger Shane," he added, "You have the right to an education. No one – not even your husband – has any business standing in your way! And you have the time. I bet you're well organised, aren't you?

Sarah smiled. Shane loved the way she organised the house.

"Then you could create time – when the boy's asleep or at playschool or whatever. A couple of hours a day, every day – you'd sail along ... Lecture over!"

He laughed. It was an infectious sound to Sarah but, to Nadine, out in the world and more aware of men like Tony Crewes, a little desperate.

"There you are, Sarah, what have I been telling you?"

"Does she bully you?" asked Tony.

"Yes", laughed Sarah.

"Feminists are like that – they've always got an agenda that has a distrust of men at its centre," he laughed.

"Over the generations, men have given us good reason to distrust them," responded Nadine, "It's too nice a day to be riled by you!"

"I'll go. I've disturbed you long enough."

"We'll walk back with you," replied Sarah, "It's time, anyway."

Nadine and Tony Crewes parted company with Sarah at her cottage door and walked on alone.

"Thanks for that," said Nadine.

"I rather guessed you'd been pedalling the same bike."

"For a long time – she's intelligent and lovely ..."

"... and wasted, totally, on that lout?"

"That's for Sarah to say – but probably."

They paused by the paper shop, about to go their own ways, but reluctant to part company. Each guessed what was on the other's mind, but neither felt able to open up such a conversation.

"How's the investigation going, then?" asked Tony, suddenly.

"The police are saying nothing. There is still a lot of forensic work to do ..."

"But you believe he did it?"

"Yes – who else would have done?"

"Exactly."

"You were on the beach that night – did you see nothing?"

"I remember I had the impression of a presence. I remember looking about me, and the sense of something coming towards me – something evil. There was anger in the air – a wilfulness. That's the only way I can describe it."

Nadine let him sweat out the memory before she said:

"There was some suspicion about Peter Vishnya and his dog, wasn't there?"

"I don't really know Vishnya. His disappearance hasn't been helpful."

"There's no chance – in your mind – that the whole thing was an accident – that it was the dog which ripped open Clive's throat?"

Tony looked at Nadine, and smiled.

"We both fear we're right," he said, "and, if we are, how will she cope with such knowledge? How could any mind get itself around such a realisation?"

"It couldn't – not and stay sane."

"Keep in touch."

"Yes."

Nadine was sombre as she let herself into her father's house. She wasn't in the mood for any of his "will of the Lord" stuff and it was fortunate that he was out when she arrived. Nadine went into their kitchen, laid the gingham cloth and set out the items for their simple tea. The kettle hissed. The latch on the kitchen door lifted.

"Hello, dad."

"Ah – Naddy – that's wonderful. I do enjoy tea-time with you."

He didn't kiss her – to his generation such an act was unnecessarily demonstrative. She knew, however, that he loved her, knew he appreciated her being there in the kitchen and would – if the necessity arose – have given his life for her without flinching; that had to be enough.

"I've been out with Sarah."

"And Mr Crewes."

"How did you know that?"

"I bumped into Necker Utting. She saw you together on the corner seat."

"We're having an affair, dad."

"If I thought that, Naddy, my heart would break."

They laughed together. Her father had got used to her wild statements. It was one way in which Nadine asserted her personality on the home when she returned from university.

"Watch Mr Crewes, Naddy – he's an unrepentant adulterer."

"How do you know that?"

"He's committed adultery and never repented."

"I said – how do you know?"

"Does he attend church?"

"I don't think he's a regular churchgoer."

"There's no such thing as an irregular churchgoer, Naddy. You either go or you don't, and until Mr Crewes has faced his God he remains in a state of sin."

"I don't condone his adultery, dad, but it isn't for me to judge him."

"I'm not suggesting that we should judge him, Naddy. If he turned up at the Bethel, at any time, I should welcome him with open arms, but until he does he has turned his face against the Lord."

Nadine had poured the hot water onto the tea leaves as they spoke and the smell of the freshly-brewed tea was in both their nostrils: it was everyday, it was calming. They sat down – Simon at one end of the table and Nadine at the side, next to him. She handed him the bread plate and watched as he spooned jam onto the slice, spread it with his knife and began to eat it in small nibbling bites.

"How is Sarah?" he asked, "It will be better when she knows the truth."

"Will it?"

"We cannot hide from the truth, Naddy. It is better to face it."

"With the help of the Lord?"

"We can do nothing without Him. Keep close to her – I know you will – and steer her through the stormy waters that await her ... which cake are you going to have - the muffin or the apricot bar?"

"I might have both."

"Don't joke, Naddy – greed is one of the seven deadly."

Nadine looked at her father; he was a witty man, but sometimes she wondered if he knew whether he was joking or not.

Tony Crewes also sat in his kitchen, being lashed by his wife's tongue. She, too, had been told of his arrival in the village accompanied by Nadine Palmester and Sarah Marjoram.

"What were you doing?" cried Beth Crewes.

He had been over it at least four or five times – repeating his explanations, reassuring her over and over again. Ever since his adultery, Beth had been suspicious of his every move, and it was clear to him that she believed his leaving work early and his meeting the two women on the cliff top had been planned. He knew that, in a moment, there would be the reconciliation – Beth wanting to "make it right", take back what she'd said and start again. It would take all evening; far into the night they would still be talking, going over the ground of "that woman" and why he had done it. He would soak it up – he knew that: soak it up and resent every minute of it. There was no escape from your past, no escape at all.

CHAPTER 3

The social scene – the Close barbecue

Beth Crewes was not relieved to be at the barbecue thrown by Sidney and Mavis Close. She had been on tenterhooks ever since Mavis rang. She was sure that everyone would know Tony had arrived in the village with those two women, and draw the wrong conclusions.

Martin was there under protest. He neither liked the Close's nor enjoyed socialising with them. Privately, he called them 'The Glums' because of the way Sidney pulled down the corners of his mouth whenever anyone appeared to be enjoying themselves. Moreover, the conversation was going to revolve around the murder of Clive Brown, and Martin objected strongly to any collision between his public and private lives. His consolation was that he would be there with his wife. He was proud of Amy and enjoyed showing her off; Amy had a lot of spark, and it showed. Secretly, Martin enjoyed watching Sidney and Boller watching Amy. Both of them grabbed other men's wives by the arse and had a good grope whenever they could; neither of them had ever laid a hand on Amy.

Ample and Billy Bassett were both looking forward to the barbecue; socialising within the village was a big part of their lives. Ample also knew that Martin and Amy Billings were going and was desperate to find out whether the police were any nearer arresting Shane Marjoram for the murder of his father-in-law.

Barry and Lianne Snooks were also looking forward to going – Lianne because she wanted to find out how far short of her barbecue Mavis's would fall, and Barry because it would be an evening away from the television and Lianne's concerns with him improving himself.

It was a beautiful evening. Mavis always seemed lucky with the weather –whether she hosted the first or last barbecue of the year, the sun shone for her. It had been a glorious summer. Her garden, like her, was somewhat prosaic; she spent little time bothering with it. This year, however, even Mavis's plants were beside themselves. Bees hummed everywhere, but would be gone by evening, and she had sent Sidney with a pesticide to wipe out any other insects that might be lurking in corners.
    Her no-nonsense attitude to gardening – and, indeed, life – was also reflected in her attitude to barbecues: keep it simple. She was providing chicken, sausages

and burgers with various salads: nothing more – except her sweets. Mavis did tend to hold the championship cup among the other women when it came to sweets. Men loved apple pie and custard, fruit crumble, lemon meringue pie, sherry trifle or sticky toffee pudding. Watching his friends tuck in to the likes of these made Sidney wonder why his wife didn't pay more attention to life's dessert. He wouldn't have wondered this had he not heard Tony Crewes make the comment "life's dessert" some years before. Crewes had pushed his jest to the edge of vulgarity, comparing "the sweetness at the end of the meal to sweetness at the end of the day". Sidney – while objecting to it – had never been able to get the comment out of his mind.

Boller and Pliny Skeat were the first to arrive, as usual, and Sidney settled them in with a glass of dry, white wine for Pliny and a beer for Boller. He noticed that Boller never groped Mavis as he did the other women – and it wasn't for the same reason as neither of them groped Amy Billings. Pliny joined Mavis in the kitchen on the pretext of helping her with the food, but actually to find out if Mavis had heard that Tony Crewes had been seen with Nadine Palmester.

"Hmm, he's let her down once – he'll let her down twice. A leopard doesn't change its spots."

In the garden, on his second beer, Boller was running down his local team – Norbridge – who were now out of the Premier League and sinking further down the First Division.

"You heard about Tony?" asked Sidney.

There was something of the 'old woman' about Sidney, and Boller, still intent on running his team down, looked surprised to be bothered with the question.

"What about him?"

"Him and Nadine Palmester."

"Well, I don't believe it and, anyway, if it's true, I wish him luck. If yer aint getting it at home look around, is what I say."

Sidney was shocked; he hadn't expected such a blunt answer from Boller. He stared at Boller for a moment and then stood up, ostensibly to turn on the barbecue, in reality to cover the expression of distaste on his face – the expression that Martin Billings referred to as 'Mr Glum'.

Martin Billings came in through the side gate at that moment, and grasped the situation in seconds. He'd always been wary of Sidney Close; apart from actively disliking him, he actually distrusted him. Martin had come across sexual repression in his work – it always burst out eventually and usually in unpleasant ways – and he sensed it strongly in Sidney.

"All right, Sid?"

The comment was deliberately provocative forcing, as it did, Sidney to look up and answer. Amy soothed the situation by going across and kissing both him and Boller on the cheek.

"Where's Pliny?"

"In the kitchen, with Mavis."

"What – leaving you boys on your own?"

"It's the only chance we git to talk abart page three," said Boller.

"No good talking about it, Boller – get out there and grab it," said Amy.

"Yeah – chance'd be a fine thing," he laughed.

Martin looked across at Sidney, whose back was now firmly turned, and said "Are them sausages firming up, Sid. I find the heat blows them up a bit."

"Yeah," said Boller, "Heat blows everyfing up, but I like my sausages firm."

Sidney Close didn't speak; he gripped the slice and turned the sausages.

"Just be careful what you get up to with Martin Billings," said Beth as she and Tony Crewes walked down High Path towards the Close's house.

"With Martin?" said Tony.

"When you and he get together, things get out of hand."

As they entered, Tony caught Martin's eye and his friend flashed a glance at Sidney's back. Neither Beth nor Amy missed this and both tapped their husbands discreetly on the ankle with the toe of their shoes. Both men yelled in mock pain and gripped their ankles in exaggerated agony. Beth and Amy exchanged glances – Amy with a twinkle in her eye, which was not returned by Beth, who saw nothing amusing in her husband preparing to wind-up Sidney Close.

"You lads bin stung?" asked Boller.

"I thought you'd dealt with the bees, Sid," said Mavis.

"Perhaps it's the birds, rather than the bees, causing the trouble," said Tony.

"We shouldn't have much trouble wiv the birds and the bees at our age," laughed Boller.

"Boller," said Pliny.

"Cor blimey, a man can't say nuffin."

Sidney concentrated on his cooking. He was going to speak with Mavis when all this was over; it was time to find other company.

Bishop Twiddle was enjoying one of his frequent visits to the rectory at Dunburgh, much to Esther Unwood's annoyance. Since Corvin's elevation to rural dean, the bishop had found it necessary "in his pastoral capacity" to come to dinner more often.

Corvin had asked the bishop's advice about which port he preferred, but Peter Twiddle had suggested that they "simply open another bottle of wine – the Muscat de Beaumes de Venise is always very acceptable". As he drew the cork, Corvin wondered what Esther would have said about the bishop's use of the word "simply".

"Rocquefort and Muscat might seem like a strange combination, Corvin, but they go well together – the sharpness of the cheese balanced by the sweetness of the wine ... Balance, Corvin – so essential for the calm and ordered life of the church."

"Certainly, your lord ..."

"Peter, Corvin – please."

When they were settled comfortably, Bishop Twiddle asked:

"And how are we finding our elevated position, Corvin? Does the post of rural dean suit you?"

"Indeed ... eh, Peter ... I find the challenge ... exhilarating."

"Good, good. I told the Diocesan Council you were the man for the post. Exhilaration – a good choice of word, Corvin. Exhilaration is what the church needs today."

There was an elegant silence while the bishop tilted his glass. Corvin watched with all the envy and anger of a man from the working class who had risen in life but knew he would never be part of the social order to which he now belonged. The bishop's glass had been swirled and his nose was thrust beneath the rim – 'calibrating his nose' Corvin believed it was called. The bishop's eyes closed in ecstasy and then the glass was transferred to his mouth, and it seemed to Corvin that he began chewing on the wine; his lips puckered, the cheeks were drawn in and there began a genteel puffing and blowing as the bishop inclined his head backwards and the drink finally trickled down his throat.

"So much 'backbone' for a white wine, Corvin – so very heavy and sticky but grapey, scented, lots of fruit flavours. I think we may sample the Rocquefort, now."

The bishop's use of 'sample' annoyed Corvin as much as his previous use of 'simply'. There was no question of 'simply' opening the bottle of wine – it was no simpler to do that than pour a glass of port; they were going to drink it! Likewise, they were not going to 'sample' the cheese; they were going to eat it – and probably eat it all! There was hypocrisy here that smacked of the self-indulgence of the upper middle classes. It wasn't why Corvin had come into the church.

"I understand you are proposing to combine the eight o'clock communion for Dunburgh and Gislam, Corvin?"

The question came suddenly as did all the bishop's enquiries – when one least expected them – and Corvin was nearly taken off-guard.

"Eh – yes, Peter. It seems to make sense that the two neighbouring parishes should worship together especially as the eight o'clock tends to be the preference of the older congregation."

"Is it a popular move?"

Corvin knew very well that someone from Gislam had been on the telephone as soon as the bishop spoke, but he was angry and not to be dissuaded.

"It wasn't done for popularity, Peter, but to bring the two sets of worshippers closer together – one Sunday at Dunburgh, the other at Gislam."

"Admirable ... admirable, Corvin ... but we should always consider the sensitivities of our parishioners. I imagine Gislam is a ... a ....."

He waited deliberately, hoping to draw Corvin into agreement, but the rural dean remained silent.

"... They are proud of their church, Corvin. A labour of love, I understand?"

"Indeed, your lordship – but a trifle ...."

He paused deliberately and then went on:

"... elite."

"A nightcap, Lianne?" asked Barry Snooks, when they arrived home.

"It depends what kind of nightcap you have in mind."

Lianne said it flirtatiously. It was important to her to know that she could still be attractive. Barry Snooks looked at his wife. He was experienced enough to realise that she was feeling frisky, and that to take her up on that might cause less fuss than to turn on the television and let her go to bed on her own. He put down the bottle of brandy he had been about to open, whipped a cushion from the kitchen chair and placed it against his wife's belly (so that the table wouldn't hurt her), turned her round and bent her over the table. He then waited until she spoke. "Barry?" The tone was right. He had not misjudged her feelings, and Barry Snooks wasted no more time.

Lianne turned to him when they had finished, and her face was full of the joy she felt. He looked at her and grinned, but he didn't take her in his arms and kiss her; he hadn't done that for over ten years.

Ample helped her husband up stairs and he flopped, giggling, on the bed while she undressed him and folded his clothes; he couldn't have managed himself. She didn't bother with his pyjamas, but rolled him in under the duvet and then undressed herself. She pulled on her Past Times nightie – it was voluminous and covered her nicely – and climbed into bed beside him. She felt Billy stir and reach under her nightdress; he was still giggling. 'Oh well, why not?' Ample helped him lift it up, and then hauled him onto her. Billy had always been very fond of her huge breasts, and now burrowed his head down between them. 'A man could get lost in there.' Billy now did, blowing and puffing his cheeks with delight as he nuzzled deeper.

Boller was always in a randy mood after a get-together and he knew Pliny wasn't going to refuse him; it wasn't part of their routine. She was already in her nightdress when he reached the top of the stairs, two steps at a time.

"Cor – Ov bin waitin' for this all night, babe."

So had she – since she knew it was coming and, anyway, Pliny liked a bit of slap-and-tickle. Boller was hot when roused; his whole taut body seemed like a furnace. There wasn't much spare flesh on him – Pliny saw to that – and they came together in a kind of dry heat. Boller's lovemaking was both abandoned and intense; he threw himself into it heart and soul. Once on the way, he never paused for reflection. The rattling of the bed against the wall grew louder and louder and he came with a great shout of joy, bringing Pliny with him, and all before him.

"Did you have to get them going? You know what Boller and Billy are like!" said Beth Crewes, as she and Tony walked up their driveway.

"I thought everyone rather enjoyed themselves."

"You may have done. Sidney and Mavis were on edge all night."

"Why? We got a running gag going about Billy's wine. He enjoyed himself – so did Ample. Nobody was offended."

"It's always the same when you get together with Martin Billings. You never know when to stop. Not everyone likes that kind of language."

When they got in, he went to his study and sat down at his desk; here, at least, was a peaceful place. He leaned forward, praying that Beth would get into bed and fall asleep – but no, she was at the door.

"Well – are you coming to bed?"

"Yes – I'll be up in a minute."

It wasn't going to go away – not tonight. Tony Crewes got up, quietly, and let himself out of the side door. It was a warm, beautiful night; somewhere, something – or someone – was waiting for him. He didn't know where, or who, or when he would find what he was looking for, but it was pleasant along the beach: the moon was full, the days were long. As he listened to the swish-swish of the waves on the pebbles he felt at peace with himself – at least for a while.

Mavis was already in bed when Sidney came into the room. All was quiet; Mavis was already tucked up in bed with the duvet round her ears. Sidney undressed quietly, folded his clothes and stood naked in front of the dressing table mirror. He felt his balls; they were rock hard. He turned and looked at Mavis whose eyes were shut tight, and then he approached the bed and knelt beside her. He slid his hand under the duvet and felt for her; she was warm and soft. He ran his hands up and over her hips. Mavis stirred, and puttered:

"Not tonight, Sid. I'm too tired."

She turned without opening her eyes, and adjusted the duvet round her neck. 'Not tonight, not any night.' The thought passed through his mind like a curse.

"Martin – what are you doing?"

"Just checking."

Martin was in his station, checking for messages on the 1950s bakelite telephone, which he'd had adapted. When Amy came in he replaced the beautifully heavy receiver onto the rest, listened to that distinctive click and turned to her:

"I won't be long."

"You won't be any time at all, Martin Billings, or I'll have you here in your antique police station. What would Superintendent Junket say about that?"

"There's a time and place for everything, Amy, and police stations are not for what you have in mind."

"Is that what your Superintendent would say?"

"That's what I'm saying."

"Are you? Have we ever made love on a leather chair, Martin?"

"That's a leather padded Windsor chair, Amy! You don't make love on a leather padded Windsor chair!"

"Don't you?"

The bishop was safely tucked away in bed and Corvin made his way slowly up the stairs with a mug of Ovaltine in his hand. Esther was already in bed, a night-cap holding her hair in place.

"Thank you, Corvin. You're very kind."

He usually brought her a mug of something at the end of the day. Sometimes she fancied Horlicks, and at other times drinking chocolate or even a cup of tea – tonight it was Ovaltine.

"You're very good to me, Corvin."

"You're my wife."

"I know but ..."

"But nothing, my love."

"You've never regretted marrying someone twenty years older than you."

"No, Esther, I have not."

It wasn't true, but the truth wasn't what Esther wanted to hear. There had been times – there were times – when he wished that Esther was younger. He may have wished that but he had never regretted marrying Esther: there was a difference, and it was a huge one.

Horst Brultzner stood in his 'bedroom' looking out over the front of his house towards the rectory. He had just seen the last lights turned off and knew that Corvin was on his way to bed. The sash window was up and he rested his hand for a moment on the back of the Sheraton chair – just for the pure joy of touching it. The rectilinear lines were beautiful, and he ran his long fingers lovingly over the chair – from the seat to the shoulder.

He would visit Rebecca Unwood tonight. He had not spent time with her alone since his early days in the village when he had come to her window and saw her, naked on the bed, gently massaging herself. If only he could have touched her then, and made love to her as a man would have done.

The large bat flitted across the trees that divided the Old Vicarage from the new rectory. He had been invited in on that first occasion, and could now come and go as he wished. The bat settled for a moment on the open window-sill and then flapped down to the floor of Rebecca's room. As a bat, Brultzner could travel discreetly in the dark and he had to enter the Unwood's home unnoticed. The young woman was sound asleep. Slowly the bat diminished and became one with the shadows. As it faded, a white – almost transparent – mist seeped slowly from the body and poured into the room. As the mist grew so it thickened, reached up and contracted until dark shapes became visible within the swirl. The progress of the mist was leisurely, but filled with a fearful energy that tugged and twisted it into shape.

Brultzner stood in the room looking down at the young woman, knowing she was helpless on the bed. She didn't stir; as on that first occasion, she was stupefied with sleep and contentment. He was filled with desire and desperate hunger. He sat next to Rebecca for a long while, however, wanting to be held by her beauty. He adored the freshness of her complexion, and the way her blonde hair, cropped to neck length, swayed and bobbed when she tossed her head. The large blue eyes were closed now, but he could imagine them under the lids. He pulled the duvet down. She was wearing one of those old Victorian-style nightdresses. Brultzner smiled; she might almost have dressed for him. He ran his fingers under the low neck, opened the little buttons which led down to her breasts and slid it off her shoulders. He had always loved the bare shoulders of women. Her chest and breasts were good, and her muscles young and supple. Her neck was fluttering lightly, and he could feel the warmth of her body as he leaned over to feed.

CHAPTER 4

The absence of good

Grise Culman had been making love with her husband, Owen, all night. She gave him no rest until he satisfied her again and again. Owen collapsed exhausted on the bed, relieved that he could now fall into a deep sleep for a few hours. It was five in the morning and the sun was rising over the sea. Grise pulled on her silk gown and walked out onto the terrace. She loved the summer, wandering round half-dressed with the warmth of the sun on her body. She wondered whether to swim, or to walk down to the cliff edge, brushing her bare feet through the grass; the call of the grass proved stronger. It was warm, even at this hour. She breathed in, filled her lungs, opened her wrap and let her breasts and stomach feel the first, tender warmth of the morning sun. She reached the little gate which let her out onto the cliff top. Grise closed her wrap, and sat for a moment on the seat they had placed there for guests.

It would be hot by late morning and almost unbearable by mid afternoon. It had become impossible to be out of doors by three – well, almost impossible. She still walked up through the village, and one afternoon she had walked the fields with Nin Chambers. Apart from Nin and herself, the only things moving were the butterflies. She still kept in with Nin, despite Mark; staying in with Nin kept her close to Mark.

Grise glanced only quickly along the footpath before making her way down to the beach; she wanted the feel of the warm sand between her toes. What she liked about the heat was its violence; it struck down at you from a blue sky, bringing the heat out of your body, turning it that lovely golden colour.

The sand was no disappointment. Still warm from the previous day's sun, it struck upwards into the soles of her feet, and then enclosed and enveloped them – wrapping her like a lover in its warmth. There was nowhere to hide here on the wide beach. Grise strode out across the dunes towards the edge of the sea, and there she delighted in the water lapping over her toes. She stretched her arms and spun round; her wrap, caught by the breeze, was whipped from her and she stood naked. She laughed, watching the silk cloth as it fluttered along the beach. Grise wasted no time; she ran straight into the sea and allowed the swell to draw her out.

She took her morning pleasure in the waves before walking, casually, back to the cliff top, picking up her dressing gown on the way. An early shower washed the salt from her body, which was glowing from the sun and the swim. It was nearly six thirty and Owen was sound asleep after the exertions of the night. She wondered whether to wake him, but decided against it. Grise hungered, but was not a selfish woman.

The object of her desire, Mark Chambers, was not facing the day with quite her degree of equanimity. He had to visit the Beachlands Health Club – another contract was under discussion – and was not looking forward to it at all. The only consolation was that Owen would be there – his plans for the larger gym, badminton courts and restaurant were now a distinct possibility following his election to the council and, more importantly, his offer to serve on the planning sub-committee.

He glanced proudly round his garden as he left – the climbing roses golden yellow and scented, the wood spurge with its red leaves and greenish flowers, the cotoneaster with its small, glossy leaves and white flowers, the white-flowered potentilla, the purple-blue spikes of the salvia, the trumpet-shaped flowers of the convolvulus, the silky-pink cistus and the feathery wormwood. He remembered Nin planting each of them. Perhaps summer wasn't so bad after all; soon the butterflies and bees would be swarming around them. He smiled at Nin; it was good to be alive and have a home.

Owen had woken late – not surprisingly – and showered in a hurry. When he arrived in the kitchen, Grise had his boiled eggs ready. She came to him, reached up with her arms, pulled his mouth down to her and gave him one of her deep kisses. The children were already off to school and so they sat together, alone and quiet. Grise wanted Owen to say something about last night, but his conversation and thoughts were all about larger gyms, badminton courts and restaurants.

She watched Owen as he ate. She remembered the cricket match where they had first met, how she had dumped her current boy-friend on the spot and watched Owen. She remembered the way he had looked in his white flannels and how attentive he had been. She remembered how their love-making had always been on her terms – quickly if that was the way she wanted it, or all night when the mood took her.

Some summer evenings, when Grise and he were sitting outside with the children, Owen felt that this must be what Heaven would be like – sitting around with those you loved in the warm, wearing light clothes and with tiled floors heating your feet. He knew his children loved him. This summer the beach had been wonderful. He took them down into the dunes when they got back from school, and they would spend an hour in and out of the waves while Grise cooked their tea.

He took pleasure, too, in watching Grise whose natural beauty the summer enhanced. He couldn't make up his mind whether she adorned the summer or the summer her, and decided it must be a bit of both. Her beauty seemed to sparkle then; it was as though the world had always been like this, as though there had never been a life beyond Grise.

"What are you thinking?"

"How lovely you are – especially in summer. Summer suits you, Grise."

Mark Chambers drew up on their driveway and walked onto the terrace he had built for them. He had never been quite sure whether or not Owen knew about him and Grise. His shame extended, beyond the sense of betrayal he felt regarding his own family, to Owen – a man he had hurt immeasurably.

"Hello, Mark. Good to see you. Everything's ready."

So it was: the initial drawings and plans were spread on the table where Grise and Owen had sat for breakfast. The sun was now rising; the azure sky was like a mirror reflecting the sun downwards over the earth; the terrace was bathed in a glowing sphere of warmth. Grise came out onto the terrace, carrying a tray with cups and a cafetiere. She was wearing nothing but skimpy trousers and a bikini top.

"Hello, Mark – long time no see."

Mark Chambers fumbled awkwardly with the papers, not daring to look at her in case Owen saw the expression in his eyes. He hadn't seen her closely since April. Everything came back to him – she was attractive, she was exciting. The dark brown eyes, the short black hair, the way she had of looking down and then up under her lashes, and the smile that lit up her whole face struck at him like a hot sun. Grise came close and kissed him on the cheek as one would greet an old friend.

During the affair he had given Owen no thought at all, but gradually he had crept into Mark's consciousness and Mark's shame had swelled accordingly. He felt the desire to do something for Owen, to make amends in some way while knowing that he never could. There seemed no escape from the road along which his lust had led him; he was doomed to walk it forever until he reached those green hills far away.

The sun was at noon before they had finished their discussions and Mark promised to draw up some estimates. They sat quietly and Grise brought them all a cool drink. The terrace was already warm – almost hot to the feet. House martins flitted back and forth to their nests under the eaves of Beachlands. On the beach, gulls shrieked; they seemed far away. There was the faint hum of cars from London Road. They waited as though there was nothing to do.

After a while, Owen excused himself – he had to see the Fat Councillor. Mark said he must go too, but Owen said there was no need – why not have a spot of lunch with Grise? Grise said that she could do a quick sandwich. Mark had no obvious reason to refuse; anyway, to refuse would have drawn attention to the very thing Mark wanted to hide.

In the kitchen it was cool, but the unreal sense of being in another place still pervaded the air. He remembered thinking how easy it was in her company.

"Why fight it, Mark? You know you want me, and I'm damned sure I want you. Why did you stay if it wasn't for that? You could have gone when Owen did."

He had wanted to stay; he had wanted to be with her and near her again – alone. Her eyes wandering over him seemed to be part of the heat of the day – part of the dappled light on the pool, part of the chirruping birds, part of the shade of trees with their rustling leaves, part of the bees pursuing their honey from blossom to blossom, part of the golden roses and the red-green wood spurge ... Mark shook himself.

"It's over, Grise. I shouldn't have stayed."

"But you wanted to?"

"Life isn't just about what you want – is it?"

"Then what is it about?"

"You know as well as I do."

She made no attempt to move towards him, but laughed.

"Don't look so nervous – I'm not going to force you."

"Does Owen know about us?" he asked, without really knowing why.

"Why do you ask? What has that got to do with it?"

Her eyes flashed, and Mark realised just how single-minded she was; she moved towards him and, in that way she had, touched him very lightly on the chest where his shirt was unbuttoned.

"I enjoyed it with you, Mark. I enjoyed your energy, your briskness. I felt wonderful – and you were transformed. People all said how happy you looked during the time we were together. It's up to you."

"I know. I enjoyed it, too, Grise – you know that – but I made my decision."

He tucked their plans and drawings under his arm and walked out of the kitchen. Outside, the sun was still shining, and the smell of the sea still wafting in on the breeze. The heat seemed less brutal than it had, less demanding, less insistent that he strip off and bathe in it. He was relieved and careful not to look back.

Grise smiled to herself as he almost ran out of the kitchen. She just knew that her time would come again. She picked up the telephone and called Sandra Bint.

"He just left – quickly," she told her, and Sandra laughed.

"Men never know what they want. You have to show them."

Sandra Bint had been through three marriages, and so was considered quite an expert on the subject. Sandra's first marriage had been one of those disastrous teenage things. It had been a disaster from day one, but at least her child 'had a name' and in those days you were an 'unmarried mother' not a 'single parent'. She'd soon found that her husband was "having it off with a little tart from his office" and ditched him – on condition that she kept the house. She promised not to bother him again.

She worked hard to keep herself and her child – pubs, clubs and the like where she honed her street wisdom – and then fell in with a rig worker. He was a decent bloke and well heeled. All her friends liked him, and Sandra's social life had taken an upward turn. She found herself invited to Lions Club dos, began to make a better class of friend and joined the Conservative Party. She and her rig worker also bought a house with his money, and Sandra was wise enough to "have it put in both names otherwise her self-esteem was nowhere". Her rig worker had agreed and so, when divorce number two came round, Sandra found herself the proud owner of half a house which hadn't cost her a penny.

She'd been fond of her rig worker but he'd been away a lot, and she fell in with a Conservative councillor who also happened to be a Lion; dinners out and evenings in took their toll on the marriage. The Conservative councillor had divorced his wife and married her; she was penniless, of course, and so he bought the house with his share of his own divorce settlement. Property prices were rising fast at the time and so, when divorce number three came round because the Conservative councillor found out that she was still seeing her rig worker, Sandra gained half of the "very nice" profit they had made when the house was sold. She'd come out of three marriages with at least part of three houses, and Sandra certainly had a smile on her face. She now had her own house – more or less paid for – and was looking for "Number 4".

Her smile won her many friends; Sandra Bint was extremely popular wherever she went. During her rig worker phase, she had won Corvin Unwood's heart and done sterling work for the church in Dunburgh. It wasn't just her smile, of course, which won her friends. Sandra was always ready to "take people as they are", and it made her "easy company". It was this readiness of Sandra's to accept the "ways of the world" which brought Grise Culman to her door. Grise wanted to re-ignite her affair with Mark Chambers and – because she had doubts about the rights and wrongs of this – she needed to talk to someone who would encourage her.

"I wouldn't think twice about it. This isn't a rehearsal."

Grise had heard that before, and it was easier to agree with such a statement than to challenge them; after all, it was true – you don't "get a second chance". They were sitting on her patio sipping cool, dry white wine.

"I do have Owen and the children to think about."

"What the eye doesn't see?"

"I'm not like you, Sandra. I don't take things quite so ... lightly."

"Enjoy it while you can! Have a little fun along the way. Owen loves you – everyone says so! He isn't going to divorce you for one mistake ..."

"Two 'mistakes'".

"One mistake – it's the same man! Tomorrow is the first day of the rest of your life, Grise!"

"I know that."

"It happens all the time ... Do you fancy something to eat – this wine is going to my head a bit," said Sandra.

"I wouldn't mind – just a small bite, that is."

Sandra disappeared through the back door and Grise closed her eyes, inviting the heat to bear down on her. It was mid afternoon, approaching four, and the summer sun had been high for hours. Sandra's garden was small and enclosed so the heat pushed downwards until you could hardly breathe under its weight. She was as clever a gardener as she was a caterer, and had filled the little space with sun-loving plants so that the raised bed which bordered her patio was filled with sweet scents, blue flowers with white eyes, dreamy creams galore, intense scarlets, lavender-blues and clusters of pink. It was a woman's garden with colours that shimmered and splashed, shone and sparkled.

"You can smell the heat indoors," said Sandra as she came back with a plate of olive and anchovy bites. "I'm not sure that these are going to go too well with the wine, but they'll melt in your mouth. Ainsley loves them! More wine – best drunk young and fresh! ... Did you hear about Rebecca Unwood?"

"She's not getting married at last?"

"No – though you'd think there was someone with enough about him to snap her up, wouldn't you? No – she's had that funny turn again."

"Funny turn?"

"Like you were that time – bloodless and weak."

"How do you know?"

"Liz Shaw told me. She was at the rectory this morning and Alan Read was there. Evidently, her mother – Rebecca's, that is – had insisted on getting him in. She hadn't got up for work this morning, and they found her in bed – white as a sheet and with those funny bite marks on her throat."

Esther Unwood had knocked several times on Rebecca's door before entering her bedroom. Getting no answer, and realising that Rebecca would hate being late for work, she had persuaded Corvin that it was the right thing to do.

The scene in their daughter's room had horrified them. The duvet had been folded back and Rebecca was in a deep, unnatural sleep with her nightdress pulled down to reveal her chest. A small trickle of blood had run into the fold of her breasts; this came from two small puncture wounds on her neck, but had long since dried. Her face was pallid – a terrible pallor which gave the impression that she had been drained of all her blood. Corvin had attempted to wake her but to no avail, which was so unusual that he began to fear she was dead. He leaned over and listened to her heart, which was still beating. He cried out to Esther to fetch the doctor. While Esther was gone, he examined the two little wounds – they were clean and fresh, not what one would have expected from the bite of a rat or a bat. There was no tearing of the flesh, no dragging of the skin.

Alan Read came, as always, quickly. His bag was a reassuring sight, and Corvin and Esther relaxed almost as soon as he entered the room. He took Rebecca's pulse, listened to her heart, extracted a sample of her blood and turned to her parents with a smile.

"I don't know what is wrong with Rebecca, but my inclination is to let her sleep. Keep her warm, Esther – but not too warm. This room faces ... what ... north-west, doesn't it? So this weather shouldn't bother her too much. I'll have my mobile on – keep in touch. If there's any change in her condition, let me know at once. I'll be in the village more or less all day. Don't worry about the blood sample. It's just a precaution. I'll send it for testing ... Has anything like this happened before?"

Esther hesitated only for a moment and then said:

"Yes – just a few months ago, in March. I went to wake her up with a cup of tea, and her door was locked, so I knocked. When she came to open it, I noticed a few drops of blood on her nightdress. She was quite snappy about it. She was weak for days – unlike Rebecca! She's normally a picture of health. There were the same two marks on her throat – she had clearly been bitten. I thought it must have been a bat that had escaped from the wildlife park."

"And Rebecca recovered in a few days?"

"Yes – within a few days she had returned to normal."

"We can only keep our eye on her, Esther. I see no point in prescribing medication at the moment. As you say, she's a healthy young woman and I am sure she will recover."

"You've had too much to drink to fetch the children, Grise. Give Owen a ring and have another glass of wine," insisted Sandra Bint.

"Do you know, I think I will?"

The heat of the afternoon had softened them; both women sat in a kind of dazed heat, broiling luxuriously and very disinclined to move.

"Are you still seeing your rig worker – we all liked him?"

"I'm seeing a policeman in Lowestoft. He's married, unfortunately – but, then, that's his problem not mine."

"Don't you ever feel a bit guilty?"

"Why should I? His marriage problems have nothing to do with me."

"That isn't the way the world will see it. Everyone will say that it's you who broke up the marriage."

"I don't know what his problems are with his wife, but they started before I came on the scene. Wives are fond of blaming the 'other woman'. Most of them need to ask what went wrong with their marriages in the first place. Women like me often keep marriages together. When my copper's had a night out with me, the pressure's off at home."

Mark Chambers had just enjoyed haddock with soured cream and mushrooms, sitting on their patio with Nin and the children. He enjoyed his son's company; the 'boy' was still living at home, but about to marry. After he'd gone, they'd still enjoy a pint together on a summer's evening. It had been a close thing this morning. Mark laughed with relief; he was pleased he'd turned his back on it.

"Penny for them?" said Nin.

"Not worth that."

"Were you thinking about Owen's extensions?"

"Yes – it'll be a big contract."

"Why don't you let Markie handle it?"

Mark looked at his wife closely.

"You've only to say the word, dad."

"It's just a habit with me, boy – you'll be the same. It's not a question of not trusting you, it's simply ..."

"Simply what, Mark?" asked Nin.

"Pride in your work," said her son, "I'll be the same."

"I hope so – but your mum is right. Do you fancy handling this one?"

"It'll be great."

Mark smiled at his son and his wife; a great weight suddenly slid from his shoulders.

Corvin and Esther sat in their 'refectory', the evening breeze blowing in through the french doors. They had eaten little, tempting Rebecca with spiced vegetables and rice since she wouldn't think of meat, even now.

"You're anaemic," insisted Esther, "You need some red meat."

"You might as well offer me blood, mum. That's it – I'll have a pint of nice, red blood – warm and refreshing, straight from the cow."

"Don't be silly, Rebecca. The old doctors used to prescribe steak and kidney puddings if you were run down. They knew what they were talking about."

She had nibbled at the spiced vegetables as had Corvin who found no nourishment at all in food without meat. Esther, too, had barely touched her meal – such was her concern for Rebecca. Alan Read had dropped by at the end of the day and chatted with Rebecca who perked up in his company, but he had noticed that the colour was yet to return to her cheeks and insisted, to Esther's relief, that she made no attempt to return to work until he gave the all clear. Esther had other things on her mind as well, and when Rebecca had returned to bed she spoke to Corvin.

"Corvin – how do we stand on 'evil' these days?"

"I wasn't aware, my dear, that our 'stand' had changed greatly."

"You sound like Twiddle, Corvin – give me an answer."

"It remains the problem it ever was – as formulated by Epicurus. Either God can prevent evil and chooses not to – and, therefore, is not good – or chooses to prevent it and cannot – and, therefore, is not all-powerful."

"But it exists in the world, doesn't it?"

"Evil is that which is morally bad or wrong, or causes harm, pain, or misery."

"You're still skirting the issue, Corvin. You're giving me textbook answers."

"What is troubling you, Esther?"

She looked at her husband with muted terror in her eyes, and he was frightened.

"Tell me more, Corvin. It is years since I gave this any thought at all."

"St Augustine argued that evil is the absence of good ..."

"Isn't that begging the question?"

"... in the same way that darkness is the absence of light"

"A nice image, but where does it get us?"

"Evil creeps in when we turn away from good. Something created 'good' can, therefore, become 'evil' but – in the context of the whole of eternity – what appears to us to be evil may be seen as good. To put it another way, from God's eternal perspective everything is good."

"So evil may – in that sense – return to being good."

"That is the Christian message, Esther."

She was silent for a long while, and Corvin enjoyed her silences.

"Aren't you interested in why I have asked you about evil, Corvin?"

"I am waiting, my dear. I knew you'd tell me when you were ready."

"Have you ever been aware of evil, Corvin – aware of its presence?"

"Yes – in some places I have been."

"So have I – sometimes in people, but more often in places. I suppose some people are more susceptible to its presence … I sensed it this morning – in Rebecca's bedroom. Call it a lack of good, if you like – that, at least, makes some sense of it. Let me finish! There was a lack of good – there was evil – in our daughter's room, Corvin. I even sensed it – for a moment or two – in her."

"Esther!"

"I have to say what I feel. Who can I speak to if not to you – you are my husband and my priest. Believe me, love, I would not even begin to let these thoughts enter my mind if I had not felt as I did. It is no good turning away, Corvin – these things must be faced! … I am old, Corvin. I have been on this Earth for seventy years. I go back a long way and this was an old evil – subtle."

"Subtle?"

"The word came – I don't know why. I'm going up to see Rebecca. Will you make me a cup of cocoa – I'm cold?"

"What's wrong, Alan?" asked Penny Read.

"Nothing … nothing."

"So it's quite normal for you to eat your dinner with only a mumble, sit staring at the rhododendrons, ignore the children when they say goodnight and let me put all four to bed, is it?"

Alan Read laughed, jumped up, grabbed his wife and whirled her round in his arms. When he came back downstairs from saying good night to his children, Alan smiled at his wife.

"Do you want to talk about it?" she asked, "it's better than sitting there brooding, and I'm Mrs Confidential – remember?"

"It's not that. I haven't really got it straight in my own head yet."

"Got what straight?"

Penny Read loved her husband dearly and let him know it every day of her life; no twenty-four hours went passed in which she did not put her arms round him for a hug and a kiss or both. They had four children aged twelve, eleven, nine and eight; her father had enquired why they skipped a year and she had pleaded a hot summer. It was just the way it had worked out; she could remember when each one was conceived and they had all been a joy. They had given them straightforward, family names: Amos was the eldest and named after her father, Anna-Maria was the second born and named after Alan's mother, George was the one who had skipped a summer and was named after Alan's father and Helen simply had to be named after her mother

Penny not only loved Alan – she admired him. He had come to Dunburgh as a young doctor, straight from medical school and – within a few months – made his mark on the practice; many people simply do a job, others – like Alan – have a vocation. He had established from his first day that he was on duty twenty-four hours a day, three hundred and sixty five days a year – for those patients who really needed him, but God help those who called him out unnecessarily. He considered general practice to be pinnacle of the profession – the only reason for which any serious doctor could exist – and everything else in the medical world to be a "support service".

She had been a teacher at the local school when he arrived – in trouble with a boyfriend she had followed down to Suffolk from college. She confided in Alan one night over a pint at a village dance, and he had said – "He's a waste of time. Give him the elbow and marry me." She hadn't laughed – it had sounded too ridiculous for that – but they were married within three months and their first child arrived a year later.

She watched him twist his long frame into the chair, curling his right leg over the arm. She smiled at the wavy hair, now thinning prematurely, and waited. It was Penny's favourite time of the day – when the children were safe in bed and she could sit and talk with her husband. They'd had the conservatory built to run off their sitting room, extending the home into the garden even through the winter months. It was a large house – three cottages knocked into one; there were two ways in and out of every room.

"This morning I attended a young woman who appeared to have lost a lot of blood. She was very pale and her pulse was weak – although not critically so – and there were what appeared to be bite marks on her neck. It was from here that the blood appeared to have trickled, but there was no significant amount on the pillow case. When I asked her mother if anything similar had occurred before, she said that it had – in March. So, we have now had six such incidents in the village in four months – to my knowledge. What the hell's going on, Pen?"

"Six cases? I take it you're referring to Amy Billings, Grise Culman, that young hairdresser, this morning's young woman – who was it?"

"Rebecca – who has been bitten twice."

"And who else?"

"You."

Penny Read blushed, and looked angry for a second.

"How did you know?"

"How did I know my wife was listless and bloodless?"

"I didn't want to make a fuss. I was OK after a few days."

"Did you notice any bites on your throat?"

"No – yes."

"There you are, you see – almost a lie, wasn't it?"

"Alan!"

"None of the women have been keen to acknowledge the bites. You've all tried to hide them and were a bit snappy when they've been mentioned. And there's one more thing – all of you have, in your own ways, been attractive women."

"What difference would that make?"

"I don't know – unless we've got a particularly picky bat!"

"Do you mean you think I was bitten by a bat?"

"I don't know, Pen, but it's time to start collecting some data. There'll be a common factor here somewhere."

Penny walked over to him and knelt at his feet, leaned her head on his knees and looked up at him: most of their children had started this way.

"Is it just possible, Alan, that you are seeing a pattern where none exists? You didn't see the marks on Grise or Amy did you? They were something you heard about. And you didn't see those on me because I didn't want to bother you."

"Is this the curse of the analytical intelligence – chasing ideas up blind alleys?"

"Maybe – come to bed."

CHAPTER 5

Mother and son

Sandra Bint was branching out yet again; her little catering business was a hit in the neighbourhood, but she needed more serious finances. Normally, a blooming business would approach a bank, but Sandra's instincts told her that a man would be cheaper – provided, of course, he was a man with money and her amorous policeman was; he had a good salary, the prospect of an early pension and fat lump sum.

He had told her this while they were sweating, deliciously, in her little bedroom after all the frenzied activity. He had taken her out and surprised her at the restaurant table with the little gift of a handbag he knew she wanted. Sandra took this as a good sign – he obviously knew how to treat a woman. She had always avoided men who "just wanted you for sex"; they had to be prepared to give something in return. He looked a very promising prospect, and Sandra was keen to cultivate his friendship.

They'd had a good night; he was an energetic man in desperate need of physical release from a very stressful job, and Sandra was happy to oblige. Her little house was quite rejuvenated by the unaccustomed activity; things had been quiet since her third divorce. She had a few doubts about how many other women he'd been with – since he'd said that his wife had never been remotely interested in sex – but Sandra was, if nothing, a pragmatist and she shelved that thought in the wider interest.

As yet, of course, she couldn't introduce him to her friends, which was always a bit of a social inconvenience – it is, after all, a couple's world – but that would come with time. As soon as he made his move or the wife found out and made hers, Sandra could bring things out into the open, which would be much nicer all round. Everyone found her a bit of a laugh and she was looking forward to waltzing into one of their barbecues or parties with a new man on her arm.

So Sandra dressed for church that Sunday morning feeling 'bright and breezy, free and easy' – as the song goes. The only slight shadow on her mind was her son, Ainsley, who had confided to her after Horst Brultzner's luncheon party that he was thinking of splitting from his young wife.

Ainsley had wasted his time at school – like a lot of his year group – because the teaching had been poor, but Sandra had managed to get him on a business course at the local college. Armed with his NVQ2 in business management, Ainsley had been able to set up as a Financial Consultant. His future mother-in-law had seen him as a bright prospect and invested some capital in an office in Norbridge, so that "he would have credibility". She had also provided the deposit for a home for Ainsley and her daughter. There was, therefore, a lot at stake, and if Ainsley handled it badly he could find himself worse off than when he got married. Besides, Sandra rather liked her daughter-in-law and thought it was a shame that the marriage was nearing the rocks after only nine months. Still, he was taking her out to lunch after church and Sandra had high hopes that she might persuade him to think again.

It was a wonderful Sunday morning – a morning that made going to church worthwhile. The sun had risen early and, by ten thirty, the air was warm and inviting without being stifling. Sandra's dress swayed as she strode up the sandy path from the lych-gate. How she loved summer dresses! It was sleeveless to show her slender arms, thin to hang invitingly over her slightly large buttocks and short to give her shapely legs an airing. Her outfit was topped by a hat from Zara. Anyone with a smidgeon of respectability wore a hat for church and broad-brimmed summer hats really suited Sandra, setting off her thick, cropped dyed-blonde hair to perfection. She smiled at everyone and they smiled back; it was good to be alive.

The bells rang out over the village, summoning the faithful to prayer, and Sandra was glad to be one of them; the church was, after all, a social venue and should be appreciated as such. She'd noticed that most people who rarely came always sat at the back, and it gave the wrong impression. You needed to be sufficiently near the front so that you showed confidence, but sufficiently near the back that you could make a sweeping walk to the altar rail when communion was served. It wasn't often that Sandra took a middle road but, in church, that seemed to satisfy both worlds.

The church was filling quickly. The morning service was popular in the summer when the weather invited you out and there were new summer dresses to show off. Sandra knew how much Corvin appreciated this; he worked hard round the village and deserved a full church. She had taken to him when he welcomed her "into the fold" after her first divorce, and he had been a strong supporter of Sandra ever since. She and her rig worker had been a familiar sight at all church socials during their time together, and Corvin had "understood the strain which having your husband away so much of the time" placed on the marriage. Sandra appreciated this.

The organ struck up, and the choir – followed by Corvin – began to process down the aisle. Everyone stood for the first hymn. It was one of Sandra's favourites:

> "Father, hear the prayer we offer:
>> Not for ease that prayer may be,
> But for strength that we may ever –
>> Live our lives courageously."

She sang heartily and with feeling; it was a bit old fashioned she knew, but it reminded her of school days. Sandra expected that Clara Gobley had chosen it. She always chose hymns like that whereas Penny Read would have things like *Little Yellow Sunbeams*. When Corvin said:

"Almighty God, to whom all hearts are open, all desires known, and from whom no secrets are hidden ... "

Sandra wondered whether he meant it. You wouldn't really want God to know everything, would you?

Soon, however, her attention was taken up with something more interesting than the service, and the words, as usual, washed harmlessly over her. She noticed that Penny Read was getting the Junior Church children into a group on the steps that led up to the choir stalls. Corvin always liked to involve the children – usually near the beginning of the service so that they could leave for their own activities when they had done their little piece. Penny was saying something about "repeating the lines after the children"; it was going to be one of those songs. They began:

"From the tiny ant ...." and then Penny ushered in the congregation who repeated the line – well, some did but evidently not enough because Penny stopped the children to run over the words of the verse. Only, the organ didn't stop; it blasted on at full volume.

Penny looked at Corvin who smiled back but did not move, so Penny walked across to him and whispered something. He inclined his head but remained still, and the organ continued playing. Penny smiled at the congregation and lifted her hands to the Lord – and waited while the organ, now a passionate crescendo, played itself out. There was a silence, and then both Corvin and Penny spoke at the same time – he to introduce the Old Testament reading, she to re-introduce the children's song.

Sandra – ever a casual student of human nature – leaned forward to watch people's reactions. Esther Unwood was frozen stiff in her pew, Sydney Close glared angrily at Penny, Bernard Shaw blushed to the roots of his thinning hair while Liz wrung her hands and looked anxiously at Esther, Tony Crewes was smiling to himself and Beth was giving him daggers, Lianne Snooks smiled discreetly while her Barry puffed out his cheeks and looked resigned, and Corvin appeared thunderstruck, continuing to talk like a machine but gradually losing his volume. Sandra, looking frantically round, had no time to observe anymore because – at that moment – Rebecca Unwood, paler and more drawn than Sandra had ever seen her, stood up and walked across to the piano, which was kept by the lectern. She passed a quick word with Penny, took a book from her, and began to play the melody softly and gently. She gave Penny a nod, and Penny turned to the congregation.

"Thank you, Rebecca – now, perhaps, we can try again. This is the children's contribution to our end of term service. They will sing a line and we would like you to repeat it. Let's run over the first verse so that everyone gets the idea."

Corvin hadn't moved, and nor did he join in the clapping at the end of the song. He appeared rooted to the spot, struck by arrows from several directions and transfixed to the wood of the rood screen.

Sandra was so excited that she could barely wait to leave and talk with Ample, but she had composed herself by the time they reached the bit where everyone walks down to the altar to receive the bread and wine. Sandra always enjoyed this moment; she missed being married to her rig worker at times like this because he always said how much he admired her "arse" as she strutted down the aisle – and Sandra was always most careful to select an outfit which would show this off to its best.

Outside in the beautiful sunshine, everyone heaved a sigh of relief; say what you like, churches are always cold in summer and freezing cold in winter. It was almost as though they were built that way as a punishment: a punishment for your sins, no doubt, but Sandra couldn't be bothered with that – life was too short.

Alan Read stood on the church path, waiting, and Sandra couldn't resist going up to him. She left Ainsley and Milly with Grise – "just for a minute".

"I thought Penny was wonderful," she said.

"Thanks, Sandra – I'll tell her. To be frank – so did I, but I cannot imagine that everyone will agree with us."

Sidney Close was almost at the lych-gate when Miss Mealey and Mrs Teale waylaid him. He was rather pleased when Mrs Teale said:

"Miss Mealey and I thought it was disgraceful, Mr Close."

"Disgraceful," agreed Miss Mealey.

"It's not for me to say, ladies," said Sidney with an exaggerated shrug of his shoulders, "I'm nobody now."

"The rector was a fool to let you go," said Mrs Teale.

"It's a crying shame," said Miss Mealey, in support of her friend.

"A matter of principle, ladies, cannot be ignored!"

Sidney enjoyed saying that; he paused on the path to soak in the warmth of their adoration.

"I can't but think that Dr Read is very embarrassed by the whole thing," said Mrs Teale.

"Not everyone sees it like us, ladies."

"Look – he's talking to the rector's daughter. I expect he's apologizing."

"If that is the case, which I'm afraid I must say I rather doubt, he'd be better apologizing to the rector."

"I feel sorry for the rector," said Miss Mealey, "If only you were still rector's warden, Mr Close."

"If only," agreed her friend.

"Have a word with Mister Shaw, ladies. I'm sure he'll be only too pleased to listen."

Having listened to so many such complaints during his time in the post, Sidney's concern for Bernard Shaw can only be described as touching.

Alan Read had not stopped laughing since he and Penny arrived home; over and over he had reassured his wife that she was magnificent.

"I didn't do it deliberately, you know," she said for the – was it tenth time?

"I'm sure you didn't, Pen," her husband responded for the tenth time.

"No, I really didn't. I just couldn't let that woman drown the children out. We'd practised that song and they were looking forward to performing it. I thought it would be a good choice because the congregation could join in, and when they didn't and she played on, I was just determined to start again."

"Corvin will have to sort Clara Gobley out. He can't have that kind of thing going on in his church. It's simply not acceptable."

"Do you think he will?"

"He has no choice."

"Thanks, Alan."

"For what?"

"You know – for supporting me. I know this is a small thing – a little Junior Church in a little village with little minds. In the big scheme of things ..."

"...it doesn't amount to a hill of beans? *Wrong*. If we all took more care of what you call the "little things" – our patch of the world – if *everyone* did that then the world would – per se – be a better place on the larger scale."

"What do you think Clara Gobley will do?"

"See Corvin – just as she did last time when you wanted to choose the songs."

"But it didn't do any good. I got my way, if you like and chose the songs, but then she played the wrong tunes."

"And Corvin let it go – having told her that you must choose the songs for the children."

"Yes."

"He'll have to make a stand sooner or later – and better sooner."

"But then he might lose his choir mistress and organist."

"Pen."

"Yes?"

"Stop being so reasonable – if you persist in seeing everything from everybody's point of view, you'll get nowhere."

Penny Read laughed and slipped off his lap to take a look at how her Sunday roast was going. Alan followed her into the kitchen.

"I must say I admired Rebecca. She had a difficult decision to make, and she made it quickly."

"She saved the day for me. She knew full well that I could have played the piano myself. Her getting up to do it was an act of solidarity."

"Did you get a chance to thank her?"

"Oh yes – as soon as I'd seen the last child safely off with its parents. She came over to the Church Centre."

Alan laughed again and said:

"So it isn't only the roast that will be hot in the Unwood house this Sunday lunchtime?"

Alan Read could not have been nearer the mark. It wasn't simply "hot" at the rectory – there was an air of attrition which had turned a warm summer's day into one which burned.

Corvin was wretched on several counts: he had been chastised by three women in less than the space of an hour and the situation was still unresolved, the future held nothing but the prospect of uncertainty and humiliation, still to be faced was the backlash from other parishioners. If only, if only – he thought as he sat in the back garden, taking refuge from his own home – we could really live in peace with one another; the burning selfishness of the ego was responsible for so much destruction.

His wife had wondered why on earth he hadn't ignored Penny Read and continued with the communion – as a priest it was his simply duty.

"I have nothing but admiration for the way Penny Read stepped in and ran the Sunday School – or Junior Church as they choose to call it now – but the audacity of the woman – to stand up in the middle of a Holy Communion service and refuse to let it proceed until her children had finished their song!"

"It wasn't quite ... "

"Wasn't quite like that! That's how it seemed to me and everyone else sitting there wriggling with embarrassment – a priest having the Church's most sacred service put on hold by a Junior Church teacher! You need, Corvin, to sort your priorities out! Progress is all well and good but we have a tradition to uphold. There's been enough meddling in the church by the modernists. They've jettisoned Cranmer's Book of Common Prayer – with all the beautiful ritual of its language – in favour of this Alternative version – and now, we've got members of the congregation telling us how to run the service. She was interrupting a most holy ritual, Corvin!"

"It was simply a chance for the children ... "

"Why? Why did they have to sing during the communion service – because Penny Read thought it was a good idea?"

Corvin knew he'd been foolish to do anything but absorb the flack; any explanation he attempted simply provided more fuel for Esther's anger. In fact, the whole business had been a mix up. Penny Read had asked if they could have an end-of-year service with the children, or if the children could do something before the communion. He had been reluctant to waive the ten-thirty communion service so an unhappy, and ill-fated, compromise was arranged. Clara Gobley's resentment at "her interference with church music" had not helped.

His daughter had also laid into him on the opposite tack – why hadn't he supported Penny Read – were the children not important to him?

"You either live in the past or you move towards the future and the children are the future! You either side with the Penny Reads of this world or the Clara Gobleys – you can't have it both ways! Stop sitting on the fence, dad! Strap on your armour, pick up the sword of your faith and get out there into the battleground! The battleground is to win hearts and minds and you'll only do that by looking Clara Gobley straight in the eye – without flinching!"

She'd been right – he hadn't met Clara Gobley's gaze; the woman had the eyes of Medusa and he'd been turned to stone as she attacked him in the vestry.

"I am the choir mistress here, rector! I choose the music – not your Junior Church teacher! I choose what will be sung! I will not have the Holy Communion turned into a kindergarten! Make up your mind what kind of church you want!"

Simple statements delivered with almost supernatural venom. The woman terrified him – the baleful eyes, the aquiline nose which made her look like a hawk, the tribe of cats, the crow, the stench rising from the faeces, the cups in which she offered you tea, the white rats running up and down the sloping candlestick, the jackdaw and the hedgehogs lapping milk. Corvin had seen them all – and more. He didn't really want to face a battle in there – a battle he was doomed to lose.

Rebecca had then turned on her mother for supporting Clara Gobley against Penny Read, accusing her of being "two-faced", of actually wanting "a progressive church but siding with yesterday's people" and that she too needed to decide "which side she was fighting on."

Over and above all this verbal abuse, however, was something that had disturbed him even more. He was aware that Rebecca had a sharp side to her nature, but it showed itself rarely and only in slight flashes of anger. He had never seen, or ever heard, her lash into either him or her mother before – not with such spleen. Her face has been colourless with the skin drawn taut across the high cheek bones, and her lips had been drawn back into a snarl, showing sharp, white teeth that gnashed. It reminded him of wolves tearing into their prey. Corvin could smell the dinner cooking but was not looking forward to his Sunday roast.

Sandra Bint normally slept heavily but the warm day became an even warmer night and she tossed and turned in her bed, unable to wake and yet unable to sleep dreamlessly. The open window brought no cooling breeze. She had also drawn back the curtains before she got into bed, but it made no difference other than that the moonlight played on her body as she reclined on the bed waiting for sleep.

When she turned out the lights, Sandra noticed a strange mist in the garden. It wasn't the infamous sea mist of Dunburgh (she was too far from the beach for that), and it was too dry for the ground mists of summer which form during the night. This mist seemed to creep – across the lawn between the shrubs and up to the wall of the house where it struggled for a while, and then climbed the wisteria that grew beneath her bedroom window. It seemed in no hurry, but hung there waiting. Sandra shrugged it off and climbed into bed. She always slept naked and, in this hot summer, had only the covering of a thin sheet. She curled into this until it wrapped around her, drawing sweat, and then she kicked it to the floor.

She thought she had dropped off when a movement at the window seemed to wake her. The mist was outside the window now – hanging there against the glass – and the heat in the room had become intolerable. She slipped from the bed and went across to look out into the night. The mist became sinuous, like a man naked and writhing. It appeared to grip the half-open window as though wanting to pull itself into the room. Sandra smiled to herself – 'give me a man after midnight' – and reached out. It was cold – the fingers of mist closed upon her, cold and inviting on such a hot night. She thought perhaps it might be cooler in the garden, and decided to sit out for a bit.

She slipped on a robe, went downstairs and through the back door. There was a little seat near the fence under the overhang of her neighbour's tree. It was warm under her buttocks, and she sat there looking round the garden, feeling proud with what she had created. The mist had cleared now; there was no trace of it anywhere. It was still hot – even outside – and Sandra thought she might remove her robe and wander naked – like Eve in Paradise.

Around her the shadows grew, cast by the moon through the leaves and branches of the old tree. The leaves rustled slightly as though it were autumn; Sandra looked up over her shoulder. A face was staring down at her – a face that seemed to be made up of leaves which sprung from the eyebrows and the tear ducts. Sandra couldn't make out whether the face was crying, or whether the grimace was one of anger. She was held by the eyes which pulsed from the tree, and watched as the shadows around her deepened and took the form of a man. He stood behind her and leaned over in a gesture almost solicitous were it not for the teeth which became prominent in the leafy mouth – teeth like those of giants in her childhood fairy story books.

He lifted her from the seat and tore her robe from her so that she stood naked in the moonlight. Her body was full and sumptuous; she felt the blood pulsing in her throat and her love juices run. The man – human now and dark with desire – lifted her mouth to him for his first taste. She felt his tongue lapping on her throat and then he drew back, sniffed the air like a wolf on the scent and threw her to the bench.

Horst Brultzner stood in the shadow of the driveway to Beachlands Health Club, hungry and frustrated. The Bint woman had promised him a rich feed. Unable to enter the house uninvited, he had successfully lured her into the garden for his satisfaction but, as he leaned to take her, the vampire had smelt the corruption within. She was polluted, like bad meat. She offered only contagion, and his dependence on blood made him susceptible to such diseases.

He dare not return to Rebecca. His excitement the other night had drained her too fully. She needed time to recover. He did not want a death on his hands – not more of his kind roaming the village for sustenance. He had come home for a quiet life.

He must find another, and be more cautious. His dark shadow passed along the road, flitting between the trees in the moonlight. Only the dogs saw him as he went on the prowl. There was a woman – the tall, dark beauty on Shoemaker's Lane. Her angular shoulders and the droop of her neck attracted him, and – one coffee morning at St George's, sharing his joy of antiques – she had invited him round at anytime.

CHAPTER 6

Sarah Alone

It was a Thursday night and Sidney Close was hurrying home from bell ringing practice. Apart from the sheer physical pleasure of controlling the great bells, he enjoyed the company of the small, select band who comprised St George's bell ringers. It gave him the chance to meddle in the church in that underhand way he found so pleasurable – a word here, a hint there and Corvin Unwood's life could be made just a little bit less enjoyable. Tonight had not been that successful. John Barker for one would hear nothing against Corvin – he was the rector and that was that – so Sidney walked quickly down the hill, hoping to work off his feelings with his dumb bells and chest expanders.

It was a hot night again, and the sweat poured from him. In a couple of hours, behind the bedroom windows, half the village would be lying awake, perspiration caught in rivulets as it trickled between their thighs and through their matted hair to the pillows and sheets beneath. The nights had brought no relief from the sun; it may have disappeared for a while, dust and insects may have settled, but it was still there, lurking in your crotch and armpits.

He was alone: most of the others would be going to one of the pubs and that wasn't where Sidney wished to be seen. He remembered the years he had walked down Church Hill with Clive Brown – saying goodnight at his gate as Froggy went on to the Jolly Sailors. It seemed a long time ago, but it was only two months since he had been murdered.

As he passed the corner of Shore Lane, Sidney noticed a figure slumped on the bench seat. It raised its head as he came into view, and Sidney recognised Shane Marjoram. The moon was weak, in its first quarter, and Sidney couldn't make out the details of the face but he recognised enough to know his assistant.

"Mr Close ... Mr Close?"

The voice was insistent – too much so for Sidney to ignore.

"Mr Close!"

It was almost as though his name was a talisman – holding the key to some great mystery. Sidney walked across to the bench, but didn't sit down. He could smell the drink on Shane and wanted to get away as quickly as possible.

"How's Sarah?" he asked, groping for a quiet topic of conversation.

"My Sare's fine – don't you worry about her. Why – what are people saying?"

"People aren't saying anything – everyone feels sorry for her ..."

"No need for that! I look after my Sarah. She's all right."

"I'm sure she is, Shane. How's your son?"

"Matthew's all right. What are people worried about?"

"As I say – they're not. I just wondered ..."

"Right – well that's OK then. They'd better not be – that's all."

Shane stood and leaned on Sidney, who flinched.

"Oi'll walk back with yer, Mr Close. Keep yer company."

With the drink, there came an aggression that Sidney never noticed during the day. He could feel the strength in the young man's body as Shane tottered to his feet; he wasn't someone with whom you would want to tangle. They stood together, on the small rise at the junction of the two roads, like old friends – drinking mates who had just come from the Jolly Sailors. Sidney looked about him; the sooner they set off home the better.

Then – to his dismay – Sidney saw two more figures coming towards them from the direction of the beach. One sauntered in a fashion so lazy that it irritated Sidney beyond reason; the other was alert, his ears pricking like a dog's for any sound that might be unusual, his gait easy but poised and his stance heavy. It was Tony Crewes and Martin Billings – both men he detested. Tony Crewes didn't seem to have noticed them, and was deep in the exposition of something, but Martin Billings had sized the situation up before he was within two hundred yards of the seat.

It wasn't until both pairs of strollers drew abreast of each other that Shane and Tony looked up and their eyes met. The story of the "head wetting" – as Tony Crewes liked to describe it – was well-known in the village. Spread, as it had been originally, by Liz Shaw it had since taken many forms – none of them flattering to Shane Marjoram. This wasn't the moment for a showdown, but both Martin and Sidney felt the tension in their companions. Shane's took the form of repressed anger, Tony's of an assumed nonchalance, which only further irritated the younger man.

"Oive got sumfin ter say ter yew, mate. Yew an' me hev got a score ter settle."

Tony Crewes only response was to run his eyes over Shane as though he was surprised by his choice of clothes.

"A score ter settle – and oim lookin' forward to it."

Martin was used to the expression of violence by drunken louts – in his village, when he was around, it usually came to nothing – but Sidney wasn't and the threat took him by surprise. It delighted him, and he hoped that Shane would throw a punch at Tony Crewes and break his jaw.

"Have you been home to dinner yet, Shane?" asked Martin.

"What's it ... no! Why?"

"Sarah will have it nice and warm for you."

Tony smiled to himself at his friend's inept choice of words. This infuriated both Sidney and Shane – Sidney because the image of a 'nice and warm Sarah' was more than he could bear, Shane because he thought Martin was taking the piss. Tony Crewes, assiduously avoiding Shane's eyes so that he would give the impression he didn't acknowledge his existence, saw the expression in Sidney's. Here was a man who spent many waking hours with Sarah on his mind. He'd known lust himself – thank God – and could see it in others; for a second or two, he felt genuinely sorry for Sidney Close.

"What's it ter yew – copper?"

"I have a care for everyone in our small community, Shane."

"I don't need your care."

"I don't think I've ever heard anyone say that before," said Tony.

"Say what?" asked Martin.

"Copper. I thought it was a term which had gone out of general usage. Is that what comes from watching television all day, Sidney? Do you know – you chaps are probably more au fait with outdated terminology than anyone else in the village? I suppose you just pick it up, do you, when you're tuning the sets?"

Martin knew that his friend was deliberately taunting both men – although he was unsure why. He couldn't have realized the depth of Tony Crewes's anger when he thought of Shane and Sarah.

To Tony Crewes, it was simply a waste of niceness and decency and education that she should be saddled for life with such a piece of nothingness. He had said so to himself many times – ever since seeing her in church at her mother's funeral. He would not have admitted that he was fascinated by her, and the fascination was certainly not sexual as it was with Sidney. He had avoided Shane's eye since that first glance and addressed his comments to either Martin or Sidney. He knew this would annoy Marjoram even more and he wanted the younger man to hit him – not, perhaps, to actually land a punch, but the effort would have been appreciated. He could then, with some impunity, have driven his own fist into the drunken face; this would have given him immense pleasure.

"I think Mr Close had better get his apprentice home, don't you PC Billings – before our young friend topples over on his face?" he said, and then added as though by an afterthought, "You seem able to hold your drink a little better, Sidney."

Before Sidney or Shane could answer, or Martin interrupt, he continued:

"Is this a modern personnel technique, Sidney - 'Management' and 'Worker' drinking together – hmm? Team building, is it?"

Two things saved Tony Crewes from being beaten to a pulp by both Shane and Sidney at that moment – the fact that Martin was there and Sidney's upbringing which had taught him to abhor violence.

Shane found it difficult to order his emotional thoughts with anyone but Sarah; his instinct was to strike out, if he felt anyone was set on offending him. As Tony Crewes talked on, his mind framed the thought that this man disliked him intensely, and yet he could not begin to understand why; all he felt was that Crewes had the patronising air of a school teacher. He'd get his own back, but that would have to wait. In the meantime, he knew his anger was rising uncontrollably and he turned on Tony in the only way he knew how – by meeting abuse with abuse.

"I don't know what you're getting' at, mate, but Mr Close and me haven't bin drinkin' together. Anyone can see he hasn't touched a drop. Mr Close aint the drinkin' kind. He's respectable. He aint the sort to go round pouring buckets ov wa'er over people's heads, and that kind of thing. Yer need to mind your manners when you speak ter respectable people."

"Well, I must say I haven't had much faith in that kind of approach myself, Sidney," said Tony – deliberately ignoring Shane – "My firm sent us all to Dublin on a 'team building weekend' once, but we just drank too much Guinness, whereas your young friend here has an allegiance to you that one can only describe as admirable."

"Yer think yer clever don't yer?" said Shane – "all the big words and fancy talk but, when it comes down to it, yer no be'er than anyone else. Ov sin yew drunk. Yew got no cause to stick yer nose in the air at me."

"I can assure you ..."

"Yew don't have to assure' me of nothing – I don't need your assurance. Ov got my Sarah. Yew was down there on the beach that noight her dad got killed, weren't yer? Heh? What were yer doin' there? 'as your copper friend asked you?"

"Now, Shane ...," began Martin.

"Nar – never moind that. It aint 'Now Tony ....' when 'e gets going is it? You let him prat on an' say what he loikes, but the minit oi gets goin', it's 'Now, Shane ...' Don't oi hev the same rights of free speech as he does?"

"Come on, Shane. Let's get you home," said Sidney.

As he spoke, Shane's voice was rising in volume. Sidney could see that they would soon have a slanging match going on in the middle of the road.

"Nar – wiv all due respects, Mr Close, let me finish. Oi know Oi've bin drinkin' – but so have they, and just because this one has got the gift of the gab don't mean he should be allowed ter get away wiv it. Or right – so I don't speak like 'im, but Oi've still got the roight ter say my piece."

Shane was warming to his attack on Tony Crewes. He hadn't expected to silence the older man who now stood looking at him – or rather over him – in that snobbish way that teachers had when they gave you a dressing down. In Tony Crewes, at that moment, he saw every teacher who had ever hounded him.

"Well – what yew gotta say fer yerself then?"

"You seem able to say enough for both of us," said Tony, taken aback. He had been taunting the younger man – he accepted that, but perhaps Shane Marjoram had a point. After all, education wasn't there to be used as a battering ram, was it, and was his superior education all that separated him from this lout? Tony Crewes felt ashamed then – only momentarily, but long enough to cast his thoughts back.

"Don't tell me you're at a loss fer words, Mr Crewes."

"It just might be a good idea if you sobered up."

"Why – Om not that drunk – and yew know it. Some ov your writers did all their best work when they were pissed. Oi don't remember anyone tellin' them to 'sober up'. Oh no – it was drink up, Dylan, and write us anuvver poem."

Despite himself, Tony found that he was warming to Shane – anyone who could ridicule writers and drink must having something about them; he began to regret the bucket of water. He turned his attention to Sidney.

"You seem to be successful, Sidney."

"Successful?"

"As an employer – broadening the horizons of your workforce."

"He's being sarky again," rejoined Shane.

"No, no. I can count on the fingers of one hand the number of people I know who have raised Dylan Thomas as a topic of conversation with me in the last twenty years."

"Yeah, well we usually chat about him on the way to fix annuver telly – don't we, Mr Close?"

Martin Billings had never seen his friend so put down and laughed. He'd always found that laughter diffused situations – if you could get all parties laughing together. Catching his eye, Tony Crewes also burst into laughter. Ever since his copper' remark, he had been attempting to annoy both men. He was the first to admit they had out-manoeuvred him.

"What yew fuckin' laughing at?"

"The laughter is to cover their embarrassment," said Sidney.

"Over what?"

"People like Mr Crewes do not credit people like you and me with any kind of intelligence. They don't think it likely that we might actually read anything which they would consider worthwhile. So when you brought up Dylan Thomas, he was thrown. Isn't that right?"

He addressed his question to Tony who smiled and said:

"You might have hit the nail on the head – as they say."

"Nar – not might have done – have done. Goodnight PC Billings – take yer friend 'ome before he falls over."

As they moved off, Sidney was exultant. He, like Martin, had never seen Tony Crewes so dismissed before. All that spoiled it for him was that the initiative should have come – by accident – through the likes of Shane Marjoram.

"Shakespeare didn't drink."

They heard Tony Crewes's voice and the sound of his laughter. The thing about educated people was – they didn't mind being 'put down'.

"We had 'im, Mr Close?"

"Yes – we had him. Let's get you home – Sarah will have your tea on."

Sidney had seen Tony Crewes humiliated. Yet, he'd not seemed bothered and shrugged it off with that over-bearing nonchalance. He didn't like his assistant on a personal level, but he was a good worker and you had to admire the lad. What he had he'd earned honestly with the toil of his own hands whereas the likes of Crewes simply drifted in and out of university, and then found a cushy number somewhere – an easy billet that brought them lots of cash for doing next to nothing.

Shane paused by his gate, hoping Sarah wouldn't call him in. He felt good with himself and wanted to celebrate – if the tart at the Jolly Sailors would give him a pint. He'd been meaning to get the Crewes bloke for a long time, and tonight he'd come out ahead on points. One day, he'd find him alone and go for the knock-out.

"What got into you? Why on earth did you try and rile them?"

"They irritated me – although I must admit that I shall respect Shane Marjoram's 'rights to free speech' outburst for some time. He had a point, didn't he Martin? Do educated people use their word power to batter others?"

"You don't set out to rile people like Shane Marjoram."

"I bow to your superior experience."

"Never mind the sarcasm ..."

"I'm not being ..."

"Yes you are! It's a favourite ploy of yours. You say something outrageous, and then pretend you didn't mean it in the way it sounded."

"I didn't know you had an interest in linguistics, Martin."

"You're doing it now – that wasn't a straightforward comment anymore than your interest in Shane Marjoram's use of the word 'copper' was."

"Really?"

Martin laughed. He enjoyed Tony Crewes's company. The man was a frustrated wit who often simply said – out loud – what everyone else was thinking, but felt unable to say: long may he continue to do so.

Since her father's death two months before, Sarah Marjoram hadn't slept. She would lie awake beside Shane, praying that he would drop off into a deep sleep quickly so that she could steal downstairs and make herself a cup of tea, or creep outside for a walk. She had long since stopped leaving him notes – he never woke anyway, and Matthew was as safe asleep with her out of the house as he was with her unconscious in bed. The walk along her parents' funeral routes had become almost a nightly ritual. It wasn't far to the graveyard and she rarely met anyone; not since that first time had she come across Tony Crewes. Once or twice she had bumped into the new man who lived in the Old Vicarage – Mr Brultzner. He kept late hours – said he couldn't sleep and liked to walk in the quiet of the night. He had spoken softly to her; he had listened to her sorrow when he surprised her by the graveside.

Sometimes, usually during the day, she found herself crying uncontrollably. It was so unlike her, and Shane – had he popped in on his way to a job – would not have understood. She would sit in the garden and the tears would come, unbidden, and course down her cheeks. Sometimes it was worse than that and her body shook – setting tremors going in her left arm and right leg. Her breath came in fits and gasps and, when she could cry no more, her body collapsed onto the table or bed – wherever she was sitting or kneeling – and dropped into a ragged sleep. She would wake suddenly, not knowing what time it might be: it could be that hours had passed, or minutes. Once or twice Matthew had tugged her arm with an insistent "Mummy"; at other times, she would wake with a start and rush off to the playgroup, or hear Nadine knocking on the door.

She felt worthless. She had a sense that, in some obscure way, her parents' deaths had been her fault. It didn't seem right that they were gone, never to return. A child looks after their father and mother when they grow old, and Sarah felt that she had failed them. Her father that night had not come to the house, and she had done nothing. Was he being killed while she sat at home waiting? Her lovemaking with Shane had become one-sided: it was no longer a mutual pleasure.

Her walks with Nadine restored her for a while, but would leave her tired and weak – wanting only to seek the sleep which nature now denied her. The house was still as lovely as ever – still as neat and clean and tidy the way she liked it – but the housework which she had once loved was now a chore: an effort – a huge effort – to be made with no joy at the end. Cooking for Shane and herself fell into the same malaise; no longer would she pour through her mother's tattered cookbooks, but rather she reached out for the ingredients and did what she could from memory, and without love.

Perhaps what frightened Sarah most of all, however, were her mood swings. She had never suffered from these even during her teenage years. Her mother used to say, with pleasure, how Sarah had never given her a moment's sorrow: only once could she remember Sarah having "a little sulk". What the onset of her periods had failed to do, the death of her parents had now brought about. She even found herself becoming angry with Matthew. Suddenly, her "little love" had become demanding. After she lost her temper with him, Sarah felt so guilty that she would hug him until the little boy yelled for breath. She would then rush round the house grabbing at anything he might like to distract them both from what she had done.

Living had become an agony for her. The joy was gone and the road ahead, which a few months before had been filled with hope, now stretched endlessly into greyness. It had always been an effort, with Shane like he was, but one that was worthwhile. Now, it seemed to Sarah, she had lost everything – not just her parents but her little boy and her love for the future.

No one – except Nadine – noticed any of this; those qualities which had always attracted people to her appeared still to be there, but her inner fancies were now dark and menacing. Sarah was frightened by them.

It was in this state that Shane found her that night – after his confrontation with Tony Crewes and after further drinking to celebrate putting him down. He relayed this to Sarah, as she brought him the habitual cup of tea and knelt by his feet. As he talked – boastfully, expanding on his put down – Sarah sunk deeper into unhappiness. She had reached the point where she could no longer pull back, where the truth she and Nadine had avoided was slapping her round the face almost in ecstasy. Those thoughts left unsaid were now churned to the surface; the fears they raised had now to be faced. Gaps were opening in her world; her thoughts now free to terrorise her.

"How did you know that, Shane?"

Even her voice sounded unnatural as she asked her husband the question. He had just told her how he goaded Tony Crewes about being on the beach the night her dad was killed.

"Know what, Sare?"

"That Mr Crewes was on the beach the night dad was killed."

"You told me."

"No I didn't, Shane."

"I only said it 'cause he weren't questioned – his mate bein' Billings, the copper."

"That's not what I'm saying, Shane. How did you know he was there?"

"Fuck me, Sare – what yew mean?"

"You know what I mean. You always said you were drunk and sleeping it off up by the Beachlands. You never mentioned Mr Crewes or anyone else."

"Fucking hell, Sare – you told me."

"I never mentioned Mr Crewes to you."

"What yew saying'?"

"You know what I'm saying, Shane. I've always known, but I couldn't bring myself to admit it. To admit that would ... break my heart beyond all imagining."

"Fucking hell ..."

"Stop saying that, Shane. We don't have swearing in the house."

They sat in silence: he unable to find the words, she not wanting to utter them. Sarah got up and made them both a cup of tea. Afterwards, she never understood why she did that; at the time it seemed right. They sat sipping their drinks for what seemed like hours, and then Sarah said:

"It was the only thing which made any sense. We all knew that – everyone. dad had no enemies, no one who hated him – except you ... I suppose I kept hoping that the police would do it for me, but they can't, can they, Shane? There's no evidence, is there? Only I knew ... and Nadine ... and PC Billings – everyone, but we couldn't do anything or say anything, could we?"

"What are yew gonna do, Sare?"

"I don't know. What are you going to do?"

"What?"

"You've killed a man. You killed my father. What are you going to do?"

"Fu ... I don't know."

"Do you want me to think for you? Hmm? Do you want me to ... steer you through this?"

Her voice had risen, slightly – only slightly (tiredness was keeping her quiet at present), but it had an edge to it that Shane had never known. She wanted to just walk out of the house, to get away with her child and to walk forever until she dropped on some road and faded into oblivion. This was a feeling with Sarah, not framed as a thought or a wish. Something else in her wanted to go to the kitchen drawer, take out her steak knife and deal him a blow he would never forget. 'Lizzy Borden took an axe, gave her father forty whacks'. Her granny used to sing that when she was a little girl. Sarah had never understood what it meant, but it sounded funny.

"Perhaps you can start by telling me why?"

"Wha'?"

She realised as he said that how much his 'Wha'?' had irritated her over the years. Her voice racked up a notch in volume.

"Tell me why you did it!"

"He wound me up, Sare."

"Don't call me that!"

"Wha'?"

It was put on – the 'Wha'?' He used it when he didn't want to think of an answer, when he didn't want to have to explain.

"Don't call me 'Sare' – ever again. My name is Sarah – Sarah Brown."

"Mar ..."

"Brown – Sarah Brown."

Her maiden name gave her a sense of release – of freedom – that she found, notwithstanding the awful circumstances in which she had found it, exhilarating.

"My name is Sarah Brown. Now tell me why you killed my father."

"He wound me up. I met 'im when he was comin' back along the front. He was going the uver way round, 'e said – uverwise we wouldn't 'ave bumped into each uver. I was soberin' up. We took each uver by surprise. I arst him to lend me a fiver for a couple of pints so I could drink meself sober. Yew should hev heard wha' he said ...."

"What did he say?"

"He said I'd never be sober, said me muver must have fed me on beer from the bottle. 'e said I was a drunken lout from a family of drunken louts, and it would do us all a favour if I jest walked into the sea."

"So you hit him – hit my dad with a piece of driftwood."

"I couldn't stop meself. He riled me up ..."

"And you left him there – that poor old man, bleeding to death, in agony, alone on that beach?"

"I didn't mean to Sa ... I din't mean to ... kill him."

"No ... I'm going now ..."

"Yew what?"

Sarah heard the panic in his voice; the rising anger fired by his re-telling of her father's murder was now fuelled by panic. She'd always known he was dangerous, had prided herself on 'containing' his anger, of 'drawing it to her own purpose', but now she feared it – feared it for herself and for Matthew. Sarah knew that she must get out of her house, leave her home and go, as quickly as she could – without thinking too much about it, without hesitation, without giving him the chance or the excuse to stop her. If once, just once – however inadvertently – she roused his anger then there was no knowing what might happen.

"I just have to go ... Shane ..."

She uttered his name and almost choked. It wasn't a name she would ever use again, but it might soothe him now to hear it from her lips.

"... Shane ... You must see that ... that I need to get my head round this ..."

"The police! Yew goin' to the fu... p'lice?"

"No ... Something you've said is not evidence and, anyway ... a woman can't testify against her husband ...and I wouldn't want to ..."

"Where yew goin' then?"

"Out – just out. I need to walk."

She didn't dare suggest that she was taking Matthew as well; he had to believe that she was coming back. How was she to take the baby?

"How long?"

"I don't know – just out."

"Yew scared of me, Sa ... Sarah. Is that why yew want out?"

He moved closer to her, staring into her face – as though he'd know a lie if she told one, but Sarah looked him in the eyes as she had always done when he came in drunk and angry.

"No ... Shane... I'm not scared of you. I never have been. Maybe I'm the only one who hasn't, but I haven't. I've always known you wouldn't lay a finger on me."

He still watched her – like a fox stalking a rabbit, waiting for it to make a wrong move, to come too close to the bush behind which it lurked.

"I'd never hurt you, Sa ..."

He reached out for her then in the way he always did and Sarah knew, by the look in his eyes, the one sure way of leaving the house forever. The gorge rose in her throat, but she knew that when it was over he would sleep – soundly – and she could leave without molestation: once it was over.

She wanted to wash him out of her afterwards but there wasn't time. He lolled on his back as always after ... after what used to be love-making, and she rose quickly from the bed, rubbed herself on a nightdress, dressed and then packed a holdall. Sarah didn't know what she was doing or why; she didn't know what she was feeling. She did know that the activity was good – that it would keep her focussed.

In Matthew's room, she packed another holdall and gently lifted her son from his bed. If she could just get him to safety now then everything would be all right. Sarah dressed him while he slept, putting a light summer coat on over his pyjamas and some socks and trainers on his feet.

Then she went back into the bedroom; he was still asleep, deeper than ever. What did he imagine she would say in the morning? Unreal world that has such people in it; that was a quote – or two quotes in one; she remembered one of her teachers saying that at school and, at the time as a young adolescent, she had thought 'How true!' Now it was. Sarah took her purse and credit cards and left.

One of the holdalls she slung over her shoulder, the other she carried in her left hand, propping Matthew over her shoulder with her right. She couldn't go far like this, but then she didn't have to; a plan was already forming in her mind. The pushchair – the pushchair would be useful. The front door opened easily, and she was outside in the fresh, warm night air. She rested the bags on the step, leaning Matthew against them and went back inside. Everything she ever loved was in this house – and the memory of everything she ever loved. She just had to take one thing of her mothers – one thing. Something she could wear – the brooch, the silver brooch. She was suddenly tired – very tired, and wanted to push on. If she stayed now and looked for more, she would never leave, but simply curl up and die here.

Sarah closed the front door of her lovely cottage behind her for what she knew would be the last time and, with the holdalls resting on the buggy, walked quickly along the road to Nadine's house. Halfway, she turned back, realising that she couldn't possibly explain to Nadine; she would have to write it down – briefly – and her notepaper was in the house. It made no sense to her that she was returning, except the simple logic that she knew he wouldn't wake and she could write down what she had to say in peace – if Matthew stayed asleep.

Once more inside her home, she rested her son on the little settee in the front room and sat down with her notepaper; it only took her a few minutes to write down what had passed between her and ... him. Sarah took a quick look around the room – the low stool by the fireplace, the old fifties tiled surround, the arched rustic bricks, the wooden mantle-piece on which she had arranged her mother's old Napoleon clock, the brass hotel bell, her grandfather's cartridge cases, the photographs of her and him and Matthew and of all three, the niches within the fireplace she had persuaded him to build for the small copper kettle which belonged to her grandmother and her father's glue pot and the arrangement of fresh flowers that always filled the fireplace in summer – and then, taking the Napoleon clock and stuffing it into her holdall, she really did leave.

Nadine answered immediately and Sarah, without hesitation, placed Matthew in her arms, telling the startled journalist that she must look after him. She was feverish now, bent on some ill-defined purpose and needed to hurry. Nadine's protestations were of no avail. Before she knew what was happening, Matthew was asleep on her chest; his holdall was at her feet and his buggy on the doorstep. Her call - "Sarah" – did nothing to stop her friend who hurried back along Shore Lane.

Afterwards – for ever afterwards – Nadine wondered how differently things would have been if she had hurried after her friend that night. Her only comfort was that, at the time, Sarah had desperately needed to be alone and to heed her urgent cry – "Read the letter in the holdall" – seemed the right thing to do. There are times when we all need to be detached, and Nadine, knowing her friend, respected Sarah's wishes.

Sarah barely knew where she was now. The relief of knowing Matthew was safe poured through her, and freed her for the second time that night. The relief washed her mind of every thought except the need to move on. Dark trees and burnished lamps lit her way as she rushed headlong up the hill towards St George's Church. Clear, clear – now she could think, start to think afresh and begin to make some sense of what had happened. Nadine would understand; she would make those people who knew her understand. Somewhere, Nadine would always be there for her – understanding what she must do. The night was long and she had time, away from it all, to think – to bring her thoughts together, to come to terms, to learn to live with an unimaginable grief.

The churchyard welcomed her like an old friend, a well-known visitor. Here was safety for a while: from here she could be delivered. She had come here often since March – sometimes with Matthew, but usually on her own. Since her father's death, her visits had been frequent: to escape or to understand – Sarah couldn't decide. She hadn't accepted the idea that the man she loved, had loved devotedly, to whose child she had given birth, had really murdered her father. It might have been a drunken tramp or a drug addict on a high – much more likely this than the man she once called husband. What he had said, the way he had spoken the words, however, left her in no doubt. The man she called 'husband' had beaten her dear father to death, brutally. There had been no mercy on that night. Her father's neck had been so savagely beaten that the marks looked like those left by the teeth of a wolf. Alone he'd been with no one to love him, to hold him in their arms in his last moments of life, bleeding surely to death on the hard pebbles of the beach. 'Lizzie Borden took an axe, and gave her husband forty whacks'; then the circle would be complete. He would still be asleep, oblivious until he woke for his breakfast tomorrow morning. Tomorrow could be another normal day for him – going to work, having a drink, coming home to his family in the evening. She began to see sides of her husband – her ex-husband – which she had never acknowledged to herself; the world was OK provided things were going all right for him. How much love had she spent on him; how much love had she squandered?

Sarah's mind see-sawed. Nothing settled, nothing lifted her from the ground where she knelt by her parents grave. She read the inscription as she had done a score of times – 'All is well' and all would be well for all of them tomorrow; all she had to do was collect Matthew and go home. She felt unable to move. Her thoughts held her on the spot; to move was to decide. Fear invaded her again: fear of repercussions, fear of her own nature. She tried to move her right arm but it was frozen there, the index finger pointing at the inscription, like some spirit. Her head would not turn and she could not lift it further than to read the gravestone. Sarah began to rock backwards and forwards, and as she moved sobs racked her body, torn from her throat. The muscles of her jaw were cracking as her mouth was wrenched open, further and further, to allow the sobs room to escape. They were agonising sobs, tortured from her in the deep pit of her despair and helplessness. If only someone would come to her aid – someone to lift her up and cuddle her closely and take her home: else, she would be here always – forsaken.

She could not move her head, but knew the churchyard and its ways – the old tombstones like shadows against the light of the sea, marked by time and wind and tumbling into the earth, hedged by the long, rough coastal grass and brambles to the west. She was bent now, aching in her suffering. Twisted shapes of blackthorn trees rose up and leaned over, but did nothing to comfort Sarah. Surely, from the darkness someone would speak words of comfort? Was that the crunch of feet on gravel along the pathway of the churchyard? Was that her dad caught in the pale light of the lantern, stooped and straining. She wanted to cross herself but could not; her right arm was still fixed at that ridiculous angle, pointing to the gravestone. Quietly her mind intoned 'Since we believe that Jesus died and rose again, so will it be for those who have died: God will bring them to life with Jesus.' An uneasy silence crept in upon her; the warm, summer wind ruffled her, but against that comfort came the howling of wolves from the Wildlife Park. The lych-gate creaked but she could not turn her head to look; the street lamp cast its light darkly along the path. As a child she had run to her mother's arms but they were not waiting for her now in the darkness. Terror waited in the coffin; the figures of her mother and father retreated and were turned into shadows by the lamp as it shone through the arch of the gate. Sarah felt their sadness heavy upon her own, and then the voice spoke – "Sarah!" – and she knew he had come for her.

His hand had touched her shoulder as his voice soothed her mind, and Sarah found that she could move again; her gratitude was enormous. Slowly she rose to her feet and looked up into the yellow eyes, as sear as an autumn leaf, without lashes and reddened. Steadily they looked into her as she struggled to make sense of what was happening, to find the words to speak. He had held her before, safe in his arms. Sarah knew that as soon as she saw him, but could not think where or when they had come together. He led her from the churchyard, down the hill and into the grounds of the Old Vicarage.

She wanted to float, to drift away on the tide of the night and never be seen again. The old elms swayed for the young moon, peeping at her through their summer foliage and Sarah was happy, relieved of responsibility. They had passed in shadow along the road, none had seen them; they were alone in the dark. She was aware of him – the pale face tinged with greyness and the silver hair – running his silent fingers over her throat. She was aware of the lean old muscles in his gaunt neck. He seemed to be helping her to make her way up steps, stone and green, and then there was light and the opening of doors. Sarah felt herself lifted to him and his teeth on her neck and then there was that sweet, sharp pain and the slow sinking into sleep; peace swept over her. She was a long way now from the nightmares that haunted her; if only … if only she could drift into such unconsciousness herself, and lie there waiting for dusk.

When Sarah woke, she was in a room she had never seen before. The furniture here was light in style. There was a rush-seated chair and a black, occasional table with gilt decoration; there was also a larger table, beautifully decorated with a tall mirror hanging above it; the walls were light. She sat on an easy chair by the little table; at her side was a glass of red wine. Terror seized her again. She tried to force her mind back, but it remembered no further than the steps. This, she knew, was a dream – no, an hallucination. It was the kind of thing drugs did to you. She struggled to her feet and fell, knocking over the glass of wine and falling against the table. She had never known herself so weak. Her arms twitched, and her head jerked. She felt like a puppet being pulled this way and that by madness.

Outside somewhere was the night. Darkness and oblivion were all she wanted, and she crawled along the floor to the door. Brass and turning: she was in the hallway. Never had such a lassitude overcome her. Somewhere, out there in the night, was Matthew. Graves rose before her; her parents smiled – together again. If only she could find rest; rest in the coffin.

It was nice in the driveway. She knew she had to get clear of the house before blackness overwhelmed her. One last, one supreme effort and there was safety. Her home beckoned. Once she had loved there, fondling her child on the Pooh Bear rug with the sun dappling them, his tiny hands reaching up and pulling her hair gently. She smelt summer flowers – cranes-bill and honeysuckle. There was a yearning deep within her, and a terror that she had lost this forever. Sarah was so weak now that she found herself having to clutch the trees as she made her way to the road. Her neck throbbed; reaching up to stroke it, her hand warmed with fresh blood. One last ... one last ... effort; nothing worthwhile comes without effort. Her dad used to say that; where was he now? And then she knew – just for a while – where she was and who she was; unbearable memories flooded her mind. Ahead was the lane and shadow. Confused, disorientated and staggering with bewilderment she reached it and collapsed to her knees.

Calmness overcame her in the lane and she waited – expecting something to happen, but no one came. She thought about Nadine and Matthew, in the bungalow just along the road. They seemed a long way from her now – far away and out of reach. The weakness made her tired, so sleepy she wanted to close her eyes and dream forever. Somewhere beyond her was the sea, lapping peacefully on the shore. Sarah's eyes lifted. An image gelled in her mind, and she wondered what was coming that could give her comfort. She heard Corvin's voice "And just at the moment when someone at my side says, 'There, she is gone!' there are other eyes watching her coming, and other voices ready to take up the glad shout: 'Here she comes!'" And whose voice will cry for ... her ...'Mary' !

Sarah knew what she had to do now; amidst all the confusion, she understood. Getting to her feet she rushed up the little slope, crossed Ivy Lane and stumbled gratefully down the little track known as Sea Row Lane. She passed Coastguard Cottage: all were asleep – no lights anywhere. So she came at last to the steps and the beach; here her father had died and she was coming home. The pebbles crunched and rattled under her feet; she slipped and fell, but reached the edge of the water. It was cold. Even in summer, even after so hot a day, this east coast sea was cold, but Sarah didn't mind. Here was the salvation she sought.

There was fear, and she did turn back, crashed back towards the sea wall and huddled herself in the dunes. A terrible cry came from her lungs. She found herself, threshing backwards and forwards, helpless to stop the incessant twisting and turning of her body as her arms wrapped around her chest and her head beat the ground. The screaming seemed to clear her head, to calm her again. Suddenly, utterly exhausted, she was at one with herself.

The waves rose to meet her as she glided into them. There was lightness in her step despite the pull and tug of the sea, and suppleness in her shoulders when she leaned into the water. Her legs swung easily from the hips at first and then became one with the tide until she turned, resting on its pulsating surface, gave herself to its peace and drifted from the shore.

CHAPTER 7

The spider and the fly

Sarah was the first woman Horst Brultzner had taken on the streets since his arrival in Dunburgh, and he now regretted it, bitterly. His whole strategy – to preserve his peace in this village which held so many fond memories for him – had been to contain the situation, because once he was discovered he knew that, as the English say, 'the game was up'. He would become very vulnerable. He had visited many of them, but always in their homes where, after he had slaked his thirst, they could rest, recover, and become themselves again. He had always been careful never to drain any of them to anywhere near the point of death.

Sarah had been a particular delight to him: a young, fresh, healthy woman who had made him welcome and encouraged him to be playful with her son. Later, he had come to her at night, speaking soft words at her window, and she invited him in – unknowingly the first time, and then with a soft eagerness which always pleased him. Like the others, she was unaware of this, and her daily life continued as normal. It was an arrangement which suited everyone admirably.

Finding her in the churchyard, however, had seemed too good an opportunity to miss: a few steps down the road and they were in his driveway, and then the peace of his morning room. It was good to see her sitting there – in a room the Victorians designed for women – and when he had finished, Brultzner had left Sarah with a glass of red wine to sleep for a while before he took her home.

The village was in summer darkness, Church Hill was quiet and he foresaw no problems. Slipping into the house, he had checked that the husband was asleep and then found the key – expecting to return, walk Sarah home, put her to bed and then leave, unobtrusively. He had travelled carefully, of course – keeping to the side of the road, flitting rapidly from shadow to shadow in the way of vampires and he had enjoyed a brief look at Sarah's home which he remembered, from a previous visit in 1810, as a fisherman's cottage.

He had not expected her to wake and leave alone. He would not have known (nor, indeed, cared) when he found her at her parents' grave that Sarah was on the verge of a breakdown. Shock and anger turned his mood to violent resentment; he was not a creature who appreciated his plans being usurped. He stormed from his house and stood in the driveway. He had lingered too long before returning, and Sarah now seemed to have vanished without trace; but her smell was in the air and like the hungry wolf he was, Brultzner followed it to the lane where she had fallen. Here, where she had lain near death, it was strong; he paused only for a moment and then tore off along the lane as though on the trail of meat.

On the beach he found her holdall, abandoned where her father had met his death, and Brultzner loped to the shoreline where he paused. He must assume that she had entered the water; the tide would be carrying her out. He peered across the water, sure that he could see her bobbing in the moonlit hollows of the sea. Dawn approached on what was set to be a hot, bright summer's day, and Horst Brultzner knew he had to seek help. It would soon be sunrise; he had no choice but to wake Crafty Catchpole. Better that she should live than die with his mark upon her, or by her own hand in that state. He could not have her body found dead, washed up further along the shoreline; they would bury her and then his troubles really would begin.

Crafty Catchpole woke, with what can be mildly described as a 'start', to find Horst Brultzner standing by his bed. Brutzner had secured access to every possible house in the village in case he should ever need to do so; the ritual by which his kind could not enter unless invited was a serious inconvenience at times.

"You will excuse my intrusion, Mr Catchpole, but I have need of your services, and did not wish to wake your neighbours with my knocking."

"How ...?"

"Doors hold no mysteries for me. Come, get dressed – I need a boat."

"I can't see my way clear ..."

"It will be clear enough. Come."

He pulled the blanket and sheets back and lifted Crafty from his bed in a single movement. Crafty dressed without his usual circumspection – finishing with his father's dark-blue seaman's jacket, the peaked cloth cap with the piece of braid along the base of the peak and the Clint Eastwood cigar. Before Brultzner spoke again, they had left Coastguard Cottages, made their way down the lane and were running – breathlessly, towards the fishermen's boats moored further along the beach – with a pair of oars and rowlocks under Brultzner's arm.

"A young woman has thrown herself into the sea – I found her holdall on the beach. The tide is going out and we need to find her – we may already be too late."

"We can't roightly ..."

"Come – release the boat from the winch and push."

Crafty had never seen a boat moved such a distance without wheels before, nor so easily and never by two men. He marvelled at Brultzner's strength, as the boat scraped its last few yards into the sea and Brultzner leapt aboard, avoiding the water with an agility Crafty had only seen in gymnasts.

"Mr Catchpole – give me your hand!"

Crafty found himself yanked aboard the long-shore fishing boat, his feet also barely touching the water, and then Brultzner had fixed the rowlocks, turned the bow to the open sea and taken his position so that he could peer out over the waves.

"Row, Mr Catchpole, as you have never rowed before. The tide is with you."

Excitement was not a priority in Crafty's life; he preferred to bide his time and see his way clear, but even he felt a surge of the past burning through his muscles as he pulled at the oars and took the boat out onto the waters. The cigar had not moved from his mouth and he rolled it from side to side across his lips as he put old skills into the rowing. He grunted and sweated in the lure of the chase and the warmth of the early summer morning. Occasionally, Brultzner rapped out a command and he adjusted his pull to change direction; otherwise, he found himself immersed in the work as if he were a machine rather than a man. It was still dark, and they had a while before the sun would show them the way. In the meantime, Brultzner's eyes were their guide and – glancing, once in a while, over his right shoulder – Crafty could see that they had cleared the groynes and were well out on their way towards Lowestoft.

He knew that, for a time, while it was on the turn, the tide would be slack and the waves calm or at rest, but soon would begin to ebb; their best chance of finding the girl's body – Crafty did not think she would be alive – was during this period of slack water. He also knew that the beach shelved deeply not many yards from the shore and that the undertow could have pulled her down and thrown her in against the breakwaters. She could, as they hunted for her out on the open sea, actually be nearer the shore than their boat. The tidal currents here were strong and flowed alongside the beach; there was no telling where they might find the body – if they found it at all.

He told none of this to Brultzner who had not moved since the boat left the shore, and who stared fixedly into the darkness. The moon was weak and Crafty could see little – just the silver topped waves lapping against each other – but Brultzner's eyes seemed to pierce the veil of blackness. Their progress in finding anything, however, was painfully slow. The waves slapped and buckled back, lazily stroking each other; their very calmness seemed to taunt the search. Where they broke against the groynes, the spume was little more than a puff of cigar smoke. In one respect, Crafty was grateful – it made the job of rowing easier; in another, the tedium of the search allowed his adrenalin to fall and he began to feel tired. The slight breeze, still warm, was now off-shore and dried the sweat on his brow. A sense of calm overcame him, and the bobbing of the boat – drifting slowly out to sea – had an hypnotic effect.

During moments of rest, Crafty stole quick glances at Brultzner and saw that he was crouched in the bow of the boat, poised like a wild animal about to make its strike. He seemed not to have moved at all, but rather had become fixed to the hull of their craft, like some savage figurehead that was to hold the fate of the boat in its hands. When he moved at all it was only to bark out a command. He seemed to know such terms as 'port' and 'starboard' and referred to the boat as 'her', and he knew how to hold a boat steady by putting her bow into the run of the tide. But he was anxious and irritable, and kept glancing towards the horizon. Crafty put this down to his concern for the girl, knowing that the longer she was in the water the less chance they had of finding her alive.

"Swing her round, Mr Catchpole!"

The cry roused Crafty and he drove in deeply, but slowly, with his left oar. The boat shivered, there was a bump and Brultzner leaned out over the starboard side. He reached into the water. Crafty heard the hissed intake of breath.

"The feet, Mr Catchpole – take the feet!"

As he spoke, Brultzner leaned further over the side and brought all his strength to bear in lifting something heavy from the water. Without looking, and keeping his eyes closed tightly, Crafty gripped and lifted the legs of the body. It fell into the boat with a thud. Brultzner turned the body over and pumped away with its arms.

"The shore – row like Hell, Mr Catchpole – we may yet be in time."

The return was a harder row. Although it was still slack water, the pull of the tide from the shore was strong and Crafty's hands, unused to the oars, began to chafe and blister as he put his back into the work. All the while, Brultzner seemed to work on the body, but his voice never stopped chiding Crafty to make greater efforts and his eyes never ceased from roving the horizon for the first signs of the sun's rays. Eventually, apparently exasperated, he wrenched Crafty from his seat and took the oars. Crafty took the tiller but his eyes could not help straying to the body and, for the first time, he realised that the young woman was Sarah Marjoram. He wasn't given to a great deal of empathy, being largely absorbed in thoughts for his own welfare, but tears rose to his eyes as Crafty saw the young body slumped in the bottom of the boat. Her skirt and light summer coat were riled up above her knees, and her arms were twisted out to the side at unnatural angles like some rag doll thrown into the corner by a child. Her hair – always so beautiful with its honey-coloured flow to her shoulders – was matted and twisted like so much old rope found on the beach, beaten and bleached by the sea. Her head was pulled to one side and water trickled from the mouth. If she were alive, he thought, Sarah Marjoram must have risen from the dead.

"Keep your eye on the shore, Mr Catchpole. Guide me in. We have no time."

The boat had sped like the devil against the run of the tide and was now about to beach herself. Brultzner shipped the oars and leapt ashore, clearing the water with the same agility he had managed well over an hour before. He attached the winch cable, and he and Crafty Catchpole returned the boat to where it had been found.

Brultzner looked around him. The village was still quiet, even dead, in the weak moonlight and nothing stirred along the beach. He breathed what Crafty took to be a sigh of relief and then his eyes – those awful eyes that turned your mind over and dumped it back into place – turned upon his servant.

"Listen to me, Mr Catchpole. I am taking Sarah Marjoram to where she may stand some chance of recovery. You will say nothing. Do you understand me?"

Crafty nodded, but his eyes were dull and Brultzner knew he was not listening.

"You will say nothing to anyone, Mr Catchpole. Her life may, and your life certainly will, depend upon your silence. Do you understand me?"

Crafty's eyes were now meeting the vampires, but were dim with incomprehension, their natural furtive look cast aside by what he had seen in the boat. Suddenly, Brultzner slapped him so hard it felt as though his head was leaving his shoulders. Crafty had never been struck like that before in all his life, and then a second blow rocked his head from the other side; it had been delivered with the back of Brultzner's returning hand and the knuckles took the flesh from Crafty's cheeks.

"Do you understand me – your silence is your life."

"Moi silence is moi life."

"Come to me this evening – before sunset. I will have need of your services."

"Hev need of moi services."

"You understand?"

He did: not to have done so would have brought the hand across his face again and, more than anything, Crafty did not want the pain of that blow.

He watched Brultzner carrying the young woman's body up from the beach, and along the sea front towards Sea Row Lane. Crafty turned to pull the cover back over the boat. Apart from the watery stain in the bottom, there was no evidence that she had been there, or that they had ever pulled her from the clutches of the sea.

Although he had commanded men through many ages, he had done so with the haughtiness of an ancient aristocracy, and Brultzner's essence made it difficult for him to understand the subtleties of human nature. Just as he had, unknowingly, made an enemy of young David Stokes with his slaying of the white bull so he had made an enemy of Crafty Catchpole with the slaps around the face. A shake of the shoulders, an insistence upon his listening, even the use of menace would have steered Crafty along the road Brultzner intended, but the physical violence had angered him – a slow anger, perhaps, one that simmered rather than boiled, but an anger no less.

So, with the coming of dawn, Crafty made his way to Clara Gobley's bungalow on Church Hill. Their little arrangement had not, as yet, come to anything; but now he had much to tell and, possibly, something to learn, for Clara Gobley or her partner Bert may have been watching through their telescope the previous night. His knock on her door brought the hawk-like eyes to peer at him, and then the harsh voice which bade him enter.

"I have been expecting you, Mr Catchpole. Bert has the tea on – whatever we are drinking is your choice, I believe."

"Oim seein' moi way clear, Mrs Gobley."

"I'm sure you are, Mr Catchpole."

The crow had long since disappeared from the television set, having been returned by Clara and Bert to the wild, but its pile of excrement remained festering on the table. The other objects still cluttered the room, but Crafty barely noticed them now. He had grown used to the inevitable white rats, the lounging cats and the odd bird in a cage. He took the proffered seat, clambering through the usual arrangement of chairs, avoiding the saucers of milk and the assortment of legs. Clara listened, without interruption, to his rambling tale which he interjected with his own surmises and fearful wonderings. While he spoke, Bert – still dressed in the old short-sleeved pullover and cracked leather shoes – served tea and biscuits.

"Orange Pekoe, Mr Catchpole."

When Crafty had finished, Clara Gobley, watched by Bert, spoke.

"And why do you think he went to all that trouble, Mr Catchpole? Why not simply telephone the coastguard?"

"I don't roightly know, but what I do know is – she were dead when he took her from the sea."

"And he has her at the Old Vicarage now?"

"Oi can't think where else he ken hev taken her."

"No – and you would be right. We saw him arrive. Bert was up early, splinting the leg of a hedgehog, and took a look from our turret."

She looked at Bert who smiled. They had obviously been talking about Horst Brultzner at length ever since Crafty's proposal, and particularly since the incident of the grey wolf. They had, also, decided to take Crafty, partly, into their confidence.

"Bert and I have been meaning to talk to you, Mr Catchpole. Your employer is a most interesting man. Would it surprise you to learn that he has a pet bat which he regularly sends out over the village at night? It is a large bat, too – larger than any Bert has been able to find in his books.

"Where does it go?"

"A favourite place is the rectory. I wonder if our good rector is aware he has such a visitor?"

"But whoi?"

"That is what we hope you can find out for us, Mr Catchpole."

"Oi don't see ..."

"You will. Would it surprise you to know, also, that he keeps a wolf – the large, grey wolf I pursued around the village?"

"That's not possible – Oid know."

"Nonetheless it is true – the creature is often about at night, prowling the grounds. Bert and I have lost several cats, Mr Catchpole, and we are not at all amused. It is time that we did something – time we took you up on your proposal – but first we need to pool all our mutual knowledge. Knowledge, as you rightly said, is power."

Crafty sat for a while expecting Clara to continue, but she just stood watching him, over the bridge of her aquiline nose, with those piercing eyes.

"Well, Mr Catchpole – you do have more to tell us?"

"Do I?"

"What do you make of him entering your cottage as he did?"

"I can't say as how I was amoosed."

"You're sure he didn't have a key?"

"I never saw my way clear ter givin' him one. Whoi would I ...?"

Clara could see that questioning Crafty was going to be a long process so she turned to making statements and suggestions – something which better suited both their temperaments.

"You say he had been round before and that you had invited him in, but that he had no key and the door was definitely locked? Nod if you agree, Mr Catchpole!"

Crafty nodded.

"So he entered your locked house through closed doors and windows?"

Crafty nodded again.

"He moved a boat down one hundred yards of beach, and back, without the benefit of wheels – a task that usually takes six or seven men, with wheels?"

Again the nod.

"He finds the girl in the water – at night, without lights – using only his own eyes, and then lifts her into the boat with little assistance from you?"

Crafty gave his fourth nod.

"And he threatens to kill you if you tell anyone?"

And his fifth.

"An unusual man, don't you think, Mr Catchpole."

Clara ignored the sixth nod, and turned to Bert with a smile.

"Mr Catchpole," said Bert, "we need a closer look at Mr Brultzner's activities. I take it that certain internal doors are locked? But they are old Victorian tumblers, aren't they – easy enough to open?"

Crafty gave his seventh nod.

"We need access to the house, Mr Catchpole, and this is what I want you to do. Firstly, take a look at those locks and see if you can find the name of the maker. Secondly, take a look at his security system – PC Billings had one installed – and find the master switch. Thirdly, we have noticed that Lord Wangford's car sometimes calls for him – let us know when this next occurs. That will be our chance to look around."

Normally, Crafty would have been outraged by these suggestions. Refusing them would have put him in charge of the situation, making it clear that he – not the Gobley's – was master of the Old Vicarage. Despite his keenness to gain control over his pigeons, which is what had inspired him to consult Clara Gobley in the first place, he had been prepared to play the game slowly. The slap around his head had altered all that; he was now prepared to 'face off' the man he considered to be his opponent.

"I see moi way clear," he said, drank his Orange Pekoe and left.

Neither Clara nor Bert had spoken all day – at least not about the Old Vicarage and its strange inhabitant – but when they retired to bed that night, early, with their usual box of Turkish Delight, Clara said to him:

"Well ...?"

They had both considered Brultzner, deeply, and Crafty's information of the day had decided them to think the matter through to its conclusion.

"We have a vampire in the village, my dear – possibly two. I have been reluctant to come to this conclusion, but I am afraid there is no other."

"And he has been here since March – five months. A subtle vampire, Bert!"

"Very subtle, my dear, and I rather think an anxious vampire at this moment. It was not his intention that the young woman should join him."

"Share your thoughts, Bert. You know more about these things than I do."

Bert was a great fan of horror movies and had been an avid viewer of the BBCs double horror bill in the early eighties. When they had abandoned this policy, Clara – on Bert's behalf – had demanded to see the Director General and her interview with him, after a series of fascinatingly vituperative letters, was one he had never forgotten – despite his inurement over the years to unbridled verbal abuse – but the policy stayed firm.

"His ability to enter Mr Catchpole's cottage – despite all doors and windows being locked – finally decided me; that, and the strength needed to push the fishing boat down to the sea, and the fact that he can see in the dark. You and I have long wondered why he had a wolf and a bat or, indeed, whether he was the wolf and the bat. Certainly, the wolf was playing with you that night as only a human would have done. So – vampires would appear to be the order of the day."

Bert paused a moment and then said:

"Now, the young woman who Mr Catchpole is sure was brought dead from the water. Let us suppose that he has been drinking her blood for some time – drinking, but never to the point of death. So, each time she recovers, and never joins the ranks of the Un-dead, never becomes a vampire herself. Why? Well, a village of the Un-dead would bring him enormous problems if he wants a quiet life here. But tonight – for reasons we shall come to hear, no doubt – she drowns in the sea, while his mark is still upon her. If she was the victim of a vampire, to die in such a state would make her one, too – as surely as if she had died from loss of blood by his bite. So – unless he wants her found, and buried, Un-dead – he must rescue her from the sea and conceal her himself ..."

"Before you go on, Bert – explain the term, Un-dead."

"Vampires never die – they are immortal, but cursed with the need to live off human blood. Each night they rise from their graves and suck the blood of the living. The last thing Herr Brultzner would have wanted is this young woman wandering through the village each night hunting for a victim. Un-dead, my love, means just that – vampires never die, but neither are they alive in the sense that you and I are alive. Each dawn they must return to their coffin and sleep until sunset."

"But we have seen Horst Brultzner around during the day."

"Yes – and I do not understand that, but we will in time, no doubt."

"And their souls?"

"Their souls, my dear, are never free, but trapped for all eternity in what must be a kind of Purgatory."

"So what will he do now? The girl cannot simply disappear, Bert – even here."

"People disappear every day, my love. We wait and keep our knowledge to ourselves for a while – especially from Herr Brultzner. If he were to suspect that we knew about him, our own lives would be at great risk."

"More than that, Bert, so would our immortal souls."

Bert's wisdom had led him to more or less to the right conclusions regarding Horst Brultzner's concern for Sarah Marjoram. Once he had Sarah safely inside the Old Vicarage there was little he could do, but wait until night fell. She was dead as

Sarah Marjoram – killed by her own hand – but he knew she would live on as one of his kind. He also knew that she would be both terrified and exhilarated, as she entered this strange new world. His anger had subsided, and he had decided not to have her destroyed and buried. Other schemes pulsed quietly through his mind, as he watched the young woman while her extraordinary, unspoiled beauty returned. What troubled him were those things he could not know – why had she thrown herself in the sea, where was her child, when would her husband begin to look for her? These, he hoped, would become clear after they had spoken, and then he could take whatever measures were necessary to secure his peace and quiet.

She was dead, but had to be reborn as a vampire. He had removed her salt-sodden clothes and burned them. All day he had watched as her body cleansed itself of its human poisons and the skin took on that clear, ethereal tone. She would be more beautiful than ever, when once re-born – any slight blemishes on the skin would disappear, any signs of age fade from her; her eyes would brighten, her lips redden, her teeth become whiter than they had ever been, and she would be filled with that inner radiance which vampires never lose and human's have for so little time.

Afterwards, he washed, dried and powdered Sarah. He re-dressed her in clothes from the holdall; he combed and brushed her hair into its shining honey-coloured beauty, and then rested her on the Eastlake day-bed in the morning room.

He would oblige Catchpole to bring soil from the churchyard that night, undercover of darkness – a barrow-load or two would be enough – because she must have her native soil, consecrated, within her bed or coffin. For now, it must needs be a coffin or box such as he used; later – if the plan forming in his mind worked – a bed. He would find the coffin and line it for her with cloth from his homeland.

Above all things, he must calm her panic when she woke this evening for the first time as a vampire; he would help her accustom herself to the new world she had entered. Unsure of their powers at first, fresh female vampires hesitated to approach young men and, as often as not, would select children upon which to feed; this would be disastrous. They also had a desperate hunger which she would need to learn to control; failure to do that would create ever-increasing numbers of their own kind, and destroy his influence at the centre. For the time being, however, he was happy to wait; her beauty and her presence – if he could manipulate them satisfactorily – would enhance his life and his house.

Crafty Catchpole had been and gone – his instructions clear and the man sworn to silence. The vampire closed and locked his front door, and returned across the hallway to the morning room; he knew that, within the hour, Sarah would wake. He was tired himself – having stayed with her all day – and knew that a long night was ahead, but he was excited as he had not been for years.

When Sarah finally opened her eyes, the first thing she saw was Brultzner. She recognised his face immediately. Sarah knew that this was the one who had come to her at night, while her husband was sleeping; this was the one who had whispered sweet things into her ear, and then bared her throat and taken what he wanted. He was fearsome, but she was no longer afraid of him; the nightmares he had sometimes left her with did not return. She laughed: it was a cruel laugh, not the kind that had ever come from the mouth of Sarah Marjoram or Sarah Brown.

"Welcome to my house. Leave some of the happiness you bring."

Sarah showed no recognition of his quote. His heart skipped a beat of joy; here was an untutored mind – one he could, over centuries, introduce to the worlds of art and culture.

She laughed again as though unsure of the sound, and then stood and walked passed him to the window; she felt free in a way she had never done before. The burdens of her life had slipped from her; she felt the same sense of wonder and freedom as she had after sex with her husband. She felt in control, knowing she had tapped a source of power – had come into her own at last.

It was now dark outside, and she caught her reflection in the window. Her face, even in the dullness of the night, was radiant – like a bride on her wedding day. Sarah turned and looked back into the room. Brultzner had not moved from the chair he had placed by the day-bed, but sat watching her; he knew what was going through her mind. The colours in the room had not changed, but were cleaner. It was the same apparent change that one experienced at the poles when looking at the night sky, or on a mountaintop when grass, bushes and rocks came to life and took on a clarity they had never before possessed. Sarah thought she was seeing everything for the first time – the gilt binding on a book, the detail of the embossed tapestry in the fabric of the day-bed, the pattern of each motif on the wallpaper; even her clothes, which she had worn many times before, looked fresh and new. She was also aware, however, of a gnawing hunger in her stomach and the need to satisfy it.

"What has happened to me?" she asked, turning to Brultzner.

"What do you remember?"

She remembered everything, and Brultzner listened attentively as Sarah told her tale; the pieces of the puzzle fitted exactly and, like Crafty Catchpole, he now 'saw his way clear'. The vampire smiled to himself; less than twenty four hours ago, his world had seemed on the edge of ruin – now he could begin to pull it together. She had much to learn, but he had time and Sarah was exultant in her new world. He would introduce her to it gradually so as not to frighten her; step by step she would come to know what it was to be a vampire.

"You have left one world and been re-born in another," he said, "At first it will seem strange so do not rush to understand it, or fight against it. Be calm and all will become clear. Your child – the love of your life – is safe. For now, for a short time he must remain with your friend, but soon – when you are ready – he may join us here. You have become immortal – do not start ..."

He had seen the moment of panic in her eyes and rushed to calm her.

"You will see him grow and prosper – through all his life. Think of that, Sarah – for all of his life your child will have his Guardian Angel – you, always at his side."

Brultzner paused, while the momentousness of this dawned in Sarah's mind.

"... but first you have to learn of your new life, and we must begin tonight."

Her mind was completely calm – the timbre of his voice, the reassurance of his words had lifted the troubles from her shoulders; only, there was that gnawing in her stomach. He seemed to understand that, also.

"You are hungry?"

"Yes – and yet I do not want food."

"All creatures have to eat – your villagers spend much of their time doing just that – but for us it is different. Come!"

He drew Sarah to him and took her in his arms as a lover might have done – stroking her hair, paying her compliments and kissing her gently. He opened his shirt, slit his chest and brought her mouth to the run of blood. "Drink and be satisfied," he said. There was a few seconds revulsion, and then she brought her lips to his chest. It was like suckling her own child when he had been a baby – she drank the warm blood, as Matthew had sucked the warm milk from her breasts. Sarah felt it coursing through her, filling her and passing into her veins; she felt warm again and happy. He held her close and when she sank her teeth into his chest a sigh came from him.

The following morning, Peter Vishnya walked slowly up the driveway of the Old Vicarage; he had come to make his first report on their business dealings in Estonia. All was quiet. The once gloomy trees were expertly pruned, and the brambles and scraggy grass cleared. He came to the terrace; the stone urns on the buttresses bloomed with fuchsias. The terrace was neatly divided symmetrically by flower beds and surrounded by low, neat privet hedges in the Italian style.

Peter looked up at the house, impressed with its grandeur. He noticed, as Crafty had noticed, that the front door was ajar, and was reaching for the bell pull when the door opened.

"Mr Vishnya – welcome! I have been waiting for you," said Horst Brultzner, thinking, once again, how a parlour-maid would strike a more authentic note. As yet, his household did not stretch to such a luxury but, in a very short time, it would.

CHAPTER 8

Rebecca uses a long spoon

The only thing which had delayed Nadine Palmester taking Sarah's letter to Martin Billings was the thought that her friend might turn up before morning and recant the whole story. When she hadn't arrived by daybreak, Nadine walked round to Martin's house and then accompanied him to Shane's cottage. Martin's knock on the door woke Shane who eyed Martin suspiciously when asked if he knew Sarah's whereabouts.

"We've a letter, see, sonny," he said, "Your Sarah seems a little upset."

His usual vocabulary when under stress not being up to the occasion, Shane was at a loss for words. He stood, silent and sullen, on his doorstep – still in the dressing gown he had pulled on, hurriedly.

"Get yourself dressed – I'll wait."

When Shane went in, Martin turned to Nadine and said:

"Try to find her – phone anyone who she may have gone to. I'll phone HQ and we'll start a search – the beach and so on, just in case. Keep in touch – you have my number and the mobile phone is always on ... Don't worry about Marjoram. Keep your doors locked just in case, but I'll sort him out."

What happened inside the cottage remains the stuff of folklore. Needless to say, when Martin finally emerged with Shane, Matthew's quietude was guaranteed and Martin had a statement already in his possession.

"We shall have to visit HQ, sonny. They will need a little chat with you – just to set the record straight, you understand?"

Shane nodded.

By noon, it was known that Sarah had disappeared and that Nadine was, temporarily, looking after her son. Nadine's editor in Lowestoft had been most understanding and hoped, anyway, to obtain a first hand account of what might turn out to be the resolution of a murder. Nadine was distraught when none of her phone calls located Sarah.

"She could be anywhere, Naddy," said Simon, "The Lord will provide."

"She had no family, dad, and none of her friends have heard from her."

Nadine took Matthew for a walk late in the morning. Her father came with her and she felt safe with him. At the back of her mind was the notion that, if Matthew was out and about, Sarah might appear.

Martin's request for a formal search drew a blank at HQ – Superintendent Junket deemed it too early – and so Martin made a few phone calls. The first was to Harry

Bailey, of the Fishermen's Hut, who organised a thorough search of the whole beach from Pakefield to Blacksands Ness. The second was to Mark Chambers who halted work on his current site and joined Harry's group. The third was to Corvin Unwood who cancelled all church engagements, including a telephone conversation with Bishop Twiddle, and changed his cassock for trousers and gumboots before making a few calls of his own. A fourth call to Tony Crewes drew in most of the Inn Crowd and so – by early afternoon – the search had also moved inland and covered the marshes along the River Cassyn as far as Dunburgh Dam. A fifth call to Owen Culman, who contacted members of the Health Club, covered the village – every street, lane and piece of spare land. A sixth call to Lord Wangford extended the search across his lands, as far south as Coveacre and as far west as Sotterley.

All this time Sarah was on the day-bed in Horst Brultzner's morning room as the last vestiges of human life passed from her. Among the villagers, only Crafty Catchpole, Clara Gobley and Bert knew where she was, and they – for their own reasons, and in fear of their immortal souls – kept quiet.

Shane Marjoram was released late in the afternoon. An allegation by a missing wife doesn't constitute evidence and the signed statement handed over by Martin Billings, in an attempt to hold him for a further night at least, was seen as "inadmissible evidence obtained under duress". He returned to a village rife with speculation, rumour and enough gossip to bar him forever from its firesides. He went back to his cottage and locked the door.

Sarah had been his bulwark, and she was gone with his son, leaving him alone – and all because of what he hadn't meant to do. The old man had come on him that night. When he called out (yeah, all right, drunk!) the old man had tried to ignore him. No one, but no one, ignored Shane Marjoram, but he hadn't meant to hit him – not that hard, nor kill him, and now Sarah had fucked off too, and Nadine cunt-face had got his son.

He crouched in the cottage, but knew it was going to be too much for him. If only it wasn't summer, if only the fucking sun wasn't out all fucking night he could get out for a drink. Shane went into the kitchen and opened the door of the fridge; there was nothing there, nothing you could just eat, anyway. He'd never had to fend for himself – first his mum and then Sare … Sarah. He took a lump of cheese and some bread from the bin and made a rough sandwich with some chutney; this oozed from the sides and slopped onto the fucking floor. Shane ground it in with his toe; there were a few fucking faces he'd like to do that too. Too fucking right!

He went upstairs and into Matthew's bedroom and drove his foot into the side of the cot. He sat on the Lloyd Loom chair, throwing his wife's old-fashioned nightdress across the room. His eye caught the rocking chair. She used to cuddle the boy there, rocking him backwards and fucking forwards. Matthew's hands used to reach up and pull her hair. Fuck me! He stood up suddenly, went over and picked up the vase of flowers. They were buttercups – even he knew that – and Sarah had picked them only yesterday and put them in their son's room. He'd meant to throw them against the wall but replaced them; then, he sat in the chair and cried. Even as the tears ran from him, he wouldn't have admitted he was crying; it was more an outburst of rage against the world, which had always been against him. How quickly things can change – just in a fucking day.

The cottage shrank as he sat there. It crowded in on him and Shane knew he had to get out – people or no people. The street was more or less clear. It was early evening, and the men were home having their tea. The Jolly Sailors was only a few steps from his door and he entered quietly – not wanting to attract attention, only wanting a drink to settle him down. "Out!" She never looked at him, never took her eyes from the glass she was shining, and she never knew how close she came to having it ground into her face that evening. Shane's eyes flitted round the bar. The few men there fixed their eyes upon their cards and never looked up, never acknowledged that he stood in the doorway. He saw Plumptious Walters's hand move towards the phone, but he didn't feel like 'turning on the charm' and left.

Right across the fucking village now he'd have to go to the fucking King's fucking Head and the beer wasn't as good – nowhere fucking near! As he walked, Shane noticed that his side of the road cleared – even if it meant people crossing to walk in the road they avoided him. He stopped at Sidney Close's house and knocked. The door opened only slightly. "Take a few days off, Shane. I can manage. I hope they find Sarah soon." Then, the door closed. Soon he'd have no fucking money left. What the fuck was he to do then?

He paused at the corner of Shore Lane, remembering his meeting with Tony Crewes and Martin Billings. Nadine Palmester lived down there with her Bible-bashing dad – the git at the Bethel who thought he could tell everyone what to fucking do. Shane wondered about smashing her door in and just taking Matthew home – he'd be all right then – but he thought of Billings and what he'd said, and thought he'd better have a few drinks first.

Martin Billings, too, was thinking about what he had said and done that day – obtained a signed confession concerning an unsolved murder, organised a thorough search of the neighbourhood and received a disciplinary caution from his 'superior' officer. "The Book, Billings! You do it by the Book. That way nobody can point a finger. Follow the procedures and you're home and dry – nobody gets pilloried by the press, nobody loses their pension." "The day of the maverick is over, sir?" Martin had said it for him to save his chief the trouble, and then gone home.

He knew he wouldn't sleep that night – Nadine's safety had to be secured and drink might loosen his grip on Shane Marjoram. Martin knew he would have to be about to guarantee her welfare. Then there was Sarah – where the hell was she? Had she gone into the sea – would they find her washed up on the coast somewhere north of Lowestoft? He'd kept his patch so quiet – and now this: a murder and a missing person all in the space of a couple of months. Where would it all end?

It was two days after the search for Sarah that Rebecca Unwood paid a visit to Horst Brultzner. She wouldn't have admitted why to herself – but she had heard that Peter Vishnya was back in the village and had called at the Old Vicarage. She didn't expect to meet him there but would find out he had returned, and then it would be only natural to call round and say hello.

Horst Brultzner did not answer the door immediately, as was usual with him, but eventually she heard his footsteps on the stairs and the door opened.

"My dear, Miss Unwood – Rebecca – how pleasant to see you."

"May we not sit in the garden, Herr Brultzner – Horst? It is a lovely day."

"Alas – my skin."

"Of course – I'm sorry. I have a day off and thought I would just drop in for a moment. It is a while since we met – the day of your now famous luncheon, in fact."

Brultzner looked tired – as though he had gone several nights without sleep – and Rebecca said so when he took her into the morning room.

"The vicissitudes of the entrepreneur, my dear – your Mr Vishnya has been doing sterling work in his native Estonia."

"He has returned?"

Rebecca wasn't sure why she feigned the question, knowing Brultzner wouldn't have been impressed or remotely interested.

"Returned with a wealth of interests to discuss. He is 'My Man in Estonia', as they say, and he has been busy on my behalf – and, of course, his own. Artistic, cultural, industrial – our interests spread far and wide in his little country. We may have a plant to modernise – textiles, forestry or fishing! What would you choose, Rebecca? Do sardines have any attraction for you?"

She laughed and was pleased to do so; any contact with Horst Brultzner was a step nearer Peter Vishnya.

"I quite like sardines. On beaches in the Mediterranean, the fishermen barbecue them for you as you watch."

"Aah … the Mediterranean … Sardinia – my island."

"Your island?"

"I use the word in its …..eh generic sense. I once loved Sardinia, and was loved there – during the time of the Empire, you understand? And then, when that fell and we were all called back home, my little island was overrun by the scum of the earth – the Vandals, Byzantines, Saracens … the Spanish, the Austrians, the … all of them gone."

Rebecca thought his mind was wandering. Her father, who would remember nothing of yesterday, drifted back into the years immediately after the war.

"You have a wonderful sense of history, Horst."

"And all because of a sardine! Hah! I am capturing the English sense of humour, am I not?"

"Sometimes I think you are more English than the English."

"But only when I am here – in Germany I am more German than the Germans, in Switzerland more Swiss than the Swiss – although I do have difficulty in Spain! Ah – the Spanish temperament is too torrid for me."

"But you are at home in Italy?"

"Yes ... but it is many years now since I was at home."

He looked at her as though an idea had come to him, and there was a gap in the conversation. Rebecca's mother had taught her this was embarrassing, and so she said the first thing that came into her head.

"How long will Peter Vishnya be here?"

"A few days – he has some things to see to in London and then he is off again. You must see him, Rebecca. He is a changed man – no longer toddling round the village doing odd jobs. He has entered the world of business!"

Rebecca hoped that he would not be too changed; she was fond of the image she had of him – a thin and rather gangling figure in cricket whites. Not that she had ever seen him dressed like that; it was just an image – a picture of a mental state.

Brultzner, normally a man courteous to the point of embarrassment, was suddenly quiet. He seemed to be far away, the talk of Italy having distracted him. Rebecca felt that he wanted her to go, and yet she was drawn to stay. They'd had little contact, but he was compelling. She could have walked over, sat on his lap and put her arms round his neck. She could have drawn his head up to her, placed her lips on his and ... He was smiling, vaguely. Rebecca shook herself, and he noticed her again.

"Rebecca – please forgive me! You came – we sat talking – I was entranced as always, and I forgot my manners. Please – you will have a coffee?"

"No – I ...."

"You will – I insist. I should not forgive myself if you were to leave without having had a coffee. African will please you?"

She laughed, so pleased he had asked her to stay.

"Whatever you suggest – I really know nothing about coffee."

"I will fetch us the coffee ... I really could do with a servant, Rebecca."

Horst Brultzner returned with the Wedgwood cream-ware coffee pot and matching cups, saucers and jug on the papier mache tray.

"How lovely!"

"So your Mr Vishnya thought."

"You have heard of the trouble in the village, Horst?"

The question came out of the blue, and Rebecca was not sure why except that it was on her mind, whatever else she might be thinking or talking about. Brultzner smiled, but said nothing. Rebecca explained everything that had happened concerning Sarah Marjoram.

"Ah – Mrs Marjoram – Sarah – I think now she is Miss Brown again."

"What do you mean?"

"Is the young lady likely to want the name of the man who killed her father?"

"No – I suppose not."

"Do not worry yourself about Sarah, Rebecca. This has been her time of trial. She is resting ... I expect she is resting. She will return. She thinks of her child."

"You seem very sure."

"If I were a gambling man I would place a bet. Give her time. She ... has experienced many changes in her life. She will return to her roots. We all do."

"It will be a great relief to everyone just to know that she is still alive."

"Rest assured."

After Rebecca had gone, Horst Brultzner walked quietly back to his bedroom. He went in and locked the door behind him. He was not sure why – no one was likely to interrupt them. He just wanted to be alone with her – undisturbed.

Sarah was asleep in the coffin they had stolen for her from the village undertaker two nights before. Her beauty was breathtaking. Horst had lined the coffin with a golden silk from among his native cloth. The choice set off her honey-coloured hair to perfection. It spilled over the silk and surrounded her face which had, in death, grown more beautiful. The skin, which had been pale, now shone with a light tan as though filled with an inner radiance; it was flawless. The red lips, closed in sleep, covered the sharp, white teeth, but Sarah's mouth was gently curved as though, at any moment, the eyes might open and smile upon his gaze. He realised that any human looking at her would not believe that she was ... dead; this was the fatal attraction of the vampire in sleep – their lingering seductiveness. The dreaminess which had blessed her in life was now intensified.

His anger was replaced by a greater excitement than he had felt for decades. She promised, when he had broken her into the world of the vampire, to be a fascinating and worthy companion. Sarah would have no trouble feeding and remaining unknown, provided the insatiable hunger young vampires always felt was restrained.

She had made a good start under his tuition although he was now greatly fatigued – this was his third day without sleep. The vampire sleep is a ritual rather than a need, and his fatigue sprang from the remorseless need to stay awake, yet inactive. Boredom had always been his bete noire, but he dare not leave her in case, in these first few days, she should wake unexpectedly and wander. Once the pattern was established – once the ritual was hers – then he would close his eyes.

Their first two nights had passed successfully – she was an intelligent young woman and learned quickly. They had passed out into the night and he had taken her to the bedroom of the young hairdresser. He re-lived his own first excitement again in her delight, as she drifted with him to the window and tapped lightly upon the glass. The young girl had come willingly, eager for his touch, and he had laid her gently back on the bed and shown Sarah where she must bite so that the blood would flow easily and the wound would be neat. She had not questioned the need; few of any species willingly go hungry and she found the warm blood satisfying. He had explained that rarely did their quarry complain to anyone if they felt tired or weak the next day; rather, they would hide the little wound until it was healed. Sarah's only distaste, he noticed, had been in drinking from a woman; this she had felt unnatural and he knew that, before long, the desire would drive her to seek men.

He had walked her round the village, moving in the shadows. Sarah saw, for her first time, in the dark. She could scarcely believe that the night was as day to them – the veins on a leaf as clear, the running bubbles in a stream as bright, or the flowers she had always loved as beautiful. Her delight was child-like; the warmth of the summer's day was still in the ground and she danced, barefoot, along grassy verges. Down the back lanes she leapt roots and bushes, marvelling at her agility. Barn owls – formerly a flash of white in the dark – she now saw in all their tawny beauty. Bats – the village was home to the pipistrelle – circled clearly overhead, chasing moths across the sky. She ran under blossoms that rained upon her like confetti and savoured their delicacy. She lifted roses to her nose and drew in their scent. She caught insects as they jumped from her path.

Horst had rarely, if ever, seen a young vampire so in love with the world. He was enraptured by her – as she leapt gates without using her hands, stood tiptoe on fences, glided majestically to the clock on the church tower and tied a sprig of laurel around its minute hand.

She soon learned the knack of speed – one second walking with him, the next waiting by the newsagents. Once a group of teenagers, staggering home late from the Duke's Head, passed them in the street, but so fast were the vampires that Horst and Sarah remained as shadows – unnoticed. In was in this way, on her second night that Sarah took her second victim. The youth lingered too long behind his friends who called, laughed and moved on without him. By the time they returned, he was slouched against a hedge and they had to carry him home. Horst had been impressed with her – the speed with which she took her prey and the neatness with which she left him to be collected.

All she lacked he realised was the venom. Sarah, who he took to have been gentle in life, was also gentle as a vampire. She had taken the young woman softly, and laid the young man gently against the hedge where he would be found. It was not unknown, of course, for the personality of the human to pass over, but vampires were usually marked by a certain malignancy of purpose – an intensely selfish desire, in human terms, to have their will. She was young, of course – he kept reminding himself of that – and centuries were before her; she would change, she would coarsen as the nightly feedings took their toll. 'It's always the quiet ones' – the human aphorism passed through his head several times during those first days. He had come early one night to her window and watched as Sarah and her husband made love and she had been vigorous and eager – taking control, steering the action. He looked for that energy now in her new life, but had yet to find it. In some respects, Horst was glad – she needed to learn restraint: in others he was troubled. 'It's always the quiet ones.' Behind those placid eyelids there might lurk a purpose, and the ancient vampire worried that her revenge would be brutal and bloody.

He had tutored her on their return the second night – just enough to make her careful, just enough to teach her the limits of their powers.

"Our kind is immortal. We do not die … unless we wish to do so …"

He was unsure why he added that: no vampire had ever so wished. He was aware, perhaps, of her human longing for her parents.

"…. or are careless. Listen carefully to me, Sarah, and you will see your son grow up. We must have blood as humankind must have food, but we do not need to kill for it. We take as much as we need, but are always careful not to drain our prey to the point of death. If we do that, then they become as we are. A vampire might kill one human for every day of his life – and where would we be then? Overrun by vampires?"

He smiled at his own little joke, but Sarah ignored him, so intent was she on listening.

"We cast no shadows – we are shadows – and we have no reflection in a mirror. Aah – you do not favour that? Sometimes we may see ourselves reflected in the night – as they say, 'through a glass darkly' as you did. But, be wary of mirrors lest you give yourself away. We have tremendous strength – do not underrate it. Many killings have occurred because a vampire did not appreciate the power of their arm. Later, as you grow in skill, you will be able to transform yourself into other creatures – the wolf, the bat – but not yet; that is a pleasure to come. Mr Catchpole would have me transform myself into a racing pigeon – if he had his way!"

Brultzner laughed; he was enjoying himself – it was a long time since he had tutored another vampire.

"We can become mist, which shields us, or dust which transports us – there will be times when you may need to pass through the crack in a door, or the gap in a sash window. And, as you have already discovered, we can see in the dark. We can move quickly, as you have seen. So quickly, in fact, that we appear as shadows and are, to all intents and purposes, invisible.

But we are vulnerable, and there are limits to our powers. We cannot, for example, enter a house unless first invited – although this is not usually a problem because our powers of persuasion are seductive, as you saw with the young hairdresser last night. We cannot bear sunlight – it will destroy us – although, as you mature as a vampire, you will be able to venture out on shady days, as I do. We sleep at night and this must be in a ... vessel – coffin, box, bed ... whatever – which contains consecrated soil from our homeland. So, I brought mine over with me and Mr Catchpole obtained yours from your local churchyard. What you must remember, as your abilities develop, is that such powers cease between sunrise and sunset – so, should you be bounding round the village as a wolf when dawn breaks, a wolf you will remain for the day!"

He laughed again and Sarah enjoyed his enthusiasm.

"I am not joking – be sure to return to your ... vessel at night – I will have bedrooms created in the Victorian style when Mr Chambers and his men move to the first floor. Do not be caught out in daylight other than on your own terms – you will be at great risk. Running water we cannot pass except at the slack of the tide – it was a close call the other night."

Sarah smiled and then frowned; he noted both her reactions.

"You will know from your films that garlic poses a problem for us – although, to my mind, the smell of garlic poses a problem for everyone! It bars doors and windows – again for a time. The rowan has the same power – placed on our coffin it traps us there. For you – the cross will be a barrier, as will the holy wafer of your communion. Your beliefs and upbringing are such that you will yield before these things. Not so for me, of course – my faith is older. We can be destroyed – you will know this again from your films – the stake through the heart, the cutting off of the head, and stuffing the mouth with garlic …"

He paused, thoughtfully, and laughed to himself.

"… So we mix with the humankind but quietly, unobtrusively, going about our business as they go about theirs."

Sarah listened silently to all he said, only nodding to show her understanding if he glanced or paused. When he had finished, she said:

"You said that I might have my son to live with me."

"Yes, but be patient. He is safe with your friend at the moment."

"But he'll wonder where I am."

"Mummy is having a little holiday. She is tired. Children understand. Trust me Sarah – it will not be long."

"But how will I …"

"… look after him? How have I restored a Victorian house? There are ways – it just takes time to get used to your new world."

Rebecca Unwood sought Peter Vishnya out as soon as she left the Old Vicarage. His house, on the London Road, was still welcoming.

"Your move was so sudden," said Rebecca.

"There was nothing to make me stay. Herr Brultzner made his offer and you made your feelings clear."

His bluntness took her breath away, and Rebecca, unused to anyone but her mother speaking to her in such a manner, looked startled. Peter noticed this, but said nothing as he placed a plate of tuna-bean toasts in front of her.

"There was no …"

"There was every need. It's lunch-time and I'm hungry, and I could hardly eat while you sat and watched. Here …"

He poured her a glass of Entre-Deux-Mers, without asking whether she liked it or not.

"Between two seas," he said.

"Pardon?"

"Between two seas – the Dordogne and the Garonne. Rivers, really, I suppose but there you go – translation is an imprecise art. But the wine isn't – crisp, grassy, clean and fresh."

"What are …"

"The toasties? Yevgeny loves them – fresh french bread, thinly sliced, cannelloni beans, tuna, parsley from the garden roughly chopped, tomatoes on the vine bought today, red onion and a drizzle of olive oil."

"They're very nice …"

"… but messy - you're dropping the onion slices down your dress."

"Oh …"

"Get if off, and I'll soak it quickly in salt."

Before she quite knew what was happening, Rebecca was back on Peter's patio in his dressing gown, enjoying the lunch while her dress soaked.

"Things are going well for you in Estonia, I hear."

"I think so. Herr Brultzner is pleased ...."

"... and you are excited?"

"Yes – it is good to be doing something, at last."

"And Yevgeny?"

"He has settled into school and is learning fast."

"And Anton?"

"Anton is Anton – happy to be where Yevgeny and I are living."

"Well – that's nice. I'm pleased things are going well for you ... Peter. Mr Brultzner's 'Man in Estonia'."

"Better that than 'Nobody's Man in Dunburgh'."

"Yes – well I think I'd ..."

"... better be going? You can't – unless you are intending to walk home in my dressing gown. I gave you the messy onion to keep you here – enjoy your lunch."

She looked him up and down and knew that a 'normal' woman – whatever that might be – would take him in her arms and lead him to bed. She also knew that she wasn't 'normal' and neither was he; such a move would simply cheapen both of them in each other's eyes. Rebecca laughed. It was a joyful sound; she had never felt happy, in quite this way, in all her life. Something was settled between them at that moment although neither would have said what; they smiled at each other, and suddenly Estonia didn't seem so far away.

They talked all afternoon. He of Tallinn – the upper town on its steep hill topped by the citadel, the lower town with its medieval walls, its port and industries, its Academy of Sciences, its theatres, orchestras and operas, its churches ... It wasn't what he said but his enthusiasm which entranced Rebecca.

"What do you do? What interest can Horst Brultzner have in Tallinn?"

"He is an entrepreneur. I make contacts – we invest in failing industries or industries that need modernising. I translate, I hustle – I am of use to my country. I am invigorated, Rebecca. New life flows through me."

"Will you sell this house?"

"No – I think not. My wife's relatives would be hurt. They need to know that Yevgeny has a home here, too."

"And he is really doing well?"

"Oh yes – children are so resilient."

"And his new class mates – they are kind to him?"

"Yes – oh, yes. Anton meets him every day, if I am detained."

"The dog can tell the time?"

"Oh yes – and you? Tell me about my second home – Dunburgh."

Rebecca ran over all that had happened, ending with Sarah's disappearance.

"You say her husband has been freed?"

"There was insufficient evidence on which to charge him."

"Hmm – but everyone knows?"

"Yes."

"He is a danger in the village, Rebecca – a danger to Nadine, to his son, to anyone who stands in his way. And no one knows where Sarah has gone?"

"No – it's been three days now and no trace of her – the search was fruitless."

"The search found nothing and it was thorough – so the search was good. Sarah has been taken in somewhere otherwise you would have discovered the body."

"Unless the sea has her?"

"Yes – and the sea gives up its dead in its own time."

"There was one funny thing – one of the boats had been taken out."

"Go on."

"No one saw Sarah after she left Matthew with Nadine, and that was late. By the next morning she had disappeared and a boat had been out to sea and back again. It had been moved without wheels and that would take many men ..."

The conversation drifted off again then, as conversations do, and Peter Vishnya thought nothing of it until later that evening.

He walked her home at dusk, having washed, dried and ironed her dress. It was another beautiful twilight; well into August, the summer was as relentless as ever. The sun cut at them through the summer leaves, dazzling and warming. They took the long way round and the sweet smell of the harvest – early because of the fine weather – blew down from Podd's Field. They turned into the rough lane where they had held their previous conversation. Now, there were corn poppies with their bristly hairs and bright red petals, purple and yellow field pansies and the broad leaves of the bladder campion. Hedge sparrows shot across the path, narrowly missing their heads, flirting as though for a late nest. They came to the little bridge over the River Cassyn where Rebecca had said goodbye to him. He smiled and they continued down Marsh Lane.

Corvin and Esther were sitting outside their french windows, taking in the last of the sun. Corvin leapt up when he saw Peter:

"My dear boy, I heard you were back. How are things in Estonia?"

"Let him sit down first, Corvin," said Esther, "You'll have something to eat, Peter? You may as well. Rebecca's tea has been going cold for two hours."

"Yes – I'm sorry, mum. I should have phoned. Time slipped away."

Esther looked at her daughter and gave Corvin a quick glance, but said nothing.

"You look very prosperous, Peter – new clothes?"

"Yes – I can no longer slop around and ... I'm in a position to buy new clothes. You've yet to see me in my business suit – or suits. Appearance in the modern Europe is everything."

"You are enjoying yourself, my boy?"

"Oh yes, Corvin – the opportunities are immense. Translation is a real issue and I have carte blanche to use my skills wherever they are needed – provided I put Herr Brultzner's interests first."

"We thought he might require that!" said Esther.

"He does pay my salary, and I do live in an apartment purchased by him."

"Where does he get his money from, Peter?" asked Esther.

"Mum!"

"It's a reasonable question – and I'm curious."

"I don't know. All I do know is that he pays cash for everything – businesses, houses, museums …"

"He owns a museum?"

"In what used to be East Germany – yes. Not, as yet, in Estonia, but we are working on it."

Peter Vishnya laughed; everyone he had met was puzzled by Brultzner's wealth. There was always the assumption that if a man was wealthy he must have come across his fortune dishonestly, but Peter could find nothing of this in Brultzner's dealings. He did not, of course, 'own' museums, but he certainly supported several across Europe. In the quiet of his evenings, once familiar with Brultzner's business transactions, he had made some discreet phone calls. He was unknown in Estonia but well-thought-of elsewhere, especially in Germany, France, Spain and – above all – Italy. This much Peter had gleaned through conversation with his business associates. They all trusted him; little was ever written down – except when this was really necessary. All was done by the shake of a hand, and Peter had closed several discussions in that way. He felt that no one ever crossed Brultzner; his word was his bond, and those with whom he did business would be expected to honour their agreements. Like Esther, he had taken an instant dislike to the man but could find no reason for it – only his instincts. Esther placed more reliance on those and stuck to her point of view.

"I am at present negotiating the purchase of an island for him. There are many of them and he would like to buy one."

It was a pleasant evening and Peter stayed longer than he had intended.

"And you don't miss England, Peter?" said Esther.

"Oh yes – of course I do. I was happy here, but my future must lie in my own country. We have far to go."

"As long as you can be of use to Horst Brultzner?"

"As long as I can be of use to my country – there is much I can do."

"So you have no plans to return?"

"Mum!"

"I do not mind, Rebecca. Your mother's concern is flattering to me. It was not until I went that I realised what use I could be, Esther. It would be difficult now to turn my back on that."

"Of course," said Corvin.

"Well – we shall miss you. That's all I can say."

"And I, you. I have valued your friendship and your fellowship."

Corvin had listened to Peter and the women, saying little. He, more than anyone, valued Peter's friendship and would miss him. He remembered thinking how he trusted him, knowing his words would not be twisted. Peter's eyes were kind and his smile steady. His visits put their home in an easy mood and widened their family. Esther did not interrupt him at every opportunity, and Rebecca relaxed. Talking to Peter Vishnya made all things seem possible.

"Might we share a few words together," he said.

"Of course. I should be delighted."

Sitting outside, the darkness now around them, Corvin said:

"Lord, bless all our endeavours – at home and abroad, whether they be large or small, of great moment or of apparent unimportance. Guide us, Lord, to make those choices we must make in the Light of the teachings of your son, Jesus Christ, and grant that we may be filled with your Holy Spirit. Let us know, Lord, that your hand is always there to guide us wherever we may be, and let us know that whatever we do is of significance to you. Extend your hand over us, Lord, and give us shelter that we may always feel part of your caring community of love – in the name of the Father, the Son and the Holy Spirit."

"Amen … Thank you, Corvin. I shall treasure that prayer."

When he left – finally – Rebecca saw him to the gate and then insisted on walking him "at least to the church". It was a summer's night and he thanked her.

"Dad was very moved, tonight. I haven't seen him like that since his mother died. He values your friendship, Peter."

"And I, his."

"He's such a complex man – a hero and a coward. He has faith, he holds the right ideas, but he won't stand up for them against …"

"… against people?"

"Yes. If he thinks there's going to be conflict he'll wriggle around, back down – even change his mind and let people down. Look at him with the bishop – 'Yes sir, no sir; three bags full sir'."

"Your father doesn't like conflict – especially in-your-face verbal assaults, and he's too much of a Christian to tell those who deserve it to sling their hook."

Rebecca laughed with pleasure; it was good to find someone who supported her father without reservation. At the lych-gate they said goodnight, without a kiss but with enough shared understanding to fill both their hearts. It was just sad that now, of all times, Peter needed to go to London, and fly back to Estonia.

"One of the boats had been taken out? A fisherman told your father?" he interjected, suddenly,

"What? Yes."

"By the next morning Sarah had disappeared, and a boat had been out to sea and back again? It had been moved without wheels and would have taken many men?"

"Yes. What made you think of that?"

"It's been on my mind all evening. Why would anyone steal a boat?"

"To take something somewhere … to collect something?"

"Or to bring something back."

"I don't understand."

"No – nor do I, but I will."

As Rebecca made her way down Church Hill, two figures emerged from the dappled shadows of the church wall. Horst, in his 'briefing' had forgotten to mention how acute a vampire's hearing was – he and Sarah heard every word that passed between the lovers.

"He is an intelligent young man – this Peter Vishnya. It is as well that I have him working for me in Estonia – better there than here."

He enjoyed the rough humour, but it was lost on Sarah who wanted only to leave the graveyard where her parents were buried. She had, however, fed. A young man, working by floodlight in the harvest field, had taken a short break and was now propped against one of the cylindrical bales "sleeping it off", as the farmer who employed him said with feeling the next day. His blood had been good – fulfilling, satisfying – and Brultzner envied her the pleasure. He had not fed for three days and eyed Rebecca, covetously, as she walked home. Sarah saw his look and smiled.

"Take her. I know the rhythm of the night – you have taught me well. Enjoy her while I wander. I shall return before the cock crows thrice."

She laughed: it was a cruel laugh, uncharacteristic of her in life. She was unstable – the shock that led to her suicide had yet to be expunged and her mood swings continued beyond the grave.

"You feed no more, and keep to the shadows. Now watch."

He did it to impress her with his power, as a warning that she should not defy him. The mist grew from, and surrounded, him. It ducked and dived within itself, absorbing shape and form until he seemed like a guy on a bonfire, but with mist rather than smoke pouring from every orifice. When the elemental mist had buckled and consumed itself, the great bat flew upwards and forwards. It neither flitted nor circled, but passed through the darkness straight for the house of its prey.

Her sense of freedom was enormous, but she had no intention of disobeying his commands. She was young again – a teenager: irresponsible, devil-may-care, on the town. Sarah knew she could be seen, but was never in one place long enough for anyone to believe she was there; her speed of movement was awesome. It was late, but it was summertime and there were still groups of people about, sitting in the gardens under patio heaters or enjoying the night through the doors of their conservatories. She visited many – lurking in doorways, sliding through the gaps in fences, all the while testing her powers of coming and going. She stood on the edge of a group of youngsters and was almost unnoticed; "Who was that?" one of them had said and another "Wha' …. who? I dint see no one."

Emboldened, she ventured to Nadine's house. The lights were out and, when Sarah tried to slide in through the door jamb, she found that she was barred. Many times she had entered here, but had never been invited as a vampire. Her temper flared, her eyes blazed. She tossed her head in rage, running fingers through her hair like a teenage girl who cannot get her own way, and the beautiful lips drew back over the teeth in the snarl of a dog. It was over in seconds, but left her terrified. She already knew that vampires had a malign nature and that their moods were unpredictable, but feeling it in herself was, nonetheless, frightening. 'Lizzie Borden took an axe, and gave her husband forty whacks'. Human memories flooded back – 'Alone he'd been, with no one to love him, to hold him in their arms in his last moments of life, bleeding surely to death on the hard pebbles of the beach.'

She made her way to the beach, turning into the lane where she had stumbled, and reached the sea, lapping peacefully on the shore, in no time. There were still strollers on the sea wall – married couples arm in arm with young children, youngsters pushing and shoving each other. Sifting between them, unnoticed, she arrived at the Jolly Sailors. Plumptious was behind the bar – open late for the tourists, with the locals taking full advantage of the extended drinking time. Sarah knew that she couldn't go in – not at the moment: perhaps tomorrow or the next night? Sarah sat on one of the benches and watched people coming and going. A woman brought a little boy out, and dumped him in a push-chair.

"You wait there a minute," she said, and went back inside.

Laughter and shouting spilled through the doorway. The little boy was too old for the buggy and resented being there while his mum collected the other children. He wrestled himself out and ran over to Sarah who caught him before he fell. The mother came out with a second child and told her to stand by the push-chair. She saw Sarah with the little boy and said:

"Wha' – the little bleeder tried to git out did he? You stay wiv the nice lady. I won't be a minute."

Sarah cradled him in her arms, nuzzling his neck playfully. It was like bringing her own child to her when he had been a baby. She sucked the warm blood, as Matthew had sucked the warm milk from her breasts. Sarah felt it coursing through her, and passing into her veins; she felt warm and happy. It was a while before the mother came out with her husband and third child in tow. The little boy was asleep in the pushchair.

"Thank Gawd fer that," said his mother.

"The nice lady put him back," explained her daughter.

CHAPTER 9

Martin Billings at bay

Martin Billings, feeling peaceful as he poached two eggs for his and Amy's breakfast, was startled by the hammering on his front door. He had fixed a perfectly excellent Victorian pull which should have set the bell ringing in his office with a gentle tingling sound. He looked up, sighed, placed the lid back on the poacher to keep the eggs warm and went to answer it. Rollie stood there, his eyes starting from his head. He growled at Martin from under a pair of bushy black brows.

"You've gotta come. Necker says you've gotta come. Someone's dead."

"Who is this, Rollie? What are you talking about?"

"Necker says you've gotta come. It's her neighbour."

"Mrs Turrel?"

"Ye-es."

"Mrs Turrel's dead?"

"No – the boy."

Martin went to the phone, called Alan Read and asked if he would make his way to the Turrel's in Shore Lane; he called to Amy, and set off with Rollie in the car.

At the house, one of those that sat on the edge of the marsh, Necker Utting was in charge. This was something she enjoyed whatever the circumstances; put Necker in charge of just about any institution in the country, and it would be run more effectively. As it was, she had to content herself with living off the state, doing casual jobs and helping out with the Cub Scouts.

"He's upstairs – whoite as a sheet – nart a drarp a blood left in 'im – poor little beggar. Oi don't know what this villij is a-cumin to!"

As he entered the house, Martin felt a mixture of resentment and compassion – compassion for the family in these dire circumstances, resentment because he cared for his patch. In the last few months things had gone haywire, and Martin felt himself going down the same road. A murder, a young woman missing and possibly dead, a killer at large – released by his own force into the community – and now this: things could only get worse. He hoped Alan Read would not be long.

In the child's bedroom, his mother sat on the edge of the bed – her face a tortured image of bewilderment, disbelief and anguish. The death of loved ones is always painful, and that of a child particularly so; it is unnatural for children to pre-decease their parents. Martin touched her shoulder, gently, in what he felt was a futile gesture of compassion, and then looked at the little boy.

"I don't believe it, Constable Billings. He was right as rain last night."

"Why is he still in his clothes?"

"I didn't like to change him, poor little mite. He was that tired when we got back from the pub, I just put him to bed as he was and drew the duvet up round him."

The little boy was chalky white. In all his time in the force, Martin had never seen death like this – even road accident victims who had lost a lot of blood retained some semblance of colour, but this child was ashen. He touched the neck to check the pulse; it was a move that made him feel stupid, but it had to be done. As he expected, there was no pulse. He sat down to wait for Alan and keep Mrs Turrel company. He caught her eye; she was hoping that he would say the boy was all right, would wake up in a minute and run round the room.

"What can have happened, constable?"

"I don't know, Netty. Let's wait for Dr Read to get here."

Alan Read arrived more or less as he spoke. He smiled at Mrs Turrel and then examined the child carefully and slowly. As he did so, he asked her how her son had been, what he had eaten, had he shown any signs – anything that could help him to a diagnosis. When he had finished, Alan drew the cover up over the child and sat beside the mother.

"I'm sorry, Mrs Turrel – there is nothing I can do for him. Would you like me to make the arrangements?"

Mrs Turrel nodded. She was grateful; her mind had just stopped functioning. Alan paused and then went on, speaking slowly; this was something he didn't want to repeat or explain.

"There will have to be an autopsy. Do you understand? We need to know what happened to your little boy."

"Oh yeah ... I want to know that Dr Read. They won't ...?"

"No ... Before I go, is there anything I can do?"

"No thanks, doctor. This is no time for pills. You have to learn to face up to these things."

She was already coming out of her mindless state; the stoicism made Alan want to cry. He knew she wouldn't accept help – not even after the realisation of what had happened set in, not even after the shock had come.

"How about your husband – we can offer your family counselling."

He felt foolish saying it; generations had existed without it – generations more would do so. Mrs Turrel smiled; words would have been wasted.

Outside in the street, Alan Read turned to Martin Billings. His tone was completely at odds with the professional demeanour he had assumed in the house.

"You'll arrange the autopsy? I want to know what's going on, Martin. I have never seen anything like this. There wasn't a mark on the little lad's body, and yet I don't think he had one drop of blood left in him."

"No marks anywhere – not even on the neck?"

"Why do you ask about the neck?" asked Alan.

"There have been one or two instances recently where women have been listless – bloodless, if you like – and they have had this bite on their necks."

"Not a mark. There's no way the little lad could have lost any blood in the normal way and yet every vein I could find had collapsed. It makes no sense at all. It leads a rational man to irrational conclusions."

Martin stood looking at his local doctor, and recalled Tony Crewes's words, spoken in jest, during their conversation on the night Corvin had joined them. Necker Utting interrupted their thoughts.

"You warnt me ter see ter this, Darcter Read," said Necker.

"If you'll be kind enough to stay with Mrs Turrel for a while, that will be good. I'll call in at the undertakers myself."

"It's a rum un, int it?"

"As you say – a rum un."

"If yew ask me, there's somethun' weird goin' on."

"Such as?"

"That'd be sayin', woon't it?"

Knowledge is power to these people, thought Alan – but not if you share it.

"Has Mrs Turrel said anything to you that makes you think that?"

"That int fer me ter say."

"It is for you to say, if it throws any light on what has happened to that little boy," said Martin, sharply, "Withholding information is a serious offence."

"I int offending no one. Oim jest sayin' it's a rum un."

The autopsy revealed nothing with regard to the blood loss which was, as Alan Read had suspected, enormous. In addition, there were no internal or external injuries, and the samples he took revealed nothing. The only thing that puzzled the police surgeon who carried out the post mortem was the fact that the body showed none of the initial signs of decomposition. Rigor mortis should have set in five to ten hours after death but had not done so, and there were no signs of the usual discoloration that occurs on the underside of the body. Organs died at different rates – the brain cells after five minutes, the heart after fifteen and the kidneys after thirty; there were no indications that this was happening.

"But the child was dead?" asked Martin Billings.

"Technically, death occurs at several levels," replied Alan Read, "Somatic death is the death of the organism as a whole. It is indicated by the cessation of heartbeat, respiration, movement reflexes and brain activity … All these had occurred except one – there was an indication of brain activity."

"Then the child was alive?"

"Well, as you know, the concept of 'brain death' as the reliable indicator has gained favour in recent years. So, should we have restored respiration and cardiac functioning? Should we have been quicker to go for a transfusion? The child had been dead – in the somatic sense – for anything up to ten hours when we got there."

"But there was no irreversible loss of brain activity?"

"That is the case."

"Could we have restored him to life?"

"Could we have spared that family what they are now going through — and will continue to go through for the rest of their lives? I don't know. In recent years it has been well-established that a person can lose all capacity for the higher mental functions while the lower-brain functions such as respiration and circulation continue. It is now argued, by some authorities, that the only certain sign of death is the absence of activity in the higher centres of the brain — those which give us our capacity for consciousness and social interaction."

"Those things which make us human?"

"Yes."

Necker Utting enjoyed her work at the undertakers — laying out the corpses. It brought what she lacked in her everyday life — an intimate contact with the village. It also brought her gratitude and respect; it was a job which had to be done and which, nowadays, nobody wanted. She enjoyed it through the patronage of Old Strowger who, though he no longer took an active part in the business, had known her mother and had a soft spot for Necker. In the past, the job had been done in the home of the deceased and then the body was placed in the coffin, usually in the 'front room', for everyone — neighbours and family — to see and to pay their respects. That happened only rarely, now.

She looked at the little boy before her and wondered how he could be dead; more than that, she wondered if he was dead. The whole body, though unnaturally white, seemed alive and some colour was returning to the chest and legs. The coroner's men had done a neat job; there seemed hardly a mark on him despite all the cutting and poking about. There seemed no need to do anything but wash him down and dress him nicely, but she knew her business and the tools of her trade excited Necker — she found nothing distasteful in the removal of the blood and gases, the insertion of the fluids and the dusting with the preservative powders. When she had finished, the little Turrel boy looked lovely. Necker arranged him carefully in the coffin, ready for the men to carry him through into the little Chapel of Rest. It wasn't really a chapel, of course — just a small room where the family could be quiet and uncluttered with their thoughts.

She then checked that things in there were just so — the flowers and the little wooden cross; then she locked the mortuary door and went home for her tea.

Nadine was enjoying the Matthew's company and looking after him. Having a career was all very well — and she loved it — but this little boy took her into another world. Her father delighted in the child's company, cared for him most of the day and even put him to bed when Nadine was working late. It had shown his congregation another side of Simon Palmester. The fundamentalist preacher from the village Bethel now seemed more like everyone's grandfather

He had been particularly busy over the past few days with the untimely death of Luke Turrel. The Turrels were one of those families who moved their children round the churches — according to who was offering what and when; at present they were attending the Bethel, which had been handing out free books, and so

Simon was to take the funeral service. He and Nadine agreed to differ over the boy's death.

"It cannot be the will of the Lord, dad, that a little boy is dead."

"God moves in mysterious ways, Naddy ..."

"... and it's not for us to question his will – I know that! I also feel, in my heart, that such a death cannot be part of any 'grand plan'."

"I love you Naddy, but I sometimes wonder what I have taught you over the years. The Christian – our kind of Christian – has only to put their faith in the Lord. Have I not shown you, many times, the greatness of his power? You remember the crippled child we prayed for? The Lord straightened her legs! You remember that bitingly cold winter when old Mrs Strowger was short of coal? What did she find on her doorstep when her need was greatest? I cannot tell you – or Netty Turrel – why the Lord has taken her child. We may never know – not in this life – but He does. His hand – his mighty hand – is everywhere in this child's death and, when our solemnities are complete, He will welcome little Luke Turrel with open arms. He will hold him to his bosom and say "welcome – my true and faithful servant". When we send him to his Maker tomorrow, it is with joy and thankfulness."

Horst Brultzner struck Sarah such a blow across the face that she reeled backwards over her coffin and sent it crashing to the floor. The news of the child's death had reached him and her guilt had been written all over Sarah's face. His anger had known no bounds.

"I couldn't resist him. He was so warm and tender on my bosom. His blood was so fresh in my mouth ...," she screamed.

"They are always so – the tenderness of children is ever a temptation to our kind, but I told you – never drain them to the point of death, and you have disobeyed me. Our safety lies in our secrecy. Once we are known to the world – despite all our great powers, we are vulnerable. We lie, helpless, by day. It is then they will come, drive stakes through our hearts, cut off our heads, stuffed our mouths with garlic and burn us."

"I'm sorry."

"Your sorrow is meaningless! Its very expression is a human frailty. Your greed has exposed us."

"I don't understand."

"You have created a vampire. A human killed by a vampire becomes one. I have told you this!"

"The child?"

"Yes! Now, can you imagine what will happen once his funeral rites are complete? He will rise from his grave and seek blood. A child – wandering the village, not knowing what or who he is and needing to feed ... When I heard from Catchpole, I hoped – I almost prayed! – that he might be cremated. That would have solved our difficulty. But no – the mother does not want her son given to the flames."

"What are we …"

She never finished the sentence. The look that Brultzner cast upon her was so hellish it silenced her and she knew – knew the answer to her unspoken question.

"We could wait until he is buried but that would mean exhuming the coffin in the graveyard – your rector has given permission for the child to be buried there, in St George's. It would be dangerous. We must act before the funeral tomorrow."

He looked into Sarah's eyes, reading her thoughts.

"No – you will not drive home the stake, and neither will I. It is forbidden for vampires to destroy their own. Some have been forced to it but even I – even I – recoil from that desecration. But you will watch – you will know the meaning of what you have done and, thereby, you will learn."

His voice was quiet now; he had decided his course of action, and an unearthly silence surrounded him.

"We shall, once again, break into the undertakers and take Mr Catchpole with us. He is taciturn by nature. Now his life – his very soul – depends upon it."

It was late in the day, when Martin Billings stood by the freshly-dug grave. So small – a child's grave is so small. It's an obscenity that he was to be buried at all. Martin looked down into the hole: six feet under just like a grown-up. A movement distracted him. Somewhere beyond the graves a shadow had stirred beside the hedge that separated the graveyard from the farm.

"Can I help?" he said, quietly.

Martin had found that people responded to a quiet voice or an offer of help; even if they were up to something, it calmed them. Rollie emerged from the shadow of the wall grinning in his inane way. The youth's head – which hung forward, sullenly, like a dog that has been told off – shook from side to side and the eyes rolled. He appeared to be looking around him, but his gaze was fixed on Martin. It was a cunning movement that said 'I know something. I have the knowledge and the power.' It was the classic defence of the isolate, the one with no friends: knowledge was power, power was influence, and influence was people.

"You seen her?"

"Seen who, Rollie?"

"Her."

"Do you mean Necker?"

"Necker – her – what does she know?"

"What do you know?"

"I know," said Rollie, with his cunning look.

"Really?"

"I keep my eyes open. I don't miss much. I know what goes on."

"Perhaps we ought to have you in the police force."

"I know."

"I know you know, Rollie, but I'm not sure what you know."

"Ask her."

"I already have."

"Not her! Her!"

Again Martin felt the desire to strangle the youth, but remained ... tranquil.

"Which her is that?"

"His sister."

"Luke's sister?"

"Her."

Martin set off towards the lych-gate, but before he reached it Rollie was in front of him, barring his way.

"I know. I can tell you."

"Then bloody well do so."

It was a calculated profanity – calculated to shock and it did. Rollie's eyes popped and his mouth opened.

"She saw her – the bootiful lady."

"The what?"

"That's what she called her – the bootiful lady. She meant beautiful. She came to them at the Jolly Sailors and held Luke in her arms."

"When was this?"

"The night he was killed ... She came to him the night he died – the bootiful lady. Luke's sister told me."

"And who was this 'bootiful lady'?"

"It was her. Her what's missin'."

"Sarah Marjoram?"

"That's her – she's about."

"You must be mistaken, Rollie. Sarah is missing, but she's not been seen in the village. If she was here someone would know."

"What I'm tellin' you is right. She sucked his blood. You'll see – you'll see I was right."

"Good night, Rollie."

"You'll see. I seen her!"

Martin was already on the way home, laughing to himself. He'd been worried unnecessarily – they were all talk; neither Necker nor Rollie knew anything.

Crafty Catchpole woke to find Horst Brultzner by his bed for the second time.

"You will excuse my intrusion, Mr Catchpole, but I have need of your services and did not wish to wake your neighbours with my knocking."

"I can't see my way clear ...."

"It will be clear enough. Come."

Crafty had an awful sense of déjà vu as once again Brultzner pulled back the bedclothes and lifted him up in that single movement. This time, however, Brultzner took Crafty's head in his hands and made him look into his eyes.

"Listen to me, Mr Catchpole – very carefully."

He dare not look up – but he did, into those ancient eyes of the autumn leaf. The yellow irises gripped him, tightened into his mind and held him there, chilled, unwilling, but unable to resist. Crafty felt as though he were being dragged down into some pit of perdition, some awful place where his soul would rot forever, never to see his parents again. This terrible fear came to him unbidden and almost uncomprehended, but stained deep in his thoughts like a dark shadow.

"Tonight you will come with me, and do what I bid. Each thought, each action you will undertake without question – we have no time for questions, Crafty." It was the first time Brultzner had used his Christian name, and the effect was strangely soothing. "As each task is accomplished, the knowledge of it will pass from you."

"Oim seeing my way clear."

"Of course you are."

The hands eased their grip upon his cheeks and Crafty felt his head sink back into his shoulders; once more he saw the whole of the face – the lashless and reddened eyelids, the aquiline nose, the pale lips and the silver-grey hair.

Outside in the lane there was a woman and Crafty knew her as Sarah Marjoram, and wondered. Like Brultzner, she was dressed in black and they moved quickly, part of the shadows of the night, with Crafty between them. It was very dark, and the new moon only intensified this as they made their way passed the church. Eventually they were standing outside the undertakers. Crafty looked up at the name over the shop, which also served as the village hardware store – *Strowger's*; the name went back generations in the village. A narrow alleyway ran alongside the shop and Brultzner, without a glance into the street behind them, walked down this until they stood by the padlocked gate. Brultzner gave Sarah a nod, so brief as to be almost unnoticeable, and she took Crafty's arm. He flinched with the coldness of their touch as Brultzner took the other, and then found himself drifting upwards, onto the wall and then down into the yard.

Brultzner relaxed now – out of sight of the main street he clearly felt safer. Again he nodded to Sarah; there was a flurry of mist – a heavy, sullen mist which disappeared under the door of the chapel of rest – and Crafty found himself alone with the woman. She didn't look at him, but seemed transfixed by the door. He heard the turn of a key from within and the door opened. Brultzner ushered them in roughly and she pushed Crafty ahead of her; Brultzner then locked the door from inside. Afterwards, as his brain struggled to see clearly what had happened, Crafty recollected a key safe on the wall but that night his eyes were watching Brultzner too closely to be conscious of this.

The chapel was lit only by a small artificial candle in a niche to the side of the coffin, but this didn't seem to hinder Brultzner who approached it and placed what looked like a doctor's bag on the side chair. He took from this bag a screwdriver and began to unscrew the coffin lid – handing another screwdriver to Sarah and beckoning her to do the same. Her eyes opened in fear, her mouth curled back exposing the sharp white teeth and she hissed like a cornered cat. Anger flared across Brultzner's face for a moment and then, following her stare, he became aware of the little wooden cross at the head of the coffin. He smiled, picked it up and tossed it into the corner. Sarah shuddered, but moved to the left hand side of the coffin and worked urgently.

Crafty struggled to comprehend; that sense of perdition he had felt when Brultzner looked into his eyes increased. He wanted to pull back and run away. He wished he had never made his first journey up the path to the Old Vicarage, never peered through the front door into the hallway, never wanted his pigeons to cheat on their flight home – but it was too late for such qualms. The coffin lid was lifted off and placed against one of the walls. Brultzner gestured him forward and Crafty found himself, unresistingly, looking into the coffin. Brultzner reached into the bag and this time brought out a powerful torch which he hung over the side of the coffin.

The little Turrel boy lay there, several days into death, waiting for his funeral and looking as fresh as he had when running down the village street with his sister and brother. His face, if anything, was fresher and healthier than it had ever looked – just as though the boy was awakening into new life. Necker had done her work well; the child's hair had been lovingly brushed, but still flopped carelessly across his forehead as it had done in life. He had been dressed in his favourite clothes – trainers, jeans, a T-shirt with a spaceship blazoned across the front, and an open sweatshirt. The smile on his face lacked innocence, but Crafty did not notice that; he was captivated by the boy. When he looked up, Brultzner was watching him; he knew that Crafty was under the charm of the vampire and would have lingered there until the child woke on the morrow. Sarah's eyes, too, had never left the little face, which was so alluring in death. A few tears trickled gently down one of her cheeks.

When Brultzner's hand reached into the bag for the third time, the gazes of both Sarah and Crafty attended it. He took out a bunch of garlic flowers and then a long, sharp knife; both these things he placed near the coffin on the white altar cloth. Next he drew out a short stake, pointed at one end, and then a coal hammer which he handed to Crafty. Brultzner seemed disturbed now, but the determination in his face never wavered. He lifted the body, removed the sweatshirt completely and raised the child's T-shirt clear of his chest. He then placed the point of the stake over the boy's heart, took Crafty's left hand and brought it forward until it gripped the stake. Brultzner never spoke and Crafty was surprised that he knew what was expected of him. He saw the sharp end of the stake score the boy's flesh and then he raised the hammer and struck – struck with all the strength he had, struck as though one blow would do it and the whole horror would be gone.

Sarah could not take her eyes from the child's face as Crafty drove the stake into him. The mouth opened and she saw, for the first time, the sharp teeth; they gnashed and the body writhed as it tried to pull back from the blows. The boy's arms reached towards her in a gesture of supplication, as her own child's had so often done, and his eyes opened. There was fear in them – a terrible fear – and anger, as though he knew something was being denied him. He opened his mouth, earnestly asking the impossible and the neck muscles tightened. Crafty struck again and then a third time; a small cry came from the mouth – it sounded to Sarah like the cry of a child who had got its own way – and then he gasped and the mouth closed, the arms dropped and the body was still. She saw Brultzner looking at her and cast her eyes down.

Crafty stepped back, the hammer in his hand, but Brultzner drew him forward again and handed him the knife; the nightmare had to find its own conclusion. Brultzner nodded Sarah forward as Crafty drew the blade down into the throat and cut off the head. It took all his strength to sever the bone but at last the head lolled back and he stuffed the mouth with the bunch of garlic flowers Brultzner gave him.

Brultzner drew down the T-shirt and replaced the sweatshirt. He drew it up, tightly, round the boy's neck so that the shirt and the coffin lining held the severed head in place. When Sarah helped him replace the lid she looked at the Turrel boy for the last time in his coffin; there was a smile on his lips and this time there was no malice. As they prepared to leave the chapel, Brultzner looked at her and said, quietly:

"This child's downfall was due to your greed. Learn from tonight."

Outside it was still dark. It shrouded Crafty's mind and kept him from thinking though he still struggled to see things more clearly. Each time he tried to frame a thought, however, it flew from him into the night. Brultzner saw him to bed, leaving him to his dreams. Blackness cloaked the village and all was peaceful, waiting for the day of Luke Turrel's funeral to dawn.

CHAPTER 10

An angel at your side

Simon Palmester had long since come to terms with death – his own and that of others; his implacable faith in his Lord left no room for doubt – or sadness. Young Luke Turrel had gone to his maker; here was every reason for the family to rejoice. He had been in constant touch with the family since Luke's death, either personally or through another member of the church. The family had never been left alone to grieve. It was then, he had found, that feelings of alarm, anger and distress set in; it was then that the family had difficulty sleeping, lost their appetites and spent much time crying. Loneliness led to depression, depression to doubt, doubt to disbelief; it was against this that his flock had to be guarded. He was expecting his little Bethel to be packed, and was not going to let the opportunity to evangelise elude him; this would have been tantamount to a sin.

"Young Luke Turrel is to be envied today for he is wrapped in the arms of Jesus – an angel forever at his side. Brothers and sisters, I ask you to join me now in praising the Lord that he has seen fit to welcome his child back home. Be not sad, brothers and sisters! Who are we to feel sorrow for one so blessed? Lord, we thank you for taking Luke up into your tender, loving care! We who are left here in this vale of sorrow look up and say – Luke, in the smallness of our hearts we envy you! Yes, brothers and sisters – envy! For who would not, this day, rather be with young Luke, safe in Paradise, running through the green fields of Heaven with the other angels, in the land of milk and honey! Let us sing together – Tell out my soul, the greatness of the Lord!"

They all knew that one, and they all sang – those who shared Simon's faith, those who had no faith at all, those whose salvation lay along other paths, those who had come because they knew the boy, those who had come out of pity for his parents, those who had come simply to show solidarity. They all united in one voice with Simon's baritone booming from the pulpit. He had been right – the church was packed to overflowing and the doors were open and they spilled into the street and across the road and onto the grass verge where he had played, but their voices were as one when they sang. Crafty Catchpole was among the congregation, his memory of the previous night a blur but with sharp pangs stabbing through him. Corvin sang with the others, but his mind was elsewhere; he was lost in grief, which his compassion enabled him to share with the family. Nadine listened to her father and resented his composure, his almost smug certainties, but he was her father and his faith was sincere. She knew that, and if it was her in the coffin his joy would have remained the same. Alan Read sang beside his wife, Penny, and wondered about the higher centres of the brain – the neocortex. Martin had no taste for funerals and was re-directing traffic to avoid the overspill of mourners on the road. Necker Utting sat behind the family with Rollie, who spent the service muttering to himself, fearful of Simon and yet knowing that he knew, better than anyone else in the Bethel, what was going on.

Among the congregation was Lord Wangford who had a habit of appearing at key moments in the life of the village, but whose attendance at the funeral of a boy unknown to him was strange. Alan Read had telephoned asking to speak with him, and Charles Wangford was worried. The doctor, when pressed as to why, had said he was concerned about some matters possibly connected with Horst Brultzner and he understood that Wangford was a personal friend. The last thing his lordship wanted was speculation about Brultzner, and he determined to attend the funeral so that he might allay any fears in the village and kill any undesirable speculation.

He had arranged to see Alan Read after the funeral and they walked together to the doctor's house which was on School Lane. Penny Read had excused herself and left the men to walk alone. It was a glorious summer day, and Charles breathed in the warmth and the scents of the season. He loved the village in all its moods; he was glad to have been born here and could think of no better place to die when his time came.

Alan Read made them both a coffee and they sat in his conservatory. Both doors were open and a soft breeze drifted by them. Alan was the first to speak as they sipped their coffee and munched quietly on the chocolate marzipan cookies which Penny had left ready in the little "coffee tin" – as she called it. Alan had a sweet tooth.

"Charles – how well do you now Horst Brultzner?"

Directness is all very admirable in a doctor at times, but this was not one of those times and Charles Wangford – despite rather expecting the question and having prepared himself for it – stiffened.

"Why do you ask, Alan?"

"To be absolutely honest, I'm not sure. Let's just call it the 'elimination of possibilities'. I'd like you to listen carefully to what I have to say, Charles, and grant me the benefit of not calling the local mental hospital."

Alan Read then outlined his observations, while Charles Wangford listened without saying a word. Now under control, the expression on his face and in his eyes did not falter. When Alan had finished he asked:

"What has all this got to do with Horst Brultzner?"

"Perhaps nothing, but the condition began soon after he arrived in the village."

"You've eliminated all other changes occurring around that time?"

"No, Charles. I have simply collated dates and, since a rational explanation is beyond me, I am drawn to irrational possibilities."

"Horst Brultzner is a most respectable businessman, Alan. He is not in the business of blood-letting."

"What do you know of him?"

"I really cannot share that confidence with you, Alan."

"But your links with him are more than business ones, are they not?"

"What do you mean?"

"As I understand it, Charles, you have been very instrumental in arranging matters for him – his coming to this country, his residence here, his house ..."

"My family owed him a debt – although why I should tell you this is rather beyond me, Alan – and assisting him is my way of showing gratitude ..."

The asperity in his voice did not escape Alan, and Charles Wangford knew this; he decided to bring matters to a close.

"... I really do not see what this has got to do with your medical problem!"

"What do you know of his personal life?"

"You are persistent, Alan – if I may say so, quite discourteously so!"

"Then I apologise. I am groping in the dark. I simply supposed that you had a personal connection with Herr Brultzner, and might be able to put my mind at rest."

"You may put your mind at rest, Dr Read. Further – let me advise you that Horst Brultzner is not the kind of man who would tolerate any enquiries into his private life. He is of an old European family. Such people do not take lightly to your sort of enquiries. Be warned, by a friend, you would do well to stay in the light on this one. You must excuse me now. Please thank Penny for the cookies."

Charles Wangford made straight for the Old Vicarage. Charles was frightened and he was ashamed, but his oaths bound him and that was all there was to it. By the time he reached the door, he had made his various decisions – ones that would remove the heat from the situation and allow matters to return to normal. The bell rang deep within the hall and within seconds a young woman dressed as a parlour maid opened the door.

"Good morning, my Lord. Mr Brulztner is waiting for you in the study."

Charles Wangford knew immediately who she was and, as he stepped passed her into the hallway, the events of the previous few days unfolded in his mind. The nature of her disappearance and the death of the child – neither of which, until that moment, he had attributed to Brultzner – now became clear to him. Sarah ushered him into the study and left him with Brultzner, who rose from his desk, smiling broadly.

"My dear Charles, to what do we owe the pleasure of your company?"

"I am not sure that 'pleasure' is quite the word I would have chosen."

"My dear fellow, what possible cloud could there be on such a day as this?"

"The cloud of a young child's death?"

"Ah – I might have known that you would make that connection. The English aristocracy is not known for its intelligence but – as always, Charles – you are an exception to the rule ... the matter is, shall we say, expedited ..."

He walked to the mantelpiece and leaned his elbow upon it before continuing.

"I have taken Miss Brown – she wishes to return to her maiden name – under my wing. That way we can be sure nothing ... untoward will happen."

"You would not consider the child's death ... untoward?"

"That was unfortunate, but it will not occur again and we have ... dealt with it. There will be no repercussions."

"There already have been."

Charles Wangford outlined Alan Read's concerns.

"You must leave the village – at least until things settle down."

"Must?"

"Must – you have no choice. It is the only course of action which will, in the long run, enable you to return here with impunity."

Brultzner did not enjoy being told what to do, but his brain was quick and he respected Wangford's judgement. He also knew that the aristocrat was bound to him by loyalties almost beyond blood itself. He trusted that any decisions to which Wangford came would be in his own – Brultzner's – best interests.

"I appreciate your concerns, Wangford. I shall give them some thought."

"There is no immediate hurry. Dr Read does not pose an instant threat – he scarcely believes his own conclusions – but there must be no more instances which will compound his fears. Do you understand?"

"Oh yes, my dear Charles. Indeed this very evening we are to take steps which will – shall we say – curb any likelihood of Miss Brown straying further."

When Nadine Palmester opened her door and saw Sarah standing on the step she was bewildered beyond any imaginings.

"I'm sorry, Nadine – I should have rung first," said her friend, laughing.

"Sarah?"

"Yes it is me."

"We didn't know – we had no idea where you were."

"I couldn't get in touch," said Sarah, "... may I come in?"

"What – oh yes, of course. You don't have to ask – please. I'll make you a cup of tea. You must tell me everything that has happened."

"Is Matthew all right?"

"Of course. He's asleep. I'll take you up to him."

Sarah stepped across the threshold and stood in the narrow hallway of the bungalow. A short flight of stairs took her to Matthew and for the first time in so many days she looked upon her son; the love she had always felt was still within her, and Sarah heaved a sigh of relief. She watched him while Nadine made the tea and then went quietly downstairs. The two women, who had always been so close, stood looking at each other.

"Let me give you a hug," said Nadine.

"I've not been well – you may find me a little chilled."

Nadine shivered as she pulled Sarah close. Her friend felt like ice and, try as she did to prevent it, Nadine recoiled – however slightly.

"Are you not well – what is it? Sit down. Tell me."

"Let me start on that night – the night I disappeared. I wandered forever – or so it seemed – and found myself in Beccles. I didn't know what to do, but eventually I plucked up courage and knocked on the door of an old friend of mum's. She let me stay there."

"Why didn't you ring?"

"I couldn't – not after what had happened. I didn't want to talk. I just stayed in my room until the shock had worn off a bit. I came back a few days ago and bumped into Mr Brultzner. He was very kind and offered me a job – he wants what he calls a parlour maid. He said I could stay there and have Matthew with me. It'll be difficult for a while but I can get someone to take him backwards and forwards. Some days I'll be able to take him myself."

Listening to herself, Sarah was amazed how easily the lies mixed in with the truth. She and Brultzner had rehearsed the deception, and now it trotted glibly from her tongue. In her human form she would have felt ashamed, but her conscience was barely tinged with that feeling now.

"Mr Brultzner is going to have one of the rooms turned into a bedroom for Matthew but, in the meantime, he says he can sleep in the morning room."

"Do you want me to arrange to get some of your old furniture from ..."

"No. I know Shane is free again and you don't want to go near him, Nadine. Besides, Mr Brultzner wants Matthew's furniture and mine to be in keeping with the rest of the house. Eventually, I will have a room of my own."

When she went, having broken the ice with Nadine, Sarah left Matthew sleeping. It was arranged that Nadine should bring him across to the Old Vicarage in the morning rather than startle the little boy awake. She kissed him lightly on the forehead before she left and then gave Nadine a brief hug and kiss on the cheek when her old friend saw her out. As she reached the gate, Simon Palmester arrived home.

"Sarah, it's good to see you!"

He took her hand and shook it firmly.

"I'll explain, dad," called Nadine from the doorway, "Sarah doesn't want to go through it all again."

"It's good to see you back, Sarah. Welcome home."

Some days later, Rebecca Unwood sat at her dressing table writing her daily e-mail to Peter Vishnya. She still could not quite understand what had happened between them, but she felt happier now than she had for many years.

"... Dad and I went to visit Mrs Turrel this afternoon and she seems to be taking it very well. These Suffolk women are so stoical – perhaps it helps them to get through life. I walked up Marsh Lane with her afterwards and we picked some wild flowers – corn poppies and field pansies – which we put on the little grave. They have placed the stone already. Mrs Turrel wanted it done quickly. Dad just said yes, although it's usual to wait. It has a lovely inscription, 'Dear Luke, may you always have an angel at your side'. Isn't that beautiful? I sometimes think that a simple faith is best. We ask too many questions these days. Mum has always said that. Do you believe in angels, Peter? I think I do, but they're strange beings, aren't they? It comes from the Greek – but I expect you know that. The word is 'aggelos' which means messenger and that's how we think of them, but they are also guardians. I think every child should have one!

Oh yes - the biggest surprise of all is that Sarah Marjoram is back and working for your employer at the Old Vicarage! Can you believe that? He said he wanted a parlour maid, and we all thought he was joking. Maybe it's just to help Sarah out for a while, but Nadine said that she is quite happy there. If only they could prove that husband of hers is guilty. The whole village is shunning him, you know, and it doesn't seem right somehow. It certainly isn't Christian! After all he hasn't been found guilty of anything! Dad talked about going round to see him, but Shane is such a foul person. Mum was dead against that, of course, and eventually dad caved in. I must say I am relieved – although I shouldn't be! I think he's lost his job, too. There's talk that Sidney Close isn't going to have him back.

Oh dear, I have just read over what I have written so far and it's all funerals and gloom. I'm sorry. How are Yevgeny and Anton? I do miss you, Peter. It will be so nice when you come back again for a break. Perhaps next time, you can bring them with you? I'm sure your little boy will love to see the village again. Do you remember that afternoon – how we sat talking, me in your dressing gown, and I think I drank more wine then than I've ever done before. I laugh to myself now, just thinking about it. And I remember you walking me home and how we sat, and dad prayed.

I stopped by the little bridge when I was out for a walk this afternoon, and it was nice just being quiet and thinking about you. Thank you for saying what you did in your last letter. I needed to read in words what was accepted between us that afternoon and evening. I shall treasure that letter always ... "

Alan Read also sat writing – or, at least, leaning – on his laptop, but there was no joy at all in what was doing. He had been surfing the net for information about vampires, and feeling increasingly silly as he did so. It was interesting enough in its own way – the 'Un-dead' rising from the grave to suck the blood of the living at night. Well – everyone had to eat. According to the statistics, the country threw half the food it bought each year into the rubbish bin. Perhaps vampires were less wasteful?

Yes – he could accept their origins –'nosophoros' the plague carrier becomes 'nosufuratu' the vampire. Disease and blood had always been linked in the minds of humanity – and with good reason. Stories of such creatures pervaded folklore, were carried across continents by travellers and then turned into stories to keep the children quiet at night. Suicides, people born under a curse, witches (and even a dead body over which a cat had jumped) becoming 'infected' he could understand. But pumpkins left out in the sun too long, door latches left unlatched and watermelons as vampires? And the ability to turn themselves into mist, bats or wolves and the capacity to fly? The methods of destruction he had picked up from films, except the one where you stole the vampire's left sock, filled it with stones and threw it in the river; somehow he couldn't see Peter Cushing doing that – not without a smile.

Alan had hoped to find something about vampirism as a perversion because, undoubtably, there would be people who would turn it into a cult – people who needed to convince themselves that they had special powers that placed them above others, or outside the constraints of common law. He could find nothing. There were a few 'vampire dating agencies' but nothing else. He closed his laptop and pushed his notes into the bottom drawer of his desk – the place he reserved for anything he would probably never look at again and, eventually, destroy as rubbish.

Perhaps he was barking up the wrong tree – groping in the dark. Perhaps there was a simple, medical reason for what had happened to Luke Turrel and almost happened to the women.

He went upstairs and looked at Penny who, by now, was fast asleep. He loved her so much; even looking at her in sleep made his knees turn to jelly, and his heart turn over in his chest. He had been driven by fear, he realised. When your loved ones or those for whose care you are responsible are threatened, and you can find no answer to their plight, you turn to irrational solutions as a defence.

Crouched by Luke Turrels graveside, Rollie had no such doubts. The boy had been sucked dry by a vampire and would become one himself. Rollie wanted to see that and had armed himself in readiness. Garlic flowers, holy water and communion wafers were virtually impossible to come by, but he had 'borrowed' his mother's crucifix – or, in truth, taken it from the wall.

It was dark in the graveyard. Even in summer, once the sun had gone to rest, darkness descended on the world, but Rollie was not frightened. He had read the books, seen the films, played the games and he had his crucifix in his hand. He looked at the stone – 'May you always have an angel at your side'. That was a bit soppy. If only they knew what had really happened – he could tell them! He had told them, but no one listened – not to him! Angels weren't necessarily good beings. It was often difficult to tell the difference between an angel and a demon. The difference was not always very great, and this child certainly had a demon by his side.

The copper hadn't believed him, and he'd show the copper. A crucifx and a camera – wouldn't they choke when he got a picture in the paper? He'd told them and no one believed him, but he would prove it – hold the vampire back with the cross and photograph it. No one had ever photographed a vampire before; he could open a web site and become famous.

So intense were these thoughts as they ran through his fevered imagination that Rollie was unaware of being watched. He remained unaware as the figure approached him in the shadow of the church, disappearing for a while as it made its way along the south side of the building to reappear by the west door. A light flickered across the figure, and smoke issued from its mouth. The smell of a cigar was carried on the warm air, but still Rollie remained unaware. Suddenly, Crafty Catchpole was behind him and said "Boo!"

Terror takes us all in different ways. Rollie struck out. He yelled in absolute fear and struck out, arms and legs lashing the air and pounding into the figure behind him. Crafty took blow after punishing blow to his legs, groin, chest and face. His yells only made it worse; shouting at Rollie was a bit like shouting at a dog. Rollie barked back and struck at this horror with all his strength. It was only when he was exhausted that Rollie collapsed to the shingle path, and rocked back and forth in terror. By then, Crafty was also rolling around, clutching his body and groaning in agony.

At last, they quietened down and stole a look at each other, and the realisation that neither posed a threat removed the terror. After a while, Crafty, still bruised and aching but mollified, stood up and offered Rollie his hand.

"Om sorry, boy. I din't mean to startle you."

"That's all roight. I din't mean ter hit yer."

"What yew doin' here?"

Rollie, too exhausted for evasion or cunning, told him.

"Well Oim blowed – if that ent funny," said Crafty.

"What yew mean? Yew don't believe me?"

"Well it's a rum un, int it, but yes I dew – and I don't know whoy."

Flashes of pain passed through Crafty's mind: images that made him want to scream out seemed lodged there.

"He's in there," said Rollie.

"No he int."

"Howd yew know?"

"Oi don't," replied Crafty, "but he int."

'He had been dressed in his favourite clothes – trainers, jeans, a T-shirt with a spaceship blazoned across the front, an open sweatshirt.'

"There were a smile on his lips," Crafty sighed.

"What?"

"There were a smile on his lips."

"What yew sayin'?"

"I don't know. I can't see no more. Oi'm goin'."

Before Rollie could say anything else, Crafty Catchpole, clutching his bruised body, was running off towards the church.

Matthew Marjoram – now Brown in his mother's mind – was asleep in his new home. He had settled in well. A nice little boy, never any trouble, he understood that mummy could not always take him out in the daytime because the sun hurt her skin now. On those days he would play in the garden, but must go no further than the gate. In the mornings, one of mummy's friends took him to the play group and in the afternoon he came home and she played with him. Sometimes, Mr Brultzner – who he could call 'Uncle Horst' – played, as well. Sometimes he could have friends to play – if the weather was nice, and they could play in the garden.

He knew that soon they were going on holiday with Uncle Horst to see some of his houses in Italy, Spain – everywhere! He was looking forward to that and so was mummy because she said so. They couldn't go quite yet because there were lots of arrangements to make – mummy had told him it would be in a few weeks, in September.

Mummy laughed and smiled when they talked together. She had always been beautiful, but now she was more beautiful than ever. Her whole skin glowed as though she had the sun shining from inside her. Sometimes, though, she was so pale that he thought he could see right through her skin, but it was still beautiful with a strange blue light. Her teeth were much whiter, too, but sharp like the wolf in the story, and when she smiled or laughed out loud they might look pointed.

CHAPTER 11

Birds of a Feather

Her son was right. Sarah Brown was looking forward to the holiday Horst Brultzner had promised them. She had never been abroad before: finances simply wouldn't have allowed it. Now, she felt more certain of what life held for her. She realized that the arrangements would be complicated – earth from the churchyard had to be shipped abroad for her bed, and Crafty Catchpole had once more been busy in the darkness with his wheelbarrow and spade before Lord Wangford was called in to organise the shipping. They would also be more comfortable travelling at night. Although this was not strictly necessary, such a precaution would avoid any danger of them being exposed to an excess of daylight.

In time, Horst had explained, she would be able to reside anywhere, but for now he proposed just one place for this holiday – Prague! Yes, he said, the housekeeper was one of their kind; she was a Czech, and knew the city like the back of her hand. She had been responsible for ensuring Herr Brultzner's comfort there for many centuries past. The earth was to travel ahead of them and his housekeeper would prepare their welcome – and, to free them to enjoy themselves, would look after Matthew.

It was the coming of the autumnal equinox, he explained – that cooler time at the close of summer when fruits ripened and harvests were gathered. It marked the beginning of the darker days which, now until the turn of the year, would become progressively shorter. This made life easier for the vampire and was celebrated with a masked ball. It was to be Sarah's first ever ball; young women of her class in England did not attend masked balls as a matter of course.

One morning, as Sarah was dancing through her housework, relishing this holiday to come, the doorbell rang. Lord Wangford's Bentley had arrived for Horst Brultzner soon after dawn, and Sarah – too happy with the prospects of her holiday to retire at once – had been flicking a feather duster around the ornaments in the ground floor rooms. She glanced out of the morning room window and saw Sidney Close standing on the terrace. She had long since surmised that he desired her in that buttoned-down, secretive way of his, and smiled to herself as she crossed the hall to answer the door.

"Good morning, sir!"

Sidney knew about Sarah – the gossip had spread like wildfire around the village – but it was still a surprise to see her and he stood speechless.

"Can I help you?"

She enjoyed playing the part; it was quite wonderful being in control, and with so little effort. Sidney stared for a moment, feeling quite foolish and then said:

"I've come to see Mark Chambers. I thought he would be here. There's some electrical work needs doing."

"Mr Chambers normally arrives early, sir. If you would care to come in and wait for him, I'm sure Mr Brultzner would have no objections."

Playing with the language was a delight; it perplexed Sidney Close, and Sarah wanted to laugh out loud, but a parlour maid would not have done that.

"I'll wait outside."

"Mr Brultzner would be most upset if I made you less than welcome. Would you care to come this way, sir?"

Sidney followed with a smile, watching her hips sway from side to side in the ankle-length, black dress. She led him towards the front parlour. Sarah realized that the white pinafore would excite him – that and the little mob-cap, and the fact that she exposed nothing; less is always more enticing. Sidney felt the lust she expected of him; he wanted to reach out, take hold of the apron bow and pull it undone, gently, so that it slipped from her waist to the floor. She would turn then and ... Sarah turned and smiled as she opened the door of the front parlour.

"Would you care to step inside, sir?"

It was the dress and pinafore that did it; he wanted to take her with her parlour maid's dress on. He'd be rough and leave her crumpled on the rug, stand back, pour himself a whisky and then come for her again ...Sarah laughed, and the spell broke. A slight, cool breeze drifted in through the window, and Sidney shook himself.

"Tell Mark – when he arrives – that I'll come back later. I've a job pressing."

Sidney barely knew what was happening as he staggered back from his desires and made for the front door. He wrenched it open, fell out onto the terrace and breathed in the morning air. He had escaped – he was lucky; his testicles were like rocks, but he was a fortunate man, free to savour the true pleasures of life.

In the doorway of the front parlour, Sarah straightened her dress and settled her cap. She had held Sidney Close in the palm of her hand and released him only when she wanted to do so; had she sighed instead of playing that laugh, she would now be sucking his blood from him. She had always had this power with her ex-husband; now she had it with all men.

Back in his shop, Sidney made himself a coffee while he collected his thoughts. He couldn't quite remember – didn't want to remember – what had nearly happened. She'd enticed him, of course; that kind of woman always did that – drawing men down to their way! The main thing was – he'd resisted and come away, clean. He gulped the coffee – black, hot and sour – and it was just what he needed. It was time to act – to sever his connections with the Marjorams once and for all.

The shop door bell rang and he sat bolt upright. It was the two old women – Miss Mealey and Mrs Teale. His heart sank, as a smile rose to his face.

"Ladies – lovely to see you, to see you ..."

"... lovely!"

They chortled with joy as always, and Sidney was nearly normal again as he moved into his routine; there is much to be said for the repetitive nature of everyday life. The pink phone had been a great success – as pink phones always are, said Sidney. They giggled and looked at each other, each wanting the other to "wonder about Mr Marjoram". Sidney enjoyed this kind of banter, and wondered "who told you that, ladies" – referring to the gossip that foresaw Shane's sacking. They liked Shane – "we always called him Shane, didn't we, Mrs Teale", and Sidney was pleased because "Close Electricals aimed to give satisfaction". Nothing was too much trouble for Shane, and "he never asked for anything in return. And what he didn't know about antiques wasn't worth knowing," Miss Mealey was quick to reassure Sidney. Her friend added that he always had an eye for a bargain, "and his London friends could not have been more obliging."

Sidney groaned: he'd had no idea that Shane might be part of the antiques scam which Martin Billings detested with particular venom. He decided to steer the conversation away from Shane and get the old girls out of his shop as quickly as politeness would allow. Was there anything he could get them while they were there – a customized fascia for their phone, perhaps? Free! Free? Free!! Sidney concluded the sale on his usual exclamation marks, and Mrs Teale took out her little purse and scrabbled about among the notes and coins. It had been a close call; he nearly hadn't made the sale. Sidney heaved a sigh of relief – for the ladies to have left without buying anything would have amounted to an insult to his establishment.

The shop door rang as he held it open for the ladies – both immensely satisfied with Mrs Teale's purchase – to leave. He looked at his watch; it was only nine thirty – he couldn't believe it! He'd drop Shane's cards through his door tonight and that would be the end of the matter: only his sense of right and wrong was affronted. The police had released Shane and he was innocent until proven guilty. 'Let him who is without sin among you cast the first stone.' What if he wasn't guilty? It was only the say-so of his wife, and she wasn't exactly as pure as the driven snow.

His thoughts were tumbling along these lines when the shop door bell rang again and in came Nadine Palmester. She was a friend of Sarah Marjoram and the last person Sidney wanted to see at the moment. Could she have a word with him? It wasn't for her to tell him what to do, but Shane Marjoram was not an asset to the village and he was a danger to his wife. "She's no longer his wife – even in name," Nadine was quick to reassure Sidney, but "that's not for you and me to say, is it" he replied, and what would "laying him off achieve?" Were his wife and child to lose their home because Nadine didn't like Shane? And. after all, "He is an innocent man, Nadine – until a court of law proves him guilty". He thought she, as a journalist, might have taken a "more detached view." He enjoyed that little jibe. But Nadine was speaking as Sarah's friend, and "had her interests at heart." When Sidney re-iterated his concern over Shane being unable to pay the mortgage, Nadine reposted that "Sarah has inherited her mum and dad's home, hasn't she? One will pay for the other." Sidney hadn't thought of that: fancy inheriting a house! Anyway, he couldn't discuss it with her — "it wouldn't be right, would it?" Nadine gave him a nod and left the shop; it wasn't until she had disappeared from sight that Sidney realised he hadn't sold her anything.

When Sarah heard what Nadine had done she was furious. Her friend — her one time friend, perhaps — came to visit her at the Old Vicarage late one evening just as she was putting Matthew to bed.

Horst Brultzner had been as good as his word and the morning room, which at the opening in June had been his pride and joy, was now converted into a room for the child, temporarily. When Nadine first arrived, Sarah had been over the moon:

"Look — just look! Isn't this beautiful?"

She showed Nadine the bed which had been settled discreetly in the corner of the room. Matthew seemed happy, too; she missed him, but he seemed content romping on the bed, playing with his toys.

"Why are you wearing those gloves to get Matthew ready for bed?"

"My touch is still cold."

"Oh, Sarah — you are all right, aren't you?"

"Of course I am."

The little boy had always been so warm — so cuddly — that it seemed strange for Sarah to be covering her hands when she touched him, and when she kissed him it was on the forehead, through the hair, as though she didn't want her lips to come near the boy. He smiled. Like most children, he accepted change as normal once he felt safe.

It was on the driveway that Nadine told Sarah what had passed at Close Electricals; it was on the driveway that Sarah exploded.

"You had no right, Nadine. When I want your interference I will ask for it. Shane Marjoram is mine, and I want him where he is — where I can find him when the time comes. Do you understand me?"

Nadine had left — half thinking that Sarah simply did not want Shane missing when the law came for him, yet knowing in her heart that there was more to it than this: so much venom, so much anger from one she had held in her arms.

Shane Marjoram had heard the cards drop onto the doormat and seen Sidney Close shut the gate behind him. He shoved up the window and bellowed across the road.

"What yer doin' Mr Close? Aint yer gonna come in?"

"I have to get home to tea, Shane."

"Yeah? Is that it, then? Thanks fer all yer hard work, Shane — now fuck off."

"No need to be like that, Shane. I've a business to run. You know that."

"And who helped yer build the business up then — hey?"

"Take my advice, Shane — move out of the village and make a new start."

"Without me kid or me wife? Fuck off! Why should I? I aint done nothing — and no one can say I have. There's no good you goin' ter church on a Sundy, Mr

Sidney Fucking Close and droppin' a good workman's cards through the fuckin' door on a Mondy! If you're a fuckin' Christian, yer need to be a fuckin' Christian seven days a fuckin' week!"

Sidney Close had almost run along the road to his house and was nearly out of earshot so Shane slammed the window down, catching the delicate lace curtains beneath it and ripping them. They looked in keeping with the rest of the house which had gone to the dogs since Sarah left. The wall panels in the kitchen were smeared by dirty fingers; the collection of china plates shoved aside or broken on the floor; the gingham cloth was crumpled on the table and was covered with crumbs and empty food cartons; around the sink unwashed crockery gathered; on the oven top a few saucepans, a frying pan and a wok attracted the insects of the summer. In what used to be their sitting room, dust had settled on the wooden mantle-piece, perched on the Napoleon clock and lingered around the brass bell and cartridge cases; the photographs, dusted daily by Sarah, were stacked aside or smashed in the hearth; her father's glue pot was slung in the corner; the summer flowers were dead and shrivelled. In the bedroom, Shane's boot print still dented the cot on which had been thrown the Pooh Bear rug; the buttercups had withered and the chair, on which Shane had cried that first night after Sarah left, lodged where he left it. No one listened now from the bottom of the stairs to the sound of a child sleeping.

After Sidney had gone, Shane waited until it was just dark and then went out into the village. He found that he was pleased to be outside. Indoors it had been stifling, with the stale smells of the house covering him like a grubby blanket; in the night air it was cooler. He walked rapidly to the corner of Shore Lane, having decided to take the long way round and make his way towards the far end of the village. He perspired and felt good about it as he turned into Gylde Hall Lane and strode up the slope towards the village school. He hadn't exercised since the police let him come home – nothing: no cricket, no work and no sex. It was the latter he missed most of all – not just the sex, but the exercise you got doing it. He and Sarah had always been very physical. It was good to feel his muscles being stretched again. Reaching the top of Gylde Hall Lane, he turned out of the village and strode off towards Lowestoft. He soon reached the bypass, passed the toxic pit and made his way into Pakefield. No one knew him there. Away, if they did, they could get stuffed.

When he came to The Crossways, he walked in and ordered a pint. Nobody batted an eyelid so he downed it (in the space of time it took the landlord to put his money in the till) and ordered another.

"You've got a thirst on yer, son."

Shane nearly said "Fuck off" but decided to stay with a "Yeah", and then he sat down in the corner seat. It was an old pub. No one had messed it up yet with poncy bar stools and table snacks. He slumped back into the upholstered settle and enjoyed the comfort of his second pint. He was hungry. After the second pint, he realised just how hungry he was; he hadn't had a decent meal since Sarah left. He'd lived off stuff you could heat up – so he ordered some steak and kidney pudding.

"Yeah – pudding, son, this is the real McCoy, the proper suet crust. Get that inside yer, you'll be ready fer anything. Mer wife makes it – it's lovely, jest like her!"

Shane wasn't there for the conversation and didn't want to stand listening to the old bloke going on about his missus so he paid, grunted, and sat down again in his corner seat. He felt at home here, in a way he hadn't done in his own house for a long time. When the meal came – brought in by a young girl showing off her belly and boobs – he virtually grabbed the knife and fork. She leaned over him to place the condiments by his plate and make sure he got a full view of her breasts, and then asked, archly, if he wanted anything else. Shane looked at her, cast his eyes up and down her body and went back to his meat pudding without saying a word. The look and gesture had said everything. 'What's a little girl with big tits got to offer me?'

"Well fuck off then," she said, and stormed back to the kitchen.

Upsetting her was the relish on his meal. He ordered a third pint and looked around. There were several people in the bar – mainly men in the company of other men: there for the drinking, the chat and a quiet game of darts. None of them looked at Shane and he felt free at last. Not a man for sentimental memories – except those associated with his wife – Shane enjoyed that evening as much as any he could remember. He dozed peacefully, as you only can in an English pub where nobody seems to mind or notice, and listened to the soft thud-thud as darts hit the board. It was peaceful, like listening to Sarah singing the boy to sleep.

He tried not to think about her – it didn't do any good and only upset him. His time would come to get even, and get even he would. Brultzner didn't scare him, and neither did Billings. Once the heat was off, he'd sort them out for good. When the landlord called time, Shane had downed at least six pints, enjoyed a dessert – spotted dick and custard – and felt content and full.

The physical release he felt on the walk back was just as invigorating to him as the walk out. He chose the longer route and marched along the bypass. Cars and lorries roared by him at close quarters, threatening to throw him into the ditch. He stumbled, and sometimes fell, on the rough tussocks of grass which sprouted there, but enjoyed this cut and thrust with the earth.

Shane lifted his head as he reached the turn into Shoemaker's Lane, near the wildlife park, and howled like a wolf. The cry started deep down behind the muscles of his gut and rose as though hauled from some primeval pit – a protracted column of sound that he ejaculated into the air. The timber wolves from the park caught the cry and howled back, setting up a devilish chorus of panic across the Blacksands Marshes which startled every animal in the vicinity. Oh to be a werewolf and tear the throats from your enemies before loping furiously away into the darkness. Shane sprinted off down Shoemaker's Lane and passed the church, giving way to great leaps in the air as he crossed Podd's Field. There wasn't one muscle, bone or sinew in his body which wasn't vibrant with new life.

He paused at his cottage door, eager to enter – eager as he had not been since the cops pissed on him. Standing outside, he sniffed the air. Someone was in there – in his home. He unlocked the door and walked in quietly. There was no sound, and only the moonlight shone through the little window which overlooked the marsh. He looked around the sitting room and saw nothing at first – just the dappled shadows of the moon through the torn, lace curtains bathing the room in its cold, blue light – and then he saw the woman sitting by the fireplace on a low stool, her legs curled to one side. She looked up as he closed the door, and smiled. He thought it was a ghost at first, something from the dead come back to haunt him, but then realised that it was Sarah. "Hello Shane." He wasn't sure, afterwards, whether she had said it or not – whether he had, in fact, simply remembered how she used to greet him. Certainly, the voice seemed to be merely a part of the room that night – no more, no less than the shadows which lurked in every niche and corner. It was unnerving that she did not move, but sat waiting quietly as she had always done. 'Was the boy asleep upstairs?' The thought passed through him, unbidden.

He approached her, slowly – not sure that she was real, so still she sat watching him. Her beauty was astonishing – the honey-coloured hair shone to perfection, spilling over her shoulders and framing her face. Since leaving, she had grown more radiant. Her skin shone with a golden tan, and yet beneath the glow she was so pale that he thought he could see right through her skin which seemed to harbour a strange blue light. The red lips smiled upon his gaze – but faintly with no laughter in the eyes – and, as the lips parted slightly, he saw the very white teeth. He realised, more now than ever, the attraction she had always held for him – that dreamy look, which meant she always kept something from you, was intense.

Without realising it, Shane had approached to within two feet of her – so close that she could reach out and touch him. It was then that he saw the axe in the hearth, but it didn't disturb him, despite knowing that she must have brought it in from the yard. Sarah slipped from the stool, knelt at his feet – as she had often done before – and reached up to undo his belt. His trousers and then his pants were round his ankles in seconds, and then her hands, cold as ice, tightened on his buttocks. He felt her rise against him, her soft breath on his thighs and then around his crotch. He felt her tongue flicking over him, and the power rising in him as the moment came when he wanted to lift her from the floor and explode into her. The moment arrived, and he felt her teeth on his stomach and a sharp pain as she bit into him and sucked.

Sarah had always been a good lover – she had no secrets, she simply enjoyed it – but rarely had he known her like this. She'd taken him, held him to her purpose, and now she controlled him. He could do nothing but take the ecstasy she offered. Her teeth clenched harder and he sensed the warm blood springing from him and into her mouth. Her sucking seemed to draw the fluids from him. His balls softened and relaxed into the scrotum, his penis sagged with satisfaction and – when she had finished – his knees buckled and he sank to the floor. Sarah moved across him, ripped open his shirt and sank her teeth into his chest. The rising tide of pleasure swept through him like waves. His head swam and he was adrift. There was fear there, and he wanted to turn back, wanted to push her from him as his mind lost itself and he floated into unconsciousness. A terrible swoon came over him and he found himself twisting and turning in her grip, and then a great groan rose from his abdomen and his shoulders twitched as the tension went from them. He felt exhausted, but the lightness in his head was wonderful and he seemed to glide up and out and over the waves on which he had drifted.

When he woke, Sarah was kneeling by his side, blood trickling from the corners of her mouth – a repulsive light in her eyes. In her hands she held the axe which he had seen on the table. She didn't speak, but he heard the words clearly as though his mind and hers held a common thought – just like it had been after good lovemaking when they had come together and shared each other's sweat and joy and consciousness. 'Lizzie Borden took an axe, and gave her husband forty whacks.'

He pushed her away and laboured to his feet. He was weak now from loss of blood and, as he stood, tripped over his trousers and pants which were still round his ankles and clung to him like bindweed. Sarah never moved as he fought to clear his head and get away from her; moreover, she appeared unperturbed by his struggles, but knelt watching him as a child might watch a fly struggling in a web, waiting for the spider to come out of the corner. His fitness and strength seemed of little use to him now, and he sank back down to his knees.

It was only then that she stood and walked over to him. Sarah had held him since he came into the room, and Shane Marjoram knew that, and in his knowledge there was contentment as well as terror. She still had that lightness in her step, that seductive swing of her hips and that, now horrifying, suppleness in her shoulders as she leaned over him and spoke so softly.

"Did you enjoy yourself?"

She waited while he looked up at her, his eyes pleading for more.

"Answer me."

Still the voice was soft with a deep yearning he could not understand. He nodded, and she smiled and there was joy in her smile now. He saw the axe in her hand and knew – or thought he knew – her intentions. Shane Marjoram – kneeling before his own executioner – understood, in that instant, the hate she felt for him. The waves of redemption rose within him and he glimpsed a kind of peace at last. Sarah stood quietly, still smiling, still with the blood running from the corners of her mouth, still not lifting the axe to strike him. She knelt beside him and took his head in her hands, lifting his face to her.

"Good. I am glad you did, and there is more – more delights than you have ever known, more dread than you can ever have imagined. I shall return and I shall take you there, but you must wait for me – wait, unfrequented by troubled dreams, until I am with you again. Do you understand?"

He nodded and Sarah stood, placing the axe back on the table. Still he expected her to strike, but she moved serenely into the kitchen and, when she returned, his blood had been wiped from her mouth. She glided passed him to the door with that familiar lightness in her step – a woman who had made a decision he could not begin to even guess at, a decision that had lifted the suffering from her mind. She leaned into the doorway, her legs swinging easily from the hips and then became one with the air. She turned and let her gaze rest upon him, kneeling there, for a while, and then was gone – wafting through the doorway like mist.

CHAPTER 12

Sunday school

Penny Read sat on the bench on the little grassy mound opposite St George's Church, and waited for her husband to arrive in the car. By her side sat her eldest daughter, Anna-Maria (known to all, for no apparent reason, as Nell). Junior Church had re-started and, with her four children, she had just come out. Their dog, Leo, was with them, stretched out on the grass by Penny's dress. George (her youngest son) sat by the dog, ignoring Amos and Helen who ran round their mother in circles. Leo was a Labrador – creamy-white with a broad head and chest, a classic of his kind.

Penny's beauty was also a classic of the English kind – what is called the 'English rose look'. She accepted this without undue vanity. The loveliness of her looks sat as easily with her as did the loveliness of her nature. She was so apparently perfect that Penny was a constant source of irritation to other women, and yet few could honestly say they disliked her – such was her charm.

Tony Crewes stood by the lych-gate, waiting for his wife to finish busying herself with something trivial like next month's flower rota, and watched Penny. He was reminded of a picture he had once seen; a woman appeared over a sand dune, her summer frock billowing in a light sea breeze and her children ran out from behind the dress so that they appeared to come from it; the expression on the woman's face was one of utter fulfilment. Penny saw him, waved, and so he walked over.

"Aren't we lucky – our glorious summer continues into September?"

"We can enjoy a few more weeks of patios and barbecues." replied Penny.

"Sunday school ..."

"Junior Church!"

"Junior Church started back today?" he asked.

"Yes, and I took Leo in to talk about pets and how we need to care for them."

Between them, as they spoke, was a mutual consciousness of the summer past: Luke Turrell's death, Sarah's disappearance and 'resurrection' (as he had phrased it to Beth) and the impending comeuppance of Shane Marjoram. Their conversation drifted into, and out of, these concerns that had tugged the village by its ears. They both felt pleased for Sarah who could, at least, start a new life more suited to her intelligence and nature. The law was closing in on Shane – "surely it couldn't be long now?" When it did, Sarah would be free and safe.

"The Harvest Festival will soon be upon us," said Penny, with relief.

"Will the children be singing?" Tony said, laughing.

"Of that you can be sure!"

"And you have the backing of our esteemed rector?"

Penny Read genuinely liked Tony Crewes, but felt that remarks like that spoiled him. There was spitefulness in the man – a small-minded vixen-like quality that emerged suddenly, and was unbecoming. She said so, but not in so many words.

"The rector's all right, Tony. I thought you were an ally of his."

"I am, really. At least, I prefer him to those around him!"

"He is put upon – if you take my meaning?"

"I stand corrected."

"Good. Corvin needs all the friends he can get."

"You really like the man?"

"Yes. I know he won't stand up to people, but that's more a personal failing than a lack of faith. He simply doesn't like confrontation … it can't be easy for him."

"No – I suppose not."

"There – did I sound very school-marmish?"

"Not too much!"

"We're going out to lunch," she said, "we've got a picnic in the car and we're taking advantage of this lovely weather. Once the children are back at school, routine seems to take over so we're making the most of our freedom while we can."

As she spoke, Alan Read arrived in the Volvo he drove. 'It would have to be a Volvo, wouldn't it?' thought Tony, 'safe, secure, solid.' He shook hands with Alan, while the children climbed into the back and Leo jumped under the hatch to settle by the picnic basket.

"How's Beth?"

Dr Read even said the right things! Tony watched as he walked round the car to open the door for his wife. He ignored the question.

"Enjoy your picnic," he said.

"Thanks – we shall."

Tony watched them as they drove off to their faultless picnic in the forest.

"Where have you been?" said Beth, as he arrived back where she had left him.

Ever since the affair it had been like this; he couldn't take one step outside her recognisance without being questioned about where, why and with whom. He liked to think he was a patient man who simply lacked patience. Tony Crewes drove his foot hard into the gravel path.

"Be careful!"

"Hmm?"

"Be careful! The path!"

Was it that delicate, that likely to be damaged by one jab of a man's toe? Patently not!

"Yes, of course," he said, and looked across her at Corvin Unwood who was approaching them along the path.

"Tony – hello!"

"Hello Corvin. I've just listened to Penny Read singing your praises."

"It's nice to hear someone is! Beth has offered to take on the flower rota."

"I'm sure it's in safe hands, Corvin."

The hours of anguish he was now to face for twelve months sat heavily upon his heart and his shoulders, as Tony smiled first at Corvin and then at Beth; his wife never made light of anything, never took joy in the simplest task.

"It seems a long time since our little chat," said Corvin.

"Chat?" questioned Beth.

"Your husband and I were discussing the concept of the soul, Beth."

"You never told me, Tony."

"It must have skipped my mind ... When Mary talks of the 'soul' she means her whole self and it is the whole 'self' which, after death, lives on with God. So our eternal life, which we are living now, will continue into 'eternity', but we shall inhabit eternity in our spiritual body. Our spiritual body grows out of our earthly life as a plant grows from a seed. Our spiritual body expresses the personality we have developed in our earthly body and lives in a state of consciousness with God. It is that state which we call Heaven. Awesome?"

He directed the question at his wife because he knew that it would 'scare the shit out of her' and shut her up. Beth stood in silence, and Corvin smiled benignly.

"If only all my parishioners listened so carefully!"

"Occasionally, rector, the state of my soul perturbs even me."

"So it should – remember St Paul's image of the seed and the plant."

Tony was now indulging in that 'vixen-like quality' disliked by Penny Read. Beth knew this, but did not know why he behaved in such a manner. Tony went on:

"We are conscious of God – and of each other – through all eternity!"

"But we only come to the Father through the Son, and in accepting Him as our Saviour our sins are taken from us," said Corvin.

"Ay, there's the rub," laughed Tony.

"It is no sleep of death, but of everlasting life," said Corvin.

Corvin was confident now in the face of the other man's gentle taunts. Tony knew that, and realised that Penny Read was right; the rector was a man of faith. He knew his own mind and his own path, but he lacked the emotional stamina to ... what was the phrase – 'stride the rugged pathway'? When Corvin left them, Beth said:

"There was time when I could trust you, Tony – when I knew where I was, when I could rely on you to say the right thing!"

Corvin hurried towards Martin Billings, eager to enlist his help with the Harvest Festival. There had been mumblings among certain elements of the congregation about the 'pagan origins' of Harvest, and Corvin wanted to squash these in the bud. Martin was not a particularly religious man – seeing the church more as one spoke in the community wheel rather a source of spiritual enlightenment. He did, however, like Corvin because he could be seen wearing out the shoe leather.

A relatively new element in the congregation – a small group influenced by visits to a 'charismatic' church in Lowestoft – was attempting to return the church in Dunburgh to the Word of the Lord. They objected to the Harvest Festival on the grounds that it represented the worship of pagan gods. Corvin's protestations that the church had always embraced the cultural traditions of the communities it evangelised had carried no weight with these people who saw such traditions simply as a perversion of God's Word. A member of this group had now wormed his way onto the Parochial Church Council and planned, if Corvin's sources were correct, to put the kibosh on the festival.

St George's Harvest Festival had always centred round the once thriving fishing industry based in the original Dunburgh Beach village and, in the week leading up to Harvest Sunday, men from the Fisherman's Hut assumed the traditional right to decorate the church; indeed, Boss Wigg held a key which he never relinquished. This decoration was spectacular, thoroughly enjoyed by the adults, held in awe by the children and never varied. Oars were lashed to the pews and formed an archway down the aisle under which everyone processed to their seat, drift nets hung from the rafters and ship's lamps adorned the window sills. Other nautical accoutrements seemed scattered (although their position remained exactly the same each year) about the church; anchors encircled the font, lobster pots lined the chancel, rope was coiled strategically in both porches and by the vestry steps, a tiller rested by the lectern, green glass floats hung from the pulpit, a trawl net was draped from the coat of arms on the north wall and small piles of rowlocks were located by the choir stalls. Even had he wished to do so, Corvin would have found it extremely difficult to stand against such an array of custom.

Martin, of course, was appalled that anyone should wish to do so. The idea that the men from the Hut would not be arriving in early October with their trailer loads of fishing gear was anathema to him and he undertook to have a word with them on Corvin's behalf. He was a great believer in community pressure and 'the Charismatic' could look forward to a few disconcerting weeks as he walked about the village exercising his Cocker spaniel. As Martin said:

"There are always other churches more suited to the taste of the pious."

He also re-assured Corvin that John Barker and himself would be on-side at the next PCC meeting, and he would make certain that Yammer Utting, who usually only appeared when he had a grudge, came. Yammer – in his suit jacket, split-crotch trousers and Norbridge supporter's bobble hat, bursting with his leathery anger – would be a match for 'the Charismatic'. Corvin wasn't sure that Yammer – red with drink and bursting with ire – was what the PCC needed, but he would be on the right side.

"Have they complained about the sheaf of corn, too?" asked Martin.

They had. In a well orchestrated attempt to involve both communities – the farmers and the fishermen – Corvin had introduced the sheaf along with plaited loaves and gifts of food, which were sent to the Cedars of Lebanon retirement home. Gifts of food had long been a tradition in the Junior Church, and in a titanic struggle against overwhelming bigotry, in which he was joined by Penny Read,

Corvin had been victorious in his attempts to have these "gifts of the earth" placed prominently in the area next to the font and on the lady altar to the left of the chancel steps. The Podds, a long standing farming family, provided the sheaf and the plaited loaf. Penny Read had gone so far as to suggest that, after the service, the sheaf should be re-buried in Podd's Field, but Corvin had blanched at this idea. It wasn't so much that he had reservations about what amounted to this return to a symbolic human sacrifice, but his scars from the 'Battle of the Sheaf' had not yet healed and he was tender to the touch. Esther had been against it, feeling that Penny needed "reigning in". The advice of his oracle had been enough to convince Corvin that they would be better to hold the ground over which they had fought than to fight on, and risk losing what had been gained.

"It's a shame they'll miss the Harvest Supper," continued Martin, building his resentment at their attitude into a bullish stance.

"Miss the Harvest Supper?"

"The Charismatics – presumably they will not want to be seen there?"

This was something Corvin hadn't considered. Lots of people who were never seen at church from one year's end to the next appeared at the Harvest Supper – tickets were at a premium. The serving table ached with food, almost buckling under the weight of beef joints, pork pies, hams and Totto Briggs's famous sausages. His family business, which went back generations, always provided the Harvest Supper – free to the church. He considered it his contribution to the religious life of the village. Corvin doubted whether 'the Charismatics' would grace it with their presence, but he wasn't sure; they might consider it more a family occasion than a spiritual sortie. In a way it was: before the nights finally darkened through autumn into winter, it brought the congregation – and their acquaintances – together in a warm, festive celebration of the "fruits of the earth of which we, in this country, do not go short" as Bishop Twiddle always sighed when giving the thanksgiving speech on a full stomach. They might, on second thoughts, object to the corn dollies – those last vestiges of pagan sacrifice – with which Penny Read and the young teenagers who helped her with Junior Church insisted on decorating the Church Centre where the supper was always held.

"We had better ask her to make a big one this year, then," said Martin, warming even more to the challenge of fighting the good fight and keeping "the Charismatic brigade" at bay. "Perhaps she could use a whole sheaf? Imagine that, Corvin, a corn dolly the size of a man standing in the doorway of the Church Centre welcoming the faithful!"

Martin clearly sensed a fight was on and, grateful though he was for support, Corvin wanted to avoid any outright conflict with the 'Charismatics' or anyone else.

When Martin had said his farewell and reached the gate, Esther Unwood was waiting for him.

"Did you re-assure him, Martin? These people are the limit."

"I think it's wrong to lose traditions. They're part of our heritage. The rector said that Penny Read wants to bury the corn dolly in Podd's Field after the service."

"I think Penny gets a little over-enthusiastic sometimes. I believe that the old country folk used to bury the last sheaf of corn in the field as a gift to their gods."

"As a way of saying thank you for the harvest?"

"Yes. I expect that before corn dollies they made human sacrifices, and buried some poor young man. We don't need reminding of that, although there are some young men could do with being buried."

Martin ignored the remark, but Esther persisted.

"Are you any nearer charging him?"

"You know I can't talk about that."

"In the old days the villagers would have taken the law into their own hands."

"We must thank God that it's not 'the old days'," said Martin, quietly. "If it were we'd have the Charismatic shot, the young men buried and suspects … hanged?"

"I was only joking, Martin."

"Were you? I've always thought that there was only a small jump from the thought to the deed. An idea is like a seed – once it takes root, there's no stopping it."

"Are you telling me off, Constable Billings? Are you giving me a caution?"

"Not a caution: simply a comment. It's not so long ago they were burning old women at the stake around here – just in case they might be witches."

"It was over three hundred years ago, Martin."

"Don't answer this next question – just think about it in terms of how short a span of time is three hundred years. How old are you, Esther?"

Esther laughed: in the scale of time, three hundred years was nothing.

"I take your point. I promise not to shoot anyone on the way home."

"As long as they're kind to Corvin?"

"Talking of bigotry, I want a word with Clara Gobley," said Esther.

"You must be a glutton for punishment."

"We can't have a repeat of what happened at the end of term service in July during the Harvest Thanksgiving. Penny Read may be a little single-minded, but her heart is in the right place."

"But Clara Gobley's is not?"

"No," said Esther.

"What are you going to say to her?" asked Martin.

"I'm not sure. I just know that I am not going to face another catastrophe in the church. Penny Read won't budge – and, after all, a Harvest Festival should involve the children. Clara Gobley will have to … to …"

"Give in? Come on-side?"

"You're laughing at me, Constable Billings."

"No – but you have my number if you need it. Good luck!"

Esther watched him walk off along the path. She really did like meeting people after the Sunday service; perhaps Clara Gobley would have mellowed?

As she turned into the driveway of the bungalow on Church Hill, Esther Unwood did not really believe that, but she had determined to confront Clara Gobley. The front door was slightly ajar and, like Crafty Catchpole several months before, she pushed it open. The tidal wave of cats poured through the gap, spitting in all directions, and Esther watched them disappear through the unkempt hedges on the far side of the road. The odour followed them and, again like Crafty, Esther gagged and turned away. Despite her own garden being anything but neat and tidy, Esther was astounded at the state of Clara's.

"You don't seem to like my garden, Mrs Unwood, but it suits the animals and they're the ones who matter. Don't you agree?"

"Of course," said Esther, "It must be paradise for them."

"To what do I owe the pleasure of this visit?"

"I've come to ask you a favour."

"I thought you might."

It was a lie. Clara had given the matter no thought at all but, once Esther had spoken, the organist and choir mistress grasped the situation immediately.

"Come in. Bert will make us some tea."

Seated uncomfortably on one of the settees, sipping her tea carefully and watching Clara attach splints to the leg of a hedgehog, Esther waited.

"You want me to agree to allow Penny Read to choose the music for the Harvest Festival?" said Clara, at last.

"No," said Esther, "I don't think that would be right. You are the organist and the choir mistress – the choice of church music is yours. What I would like is for you to agree that the children sing one song, at any time of your choosing, during the service and ..."

Esther paused, deliberately, and then went on:

"... that you will accompany them on the piano."

"I've never refused to do that!"

"I know."

"I've never been invited."

"I'm inviting you now."

"Have you discussed this with Mrs Read?"

"No."

"So how do you know that Mrs Read will agree to this?"

"She will have no choice."

Again, Esther received that hard, hawk-like look. Clara prided herself, like many arrogant people, on being impossible to deceive. She liked to believe that she could read minds and detect truth in anybody. She wanted to refuse Esther's request, but knew that would make her look small; it had been couched as a request – a favour. She saw Penny Read's face when the rector's wife told her what had been arranged.

"Very well," she said.

"Thank you," said Esther, "I will see Penny Read and tell her to let you know which song in good time."

"You said that I was to choose the music, Mrs Unwood."

"Of course, and the when and where in the service that the children will sing, but they have a limited repertoire of songs and will sing best what they know well."

Clara's anger didn't show, and the hand that held the hedgehog didn't tighten. At least the compromise would put her in charge, and the singing would do the church justice. She looked harshly at Esther, who returned her stare with a discreet smile on her face, and then went back to her work. There was still the chance for many a slip.

Taking the short walk back from Clara's bungalow to the rectory, Esther felt pleased with herself. As she turned into Shore Lane, Crafty Catchpole passed her on his way along Church Hill. She smiled, and he waved back before bending his head down over the handlebars of the old butcher's bike and peddling furiously up the hill.

Crafty was convulsed with both fear and excitement. Horst Brultzner and the woman and her child had gone, and the Old Vicarage was empty. He had mastered the security system. The power to command animals was in his hands. He had carried out Bert's requests to the letter – the Victorian tumbler locks had been identified and keys made, the workings of the security system had become clear to him and he knew that they had sixty seconds once the alarm was activated to switch the device off. Moreover, the man who slapped him round the head had left the previous evening.

Bert listened to him carefully and with great respect; then, much to Crafty's disappointment, sent him home, telling him to return that evening – when the road was quiet enough to approach unseen.

After Crafty left, Bert made his preparations. He knew that the vampire had left, but Bert – having watched so many double-bill horror films – was taking no chances. He took an old, doctor's bag and placed in it a crucifix, some garlic flowers, holy water which Clara had lifted from the church's stoup, holy wafers which she had 'borrowed' from the aumbry cupboard and a knife with a long, thin blade. They could not be better protected. He also placed a long iron spike by the bag. Bert's researches had shown him that the metal vampire's feared was common iron – that which bound them to the earth. Three heavy torches, some sacking, a plastic bag and the keys he'd had made completed his preparations.

He and Clara ate well that evening before setting out – a beef goulash made with plenty of garlic cloves. By the time they left their bungalow, both were sweating garlic, profusely. She had also agreed to wear her mother's necklace with its small, golden cross, but had refused the rosary beads because they were "Catholic". Since Crafty's earlier visit, when Bert had drawn his final conclusions about the nature of Brultzner, he and Clara had cleared a discreet pathway through the debris of their garden and along the back of the chemist's house, which separated their bungalow from the grounds of the Old Vicarage. They were thus able to make their way unseen into the garden, avoiding the shingle driveway over which "no one can walk ... without making a noise".

When Crafty arrived, Bert took the crucifix from the bag and handed it to Clara before draping all their necks with the garlic flowers. He then handed Crafty one of the holy wafers and told him to hold it before him, which Crafty did to the letter of the instruction – gently and straight in front of his chest. He also gave Crafty a key which he hoped would fit the internal doors. Bert himself had a phial of the holy water in his left hand, held between finger and thumb. He nodded at Crafty and they walked to the back of the house, leaving Clara by the front door. Bert had briefed Crafty that morning, and he knew what was expected. Once Bert had slipped the blade of the knife between the lower and upper frames of the sash window – which opened into Sarah's morning room – released the catch and pushed the window up, Crafty had sixty seconds to reach the master switch in the wall cupboard in the hallway.

Bert slipped in the blade of the knife, lifted the window and placed the sacking over the sill so that the non-drying paint ... DNA coded to Brultzner's premises and which they couldn't wash off would not take the buzz out of their burglary by covering them in sticky paint. They heard the thin trill of the alarm as it counted down the seconds, and Bert eased Crafty over the sacking into the morning room from where he made his way quickly to the inner door. The first key fitted as Bert had known it would, and Crafty rushed along the hallway. He opened the little cupboard that housed the system and pressed in the master switch – the little button marked with the cross. The trill ceased and he heaved a sigh of relief. Bert was behind him and when the alarm died he opened the front door and let Clara in – unsprayed by the green paint which the light sensors over the front door would have activated.

He raised one finger to his lips, having closed the door, and then went back through the morning room to remove the soiled sacking, place it in the plastic bag and close the window. The standard alarm with its movement sensors built into the light fittings and contact sensors built into the door jambs was now de-activated. They were in, able to move around, and with no intention of spoiling the ambience of the restoration. Bert smiled to himself. Prior to meeting Clara he had indulged in a little, minor burglary. In fact, it was coming together with her at a revivalist gathering that had weaned him from "his sinful ways" and "placed his foot on the straight and narrow pathway". That was years ago, and this was the first time since then he had exercised his professional skills, but he knew Martin Billings and his attitude to crime, and the smile was one of pleasure.

Bert knew that the study was on the ground floor – gossip following Brultzner's luncheon had informed him of that – and he decided to return there last of all, once they had satisfied themselves concerning the rest of the house. He could then close the thick, heavy curtains and read through Brultzner's papers at his leisure. He nodded at Clara and Crafty, and then led the way round the downstairs' rooms.

Clara wasn't sure what she had expected to happen when they stood, at last, in Brultzner's house. She had crossed herself while she waited – though normally she was against such "showiness" – and did so again, as they waited for Bert to lead the way. She noticed that Crafty followed suit. The door was now closed behind them, but she double-checked and then cast her eyes on those that led off the hall: nothing stirred, no knob turned, no tumbler clicked. The only light in the hallway was cast through the front door, and the colours from the stained glass window were thrown along the black and white tiles. She had expected demons to be guarding the house and clutched her mother's crucifix tightly, but the atmosphere did nothing to encourage her fear; all was peaceful and quiet. The thing of which she was most conscious was the smell of beeswax polish on the hat-stand, which stood just inside the front door: there was nothing rank, no smell of the dead or decaying.

Bert paused at the top of the stairs that led down into the scullery, cellar and kitchen. His torch picked out the door at the bottom and one of his keys unlocked it. 'You have not seen my house, Mr Catchpole? Come.' Crafty remembered Brultzner's enthusiasm and sensed he heard his voice. 'Surprisingly for a country vicarage the original kitchen is in the basement, which creates a fourth floor.' Below stairs, it was now pristine, 'lit only by the light able to pass through the grid in the yard above' until their torches picked out the shining tiles and slabs and their glow was reflected back. The black-leaded range was restored to its original shine with the use of real black lead – poisonous and unobtainable in Britain. On the wooden shelves there were apple corers, cherry pippers, knife polishers, a mincer and a range of heavy iron pots and pans. Clara could not imagine anyone cooking down here and wondered how Sarah Marjoram fed her son, but she did detect the smell of fresh bread lingering on the air; it was clear that the oven had been used.

In the cellar there was no dust – the racked rows of dusty bottles had been complemented by many more, all shining in the light of the torches. 'Your last rector enjoyed his wine, Mr Catchpole. He kept a fine cellar by all accounts.' Brultzner had now returned that cellar to ecclesiastical correctness. In the scullery there were no longer cobwebs hanging everywhere covered with grit and coal dust, and no spiders lounged in the webs waiting for their prey. Crafty whispered in the stillness.

"You are already under the spell of my house, Mr Catchpole. Good."

"What was that?" asked Bert.

"That's what he said to me – Him."

Crafty remembered the sensation of being rendered powerless by the man's enthusiasm and the chill of standing next to him in the confined space of the basement hallway. At one end, the steps led to the yard above where the outside stairwell was surrounded by spiked railings to prevent children falling. 'I shall transform the old house, Mr Catchpole.'

"Oi don't like it here."

"There's no good you getting cold feet, Mr Catchpole – in for a penny, in for a pound. Think about your pigeons!"

"He's here! He's everywhere. Time is nuthin' to Him."

Once again, Crafty feared for his freedom.

They made their way to the ground floor where Lord Wangford had sipped coffee in the hallway and where the davenport had stood. Bert indicated the stairway to the first floor and led the way. Here, the bathroom had been re-furbished 'not only beautifully but with flamboyance and wit' – the cast iron bath standing on four claws and the geyser, now working, over its narrow end. The bedrooms yielded to Bert's keys as readily as the other rooms had done. Signs of Mark Chambers's men were everywhere. They turned off the torches for fear of attracting attention from the road. There were no curtains as yet, but the bricklayers, carpenters and plasterers had been busy and the bedrooms waited only for the painters.

They made their way to the second floor where the dust of decades still lingered. They could see footprints where the builders had come and gone. There were four rooms off the landing and each opened to Bert's keys. In the largest of these rooms, amongst the dust and cobwebs, was Brultzner's 'box'.

"Don't touch it!"

"He has gone, Mr Catchpole."

Bert lifted the lid. From beneath the red silk lining came the faint, vaguely miasmic smell of earth. Bert and Clara exchanged glances; they had discussed this moment many times following Bert's revelations about vampires. A holy wafer in this chest would render it useless to Brultzner. Unless he had others to which he could fly for refuge, the vampire was lost without his coffin. On his return, they would have him at their mercy. He would be on the run, banished from their world forever – or in their power. Bert handed the little casket, in which the wafers were stored, to Clara. She gave him one of her hawk-like stares and then, taking the wafer from the pyx, she placed it carefully on the silk. Crafty watched in amazement.

"Fear brings order to society, Mr Catchpole. See how well the old house has resisted any attempts at vandalism."

"Did you speak, Mr Catchpole?" asked Clara.

"No. I was thinking. He said that to me."

In Sarah's room they found her coffin and, when Bert raised the lid, the aroma of earth was stronger – even malodorous. Crafty remembered the smell. 'You will bring soil from the churchyard this night, undercover of darkness.'

"I did it!"

"What, Mr Catchpole?"

"I brought it – the soil!"

"She had to have her native soil, consecrated, within her coffin," said Bert.

"What's it all mean," yelled Crafty, "What's this got to do with his power?"

"Sshh, Mr Catchpole. I'd forgotten we'd not taken you into our confidence. I will explain later – when we get home."

Bert's use of the word 'home' must have reassured Crafty because he watched in silence as Clara placed a second wafer in Sarah's coffin. When they stood again in the hallway, he watched while Bert unlocked Brultzner's study, entered, drew the heavy curtains and beckoned to Clara.

"I shall be here for a considerable time," said Bert, "There are many books and papers. Be sure to replace anything you touch exactly as you found it – just in case we decide to go back on our plan."

Crafty looked back into the hallway. At the far end he saw what had been the back parlour, but was now Sarah's morning room, where Harry Bailey claimed he had seen the Monet. His curiosity was roused. While Bert read, he'd take a look in there.

"Oim seein'my way clear ..."

"You do that Crafty," interrupted Bert, who did not want to be disturbed.

In the morning room, Crafty's eyes were drawn to Matthew's little bed. There was just enough light to see it there, nestled discreetly in the corner. Crafty imagined the child within it. 'Tonight you will come with me, silently, and do whatever I bid.'

Crafty felt his head sink back into his shoulders. Once more he saw the whole of the face – the lash-less and reddened eyelids, the aquiline nose, the pale lips and the silver-grey hair. Outside in the lane there was a woman and Crafty knew her, recognised Sarah Marjoram ... the little Turrel boy lay there, several days into death ... looking as fresh as ever ... Crafty became aware that he was staring into Matthew Marjoram's bed ... there had been a child ... a boy ...

He stumbled from the room, down the cellar steps and out into the yard. 'You will find me a good master, Mr Catchpole.' He hadn't – he hadn't at all. He gulped down the warm air of the summer night and leaned against the spiked railing.

"Mr Catchpole?"

It was Clara Gobley's voice. She had come to find him – she and Bert were worried. Would he like to accompany her into the second floor rooms, while Bert finished his reading, and they could look at those paintings? Crafty followed her like a zombie.

They found the paintings which had moved ever upwards – Monet, Cezanne, Gauguin, Van Gogh ... just names to Crafty – names muddled in with screams and hammer blows and blood and a smile of innocence.

Dawn approached as they left the Old Vicarage. Bert wore a smile upon his face and carried a number of books under his arm. The holy wafers had been left in the coffins, and Bert had written a note to Horst Brultzner – a note requesting him to present himself at Clara's bungalow upon his return.

"They will return at night and find themselves banished from their home forever – unless we decide that they shall return and under what agreements. The day of animal power is with us, Clara."

Crafty listened but did not understand although they explained everything to him. That night, and for many nights, he was with his computer and the words he typed into his search engine were words he had never imagined before – vampire ... Un-dead ... nosferatu.

CHAPTER 13

'The pale cast of thought'

Far away, in Estonia, Peter Vishnya also spent sleepless nights thinking of Horst Brultzner. He had suspected the man from the beginning. As early as their first meeting in spring – in a sense, before their first meeting in spring – his instinct had told him all he needed to know; but he had suppressed that instinct, surrendered it to reason, knowledge and intelligence. Even now, after his visit to Leipzig, he was unsure whether to accept what he must know to be true.

He was a visiting a friend in Parnu, a seaside and spa town in the south west, located at the mouth of the River Parnu on the Gulf of Riga about eighty miles from Tallinn. It was a well-known spa – renowned for its healing waters and mud baths – and Peter had spent his morning in the Health Rehabilitation Centre, an echo of Soviet days, where a medical team weighed him and gave him a white card that he was told to keep with him always.

His mud bath had been the usual unforgettable experience, but one that seemed obligatory in Parnu. He had been coerced into stripping naked in a white tiled alcove while the attendant – powerful in a dirty, white doctor's coat – had poured mud onto a khaki sheet. Peter had then been required to lay in this, while more mud was poured over him, leaving just his face and chest clear. The mud was real – it was full of grit and smelt like compost – and Peter hoped that it was not re-cycled from the previous patient. Afterwards he showered and dressed, and had to admit that his skin felt warm and smooth as he strolled along the promenade.

He was on his way to Munga's – a homely restaurant where they would get a three course lunch for two, including drinks, for about fifteen pounds. He was looking forward to bacon collar with mouldy cheese and a Pallas Athena salad. Peter realised that the ambience of the place was taking him over; Dunburgh-on-Sea seemed far away, and getting further. The Estonians, his own people, were reserved and courteous. A smile did not always bring a response – it might take two or three – and, in the restaurant even families or groups of friends would sit quietly conversing.

The previous day they had driven out into the countryside – his friend, Omar, with his wife and young daughter, Vera, who had played with Yevgeny in the endless pine forests around their summer home. Peter had laughed and said, "Summer home, what wealth!?" knowing that this was not so. The place had been commandeered, for no apparent reason, under the Soviets, and Omar and his family moved to what amounted to a council flat in Parnu. When the Berlin wall

293

came down, Omar – now working in the town – found he had a summer house in the country! "It caused much amusement!" It was dilapidated and dirty – at some point a tree had fallen through the roof and nobody had bothered to remove it and make repairs – but it possessed a kind of rustic luxury which Peter found comfortable. Omar had created a barbecue in the peasant style. Starting with dry wood he had made a bonfire and actually cooked over the embers. Valya, his wife, had marinated the meat all day, and they could squeeze the juices from it because of its succulence. She had served it with a sharp sauce, peppers, small cucumbers and fresh bread from the oven.

Here, on the salary Horst Brultzner paid him, Peter would be a wealthy man. He could afford to buy a country house like Omar's and renovate it to what, in England, would be a standard of unimaginable luxury. Peter Vishnya had relaxed in the knowledge, watching his son and Omar's daughter in the glow of the fire, talking with his friends and rubbing the ears of his wolf, Anton.

Now, the promenade stretched before him, with lawned gardens to his left and the sandy beach to his right. Between the line of palm-like trees, he saw a few fishing boats. 'By the next morning Sarah had disappeared and a boat had been out to sea and back again. It had been moved without wheels and would have taken many men?' 'Yes. What made you think of that?' 'It's been on my mind all evening. Why would anyone steal a boat?'

On his first night here, Peter had witnessed a strange ritual. The beach had been packed with people of all ages, but the action had taken place around the young. There had been fire everywhere – anchors and torches alight on the sands and out to sea – and lines of young people dancing and waving. They had eaten fish barbecued on the beach, the oils running out through the bread onto their arms. The tanned skin of the youngsters had glistened; all had been highly-charged and excited. Peter remembered thinking that they would pair and mate that night – as the English had once done on May Day, but here it would be somewhere along the beach among the boats. One young man had emerged from the crowd, and passed down one of the lines of dancers. In his hand he had carried a flaming torch. He was naked from the waist up, and walked with the flame into the sea – further and further out until he disappeared completely, and the flame died in the waves. It reminded Peter of the slaying of the Corn God. Was this ritual such an event – ensuring the success of next year's harvest: sacrifice one young person to the god of the sea, to be re-born next season? But what had this ritual, in his own land, to do with anything?

Where should – where could – he start? What did he know? He had already been over that day in St George's churchyard many times and knew that he had acted out of instinct. Brultzner had provoked him. "The god who dies for his people is not a Christian idea." And then he'd said, "I sense a power in you, Mr Vishnya, but I do not sense it in this church … Why have you brought me here?" Yes – why – as a warning – a warning of what? He knew now, as he knew then, that he had played his hand very badly – and to what purpose?

Once familiar with Brultzner's business transactions, he had made his "discreet phone calls". Brultzner was known throughout Europe, and all thought well of him. Brultzner was trusted; his word was his bond.

'By the next morning Sarah had disappeared and a boat had been out to sea and back again. It had been moved without wheels and would have taken many men?'

'Oh yes - the biggest surprise of all, though, is that Sarah Marjoram is back and working for your employer at the Old Vicarage! Can you believe that?' And the little boy had died from a total loss of blood!

Instinct – intuition – feelings? There was no reason to suppose that it was Brultzner who had borrowed the boat, or that Sarah's working at his vicarage was anything but normal. But there was Leipzig and what had happened there – or what he supposed had happened.

Peter Vishnya had gone to Leipzig on Horst Brultzner's orders to collect a chest of papers and deliver them to an address in Prague. It had been no more than a business trip. Peter was to stay at Brultzner's house in Leipzig where his housekeeper would look after him during his stay. Peter was to enjoy himself in the old city. His housekeeper, whose name was Eva Schulz, would furnish him with a list of contacts – friends of Brultzner's who would make him welcome as a stranger in their city.

He had flown into Leipzig/Halle Airport and, via the extremely efficient Airport Express train, found himself at Leipzig Central Railway Station within fourteen minutes. Frau Schulz had offered a car, but Peter preferred to find his own way, knowing that Brultzner's house was somewhere in the city. The station forecourt was the focal point of all transport systems and the gateway to the city.

He knew Leipzig only by repute. He had heard of the Leipzigers proverbial love of coffee, which gave rise to the nickname 'kaffeesache' and he, sharing this love, hoped to find the old coffee houses which had been popular meeting places since the seventeenth century. He headed for the Old Market Square situated right in the city centre.

Kleine Paris – the city's nickname in the eighteenth century – attracted many prominent artists, among them Goethe, Schumann and Bach. Leibniz and Wagner had been born in the city. Mendelssohn conducted the Gewandhaus Orchestra from 1835 to 1847. Luther debated in public on the site of the present Rathaus. Peter, who had only ever travelled to England for his marriage until now, was excited. He turned off the main square and into one of the many side streets where he found his coffee house. He sat down and ordered – through a clean, immaculately dressed waitress – a streusel made with cranberries and blueberries, served with whipped cream.

This evening, having introduced himself to Frau Schulz, he would wander out into the city, once more, and find the Auerbachs Keller, immortalised in Goethe's *Faust* and where, he understood, he might find the famous Leipzig Gose – a top-fermented beer, forgotten for centuries, until revived by an enterprising Leipzig landlord.

Thinking that he had better let his landlady know he had arrived, Peter took out his phone and rang the number given him by Horst Brultzner. The housekeeper's voice was (he forgave himself the cliché) musical. The nearest instrument to which he could equate her voice was that of a Welsh harp and he felt caught, somehow, in the middle of a long glissando. He was to enjoy himself, there was no hurry, she would have a meal ready for the evening, Herr Brultzner always served his guests at eight if that was convenient and then – perhaps – he would like to see their beautiful city? No, thank you, she would not join him at the café despite it being a lovely sunny afternoon in late summer. He was pleased that his German was of such a high – if theoretical – standard. He was looking forward to the evening.

Having finished his coffee, Peter – the housekeeper's voice still singing in his head – made his way towards the address he had been given. He knew that it was somewhere behind the Old City Hall, off the Naschmarkt, near the Old Stock Exchange. Here he found the sculpture of Goethe – the one which commemorates his student years and sweethearts – and, beyond, a maze of small streets. Eventually, he stood in front of a tall building; he assumed it was Renaissance, but couldn't be sure. It was three stories high with sets of double windows, each with a decorated pediment – was that the word he wanted? It seemed to be part of a long terrace of houses and he wasn't quite sure which of these belonged to Herr Brultzner. In front of him was an open archway which led into an interior courtyard; above him, a balcony encompassed two french windows. He was staring in a bemused fashion when a side door under the arch opened, and a woman stepped out and greeted him:

"Herr Vishnya?"

"Frau Schulz?"

"Welcome to Herr Brultzner's house. Enter freely, go safely!"

The housekeeper obviously shared her employer's sense of humour – or perhaps this was the greeting she had been taught to use. Peter Vishnya smiled and entered the Leipzig home of what he was beginning to think was a remarkable man. He knew what to expect – a Renaissance house decorated and furnished in the German Renaissance fashion. He was not mistaken – everything from the cutlery to the furniture, as he learned during his stay, was entirely in tune with the period of the house. In the light of the hallway, he looked at the housekeeper, closely.

He couldn't remember seeing such a beautiful woman ever before in all his life. She was tall and statuesque with a figure that was entirely Greek. Her hair, which was soft and flowing, was honey-blonde and rippled over her shoulders in a full, glowing mane. Her face was pale and radiant with an inner light – a light that seemed to him, in the hallway of Brultzner's Leipzig home, to have a blue iridescence. He looked into her eyes, and they engulfed him. He thought, at first, that they were turquoise in hue but then decided that the blue was tinged with red, and he settled for purple. They were liquid, of course: Peter thought that all such eyes must be liquid because they shone so brightly. If only those eyes would stop looking at him, but the gaze of Frau Schulz was unflinching. The pallor of her face was enhanced by her mouth which was gently curved in lips of reddish-gold. Despite all this, Peter knew that she was not a young woman. He was reluctant to guess her age but it must, judging by the trim lines around her eyes, have been about fifty. Yet, within her and from her, there shone an eternal freshness.

"Let me take your bag, Herr Vishnya. You must be tired."

"No – not a bit – I have enjoyed your city. It has been a pleasant welcome for me this afternoon."

"I will show you to your room. Please rest before your dinner is served."

"Thank you."

He stayed in his room, the balcony of which overlooked the city, until a bell summoning him to dinner. The meal was served by Frau Schulz and had, obviously, been cooked by her: he enjoyed fischsuppe mit krabben, muscheln and heilbutt, westerlandertopt and frische erdbeeren served with a Reisling Spatlese Mosel. Peter loved the German sound of the food, each course of which was presented by the housekeeper with pride, and relished each mouthful. By the time he had finished eating, he was satiated, tired and ready for an early bed, but the "night was still young" Frau Schulz reminded him and Herr Brultzner wished him to see the beautiful city by night. When would he be ready to go out into the night?

Peter had never come across such a woman in all his thirty years. She seemed utterly composed and the smile, which never left her lips, sparkled from her eyes. Simply looking at her filled him with an inner contentment he felt he had never known before; he raised his own eyes and looked into hers with a longing that filled him with shame.

"Would you allow me to show you our beautiful city, Herr Vishnya? It would bring me great pleasure."

He could not have refused even had he wanted to; besides, the very idea of having her company into the night fascinated and enlivened him.

"Of course – thank you. My name is Peter."

She inclined her head slightly, and her high cheekbones seemed to lift as she smiled.

"I am Eva and I am pleased to know you."

It was a warm night, but he noticed Eva wore a dress of purple velvet flecked with gold. It was tight upon her body, but long sleeves hung loose about her arms. On her hands she wore light, golden gloves which rested gently on him, as she ran her arm through his so that she leaned slightly into his shoulder. Her neck was slender, with the faint wrinkles of her age, and rose proudly from strong, finely-shaped shoulders which were revealed by the low neckline of her dress. Her breasts glistened with the same blue light which irradiated her face, giving the impression that her skin was translucent. Had she been sent to seduce him, Eva Schulz could not have had a more devastating effect on Peter Vishnya; but there was nothing coquettish in her manner, which was open and honest. She laughed and said:

"There is a nightspot here which I love, but where it would be difficult for a woman to venture alone. I am so pleased you have allowed me to escort you, Peter."

She laughed, quite girlishly, as though she were going somewhere somewhat risqué for the first time, and Peter found this charming. There was nothing pretentious in her manner as she took his arm, and they made their way through the narrow passageways and round the corners where people teemed on their night out.

As they walked, Eva talked about her city. They passed through the Specks Hof arcade, one of the most architecturally outstanding premises in Leipzig.

"It was a simple trade yard owned by a man called Speck! Then – at the turn of the last century, Emil erected the Trade Fair House. It was run by the Baron ..."

"The Baron?"

"The Baron of Speck. He was a wonderful man – big, virile, everything a man should be. And so many sheep. He was rich – so rich. They extended it almost as soon as it was built and connected it to the Hansa House Messehof by means of the passage. I love it! There are so many shops – so wonderful! And now – after all those years of Soviet dullness, it has come to life again."

"Where are we going?"

"The Moritzbastei!"

She laughed again, and he felt that he was taking her on a night out, so pleased was she to be in the city on the arm of a man.

"It was designed by Hieronymus Lotter in ... oh the 1550s. He was so efficient – all a good German should be, Peter Vishnya," she laughed, "But it was abandoned – like so many old buildings, and then in 1974 students from the university excavated it and turned it into a trendy night club. There are battlements where we have theatre and concerts and open-air movies, and vaults going three stories underground! So many young people, it giddies the mind!"

"You like the young?"

"I love the young – they are the future of the world. So many lovely young people, and all in love! You will take me there, Peter, and there we will start our night out together."

They moved on through the passageways of the city and the walk was as exhilarating as riding out on a fresh, young horse. Each step that took them nearer to the nightlife of Leipzig was accompanied by the restless pawing of the cobbles beneath their feet. Her heels clipped the ground like finely shod hooves, seeming to strike sparks from the cobblestones, and Peter half expected to see a trail of fire behind them. Yet their progress was stately, even slow, and he realised that the excitement of the journey was within him. Eva but glided until they came to an iron gateway beyond which danced spots of light, and they made their way along a vaulted passage into the heaving throng of young bodies dancing and talking and simply being alive. The animation was intense and Eva fed from it. Waitresses hurried backwards and forwards with steaming, slopping tankards of beer. Peter had the sensation of being hurried through the courtyard of a castle towards his fate in some deep dungeon. Down and down they went, stone walls rising on each side as they twisted and turned along spiralling stairways.

He drank little and Eva drank nothing; the intoxication was within them both as they danced. Nothing is more flattering to a man than having a woman excited in his company. It is not the expectation of what might be, but the thrill of what is happening at that moment, suspended from all other moments in time. She looked into his eyes in that direct way she had, and her gaze lit his heart with brilliance. He was not himself, he realised that, but could not draw back from what was happening. Euphoria swept over him until, at last, she led him to a cool bench in a quiet corner, and they sat with the stars above them shining against the darkness.

"You like to dance, Peter?"

He didn't answer: he couldn't – the things he wanted to say were unspeakable to him and a simple "Yes" seemed trivial.

"I am enjoying myself so! This is a chance I do not often have – to be taken out by a handsome man who thinks only of me. One night in an eternity of nights is not much to ask from life – is it?"

"No."

Her head tilted back and she looked up and across at him, her neck stretched gently until it was as smooth as carefully folded cream. He felt his head moving towards her throat as his eyes watched the blood pulsing under the satin skin. His lips brushed against her, softly. He felt her breathe warm on his cheek; it was audacious in a way he could not comprehend. 'Peter.' He wasn't sure whether she spoke his name or whether he simply heard the sound of her voice within him. He seemed to swoon for a while, and when he came round his head was resting against the back of the seat, and Eva was looking down at him.

"It was the heat."

"I fainted?"

"For a moment only – come, we will walk. It will be cooler away from here."

They left the Moritzbastei in a dream, and Peter felt she knew of the spell she was casting over him and it was as though she, too, was incapable of withholding its enchantment. Without a word, she told him that she had waited for him so long, had dreamed of him coming, that the love between them was 'stronger than death', that she would 'follow him to the ends of the earth', that he would 'live in her heart forever' ... He was beguiled, as he walked.

They arrived in the oldest part of the city – the area around Barfussgässchen, where the buildings stand shoulder to shoulder. She knew them all, intimately, and led him round numerous picturesque corners and down winding passages.

"Drallewatsch," she said, "We must dance again! I love the atmosphere!"

They ordered food which only he ate and beer which only he drank. Peter never noticed this at the time – it was only afterwards, thinking back, trying to piece the events of that evening into some sort of sensible understanding. They were only snacks, of course – something to soak up the beer – and what they left, the students, who swarmed through the pubs, seized. Eva loved this, and said she only ordered the food so that she could watch the young people enjoying it.

They walked back to Horst Brultzner's house, languorously. The sense of weakness was wonderful – all energy seemed to drain from his body and Peter offered himself up to the night. He was light; he could float. Eva had welcomed him as a housekeeper, but taken him out on the town as a lover. She had a taste for the grand life, a feeling for style. No one seemed to know her, but she was known everywhere. It was late or, if you prefer, early when they returned to the house behind the Naschmarkt. Eva unlocked the side door under the archway, and he bowed her in before him.

"Such a night, such a night – I do not know when I have enjoyed myself more in recent years. Thank you, Peter."

"Thank you."

"You are here for a few days – I will show you more of the city tomorrow."

"I would love that."

"You know your room. Would you like a night cap?"

"Thank you – no. I am very tired. I think I will just sleep."

"There is no rush. Sleep all day if you like. There is a bell in your room. Summon me when you want to break your fast."

His beautiful bedroom, with its wooden panels and white walls, had inspired him when he arrived, but now he was so tired Peter scarcely noticed it. He did remember, afterwards, noticing that the heavy curtains had already been drawn and wondering by whom, but this was all. There was a key – a heavy iron key – on the inside of the door and this he turned, climbed into bed and slept. He did not know how long he slept – it may have been well into the next day because little light entered through the curtains – but he did recall, or thought he re-called, waking once.

The sleep of exhaustion (he had travelled all the previous day) may have fuddled his memory, but he thought he saw Eva standing by his bedside. This could not have been, of course, for he had locked the door, but it seemed as though she stood watching him sleep. She was wearing one of those old fashioned nightdresses, held loosely on the shoulders by a ruffled neck, and flowing to the ankles. She stood a long time observing him, and he was consumed again by that over-riding passion for her. The expression on her face was one of utter contentment, and all he wanted to do was reach up and hold her to him.

She sat by him on the bed, reached out and ran her fingers across his brow and through his hair; the gesture was tender, infinitely delicate, and full of compassion. Her eyes, even deeper purple now in the half-light of the bedroom, were full of tenderness. They shone with a kind of gratitude – as though she had waited for him a long time and her patience had been rewarded. Eva seemed satisfied to sit there gazing upon him as though his presence in the house fulfilled a long-felt need. How long this went on, Peter could not remember.

Eventually Eva stirred with a small sigh, shifted her position slightly on the bed and drew back the sheets – for they were sheets, white cotton sheets under a summer blanket! He later recollected their coolness on his body. He was naked, but it was not by this she was roused. Eva merely passed her hands over his chest once or twice and then turned to his wrist, which was spread open on the nightdress that covered her thighs. She took a pin, then, which she seemed to have tucked into the night dress and made two small pricks in his wrist. The blood trickled, and she stooped over his arm and sucked hard. The feeling of weariness he had on the way home returned, and a soothing drowsiness swept through him, drawing the ache of tiredness from his limbs, leaving him refreshed and dazed. The more she sucked, the more blood she took from him, the further he drifted into an untroubled sleep. His mistress had need of him and he was giving her satisfaction.

When he woke later in the day, he bathed, dressed and went downstairs. It was already well after noon, and Eva was waiting for him in her housekeeper's black dress and white apron. She smiled.

"You have slept well?" she asked.

"I had no idea it was so late."

"You are on holiday. There is no rush. I thought perhaps you would prefer a light lunch to a hearty breakfast?"

She laughed again, and his body tingled outwards from the groin.

"Thank you."

"The courtyard is pleasant at this time of the day. There I have set your meal."

She led him to the courtyard, and he ate by the fountain while Eva served him, course by course. On her comings and goings, she talked quietly all the time, clearly taking pleasure in his company. When the meal was finished, they sat over coffee.

"Are there any particular parts of the city you would like to see?"

"It is your city – your joy! I leave it to you," he replied.

"Then, this evening, after you have eaten, we will set forth!"

For the four days of his stay in Leipzig, at the house of Horst Brultzner, he went out each evening with the housekeeper, Eva Schulz. He felt all the excitement of a man on his first affair. She took him to the famous Auerbachs Keller; the cellar was, she said with a laugh, a "wine bar" in 1519. She obtained tickets for a performance of *Cosi fan Tutti* at the Opera House on the north side of Augustplatz. "It is the oldest musical stage in Germany, Peter – it goes back to 1693!" They stood together in front of the south portal of St Thomas's Church and admired the statue of Bach, and there they listened to a Monday concert of Bach's music. They visited the Bose House "where Bach and his family had been guests of his friend, George Bose".

"Coffee, Peter – I know you love coffee. I have saved this for the last – Zum Arabischen Coffe Baum. It is the centre of Leipzig for three hundred years – can you imagine that? Here have been Hoffman and Wagner and Bach and Grieg and Lessing – and, of course, Goethe! Schumann had his own table! In and out they would go – just as you and I are doing now! And here Helmut Kohl and Lothar de Maiziere talked about bringing Germany together again."

Over the doorway the sandstone sculpture showed an Ottoman offering a cupid a cup of coffee. Peter smiled at the innocence of the carving – the Christian West and the Islamic East together over a cup of coffee.

On their last night – and all their excursions had been at night – Eva was quieter than usual. They had been to listen to the Gewandhaus Quartet – "the oldest string quartet in the world" she had said in a rare moment of excitement that evening – and were standing outside St Nicholas's Church where the prayers for freedom were said, and the German people waited for the coming of a peaceful re-unification.

"We were so happy that night – all together, waiting in the darkness. I was, for a while, at one with my people again."

Back at Brultzner's house, she kept him from his bed drinking and talking.

"Must you go today? Can there not be a few more days together? I have so much enjoyed your company, Peter Vishnya, I do not know what I will do without it. I would not take you from your life, but I would detain you a while longer that you might be with me and bring me comfort. Is that not a good kind of friendship – almost a kind of love? What normal woman would offer her man such a freedom? You have nothing to fear from me – I have only the warmest affection for you. Will you not miss me? Will you not be a little less happy without me? Is there not just the tiniest regret in your soul that we are to part?"

In his soul – and in his heart – he had to admit there was more than a normal grief. When he went to bed that night, Peter Vishnya left the door unlocked. He was tired of what he saw as the dishonesty – the pretence – and he tried to stay awake until she came. This night, after she had sucked from his wrist, Eva did not sit by his bed, but pulled her nightdress off – over her head so that the golden hair tumbled down over her beautiful shoulders – and settled down by his side. He fought against it, but drowsiness overcame him and he drifted into sleep.

Omar looked at him as Peter completed his story. They had finished their three course lunch; the gulaschsuppe, the bacon collar with mouldy cheese, the Pallas Athena salad and the frische Ananas were being "settled" in his stomach by a string of vodkas. Omar saw his friend's dilemma, and thought it ludicrous.

"You have done nothing wrong, Peter. You are being morally fastidious. Each night you go out with this Eva who is a lonely woman, and enjoys your company. Each night you return with a full belly, and you dream – that is all! So you liked her – she is a beautiful woman! Maybe you felt a little desire for her, but you turn over and sleep. Is this morally reprehensible? For this you will make a "clean breast of it" to your Rebecca? I don't think so. You have nothing to make a clean breast of – did you even kiss this woman? No!"

"What about the sucking of the blood?"

"I have said – a dream. You had eaten well of foreign food, and drunk."

"Not so much."

"It was a dream – strange surroundings, unaccustomed feelings and the excitement of a remarkable city. Add to these the closeness of a beautiful and unusual woman and what can you expect? Was there a mark on your wrist each morning?"

"No."

He had been puzzled by that, but assumed that it was because of the tiny pinprick.

"There you are then! You have not said what happened in Prague."

"Nothing much – I stayed only a short while, was welcomed by his housekeeper, met Horst and Sarah – that is all, really. He was pleased with his chest of papers, and asked me to do a few things in Tallinn when I returned."

"He seems a remarkable man to me – so much energy!"

"Yes. The house in Prague was renovated in the style of its original period."

"Peter – you would not be working for this man if you genuinely suspected him of vampirism. Your instincts have led you astray this time. Besides – you're not telling me you believe in that superstitious nonsense, are you? ... What does Anton think of him?"

"He looks him in the eye and sits watching. I think he is the only creature who has met Herr Brultzner who is not either charmed or perturbed by him," he replied.

"There you are – trust your ... wolf. What did Socrates say of dogs?"

"It was Plato. He said that they were the only true philosophers ..."

"He said – I remember now – that they had the soul of a philosopher."

While Peter exorcised his demons with Omar over vodkas in Munga's, Rebecca Unwood was serving tea at the church fete. She enjoyed this – it was an essential part of her father's work in the community.

There was an unspoken promise between her and Peter Vishnya which, she knew, he would honour. What was uncertain was the form that honour would take, and how it might change her life. 'It was not until I went there ... that I realised what use I could be. It would be difficult now to turn my back on that.' So would her future lie in Estonia among people she did not know – away from her own family? That night she wrote her usual e-mail to Peter.

The church fete was really enjoyable. Everyone had a good time and dad was pleased because the churches came together for this one. It seemed to bring the village a little harmony after the awful summer we have had. First Clive Brown and then little Luke Turrell! When do you think you will be able to pay us another visit? It seems so long since you were here. Was your visit to Leipzig successful?

Rebecca looked at what she had written – it was all questions and misery and wanting. She deleted it and sat looking at her laptop, and then she used the little blue arrow: if she couldn't say what she felt at this stage what was the point?

"Dad has lost his way a bit, you know. When he came into the ministry, he expected it to be dynamic. He doesn't really want his time to be spent on fetes and the like. He seems always to be on the run from something or catching up but never, he feels, moving forward. I try to tell him that people are caught not taught."

'Thank you for saying what you did in your last letter. I needed to read in words what was accepted between us that afternoon and evening.' He had written, quite simply, that he loved her; and that when he returned they would talk about this – but he hadn't returned, and she was no good at writing letters of love because she had no experience. Besides, the situation between them wasn't straightforward; they had Yevgeny's feelings to consider.

Have you spoken to Yevgeny yet? I do not want to make things difficult for your little boy. And you must also consider Anton!

Rebecca laughed when she wrote that, but she was rather jealous of the wolf and Yevgeny; they were with Peter in Estonia – she was alone in England. She deleted the bit about Yevgeny and Anton; it sounded silly and possessive. How could you unfold intimacies in an e-mail? Rebecca looked over what she had written. It was unconnected ramblings that led nowhere. She deleted the lot and turned to her diary.

Dear Peter,

I love you very much. I know that now, and can't wait until we are together again. It seems so silly when life has suddenly become so meaningful for me that I cannot touch and talk to the man who has helped to make it so. Wherever I go and whatever I do now you are always with me, by my side. I think of you, constantly, day and night.

I never realised until we sat together that afternoon in your garden that love frees. I should have done because the love of Jesus frees the soul, but it wasn't until then and the lovely evening that followed that I felt FREE in a way I had never done before. I feel it now, sitting here writing to you. There is a real sense that I can find love only in you and – I hope – you will find a new love in me.

I am so pleased you mentioned marriage in your letter because it is only in marriage that love can find true fulfilment. It isn't until a man and woman have made their commitment to each other that they can forge a love unique to themselves. I felt, that afternoon, that you accepted me for what I am and it is only from there – from what you are and what I am – that we can begin. We should not have expectations of each other but trust each other to have goodwill.

I do not just want to be your wife, Peter – I love saying and writing your name! – I want to be your lover and friend as well. I sometimes think that is the hardest part of a marriage – to treat your husband or wife as well as you would treat a friend.

Do you know what I want to do when you get back? I want to be alone with you. I want us to go out for the day – say London, or somewhere we are not known and can mingle with the crowd, unseen. I want to wander through Covent Garden with you and have fresh melon and orange at Ponti's, just simply to laugh and chat. I want to see you smile, and watch the glow of the sun on your hair. There are too few mornings like that in life. I want to plan a day for you that turns out to be a day for me as well! Does that make sense? I want to walk and talk and shape our future together.

I know that you loved your first wife and I respect you for that. I don't have any feelings of anxiety, let alone jealousy, regarding her at all. I do not see myself in any way standing in the light she shone for you. I hope to be able – through our love for each other – to be able to shine a light of my own. I know already that you will be a kind husband and a tender man and I desire that more than you might imagine, Peter.

I shall feel proud being Peter's wife. Your attractiveness drew me to you right from the first time we met – although I refused to acknowledge it even to myself! How proud I shall feel whenever I stand by your side, wherever it may be – in sunny wood or rainy street. You raise my expectations of myself and I am glad of that, and I know that you will stay by my side and speak up for me should I ever be beset by the troubles of this world.

We must be honest with each other – without fear or favour of the consequences. Looking back after many years we should be able to say that we were true to our ideals and that they were realised in each of us. For both our sakes we should never be less than sincere with each other – without rancour and in benevolence.

We should not fear the changes that will, inevitably, occur between us. Love and marriage are about change, and we should embrace it with joy and fresh understanding – give one another an active voice, encourage one another to walk proudly, nurture our neglected talents.

Oh, Peter – the unexpectedness of it all! Hold me – we have the day! My spirit soars when I think of you - summer on your skin, and evening light. The memory of this fills my heart for the day!

Love you more than the entire world,

Rebecca."

Eva Schulz stood looking at her bed; to all intents and purposes it was a bed. It looked and felt like a bed – four-posted with green-gold satin curtains that slid open along shining poles at the touch of a hand. When she slipped in between the silken sheets, they would caress her body as lovers had done in the past and for a while, before she drifted into sleep, she would tingle with the excitement of what had been. In truth, however, she saw it for what it was – her coffin.

She had enjoyed the company of Peter Vishnya as much as she had told him – 'Must you go today? Can there not be a few more days together? I have so much enjoyed your company ......I do not know what I will do without it.' Walking and talking with the Estonian in her native city had brought her an inexpressible joy. For her, it had been an unnatural joy for she kept awake by guile and could not share in many things which brought him pleasure; but it had been enough, and so much more than she had known for so long.

The company of men had always delighted Eva – the company of men and all that went with it: the dancing, the feasting, the lovemaking, the sharing. All eternity was now hers, but she had lost the satisfaction of the moment – that happiness she had felt in the company of a man who was hers and hers alone. She could not live now as she had once done, but must flit through her 'life' as a creature of the night – destined, in the end, to be alone forever.

CHAPTER 14

The masked ball

The affect of Prague upon Sarah was even more breathtaking than Leipzig had been on Peter. She was a village girl who had never travelled far – the environs of Dunburgh-on-sea had been the limit of her world. Horst Brultzner realised this, of course – it was part of her attraction – and, prior to the night of the ball, he spent time introducing her to one of his cities.

On their first night, he walked her along the Royal Route, following the coronation processions of Czech kings since 1458. He was excited by the splendour of the buildings; she, by the golden sheen of the lamp light on the cobbles. They followed the mysterious paths and the narrow streets and passed through the Old Town Square. Sarah saw splendid murals and interesting facades, and was bombarded by such exotic names as The House of the Black Madonna. Horst Brultzner watched her with fascination, once again able to see everything fresh as though for the first time. There were the souvenir shops on Celetna Street offering toys and dolls in amber and garnet as well as porcelain and wood. She bought Matthew a wooden soldier painted in bright colours, and Horst bought her a jewel case made of Bohemian crystal. They climbed the Tower of the Old Town Hall with ease, drifting by the other walkers, and she made herself a souvenir, paying with her first foreign coin – 20 krona.

They passed through narrow streets and came, at last, to the one landmark of which she had heard – the Charles Bridge. Here, there was a brief, unpleasant incident when a pickpocket grasped her shoulder bag. Sarah, unused to these things, gasped and attempted to pull against him, but Horst, with that vampire speed and strength to which she was becoming accustomed, twisted the man's arm and tossed him over the bridge. The movement was so quick that no one but Sarah noticed until passers-by heard the splash and scream. There was a brief commotion, but she and Horst walked on without batting an eyelid. The bridge was alive with portrait painters – they were to return and have Sarah's painted for the Old Vicarage in Dunburgh – jazz ensembles, caricaturists and singers. She touched the statue of St John and made her wish at Horst's behest; he smiled but did not ask her what she desired. The final steps to the castle were anything but tiresome to them, and they stood together watching the wonderful view over Prague.

The following morning he took her to Wenceslas Square, and to a tailor's he had long known who was to make her gown for the masked ball. The tailor himself stood smiling and imperturbable, while three or four women fussed around Sarah, measuring her for the gown. Horst sat smiling, drinking coffee and eating dainty sweet cakes. He did this parsimoniously, and told Sarah afterwards that they would keep him awake later, but that it was expected. The tailor watched Sarah while puffing quietly on a cheroot and then, when the women had no more to measure or fuss about, he said:

"Fraulein – we shall create for you just the dress of the ball. Red ... in at the waist – you are lovely – and clinging your figure. Perhaps, off one shoulder and sheathed to your ankles? There will be freedom of movement for the legs – trust me."

He spoke quietly, without exclamation, and Sarah understood that he had been chosen by Horst because he would, without fuss or consultation and with perfect taste, create, for her, the "dress of the ball". Sarah had never had a ball gown, never known anyone who would have thought she might need one or want to be taken to a ball.

The night came and, that morning, the dress was delivered accompanied by the fussy little tailor and one of his women. The housekeeper, a rather dour woman who stood aloof from the proceedings but observed them with interest, let the tailor into the house and then kept close to him until he left. She had been nothing but friendly to Sarah – although this was to be expected – but Sarah could not make her out, could not see where she fitted into the world of Brultzner and doubted whether she would have been welcome without him.

Quite where the ball took place, Sarah never discovered and did not, afterwards, dare to ask. She was coming to understand that had Brultzner wished her to know she would have been told.

A large black car – the old type her father used to refer to as a "sedan" – arrived at the house. The housekeeper, Frau Schnell, assured her that Matthew would be perfectly safe, and Sarah was whisked away. She had half-expected a horse and carriage, like those on the main square, but the sedan was old-worldly enough to impress her. They sped through the dark streets and arrived, rapidly, at an imposing building with a long flight of steps that narrowed as they rose towards the two Roman-looking pillars which flanked the doorway. Servants were everywhere: from the chauffeur to the cloakroom attendant, they fussed and guided.

Sarah took the building to be some kind of mansion – the nearest thing she had seen to it in England was a stately home which she and her parents had visited one weekend. Room opened on to room through wide and gilded double doors. She felt splendid and relaxed in a way that was unfamiliar to her, and was unselfconscious about how she might appear to other people. With her honey-blonde hair sweeping her shoulders and the red dress hugging her figure from the breasts down to the ankles, Sarah knew – and her demeanour showed she knew – that she was, without any doubt, the most beautiful woman in the room. That dreamy look in her eyes which softened her expression, contrasted strongly with the hard, hungry looks of the other women. However beautifully dressed, however ornate their masks, they could not hide what lurked behind their eyes.

Horst led her from room to room – or, more appropriately, from suite to suite because 'room' was too inadequate a word to describe each chamber through which they passed. Each was complete within itself – its own amenities, its own style, its own décor; on this evening, also, each had its own chamber ensemble of musicians – a string quartet. The suites led one into the other, so providing an endless vista of opulence which receded far into the distance. Sarah had the impression that she was looking into a series of mirrors which reflected each other's images into eternity. The light glittered from every surface, provided as it was by a multitude of chandeliers and wall lamps whose rays were caught and cast from white walls, gilded doors and panelling and mirrors.

She was conscious of being watched as they passed the other guests. All deferred to Horst and, by association, to her; once again she had that unfamiliar feeling of being the centre of attraction, and Sarah revelled in it. Her dress stood out from those of all other women – partly because of the perfection of its fit but chiefly due to its colour. No one else had a red dress; most of the women wore dark shades of green, blue or purple. All the men were in evening dress although the period style varied greatly; some could have come from the latest Hollywood movie, others from centuries past.

She had been worried about the dancing, although she had danced as a child. Girls of her class in England no longer learned to ballroom dance as part of the ritual of growing up, but he assured her that "there was no need to be concerned." She would dance beautifully because he would lead her and "should her card be marked by any other gentleman" he, too, would be a dancer!

The dancing had yet to start, however, as they processed through the chambers. Groups eyed them as they passed, all giving Horst a slight bow of recognition. Sarah noticed that, while all acknowledged him, none approached unless he made the first move and then their attitude was one of respect – even servility. His demeanour was patriarchal – paternal to the point of condescension, but for each he had a few words and a smile. Sarah wondered about that; was it a smile? A smile had warmth; all these people smiled, but few showed any warmth. The twitching of the mouth was unaccompanied by any affection in the eyes; the 'smiles' were scarcely even social. She felt chilled amidst the glamour and the opulence; none of these people had any tenderness for her – that was an emotion they had left behind somewhere in another world.

The look in the eyes of most women was one of envy, as though they were watching the latest film star parading on the red carpet. The look in the eyes of most men was one of lust – a desire doomed to be unrequited. Sarah laughed; the look of abandon in them all only made her feel more elegant, more captivating.

She was, as yet, ignorant of classical music so nothing that each of the seven quartets played meant anything to her, but she did recognise that each chamber had a different ambience, and that this was due, at least in part, to the type of music played. Some was restful – sweet swathes of strings that swept her in and held her there, quietly. In other rooms, the instruments played violently, racking the feelings, drawing ire from the brow. In yet others, there was joy or exuberance or

– in a phrase she had heard from her mother – "gay abandon". In one, the strings were pensive, and in the final suite the music was even menacing.

As the evening progressed, Sarah realised that there was a pattern. The early music set the mood – set several moods depending upon which room you might be in at any time. Then, groups of players appeared – some in festive fashion like jugglers at a medieval fair, some reciting poetry, others acting out small plays or performing tableaux. In one chamber a group of dancers performed an arabesque and Sarah was impressed by the ornateness of the melodies and the intricacy of their movements; they seemed hardly to be the art of humans. The mime artists entranced her; dressed in black and white with their faces made up to look both ludicrous and frightening they expounded quietly their stories.

Brultzner's delight in her pleasure was evident to all. They knew him – over the centuries he had appeared with many women, all of whom later vanished somewhere into his realm, all of whom he treated with an almost antique courtesy. Like Sarah, they had worn red and been dressed in classic style; like Sarah they had danced with all night – inexhaustible until just before the cock crowed.

There was, of course, no food; waiters circulated with glasses of red wine on silver trays, but even this was drunk with moderation and not at all by some present. The evening was a celebration of the arts down the centuries and a welcoming of autumn and the dark nights to come.

Sarah's first dance, when it came after midnight, was with Horst Brultzner. It was one of the Strauss family's complicated waltzes and she knew, as soon as his arm circled her waist, that what he had said was true – she had no cause for concern over the juvenility of her dancing. He led her with precision, like an old dance master, and her feet and body found the pulse and she was away. Where they led, others followed and soon each suite – save the far, pensive one where those who preferred to talk gathered – was a swirl of dresses. The quartets provided waltzes, polkas, quicksteps, cha-chas, foxtrots (and some dances of which Sarah was unaware) to suit all tastes.

She danced all night from suite to suite and from man to man. Earlier, as they had moved from party to party conversing, a polite request had 'marked her card' and now each claimed his right. It was a ball as romantic as a young woman's dreams, and yet it was not about romance, and certainly not about love. The passion at this ball of vampires was cold and insular – detached, remote, aloof. Sarah sensed it in each of her partners to varying degrees; their interest in her was … communal. For them, she was not so much a person as an … item. She was part of this … collection of vampires, none of whom owed any allegiance, other than the loyalty of fear, to any of the others. Sarah struggled to find the words to explain this, but knew what she meant in her heart and – amidst the grandeur and affluence – she was repelled.

Horst was unaware of this and would have been either indignant or enraged had he sensed such a feeling in Sarah. She was a vampire now – one of the thousands who stalk the world – and there was no escape from her state other than the stake, the fire or dismemberment. He had long ceased to look upon his condition as a plight from which one might escape, but saw it rather as one might look upon one's ranking in society; you ignored or engaged the difficulties, and embraced the advantages. Each year the Masked Ball of the Equinox held the promise of long, dark nights and easier feasting ahead. Just as the humans gave thanks for the harvest stored, so the vampires gave thanks for the harvest to come. He liked this mansion in Prague but, in other years, had been equally pleased when the celebration took place in open fields surrounded by fire; then the costumes changed, and the vampires colluded with the wildness of the peasantry.

Here the 'mask' was twofold – the one they all wore and the one which shielded their passions. It amused Brultzner. He had always been fascinated by the terror which lurked beneath the skin. Dress a body with whatever luxury, disguise a face with whatever make-up – there was no camouflage for what humans called the 'soul'. Look through the mask into the eyes, and that was visible for all to see. It was her eyes that held a great part of Sarah's fascination. It was through them that Horst had been drawn to her and by which he was still, though her 'master', held. Watching her dance, he enjoyed the sheer exuberance of her movements. This enjoyment was heightened by the knowledge that all her partners would see what he had seen and captured forever – desires they still held, but could never consummate.

The celebration each year fell to one or other of the oldest vampires to arrange – according to his lights and his cultural roots. This year, wishing to present Sarah in surroundings of elegance, he had exerted his prerogative and commandeered the festivities. His people in Prague had been excellent, sparing no effort to create this occasion under his direction. He had taste and refinement. His people had long ago conspired to please him, and – with that terror he loved to see beneath the skin – they collaborated to display his extravagances. 'A good friend I have been to many, but few would choose me as an enemy.' He smiled to himself, thinking of Peter Vishnya safely entrapped in Estonia and enjoying himself with Eva in Leipzig.

Despite her repulsion, Sarah gave herself over to the night. She enjoyed being wanton – abandoning herself to the pleasure of the time. She had never been like this before; as a school girl she was what they called chaste until ... until her ex-husband came along and she got caught up with him. She'd enjoyed him, and him only, but that was of the past. Sarah felt the pull of her new kind. She danced, wondering what these vampires had been like as humans. They were all beautiful in the way vampires are – drained of all human toxins and waste, their skins glisten and possess that wonderful translucence as though a light was shining permanently from within; a light tinged always with the blue centre of a flame. They all seemed to have fed earlier in the evening because they had warmth – just as she and Horst had gone out for food before they dressed for the ball. Whatever their personalities had been in life, appeared intensified by their vampirism – intensified, burnt out, lost forever? Sarah shuddered, and saw Matthew asleep in his strange bed looked over by Frau Schnell. Abandoned? She turned into the night and the moment and the dancing.

Her partners had varied; this one was a violent man – one who took pleasure from the pain of others. Although it posed no threat to her, Sarah knew this from his dancing. Each step, each dip of his body, each corner of the dance floor was a chance to yank and tug and twist; in his eyes, as he made these moves, was a smile of relish. Her previous partner had a touch of the bizarre; his steps had been outlandish, his turns fantastical, his cornering grotesque as though he meant both to scare and embarrass her. Another had disgusted her; in life such a man would have made her flesh crawl and sent her running to the ladies room to vomit – his leer, the press of his paunch against her stomach made it churn.

They not so much danced as stalked the floor, like hunting animals. Once, she had watched a cat creeping in on a group of young rabbits enjoying the early morning grass. Nearer and nearer the cat had slid until the rabbits had nowhere to run. The cat had no need to hunt; his breakfast had been waiting for him. It was nature that called him – the instinct of his kind. Vampires were like that; they couldn't help what they were and each played out their role within the personality they had brought from life. Where had she heard that before? The rector had talked about that one Sunday in his sermon. 'Our spiritual body, after death, grows out of our earthly life as a plant grows from a seed. Our spiritual body expresses the personality we have developed in our earthly bodies.' She wasn't quite sure what he had meant, but he seemed to mean that nice people continued to be nice after death, throughout eternity; whereas those who had been unpleasant in life remained so. 'The kind of person I am now will continue into eternity. After death, I shall have a spiritual body.' But she wasn't dead; she was … the word stuck in Sarah's throat.

She looked at her partner; this one simpered round the floor. She could imagine him approaching a victim almost with an apology on his lips – but needing to feed just the same. She had heard of men apologising before they raped their victims, as though in some way that atoned for what was to happen.

How did she approach her prey? Were they dupes, scapegoats for her needs or was their suffering necessary in the great and grand scheme of things? At the moment she took them, they wanted her; Sarah believed that … she had to believe that or she would …. They wanted her; she had seen the desire rise in their eyes, had felt their erections against her thigh. She took them gently, caressing their pleasure as she drank. Even … even the child had come to her as it would have approached its mother to suckle as a baby.

She was one of them, dancing out her own destiny in this masked ball of the vampires. She writhed with them, taking on their shade from suite to suite, partner to partner – moving from violent waltz through disgusting tango to bizarre foxtrot, without demurring. The musicians played on and she danced on – capering, gambolling, prancing: whatever was demanded by the moment. She watched each ensemble of musicians engrossed in their playing. Whether violinist, cellist or viola player, everyone was entranced by their own virtuosity, engrossed in their own skill. As the night wore on, the dancing became wilder – not manic but intensified, so that the violent dancer wrenched, the bizarre dancer frolicked, the disgusting dancer drooped. Sarah danced in a nightmare of the emotions – writhing, squirming and twisting herself into her partner's pattern until each suite, each ensemble of sound became a corruption of the ballroom. The lights sparkled from chandeliers and the gilded walls, but the dance itself was a distortion of pleasure, an affront to the light.

As the night bore on towards dawn, the effrontery increased with each personality imposing itself on the dance, slashing into the rhythms in a dark riot of greens, blues, purples and blacks. Yet the similarity of the women's colours blended into bands of colour which draped and enfolded themselves around the rooms so that individuals became lost in the mob. The dancing of the women became wilder – riotous, stormy, tempestuous, and, even among this veneer of sophistication, rough. At a village hop, spurred on by drink, young couples would now begin to leave the room – drifting into the darkness to take each other as their desires dictated. Here, in this mansion of refinement these desires could not be satiated, but only turned in to feed on themselves – or so Sarah had thought, but this was yet another introduction to the world of the vampire. She noticed that couples did drift away, green and black by purple and black, by blue and black; drift away until the floors were less crowded and those that remained danced more freely.

Staircases led upwards from doorways that served each suite and the vampires left through them – warm now from their earlier feeding they could indulge in what humans called ... lovemaking. Sarah hesitated to use the word – once it had meant so much more to her than it did now. Their flesh afire from the blood and the dancing, they could couple themselves – before the cold and revulsion returned.

Below, the dancing continued: the intensity of their rhythms almost uncivilised, the sedateness of the ballroom became primitive. They were vampires, and the enhanced speed of their movements now translated into the dance – serene waltzes were abandoned in favour of unbridled polkas. The musicians were forced to increase their tempo to unbearable limits as the dancers – now riotous – raced from suite to suite in agonies of pleasure. Sarah was spun from partner to partner by a single tap on the man's shoulder. A simple "Excuse me" and she was off again in another direction with another vampire. She realised, with horror, that she was not tiring – that this unruly madness could last forever, that she could (daylight allowing) dance her way, un-jaded, through all eternity.

Horst, she noticed, danced little, but stood passing the night in conversation, and watching the proceedings with a paternal eye. There was a feeling within Sarah that they were building towards some climax to the evening, but she couldn't imagine what this might be – an entertainment, a spectacle? She couldn't decide. Some of those who had left for the bedrooms above returned to the dancing, others faded into the night that was now showing the first signs of day – the cold blueness which creeps over the horizon before the sun rises. They left singly, like disgruntled lovers, or embracing in pairs to find a final 'feed' before returning to their coffins. Others remained where they were – in the bedrooms, their passions bringing fresh horrors to the night. Sarah realized the complexity of what Horst had achieved with this ball; each of those above would have to retire to their 'grave' before daylight. Each bedroom would, therefore, have to harbour at least two coffins – each one of which must have been brought here by … she couldn't imagine how this had been achieved.

She realized, as she danced and pondered, that the chambers were filling again with fierce dancers. The musicians roused themselves to a final, strenuous exertion as the vampires returned from bedrooms and platz like feral cats. Once again, the brilliant lights captured the riot of dark colours – the rhythms of green, blue and purples cut through by the blacks of the men – as they invaded the mansion. Now, the dancing became uncivilized, even lawless, taking them back to those pagan harvests in field and farmyard where once they had propitiated their gods with human sacrifice. Horst came to her, and took her from the one with whom she danced and led her out onto the floor. He led her down to the far room where the music had – earlier in the evening when actors, singers, musicians and dancers entertained them – been pensive. Now it took on a solemn note, at least at first, as he danced her in a stately polka amongst the others. All were on the floor, with partners or in groups. Among the dark hues, saturated with the night, Sarah's red dress blazed like the sun.

He danced her round the far room and, as the tempo increased, the other dancers fell aside like so much corn cut under the sickle. They ceased dancing and stood to watch Horst's progress through the seven rooms. In each, he and Sarah out-danced them all, spinning them into a silent semblance of sheaves of grain. The blue of dawn was over-running the mansion as they cut their way through the vampires, room after room. There was expectation in the air; many of those present had passed, before, through this ritual. Sarah's exhilaration only increased as her understanding grew, and she laughed with pride, seeing the golden flame of her dress sweeping them all aside until, in the first and final chamber, she and Horst came to rest in the centre of the seventh floor. All was still, watching and fateful.

A wolf stood before her in the mansion – a creature so huge that Sarah realized it could not be a real wolf at all; but it was alive and waiting. She looked around and there no pity in any of the eyes that watched; indeed, there was fierce exultation as they gazed. She looked at Horst and he stepped back, making way for the wolf to spring and do what it was to accomplish. It rose from its haunches and made ready to spring upon her in a single bound, mouth wide, drooling with anticipation. She expected to feel its teeth rip into her body and tear great chunks of her flesh from her: she had read about how wolves fed. She saw the hair bristling along its back, and her own stood on end in terror. She saw only betrayal here: Horst had brought her to this annihilation just when he seemed to be helping her come to terms with the awfulness of her death. The wolf snarled, circled her once as though deciding where to bite, and then leaped, striking Sarah's shoulder and throwing her to the ground. She fell onto her back and the wolf, true to its kind, went for her throat. She struggled, piteously, for a short while, and then all was darkness.

A great cry of elation went up from the vampires. The sun had been destroyed for another year and they were free to roam the streets of their cities, towns and villages without qualms: easy in their minds, free in their spirits. The god of their darkness had been propitiated once more. They fled, as the sun touched the horizon, most to their coffins above, others – who lived in the city – to their homes.

Rebecca Unwood stood in her father's church and watched while it was decorated for the Harvest Festival. She loved the Harvest – had always loved it, ever since she brought her first gift as a young child – and this year she and Penny Read were to have the children centre stage for at least a time. Like her father, Rebeccca had no reservations over the pagan elements, and had – with a great deal of mischievous humour – taken up Martin Billing's suggestion of "a corn dolly the size of a man standing in the doorway of the Church Centre welcoming the faithful." This was already in hand, thanks to Penny Read, who was to provide the expertise, and the Podd family, who were to provide the sheaf.

"It's coming on nicely."

Penny Read's voice broke into her thoughts and she was relieved. The oars were lashed to the pews, the drift nets hung from the rafters, ship's lamps adorned the window sills, anchors encircled the font, lobster pots lined the chancel, rope was coiled strategically in both porches and by the vestry steps, a tiller rested by the lectern, green glass floats hung from the pulpit, a trawl net was draped from the coat of arms on the north wall and small piles of rowlocks were about to be located by the choir stalls. Boss Wigg and his men from the Fishermen's Hut had almost completed their usual spectacular adornment of the church.

"Isn't it just, Penny? How are the corn dollies coming along?"

"The children are fascinated – and so are the mothers! I think we shall have more than we can handle. We might even have to place some in the church!"

"What do you tell the children about the pagan origins of corn dollies?"

"That it was a way of saying 'thank you' to the gods for a good harvest in pagan times, and it's our way of showing that we are grateful for the food we eat."

"Were you really keen on burying one in Podd's field?" asked Rebecca.

"I still think it's a good idea. It's a link with our pagan past."

"Do we need reminding of that?"

"Rebecca! Have you had a change of mind?"

"No! – and I know – I'm beginning to sound like mum!"

Both women laughed loudly. They were fond of each other, shared much the same religious views, and were allies against the encroaching seas of bigotry that always surround religious matters.

"Peter wrote to me recently about something that he saw in Estonia."

Rebecca went on to describe the ritual on the beach involving the young man with the lighted torch. Penny listened in silence, wondering whether she should use the story with the children, and deciding that it would be a good idea.

"We're never far from barbarism, are we?" said Rebecca.

"In what way?"

"How big a gap is there from the thought to the deed?"

"Talking about corn dollies isn't going to lead to human sacrifice, Rebecca."

"No ... but we are drawn to it, aren't we – drawn, almost inevitably, back. It has a fascination for us – so what separates us from our ancestors?"

"A hundred and fifty years of education."

"You're so certain, aren't you, Penny?"

"It's why I teach. Education takes us forward by valuing the best of the past, while moving attitudes on. What's wrong, Rebecca?"

"Nothing, really – I'm just beginning to see everyone else's point of view."

"It's only because you're beginning to question your own."

"What do you mean?"

"You're thinking about Peter and all that marriage to him would mean. You're realising that you may have to begin questioning the values you've held all your life. You've realised that marriage means compromise ... Some women never realise it."

"You're wise, aren't you?"

"I've loved a wonderful and ... ethically difficult man for a long time. Our marriage has survived because we accept the differences in each other."

"What has this got to do with corn dollies?"

"It isn't the corn dollies. It's you questioning cultural differences and assumptions. Don't draw back. Learn from the past, but embrace the future."

When Sarah woke, Horst Brultzner sat smiling down on her and she understood. Her vampire instincts were sharpening, as was the horror of her condition.

"Where is Matthew?"

"He is safe with Katerina – Frau Schnell."

"Why did you allow that to happen, Horst?"

"It is our custom."

"I thought the red dress was to show off my beauty."

"It was – and did. You are honoured among our kind. There are none who will not, now, defer to you."

"What do I look like?"

"As you have always done – since you became a vampire."

She looked in the dark glass of a window. It was true; her face and body were beyond any perfection she might have imagined as a girl when she dreamed of being a princess. Her natural beauty remained accentuated by her vampirism. There were no signs of the ravages of the wolf except where the red dress had been rent.

"We are immortal and each dusk our beauty returns."

"Where are we?"

"We are in a room above the seven suites of the mansion."

"What was that creature?"

"It was one of us."

"Not a real wolf, then?"

"It was real enough when the moment came … All vampires have an unnatural beauty, but those who are unusually attractive in life even more so. You are such a one, and you are one of mine. It is why I chose you for tonight."

"I want to leave here … Have you sat with me all day?"

"Yes," he said, and there was affection in his voice, "It is dusk now and the others will be waking, too. I will call for the car."

"No – we will walk."

He waited while she bathed, quickly, and then put on the dress of midnight blue he had arranged to be delivered from the fussy little tailor whose shop was just off Wenceslas Square. They walked along the corridors of the mansion – he just behind her, attentive to every door and turn. The wallpaper was heavily embossed, the floors richly carpeted – as of another era. The night had changed her – Sarah knew that; the ravages of the wolf had left no physical scars, but Sarah now saw her existence differently – revealed in another light.

They passed doorways to the staircase that led to the suites below and she was aware of the vampires stirring within; she and they had become as one. Sarah had once seen the inside of a brothel in some film she had watched with … her ex-husband. She remembered being nauseated by the sumptuous furnishings and garish colours as they struggled to conceal the sordidness of what was happening. Now, beneath the cool exterior of her beauty, Sarah's own flesh was afire with the blood and the memory of the dancing – rapture untamed, ardour ferocious, infatuation turbulent, enjoyment barbarous.

The city was beautiful in the early evening – the splendour of the buildings, the mysterious paths and the narrow streets, breathtaking murals, interesting facades and exotic names all lit or thrown into shadow by the golden sheen of the lamps on the cobbles. They passed through squares and across bridges like young lovers returning home.

CHAPTER 15

Retribution

It was Frau Schnell who told Sarah the story of the wolf who swallowed the sun. She seemed to understand what Sarah had been through, and wanted to offer reassurance

"Your ordeal is over, child. Once they have completed the ritual, they are happy – enjoy the rest of your stay. The story goes that, at the end of the world, there will be a great battle between good and evil – and evil will win. A great wolf will emerge from the ranks of those who oppose the gods and that wolf will swallow the sun. Once the sun is vanquished, all evil things will hold sway upon the Earth. In Horst's little tableaux you were the sun this year. Now you may join the Un-dead!"

"How long have you been ... Un-dead?"

"Time means nothing to us. You know the carol – Good King Wenceslas? I was here when he was king."

She laughed at the expression on Sarah's face.

"He was a weak, bedevilled man – harried by his family, imprisoned by his nobility – who did nothing to support his friends or allies."

"When was this?"

"About the year 1400 – yes, I am over six hundred years old!"

Sarah knew she would see her child grow and prosper. She had never really considered the implication that she would also see him age and die. Katerina Schnell laughed again.

"You will get used to it. You will never be older than you are now. You will always entrance men and bewilder women. Horst is careful. He is not a wilful killer as are many vampires. You are intelligent and he has chosen well. Every distinction in the world is at your command. You will be 'reborn' many times."

"Reborn?"

"You will see."

They arrived 'home' in Dunburgh late one evening and Sarah put Matthew to bed, quickly. The child was tired and so she undressed him, pulled him into his pyjamas and tucked him up in the morning room where he still slept, waiting for the completion of his own room upstairs.

Horst had wandered out into the night. He had always loved the night – even as a child, long before his 'conversion'. For him the sight of the moon never palled. He had dreamed of going there and the American space programme had, at one time, given him hope, but now he knew he would have to wait. For him, however, the day would come. He was a contemplative man. He had watched the harvest moon in Prague, as they waited for the equinox, and now there would be several successive evenings when the moon rose beautifully close to sunset and there would be strong moonlight all night. He would watch the harvest being gathered and teach Sarah how to pick her farm-workers with care at the right moment. He smiled to himself – dark humour had always been one of his idiosyncrasies. When the hunters' moon appeared, a month later, he would be out in the woods waiting for the poachers. He had, at times, done this in anger. As they tracked the game on one of his many estates, so he would stalk them – a view to a kill. They never knew the risks they took. Now, having mellowed with age, he pursued them for fun. Poachers – those thieves in the night – were almost always what the English called 'cocky', and he had hunted them down until they were witless with fear. It was always good to see brazen cheek replaced with pop-eyed terror.

It was while he stood contemplating such nights that his mind returned to Sarah. 'Have you sat with me all day?' 'Yes.' She had looked at him, in that way of hers, and he had been overwhelmed with affection for her – he who had known so many sophisticated beauties was attracted to this simple, country girl. Guilt, or remorse, were not emotions of which he was capable, but it wrinkled his 'conscience' (as humans would have called it) just a little that he had faced her with such an ordeal. Horst re-called the expression on her face as the wolf had bitten into her, and she had fought, quite pointlessly, to protect herself. It was while these thoughts were passing through his mind that he heard her scream. It was a fearful sound, even to him, as though Sarah was being tortured. His ears told him exactly from where the scream came, and he was with her before the next one died on the air.

Sarah stood by her 'coffin', the fingers on her right hand bearing the marks of the holy wafer placed there by Clara. It had burnt into her flesh when she touched it.

"I came to change, and saw that in my resting place. What does it mean?"

"It means that someone has been here while we were away. We are discovered. Our home has been violated ... See that your son still sleeps. I will look round."

"What about that?" said Sarah, pointing to the holy wafer.

"It is everything to you – a mere nothing to me!"

He reached in and crushed the wafer in his hands, strode to the window, threw up the sash and tossed the wafer out into the night. He found his own chest equally violated, destroyed the wafer and ran from room to room in a frenzy of anger. The hunter does not enjoy being hunted, and Brultzner would not be frustrated or challenged without a fierce and terrible fight. Eventually he came to his study, and found the note Bert had left him. So now they were mocking him! How many had they told? He found Sarah in the hall, rubbing her fingers. The pain cutting through them was one of belief rather than nerves. Brultzner took her hand and stroked it, gently.

"The pain will go after you have slept tomorrow. See that your son remains undisturbed for the rest of the night. Feed if you must, but return quickly to him. I do not know what the night holds for us but, by dawn, it will be settled."

She knew his anger, and saw it written all over his face which was vindictive with rage. The yellow eyes flamed like dying suns, the red-rimmed lids burned, and the pale grey face was flared by the purple hue of his temper.

He stood in the driveway of Clara Gobley's house and waited. He knew that they would have watched him return – watched in anticipation and dread at their audacity. As far as humans went she might have made an interesting opponent, but Horst Brultzner had not devoted time, money and love in his Victorian house to have his desires thwarted. The woman and her man had made a fatal error – so sure were they of themselves – and tonight it would cost them body and soul.

The door opened, and Clara Gobley stepped out.

"Herr Brultzner, we have been expecting you. Come round to the back. It's a pleasant night to sit in the garden. You will excuse us if we do not invite you in."

The man, Bert, was sitting on an old iron bench, nursing a tarred gull. He appeared composed, but then fools often felt like that – confidence in their own folly was a sure hallmark of the stupid. At his side was an open doctor's bag.

"Before we begin, Herr Brultzner, might I offer you a cup of tea – late though the hour may be? You do drink tea?"

"Occasionally, Mrs Gobley – that would be delightful."

Her manner drew his anger from Brultzner. He sensed the English flippancy in the face of danger, and it calmed him. Unusually, Clara did not expect Bert to provide the refreshments, but rose and went into the kitchen.

"We have sent for a third party, Herr Brultzner. He will only be a short time."

"Sent?"

"By carrier pigeon!"

"Ah – so out-dated, yet so satisfying," Brultzner smiled.

He was enjoying himself. No one had seen him arrive, and most of the night was still before them. The anticipation of some English badinage soothed his anger, and he had time on his side – time, and their ignorance.

Before Clara emerged with the tea (all set beautifully on a silver tray), Crafty Catchpole appeared in the driveway, his face ashen, his whole body shaking. Horst Brultzner sighed with relief. At least he understood how they had gained access to his house, and with whom he was dealing. The night could be concluded satisfactorily, and there would be time for some banter along the way.

"Good evening, Mr Catchpole. I am somewhat surprised to see you here."

"Oim seein' moi way clear," said Crafty.

"I'm sure you are," replied Brultzner, his eyes never leaving his servant's (soon to be his former servant's) face.

"Perhaps we had better start with an apology, Herr Brultzner?" said Clara.

The vampire had already satisfied himself that they considered him to be at a disadvantage, but was still curious as to their motives and so decided, for his own amusement and edification, to play what he saw as the 'humble card'.

"If you consider it necessary, please go ahead."

"We needed to satisfy ourselves that certain things were as we suspected, and this necessitated us breaking into your house."

"Of course."

"It was also necessary that you should call upon us on your return so that we could place certain requirements before you."

"Naturally."

"It was preferable that we met – this first time – on our own ground."

"I quite understand."

"We are aware of your special ... powers. You need to be aware of ours."

"That would give me immense gratification."

"It is not our intention to thwart you, provided you agree to certain stipulations and abide by certain agreements which we shall lay down this evening."

"I am pleased to hear that – and what might be those stipulations?"

"You have conducted yourself with extreme care – that will continue."

"I seem to have met your first stipulation, Mrs Gobley – are there others?"

"You will confine your activities to those who do not attend church."

"Some churches, or all churches, Mrs Gobley?"

"All churches," cut in Bert, "We're not here to discriminate."

He and Clara had discussed at length the possibility of curbing Brultzner's activities' – as they eventually got round to calling them – almost entirely. Bert pointed out that vampires could, if necessary, live off animals such as rats and this seemed preferable to allowing him to continue feeding from humans. Clara, however, had pointed out that she saw no reason why animals should suffer at the expense of people. Since most of the village was damned anyway, the vampire could be trusted to select his food as he seemed to have done since he arrived – that is, with care.

"Oi don't go ter church," said Crafty.

"Then perhaps it's time you did, Mr Catchpole," said Clara.

"You will also see to it that the woman does likewise," said Bert.

"I think you can rely on that. Are there further stipulations?"

"No. We come now to the conditions upon which you will remain."

"Which are, dear lady?"

"That you teach Bert and me how you command animals ..."

"... and show me how to hurry moi pigins up."

"To what purpose do you require this power?"

"Animals are exploited in this village, Herr Brultzner. Bert and I spend our lives fighting their oppression. Did you know that fox-hunting still goes on? Did you know tankers still pour their filth into the sea? Helpless creatures lie injured everywhere, birds drown, and young foxes die of hunger in their dens. Once they come to our command, we can help them better."

"And oi want ter breed a champion pigin."

Brultzner had decided, before he left his home, that he would kill whoever was involved in what he saw as an invasion into his life and sanctity. He had known he was dealing with cunning people, but not that they were mad. However, listening to them speak had led him to wonder whether he was under any immediate threat – provided their greed held sway, he would be in control. He could then see to it that they died suitably. He was still unsure whether to continue the humble card, or make stipulations of his own. Catchpole was a slightly different matter. The man had been his servant, and Brultzner could not countenance betrayal by a servant. The idea of lying in his 'bed' each day at the mercy of such people also troubled him – despite the power of their greed.

"You have me at a disadvantage. It appears I have no choice in the matter."

"We are so glad you appreciate that, Herr Brultzner."

"So what happens to me once you have the powers you desire?"

"You will continue to be free to... live as you wish."

"What assurance will I have of that?"

"Our word," said Clara.

"Upon what oath will that be?"

"The Bible – it binds us, and holds even you in sway?"

"Then perhaps you would be good enough to fetch your family copy?"

Bert toddled off, and returned, shortly, with a large, tattered brown volume – its covers and spine marked with the scratches of more than one hundred and fifty years of use. On the cover were the words 'Sold Under Cost Price – British and Foreign Bible Society – Two Shillings and Sixpence'. Horst Brultzner smiled to himself as Bert placed the book carefully – but with casual reverence – onto the wooden table where their tea cups stood. Both placed their hands upon the book and, when Crafty hesitated, glared at their accomplice.

"Om not seein' ..."

"See or leave, Mr Catchpole. We need you under oath," said Bert.

"Moi conscience int clear on this."

"But is quite clear about cheating in the pigeon racing, I suppose?" said Clara.

"Oi ent cheatin' – om breedin'."

"Swear or leave!"

"I swear under protest."

"Then you are best to leave."

"Oi'll swear."

He placed his hand upon the Holy Book, and began to repeat Clara's words.

"I swear by Almighty God ..."

"One moment," said Brultzner, cutting into their righteousness, as he reached out and took the book in his right hand, "I think that it might be open at an appropriate page?" he mused, flicking the pages, while they crackled under his touch, "Perhaps St Matthew, chapter 19, verse 18 – Christ's exhortation to the young man who sought eternal life?"

"Thou shalt not bear false witness," said Clara looking at Bert, who also stood in awe of Brultzner. Neither had expected him to be able to touch the Bible, let alone turn its pages and know its message.

"We are ready now?" he said, smiling as they nodded, "Then repeat after me – I swear by Almighty God ..."

"*I swear by Almighty God ...*"

"That I shall hold true to my word ..."

"*That I shall hold true to my word ...*"

and so he, and they, continued to the conclusion of the oath:

"...regarding the person of Horst Brultzner ...and all who appertain to him ... that they shall remain inviolate ... from any hand of mine ...or my accomplices ... This I swear before my God."

Brultzner's demeanour remained 'humble' throughout. He felt like a priest leading his flock along the paths of righteousness – even 'for thine own name's sake'. He smiled to himself. He had them now – humbly, but as securely as if they were housed in the deepest dungeon. He would play with them for a while – hold out false hopes, teach them to call certain animals, perhaps – and then destroy them one by one. As he left, he assured all three that there was no need to "attend him". If Mr Catchpole could fetch a few more barrow-loads of soil that would be sufficient, since they had corrupted Miss Brown's resting place. He had, he explained, "an Indulgence" and left them, victorious but wondering.

Sarah had decided what to do about Shane Marjoram before she left for Prague. Her ordeal with the wolf only hardened her resolve. She remembered his pleasure when he had found her there that night. He had always been the same – a victim to his own pleasures.

He had begged her for it when he hardened and felt her ice-cold hands on his buttocks. She had wafted her soft breath around his delicate parts, flicked her tongue over him, felt his need to explode into her, and then bit and sucked. She knew she had always been a good lover, and now her power was increased beyond imagining. She could offer ecstasy, and she would control. He would cry out for her, and she would take him, night by night, moment by moment until she was ready to deliver him into Hell – the joy, and then the terror of an eternity's consciousness. 'Lizzie Borden took an axe, and gave her husband forty whacks'; but she had greater powers than Lizzie Borden ever dreamed possible. 'Did you enjoy yourself? Answer me.' He'd felt he was kneeling before the axe-man that night, and he still wanted more. She thought again of her dear father's body on the hard pebbles. '... more delights than you have ever known, more dread than you can ever have imagined. I shall return and I shall take you there, but you must wait for me.' She knew that was just what he was doing.

While Sarah had been in Prague, Shane's pattern had changed in only small ways. Each night he had ventured out after dark and visited The Crossways for his evening meal. He found that it was always a relief to leave the house, and he always walked rapidly. The sweating felt good each time, and his muscles came to life. When he got there, he always downed the first pint at the bar and ordered the next while he was drinking it. He always had steak and kidney pudding, or something like it – shepherd's pie or beef and ale pie. They came to expect it of him.

The little tart with the big tits got what she wanted. She'd waved them around in his face once too often, and he shafted her – outside, in the alley, up against the wall. The blokes in the pub – the drinkers and chatters and darts players – gave him a wink after that; otherwise they continued to ignore him, and that suited Shane. He didn't always have a sweet (money was running out), but the little tart was sweet enough. He always did his wolf howl on the way home – it got the buggers from the wildlife park going every night. He loved that! Of course, he always got home to an empty house, but she said she'd come and he knew he could rely on her – Sarah had always been reliable. It'd be nice to have a real woman again – the shag at the pub wasn't a patch on his ... on Sarah.

He knew that she was there before he ever arrived home that night. No sooner had he reached the top of Shoemaker's Lane than he sensed her waiting for him. There was no time for wolf howls. He ran like fuck along the lane, and then down Church Hill and Beach Road to his house. Sarah was home! When he opened the door, it was just like old times – the lace curtains had been stitched where his slamming of the sash window had ripped them, the kitchen walls had been wiped clean, the collection of china plates were back in the place Sarah had always put them, her gingham cloth was smoothed out and the crumbs and cartons gone, around the sink was clear of unwashed crockery, the oven top looked ready to cook a fresh meal – in fact, some soup was simmering. In what used to be their sitting room, the wooden mantle-piece shone with polish and the brass bell and cartridge cases glistened, the photographs and glue pot were replaced and in the vases were sweet peas and ... mallow! He recognised those – his ... Sarah had loved those!

She was home – but not sitting by the fire as she had been last time. Shane knew she'd be waiting for him in bed. He ran up the stairs and she was there – under the duvet in their little bedroom. He remembered the last time – her beauty had taken his fucking breath away. He couldn't wait to get that nightdress off her shoulders and plunge his face into her mass of hair – her fucking skin was like silk, and that smile of hers and those eyes.

"Fuck me, Sare."

She didn't admonish him this time; she was gagging for it! He could see right through her skin and the red lips smiled like before, and then they opened – just a bit, just a teasing, fucking bit! Cor – she'd always been the best tart in school with that look of hers; it got right into a bloke.

"Hello, Shane. I'm pleased to see you again."

"Fuck me, Sare."

"That's just what I'm going to do, Shane."

"Fucking Hell!"

"You're fond of that word, aren't you Shane?"

He hauled the duvet aside, and jumped into the bed with her – she was as cold as ice, and he shuddered. The disappointment in him assuaged the fear. Common sense told Shane that something was abnormal; his lust told him that everything was fine – she just needed warming up. His trousers were partly unzipped, and his shirt was partly off his shoulders. Sarah sat up, and ripped the shirt from him. He'd always loved her undressing him, and he fell back with a groan as she yanked down his trousers – tugging away his shoes and throwing them to the floor.

"Now, Shane."

Her teeth – those sharp, white teeth – sank into the top of his thigh, just above the groin and he came. Shane felt the semen shoot from him, so intense was his excitement. She took him then at her leisure, sucking the life from him as he swooned and then blacked out.

When Shane came to, Sarah was sitting on the edge of the bed watching him. She smiled and spoke in that old, familiar way of hers. 'Life means all that it ever meant.' He'd heard that somewhere – where? He felt himself drifting into and out of consciousness, but still she sat, waiting patiently for him.

"I've brought you some coffee, Shane."

"Thanks Sare ... Sarah."

He'd corrected himself that time. Was it the way she was looking at him – with no laughter in her eyes?

"I want you again, Shane. Don't keep me waiting – I'm gagging for it."

She seemed to be mocking him, but she'd just done him proud. As he drank the coffee, Sarah began stroking him She caressed him in long, shafting moves so tender he could hardly bear it.

"Come on Shane – I'm waiting!"

He couldn't – it hung there in her hands, drooping. He was knackered; he couldn't help it – he couldn't do it for her.

"Don't disappoint me, Shane. I'm hungry for it!"

It was the way she kept saying "Shane" – just as though she was laughing at him, and she didn't talk dirty like that, not his ... not Sarah.

"If you can't get it up, Shane, I'll have to do it for myself."

"Fucking Hell!"

It had never happened to him before; he'd never been impotent in his life. The more he tried, the worse it was; she looked down on him with a kind of contempt on her face, and Shane grabbed her in anger and pushed her back onto the bed. She laughed up at him. She was warm now, and he wanted her badly. He couldn't get over her beauty. The way her hair and skin shone, the press of her young breasts against his chest and the nipples hard against him, the curve of her mouth and that faraway look in her eyes tormented him. He wanted to shag the arse off her and he couldn't ... he couldn't get it up!

"There's some soup on the stove, Shane – perhaps you're hungry. Shall we go downstairs for a while, or would you like me to give it to you in bed?"

Still that taunt in her voice – and she was there under him, his legs between her thighs like it had always been, and in that nightdress he loved. Shane felt so weak he just wanted to sleep for ever, and yet he wanted her to do what she did, again. It was great being sucked by someone you loved. He realised, perhaps for the umpteenth time, how much he did love her: they'd had good times, and she'd woken him in the night many times so they could make love. He knew she desired him, and wanted things to be right between them. When she put her hands on him, he still trembled.

As they lay there, she continued stroking him – running her fingers, warm now, over the curve of his buttocks, and he shuddered with longing under her touch. Her fingers probed that little place where the top of his thigh met his buttocks – that little place where he was particularly sensitive, and he knew she was trying to please him. Sarah eased him slightly away from her so that his chest was stretched. While continuing the slow circular movement on his buttocks, she began to massage his chest with her other hand. He felt himself stiffen at last. She turned him on his back, and Shane thought she was going to mount him. The soft, quivering ran along the inner side of his thighs and Shane felt good – manly again. Sarah leaned over him and he could smell her perfume. Better still, he could smell her – smell the warmth of her. He reached up and pushed his nose into the little well between her shoulders and collar bone. She always smelt good there; it was sweet like fudge. He put his hands up onto her buttocks to heave her across, and looked up. Sarah's hair hung around her face, and he remembered how she used to lean down and tickle his chest with it. Her red lips were parted and the white teeth shone. Then, she lunged and they sank into his neck. He felt himself come again but not with her; his life fluids spilled out, uselessly, over his chest. Shane felt her pulling on his neck and the life going from him and darkness overcoming him, and he wanted it to go on for ever.

When he woke, it was morning and Sarah had gone. He wanted to go to the toilet, but when he twisted his legs over the side of the bed and tried to stand Shane almost fell over. In all his life, he had never felt so weak.

In the bathroom mirror, he saw that his face was pale – worse than pale: white as a sheet. On his neck were the marks – just two bite marks – of her teeth. They were quite neat little holes, and closing. He rubbed them gingerly, but there was no pain. He looked down at his groin and saw two more, also closing. He showered. Until Sarah left, he had always been scrupulously clean, and wanted to be again. He dressed, with difficulty, in a T-shirt and jeans, made the bed the way she liked it and went downstairs. There was a note on the kitchen table.

Shane,

I've put the soup on the side to cool. You might like it, with some fresh bread, for lunch. You'll find some porridge in the pot on the stove. It's just the way you like it. I'll see you tonight.

The note was unsigned, and he registered the lack of 'Dear' – but it was a note, and she had made him breakfast. He wolfed it down. There's something about breakfast, or any meal, when someone else has made it for you.

He didn't know how he stopped himself from going to the Old Vicarage and knocking her up. The day dragged endlessly for him, and he skipped going to The Crossways that night for fear that he would miss her. It was after dark when she arrived.

"I've just put the boy to bed, Shane. He wanted to play out longer while these nice nights last. We shan't have summer for much longer now. It's as good as over."

She sounded like the old Sarah – concerned about her home and family. She had arrived suddenly. He'd been sitting in the living room, looking at the space where the Napoleon clock had been, and suddenly she was standing beside him looking down, running her fingers through his hair. Against his face, her thigh felt cold – not ice cold like last night, but without warmth. He wanted to run his hand up under her dress, but decided it wouldn't be the same as in the past.

"I wish I could see the boy again …I miss him."

"I expect you do, Shane. He's a lovely boy."

"Do you think …?"

"I haven't come to talk, Shane. I've come to fuck."

The obscenity coming from her sounded even viler than he could have expected. Shane looked up at her, and was ashamed.

"Are you taking me up, or perhaps you'd prefer we did it here?" she said.

Upstairs, standing by the bed, he felt as whores must feel, compelled to satisfy man after man with no break all day. Sarah had always enjoyed sex and he'd appreciated that, but now she was insatiable. Before he'd had time to make any gestures of affection, she'd pulled down his jeans, torn off his shirt and thrown him back on the bed. She watched him lying naked, roused by her desire for him, as she undressed, slowly. Off came the light summer dress, and off came the bra and knickers. He noticed that neither left a mark on her body. Her skin was flawless and once again he saw that strange blue iridescence as she leaned over him and ran her tongue quickly over his stomach muscles.

He almost came when she did that, but controlled himself. They'd always liked long nights of love-making, and this was going to be one to remember. Her body hadn't touched him when she came down onto him, leaning forward on her hands which were placed either side of his head. He felt himself enter her for the first time in so long and closed his eyes in anticipation of the sweetness of it and the warmth and sheer delight of being inside her. He wanted nothing more than to be at one with her, again. Then, in seconds, the shock took his breath away. She was cold – every muscle within her seemed chilled. She tightened on him, momentarily, and he pulled away.

"You need to warm me up, Shane. I need to drink."

She brought her mouth down onto his throat, and the warm blood flowed. He felt it going from him as it coursed through her body. Her hands gripped his shoulders for support, and then he passed out and life faded from him for a time.

It was after midnight when he woke – weak, exhausted from her replenishments – and she was sitting on the side of the bed watching him, silently. She was still naked in the warmth of the late summer night and, against all hope, he raised his hand to stroke her breast.

"Let's see what I can do for you, Shane."

She was relentless: hard as nails in her desire for him, adamant in her lust. He'd never thought of her like that before. They were both naked – something that would have excited him beyond measure once – and she stroked him remorselessly, leaving no part of his body untouched by her probing fingers. Her very stillness and composure were disconcerting. There was no sweat on her and no excitement in her manner – just that relentless brushing of her fingers. He stiffened under her touch but sagged again, flopping uselessly across his own abdomen, as she mounted him.

"Shane."

It was all she said – his name – but every disappointment in the world was within the sound of her voice. Again and again that second night she roused him, and each time he failed her. Sarah would lean over, sink her teeth into some new place and satisfy her craving for blood, and each time Shane felt weaker.

When he woke he found himself tucked safely into his bed with the duvet pulled up round his neck and, when he eventually struggled downstairs, there was a note saying *'Just to keep your strength up'* and a plate piled with toast and bacon to warm through for his breakfast.

His body had several new love bites – all in places only a lover would find – and he looked at them with a kind of forlorn, even stupid, admiration.

For a week or more – in all the time he had to think about it, he could never make up his mind just how long she came to him by night – the same thing happened. The darkness was laden with unfulfilled desires; and the daylight, by obsessive longing and exhaustion. During this time, Shane remained cleaner, and the house remained tidier than it had been since she left. In many ways, he felt happier – life returned to a sort of normality. In simple terms, it was nice to have her back again.

Each night she came to him chilled, and he recoiled from her. When she had satiated and warmed herself from his veins, he was too exhausted to find any gratification. At times he felt that she was playing with him, at others he convinced himself that she wanted him and was returning to the family home. He would watch from the little window which over-looked the marsh, and half-expected to see her gliding along the road, hips swinging in the way they always did, with Matthew by her side.

It was only occasionally that he would admit to himself that the coldness in her was more than the chill of her body when she arrived, and that the indifference was deeper. Never did it occur to him that Sarah had, in all she did, a deadly purpose. As the time wore on, his obsession grew. The more he wanted her, the greater became his exhaustion.

At last, one night when his fatigue and lust had burnt each other out, when his body was covered in more bites than he could count, Sarah grabbed his hair and twisted his head round to face her where she sat on the edge of his bed.

"I'm going to kill you now, Shane," she said, "I'm going to suck the last drop of blood from your body and leave you to die. Only it won't be an ordinary death – you'll wake this evening as a vampire. Your body will be cleansed of all poisons and you'll be more handsome than you ever were in life. Everything lovely about your body – and it is a beautiful body, Shane – will be enhanced, just like mine. You will become ravishingly attractive – there isn't a woman alive who will be able to resist you. The whole world will be at your feet for all eternity."

He looked up at her, his eyes glazed, in disbelief.

"All those marks will be gone and you'll never suffer a blemish ever again. Can you imagine being as glorious as that for all eternity?"

She paused to let him ponder on his good fortune, and then continued, slowly.

"Only it won't be quite like that for you, Shane. After you're dead, I shall dress you to cover the marks, and then go home and tell Crafty Catchpole that I want something from the cottage. He'll find you and call the doctor – or ask me to – and we'll have you certified as dead and taken to the undertakers. As 'next of kin', I shall be in charge of the funeral arrangements and I won't want to hang around – not after what has happened. I've already written a note to Necker saying that we don't want embalming, but to get you in your coffin quickly. Do you like the sound of that, Shane? It'll be a nice coffin – silk lined, brass handles – you know, nothing but the best for … my ex-husband."

Shane heaved himself up from the pillow, a look of bewildered terror playing across his face, but Sarah, far stronger than him now, yanked him back by his hair.

"There's nothing you can do, Shane. I have a vampire's strength – even if you weren't weakened from loss of blood, you'd be no match for me."

She looked at him with such contempt, such hatred, that Shane – in those last minutes of his life – couldn't believe what he was seeing or hearing.

"You've lived your life exactly as you wanted, haven't you Shane – without any real regard for anybody or anything – even me, who loved you once! Your temper – what Shane wants, Shane gets! – has ruled you and everyone you've come in contact with, hasn't it? When you took dad's life on that beach, it didn't trouble you one little bit, did it? You never gave a thought for me – left without a dad. You never gave a thought for Matthew – left without a granddad."

She paused again, waiting for the words to sink into his dull brain. It was difficult communicating with him at the best of times; in his weakened state he needed more consideration than usual.

"But I've given you a lot of thought Shane – I cared for you in life, gave you more love than you deserved, more kindness than you ever appreciated. I've always been thoughtful where you're concerned, Shane – in life, and now, in death. I'm going to ask Crafty to do one other little thing for me – as well as finding your body. I'm going to ask him take some garlic flowers he was given, and get Necker to seal your coffin with them – just so nothing nasty can get in … or out …"

She paused again. There was a lack of comprehension in Shane's eyes, and she wanted him to grasp her meaning in its entirety.

"And just to make "assurance double sure" – remember that quote, Shane, or were you messing about at the time? – I'm going to ask him to have mum's crucifix – the one she kept on her bookshelf and which I had in the cottage – fixed on the top of your coffin."

He pulled away from her; she jerked his head round and looked into his eyes.

"Get it, Shane? We shall bury you quickly – the Reverend Unwood will oblige me, I'm sure, under the circumstances – and then you can spend eternity thinking about what you did to my dad. How does that sound to you – fair? ... If it wouldn't desecrate his memory, I'd have his photograph pinned inside the coffin lid so that when you wake, at dusk, you could look at him all night long. Vampires can see in the dark, Shane ... not that you'll have much to see ... six feet under ... for all eternity."

Her eyes were unflinching as she looked into him, and he knew there was no mercy for him in her heart.

"Well come on Shane – say something – don't I even get a 'fuck me'?"

He made one last, futile attempt to free himself, exerting every ounce of strength he had to wrench himself clear of her and the bed, but he was like a baby wriggling in her arms, and she eased him back onto the pillow. Even then, the desire poured through him – reminded, as he was, of other times she had pushed him back in their love-making – and he felt himself stiffen. He'd read somewhere that the last thing a man has before he dies is an erection. Sarah looked into his eyes, once more, before curling her head round to his neck. He felt the teeth bite into him, and heard the sucking sound as she took his life.

Necker Utting looked at the young body before her. She'd been told not to embalm him – that the family wanted him buried quickly. Necker thought she knew why. Shane Marjoram wasn't the sort of person you wanted hanging around too long – even dead! No one had told her about the marks on his body, though. She'd never seen anything like that before in all her life. "Get on with it!" her boss had said, and she thought he was right – 'least said, soonest mended.' That was an old saying and sure to be true. Still, you wouldn't want to think that there were rats around that could do that to a man – although everyone knew they were getting bigger these days. Still, the doctor had seen him and signed the death certificate so it must be all right. It hadn't been that young Dr Read, but the proper one so he knew what he was doing. Necker didn't like Alan Read – he was too free with his opinions for her liking; he'd told her once that she was wasting his time and NHS money, coming for medicine she didn't need! The rector wanted the funeral the day after tomorrow, and Crafty Catchpole was coming in a moment with some special things for the coffin. She supposed you couldn't blame the young woman. Everyone knew that her husband had killed her father – the sooner he was out of the way the better.

Crafty had had the shock of his life when he found the body. Miss Brown (Miss Brown? Everyone knew she was Sarah Marjoram!) had asked him to get her a couple of cookery books from the cottage, but he'd found more than she'd bargained for all right! Then everything had happened quickly – the old doctor had come and the rector, and then the undertaker. Necker had been almost drooling when she heard about it! Then Miss Brown had asked him to go back to the cottage. She couldn't go herself – she didn't feel up to it, although she looked fresher than ever to him. She'd asked him to get her mother's crucifix from the bookcase and take it to the undertakers, and would he also take some of those garlic flowers Bert had given him. She seemed to know everything! He'd been dashing round everywhere – doctors, undertakers, rectors – just as though he was some errand boy!

When he arrived for the second time, Necker looked at the cross and frowned.

"It's not usual," she said.

"Usual or not, it's what she wants and she was his wife – not yew!"

"Thank God fer that – I wouldn't hev wanted ter be – but it's not usual."

"End Oim ter fix it – end dew the flow-ers.!"

"Hev yew spoken ter ...?"

"Yes oi hev end he ses ter carry on."

Necker would moan endlessly about authority – her boss, the rector, the doctor – but would not actually defy them, and so she stepped reluctantly back while Crafty wiped the flowers of garlic along the edges of the coffin and then placed them on Shane's chest. He was a good looking boy all right – shame he went to pot. He could have done himself proud if he'd stayed off the drink. It was the curse of the world – drink. If he hadn't been drinking he'd never have lost his temper and killed Froggy Brown, and the family would still be together.

Necker insisted in helping Crafty place on the coffin lid and then they screwed it down – the reek of the garlic sealing the joins forever. The undertaker had already pierced four holes in the lid where the crucifix was to go and so Crafty had no difficulty in securing the crucifix with the slim screws Sarah had asked him to get from the hardware store. She hadn't touched the cross herself, he'd noticed, but fussed around while he drilled the tiny holes in the upright and then in the cross piece where the arms of the figure of Jesus were nailed.

"It aint usual fer a coffin ter be closed loike this, so early. The relatives loike ter see the bardy fust."

"Well she woont want ter see him, would she – not arfter what he done!"

"Oi spose nart," said Necker, reluctantly.

Corvin Unwood had not hesitated in meeting Sarah's request that the funeral be done quickly. The poor girl's memories of husband were heinous. She would have to live with them and, somehow, explain them to her little son one day. He didn't even really expect her to come to the funeral – unless she felt up to it. Everyone in the village felt relieved that he was gone; it was as though a painful thorn had been withdrawn from a toe or finger. The sooner he was under the ground, the better.

The day of the funeral was slightly overcast, but warm as September moved gently into autumn. Although he had expressed his support for her absence, Corvin was a little surprised when Sarah did not arrive. Esther was outraged – it being "Sarah's duty to attend her husband's funeral whatever he had been like". However, Horst Brultzner turned up "to represent his housekeeper who was in a state of shock".

There were no special poems and no requests for a special hymn, so Corvin kept the service as simple and unadorned as the ASB demanded. Those present sang the twenty third psalm and followed the coffin to the graveside. Corvin intoned:

"*We have entrusted our brother, Shane, to God's merciful keeping, and we now commit his body to the ground ... in sure and certain hope of the resurrection to eternal life ...*"

Shane's ex-wife had seen to it that he could be sure of that. She had also seen to it that he would be denied *"the fullness of joy"* for all eternity.

When night came, Shane woke and opened his eyes and saw the lid of the coffin – just as Sarah had told him he would. He felt the oppressive stench of the garlic flowers upon his chest, but could not bring his arms to touch them. He yelled and screamed. He kicked at the coffin lid, but could not move from it. Even as he sensed his power to rise from the grave, he also knew that the coffin was sealed against his escape. He was aware of the cross that held him. Its awful power stemmed from his fear, but there were no prayers he could utter – his lips had never framed them with ease, and now the gift of redemption was taken from him forever.

His consciousness was limited to the night. During what was daylight for the world above, he could neither move nor shout. When dusk had fallen, his torment filled the churchyard and there were those who passed who swore – much to the scorn of others – that they heard him shouting from below the earth, shouting much as he had done in life, when drunk. Sarah visited him that first night, as she did sometimes afterwards, and spoke softly with him – for a vampire's hearing is as acute as its sight – but there was no hope for him in her voice. Shane Marjoram had made his choices in life, and now he must abide by them.

CHAPTER 16

The social scene – the Harvest Supper

The tables at the supper did, indeed, buckle under the weight of the food. Everyone was pleased to see Sarah Brown there – it was good to see her getting over that dreadful husband of hers, although some commented that she ate little. She was accompanied by Horst Brultzner who, everyone also agreed, was fitting nicely into the social life of the village. He, too, ate little, but then it was generally accepted he was an abstemious man. However, the occasion was as joyful and festive as it had always been with most people ready to tuck into the surfeit of food provided by Totto Briggs and his family.

Bishop Twiddle had found himself in the village and felt obliged to come along when the rector pressed the invitation upon him. He was most welcome; it was good to see the hierarchy of the church – usually so aloof – taking part in the normal life of the majority of parishioners. The issue of the combined communions of Dunburgh and Gislam was still twitching under the surface but Corvin – supported by Esther's concern for his health and Rebecca's aversion to middle-class snobbery – remained adamant. He had welcomed several Gislam church members to the Harvest Supper, reminding everyone in his opening speech that "we are concerned with creating a spirit-filled, caring community of love." Bishop Twiddle had nodded in sage agreement and smiled – with, he hoped, an expression of immense tolerance – at the retired teachers, vets and gentleman farmers present. Since Corvin's elevation to the rural deanery, Peter Twiddle had found that not only had his visits to Dunburgh become more frequent but that his contemplative musings – as he liked to call them – had begun to take a more practical turn. He had also been introduced to a Peter Vishnya who insisted on talking to him about the state of the church in Estonia – something about which he would have preferred to remain blissfully unaware. Awareness obliged one to action which was, at all times, to be avoided.

Still, he had been able to re-acquaint himself with the most estimable Horst Brultzner – a man who England should be pleased to welcome and call friend. His interest in the traditions of the country and in the preservation of its heritage could only be admired. Moreover, he had been able to chat with Charles Wangford – another stalwart of the Anglican tradition – and had received an invitation to spend some time on the Wangford estate. Peter Twiddle was looking forward to that; it would make a welcome weekend break from the Sunday turmoil at the cathedral, and he would be able to apprise himself of the condition of the Wangford cellars, which he remembered with fondness.

There had been one or two strange people at the supper – people whose presence may have afforded a certain cosmopolitan air to the village, but whose credentials must remain suspect. He had not, for example, welcomed the interest of one Tony Crewes in the concept of the soul. Peter had been disturbed by this, and couldn't decide whether the man had been drunk or deranged. Fortunately, Crewes's wife – a small, dark woman who clearly knew her own mind – had drawn him away from such topics, and led the conversation down the more agreeable paths of food. Also, he had not welcomed the concerns of the village bobby over community policing. It was true that the church was often consulted on such matters, but only in an advisory capacity – there was never any expectation that he would actually have to do anything, which was what this PC Billings seemed to be proposing. It might pay to have a word in the right ear.

Grise Culman's enjoyment of the Harvest Supper was infinitely more practical – it was simply good to be seen there meeting the right people, and Charlie Wangford fell into that category. It didn't take much to flatter the old aristocrat, and you never knew where that might lead in the business world. She'd hoped to bump into Mark again, but he and Nin weren't here. Once his son had taken over the extension contract, Grise had realised that Mark was not going to oblige. Shame!

Owen was tucking into his soup – he'd gone for mulligatawny while she had chosen carrot and coriander. He was wolfing down the warm bread. She had to admit that the food – though simple – was good. There was something wholesome about it – unfussy. They could eat like peasants. Across the table from her sat Tony Crewes. It was he who had used the word 'peasants', but then he would. He read a lot (everyone knew that) and thought he was clever. Grise quite liked him.

Grise thought she might have a go at a meal like this – perhaps on Bonfire Night. It would suit the occasion and be simpler than a barbecue, which is what she usually put on. There was something very attractive about the cold meats set out as Totto Briggs had done them – and with hot soup and fresh bread, who could ask for more? Perhaps some dishes of hot vegetables – tomatoes with Parmesan and cream, swede and apple casserole, pineapple parsnips, red cabbage with apple, stuffed cabbage … the list was endless!

Corvin was pleased with how the evening was going. His opening talk had, he felt, brought things together nicely. He'd got in his favourite phrase about the "spirit-filled, caring community of love" and he was contented. Despite his working class credentials, Corvin quite liked the top table concept – especially when it placed him there with the bishop and Lord Wangford. There had been considerable growing opposition to it over the years – supported by his own daughter – but Totto Briggs had refused to budge. It was "*his* supper, *he* paid for it and he'd do it *his* way and, if anyone didn't like it, they could stay at home". Corvin felt compelled not to argue.

One of the Briggs family hovered around the top table offering a second helping of soup – "if anyone should want it". Corvin and Charles Wangford did, but the bishop made a point of refusing.

The top table, having been served first with their soup, were asked to lead the queue for the meat. Corvin and the bishop both deferred to Lord Wangford who deferred to Horst Brultzner as "his honoured guest" who capped them all by deferring to "the ladies". It was Esther, therefore, who found herself escorted to the meat table by Horst, followed by her daughter. Esther, too old to want to eat much, wondered whether Totto had not overdone it again. The usual huge range of cold meats and pies was supported by salads galore – new asparagus with pesto dressing, tomato and mint, fennel and celery, Italian bean, warm carrot with cumin, lemon and coriander couscous, Asian rice, cracked potato and salsa potato. There had been some discussion the previous year about the lack of provision for vegetarians, a species which Totto himself did not understand, but for which his daughter, a growing force in the butchery business, was determined to provide. Both Rebecca and her mother saw a woman's hand in the range and number of salad dishes.

Sandra Bint, without her son Ainsley who still found Harvest Suppers boring, noted them all. She was still sleeping naked as summer wound to a close, and had spent the night with her amorous policeman. She could still remember waking that night, lying in the garden against her bench, and wondering why; she'd told Grise about it, but her friend was no help. She'd wondered if the amorous policeman had left her there! Sandra was sure that it was someone else, but couldn't think who – she was usually so careful and only carried on with two men at the same time if she was sure they wouldn't meet. She couldn't believe that she had invited another man round to her house while still pursuing the policeman – just in case he had turned up unexpectedly for a nibble. Never mind: that was in the past – life moves on. It was a pity she still couldn't bring her policeman with her – he would have looked nice on her arm – but you can't have everything.

She was still determined to get Grise and Mark Chambers together – they were made for each other and she could see that Grise was lonely. Things would be looking up in the village then – what with Rebecca Unwood getting married. Her man was quite dishy in an intellectual sort of way: still everyone to their own! Personally, she wouldn't want a man who thought too much. Being able to listen, chat on about nothing much at parties and throw in the odd 'funny' was enough to keep the social wheels turning without boring your pants off. Not that she'd ever dropped hers for that kind of man, anyway.

"Penny for them, Sandra," said Tony Crewes.

"They aren't worth that, Tony."

"Thoughts that flutter through even the most trivial mind are worthy of consideration."

"And my mind's trivial?"

"I didn't say that."

"But he meant it," cut in Martin Billings.

"I meant nothing of the sort, Martin. You policeman are too quick, sometimes, to rush to conclusions. I meant what I said – that whatever anyone thinks is worth consideration – so …?"

"You bugger," she laughed, quietly, across the table.

Martin Billings slumped back in his chair. His friend had disappointed him – not just by making that crack about policemen, but by stemming the flow of what might have been a disruptive conversation. Tony could usually be relied upon to stir things up. Martin was feeling hemmed in, and there was anger in him which wanted to break out. It was time to get away for a while. The Brown-Marjoram case still haunted him – in particular the failure of the force to bring things to a swift conclusion. Years ago it wouldn't have been like that – Marjoram had done it, everybody knew he had, there was a signed confession and he'd got away with it. He might be dead, but they'd never pinned the murder on him and, now, it was unlikely they ever would. He'd escaped justice, and that galled Martin.

Then, there had been the little Turrel boy – Martin had felt so helpless sitting in the child's bedroom with the mother on the edge of the bed. He'd never forget her face – tortured with grief. He remembered touching her shoulder and feeling what a pathetic gesture that was in the face of her bereavement.

Amy knew how he felt, of course, and suggested that they should get away in the autumn, but Martin wasn't sure that was what he wanted. He felt like something different – something that would test his physical fitness to the limits: a break with some mates – or a single mate, doing something. "Then why not take up cycling?" Amy had said. But who the hell would go with him? Not Tony for sure; too strenuous for him! "Alan Read?" Amy had suggested.

Penny Read was feeling smug, although she fancied she shouldn't. Her side had, more or less, got its own way. The church hall was decorated with the children's pictures, and festooned – well, hung at least – with corn dollies. They, also, had that life-size one outside to greet everyone. Mrs Podd had made that with great joy, and the teenage girls had helped her. Many of them were here tonight, and Penny was determined it would be an evening for them to remember. She laughed quietly to herself, as she and Alan tucked into their supper, at the memory of the Charismatics' arrival. The had tried to pass the giant corn dolly without noticing it, which was impossible since the girls had placed it with one hand stretching half-way across the doorway. Only girls of that age could have done that! But the bigots had been routed for the night, and another tradition resurrected. She was still half-intending to bury it in Podd's Field with the older girls. It would be fun, and there was no harm in these old customs – not now. Martin Billings had been a great help. He'd stood up for Corvin at the PCC meeting and bullied through both the pagan traditions and the children's participation in the Harvest Festival. She liked Martin. He was to law and order what her husband was to medicine in the village.

She knew that Esther had gone to see Clara Gobley. She realised that it wasn't so much for her sake as for Corvin's. Esther was only behind progress in the church when it couldn't be avoided, or if to oppose it brought Corvin into conflicts he couldn't resolve. It made Penny smile that his great arena of conflict was Esther herself! But she had 'faced off' the organist, and that was to be admired. She was looking forward to the entertainment. It was always so (what was the word) rustic? When she'd left her own village for university, it was with relief at leaving all that behind. Now that her own children were growing up she welcomed it, and hoped that the youngsters there tonight would see the funny side!

Penny herself had offered to call a few dances to round off the evening and when the 'sweets' – a choice of lemon and apple pie, mandarin meringue, apple dumplings, cheesecake, spicy rhubarb crumble or pineapple upside down pudding – had been consumed and the tables cleared and stacked she had everybody up on the floor with Circassian Circle.

Tony Crewes was always slightly cynical of this sort of thing – harping back to a mythical past when the farmers and fishermen of Dunburgh had been exploited by their masters – but even he was soon caught up in the spirit of the evening. It was not, even, as though the music was real (Penny had brought tapes and CDs from her school) but the sound of the accordion and the violin racing their feet along was intoxicating, and Penny called well. As he danced, Tony watched her. She was still in a cool summer 'frock' (he loved that word) and fresh as a breeze on a hot day. She stood on the stage, commanding the microphone, while everybody else danced to her bidding. Tony laughed. His wife was going to have something to say about that when they got home.

Tony found himself dancing with anyone from nine to ninety. His own children passed him by followed by Penny's, and then he found himself in the arms of Sarah Brown. She'd gone back to her maiden name, and he didn't blame her for that – not after what her husband had done. That bastard was well under the earth.

She smiled at him as they did their turn. He had been kind to her once or twice, and there was an unspoken gratitude between them. He recalled the first time he had actually noticed her – at her mother's funeral in March. Her eyes had been upon him when her husband arrived drunk at the church. The second time had been on that dreadful night when they had found her father's body. He'd been woken from a drink-induced sleep by the sound of her voice, and been taken by her beauty – that dreamy look which, that night, had been haunted by anxiety.

"You're pulling your life together, Sarah – for you and your son?"

"Yes. I remember what you and Nadine said that afternoon."

"Tomorrow is the first day ..." He left the platitude unfinished.

"Horst has been very kind. Matthew and I have security now."

"And a future?"

"Yes – for always."

They danced on to new partners and Sarah found herself in the arms of Sidney Close. She was warm tonight – she and Horst had supped lightly before coming to the Harvest Supper – and Sidney smelt the heat in her body. His grip tightened on her waist as he spun her round, and he drew her in to his chest. He had that tight-lipped smile on his face which Sarah hated. She'd never liked nor trusted Sidney.

Given half-a-chance he'd have ... whatever men of that age did when they got their hands on a young woman. He always reminded her of the 'Sir Jasper' character she'd seen in village music halls. If they couldn't have you, they tied you on the railway line. Sarah had never understood why they did that unless it was ...

"I was sorry to hear about Shane," he said, insincerely.

"Thank you."

"It was so sudden in the end."

"Yes – I don't think ... I don't think Shane expected it."

She had no remorse over what she had done to Shane and found herself (when she thought about him at all) indulging in what she remembered her English teacher calling 'black humour'. Horst had never spoken to her about it. He would not have approved, but Sarah felt that he would have understood her anger was righteous.

"You'll have to start getting back into the life of the village again, Sarah – you've had a bad year."

"Yes."

"The autumn is coming on – there'll be a lot happening."

His grip tightened – just that bit too much across the small of her back, just on the buttocks. Nadine had warned her about Sidney; 'I don't trust him – watch out – he's a lecher. He resents others enjoying sex because he's frustrated himself. If they were still hunting witches here, he'd be up there alongside Matthew Hopkins, 'interrogating' female suspects.

Sarah remembered the day he had come to the Old Vicarage looking for Mark Chambers. He'd been on the point of tearing her dress off when she laughed, and then he'd pulled away from her and stumbled out onto the driveway. There might be some mileage in Sidney Close. She wouldn't enjoy it – yes she would! – taking him, drawing her pleasure from him. It would teach him a lesson – just enough to have him simmering forever.

Bishop Twiddle enjoyed a short but meaningful discussion with Lord Wangford who had endorsed his opinion that Corvin was doing a good job in what was, after all, a difficult village.

"Godless times, Peter – you shouldn't expect too much of your clergy. If they can keep their feet on the ground, moving forward, that's an achievement in itself."

"The diocese expects just a little more than that, Charles."

"Then it shouldn't! Corvin does a good job here just holding things together, and he has a vibrant Sunday School ..."

"Junior Church!"

"Call it what you will – look at these youngsters tonight. They're the future – not that bunch of grey-heads against the wall."

Peter Twiddle – from the ranks of the upper-middle class – had never quite got used to the bluntness of the aristocracy. Indeed, he often found the Duke of Edinburgh rather outspoken, but he knew Charles Wangford's heart was in the right place.

"What say you, Horst?"

Charles Wangford threw his remark to Horst Brultzner, knowing that he would be pleased to be drawn in to the bishop's musings, and deliberately using his first name to increase the sense of informality. Something he would never have done had they been alone.

"Sometimes it is necessary to ruffle feathers to create change, but that is not the English way, is it, my lord?" replied Brultzner.

"Eh – no – indeed."

"The life of the English village trickles on as gently as its streams, the future being shaped almost imperceptibly by its meanderings."

"You have a poetic turn of mind ... Horst."

"I try – but poetry, I fear, is a gift. A man may conquer nations, yet fail to write a poem."

All three laughed. Horst's comment contained a mixture of arrogance and humility that puzzled the bishop and delighted the aristocrat.

"I always thought it a shame that your church did away with Cranmer's *Book of Common Prayer*, to be honest, my lord. It had a beauty – bought at a terrible price – which far outweighed its supposed 'shortcomings'."

"The church must move with the times, Horst – and I would point out that the...eh, new version is only an 'alternative'. We had no intention that Cranmer's ...eh...rendering should be phased out completely."

"And what have you achieved by it – by this 'new' version?"

"It was hoped that the use of more modern language might attract into the church a new and future generation."

"And did it?"

"Perhaps not with the ....vigour we had intended."

"You tamper with traditions at your peril. Watering down your religion leads to confusion and weakness – the people without leadership, the clergy without faith."

"You find our faith less than full-blooded, Herr ... Mr Brultzner?" queried Corvin, cutting lightly into the conversation.

The interpolation surprised the other three in equal measure. Corvin rarely addressed anything so directly to the bishop let alone the aristocracy for whom, Charles Wangford had noted, he had what appeared to be an almost fawning respect.

"I can recall times, rector, when men died for their faith and, indeed, killed for it. The man we have just spoken of – Archbishop Cranmer – died in agony at the stake for his beliefs."

"Despite his previous recantations," said Corvin.

"You doubt the integrity of your first archbishop, rector?"

"He was burned by the Catholics – nothing could have saved him, not even his recantations. They were determined he should die. It is not a time, I feel, to which one would wish to return."

"You know of no-one who would wish to die for their faith today?"

"I would hope not – we have reached an age of love and reconciliation in the Christian church. That is what we need to take forward."

Bishop Twiddle felt rather proud of Corvin – even if he did sound like his wife speaking. No, that was unfair – Esther Unwood was not a conciliatory person. Corvin had spoken from the heart.

Rebecca Unwood and Peter Vishnya were entangled in a web of speculation which tugged them forward in the direction of marriage. Despite the fact that they had only touched upon the possibility themselves, there was an assumption in the village that they were to be married. Peter seemed at ease. She had given him her diary and he had read, in the untidy peacefulness of the rectory garden, what Rebecca had been unable to say in her e-mails. She had then written it out for him on pieces of handmade paper, and he had placed it unfolded in the drawer of his desk in his house on London Road. He spoke to her, assuaging any worries she might have had about his first marriage, about Yevgeny and about Anton. "I do not have any worries. So long as you have talked to your boy about it, then I am happy."

She wanted to marry that autumn with the fruits and flowers of field and hedgerow adorning the church and reception, but Peter cautioned her to wait. There was her mother, her work, the coming chaos of the festive season. Spring, with its new life, and with all winter to make plans, would be a better time for starting an eternity together. She laughed at the word 'eternity' and Peter said, "Talk to your father: ask him about your soul and mine."

"We have nothing definite planned," she said, laughing, to Sandra Bint.

"Everyone's saying it will be before Christmas."

"In that case, everyone's wrong."

"So it will be in the spring, then?"

"Yes – but we don't know when."

"And how does Yev ... your little boy feel about it, Peter?"

"Yevgeny is delighted. Rebecca is to spend a little time in Estonia with us ..."

"He's not here tonight?"

"No – he preferred Anton's company at home."

"Are you keeping your home on here?"

"I expect so."

"I think that's very sensible," said Sandra, now armed with a month's gossip.

"You now know more than we do, Sandra," cut in Esther.

"You must be over the moon, Esther!"

"We are very pleased for both of them – and for Peter's little boy."

"Estonia's not far away – not these days."

"No – not far."

It was, however, to one of Esther's generation, far enough: endless miles of sea and land to be crossed, and her daughter gone from her. She was pleased for Rebecca (of course she was) but she was sad for herself. If only Peter could have found work at home.

"I don't want her to go, you know," she said to Corvin, as they sat in a late garden when the Harvest Supper was over.

"I know, my dear, but you do want her to be happy, and her future lies with Peter – not with you and me. We have been lucky to have her with us for so long."

"Yes."

"You say 'yes' without conviction, my dear."

"Is the bishop asleep?"

"He was too tired – even for his bottle of "hushed Beaujolais"."

"Will that be our life after Rebecca, Corvin – bishops and Beaujolais?"

"You mustn't think along those lines, Esther."

"I'm a mother, and I shall miss my daughter – that's all I'm saying!"

Penny Read, against her better judgement, had allowed herself to be persuaded by the enthusiasm of the teenagers from the Junior Church. After all, there weren't many of them, and they were the years, thirteen to fifteen, when they left the church. She had told Alan to take their own children home, convincing the oldest (who was twelve and "nearly a teenager") that he was still too young to stay behind after the Harvest Supper was over. When the clearing up had been done, she and Joanne Podd took the girls into Podd's Field. With the bishop's final blessing – "May the peace of God, which passes all understanding ... be among you and remain with you, always" – ringing in their ears, the two women, giggly as schoolgirls again, led the digging. Penny marvelled at how paganism and her own faith marched hand in hand.

The field had already been ploughed for a winter crop and the digging was easy as they plunged spades into the deep furrows left by the tractor. The girls were eager, and took more than their share of the work. Once the hole deepened, Penny and Joanna did little more than watch as the 'grave' opened up. They had jostled and almost squabbled as the human sheaf was carried across from the Church Centre, and this was repeated now the time had come to bury it.

"What shall we say, Mrs Read?"

"Say?"

"We can't just bury it in the hole. We ought to say a little prayer."

"How about that song they sang in church, Penny?"

"*Lord of the Harvest?*"

"Yes."

"We'll sing it together then."

Their unaccompanied voices were beautiful on the night air. They began in almost a whisper but, as the words took over, they became less inhibited by the secretiveness of their mission, and could be heard – faintly but audibly – by those who passed along the road home.

"Lord of the Harvest, lord of the field,
our thanks now to God in nature revealed ... "

Penny, who loved teaching the song, was almost in tears as they finished singing: Joanne and the girls were. The corn dolly was lowered gently into the grave, and they shovelled the dark earth back upon it.

"It's like burying someone, isn't it Mrs Read?"

"Yes, I suppose it is."

"Saying goodbye."

"Yes – you're right."

"But somehow knowing you'll see them again."

"In next year's harvest?" asked Joanne.

The girl who had spoken was quiet. She knew, intuitively, what she was thinking, but couldn't express it in words. It was a thought apprehended rather than framed in language. Penny smiled at her in the darkness. One of the beautiful things about teaching was sharing those moments of understanding with a child.

"If only it was real," said the girl.

"Real?"

Sometimes only a word, a quiet expression of interest and trust, was all that was needed to encourage the thought to grow.

"Real – that we will meet again."

They stood for a long time together, not one of them wishing to move and break the moment. They were all unsure what it was they had shared – this old ritual to appease the god of the harvest, the giving of a life that others may live. Was it simply a fantasy – the human race's attempt to come to terms with the forces that raged around them – or was there more to it than that?

Penny and Joanne insisted that they were all accompanied home.

"I know you walk home though the village every night, but not tonight! Your parents have trusted me to look after you and that is what I intend to do!"

Each girl was taken to her door, each door was seen to open and close as voices welcomed the homecoming child, and then the two women drove themselves back to their families.

"Did it go well?" asked Alan, as he handed Penny a gin and tonic.

"Yes – it was fun ... and thought-provoking."

Alan was quiet, swirling his whisky round the glass, inhaling its clean aroma.

"People are very complex, aren't they Alan? ... I see those girls every Sunday and I think I know them, and then something ... almost magical occurs, and I see them in a completely different light. You wouldn't think, would you, that they had this capacity to understand things beyond ... beyond understanding. There was a girl, tonight, who glimpsed beyond the grave."

"What did she say?"

"Nothing too much ... it's just that suddenly we all – all of us there in the field – had this shared understanding of the ... of the continuity of life and death."

Book Three
Autumn Falls

CHAPTER 1

The call of the wild

Horst Brultzner had made his decision; in the idiom of the English he loved –
'enough was enough'. He had worked with Clara Gobley and the one she called
Bert. He had worked with Crafty Catchpole whose pigeons were now homing
with a reliability of return that made the other members of the club suspicious.
Horst hadn't been sure why he agreed to their requests, but killing them at that
time would not have been sensible – too much had been going on in the village.
Things had quietened down now as they always did with the coming of autumn,
and the odd death would attract only the attention it should – and, certainly, no
undesirable speculation.

He admired Clara Gobley and her man, Bert – in his own way, as much as he
admired anybody – but he could not live on in the village with their knowledge
hanging over him like the Greek's sword. He had taught them the calls to which
animals came and watched them as they stalked the village seeing to the injured,
the threatened and the abused; abandoned cats, parent-less fox cubs, chained dogs,
ducks injured by the occasional joy rider, and fledglings that had fallen from nests
all drew the compassion of Clara and Bert. With the powers he had given them,
they were able to charm parents to their young, the endangered to a haven and the
stricken to nursing. He admired them, but they needed him no longer and they had
religious scruples about what he was and how he lived. Horst worried that they
would make peace with their god, break their oath accordingly and destroy him;
he had to act.

October had arrived with all the beauty of autumn. The wet earth harboured
mists, which rose into the air each morning; the wet air engendered fogs, which
drifted across the fields at night. It was a good and peaceful time; autumn was soft.
He enjoyed watching the leaves turned to red or gold and drift to earth before
finally rustling russet under the feet. The harvests were safely in, and the fields –
brown again and stiff with yellow stubble – waited for the plough. Birds gathered
on the wires, preparing for their flight to a warmer winter. Food was plentiful with
fruits and berries ripe: apples, pears and plums were picked, nuts were stored,
larders filled. Horst still enjoyed this, with long memories of provisioning his
soldiers.

After saying farewell to Sarah, he strolled out into the night. Already it was
quite dark, and there was a light in the church. It was Friday and the choir would
be practising their songs for the Sunday services. He could hear the sound of the
organ with its dark, gothic threat. It was forever associated with melodrama and

345

madness in the popular imagination, despite the wonderful Bach. He drifted, like the mist, into the graveyard and sat on one of the bequeathed seats so that he could listen while the smells of the warm earth and damp grass stirred his nostrils. He smiled and ran his hand along the wooden seat; the lights from the church shimmered. His finger touched the web of an early spider and he took it gently on his finger before blowing the creature back against its own web as a child might have blown a dandelion clock.

He had played with Sarah's son in the early evening, bombarding the boy with handfuls of fallen leaves and chasing him around the little wood that lay between them and the rectory. Sticks cracked under their feet, and they kicked the leaves skywards. The garden had attracted squirrels during the summer, and Horst had made it a haven for English red squirrels, which Matthew had shown his friends. Now, they prepared for the coming winter, and the vampire and the child watched them, each overwhelmed by the wonder of the natural world. In his own mind, Horst had already decided that this would be the boy's destiny – to know more about the world of animals and plants than any other living soul had ever known. Sarah had watched them. She was delighted that the boy already had the knack of 'calling' and that the animals in the garden watched him as though he were one of them.

Horst made his way down the road, passing gently in the shadows of the field where he had observed Penny Read and the young women bury the sheath of corn. He had enjoyed their singing, their youth and their eagerness for life. He lived through the excitement of others, especially the young, and looked forward to holding each of them in his arms while he slaked his thirst. There was vibrancy in their slender bodies which filled him with desire and longing. He had long-since overcome the vampire's urge to possess and conquer, though such instincts had been in his very nature when a man. For centuries, he had gained so much more by insinuation, by becoming central to the lives and loves of his women through the adoration of their bodies.

As always, the garden of Clara's bungalow was well lit from the house. The vampire knew that Bert would be waiting for her return from choir practice and would be tending to one of the many animals they had saved. Tonight, through the window, Horst could see that it was a rabbit which Bert held – a young one with a snapped leg bone. The man was crooning gently to the little creature, and the rabbit was quite still on his lap, as though hypnotised by the sound.

Horst turned and walked into their garden. He had never enjoyed killing. It had always been a craft to him, undertaken with the same care and precision with which a cabinet-maker would construct tables and chairs. He looked around the garden as he prepared himself, and didn't see the mess others saw. He noticed only Bert's herb garden and the rows of vegetables – cabbages, turnips, parsnips ready for the winter; the last of the beans were withered now and rotting for compost. He noticed the donkey's stall and the pens where they kept the injured animals – there was a fox and several rabbits. He sniffed the air: musk and rotting vegetation – the life for the coming year. A huge moon filled the sky, silhouetting a horse chestnut whose leaves were always the first to drop.

He turned and looked up at the bungalow; the attic windows were still open. Ivy clambered all over the roof, spreading itself across the red tiles and hanging in pendulous clumps from the end gables; it seemed also to be clinging to the sill, and making its way into the house. Horst looked carefully around the garden. He had seen an old rope slung by a water butt, and he smiled when he saw it still there; the vampire walked over, picked it up and swiftly made a running noose in one end.

He walked in through the door of the kitchen. It appalled him as it had appalled Esther Unwood. It was a few moments before Bert became aware of him, so absorbed was he in splinting the young rabbit's leg. When he did, his nose twitched and a spasm of fear passed over his face. He smiled, but not with confidence.

"How did you get in here? I thought ..."

"You tended a stricken rat some weeks ago, Bert – remember the one you found breathless by the gate? ... I have to be invited, of course. You were right about that, but the form is not material and I knew that one day I should need to see you."

"Clara is at choir practice."

"I know, but it is you I wish to ... see, first."

The slightest of pauses between 'to' and 'see' was enough to terrify Bert – enough to burnish the innocent 'see' with the meaning of a hundred imaginings.

"I'll do what I can ...."

"I'm sure you will but ... please ... finish seeing to the rabbit first."

"Would you ...?"

"I think not."

The thought of tea rarely enticed Brultzner, and particularly not in this house. Bert's hand shook as he finished tying the bandages that were to secure the splint. The rope was hidden by Brultzner's coat and Bert didn't notice that; had he done so, his terror would have been confirmed.. The vampire's manner was nonchalant, and yet there was nothing flippant in his demeanour. He watched Bert's administrations with interest and care, and this raised the hope that was fading fast from the man.

"You might have made something of your life in the veterinary service, Bert."

"Vets need paying. Wild animals don't have the wherewithal."

The phrase – and the humour – made the vampire smile.

"So how do you sustain yourselves – and the animals?"

Bert's look suggested that Brultzner might mind his own business, but he thought better of it and answered.

"Clara was a teacher. She has a small pension. I put a bit aside."

"What did you do?"

"This and that – we manage."

The vampire, haughty landowner that he was, had always admired what the commoners called 'grafters'. He thought to himself that things might have been different had not Clara, Bert and, of course, Catchpole not dictated the circumstances. When Bert finished, he looked at Brultzner.

"I have to put her in a hutch now – there outside," he said.

"Of course."

In the back garden, Bert heaved a sigh of relief. He was free of the vampire's presence because Brultzner had made no move to stay with him. Bert placed the young rabbit carefully in the freshly-prepared hutch, nestling it gently down in the fresh straw before glancing over his shoulder. He saw through the kitchen window that Brultzner had not moved and decided that he might walk casually – very casually – towards the gate. He saw Brultzner as he passed the side window, still as a shadow in the living room, and in a few steps he had reached the road. His fear dropped from him like sweat in summer and he breathed an unexpected sigh of relief. Clara was not far away; choir practice would be over in half-an-hour or so.

He wanted to step further, into the road and across, and run like hell to the church and sanctuary, but he couldn't do that; his feet wouldn't move – not beyond the gate. The longer he waited the more suspicious the vampire would become and yet nothing – not fear, not relief, not even common sense would make him step into the road. 'Rooted to the spot.' He knew what the phrase meant now. It was as if his gaoler had opened the cell door and gone for lunch, leaving him free to escape, and yet he – like a prisoner long held captive – dare not make his dash. He heard the organ; he imagined Clara, imperious with the choir, fidgeting on the organ stool. All this started that day in spring when Catchpole had come to them with his ludicrous proposal. If only they had then thrown him on the compost heap!

"Bert – you are taking the night air?"

Brultzner stood at his side. There had been no sound, and no sensation of movement. One moment he glimpsed the vampire through the living room window, and the next he – It – was by his side, faster than his last thoughts had flown.

"I love the night. Listen."

Brultzner raised his head and from his throat came a low, keening whine which evolved into a soft but piercing howl. The sound was full of longing for a life that once was and now could be no more. It was taken up by the wolves from the wildlife park as they answered Brultzner's cry.

"You and me both, Bert – as the Americans say – love animals in our own way. What music they make."

He looked at Bert as he uttered the quote and was gratified when Bert's look acknowledged the reference.

"We will go inside now."

There was no refusal Bert could make; he turned and shuffled alongside Brultzner as though the vampire had him on a leash. He gazed around the cluttered living room. It was home to him: the cobbler's last had belonged to his father, the Marconi radio had filled the evenings of his childhood, the hard-backed books were from their home library, the 78s – with their sentimental Italian music – had been his mother's favourites and the apple basket in which they stood she had used to collect the fruit from their own garden.

"You took papers from my study at the Old Vicarage when you and your companions violated my home. Where are they?"

"Upstairs – in a chest. They are unharmed."

"That is fortunate. You have read them?"

"Yes."

"Then you will know much of my business. Who else has read them?"

"No one – Clara wasn't interested. I just thought that they might help."

"Help?"

"Help us get what we wanted from you."

"You will fetch them, please."

Bert looked at the vampire whose face was still unperturbed and felt another false glimmer of hope. He felt impelled; his feet were on the stairs before he knew it, and Brultzner was waiting for him. Bert opened a small door at the top of the stairs, reached in and pulled out a small brass-bound chest of the sort sailors traditionally used in the days of sailing ships. It was free from dust – almost pristine, and strangely at odds with the rest of the house. He unlocked it with a small key which hung from one of the handles and handed Brultzner his papers.

"We only did it to help the animals."

"Of course."

"We have what we want. We have no intention of welshing on the deal."

"Would you wish to lie in your bed at night ... Bert, knowing that someone had the power of life and death over you?"

"No."

"No. What is in here?"

Brultzner looked up at a small trapdoor, which he assumed led into the roof, and then gestured to one room that went off the small landing at the top of the stairs.

"It's an aviary. The birds convalesce there. When they are ready, they fly to freedom through the window."

He opened the door and they both stepped inside what in a normal house would have been a bedroom. The window Brultzner had noticed from the garden was opened outwards and through it shone the moon which was the room's only light. Feeding troughs, liberally filled with seed, were scattered casually around the walls; small perches were supported by brackets and larger ones, presumably for the occasional rook or gull, stood on stout wooden frames obviously built by Bert. Along one side of the room there were cages, but only one was occupied – by a pair of dunnocks. The floor was covered with a blend of newspaper and straw, which was liberally coated with excreta. Water troughs hung from the perches or stood around the floor.

The ceiling had been removed – or, rather, smashed aside – so that the flight area was increased as much as possible for the birds. From where he stood, Brultzner looked up into the very roof of the house through the exposed beams that held it in place. What occurred, as the vampire saw the beams, happened so quickly that Bert was only partially aware of his own death. One moment he stood gazing into the roof space with Brultzner, and the next he was sitting on one of the beams in the vampire's grip. The few birds perched there disappeared in a flurry of feathers and squawks, and then Bert dropped through the air with the noose around his neck. It pulled tight before he reached the floor and his neck snapped. His body swung to and fro for a while and the feet and hands twitched, as Brultzner tied the other end of the rope to a beam, and then was still.

The vampire scuttled across to the trapdoor, opened it, dropped the loft ladder to the landing and glided to the floor. Clara's companion had committed suicide, hanging himself in their aviary. 'There's no accounting for the things people will do.' Brultzner smiled as the colloquial phrase drifted into his head. He checked that the body was dead, although the angle of Bert's head (Brultzner had placed the knot with care despite the speed with which he moved) left no doubt in the vampire's mind. He shut the aviary door behind him as he went downstairs to wait for Clara.

Clara disappeared from choir practice slightly later than usual and hurried home. She and Bert had a lot on at the moment. She had left him tending an injured rabbit some motorist had thrown to the side of the road to die. Ripe with her customary anger at the carelessness of the world, she stormed down Church Hill to her home.

She had been flexing her right elbow at ninety degrees for the past hour or so and had felt her body pivot on the stool. She had dropped her shoulders, but this had not prevented the tightening of the trapeziums and she was feeling her usual irritable self – fatigued and agitated.

The house was usually quiet, except for the sounds of the animals. She liked it that way. Tonight there were no sounds at all. She always had a sense of Bert's presence, always walked in to a cup of tea, but he wasn't at the door. Clara paused in the driveway. Unconventional but wedded to her routines, Clara did not welcome change.

"Bert?"

She hurried across the living room, passed through the kitchen and out into the back garden. The injured rabbit was in its hutch, but there was no sign of Bert. She called again. Ever since they'd met in her late forties, he had always been there for her.

"Bert?"

Despite her deserved reputation for irascibility, Clara had never raised her voice to Bert; theirs had been an harmonious relationship.

"Bert?"

She was worried now, and went deep into the garden thinking that perhaps he had fallen and injured himself.

She had retired early from teaching, at Bert's instigation. Since then they had dedicated their lives to helping animals and making life as unpleasant as possible for anyone who got in their way. The young man joy-riding down Gylde Hall Lane with his latest girl, spinning a duck from his wheel and leaving it with a broken leg to die a lingering death at the mercy of cats had wished he hadn't when

Clara laid hands on him. The next morning he was found taped to a lamp-post with a sign hung round his neck. The sign read 'I didn't give a fuck about the duck so the duck's friends didn't give a fuck about me.' Bert had written the notice (he had a way with words when the occasion demanded) and Clara had made sure that a photograph appeared on every lamp-post around the village.

She rushed back into the house; it appeared empty. Why weren't the animals talking? There was no chirruping from the hedge sparrows upstairs, no squeaks from the white rats, no calf-rubbing welcome from the many cats, no caw from the jackdaw which they'd had so long, no lapping of milk by the hedgehogs who seemed to live permanently in the garden. The fox was restless, and the ears of the rabbits were cocked at a listening angle. As always when upset, Clara became angry – not with Bert but with the situation – and she wanted to put things right. Bert had come into her life after so many years of no one wanting her. She knew what the world thought of her – ugly, belligerent, vulgar-mouthed. Who would desire such a woman? Bert did; he moved in and cherished her as a true lover will cherish the woman he loves however unusual that love might appear.

"Bert!"

There was anguish in her voice as she rushed upstairs to the aviary. The door was closed but the ladder to the loft was down. Why? Had Bert gone into the roof space to tend to an injured bird? She trod quickly up the ladder, but saw nothing and shinned down again. On the landing she paused before reaching for the handle of the aviary and then, with habitual forthrightness, pushed the door open. Bert's body still hung with his head at its grotesque angle, his arms dangling helplessly by his sides. The face was blue and the eyes shut tight, but he seemed to be looking at her for assistance. Clara approached the body and lifted the legs gently as though wanting to ease the pressure on the neck.

"Bert?"

Clara could not accept that he was dead – especially by his own hand. Was the only man who had ever loved her (and come anywhere near understanding her) hanging by his neck – dead? The word framed itself in her mind, which then rejected it. Tears rose in her eyes and anger rose in her heart. Someone had done this to Bert; someone had murdered him. Clara lifted her head and howled. She dropped to her knees, still holding his feet, and hugged them to her face and to her breast. 'Bert – fierce, gentle Bert who had never harmed anyone who didn't deserve it, whose heart went out to any stricken creature – hanging on the end of a rope, his neck broken ... his lovely, ugly face blue with dead blood ... his life in tatters.'

Clara was incapable of feeling sorry for herself. The thoughts came in outbursts of anger against his killer, as the identity of that killer became a picture in her mind. Bert might have upset many people in his time but there were none with the guts to kill him except Brultzner. It was night and the vampire would be abroad, but when morning came she would find him and destroy him as they should have done long ago. Only fools make deals with the Devil, and their folly had taken Bert's life.

She was a heavy woman plagued by the onset of arthritis but she would climb the ladder, make her way across the beams and cut him down. Then, at least … at least the … at least his face would look as she remembered it. He had loved her well and unselfishly: teasing her in that pedantic way of his, pretending to be servile for their amusement and their 'guests' bewilderment. Clara, her face contorted with grief and stained with tears, smiled as she thought of him she had loved: the man who had come to her and accepted her for what she was – and loved her. She was bitter, and the bitterness concentrated her mind.

Leaving the dangling body reluctantly, for the moment only, while she climbed to the rafters, Clara stepped out onto the landing and clutched the ladder. A shadow passed her. She was aware only of a presence and a sense of unspeakable evil, and then she fell backwards through the air. Her body crashed and blundered from stair to stair and from wall to banister until it hit the bottom step. It collapsed, twisted and slumped, looking more like a heap of old clothes than a human being except for the head which peered from out of the grubby cardigan and turned to look upwards. She was only partly conscious at that moment. The blows she suffered, as she stumbled backwards, had concussed Clara. She felt her body being lifted and then the back of her neck was brought down hard on the banister, and there it snapped. Brultzner let her go and she fell, for a second time, into a heap of ragged clothes.

He knelt over the body and assured himself that she was dead. 'Seeing Bert's body hanging from the rafters, she stumbled backwards in shock and broke her neck as she fell down the stairs.' Brultzner heaved a sigh of relief. There was nothing to link their deaths to him. No one but Sarah knew of their infamy except Catchpole, and he would soon, as a faithless servant, meet a well-deserved end.

The vampire returned to the aviary. He did not look at Bert's corpse. He only paused to retrieve his papers and return the small brass-bound chest to the small loft cupboard at the top of the stairs. He moved quickly down, stepped carefully over Clara's body, and looked around. All was as it should be, except for the quietness of the animals. When he was gone they would stir, looking for food.

Outside, the autumn night closed comfortably around him. It had been a warm day and the mists would soon start to rise from the grassy banks and from the fields. He would disappear into them and become one with them. He began to feel easier in himself. The weeks since they had returned from Prague to find the holy wafers in their coffins had been a strain. Lying helpless during the day, and knowing that others held the power of death over them had not been easy. Although Horst was sure that it had been wise to wait, he had realised the risk. His patience had been rewarded, however. Their deaths would appear natural; they had been an eccentric couple who had met an eccentric end, and the villagers would raise no questions – especially with PC Billings out of the way.

Penny Read had been really excited when Amy Billings suggested the cycling holiday. She knew her husband worked too hard, and a short break cycling through France would do him good, so she persuaded him to take the time owing to him and go. "No questions, Alan – go! Martin needs a break and it will do you both good. You're putting on a bit of weight, anyway – you can work it off!" He'd tapped her backside for the cheek of the remark, they'd laughed and kissed and he'd popped round to see Martin who'd been both pleased and surprised. By the time he got home, Penny had also popped round to the surgery and had a word with Jim Maxwell, the senior partner in the practice, who succumbed quickly to her English rose charms and arranged to cover Alan's work. The next day she went into Norbridge and bought him a bike that was delivered that evening. "It's a fait accompli, Alan – now you'll have to go. Ooh – and no mobile phones! You can phone me, and only me, on the house phone each night. The practice can manage without you for a week and the constabulary can manage without Martin."

She and Amy had laughed about it over coffee each morning. Neither of the men liked being organised, but once the choice was taken from them they had "succumbed gracefully" and planned their trip with eagerness. Maps appeared, routes were sought, inns were telephoned and ferry tickets were booked. Within a week, they were in France cycling along the coast roads of Normandy, visiting Ault, Le Treport, St Valery-en-Caux, Veulettes-sur-Mer, Fecamp, Yport and Etretat. They had escaped the rigours of their daily lives and would return refreshed.

Both Penny and Amy were excited for their husbands and followed their route with avid interest. Besides, it gave them an excuse to meet up each morning and to share one lunch at the Trattoria Rustica in Norbridge.

On the day the news broke in Dunburgh about the deaths of Clara and Bert, Alan and Martin – their bikes propped against a beautiful stone bridge on the road to St Valery – were sipping chilled cider in the shade of a cafe umbrella, while the auburn sun of autumn glared from the white walls.

"Crafty found them," said Sandra Bint, "They'd been dead for days!"

"No," said Nin Chambers, "How awful! He must have been shocked."

"The cats had started to eat her!" said Sandra.

"They hadn't been fed, had they? I suppose the poor things were hungry. What's going to happen to the other animals?"

"Ainsley said they called in the RSPCA. I suppose they'll find homes for them and release the rabbits and foxes back into the wild."

Superintendent Junket had been annoyed when the news arrived on his desk. Without Billings on the scene (much as he disliked the man's maverick approach to policing) there was the possibility that things would get out of hand. After all, the village should be settling down for the winter. An apparent suicide didn't calm matters, and the press was rife with wild speculations. He'd expected more of the Lowestoft Gazette, but even they had indulged in fanciful journalism and, of course, the nationals and television had a field day. The woman's corpse had excited a lot of attention – especially when it leaked out that she had been partly eaten by her own cats. The force could have done without such an incident. There was enough to worry about, with the teenage drink problem and drugs filtering in from the continent through Eastwold, without respectable people dying in strange circumstances.

He had worked hard to convince the bloody journalists that there were "no suspicious circumstances surrounding the case". The "forensic boys – oh, yes, and girls" – had given him their assurance. The man had, for no apparent reason, hanged himself by climbing into the loft, putting a running noose around his neck, tying the other end to a rafter and then dropping down. His ... (partner?) ... had, clearly, found him there and stumbled backwards down the stairs in shock, breaking her neck in the fall. Yes – the animals would be looked after. The Cats Protection League had taken care of them, the RSPCA would see to the mice and other pets, and one of the villagers – a newcomer, Herr Brultzner from Leipzig – had offered to care for the wild animals until they were well enough to return to the wild. His grandson was good with animals, and it would be a pleasure for him and the boy to nurse them back to health. No – the cats would not be put down. He had been assured of that – they were only following their natural instincts, after all. Billings might be annoying, but he did deal with that kind of enquiry without fuss and with the minimum of leaks. Paperwork, paperwork – it piled up over nothing and always in triplicate. Why the hell did the Chief Constable or the government need to know about what happened to a few injured animals in a Suffolk village? Superintendent Junket mopped his brow. He was worried – he was beginning to sound like Martin Billings.

"I'm glad they're both away," said Amy to Penny over their lunch in Norbridge, "Martin would be bustling around now, fending off the press, and you can be sure that your Alan would have been the first to be called to the scene."

"And there's nothing either of them could have done, of course – nothing, that is, that others can't do."

She paused and looked up from her radicchio and chicory gratin.

"Mind you – I do feel rather bad about Clara Gobley. She and I had been at daggers drawn for some while, as you know ... it just shows how small one's world can become, doesn't it?"

"Oh, come on Penny. She didn't deserve to see her man die like that and nor did she deserve to die herself so horribly ... but she was an awful woman."

"Umm – I just wish we'd got on better – that's all."

"What's going to happen to their house then?" enquired Ainsley Bint.

"Their house?" said Sandra. "What are you thinking, Ainsley?"

"It can't be left derelict, can it? The council will have to do something."

Sandra had been proud of her son – with the slight reservation that he was not treating his young wife, Milly, very well – ever since his success on the business course at Lowestoft College. His NVQ2 in Business Management had armed him as a 'Financial Consultant', and he'd managed to give ruinous advice to several local firms and private individuals that had paid very well. He now clearly had his eye on the housing market: not a boy to miss a chance.

"I don't know. I'll ask Owen, or one of his councillor friends."

"Any chance of your amorous policeman stumping up some cash? We could make a tidy profit on that bungalow and pay him back in no time – once we'd got Mark Chambers to patch it up a bit."

"Keep your hands off my policeman, Ainsley – I need him to finance my catering business! Try Milly's mum again."

"I've soaked her already and she's a bit pissed off at the moment."

"Don't throw away your chances, Ainsley – they don't come easily. If you want Clara Gobley's bungalow, you'll have to work for it!"

"She'll go to her Maker, Corvin, and settle her own account with Him," said Esther when her husband expressed concern that he had failed Clara Gobley. "There's no good sighing like that, Corvin. There are some people who just have to 'cure' their own souls. You can't be responsible for them all."

"But I am, Esther. I'm a priest – their priest."

He got up from the breakfast table and walked away. Esther knew that she had overstepped the mark and, against her every instinct, said nothing.

In his study, Corvin knelt and prayed. He was secure here, with Martin Luther looking down on him. Before he closed his eyes, he looked around for reassurance. The re-birth of hope and faith he had preached at Easter seemed no nearer – he had not even brought his choir mistress and junior church teacher together in harmony. A sigh came from his heart and the tears rose to his eyes.

"Oh my God – have I forsaken you? Where are the souls of Clara and Bert now? Do they reside in your safe arms? *The soul is not an aspect of the person but the whole person as a living being.* Where did Clara and Bert fit into your scheme of things? Have they found eternal peace at last – now their rancorous lives are over? Why could I not bring them together with the rest of our community? They were members, but forever on the edge. I tried, Father, but did I try hard enough or did I draw back when the conflict became ... unpalatable to me? Bert had his good side. I know, Father, that is all you want of us – to 'trust in you and let our good side through. Clara and Bert were trapped within their own selves, and I could not bring them to you. I am charged, Father, with this awesome task – to lead my flock to you, to lead them to eternal life that they may spend eternity with you. *Our spiritual body, after death, grows out of our earthly life as a plant grows from a seed. Our spiritual body expresses the personality we have developed in our earthly bodies.* How are Clara and Bert to express their personalities in your Kingdom? Look kindly on Bert, Father. He was not the man to kill himself, and we may have more to learn – but what we seek you will already know. I pray, Father, that Bert is with his Clara wherever you may see fit to look after them. *Heaven is the state of being with God. It is when we are with God all the time and consciously aware of his presence.* How awesome is that thought? My doubts, Father, are the doubts of a mere man – even my priesthood cannot keep them from me. I ask my questions in utter humbleness – not knowing the full magnitude of Your compassion, yet not doubting it. Keep Clara and Bert – if that is Your will – in Your knowledge and love, with You and Your Son, Jesus Christ our Lord, that they may remain with You – Father, Son and Holy Spirit – always."

Matthew, no longer Marjoram but Brown in honour of his mother's parents, came to know and charm the wild animals Horst Brultzner had rescued from Clara and Bert's garden. His mother had read him an abridged version of *The Pied Piper of Hamelin*, and this is how he saw Brultzner and came to see himself. It was not with pipe that he called them but with sound and authority. He did not talk to the animals so much as captivate them as one might calm an angry dog with voice and touch. His mother's master soon became his teacher and Matthew learned to trust in him and seek his guidance.

He learned from Brultzner the enchantment of food and the freedom from fear so that the animals came to trust him as they once trusted their own parents. Each day he fed them and each day he spent time with them and, when their moment came, it was he who opened the final cage so that they might explore the garden. Through them he came to know other animals until, to the little boy, the garden of the Old Vicarage became an enraptured place.

Strangest of all to him was the fox that had been rescued by Clara and Bert almost from the very mouths of the hounds. The fox returned each night to the garden and hovered in the presence of the child, seeking his company even when the wild called. Sarah watched from the window of the morning room as her son walked out alone to speak to the creature, and she smiled to herself and her heart was gladdened by her son's power.

Brultzner took the same delight in the child as a grandfather might have done and looked forward to each evening they spent together. He ordered picture books to supplement the boy's knowledge, and a life – such as he had never known – formed slowly around him as the days deeper into autumn.

"He has a destiny, Sarah," said Horst, as they stood together watching the boy, "He will learn from books and he will learn from the great educators of his time but he will finally know more than they can ever teach him. He will have the power and the cunning."

Sarah smiled up at him; her son seemed free as he had never been when the son of Shane Marjoram. Sarah felt easier in her mind now that nothing would stand in his way – not violence, not ignorance, not bigotry.

CHAPTER 2

Evil is as evil does

Sarah had visited Sidney Close for the first time after the Harvest Supper – remembering the day he had wanted to grab hold of her, grip her hard and bring his mouth down onto hers. Relishing the gleam of lust in his eyes, the sweat on his forehead, and delighting in the knowledge that he was on the point of tearing her dress off when she laughed, Sarah had stood at his back door and tapped.

She needed to feed and had always been reluctant to take the young men – although sometimes there was no choice. Instead, she would enjoy herself with Sidney. He deserved a kind of punishment – forever enticed, never satisfied. If she must feed from someone, then better him than those still with their ... innocence; it was a notion she seemed to be straying further from each day into her eternity.

"Hello, Sidney."

She said no more than that to start with, but stood watching his utter bewilderment. She had come to realise, through her vampire state, that men like Sidney Close dream about having it handed to them on a plate – that they spend much of their waking lives fantasising about how they will enjoy it when it comes. She could accept that – Shane was driven in much the same way – but what she disliked was the hypocrisy: not only the pretence that they were not like that, but the self-righteous indignation when others were. She had read about such men, of course. Sarah had read voraciously and met Dickens' Bradley Headstone, Balzac's Baron Hulot, Charlotte Bronte's St John Rivers, Fielding's Blifil and the dark men who filled the life of Defoe's Moll Flanders. Now she watched Sidney Close desiring her, thinking he could have her, but realising his wife was only just asleep upstairs.

"It's late," he said.

"Not too late, Sidney. I can feel your hand on my buttocks."

He blushed and the anger showed in the glare he gave her.

"You're not going to leave me on the doorstep, are you?"

"Perhaps you could come back in the morning – not here, come to the shop."

He didn't know what he was saying, of course – just anything to get rid of her, anything to make her disappear from the back door so that he could close it and get to bed. He was trying to pretend that she hadn't said what she'd said, that he hadn't thought what he'd thought; to fantasise was one thing, to sublimate those desires was quite another.

"I really think you should go home, now," he said.

"You mean I misinterpreted your touch?"

"We were dancing. I didn't mean anything."

"No? ... Why am I standing on your doorstep, Sidney? You can't believe it, can you? You may have dreamed it, but the reality is so different, isn't it? Do you remember the day you came to help Shane fit the satellite dish? ... What were you thinking as you stood in the bedroom?"

She smiled, and it angered and alarmed him. This woman knew her power, and was using it. The soft swoon of her vampirism was overcoming him.

"Mavis is asleep. I must go, now. I'll .... We'll speak in the morning."

"Sidney."

There was a pleading in the voice – 'just a cup of tea.'

"Come in then – quietly."

So she stepped over the threshold, and the house and home became hers. She decided to let him know – for the first time ever in his life, she realised – what he had been missing all those years.

He did not resist, but was trembling as she removed his clothes until he stood naked on the tiled kitchen floor before her. Sarah tossed his clothes aside, looked him over and then undressed herself. Somehow, Sarah's eyes seemed to tell him that Mavis would not wake.

"Come to me," she said.

She reached up and drew his head down, pulling him in against her, kissing him and then forcing him to the tiled floor where she sat astride him. Sidney, beyond himself with excitement, felt the physical release as he looked into her eyes. A slight, cool breeze drifted in through the windows and she shook herself.

"Nice room," she said, as she left, leaving him spent and on his back on the tiled floor, his clothes strewn around him in a tangled heap.

That night they both returned to their own 'beds' in turmoil. Sarah had drawn him on, but felt be-smirched by him. She had not realised she would feel like that – not from the mere taking of his blood. Her only consolation was that – for Sidney – there would be that half-knowledge of what was happening, all the guilt of extra-marital sex. By day, he could never escape that intense longing; if it were assuaged at night, he would be swamped by guilt the following day.

Sidney had folded his clothes carefully, with that old-maidish neatness of his, and then gone quietly up to bed. He stood naked in the bedroom looking at Mavis, in her brushed nylon nightdress, sleeping soundly.

For that brief moment, before all the recrimination that was to follow, he acknowledged to himself that he had enjoyed what happened in the kitchen. Then, he climbed quietly into bed beside Mavis and the waves of guilt washed over him.

Nadine Palmester bumped into Sidney Close as he came out of the Bethel. She'd noticed that he always hovered around there – its fundamentalist outlook appealed to his black-and-white nature – but she hadn't heard her father speak of him for some time. He was walking with a spring in his step but with a glance over his shoulder – as though, she thought, he might have enjoyed himself and wondered whether the Devil had seen him. He looked at her, furtively, and she could see that he didn't want to speak but he had no choice. He acknowledged her with the briefest of nods.

"Good morning, Sidney – joining the ranks of the saved, are we?"

She guessed that he knew her views on religion, and had expected that tight smile. Nadine only wanted to irritate him, and was shocked when he turned on her.

"I don't need saving. You'd be better off saving that friend of yours."

"Friend?"

"Sarah Marjoram – or Brown as she calls herself now."

"Why would Sarah need saving?"

"Ask her."

He stormed on by, angered by his own outburst, and frightened by his near confession. It was always there, in the fore-front of his mind – guilt and salvation. Unknowingly, Nadine had touched a sore point and triggered an ending.

She watched him walk on down the street and then went into the little chapel. She didn't like it; the place always smelled of damp, decay and the teachings of old books. The pulpit reared up before her, looking down on a dying congregation. Fewer and fewer came as the years went by, fewer and fewer still succumbed to its lies and half-truths. She had sat there as a child listening to things she knew could not be true, yet having to believe them because they came from the lips of her father. "I love you Naddy, but I sometimes wonder what I have taught you over the years ... You remember the crippled child we prayed for? The Lord straightened her legs! You remember that bitingly cold winter when old Mrs Strowger was short of coal? What did she find on her doorstep when her need was greatest?" Perhaps it didn't matter as long as these half-truths and outright lies hurt no one – and they were only 'lies' in that they went against the facts. Her father believed them with his intense sincerity. Simon was standing just inside the doorway, tidying books. She went over and kissed him lightly on the cheek. He smiled with genuine affection.

"Hello, dad. What was Sidney Close doing here?"

"What would he be doing in the House of the Lord, Naddy? Praying!"

"Is he returning to your flock?"

"When a man is in a state of sin, Naddy, he needs a strong God."

"Stronger than the one offered by the Reverend Unwood?"

Simon looked at her, almost with a sneer on his face. He would not belittle another priest but his eyes said 'Yes, that is the Truth.' Nadine knew Sidney's background – his father was an elder in the Baptist church in Eastwold and Sidney had always felt the pull of the Baptist community and had attended the Dunburgh Bethel. His parents had taught him that Christians of their sort had only to read the Bible; all the answers were there, in the Good Book.

"He seemed troubled and he mentioned Sarah."

"Your friend hasn't been seen in church since before her husband died."

It was true. Nadine saw less and less of Sarah as the months went by – since the death of Shane, she hadn't seen her at all. She'd come home early for the funeral and wanted to take her father out to lunch, but decided otherwise. She gave him a smile, touched his arm lightly and walked out of the Bethel. Simon watched her go – knowing what was in her mind.

The Old Vicarage was ready for planting now that autumn was here – giving the plants the whole of the winter to gain a root-hold in the earth. Crafty Catchpole and Horst Brultzner's landscape gardener, Mr Dix, had worked hard through the spring and summer clearing the dead growth and preparing the soil for the new plants.

Despite Brultzner's insistence on spring planting, Mr Dix had held out for at least some of the shrubs to be planted in the autumn. Crafty was sweeping leaves from the shingled driveway when Nadine walked through the gate.

"Hello Crafty."

"Miss."

"The garden looks lovely."

"It will that. We held out, see."

"Held out?"

"The governor wanted everything done in the spring but we said 'No' – wait fer the autumn when the roots hev got a chance – and it were as well, seeing the summer we hed."

"It was hot."

"It were that."

"Is Miss Brown about?"

"She were earlier. Stays out late these days."

"Late?"

"At night. I've seen her about."

"In the village?"

"Least said."

"It's nice to see her enjoying herself. She's been through a very bad patch."

Crafty looked at Nadine from beneath the cloth cap with its piece of braid along the base of the peak. He had dark reservations about Sarah – nightmares still haunted him.

"She ent roight," he said, pushing the nightmare from him.

"What do you mean?"

"Least said."

Nadine smiled and walked on to the front door. Sarah must have been watching her from the front parlour because before she had the chance to ring the bell her old friend was smiling at her. Sarah was dressed in her parlour maid clothes.

"Mr Brultzner is unavailable this morning, miss."

"It's you I've come to see, Sarah."

"Come in then – and welcome."

Over a coffee – which, Nadine noticed, Sarah did not drink – they chatted only briefly before Nadine, with journalistic ease, brought the conversation round to the purpose of her visit:

"I bumped into Sidney Close just now."

Sarah said nothing for a moment and then, simply:

"Oh."

"He mentioned you."

"Oh."

"He'd been in the Bethel – praying. I made a little joke about him 'joining the ranks of the saved' and he rather flew at me and said I'd be better off saving you. I just wondered what you'd been up to – how you'd annoyed him."

In a world hostile to them, vampires learn quickly to defend themselves. Previously, Sarah would have laughed the matter off or launched into a conversation about Sidney's hypocrisy. Now, she was nearly silent; entering less into conversations with old friends was one means of defence. She was aware how taciturn she must seem to Nadine; she was unaware of the cunning smile that pervaded her once amicable face. Nadine almost recoiled, but covered her alarm by saying:

"He's not been bothering you, has he Sarah?"

"I have nothing to fear from Sidney Close, Nadine. Perhaps he's been dreaming again."

"And he has no reason for imagining you need to be 'saved'?"

"Let him save himself."

"From?"

"From himself," she replied, and the cunning smile becoming hostile.

"I haven't seen you out and about lately. Do you fancy a little walk? It's still nice along the cliff path. We could take Matthew ..."

"Matthew will be home from nursery soon and he'll want a little sleep."

"Of course – are you collecting him?"

"No – we have a girl who does that."

The riposte was snapped out, but Nadine persisted:

"You don't feel strong enough to fetch him yourself yet, Sarah?"

"I'm a working mum, Nadine. I have a house to look after. Don't worry about Matthew. He is well cared for."

"And he and 'Uncle Horst' still get on well?"

"Horst is more like a grandfather than an uncle, now. Matthew is only little but he's learned so much from him."

Sarah became animated again – her facing shining as she talked of Matthew, the animals and Horst. When Sarah spoke of the fox, Nadine said:

"I've just come back from their funeral."

"Ah, yes – the Gobleys. No loss to the village, are they?"

"Who can say? No one deserves to die as they did, Sarah," retorted Nadine, shocked at her friend's callousness – something so foreign to the Sarah she'd known. "Matthew likes Horst?"

"Loves him – admires him."

"Would Horst look after him for you?"

"Why do you ask?"

"I thought perhaps we could go out one night."

Sarah's hesitations were becoming painful to both of them: again the cunning smile crossed her face, again the flare of anger crossed behind her eyes.

"I'll see. I'll ask Horst – he is my employer, after all."

Nadine began to wonder whether there was more to the relationship. She looked at Sarah closely, wanting to avoid her eyes, wanting not to see that baleful look, but drawn into them with only a token resistance.

Sidney Close was pleased that he now had no assistant, although the work-load was too much for him; at this moment in his life, Sidney needed to be alone. She had come to him each night since that first night, and each night she tormented him,

Each night, she stood by his bed and removed her clothes slowly while he lay there helpless, unable to touch her unless she wished it. She would kneel by his side or sit on the edge of the bed, when she was naked, and run her lips over him. He trembled at her touch, knowing what she was going to do, yet desiring it and fearing it. He was in torment, and his desire was un-satiated. When she was ready – when she had watched him long enough – she always drew back the bed clothes and removed his pyjamas so that he too lay naked at the mercy of her hands, which knew where to stroke and where to probe until his pain became excruciating. All the while Mavis slept beside him, snoring quietly, subdued by the vampire's will.

Sometimes she beckoned him from the bed and led him naked round his own house until every room was contaminated by her lust. Always, she took him to the point, the very acme, of fulfilment only to leave him gasping in an agony of frustration. At the close of each night, when she appeared to have finished with him, she would drape herself around him and sink her teeth into his body. Then he came, while she sucked what life she wanted from him, and left him limp, and helpless – a prey to his own mortification.

He could not sleep after she'd gone. He could only lie beside Mavis, or wander from room to room, pausing by chair or table or rug or bath – wherever she had roused him, wanting her back, looking forward to the next night. Without sleep, he became more and more haggard. He neglected himself, and only the nagging of his wife kept Sidney clean, but even Mavis could not prevent the darkness gathering around his eyes and the whipcord tension straining his every muscle. At times he looked at Mavis with intent, and only his upbringing, only the sense of decency bred in him, prevented Sidney from venting his lust on his wife.

Each day, released from the terrors of the night, he prayed. He chose the Bethel because there his God was stronger; only the God of the Absolute could save him from what he knew to be mortal sin – a sin willingly committed, the sinner knowing it to be sinful. He loathed her, he detested her, but he craved her coming. If she was late, he would creep from the bed and wait by the window and her step on the stair was like balm to his ... his yearning. The more she gave him, the greater the excitement she aroused within him, the deeper went his lasciviousness. Sidney knew this, but could not help himself. Each night he turned further from God, each night the Lord's sanctifying grace became lost to him, each night his immortal soul crept nearer and nearer to perdition. Each day he prayed for his own redemption, but the act of contrition was false – he knew that and could not help himself.

"Yew roight, Sid?"
  "Why'd you ask, Scrub?"
  "Yew look kind of sweaty – like a man whose moind's on uther things."
  "Is that right?"
  "I seen you drop a glance or two at Plumptious's neckline, meself," laughed Harry Bailey, picking up the drift of Scrub's comment.
  Sidney was in the bar of The Jolly Sailors fixing a new, larger screen at the end of the room. He'd nodded to those sitting there but moved on quickly to the job he had to do – not wanting their conversation, not wanting them to see the look in his eyes: the look which had watched him from the shaving mirror that morning, the look that saw Sarah's naked body hovering tantalisingly before him. Plumptious had been leaning over the bar when he came in, her breasts on full view for the benefit of the customers. He'd noticed she always changed into a low neckline when she was serving. She'd brushed against him, smiling, as she showed him where the screen was to go, and then she'd disappeared into the kitchen.
  "She got a noice pair, ent she Sid?" offered Jumbo Gooch.
  "If you say so, Jumbo. I'm too busy to notice myself."
  "A man ent never to busy fer that, Sid. You tell me yew aint noticed them big breasts of hers and Oim tellin' yew, yor strayin' from the trewth."
  "Come on admit it, Sid, breasts loike that'll fill your balls."
  The card players guffawed. They loved ribaldry – once started, there was no stopping them. They all knew Sidney's reputation for "quiet lust" as Dick Utting had once said to Deaf Charlie, and were determined to have a laugh at his expense.
  "You get on with your card game, Dick – leave those of us who work for a living to get on with our jobs."
  "No need ter get nasty, Sid. It's jest that yew look loike a man who needs ter get his end off!"
  Again the laughter rollicked round the pub.
  "Toime to mount your steed and get roiding."
  There was more laughter – more excruciating embarrassment. Sidney struggled to keep calm, strove to fight the good fight against his own demons but the forces of mirth were against him.
  "It's not respectful," he said.
  "Respectful be buggered," said Scrub, "There ent many women who doint loike a bit o' slap and tickle ..."
  "... or a good rogering," roared Dick.
  Tears were streaming from their eyes, now. Even John Barker, who normally avoided any involvement in "dirty talk", smiled broadly.
  "A little bit of 'How's yer father?' never hurt no one."

"There's some do it ev'ry noight yer know," said Deaf Charlie, quietly.

"Well don't yew then?" cut in Harry, amidst more raucous bellowing.

"We thought that was what sent yew deaf!"

"No – yew got it wrong there, Jumbo. That sends yer blind!"

Exclamations of merriment resounded around the bar. Sidney gritted his teeth and clutched the top of the ladder. In a moment he'd kill someone.

"I woont moind bein' both blind AND deaf fer a roll in the hay with Plumptious," said Harry.

"I meant it, yer know," said Deaf Charlie.

"Meant what, Charlie?"

"Some dew it ev'ry night."

"Well there int many noights Oi don't go round the block a few toimes."

"No, Oim serious. There's a little, quiet bloke lives down Holly Grange Road. Me daughter lives next ter him, see, and she was tellin' the missus that his bed's always goin' twenty ter the dozen."

"That right, Charlie?"

"It's always the quiet one's ent it?" said Harry.

"You're a quiet one, ent yer Sid?"

"But he aint little, are yer Sid?"

More laughter: by now, both Harry Bailey and John Barker were choking.

"Yer a big boy, are yer Sid?"

"Big where it counts, eh Sid?"

"Got a big tardger!"

"Yew ken go ter town with one of those!"

"Yer ken go on the town with one o' those!"

"Wimen loike a man who don't get tired too quick."

"It ent the size what counts – it's what yew do with it."

"Ent no good hevin' a Sergeant Major of a tardger if it's only doin' the work of a Private."

The laughter had, by now, reached hysterical proportions. There wasn't one of the group who was not convulsed with hilarity. They were boys again, in the playground full of glee and daring to use 'the filthiest words in the world.'

"It's a funny old word, int it?" said Harry.

"What's that, Harry?"

"Tardger."

"Oi always preferred 'dick', myself," said Jumbo, deliberately, and achieving the laughter for which he'd aimed.

"Give me 'shaft' any day," riposted Dick Utting.

"What yew call your 'old man', Sid?" asked Harry.

Sidney hit the foot of the ladder and reached the card table before any of them realised what was happening. He grabbed Harry Bailey by the collar and lifted him from the ground, his strength surprising even himself. With a furious roar, he pulled the card player from his chair, which clattered back across the room, and threw him over his shoulder towards the bar. Harry hit it with a thud and fell with a groan. Sidney was on him before he could gasp for breath. He yanked Harry to his feet, held him with his left hand and drove his right fist into Harry's shocked face. There was a crack as his nose went, and blood spattered everywhere.

The rest of the men just stared in disbelief, not one of them moving. Their outrage would come later; all they could do now was try to grasp what was happening. In the meantime, Sidney's fist pummelled Harry's chest, shoulders, neck and stomach. The expression on his assailant's face was so bestial that Harry thought he was doomed. His hands flailed in the air, but Sidney was bigger than him and his reach was longer so that Harry's blows, ineffectual in strength anyway, merely fell uselessly onto Sidney's arms.

Before any of the men could rouse themselves from their stupor, Plumptious was in the bar pulling at Sidney's back, gripping deep into those hard shoulders. She had a walking stick in her hand – thick, solid, gnurled at one end – and she brought it down onto his head. Sidney groaned as the blood sprang from him, and sank to his knees. The next moment, before Plumptious could deliver another blow, he collapsed, the life going out of his muscles as he hit the floor.

"The police – call the police."

"Be quiet, Scrub Turrel," snapped Plumptious.

"Anyhow," said Dick, "PC Billings is away."

"He ent ...."

"I said be quiet," said Plumptious.

Sidney rose and looked around him, realising what he had done. A great cry came from his heart and he reached down and lifted Harry from the floor, rocking him against his chest.

"Call the ambulance! Call the ambulance!"

"It's only a scratch," muttered Harry, his mouth cradled deep against Sidney's shirt-front.

"Give him here, Sid – I'll see to him," said Plumptious.

As she eased Harry away from him, Sidney's grip slackened and he stood, seeing the eyes upon him as he looked round the bar. These were men he had known all his life.

"You all right, Sid?" said one voice.

He turned and looked at the speaker. John Barker's face was creased with concern. Sidney felt sick; he looked wildly about him, once more, and then rushed from the public house.

CHAPTER 3

Sidney taken

"Do you want to talk about it, Sidney? You've come every day this week."

Simon Palmester stood at the end of the pew looking at Sidney. Blood was running freely from the wound Plumptious had inflicted, and Harry Bailey's blood was all over his shirt. He dare not go back to the shop, which was his only refuge.

"I've committed a sin, Simon – a mortal sin."

"Nothing stands between you and God, Sidney – on your knees before your Maker. Confess your sins to Almighty God."

Simon knelt beside Sidney and brought his hands together as clenched fists.

"O Lord, look down upon thy servant in his wickedness and lead him unto the path of righteousness. If he is tempted again, Lord, remind him of the pains of Hell – the fire and the torture. Purge his sins, Lord – that he may turn again to you, and redeem his immortal soul."

They prayed for an hour on the decaying floor of the little chapel, and then Simon took him into the room that served as a vestry and washed away the blood as well as he could. Sidney looked up into the preacher's face and saw only compassion.

"It was her – Sarah ... Marjoram."

He couldn't bring himself to utter Clive Brown's name alongside hers.

"We bring about our own damnation, Sidney. The Lord gave us free will – it is up to us to choose the path we tread. Your temptation is of the Flesh – these are good desires, which God has given us, used in sinful ways. We cannot blame others – even Satan, even Sarah Marjoram – for our sin."

Corvin Unwood came across him in the churchyard where he had gone after his prayers with Simon Palmester. Sidney had sought it as a refuge when dusk fell. He sat in the older part, waiting for the darkness that would take him to his shop where he would find a change of clothing away from prying eyes, and away from Mavis and her questions. He wondered what had happened at The Jolly Sailors. How was Harry Bailey? How would he face him tomorrow? Would there be a tomorrow?

Corvin listened, while he poured out the whole story. He listened with growing dread that no one would believe him, and Esther would call him a fool for listening to the ravings of a man who must have been drunk. Corvin wanted Sidney home, knowing him not to be a drunk but recognizing his deep licentiousness. He wanted it to be tomorrow when everything would be all right. He couldn't carry this story to the bishop. 'Don't look under stones, Corvin. Dark things hide there.' His mother had told him that; he believed her. He took Sidney's hands in his and they prayed together, and then Corvin walked with him to his shop and waved farewell.

Once home, Sidney felt better. Simon had washed the blood out of his hair and the wound didn't show. No one had come knocking. Mavis asked no questions. He sat down and they ate the evening meal together.

"You were late today, Sid. Plumptious rang – said not to worry, everything would be all right. What did she mean?"

"I left a job part finished. It was one of those days."

"I'm out this evening – WI. I won't be late. Will you do the washing up?"

Would he? Sidney wanted to: normal domesticity beckoned. His hands relaxed in the warm suds and he felt the rinse water wash him clean. 'Like Pilate.' The house was quiet after Mavis had gone and Sidney picked up the phone and rang Harry Bailey's number. His wife answered, and Sidney put the phone down. A few seconds later it rang. He hesitated, and then grabbed the receiver.

"That yew, Sid?" asked Harry, "Sid?"

"Yes."

"Good of yew ter ring. No damij done – thanks – jest a few stitches. Plumptious called the doctor. He soon fixed me up. Sorry about what happened."

Sidney could tell that Harry's wife was listening. Everything the man said was hesitant and guarded. She could read into it what she might.

"It's me who should apologise, Harry."

"No – these things happen. Things ..."

He paused. Sidney could hear the unspoken 'get out of hand' but Harry actually said:

"... don't always go accordin' ter plan."

"I'm sorry, Harry. I'll make it right. I appreciate the way you've taken it."

"Friendship's more important than a broken nose, Sid."

"Yes – thanks again, Harry."

"Yew moight ring Plumptious. She were a bit worried."

He did, and Plumptious apologized and asked whether he'd finish the job tomorrow. Sidney said he would – first thing in the morning after he'd popped round to Harry's with a new television set.

"State of the art, Sid?"

"State of the art."

He felt unreal. It was as though nothing had happened or, if it had, everyone concerned wanted to keep it quiet – 'under wraps' as they say. Harry and Plumptious had dismissed it as of no importance. Simon had referred it to God – not excusing Sidney his sin, but stressing his need to confess it and accept the redemption offered through God's son. Corvin had wanted it to go away, and stepped aside from the splintering repercussions he expected.

Sarah had slept because Matthew was going round a friend's house for the afternoon and would not be back until after dusk. Horst had shown her how she might avoid the need to sleep at all during the day, but it was always a relief to retire to their coffins, and she felt refreshed and more ready for the night after she had slept. When she woke, her first thoughts were of Sidney. Her purpose had been to torment him – to push him to the point where his desire for her would drive him to … attempt rape. She knew, in wanting this, she was giving way to the vampire side of her nature, but she enjoyed it. The other side of her, the human side, the side that still cuddled Matthew, pitied him. Here was a man whose sexual needs were powerful, and whose wife offered him nothing.

Sarah felt it more and more difficult to reflect quietly on herself – something which had been her life-saver during her marriage to … Shane. The name was distant now – a festering corpse. She felt as though she were entering adolescence again – a teenage vampire with all that angst! She laughed to herself, but was still human enough to feel frightened. What would happen when she no longer felt the desire to cuddle Matthew?

At times, Horst seemed to show more tenderness than she did towards the boy, and had more need of his sweet company; but Horst was an old vampire – he had become used to living in the selfishness of his own skin. Sarah had not, but the masked ball had been a pivotal moment for her. It was then she realized she stood alone just as they all did. There was no companionship, no compassion and no tenderness in the world of the vampire – only the hard-edged, self-seeking need to survive. She had felt herself becoming remote from Horst – keeping things to herself, consulting him less, going her own way. Her bond with him was Matthew; the boy's developing needs held the old vampire and his protégé together.

She had never been wilful, but she enjoyed it now. Teasing (no, torturing) Sidney to the edge of madness gave some part of her nature great satisfaction. Was it human or was it vampire? She had felt vulnerable with Shane. Holding things together had not been easy, but with Sidney she was in complete control. Sarah knew, with a fierce gladness in her heart, that there was no way that this man could harm her; she held him, effortlessly, in the crook of her little finger.

Sidney could not believe he had got away with the day. All his life had been devoted to doing it right, being a role model, setting an example in a godless world. He'd strapped in his lust, buttoned down his anger, buckled on the armour of righteousness and fought the good fight, while others had got away with it; and, now, so had he. There were good people out there – the Harry Bailey's of this world – and they had recognized the goodness in him; there were bad people, too, and they led you astray, and needed teaching a lesson. Sarah Marjoram was one of them. He hadn't asked her in, and now she'd taken over his house. It was as though she bewitched him every time she entered. He'd teach her a lesson, and pack her off once and for all.

Mavis had returned from WI and gone up at her usual time and they'd kissed 'goodnight' in that way married couples do. He waited in his room, working out with his exercise equipment – the chest expanders, the dumb-bells. He was working up, not working off, the tension in him. He wasn't sure what was going to happen, but it would be decisive. He told himself that, although he knew very well what he had in mind.

She was later than usual when she arrived, but as seductive as ever. After that first night, she always came with nothing under her dress, so that he could see and feel every curve of her body, and she was so firm. He would see her husband's – her dead husband's – hands on her and that craving in her eyes. Some women had an abnormal longing for sex, and she was one of them. They aroused a hunger in a man that had to be satisfied. Before she could look at him, before he could be drawn into her and come under her sway, Sidney grabbed Sarah and unzipped her dress. She turned, taken by surprise and, under his weight, crashed backwards to the floor. He was naked and, before she knew it, was kicking away her dress. His right hand reached up and pulled her hair back, harshly. He held her, his weight on her body, his right hand keeping her head down, his left pinning her shoulder to the floor.

"I'm going to teach you a lesson, my girl, you'll never forget. You won't be so keen to torment other decent men then, won't be so keen to bring them down when I've finished with you."

He said it quietly, between clenched teeth and his tight lips. There was spite in the words – venom she'd never known; Shane at his most vigorous had never sounded like this man. This was something he'd always dreamt of doing, and her lust had released his power. He'd sort her in a way she'd never been sorted before. She'd think twice before she felt the urge to taunt a man, again; this was God's work.

Sarah shuddered; the coldness of her made him gasp. He released his hold on her hair – only momentarily, but long enough for her to raise her head and sink her teeth into his neck. Sidney screamed, slackened his hold on her shoulder and then Sarah was on him. Her strength shocked him. He felt his whole body – all that toned muscle – pushed over onto its back, and then the woman was astride him and his blood flowed languorously and willingly into her.

When she had finished, Sarah stood and listened. There was no sound from upstairs – the spell she usually cast over the house was intact and Mavis slept soundly. Sarah was breathing heavily. He was no match for her vampire strength, but his assault had been unexpected. Now he was still, but she had only drained him of some blood, and soon he would wake. She wasn't angry – not now she had the better of him – but he had scared her. This man had almost succeeded; she had almost been violated. She slipped her dress back on, smoothing it down her thighs, wondering what to do. She'd taken Shane, night after night, to the point of death, but this man couldn't share his fate – she couldn't bury another vampire for all eternity. Sarah was relying on holding him in thrall, as Horst had taught her. 'Their desire for you will be overwhelming, but they will never quite know who you are or when you will come. They will be in love with you forever – enthralled.' She had, though, roused this man sexually – deliberately playing with him, not contenting herself with the taking of blood, but wanting to make him know what he was missing. He was aware of her in a way uncommon in the victims of vampires; he was conscious of her as a person.

Sarah went to the window that opened onto the Close's back garden. She sat on the window ledge and waited for him to stir. She couldn't hold him in a state of permanent weakness. She couldn't kill him, but she couldn't have his yearnings bringing him to the door of the Old Vicarage. She felt sure that he did not know her nature; he may have guessed, but she thought not. The bites were love bites to him, part of the perversion they had enjoyed.

When Sidney stirred, he did so suddenly and was sitting bolt upright watching her before Sarah realized it. He was strong for a human – strong and determined.

"What are you?" he said, casting his eyes about the room.

"I am your lover, Sidney – that is all you need to know."

"You're not human, are you? You were. I knew you as a girl, as Clive Brown's daughter. You were human, but you're not now."

He was breathing heavily as he spoke, and his hand went to his neck where he found the trickle of blood.

"You did this?"

"You liked me biting you."

"You made me like it. Years ago they used to burn women like you – burn out the rotten wood to keep the tree wholesome!"

His anger roused him again and he sprang from the ground straight at her, a dumb-bell in his right hand. He swung it round, but Sarah wasn't there and it crashed through the window, shattering glass into the garden. Still the house did not stir – not Mavis, not their daughters. Sidney whirled round. Sarah was standing behind him on the far side of the room. He rushed at her, not knowing exactly why – just knowing that she was someone who had to be smashed into the ground. Sarah again moved with vampire speed, bewildering Sidney who – not seeing her where a few seconds before she had been – spun round himself. He caught his foot on the second dumb-bell that shot forward taking his leg with it, and throwing Sidney backwards. His head collided with the pile of weights; his skull cracked and his neck twisted to one side.

Sarah stared at his body and she went to touch him. She knew, before her hand rested on his throat, that Sidney Close was dead – killed by accident, but with the mark of the vampire (her mark) upon him.

CHAPTER 4

Cure of souls

"You left him just as he fell?"

"Yes, sir," replied Sarah, as Horst Brultzner questioned her.

This time he did not strike her – did not send her reeling across the room in his anger. He smiled; it was his calm smile – the one he assumed when under immense pressure.

"You did well to tell me, Sarah. It was very wise of you. You see the dangers, of course – this threat to our life here. It is as well to be prepared. We will, for the time being, await the outcome of events. Let us hope that the family require a cremation. I will see the rector this morning – let us hope the weather is suitable."

Mavis Close came to see Corvin in that calm Suffolk way of hers – stoical almost to the point of callousness – and poured out her story. The priest listened quietly, and she found that soothing. Whatever they might say about Corvin Unwood, he was a kind man, and she left knowing that he would take care of the details. The girls had to have breakfast (a neighbour was looking after them) and they had to be got off to school: that would be best this morning, while she sorted things out. Mavis had woken in the night, found Sid on the floor of his room, still warm, and called the doctor and Corvin. She had then phoned a neighbour who had come to keep an eye on the girls (both sound asleep still) while she saw to the doctor – the old one; Alan Read was still away. It had been a relief to walk round to the rectory. Corvin had been waiting at the gate, and taken her into their sitting room. She had cried then, but now – with the sun rising over the sea – she was peaceful again.

As he stood at the gate, watching her walk home to her two girls, Corvin was overwhelmed by guilt. He had hesitated, he had pulled back from doing anything – despite all that Sidney Close had told him – not because he was uncertain about what was right, but because he was unsure how others would react to his decisions. 'She comes each night ... I'm tormented. She kneels by my side, or sits on the edge of the bed and all the while Mavis is asleep. Sometimes she leads me round the house ... there isn't a room where we haven't ... every room is contaminated by her lust ... and when she's finished she leans over me and sinks her teeth into my body ... sucks the life from me ... I'm left ... mortified.' How much courage had it taken for a man like Sidney Close to confess all that – yes, confess! He was a low church Christian who confessed straight to his God – not through a priest. Yet he had come to St George's and sat in the churchyard and prayed for a priest to come and when the priest had come ... nothing. 'Let me walk you home, Sidney. You'll feel better in the morning.' He hadn't given a damn how Sidney felt in the morning – hide it away, wrap up the problem. It might go away but, if it didn't, he couldn't be blamed for making the wrong decision. Better do nothing than do the wrong thing.

One good thing – Esther was still asleep: those tablets kept her knocked out, oblivious to the pain of her arthritis. At least he wouldn't be faced by a barrage of questions and advice on how he ought to act. Martin Billings was away, but he had the telephone number of Superintendent Junket. Martin had given him that when he and Alan Read left. Corvin wasn't sure why it had been handed over with a smile and the comment – "It will get you straight through, Corvin. You won't have to listen to Mozart mangled on various switchboards". He'd wait, make a cup of tea and then phone – once people were up and about.

In his study Corvin reached into the back of the wall cupboard, pulled out the small kettle from beneath the pile of vestments, fill it from the cold tap in the toilet underneath the stairs, went back into the study, took the one-ring gas burner from the bottom of the wardrobe and struck a match. The tea was good, and so was the chocolate biscuit he dunked. Corvin felt the drink flow through him, and open up his mind as the taste rose over his palate. The ritual soothed him. He took the wooden cross from the bookcase and gripped it; then he knelt, leaning against his desk, and prayed.

"Oh my God, I have failed one of my people. He came to me asking the way forward and I could see it – knew the path he should take and yet cast no light along the way. Each night he wandered further from You, each night Your sanctifying grace became as a speck far back along his road and each night his immortal soul journeyed nearer and nearer to perdition, and I left him to travel on alone.

I am weak, Lord – a man of faith but a priest of no substance, a priest without a backbone. I am indecisive, irresolute, wavering – a thing of no determination, and in my lack of firmness I have stood aside and watched a man walk to his death.

Your staff, placed in my hand, could – and should – have been his. It stands now in the corner – unused, abandoned by your priest ..."

He couldn't go on; he wanted to, but his own wretchedness overtook him. He knelt until the sounds of the house woke him – his wife coming carefully down the stairs, his daughter stirring in bed. It was morning and there was the day to be faced.

In the end, Mavis was glad that she had not insisted on the girls going to school; it had seemed the sensible thing to do while she got on with the business of putting things to rights but the news of Sid's death travelled fast and, by coffee time, it seemed that the whole village knew. It seemed good, then, that her girls were with her. The undertakers had come and gone. Sidney was to be laid out and she could take the girls to see him that night; it would be better like that – all three of them together. Mavis had seen the wound on his neck and thought that perhaps some animal had got in through the broken window. She didn't like to think about that, and didn't want her girls to see it; Necker would put things to rights. The truth had yet to sink in, of course: making arrangements, restoring of the status quo was everything at the moment, but in a few days the shock would come and pull them down.

Corvin dialled the number Martin Billings had given him and he heard the receiver lifted, immediately. He recognised the voice and introduced himself.

"Ah, Reverend Unwood, it's good to hear your voice again. How may I help?"

Corvin patiently explained his predicament, detailing everything that Sidney had told him without drawing conclusions, but suggesting that the circumstances of the death might warrant investigation. When he had finished there was a long pause before Superintendent Junket said:

"Have you spoken to PC Billings about your concerns?"

"He's still away – with Dr Read. That's why I am phoning you."

There was another long pause and then the Superintendent said:

"Yes."

Corvin waited. Help, he felt, was at hand – the Superintendent was clearly giving the matter considerable thought, and then the voice said:

"Have you spoken to anyone else about this?"

"No."

"Good."

Again the long pause: there was no movement on the other end of the line. Corvin imagined that the Superintendent might be consulting a manual – flicking through the procedures in such a case – but there was nothing. Eventually the voice said:

"Reverend Unwood ... I think it might be a good idea if you kept this to yourself – oh, and don't mention this call to me ..."

There was a tension in the voice now – almost, Corvin thought, a bullying insistence.

"... Do I have your word on that?"

Corvin hesitated, and then persisted:

"Superintendent, I really do think that this matter should be taken seriously."

"The force takes all such matters seriously, Reverend Unwood, but (let me advise you in your own best interests) these things are best handled properly – by experts, by the people who know, by those trained for the job. This is not an area for amateurs – apple carts and all that. You take my meaning? This needs a man on the job – a local man – someone who knows the ground. It would be a good idea if PC Billings were involved. Take my advice and give him a ring when he returns ... and don't mention this call to me – undermining the man on the spot, that sort of thing ... do I have your word? Matter of protocol, you see – formalities, the right way of doing things – conventions – what you would call etiquette. If PC Billings decides the matter needs taking further, he will – quite naturally – seek my advice. At which time it would become proper for me to intervene. These procedures are put in place to serve our best interests, Reverend Unwood – don't buck the system – it's there to protect you. Take my meaning? Good."

"The funeral will take place in a day or two – after that …"

"We can't rush these things to suit individual whims, Reverend Unwood."

"No, of course not."

"If you feel it necessary, perhaps you would care to phone your own immediate superior – Bishop Twiddle, isn't it? I'm sure he'll offer you appropriate advice – but, once again, it would be in the interests of decorum not to mention this call to me … by the way, where did you get this number?"

"PC Billings …"

"Really? … I wonder … I'll speak with Martin when he returns."

Corvin heard the receiver replaced. He didn't see Superintendent Junket make a brief note to the effect that a certain call had been referred to the local officer, but he was left with the impression that he had made a fool of himself.

Simon Palmester shared none of Corvin's doubts. Sidney had said less to him. He knew that there was a woman involved (that was often the case) and that she was Sarah Marjoram, but Sidney had not involved him in even the sketchiest details. "I've committed a sin, Simon – a mortal sin." Simon knew his advice had been good – "Nothing stands between you and God, Sidney – on your knees before your Maker … We cannot blame others – even Sarah Marjoram – for our sins."

He believed that – otherwise 'free will' made no sense at all. Men were fond of blaming the woman when their passions led them astray. Sex was given by God for the mutual comfort of men and women, and for the procreation of children in a permanent union between one man and one woman. Any other use of sex was a sin. It was as plain as a pikestaff. The modernists could fudge and wheedle, but the Truth was there, in the Good Book, for all to see. Sin – sexual or otherwise – is simply disobedience to God's will. There was no point in making it difficult, in deliberately obfuscating the matter. Sin was sin – and Sidney had sinned … and then repented. Was his repentance contrite? Simon hoped so for now Sidney was dead and to die in a state of sin was not … was not something to be welcomed! Sinning against the Creator was spiritual death. The sinners in the gospels were not wicked people – not in the way the world sees wickedness – but they were people who had broken their relationship with God, wounding His love for them. Repentance brought immediate forgiveness from the Lord. Had Sidney died while repentant?

Simon was annoyed that Sidney was to be buried in the graveyard at St George's, and he was annoyed that Corvin who was to take the service. He had spoken to Mavis Close but she was she was adamant – Sid had been the rector's warden and it was there he was to be buried!

'Sins of omission' – Corvin could hear the phrase running like a death knell through his head. 'The failure to do what is right.' He knew that; oh, what a dreadful thing it was to be aware – the ignorant were truly blessed! The least he could have done was to accompany Sidney home and pray with him – and stay with him, if the man was troubled. Instead, he had sent him on his way, glad to be rid of anything which might ripple the waters, which might be confrontational to handle. He could hear Esther's voice now – 'What a ridiculous notion, Corvin! You have better things to do than pander to such nonsense!! It's utterly ridiculous!!!' No one used exclamation marks as viciously as Esther.

"Did you go and see your friend?" asked Simon Palmester.

"She's changed, dad. It isn't the Sarah I knew."

"Go on."

"There was a callousness about her. The only time I saw the old Sarah, during our conversation, was when she talked about Matthew."

"I went to see Mavis this morning …"

"With our condolences?" responded Nadine, knowing this not to be the case.

"I wanted to persuade her to have Sidney's funeral service at the Bethel."

"To give him a sunny send-off?"

"Naddy."

"Sorry."

"When I was there, Mavis told me that when she found Sid. He had bite marks on his throat – just as though a dog had bitten him … Now I know that your friend Sarah was somehow involved with Sidney. There'd be no reason for him to mention her if that were not the case – right?"

"Go on."

"But we'll take it that their involvement wasn't sexual."

"I'm sure of that, dad. Sarah had only ever been with her husband – God bless her. She wasn't someone who put it about."

"So what was their involvement?"

"I don't see what you're getting at, dad."

"You will. When Luke Turrel died, there wasn't a drop of blood left in him. As you know, I did the funeral and I spent some time with the family. His sister talked of this "bootiful lady" – she was a Norfolk girl, see," he smiled.

"Go on, dad."

"The doctors thought that Luke had died of some strange illness but couldn't account for the loss of blood …."

"There was no mark on Luke, as I remember."

"No, but that would have healed over night – after he died. Mavis found Sid almost immediately he fell. It was probably the fall that woke her."

"I don't follow, dad."

"Only because you don't want to … think, Naddy!"

"You are saying that Sarah is the connection. She was the "bootiful lady", and we know she was involved with Sidney."

"The boy was drained of blood and Sidney had been bitten on the throat. It doesn't take a genius to work out how and why, does it?"

"Oh, dad!"

"The Devil's at work here, Naddy. You spoke just now of blasphemy. Jesus said that all sins can be forgiven except one – blasphemy against the Holy Spirit. You know what that is, Naddy?"

She didn't answer: Nadine Palmester could not believe her life-long friend had anything to do with these deaths, but her father's face was ashen with fear.

"Blasphemy against the Holy Spirit is rejecting good deeds – done in the power of God – as being works of the Devil. If my fears are right, Naddy, this death and that of young Luke – both of which I first saw as the will of the Lord – might well be the work of the Devil. I wouldn't want that – not Simon Palmester seeing the work of the Devil as the will of God. That would be a blasphemy, indeed – what you might, laughingly, call a double-take. He would have me in his grip, then, wouldn't he Naddy? Me – of all people – working for him!"

"What are you going to do, dad?"

"I want to persuade Mavis Close to let Sid lie at rest here – in the Bethel – before the funeral. He was a Bethel man – before he got involved up the road. I don't think she'll refuse, seeing as though the funeral is at St George's. I can't see the difference between him lying here and him lying in the chapel of rest at the undertakers. Anyway, I'm off to Eastwold this afternoon to see Sidney's father. I think he might be the deciding factor."

"Why here, dad?"

"Here, I can keep my eye on things – *and I can pray!* If I were a gambling man, Naddy – which, of course, I'm not – I'd lay all I own on those marks having gone from Sidney Close's throat by tomorrow morning."

Simon Palmester met with the success he expected, talking to Sidney Close's father, who was both admired and loved by his daughter-in-law. He had welcomed their courtship, he had enthused over their marriage and sorted out his wife over the choice of church, he had helped them financially over the years, he loved their children and he supported Sidney in his role of rector's warden. When Simon phoned, he was told that Sid's father was actually in Dunburgh, comforting Mavis.

Under his guidance, Mavis saw not only the sense but the "niceness" of having Sidney lying at rest in the Bethel. Members of the Bethel community would feel able to come and go more freely and – the Bethel being almost next door to their house – Mavis would be able to visit in when she wished.

With Mavis now beginning to realise her loss, she left the arrangements to Simon and her father-in-law. By mid-afternoon, the undertakers had been advised and – if Necker completed her work in time, which she would – Sidney's body could be escorted to the Bethel that evening.

Simon returned home and prepared himself: there was praying to be done, weapons to be gathered. What form his enemy would take he had no idea but Simon had wrestled with the Devil before, had struggled for the souls of his flock, and he intended to be ready for the fight. Indeed, he relished the very thought of the conflict.

After lunch, Rebecca and her father left Esther to do the washing-up and went for a walk. Rebecca took her father towards the church and then along the lane where she had walked, fallen in love with and then rejected Peter Vishnya. In her certainty, now, of his love she smiled with pleasure. Autumn had made its mark: gone were the stitchwort and the purple loosestrife under the hedges and the yellow flag flopped along the river bank. They paused by the bridge and Rebecca turned to her father.

"Come on, dad. You mustn't bear this alone."

Corvin sat on the end of the wooden bridge and sighed. He was pleased his daughter loved him enough to want to listen. Slowly, broken thought by broken thought, he poured his grief out to her. She never interrupted him, but leaned against the rail of the bridge, on the verge of tottering back into the river, and watched him with her large, blue eyes. When he had finished, Rebecca sat beside him, put her arms round him and kissed him on the cheek.

"Oh dad," she said, "Stop torturing yourself. You're a good man and a good priest. You just don't like emotional conflict."

Horst Brultzner had discovered by late afternoon that Sidney's body was not to be cremated and that it was to lie at rest in the Bethel until the funeral that was to take place within two days. He didn't blame Sarah as he had when the Turrel boy died; he could see that she had a right and a need to feed, and assumed that Sidney Close's death had been an accident. He had no reason to know that she had toyed with Sidney, and made herself known to him.

"There is no need for you to accompany me tonight, Sarah. I will take Catchpole, who will do what must be done."

"Is there no other way? Can't we seal him within the coffin?"

"For all eternity? The vampire's nature is growing strong in you, Sarah. When I leave here – as one day I will – Dunburgh will be in good hands!"

"You plan to leave me here?"

"We have much travelling and learning to do, but you may one day, a hundred years or so from now, wish to become housekeeper of the Old Vicarage – hmm?"

Sarah smiled. The thought had never occurred to her – she who was used to thinking only in years – not decades, let alone centuries!

"But tonight we have other business afoot. I will see Catchpole – we seem to be dependent on him again. Perhaps there is a more loyal servant who could take his place? In the meantime, he can make himself available after dark. Now I must prepare the implements."

"May I come?"

"You wish to?"

"Yes. If one day I am to be the Lady of Dunburgh ...."

She laughed and Brultzner joined her; she was so young – so full of fun – and one day the viciousness would settle down.

"... I would like to be with you tonight."

"Very well – the pleasure will be mine!"

"Do you know where the body is to lie at rest, Corvin?" stormed Esther.

"Yes, my dear."

"And you've done nothing about it??"

"What should I do about it, Esther?"

"It's a deliberate insult."

"I think not, my dear."

"Then why can't Sidney lie in the chapel of rest at the undertakers, like everyone else?"

"I imagine Simon felt Sidney had been a member of the Bethel community, and this would be an appropriate way of showing their respects to him."

"Respects, my foot! This is one in the eye for you!"

"I don't think so, my dear."

"I know so!"

"Everyone is welcome, Esther. I shall probably go down to the Bethel myself during the course of the evening."

"You'll do what!"

"I said ..."

"I heard what you said – I just couldn't believe it!"

"Esther, we have attempted, in Dunburgh, to create a caring, spirit-filled community of love. The coming together of the three churches is very important."

"You realise that Simon Palmester attempted to have the funeral changed to the Bethel, don't you?"

"Yes, my dear."

"Yes?"

"Yes."

"Corvin – don't keep repeating yourself. Weren't you ... flabbergasted at the cheek of it?"

"Simon feels strongly about these matters, Esther."

"So you would have been happy to have him usurp your prerogative as priest of the parish and attend one of those awful 'Glory, Alleluia' services?"

"I don't think ..."

"Exactly ... you've said it for me!"

"Esther ...."

"Don't Esther me, Corvin – I'm annoyed. These people pretend to want the integration of the churches, and take every opportunity to undermine your position."

"I do not see, Esther, that this undermines anything. In fact, I find it quite moving that such a vigil should take place ..."

"Moving?"

"In the past, Esther, families did not get rid of the body before it was cold. The body was placed, usually, in the front room of the house. Everybody – family, friends and neighbours – would come round to the home and pay their respects. It was a way of saying goodbye, and far healthier – in my view – than this modern obsession with getting the body out of the way so that no one is upset."

"Well said, dad," cut in Rebecca, who had been listening to the altercation and waiting for her moment to intervene.

"Both my parents – and I am sure yours, Esther – spent their last moments in this world in the bosom of their families – as Sidney Close will do."

"I still say that sly Simon Palmester's motive is to give you – and the Anglican Church – 'one in the eye'! I can't imagine what Bishop Peter will think."

With this final shot Esther left the room, not wanting to take on her daughter in full sail – as she clearly was, judging by the expression on her face. Corvin looked at Rebecca – he'd forgotten the bishop.

Bishop Twiddle listened patiently on the other end of the phone to all that Corvin had to tell him and the parish priest outlined once again, as he had to Superintendent Junket, his concerns about the manner of Sidney Close's death. He wondered whether Corvin was serious in his suggestion that old cults were alive and well in Dunburgh. He wondered whether Corvin was suggesting that the estimable Horst Brultzner was somehow involved in these, since Sarah Brown was his housekeeper. We had to be careful, you see, about the ethnic implications of such accusations. Other cultures had different customs – it was not to say that they were … in any way suspect.

Yes, he appreciated Corvin's concern – certainly the teeth marks were troubling, but they only had Sidney Close's word for that; indeed, not so much his word as his … confession. Confession wasn't something which the Church of England saw in the same light as … other members of the Christian community and perhaps we were not so circumspect about the manner in which we listened? Corvin would be aware that the very word 'confession' came from the Latin for 'complete speaking'. It seemed to him that perhaps Sidney Close had been – to use a modern word – 'stressed' and that his speaking was anything but complete. It would not pay us to jump to conclusions. It was safer by far for members of the church to make their confessions as part of a 'corporate act of worship' or quietly and privately during the sacrament of absolution.

He would advise Corvin to monitor the situation but keep his concerns in the main to himself until there was some other corroborative … material. The bishop hadn't liked to use the word 'evidence', but it nearly slipped off his tongue.

Yes, he did feel that it would be a good idea to pay his respects to the deceased during the Bethel's night vigil. It would be further evidence of the churches coming together.

When he put down the phone, Corvin felt both relieved and isolated. The bishop hadn't castigated him for the phone call; at the same time he had offered no help at all. It was clear to Corvin that he was the priest-in-charge and that any decisions must be his – but preferably made in 'accord with church policy'. Corvin, however, wasn't clear as to the nature of that policy; he didn't like to worry Rebecca again – he knew her views on policies.

Mavis Close and her daughters and in-laws were the first to see Sidney after he was brought to his final resting place. Mavis saw him again as a young man

– good-looking, well-built with a fine head of hair; if anything he was more handsome than ever. His skin seemed clearer and almost shone with an inner light. One of the girls commented how his skin had no blemishes, how red his lips were and how white his teeth; they were at the age when these things first start to matter.

Mavis smiled. Sidney had been a good husband – a good provider, kind to the children and faithful to her; they had insurances, she would sell the shop and take a little job. She and the girls would manage quite nicely. Her father-in-law, anyway, had promised to give them any help they might need.

She was glad that Simon Palmester had suggested the coffin should be placed in the Bethel; it would be like it was in the old days when people did drop round to pay their last respects. While she was there, the rector came in and shook hands all round; it was strange how something like this brought people together. Simon and the rector and her father-in-law talked like old friends; Sidney was in good hands.

Mavis's faith was simple – people could skit it as much as they liked and talk about 'timelessness' and 'a state of being with God'. Heaven, to her, was a place where – one day, God willing – she would meet up with Sid again and sit and chat on a white bench in a green park. She had told the girls this and it had brought them comfort – to know that they would see their dad again and that, after the funeral, he would be at peace in a beautiful garden.

That Russian pig (what was his name? – Kruschev or something like that) had mocked the idea. What did he say – "Our spaceships haven't found this Heaven of yours yet!" Well they wouldn't, would they? If you didn't believe in it, you were unlikely to find it. You can't see what you don't believe to be there! Anyway, you weren't likely to get there in a space-ship! "Heaven is a place so much better than this one that we have no words to describe it." That's what her parents had said and also what her father-in-law believed. It was enough for Mavis; she had no doubt in her mind that her husband was on his way to Heaven.

Alan Read listened while his wife told him about the arrangements surrounding Sidney Close's death. Sitting outside the little French café on their way home, he and Martin Billings felt a million miles away. Death must have been instantaneous – cracking your skull on a stack of weights. He was a big man, heavily muscled – he must have fallen like a pile of bricks.

"There were no other wounds?"

"No Alan – not that I've heard of – Jim Maxwell was the one they called in – you can ask him about it when you get back. Enjoy the rest of your break."

"If there had been any suspicious circumstances, Alan – the police would have been called in. Don't worry about it – have another glass of vin blanc," said Martin.

" … No, I don't suppose there is …," said Alan, on the phone to Penny.

"Is what?" said Martin.

"No point in rushing home for the funeral."

"No," said Martin, "certainly not."

He poured another glass of Vouvray – they had forsaken the local cider.

"Just give Jim a ring and ask him," Alan suggested to his wife.

"Come on Alan – let's enjoy our last few days here. You can't be had for being drunk in charge of a bike – at least not in France! This is wonderful – light, airy, actually tasting of grapes, soft on the palette, slightly ....buttery...."

"Shall we order lunch?" said Alan, as he switched off the phone.

"Why not?"

"Look at this menu, Martin – fillet de sole Normandie, crevettes au cidre, escalopes cauchoises ... are we spoiled or are we spoiled?"

Nadine Palmester telephoned Tony Crewes in the early evening. His wife, Beth, answered, and relayed the message to Tony when he arrived, and just before he poured his usual glass of wine.

"What does she want?"

"I've no idea. Did she leave a number?"

"You mean you don't know it?"

"No – now can we stop the word games so that I can make this call before I flop down for my dinner?"

"There's no need ...."

"The number, Beth – please. Nadine and I know each other, but how often does she ring here? This must be important."

Their conversation was brief – just an arrangement to meet at the Bethel where Sidney Close was lying at rest.

"What was that about?"

"I don't know. She seems to want to talk to me about something."

"I didn't know...."

"We're not. Christ!"

"Thanks for coming, Tony. I hope ...."

"It's all right – if it wasn't this, it would be that," he laughed.

They were standing by Sidney's coffin and Tony was wondering why he had invested so much energy into despising the man; it seemed so pointless now that he was dead.

"Have you seen Sarah recently? I'm worried about her."

They left the little chapel and walked along Harbour Road towards the sea, while Nadine recounted her meeting with Sarah and the subsequent conversation with her father. Tony listened, recalling conversations with Martin and Corvin.

"You don't subscribe to the sexual theory? It would be much easier."

"Tony! Can you imagine ...?"

"No – but your father doesn't believe in vampires – not the movie-style vampire, does he? Is he thinking that this is a cult – a group of perverts?"

"He says it's the work of the Devil. Dad does believe in demons so there's no reason to suppose he doesn't give some credence to the existence of vampires."

"Not Sarah! – you don't believe ...?"

"I don't know what to believe, Tony. That's why I gave you a ring."

They walked on, came to the Seaview Café and went in for a coffee. While they waited, Tony recounted his conversations with Martin and Corvin. Nadine's face slackened and her eyes brimmed with tears as she listened.

"It's only a few months – or is it weeks? – since we were talking together on the cliff path. Sarah was planning – or talking about – an education. It's not … conceivable, is it? Do you know why dad asked for this vigil? … He must believe that there is something in all this. If it wasn't him, I'd just dismiss the whole business as religious nuttiness, but he is so serious, Tony. He believes that, by morning, the wounds will have disappeared from Sidney Close's throat."

"Are you concerned for your father, Nadine – or do you think he will spend the night sitting quietly by a corpse?"

"I'm concerned for Sarah, Tony."

"Do you want me to call in on the Bethel tonight, Nadine?"

"Would you?"

"Yes."

"Then … please – if you would – if only to see that dad's all right."

When he arrived home, Beth said:

"What did Nadine Palmester want?"

Tony was amused – it was the full name that got him – "Nadine Palmester" – as though her name was a recognised term of abuse. He said:

"Nothing."

"Nothing?"

"Nothing much."

"Nothing much?"

Tony wondered how long the game could go on, but he was tired and so he said:

"Nadine is concerned that Sarah Brown might be a vampire – and, if she is, who the King Vampire who created her was – was it …"

"Oh, don't be so utterly ridiculous," said Beth.

"Precisely," said Tony.

CHAPTER 5

Vigil

Simon Palmester had prepared himself well for the night's vigil. In a sense, however, his preparations were decoration; his principle weapon lay in his faith, and this was unshakeable. Come what might he was ready, and his trust lay not in the 'weapons' in his bag, but in his belief in the Lord God. He entered the Bethel without a moment's trepidation; come Hell or high water, in the morning he would rise triumphant from the ashes of the night.

The chapel was a second home to him; at night, others might have found it fearful, but not Simon. Sidney's coffin had been placed on its trestles so that the corpse's feet faced the door and its head was towards the small, simple altar. Simon wasn't one for candles but this night he had made an exception. His first task, as night began to fall, was to light several: two burned on the altar, others were placed at the end of each pew so that the aisle was lined with fire, and he had two, resting on the trestles, at each end of the coffin. This wasn't out of fear. Simon had a sense of the theatrical and he wanted Sidney's visitors in awe of the Lord: somehow, candles achieved this better than electric bulbs. The effect was to make the corners and doorways of the small chapel gloomy, while the candles flames danced like devils, throwing shadows along the walls. Each visitor who entered set these off with the breeze from the open door.

Sidney's wife and two girls had come and gone. The chapel had been lit by daylight when they were there, and Simon's comforting arms were placed round all their shoulders. Mavis had been quiet, but the girls almost excited. Children accepted death, even the death of a loved one, more easily than adults; they had less about which to feel guilty. Simon smiled grimly to himself; he had a deep awareness of the frailty of human nature, but it aroused no pity in him. There was no need for pity once the Lord had entered your life.

Since Sidney's family, there had been a steady stream of visitors, all paying their respects to Sidney in the time-honoured way: his parents, both on Simon's wavelength and grateful to Simon for offering the chapel as their son's last resting place: Sidney's close friends from the village – the non-believers with bowed heads and heavy hearts, the faithful with joy in their eyes: the men from the Fishermen's Hut, their earth-bound natures suspicious of what they saw as the supernatural, but good men, men sure of their duty towards the deceased: Miss Mealey and Mrs Teale together, remembering what a nice man Sidney had always been when they rang the bell of his shop: members of the congregation of the 'other church' all curious about the Bethel, all wondering whether its power was greater than their own place of worship: Plumptious and Benny Walters, remembering one who rarely graced their establishment but who could be relied upon when their need was electrical: Crafty Catchpole had slunk in, as though taking an interest in something forbidden: Bernard and Liz Shaw, the new rector's warden feeling guilty that he had supplanted Sidney in his post: Sandra Bint, over-awed by Sidney's beauty in death, eager to hurry off and gossip, a woman "steeped in sin" and "as ready for damnation as any" Simon had seen: Harry Bailey and his wife, Harry still bearing the bruises from the beating Sidney had given him but forgiving and full of genuine grief: Penny Read, out of respect and apologising that her husband was still in France, with Jim Maxwell the senior partner in the Dunburgh-on-sea surgery: Necker Utting, admiring her own handiwork, with Rollie whose ghoulish interest in the corpse earned him a speedy exit from Simon: Gris and Owen Culman with Mark and Nin Chambers, an "uneasy and unholy foursome" (according to Simon) on their way elsewhere. Simon greeted them all with equal forbearing, concern and spiritual curiosity.

He noted that some had not arrived even though the evening was well on – his own daughter among them: notably, however, Corvin Unwood with his family. When Corvin did arrive it was with both wife and daughter, but Esther Unwood looked around her as though she had entered a house of ill-repute. Simon smiled his grim smile and greeted her warmly.

"It has been a great success, Corvin," he said, "and attracted those who have forgotten what the inside of a house of God looks like."

He caught Esther's eye as he spoke. Simon was a bigot who found other people's bigotry amusing.

"I am pleased, Simon. It is good that we should come together in this way, even on such an occasion. The fear of death is an unnecessary burden."

"What they fear most Corvin is not death, but life after death. They are unsure – the unbelievers, that is – what awaits them!"

He said it with relish, secure in the knowledge that he was saved.

"Would you like us to pray with you for a while?"

"I would welcome it. You may stay all night if you wish. The company would not go amiss."

All four knelt in the front pew – Esther ill-at-ease – and prayed, at first quietly, each in their own world, and then Simon's voice boomed throughout the chapel.

"O Lord, accept Sidney Close into the bosom of your Heavenly family. He came to us, Lord, his hands stained with sin, his mind polluted with vileness, but our ministrations fell on deaf ears. He did not want to talk about his spiritual abyss, Lord, so deep was his shame, yet nothing stood between him and You, Lord. We knelt here before You, Lord, and he was cognisant with the pains of Thy Hell – he knew what was expected of him, knew where his duty lay and yet – weak in his humanity – drew back from Your everlasting salvation, enticed by the temptations of this world. Purge his sins, Lord, for he was – at his best – Your faithful servant ..."

"Amen," said Corvin.

"... and redeem his immortal soul. Were it as easy, Lord, for the living to wash away the offence of the soul as it is to remove the stain of blood from the murderer's hands then we would not be worthy of Your everlasting Kingdom, for the virtue of redemption lies partly in our own struggle to be pure. Sidney struggles no longer in this mortal coil. His soul, Lord, is in Your hands and we who loved him pray for him now. He knew, Lord, that we all bring about our own damnation, that free-will is a gift, not a trinket for a wilful child. Each of us treads the path each of us chooses, and Sidney's appetites led him along the path of perdition. His temptation of the flesh was a corruption of the good desires You give us, Lord, but we pray for him now ..."

"... in sure and certain hope of the resurrection to eternal life," said Corvin, angered by what he saw as Simon's self-righteousness and lack of compassion, perturbed that someone might enter the chapel while its priest's prayers grew ever louder.

Esther stood and, without speaking, left the chapel; Rebecca followed her quickly but not before casting a quick, reassuring look at her father. Corvin stayed and spoke when Simon rose from his knees.

"He came to you, as well?"

"He knew the path he should take and yet each night he wandered further from the Lord."

"There but for the grace of God go I – or you, Simon?"

"It does no good to pamper the weak, Corvin – they grow only weaker. I fear the Devil's hand in this – he is after my soul and yours and Sidney Close is his bait."

"I do not understand, Simon."

"I see the Lord's hand in all things, Corvin – the death of Sidney, the death of that young lad – and I do not question the Lord. But what if this is the work of the damned? Where would I stand, giving this my blessing? I will not be tricked, Corvin. I will not be seduced from my chosen path. If my fears are right, I am here tonight fighting for my very soul – as well as that of Sidney."

Corvin stared at him as though the Bethel priest was mad, but he could see the fear in Simon's eyes. If he were to hail Sidney's death as the will of the Lord it would be blasphemy, if it was the work of the Devil; accepting bad deeds – done in the Devil's name – as being the works of the Lord was the same as rejecting good deeds – done in the power of God – as being works of the Devil.

Corvin smiled – he could think of nothing else to say or do. Simon's thinking was not his, although he shared the same knowledge and the same concerns. Simon watched him leave the church but heard no voices in the road, and judged that Corvin's wife and daughter had already returned home.

Evening was well advanced by now and soon the last rays of the sun would be gone; somehow he knew that Nadine would come again but he hoped it would not be yet. He walked over to the coffin where Sidney lay and looked at the corpse. His worst fears were realized; when he moved aside the collar to look at the neck, it was smooth and flushed and, beneath the sallow skin, a bluish light glowed.

Moreover, the marks of the bite had vanished. The smirk which had always lingered somewhere – beneath his eyes, around the corners of his mouth – now possessed an almost aristocratic arrogance. The corpse had a confidence in death which the man had never possessed in life. Then, he had been restrained by his upbringing: now, that restraint seemed to have passed away. Simon looked down on a face both disdainful and cruel, the face of a Being that would have its way. He knew that it was watching him, not consciously perhaps – for the Thing that had once been Sidney Close was still struggling with its own awakening – but with purpose. Simon had no sense of panic; he knew that calmness was essential if he was to win the contest which he faced.

He put his hands together and began to pray again, silently this time, his mind's eye focused on an image of Christ, which he had seen in a child's picture book. He tried to hold in his imagination the purity of the expression on the Holy face, and see the selfless love pouring from the eyes. He wanted to feel that love around him, protecting him like a knight's armour. Without opening his eyes, he turned and walked to the altar. Prayers raced through his head; the long-remembered words flowing easily from his lips. Had the words always come so easily? Was he guilty of glibness? Simon dropped to his knees, his hands still pressed tightly together, palms aching. He realized his head was lowered so that his nose rested lightly on his fingertips. The tightness in his hands soon spread along his arms and across his shoulders until they felt sore with the stiffened muscles. His neck throbbed, and his head twitched in grief. Simon opened his eyes and looked around; he turned his head quietly. The church was peaceful: nothing stirred.

He looked at his watch; it was less than an hour since Corvin had left, but now the church was in darkness except for the guttering light of the candles. Simon felt distracted. He had spent many nights in prayer, on his knees, at one with his God and his concentration had never failed. Dawn would arrive and he would stand refreshed despite the rigours of the night: yet now he felt bewildered, his composure gone. Simon was no longer 'at one' with his God; slowly, the fear that he might be 'found wanting' crept into his consciousness. He heard the latch on the chapel door rattle. He heard a voice calling to him but could not bring himself to think who it was; the voice was just a sound in his head. His own voice, as he answered, seemed like a trick.

Simon looked up and found his daughter smiling down at him. She had entered the Bethel without a thought for herself and found him kneeling by his altar. He heard himself saying "You must go, Naddy, this is a dangerous place." He heard her answer "Dad – this is your church!" He felt her lift him, and realized that they were sitting in the front pew. Her arms were round him. He felt lost and saw the puzzlement in Nadine's eyes. She had never seen her father so shaken; it was almost as if his confidence had gone. 'Yet my ordeal has scarcely begun.' Simon was certain of one thing; he must convince Nadine he was himself and get her to leave the chapel. He told her that he would explain in the morning, that he had been lost only in the company of his God and that he needed unbroken communion with Him. Nadine understood and left quietly, hearing her father's voice calling.

"Go quickly, Naddy: go safely."

When he turned from the door, he saw the corpse of Sidney Close watching him from the coffin. It – whatever it was – sat looking at him. 'If I were to hail Sidney's death as the will of the Lord it would be blasphemy, if it were the work of the Devil.' The sight and the knowledge gave him back his strength and his will to fight; he had been right as, all along, he knew must be the case. You can fight the Devil, once you can see him. Sidney's corpse grasped the edge of the coffin, its hands blue and trembling, and hauled itself up and over the side. It stood like someone recuperating from a deep illness; the head hung forward, the shoulders shook with cold, and sweat poured from the face. It had been dressed in one of Sidney's favourite winter outfits – jeans, open-necked check shirt and a brown leather jacket. It seemed unable to bear the jacket and pulled it off, letting the garment drop to the tiles. Simon saw that it wasn't merely sweat in which the corpse was soaked; other fluids were oozing from the hands and feet, and suppurating from every pore. The pus was green, tinged with yellow; occasionally Sidney's corpse would retch and the same viscous liquid would be propelled from its mouth. As it wretched, the corpse stumbled and grasped the pew ends for support.

'As in life, even so in death.' Simon, composed now, smiled to himself; his humour had always been tinged with darkness. The smell in the little chapel was appalling; it was that of putrefying flesh. 'Bad meat has nothing on this.' He wanted to reach out and help the creature, which had now sunk to its knees but the vile smell held him away. He had come across many a rabbit on the point of death and helped it over to the other side with a blow on the neck, but Simon could not approach the corpse even though it now lolled forward vomiting copiously onto the tiled floor, its neck exposed and vulnerable.

He had seen bodies in the early stages of decomposition, but his wasn't like that; Sidney's corpse seemed to be fighting for life. Simon reached for his Bible, opened it and turned to *Corinthians 15: 42 – So also is the resurrection of the dead. It is sown in corruption; it is raised in incorruption.*

He ran his eyes down the passage and came to *15:53 – For this corruption must put on incorruption, and this mortal shall have put on immortality.*

The corpse was shedding its body fluids, ready to rise again. He looked again at his Bible; this time he read *15:49 – And as we have born the image of the earthy, we shall also bear the image of the heavenly.*

As Sarah had been reborn under the tender gaze of Horst Brultzner, as thousands before her had been reborn in the security of their coffins, so Sidney's corpse was now clearing itself of its human poisons on the floor of the Bethel. Simon knew little of vampires. He could not anticipate what might happen next; he saw only what once had been a human body struggling in a mess of putrescence.

What he did know was that this was his fight, now: his fight alone. He could not let anyone else enter the chapel, especially his daughter should she return – and Simon suspected Nadine would do just that, sooner or later. He walked quickly to the door, turned the key and locked himself in with the corpse.

Time passed and the corpse did not move from its prone position against the side of the pew, as Simon intoned prayer after prayer. He was filled with a dreadful sadness, knowing that somehow he must destroy the Being which was helpless on the floor of his chapel. He was certain that it would rise again in some kind of devilish resurrection and that it would no longer be human. Sidney Close had died; there could be no doubt that the corpse was no longer Sidney. It was equally certain that it was taking on some form of life after death. He reached into the little bag he had brought with him and took from it the large cross he kept at home; this had been his wife's and, though not a man who had much respect for what he called "idolatry", Simon cherished this cross.

He heard the beery laughter of drunks as they passed by on their way from The Jolly Sailors; there was a rattle as one of them tried the door. Knowing that a body was at rest inside, their curiosity was aroused. Simon was glad he'd had the forethought to turn and remove the key: such knowledge as his was best confined to the few. The time must be after eleven, he guessed, but this side of midnight. Plumptious kept traditional time. He took a flask from the bag and poured himself a coffee; he was more confident since Nadine had roused him, and felt comfortable. The coffee was good; it was one of the few luxuries he allowed himself. One cup in the morning was his usual level of sin; today he had indulged himself to sustain his concentration through what he had expected to be a long night.

When he looked up from where he sat on the altar steps, the corpse of Sidney Close was standing in the aisle watching him. The plastic cup almost slipped from his fingers but Simon gripped it at the last moment, poured the remains back into the flask, screwed on the cap, placed the flask back in the bag and stood. The simple series of actions composed him. In one hand he held his Bible, and in the other the cross of his late wife.

For a while he wasn't sure that the corpse had seen him or, to be more precise, was aware of his presence, but then it took a few, tottering steps forward and reached out with its arms. The mouth opened, dribbling the sickly fluid, and Simon saw that the teeth were sharper. The mouth twitched and the whole face quivered. When he looked into the eyes, Simon realised that the Being was still in some comatose state between life and death for the eyes were blank; there was in them, neither sight nor understanding. The corpse began to fling itself about, the arms flailing in front of the body as though to grip whatever came its way and Simon knew he had to stay clear of those arms. He feared that, as yet, there would be no power in the cross; nothing can fear what it cannot see. He stepped carefully back into the little sanctuary before the altar and knelt down to pray. As he did so, the corpse moved towards him but stopped at the altar steps. It jerked backwards, screaming and shaking its right hand – the one which had reached out, seeking – as though the fingers had been burned. In the air was the smell of seared meat. The corpse staggered backwards and collapsed into the front pew where Simon had placed his bag.

Simon moved forward, his outstretched arm holding the cross but, although the corpse's eyes looked at it, they obviously saw nothing and it sat staring helplessly. Simon was tempted to reach for his bag, take out the iron stake he had brought and drive it through the Being's heart; he knew that iron pinned evil to the earth. He also knew that, should he fail in his first thrust, the corpse would lay hands on him and hold him tight.

The corpse shuddered and a chill wind passed between it and Simon, who drew slightly back, waiting for whatever was to happen but the corpse made no further moves. It seemed exhausted and grateful to be sitting quietly. Sidney Close was barely recognisable within the Being in front of him, but Simon knew he lurked there somewhere, awaiting deliverance. He could see it struggling for breath and the eyes, shut tight, seemed to express through their sightless lids a bitter fight against pain. Simon had seen terminally-ill people in such a state as they contested death in a vain attempt to drag themselves back into the world.

How long this continued Simon had no idea, but he knew that he was not locked in a desperate struggle for Sidney's soul as he had expected to be; Sidney had already passed beyond any such help. Simon could do no more than watch until his moment came and he could drive this Being back to its coffin and destroy it. In the meantime, he needed to stay clear of those hands.

All the time he chanted his prayers quietly, and eventually the corpse looked up as though it had heard something and its teeth champed and its head rose as if peering at some dark and distant sun; then the eyes opened and there was a glimmer of recognition. The corpse took up Simon's chanting, twisting the sounds of the words round into some devilish incantation. He realised that the phrases might be Latin or Greek but had no idea what they meant, feeling only that they were some corruption of his own prayers. He raised his voice and his words boomed around the chapel; the Being followed suit until both of them were locked into a battle of the baritones. He stood and the corpse stood with him; there was no distance between them now and either could have reached out and grabbed their opponent.

As he stood, the slime of death began to fall from Sidney's corpse. The fluids were expending themselves and, beneath them, the body took on the inner radiance of the vampire. There was another noise now, but Simon, engrossed in his battle with Sidney's evil spirit, had no time to wonder what it was: later, near to death himself, he was to remember it as a monstrous thudding as though millions of hands or wings or talons were banging on the windows, doors and walls of the chapel. He would wake, screaming, and imagine that unearthly creatures were attempting to batter their way into his sanctuary. At that moment, however, his thoughts were focussed like a beam of light from Heaven on his enemy. There was no shaking in his hands as they held the Bible and the cross; there was no tremor in his lips as he chanted the words, and the words themselves became a hymn of defiance against all evil things. He found himself singing Montgomery's battle song:

"A holy war those servants wage:
In that mysterious strife
The powers of heaven and hell engage,
For more than death or life."

As he sang and the words rose from the wells of the spirit within him, Simon was more or less unconscious of any effort to recall them. His mind held only one image – that of Christ's face from a child's picture book: a face full of compassion and wisdom, a face fearless against any onslaught, a face exuding only light and hope into the darkness of the world.

It had become cold in the chapel as they sang their battle of words, and the intensity of it made Simon shiver. His fingers 'glowed' as on a winter's day and he brought his arms across his chest and rubbed them against each other, huddling his upper arms. The corpse tore its clothes from its body and used them to rub off the sweat and pus, and then it appeared conscious of its nakedness and looked around. It could see now and turned a glittering pair of eyes on Simon. It smiled, turned away and staggered towards a small cupboard at the side of the chapel where various clerical robes were kept. Like a wayward child, it selected a cassock and dressed; then, once again, it turned to smile at Simon. It seemed aware of him and yet bemused. Simon felt no immediate threat, but sensed that soon the Being would turn on him. He could not know that Sidney Close had no understanding of what had happened to him, that – as he stood watching the priest – he too could only wonder as Sarah had done when she woke in the morning room at the Old Vicarage.

Sidney's eyes were clearing now and he realised that the colours in the room were clearer and brighter than he had ever known them: it was like putting a polarising filter on your camera – suddenly the glare had gone and you could see the surface. He noted knots he had never seen before in the wood panels, he saw the stains of human hands on the backs of the pews; he followed the grain of the wood in the altar cross. This cross seemed frightening, but he was barely conscious and he could not comprehend why; it, like the man who stood before him, was something to be avoided. He looked away from the cross at the curtains which draped the screen behind; they were dirty, caked with the dust of ages. He had never noticed that before. Swinging his head painfully to the right, he looked back at the man. Behind this man – on the altar – he noticed the white cloth which covered it and vague memories stirred. He saw a woman – she was wearing a brushed nylon dressing-gown and working on some embroidery, and she smiled at him as he came in and rose to make him a cup of tea.

He walked across to the pews and rested on them. Everything was clearing a little, but he felt so tired. If only he had the strength to ... kill the man, he would be safe, and could rest. Something told him that the man who watched so quietly was dangerous: one last effort before he slept! Sidney whirled round and leapt at Simon. He was surprised at his own speed and found himself soaring through the air, over and above the altar sanctuary and clutching at the pulpit. He climbed into it as Simon turned to face him. Sidney felt the strength bristle and fade in his muscles, but his working-out when human stood him in good stead now. He took his time walking down from the pulpit. It pleased him to think that he was mocking something. Standing at the bottom, he flexed his fingers and lifted his head to stretch his neck. He opened his mouth and yawned.

Simon was appalled at the speed with which Sidney had moved: one moment he was standing by the gown cupboard looking priestly in the white and black robes, the next he was in the pulpit, looking down at Simon with a gloating smile on his face. 'I must show no fear; I must allow no fear to distract me from the work of the Lord. Lord let your face still shine upon me.' He kept his eyes on Sidney, but suddenly the vampire vanished, dispersed into the shadows and stood by his side. The vile hands took him, lifted and threw, and Simon felt himself crash into the side pews. He was stunned and blood ran freely from a gash in the side of his face. He vomited and almost passed out, but the cross was still pressed to his chest and the Bible was still clutched in his hand. 'I am prey.'

In that thought he was wrong. Sidney had scarcely woken, let alone woken hungry; the time of gnawing hunger was yet to come. Now, he only needed rest but first he knew the threat of the priest had to be removed. He leapt upon Simon and pulled him to his feet. The priest was dazed, but still with enough strength to push against Sidney as he placed his hands around Simon's throat, ready to strangle him. His wife's cross was squeezed against Sidney's chest. Simon smelt the burning fabric and then the grilled flesh. Sidney screamed and jerked backwards, loosing his hold on Simon, who stared in disbelief at the mark which the cross had cut through the robe and at the seared flesh beneath.

Sidney was bewildered: the pain was nothing compared to his utter amazement. He turned and glowered at the priest, anger and bemusement struggling for a place on his face. The look was hellish. Simon had seen it on the faces of demons in books; he had laughed at it on the gargoyles of churches. Now he faced it in his own chapel; he was matching the Devil's own, looking directly into the depths of the Inferno. Flames seemed to leap around the head of Sidney Close and shoot from the mouth as it opened to reveal the sharp, white teeth – the canines long, curved and pointed like those of a rattlesnake.

Simon raised the cross in his right hand, holding it at arms length between him and his enemy and lifted his head to his God in a prayer of supplication. He stretched his left arm and held it Heaven-wards, still clutching his Bible. Sidney recoiled. Here there was power: he knew that, somehow felt it throughout his whole being. Here there was right and wrong, good and evil. He'd thought about it a great deal. It was something he had grown up with; his parents had taught him and the church had re-enforced it. 'Christians always have the Bible, son; it makes life simple, it irons out the creases, it gives you a basis on which to bring up your own children and it gives security to the community in which you live.' His father's voice, over all those years!

Sidney screamed: it was his final scream as a human being, his final scream of anguish at what he knew he had lost. It was a realisation that he was not to have again: in future, such screams would be screams of anger at having his will frustrated. His transformation was almost complete; the slough of humanity had almost slipped from him. He moved slowly towards Simon, meaning to glide suddenly into the shadows, take the priest from behind and pull his head from his shoulders. The moment never came. His eyes caught the wooden cross – they couldn't do otherwise, his whole upbringing forced him to this – and he felt the power burst from it. The cross glistened, wooden though it was, and a shaft of celestial light caught Sidney in the chest and flung him backwards with such force that no scrambled grasping at the pew ends could prevent his fall. He was stunned as his head cracked against the altar rail.

Simon felt it, too: that surge of power which seemed to come through his outstretched left hand and shoot out through the cross in his right. He saw the light – a beam of goodness through the darkness – and felt his wife's cross quiver in his hand. He saw Sidney's body propelled backwards, saw the force of the Lord lift him from the earth and hurl him into the altar rail. 'So perish all those who set their face against the Lord.'

He collapsed himself, emotionally exhausted by his battle of the night and physically wounded by the blows he had received as he crashed into the pew. Simon, although spiritually exhilarated, found himself sitting on the tiled floor of his chapel, leaning his back against a pew. He stared in front of him, but could make no effort to rise; he was utterly spent. His whole body ached with God's work, as if he were a soldier at the end of a long and weary battle; his sword arm still clutched the cross and he looked with pride at the scorch marks upon on the wood. His hand and arm too were burned, and he looked with pride on the scars before he passed out.

Simon came round to the sound of voices. He thought they were outside his chapel and disputing in hushed tones, but when he looked up he saw that there were three figures by the coffin of Sidney Close. Simon didn't move: there was fear and quiet anger all around him. He would wait and see what occurred. He closed his eyes, like a child who stays awake waiting for his parents to leave the room; pretending to be asleep, he needed to see what was happening. The body of Sidney Close had gone: that was his first apprehension.

His second was the recognition of the voices. Horst Brultzner (the author of all this turmoil) was one: another was his disciple, Sarah Marjoram now Brown (the one who had brought Sidney to perdition) and the third was Crafty Catchpole. It was the woman's voice which was raised in hushed anguish; she was frightened and wanted to be away from this place. Brultzner's voice was soothing, assuring her that all would be well if she put her trust in her new world rather than the "childish" teachings of the old. Catchpole did not speak; he stood like a somnambulist, waiting. It was clear from their conversation that their interest was in the corpse which Simon supposed they had replaced in the coffin. He didn't understand enough and wished that he'd read more about these creatures. All he did know was that vampires were corpses who rose from their graves in the dark and sucked the blood of the living. He could only think that they were awaiting some vile resurrection and knew he couldn't wait.

He stirred slightly, only slightly but the movement caught the sharp hearing of both Brultzner and the woman; they turned and looked at him.

"What a shame you had to wake, priest."

Neither moved, but Simon knew they were in no hurry. He had seen the speed with which the corpse of Sidney Close had reached the pulpit and these were healthy vampires. He tried to stand but the pain in his ribs at the back was excruciating, and he cried out. He realised that several bones must have broken when Sidney Close flung him across the chapel. Simon gasped and leaned forward. He thought that if he could just get to his knees he would be able to pull himself up on the end of one of the pews, but he couldn't hurry. Each move sent the stabbing pain across his back. 'If only they will let me stand.'

They did: both vampires seemed attracted by his efforts and waited until he was leaning heavily against the pew. Only the woman's face showed an immediate terror when her eyes fell on the Bible and cross which Simon held.

"You are in no fit state to fight – sit, rest, sleep."

Simon felt his eyes become heavy and he tottered slightly.

"Sleep and forget; deep, deep sleep."

"I am a weapon," said Simon, "merely the sword arm of one who is greater than you, whose power transcends yours and that of all evil things."

"You take him. Enthral him and overcome your own trepidations," said Brultzner to the woman, "but remember, enough is enough – enthral but do not kill."

The woman moved slowly and, as Simon could see, with reluctance. She was frightened of him: despite all her supernatural powers, she was scared. Sarah glided from the coffin and her eyes never left Simon's face. He was aware of her extraordinary beauty, but it was more than that: the woman was, simply, unbelievably seductive. Simon was taken by her petite figure and the strength in her; she possessed the vibrancy of the vampire – a dead creature pulsating with life! Simon had to remind himself, as he was drawn into that mane of honeyed hair, that she was dead. The lightness of her step as she passed in front of the altar, the suppleness in her shoulders and the way her legs swung easily from the hips all added to her attractions. Her movement was so unaffected, and that dreamy look in her eyes ... Simon shook himself, and thought he saw her smile. He hoped she wouldn't speak; her voice was so soft, so gentle, so coaxing

"Simon."

It was all she said and it was enough to shake him from the binding of her spell. 'Simon Peter said unto him ... I will lay down my life for thy sake. Jesus answered him, the cock shall not crow, till thou hast denied me thrice.' "Simon" – his Lord's voice in the mouth of this demon! Simon Palmester, Man of God, raised his wife's wooden cross again and lifted his eyes and left arm to Heaven. She screamed – the Thing that had once been Sarah Brown screamed as the teachings of her childhood shattered her. She fell to the floor and lifted her arms to Heaven, her mouth stretched in a cry of unmitigated distress. It was then that the power of the cross lifted her and threw her body backwards into the far corner of the church. Simon felt the glory as it once again coursed through his body, using what little strength remained to fulfil its purpose. Sarah's body hit the far wall of the chapel and then collapsed onto the floor, looking like a puppet which had been tossed aside, its strings tangled, its arms and legs criss-crossed in abandonment.

A slow hand-clap brought his attention back to Brultzner. The ancient vampire bowed, not mockingly as he might have done but in genuine admiration.

"I applaud you, priest. Your faith is authentic and I see the power of your God in the strength of your arm but what are you to do about me? My god walked this earth before yours, and your people destroyed his temples in their envy and greed for power. This very year we have commemorated the slaying of the white bull and so released its power for all mankind. '*Viros servasti eternali sanguine fuso*' – you are familiar with the quotation? Ours was a man's religion, priest – rigorous and virile: unlike yours which has fallen into disuse, overcome by the lassitude of an easy life. I exclude you, of course, from the term 'disuse'. I see in you the power your God once loosed upon the world."

It was spoken calmly, but to Simon the vampire's words sounded like the ravings of a madman. Simon had no knowledge of Latin, nor any extensive familiarity with faiths other than his own. He sensed, however, the power in his enemy and knew he would not be defeated as Sidney or Sarah had been. Simon raised the cross.

Brultzner walked towards him across the chapel. The cross lifted in Simon's grip as he felt the pulsations along his arm, divining the threat of the vampire, but there was no celestial light issuing from the cross nor the slightest apprehension in the vampire's face. He took the cross gently from Simon's grasp and placed it on the shelf of one of the pews. He spoke softly.

"I wish you no harm. The followers of my god are forever pledged to fight evil; we, too, view life as a constant struggle between light and darkness. I cannot, however, allow you to frustrate our purpose. We came to destroy Close just as you came, presumably, to redeem his soul – a soul already lost to your God. You have been a worthy opponent and you shall now be a worthy ally – should I ever need to call upon your services. You will sleep now and when you wake you will forget what you have seen tonight."

Even as Brultzner spoke, Simon had no idea of the vampire's intentions so absorbed was he in what the devil had to say; but when he was silent there could be no doubt. The vampire lifted the Bethel priest gently and bared his neck. Leaning over him, making futile his already feeble struggles, Brultzner sunk his teeth into Simon's neck, sucked and drank. Simon could not struggle; his energy was spent. He sank further and further into unconsciousness until all he heard was the vampire's guzzling of his blood and then what he thought were voices, but these faded as he collapsed onto the tiles of the chapel floor.

Brultzner looked up as he, too heard the voices. It was now well after midnight, and he had thought himself and Sarah to be safe from interruption; whatever happened, they could not be found in the chapel. The voices were those of a man and a woman. They were rattling the door and he heard the sound of a key in the lock. He had to decide quickly what he must do; retreat or stay and fight the newcomers. The victory would be his, but at what cost? How many more of the human kind could he draw into his plans without the certainty of eventual discovery? Catchpole must stay - his fate was, anyway, already decided – but he and Sarah must leave without trace. They would deal with Close when the opportunity arose; he would not leave his coffin until after the burial. They had two more nights to drive home the stake.

He was a whirl of shadows as he passed across the chapel and lifted Sarah from the floor. When the door opened and Nadine Palmester and Tony Crewes entered the chapel, they saw only a strange mist which made its way, sinuously, across the floor, engulfed their feet and then passed out and dispersed into the night.

Tony Crewes had come as he said he would, first calling at Nadine's house and – finding the lights on – tapping at her door. She had been relieved to see him, and together they made their way to the Bethel. The light of the flickering candles was all that they had seen but they had heard voices, a scream followed by a slow hand-clap and then more voices as they rattled the lock and used Nadine's key.

They barely noticed the mist at that moment. Simon's body crushed against the pew and the still, silent figure of Crafty Catchpole by the coffin were enough to absorb their attention. They noticed, too, the stake and coal hammer in Crafty's hands.

"Crafty, what are you doing here?"

"Oi don't roightly know, Miss. Oim seein'moi way clear."

Nadine passed a glance with Tony Crewes, and then walked across to the stooped figure by the coffin.

"Go home, Crafty, and think about it. I'll come and see you in the morning."

"Roight miss."

He walked from the church, a figure seemingly drugged. Nadine saw him as no more than the servant – at the most, accomplice – of more powerful figures. She thought it best that he was out of the way before they gave all their attention to her father whose pitiable state had brought tears to her eyes. As a last thought, she said:

"You'll be able to find your way all right, won't you?"

"Yes, Miss, oi'll be able ter find that all roight."

She took the stake and coal hammer from his unresisting hands as he left. It was the last she was to see of Crafty Catchpole, but Nadine was not to know that as she turned to Tony Crewes who was staring at Sidney Close in the coffin. Sidney had been good-looking in life and what people call 'a fine figure of a man'; in death he was handsome. Gone now were the fluids he had expelled as his human body took on that of the vampire. His skin shone with that inner light and, although paler than it had been, the complexion was flawless. Watching him, Tony Crewes could not believe that his old sparring partner was dead. 'Nadine is concerned that Sarah Brown might be a vampire – and, if she is, who the King Vampire who created her was … Oh, don't be so utterly ridiculous.'

"What are you laughing at?" asked Nadine, seeing the smile on his face.

"Nothing. Are we still dealing with a vampire?"

"I don't know."

"Let's take no chances."

Without another word, Tony Crewes placed the lid onto Sidney's coffin and tightened the screws with his fingers. He then went to the altar, picked up the cross and placed it on top of the coffin. He didn't feel able to use the stake and coal hammer, which Nadine held in her hands. You had to be very sure of yourself to do something like that, and he still had the uncomfortable feeling that some form of hysteria was at the bottom of their troubles.

"He won't escape from there. Let's see to your father."

Simon Palmester groaned as his daughter and Tony Crewes attempted to move him. The pain in his broken ribs where the bone pressed into his lungs was excruciating. Faint as he was, however, from the draining of his blood and his brutal treatment at the hands of Close and Brultzner, Simon was grasping at consciousness. Men of his sort do not allow their souls to be threatened and, although Brultzner had tainted his memory, the priest knew that he was in the direst peril. He coughed blood and the retching stirred him into a subdued wakefulness: enough to recognise his daughter and the man who he had pegged as an atheist.

"Naddy – it is you? Get me upright, get me seated."

"Dad, you need an ambulance."

"Call Jim Maxwell – please, I mustn't leave here tonight."

It was as he pleaded with her, knowing her stubbornness, that she noticed the mark on his throat.

"Oh no, he's put his mark on dad."

The exclamation was a cry of pity, forlorn and helpless in the face of her adversity.

"His mark, Naddy?"

"The mark of the vampire is on you, dad."

The sob that came from Simon had more determination than desperation about it. He remembered only little of the night, but the fear which had brought him to the chapel, the fear which had informed his vigil, was still strong within him.

"Get me home, Naddy. Your friend will help – the Lord uses the most unlikely tools to do his work."

Nadine smiled at Tony as he bore the mild insult.

"Dad, you're in no fit state …."

"Get me home, Naddy! I'm too weak to explain and, anyway, some devil has impaired my memory, but I know I must get home. Get me home and call Jim Maxwell – no, not yet. Get me home and light a fire."

"Dad …"

"Don't argue with me, Naddy. My very soul is in peril. Get me home, light a fire and make sure you have one branch I can grip protruding from the flames."

They argued with him no further; his tone and his deadly purpose made any debate superfluous. Even his screams as they helped him from the floor of the chapel did not deter either Nadine or Tony; the old priest would have his way.

They sat in Simon's kitchen, the fire burning brightly in the stove. Nadine had made them all a cup of tea and they were gathered round the table. The chapel seemed far away and, thought Tony, may never have existed, but Simon's groans and cries on the way home were still fresh in Tony's mind. The priest's agony was all too apparent. The gasps for breath, the yellow complexion, the sweating, the tightly closed eyes, the final collapse as he reached his own front door and the painful sigh of relief as he was helped into his chair all showed what an enormous effort of will that short walk had taken out of Simon. When he looked up, his eyes were drawn into themselves: bleak, distant and shielded from the wounds to his body.

Tony had some idea what the priest was going to do, but preferred not to think about it. He had asked them to pray with him and Tony had sat and moved his mouth, wordlessly. It was the best he could do. He had been surprised Nadine had no difficulty praying, picking up her father's words so easily, but then realised this was Nadine's past playing its part.

"I shall pass out when it happens," said Simon, "be careful of the brand. Nadine, if ...."

"Dad!"

He smiled at her, father to daughter; it was a complicity which Tony envied. He wasn't that close to anyone, not even his own children.

The sound of the priest's wincing was unbearable to Tony when the moment arrived, but he noticed that Nadine made no effort to help her father. It was clear from where she got her independent streak. He tapped aside the stove doors with the poker, spitting blood as he leaned forward. Simon then reached for the oven glove, which he had placed ready on the table. He picked out the burning branch, tapping the white ash from it so that the red hot core shone clearly. Smoke rose from the ember and Simon reached for the mantelpiece with his left hand; there was a mirror on the little shelf. He needed that to see the marks of the vampire, clearly. He didn't pause once he had a firm grip, not even to look at his daughter. Tony could already smell the heat from the open stove scorching the olds priest's trousers as he brought the fire-brand onto his throat. Tony looked away, but remained ready to catch him. Nadine never took her eyes from her father. The old man didn't so much as scream when the branch burned into his flesh, searing out what he had called "Satan's stain" in his prayers. His teeth clenched, the ember dropped from his grip and he collapsed yet again that night. Nadine could smell her father's flesh burning as she and Tony caught him.

"How did he get this burn mark?"

"Don't ask, Doc. You wouldn't want to know. How are his ribs?"

"There is no possibility of my 'strapping him in'. Your father will have to go to hospital. He needs an x-ray and proper care. If his lungs aren't punctured, I'll be most surprised," replied Jim Maxwell, who had arrived within minutes of Nadine's call, "I'll arrange for an ambulance to come and fetch him. The paramedics will look after him so there is no need for you to go. Even if he is conscious, he'll not feel like speaking. Anyway, after the injection I've given him I imagine he will sleep until morning. How did he come by his injuries?"

"Will the hospital need to know?"

"They will most certainly ask."

"We're not sure about the ribs. We found him slumped against one of the pews in the Bethel."

"And the burn?"

"Self-inflicted – he had an accident with a piece of burning wood."

Nadine took no notice of Jim Maxwell's advice and went to the hospital in the ambulance after asking Tony if she could call him when she returned. He said he'd keep his mobile on, and would, anyway, wait for her to return. She didn't argue.

While Nadine was away, Tony strolled back to the Bethel and used her key to enter. He unscrewed the lid from Sidney Close's coffin. The ex-rector's warden had not stirred; even his hair flopped across the forehead as it had done when they left him. Tony touched the flesh; it was cold. He prised back the upper lips; the teeth were sharper than they had been in life but didn't the gums shrink and wouldn't the teeth look longer? He trod round the mess on the floor; it was similar to the trail left by slugs but had been spilled in patches. He picked up Sidney's clothes; they were clammy with sweat and excreted juices. He wondered how they came to be there. Simon wouldn't have removed them – would he? These religious people had some strange ideas; perhaps Simon hadn't approved of Sidney appearing at the Pearly Gates in jeans and a leather jacket. Tony folded the clothes neatly, placed them on the front pew and went back to the coffin. Sidney certainly looked more his old self in the cassock. Tony could remember him walking down the aisle in front of the rector, holding the cross and with that smug look on his face. It was more so, now. Like Simon, Tony thought the face was arrogant and cruel. 'What does it take to turn a smirk into a sneer?'

The last few candles were guttering to a finish in the chapel and the shadows had now grouped into a pervading gloom. There was a deathly, dust-of-ages smell about holy places. Being shut in one would give you the creeps, so what was it like, locked forever in a coffin? Cremation for me, thought Tony Crewes, and realised he was being flippant because he was frightened. What was this fear of the dead? He had been terrified on the beach that night when he had stood guarding Clive Brown's body, but that was from fear of something tangible – the lurking killer. In this chapel, where so many terrors had been paraded before so many congregations, it was the fear of a what – a break with the tradition of death? We surrounded it with custom because we wanted to be in control, wanted to be sure it wouldn't … surprise us? Bury the dead: that's where they belong – safely underground or burned to a crisp but not … waiting to spring surprises on the living. He realised that the sweat was pouring from him on this chill autumn night.

Why had he come here: to convince himself that the dead were just that – not a threat to those who would wake naturally in the morning?

"Did he say anything?"

"No, apart from some rambling. He's badly injured. The lungs have haemorrhaged."

"He will live, Nadine?"

"I hope so, Tony. He's all I have in the world and ... despite what he is ... what he appears to be ... he is a good man. Whatever he fought tonight – his own fantasies or a horror unimaginable – he fought it alone and for the good of his ...."

"... flock."

"Yes – that's how he saw them – sees them."

"What now?"

"We wait until he regains consciousness, and find out what he has to tell us."

"We need someone to pull this together, don't we? There's so much happened when you think about it and yet there's no one who has their finger on everything, no one who could make out a case for the utterly ridiculous, and make intelligent people believe it sufficiently to do the unthinkable."

Nadine had been brought home by Jim Maxwell, and she and Tony now sat in her kitchen, leaning on the wooden table, facing each other over a cup of coffee. They were comfortable in each other's company, drawn together by their affection for Sarah Marjoram – she out of friendship, he out of sympathy.

"I went back to the Bethel while you were gone."

"Tempting providence?"

"Wondering why."

"How was Sidney?"

"Just a corpse."

"And the marks on his throat?"

"He was without blemish."

"So we go and drive a stake through his heart?"

"No."

"Why not?"

"You know why not – one doesn't desecrate a corpse," said Tony, "Neither you nor I are sure about this business. Neither of us believes that Sarah is a vampire and, therefore, Sidney's death was an accident."

"And Luke Turrel?"

"The only connection is in your father's mind."

"So what happened to him tonight?"

"I don't know. Did he say nothing?"

"He mumbled a lot – that's all – but he was sedated."

"What did he mumble about?"

"Bulls."

"Bulls?"

"Yes."

"Your father can't have been gored by a bull – not in a chapel!"

"He mumbled about a white bull and some Latin phrase – *Viros servasti* ...? I couldn't catch it."

"*Viros servasti eternali sanguine fuso?*"

"*Maybe – why? Does it mean anything?*"

"Yes – 'You have saved men by the spilling of the eternal blood'."

"Where does it come from?"

"Did you father say anything else?"

"He was rambling – things like 'My god walked this earth before yours and your people destroyed his temples' – nothing that made sense. Do you know where the phrase comes from?"

"Yes – but it has nothing to do with vampires. It's an old religion – older than Christianity. It was militant; it viewed the world in terms of a constant struggle between good and evil. It was popular with Roman soldiers."

CHAPTER 6

The 'Wild Hunt'

Crafty Catchpole had walked slowly back to his cottage when he left the chapel, barely knowing where he had come from or where he was going. It would all come back, once he sat quietly and thought it through, calmly.

He remembered something heavy falling with a thud into the boat ... her hair was matted and twisted like so much old rope found on the beach, beaten and bleached by the sea ... her head was pulled to one side and water trickled from the mouth. He remembered being slapped so hard it felt that his head was leaving his shoulders. He remembered a narrow alleyway ran alongside the shop and flinching with the coldness of their touch ... the chapel was lit only by a small artificial candle in a niche to the side of the coffin ... the little Turrel boy lay there, several days into death, waiting for his funeral ... there was fear in the boy's eyes. He struck ... it took all his strength to sever the bone ... the village was cloaked in darkness.

For many nights, he was with his computer and the words he typed into his search engine were words he had never imagined before – vampire, Un-dead, nosferatu, uber and witch. 'There's no good you getting cold feet now, Mr Catchpole – in for a penny, in for a pound. Think about your pigeons!'

Ever since he'd been working for the new man at the Old Vicarage, Crafty had felt dominated by him and he couldn't understand it. After all, it was he – Crafty – who had made the first approaches, he who had called that day, he who had helped his lordship and he who had restored the garden.

He stood in Sea Row Lane looking at the old Coastguard House. He was tired and wanted to go to bed. It was only a slight walk along to his cottage, the cottage that had once been his parents' home, where everything was still in its place – his mother's soup ladle, the Welsh dresser, the pickle jars, the deep earthenware sink, her baskets ... He wanted to see his possessions again, to touch them and know they were still there – the stereo system, the range cooker, the computer and – his pride and joy – the pigeon loft, which he scrubbed with the same love his mother had once expended on the house. He just wanted to go to bed.

"Good evening, Mr Catchpole. Are we taking the night air?"

It was the one voice he didn't want to hear – the voice with the faded, yellow eyes. He looked up. A face was staring down at him – a face that seemed to be made of leaves that sprang from the eyebrows. He was held by the eyes, which seemed as old as creation. There was something savage about the man that struck fear into Crafty's heart, but the voice was soothing.

"I think it time, Mr Catchpole, that you share my joy of the animal world."

"If it's all the same to yew, sir, oid pr'fer ter keep moi own counsel."

"It isn't the same to me, Mr Catchpole. I much desire the pleasure of your company tonight."

It was a short walk, and a quick one. Off the beaten track they went, somewhere down beside the church and then along Dovehouse Close beside Cassyn's River. Its very name recalled days, long ago, when the neighbouring farms kept doves that were essential as a supply of fresh meat in times when cattle could not be over-wintered, and before fridges hummed in kitchens. The lanes became tracks and the tracks disappeared. They kept to the east of the river and followed its course towards the north-west. The reed beds were thick here, and the river invisible; beyond it, stretching towards Blacksands Ness, was the marsh. Every now and then, Horst Brultzner turned and smiled. His sharp, white teeth glinted in the night like those of a wolf. The place was desolate – a quiet backwater where children played against their mothers advice and where lovers strolled. It was a place where you could be alone, away from the prying gaze of the villagers; it was deserted, but not forlorn. Crafty remembered it from his own childhood, remembered how he and his friends had enjoyed playing on the out-dated and abandoned farm machinery that rusted there and was eventually over-grown with grass and brambles. They used to call it 'The Wreck' and imagined they were the only ones who knew of its existence. At this time of the year they found blackberries to eat and, in the summer, wild plums.

Beyond the The Wreck, hidden by hawthorn hedges and willow trees was the Dunburgh Wildlife Park that specialised in European animals: among these was the timber wolf. A pack of them roamed in the woods to the north of the park, fenced in and fed daily on dead rabbits. They could be heard howling at night, and the villagers took delight in fearing them as much as Horst Brultzner took delight in their company. He had visited the park many times, at first scaling the fences but later creating a hidden entrance, always avoiding the security patrols, his heart forever going out to these creatures of the wild, kept here like pets in hutches. Once they had been sacred to the gods – strong, kind, intelligent animals; now they were obliged to bear, each day, the gawp and garrulity of the ignorant.

When they arrived at the fence, Crafty found himself being pushed through a mass of gorse bushes and following a twisting tunnel into the park.

"I think of this as Wolf Run, Mr Catchpole," said Brultzner, his voice exultant.

He grasped the padlock on the gate, twisted it off with one turn of his hand and ushered Crafty inside the enclosure. It was dark under the trees, but almost immediately Crafty saw the glint of many eyes upon him. A dark, heavy wolf loped towards Brultzner and inclined its head for Brultzner to tickle behind the ears. The wolf had a spring in its step and its tail wagged happily like that of a dog. Crafty somehow knew that this was a male wolf. A moment or two later its mate followed; she was more slender and her movements graceful. She, too, lowered her head. Beyond them a dozen or more pairs of eyes watched; red tongues lolled over sharp, white teeth. There was something terrifying about their very stillness but Crafty, despite all the stories he had heard as a child, was not frightened. The heavy mane of the pack leader shone like silver and the dark face of the female reminded Crafty of a picture he had seen of a beautiful woman wearing a mask at a ball.

Several other wolves joined the pair around Brultzner – a light-grey male, a red-buff female and a young wolf that was slim and black. They held their tails high, rolled on their back and barked, licked each other's faces and hugged each other with their paws. Others in the pack then moved forward – some crawling, some slinking – until they formed a group about Brultzner and Crafty; it was like being part of a family. Once welcomed, the wolves chose to sit or lie down; some even curled about themselves like dogs. All the time they touched each other, nuzzling and nose-rubbing. They were excited – Crafty could sense that – and soon began to dance about; the younger wolves yelped or growled for the sheer joy of the vibrations in their throats. The older wolves joined them, pointing their noses towards the autumn sky and giving a long drawn-out call to the stars. The call became a howl undulating through the night, sometimes a musical series of barks, at others high-pitched with yearning, and always joyful. Brultzner lifted his head and joined the howling; the wailing came from deep within him and, together, he and the wolves sounded like a choir singing out its soul.

Crafty was alone then: his sense of family vanished abruptly and he was the stranger in the camp, the odd-one out. He fidgeted and reached in his pocket for one of his cigars but as soon as he struck the match all eyes were upon him and the cheroot hung, unlit, between his lips. Brultzner smiled as he spoke:

"The fumes would upset my friends, Mr Catchpole. Their noses are very sensitive. How do you find my friends?"

"Oi doant roightly know. Oi aint never bin this close afore."

"And your fairy stories haven't prepared you for this?"

Crafty looked at Brultzner, blankly. His mother had been an admirable woman in many ways, but those ways did not include the reading of fairy stories to her child: that was the business of the teachers.

"They are much maligned, you know. 'Who's afraid of the big bad wolf?'" Brultzner chuckled, "They are killers, of course, but they have no one to kill for them as do your kind. When your joint of beef arrives on the table for Sunday lunch it has already been butchered for you, but these noble creatures do their own butchering. You see how the younger ones revere the old? In the wild they would soon leave the family, but they are only last year's cubs and still have much to learn. You sense their excitement now? They know a hunt is imminent because I am here. Let us not keep them waiting."

Without another word, the vampire took Crafty by the arm and led him out through the gate towards Wolf Run; they were followed by the pack. They seemed in no hurry, trotting along at about five miles an hour, and Crafty found he could keep pace with them quite easily. The wolves were obviously enjoying themselves, stretching their legs and looking about with excitement. Frequently, they stopped to sniff the plants and stones they passed, but made little effort to pursue any animals roused from hiding; their pleasure seemed to be in the running. Brultzner led them along the river to the farmland north of the village until they reached Tunstead. Here there were sheep in the fields and the flock scattered as the pack drove through them, but the wolves made no attempt to kill. They paused by the gibbet tree where the local hangman had done his work by moonlight. Crafty's father had told him that they dispatched malefactors quickly in those days: 'Condemned by lunch-time, hanged by supper.'

Brultzner took Crafty by the arm again, as the pack rose and made its way across country. Their pace remained the same, but Crafty had none of the tireless energy of the wolf and soon the vampire was running for both of them. The wolves sniffed the air, persistently. Their muzzles were up, their tails stiff with expectation and their nostrils dilated. The younger wolves would sometimes dart to one side after a rabbit and the older ones watched them with what, in humans, would have been a smile on their faces; they were waiting for bigger game. The young of the pack would fight over the kill. Crafty heard the crunch of bones and saw the rending of the flesh as the prey was devoured, still warm with life, by the wolves. They licked their faces afterwards and then cleaned each others, in a gesture of sociability, before rolling in front of the leader or approaching him, their tails wagging and their heads down. They barked, in such a way that Crafty was reminded of dogs on the beach, and then they joined together in long howls that floated over the night air. Always in their howling there was rapture.

It was the dark, heavy male who always signalled a new start to the hunt – never Brultzner, who allowed their instincts to determine the journey. They raced towards Willowmere across newly sown fields, their paws uprooting the shoots of winter wheat. Sometimes they skirted hedges or slipped down into ditches and broke through them where the foliage was thinnest; at others they jumped and seemed to float over them like race horses. There was something almost supernatural in the way they did this; Crafty had seen dogs leap fences, but not in this way – not as though they were almost flying. At Willowmere they paused for a while at the Cherry Tree public house and sniffed around the chicken run, but a glance that passed between Brultzner and the leader of the pack prevented any attempt by the young wolves to raid the coop.

Crafty noticed how the leader's mate never left his side. They ran, shoulder to shoulder, occasionally snapping at each other in a playful manner but otherwise content in each other's company. When excited, she would raise her black face into the air and howl and he always answered her call. There was the kind of affection between the two animals that Crafty had seen in newly-married people.

Beyond Willowmere they came to Gislam. There, the pack turned on its journey and headed west, slipping through the dark woods, which edged Wilford, and then on to Muttingham. Scattered copses were a more or less natural hunting ground for the wolves, and the yearlings snapped up several squirrels and mice as well as more rabbits. Crafty noticed, however, that they ignored the larger prey such as cows and sheep; sometimes the younger wolves seemed tempted and there was no doubt that the pack could have outrun any of the cows easily, but the leader would always bark and press on with their journey.

By the time they reached Muttingham, Crafty guessed that the pack had covered the best part of twenty miles and yet they showed no sign of exhaustion. They tended to ignore roads, preferring the shelter of hedges or woods. The trees were losing their leaves by now and many had become dark silhouettes against the dark sky. The night was intensely quiet. All movement was secretive, and there was an autumnal chill in the air. Crafty was excited but within him there grew sadness. The pack was aware of him and yet ignored him. He grasped, dimly, that if he were to fall only Brultzner would feel obliged to stop and urge him onward. He was of no importance to the wolves and, having been the centre of his own universe for so long, Crafty could not understand.

They regained the course of the Cassyn River, and the wolves were thirsty. They dipped their noses into the stream and drank noisily – slurping the water like dogs. Crafty felt that he could have done with a pint himself, and when Brultzner offered him a handful of the river water he lapped it up.

After the drink, as they headed south-east through Sottingfield towards Blacksands Ness and the sea, the wild chase took on a different tone. The leader became tense and was, suddenly, on a quest. Crafty could see this as he watched the thick, silver mane twisting and turning from side to side. The great wolf led them across a road and then, in one long leap, over a low fence bordered by a ditch. They were in parkland. The grass had been chewed close and they ran under carefully spaced oak and chestnut trees which gave shade to the grazing sheep. The pack ignored these, however – easy prey though they were – and raced towards a belt of woodland.

Suddenly, Crafty saw their prey. A herd of deer was feeding at the edge of the trees and the wolves ran straight for them. The herd bolted, easily outrunning the wolves, but one older deer – confused by the sudden onslaught – lingered, looking about wildly. The leader of the pack went for its throat. The deer, desperate for life, kicked out with its hooves and drove its antlers into the pack, which gathered around it, biting. The deer was large and strong – it tossed them around and stamped them into the ground, it broke their heads and ripped open their sides – but it was no match for a dozen wolves who were already tearing off chunks of its flesh, even as it fought. The bloody fight lasted only minutes, and when the old stag fell the wolves gorged themselves. Brultzner stood to one side, with Crafty, watching.

"They will save some of the meat for later, Mr Catchpole. Watch how they chew off large chunks, which they will take with them to hide. They head home now and will bury the remains of their kill as they go, probably by the river. Nothing is wasted in nature, Mr Catchpole. After we leave, other creatures will feed here – foxes will come and the crows will pick the bones clean before morning."

The wolves licked each other's wounds before they left the park, clearing the blood from their thick coats, and then made their way homeward, slowly, because all they wanted to do was sleep and rest; their stomachs were full. In this way, burying their caches of deer as they journeyed, the pack arrived at Blacksands Ness. The young wolves curled up on the sands and the leader's mate stretched out on her belly, while he trotted to the crest of a small rise, instinct warning him to keep watch. Crafty was less exhausted than the wolves because Horst Brultzner had propelled him along in the midst of the chase but was, nonetheless, glad of a rest and wished he had a pint of beer in his hand. Never mind, he thought, the madness of the night would soon be over, and he could escape his employer's clutches and return to the peace of his cottage where a drink would be waiting.

How long they rested at Blacksands Ness, he couldn't tell, but it seemed no time before Horst Brultzner stood behind him.

"You enjoyed our wild hunt, Mr Catchpole?"

"Oi can't say its sumthun oi'd want ter do evry noight, but it was OK as far as it went."

"I thought at one time that you had a certain affinity with the animals, Mr Catchpole."

"Oi dare say I do."

"What a pity it was that you decided to cross me."

"Oi can't roightly say that was my intention – oi jest warnted to breed faster pigeons."

"Why didn't you ask for my help instead of desecrating my home?"

"Oi weren't shewer we'd see oi to oi."

"One thing you can be sure of, Mr Catchpole, is that we do not see eye to eye now. It is bad enough that you helped the Gobley's to desecrate my home; it is even worse that you were in my service when you did so. There is nothing worse than an unfaithful servant."

His tone had remained steady throughout the conversation; the intense anger he felt at Crafty's betrayal showed only in his choice of words, not in the manner with which he delivered them. Crafty had stood when Brultzner approached, but remained looking away: now he turned to face his master. The yellow eyes did not flicker as Brultzner spoke:

"How long do you think it will take you to walk home from here?"

"About twenty minerts, oi'd say, so long as oi'd no wind in mer face."

"We'll give you fifteen, Mr Catchpole, so you had better – as they say – get a spurt on."

"Oi don't roightly see moi way clear as to your meanin'."

"It's quite simple, Mr Catchpole. We're going to hunt you down, but we will give you a sporting chance – how wonderful these English phrases are! – which is more than you gave me when you invaded my home."

"You're gonna send them wolves arter me?"

"You have it – in a nutshell. They're not hungry, of course, but – if they catch you – they'll bury your meat for another time. Normally, they wouldn't bother to hunt now, but they'll do it if I ask. Your fifteen minutes has started."

The terror Crafty felt filled his stomach and weakened his knees. He collapsed onto the beach and looked up, but Brultzner was already disappearing, enveloped in the elemental mist, which accompanied his shape-shifting; all that was left of him, in his human form, were the yellow eyes which burned like an old fire from the centre of the mist. This folded and twisted in upon itself, darkening and becoming as thick as smoke from a bonfire; within it, patterns of muscle emerged and limbs stretched in pain. The writhing was horrible to watch but, as his time ticked away, fear mingled with fascination rooted Crafty to the dune. Other than the yellow eyes, red was the only colour within the distorted mist – red blood coursing through veins, red muscle squirming into place, a red tongue lolling from a mouth full of those pure white teeth. Crafty shuddered as he gazed. Inside him was the belief, which he knew was hopeless, that Brultzner would change his mind, or that he could be 'warmed up' to Crafty's point of view like any other prospect. It was a big wolf that began to emerge from the mist; it had a grizzled coat with coarse hair, a jet-black face and silver mane. Crafty backed away as the claws flexed themselves and the great creature stood and stretched itself like a waking dog. The beast lifted its head and howled in ecstasy; its mouth was cavernous – large enough to swallow a man's leg in one gulp, thought Crafty – and the howling matched it in volume. The pack took up the cry and soon the 'call of the wild' echoed and re-echoed around the Ness; it stopped as suddenly as it had begun, and their eyes turned on Crafty who still had not moved. 'Ten minutes.' The voice spoke in his head, and he stumbled to his feet. He knew that it would be no use to plead; the eyes of the wolves were implacable, even quizzical. He was, to them, simply meat, and worth no more consideration than the deer they had just slain.

Crafty turned and ran. Looking back over his shoulder, he saw with a foolish relief that none of them had moved. Much as they, like dogs, loved the chase, the pack simply watched him run. Later, the wolves would pursue him, following his scent across the dunes and beach of his home village. 'Fight or flight?' He had no choice, but terrified as he was, with the lump gorging his stomach, Crafty began to think. Thought, now, was his only chance if the picture he had in his mind, that of a wolf running alongside him and leaping for his throat, was not to become reality. He turned and made his way towards the sea; he knew that water covered scent. He reached it quickly and, below the shingle line, he was running on wet sand. He looked back; they were still watching him, but soon he would be out of sight and Crafty planned to run inland, then, wasting precious time but gaining the protection of the salt-water lagoons. He would find a raft there – a rough contraption, knocked together from palettes, on which the local children played. He could then drift across the lagoon – quietly, he hoped – while the wolf pack searched the shore-line and ran on towards the village. If the worst came to the worst and they discovered him on the water, at least they would have to swim out to him and he would, striking at them from the raft, have a better chance than if he were running.

His plan worked well. He had already reached the centre of the lagoon when he heard the pack in pursuit. They yelped and barked their way along the tide-line, but Crafty's scent had vanished and the wet pebbles held no apparent trace of their quarry. The pack moved steadily along and reached the sluice but, finding no sign of him, they turned and re-traced their steps.

Crafty was tempted to stay; it seemed safe out there on the water. As the howling died on the distant beach, however, he decided to make his way home. He paddled the raft silently to the far side of the lagoon and slipped ashore. He was surrounded by gorse bushes, and felt impregnable. The shore of the small lake offered him a route to the River Cassyn, and Crafty took his chance.

He wanted to sleep, badly, and became aware of his body for, perhaps, the first time in years. He was not a man who reflected much about that kind of thing. He lived with an intensity of purpose (not unlike the wolves that now pursued him), focussed on whatever held his interest at that moment: general reflection about his person was not something in which he indulged. Now, fearing death as he did, his body suddenly held a morbid fascination for him. He watched his feet racing through the grass, felt his hands caught on the spiky gorse and became aware of his fingers gripping the heavy branch, which he'd grabbed as he pushed off with the raft. He remembered watching children playing fight games with such pieces of wood, pretending they were swords, and he had envied their carelessness. There was no pretence now: the gnarled, sea-whitened branch was a weapon.

He ran with the same pugnacity with which he'd lived. Crafty was surprised how fit he was, and how quickly he was able to cross the open ground between the lagoon and the river. He made first for the rough road, thinking this would not hold his scent as clearly as the earth. He ran along this for several yards, crouching low, and then slid quickly down the bank, between bushes of gorse, and listened. Some distance away he could hear the whimpering of the wolves. Occasionally one would snarl or yelp, excited by a new scent. They must be running about where he had left the shoreline, seeking his smell; soon they would find it and then arrive at the eastern edge of the lagoon.

Crafty had wondered whether he would find a small rowing boat in the river – the men from the water-board sometimes used one to examine that side of the sluice – but he was out of luck. Crafty almost lit a cigar at that moment. He wanted to chew on the end, draw in the smoke and 'see his way clear' but he resisted the urge and, instead, took off all but his pants and vests. With a quick glance over his shoulder, he slid into the Cassyn, holding his clothes at arms length above his body, and used his legs to scull himself across the river. Should they appear now, on the far bank, he would be seen and they would pour through the gate, which was the one gap across the Cassyn, and reach him; so Crafty scuttled up the bank onto the village side of the river and hid. He pulled off his wet underclothes, dressed quickly, wrung out the wet pants and vest, and was off towards the dunes that bordered the marsh. His main hope was to reach the caravan site. There would be no one there at this time of year, but there might be an unlocked door, a shed – any place in which he could find shelter.

The pack had lost his trail until one of them picked it up at the top of the beach and howled for the others. There was a moment of intense excitement, with all the wolves joining in a chorus of snarls and yelps, and then they followed his trail to the edge of the lagoon.

Brultzner ran with them. Having once been human himself, he could understand Crafty's reasoning and guessed that he had made for water. When he saw the raft on the opposite side, the vampire knew that Crafty had tricked them and would probably make for the river. He was a sporting man, however, and waited for the wolves to discover this for themselves. They split into two groups and each group sniffed its way along the edge of the lagoon in different directions.

The deer had satisfied their hunger, but now they had an appetite for the chase. Besides, the pack had a loyalty to Brultzner, who they saw as one of their kind, but wiser and more powerful. He had never tried to lead the pack, but they had always come to his bidding.

The lagoon was edged by small beaches at each end and reeds, through which the wolves could not go, along the western bank. Those who had made their way south now found their route blocked and wasted much time attempting to pick up the trail. They found the scent of many rabbits, which had a warren amongst the gorse that stretched from the reed beds to the edge of the farmland. They startled the occasional partridge and the younger wolves pursued these for the sheer delight of the chase. They sniffed more deer on the Wangford estate. They went to the fences, poked their heads through the rails, and watched the cows. These, however, were all distractions, and the older wolves called them back time and again.

The group who had made their way north reached the raft more quickly. They'd been confused only by the multiple scent of humans on the small, northern beach where the old pill-box shelter provided a playground for children. They spent some time running around this, in and over the shelter and then back to the beach itself, but the smell of Crafty Catchpole was not among the many trails and so they moved on until they came to the raft and there was the sign of their quarry! They howled again into the night; it was a howl of triumph and eagerness to be on the hunt.

Before the rest of the pack reached the raft, the jubilant ones were off and reached the river at the point where Crafty had swum across. Brultzner now saw Crafty's intentions clearly, and watched, with rising exasperation, as the pack once more split and scoured the southern bank of the Cassyn.

Crafty, like the wolves, was jubilant. He had not expected to reach the caravan site. Once within its boundaries, he paused. He had got so far. Could he get further? Could he actually get home? It was a familiar distance; he had cycled it often. He could cross the camp-site on the hard tracks, and then he would be on Beach Road, and the Seaview Café would be in sight.

The swim had cooled him; he was no longer sweating. His purpose had removed his anxiety – that terrible lump in his stomach, that horrific ache in his trembling legs had, for the moment, gone. Exhilaration swept through him. What a story he would have to tell when this was over! He decided to go for it and ran.

He dodged between the caravans until he reached the far side of the site, ran passed the communal block, where the pool tables were, and down to the hard promenade. He felt his heart pounding in his chest, as much as with the success that now seemed within his grasp as with the effort of running. His body was a series of knots of hard muscle; at that moment he could have joined Clint on the empty street of that western town and gunned down the marauding bandits.

At that moment, the wolves gave up their scrutiny of the river bank and prepared to disperse, but Brultzner had other ideas. The idea that Crafty Catchpole might escape the fate he had in mind for him angered the vampire. He lifted his head and howled, eyeing the leader of the pack who came towards him, head lowered. Grunts, snarls and yelps passed between them. The black wolf was confused but he knew it was the river that barred their way. Eventually he led the pack eastwards to the one point at which the Cassyn could be crossed, and the whole pack poured through or over the style. Their crying was frantic. The pack split again. Some ran towards the marsh, while others explored along the north bank of the river until they came to the point where Crafty had swum ashore and dressed. His scent was strong and they wasted no time, not even waiting for the rest of the pack to catch them up, before they dashed across the open ground towards the dunes and the caravan site, their noses to the ground. If only they could see their quarry – if only, but until then they had to rely on their sense of smell.

Crafty now had only the length of the promenade to run. The old Sea Sailing Clubhouse was to his left. Houses bordered the whole of his route, but these were holiday homes and there would be nobody to offer him shelter. He cast his eyes over the beach. 'Fire!' Was there anything there which he could burn? Wolves hated fire; they were terrified of it. You could keep wolves off with fire; he'd read that in a book. It had been a dry autumn so far; the abandoned and broken old fishing boats would burn, the tarred rope would light easily.

The first cohort of wolves – those which had picked up his scent on the north bank of the river – streamed through the gap from the caravan site. They set up a howling, which alerted their comrades that the prey was now in view, and tore after Crafty. He saw them, grabbed a coil or two of rope from one of the wrecks on the beach and scrambled on top of the winch shed. He was just in time. The first wolf snapped at his foot, biting off a lump from his heel and taking his shoe with it. Crafty screamed in pain, turned and brought the rough branch he carried down onto the creature's skull, which cracked. The wolf fell, stunned or dead, between the old fishing boat and the winch shed. Terror and exultation flowed through Crafty. He saw the vulnerability of his position, but was cheered by what he thought was his kill.

Crafty took a match from his pocket, lit a cigar and fired the tarred rope. Flames burst from it, immediately; the dry summer was on his side. Despite his fearful predicament, Crafty laughed and tossed the burning rope into the dead wood of the boat just as the second wolf leapt at the winch shed, its front paws scrabbling for a hold. For a second time, he brought the branch down, viciously, onto a wolf's skull and heard the crack; for a second time, a wolf dropped. He'd seen a film once where a trapper escaped from wolves, beating them off with his rifle butt. What was the film – *The Trap?* Was that it? Crafty lit another length of rope as the third wolf launched itself at him and swung the flaming weapon into the creature's thick mane. It squealed in agony, and raced off across the beach pursued by two of its comrades.

The remaining wolf from the first cohort circled the shed, wary of this prey, which fought back with such cunning. He had killed two of their pack, possibly three, and distracted two others from the kill. The rope burned in Crafty's hand; it would be of little use to him once it was charred to nothing, and so he tossed it at the wolf. It yelped angrily and drew back, as the burning rope struck and scorched its fur. Crafty lit his final piece of rope.

They could only attack him from three sides now because the boat was well alight on the fourth; that would give him a slight advantage, provided the flames did not catch the winch shed. Crafty began to feel successful. If only he could last out until daylight, he somehow felt that the pack would leave.

The second cohort appeared at that instant – they had come from the other direction, from the northern end of the promenade, from the direction of the Fishermen's Hut. They had intended to head him off! Crafty's heart sank again. Here was an intelligence, a communication through their infernal howling, which he had not anticipated. If they could plan to hunt like that, they could plan to bring him off the shed!

The burning wolf on the beach was still yelping in pain although by now it had reached the sea and doused the flames. Three down, but he was still faced by nine of the creatures. Crafty knew he had no place to run and dreaded the moment when more than one of the wolves would attack him at the same time.

They circled the shed, keeping well clear of the burning boat, and he could see that they were angling for a distance from which they could leap onto it without having to scramble up the side. He had been lucky with the first two; their hurried attack had been their downfall. The pack was calmer now and the circle of wolves around him was tightening. Crafty couldn't keep his eye on all of them, but by moving back to the far corner of the shed – the corner nearest the flames of the boat – he could watch those on the promenade and on one part of the beach. He knew that it would be from the promenade that the surest spring would come. It had to be – concrete would give them a firmer footing. The heat from the boat scorched his hair and he felt his back burning despite the thickness of his seaman's jacket. He wished it was over – one way or the other.

All the time, the huge grizzled wolf which was Brultzner had stayed back, watching events as they evolved. He had not expected having to contend with bodies. After the killing of Crafty, he anticipated that the pack would make its way back to the wildlife park, leaving no traces. The villager had surprised the vampire with his courage and resourcefulness. He was stupid and uneducated but had fought with a cunning and tenacity that Brultzner, once a soldier of Rome, could only admire. He had the power, the influence with the wolves, to save his unfaithful servant as a reward for having fought bravely; but forgiveness was not in Brultzner's nature and securing his own safety in the village was of paramount importance to him so he watched and did nothing in the closing phase of the wild hunt.

The pack leader lowered its head and yowled as a signal to one of the yearlings on Crafty's blind side. The young wolf leapt, almost taking Crafty off-guard, but he turned quickly, swung his last piece of rope up and under the wolf's belly while, at the same time, ramming his branch through its soft and exposed chin. The young wolf yelped, hung in the air for a second and collapsed backwards, singed and with its mouth injured. The assault knocked Crafty off-balance, however, and then the leader struck, bringing him down and tearing out his throat. As he lost consciousness, his body, coughing and spitting blood, was hauled from the winch shed and the pack was on him, ripping open his flesh and devouring the meat until he was no more than a stain and a few bones on the beach which – later that morning, before anyone was up – the seagulls picked clean.

Rebecca Unwood heard the night's news when she arrived home from work the next evening; a chorus of gossip had reached her father during the day and he poured it out to her in his study after dinner. She phoned Nadine Palmester immediately and learned that Simon was being detained in hospital. He could not explain what had happened to him, but Simon was sure that his memory would return. Rebecca also learned that he had agreed to stay in hospital only on condition that members of his congregation, led by Nadine, mounted the second night's vigil "with as many villagers as are willing to join you. You are not to stay in the chapel alone." Nadine agreed and had then contacted everyone she knew.

Corvin was eager to join the vigil and it was while he was discussing this with Rebecca that he told her of the escape of the wolves. They had, he said, "found only Crafty Catchpole's cloth cap with the piece of braid along the base of the peak and a few bones together with the bodies of two wolves" but "it doesn't, unfortunately, take much imagination to piece together this terrible tragedy". She also learned that the owners of the wildlife park were under enormous pressure to have the creatures put down but that Horst Brultzner had objected to this, strenuously.

The second night's vigil was uneventful; the Bethel had been ablaze with light – both electric and candle. During the night, people had come and gone as they pleased, although Mavis did not bring her girls to see their father's corpse again. Rebecca noticed that Horst Brultzner was among the congregation and decided to take a 'rest day' owed to her and visit him; it had been a long time since they talked.

She found him "pottering around his garden"; he was pruning an everlasting sweet pea which had climbed along the trunk of one of his silver birch trees. He took her hand and kissed it gallantly.

"Mr Catchpole will be missed my dear – though it is, perhaps, selfish of me to say so under such tragic circumstances."

"I understand you have spoken out against having the wolves put down."

"Naturally – they are animals; they have no evil in them. The papers are making much of their 'vicious nature'. I deplore this kind of sensationalism; do they think the creatures are going to 'huff and puff and blow our house in'?"

"Feelings and fears are running high."

"Possibly, but it was your kind who put them where they are and it is your kind who must shoulder the responsibility for what they do in, what is to them, an unnatural environment ... You will join me for coffee?"

"I'd love to."

Sarah Brown opened the door as they entered and gave Rebecca a smile as she curtsied. Rebecca looked at her; it was hard to believe that this beautiful young woman, who had suffered so much and struggled so hard to bring up her child decently, could have had anything to do with the death of Sidney Close. Horst waved Rebecca into the morning room. Their conversation glided smoothly and sadly around Sidney and Crafty, and Rebecca explained how her father would, in the absence of a body, arrange a memorial service for Mr Catchpole. Once Sarah had placed the coffee tray by her employer, however, Rebecca turned the conversation, quickly, to what was on her mind.

"Horst, I have come to ask for your help."

"You have only to ask," he said, opening his arms in a gesture of solicitude.

"What I am going to say will seem strange – impossible, unbelievable – but I want you to hear me out ..."

She looked away into the autumn garden, and then back to her host.

"Before he came to trust you and work for you, Peter was suspicious of you. Do you remember?"

"With pain in my heart, Rebecca."

"He said to me once that you were from the Old World and that things were different there, things we know nothing of in our cosy English villages. He had great faith in your knowledge of ... of the obscure ... I want to tell you what dad told me about Sidney Close ... about what Sidney Close told him ..."

"Please – you are troubled, and I have all the time in the world on my hands – and your Peter is right. I do know of things which have passed beyond the understanding of your modern man. If I can help ..."

He opened his arms again in a gesture of solicitude and Rebecca unburdened herself to him. Horst Brultzner listened without taking his eyes from her; she was not a stupid young woman, and yet she had made none of the connections that he feared as obvious. Her only suspicions resided with Sarah Brown and these could be easily remedied. When Rebecca had finished, he smiled and rang the bell. Sarah came into the room, curtsied as he had taught her and reached for the tray, but Brultzner stopped her with a gentle touch on the wrist.

"Miss Brown, may I ask if Mr Close was ever ... how shall we say? ... forward with you at any time. Miss Unwood has expressed some concerns."

He said no more, but Sarah sensed that he wanted an honest answer. He was, she knew, covering their tracks although she had no idea what suspicions Rebecca harboured. Her voice was steady, since deceit was second nature to her now.

"There was an incident, sir. I could see no purpose in making too much of it so I said nothing. May I ask why you have asked this now?"

"There has been some confusion over something, which I believe may have happened prior to Mr Close's accident. He was very muddled just before he died and expressed his confusion to the Reverend Unwood."

"I see," replied Sarah, "It was only a small thing. He made a pass at me when he came to the house one day. That is all ... it seems wrong to speak ill of the dead."

"Of course. Thank you, Miss Brown."

Sarah curtsied. Horst Brultzner turned to Rebecca.

"You will excuse my being so direct, but it seemed important that we understood what might have been in Mr Close's mind. He was a ... passionate man?"

"There were stories – innuendo, mainly."

"I understand. You can see, however, where his ... inclinations led him. Miss Brown has worked for me since her disappearance, following her tragic discovery about the perpetrator of her father's death. She is still in a delicate state, of course, but much better. I do not see how she could have become involved with Mr Close for she rarely leaves the house. Her whole life revolves around her son and her work."

"And the other matter?"

"Vampirism? Now there I may be able to help you, but I can scarcely believe that here, in twentieth century England, such things could exist. It is an old belief and comes out of the plague years in Europe when corpses – some dead, others dying – piled up in the streets. It is easy to understand how such beliefs came about, and our fascination with the dead has sustained them. A vampire, tradition tells us, comes about through suicide when the soul cannot rest but must forever hover in the world of the living, sustaining itself on blood. A black cat crossing the path of a corpse will also bring about the condition – if you can believe such a thing, Rebecca."

He paused and looked at her for a moment and then continued:

"The cure, of course, is well-known – a stake through the heart, or burning. If your father is truly worried about this, is there no chance that Mr Close could be cremated? Not – you understand – that I am suggesting there can be any truth in these worries, but might it not allow everyone to sleep easily in their beds?"

"It does seem silly. I suppose I just wanted you to put my mind at rest."

"Simply exposing Mr Close to the sun would be disastrous for him were he indeed a vampire."

"You're laughing at me."

"No, no – you are wrong. I do believe such creatures might exist. There are 'stranger things in heaven and earth' as they say ... Your friend had no interest in the occult?"

"I wouldn't think so – it's hardly Sidney," laughed Rebecca, "thanks, Horst – I'm sorry to have wasted your time."

"You have not wasted it – it was my pleasure and I hope I have put your mind at rest. You will be there again tonight – at the vigil?"

"Yes – it's the funeral tomorrow."

"Then I shall join you. I might ask Miss Brown to come with me. She was once a member of Mr Close's church, I believe?"

"Yes – her father, Clive, was people's warden."

"Then we shall add our prayers to those of his friends. In the meantime, Rebecca, do consider my suggestion regarding cremation – if only to put your father's mind at rest."

Horst saw Rebecca to the door and stood in the driveway waving her goodbye as she walked to the gate. Her visit had been a possible relief. If the fears of Sidney Close's community led them to cremate his body then everyone's worries would be over and life in Dunburgh-on-sea could return to normal: if not ... then he would have to find someone to take over Mr Catchpole's role.

Rebecca sat in her room, sending her daily e-mail to Peter Vishnya:

......I must say it took my breath away a bit when Horst asked her point blank, but Sarah didn't seem put out at all. She just said yes, Sidney had tried it on with her when he came to the Old Vicarage. It didn't come as too much of a surprise, really. I had heard one or two whispers that he was a bit free with his hands. Anyway, it explains his obsession with her and why he went on as he did with dad.

There were fewer people at this last vigil. I suppose the novelty has worn off and it isn't everybody who can stay up all night, but Horst was there and Sarah, as well as Nadine and Tony Crewes. Several of the old boys came along too, including Harry Bailey with who Sidney had some kind of tussle. Dad said the prayers and we sang. I think we all enjoyed it in a strange sort of way.

They are going to give Crafty a memorial service. There is nothing much left to bury. Hasn't it been awful - so many deaths in the village? Can you imagine what it would be like to be eaten by wolves! Sometime ago I read an article about fox-hunting, and one man described the fox – at the end, when they killed him – as a 'piece of living string'. It must have been like that for poor Crafty.

Nadine said that Simon was awake and taking nourishment, but could remember very little. He kept repeating some Latin quotation which Tony Crewes seemed to understand, and Simon had what Nadine said he called the mark of the Devil' on his throat. When they got him home from the chapel – before he went to hospital – he burnt it off with a red-hot ember. It's very puzzling. Whatever happened in that chapel must have scared Simon silly and you know how tough his religion is!

Did I say – dad is taking both services tomorrow. Mum has had nothing to do with the vigil. She didn't approve of Simon holding it in the Bethel – thought he was upstaging dad!

Anyway, I'm almost asleep now and I love you very much so I'm going to bed with your picture under my pillow.

CHAPTER 7

'Death is the path to life'

Tony Crewes had been more than puzzled by Simon's ravings about a "white bull". As a young man he had read widely and, when Beth and his children permitted, he still did. He knew the part bulls played in many old religions but none of these, as far as he knew, had anything to do with vampires. He was sure, however, that white cattle were bred in the area. He had heard some tales about a prime herd on the Wangford estate. On the Saturday morning following the funerals, he slipped quietly out of bed and went for a walk. Beth stirred slightly, but she was a heavy sleeper and he was able to dress without disturbing her. He left a note, saying simply that he had fancied a quiet walk, on the kitchen worktop.

He followed the shoreline, dodging the waves as they rippled on the beach, until he came to Blacksands Ness. He made his way inland. Tony enjoyed the autumn; it always seemed such a restful time of the year. After the hectic rush of summer, everything – and everyone – was settling down: people to work, nature to rest. There was a drawing-in of energies as the world made ready for winter. If you were tired – and he was tired of just about everything – this was the time to recuperate. He passed through the gorse, which stretched from the lagoons. Some of the bushes still sported their yellow blossoms but most had settled for green. The horse-chestnuts were already bare of leaves, and the silver birches were close behind. He pushed his way through bracken, sliding the leaves between his fingers. It was damp underfoot but pleasantly so, and he pranced about, leaping from tussock to tussock as he made his way, along footpaths of his own devising, onto the Wangford estate.

Sheep still grazed on the parkland, which was lush, and Tony paused to gaze at them. He wasn't sentimental and realized that they were only there to be eaten, but couldn't help admiring their tranquillity as they ignored him and concentrated on their feeding. Once or twice he had wondered about becoming a vegetarian, but custom and need helped him to shrug off the thought. Beyond the sheep he came across a herd of rich-brown cows that paused to eye him in the way that cows do, but never paused in their chewing. Tony felt at peace with the world, despite knowing that – when he arrived home – Beth would wonder where he had been, would not believe his answers and had really expected that he might wait for her and the children. It would be impossible to explain that had he done so his walk would never have happened.

Everything was slightly damp at that time of the morning – gates, fence-posts, tree trunks, leaves and water troughs. The damp suited him, as did the low-lying mist that shrouded the parkland. There was little wildlife about as yet, but he met one fox – a large, scrawny, beast – returning to its den. Occasionally, an early finch or hedge sparrow would shoot across his path. He could see Wangford Hall to his right, rising above a copse of trees; to his left, the sea was now a distant hiss on the shore. Tony slowed his walk, out of respect for the fact that he was trespassing and because he sensed he was near his quarry. He entered a belt of trees that skirted a large field.

The mist still hung low on the meadows. Through it, across the parkland, on a slope that ran down to the Cassyn River, he saw the first of the white cattle, moving like ghosts under the oak trees. They seemed proud animals, and looked up almost disdainfully as he approached from the trees. Beyond them, near the far rail of the field, he saw people moving – a man and a boy. They worked in such harmony that Tony surmised they were father and son. They seemed to be feeding the animals, but Tony could not understand why; there was plenty of natural grass.

Standing and watching, he suddenly became aware that he didn't really know why he had come. If he found a white bull what would it prove – that there was somehow a link between what had happened to Simon Palmester and the local aristocrat, Lord Wangford? If that were so, would Charles Wangford be able to throw any light into the darkness? 'Nothing ventured, nothing gained.' Tony Crewes walked along the edge of the belt of trees and joined the shingle track that wound its way beside the field along the rise of the hill. As he approached, the man and boy looked up; it was the man who spoke.

"Morning, sir," he said, "Is there anything we can do for you?"

"I came to see the white bull."

"And what makes you think we have such a beast here?"

"This is an unusual herd. You must have a bull among these cows."

"We did, sir, but he's passed on, shall we say. The new leader of the herd has yet to emerge. They are only young bulls at present."

"The bull died?"

"Yes, sir."

"I'm sorry to hear that; it must have been a magnificent animal."

"Yes, sir – a god among cattle."

"You are the herdsman?"

"Yes, sir – John Stokes by name, and this is my son, David, who will one day, God willing, take over from me."

"Hello – John, hello David. My name is Tony – Tony Crewes."

"We're pleased to meet you, sir, however unexpected the pleasure."

"I know I'm trespassing, but I did come in on the public footpath. I just couldn't resist having a look at these cattle."

"I'm sure his lordship won't mind, sir."

"Are these the only white cattle of their kind in the country?"

"Oh no, sir, that would never do – you'd have too much in-breeding. We regularly exchange cattle with other breeders."

"I thought so. I saw a herd like this once ... only I can't remember where; we were on holiday, I think."

"Ask your wife, sir. She's sure to know."

There was no sarcasm in the advice such as there would have been if Tony Crewes had offered it. He smiled.

"Yes," he said, "they tend to be hot on details, don't they?"

While they were talking, the boy – who, Tony thought, seemed agitated – had wandered off. He strolled into the field among the cattle, and then down to the far side where Tony had walked from the trees. When John Stokes proffered his hand and turned to leave, he called to the boy who answered.

"I'll be there in a minute, dad."

"As I say, sir, his lordship will be only too pleased to answer your questions, I'm sure, but I must be off. Tell my boy to hurry along when he gets here, will you?"

Both men laughed as they watched the boy dawdling towards them along the side of the fence. John Stokes strode off towards the main hall. When he had gone, the boy's pace quickened, and he was at Tony's side in seconds.

"I saw what happened to the white bull," he said, excitedly, "They killed him."

"Who?"

"They were thirty of them – thirty one. I saw them do it."

"Does your dad know about this?"

"Yes – but dad wasn't one of them. He loved the bull – like me."

"Tell me about it."

"I can't now – there isn't time. I walk the dog at night – before it gets dark. Can you be at the Ness about half-past four?"

"Of course – but you'd better ask your dad first."

"Dad is faithful to his lordship. He wouldn't want me to tell you."

"Then why are you?"

"I loved the bull. He never harmed no one."

With that, David Stokes ran after his father along the top of the field. Tony Crewes watched him and wondered what it was that would goad a child into betraying the father who he clearly loved.

Rebecca Unwood read over Peter Vishnya's e-mail yet again:

.... *Horst was right about vampires and plague: in Greek the word for them is 'nosophoros' which literally means 'plague-carrier'. You find versions of them in all mythologies, but they are most common among the Slavonic peoples from whom we get the word 'nosufur-atu'. You see the connection with the Greek? This has become 'nosferatu' and we use it to mean the same as vampire, but this may not be the case; the creature changes from country to country. It is generally accepted, among those who study these things, that the stories were carried by gypsies travelling north from India where they have a number of bloodthirsty gods such as Kali. The stories get picked up and changed to fit local customs.*

If you dig back into the records of your own village, you will find some 'evidence' of such things. My wife was a Morling – you remember? Her father, who was born in 1916, acted as a local reporter for the Lowestoft Journal and he was a mine of information about Dunburgh. His own father had been born in the 1880s and his grandfather about 1850. The grandfather's memories – through his own parents – went back almost to the beginning of the nineteenth century. You see why I am fascinated by your history?

Well, around 1815, Dunburgh had what amounted to a lifeboat. There are treacherous sands off Dunburgh – the Barnard and the Newcome to name but two – and ships were often driven onto these. On this occasion, a ship carrying salt from Liverpool to Rotterdam sprang a leak and after fifteen hours toil at the pumps the crew of seven had to admit defeat. There was an easterly wind blowing and the ship was driven onto the Newcome Sands in very heavy surf. The villagers had been watching the vessel's struggles and they dragged the lifeboat down the beach – men, woman and children! Can you imagine? Someone had already brought the mortar from Lowestoft and this was carried out towards the stricken ship.

The wind was from the east and blowing strongly so they fired the mortar when they were as near as they could go. The crew of the cargo ship had already lashed themselves to the bowsprit, and the shot and line from the mortar fell in the midst of them. They fastened themselves to this, about six feet from each other, and dropped into the sea one by one. It must have been horrendous. They were constantly bobbing up and down in the swell, sometimes completely out of sight from the shore, but all seven were, eventually, hauled safely into the lifeboat: all that is except the captain who had taken shelter in the shrouds. A second mortar was fired for him and the rope fell onto the very yard of the ship where he was standing but, for whatever reason, he seemed reluctant to take it. There was anguish on all faces – the captain himself and those who seemed doomed not to save him. They fired a third shot but, at that moment, the masts gave way and the captain was sucked down in the midst of the wreck.

The mariners were billeted with local families for a while and that very night, as one of them sat down to supper with his hosts, the captain appeared at the table and asked for food. He was given a bowl of stew and disappeared. You can imagine the alarm among the family who had befriended the sailor! The next day, the mariner told his shipmates what had happened and each told the same story; the captain had come to each house and demanded food. He left once he had been fed.

The next night the captain appeared again and demanded food; this was repeated on the third night. There was a feeling that he should be refused: at which he nodded to each mariner in turn in each of the seven houses he visited. Over the next week all seven seamen were found dead in their beds, one after the other on successive mornings.

The funerals took place one after the other and, within three days of each burial, each mariner appeared to the family who had given him bed and board. The ritual of the visits was always the same – always the men appeared at meal times and, within three days of their first visit, a member of the household died. The situation deteriorated rapidly. Night after night in the village there was clamouring and uproar as the seamen struck villagers down, seized them by the throat and squeezed their stomachs until they nearly suffocated. The people of Dunburgh were in a pitiable state: bruised all over, pale, thin and exhausted. They would be found in the morning – hot, sweating, gasping for breath and covered with lather.

There was a young soldier in the village at the time – home on leave from the Canadian War against the Americans and courting one of the local girls – and he decided to take a hand in this business by waylaying the captain who was still appearing in the village at night. He apprehended him on the beach and drove a wooden stake through his body with the help of a gang of frightened villagers, but the captain only laughed at them and set about beating each of them round the head with the stake. The soldier was undaunted. Fresh from the Battle of the Queenston Heights, he forced the captain onto a cart and held him down, while the cart was wheeled out of the village to the place known as Black Clump. There they drove more stakes through the man, who "shrieked and waved his arms and legs", and burned his body.

They returned to the village the next morning and disinterred the corpses of the seven mariners. The bodies were flushed, the limbs soft and pliable, their blood was still fresh, in some cases their eyes were open, in others the respiration was normal and others cried out as their bodies were pulled from the grave. A great fire was built and the corpses all reduced to ashes.

Peace returned to the village and the young soldier, whose intervention had removed months of terror and hardship, was hailed as a hero, but his fame was short-lived. Within a week of the terrible conflagration he was sentenced to five hundred lashes for being found drunk on duty at the local garrison. It was, of course, a death sentence. The villagers were outraged at his treatment and the local vicar offered a plot in the churchyard. He is buried in the old graveyard and his headstone bears the inscription 'Death is the path to life'.

You can see the muddle of history here, Rebecca. Did those seamen bring some fatal illness ashore with them when the villagers undertook their rescue? It certainly wasn't 'the plague', as we know it, but it could have been a similar disease. Burning of corpses was common in such cases; it was the only way to wipe out the infection. Were the bodies actually dead when they were buried – who knows? Was the 'appearance' of the drowned captain a later embellishment? How strange, too, that the young soldier's life should be ended so brutally. Flogging was common enough in the army, but five hundred lashes for being drunk? Anyway, are the stories actually connected or three separate strands woven into one by the memories of those concerned?

Rebecca felt exhausted by the account: exhausted and demoralized. It was easy to forget that the world – not so long ago, in the time of her great-great-grandfather – was so uncivilized. Each day you walked through the village, each day you believed that the world was a better place, and then something brings it home to you that just under the surface lurk behaviour and forces that threaten your existence.

Corvin Unwood stood by the grave of the man he had buried and wondered. He had visited Simon Palmester in hospital, 'two old rivals chin-wagging together', and the Bethel priest had been grateful. Corvin recalled their conversation.

"'There are evil forces at work in the village, Corvin. The duty of care we have for our people is being tested."

"Sidney Close now lies within his grave – at peace with God."

"Stop evading what faces us. Stop trying to calm things down. This is a time for rousing men to action – not tucking them up in bed. My memories are fitful and broken, but we can piece them together with the Lord's help."

"No memory has returned to you?"

"Some – I told Nadine about a white bull, and I have this image of a figure kneeling against the pew and I am filled with a dreadful sadness. I have to destroy the figure, and it seems to be a child, and there is an appalling smell in the chapel ..."

"And was this figure Sidney Close?"

"I wish I knew. Keep your eye on the grave, Corvin, and keep your Bible and your cross in your hands.'"

Corvin felt like a soldier awaiting battle, or thought he did. Men of Corvin's generation had never faced mortal conflict – that had been the lot of their fathers and some of their sons. The feeling, though, focussed his mind and defined his purpose. He feared the tongues of women, but he did not fear spiritual evil; the Devil gave you something to fight. If you lost, then God would stretch out his hand; if you won, you could go home to a quiet tea.

He realised that he had already stopped sharing his thoughts with Esther. He wondered whether it was worth confiding in Martin Billings as the cowardly Junket had suggested. He had no doubt that phoning the bishop would be an absolute waste of time. There was, of course, Alan Read; he was sensible and open-minded. Rebecca must be kept away from whatever happened if for no other reason than that she was friendly with Horst Brultzner. Corvin was shocked by his own stray thought. Brultzner could not possibly be involved. He was a man of standing in his own right and on first name terms with the aristocracy and the church: both Lord Wangford and Bishop Twiddle stood in awe of him.

'She comes each night ...She kneels by my side or sits on the edge of the bed and when she's finished she leans over me and sinks her teeth into my body ... sucks the life from me ... I'm left ... mortified.' Sidney's words kept returning to haunt him. Sarah Brown was involved. Her liaison with Sidney Close was more than sexual, more than simple lust: it had all the corruption of the vampire. There he'd said it! Mustn't Brultzner also be involved; how could it be otherwise?

Sidney Close stirred, not knowing himself. Around him there was nothing; he could see the nothing. Nothing was a red silk cloth, red as blood, soft as a woman's skin. He wondered where he was – awake and so alert, so alive to the world and so hungry; he needed sustenance. Never before had he experienced this awful gnawing sensation in his stomach. He could scarcely breathe here, but that did not matter. Confined as he was, Sidney felt unrestricted. He saw himself rising to earth, a thin vapour of potent mist rising up through the soil to the world above.

Tony Crewes looked at his watch. It was almost five-thirty and the sun would soon be gone. He decided he must wait until dark was almost upon him and then accept that the boy wouldn't come after all. He didn't blame him; in fact, he rather admired the boy's loyalty, but it was frustrating to have arrived at what might have been an answer to his question.

"Mister?"

David Stokes was within a few feet of him and Tony was startled by his sudden appearance. Lolloping beside him was the family dog: a black Labrador. It ran up to Tony and licked the hand he proffered.

"Sorry Mister. I didn't mean to startle you."

"It's all right."

"My mum's always saying not to creep up on people."

"I used to do it. Boys will be boys!" said Tony, uneasily. He didn't know how he would account to the boy's father for being here if he should come upon them. "Are you sure you want to tell me this, son? I wouldn't want you being disloyal to your dad."

"I don't know what else to do. Dad was as upset as I was about the bull. He didn't say so. He just said 'That's not for us to ask' and 'It's not in every lifetime we see this' but he didn't mean it."

"So your dad would want you to tell me?"

Tony wondered why he was being so scrupulous; the boy was willing to speak so why didn't he just listen?

"Do you want me to tell you or not, Mister?"

"My name is Tony, and yes I do want you to tell me."

David told his story well and, long before he reached the moment of the slaying, Tony's mind was dancing with the weird figures of the ritual.

"I couldn't see any colours – it was moonlight ... Last in the procession ..."

The boy's voice tailed off, and then he seemed to collect himself. "... was his lordship. I could tell by his round shoulders. He was dressed like the first one, the one who killed the bull, but he carried a flat dish and a long staff."

Tony looked at the boy with tears in his heart. He knew the child would see that awful procession until his dying day – the thirty one figures silhouetted on the slope against the night sky.

"Afterwards they all moved forward in a circle around the ... bull."

"Yes ... I'm sorry, son."

"Will you do something, Mister?"

"Tony."

"Will you do something, Tony?"

"Yes – but I'm not sure what. There's a bit more to all this than the ... things you saw. In fact, what you have told me just deepens the mystery. I'll have to think about it ... and get back to you ... I shouldn't tell anyone – even your dad – that you've told me this."

"There is something else ... Tony."

"Go on."

"There's a place ... on the estate ... that they go to."

"A place?"

"No one ever goes in there – not even dad."

"But you know where it is?"

"Yes – but I don't know where the key is. His lordship must have it."

"You've done enough, son. Leave this to me now. Don't try and find out where that key is."

"Are you sure, Tony? I don't mind."

"I do. I'm not sure what's going on yet and there is no sense in you getting yourself into trouble. If I need your help again, I'll get in touch. OK?"

"OK."

Tony wasn't sure whether the boy guessed his insincerity. Naturally, he wanted the key and the boy was the obvious one to get it.

Horst Brultzner had been in a quandary. He'd had no choice but to dispense with Catchpole; the man knew too much and was not loyal. The killing, however, had left him – at this critical moment – with no one to deal with Close. It had seemed straightforward enough, even after the Bethel priest's meddling on that first night. The possibility of cremation had raised its head but he had been thwarted. Then the village continued the vigil, making any further action impossible before the funeral.

He had known Close would rise from his grave tonight and Brultzner could not have him loose in the village; at the same time he did not want to take him under his wing. The woman was one thing; women were always biddable. Male vampires, however, were far more likely to rampage. The sexual urge was always there, heightened by their new-found powers, and men of Close's disposition never failed to take full advantage of the change.

So he had come to the graveside just before dusk and performed a little ritual with four Christian crosses, which were all he could obtain in a hurry. He would have preferred some garlic flowers and a young rowan tree with its red berries. However, the ritual was complete and would hold Close until he had time to find a new gardener. Then, they would come, raise the coffin and destroy the vampire within – or, at least, Catchpole's replacement would; Brultzner never broke the age-old lore.

As he left the churchyard, however, a figure emerged from the shadows. Rollie was ever-watchful, his mother's crucifix in one hand and a camera in the other. He hadn't come every night since the Turrel boy's funeral, but he always came after a fresh burial. Now he had acquired holy water and communion wafers to add to his weaponry. His role as altar boy had its advantages, and he was engaged upon a Holy War.

Rollie was puzzled by Brultzner's little ritual. He had seen nothing like it in any book he had read, film he had seen or game he had played. Even in the film with all the bats, where the old man had drawn that circle with chalk on the floorboards, it hadn't been like this. He'd often wondered about the German, but he handled the crosses with no bother at all. Rollie thought he might a vampire-hunter. He had simply buried one at each end of the grave and one at each side, muttering some foreign phrases as he did so. He'd done it all very exactly, but there'd been no pentagons or signs of the zodiac.

Rollie waited until Brultzner had left the churchyard and then made his way to the grave. Gingerly he reached out for the last cross which Brultzner had placed – the one to the left of the grave – and removed it. The sacred symbol came easily into his hand. Emboldened, Rollie removed the second cross and then the other two with increasing confidence. Nothing stirred but a faint mist above the grave, and he retreated to the shelter of a yew tree and waited.

Corvin sat and listened to all his daughter had to tell him. She had printed off her fiancé's e-mail and he had read that through at least twice. He wanted this whole, horrible business to be done with; he wanted tomorrow's sun to rise on a happy world. Where now was his "spirit-filled, caring community of love"? He heard his own conscience; he heard Simon's insistent voice.

Sidney felt his chains snap as Rollie removed the crosses, one by one. He felt the power surge through his muscles as it had done when he first woke, before the muttering and the awful burden on his heart and chest. It was dark, inky black, but he could see in the dark, he could see the red cloth of … his coffin. Terror overcame him; he screamed and then grew calm. He felt purposeful and vicious; he needed to feed. The calmer he became, the more he felt at one with himself. His body relaxed, a thousand worries drained from his head and his body seemed lighter, light enough to drift upwards. So he passed through the soil of his burial and was once again on the pathway of the churchyard.

Sidney shuddered and looked about him. He had often dreamed of Heaven, dreamed of what it would be like when the corporeal body was cast away forever, when that awful sack of lust and perverted desires fell at last from his shoulders. This wasn't Heaven; he knew that, but it was a … state of freedom. Behind him, down there in the dark earth, was home. He could return there whenever danger threatened.

He looked at himself. Why was he dressed in the robes of a priest or a chorister? Where were his clothes? Home – they were at home. Sidney looked about him; there was nobody watching that he could see, and yet he sensed a presence. He ignored it – ignored Rollie, who crouched behind one of the large, old gravestones, too frightened to take his photograph. He'd let the genie out of the bottle and now it was free in the world.

Sidney moved quietly, surprised at the ease with which he glided across the churchyard. Vague memories stirred within him as he moved. He recalled the pulpit in the Bethel from where he looked down on … on Simon Palmester. The Bethel priest had hurt him, sent him flying backwards into one of those … those pews. He did not struggle to recall anymore. There was pain there – pain unimaginable and a separation that was almost unbearable. If he was to survive this, he had to … to harden. He needed resolve and … ruthlessness.

He had walked this way many times before, making his way home to … to … in the brushed-nylon nightdress; he hated that brushed-nylon nightdress. Tonight he walked in the shadows. No one seemed to notice him. He was there one minute, and ahead the next. A group of teenagers passed him as he stood by the allotment gates. They were all tarts these days – teenage girls. He had tried to keep ... to keep ... to keep ... He couldn't finish the sentence. He had two girls once. They had been growing into the teenage years; he didn't want them lured into marriage with the ... with the likes of Shane Marjoram. He'd tighten the religious coils around them ...

Sidney stood in front of his house. The lights were still on; he could hear voices. He swept to the back door, along the side of the house. His hand was on the latch, but the door wouldn't move. He couldn't get into his own house!

"Dad – come in, dad."

"What is it, Wendy?"

"I thought I saw dad at the door."

Mavis opened the door and looked across the patio at the barbecue where Sid had so often stood; the men always cooked at barbecues. She didn't see him. Sidney was just one of the shadows of the autumn night.

"You're imagining things."

Mavis put her arms round Sid's eldest daughter and hugged her. There were tears in the eyes of his three women. It was at that precise moment Sidney realised the gulf between him and all humanity. He knew that he was unable to reach out and comfort his own family. They either wouldn't see him, or they would be terrified of him. He didn't understand how he knew this – realisation, and the gathering of his memories would take time – but he understood, with a dreadful clarity, that he was in, and of, another world. 'In the world, but not of the world.' He didn't understand what he was, but he knew that he was no longer human – not in the ordinary sense of that word.

He waited until they had closed the door, and turned to leave his home forever. It was then he noticed that the upstairs window was open – Mavis had always been one for fresh air – and he remembered why he had come. He needed a change of clothes. Sidney didn't think about how to get to the window: it simply happened. While his mind was juggling with the problems of using the water-butt to reach the eave-board, his body had left the ground and was crouching on the ridge. The window was only partly open, but he slipped in easily and stood by his wardrobe. He could still hear the women talking below. Quickly, he pulled off the clerical robes and found himself clothes to wear – a check shirt, jeans, builder's boots and ... where was his leather jacket? 'The floor of the chapel; it was lying on the floor of the chapel and Sly Palmester was watching me!' Damn it! He'd particularly liked that jacket – It had an animal quality about it – but the brown suede one would have to do for the time being.

His first evening, resurrected Un-dead, was a joyous one. Like Sarah before him, he learned quickly. The hunger was gnawing at him. He drifted by the Jolly Sailors. A group of teenagers staggered out – half cut and giggling inanely.

Sidney followed them home, a shadow in their wake. The girls were the tartiest he'd seen: a real bunch of slags – jeans just above their fannies, tits pushing out of their jackets. 'And they wonder why women get raped!' He picked out a buxom blonde who he thought would struggle nicely in his grip. He watched her kiss her boyfriend goodnight, grinding her pubic bone into the grotty little tyke in that squirming way they do, their mouths going round and round as though they were winding up a clock: then he followed her home. She became aware of him as she turned into her driveway. No doubt her mum was waiting up for her, but Sidney knew how quietly it could be done. She gasped when he approached her and looked startled, but only for a moment. 'As soon as these little tarts think someone fancies them, they wet themselves.' After the fear, came that 'bedroom eyes look'; she was still apprehensive, close to home as she was, but something in his eyes was reassuring.

"What do you want," she said, reaching automatically for her rape alarm.

He took the front of her denim jacket in his hands and ripped it open. The bra came with it and Sidney was down into her breasts, sniffing her like a hungry wolf, and then sinking his teeth into her throat. He 'came' as he sucked. The girl gave the kind of sigh he'd heard in certain films he'd watched late at night after Mavis had gone to bed. The girl gripped his head with her hands and pressed him onto her, stretching back her throat. When he'd finished, she went limp, and Sidney lifted her up and she was no weight at all, such was his strength. The girl's arms went round his neck and she kissed him full on the lips. Sidney had never been kissed like that – ever. He had dreamed about it, been hungry for it, but this was the first time it had happened in his life, in all his forty years.

He left her on her doorstep and ran off like an adolescent boy: his was the power, his was the glory! The sense of release in Sidney was enormous; every trace of tension left his muscles. He felt that he'd had his first kiss, and knew she was waiting with more when he returned. His vanity told him that this was him – the real Sidney Close. His instinct told him that this new power over women, this ability to have them desire him and clamour for him, was due to something else altogether – the changes through which he had passed. He was to learn quickly that the vampire's quarry rarely complained. They might, afterwards, live in a state of tremulous fear, but they were always waiting.

He raced quickly round the village, seeing in the dark for the first time. His pleasure was vigorous. He leaped five-bar gates like a young man, he turned a car – which he thought badly parked – onto its side, he jumped up and over the low-lying autumn mist as though vaulting a wooden-horse and he crashed down into puddles – boot heels first. He was in love with the world again as he had been when a young man. In the churchyard, he took hold of an old tombstone and wrenched it from the ground. Like Sarah before him, he eyed the bell tower and floated upwards towards the night sky. He pulled out the wooden slats and slid in. He rang the bell – the largest bell – with the yank of a single hand, and then leaped from the top of the tower, reaching the ground before the peals died on the night air. No one would see him; he was invincible. His mind was clearing with all the activity. Someone had done this to him; he needed to know who it was who had bestowed these gifts.

He looked around the graveyard. It had been a fearful place in the past, best avoided at night. The yew trees cast darkness over the gravestones so that, even with a full moon, they were always in shadow. The hedges that bordered the churchyard were alive with creatures he had never seen before. Even the headstones told their own spooky stories. 'At rest. At peace.' How did they know that? The graves had always seemed so still before; it was that and the unearthly silence that was so frightening. Shadows lurked rather than hung, however pale the moon. The stone decorations on the older tombs seemed more demonic than angelic; they were always watching with their sightless eyes. Sidney could see them clearly. He could even see the glistening trails of slime left by the snails of the night. He smelled the earth, and the aroma of a freshly dug grave was sheer gratification. All around him were corpses – creatures who had embarked upon their final quest for happiness. The silent churchyard was thronging with sound. He heard birds shake their feathers, spiders spinning their webs, field mice snuffling through the rank grass around the stones and the flap-flap of an owl watching them.

Here was nature and he was part of its eternal cycle of life and death. This was the adventure he had craved. This was his journeying forth on a ... noble (he paused at the word) cause; legends and knights and maidens jostled for dominance in his mind. The graveyard was his home. 'Death where is thy sting-a-ling-a-ling, or grave thy victory?' He heard the voice of Tony Crewes singing the words facetiously. The clever dick had heard it somewhere – in a play or a song – and thought it funny. Blasphemy was nothing to a man like Crewes, but now Sidney had these superhuman powers he would have his day with Tony Crewes.

He couldn't sleep. He was too full of ... life. Was that the word? He would sally forth and find another woman – nubile and fresh. He fancied a young one tonight, and he had one or two in mind. Everything was taking on a new meaning!

CHAPTER 8

Cowardice

Necker Utting waited with her usual feigned impatience until Rollie joined her; she liked bossing people about, and making them feel ill-at-ease was one of the techniques she had imbibed at her mother's breast.

She was the most important person in her world (but liked to be seen giving her services freely) and adopted, habitually, a martyred expression of face and tone of voice. She helped with the Cub Scouts, didn't she (although the boys would have preferred otherwise) and her nickname had been bestowed due to her obsession with their neckerchiefs.

Apart from her work for the undertaker, how she made her living wasn't apparent; she seemed to be everywhere and nowhere, doing everything and doing nothing. It was quite clear to her that the village would come to a grinding halt without her services; it was equally clear to the village that she was, simply, a nosey-parker. Her presence at everything was an absolute necessity; her presence at anything was tiresome – indeed, she had been the reason for the resignation of two Cub Scout leaders. Necker was not aware of this; she would have been hurt had she known. The District Commissioner had wrung his hands on several occasions but couldn't bring himself to broach the problem with Necker. "Her heart," he always said, "is in the right place."

She was more chapel than church, but never missed a fete at either. Simon Palmester took the line that she was "half-witted but typically silly Suffolk" and treated her accordingly. She got on well with Simon because Necker liked to know where she stood and realised, from his avuncular manner, that he both liked her and appreciated her contribution. Corvin Unwood was more charitable; there was no way that he could look upon another human being in such dismissive terms, and so he tried to avoid any confrontation. In doing so, he appeared to be avoiding Necker herself, and so they didn't get on at all because, as Necker complained, "you don't feel valued".

She liked to be out and about early in the village, just in case she missed anything, and the morning after Sidney's funeral found her wandering up Church Hill for no real reason. It's true she carried a letter in one hand and a shopping bag in the other, but these were simply to give her an excuse for being out and about. Necker knew, more or less, the time everyone left their beds in the morning – especially at this time of the year – when it was still dark at half-past six.

The mist had been sliding down the bank from Podd's Field and had crept across the road, winding itself about her feet. It hung in layers over the field itself and the church seemed to rise from it. The sun was coming up over the sea behind her and cast an orange glow through the mist. Under her feet, the damp leaves clung together, providing a soft carpet on the footpath. She was making her way towards Market Place where Totto Briggs had his shop and slaughter house on the corner. Some new people had moved into one of the cottages there recently and rumour had it that they worked in London: Necker wondered how they travelled back and forth to work each day.

As she had passed the church, a figure emerged from the graveyard: it was Rollie. He was twitching about looking over his shoulder; he was in a state of uncontrollable excitement, not to say fear. Necker smelt news in the air

"Whut on 'arth a' yew doin' out here at this toime o' the mornin'? You'll ketch yer death o' cold."

Rollie hated her. Despite all her kindness to him, Rollie just wished that she would go away. She'd straightened his 'necker' too many times for there to be any chance of reconciliation. When he found her that morning after Sidney Close's funeral, however, he was relieved. Rollie just had to tell someone and his mother would simply have boxed his ears.

"I saw his ghost."

"Yew whut?"

"I saw him – Sidney Close – he was out and about in the village last night. He's back in his coffin, now."

"Yew wanna wotch whut yorer sayin', boy, sayin' things loike thet. You'll be gettin' yourself in trouble."

"I tell yer, I saw him."

They were both hooked now – Necker because of something she'd been thinking about ever since she'd laid out Shane Marjoram, Rollie because he wished he'd kept it to himself – knowledge was power: share it and you lost it.

"Go on," she said.

She was remorseless; he'd known she would be, just like his mother – on and on until they'd wormed everything out of you.

"Come with me?"

"Whut? I ent goin' in there," she said, as Rollie nodded to the graveyard.

"Then I ent goin' to tell you."

Rollie was learning her cunning ways, and so, reluctantly, she stood beside the fresh grave of Sidney Close and listened.

"He came out of the ground like fog, see. That's what it was like, a great pillar of fog rising out of the ground and it took on human form – his form. It just sort of twisted itself into his shape."

"Yew mean his spirit?"

"No, it was him. He went off after a group of them kids. I couldn't follow him, but he came back. You look – he pulled out one of them old tombstones and then he flew up to the tower and rang the bell."

"You're hevin' me on," said Necker, but suddenly knew he wasn't. She'd woken in the night to the sound of the bell. One ring was all it was, but she didn't miss much; she'd stay awake sometimes just so that she didn't.

He took her across to where the tombstone rested on its side across the footpath, which led into the old graveyard.

"Yew sure that weren't them yobbos?"

"I'm sure and so are you," he said, with a sly look at her. He was enjoying himself; he felt superior to someone, and this wasn't a regular occurrence in his life. He was right that she was hooked on his every word although he couldn't know the reason.

Necker was remembering the body of Shane Marjoram. She remembered thinking how handsome he was, and all those bite marks over him and how everyone had been in such a hurry – her boss, the rector, the doctor, the wife … everyone. They knew: those sort of people always knew and thought the likes of her were ignorant. Even Crafty Catchpole knew – God rest his soul. There was no body to lay out with him: the wolves had that! He'd been a hurry to do what he had to do, too. *She* wanted it done and now we know why! The place had stunk of those flowers for days. Screwing the coffin down like that before the relatives had time to pay their respects. You can't hide that sort of thing – the truth will out in the end.

"Dew yew knows what you're sayin'?"

"I do," replied Rollie.

She looked at him – the one the other kids called "the freak". He was beside himself with pride and joy. He rolled his dark, bushy eyebrows in a gesture of cunning and power. He twisted his head to one side, and then pulled it down inside his jacket as though hiding from the world.

"I know something else, too."

"Goo on."

"He's one, too, but he ent come out yet."

"Who?"

"The little Turrel boy. She bled him white. His sister said so."

"Who did?"

"Yew know. Her. She came to them at the Sailors, and held Luke in her arms."

"Hev yew told anyone this?"

"They wouldn't listen. I tried to tell PC Billings but he went off, laughing."

"Yew need ter be careful whut you're sayin'. Yooll get yourself inter trouble."

"I sit by his grave sometimes, but he's never come out."

Necker was frightened; she didn't want to handle this herself. She wanted to know; she wanted to be the … the fountain of all knowledge, but she wanted somebody else to do something.

"We'll go and tell the rector," she said.

"You can. I int," replied Rollie, falling into Necker's mode of speech.

"He ought to know."

"You can tell him now then, 'cause here he comes."

As they spoke, Corvin Unwood strode along the south path of the church, his paunchy figure showing concern. Necker turned to meet him and, as she did so, Rollie ran off passed the west door and out through the lych-gate. She was alone with her knowledge and her worries, but not for long.

Corvin could not avoid her – to turn and go back would have been rude – but the last thing he wanted at half-past seven in the morning was Necker Utting doling out her measure of rustic wisdom. He was sure the church bells were all right and had told Esther as much, but she had insisted that he came "to just have a look". The ringing had woken her in the night, and neither of them had slept since. He'd made her a cup of tea, creeping down the stairs to avoid waking Rebecca, but this, soothing as it was, had failed to send her back to sleep. By half-past six, he'd been ready for breakfast, which he had taken to Esther in bed, and his inevitable walk up Church Hill. He'd seen Necker and Rollie as he reached the top of the steps on the eastern side of the church.

"Good morning, Necker."

"Morning, rector."

"And how are you this morning?"

"None too pleased, I ken tell yew."

"Can I help?"

"Yew ken lissen."

Corvin did, with growing dread. What Simon would have called "a web of devilry" was spreading wider and wider. 'First there was Sidney and Sarah. Now, Luke Turrel and Sarah, and Shane Marjoram and Sarah, as well? In the middle of it all – at the very centre – Horst Brultzner! Could there be any doubt?' Nobody was going to believe him. He had already telephoned Superintendent Junket and the bishop: neither wanted to know. He was alone: to whom could he turn?

"Are you lissnin' rector?"

"Yes, of course. Young Rollie has a wild imagination."

"It was me saw the bite marks on Shane Marjoram, rector – not Rollie. He was buried quickly ..."

'... With a cross screwed to his coffin,' thought Corvin, 'Why? He wasn't a religious man. And the church reeked of garlic. I remember now.'

"Whut yew go-in ter do?"

What he wanted to do was to see that the bell was all right and then go home for – perhaps – a second breakfast.

"I shall consult the proper ... authorities."

"And whut will they do?"

"In such cases – given that such cases exist – there are ... procedures ... We only have Rollie's ... speculations about the little boy."

"He wus as whoite as a sheet, rector. There wont a drarp a blood left in 'im ... Even the darctor said so. And that Shane Marjoram, he wus bitten all over – in places oi wouldn't loike ter mention ... It's a pleec matter if yew ask me. There's some funny goin's on."

"Have you mentioned this to PC Billings? I believe Dr Read and he are home from their cycling tour."

"It woont be no good. If yew wont lissen, why should he?"

"I am listening, Necker."

"So whut yew goin' ter do?"

Corvin looked down at the grave of Sidney Close. It did seem hard to believe that anything had risen out of the crumbled earth. Theological college did not prepare one for these extremities.

"And that Rollie – he needs guidance, rector. He's all wound up about this. There's no tellin' what he moight dew."

"You say he watched the grave all night?"

"He did. He's at risk an' he 'ont lissen ter me. Yool hev ter speak ter him."

"Yes, of course. I noticed him run off. Perhaps when he feels able …."

"He's a wild one, rector. His too intelligent fer werds. He moight take it inter his head ter dig the bardy up!"

"I would strongly advise against that, Necker. He has never tampered with the grave of young Luke, I take it?"

"Nart so far as I know, but there's no tellin'."

"I'll leave it to you, Necker, to get Rollie to come and see me."

"There ent no good leavin' it ter me. Oim askin' yew to do somthun."

Corvin had had enough. He excused himself on the pretext of "seeing to the bells" and watched Necker toddle off down the path to the lych-gate. When she reached the gate, she turned and called back:

"Oi'll leave it ter you, then, rector."

Corvin turned away and walked into his church. He felt safe in there, safe from the world, safe from having to do anything too precipitant. Before climbing the spiral stairway to the bell tower, he went to the front of the church, leant on the altar rail and tried to pray, but the words wouldn't come. All he could find in his head was Bunyan's line 'I see myself now at the end of my journey; my toilsome days are ended.' He had no idea why they had come into his head at that moment: perhaps, too many funerals?

Esther was more conciliatory than he had expected; she listened attentively while they drank a cup of coffee and Corvin devoured two of the chocolate muffins she had made while he was seeing to the bells. There had been no outburst as he'd expected, no 'What a ridiculous notion, Corvin! You have better things to do than pander to such nonsense! It's utterly ridiculous!' Far from it: Esther never spoke until he had finished telling her everything.

"Bishop Peter was no help, of course?"

"No, my dear."

"No surprises there then, Corvin."

He looked at her but felt reluctant to defend Peter Twiddle at that moment.

"I do not see what you can do, Corvin. Exhumations are out of the question – you have no reasons for requesting them, no reasons that would cut any mustard with the authorities, and you can hardly dig them up yourself. At the same time, you cannot simply leave things as they are. You must get help. You must enlist allies."

"But who, my dear? Who is going to believe such nonsense? I must say, I did not expect you to take all this on board, yourself."

"I may have decided views, Corvin, but I am not a bigot. Besides, I love you and can see that you are troubled. I do not, of course, believe in vampires but I do believe in human evil and there are, undoubtedly, groups of perverted people who would take a delight in this kind of thing. I have never liked Brultzner – not from the first day he insinuated himself into our home and swamped you all with his 'charm'. I use that word in the loosest possible sense, you understand?"

"Yes, my dear."

"I think you should approach Alan Read. He was the doctor on these cases."

"Not all, my dear."

"Some, then! There's no point in approaching Jim Maxwell. He'd simply tell you to take a holiday ... but I think Alan might listen. His wife is a bit above herself, but he seems a quiet, sensible man. He's friendly with Martin Billings, isn't he? I'm not sure about Martin. He's a maverick, but I wonder whether he would, when the fat was in the fire, actually defy protocol and go it alone. Anyway, you can discuss that with Alan."

"Anyone else, my dear?"

"Not Simon Palmester – he's too extreme, but his daughter Nadine was a great friend of Sarah Marjoram's. She might be of help – but avoid that friend of hers ...what's his name?"

"Tony Crewes?"

"Yes – he's an atheist; it stands out a mile. You need committed Christians on your side, Corvin – people who recognize evil for what it is – not the liberated left!"

"Yes, my dear, but what are we to do."

"I don't know, Corvin, but you need allies before you can make that decision. Ooh – and you telephone Bishop Peter."

"But ...."

"No buts, Corvin – the bishop is rather like you. He'll not do anything if it promises a quieter life to leave it alone, but there's no reason why he should wriggle out of his responsibilities here! You have approached him on a spiritual matter and he should be (what's that terrible word Rebecca uses?) pro-active! Yes, he should be pro-active. In fact, it might be a good idea to put it in writing. He can put the phone down, but he cannot ignore a letter!"

"He might conclude that I am insane, my dear."

"He might."

"You don't think that, do you, Esther?"

"No – I have said that I do not believe in vampires per se, but I do believe in what inspires people to want to believe in them. Now, you go and write your letter."

Corvin screwed up his seventh attempt at a letter to Bishop Twiddle. He was overcome with relief by Esther's support but still fearful of what the 'powers-that-be' would think of his 'concerns'. He had realized, as he sat in the quiet of his study, that Lord Wangford would also be involved if Brultzner was – however marginally.

The aristocrat had been very instrumental in securing Brultzner's passage to England, in purchasing his home and in supporting him once he had arrived. Besides, he wanted to consider who would be his allies. He felt Esther was right about Alan Read and wrong about Martin and Tony; Corvin felt that both men would rally round. He also felt that Peter Vishnya should be approached and wondered why Esther had not mentioned him. He was dubious about approaching Nadine Palmester but felt that he ought to consider her father. Esther did not like the Bethel priest, but Corvin was aware of the passion with which Simon believed in his God. There was still much to be considered before he committed pen to paper.

He knew Esther would not disturb him while he was in his study and so, waiting until he heard her upstairs, he slipped out, closing the door quietly behind him. If Esther thought he was composing the letter, she would leave him alone but her attitude, if he suggested a walk, would be quite different. He wanted a breath of air and he wanted a credible ally. He felt that both might be obtained by walking through the village towards Alan Read's house.

As he passed the church, he noticed Rollie making his way into the graveyard and wondered what the strange lad was doing. At that moment, however, Corvin did not want to get involved – not until he was sure of his friends – and so he pretended not to see him and carried on along Church Hill.

Rollie was playing god. He had removed Horst Brultzner's crosses and released the 'enie from the bottle. He now wondered whether he could put back the cork, allowing the vampire freedom only when he, Rollie, wished it. He replaced the crosses carefully, closing the tomb of Sidney Close. Rollie's amusement exhibited itself in the usual manner. He rocked back and forth, holding his chest and sides as though they would split open. He laughed until his laughter took him hurtling along the shingled footpath to the lych-gate, all the time muttering to himself. He couldn't wait for night to come; he'd wait by the grave as darkness descended on the churchyard. His power was growing daily – he who controlled demons.

Alan Read was at work, but Penny, who had a job-share post at the local school and was at home that morning, welcomed him to a cup of coffee. Corvin was reluctant to accept – not because he disliked Penny Read's company but because he wanted to talk to Alan, urgently. However, courtesy won the day and he found himself sitting at Penny's breakfast bar chewing over the problems that faced the Junior Church. They seemed a long way from the problems that beset him now, but Corvin listened because, after all, this was the centre of his work here in the parish of Dunburgh-on-sea.

When he left, elevated by Penny's enthusiasm, he was more bewildered than ever. How could these things be happening? Oh, if only they would go away and allow him to concentrate on what really mattered to the parish!

Necker Utting left the Church Centre that evening and made her way home. The boys' neckers had been checked and found wanting and she was pleased with herself. Church Hill was in darkness but she had her torch and its beam lit her way. It was the heavy torch her father had given her – what he used to call his "burglar's torch". One blow with that would lay anybody out cold. She walked alone, not having yet cottoned onto a replacement for Rollie, who had left the Cub Scouts long since. She was thinking about him as she passed the church and, throwing caution to the winds, she crossed the road and walked into the graveyard. It was spooky all right – all those grey stones sitting hard on the dead, holding them down.

She was as frightened as anyone else (with an imagination) by graveyards, but was blessed (or cursed) by her Suffolk stoicism. Besides, she was concerned for Rollie. As far as she knew the rector had done nothing all day and the night was once again upon them. Was the boy going to be there? Sidney Close's grave was as undisturbed as it had appeared in the morning; the earth had, if anything, settled a little more.

She'd noticed before how graveyards always seemed to enclose you. It was as though you had walked into another world, and retreat from it might not be an option. Necker looked at the light of the street lamps beyond the lych-gate. One or two cars passed, taking the boys home; she wasn't far from the road, but it could have been a hundred miles away at that moment. Rollie wasn't there, and so she decided to walk on, round the church – her pride wouldn't let her turn back and hurry through the gate – and out by the steps on the eastern side. The far side of the churchyard was certainly gloomy, disappearing as it did towards the war memorial under the black tunnel of the yew trees. Beyond, there was the glow of the houses along Beach Road, and the sky seemed to reflect this light back onto the church so that the stones in the old graveyard were picked out as silhouettes. The quiet was deathly. It was always the quiet that got to you: out of the silence, demons would leap.

As she reached the buttress of the west porch a figure appeared, walking slowly along the path. It was a woman, neatly dressed in the modern style with jeans, calf-length boots and a body warmer over her light jacket. Necker, bundled up in skirts and cardigans, noticed the trimness immediately. It was a young woman and she moved with an easy swing of her legs from the hips. It was Sarah Marjoram – the one who now called herself 'Brown'. Necker moved back into the shadow of the buttress and waited. Sarah passed her, apparently deep in thought and unaware of Necker's presence, making her way to her parents' grave, where she stopped and looked down. Necker dare hardly breathe: it was so still, and she was sure that the woman would hear the slightest sound. Minutes ticked by and became quarter, and then half, hours. The figure that watched her parents' resting place never moved. Her head was inclined slightly and she might have been praying.

Necker was not frightened by the figure – there was nothing ghostly about the young woman – but she did not trust herself to move or speak. The figure was at home in the churchyard. It was clear that she came here on many nights – and that was unnatural. Eventually, Sarah turned and Necker could see that her face ran with tears. Sarah lifted her head and her eyes fell upon Necker in the shadow of the porch.

"How long have you been watching me?" she asked.

"Ever since yew came – I meant no 'arm."

"This is my private place and my private time."

Sarah's attitude stung Necker. She had a decided view of her own virtuousness.

"There's nothin' private 'bout a graveyard. Anyway – yew've got nuthin' ter get high and mighty about."

"What do you mean?"

"I sorer him."

"Saw him?"

"I laid him out. I saw what yew done. There's no call for you ter get high and mighty. I could tell a lot of people about yew and then where would yew be?"

"What people would you tell – and what would you tell them?"

"I've only got to say. Yew were seen – with the little boy, as well."

"You're not threatening me, are you, Necker?"

The voice came from behind her. She could no longer see Sarah Marjoram, who was in the shadow of the porch and Necker dare not turn round, but she spoke with an inherent stubbornness.

"I know whut I saw and I know who'd be int'rested."

Sarah saw Horst's anger and felt his blow across her face. She saw herself and Matthew out on the street, seeking shelter, or dead by the old vampire's hand. Her master knew nothing of how she had punished Shane, was totally unaware that he lay, Un-dead, in the graveyard, gnawing at his burial clothes for want of blood, for all eternity. She saw herself at the mercy of this dull, cloddish woman – this village half-wit. She saw her whole future, and that of Matthew, destroyed. Horst had shown his ruthlessness in taking her to Prague and offering her as a ritual sacrifice before the others of their kind. The woman had to go, had to be silenced; she would worry about the consequences later. There was no family – Necker lived alone; a quick cremation, and all would be well. Sarah took her enemy's head in her hands, yanked it round and sank her teeth into the fat neck. The taste was appalling – the flesh old and sallow, the blood lifeless. It was like sucking on the juice of an old apple; there was no crunch as she bit and she seemed to be drawing juices from a floury pulp.

Necker fought with all the strength she could muster, swinging her father's torch up and over her head. It struck Sarah across the skull but her teeth held firm. She slipped her right arm onto Necker's chin, holding her in place and grabbed the torch with her left hand. She wrenched it from her victim's grip and flung it across the churchyard. Dropping her hand back to Necker's shoulder, she tightened her grip. There was no delight in the seduction here. This woman lacked the sensuality to take pleasure in what was happening to her. Never having been roused sexually, she was un-moved by the touch of lips on her throat, by the erotic kiss of the vampire. She only saw herself vanquished and fading. As the blood was drained from her, Necker's struggles lessened and she collapsed into Sarah's arms. The vampire continued to batten on her, drawing the life-blood. This one had to die – Sarah knew that and, not until she felt all life pass from the body, did she relent.

Necker dropped at her feet, under the shadow of the west porch, and Sarah glided quickly away, leaving her victim to be found in the morning.

Rollie had watched everything from the dark shadow of the wall where, months before, Martin Billings had found him when the policeman came to gaze on the freshly dug grave of Luke Turrel. Neither woman had been aware of him – one so intent on destruction, the other on survival. Once he was sure that Sarah had gone, he made his way across to the body, his head held forward and lolling from side to side, his eyes rolling. His excitement was intense, overcoming any fear he may have felt. This was his first dead body – ever!

The whole … scenario rolled out before him; he was in the film. Necker had become a vampire, and he had seen how you destroy vampires. Even if they cremated her, it would be best if she were staked first – to 'make assurance, double sure': that Shakespeare knew his language.

No one else would suspect, not if he covered the mark of the vampire on her neck by pulling her collar up, not if he got the torch back to the body. Not that they'd suspect, anyway – they all knew nothing! She was still warm and there was a faint trickle of blood from the wound. He ran his fingers over the mark and nearly wet himself in his enthusiasm. He felt like Van Helsing coming upon the King Vampire's latest victim, and he was the only one in the village who knew everything. He'd bide his time. Here in the churchyard wasn't right. She would have to be in her coffin. Who'd lay them out now that she was gone – the undertaker himself? Rollie knew where Necker kept her key to the … to the morgue! He'd get that and be there after she was removed from the Chapel of Rest.

It was the following night that Rollie set out on his adventure. If only it was Hallowe'en, if only he could go through the village dressed in a cape! Rollie stood in front of the mirror in his bedroom. It was a small mirror but by standing back and jigging about he could get a complete glimpse of himself. He had borrowed his father's farm labourer's leather jacket, which had many pockets, and fastened it round his waist with a wide, leather belt over an old shirt which was open at the neck. He wore a neckerchief – not the scout one, but a red-spotted one he'd got from his granddad. He tied this in a knot and the humour was not lost on him. In the pockets of the jacket he had placed a screwdriver, his crosses, a tube of instant glue and his flask of Holy Water; the flask was a hip flask he'd taken from his father's bookshelves and he'd have to get that back before morning or face a beating. He didn't like his jeans but there was nothing else to wear and the jacket did cover them pretty well, especially with his black Wellington boots pulled on up to his knees. The old cricket bag his father kept in the loft had been a stroke of genius. Rollie had seen it many years before on one of his prowls around the house, when his mother had thought he was out playing. He had crept in there when he arrived home, emptied the bag carefully and then placed it under his bed. Now it contained sharpened stakes and the family coal hammer as well as his grandmother's old carving knife, the garlic and his granddad's hurricane lamp.

Rollie had thought through his evening's work with great care. Many times, his imagination had lived through this moment in his life. He had pictured it in detail – he, the all-knowing adventurer, pitting his very soul against the devil and all his works. The house was deathly quiet before he made the first move. He could hear his parents snoring in their bedroom as he crept down the stairs to the kitchen. He placed the cricket bag by the back door and hung the labourer's jacket over the back of the kitchen chair. He then set to, preparing himself a meal, having carefully closed the kitchen door to the house, beforehand. The egg and bacon sizzled in the pan and he added tomatoes and mushrooms; it was important to dine well, and he opened a bottle of his father's beer to complete the meal. Finally, he fried a round of bread in the pan juices and sat down to consume his repast which was laced, liberally, with brown sauce.

It was very dark when he eventually closed his parent's back-door quietly and set off on his mission. Lights still glimmered from some houses but this only intensified the blackness, much to Rollie's delight. They were all safely tucked up in their beds; he was on an errand of valour. A few people passed him and he paused in the shadows of the hedges to avoid being noticed. The churchyard was not on his way at all, but Rollie was determined to pass through this by climbing the southern wall and making his way to the undertakers through the lych-gate. He walked briskly down Marsh Lane, turned across the field where the scouts had their hut and clambered through the brambles into the old graveyard. It was a matter of minutes before he was out once more on Church Hill, having passed the graves of Clive Brown, Luke Turrel, Shane Marjoram, Sidney Close and the small memorial plaque to Crafty Catchpole on the way.

He passed the Duke's Head and saw, through the misty windows, a group of the teenagers who had made his life such a misery. They were playing pool in a way that he never would, but Rollie merely smiled at their ignorance. Eventually, with a quick glance along the road in both directions, he stepped into the alleyway alongside the undertakers. He took the set of Necker's keys, which he had stolen from her house, and unlocked the heavy gate into the backyard with the longest of them. His excitement was palpable, and it was all he could do to stop himself shaking with joy. Inside the yard the hearse was parked, and behind this was the neat little building which they called the Chapel of Rest; beside this was the morgue. Rollie selected the smallest key, inserted it in the lock and turned. It opened easily and he saw that the chapel was lit only by a small artificial candle in a niche to the side of the coffin. He placed the cricket bag carefully in front of the door before opening it and then removed the lamp. He deliberately fumbled in one of the leather pockets, although he knew full well that the matches were there, and then he raised the glass and lit the mantle of the lamp. This he placed carefully on the altar so that the light which hissed from it shone obliquely onto the coffin.

He needed a companion now – someone to admire his knowledge and courage; a Dr Seward to his Van Helsing. There was no one, and Rollie chatted to himself as he had done since he was a child.

'What are you going to do?'

"I'm going to open the coffin."

So saying, he took the screwdriver from one of the pockets and proceeded to undo the coffin lid, which – like Brultzner before him when they had come to stake Luke Turrel – he placed against one of the walls.

Necker Utting lay there, younger but uglier than ever. She had appeared to the boys to be simply a fat old lady (although she was no more than thirty-something) and age had softened her features. In death, her skin had tightened and her face regained the pastiness and podgy cheeks and nose of her adolescent years, so that she appeared to be a gawky girl – the least attractive in her class, the most eager to get her hands on a boy. She was dressed in the shapeless skirts and cardigans she always wore. On her feet were brown lace-up shoes of the type known as brogues. The smile on her face was one of self-satisfaction. It lingered, enticingly – even on Necker's face – around the corners of the mouth. Rollie – despite his hate for this meddling woman – was fascinated; he had come under the allure of the vampire. He shook himself.

'Is this really Necker's body?'

"It is – but a nightmare of her former self. This is the Devil's spawn!"

Rollie reached into the cricket bag. He took out a bunch of garlic flowers and then a long, sharp knife; both these things he placed near the coffin on the white altar cloth. Next, he drew out a short iron stake and then a coal hammer which he placed beside the stake. He looked about him; this was a moment to savour. He leaned forward onto the trestles that supported the coffin.

Rollie's eyes glistened with a fanatical look as he picked up the stake in his left hand and gripped the hammer in his right. He placed the point of the iron stake over where the heart would be, took a last look at Necker's face, and struck with all his might. Her body trembled from head to toe; the shuddering ran in spasms throughout her entire frame. The hands and arms twitched and the legs jerked upwards, kicking her feet out into the air. Necker opened her eyes and Rollie stared into them as he brought the hammer down onto the top of the stake again and again; he knew he dare not waver in his task. Her hands reached up and grasped the stake as though she would wrench it out, and he felt the iron bar move upwards in his left hand. Frantic, Rollie re-doubled his blows.

"The Lord gives and the Lord taketh away, blessed be the name of the Lord."

Her eyes rolled over into themselves so that only the whites could be seen; she looked like something from a zombie film. She squirmed, trying to pull away from his blows, while at the same time pushing hard against the stake. Her neck stretched back as though she were offering the softness of her throat to a lover, the mouth opened and one long cry of anguish rose from it, a cry that suggested she had seen beyond the green hills and been denied a place.

"My soul looks for the Lord: more than watchmen for the morning."

Blood issued from her mouth, blood and a white fluid from her nostrils and ears. As her cry mixed with these, Necker seemed to choke and the cry became a splutter and then there was silence. Rollie let the hammer drop from his grasp.

He looked into the coffin. The 'Thing' which had been Necker lay still and there was a smile, a contented smile now, upon her face. Rollie took the carving knife from the bag, the very knife with which his grandmother had carved the Sunday joint on so many occasions when he was a small child, and cut off Necker's head. It was not accomplished with the ease he had imagined. The bone in the neck avoided all attempts to snap it, and he had to poke and twist with the point of the knife before the head was finally severed from the body. He had rolled up his shirt sleeves, which was as well because his hands and forearms were covered by blood before he had finished.

Rollie wiped them clean on his neckerchief before he took the garlic and stuffed her mouth with it.

He felt sick; it hadn't been quite what he thought. He was left with a sense of ordeal faced rather than duty done. As quickly as he could, Rollie tidied her body, replaced the coffin lid (screwing it down as tightly as he could, having first dipped each one in the glue), fetched together his implements and left the chapel, remembering to lock the door behind him. He let himself out through the gate, locking it likewise, and made his way down the village street.

Outside the chapel everything was quieter than it had been; the pub was closing and the pool players rolling home. He avoided them all, cutting through Market Place clutching his cricket bag and then making his way down Shoemaker's Lane and Church Hill. He kept to the shadows and as the distance between himself and his deed increased he began to feel relieved. There were no birds singing, no dawn chorus, just the far-off singing of drunks. It was still dark night and the sun had yet to rise but his heart was lighter as he made his way home to bed.

CHAPTER 9

Home to roost

Corvin Unwood's voice opened Necker Utting's funeral service, although his mind – on the verge of being shattered – was far away.

"Jesus said I am the resurrection, and I am the life; he who believes in me, though he die, yet shall he live, and whoever lives and believes in me shall never die."

The Cub Scouts were all in place, their neckers folded perfectly and their woggles straight. They had all disliked her and now she was dead they all felt bad. The leaders, who had also found her 'help' irksome, felt likewise and had lectured the boys on their duty. This amounted to attending Necker's funeral and parading smartly with the flags, which preceded the coffin down the aisle. Now that she was gone forever, Necker Utting was "going to be missed". Even those who disliked her – perhaps, especially those who disliked her – would miss her most. She had no relatives and so cremation was decided upon between the rector, the undertaker and the Cub Scout leader – all of whom seemed surprised to be consulting each other, but all agreeing that she would want cremation and a small plot in the churchyard; the "small plot" was significant because no one was going to tend it.

Corvin spoke of her in subdued terms. She was someone who had – apparently – appeared in the village one day, gone to school there, grown up there without noticeably being a teenager and eventually entered adulthood. No one seemed sure who her parents might have been or where they might have been buried – if they actually died in Dunburgh-on-sea. She was "Necker" to everyone, whether or not they knew the reason. She irritated everyone in more or less the same way, but – it was unanimously agreed – she would be "sorely missed", irreplaceable. They didn't make her like anymore; after she was cast, the mould was thrown away.

The funeral was well attended – surprisingly well attended in Esther Unwood's view – especially by the members of the Fishermen's Hut. These included Deaf Charlie Utting, Dick Utting and Yammer Utting – not one of whom claimed any relationship with the dead woman; indeed, Yammer denied – vociferously – that his family and hers were in any way related, which made people think that, perhaps, they were. There were even rumours that he had approached the Cub Scout leader and offered to pay for the little do she was putting on for Necker, as a mark of respect, at the Church Centre after the funeral.

The Cub Scout leader was, as it happened, related to Ample Bassett who was a fount of such information. Jim Maxwell, who had certified the cause of death as

441

exposure brought on by anaemia, also attended since Necker had been a patient of his as long as he could remember. The Inn Crowd were also present. All their children had attended Cub Scouts and they felt it right to be there; most of them had contributed something towards the little do. The Church Centre wasn't Lianne Snooks's idea of a proper venue but it was OK for Necker Utting. Elders of the Methodist Church came along because Necker often went to the youth events, helping and advising where she could. Simon Palmester was still in hospital – much against his wishes – but Nadine came in his place to represent the Bethel.

The range of emotion that rippled through the onlookers as the hearse departed for the crematorium was varied and complex. Corvin and one Methodist elder went with her, as did the undertaker. Everyone else descended on the Church Centre. No one had really known Necker well enough to attend the little cremation ceremony at the crematorium, and there were no immediate family. "Paying your respects did not have to verge on hypocrisy", as Lianne Snooks pointed out. At the last minute, however, Nadine Palmester decided that her father would wish her to go, and so she claimed a place in the hearse. As she did so, Rollie joined her, much to everyone's surprise – darting into the hearse as it was about to drive away.

"He was fond of her," said Joney Chine, "they spent a lot of time together."

Rollie sat in the front of the hearse, squeezed against one of the pall-bearers, and everyone said how dignified he looked. It was true; he wore a black suit, which had come from somewhere in the family wardrobe, and sat poised with an unusual dignity – his back straight, his head high, his hands relaxed in his lap and his brow smooth. His mother had made a futile attempt to stop him but, remembering the incident of the holly bush outside the school, decided – as he dodged her hand – not to persist in her efforts. Roland van Wiggs, vampire-hunter, was seeing his task through to the end; besides, he'd never been to a cremation and was looking forward to finding out what it entailed.

On their way home from the funeral meal, Bernard and Liz Shaw met Sarah Brown nee Marjoram. It was a clear, bright and crisp November morning and she stood in the driveway of the Old Vicarage, shadowed by the beech trees which were, by now, almost without leaves. She hovered there, and seemed unable to "venture further", as Liz Shaw indicated to her husband when they got home.

She'd changed since her husband died, thought Liz. She was once a bright young mother who it was a pleasure to see out and about with her baby boy. Now, although her beauty was breathtaking, she often looked drawn and fretful. Such was the case that morning when she almost waylaid the rector's warden and his wife.

"So they've taken her for cremation?"

"Yes, dear – it seemed the best thing, all round."

"I was worried about her. She seemed to be alone. Did she have no relations?"

"No … the rector went with her to the crematorium."

"And no one else?"

"Are you not well, dear?" asked Liz, irritated by Sarah's manner. If she were so concerned, why hadn't Sarah come to the funeral herself?

"Why do you ask?" replied Sarah, peering at Liz Shaw from under her eyebrows. This gave the impression of shyness, but the look was hard and suspicious.

"I wondered why you weren't at the funeral ..."

"I'm fine, thank you. I'm not a relative. I hardly knew her."

"So how do you like your new job as Herr Brultzner's housekeeper?"

"It's wonderful and so convenient for Matthew and me."

"And how are Herr Brultzner's renovations coming along?"

"Almost complete – the bedrooms are finished."

"How nice it would be if he held another of his soirees at Christmas. We could all come and see how wonderful it looks."

"I'll mention it to him," said Sarah.

She knew the idea would appeal to her master; it would set the seal of respectability on their presence in the village, and remove any doubts that people might harbour about the events of the autumn. Sidney Close's death had nearly been a fatal setback and Horst, she knew, had yet to settle the issue; if only they could pull through this one, people would be reassured.

Horst smiled at the suggestion.

"Your duplicity, Miss Brown, does you credit. I will approach Mr Briggs. I am sure he will be only too willing to provide us with a suitable repast. We shall do the royal thing and open up to the public. Mr Chambers and his men have so nearly completed their work. It is a muddy time of the year, of course, so we must order enough slippers for our guests to change into – a little custom from the Old World! Perhaps a more select gathering this time? But no, it is important to welcome all – the village, after all, is our home, the centre of our little world for a while. A traditional English Christmas in a nearly-restored Old Victorian Vicarage – how Dickensian!"

His delight was over-whelming and the joy she had first felt during those heady days of midsummer, when she and Matthew had first come to the Old Vicarage, began to return. Shane deserved his fate, Sidney's had been a terrible accident and she'd had no choice with Necker. Any good mother would have done the same to defend her child's future. 'What about little Luke Turrel?' An accident, an accident: she hadn't realized what she was doing! She and her son had a home and a future. Matthew would probably be very famous one day; his expertise with animals was unlike anything anyone had ever seen. His teacher had put him in sole charge of all the pets in the nursery; his rapport with them was, she said, uncanny.

"You're thoughtful, Sarah."

"I was thinking about Christmas. The whole house will come to life!"

"We do not have much time – what is it – November 15th, already? Let us arrange the invitations for three weeks time – December 7th – yes. You must have a little nursery party for Matthew, too – perhaps the following week, when schools will be reaching their most festive moments. I will show you a children's German Christmas for your son – the Germans have wonderful festive ideas for children."

While they were speaking the telephone rang and when Sarah answered she found herself speaking to Lord Wangford. To Horst's amusement, she curtsied in the hallway when she realised to whom she was speaking.

"Lord Wangford, sir."

"Thank you, Miss Brown. Charles? Good … I am obliged, Charles … and he is reliable? Tomorrow would be suitable but there is no immediate hurry. Seasonal … no Charles, the seasons have little to do with my present need for a gardener … I am obliged to you."

"We have a replacement for the unfortunate Mr Catchpole, my dear," he said, smiling as he turned to Sarah. "One of Lord Wangford's 'old retainers' – I believe that is the English expression. He is a retired man looking for congenial employment. Hopefully, we shall have settled the problem of Close before Christmas."

"Isn't he …"

It was rare she questioned Brultzner; it was something he never appreciated.

"Close is secured for the time being, Sarah, but I would prefer a final solution of his problem and our new gardener will provide that for us."

Esther Unwood, much as she wanted her daughter's happiness, was not amused by the sudden arrival of Peter Vishnya who, having completed some business for Horst Brultzner in Belgium, had crossed the channel overnight and stood on their doorstep, smiling, by early afternoon. Rebecca was down the stairs and in his arms in a trice, Corvin felt an enormous weight fall from his shoulders as he looked forward to a quiet chat with his prospective son-in-law, but Esther stood in the kitchen doorway with a subdued scowl on her face.

"I couldn't resist it. I phoned Horst and he said to come over as he wanted to see me anyway. I have to return to Estonia in a couple of days but I'll be back – if that's all right with you, Esther – for Christmas."

"My dear boy – need you ask?" said Corvin.

Esther was delighted – of course she was! It was what they had wanted for Rebecca for years, but … she didn't want to lose her daughter. She didn't see why they had to go to Estonia. Where on earth was Estonia? She would still have Corvin. She knew that, but a husband wasn't the same as a daughter. Esther was aware, too, of her age; she didn't want to die and not have a chance to say goodbye to Rebecca – and how would she do that, if death came suddenly? And, if Rebecca had a family, would they ever see the children? What about Corvin? He was as dependent on Rebecca as anyone. Surely, Peter Vishnya could work for Herr Brultzner in England?

Everyone seemed to be pushing the wedding on; the whole village had whispered about it ever since the Harvest Festival. That wretched Bint woman talked of nothing else whenever they bumped into each other. "Everyone's saying it will be before Christmas." Well, everyone was wrong – as usual. And yet she knew they were happy. You could see it in the way they were together. And Rebecca had said "I do not have any worries. Peter has talked to his son about it, and I am happy." At least she had talked them out of getting married that autumn "with the fruits and the flowers of field and hedgerow adorning the church and reception." It would have been lovely but ... too soon. Peter had seen that: at least he was sensible.

Now, spring seemed just around the corner and it looked like being an Easter wedding so Rebecca would be gone by the summer. They were keeping on the house in the village – but they wouldn't need it. They would stay at the rectory when they came over. "You must be over the moon, Esther!" Silly woman – would any mother be over the moon at the prospect of losing her daughter? "Estonia's not far away – not these days." Far enough: endless miles of sea and land to be crossed and her daughter gone from her. Corvin had been nothing but irritating about it – expressing a joy he could not possibly have felt. "Will that be our life after Rebecca has gone, Corvin – bishops and Beaujolais?"

"Hello, Peter," she said, with a broad smile, "We'll open one of the bishop's bottles of Beaujolais to celebrate your flying visit."

"Esther!"

"Corvin!"

They all laughed. As Corvin often said, she wasn't really worried for Rebecca – she knew her daughter would be safe with Peter Vishnya.

They shared a light, pleasant lunch – broccoli and poached egg toasts – and then Peter and Rebecca went for a walk.

"Your mother's coming round?"

"Yes," laughed Rebecca, "slowly, but she'll get there."

"And you've no second thoughts?"

"Why do you ask – have you?"

"No – just checking!"

They kissed as he finished his sentence. Their lips were cold in the November air and there was the slightest of tingles on their noses as they touched. He held her so gently that her body seemed to float as it rose to him and his left hand rested lightly on her right hip. How long their lips held she could not remember, but it was their first 'cold' kiss and Rebecca loved the sensation which tingled throughout her body. They were standing in the middle of the track which led down to Marsh Lane, and the world could have passed them by on either side for all they might have known or cared. Their lips lingered: there was no attempt to push the kiss beyond the sheer excitement of the touch – the feather-like caress they gave, each to the other. His right hand sought her left and stroked her fingertips gently, completing the circle of their union.

"We will make it an Easter wedding, then?" asked Peter.

"Yes – I would like that."

"Then you must come over to Estonia after Christmas and see whether you like my apartment. If not, we shall need to start looking for a larger house."

They walked on in a lover's silence until they reached the bridge where, once, they had gone their own ways and, later, come together.

"You've read my letters – e-mails? Do you believe in vampires, Peter?"

"Yes – but not here. I must confess that, at the beginning, Horst Brultzner struck me as … uncanny. I thought he would …refuse to enter the church. Since I've have been working for him, however, I've found nothing in his business papers or his dealings with the world that suggest he is anything but an entrepreneur."

"Nothing?"

"A priest died in Leipzig while he was there – but…?"

"And the lady you met in Leipzig?"

"Eva Schulz?"

"Yes."

"Did I tell you about her?"

"Why do you ask? You tell me everything, don't you?"

"Yes."

It was a lie – his first lie to Rebecca, but he couldn't correct it; there was no drawing back from the untruth. He couldn't begin to tell Rebecca what he had felt for Eva Schulz or what she had meant to him during his too-brief stay in Leipzig, and yet he had done nothing … dishonourable. It was simply that he had felt … Peter stopped his thoughts. He'd had all this out with Omar; he had done nothing wrong! But the desires within him had been wrong.

"Peter?"

"Hmm?"

"What's wrong?"

"Nothing."

"Are you sure?"

"Yes."

"You went very quiet when I mentioned Eva Schulz."

"She was a strange woman – that's all."

"Strange – in what way?"

"It's hard to explain. She was … other-worldly."

"Like a vampire?"

He laughed – very loudly: deliberately loudly.

"No," he lied, "not like a vampire – more like one of Rackham's fairies."

Eva Schulz had been nothing like Rackham's fairies. He mentioned fairies just to throw Rebecca off the scent of his true feelings at the time. She trusted him and so she believed him and did not pursue the conversation further. It is always easy to lie to those who trust us. Peter felt ashamed but convinced himself that there was no ultimate deceit in what he had said. This was a happy evening together – the beginning of a happy and fulfilling future. Why discuss one … indiscretion?

"You are funny!"

"Funny?"

"Fairies!"

They both laughed as they dropped twigs into the river; the moment had passed – it was salvaged from being wrecked by time – and they were happy again.

"Your mother is happy with an Easter wedding?"

"Yes … mum is going to miss me, but she'll get over it. It's dad I feel sorry for – mum will take it out on him. I came late in their lives and am doubly precious for that … Mum has a sharp tongue, and life cannot have been easy for him. I provided an intimate link between them. I am one of the ways through which they can express their affection for each other – and they do have affection for each other, a deep and abiding love."

"They also have their faith."

"Yes. She comes from a family whose unshakeable belief and daily worship runs back through the generations. It's second nature to her – something so deep in her bones. She doesn't think about it. Dad's faith is more thoughtful, but also rock solid. He came to it through his mother. Granny, of course, is one of the reasons he finds it difficult coping with … strident women. He loved her, and she him. She was all women to him until he became a man – and she was only ever gentle and kind. He simply wasn't prepared for a different reality."

Horst Brultzner was immeasurably pleased to see Peter when he duly called the following day; he had been surprised by the success of their relationship. Never before had he trusted anyone as he had trusted Peter Vishnya, and the Estonian had repaid him, as they say, a hundredfold.

"My dear fellow," he said, as Sarah opened the door and ushered Peter into the hallway, "it is so good to see you. Come in, come in. I understand that you are going to be married? I hope I can continue to rely on your expertise?"

"I hope so, too, sir. You might say that I am depending on it."

"You and your future wife will live in Estonia, then?"

"That is the plan."

"Then you must allow me to offer you a larger house as a wedding present."

"Rebecca and I had planned to look for one in the New Year."

"It will be my pleasure. Keep your eyes open for one that appeals to you and is large enough – yes?"

"Thank you, sir."

"It is I should thank you. Your Estonian citizenship has been the key factor in our entrepreneurial expeditions in that country."

As they spoke, Matthew Brown came running down the stairs and along the hall straight into his mother's lap. The little boy then turned to Brultzner and smiled.

"Can I show your friend the animals?" he begged.

"Not now, Matthew," warned Sarah.

"How can we say no to the boy? Come, Matthew."

The boy took Brultzner's hand as he would have taken that of a grandfather. Peter noticed the gloves – but it was autumn and the November mornings were chill. In the garden, Peter noticed that the outhouses had all been renovated and that, further down in the garden, deep within the copse of trees, there were wooden buildings similar to stables. Sarah's boy ran ahead, straight into what had once been the wash-house of the Old Vicarage. An old crow with a broken leg in splints sat, stiffly, in a large cage and looked up as the boy entered. Matthew went to the cage immediately, opened the door and the crow hopped onto his arm.

"We only keep him in here because Grandpa says he will fly away – but he won't."

"Matthew!"

Sarah's voice carried a note of admonition, but only because Brultzner was her employer. It was, in reality, filled with pride.

"Your son is right, Sarah. Show us, my boy."

Matthew took the old crow into the garden and walked with it to the front of the house where he helped it to hop onto one of the large, terracotta pots. The bird looked around at the open garden and the sky beyond the trees and, with an effort because it was clearly an old bird, the crow flapped raggedly away and along the path towards the gate until the boy made a cawing sound. When it heard him the old bird lifted its head to one side, quite askew and looking almost as though its neck was broken, and hopped back. At that moment, a cat appeared round the corner of the house and raced towards the bird. Matthew hissed quietly and the cat stopped and came over to him, its head lowered waiting for a scratch between the ears. It continued to eye the crow, but made no attempt to rush at the bird; for its part, the crow seemed unperturbed by the cat's presence. Both animals had their attention on the boy.

"They play this game every morning," said Matthew.

"How old is your son?" asked Peter, quietly, to Sarah.

"He's at nursery school. He's four."

"His language is so advanced."

"He spends a lot of time with Horst, and we read to him."

"You have a gift, my boy," said Peter.

"Horst has taught him the way with animals."

"But it is still a gift," interrupted Horst, "Peter is right."

"Would these animals hurt each other if you were not here?" asked Peter.

"Yes," said Horst, speaking for the boy, "he is their master."

"And their friend," said Matthew.

"And their friend," re-iterated Horst.

"Can we show him – you know what?" asked Matthew.

Horst laughed and Sarah followed suit, laughing with a certain relief, Peter thought. They made their way through the copse until they came to the building, whose door was open, that Peter had supposed was a stable. On the straw within lay a wolf, its fur partly burned away. Peter realised that it must have been one of the pack from the wildlife park – the one which Crafty Catchpole had fought off.

"A nasty man did this to him."

"I was told that the man was fighting for his life."

"He would not hurt anyone," said Matthew, and he walked up to the wolf and rubbed its muzzle.

"They were going to have him put down but, as you see, he is with us still. Under the boy's nursing care, the wolf has thrived."

"And when your wolf is better?" asked Peter.

"Grandpa says we can keep him."

"You'll certainly never have to pay baby sitters, Sarah," laughed Peter, "My Yevgeny is at home in Estonia now, and Anton walks him to school every day – and probably tucks him in at night!"

"Your Anton is – as I remember – a remarkable creature, Mr Vishnya."

"He has a mind of his own."

"Do you think he would listen to me, Mr Vishnya?" asked Matthew.

"Watching you with the animals, my son, I do not think he would have any choice," laughed Peter.

Rebecca called on Sarah Brown at Peter's suggestion and found her alone in the house. She had never been intimate with Sarah. She knew her as someone nice in the village, the daughter of Clive and Mary, who had both supported her father, and as a bright young woman who had got mixed-up with a bad husband, but had tried to bring her child up properly. Sidney's allegations had cast a shadow over that image, but Sidney was known as a man prone to ….well, it was not good to speak ill of the dead. The young woman herself had been open and honest when Horst Brultzner had questioned her about it in circumstances which would have thrown most people. Rebecca had no reason to think anything but good of her and, when Peter suggested she should call on Sarah, Rebecca had few reservations.

They went into the morning room and Sarah waved her to the Eastlake day-bed, as Horst had done, and sat herself on the William Morris chair. There was a stillness about Sarah that was unsettling. Her self-composure was extraordinary and it exuded a charm, which was instantly attractive. Simply sitting, Sarah drew Rebecca to her; the priest's daughter thought she had once known this person, long ago, while realizing that it was impossible. She felt relaxed in her company even though hardly a word had been spoken; she felt relaxed to the point of drowsiness. He father had once said that part of Sarah's influence over her wild and brutal husband had been the young woman's ability to emanate a soothing aroma. Rebecca felt that Sarah could transport her to far away places. She looked up and saw that she was being watched, intently.

"I'm sorry. I was day-dreaming."

"I do it all the time," replied Sarah, "Dad used to say that I would day-dream my way through life."

"Was he right?"

"It helps. You should never lose touch with your dreams. Sometimes they are the only things you have left to cling onto."

"You still miss your husband?"

"No – I visit him often and we talk, but it is better for Matthew that he has this life with Mr Brultzner and me."

"Peter said that Horst is like a grandfather to him."

"At first he was 'Uncle Horst', now he is 'Grandpa'."

"Children need family."

"Yes – I can only do my best now to see that Matthew grows up well."

"You have no desire to marry again?"

Sarah threw back her head and laughed. It was a heartless sound, so unlike the young woman's appearance suggested. It was a laugh that jeered, and derided life.

"I'm sorry; I didn't mean to be nosey."

"I'm not offended. I have a life for which women will pay fortunes."

"I don't understand."

"What is it that women most desire?"

"Tell me," replied Rebecca.

"It is to remain forever attractive – beautiful."

"Is that so important ... Sarah?"

"It would appear to be."

Again, Rebecca was overcome by that drowsiness that seemed to flow throughout her body as Sarah talked of the everlasting search for eternal beauty. Although Sarah did not move, she overwhelmed Rebecca, casting a spell that was fairy-like. She felt that she could listen to this young woman's voice forever. She felt caressed by her arms and kissed by her lips: gently kissed, as though a spider was walking over the sensitive skin of her neck. It was an embrace that you could sink into, deeper and deeper, lower and lower. Yet she never moved. Rebecca could see as she watched her through the mist that Sarah did not move from the chair, but sat very still and gazed upon her with those deep and dreamy eyes.

"And you have this gift – this gift of eternal beauty?"

"Yes."

"How can you be so sure?"

"Horst told me and I have felt it in my whole being since I came to work for him. This house is an enchanted place."

"The Italians talk of beauty in that way," said Rebecca, "They see their old folk as beautiful. The body for them is not forever trapped in the smoothness of youth. They allow themselves to grow old gracefully."

Later, thinking back, Rebecca wasn't sure whether any words had actually been spoken or whether she had imagined the conversation. She only remembered, vividly, the effect that the young woman's beauty had upon her as she spoke. She had never before been attracted by other women – never admired any who had been acknowledged as beautiful, never felt any tinge of envy towards them – but she was drawn to Sarah as some of her school-friends had been drawn to each other when they 'slept-over' at each other's houses. They talked about sharing their beds, laughing and cuddling together in a way that was quite different from how they behaved with a man. She felt that now, as Sarah gazed upon her. She wanted to throw her arms around her, rub cheeks and pull her close. She was so beautiful – the easy grace of her stillness, the huge mane of honey-coloured hair, the translucent skin, the fire that burned within, the smoothness and gentle pulse of her throat, the red lips curved forever in a gentle smile ... and the power! There was an irresistible power which emanated from her and Rebecca realised that Sarah was aware of this.

"I'd do anything you commanded," said Rebecca.

"Yes."

"What did I say?"

Rebecca moved slightly on the day-bed to make room for Sarah, who she wanted to sit beside her. She wanted the other woman to come close and put her arms around her, ease her dress down over her shoulder and nuzzle her neck. She felt the need for a female companion – someone with whom she could share her deepest thoughts. Sarah never moved and, before she realised what was happening, Rebecca felt herself stand, walk over to the other woman and take her hand. She squeezed it tenderly.

"We can be friends, can't we?" she asked.

"For always," replied Sarah.

It was like waking from a dream, to find herself standing beside the other woman. Rebecca was embarrassed, and so she laughed.

"Mum always said that women need a female friend – that there are some things you just cannot talk about with a man."

"Yes, I think that's true," replied Sarah.

Suddenly, everything seemed natural between them just as, a moment before, it had seemed … perverse.

"Horst is going to hold a Christmas party in the Old Vicarage," said Sarah, excitedly, "it was Liz Shaw's idea. He is over the moon about it. The whole house will be open and trimmed and alive. I can't wait. You will help, won't you Rebecca. I'm sure he'd love that – if you offered."

"If you think …"

"Of course he would. It would tickle him pink to think that the rector's daughter had offered. He wants it very Dickensian."

"I'd love too."

Suddenly the village seemed alive again, and thriving with everything possible; the gloom of too many funerals was shed. The two women walked across the room and looked out of the window. Matthew was in the outhouse, so Sarah tapped on the window and he turned to her with a quick smile.

"Can you imagine how I feel, Rebecca? My son, so young, potters about the garden, safe and sound. For the first time in my life – and I realise that now and can speak of it – I am free from the tension of not knowing what might happen when Shane came through the door. He had never hurt the boy, you understand, and never laid a finger on me, but there was always the feeling that, one night, he might just have too much to drink."

"It must have been awful."

"Not at the time – I always felt in control – but, thinking about it afterwards, I know that, at times, we sailed very close to the wind."

"People shouldn't have to live like that."

"No – and now we don't."

451

They stood in silence for a long while, watching the little boy as he toddled back and forth between outhouse and woods.

"And you're not afraid of him being alone with that wolf?"

"No – and I don't know why, I should be."

The two women laughed together – conspiratorially, as women do. Suddenly, to Rebecca, Estonia did not seem so far away. She saw mutual visits between the two countries, as the women's friendship grew and her children came onto the scene. Outside, she imagined snow covering the grounds of the Old Vicarage and the children playing together. Christmas was coming: the time when families got together and friends exchanged gifts.

"It will be nice," said Sarah.

"Yes, it will," replied Rebecca with a shudder, and shook herself, "Day-dreaming again! May I go? I'm cooking the evening meal?"

Sarah saw Rebecca to the door and watched her hurry down the path. "May I go?" It was the first time she had exerted her influence in the quiet of a drawing room, and it had been so easy. There had been moments when the other woman was completely in her power. She had seen Horst with Crafty Catchpole, mesmerising the other man so that he would do whatever was commanded, but she had never tried such a skill herself. She held young men helpless when she needed to feed, but never as she held Rebecca. It was frightening, but wonderful. The knowledge surged through her; there was a sense of completeness about it.

Rebecca slammed shut the bathroom door, rushed to the sink and vomited. Whatever she had eaten at breakfast or lunch piled into the bowl, and she turned on the tap to wash it away. 'May I go?' Why had she said that? She felt her stomach clench and the sick dribble over her chin. She retched and retched until she could throw up nothing but bile. When it was over, she sat back on the edge of the bath and was glad to feel the hard reassurance of the cold edge on her buttocks. She slumped forward, her head between her legs, sweat pouring from her every pore. She shivered, and was unbelievably cold. What was happening?

Had Sarah Marjoram behaved abominably, Rebecca could not have felt more resentment then she did at that moment. In some strange, unnerving way she had been in the woman's power; for a while she had been confused, unhinged, at the mercy .... at the mercy of what? They had talked of the years to come, of being friends. They had imagined their children growing up together. Why was there this feeling of ... revulsion? She had been entranced by her – was that such a bad thing?

Rebecca tried to recall the conversation but the words eluded her – not only the words, but the feelings also. How had she felt? She hadn't lost control like that since she was a young teenager. She had felt possessed, as though she were not in control of her emotions and her possible actions. More than that, there had been the feeling that Sarah Brown was in control; the idea that somebody else could make you do something against your will was abhorrent.

Rebecca couldn't think any further, she didn't want to think any further along those lines. Peter had asked her to see Sarah; now, Peter must listen to her while she talked her way through what she had felt. She wasn't hysterical; she wasn't imagining any nonsense. She looked in the mirror. Her face was pale and her eyes haunted. She would have to go to her room for a while; her mother mustn't see her face until it was under control.

"Peter, you never finished saying how Eva Shulz was 'strange'."

They were, once again, walking along Marsh Lane. Peter was due to return to the continent for a few weeks. He looked at her and smiled, evasively.

"I said – she was like one of Arthur Rackham's fairies."

"So you were never sure whether she was good or ... bad?"

"She was a lovely woman. I don't think she was 'bad' in any way."

"How old was she?"

"In her fifties, I believe."

"Did she look fifty-something? Don't be evasive, Peter."

"She was beautiful but ... you would have recognised her as an older woman. She wasn't 'mutton dressed as lamb'. Her beauty pervaded her whole person."

"Did you fall in love with her?"

Peter knew that he couldn't answer that question with any honesty. Desperately, he groped for the memory of Omar's words. 'So you liked her ... you felt a little desire for her ... Is this morally reprehensible? For this you will make a clean breast of it to your Rebecca? I don't think so. You have nothing to make a clean breast of – did you even kiss this woman? No!'

"Answer my question."

"Looking at her filled me with ... contentment and shame."

"And longing?"

"I did nothing wrong, Rebecca."

"I didn't say you did. Go on."

"She possessed an eternal freshness. It was intoxicating."

"You felt that you could refuse her nothing?"

Peter looked at Rebecca with anguish in his eyes.

"Her effect on me was devastating, but there was nothing coquettish about her, you understand? She made no advances to me. She was open and honest. It was just that simply being with her was fascinating. Do you understand?"

"Yes," said Rebecca, "I understand."

CHAPTER 10

True Colours

Tony Crewes closed his back door quietly behind him. 'Thank God the weekend is over. Even work seems attractive at the moment.' He had arranged to meet Nadine Palmester in town and to visit her father who, two weeks after his near-fatal vigil, was still in hospital. He was looking forward to that; he was looking forward to anything that would take him out of the rut of his life. He'd had a bad weekend with Beth – one of those "Can I have a word with you, quietly?" weekends.

The note hadn't helped, of course, slipped as it was through the door in the early morning. Beth had found it, left it on the hall stand and then wondered who "would be slipping notes through our door at this hour." He couldn't explain to her – only assure her that it was all right and "No, it wasn't from a woman" and "No, she couldn't read it." He didn't dare let her do that; the note was from David Stokes and Tony feared for the boy's safety.

He had met David Stokes on the beach at Blacksands Ness on Sunday morning, as the note requested. The boy arrived on time with his black Labrador and the key to 'the place'. The boy had guessed his insincerity and brought it.

"His lordship is away. I took it from his study."

"When will he be back?"

"At the weekend."

"I'll get a copy made and return this to you. You're sure about this, son? You can always change your mind."

"Do you want me to?"

"No."

"Right then. Mister..."

"Tony."

"Tony, do you know anymore than you did last time?"

"No, but I am going to see a friend of mine on Monday afternoon. He hasn't been well. He lost his memory, but I think he might be able to help."

"What's this place?"

Tony looked at the boy and looked at the very old, very heavy key in his hand. It would be difficult getting a copy made of that, but there was a locksmith in Lowestoft – one of the back-street shops where old crafts lived on – and he would go there early on Monday morning, before work.

"Tony! What's this place?"

Should he take the boy into his confidence? The lad had every right; he was the only one who had done anything, as yet.

"Will you take me with you, when you have a look?"

"Son ..."

"David."

"David ... I don't know anything for sure yet, and what I suspect about this killing of your white bull would seem to have nothing to do with an even greater mystery over-hanging the village. I'm not keeping quiet because I'm a grown-up and you're a child. I'm keeping quiet because I'm not sure what is going on – and neither is anyone else."

"But you know about the place?"

"Possibly. I'd be a little worried taking you without your dad's permission."

"Dad would say that I was betraying his lordship's trust in us."

Tony remembered how he as a child had often thought he saw, clearly, to the heart of things, while the grown-ups around him talked endlessly in circles, unable or unwilling to make a move.

"I want you to promise me that you'll do nothing, alone."

"I promise."

"Let's sit down, son – David – and I'll try to explain. Long ago, in the time of the Romans, there were many religions – one of them, long since dead as I thought – involved the slaying of a white bull. This particular religion was very popular among Roman soldiers and this country was once occupied by the Romans so they built sanctuaries to their god over here. Not many remain, but we know – from piecing together what we have found and what we can read in their histories – what these places looked like and, to an extent, what happened inside them. All of this was secret, of course, and much remains a mystery. The god was a god of light and wisdom and he is always represented, on the marble reliefs we have found, as a handsome youth with ringlets of hair, wearing a tall red cap, a flowing cloak and a long-sleeved tunic. On the carvings he is seen plunging his knife into the shoulder of a huge, white bull. A dog and a snake ...."

"Symbols of good?"

"Yes – the dog and the snake are drinking the bull's life-giving blood while a scorpion – a symbol of evil – attacks its heart, liver ... and so on. The bull, you understand personifies ...." He paused as he used the word, but the boy's eyes only flickered with irritation not with a lack of understanding, "... personifies a primeval vitality ...."

"In some mythologies a bull, or a cow, were the first living creatures created."

"Yes. The god pursues, captures and, after a dreadful struggle, brings the bull back to his cave. He has tamed the primeval force. He slays the animal, releasing its concentrated power for the benefit of mankind. From the dying bull, new forms of life spring up – from its body, useful plants and herbs, from its blood the grapevine and from its ... its semen all the useful animals are created. Those who worshiped this god did so in underground, or nearly underground, temples. In each temple there was some representation of this central event – the slaying of the white bull. What you saw was, I believe, a re-enactment of this event ..."

"So the place is a temple?"

"Yes – and an active one, which is unheard of today."

"So his lordship is the leader of this temple?"

"It must be so. These cults were very secret, David. We know they appealed to soldiers because they involved initiation rituals of physical and mental ordeals. Those who wanted to become members faced torments of cold and heat before being admitted. It was a tough religion, a constant struggle between light and dark, good and evil. Cult members were sworn to secrecy. To this day, much of what we think we know is guesswork – intelligent guesswork but guesswork, all the same. Roman soldiers carried it to every corner of the empire, but none who were members ever betrayed their secrets."

"So who is ... he – the one who killed the white bull?"

"I don't know – other than that he, too, is a member of the temple, and a very important one."

"He isn't the god come back?"

"No – I don't think so."

"He has strange powers. When he fought the bull, it wasn't fair – he was so quick. Sometimes it was like the bull couldn't kill him – the horns seemed to pass right through him. And he is so strong – like ten men – and he has power over animals. He is the only one who ever touched the bull – except dad and me."

"He isn't the god returned, David, whatever he might be, but he is a strange, a truly awesome, person. He is also dangerous. It would not be good should he find out that you have taken this key, and Lord Wangford must not find out either. The reason I have been so reluctant to talk about this is that these men must be linked through this secret religion. They will wish it to remain secret and will make sure that it does – whatever the cost. Do you understand me?"

"Yes, Tony."

"Before I take a look inside their temple, I want to try and find out about something else that happened in the village which must be linked to all this. I promise you that I will be in touch and, remember, you have promised me that you will not act alone – yes?"

"Yes. What is this other thing?"

"It was what brought me to the estate that morning," replied Tony, evasively, "A man I know had been rambling on about white bulls and he kept saying the Latin phrase *Viros servasti eternali sanguine fuso.*"

"*You have saved men by the spilling of the eternal blood.*"

"How ..?"

"I read it in a book on mythology."

"Ah! Well, I'd heard about the cattle. That is what brought me there."

"The spilling of blood happens a lot in mythology, doesn't it?" said David.

"Yes – and we need to be sure that yours isn't among the blood spilt. So mums the word. OK? I'll get that key back to you as soon as possible. Shall we arrange to bump into each other here on ... Tuesday night? I just hope that I can get the key copied by then and you can get the original back where it belongs."

"And you will take me with you into the temple?"

"Yes – but we shall need to make sure it is safe," replied Tony, hesitantly.

It was a partial lie – he didn't really feel able to put the boy at any risk whatsoever – but he hoped David Stokes didn't realise.

"What's your dog's name?" he asked, partly to distract them both.

"Bess," said David, and they fondled the dog's ears.

Tony looked at the boy once more and then turned away. He waved as he made his way back through the lagoons and he saw the boy standing there, on the Ness, watching him. He was very still, very determined; there would be no denying him what he had set out to accomplish.

He had found the old score easily; it was one of those rough streets that cut a passageway to what had, in better times, been the wharf. The score would have been dark in the past – a winding alleyway among many, frequented by sailors and fishermen in various stages of intoxication as they made their way either from or to work. The smell of fish and engine oil would have been everywhere and lingering wafts of salt water would have permeated the air and every crevice along the cobbled way. When Tony arrived, all that remained were the cobbles, the occasional cry of a gull overhead – and the shop, a last remnant of a dead age. It had once, probably, been a chandlery; there was still evidence of this in the coiled ropes, oars, lanterns, nets, floats and other marine items that now looked like so much bric-a-brac. Had the shop been created to look this way, someone would have achieved a magnificent falsehood; it was just that the decades had done it in a more leisurely and natural fashion. The man behind the counter looked up as the doorbell rang, and Tony entered. He didn't speak, but eyed Tony, quietly.

"You mended a clock for me once," Tony ventured, introducing himself.

"I remember – a small wall clock with a pendulum. I told you it wasn't broken because it had been over-wound ..."

"...because you cannot over-wind a clock. My wife didn't believe me."

"They never do."

"I have a key, and I wondered if you could cut me a copy."

The man took the key and eyed it as closely as he had eyed Tony.

"You'll be lucky to get one like this cut anywhere. They certainly won't do it at Minute-man."

There was a sneer on his face as he spoke. Tony noticed the balding head and thinning, wavy hair that flopped over the man's forehead. He wore a faded white shirt, folded half-way up his forearms, a leather waistcoat that would have cost a fortune in Norbridge (but which Tony fancied had simply been handed down over the generations), a wide leather belt (unobtainable anywhere, today) and a red spotted neckerchief. Tony could tell by the intensity of his stillness that he was excited.

"I'll do it for you but on one condition – you let me make a copy for myself."

Tony didn't bother to ask why; to have such a key, whether you owned the door to which it belonged or not, would be a privilege. Modern locks were safer, but didn't hold the interest.

"I don't mind that," he said.

"How soon do you want it?"

"Does tomorrow sound too soon?"

"Next month would sound too soon."

"I can't let you have the key that long."

"No."

There was a pause – a long, deliberate pause. The shopkeeper was about to confer a favour and he wanted them both to savour the moment.

"I'll do my best, but give me a ring before you come. This isn't going to be easy unless I'm lucky. I'll give you my number."

"Have you a business card?"

The man looked at him and smiled; he realised it was a joke. Pulling a brown paper bag from a nail in a beam, he wrote his phone number in flowing copperplate.

"Have you thought about selling me that clock yet?"

"It was my mother's."

"Well – if ever she decides to get rid of it."

"You'll have first refusal."

He left the shop feeling uplifted. No price had been discussed, but Tony knew that it would be a fair one, and the shopkeeper knew that also.

Tony arrived for work very late and left early. It gave him his second good feeling that day. He couldn't understand why one of the new management consultant types didn't suggest that he should be fired with a fat, farewell handshake.

He had arranged to meet Nadine in No 33 – a coffee shop where you sometimes had to queue for a table because the ambience was so relaxed, the coffee so good and where they actually bothered to warm the croissant. The young people who presided over the café obviously cared about it, and whoever cooked knew the art of providing fresh, warm food fast. It was one of only three cafés in Norbridge that offered any threat to the French and Italians. He smiled at the waitress, one of several girls who always seemed pleased to serve you, and was shown to a table where he was to wait for Nadine. She appeared promptly.

"Thanks for coming, Tony."

"I am more than pleased to do so. We need to see this out, Nadine. There's been too much time wasted already. I just hope, now that your dad's memory is returning, that we have enough time to persuade him to tell us what he knows."

"Have you had any more thoughts about this?"

Tony had decided to take Nadine completely into his confidence, and had reserved a table in the far back corner of the shop so that they would be undisturbed. He told her about his visit to the Wangford estate following her father's ramblings about white bulls, about the outcome and what he intended to do. He explained that while he saw no link between her father's suspicions over Sarah and his knowledge of the temple, he felt there must be one.

"The link is obvious," she cried, "The link is Brultzner" Her cry drew the attention of the waitress. Nadine lowered her voice and continued, "You have simply been looking for the wrong kind of link – a supernatural one."

"But that would involve Charles Wangford and the members of the cult."

"No, Tony. You are looking for a connection! It doesn't exist. White bulls have nothing to do with Sarah and Sidney."

Simon Palmester was sitting up in a chair when they arrived, several books piled on his trolley and a Bible in his lap.

"I'm only letting them keep me in, Naddy, because it gives me time to read."

"Yes, dad, of course. Meanwhile in the real world ..."

"Good afternoon, Mr Palmester," said Tony.

"Mr Crewes," was the old priest's only acknowledgement of Tony.

"We haven't got long, dad. I've brought Tony because I trust him – his integrity and his courage. You said on Saturday that your memory was returning – that you were seeing things. Tell us about them. Don't be stubborn – someone out here needs to know, and even if you were the one out here you couldn't do too much with broken ribs and punctured lungs. You need us – both of us."

"You've got a hard tongue, Naddy."

"Come on, dad. We've less than an hour. What happened in the Bethel?"

"Get me to the day room. We can't talk here – too many nosey-parkers," he said, giving the man in the next bed a stern look, as he spoke.

"It's rather unconnected and I'm not sure I understand it, but I will tell you what I remember and you can make of it what you will ... After you'd gone, Naddy, I turned from the door and he was watching me – or so it seemed ..."

"Sidney Close?" asked Tony.

"Yes – but don't interrupt my flow again, son. It comes and goes and I may lose it ... He was sitting up in his coffin ... It was a blasphemy, but you can fight the Devil ....." Simon relayed his ordeal in the Bethel, punctuating the account of his struggle with his appeals to the Lord and his fears for Sidney. "... even in that state, Naddy, his hand reached for the Lord. I tell you now, I felt pity for that creature so far was it from God's sweet mercy ... I prayed, Naddy – believe me, I prayed ... And I had the Lord's cross in my hand ... he was so near, I felt for my very soul, but I had my Bible ... I know this sounds strange but ... I had a sense that he was waiting for Deliverance ... I sang. I drove that devil into dumbness, and I held the Lord's face in my gaze ... I thought all Hell was trying to enter ... but I never faltered, Naddy, I never faltered ... I felt the power of the Lord in my arm and ... He lifted Sidney Close from the ground and threw him back against the altar rail ... It all goes then, Naddy, until you arrived with Mr Crewes."

"Tony."

"Tony," said Simon, who was utterly exhausted.

"There was nothing else, then, no one else?"

"No – at least, I can remember no more."

"Sarah wasn't there or ..."

"... or who, Naddy?"

Nadine hesitated. She didn't want to put ideas into his head. The ground was too fragile for that; they needed the truth. She looked at Tony Crewes who smiled – he hoped, reassuringly. Simon had lost his colour: he was as drained of blood and vigour as he had been the night, two weeks before, when they brought him in.

They heard the bell ring for the end of visiting and ignored it. A nurse entered and gasped at the sight of Simon.

"Mr Palmester?"

"Leave us, Nurse, leave us – or I'll discharge myself." The exchange was brief and biting but the nurse, having glanced briefly at Nadine and Tony, left them and closed the door.

"Do you remember the marks on your throat, dad?"

"Am I likely to forget?"

"You believe that Sidney Close put them there?"

"Who else?"

"And that he is a vampire?"

"He is the Devil's spawn. That is my belief and, from what Sidney told me before that night, I believe Sarah Marjoram was responsible for the loss of his soul."

"How did someone as lovely as Sarah come to be involved in vampirism?"

"The Devil enjoys corrupting the innocent. Sarah Marjoram, as she once was, would have been an attractive challenge for Satan."

"What do you want us to do, dad?"

"You don't need to ask me that, Naddy. You know what you have to do. Nosophoros – the plague carrier. How did you wipe out a plague? You burn it from the face of the earth."

"We shall need to have Sidney's body exhumed. Who will grant permission for that? Will you make a statement?"

"Is that a serious question? You've never insulted my integrity before," said the old man, a smile on his face.

"But who will believe us? The story is preposterous."

Another period of silence followed, while Nadine and Tony thought through the implications of the actions they proposed and Simon sank further into exhaustion. Who were they to approach? Simon views were considered extreme and he would be dismissed as a 'crazed priest'.

"We might speak to Corvin Unwood," said Tony.

"Corvin is a fine man in many respects, but he is frightened of his own shadow. You would do better to talk to his wife," retorted Simon, scathingly.

"We could speak with Alan Read," said Nadine.

"Better him than Jim Maxwell, who would have you both certified."

"Is there anything else you can tell us, dad?"

"No, Naddy – except to tread carefully. Arm yourselves against the Devil, and remember you will be doing God's work. There is no sin in that. The sin lies in turning a deaf ear to His call. Mr Crewes ... Tony ... I have my fears for you. You lack the protection of the Lord. I sense that in you. Nadine can protect herself against these ... Beings, but you cannot. There is no faith in you. There is no sanctuary for you until you accept the Lord as your saviour."

He paused and looked hard into Tony's eyes; there was fear in the priest's gaze, and deep concern and an almost overwhelming tenderness. Tony could find no words to reply.

"It only takes a small leap of faith, Tony. Put your soul into the Lord's safekeeping – make the jump from sinner to saved."

"Are you all right?" asked Nadine when they were once more in the city, driving towards St Patrick's car-park where Tony had left his car.

"Yes. I'm just overwhelmingly sad. Sarah was an intelligent girl. She was moving her life forward. She had a job with Horst Brultzner, her lad was soon to be in school and she would be free to get the education she deserved. Now this!"

"We cannot be absolutely sure ...."

"No – but we ...," Tony Crewes didn't finish the sentence, and Nadine drove in silence until she reached the car-park.

"What's our next move?" she asked.

"I think I'm going to have a word with Martin."

"Martin Billings?"

"Yes. He's a maverick. He might cut a few corners for us."

"Do you want me to approach Alan Read?"

"You probably know him better than I do – or, at least, as well."

"And Corvin?"

"What do you think?"

"I don't know."

"No – not knowing, and not daring to know, has been our problem all along, hasn't it, Nadine? I just wonder how many others might be in the same boat."

"Nevertheless, let's take one step at a time," she replied, "If we can get these people on side over Sidney Close, then we widen our ... concerns."

"So, we don't mention our suspicions regarding Brultzner, Sarah, Charles Wangford or the temple at this stage?"

"No – I think the idea of Sidney Close being a vampire will be quite enough for Martin and Alan to swallow."

When Tony arrived, Martin and Amy Billings were just finishing their evening meal, and before Tony could frame a protest there was a large glass of red wine in front of him. Martin was full of his trip to France, and Tony knew he would have to listen patiently before broaching the matter that had brought him to their table. Amy smiled that sleepy-eyed smile of hers and leaned forward, resting her elbows on the table and her chin on the palms of her hands. One little ray of hope, which shone through Martin's meanderings, was his friendship with Alan Read – something of which Tony had not been fully aware, and which boded well for what he had in mind.

Amy drifted away eventually and brought them a cheese-board, some french bread and a fresh bottle of wine.

"Is the Chenas all right for you, Tony? I find it rather insipid with cheese," she enquired, with a sly smile, "Have you asked Tony why he's come, Martin?"

"Hhmm?"

"Have you asked Tony ...."

"I heard you, Amy. Why have you come, Tony?"

"I need your help – professionally."

"I'll go," said Amy, "Good night, Tony. Give me a kiss. I'll see you in the morning, Martin."

"What's up?" asked Martin.

"I want you to listen to what I have to say without interrupting, remembering that we are old friends, that I am not a nutcase and that I have given this matter long and ... oh, Martin ... tedious consideration."

His old friend listened while Tony told his tale and Martin's mind became a labyrinth of his own recollections, centred on the little boy who had been chalky white and what Alan Read had said "... the only certain sign of death is the absence of activity in the higher centres of the brain, those which give us our capacity for consciousness and social interaction."

"What do you want me to do?" asked Martin, when Tony had finished.

"Arrange an exhumation."

"You need reasons for that sort of thing, Tony – good reasons, reasons that will hold water in a courtroom."

"Is there no chance you could arrange it ... with less fuss?"

"I'm a police officer, Tony. My job is to uphold the law – not defy it!"

"You've always been a little ... shall we say, unorthodox."

"My unorthodoxy doesn't extend to digging up bodies in churchyards."

"Come on, Martin – now is the time to put your courage to the test. We need a maverick. We need someone who can throw the book away when necessary."

"Does Corvin know about this hare-brained scheme?"

"Not yet – we thought he might lack the backbone for such an enterprise."

"You need a rest, Tony. You've been working too hard. Take a holiday."

"Martin – I've come to you as a friend."

Martin moved away from the table, picking up the opened bottle of wine as he went and retrieving the cork. He began to insert it in the neck of the bottle. Tony realised that he was tidying away, putting everything neatly into the cupboards and drawers, restoring order to the kitchen.

"What were we drinking there, Martin? Beaujolais was it – a light, unpretentious little number, all right for quaffing but without much body? It's almost time for the Nouveau, isn't it – the third Thursday in November is almost upon us – am I right? It should suit you, but drink it up quickly because it's light and low in tannin. That's the stuff that gives a wine its backbone, isn't it, Martin? Without that it doesn't keep very well! It isn't going to be there when you really need it!"

"There's no need to put our friendship on the line over this, Tony. You're obviously overwrought."

"Would you like me to bring Nadine round?"

"She's a feminist – an hysteric."

"No – no she isn't. You'll find no cooler, clearer, analytical mind in the whole village than Nadine's."

"She's obviously going to be hysterical at the moment – after what's happened to her father."

"What's happened to her father, Martin?"

"OK – what she thinks has happened to her father."

"Perhaps you'd like talk to Simon himself?"

"He's a ..."

"... religious eccentric? Yes – we'd thought the 'official line' would sound something like that! Back on board, are you, Martin? Cruising towards your retirement pension? Enjoy the Beaujolais Nouveau! Why not invite that inspector of yours round to dinner? There was a time when that kind of thing would have turned your stomach. Or was that just part of the carefully cultivated image? Martin Billings, maverick cop!"

"Have you finished?"

"Yes – I'm sorry, Martin."

"Never mind – I said, you're overwrought."

"I'm desperate. I need help and you're the only one I could think of. I believe all this, Martin. I didn't – I haven't for months, but I do now, and I have to do something."

"Go home – sleep on it. Take some tablets. Knock yourself out and wake refreshed. You'll feel better in the morning."

"Nadine has gone to see Alan Read. I only hope she fares better than I have."

"Do you think Alan will believe all this nonsense?"

"Do you?"

Martin Billings continued clearing the table, and recalled his conversation with Alan Read in France. On their return, he had heard nothing further; there had only been that call from Junket, reprimanding him for "handing out telephone numbers without due regard for the security issues" and reminding him that he "wouldn't be going far in the force with that kind of attitude." He'd assumed that the whole business had been put to bed. He didn't mind bucking the system, but not if it placed him in a position of weakness. Standing in a churchyard with a freshly exhumed coffin – illegally exhumed coffin – at his feet was likely to get him a dishonourable discharge rather than a fat lump sum because he was 'medically unfit'. Martin, however, didn't like looking a coward, and that was exactly how his old friend saw him now.

"If Alan Read gets involved, you can count me in. Otherwise, I suggest you do as I said and take a break."

"Thanks Martin."

"You've nothing to thank me for."

"I will have. I have every faith in Nadine's persuasive powers."

The two men looked at each other with a mixture of distrust and resentment – the distrust on Tony's part, the resentment on Martin's. It was all very well sounding-off bravely over a few glasses of wine at parties. It was quite another living up to that armchair heroism when the shit hit the fan. Things would never be the same between them again – even if Martin came over to their side. Tony knew that, and the knowledge was painful. He finished the glass which Amy had poured for him, and left with a smile. Martin finished tidying his kitchen and put out the light. Everything in the house was in order; he'd prefer to keep it that way.

Tony turned right from Martin's house and made his way along the High Street. He wasn't in a hurry to get home; Beth would be waiting with her questions to which he had no answers. He wondered whether to call in on Nadine, but was unsure whether she had approached Alan Read as yet, and his progress with Martin wasn't exactly encouraging.

The moon was in its first quarter and wouldn't rise until the early hours. 'Only five weeks or so until Christmas: still, it'll be over in six!' Tony often cheered himself up by being as gloomy as possible. The expense of Christmas appalled him; he was still paying back the 'festive loan' he had reluctantly acquired two years before. Shadows filled the street – pale shadows from the young moon, shadows that could have been anything or anybody. He would make his way to the churchyard and sit. If he sat long enough there was just a chance (just a chance) that Beth would go to bed and fall asleep before he arrived.

As he passed the hairdresser's, Tony was suddenly conscious of being followed. It was only the briefest of shadows, but it nipped swiftly into a doorway as he turned to look across the road into the window of the salon. He paused and walked over to the hairdresser's, turning his eyes along the High Street in the hope of seeing whoever it was; there was nothing to be seen. A prowling cat making its way to the fields of Willowmere was the only movement he could discern. He walked back along the opposite side of the road and peered across into the doorway of the cottage: nothing. It was odd; he could have sworn he had seen someone. He walked over the road and the shadows stirred. At first dark, then light-grey, they merged with, and then rose from, the porch; but there was nothing – nothing except the sound of voices from the Queen's Head.

Tony turned once again and re-passed the hairdressing salon. This time he paused and looked in the window of Totto Briggs's shop. It was clear of all but a few sterile trays and some bottles of pickles and preserves that Totto sold to accompany his pies. Tony decided against turning into Market Place. It was always dark there with sudden turnings into driveways and alleyways that led nowhere. He walked on as though he was going out of the village until he came to the corner of Shoemaker's Lane. He looked across at the entrance to the Wildlife Park and thought of Crafty Catchpole's awful death. What must it have felt like being pursued by wolves and then making your last, hopeless stand alone? It must be true – Brultzner must be involved; the vampire was known to have control over 'the lesser animals'. No one had thought of that! Crafty had been the gardener at the Old Vicarage. Had he known more than he should? Had this religious cult become an excuse for other sorts of blood-letting?

Tony turned down Shoemaker's Lane and decided to make his way home. Even Beth, at her most vituperative, was better than grey shadows and dark thoughts. He passed Market Place. A figure stood in the road watching him. He ran towards it – better faced than followed – and the figure turned away, melting into the darkness. Tony looked about. His eyes searched everywhere, frantically, but there was nothing. There had been a figure. He was sure he was not mistaken. He was sure he was not, in Martin's word, "overwrought".

"Martin – is that you fooling around?"

From one of the alleyways, he thought he heard a chuckle. Tony ran towards it, between the high-gabled walls of the cottages, opening gates onto garden allotments: nothing. He looked up. A figure, like that of a giant bat, climbed nimbly onto the roof above him and was gone into the light of the moon. Tony rushed back into the road so he could see the entire roof: nothing. There was nothing on the roof and yet, if he had seen a giant bat, it must still be there. Above him the clouds scudded across the lightening sky. There was a shadow against the chimney breast – a shadow which faded and then died.

Tony Crewes was frightened; he admitted it to himself. It had been a long day – an unbelievably exhausting day. He should not have visited Martin and had the Chenas, but should have stayed at home with Beth. He whirled round and walked quickly away towards home, glancing back only once. There were the allotments, the water tower, the old farm labourer's cottages, the new bungalows and the open road. There were the neat little gardens to the cottages, and the shingled driveways to the bungalows – the old and the new, hand in hand. Think prosaically – stay sane! Tony challenged himself and smiled. Nadine had surprised him with her introduction to her father. "I've brought Tony because I trust him – his integrity and his courage." That had been nice; Tony Crewes hadn't been sure of either since he was a young man.

He reached the grassy hummock at the junction of School Road, Shoemaker's Lane and Mardles Lane where, early in May, Horst Brultzner had seen Peter Vishnya watching him. Tony glanced across towards the footpath sign and saw a figure sitting on the hummock. As he watched, the figure lowered its head. Tony was angry by now and he stormed out into the road. He was half-expecting the figure to move but it remained motionless until he was near enough to see its face, and then it raised its head and looked at him. Every detail of the face registered in a single gut-stopping moment – the smooth and flushed face beneath which a bluish light glowed, the trademark smirk lingering in the eyes and around the corners of the mouth, the hair flopped across the forehead and the tight lips clenched over the white teeth that were invisible now but which he remembered from the coffin. He stared into the face of Sidney Close. He stared and stared, unable to speak while Sidney's smile only broadened into that smug grin he'd worn as he processed down the aisle of St George's carrying the cross. Here was the man who, only a few days ago (was it days or weeks?) had lain in his coffin and had been dead and buried 'and descended into Hell. On the third day ...' Here was realisation that it was not all nonsense.

"Lost for words, Mr Crewes? This isn't the first time I've seen you 'banged into dumbness'. Tell me – where did that phrase come from? That and all the other smart-arsed phrases you used to come out with to make the rest of us look stupid."

Tony Crewes didn't know whether to back away or simply stand and stare into the face. He felt that to move would invite retaliation and, above all, he wanted to avoid that. This ... this Thing sitting on the hummock had the upper hand, and Tony wanted the blow he knew was to come delayed at any cost.

"It was you following me! How long ...?"

"More stupid questions? I would have thought you might be wondering how I came to be sitting here?"

Still, Tony could find no words, and this amused Close, who smiled in the sure knowledge of his power. "I was your creature once, wasn't I – the butt of your wit in the insolence of your office ..."

Tony nearly smiled at the allusions but dare not; he was terrified at what he knew would happen.

"... something for you and Billings to mock and kick around – figuratively speaking, of course. Nice phrase, isn't it – 'mock and kick around'? Would have done you credit, at one time. Did you like it?" Sidney paused and looked at Tony. The arrogance in his smile was unnerving. He persisted in the same mocking tone, "I asked you a question – did you like it? ... Well, do I get an answer?"

"It has a certain *je ne sais quoi* about it," replied Tony, knowing that it was a mistake to use the rather pretentious, foreign phrase. He couldn't resist the temptation anymore than he had been able to restrain himself from pouring the bucket of water over Shane Marjoram's head.

Close punched him full-belt straight in the mouth and, as he tottered in the road, kicked his feet from under him. Tony fell onto his back, knocking both elbows sharply, and Close proceeded to kick him along the road. The vampire's feet, clad in the builder's boots, delivered punishing blow after blow to Tony's ribs and kidneys. The moon shot backwards and forwards across the sky as Tony tried to grab hold of the tarmac and push away from the blows. Each time he got to his knees another boot thudded into him, making him wretch and sending him breathless onto his back. Close drove his heel down into Tony's stomach, a grin suffusing his face as he watched the other man's pain, and then lifted him to his knees. He grasped him by the collar with one hand, while the other delivered rhythmic blows across his face.

"Jer" – the knuckles cut open his right cheek, "Ner" – the hand dealt a fierce blow to his left cheek, "Say" – the hand returned, widening the cut, "Qwa" – the second slap rocked his head back and forth.

Tony reeled and vomited, praying for an end to the pain.

"What does it mean?"

"A certain, inexplicable something," he managed to gasp.

Close's fist drove down onto his head once more, nearly splintering his skull. When he came to, Tony was lying on the grassy hummock, alone. He didn't think he could have been there long unless the inevitable passers-by had ignored him as a drunk. The stars were out; it was going to be a cold night. He sat up and the pain shot through him. 'Please God, not broken ribs – one set of those is enough.' His trousers were torn from the abrasions of the road, and bloody knees poked through holes that could never be darned. His shirt and jacket were pulled open and button-less; his bared chest was covered with sweat and dirt. He looked at his hands, grazed from the road and stubbled with grit. He reached for his cheek and felt the warm blood seeping from the laceration; he shook it from his fingers. Licking his lips, Tony realized that several teeth were missing. Fearfully, he felt his throat and sank back onto the grass when he realized he was clean: no bite marks. 'Thank God for that!' Close could return, of course. He would be in no hurry. Was he still in the grave, or had he moved himself to a place of safety? He must have moved, mustn't he? There were empty houses all over the village; they couldn't search every one.

As Tony struggled to stand, and as his thoughts became positive, he realized that hope was returning. He was alive, and he was thinking ahead. He could be dead now – or worse. He'd see Nadine. No, she'd had a hard day and would be asleep. He'd see Billings. No, Amy might be there and how would he explain his condition? He'd go home, go in through the french doors of his study and listen. If all was quiet, he'd make his way to the bathroom and clean himself. The evidence would still be there in the morning; his beating had clinched the matter. Both Martin and Alan Read would have to believe them now.

Every step he took was agony, but at least he was in one piece. When he reached his house, Tony saw the moon over the sea tha shone slate-grey in the light. The house was in darkness and he let himself in, quietly. Beth and the children were asleep. He knew that for certain: there was no sense of a living, wakeful presence anywhere in his home. Tony loved his home and would have known if anyone within had been awake. He sank onto his study chair for a moment to recover his thoughts and find peace. Here was a sanctuary. No one could enter here, ever.

CHAPTER 11

Hoist with her own petard

Sidney Close had inflicted all the punishment he wished on Tony Crewes, for one night. He'd given him a taste of the pain and damnation that lay in wait. Coming across him as he left Billings's house had been a fortuitous accident, but he'd other game to flush out.

He'd visited his adolescent on Pack Close as soon as the sun had gone and darkness rendered him safe, tapping at her window with a single piece of pea-gravel. There had been no need to rip off her clothes – more was the pity. She was ready for him, and gagging for it – the little slut. He'd refreshed himself from her veins several times since that first night – but not too often. It was best to keep them keen and hot. She'd been naked – young women had no style, no sense of how to entice a man – and had tugged his clothes from him as he came in through the window. He'd made her beg for it, and then denied her – he wanted to save himself – but he had taken enough blood to warm him through, and feel her come in his grip. She tried to kiss him all over before he left, but he'd let her get only so far. He hadn't wanted such intoxication – not tonight.

Grise Culman was threadbare. She seemed to drain Owen dry so quickly these days. After a couple of hours, there was nothing left in him and she was still hungry for more. She'd left him asleep on the bed and then wandered through the house in her nightdress. It was too cold to walk down to the beach in November.

She wanted Mark Chambers as she had always wanted him. The few energetic and delightful months of their affair were fresh in her mind. Whenever she felt horny, it was always Mark's hands that clutched her buttocks. At night she would toss and turn with her memories, starting with that first time in the straw when she'd felt like a bitch on heat. He was the only man with whom she had ever been unfaithful to Owen, and she wanted him again. It had been a good feeling having a man as.... natural as Mark Chambers hungry for you. Both their spare bedrooms had reeked of the smell of sex for days afterwards. She'd laughed at his dilemma, given him a fresh-air spray and told him to open the windows! They'd never had any trouble finding the place and time because both Nin and Owen trusted them. Neither had indulged in deliberate lies, either – just deceit.

She had tried to rouse Owen into being some kind of substitute, but it hadn't worked. There had been once, just once in all that time since the end of the affair, when she'd known something akin to the lust she felt for Mark. It had been after their Health Club Party when she'd ridden Owen like a horse. The next morning, the children had asked why she had called out in the night. Owen had been embarrassed and dipped another soldier into his eggs, hurriedly, but she had laughed at the memory. Sitting with her family at the breakfast table, Grise felt anything but shame. She remembered her eagerness for him and Owen bending over her and calling "Grise" as he came. His right arm had been under her shoulder, supporting her, holding her against him, and she remembered saying to him "All those promises ….." He'd loved her enough that night to terrify her; a man's ferocity could be like that – fulfilling but terrifying.

She took a bottle of white wine from the fridge, poured herself a glass and wandered over to the patio window which opened onto their terrace. The line of trees, which gave them privacy in summer, was now bare of leaves and the naked branches swayed and creaked. Grise could see them reflected in the glass; shadows danced among them. It was a pity the summer had gone; she would have loved to walk through the long grass at the edge of the cliff as she had done during those glorious days. Why not! She had a fur coat – real fur! It was one she had bought long before all the fuss, when she and Owen were young and free. It would be fun. It was a long time since she had walked about naked under a fur coat. She knew exactly where to look, and reached for her fur in the dark. It would be warm enough out there, even in November, for a short time.

She noticed a slight breeze was stirring the trees, but nothing more, when she slid back the door and stepped out onto the terrace. The fur reached almost to her ankles; it had cost a fortune but was worth every penny. The only cold she felt was on her face; underneath the fur she was 'as warm as toast'! What a lovely expression! She'd kick the fire back into life when she got in and eat some buttered toast in front of the flames. They'd done that, more than once, in the log cabin she and Owen had rented. She'd wake him. He'd have to give her what she wanted. She breathed in the sea-clean air and drew the coat more tightly around her.

The grass was dry, it being too early for the dew to have settled, and Grise felt it under her feet for what she imagined would be the last time that year. The fur felt wonderful against her naked flesh. It was funny how different things could be sexy – with Mark it had been wax coats and Wellington boots! God – she'd give anything for another autumn and winter with Mark in his wax coat!

Grise looked about her; this was her land. She and Owen had worked for every inch. It enclosed their bungalow, wrapping them in as her fur coat protected her now. She began to feel the tingle of it against her skin; she was actually warm. Her body would still be golden, too – golden and glowing under the fur. She stretched her arms akimbo and danced – the dance she had seen them do in that Russian film: the one where the peasants had twirled around the crackling fire, while the snow fell all around, settling on the black earth and fluttering down in front of the dark pines. Grise followed the drift of her raised arms and twisted her body, sinking low on the bend of the knees, rising again on her toes as they gripped the earth and took her weight. She felt her thighs slide across one another. Grise lifted her arms, opening herself to the night sky. Life didn't go on for ever. You needed to grab these moments when you could, but it was more fun to share them with someone else. It was the stretching that was so glorious. Grise spread wide her arms and spun round and round and round. How long could you keep that momentum going? She was still thirty-something; Sandra called it "prime time".

"Grise?"

She thought that it was Mark calling, and then decided it must be Owen. When she turned, Sidney Close was behind her – his legs braced, his hands clapping.

When she regained consciousness, Grise ached all over. Her blood was on fire and throbbing. She wasn't sure where they were, but it was somewhere out of the wind and he had her propped against his arm. Her coat was still pulled round her and Grise felt warm all over. She knew she had fainted and that Sidney must have caught her as she fell. He watched her without speaking, a self-satisfied smirk on his face. It was more than self-satisfied; the man knew he had her completely in his power. It was an assurance of arrogant proportions; when he wanted her again he would simply take his pleasure.

The horror of this swept through Grise as she opened her eyes, but her first conscious thought was that this man was dead. She had attended his funeral. Alive, he had lusted after her: dead, he had taken her as he wished. Grise dare not speak: not to what must be a ghost. She'd read stories about this kind of thing – years ago, when she was young, when she read. There had been one where the ghost of Don Juan had come to a woman whose husband gave her no satisfaction, and 'set her aflame with desire' – as the writer had said in the book. She felt his hand feeling for her under the coat and she was powerless to resist or even protest. Almost casually, he brushed aside the fur; he was relentless. Nauseous with shame, Grise felt herself coming before his onslaught – and that was the only word for it. When Sidney Close had finished, he pulled the coat around her in a gesture of mocking tenderness.

"You were always a hot piece, weren't you, Grise, encouraging men to lust after you? How does it feel now, to be really satisfied? I bet you've never felt before in all your life as you feel now – am I right? I've learned a lot about women recently. I never tire, see. I was watching you with Owen earlier. You shagged the life out of him, didn't you? You modern women like a good 'shag' don't you?"

"Sex in love is one thing, Sidney. Sex in hate is something quite different."

"Oh really – something quite different wasn't what you were feeling just now. I've got your claw marks on my back to prove it."

He stood and removed all his clothes, standing proudly over her. Grise realised – as she eased herself onto her elbows – that they were on the beach among the dunes where once, one glorious afternoon, she and Mark had made love. Before he had time to lift her from the ground, Grise curled her feet behind Sidney's legs and tripped him. He tumbled backwards with a laugh – a laugh that chilled her because he was on his feet again before she had gained hers. Sidney pulled the coat from her back, lifted her up and dropped onto the sand beneath her, bringing Grise down onto him.

"Close your eyes. Go with the moment. Isn't that what you want? Go on – let me hoist you with your own petard!"

When he decided to finish, Sidney released her and lay back on the sand. She did not move in case he came for her again. After a while, he leaned over her, took her head in his hands and kissed her. He kissed her with such force that Grise could not breathe and lost consciousness.

When she woke, Grise was beside Owen in their bed and she knew that he – Sidney Close, who was dead – had brought her there. She felt weak and used beyond anything she could ever have imagined. Her hand went to her throat. Blood trickled onto her fingers. Owen was sound asleep and she realised that she was, once again, in her nightdress. When she looked, she found her fur coat hanging in the wardrobe – in exactly the place from which it had been removed. When she looked in the dressing table mirror, Grise saw the bite marks on her throat and wondered why she was still alive.

Horst Brultzner's Christmas Party, swiftly prepared with Sarah's expert help for December 7th – "when everyone was still unspoilt by too much food" as Esther Unwood suggested – "went with a swing", according to Sandra Bint. No expense had been spared and Sarah, in her capacity as housekeeper at the Old Vicarage, had relished her research into the Victorian Christmas. Horst had trusted her judgement implicitly, although he was very knowledgeable himself from first-hand experience, and pride exuded from Sarah as she oversaw the occasion with love. Those who had once known her saw desperation in her 'love', but she certainly "rose to the occasion." The compliments of the villagers surrounded her wherever she went and, whatever might have been going on in her heart, Sarah could not but be pleased. Certainly, this was how Horst Brultzner saw her, congratulating himself on how sophisticated his country girl had become in the short time she had been in his employ. Sarah was duly modest, pointing out that she "could not have done it without Rebecca" who was waiting for Peter Vishnya to come over for Christmas.

On arrival, the guests were treated to a glass of mulled wine or grape juice. "We never indulge," as Mrs Teale simmered, with a smile to her friend, Miss Tealey. The drinks were served by Totto Briggs's ladies in the hallway. In each room – each of the downstairs rooms – a fire roared in the grate, and it was open house for the guests to wander as they wished. Owen Culman attended his wife all round the house as though she were in "fragile health", as Pliny Skeat chuckled to Boller. Interior decoration was one of her fascinations and people noted how exultant she was, her eyes lit by "an almost manic excitement", as Esther Unwood mentioned to Bernard Shaw.

The dining room formed the centre-piece of Sarah's arrangement. Small, silver trays carried cups of glogg, each cup with its own teaspoon. Side tables were festooned with seasonal nibbles – small roasted potatoes, chilli beef pies, goat's cheese drop scones and crab bites. The main table was decorated with cold meats, fish and pickles – hot salmon, spiced ham, pressed ox tongue, roast Guinea fowl and Totto's raised pork pie with pickled pears, accompanied by cranberry chutney and pickled beetroot with shallots. Desserts had not been neglected – walnut shortbreads, caramelised orange trifle, coffee with hazelnut macaroons and (reputedly, one of Horst's favourites) zabaglione trifle slice served with a chilled dessert wine or (for those who didn't indulge, and Corvin felt obliged to attach himself to this group) cranberry fizz.

Billy Bassett, when he could escape from his wife, spent a lot of time in here as did Barry Snooks, Ben Chine, Benny Walters with Plumptious and Bishop Twiddle who had struggled to get down to Dunburgh on time after an unbelievably busy day at the cathedral, approving the Christmas carol sheets.

The food, however, was almost a side issue. It was the plethora of Christmas trimmings that captured the eye from the moment guests passed the traditional red wreath on the vicarage door. It was here that Alan Read gripped Horst firmly and insistently by the hand, "shaking it as though he meant to shake it off" as Joney Chine later whispered to Ample Bassett. A huge tree dominated the hall from which hung baubles, bells, Christmas cones, ornamental stars, frosted snowflakes and beaded wreaths. The tree was topped by a silver angel. Father Christmas figurines, ornamental bows, nutcracker soldiers and crystalline treasure boxes littered every available surface including each of the fire place mantle-pieces. Candles – real candles – burned everywhere: tucked into nooks and crannies, perched in recesses and hung from brackets. Charles Cob, the Heritage Councillor, remarked to his wife, Myrtle, that it was "good to see someone not afraid to ignore the latest petty H & S guidelines on naked flames in public places."

Dominating the lighting, however, was a huge chandelier (in the style of Marie Antoinette, Horst explained to Lianne Snooks who took an interest in these things) which hung in the morning room. All this – this glut of festivity – was absorbed into the masses of holly and evergreens, which were spread liberally wherever space permitted. Horst had even opened up his study and hung, from the ceiling, not a twig but a huge branch of mistletoe. He had hesitated to do this, but Sarah assured him that it would provide, for the village, the "icing on the cake." It proved to be the customary lure for all, including the men from the Fishermen's Hut (Daff Mallet, Boss Wigg, and Butch Strowger) and Mark Chambers's men (Harry Bailey and Scrub Turrel). They all enjoyed a "good cuddle" when the opportunity arose.

The carpet in the front parlour had been rolled up – by the new man sent to replace Crafty Catchpole by Lord Wangford – and in the corner a violinist and harpist played English folk tunes such as Thaddy-u-gander and Sir Roger de Coverley. The music permeated the house, blending easily with the gossip and laughter which rang throughout the old building so lovingly restored by Mark Chambers and his men under the guidance of Willox and Marshall who were lost "in the throng of happy revellers" as Liz Shaw remarked to Martin Billings when he arrived late and uneasily with his wife, Amy. Sets of dancers moved neatly in and out of the room, forming groups which dispersed and reformed at will. Horst was persuaded by Sandra Bint to accompany her for a cotillion, and they made an elegant couple in the company of Mark and Nin Chambers, the Fat Councillor with Rebecca Unwood and Charlie Wangford with Joanne Podd.

The party ended just before midnight "in case we all turn into pumpkins" as Penny Read murmured to Beth Crewes, who had arrived with Mavis Close, but without her husband who, she explained, "had an accident – nothing serious, he fell over rather badly in the road." Martin Billings was apologetic about his late arrival, explaining that he "had been delayed by an incident at the Duke's Head", while Amy wondered whether, next year, Horst could arrange for "snow and a stagecoach to complete the scene" in the driveway of the Old Vicarage. It was magical – the lack of snow being countered by a crisp frost and the dark night, which awaited only the new moon in the early hours. Corvin was disappointed that "your friend, Miss Palmester, was unable to grace us with her presence" but, as Sarah explained, "her father, Simon, has just come out of hospital and still needs care." After the last of the villagers, accompanied by a trickle of local businessmen and dignitaries, had departed through his doorway, Horst turned to Sarah and thanked her, profusely. "You entered, truly, into the spirit of the occasion, my dear, and I am grateful. You have honoured my house."

Alan Read listened attentively to all Nadine Palmester said. She was amazed, and pleased, that he did not once interrupt "her flow of nonsense." When she had finished, Alan went to his desk and took out the file he had began in the summer. It contained all his notes on vampirism and the names of the women in the village he knew had borne the bite marks, with dates. She read it through quietly and then looked up.

"Why didn't you act before?"

"On what basis – none of that is evidence, and – as you said – it's nonsense ... You will respect the fact that ..."

"... this is confidential? Yes, of course ... So what do we do?" asked Nadine.

"We ignore it – or we exhume the coffin, at night, to prove to ourselves that he isn't there or is as fresh as a daisy. You say that your friend, Tony Crewes, is approaching Martin?"

"Yes," replied Nadine.

"Well, if he comes on side it will certainly make things easier."

"He'll be in touch, and then we can ... get moving?"

"No," said Alan.

"No?"

"You're in a state of shock, Nadine, and not taking everything into account."

"Like?"

"Like the phases of the moon – just a moment."

Alan left and returned with a diary which he flicked through, quickly.

"It's the 19th of November and the moon is rising. It'll be full next Monday and not wane again until December 3rd, so our first chance for a really dark night will be ... around the tenth ."

"But that's three weeks away!"

"We dare not risk being seen. Even a pitch-black night will not guarantee that, but it will help."

When Nadine discovered that Tony had actually come face to face with Sidney Close, the matter was clinched, and both he and Martin Billings were drawn, (as Alan Read said) "into the fold."

"We involve no one else – not yet – no one, not even our wives. We wait until the 9th or 10th of December and then we act. There is no longer any need to prove to ourselves that Sidney Close is …Un-dead – Tony's beating is assurance enough. We cannot dig up the coffin in daylight hours – the churchyard is a public place – so we must wait for Sidney to return to it, apprehend him and do the necessary," said Martin.

"But we wait until just before the coming of the new moon?"

"Yes."

"In the meantime …," began Tony.

"We have no choice. We shall have to render him helpless, drive a stake through his heart and then either burn or re-bury the corpse, which will return to its true state of decomposition. He is freshly dead and isn't going to blow away in a cloud of elemental dust – nothing so convenient! There will be evidence of what we have done. We shall need darkness for our deed," Martin insisted.

"Martin, is there no chance ….?"

"No chance, Tony – can you imagine what the papers would say if this was leaked?"

"Shall we involve Corvin," asked Nadine.

They had all looked at each other, the same thought going through each of their minds. Was Corvin to be relied upon? Alan answered for them.

"We shall not be strong enough to hold Sidney down, except by faith. I had considered Corvin after Nadine first came to see me, but I think …"

"We should ask dad?"

"Yes. Is he well enough?"

Nadine smiled: there was no need for an answer.

"This won't be the end, will it?" said Nadine, when she and Tony were alone, "we shall have to … deal … with Sarah and Horst Brultzner."

"Yes – it will need looking into, certainly."

"Why are we hesitating?"

"We are vacillating because neither of us is really convinced that this is happening or that the 'links' we think we have made are valid. To start involving Brultzner and Charles Wangford at this stage would be … fatal. Let's just deal with Sidney, and then start asking awkward questions."

"Do you think the others are asking the same questions?"

"Martin – no. He just wants this over and out of the way so that the village can return to normal. Alan – probably. But if this goes awry, he'll be struck off the medical register and may be certified along with the rest of us. I'm not even convinced that he believes Sidney is a vampire, but he has put his trust in your judgement and my meeting with a ghost from the grave," replied Tony.

"Have you returned the key to the boy?"

"Yes."

"When are you going to visit the temple?"

"I'm waiting for a dark night."

"Then early December could be a busy time?"

They both laughed.

It was a dark night – as dark as they could have wished for and – with the success of Horst Brultzner's Christmas Party still reverberating around the village – the group of five were to make their way to St George's churchyard within a few hours of the approach of dawn.

Tony had kept careful watch over the weeks since their meetings and seen Sidney Close rise from the earth and prowl the village. He had taken Martin with him – partly for safety (Martin was more or less a believer and the cross each of them had undertaken to carry was more likely, in Tony's view, to be effective in his friend's hands than his own), and partly to convince the policeman that things were not as they should be.

At first, Sidney had not disappointed them. Each night he had risen from the grave and set forth into the village. Towards their final watch, however, this had not been the case. On several consecutive nights he had not risen from the earth.

They met in Simon's kitchen and, before they set out, the group shared any further knowledge they possessed. In addition to Tony and Martin's report of their watch, Alan Read told them that he had been visited – confidentially – by Grise Culman. He outlined her story, indicating that she had been unusually frank with him about the details of Sidney's horrendous assault.

"You left her unprotected because we had to wait for a dark night?"

It was Nadine who expressed the disquiet they all felt.

"Grise took the traditional precautions, and he has not been successful, since."

A sigh of relief passed through the group.

"But he will be!" said Simon, expressing the fear of them all, "He will be because the vampire exerts a vile and sinful allure over its victims. Mrs Culman may have resisted him so far, but he will possess her in the end. His lust is strong and her resolve will melt as surely as a snowball in Hell. It is as well that we act tonight. I know your reasons for delay, but this will be not a moment too soon."

They sat at the kitchen table as they talked. Nadine had laid the gingham cloth and set out the items as though for the simple tea she shared, daily, with her father. This time there were five knives, five tea plates and five cups and saucers (each with a tiny spoon) as well as the cake stand, the jam in its pot with the little spoon, the butter dish with the embossed pattern of flowers, a large teapot and the strainer, the breadboard with the knife in its slot and a fresh loaf from the bin.

Nadine buttered the slices as they talked and laid them in cut triangles onto a plate which she placed on the table. She went to the cake tin and took out the date and walnut spice cake she had baked, and placed it on the cake stand. Nadine took the kettle from the hob and poured the hot water onto the tea leaves as they spoke, and the smell of the freshly-brewed tea was in all their nostrils. They could pretend it was teatime – an everyday occurrence – and calming. Before they left, Simon drew them all together in prayer.

They agreed to speak little or not at all, left the house in ones and twos, and made their way to the churchyard. The night sky was cloudy – neither moon nor stars broke through the darkness. Simon walked with difficulty, and carried nothing but his cross and Bible. Nadine supported him, while the three men brought between them the shovels, picks and ropes that would be necessary for their night's work. Alan carried the holdall that contained the long wooden stake, the coal hammer, the garlic and his sharp surgeon's knife.

The village was very quiet with not even the usual early morning traffic to disturb the stillness. Martin and Alan, who were first to arrive, crept into the graveyard and took up their positions by the equipment shed from where they could watch Sidney's grave unobserved. Martin's uneasiness with the whole business had grown throughout the evening and Alan had insisted, quietly, that they go together. He was determined to have done with the night's work, once and for all and thought his friend might backslide – although he said nothing of this to the others. Once settled, they took their crosses from their pockets and waited with a look but no word between them. Both men crouched low, thinking of their respective wives and how they would laugh if they could see them now. Each had left their houses to walk to Nadine's – both Penny and Amy had assumed that work called when the phones rang.

Tony had waited until Beth was asleep and then crept downstairs to his study, letting himself out quietly through the french doors and making his way along the beach to Nadine's house. He now appeared from the old graveyard, having approached the church along Marsh Lane, and lingered behind the buttress of the west porch. He saw himself as the weak link in the group and had the idea that if bait was required to distract Sidney Close he would provide it, giving the others a chance to surround Close with the power of their religious convictions – and weapons!

Nadine, concerned about her father's health, took him to a bench seat in the shadow of one of the yew trees. The two of them felt more secure than any of the others – Simon in his unquestioning faith, Nadine in her father's strength. Looking at her father, she thought to herself that it was he – and he alone among the five – who had made his decision rapidly once the 'evidence' was presented to him. None of the others, including herself and Tony, were so sure about their purpose in the graveyard. Nadine kept hoping that a white figure would appear and wend its way between the gravestones. This, at least, would be reassuring! She laughed gently to herself. She thought of Poe's tales of terror and his 'habiliments of the grave'. How those ghostly stories had scared her as a young woman. Yet, now she was facing her own supernatural horror she felt only a powerful desire to have the night's work finished so that she could go home to bed.

As the sun began to lighten the sky, it was Simon who moved first, whispering to Nadine that they could wait no longer. The vampire had obviously not risen to feast that night, must still be in his grave and they had very little time before dawn. She shivered now that the moment had come, but made her way discreetly to where Martin and Alan were hidden by skirting the back of the church passed the plot where the cremations were laid to rest. It was here that she had her first moment of disquiet. As she passed the line of conifers that shielded the cremation ground, Nadine knew that someone was watching her. She looked quickly round and thought she saw a figure lurking in the blackness beyond the trees. A pair of red eyes glared from the darkness? Yes – but they were not red, and they watched with curiosity rather than anger. She wondered who it was that would watch with curiosity in a churchyard at night. Then they were gone, and Nadine was left alone.

When she reached Tony, he could see that she was trembling. Nadine shrugged off his concern. He acknowledged her message and made his way to Alan and Martin who came forward to Sidney's grave. They glanced quickly round, and then began their work. The shovels clunked on two of the crosses which Brultzner had placed and then, as Simon arrived with Nadine, they found the other two. The old priest looked as puzzled as the doctor and policeman, but he took the four crosses, placed them respectfully in Alan's holdall and nodded for the others to continue digging. Martin's eyes never ceased from flickering about as he watched and twice he strode off into the churchyard, but each time returned with an angry shrug and shake of his head.

It was hard work, despite the earth being loose, fresh and sandy. Tony Crewes usually enjoyed the fact that he was unfit, boasting of it to friends during the Friday lunch hours his office staff spent in The Three Murderers pub in Norbridge, and Alan spent much of his time actually sitting. Neither of them appreciated their sedentary existence, however, during the time they were digging for Sidney Close. The sweat was soon running freely from them, and they were glad of the bottles of water which Nadine had been thoughtful enough to stuff into the pockets of her large, winter coat.

Tony stood waist deep in the grave before either of them took a serious rest, however: such was the pressure of time. When he did look up and caught Alan's eye, the doctor nodded that they should change places. It was back-breaking work throwing the heavy shovelfuls of soil up onto the side of the grave. They dug in darkness but, occasionally, Nadine would step forward to see how the work was progressing and, within an hour, she saw that the hole had reached deep into the earth. Nadine looked at her father and they exchanged frowns. Surely the coffin would be reached soon? As they looked at each other, the sound of Alan's shovel on wood was heard, and she passed the ropes across to Tony and Martin who lowered them into the grave so that Alan could loop each under the coffin handles.

Lifting the coffin was easier than they had expected – the handles had been fixed properly with screws into solid wood, and Nadine was strong. Hand over hand the four of them lifted, while Simon kept his eye on the lych-gate and pathways. He wondered to himself how they would explain away what they were doing should an early morning visitor arrive. When the coffin was placed safely beside the grave, Alan and Martin set to work with screwdrivers and undid the lid. Simon stepped forward, as they laid it carefully to one side, and looked into the coffin. Alan turned to join him. As a doctor, he was more aware than the others of what a decomposing corpse would smell like should they be wrong and Sidney Close was in a state of putrefaction. He had also read that vampires in the grave, 'full of fresh blood with loose limbs and no corruption of the flesh', smelt of the charnel house. He need not have worried on either count: the coffin was empty.

CHAPTER 12

Unclean

Sidney Close had come for Grise, on the night after she consulted Alan Read, and found her waiting. He entered the bungalow with the confidence of a successful lover, and Grise was reclining on the cream sofa with the fur throws. He had no doubt that she was waiting for him, dressed as she was in a negligee that flopped open at the breast, and with her legs stretched onto the sheepskin in front of her. Sidney imagined taking her several times on that sheepskin mat before he closed the terrace door; but, as he strode over to her, Grise raised a small golden cross. It was one her mother had worn, and Grise held it towards Close.

He dropped to his knees, not believing that such a small cross could blind him with so much light, and shielded his eyes. It had taken all the courage she could muster and all her innate pragmatism to face Close in that manner. Grise stood and walked towards him, careful to stay out of arms reach. Her relief was overwhelming. She had placed her faith in the advice of Alan Read, and he had not let her down. The man at her feet had violated her, and now she stood over him while he cowered.

"Get out of my house and do not return," she said, her voice a tremulous mixture of anger, fear and loathing, "My friends will find you and destroy you. Go!"

The words just came; she hadn't planned to say anything. No one was more surprised than Grise, when Sidney leapt backwards, his hands still covering his eyes, groped for the door, flung it open and stumbled out onto the terrace. Only then did he look up with his eyes fixed somewhere beyond her head.

"I'll come back," he yelled, angry at being denied, "and when I do, lady, look out for yourself. You cannot walk around, forever, with that ... before you. Not you!"

It was true, and she knew it, but Alan Read had assured her that Sidney Close would be (what was the phrase he used?) "Restored to rest." In the meantime, she must protect herself at night. Alan Read hadn't questioned her story anymore than she had hesitated in going to him. Grise Culman, whatever her faults, was a woman of action. She and her husband hadn't built a business by standing round and wondering why things happened, or whether they were actually happening. Her ordeal on the beach was enough to convince her that, whatever the truth surrounding Sidney Close, she had to defend herself. Alan had talked her out of going to police, saying that he would speak with Martin Billings and that there were others who knew the truth about Sidney Close.

She trusted him, but knew also that Sidney Close was a threat. She could not hide forever from him and there was part of her that wanted him – not on his terms, but on her own. She had been filled with loathing on the beach, but had woken with a sense of part-remembered sensuous pleasures when she felt the marks on her throat. Grise hated to admit it to herself, but she had enjoyed the sound of him as he drank, and her consciousness had been roused in ways she could find no words to describe.

Sidney had rushed from the terrace and flung himself into the line of trees surrounding Beachlands Health Club; his thoughts were of murder. Even as he ran from her, Sidney knew that he had the upper hand: a momentary setback was all he had suffered. He would find her again and take her as he wanted, or take what she loved most – her young teenage daughter. The girl was the spit of Grise, had just turned puberty and would be as fresh as a daisy – unspoilt! He would spoil her; she wouldn't have to wait for some spotty youth to get her to drop her knickers. In the meantime, he needed a woman and had the power to take one. Grise Culman wouldn't spoil by waiting, and nor would her daughter.

Sidney stood and brushed the wet autumn leaves from him. Something was troubling him: something other than his unsatisfied desires. It was something the woman had said – "my friends will find you and destroy you". In his urge to satisfy himself, however, Sidney Close brushed that thought aside. His mind was already on his next prey: not the compliant teenager from Pack Close – he wanted someone near at hand – an older woman, someone who would put up a fight.

Sandra Bint was getting ready for bed when she heard the latch on the gate click. Things had been a bit tricky recently and she had several men on the scene although not all 'on the go', as she liked to phrase it. Sandra looked quickly out of her bedroom window but could see no one.

She was still with her amorous policeman, but he was still with his wife who seemed oblivious to his goings-on. Sandra was a little agitated about this because she really needed the security of knowing that he would continue to fund her catering business, but it was against her principles to let his wife know. She had also been seeing her third husband again – the fat councillor – largely on Ainsley's behalf because he was desperately trying to make a go of it as a financial consultant, and had some idea about purchasing the old Gobley house. Unfortunately, Number 2 had returned from the rigs for an extended stay ashore and she had also seen him, once or twice. Sandra still carried a torch for her rig worker.

In short, she was juggling several balls in the air and finding it difficult to keep them all up. If only life were not so complicated! Still, she had to keep her business going – a girl had to earn her own living. She didn't believe in living off her man. She was duty bound to help her son and she was very fond of her rig worker. None of this made for an easy life and so, when she heard the gate, Sandra wondered who it was making a visit. She was loathe to slip on her robe and go outside, remembering that time in the summer when she had done just that to find the face staring down at her.

Sandra tied her dressing gown tightly and went down stairs. It was still warm in the little house; her heating had only just switched off for the night. Sandra checked all the windows and both doors, drawing the curtains closely together and taking the keys out of the locks; this was something she had learned to do from her amorous policeman. She was not afraid of being alone, but she didn't like unusual noises. She thought she would make a warm drink and take it up to bed with her – perhaps a cup of tea or even drinking chocolate – and so she filled the kettle. It was just as the water hissed into the kettle that there was a tap on the back door. Despite herself, Sandra jumped and then laughed. She was never fazed for long, and went to the door immediately and opened it. Sidney Close stood outside, smiling. It was a long time, she thought, since they had met and he'd never come round to her house before! Her lack of mindfulness in relation to the world was one of Sandra's attractions and she said, without thinking:

"Hello!"

She had greeted her rig worker in exactly the same way when they met at a party, while she was married to the fat councillor.

"May I come in?"

"Well ... of course!"

The hesitation stemmed from concern that one of her current interests might show up. It wasn't until Sidney stepped into the house, and shut and locked the door behind him that Sandra remembered he was dead.

Sandra was confident with men; there had never been a time since she was a teenager that she had not been able to talk a situation round, however sticky it might have been. Sidney did not move – he could not believe his luck – and so she smiled and watched him, coquettish as ever because this was her way.

"This is a surprise, Sidney."

"For me as well as you, Sandra – I never expected to be standing inside your house in quite this way."

'With the whole night before us' were the unspoken words they both sensed. Sandra held on to all her street-wise experience to avoid panicking at that moment. She had seen 'Jack-the-Ripper' movies. She had gasped as the door clicked to behind the legendary killer, and the girl realised that her life expectancy was only minutes. What she needed was to avoid anger. Anger would give him a ... motive. He was as tense as a young man in the edge of his first ... shag. Wasn't that the word they used nowadays?

"I'm just making a cup of tea," she said.

"I don't drink – not tea, anymore."

There was still within him the same sense of loss, which Sarah had never stopped feeling: the sense that he could never return to a normal life – never share tea and cakes with a friend, never sit by the fire with his ... family. It was only when the rage took over, only when he accepted the ... joys of being what he was that Sidney felt the sublime release from all his constraints.

Sandra switched on the kettle. Soon, at least, there would be hot water. She'd heard of demons – things that returned from the dead. She believed in ghosts. It always gave you a tingle when someone told a story that could be true at Hallowe'en parties. She smiled at Sidney. He was no ghost. He was solid muscle, and he had returned from the dead.

"Would you like to sit down?" she asked.

He smiled again, and Sandra wished he wouldn't do that. He'd always been intense. She'd once said to Grise – after a do at the Health Club – that "he would if he could." Sandra poured the hot water onto the teabag and stirred it, added the milk and then sat opposite Sidney, across the table. No conversation came. She couldn't say "How are Mavis and the girls?", yet she had to engage him in conversation. She had to keep him talking.

"How are things?" she said, quietly.

Sidney looked at her. This was the moment to rip her composure open, and shatter her smugness. Sandra Bint was a slut of the first water, and always had been. 'She'd had more men than most women have had hot dinners.' There was uneasiness in her eyes, but no fear. He knew a sudden move from him would scare her, but he didn't want that; he wanted her to … sweat. He wanted her to … come to realise, for herself, what was going to happen.

"Things are fine – and with you?" he replied.

"Yes … Ainsley …"

"Ainsley?"

"He's doing well."

"I haven't seen my girls for some little while."

"No."

"Do you know why?"

Sandra wasn't wandering down that conversational road. It would lead to things they mustn't talk about – not if she wanted to stay alive.

"No," she said.

"Are you telling me the truth?" asked Sidney.

"The truth?"

"You know what the truth is, don't you, Sandra?"

"Yes."

"Then I'll ask you again – are you telling me the truth?"

"About?"

"About not knowing why I haven't seen my girls for some little while."

"I don't know why," she blurted.

"No."

He seemed to enjoy the silences. The tension in her little kitchen was racked to breaking point, and all they were actually doing was drinking tea and talking … like old friends!

"I can't remember what happened to me," he said, suddenly.

Another forbidden road! Her silences were strangling her because Sandra was garrulousness by nature. She had always been able to talk for hours about nothing.

"Have you spoken to Dr Read?"

It was all she could think to say, but Sidney didn't seem to hear her. He began to ramble in his conversation.

"There was nothing but darkness and silk – red silk like a woman's flesh. At first I couldn't move and then it seemed as if my chains had snapped. I was so hungry, I couldn't tell you. How I got there I don't know, but I was in front of my house and ... and ... I got dressed ... in these. The hunger was still driving me mad and then I found the girl. I followed her home and she wanted me. I left her on the doorstep."

'Was he buried alive,' thought Sandra, 'has he been driven mad?'

"I could see in the dark for the first time. It was like being a young man again. I could leap five-barred gates. I was in love with ... with the world, and my mind was so clear. I had ... gifts! I could smell the scents of the air like an animal. I saw my way. I was on a ... quest, for happiness – the final journey. I had embarked! I understood ... the eternal cycle. I sleep during the day now, but I am ravenous for life when I wake in the evening."

Sandra felt a welcome surge of hope as he spoke. She felt that Sidney needed answers, and that she might persuade him that Dr Read was the one to give him the help he needed. If he would just let her make that telephone call then all would be well. If she could persuade him to make the call then ... she was free!

She had watched him as he spoke – watched him from under her eyelids, not daring to make eye-contact. He had changed. He was handsome, but more than that he was ... magnetic! Sandra watched the iridescence beneath his skin. The skin itself was flawless. She had never seen such peerless beauty in anyone – let alone a man. She remembered how attracted she had been to him as he lay in his coffin. The world was in turmoil when a woman could find a corpse attractive, and Sandra recoiled from the idea. Her way was the life on this side of the grave.

She wanted to move but dare not. Sidney knew this and the sense of power it gave him was exhilarating. He knew, too, that she was, as each minute passed, on the verge of pushing the table into him and making her escape through the door that led from her little sitting room to the stairs. He wanted her to do just that; he wanted a reason to pursue Sandra Bint. Yet, there was another part of him that wanted to talk.

Suddenly, she began to cry. It was so uncharacteristic of the woman that Sidney was shaken, shaken as a man would have been – not as a vampire would feel. He watched her as the tears streamed down through her fingers and splashed onto the top of her kitchen table. She was crying out of fear – he knew that; she was crying to cast out the tension within her that was, by now, unbearable. He knew he could go to her and comfort her as a man might. He knew he could go to her, gloating over his victim as a vampire might. Either way made no difference to him; motive was no longer an issue. The move brought him close to the woman and he smelt the sexuality within her. As he reached for her, Sidney still held the two images of himself in his head – the kindly man, the lascivious vampire – and there was no difference, in kind, between them. He wanted her to look up at him as he stood there by her side, and in total control of her destiny.

Sandra knew she dare not look at him. She had never been so driven into herself – had never before been in a position when she could not laugh it off, make a remark that would ease the tension and allow her to walk away. She had walked away many times before. She liked men, but knew their limitations and when it was over, it was over.

Sidney's right hand was on her shoulder and he was drawing the top of her dressing gown down and easing her nightdress over her shoulder. His hand slid down, under the clothing and cupped her left breast in his hand. She felt her nipple harden under the casualness of his touch and she wanted to vomit, and still she dare not move. "Women like you!" It was all he said and it was as though the words were thought, rather than spoken, but the next minute he had lifted her from the chair, pushed her forward over the kitchen table and ripped her nightgown from her back. She screamed, but his left hand gripped her neck, holding her down, and then he was upon her, leaning over her back and taking her from the rear. When he'd finished, Sidney slumped back onto the chair on which she had been sitting, the blood running from his mouth, and laughed. It was a laugh of exultation, the laugh of a man in his prime, at one with himself and the power he wielded over women. He threw back his head and laughed out loud, while Sandra lay crushed on the table top.

She knew anger then – anger, which was an emotion quite foreign to her nature, quite alien to her live and let live attitude to life. The fear and loathing she had felt since he arrived burst from her and she stood, turned and brought her right hand smashing backwards cross his face. It probably hurt her more than Sidney, but it took him by surprise and knocked him from the chair across the kitchen floor. She slung the chair at him, yanked over the kitchen table between them and bolted through the door at the bottom of the stairs, turning the key in the lock. It was enough to give her time to reach the bedroom door and lock it behind her. Sandra looked round, desperately, and realised that she had trapped herself. She heard Close wrenching at the door below, and went to the window. The drop was too far; Sandra realised that she would break both her legs. As she stood there, half-in and half-out of the window, she heard the lock snap from the downstairs door.

The bedroom door opened inwards! Sandra heard his feet thundering up the stairs and she pushed the double bed over the room against the door. It took all her strength to shift it, but the anger was still within her and that helped. She heard him kicking at the lock and saw the door-plate shudder under his blows, again and again until the screws tipped out onto the floor. Sandra threw herself on the bed, adding her weight. Close pushed at the door and the bed buckled the carpet as it slid across the room. He stepped in through the gap, passed her, slammed the sash window down and drew the curtains.

He looked at the bed, savouring an image of the men she'd had there. He wanted her to resist. He wanted to break her and take her. Sandra was kneeling on the bed now, the remains of her nightgown clutched across her breasts. He always realised that it could be this much fun. Her short hair was dishevelled, the lipstick smudged across her mouth, the mascara running down her face where she had been crying, and yet there was a defiance, which he relished, in her look. He was on her in one step, grasped her behind the neck, entwined his hands in her hair and pulled her down. She still clung to the torn nightwear and he wanted that; he wanted her to try to protect herself against him.

Sandra brought her feet up, instinctively closing herself as he leaned over her. Then she kicked, both feet catching him in the groin and sending him crashing back against the bedroom wall. He laughed as his back hit the edge of the wardrobe. She jumped from the bed, making for the window; a broken leg seemed the better choice.

It was what Sidney Close wanted. He was on his feet with his arms round her before she had reached the sill. He threw her back on the bed and then leapt over her, landing with his knees either side of Sandra. Her hands clawed up at his face, the nails drawing deep scratch marks across his cheeks. Sidney took each hand in his own and forced her, easily, backwards until he was leaning over her, his face inches from Sandra's own. He looked into her face and there was recognition there; he had known this woman as a friend.

Sandra couldn't move. She could only wait for what he might do and she saw the hesitation in his eyes and felt it in his grip. He released her hands, which were crushed and bruised by the sheer strength of his hold. His thighs still pinned her to the bed, but now he looked down on her with something like tenderness in his gaze. She still clutched the clothes across her breast and she saw his eyes watching these. His hands moved to her face and he began to stroke her in long, gentle strokes, his fingers following the curve of her jaw. His gaze was more horrifying than the fight had been, however, although she couldn't understand why this was so.

He bared her shoulder. He saw the veins pulsing fiercely in the neck after her exertions. He took one more look in her eyes, and sunk his teeth into her throat.

Owen Culman found his wife kneeling on the sheepskin rug, the gold cross in her hand, staring at the open terrace door.

"Grise, what on earth has happened?"

"I don't want to talk about it."

He walked over to the door and looked out onto the terrace. Nothing stirred, so he shut the door and turned to her with that quiet look.

"I want to know."

"Don't pressure me, Owen. I'll talk about it in my own good time."

"Is it Mark Chambers?"

"Mark Chambers?"

"I don't see any point in repeating the question."

"I didn't realise you knew."

Owen smiled but said nothing.

"Why didn't you say?" she persisted.

"Would it have done any good?"

"You must have felt ..."

"I felt awful, but I didn't want to bring matters to a head. We had the children to consider. I love you, Grise. I can understand that you're attractive to other men, and I know I'm not much good in that department, so ...," he said with a shrug.

"I never knew ... But it was you asked him back. Why – if you knew?"

"I thought it was over."

"It is. It has been for a long time."

"Then it wasn't him tonight?"

"No! I don't understand, Owen – why didn't you say something?"

"Mark is a decent enough bloke. Better him than some of our acquaintances."

"Thanks, Owen!"

"You did ask."

"I feel so dirty."

"There's no need. Nothing has changed. The past is the past – you can't go back and rub it out. I know you love me."

"Do you?"

"Yes – I've always known it."

He went across to her and kissed her lightly on the forehead. Grise recoiled and pushed him aside.

"Don't touch me, Owen – I'm unclean."

"What? Don't be silly."

"I'm not being silly!" she screamed.

"Grise – it doesn't make any difference. I wish I hadn't asked now, but seeing you on the floor like that ..."

"You don't understand, Owen – you don't begin to understand."

"Then tell me – I can listen."

"You're so patient, aren't you, Owen – so patient and understanding and kind and nice and honest and decent and hard-working ..."

"Grise – don't go on. You work hard."

"Owen – please, leave me alone – just for tonight. There's nothing wrong – not what you think, anyway."

It was at that moment that the telephone rang and Owen walked across the room to pick it up.

"Don't touch it!"

"What?"

"Don't touch it."

"It might be mother."

"It isn't," yelled Grise, snatching the phone from his hand, "Who's there? ... Sandra ... what now? ... all right. It's Sandra. She wants me to pop over to see her. Will you take me Owen? You needn't stay. The children will ... no ... oh, God, what have I done? I don't know what to do ... Sandra, can't you just tell me what it is? ... I will – try me, please! I'm at the end of my tether."

She had gone alone in the end; there didn't seem anything else to do. Owen had stayed with the children, holding the small cross and asking no questions and she had rushed to the four-wheel drive and driven hell-for-leather the half-mile or so to Sandra's. She had found Sandra slumped by the telephone in her little sitting room, spotted with blood and with a dressing gown pulled roughly around her. The pallor of Sandra's face told Grise all she feared to know. Her chalk-white face, the eyes running with black mascara and the bright red lips reminded Grise of the old whores you saw in seventeenth-century brothels.

"I don't know when he left. I phoned you as soon as I came round. Oh God, you don't know what I'm talking about, do you?"

"Yes, I do. Don't talk now. I'll make you a nice cup of sweet tea."

Despite what had happened, both women laughed – Grise hysterically, Sandra as much as she was able in her weakened state. They swapped tales sitting at the kitchen table.

"You must see phone Alan Read."

"No."

"Sandra!"

"No – I can't."

"You must. You've lost so much blood. You need a transfusion."

"I can't, Grise. I'll rest. I'll be all right in a few days."

"I'll phone Alan now. He's very nice."

"Please – I'd rather you didn't. Just tell me how to protect myself against ... him. I'm so scared, I can't tell you. What is he, Grise – what's happening?"

They'd talked and the talk hid their fears. Neither woman had uttered the word 'vampire' or anything like it. They'd seen the films, but only as a laugh. Watching horror movies wasn't something that appealed to them. It was hard to know what to make of it. Grise had consulted Alan Read, who had prescribed crosses and garlic flowers as he might have prescribed antibiotics for a urinary infection or a nasal spray for hay-fever. He'd told her to keep inside at night and to wear the cross around her neck and to rub the flowers – which he provided, rapidly – around the doorways and windows. He had stressed that the only danger she faced would be at night and seemed sure that the "plague" would soon be "under control." Keeping it quiet had been his bye-word, and Grise had gone along with it, except for the rubbing of the garlic around the doors (which she just couldn't bring herself to do). Now, her friend had been assaulted.

"I have to tell Alan, Sandra. It's not right to keep this quiet."

"Please Grise. I've listened, and I know what to do. I don't want to be alone."

"You can stay with us for as long as you like – you know that – but Alan needs to know about this. He needs to know that Sidney Close ...."

"... has risen from the grave?"

"Yes."

"No – well, tell him what happened to you tonight, but don't mention me."

"Tell me why," asked Grise.

"I've got the clap – as they used to call it."

She laughed. Grise was appalled, but Sandra laughed.

"I don't want the whole village to know."

"Alan won't say ..."

"Things get out. I will get treated, but at the clinic – not the GP. Those receptionists are well known for their gossip."

"Who was it?"

"Number 2 – my rig worker, I expect. I've been seeing him on and off – between bouts with my amorous policeman."

"Oh, Sandra!"

"It's all right. It's not catching, except ..."

"... through intercourse. I know. But it's in the blood, isn't it? It looks as though Sidney Close has got more than he bargained for!"

Both women laughed again; this time there was more merriment in the sound.

Alan Read sat with a double measure of Tobermory in his hand and tried to gather his thoughts. They had failed at the grave and no one knew where Close was hiding. It was a fair assumption that he had been alerted to his peril and found another lair. Tony Crewes had suggested – probably with some insight – that he and Martin may have been seen by Sidney as they watched the grave, and that the vampire had taken flight. The group had talked it through and made enquiries. Martin discovered that the undertakers had been broken into and a coffin stolen. It was assumed to be village louts, out for a laugh, but the coffin remained missing. Grise Culman had come back to him immediately and reported Close's second visit which had been on November 20th. He had not molested her since and Alan had hoped that Close had, for whatever reason, gone to ground.

He knew, from his researches, that vampires did not have to feed every night. They could, if necessary, remain within their lairs for years without sustenance and it was in Close's interests to remain undetected. Once discovered, he could be destroyed in a day.

When Grise eventually returned with news of the assault on Sandra Bint, Alan realised that Close was lying low only as far as Grise was concerned; he was now battening onto someone else. Martin Billings's efforts had been indefatigable. He had searched every vacant house (to which he could gain access without too much fuss) in the village and found nothing.

The group had met and talked, but there was no news. They felt as the police must when hunting for a serial killer – dreading and hoping that he would strike again and leave a fatal clue. The village, however, remained quiet. Tony Crewes and Nadine Palmester had suggested that others must be involved in the 'cult', as it came to be called within the group, but both Alan and Martin drew the line at any attempt to stage an attack on the Old Vicarage, on the basis of the allegations Sidney Close had made about Sarah Marjoram.

"He will possess her in the end. His lust is strong and her resolve will melt as surely as a snowball in Hell". Simon's words came back to haunt him as he sat in the quiet of his study away from Penny and the children. He knew what the old priest said was true, but there seemed no way forward until Sidney Close returned.

Tony Crewes also waited quietly. He had remained silent about the temple within the group because, as he persisted in telling Nadine, he saw no connection with vampirism and, until he did, was reluctant to suggest that they invaded the Wangford estate. Now he stood with David Stokes at the top of the short flight of steps which led to the doorway of the temple. He handed the heavy key to David, nodded, and the boy unlocked the heavy oak door and pushed. It opened, as always, silently on its hinges. Both man and boy missed nothing – the moss-covered stones of the entrance, the way in which the temple was sunk a little into the natural slope, the pristine cleanness of the stones themselves – as they paused in the antechamber. Tony tapped the boy on the shoulder and offered him the torch he had brought, but David Stokes just smiled and took one from his pocket. They made their way into the inner sanctuary. David pulled at Tony's arm and nodded to the two statues, as Tony closed the door behind them

"Darkness and twilight," he whispered, pointing to the statue on the left, and "light and dawn," as he pointed to that on the right.

Tony was thinking to himself that he was almost filling his pants, and the boy showed not even the remotest apprehension.

"This is Roman," said David.

"As I said, but keep your voice down."

"There's no one here."

"We don't know that," replied Tony and pointed to the small windows set high in the roof, "so keep your torch beam down."

He had seen a reconstruction of such temples in Newcastle-on-Tyne when he'd visited Hadrian's Wall, but had never stood in the real thing before. It was, in the true sense of the word, "awesome" – 'an emotion compounded of dread, veneration and wonder'. It was like standing in church and being over-whelmed by the sheer size of the spiritual journey men and women had made down the generations; even as an atheist, Tony was inspired by such places. It had always been of the deepest regret to him that he could not make the final leap that faith required. During services at St George's he felt he could often 'see into the life of the things' (in Wordsworth's beautiful phrase) and this place did hold a splendour of its own. He imagined Brultzner standing here gazing, along the aisle, towards the far end where the three altars stood. He imagined the curtains being drawn back and the eyes of the god staring out at them, the crown on his head pulsating with the light of the torch as it passed behind the recess. This was not an evil place. Tony could hear 'the still sad music of humanity' and knew that men had striven here against what they perceived as the forces of darkness. He was chastened and, suddenly, he understood.

He looked down at David Stokes and the boy's eyes were upon him and a smile passed between them and then the boy was off, excited, running his hands along the oak benches that flanked the aisle. He touched the altar on the left and ran his fingers reverently along the surface of each of the others where men had stood and placed their offerings; the boy was in touch with centuries past. On the central altar, lay the short sword he had seen Brultzner use when he fought the bull.

Tony raised his torch and lit the stone walls, which only just exceeded the height of a man. He stooped to examine the benches and then raised his head to the beamed, wooden ceiling. He ran his fingers from the wall along each of the beams and stroked the supporting posts as a man might fondle the mane of his dog.

How long they stood within the temple, Tony had no idea. He had felt 'suspended', 'laid asleep in body, and become a living soul'. He wandered back to the antechamber. Next to the fireplace was the grave – a stone pit six feet long. This is where men would have lain for their initiation – the cold of the pit and the heat of the fire – and they would have emerged as if from a tomb, re-born.

Outside, neither boy nor man spoke but stood and gazed down along the curve of the hillside. They could see across the meadows to the River Cassyn. A copse ran alongside the broad and to the west of this, in the shelter of the trees, grazed the herd of white cattle. A chill, east wind gusted up the slope. 'The many times I have stood here never diminish my feelings towards this place'. The words came into the boy's head as he stood with Tony Crewes. This was his home and tonight he had come to understand it better. Here, there was a presence.

"Where will you hide the key?" said David.

"Hide?"

"So that we can both find it, and come back when we wish."

"Here – under one of these mossy stones. Be careful, David You felt the peace in there – you saw into the heart of things?" said Tony with a smile.

"Yes. I'd expected to be terrified."

"But, instead, you came to understand what had been a mystery."

"And you," replied the boy.

"Yes – it came to me suddenly; it's all clear, now."

Neither spoke again until they reached the foot of the slope, where they said their goodbyes and parted.

CHAPTER 13

The silver brooch

It was the ticking of the Napoleon clock which finally turned Sarah's mind. She had settled Matthew for the night and was sitting in her own bedroom, when she became conscious of it on the mantelpiece; the sound reminded her of her own childhood home, of all that her mother and father had meant to her and the memories permeated the room. As winter approached and Christmas began to close in, her thoughts turned to what might have been if she and Shane had only managed to ... make a go of it. They had put so much love into their little cottage, and now it stood empty, overlooking the marsh. She went back occasionally, just to see that everything was in place, but it wasn't the same.

People would be calling in and she, like her mother before her, would be busy preparing for the festive season. There was always so much to do and the village came alive in a special way. There was the crib service and carol singing and the Christingle with her friends bustling everywhere, but now her life seemed as empty as her little cottage. Horst's Christmas party had been fun, but it had no meaning – no soul. There – the word was out! She found it difficult to say it these days. Its meaning had once been clear: it was that part of you which lived on after death. Her parents' souls were somewhere, but out of reach.

Matthew was all right, of course. Matthew was blooming, but for how long? How long could she keep up the pretence that everything was normal? Would she be able to walk him to Cub Scouts on a bright summer evening? Would she be able to take him on holidays? Would his mother only go to school concerts when they took place on some dark night or gloomy day?

Her delight during those summer days, when he had toddled about the garden of the Old Vicarage, seemed a long time ago – almost part of another world – as the Napoleon clock ticked on. She had genuinely felt that she and her son had a home and a future together – if only she could hold on!

But it wasn't just that, was it? Shane may have deserved his fate and Sidney may have had an accident, but what had she unleashed upon the world should those two one day rise from the grave? What about little Luke Turrel? Did Necker Utting deserve her fate? The torments of her conscience whirled through Sarah. If she could just focus on her own needs then she would be all right, but Sarah Brown had not been brought up like that. The church taught you to be in touch with your conscience; the church taught you to put others first.

Horst was in his study and Sarah wanted to be alone, but away from the ticking of her mother's clock. She would take a walk around the village. She would go, as always, to her parents' grave and try to talk with them. In the churchyard, she always found some peace, if only for a short while, knowing that she was near her mum and dad. What was best for Matthew? That was the question to which she needed an answer.

"I'm here, dad and mum – here again, hoping you'll have some answers."

She felt quiet by the graveside. Sometimes, when she let everything drain out of her mind, the answers came in a rush, but she didn't like them. She knew what she must do, but how?

"Horst is very persuasive and no one could have been kinder to me or to Matthew. He has given us a future."

If only she could hold on! Katerina Schnell had laughed and said 'You will get used to it. You will never be older than you are now ... Every distinction in the world is at your command. You will be 'reborn' many times.'

"But it's all wrong, isn't it, dad? You wouldn't be proud of me as I am now."

'You will see him grow and prosper ... Think of that, Sarah – for all of his life your child will have his Guardian Angel at his side.' 'But how will I look after him?'

"...and do I want to – like that? ... I remember the night we stood in the shadow of the church tower listening to Rebecca and Peter making their plans, and I knew I would never be able to do that ... not have a family, like that ..."

'If only I can hold on!'

"I didn't mean to hurt the little boy, dad. I didn't mean to hurt him. He ran over to me and I cradled him in my arms. I didn't mean to ... do what I did. The boy's arms reach towards me, like my own child asking for my love."

She let herself into the cottage and went straight to her kitchen. She wanted to make herself a cup of tea to hold by the fire for the last time. Looking round, she realised how much she loved the kitchen. It was always the central room in the house. It should have been one of her "treasured memories" – her mother's phrase.

After a while, she wandered upstairs to the room she loved most of all – her son's bedroom. There was Shane's pretty printed border that had given the room definition and added a splash of pattern to the plain and uneven old walls. There was the Pooh Bear rug; through the lace curtains the sun had dappled over them both, as she and Matthew played, bathing each in the same warmth. She had washed him there, her nose burrowing into his chest. Her eyes swept the room; she noted the picture of herself as a baby on the wall, and sat on the rug and cried.

Sarah went back downstairs, knowing she would never go up them again, fetched her tea from the kitchen table and sat by the fire, curling her legs to one side. 'We pulled out the old fifties tiled surround and built one of arched rustic bricks. We topped it with a wooden mantle-piece and on it I put mum's Napoleon clock ... the clock! She remembered its ticking.

She went back into the kitchen, washed the cup carefully and replaced it in the cupboard. Everything was "neat and trim" – another of her mother's phrases!

It did seem a shame: if only she could hold on! Standing in the garden of the Old Vicarage, watching Matthew's 'tame' wolf prowling around its cage, Sarah knew she wanted to hold on. "Hold on to what you've got – and think yourself lucky you've got it!" One of her dad's phrases! Vampires are all beautiful, but it's only skin deep! Sarah laughed at herself for using the old, inappropriate phrase. In the case of vampires, it was so much more.

Suddenly, she remembered Prague. They had been violent, bizarre and disgusting. They each played out their role within the personality they had brought from life. 'Our spiritual body, after death, grows out of our earthly life as a plant grows from a seed. Our spiritual body expresses the personality we have developed in our earthly bodies.' But she wasn't dead, and her spiritual body was being twisted by what she had become. One day, she would be as they had been – a true vampire, without feeling, without remorse, without conscience! How would Matthew come to see her?

Back in her room, her eyes went immediately to the mantelpiece and the ticking Napoleon clock. It was one of the things she had taken, at the last minute, from the cottage when she had run from Shane: the other was her mother's silver brooch. 'Everything I ever loved was in the cottage: every thing I ever loved and the memory of everything I ever loved. I had to take one more thing, something of mum's I could wear – the brooch, the silver brooch!' It was in the drawer. They always called it a 'brooch', but it was more of a locket on a pin. Sarah clicked the little button and opened it. She knew they would be looking at her – Clive and Mary Brown. 'Here she comes!' They were together – her mum and dad, but she would never join them … unless … unless … They were looking at her, one face on either side of the open brooch – her mum and dad as she had known them. They were looking at her and looking straight into her eyes. She could never shake them off – never!

She had prayed that the next day would be overcast. There was no telling with December weather. It could remain overcast for weeks and, suddenly, the blue sky would be there with its bright sun. But no – it was overcast, and that suited Sarah's purpose. She had stayed alert all night and knew that he now resided in his coffin. Once he'd returned there and the sun was up, he was powerless to leave.

She washed and dressed Matthew and packed all the things she could carry into holdalls from the cottage. The little boy was curious as to what was happening, wondering when he could go and see his animals, but Sarah was persistent in that quiet way of Suffolk women. She wrapped him, finally, in a thick winter coat and put a pair of leather boots, bought for him by Horst, on his feet. Sarah took her purse and credit cards (although she didn't know why) and left by the kitchen door so that she could escape round the back of the house, through the straggle of trees that led to the driveway. Matthew could walk, and they didn't have far to go. She had a holdall slung over each shoulder, and Matthew carried a little back-pack.

On the driveway, she looked back at the Old Vicarage, which only so short a time ago had seemed the ideal sanctuary for them both, while Matthew ran down to his wolf and round to his crow, fretting that he could not be with them today. The task before her seemed impossible. How could she explain to Nadine what she was doing? It would be much easier to turn back, back to her life as housekeeper with a position of respect in the village and a future with her son. Her mind, however, was made up – it had to be, or she would be returning to a life she had come to detest and fear. Matthew would come to understand, wouldn't he?

"Where are we going, mummy?" he asked.

"We're going to see Nadine, Matthew. I want you to stay with her for a while. Mummy has to go away."

"Why?"

"I'm not very well, dear. It's hard to explain. One day, you will understand, I hope."

"When I'm grown up?"

"Yes, Matthew, when you're grown up."

Her heart was breaking, but she laughed. How important to a child was the business of growing up! It took all her courage to knock on Nadine's door, but her determination was rewarded by the look on her old-friend's face when she opened it.

"Sarah?"

"May I come in?"

"Of course."

Nadine said it without thinking – out of habit, out of friendship. On the surface, it was like old times – the two of them coming together for a chat. Sarah dare not let herself think too far along those lines: the sense of loss was overwhelming.

"Who is it, Naddy?" called Simon's voice, from his bedroom.

"Just a friend, dad – nothing to worry about," she lied.

"Can Matthew stay with you tonight, Nadine – please!"

"Yes, of course, I'll ..."

"And for a little while?"

"You can have my bed, tonight, Matthew, and tomorrow I'll make you one up in the little room you've used before."

"Are the trains still there?"

"Yes, the trains are still there, but don't make a sound tonight. I don't want my dad asking too many questions."

They put the boy to bed and then went quietly to the kitchen where, out of habit, Nadine made them both a cup of coffee, and they sat looking at each other.

"I've got a lot to say, Nadine, and I want you to write it down as I do – can you do shorthand?"

"I can, Sarah, but journalists normally use a recorder these days. Just speak, and your words will be recorded. Are you OK with that?" said Nadine, with a laugh.

"Yes, that will be much better. He'll hear my voice then."

When Nadine had placed the recorder on the table between them, Sarah said:

"I don't know how much of this you already know, but I suspect very little. What I am going to tell you is really for Matthew when he grows up, as well as for you now. Don't interrupt me, Nadine – unless there's something you don't understand – because this is going to be so difficult. It verges on the impossible. When I'm finished, I want to just walk out – don't try and stop me – and I want you to promise me that you will look after Matthew and – when he is ready – try to make him understand. Will you promise me?"

"You know I will."

"It won't be easy – what I am asking you to do. I am asking you to be his mother. You will understand why when I have finished."

"Yes."

"And I want you to let him know about his grandparents – mum and dad – and I want, most of all, for you to let him know that I loved him, and that I did what I am going to do for his sake as well as mine. It was not selfish."

"I know what you're asking, Sarah. I understand."

When Sarah had finished her story – from where she discovered that Shane had killed her father – Nadine let her go without questions. She only re-iterated her promises to Sarah, who was distraught beyond any description, to bring Matthew up as well as she could and, when he was old enough, in the knowledge of all that had happened to his mother.

Sarah didn't know where she was going. She knew only that she must be out of the village before nightfall, and that she must keep to the shadows. It was still overcast – in that, at least, she felt God was on her side. She laughed. It was a stale phrase and, now, an absurd idea that the God she had once worshipped could ever be on her side again. She made for the lane that ran down beside the church – the one that led to Marsh Lane. As she reached the end, where it joined Church Hill, Sarah saw Esther Unwood, who caught her eye, coming down the steps from the church. Sarah felt obliged to speak.

"You look tired, dear," said Esther, in reply to Sarah's reluctant greeting, "Are you not well?"

"I haven't been well for a long time, Mrs Unwood."

Esther looked at the young women and 'her heart went out to her' – as the saying goes. She felt as though the words had been spoken, not by a person but by a spectre. It wasn't just the young woman's listlessness; it was almost as though she were not there at all, but hovering between this world and the next.

"Where is your little boy?" said Esther, in an effort to bring her back to earth.

"With Nadine – she's his mother now."

"What's wrong, dear? Where are you going?"

"Away, and I must hurry."

She smiled and turned from Esther. 'Ghastly and yet, through it all, that unearthly beauty – she was so beautiful, and so self-possessed. If I were a younger woman …' Esther shook herself and watched Sarah disappear beyond the large oak that overhung the lane.

Keeping the Cassyn River to her left, the young woman made her way along the edge of the marsh with and wondered where she was going. Ahead of her lay Dunburgh Wildlife Park and here she turned right and walked along the edge of the park towards Mardles Lane, and so to the open country. The cloud cover was thick and, although she looked up anxiously at times, Sarah had no real fear that the sun would suddenly break through. Wasn't that one sure way to end it all? Vampires cannot tolerate sunlight. To sit on the edge of a field – even a winter's field – and wait for a burst of sunlight might be the answer to her problem. Would she then go home, at last, to her parents? Would God collect her up into his arms if she committed suicide ... or must it be another hand which sent her finally to rest?

She came, in the late afternoon, to the little village of Frostenham, having made her way, circuitously, by lanes and bridleways where the grass was now coarse and thick and the ground wet and heavy. She had enjoyed her journey. It reminded Sarah of the afternoons when she and Matthew would go out together and she would talk to him of the plants and birds, and he would run ahead and pick her a flower. In winter they had come home together and cuddled in front of the fire. She loved his icy little fingers, and he would push them in under her armpits, against the side of her breasts until they were warm.

There was a pub in Frostenham, the Dog and Gun, and she went inside – not for warmth, but for human company. There were few people about at that time of the day, but the barmaid – a plump girl with a squat nose and a cheery laugh – greeted her in a friendly way and they dropped into conversation: children, men, a woman's lot and the last minute preparations for Christmas. Sarah hadn't spoken about such simple things since the summer when she and Nadine had walked along the cliff path.

As night fell, which it did by about three or four o'clock, more people began to trickle into the pub. Sarah had nowhere to spend the night, and nowhere to which she could return in the morning. The fire in the grate crackled and roared, sending flames shooting up the huge chimney, and so – for old times sake – Sarah went and sat by it and gazed down into the flames. Shane had always said she was a gypsy and could read their future in the flames and sometimes, when he'd been in one of his playful moods, she had pretended. She looked now, hoping that the future would not stretch too far, but the flames took her back, not forward. She saw the snowdrops in spring with their white and drooping flowers, the bluebells profuse along the shady banks of the higher paths, the daffodils dancing in hedgerows along the roadsides or clustered under trees, and the marsh marigolds with their smooth shiny leaves and beautiful yellow-golden flowers. She saw Matthew saying "King-cup", his teeth smiling on the 'k' and his lips pursed on the 'p'. She saw herself tilting the pushchair up towards her and repeating "King-cup" and then heard him giggle. The red flames flickered and white ash dropped from the charred wood of the logs.

"Are you all right, love?" asked the barmaid, coming up and standing by her.

"Yes, thank you. I'm sorry. I'm not drinking much am I?"

"You're not drinking anything, love, but I didn't mean that. You look so lost."

"I'll be on my way."

"There's no need."

Not knowing where she was going, Sarah walked, turning where the tracks led. She had no purpose, other than to get away from Dunburgh and find a place to ... die? She was already dead! She wanted to tire and drop by the wayside, but could not. Vampires never tire – their strength is prodigious, their stamina inexhaustible. At times, she seemed to drift along, inches above the ground. Try as she might, Sarah could not 'wear herself out'. She laughed as the phrase passed through her mind. She could hear her mother's voice.

She passed cottages from which the smell of Christmas cooking reached her nostrils. They whetted no appetite but jogged her memory. She climbed steeply at times – if the Suffolk landscape can ever be called 'steep' – and walked through farmyards, making her way, as she thought, south across the fields and round them through sheep, wet grass and mud. Occasionally she passed a group of locals, and asked the way to Eastwold. Going through Coveacre, with its shattered church and crumbling cliffs, she was met by a barking red setter and its mistress – a slim, strong woman who picked him up without breaking sweat and lifted the dog over the roadside style.

The trees along this stretch of the coast had been denuded of leaves in early autumn and Sarah couldn't help but feel sorry for a large, black bird which flew to the branches of a nearby tree. The bird seemed to be trying to settle in for the night, but there was no shelter. Dark storm clouds scudded across the sky; it seemed that rain was on the way and the crow was alone on the branch. An old man wished her well, "on such a cold night" as he kicked the mud from his boots and opened the door of his cottage from which the yellow light flooded out onto the road. If she'd like to come in, he said, there "was a cup of tea with her name on it." Sarah laughed and thanked him, but walked on.

The villages were often unlit but, even as the dark became pitch-black, this made no difference to Sarah, and she picked her way easily across meadows and over steams. Crossing one field, she paused at the gate and looked back. Walking across the field was a fox. It was well-fed, and one of the biggest foxes she had ever seen. He ignored her completely. This was his territory and he seemed very comfortable.

When she reached Eastwold, Sarah strolled into the town. There was a shoe shop where she spent some time gazing into the window, a Chinese restaurant, a hole-in-the-wall, an old-fashioned tea shop, a policeman's house which had been divided into five luxury apartments, a Conservative club and terraced houses going at £240,000. Sarah knew that time was going to hang heavily; she wasn't going to tire and she wouldn't need sleep and had nowhere, really, to go. Passing a wine shop, she noticed a tasting session in full swing. She turned away, walked quickly down a side-street and found herself heading for the sea and the pier.

There was the pre-Christmas noise she might have expected. It was after nine o'clock, and the youngsters were all kicking their heels and pushing each other around on the pavement. The girl behind the bar was untrained, but pleasant and attentive. A Scotsman dashed about, like a blue-tailed fly, with trays of drinks. The barmaid, sitting on the customer side of the bar and chatting to whoever came in, said to a stout and fleshy young lad that she was a bit bored because she hadn't got much to do before Christmas. He replied:

"Lucky you! I've got six hundred turkeys to kill in the next three days!"

When the music did start it was loud and Sarah, who had paused only for the company, walked on, wanting to explore the town for what, she supposed, would be her last time. It was lit up for Christmas, and as she walked passed the local school Sarah saw reindeer on the walls and Father Christmas in the doorway. By 11.30, she was tired of this and turned again to the sea, wandering in a distracted fashion between the rows of beach huts until she emerged at the edge of the dunes.

She headed inland, then, and walked far into the night, reckoning she must have covered more than ten miles when she reached a field she recognised. There was something familiar about the shape of the trees against the night sky and ... and the smell. A vampire's sense of smell, like their sense of sight in the dark, is particularly acute. The field in front of her was shrouded in fog, and she could see from the grass that no one else had passed that way, so she walked into the fog hoping to find some sign of ... of what – people, houses, life? She realised, suddenly, that it was the marsh she could smell: it was somewhere ahead and to her right. At the far side of the field she found a track.

Lost now, and glad of it, Sarah followed the track which was broken and invaded by scrub and bracken, until she came to a house. It was old, boarded-up against vandals and clearly empty. It was a place that most people would have found spooky. Sarah walked through the trees that surrounded it and tried all the windows and doors: none had been violated. It was derelict, unlived-in and, for her, ideal. She glided to the door with that familiar lightness in her step and, leaning into it, became one with the air. She turned and gazed out into the night and then was gone – wafting like mist into the empty house

There was a lot of movement during the night. It sounded like harvest mice in the loft, but Sarah thought it might have been the wind brushing the rafters or even birds on the tiles. She drifted into her ritual sleep and when dawn arrived she was dead to the world, wrapped in one of the golden, silk sheets she had brought from her bed at the Old Vicarage.

Horst Brultzner had not reached the same dawn with his mind in such an equanimous state. He woke at dusk and sauntered downstairs, expecting to find Sarah moving quietly about, settling the house for the night. He loved that because it showed that things were as they should be in a well-ordered world, and Horst Brultzner of all people appreciated a well-ordered world. He was not unduly troubled when he found her gone, but then decided, as always, to look in on Matthew. When he discovered the boy's bed empty and many of his clothes and toys gone, Horst rushed without knocking into Sarah's room. He saw where the golden sheet had been pulled from the bed, and knew that she had left him. 'Hurt' would not be the right word to describe Horst Brultzner's feeling at that moment; he did not have emotions in the way that humans do. Years of ruthless living had deadened the usual sensitivities, but his sense of 'right' was offended and the next emotion he felt was anger.

She could not escape him: he knew that. His sense of smell, sharp as any wolf's, would track her down in minutes. He followed her scent to the front door, which he opened. Outside, about to break into song, were carol singers. The astonishment on his face was comical and Penny Read, who was leading this group, burst out laughing.

"Have we surprised you, Mr Brultzner? We should like to sing you a carol!"

Without further ado, the carollers broke into *It came upon a midnight clear*. It was a well-balanced group with its blend of adult and child voices and the song rang out on the night air. Brultzner could not have asked for a more fitting contribution to his romantic notion of a 'Dickensian Christmas'. He stood in the doorway and listened; this was no time for his peremptory nature to assert itself. Like Scrooge, he wanted to attack them with something – perhaps one of the walking sticks he kept in the hallway – but this was another cherry in his Christmas cake, and Brultzner could do no more than enjoy the singing. They sang only verses one, two and five to keep the festive note cheerful, finishing with

"And the whole world gives back the song which now the angels sing."

Brultzner felt what in human terms would have been described as 'a lump in the throat'. He raised his hands to clap, and then gestured them to wait as he entered his study to find money for the collection box, which one little girl with raven-black hair was holding. He realised that he should have offered some small refreshment, but it was too late now – a faux pas that he would not forgive himself or Sarah when she was found. He slipped the fifty pound note into the box and smiled with his autumnal eyes, inclining his head to Penny and acknowledging the others in the group with whom he was acquainted.

"You must forgive me," he said, "my housekeeper is out for the evening and has omitted to leave any refreshment for your endeavours."

Penny Read loved the way he spoke and would not let him off the hook.

"You must make amends by joining us, Mr Brultzner – please, we won't take no for an answer, will we children? I would judge that you have a beautiful baritone matin voice. Am I right? Come along – fetch a scarf, an overcoat and some gloves. We'll provide you with a lantern."

The voices of the children were raised in a cheer. Brultzner looked at them, his eyes roving over the upturned, eager, expectant faces. Their hair, which poked out from under their woollen hats and flopped over their woollen scarves, was every colour and shade imaginable – red, red and gold, gold, auburn, black. He had no choice and resigned himself gracefully as Penny handed him a copy of *Hymns: Ancient and Modern*.

Penny was proud of the carol singing tradition in the village and considered it to have reached a point of some sophistication over the years. Groups of singers met at different places – the Jolly Sailors, the Queen's Head, the Duke's Head, the rectory, Beachlands Health Club and the school. Each group would then sing its way towards the church, pausing on street corners and gathering other voices on the way. There was some dispute about whose idea it was, but it had certainly started at the time of one of Corvin's early evangelic campaigns and he was generally given the credit.

Penny had originally led the group that started from the school, and it was the school that had circulated the drawing for the lanterns that were, quite simply, candles in jam-jars on sticks. The idea had been to involve the whole community – particularly those villagers who would normally be sitting quite comfortably in one of the pubs. The school had jumped at the idea. Who could resist the sound of children singing as Christmas approached, and what parent would refuse to join their child, and what self-respecting Christian would not 'lend their voice in song'?

Horst Brultzner found himself part of the 'rectory carollers' who made their way along Shore Lane and so passed the council houses on the Crescent and through the new estate to St George's Church. Penny Read was delighted with her catch, and even Horst took some pleasure in the occasion. They paused at each street corner under a convenient lamp-light and "sang their hearts out" – as he whispered to Penny between verses two and three of *Hark! The herald-angels sing.* The irony that he should be singing 'Born to raise the sons of earth, Born to give them second birth' was not lost upon him. Penny had been right about his voice; it was old, but he was a baritone with a high range and it was pleasant.

Corvin Unwood had led the group which started at The Jolly Sailors and they made their way along Beach Road passed the old fishermen's cottages and up Church Hill passed the houses of the wealthy chemist and other village stalwarts. The chemist always flung his doors wide open and offered mince pies and mulled wine to the adults, and real lemonade to the children. The smell of Christmas seeped out onto the road as they sang, looking inwards to the Christmas tree in the hallway.

The Duke's Head carollers made their way down School Road where they were joined by Martin and Amy Billings at the Police House, and Alan Read as the group passed his home. He had yet to tell Penny of his visit to the churchyard and it was clear, from the look that passed between them, that Martin had "kept to the thirty year rule." Clive Brown, as people's warden, had once led this group. It wasn't that Clive could sing, but his daughter, Sarah, had always accompanied him and her voice had carried the night. This evening they had no leader, but what they lacked in leadership they made up for in vocal aggression. The Duke's Head attracted the rowdy element that gave its all to once-a-year carolling.

Grise Culman, still recovering from her ordeal, refused to let this inhibit the tradition she had always supported. The Beachlands Health Club was a popular starting point for carollers because Owen and Grise always began with warm drinks and meat of some kind that they served – barbecue-style – in a fresh bread roll. This year it was turkey Italian-style, which Owen carved on the terrace while Grise served spiced wine punch, helped by Sandra.

It was a night that brought the village together in a flash of suddenly-open doors, chilled hands and feet, coins clattering into buckets, bundled scarves and gloves and heavy coats, welcome soups and warm pies, joyful if discordant voices, the impression of a journey being made, snapping log fires, sacred silences and raucous voices. As if by some divine intervention, they all came together at the church. The heavy doors swung back and they entered St George's.

Many came directly to the church, eschewing the walk – "but they came, believers and unbelievers alike", as Corvin Unwood proclaimed, because it was that time of year when the days were dark and there was a comfort to be had in gathering together. The church had, as always, been beautifully decorated with an abundance of holly and candles and a crib. The seraph spoke, angels came from the realms of glory and the silent stars went by; for some there would be a deep and dreamless sleep, and someone, soon, would need to reach back and find that glorious song of old.

CHAPTER 14

Esther Alone

The one-time leader of the Queen's Head group stirred in his coffin. He'd been in agony for days. A painful discharge of pus from his penis had gradually thickened, and he had been unable to prevent it. This had been accompanied by a burning sensation and the uncontrollable desire to urinate. At the same time, urinating had become increasingly painful and difficult. He had suffered severe stomach pains and the urge to vomit had taken him over in a huge sweat. His blood was on fire and he felt an inordinate craving to expel the blood. He was infected, and Sidney Close knew it. The one-time rector's warden, who had carried the cross down the aisle with a sneer on his face for the unbelievers, had what the vulgar would have called "the clap". It had always been a disease of the gutter; the clean and the righteous need never fear infection.

He writhed in agony and anger and chagrin, as the pus coming from him changed from white to yellow and then green. His testicles became swollen and the pain in them reminded him of the times when he had wanted Mavis so badly. Where was the whore who had brought him to this parlous state? Sidney wasn't sure what he was, but he knew he craved blood and he knew he had taken bad blood. Venereal disease was something he'd read about and talked about but never encountered, and he couldn't go to a doctor.

It was the singing which had woken him – the carollers to whom he had once belonged. He belonged to no one, and nowhere, now. He had moved to this vile place because no one would think of looking for him here, but he could not lay here forever in a stolen coffin. They had been watching him – Crewes and Billings. He could have crushed them both, but time was on his side and he wanted to savour his moments of conquest over each of them. He did, however, realise his peril. Trapped in his coffin during daylight hours he was at the mercy of them all – not only Crewes and Billings, but the nutty Rollie who he had also seen prowling about.

He'd have to get treatment or ... expel the bad blood himself. Where had that idea come from, and how could it be accomplished? He could cut his throat and his wrists and the blood would pump out of him – and he would heal. Sidney knew, somehow, that he would heal. He knew he needed help, but to whom could he go? He must find her – the one who had done this to him. She – Sarah – might know what to do. Before he took the knife to himself, he would find her and she must help him.

Sidney stood in the driveway, watching the carollers pass. He would follow them and maybe find someone. As he passed in the shadows across to the hedge lining Podd's Field, Sidney saw Horst Brultzner. He was walking side by side with Penny Read – a book like the Bible in one hand, a child's lantern in the other: Penny Read – the English-rose type, with everything going for her. A woman like that had never known want, pain, setbacks or heartache. She needed bringing down a peg or two, and Sidney Close was the man to do it. Could he pass this plague on like the Bint bitch had done? She'd spread herself around, and now he was the plague-carrier!

He was cut off from their world. He could only follow and watch. What was the German doing among them? He had come to the village only eight months before, and was now leading one of the carolling parties ... and she worked for him! The one who had done this to him worked for the stranger. Why had he never thought of that before? Sidney started from the mingled shadows of the winter hawthorn and the German looked his way – or so he thought. He slipped up the bank and made his way to the lane that skirted the churchyard, climbed the wall and crossed between the old graves towards the west porch where he could watch from the darkness of the yews. They all trooped in with their candle-lanterns bobbing in the night, casting slight and dancing shadows into the blackness that surrounded them.

Corvin Unwood, the weakest priest the village had ever been cursed with, led the Jolly Sailors party – and, yes, Mavis and the girls were there singing their hearts out. It was more than Corvin deserved, and it was more than Sidney could bear.

The Beachlands Health Club party arrived soon after those from the Duke's Head, and Sidney almost cried out in his torment. Both the women he could take whenever he wanted them were there. They were leading their carollers as though they had no care in the world. His howl mingled amongst the pain within him and he burned with hot pus, the searing in his penis and the stomach cramps that bent him double. He was scorching like a man held up for sacrifice in the flames of Hell; the revulsion rose within him as the Christmas lights shone out from the door of the west porch and the hundred voices sang:

"O come all ye faithful, joyful and triumphant, O come ye, O come ye to Bethlehem; Come and behold Him, born the king of angels: ..."

Sidney felt that he would never behold Him again.

Esther Unwood was concerned about Sarah and, the following afternoon, decided to do something – on her own. The young woman's face, as she had wandered off down the lane, still haunted Esther. 'The words she spoke came not from a person, but a spectre. It was almost as though she were not there at all, hovering between this world and the next.' Esther believed in spirits and the parlous state of the soul as it waited to be received. Purgatory for her was a real place, and she was sure that Sarah was there.

As she walked up the driveway of the Old Vicarage, all her forebodings went with her. Esther had never liked or trusted Horst Brultzner. She had subdued her instincts because they seemed unreasonable, but it had gone against the grain.

It wasn't only dislike and distrust that she felt. It was a heightened awareness of a sense of evil. Why had she squashed it down? Why had Corvin turned a blind eye?

She pulled on the bell and heard its sounds echo throughout the house. Esther waited, rang again and waited. She tried the door. It was locked against her. She wandered round the side of the house. The old outhouses were unlocked, and she peered inside.

"The back door's unlocked, Mrs Unwood."

The voice rocked her tottery old legs. She shuddered and reached for the wall.

"You all right, Mrs Unwood? I didn't mean to startle you."

"Who the hell are you?"

It was an old man who had grasped her arm to prevent her from falling. His eyes were kind and, feeling no threat, she was relieved enough to hold on to his arm.

"Who the ...?"

"I heard you, Mrs Unwood," said the man, who seemed eager to prevent her swearing again, "I'm Sam Cleat, the new gardener. I used to work for Lord Wangford. When Crafty was killed, Mr Brultzner asked his lordship to find him a new one."

"Yes, yes, I'm sorry I swore at you, Mr Cleat, but you startled me."

"Don't think twice about it, Mrs Unwood. Mum's the word!"

Esther gave him the kind of look the Queen might have given if someone had suggested her hat wasn't on straight.

"If you're looking for Miss Brown or Mr Brultzner, they must be in 'cause the back door's unlocked. It never is, if they're not here."

"I did ring the front door bell, but I couldn't make them hear."

"They sleep like the dead, those two do."

"I don't like to just go in."

"A respectable lady like you should have nothing to worry about. If you're sure you're all right now, I'll be going. I've finished for the day. So long."

He touched the peak of his flat cap in time-honoured fashion and sauntered off down the driveway, leaving Esther alone by the cellar steps. At the bottom, Esther paused before reaching for the knob of the kitchen door. Once inside she looked around. "Sarah?" It was so clean: the blackened stove shone, the copper gleamed, the floor tiles glistened, the wooden worktops were scrubbed and spices hung in their racks. On the air, the smell of fresh bread lingered. Esther shook herself. Why was old evil so ... seductive? Even the house had an unholy charm.

She walked carefully into the little passageway and peered at the racked rows of shiny bottles in the cellar. It took all her nerve to try the door that led up to the main hall. Esther prayed that it wouldn't open, and that she could turn and go home. The door opened quietly under her lightest touch. Why were the doors unlocked? "Sarah?" Even as the soft furnishings soaked it up, her voice was still loud and seemed to rush up the stairs, pulling her on. Esther fingered the gold cross on the chain about her neck.

She tapped lightly on the door of the morning room. There was no answer; and no answer as she tapped on each of the doors of the front parlour, the dining room and, lastly, Horst Brultzner's own study. Should she open it? She did, and the relief that flooded through her, when it was apparent no one was there, made her feel weak all over. Esther realized her hands as well as her knees were trembling. She was suddenly aware of how old she must be. 'With my arthritis, I shall be lucky to reach the top of the stairs.' She sat on Brultzner's chair in his study, partly to collect her thoughts, partly to delay the inevitable ascent of those stairs.

There was a sensation in the study of suppressed power. It was almost as though somewhere in those bookshelves there lurked a guardian – something malicious – watching her from a gap between the volumes. Esther believed in demons. She looked through the partly-open doorway into the hall, expecting … expecting what – that the door would close? It did. The door slammed shut. She had palpitations, realizing that the slam could wake the dead and that she was a prisoner. Her heart raced. She was near to collapse with the fear of it, and rooted to the chair.

It was only a little while after noon. Pale, winter daylight streamed in through the windows. There was nothing of which she needed to be afraid. Doors shut of their own accord at home. She got out of the chair and made her way to the door. It opened with the lightest of pulls on the knob, and there was nothing in the hall.

She was nearly half-way up the stairs when she heard the pitter-patter of tiny feet. At seventy-something and stiff with arthritis, she had long given up making sudden movements. She stopped and caught hold of the banisters, gripping them tightly. The sound passed her and slipped between her legs, leaving small, clawed footprints on the carpet. For two pins, she'd go home.

On the landing, she looked around. She wanted to find Sarah's room first – and only Sarah's room – speak with her and go home. More than anything, she wanted to go home. Esther was quite breathless. She didn't want to hang about on the landing. There was always the fear of a door opening. She guessed which Sarah's room might be and opened the door, but not before good manners obliged her to tap lightly upon it. She was surprised to see a bed and such a beautiful one. The golden, silk sheets were quite breathtaking and Esther imagined, easily, the young woman asleep. The room had a fireplace, and on either side of this were cupboards that were flush with the wall. These were closed with small hooks, which Esther lifted to reveal what amounted to wardrobes – built into the wall – in which hung some of Sarah's clothes. Esther knew that she standing in another world. She hadn't seen wall cupboards like these since she was a girl – and, then, in the house of an old aunt.

She was being drawn into the house again. What was it about old houses that drew you in? She crossed the room back to the door, just to test that it would not swing shut. To be sure, she moved the chair from the dressing table to hold it open. Despite its tranquil beauty, the room had a creepiness about it, and a smell which the perfumes on the dressing table could not hide. It was unpleasant: an aroma of graveyards and crypts. A draught passed over her feet and made its way up the chimney. Esther shivered. It was cold, and she rubbed her hands to keep warm. 'I haven't been well for a long time, Mrs Unwood.' The young woman's words just came into her mind, as though they were speaking together. Esther heard a light click, and turned. The door had closed, and the chair was back under the dressing table.

"Who's there? Stop playing with me!"

She was frightened. She admitted it to herself and rushed to the door. It opened easily and outside on the landing there was no-one: no pale, translucent shape, no half-human figure. 'It's my mind! I'm losing my mind!' Losing control worried her – especially in this place where her wits were her only defence. 'There is something here,' she thought, 'something that protects the house, something that guards its occupants, something that has nothing to do with my state of mind, something that is outside my influence, and something that is controlled from elsewhere.'

"Who are you? I've had enough of this!"

She had, and decided to find Brultzner. She had only come on an errand of mercy. Esther opened the bedroom next to Sarah's. It was Matthew's room. His toys were put away, tidily. She didn't linger, much as she would have liked to do so. She didn't want to sense evil here – not in a child's room.

There were only two other doors on the landing and one was a bathroom; the other, then, must be Brultzner's bedroom. Even as the thought passed through her mind, another cold draught surrounded her and Esther felt enveloped by evil. It breathed up through the floorboards, and filled the landing with 'an unspeakable horror'. She wished she was at home, in front of their fire, speaking with Corvin, but she wasn't, and some things in life had to be faced as they arose. Surprising herself with her own lack of hesitation, Esther opened the door. The room was eager to beckon her in, and the door swung easily on its hinges. Before she even stepped over the threshold, Esther saw the four-poster bed with its black and red canopies.

She walked into the room and approached the bed. Whatever evil lurked in the house knew she was there; it had followed her around, tracing her every step. Even as she stood on the threshold of the room, there was the patter of tiny feet. Esther reached out for support, but the room was sparsely furnished and there was nothing. Her feet ached, and her steps were tottering. She realized just how old and helpless she was, standing by the foot of that awful bed. There was the same mouldy smell she had noticed in Sarah's room, only this was far more ancient and far more pervasive. She was sure it came from the bed, and the thought made her feel nauseous and she had the desire to retch. Esther did not want to see what was in the bed. She did not want to find it watching her. She did not want to look into those yellow eyes – eyes that rustled like autumn leaves inside her head. Look up she must – her duty demanded that – and look up she did, her eyes taking in the red and black sheets.

In the bed lay Horst Brultzner, his head resting on silken pillows. She did not for one moment question that she was looking at a corpse. Esther re-called her mother's face in the chapel of rest, remembering her conviction that 'something had left the body'. It had seemed to her to be the soul. Later, Corvin had made her question that assumption – raising the belief that the body and soul are not two separate things divisible on death, but that the earthly body and the spiritual body were one and the same. If that were so, what she was looking at was a corpse who rose and walked the village and restored houses and charmed people.

She moved closer to him – so close that Brultzner could have reached out and grabbed her arm. With trepidation and infinite delicacy, she raised her hand and brushed the back of her fingers against his cheek. He didn't stir, but Esther shuddered at the coldness of the touch. He was a corpse, but a living corpse. So how was his spiritual body – given that he was dead – so different from her earthly one, and why was he here on earth? 'Heaven is the state of being with God. It is when we are with God all the time and consciously aware of his presence.' She could hear Corvin's words talking of eternity. So, was Brultzner damned to wander for all eternity, trapped on earth in a spiritual body? She had heard of such creatures, and Esther knew they posed a threat to the salvation of the living. Were he to wake, her own life would end and she would be damned. She would be condemned to wander in torment throughout eternity. The knowledge came to her, calmly, through the quiet train of her thought, and terror overwhelmed Esther as she thought of Sarah, disappearing beyond the large oak that overhung the lane.

A frightful need to escape overcame her. She knew that she mustn't panic, but she must leave that terrible house before he woke. Esther made herself look at the face again, fearful that the eyes would be open and watching her, knowing that any movement she made would be slow. Brultzner's eyes were closed. He seemed at peace with himself, but it was a false peace, a joyless sojourn beyond the grave. Somewhere out there, Sarah wandered in much the same state. There was nothing Esther could do. She was old and weak and had come, on the spur of the moment, unprepared. She must leave and find Corvin; he would have to know what to do.

She heard that strange patter of little feet again as she turned from the corpse, and saw those weird indentations on the carpet of the landing and staircase. Something was racing ahead of her, barring her path. The corpse was asleep but conscious of her every move. She half-sensed that she could make her way, agonizingly, to the bottom of the stairs, only to find him waiting. It was a slow descent, as always, and terror had made her muscles even more taut than usual. The stairway now seemed suffused in a grey-green light and Esther felt that she was passing through some kind of miasmic fog. The corruption nearly overcame her as she reached the bottom of the stairs and paused. Once again, she had to turn her head and look up. There was nothing, but this only increased her dread. Creeping through her like a fever was the belief that, whatever her wishes might be, she could not leave this place without his consent; it would be impossible to walk out of the front door.

As if to tempt – or taunt – her, the latch on the front door clacked, and it opened so that she looked out onto the driveway. She wanted to go that way but she was tired, so tired, and needed to rest. The wolf in the copse howled, and she thought of Crafty Catchpole and his awful death. There was no mercy in this old house, and its master would have his will. Esther made her way across the hall to the morning room. She knew that this had once been Sarah's room and the knowledge gave her a false sense of safety. The morning room was sanctuary, and she must just sit down somewhere, if only for a moment. It was still several hours before darkness would fall. She had time to rest.

He was fighting her. He was dead and asleep in his grave (make it look like a bed if he wanted, but it was a grave!), but he was fighting her. Esther imagined she could see a star in the fanlight over the front door, but it became diffused and split. She blinked but she could not hold it still and, slowly, the golden light stared down upon her like two malevolent eyes. The horror was that she knew all this was "rubbish" and yet could not help seeing it. As the eyes watched her approaching the door, they closed down upon her, and she felt as though she was struggling through thick undergrowth, her feet sucked from her by mud. A few steps and her strength passed away. She didn't want to collapse in the hall. The thought of him coming down the stairs at dusk and finding her lying there in a heap was too much to bear.   She needed to find somewhere to rest until this awful force left the hall and she could find her strength again. She was drawn towards her first thought – the morning room. It was a pleasant room and she could doze – just for a moment. How she got to the door, Esther didn't know. The weakness pervaded every muscle and tissue in her old body, but she got there and rested against the knob, with relief. As she leaned against it, the door opened, and she crossed the threshold, gratefully

"The ladies room", Horst had said, "the furniture is light in style, as befits the gentle sex". Esther sat with relief at the Godwin occasional table, "ebonized and with gilt decoration", and thanked her lucky stars that William Morris knew how to design chairs. It was a nice room, and she felt peaceful. The horror had gone. Her eyes were drawn to the space between the two windows where she saw an Adam gilt-wood pier table, and she imagined Sarah sitting there, relieved to have escaped that dreadful husband. It would only be for a moment and then she would slip quietly out the way she had come – down into the cellar and out by the back steps.

Sam Cleat had made his way to the Fishermen's Hut; he was a member by right of his father being one of the last skippers to fish from Dunburgh-on-sea. Although he had rarely visited – being a gardener all his life on the Wangford estate had kept him apart from the village – Sam was curious about one or two things at the Old Vicarage, and he knew that the Hut was a reliable repository of what he considered to be informed gossip.

When he arrived, several of the regulars were sitting at the long table resting their elbows around a pint. He nodded to Butch Strowger who, as always, sat at the door, and Sam ran his eyes over the group of darkly-dressed men. There was Jumbo Gooch, Daff Mallet, Scrub Turrell, Boss Wigg and Harry Bailey. It was a good gathering for gossip. They liked to think of themselves as 'knowing' and 'taciturn', but, to Sam, they were just a bunch of old women as far as gossip was concerned. The knack was to let them start talking, and not ask any direct questions. Once they got the idea that you were after something, all of them would clam-up.

"Long time since we sin yew, Sam," said Harry, always the most talkative.

"Got a job at the Old Vicarage. Thought I'd pop in and say hello."

"Thought you was retired."

"It's just a little something to tide over the pension."

"On a Sundee mornin'?"

"Had some tidying to do."

"Would hev thought you'd be better off in church," said Scrub Turrel, who could always be relied upon as the voice of dissension.

"Is that where you've come from then, Scrub?" responded Sam.

They all laughed, and a period of silence followed. None of them felt obliged to speak, being quite comfortable in each other's company, and there was a definite contentment in just sitting around.

"Yew gart Crafty's job, then?" said Daff Mallet, "Weren't roight about him."

"The wolves escaped, didn't they?" enquired Sam.

"If yew believe that, you'll believe anything," said Daff, "Wolves don't escape, not unless someone lets them out."

"What are yew sayin', Daff?"

"Om sayin' thet someone let them wolves out."

"Kids, you mean?"

"Kids be buggered. Him! Him as wanted to save them after what they done ter Crafty."

"Why would he do that?" asked Harry Bailey.

"Don't ask me," said Daff, "but I tell yer, it were him as let them out."

"Why?" insisted Sam, very quietly.

"That worry you, Sam, ter be workin' fer a bloke loike thet?" said Scrub.

"He's a trifle unusual – I'll give you that, but that doesn't mean to say he'd let a pack of wolves loose on the village."

"Oi reckon Crafty hed sin too much," said Daff, delivering his conversation grabber with a ponderous look around the hut, "Oi reckon he did Crafty in."

"Thas a rum thing ter say, Daff."

"Maybe, but it ent far from the truth, I'll warrant."

"What makes you say that, Daff?" asked Sam.

"He's a rum un, thets whoy. He's got a way with animals and he's got a way with wimen. Look at thet Shane's woife – what a carry on, her livin' there with him. And what happened ter her husband?"

"He died, Daff," said Harry, "we buried him."

"Bit sudden, weren't it – a healthy, young man loike that? Since that bloke cum here, yew think how many people hev gone ter their Maker."

He paused for dramatic effect. It was obvious to all around the table that Daff was on the boil. He had been cooking this one up for a long time.

"There's her husband, there was Froggy, there's Clara Gobley and Bert, there's Crafty – and there's Sid! And there int one of them as was ready to go! And they all had doin's with him – every one! Or her!"

"So what was it you think Crafty knew?" asked Sam.

"Oi don't know, but Crafty hant bin himself for a long toime and do you remember Sid that day at the Jolly Sailors? That weren't normal."

"Yew weren't there!" interrupted Scrub.

"Jumbo told me," said Daff, with a toss of his head.

"Yew are roight about Sid not being roight that day," said Harry.

"Yew got cause ter know, aint yer, Harry?" laughed Jumbo.

"Not a laughin' matter, Jumbo," said Harry, looking hurt, "I felt sorry fer Sid, that day. He weren't himself. Anyway, what yew got ter say, Sam? It was yew started all this."

Sam was taken off-guard by the directness of Harry's enquiry. They all watched him. Sam needed to earn his place at the table by providing at least one further piece for the puzzle.

"Nothing you could put your finger on, so to speak," he replied, "Mr Brultzner is friendly enough and keeps himself to himself."

"I just wondered what you knew about him."

They all continued to stare, as though he was drinking his pint under false pretences. It didn't pay to not keep your side of the bargain with the Fishermen's Hut.

"He's pleasant enough as I say, but he gives me the creeps."

Sam paused and looked around to see if he had provided enough gems as yet, but the stares of the other men did not falter, so he continued.

"And there's been several occasions when I've found him speaking to me and afterwards I haven't been sure where I've been or what I've done. When you been with him for a while, it's as though he's scratching around in your mind."

"That sounds scary enough ter me," said Jumbo, "Oi woont want someone scratchin' around in moi hed."

"And then there was the little boy – Miss Sarah's son. He was only a littl'un, you know, but he had the words of a grown-up when it came to animals. He could talk about them like a university professor. I felt sorry for him. It wasn't natural."

"There yew are, then," exploded Daff, "what did oi tell yer? It's a pound to a penny he set them wolves on ter Crafty. Sumthun ought ter be done about it."

Esther Unwood woke with a start when she heard the click of the door. Looking up through dazed eyes, she could see that dusk had fallen in the garden. She had slept longer than she had intended but it was always the same after Sunday lunch, and she had felt so weak. Esther sighed. Corvin would be dozing, too – snoring and spluttering away in his favourite armchair. She opened her mouth and tried to speak, but the words wouldn't come. It was pleasant enough in the room; perhaps she would doze a little longer. There was no hurry; Rebecca was out.

There was a sudden intenseness in the room. It was that struggle again – that awful struggle of wills, and she was too old, too tired for all that; it was horror, pure and simple. Why was there always this urge to domination? There was a need to move, to go somewhere, to get away. From what? The memory came back to her at that moment – at the moment when she remembered the force that had tried to dominate her. She remembered her struggles in the hallway of the Old Vicarage, and the weakness overwhelmed her again. All that sleep – and for nothing! Fatigue – fatigue like she had never known seeped through every old joint in her body. There was only the will left. What was it Kipling had to say? 'Except the will which says to them: Hold on!' Esther tried to hold on as her consciousness returned. It was the click of the morning room door as it shut which had woken her.

"Good evening, Mrs Unwood, how nice of you to drop in. 'Drop in' – how I love those English expressions. So quaint."

Corvin Unwood stirred in his favourite chair. He must have dropped off. Soon it would be time for tea, and then Evensong. He liked Evensong: pushed to a decision he would have voted it his favourite service of the day. 'My soul doth magnify the Lord, and my spirit doth rejoice in God my Saviour.' Mary's wonderful song of thanksgiving never failed to stir him. At any time of the year, it was a delight; approaching Christmas, it was an inspiration.

The church, it is true, was never over-full. All those years ago, *The Forsyte Saga* had rung the death knell for Evensong, but it was a peaceful hour to share with those of a like mind. He had prepared his sermon for tonight. With Christmas only nine days away, he had decided to ponder awhile on the symbolism of light. Several of the young people (children of staunch church families) had returned from university for the festive season, and would be there. Corvin felt he needed to offer them a challenge. Symbolism may have been lost on the older generation, but it appealed to the intellectual element he had attempted to nurture.

He looked across the fireplace at Esther and realised that she wasn't in her usual chair. Perhaps she had already made her way to the kitchen and was preparing tea. It was not a meal they really needed after one of her Sunday dinners, but it was welcome, nonetheless.

He closed his eyes and pictured the light of the world and then brought his hands together in the gesture of supplication, quietly mouthing a prayer for God to bless his sermon. He had chosen the reading from Malachi to stress the dual nature of fire. 'Behold, I will send my messenger and he shall prepare the way before me.' John the firebrand preacher compared with Jesus the gentle Light of the World. 'But who may abide the day of his coming?' 'For he is like a refiner's fire ... and he shall purify the sons of Levi ... that they may offer unto the Lord an offering in righteousness.'

He wondered what the young people would make of that; sometimes – after the service – some of them challenged him, and Corvin enjoyed the cut and thrust of debate. There was little of that in a village ministry. 'It shall leave them neither root nor branch.' They wouldn't like that; it was in accord with the God of his father, but not the God of their day. They had been raised on gentle Jesus, meek and mild. Esther would like it, however. She would approve. Esther considered that things had been watered down too much. 'A God of love is one thing, Corvin – and I do not deny His gentleness – but, for some, there must be retribution.'

Corvin looked up again and listened. There was no sound from the kitchen – no clink of cups, no clatter of cake tins. He stood up and walked through the hall and into the kitchen. His wife was not there and, for the first time since he had woken, Corvin was perturbed. "Esther." He called her name all over the house and then he became frightened. They had eaten dinner early, and she had excused herself from the washing-up saying that she wanted to go somewhere. She must have been gone two or three hours. It was dark outside, and cold.

"Corvin."

The front door opened and Esther came in, giving him a quick, sideways look.

"Where have you been?"

"What's it to you?"

"Esther?"

"You can't have been that concerned."

"I fell asleep."

"Exactly."

"Where have you been?"

"I've already answered that one."

"Esther?"

"For Christ's sake, Corvin, stop babbling my name."

"Esther!?"

"I'm going for a shower."

"A shower – you never shower."

"Well, I am tonight. I feel dirty. I want to … wash my sins away in the tide."

She laughed. It was a heartless sound and Corvin shuddered.

"I'll get tea, then, my love. We do not have long before we shall need to make our way to Evensong."

"Don't bother for me – I'm not hungry," she said, looking at him with an expression on her face that was a mixture of resentment and puzzlement. "Go yourself, tonight. I shan't bother with Evensong."

CHAPTER 15

A glimmering of light

Nadine Palmester 'sat' on the recording she had made of Sarah's story for several days. She wanted all five of them together: the thought of listening to it over and over again was more than she could bear. Alan Read was away at a conference, and Tony was engaged on late Christmas shopping with his wife: so she waited. When Alan picked up the message on his voicemail, he returned the call.

"I think the time has come to share this with a wider audience, Nadine. We have all been reluctant to do that because none of us really believed that it was happening. It's Wednesday, today. If I don't get back to you, take it that I've arranged a meeting, at my house, for Friday – no, Saturday the twenty-first. I might need a couple of days. We'll make it early – seven o'clock? OK. You ring Tony and Martin, and bring your dad. I'll do the rest."

Nadine didn't question him further. It was a relief that someone else was taking the lead, and lifting the burden from her shoulders. Alan Read telephoned Grise Culman immediately and found that Sidney Close had not re-appeared. He stressed to her, once again, the absolute necessity to do exactly as he had advised.

"Look upon it as a prescription, Grise, and take your doctor's advice. This is a plague and it will take time to cure it in the community. You've been able to order some more garlic flowers from the address I gave you? And crosses? Keep one in every room, and always carry one with you. Yes – both Corvin and Simon will be only too pleased to bless them. Good … Yes, yes – never mind that. Christmas it may be, but you mustn't venture out at night unless it is essential … no, nor your children … Then keep your eye on her! Teenage daughters need to do as they are told … Sandra? … No, she hasn't. Why? … Then ask her to do so. Take care."

He put the phone down and stood, pensively. The sensible thing would have been to get Grise and her family out of the village, but that wasn't realistic. Owen would never take on board what had happened and Grise, despite everything she had suffered, would never agree. He puffed in the way that would have annoyed his wife – had she been the kind of woman who got annoyed – and made several telephone calls.

"All right, Alan? Nothing serious?" asked Penny from the door of his study.

"Yes – unbelievably serious. I won't tell you about it now – please let me wait until everyone is here and then, hopefully, things will become clearer."

He looked up at her in a way that still melted her heart.

"It's the crisis, Pen – it has come. You remember what we were talking about in the summer? We should have acted much sooner – but how could we be sure, how could we believe, how could we expect anyone else to believe us? I'm going to be busy tomorrow. There'll be a meeting here on Saturday night. Can you arrange to have the children in bed – or out of the way – by seven o'clock? And can you arrange to have some food laid on – something simple, nothing that requires you to be getting up all the while ... oh – and no alcohol. We need to keep clear heads."

"How many of us will there be?"

"Ten of us," he laughed, "Quite a little party, but it won't be a dinner party. Maybe a little wine won't hurt – but nothing strong or heavy. Now, I'll have to phone Jim and call in sick for tomorrow."

He caught the expression on his wife's face as he spoke, and laughed again.

"Yes – that serious! And Pen – would you get me a really black coffee?"

Alan had arranged to have the meeting in their dining room. He thought that business was conducted more effectively around a table, and theirs was a large one, quite able to seat a dozen people, comfortably. "We might", he had said once, "even have managed the Last Supper". The dining room was large, also, and nowhere near any of the three staircases that led to the bedrooms; there was no chance of any of the children sitting on any of the stairs, listening. The room had an open fire that he had stoked well with both coal and logs. He had also drawn the heavy curtains across the french windows, which led onto the back terrace. The room was enclosed and cosy, he thought as he looked around. 'Sideboard cleared for the food, drinks in the cabinet or on the side-table, coffee and tea not a dozen steps away in the kitchen, dog sprawled across the french windows, disc player ready and notebooks with pencils in place.' At the far end of the room, three holdalls rested against the wall.

Nadine and Simon were the first to arrive. Nadine handed Alan the discs and, checking that she had copies hidden, he placed the originals on the table. Simon was healing slowly; the punctured lungs and the broken ribs were still causing him discomfort in his breathing and chronic pain, which he would not ease with medication.

"When the good Lord is ready, he will deliver me."

Simon accepted a glass of wine and was glad to sit, quietly, where Alan directed him. Alan thought he had never seen Nadine looking so distressed and overwhelmed. She smiled only wanly, as she set up her recording equipment.

"Matthew is at home," she said in answer to Alan's question, "with a neighbour. We didn't like to move him to yet another bed ... He speaks very little, just wondering where his mummy is and wondering when he can go back with Grandpa Horst and the animals."

When Tony arrived, he shook hands with Alan and Penny, but embraced Nadine. He shook hands with Simon, and the old man returned the grip. He respected Tony Crewes for his courage, but saw his atheism as a weak link in the group. Tony sat next to Nadine, leaned back in his chair and stretched his legs out under the table. He remained seated when Penny Read brought Martin Billings into the room. He liked his old friend, but doubted his staunchness. In Tony's view, Martin was now the weak link in the group and a threat to their success and safety. The policeman's eyes took in everything as he entered, even the presence of Leo – Alan's Labrador – across the doorway.

"Keeping an ear out for uninvited guests, are you, boy?" he said.

Leo looked up but didn't move from where Alan had told him to stay.

"Sit where you like, Martin, but not at either end of the table."

Martin sat at the far end on the opposite side of the table to Tony – his back to the fire and his eye on the french windows – where, by leaning backwards or forwards slightly, he could watch the expressions on all the faces.

When Corvin arrived with his wife, daughter and Peter Vishnya, all the men stood – Simon Palmester with difficulty. None of them had expected this: their early discussions had ruled Corvin out, and his presence was not reassuring. At Alan's invitation, Corvin eased Esther into the seat next to Martin and placed himself next to her with Rebecca and Peter to his right. Corvin liked the fire on his back and was now in the dead-centre position on the fire-side of the table. Penny offered drinks to anyone who wanted one, and sat next to Tony, opposite Esther. Alan seated himself at the lower end of the table. He smiled around and spoke.

"Welcome. I chose the White House," he said, with a smile, "for our meeting because it is further than most of your houses from the Old Vicarage, and I asked you to arrive at slightly different times because I didn't want to draw attention to us. All of you – whether you know it or not – have some idea of why we are here; all of you have, at one time or another, been involved with Horst Brultzner. The only exception, as far as I know, is Esther and I have included her because I feel that both Corvin and Rebecca will find her support invaluable.

Firstly, I would ask that, whatever you may hear tonight, nobody leaves until the business of the evening is complete – until we have all had our say. Is that agreed? … Good. Secondly, I must trust that, whatever the outcome, you will keep what you hear tonight to yourself. Yes?"

This time he did not take a nod of agreement. Alan asked each person to affirm in front of the others that they would say nothing to anyone outside the room.

"Thank you. It will be a long evening. Each of us here is in possession of information that will help us rid this village we love of a pestilence – of a plague, in fact. Each one of us has, over the past nine months – since March – been stirred to act against Horst Brultzner, or in support of someone afflicted by him. I have left the head of the table free so that whoever is speaking can sit there and be seen. The first person I would ask to speak is Nadine because it what she has to say – or rather what Sarah Brown has to say – that is, in my view, the decisive evidence. Each one here has either acted alone – for the most part – or simply not acted at all because something unbelievable has occurred, and nobody really wants to look foolish or risk culpability. Our vacillation has already proved fatal for many people. Nadine?"

Nadine walked to the head of the dining table. She looked into every face and told how Sarah had come to her. She then played the recording. For everyone, the voice of the stricken young woman was the penny dropping, the moment when they all understood – but, more importantly, accepted – what was happening.

"Thank you, Nadine. If Simon will now take the chair he can tell us what he can remember of his vigil, and then I will fill in what five of us here have already done with regard to Sidney Close, who is still at large, if temporarily inactive."

He ushered Simon to the head of the table: all listened, intently.

"How many of us dismissed Simon's experiences as fantasies? What else could one do?" Alan said, diplomatically, when the old man had finished.

He started his own account by apologising to his wife for not involving her earlier and then detailed their plan of campaign against Sidney Close. He finished by recounting his medical notes from the summer.

"These are the six cases we know of: there will be others."

Rebecca Unwood, who had already flinched as she listened to Sarah's voice recalling their intimate meeting at the Old Vicarage, stood angrily.

"You will excuse me," she said, sounding exactly like her mother, "but I am leaving now. This ..."

"Sit down, please, Rebecca," said Peter Vishnya, "this is uncomfortable for all of us, but Alan is right. We have all ignored little things too long and now ..."

He shrugged. Rebecca looked at him, ire flashing from her eyes, but she sat down. Penny Read stood and looked at the young woman.

"I know how you feel, Rebecca – violated. I was ...taken twice ..."

"At least twice," said Alan.

"Yes – one denies it and hides it. I never told Alan – anymore than you told your parents or Peter."

"Are you saying," interrupted Corvin, "that our ladies are still ... still under the influence of this creature?"

"They did not drink his blood as far as we know, and his mark has passed from them."

"Unlike poor Sarah who died with it on her throat," said Nadine.

"I cannot continue with this horror, Corvin," said Esther, "I must go."

"Please, Mrs Unwood," said Alan, "you must hear everything. Scraps of information have been our undoing."

"I must ... I will go."

"Please sit down, Esther. There is no turning back for any of us having heard that tape, and it is best we go forward in full knowledge of what we face."

"Thank you, Corvin," said Alan, "I would ask you to take the chair, now. Your narrative may be a series of uncertainties rather than a tale, but it is important to hear of your meetings with Sidney, Sarah and Necker – and what you did, or didn't do."

Corvin squirmed in the chair; his lack of directness and courage in the face of Simon's assurance and ordeal were an embarrassment to him. He felt like a man undergoing some kind of holy flagellation, but when it was over the relief showed in his eyes and face. He looked like a man cleansed of the most grievous sin.

"So neither Junket nor your Bishop Twiddle wanted to know," said Martin.

"They would rather not have heard," replied Corvin.

"So we are very much on our own?"

"Oh yes – hence my strictures at the start of our meeting," said Alan, "If what we must do is discovered then we face public humiliation, and loss of credibility and profession and livelihood. We face imprisonment, and the damage to our families will be irreparable. It would be far easier to simply walk away from this, now."

He paused only for a moment, and then turned to Peter Vishnya.

"I have asked you to come, Peter, because you work for Horst Brultzner and know more about him than any of us. I realize that anything you say against his interests will be a betrayal of his trust in you, but I hope you will consider the circumstances to be extenuating. Moreover, I feel you may have other things to tell us, and your knowledge of these things may go deeper than ours. You were suspicious of him in the very beginning, were you not? ... Would you like to take the seat?"

"After what has been said here tonight, I have no choice."

From the chair, Peter Vishnya recounted his initial hostility to Brultzner, how he was won round, what he had discovered working for him and his experiences in Leipzig with Eva Schulz. He was honest to the point of bluntness, despite the effect of his words on Rebecca. This was, he said, no time to be squeamish; complete honesty was necessary in the face of the immense difficulties they all faced. He also talked of historical researches and his letter to Rebecca, telling of the nineteenth century shipwreck and how 'the plague' came to Dunburgh-on-sea.

"In my view," he said, "there is a clear connection between this 'plague' and the one we have now. All accounts of vampirism have similar stories; there are too many for them to be ignored. I found Brultzner standing by that grave soon after he arrived. Clearly, he once knew the young soldier who was buried beneath it. It is my belief that he exerted as much influence in the district then as he does now. The young man was leading an assault on his kind and he had him flogged to death on a trumped-up charge of drunkenness."

"You mean he was the captain of the ship – the one who went down with her?" asked Martin.

"If that person was a 'captain' – who can tell: he may simply have been a passenger. The captain, according to legend, was staked and burned, anyway. History – especially storytelling – isn't an exact art. All I know is that he was standing by that grave with a look of respect on his face."

"But that would make him nearly two hundred years old?" said Martin.

"As would the histories of Eva Schulz and Katerina Schnell make them."

"Of course," said Martin, feeling foolish.

"These creatures are immortal. He could be much, much older," said Alan, "Which brings us to Tony's story, but first, have you anything to add, Peter?"

"Only that what we know will, eventually, involve us in dire work across Europe ... for now, perhaps both Rebecca and Penny would wish to say something?"

After Peter Vishnya's frankness, both women felt able to speak freely and recalled their feelings when what they now knew to be a vampire had visited them – their sense of arousal, their desire for secrecy, their anger when questioned. When they had finished, Alan beckoned Tony Crewes into the head chair.

"Tony's activities – again alone, which, I repeat, has been our undoing until now – have led him in a different direction, but we need to listen to him because Brultzner's influence over ages is a very significant factor in this whole saga."

Tony told his tale directly. It was, after all, a simple narrative arising from Simon's fractured memories. When he had finished, there was anger, bewilderment and distrust from around the table.

"You had no business involving the child," said Penny and Rebecca, together.

"I know."

"Is that all you have to say?"

"It's all I can say, but you might bear in mind that he would have gone ahead, anyway. He is Brultzner's sworn enemy."

"Why are you so certain that there is no evil in this temple?" Simon queried.

"I have been there – you have not. I, also, know something of its history, which, I might say, is not of credit to your own faith."

"Then, is Lord Wangford involved in this?" asked Corvin.

"I don't believe so – not in vampirism. His loyalty to Brultzner must spring from their secret society. The two, I believe, are not connected."

"I do not think that it would be advisable to involve Charles Wangford at this point. We are unsure how far his loyalty extends, and we can deal with Brultzner without his help," cut in Alan Read., "We must all accept that strong emotions are involved here, tonight – but we do have a common purpose, do we not?"

He paused, forcing an answer from each of them and then continued.

"Nadine has recorded all that has been said this evening. Each of us will receive a copy – if we wish. Now – before we proceed, is there anyone else who wishes to speak, is there anything else we need to know?"

"Esther?"

It was Corvin who spoke, unaccustomed to his wife's silence.

"I have nothing to say. Please continue."

"Very well, but before I do, I want an affirmation of solidarity. Whatever form it takes, it is binding upon us all. Agreed?"

Once again, Alan went round the group and insisted upon an answer.

"I want a symbol of our unity. I have already spoken to Corvin and Simon."

The two priests looked at each other with understanding, but without speaking. Corvin produced a cross from one of his pockets and held it forward into the centre of the table. They all reached towards it, placing their hands upon Corvin's.

"Lord, bless this, our enterprise, as we go forth against your enemy, as we strive to rid the world of the demons that would sully thy holy name and corrupt the innocence of thy people. Give us strength, Lord, to strive and conquer for we shall know fear and seek safety in retreat. Stiffen our sinews, Lord, strengthen our backbone and give us the victory, in your holy name. Amen."

They all joined with Simon on the "Amen" and then sat down.

"May I suggest," said Alan, "that we take some refreshment now? The first part of our evening is over – we share each other's knowledge. We now have plans to make and I think a break would be welcome."

It was: the simple enjoyment of sharing food and drink brought them together. Penny had provided cheese muffins, borek, leek and onion tartlets, a danish crown, and a courgette and dill tart. For the sweet-toothed, there were lemon curd tarts (a favourite of her husbands), red grape and cheese tartlets and pecan tassies. Alan poured wine, Penny made tea or coffee and their four children crept into the room at the sound of people drinking and eating. It was a pleasant half-an-hour as they broke into little groups about the house, re-affirmed friendships, shook hands, kissed cheeks and basked in the glow of the flames.

It was a cosy room. Penny and Alan loved it, as did their children, and they would often linger after a meal, drawn by friendship and fire. It was decorated for Christmas: half-logs of silver birch bore holly and candles, more holly (interspersed with wooden figurines) adorned the mantelpiece, a small tree (decorated in silver and blue by one of Penny's girls) stood by the fireplace, and a large wooden statue of a snowman (bought back from a skiing holiday) braved the flames on the hearth. One of Penny's boys showed round a reindeer he had carved from pine when the whole family spent the New Year in Scotland. Leo sniffed around, as all Labradors do when there is food about, but showed no anxiety and no desire to go out into the garden.

Everyone realised the significance of that unrehearsed moment – it could be any one of their homes, it could be any home in the village. They smiled at each other. This – whatever the cost might be, and no one could foresee a simple end – was something for which it was worth fighting.

"Our first task is an appalling one, but straightforward. We must destroy Brultzner ...," began Alan, when the children had returned to bed and everyone else was settled around the table.

"Is that so, Alan?" queried Nadine, and the others looked at her in surprise. "Whatever one may think of Brultzner, his care and his abstemiousness stands out throughout. He has been quite desperate to hide his ... condition, and will, I believe, be keen to continue doing so. It seems to me that Sidney Close is the wild card here. He is the immediate threat. We must find him."

"I see the sense of what you're saying, Naddy, but Brultzner certainly killed Crafty and we have no defence against him. The sooner he is dispatched the better."

"I think your dad's right, Nadine. We have no way of holding Brultzner once we are discovered," answered Alan.

"Before you go on, Alan, let me just say," interrupted Tony, "I will find Sarah. If you wonder about my motives, Nadine will explain."

"As you wish," responded Alan, "but I will continue."

"How do you expect to do that," asked Simon, speaking directly to Tony.

"I am aware that the feelings around this table, tonight, are tumultuous," said Alan, attempting to bring the discussion together again, "but our interests are, essentially, the same are they not? We must work together."

"May I suggest," said Corvin, "that Alan be allowed to finish?"

"Thank you, Corvin … Perhaps, if I outline my proposals and then offer them up for discussion?" said Alan, looking round the group, "I am suggesting that Peter, Corvin and I should destroy Brultzner, while others here see to the safety of their families. We shall go to the Old Vicarage tomorrow morning and hope to find him at our mercy … Nadine, Simon – I want you to remove Sarah's boy to a place of safety outside the village, and stay with him …. Penny must stay with our family and I would much rather you got them out of the way, Pen – to your mother's, perhaps?"

"It's Christmas, Alan."

Around the table, everyone laughed except Alan, who sighed and continued.

"Rebecca, I am suggesting that you stay with your mother and that you look after Yevgeny while Peter is away. Again, I would stress that we have no defence against Brultzner, and I would consider it safer for you to be as far away from the village as possible … Esther – your prayers and your council can offer support but we cannot have you involved in this butchery. You stay with your daughter and help where you can … Martin – I would ask you to re-double your efforts to find Close. Use any of us who are free, if you wish, but in daylight hours."

"He cannot do it alone," said Nadine, "I will remove Matthew to a place of safety where he will be watched and then join you, Martin."

"What about Sidney Close?" asked Martin.

"There is one obvious draw for Sidney Close," replied Alan, "His desire for Grise will bring him out."

"Alan is right," said Simon, "I will join the hunt for Close – once Matthew is in a place of safety. No Naddy – it is no use you complaining. He will need a priest, and Corvin already has his share of the work. Remember, also, who lies under the ground trapped in his own coffin! We can perhaps, save him for the New Year."

Alan's brow twitched at Simon's dark humour.

"Tony – what have you in mind regarding Sarah?"

"I think she would only have gone south from here. Towns lie to the north, and Sarah would have chosen the open country. Someone will have seen her – according to Nadine, she left in daylight. She will be found, holed-up in some barn or outhouse. Besides, there is one who watches everything – the nutty youth, Rollie. He's always prowling around. I have a mind to seek him out."

"Very well – against the wall you will have noticed three holdalls. They contain all we should need. Tony – take one. I will take the other for use against Brultzner. Martin you should keep the third one in readiness. Lastly, I take it that we all have mobile phones? If not – get one tomorrow. It is absolutely vital that we keep in touch and at immediate readiness. So that we don't phone endlessly around, we will have three key people – Nadine, Peter and Martin. If there are any emergencies, these are the people to phone. Peter will then pass on any messages to his family. Nadine will communicate with Simon and Tony. Martin will inform Pen and me."

"Tony," said Peter, "I would deem it an honour if you would take Anton with you. I do not believe you have any idea of the dangers you face – you must not go alone. Brultzner, also, will be seeking Sarah Brown. He will not let her betray him."

"What about your son?"

"Your need will be greater. Yevgeny will be safe with Rebecca and Esther."

"Very well – thank you. You'll have a word with Anton, will you?"

They all laughed – except Alan who took the opportunity to suggest they broke off to make their group arrangements. Excitement was high, and the conversation animated. It was an hour, interspersed with eating and drinking, before everyone was satisfied. Before they left, Corvin drew them together in prayer:

"None of us know what tomorrow and the next few days – perhaps weeks – may hold. There is no certainty that we shall all survive this time. Let us draw together, and asked the Lord's help – *Lighten our darkness we beseech thee, O Lord, and by thy great mercy defend us from the dangers and perils of this night, for the love of thine only Son, Jesus Christ, our Saviour. Amen.*"

They departed into the darkness of that particular night, each to their own homes where shock set in and fear stabbed at their hearts and determination. They all knew the road ahead would prove to be a steep and rugged pathway.

Grise woke with a start. She knew that he was in the house and her first thought was of her daughter. She leaped from the bed, with a backward glance at Owen who was snuffling quietly by her side, and ran along the hall to her daughter's room. She flung open the door. The moon was in its first quarter and there was little light in the room, but enough to see Sidney Close sitting on the edge of the bed. He had pulled the duvet right back and removed her daughter's nightdress. Sidney was running his fingers over her body, probing and stroking the nooks and crannies of her nakedness. As she burst into the room, Grise saw his hand slip from the cupped breast and run over the belly to her daughter's inner thigh. Every instinct urged her to yell in anger, but fear held her breath until she felt as though she would choke. The last thing she wanted to do was wake her family with her screams. Close would be pushed into a corner, and strike out against them all. Grise's voice came in a whisper.

"Leave her alone – please."

Sidney turned, looked at Grise and smiled. His hand continued to rove over the young woman's body. Grise's terror increased as her helplessness became clear.

"Forgotten your cross, Grise?"

Grise turned as though she might run back to fetch it. Sidney smiled at her vulnerability.

"Don't trouble yourself. I have what is more precious to you than life, and should you be foolish enough to hold a cross against me, I could tear out her throat."

"Take your hands off her – please. Don't do that!"

"Are you asking, Grise – or begging?"

"Begging."

"Beggars kneel."

Grise dropped to her knees, exposing her breasts further as she did so. Sidney looked at them with relish, knowing they were his whenever he was ready.

"Please take your hand off my daughter."

"That's better. They're precious, aren't they – teenage daughters? Peaches ripening and almost ready to pluck; and your little girl is a very ripe peach, isn't she, Grise? Blonde, but otherwise the spit of you – Miss Hot-pants 2000?"

"Stop it! You disgust me, Close. You were disgusting as a ..."

"Human being? I didn't know I disgusted you that much, Grise. You always seemed to appreciate me clutching your buttocks at parties. Of course, we've got to know each other a little more intimately since then."

Grise could see that he was enjoying himself, enjoying a conversation he could never have had with her as a man. He hadn't moved from the bed, but his right hand now rested on the edge of the mattress – at least, off her daughter's body. She knew that he had the upper-hand and the initiative for any move would be his. If only she could get him away from Margaret. Where was the girl's cross? She'd told both her children never to go anywhere without one.

"How did you get in?"

Sidney, relaxed on the edge of the bed, laughed.

"I was wondering when you were going to ask. You know teenage girls, Grise. Tell them to wear a cross – and will they? Rub their windows with garlic flowers – and what do they do?"

Grise was furious. She had known as much when she spoke to both her children. Margaret had stamped from the room with a pout and, obviously, removed the flowers from the windows and smothered the scent of the garlic with whatever perfume was being aimed at the teenage market that month; none of the crosses was anywhere to be seen.

"Wondering how you can get the better of me, Grise? Come over here."

She hesitated, thinking he had something perverted in mind.

"Now."

He said it quietly, without any emphasis. She scrambled from her knees and came.

"Take off your nightdress."

He didn't have to ask twice. Grise was too frightened to refuse. This was the Sidney Close she had always known, but out in the open now – no quick groping when Mavis wasn't looking, but full of the assurance he had always lacked. He took her nightdress as it slid to the floor and raised it to his nostrils, inhaling the smell of her body, deeply. He knelt at her feet and rested his head on her abdomen, closing his hands round her buttocks and squeezing them gently but firmly. Grise could feel his breath on her, felt her pubic hair flutter and then felt his hands running along the back of her legs. He stood, bringing his hands up and over her belly, under her breasts and onto her shoulders.

"You're used to having the upper-hand, aren't you Grise? Has it always been like that with you and Owen?"

Grise didn't answer, not wanting to rouse him.

"I said ..."

"Yes – mostly, not always."

"Too gentle for you, was he Grise? You like it a little rough, don't you?"

"Not here – not in my daughter's bedroom."

"It won't be long before she's doing it, Grise. They start early these days. She'll be dropping her knickers all round the village."

Grise hand slapped him hard round the face – or would have done, if Close hadn't grabbed it.

"Quietly, Grise – you don't want to wake her, do you?"

His hands explored her again, grossly, impertinently, enjoying the feel of every curve of her body. She shuddered in his arms, sick with the vileness of his touch. He stopped, suddenly, and smiled.

"Go and get dressed – and no funny stuff, as they say in the old movies. I can hear a leaf rustle a mile away and I'll be waiting here – with your little girl."

"Don't touch her ..."

"I said – she's yet to ripen. Get dressed. Oh, and Grise – no concealed crosses in your pockets. Oh, and Grise – don't forget to wear the fur coat – I like that. Oh, and – Grise, bring a change of clothes with you."

As they stepped out into the dark night, Grise had no idea what was in Sidney Close's mind. She felt in her heart that this would be the last she would ever see of her lovely home, but it was enough for her at the moment to know she had got him away from her daughter. Out here, adult to adult, woman to creature, she might just find a way to defeat him. Owen had not woken and she was glad of that, but she had scribbled a quick note and shoved it under his pillow. If she didn't return, he would find that in the morning.

Sidney Close was in what he obviously considered a playful mood. He carried her holdall for her and offered his other arm so that they walked as lovers, almost man and wife, around the village. Grise was an acknowledged beauty and Sidney would have felt proud anywhere with her on his arm – but not here, not in Dunburgh where he was known and dead. Watching her naked beauty in the girl's bedroom had awoken possibilities within him – a half-formed plan was lodged in his mind. It was a plan that sprung complete from the excitement of the idea, but it lacked detail. He wanted this walk in the dark with her – to calm himself, to calm her and to persuade. He sensed her fear: she reeked of it. She would have talked with the slut who had infected him and be terrified that he was going to pass it on, but he had other plans for the moment. He had grown used to the pain in his testicles and the suppurating pus. Something must be done – he couldn't suffer like this for all eternity – but it could wait for the moment.

"Have you ever wanted something – or someone – so badly, Grise, that your whole body ached for them? Hmm?"

"Yes," she replied, quickly, not daring to lie in case he pursued the untruth.

"Who?"

"It doesn't matter to you, Sidney – just know that I have."

"And have you ever wondered what it would be like to fulfil that desire?"

"Go on."

She didn't want to encourage him to ask "who" again. The longer he talked, the longer she had to find a way to beat him.

"I can have whoever I like, Grise. No woman says "No" to me. I take it when I want it – you know that."

"Yes."

"Don't you envy me a little – being in that position?"

"I don't know."

"Oh, come on, Grise – you're a woman and what women desire most is to have their way. Have you been denied?"

"Yes."

"I won't ask by whom – it doesn't matter. What matters, is you understanding that – if you were like me – he could deny you no longer."

"But I'm not like you."

"Aren't you, Grise?"

He stopped under the tree they had reached and turned her to face him. He put his hand under her chin and lifted her head so that she gazed into his eyes.

"Aren't you, Grise? The sexuality oozes from you – and you know it. There isn't one man in the village who hasn't dreamed of having you at one time or another. Imagine what it would be like to take what you wanted."

'I wouldn't think twice about it. This isn't a rehearsal. You don't get a second chance.' Sandra's words came back to her, or perhaps it was that they had always been there. 'I suppose I want the best of both worlds.' Her own answer seemed so foolish, now – now that Sidney Close was offering her just that, wasn't he? She ran from Sidney, scuffling down among the leaves at the root of the tree. He watched her, curiosity in his expression. He was amused and puzzled.

"You," she said, on her knees in the leaves, "you paint such pictures."

"It's you painting the pictures, Grise."

'Why fight it, Mark? You know you want me and I'm damned sure I want you. Why did you stay if it wasn't for that?' They'd stood by the pool, and their eyes wandering over each other seemed to be part of the heat of the day, part of the dappled light on the pool, part of the bees pursuing their honey from blossom to blossom ... Grise shook herself at the memory.

"Not this way – not like this!"

"I can see in the dark, Grise. I can pass through doorways. I have the strength of ten. I can move so quickly, I am unseen. I can make love without resting. I can transform myself. I can hear the rustle of silk and the whisper of women before

I see them. The world will be mine when I learn how to travel. Money is no longer a burden to me ... do I need to go on?"

"But your children and Mavis – they are lost to you forever! You can never know them again as you have always done."

Sidney Close flinched and shrugged.

"The memory – and the need – fades."

"Not in them! I don't want Owen and my children deserted."

"It will not be long before they fly the nest, Grise – and Owen will grow old and die, but you – you can be forever young."

"But be forever unloved."

Her voice faded to a scream, and she clutched at the words as the life she had known and loved slipped from her grasp.

"You have become evil, Sidney Close. You are inflicting your will on me through my own weaknesses."

"Your weaknesses, Grise – or are they strengths, which just wait for you to seize them?"

"Stop it! Owen? Margaret? William?"

She leaped from the earth, two twigs – for which she had been groping among the leaves – in her hands. The puzzled look returned to Sidney's face as she held them out before her in the shape of a cross. It was her last chance. Grise knew she had to drive him back, out of the field and on to the road. A car would pass – it had to! Help would be at hand. Sidney stepped towards her, slowly and without menace. He took the twigs gently from her hands.

"You've watched too many of those films, Grise. These are twigs – mere pieces of wood. They have no power. The power of the ... the ...the power lies in the faith and the person, not the object, unless it has been blessed in faith. Come, let us walk on."

She went with him, unresistingly, listening to his words as though he were her priest. London Road was silver with frost; the black sky was bright with stars. It was not late, not so late, scarcely beyond midnight. The 'night was young'. How many times had she heard that phrase at parties? The Christmas lights had gone out in the windows of the houses. They passed the house of Ample and Billy Bassett and saw the unlit candles in the window and the twig of mistletoe above the front door. There would be latecomers – people returning from festive parties, people she knew to whom she could call. The lights in the butcher's window still twinkled, chasing each other round the pane, as Sidney led her along the High Street and turned into School Road, where she saw the children's work in the windows.

There was still a light in the police house; the blue lamp over the doorway never went out, and she saw shadows pass over the blinds. Sidney's grip on her arm tightened, and they were passed White House where Alan and Penny lived. It was in darkness: only the outside Christmas tree sparkled, lighting the corner of the lane to the estate. She ran, faster than Sidney would have imagined possible, and banged upon the Read's door – but only twice. The dog, Leo, barked and a bedroom light came on and then Sidney grabbed her, stunned her with one blow to the neck, tossed her over his shoulder and sped rapidly along by the hedge and across the field where the white-haired lady carried her bucket of mash for the donkey every morning.

When Grise woke, she was in darkness but knew that he was close. She could feel him in the black of wherever she had been brought. As her eyes acclimatised themselves, the faint light that struggled through what looked like slits showed her a room cluttered with the shapes of old furniture. There was an odour – a dense smell imbued with stale air, cats' urine, rancid food, faeces and English breakfast tea.

"Don't be put off by our immediate lodgings, Grise. You and I will stroll through the streets of Europe."

She felt his hands on her, and the fur coat fell from her shoulders. Before Grise could scream, his mouth was on her throat and the sharp teeth bit into her neck. The blood sprang from her jugular vein, and he lapped it as a baby sucks at the breast or a cat drinks milk. Grise struggled and pushed against him, but his grip was relentless and firm as he drained her in deep, thankful gulps. Her last thoughts as she lost consciousness were of Mark and an open wax coat. She was inside, and her hips were against his groin and his arms were round her waist, down over her buttocks and he was lifting her to him. Grise reached up and clutched his mouth with hers and his left hand slid down under her thighs and he was carrying her into the barn among the bales of straw and she was naked now from the waist down and his juices flooded into her, and it was glorious.

Corvin woke with a start and felt across the bed. Esther had gone! She never got up in the night. She always had her last drink before nine o'clock so that she didn't need to go to the toilet. Stumbling around, half-asleep in the semi-darkness, was asking for trouble, with her arthritis. He swung his legs over the edge of the bed, felt for his slippers with his feet and then reached out for his dressing gown. Corvin was a man of habit. The landing light was on (it always was) and Corvin made for the bathroom door. It was open. She wasn't there! He listened, his ears straining in the darkness. There was no sound from either Rebecca's room or the guest room where Peter slept. Esther must have gone downstairs. She never did that – not alone in the night, not without putting on the light. He had a vivid image of her body lying at the body of the stairs, but knew that was foolish: he would have heard her fall.

In the downstairs hallway, he stopped and listened. There was no sound anywhere! He had half-wondered whether she had heard Rebecca stirring and gone downstairs. Occasionally, he had found the two of them sitting at the kitchen table sharing a mother-and-daughter cup of tea in the night. There were no lights anywhere! He looked in the kitchen without hope, passed his study without bothering (no-one but himself ever went in there) and walked into the dining room.

The french windows were open and Esther stood in the doorway, dressed only in her nightclothes, lit by faint moonlight. She was looking up at the sky and appeared to be talking to someone. When he entered, she didn't stir, didn't turn to greet him, but continued staring in front of her as thought she was unaware of his presence.

"Esther?"

She was partly-deaf but, even so, usually heard him. He repeated her name but there was still no response, except what sounded like a grunt from the garden and the sudden swishing of clothes. He rushed over to her and placed his arms round her shoulders: she was cold, freezing cold. As he took her hand, Corvin noticed that her fingers were icy. From the patio, he caught a glimpse of abrupt movement. Shadows swirled in a muted blaze of yellow and black and skimmed across the frosty ground, and then the night was still.

"Come inside. We must get you warmed up. What on earth are you doing?"

She did not speak but came with him without resistance, walking as though in a daze. Corvin sat her at the dining table for a moment, while he closed the window, and then led her gently into the kitchen where it was warmer, and he could keep an eye on her, while he made a cup of tea. She sat at the table staring blankly into space and, as the kettle boiled, he wrapped her in his dressing gown and put her feet into his slippers.

"Esther, are you all right? You've not had a funny turn, have you, my love?"

There was no answer, and so he placed her hands around the cup to warm them and then turned up the heating.

"Would you like some toast?"

She gazed, unrelentingly, into space. Her eyes were fixed at some point midway between where she sat and the far wall of the kitchen, as though someone stood there talking with her. He had seen the same expression on the faces of children – in a roomful of people, but lost in their own world.

Corvin sipped his own tea, hoping the familiar sound and activity would bring Esther back into the room. There was a flicker of recognition across her face but more of annoyance than joy and, as he watched her, Corvin saw the fascination in her gaze turn to terror. He dare not touch her. He felt to do so would disturb her equilibrium so much that Esther might suffer a heart attack, wrenching her from the place where she now resided. He couldn't explain this to himself. He couldn't express his fears more cogently, but knew that he was right. Esther was battling, somewhere else, out of reach of his love or protection. For a moment, he thought of ringing Alan Read – 'Our vacillation has already proved fatal for many people' – but he didn't. He wanted Esther to have a chance to tell him, first, in case … in case, what?

He went to the bread-bin and slipped two pieces in the toaster, brought the butter dish (his mother's butter dish – the one they had always used since she died) to the table with the jar of whisky-flavoured marmalade. He clattered a plate and a knife in front of her, and placed the spoon for the marmalade jar and the butter knife on the table. The toaster popped; the warm smell invaded his nostrils. 'Normality, Lord, return us to normality – but Thy will, not ours.'

When he returned to the table with the toast in the toast rack they'd been given for a wedding present (the one with the chickens separating the slices of toast), Esther was looking up at him. Tears were flowing – gushing – from her eyes and she was trembling all over, shaking like a child awakening from a nightmare. He put his arms round her. It was at times like this, when those you loved needed you most, that one realized just how deep that love ran.

"Oh, Corvin, I'm so ashamed. I've betrayed us all."

"My love?"

"I've put all our lives in terrible danger – all of us. Ring Alan."

CHAPTER 16

Christmas Eve

Alan Read came immediately. He and Penny had woken earlier at the sound of the two thuds on their door, and they hadn't really got back to sleep when the phone rang and he heard Corvin's anguished voice. Alan listened quietly while Esther tried to explain. Her thoughts came in fractured pictures as she tried to recall what had befallen her – a gardener, a pattering of feet and no answer, something lurking between books and running passed her up the stairs, winter daylight and a door slamming shut. Esther was sure she had been looking for Sarah.

"What happened when I came home?" she asked, turning to Corvin.

"My love," he answered, hesitating to go into details.

"Tell us, Corvin," said Alan, his voice tinged with impatience.

"I refused to go to Evensong, didn't I?"

"You seemed a trifle ...," mumbled Corvin.

"And tonight?" asked Alan.

"I remember sitting in the kitchen eating toast and marmalade with Corvin."

"But you asked Corvin to phone me. You said that you had 'betrayed us'."

"I said that?"

"Corvin, remind Esther of what happened tonight. Don't exclude details."

"Oh, Corvin, what would I be doing at an open window in the middle of the night?" said Esther, laughing, when her husband had finished.

"What did you see, Esther?" persisted Alan.

"Nothing – nothing, of course!" she snapped, staring at a point between her and the far wall of the kitchen, and before collapsing across the table, her head and shoulders sprawled over the toast and marmalade.

Peter heard Corvin and Alan putting Esther to bed and, having tapped on her door, he woke Rebecca. When Esther was tucked in and asleep, the four of them sat round the kitchen table and Alan relayed Esther's story.

"Were there any marks on her throat?" asked Rebecca.

"No – but it is clear that he has some hold over her. A fair guess would be that your mother went to the Old Vicarage in search of Sarah, was discovered by Brultzner, who is now using her to spy on us. She must have been called to the window tonight and they have 'talked' – if that's the word. Esther's memory comes and goes and, at times, she seems to realize what is happening to her – hence her conviction that she has "betrayed" us. It's bloody marvellous, isn't it, that she should come under his influence just as we thought we were getting somewhere?"

"His 'influence' has always been subtle," said Peter, "at times, several of the women he used would have probably betrayed their loved ones for him. May I make a suggestion?"

"Please do," replied Alan.

"Let us be aware of Esther's predicament, but without her knowing. She might be the means of feeding him false information that could be used to our advantage."

"Peter – it's my mother you are talking about!"

"I really must protest, Peter," expostulated Corvin.

"This man has charmed his way through this village. His influence is subtle, wide-ranging and pernicious. If we are to defeat him – and the odds against us doing that quickly have increased – then we must use every means at our disposal. Your mother will not be free of him until he is destroyed. If she can help us do that, however unknowingly, I have no doubt she would be only too pleased."

"Peter is right," said Alan.

"I have nothing in mind, you understand – any more than Brultzner did when he found her in his house. He plays his cards close to his chest, never missing a trick if he can help it – let us do the same."

"Yes ... yes, I can see that," said Rebecca.

"Good. So, we say nothing in front of Esther that we do not want him to know. We must tell the others what has happened and, when dawn breaks, we go to the Old Vicarage – just in case our suppositions are wrong and he is taking his daily snooze."

Alan was awoken, for the third time that night, before dawn. On the other end of the line was Owen Culman. He had Grise's hurried note in his hand.

"Yes, I do, Owen ... in general terms ... no – not specifically. I'll come over."

Penny, too, had barely slept and handed him a cup of tea as he pulled on his clothes, and rushed downstairs for his medical bag.

"Grise has gone with Sidney Close. I'm going to see Owen, now. Phone the others, Pen – let's keep everyone informed, but not Esther."

Owen raged, uncharacteristically, for fifteen minutes or so, bringing his children into their lounge with his unaccustomed anger. Alan indicated that they should stay while he let Owen "get things off his chest". When he had finished, Alan sat him down and said, very quietly and with deliberate calm.

"We could not find him. I gave Grise the best advice I could – given the circumstances. She told you nothing, I take it?"

"Except what to do."

"And you did it?"

There was a ghastly silence in the room.

"How did he get in?"

Alan looked at the two children, at Margaret angry and blushing, and then walked to her room. When he returned, she was sobbing in Owen's arms.

"Seal the house, as you were told to do and pray that we find them. Margaret – don't blame yourself. The adults in this awful business have behaved with the same blind stupidity. Perhaps if your mum had told you what happened to her this would not have occurred, but everyone has been loathe to believe what was staring them in the face, and no one has confided in anyone else for the fear of looking foolish. Let me have a look at you."

"What!?"

Alan ignored the sullen exclamation, and examined her throat as she tried to shake him off.

"She's untouched – that's one less thing to worry about."

"I still don't fully understand, Dr Read," said Owen.

"I know, and when I explain you will not believe me, but I'm going to do so anyway. Knowledge is the best protection you have."

Back home, Alan had a shower and changed his medical bag for the holdall.

"Wish us luck, Pen. If Brultzner is not in his – whatever it is he sleeps in – then we are in desperate straits. We shall have four vampires on the loose (I have no doubt in my own mind that Grise has joined their number) and an unwitting spy in our own camp. I can't protect you against Brultzner, who is our immediate threat, but keep whatever instruments of faith you have at hand against the others – and watch the children! I can't think of anything else at the moment, except that I love you and have never been so afraid for you and the children in all my life, and wish that you would go to your mother's where it might – just – be safer."

Penny Read took her husband's head in her hands and kissed him, fully, on the mouth. She gave him the look which had produced their four children, and held him tightly in her arms.

"Just concentrate on what you hope to do and leave me to worry about the house and the children."

He looked back at his home as he left, as though he were setting out on a long journey, and then hurried down the hill. Corvin and Peter were waiting on the corner by the allotments, sitting on the bench between Church Hill and Shore Lane as though they were enjoying a cosy chat. Alan smiled to himself as he saw them. 'In the midst of all this, there is humour?'

Sam Cleat was in the garden when they arrived, and barred their way by standing astride the driveway and leaning on his grass rake.

"Can I help you, gentleman?"

"Would you know if Mr Brultzner is in?"

"I would know that he isn't. I saw him leave, with what I think they call a 'weekend case' when I arrived."

"Did he say where he was going?"

"No, sir, he did not."

"I expect you're quite the general handyman, aren't you, Mr ...?"

"Cleat's the name, sir – Sam Cleat, and yes, I am – as they say – handy."

"You could mend a broken window, then?"

Sam Cleat frowned.

"We are going to take a look around Mr Brultzner's house and we shall have to break in to do that. It would be nice if you could mend the window."

Sam Cleat looked into Alan's face, searching for his sense of humour. Here was a doctor, a clergyman and someone else who looked respectable suggesting that he should assist them with what was tantamount to a burglary. There wasn't a trace of humour in the doctor's eyes, however.

"You needn't worry, Sam," said Corvin, kindly, "we are about our legitimate business, strange as it may seem."

Gaining entry to the Old Vicarage was not as straightforward as it had been for Esther. No longer relying on Sarah to keep house, Horst Brultzner had locked the back door himself, and so it was the large, sash window over the sink which they broke. Alan hit it with his elbow and stood back as the glass shattered around him. He then cleared the shards, released the catch and climbed in, careful to avoid the non-drying paint Martin had warned them about. As he did so the alarms, so lovingly installed on Martin's recommendation, rang. Alan raced towards the console and hit the cross before returning to help Corvin, whose corpulence caused him to stumble and puff as he scrambled across the sink.

"If you can tidy around, Sam, we'd be grateful. We may not be long."

Peter handed Alan the holdall as he spoke. He followed Corvin through the shattered window and across the sink. They walked without hesitation through the basement, glancing quickly into the kitchen, scullery and the wine and coal cellars. Peter led the way up the steep flight of steps to the landing and pushed open the door into the ground floor hall. Alan was waiting by the front door.

"Thank goodness for Martin's knowledge of alarms. I'll re-set it when we go."

The noise of the alarm had, momentarily, been worse than the pitter-patter of tiny feet that had so unnerved Esther. Corvin shuddered as he looked up the stairs.

"I'll go," said Peter, as he sensed the hesitation in Corvin.

He was at the top of the stairs in three bounds. Despite Sam Cleat's assurance that Brultzner had left, all three had the feeling that something nasty was to happen. All three shared the same thought: the thought that Brultzner knew they were trespassing in his home. They also had the sense that the house itself was subservient to his will – that in some, indefinable way it listened to him. Although none of them expected to see ghosts or demons, all three knew that the house was haunted. Most terrifying of all, however, was the thought that they had no protection against this evil. Whatever Brultzner was, and from wherever he came, he came from outside their realms of belief.

Any one of them would have faced Sarah or Sidney – not with any complacency, but in the knowledge that they had a chance to defend themselves and to defeat their opponent. Unless they caught Brultzner unawares, however, they all realised that he was more than a match for any of them, singly or collectively. As Peter stood at the top of the stairs about to open Brultzner's bedroom door, each of them wondered what he was doing here and what he hoped to achieve. They had walked, unprotected and with only the feeblest grasp of what they were to do, into the lion's den. Even Corvin smiled as the thought crossed his mind.

Peter flung back the door. The bed was empty, and the room was quiet. He heaved a sigh of relief and gave the thumbs up sign. Alan made his way cautiously up the stairs followed by Corvin, and all three looked at each other.

"What are we doing here?" said Corvin, "what do we hope to achieve?"

Peter looked at him with an expression that should have been puzzled but was, in fact, full of understanding and acceptance. They should know why they were here; their mission was clear.

"I'll take a look in the other rooms on this floor," he replied.

"Yes," said Corvin, "I'll wait."

Alan looked at both men and frowned. Without speaking, he turned and walked down the stairs. He felt the sigh rise in him as he reached the bottom. The door of Brultzner's study was ajar and he walked in, closing the door behind him. He did not like the idea of being approached from behind and, anyway, wanted to be alone. The smell of leather-bound books and furniture polish, supported by the warmth of wood, invaded his nostrils. He was ready to give himself up to this place. His eyes roamed along the shelves. The books had been chosen, idiosyncratically. They seemed to cover all manner of subjects – chemistry, mathematics, warfare, history, medicine, music, art, philosophy; this latter category had a whole section of the shelving almost to itself. There was a large section on natural history and here, among the old volumes, there were many books by modern authors. Alan felt that he belonged here, that he was part of this man's world.

Why had they never talked? Why had they never sat on the Italianate terrace and conversed over an evening's drinking? Brultzner had no natural friends in the village at all; he was isolated from all mankind. What a nature it was that suffered so! Alan could not imagine himself without friends; the possibility had never occurred to him. An overwhelming feeling of pity took hold of his mind, and his fingers slid along the surface of the desk. The wood shrank from his touch and something slipped out of the book case from between James and Jung, grasped Schlick and dropped him to the floor. Alan started from his trance and bent over to pick up the book. 'Such statements are neither true nor false, since they cannot be verified,' he read, 'They are simply meaningless.' The door of the study clicked as it opened, and Peter entered.

"What are we doing here?" said Peter, "what do we hope to achieve?" He was looking at the book in Alan's hand, and seeing what was in his mind, "Is that us – anything we could, or might, say on this matter is meaningless, since we cannot prove it to be true?"

"Hmm?" responded Alan, "I was merely picking up the book."

"What?"

"I was merely picking up the book."

Peter scowled at him and hurried from the room. Alan followed into the hall, and saw Corvin sitting on the bottom stair, his head in his hands.

"This place defeats me," he said, looking up at Alan, "there is such malignity here, such evil, that I cannot contend with it. It is not true, Alan, that good will always overcome evil. That is nonsense paraded as hope for children."

Alan could see the tears rolling through the priest's fingers.

"Durkheim said that every individual has the right to develop their own faculties in accordance with their own beliefs," said Alan.

"I'm sorry ..." began Corvin.

"If we accept that Brultzner is an ...."

"Stop it! Stop it!" yelled Peter, "Out – get out! Let's get out of here!"

He rushed at the front door, slipped the lock and yanked it open. The dull light of a winter's morning flooded into the hallway and the three of them rushed into it. On the driveway, they stood looking at each other, bewildered and shaken.

"Let's go home," said Alan, "we can achieve nothing here."

"One moment," said Peter, overcome by a second of decency, "we have Mr Cleat to consider."

"What's wrong, Alan?" said Penny, "What happened at the Old Vicarage?"

He had come in and gone straight to his study, slamming the door behind him. In all their married life, whatever concern was preying on his mind, he had never failed to kiss or hug her whenever he returned to the house. Penny left him for what seemed a long while before going to the study. She carried a cup of coffee in her hand and placed it on the desk by his laptop. He was slumped across the desk, his head and spread arms having pushed aside a sheaf of papers and books.

"Alan – what is wrong?"

"Nothing."

"Alan ..."

"Go!"

"Alan?"

He looked up at her. The man she had known and loved for so many years, and with whom she'd brought four children into the world, was no longer there.

"Alan, this is me – Pen. We're sort of husband and wife. It's called marriage."

"Give me time, Pen. I love you but I can't talk about this. I can't formulate my thoughts. I can't ... explain."

"We don't have time, Alan – you must tell me. Just let it come rambling out. This is no time for withdrawing into ourselves. Are Peter and Corvin all right?"

"They've gone back to the rectory but we all ... I think we all felt the same."

"Was he there?"

"No – yes, he's everywhere."

"You must tell me. Alan. If we can't talk, what hope is there for anyone?"

"He was everywhere, Pen. Why he needs an alarm system beats me. Can you imagine a presence so ... malign, so pervasive that it haunts the woodwork? I swear before God that there were creatures in that house – his creatures – that haunted us wherever we went: the guardians of his soul. We didn't expect to find him. We did expect to find out something about him, something that would lead us to where he could be defeated: but we found nothing! I don't believe in demons. In a way, Brultzner can be explained – no, accepted – as a ... natural phenomenon. I don't mean that! I mean ... he's scrambling my head, Pen!"

"Be calm, Alan. It'll come."

Penny watched him as he sat huddled over his desk, looking to her like a broken, old man. She prayed that the children wouldn't come in at that moment. After a while, without looking up, he began talking again and Penny listened, her hand resting unobtrusively on his shoulder.

"Can you imagine a will so strong that it permeates all it touches? I understand ghosts better now. Brultzner is in tune with all that has ever happened in that old house and there is no house in the world that has not seen its share of grief, misery and despair. He is using it against us. Corvin sat sobbing at the foot of the stairs. I couldn't bear to be in the study. Peter was all over the place – up the stairs, down again – in my lady's chamber!"

Alan laughed – a hollow, unpleasant sound coming from an empty vessel.

"'There I met an old man who wouldn't say his prayers; I took him by the left leg and threw him down the stairs'. Ever wondered what that meant? He's pulling us apart, Pen, like a wilful child pulling apart an insect. At the end of the day, that's all we are to him."

Penny watched, horrified. There was no anger in Alan and there should have been. He spoke like a beaten man.

"The worse thing is – I am not afraid. I could fight fear but I cannot fight this. This creature is an absolute egoist. He dominates all he comes into contact with: there is no standing against him. He has beaten us before we even move against him. He must be old. He goes back over the ages to where – how long ago, was he created? ... You know how a married couple can read each other's thoughts – complete sentences for each other? It's like that with him, only there is no affection. With him, it is simply this burning desire to survive. He can range over the world and make his mark on histories, but he has no care for any one. Nothing binds him to another, or to any cause. In him, it comes down to the will to survive. All those months ago, he called his house a 'mausoleum' meaning that he wished to preserve it intact as it once was, all those decades ago. But there's another meaning to mausoleum, isn't there? They are places for the entombment of the dead, above ground – and that is what he has done. He has re-created all that the Old Vicarage once was and has always been. He has brought its spooks to life, and they invade all who enter ... I need a drink, Pen."

"No, Alan – that's the last thing you need. You are talking yourself into a blind alley and taking a bottle with you will be no company. You have no choice in this matter. Others are depending on you and you have a duty to fight."

At that moment, the phone rang. It was Rebecca. Penny lifted the receiver and listened, her face grave but becoming more resolute as the call continued.

"They have no choice," she said, when Rebecca had finished, "our duty is clear. Demoralized, disheartened, dejected they may be – they have been corrupted by the house – but this is no time for the feeble, no place for the crushed.

You phone Nadine and I'll phone Martin – everyone needs to be kept abreast of events. Get your dad, and your fiancé, up to the eleven o'clock service. Alan and I are on our way now – with the children!"

After the service, which Corvin conducted in a dispirited (almost abject) fashion, speaking the words of Matins as though they were no more than a shopping list handed to him by his wife, they all gathered in the churchyard. The three men were fighting themselves now. Not believing their weakened state, they were both ashamed and daunted, and so the women did the speaking. Nadine has already taken Matthew out of the village to what she termed "a place of safety", but would say no more. Despite the state Alan was in, Penny had decided that the children would stay where they were: nothing would move her from her position. Rebecca had already arranged for Yevgeny to "go elsewhere". She was sure that he would be safe. Martin had confided in Amy – he "saw the need for her to protect herself, if necessary", and. anyway, "couldn't operate with his wife in ignorance of what was happening", but he was no further forward with discovering where Sidney – and now, Grise – might be hiding. Nadine had heard from Tony who was already walking south.

Tony Crewes had not confided in his wife. He couldn't be bothered with being branded "utterly ridiculous" for the umpteenth time and had set out before his family stirred from their beds, taking Anton with him. He reasoned that Sarah would have walked south or west. North was the town where she would be vulnerable; and east was the sea. He did not think that she was about to attempt suicide, knowing that it was doomed to fail. She could not kill herself. So he walked up Church Hill from the Old Vicarage and turned into Marsh Lane; here Sarah would have found shade should the sun appear. She would have found this safer than the road. He made his way to the marsh and then turned right: left would have taken him back into the village.

He followed the river, sure that he was in Sarah's footsteps, and so he also came into open country. Tony sighed with relief; she must have taken this way. Was that her plan? Was he wrong to suppose that she did not intend suicide? All she had to do was find an open space and sit there until the sun appeared; tradition would destroy her. Suddenly, he knew her intentions, but could not believe them. He then gave a second sigh in so short a time; the sun had been conspicuous by its absence.

So – she would come to Frostenham and the Dog and Gun. It was too early and the pub was closed. Tony gave his third sigh of the morning. Soon, bells would be ringing. Beth would be cursing him under her breath, as she bustled the children towards the church. Soon – but not yet! Where would she have gone from here? Open country or the coast? Why come this way if she was to return to the coast? Open country, then – towards Blythburgh? He fancied not. Sarah would have been here in the afternoon; it would have been getting dark by three or four. She would have turned to the coast, to where she knew best. He turned towards Eastwold and headed for the pier. A Scotsman was dashing about like a blue-tailed

536

fly and Tony stopped him to ask whether he had seen a young, blonde girl "about a week ago".

"Away with you, you old git – I'm busy. If you're lookin' for a bit of arse, you've picked the wrong place."

Anton had curled his lips at the harshness of the man's tone but, detecting that Tony seemed unbothered, he loped off quietly. Tony had never thought of himself as old before; he smiled and wished the man a "happy Hogmanay". Where would she have gone from here – south? To go north would have been to return to Dunburgh: it had to be south. He wandered all day, or until late afternoon turned to darkness. Nobody had seen her and he was sick of the sights and sounds of marshes and sea.

At home, Beth would be waiting (bristling with indignation) to give him a bollocking but, to be fair, he ought to get back. It was near to the Big Day now and the children would wonder where he was and might even be worried! Tony didn't feel like phoning Beth: he couldn't face the sound of that voice. He rang Martin and then sat down to wait. The Ship was open and he bought a beer – Adnam's Old; the simple pleasures were always the best.

"So you've achieved nothing," said Martin, as they drove back, Anton curled around Tony's feet, "Don't worry yourself. Neither has anyone else."

"But we're close, Martin. Brultzner must be at Wangford Hall, Sidney and Grise are somewhere in the village and I will find Sarah. Tomorrow, I'm starting from Eastwold and heading north."

"You have heard about the others? According to the women Peter, Corvin and Alan – of all people – are in one helluver state. On the verge of cracking up – breakdown time – Funny Farm, here we come! We might be close but we're a million miles from nailing this bloke."

Martin went on to relay what had happened at the Old Vicarage. When he had finished, Tony said:

"I read a story once – years ago – about the power of old houses to haunt, and the power of evil beings to inflict their will on others. Damned if I can remember the name of it but, as I recall, it required an affinity with the person cursed. The evil will had to have something to attach itself to – some weakness in the prey."

"So what's the weakness in our three comrades?"

Martin, despite everything, was beginning to enjoy the conversation; in women, he would have called it "having a bitch", but he and Tony had spent many happy evenings indulging in such chat.

"Corvin would fear being defeated by Brultzner; it would be an affront to his whole faith. Alan is a rational man; it is unlikely that he has ever considered a supernatural explanation for what is happening so when a house haunts him he is up against the unknown, the inexplicable. Peter Vishnya is deeply involved; he has been seduced (I use the term lightly) by one of Brultzner's vampire housekeepers and he works for the creature. Peter probably feels that he is being disloyal to

Brultzner – strange as that may seem – and has been disloyal to Rebecca. His mind is anything but quiescent."

"You don't mince your words, do you Tony?"

"We need to know our weaknesses. Stating those isn't being disloyal: it's facing up to reality."

Grise Culman found herself waking from what seemed a long sleep – the sleep of the dead. It had been three days since Sidney had taken her, and for three days he had watched over her as Brultzner watched over Sarah. His own transformation in the Bethel was a distant memory now, but nursing Grise triggered his recollection of that time. He had bathed her, washing away the body fluids that sloughed over her skin and marvelling as the iridescence glowed within her new body. In life, she had been a beauty: in death, this was intensified. Her attraction, however, was not the soft femininity of Sarah but arose from an altogether different kind of sexuality. Grise was what the tabloids like to call 'a sexual animal'. The same hunger that marked her in life would possess her now she was Un-dead. Sidney could see that in every line of her face, every curve of her body. She was to be thirty-something for all eternity: lithe, sensual, illusively agile, carnal, lascivious, lewd ….?

Sidney smiled to himself; he had chosen well. He had a partner who would share his pleasures, a woman who would yearn for the wider world beyond the village – and who had access to money. His mind had already conjured with the problems of coping with money. It wasn't possible to open a bank account once you were dead, but Grise was – officially – alive. They would soon be out of this filthy hole – once they had learned how to travel as vampires.

Grise stirred again, and he looked at her as she lay in the coffin he had stolen from the undertaker's workshop. It was a good one, silk-lined in red and with genuine brass handles; he wondered for whom it had been intended. It enhanced her beauty, splendidly: the dark hair (now black as a raven's wing), the scarlet lips with their little curve of a smile, the flared nostrils betokening just the right amount of anger, the cream-toned skin with its hint of the Mediterranean, the ebony eyebrows, the high cheekbones, the clear line of her jaw and the sparkle he knew would flash from her brown eyes which would now be chestnut with its hint of red.

Tonight would be the night to induct her in the ways of the Un-dead. Christmas Eve – with the village alight and full of festive colour, and villagers wandering happily to their homes ecstatic with seasonal cheer – would be ideal. They could feed, unhampered by the curious; everyone would be far too involved with their own activities. He wanted to parade his teenager before her to show how easy the seduction was, and impress Grise with his new-found skill.

The Crib Service always attracted a large and enthusiastic gathering of the faithful and the not-so-faithful: whatever, it was always a huge success. Penny Read organised it, of course, and Corvin was able to relax and enjoy this festive delight of his faith. Seeing where the future lay, he had done much to attract the young families; this had been one of his outstanding achievements in the parish of St George's. This year was to be no exception. It was impossible to detect in the faces and demeanour of either Penny or Rebecca the immense strain they were under. Their interest and their concern, as they came in through the west porch on Christmas Eve, were centred entirely upon the children.

Corvin had no choice but to attend; his absence, for any reason, would have marked him down in the eyes of the congregation. Alan would normally have followed Penny – who would have been in the church by five-thirty to "finalise arrangements" – with their own children at something after six o'clock. This year he had lingered and dithered, hidden himself in his study and wandered off into the garden. She had bullied and cajoled him and, not trusting his intentions, insisted that he came with her and the children. Only his regard for her, and his desire not to have the children involved in any hint of conflict between him and his wife, had forced him from the house for the short walk along School Road and down Church Hill. He sat slumped in one of the back pews, fearful and agitated.

Peter Vishnya had behaved similarly – finding reasons to be away from the rectory at his own house on the London Road, ignoring the telephone and pretending to be searching in the loft when Rebecca came to seek him out. She had been less insistent than Penny because there were issues between them that he now refused to discuss and over which he would offer her no comfort, but Rebecca had taken his arm and led him out into the Christmas night, hoping to reclaim the man she loved.

The village was beautiful as they walked arm in arm to the church where she was to accompany the children on the piano. She remembered this night from her childhood in other parishes. The houses were aglow with decorations; reds, whites, greens and golds were everywhere. Candles flickered, fires glowed, logs crackled, and houses were permeated with the smells and sounds of Christmas. The scents of Christmas were unique to that short, glorious time in the year. At no other time did ham smell of honey, or beef of mustard and mushrooms; at no other time did the smell of home-made mince pies pursue you from the kitchen; at no other time was cake steeped in such fruitiness; at no other time did so many sauces juggle for prominence in the kitchen. There were crackers on the sideboard in the dining room, the best dinner service had been retrieved and washed, napkins were folded and arranged in glasses.

Through one window they passed she saw a bowl of unusual fruit – figs and berries and boxes of dates; through another she saw potatoes, sprouts, parsnips and carrots cut ready for the next day; through another chestnuts, almonds, Brazils, and hazelnuts adorned a table; through another a little girl was putting the finishing touches to some decoration, watched by her brother.

Even without snow, there was a bite in the air which made the warmth of the houses so inviting and the crackle of burning logs so redolent of comfort and home. Habits die hard and, despite all their current afflictions, both Corvin and Esther had gone round the house "making it ready". Rebecca had taken a good look at the tree, hung with tinsel and chocolate coins, as she left and touched the sharp leaves of holly on the front door wreath. It was to have been such a happy time; it was to have been Rebecca and Peter's first Christmas together. Rebecca looked up at Peter as they walked but he did not return the glance; his mind was far away in other places.

The service went well; it was destined to succeed. The crib was traditional, dragged out and dusted down each year from quite where no-one, except the church wardens, seemed to know; but it always appeared on time – the roof re-thatched where necessary, the little porcelain figures placed securely in the bed of hay, the one spot light focussed (like a strange sun) on the central figures of the Christ-child and Mary and Joseph, with the other figures (the wise men, the shepherds and the animals) touched by varying degrees of brilliance. It was always placed by the font, just inside the west porch and even the large oak table, on which were usually placed books and notices and coffee cups, was moved for the occasion.

The children were dressed (some casually, some with endeavour, all with love) in flowing robes or animal skins and all processed down the aisle of the little church in their turn, bringing their particular gifts to the manger – gold, frankincense and myrrh, a lamb from the fields, presents for Jesus from the village (each according to their own lights). The songs were children's song and always had been; even when Clara Gobley had ruled the roost the choir had not dared to interfere with custom. They were there in support of the children whose voices carried the evening. There were no stars except the one star that shone over the manger. All came in common humility and all joined in singing the words remembered from childhood.

"Be near me, Lord Jesus, I ask thee to stay
Close by me forever, and love me I pray
Bless all the dear children in thy tender care
And fit us for heaven to live with thee there."

The occasion spoke of understandings beyond the words to explain them; they all came knowing or seeking a truth – the believer and the atheist alike – realising that somewhere here they were sharing a common pursuit of the goodness in mankind, that somewhere here, in all their hopes for the future, was that glorious song of old.

"Are you all right, Alan?" asked Penny, once they were home and the children were gathered about the fireplace, cracking nuts and tossing the shells into the flames.

"I am now," he said, simply, "It was a terrible malaise that settled into me. For the last three days I have actually felt ill, but I think it's passing now."

Boller and Pliny Skeat were throwing a little do and had invited along as many of the Inn Crowd as wanted to come. Christmas Eve was always a funny time: some families preferred their own company, while others couldn't wait to mingle.

Mavis and the girls had come. It was to be their first Christmas without Sid, and although Mavis had always done everything (she was one of that last generation of women who could not help thinking of themselves – whether they worked or not – as housewives) it was impossible without him. He had seemed to do nothing but who now brought in the logs, cut the kindling, collected the meat and groceries, ordered the drinks, washed the glasses, swept the floors and re-arranged the furniture? Mavis tried but capitulated; they were off to her mother's in the morning.

Ample and Billy Bassett had come. Their one child had wanted to go to friends for the evening, and they had dropped him off before settling in for some drinks and some laughs. Billy had brought round six bottles of his home-made wine.

"I told him you wouldn't want that at Christmas," said Ample.

"… at Christmas," responded Billy.

"But he insisted. I told him – he needs to keep a clear head. I don't want him moody tomorrow, not on Christmas Day of all days."

"… Christmas Day of all days."

Joney Chine wasn't there – she and Ben were off somewhere in their campervan – but had telephoned through her Christmas wishes.

"She'd wanted to come, I think," said Pliny, "but you know Ben! When he gets an idea in his head …"

"He's a funny bugger," said Billy.

"Billy!"

"I've never worked out why he wears that black glove on his right hand."

"Do you reckon he wears that in bed?" said Boller, "I can't think what for!"

He laughed: something ribald was to follow, but Pliny cut him dead: "Boller!"

"Sorry – blimey, yer can't even speak now."

"It's Christmas," said Pliny, as though that explained everything.

They all laughed. It was good to be among friends at such a time.

"If you don't believe me, ask any one of the ten people I've mentioned."

"Do you expect …," began Beth.

"I don't expect anything. I gave up expecting years ago. I've told you the truth, knowing you wouldn't believe it. Phone round and check."

"You know I can't phone. People would think I was mad."

"Exactly! Now – let's stop arguing in whispers, shall we – and go and enjoy Christmas with our children?"

Beth Crewes had wanted to go to Boller and Pliny's do but Tony had refused, preferring to stay with the children. Beth, feeling guilty, had argued that the children were old enough to leave for a while and that Tony simply didn't want to go, anyway. He had told her to go if she liked and to offer his apologies.

They went back into their lounge where the children were watching a repeated comedy show on television. Tony got everyone a drink and they sat around the fire together. Later, Beth brought in a plate of snacks – mincemeat and apple tart, some mince pies and a stollen slice. They laughed together at the old jokes, homely and clean, and sank back in the glow of the fire and the warmth of the settee.

Lianne Snooks had also wanted to go to the Skeat's do and had rowed with her husband in a similar way to Beth. She, too, had felt guilty at wanting to leave the children and had wanted Barry to make the decision to go. Barry was having none of it. He attempted no explanations but said, abruptly:

"If you want to go, go. I'm staying here. It's a family night."

"Family night! There's something you want to watch on the television."

It was true. The BBC could still be relied upon to put on a good horror film later on, and Barry was looking forward to watching *Black Christmas*.

The Crib Service had not had the same emotional impact on either Corvin or Peter as it had on Alan Read. It was Corvin's work and he saw the occasion from a professional viewpoint. Peter's natural respect for the power of the service was tempered by his greater knowledge and, subsequently, his greater fear of what they faced in their campaign against Brultzner. The shattering experience which had enfeebled them both at the Old Vicarage still held sway, but custom and tradition ruled at the rectory. Esther went about her Christmas celebrations in an almost somnolent state, plying her family with the traditional mince pies and the chocolate Swiss roll she always made. The women drank fruit juice by choice; the men, by their dispositions that evening. Rebecca was the only one among them who remained naturally cheerful, hurrying about in an attempt to inject joy into their Christmas Eve.

Martin and Amy Billings decided, at the last minute, to stroll round to the Skeat's do. He had told her everything. Amy was perplexed and disgusted, but relieved that she had not been the only one. As they left the Police House, she said:

"Have you checked the Gobley's old bungalow?"

"It's been boarded up by the council to prevent any chance of vandalism. Besides, Close wouldn't have gone there. Would you, when you had the choice of other, cleaner empty properties?"

"I suppose not, but it might be worth a look."

"I can't imagine Sidney choosing that – have you ever been in there?"

When they reached the do, it was in full swing. Billy Bassett, having drunk too much of his own wine, was crawling round the floor pretending to be a dog, and cut between Amy's legs as she came through the front door. Boller came over to welcome them, but refrained from giving her his customary squeeze. Without saying anything, Martin had made it clear that such a gesture would not have been a good idea.

The little bungalow was swirling with festive bodies; among the Inn Crowd regulars were Ticker Tyler and his wife, who was related to Ample Bassett. Also, there were members of Beachlands Health Club to which Boller and Pliny both belonged. As they tucked into their Christmas dishes, all regretted having missed their usual work-outs over the last three days.

"Owen just closed. No by-your-leave or anything. He just closed."

"That's not the way to attract new members," said Ticker's wife, tucking into a huge portion of mango and passion fruit Pavlova roulade, which Ample Bassett had brought along.

"Perhaps he had good reasons," said Ticker, quietly, "we don't know."

"Have you heard anything, Ticker?" asked Martin, glancing at Amy.

"No, but we shouldn't make snap judgements. If Owen closed early for Christmas, he may have had good reasons."

His innate sense of decency and caution put a stop on any further discussion and, as Martin and Amy spilled into the room, the group at the door dispersed among the party-goers, but the gossip continued around the room.

"I heard that Grise had disappeared," said Ample.

"... disappeared," said Billy, uselessly from the floor.

"Disappeared?" queried Boller.

"That'll make two women in less than two weeks then," said Pliny.

"You mean Sarah Marjoram from the Old Vicarage," said Ticker's wife.

"Better watch art, girls – it sarnds as if we've got a serial killer on the loose."

"That's not funny, Boller."

"Init – you watch enough of that sort of thing on the telly. They've even got it on Coronation Street now."

Billy laughed as he rolled around the floor, trying to find a way onto his feet.

"That's enough from you, Billy Bassett," said Ample.

"... enough from you, Billy Bassett," he echoed.

Grise Culman had taken to her first night as a vampire just as Sidney hoped she would. The expression on her face remained incredulous as he led her around the village. He changed his mind about showing off his teenage conquest for fear of reminding her how he had sat with his hand on her daughter's inner thigh. Instead, he walked her in shadow about the village, leaving hunger as her guide.

Grise was a born survivor. Owen had always acknowledged her as the driving force behind their business. She had grown used to taking the lead in everything; it was second nature to her now. She caught a glimpse of herself – as Sarah had done – in a glass darkly and the radiance of her beauty was astonishing. While others in her circle were turning their thoughts to cosmetic surgery, Grise had made the final leap into an eternity of beauty. She hadn't wanted to, but there was no good crying over spilt milk (as her mother used to say); what was done, was done – get on with it.

She didn't want to see her home again, but just had to make the trip. Her relief when she saw the house shut and Owen and the children gone she knew not where – but hoped it was to her mother's for Christmas – was palpable. She would see them again, she would watch them grow – her mother's instincts told her that – and she would help them in ways that ... before would have been impossible. They entered the bungalow at Beachlands and filled a suitcase or two with some of her clothes. Grise didn't want to lose those and had no idea, in the first flush of her transformation, how long she would be confined to the village. While they were there, Grise showered away the last of the slime of the body fluids and washed her hair in Crabtree and Evelyn's latest shampoo. Such luxury would always be hers now – from now on she could not be denied. Already her mind was planning trips abroad.

Once the initial delights were over – seeing in the dark, her tremendous agility, the ability to float above the ground, the turn of speed – Grise took a pragmatic delight in her new-found skills. She took her first 'feed' suddenly and fiercely, so that Sidney had to call her off and warn her that they were vulnerable to discovery if she was careless. She looked at him, malice already present in her gaze, and heeded his advice – for the moment. She didn't argue – there would be a time to sort out Sidney Close. What she wanted now was to visit Mark Chambers.

Nin's house – the envy of them all – glistened with Christmas and, as Grise and Sidney stood in the back garden watching them, the family moved from room to room, eager with expectation. Stockings were being hung over the fireplace, the turkey was being trussed ready in the kitchen, chutneys and pickles lined the shelves, Nin's flowers bloomed in every room, Mark was stacking logs by the grate and drinks were being poured. Grise did not envy them any of this because she saw now that Mark was hers – whether he wanted it or not – for ever. Soon, she knew, they would be off to the midnight communion.

"I don't feel the cold," she whispered to Sidney.

"You never will again but your touch will be cold to others unless you warm yourself through with a little blood."

She looked at him, remembering what had seemed an ordeal on the beach, recalling what he had done. She felt nothing for him: not even hatred. They were equal now and there would be time to understand what had happened. Sidney Close had not died, but become more beautiful. She was now the same and that was enough for one night. Sidney was anxious to be on his way, but Grise insisted that they stay and watch the house. The comings and goings fascinated her; she had a strange compulsion to become part of them and saw herself entering Mark's house.

"Have you returned home ....since?" asked Grise, looking at Sidney.

"I have seen them and been to the house once."

"Have you ever wondered if you might return?"

"What do you have in mind, Grise?"

"You died, didn't you, Sidney? Fell and struck your head on some weights. We came to your funeral – all of us. But I have only disappeared."

Nin was gathering her family – Mark and Mark Junior: coats, scarves and gloves were being handed round, smiles exchanged. They were like a pack, off on a journey. The Midnight Service was a big event in the village. The church – as for the Crib Service and the Christingle – was always packed, with believers and unbelievers alike. Sometimes, people stood outside the church, yellow in the light from the door of the west porch. They came from quiet family evenings and from parties, all rosy from fires and drink, with hope in their hearts.

The front door clicked to on its well-oiled lock and Nin and her family made their way, chatting together, across the gravelled driveway. They walked in close harmony, joining others along the High Street. Voices exchanged greetings – "Merry Christmas", "Have a nice day tomorrow", "Merry Christmas to you and yours". If only, thought Grise, it would snow. She took Sidney's arm and led him out onto the street so that they walked together like the others. He kept his head down but she looked up at the starlit sky, her eyes sparkling in the cold night air.

The church was lit, and its tower was visible as they rounded the corner into Gylde Hall Lane and passed the first row of older houses before turning through the estate. Other doors clicked, and other feet shuffled on footpaths. The village was coming to customary life before settling back into Christmas night. They eventually came to Boller and Pliny's bungalow. There was movement in front of the brightly-lit windows and Grise knew from old the discussions going on. The women would all want to go; the men would have preferred to sit drinking.

Ample had left Billy soporific on the settee and Ticker had 'offered' to stay with him, but Boller – far more under his wife's thumb than his voice gave him the appearance of being – was among the women as they stepped out onto Gilbert's Avenue, that ran through the estate and was named after the local builder responsible for the houses. Mavis and the girls were among them and Grise felt Sidney's arm tighten on hers as he saw them. She prayed that Owen and her two children wouldn't be there. At least she tried to pray and then realised that even those few small words of comfort were denied her; she also realised that she felt no concern for them. They would not be there – not three days after her "disappearance". They would be ... the words didn't frame themselves in her thoughts. 'The past is the past and you cannot live there.'

As they reached the end of Gilbert's Avenue, Grise could see Lianne Snooks walking alone up Church Hill. Barry had obviously put his foot down and stayed with the children. With her, came Beth and Tony Crewes with their children (who would far rather have been in bed or watching television) in tow. Beth Crewes had always been a demanding little woman – tenacious in getting her own way.

From the top end of the village came Alan and Penny Read with Martin Billings and Amy, and the Read's four children. Penny Read was the only woman in the village for whom Grise had ever known any pangs of envy. She had always seemed so 'complete', so self-assured and – watching her now with her family scuttling round her – Grise could see why and she felt the jealousy return.

It was the first time in all her life that Esther Corvin was unable to attend the Midnight Service. Her state was, in the real sense of the word, catatonic. She had seemed to be her old self during the evening, but when the moment came to don coats and scarfs Esther's manner had changed abruptly. Her snappish nature re-asserted itself and she refused, point-blank, to "even think about going to ... to ... the service". The row (with Rebecca and Corvin and out of Peter Vishnya's earshot) had "wearied her beyond words" and she relapsed into a sleep, which deepened immediately so that she lay on the settee in their sitting room and was out to the world. The trance-like state deepened until her whole body become rigid and immobile, so much so that she seemed in danger of falling from where she lay. Peter and Corvin, with Rebecca's help, carried her carefully to bed and tucked her firmly into the bedclothes. Rebecca touched her father's arm and smiled.

"It'll be all right, dad. We know what we have to do. It's only a matter of time. Pull yourself together and enjoy your service. They'll all be waiting for you."

She knew that Corvin did not want to go. Ever since his return from the Old Vicarage, her father's soul had been heavy and Rebecca shared every stab of his pain. His life and his life's work were both ebbing away. He felt unequal to the task of defeating Brultzner and his wife, who (despite her shrewish nature) had always been a bulwark for him, was now elsewhere and the servant of his enemy.

"I will stay with mum."

"No," said Peter, "I will stay. Rebecca – your father needs you to get through the service. Only you can help him now."

Rebecca's eyes did not leave her father's face throughout the whole service. From the opening welcome "The Lord be with you" to the closing dismissal "Go in the peace of Christ" she was with him, and when he stood in the porch, after the service, wishing his parishioner's a "Merry Christmas", Rebecca was by his side. The congregation went quietly and happily. Even for the atheists among them – like Tony Crewes, who never took communion – there was the feeling that they had shared something special that gave them another perspective on their lives. There was always what Crewes called "a joyous solemnity" about the Midnight Service. His tone was flippant, of course – even sarcastic – but, deep down, he had heard a glorious song of old. The members of their group (with Amy and Beth) lingered after the others had left, shared an additional instant of solidarity and wished each other well. Corvin's spirits had been lifted by the service and he offered words of comfort to them all.

"We go out into the world, now, in the power of His spirit, offering ourselves (if need be) as a living sacrifice, to do His work in the glory of His name. Remember that and may God bless us all."

It was still star-bright as they left the churchyard. Alan and Penny went with their children, together with Martin and Amy, by the lych-gate. Corvin and Rebecca went with Tony, Beth and their children by the lower steps. As they left the avenue of yew trees, Tony caught a shadow of movement in the corner of his eye. He thought, ridiculously, that it was Sarah and he turned back into the graveyard.

"My gloves," he said, "I think I've dropped my gloves."

Beth couldn't argue – not in front of Corvin and with the children dancing with excitement. He rushed back into the graveyard alone. He saw nothing at first, but then heard the hiss, almost at his feet. A pair of eyes stared at him from under dark, bushy brows. The white face broke into an inane grin, and the head lolled to one side.

"I know," said Rollie.

What stopped Tony Crewes driving his fist into the silly face, he wasn't sure: perhaps it was simple decency. He turned away to re-join his wife and children.

"I know," said the voice again, in a hoarse whisper.

"Know what?" asked Tony, quietly, and still restraining himself.

"Know."

Tony turned to look at the youth, but closed his eyes in case the face infuriated him.

"I know where she is. I've watched."

"Sarah?"

"I've seen her."

"Where?"

"Ah – wouldn't yew like ter know?"

"Where?" repeated Tony, very quietly

"Meet me by the marsh – Barxin' Day. You'll see."

He was gone, scurrying home across the graveyard before Tony could grab him. The little bastard would be wetting himself all Christmas Day, knowing he had Tony on tenterhooks. 'Was he telling the truth? He didn't miss much.'

"Tony?"

"I'm coming. I told you not to wait."

When Corvin and Rebecca arrived at the rectory, they didn't see the black Bentley at first. It had been driven in and turned, ready to leave. It was tucked back against the lawn that edged the front fence, out of sight of the road. When they did, Rebecca let out a cry and rushed at the front door. It was ajar, and she stumbled into the hallway, followed by Corvin. The house was intensely quiet and, without thinking, Rebecca raced upstairs to her mother's bedroom. Esther still lay where they had placed her. Her sleep was, if anything, deeper than ever, but Rebecca could see that she was dreaming. Although her body was rigid and her face austere, there was movement in the eyes. Wild dreams or visions were chasing themselves through her mother's mind. Rebecca reached out and touched her. Esther was cold, despite being tucked in so firmly, but 'in the land of the living.' Rebecca turned, but Corvin was not behind her as she had expected. She remembered Peter and hurried down the stairs and into the sitting room. There was no-one to be seen. Her heart sank within her as she crossed back into the hallway. The front door was still open, the house still shrouded in that deadly silence, and then she went into the dining room.

Her father was just inside the doorway looking across to the far side of the table where Horst Brultzner stood beside Peter, who was sitting in a chair by the vampire's side. She could see that her fiancé was tied to the chair at least by his shoulders, and that he had a noose around his neck, which pulled his head backwards. The end of this must have been tied to the chair rails because Peter's chin was forced upwards and his neck stretched and open. He was forced to stare at the ceiling and could only see Rebecca by dropping his eyes. Her father seemed remarkably calm. His hands were hanging loosely by his sides, and he was watching his opponent with an expression that suggested serenity or capitulation.

"Welcome, Rebecca, we have been waiting for you."

She didn't reply. More of the same was to follow, and it was more than she wanted to cope with that night. She sighed and walked towards the vampire, wanting only to release Peter's neck from that awful position.

"Come no closer, Rebecca, or I shall slit his throat with my finger nails."

"No, you won't," said Corvin.

"You seem very sure of that, priest."

"The last thing you want in this village is notoriety."

"You show more acumen than I gave you credit for, Unwood. However," said the vampire, dropping his eyes to Rebecca, "it is important to me that you hear what I have to say, so I would prefer you to stay where you are – for the moment."

"I will, but only if you release his neck."

Brultzner's left hand made a sudden movement and Peter's head flopped, gratefully, forward. Rebecca did not move. She was aware that he had agreed only because it suited him and that he still held all the cards. She realised, too, that her father was only calm because he saw that he had no choice. From this moment on, his losses could only increase. Brultzner began to speak, and Rebecca realised the anger within him was overwhelming.

"I came to this village in peace. I took only what I needed to survive. I did none of you any harm. Yet you have invaded my privacy and repaid my hospitality with discourtesy and abuse."

"You unleashed, on this village, more of your kind."

"I unleashed nothing. The girl came to me in distress. I took her from the sea and gave her a home. The death of Close was an accident, which I had under control until someone released him. I have done nothing in this village – which means more to me than it ever can to any of you – but restore old traditions and customs."

"You came to us in the night, and you drank from our veins."

"All creatures must live. Look around you. Visit the homes in the village tonight and tomorrow and for what you call your 'festive season'. Be appalled by the gluttony, be nauseated by the waste. You of all people, priest, must look upon both those as a sin – gluttony and waste – when so many of your kind are dying all over your world. And what others of the seven deadly sins will your Christmas spawn – greed, envy, sloth? And yet you presume to challenge my way of life as though it were, in some way, inferior to your own? You engage in the wholesale slaughter of millions of what you call 'God's creatures' in order to live, and then seek to end my way of life? I kill only when I need to do so and only those who betray or challenge me: no creature will do less! All of us have the right to defend ourselves."

"What do you want?" asked Rebecca, "Why have you come here in this way, tonight of all nights?"

"Your discourtesies have forced my hand. I am bound to act, and you have only yourselves to blame. I intend to do what any soldier will do under such circumstances. I intend to secure my position. I intend to gain myself some time, while we all re-consider our strategies. I have no wish to prevent your pursuits of Close and the girl. Indeed, if you will accept my help, I will assist you."

Corvin looked at Peter and then at Rebecca.

"Do not look askance, priest. Our interests are the same, whether you like it or not. They have betrayed me and must die; they pose a threat to your kind and must die. We are agreed, are we not?"

"Our motives ..."

"... are identical! We both – your kind and mine – wish to survive!"

Rebecca remembered the black sedan in the driveway and knew that Brultzner had already come to a decision. He hadn't arrived in a sedan because he, himself, needed to do so. She looked at Peter tied in the chair. He hadn't spoken since she and Corvin entered the room and Rebecca knew that he was aware of what Brultzner planned. Rebecca was frantic: she feared that he intended to kill her fiancé as some kind of reprisal.

"What do you want us to do?" she said.

"Rebecca," said Corvin, solemnly, "we do not make deals with the Devil."

"Your daughter has more sense than you. She realises you have no choice."

"We always have a choice," said Corvin, kindly but desperately, "it is simply that sometimes we lack the courage to make the right one."

The tension in the dining room was unbearable. Rebecca thought she would do anything to hurry it away.

"Tell us what you want."

"You are central to my intentions, Rebecca. You hold the key because you are loved. Such affection is the great weakness of your kind. I shall take you – tonight – as my hostage, while your friends and allies come to their right minds."

Without another word, or even the luxury of allowing himself to be distracted by a smile, the vampire strode across the room and lifted her up in his arms. She struggled, but it was only a token gesture. She lay in his arms, her legs held in one grip, her shoulders nestled in the other, while he looked down into her eyes and the old cravings stirred within her breast. The last sounds of which Rebecca was conscious were the wretchedness in Peter's scream, and her father's hopeless cry as he rushed to the rectory gate after the departing car.

Book Four

Winter Carol

CHAPTER 1

Dark night of the soul

It was the sound of the car starting-up which had galvanised Corvin into action. Until that moment, his feet had seemed nailed to the floor and his arms pinned uselessly to his sides. He reached the gate as the sedan swerved into Shore Lane, turned left and raced away into the night. In those terrible minutes during which the vampire had spoken, Corvin felt the weakness spread throughout his body. He turned, as the sedan disappeared, and ran back into his rectory; he was beside himself – Rebecca had been taken from him and there was only Esther to whom he could turn.

He reached the top of the stairs puffing and sweating. Esther lay as she had before they left for the service. Her two selves were welded into one on the bed: rigid almost to the point of death, cold to his touch, unresponsive to his plea, her life (like his faith) ebbing away into the bleakness of another time and place. 'Eternity is timelessness. Heaven is the state of being with God. It is when we are with God all the time and consciously aware of his presence.'

Was Esther aware of his presence? Who could he turn to, now? Corvin sat down on the edge of the bed, his head in his hands. It was Christmas morning – such a peaceful, joyful time, 'when the whole world gives back the song which now angels sing.' He felt 'unhinged': that was the awful word they used in American films, wasn't it? 'Unhinged!' They were right. How much more comforting the old English expression – 'beside himself – agitated, excited, unconnected.' He was 'unconnected' – with his wife, with his daughter, with his God. He looked at his wife again – his beloved wife. She was having a nightmare – quietly and desperately, somewhere far from him where no love could reach. Cold, cold – she was so cold. Corvin opened the chest where they kept the extra duvet for the winter and draped it over her.

He went downstairs to his study and closed the door behind him. Somewhere a voice was shouting: it was a noisome world, better shut out. He glanced furtively towards the door, savouring his sanctuary and not wanting to be disturbed. He reached into the back of the wall cupboard, found the small kettle, opened his study door and peeped out. The kitchen door was ajar; he crept quietly across the hall and filled his kettle from the cold tap in the toilet underneath the stairs. The tea was good, as was the chocolate biscuit he dunked. Corvin felt the drink flow through him, but it did not open up his mind as the taste rose over his palate. It began to close him down. His ritual failed him when he needed it most. Somewhere there was help; somewhere there was sanctuary.

He hadn't removed his outer garments. He was still dressed in his thick, priestly robes, including his winter cassock. Corvin opened the door of the wall cupboard, again, and took out a long, black scarf and some thick woollen gloves. It would be cold out there in the bleakness of the night, but he had to walk and walk ... and walk.

Corvin turned at the front gate and walked naturally towards the hill that led to St George's Church. Where else would he go? He passed his church, with its tower still lit in Christmas glory, and strode on up the road and along Shoemaker's Lane to where the High Street met the main London Road. Ahead were the fields and open country, lit this night by a dark and starry sky. Walk – walk until you can walk no more! Corvin strode on, up over Nab's Hill and the footpath to Willowmere. He was not a natural long distance walker, but the going was easy over ground which had remained dry for several weeks and, with unexpected excitement in his heart, Corvin soon reached Blower's Green Pit – a deep depression in the ground where the snowdrops, it was said, bloomed early each spring. He looked down into it and, sure enough, there did seem to be green shoots already appearing through the ground. 'Plants and animals renew themselves naturally each spring. Can we, Lord?' It was the kind of thing he might have said in his end-of-sermon-prayer. It seemed so shallow, now. Forever looking forward is no way to cope with the present.

Corvin knew he could go cross-country to Wilford. As long as he kept away from the River Cassyn, he would be all right. The inclines were slight, but enough for a corpulent man of sedentary preferences. 'To strive is good.' Why did these clichés keep coming into his head? Had he lived his life in the comfort of their truths? Why was he questioning himself so ruthlessly? 'Let it be, let it be.' Someone, somewhere, had already said that, but who it was he couldn't remember. Keep walking, keep thinking. Let the clichés take over and drive out the real thoughts, the real worries.

Corvin suddenly realised that he had not prayed. His daughter had been taken the Lord above knew where, his wife was in a sleep of death, and he had not prayed. There was a barn ahead. He knew that from his drives around the parishes as rural dean. He would make for the barn, and stop for a moment. As he skirted the edge of Blower's Farm, the collies barked. Corvin walked up to the fence to speak with them, but they snarled and snapped at his hands, tearing at the wool of his gloves. The bite was cursory and left only a stinging sensation, but its decisiveness was frightening. Corvin forgot the barn and passed on over the road and across another field. It was better to do something; whatever it was he was doing was better than doing nothing.

He dare not let his mind rest – dare not let it focus too minutely on his troubles. 'That way madness lies.' Who said that? This was sheep country; the county had built its wealth on sheep because the dry fields suited them well. St George's had probably been financed by a sheep merchant. It was always the merchants who made the money – never the farmers and labourers. The bridleway had been badly chopped by horses and Corvin slithered about; his cassock, whose warmth benefited him on such a cold night, was a nuisance when it came to balance. Its weight pulled him from side to side, as he struggled to keep his feet. Ahead was a church. Of course, it was Wilford with its Saxon tower! He would pause there and pray.

The church was a sad sight: it had been derelict for years. The roof was falling in and the building was no longer safe. Corvin knew that, but tried the door all the same. 'Hope springs eternal in the human breast.' Pope said that – Alexander Pope. Corvin had always been attracted to Pope's poetry, perhaps because he felt sorry for the man. A clever man (he read widely in French, Greek, Italian and Latin), but an irritable and abusive one. You couldn't blame him for that: he had been struck down by illness as a child – an illness which plagued him all his life – he never grew above four-and-a-half-feet in height and suffered from fevers and violent headaches.

It was strange how the afflictions of others always gave one hope. Corvin thought of this as he knelt in the graveyard at Wilford and prayed for the safety of his daughter and the recovery of his wife. He felt better after that: somehow he had placed them in God's hands and could press on. He knew where he was going, now. It was much more satisfactory than wandering aimlessly through the night. He was going to suffer on the long walk he had set himself, but that was good and he had a purpose.

The footpath continued northwards across the middle of two more fields, and he covered another mile or so until he reached the railway line. There was a safe crossing somewhere – he knew that – and Corvin stumbled along the embankment until he reached some gates. They were insubstantial and insignificant, but they gave him access across the line and he found himself, once more, on a bridleway freshly churned by horses. He followed this, through woodland, for what could not have been more than half-a-mile but seemed much longer and found himself on the banks of a river. He had left the Cassyn behind (he was almost sure of that) so this must be the Waveney and there was no way to cross! Once clear of the woodland, he could see marshes spreading interminably on both sides and in front of him. He was lost! While there were houses and churches and railway lines, he had felt secure; but now there was nothing except the endless marshes. He looked at his watch: it was half-past-four. Corvin had no idea when he had set out, but guessed it couldn't have been later than half-past-one – could it? He must have walked five or six miles, and he was nowhere.

He disliked water, especially at night, and the cold darkness of it made him shudder. However, he didn't want to turn back. Horrible though the cold wetness was, Corvin felt himself in God's hands by the river. Away from civilisation with the black night touching all horizons, he felt at the mercy of nature – exposed as the open sky. All the same, he shivered. This was an austere retreat, and he needed that at the moment. He knew that he would never find Rebecca, or help Esther back to life, without divine help and that was to be found out here, on one's own, through suffering. This was his time for reflection, and he knew his God would give him that: not through painting, sculpture, calligraphy or any other of the fine arts but through striving and suffering and – finally – sanctuary. Corvin knew he had to keep telling himself that this was true. He could not allow himself to believe otherwise. In His own way, in His own time, Corvin's God would lead him to his daughter and it was out here where he would find the answer – alone with his Maker.

If only the reed-beds would not stretch so endlessly! In summer there would have been geese, swans, grebes, cormorants and – if he was lucky – those shyer birds, the bittern and the marsh harrier; but now there was only endless lines of cold grey and tawny stalks poking up from the water – moist, clammy, chilly and dank.

He closed his eyes to think. He must turn west and follow the river wherever it might take him. It was wet here, despite the dryness of the season so far, and Corvin slipped and fell more than once. The reed beds that lined the river were a dirty mixture of brown and yellow. They poked up from the water, shrouding its propinquity and giving the appearance of safety when there was none. Twice, Corvin actually slid down the bank, and felt his feet touched by the cold wetness of the place. 'He sees even the smallest sparrow fall.' Where they had snapped off, the reeds were harsh, and stabbed him when he fell.

Beyond the river, to his right, as far as his eye could see, stretched drab drainage ditches. Beyond these, the lights of farms and scattered houses twinkled, but they were far from his reach. As he walked on and dared to look up, Corvin saw the same remorseless pattern repeated to his left – reeds and dykes broken only occasionally by alder woodland. The trees seemed besieged as though a subtle and remorseless enemy was bent on their destruction. In places the river bank had been breached, allowing the tidal waters to encroach on what had once been grazing marsh. All man's efforts to prevent this had failed, and the interminable, cold waters clutched at every good around them. Corvin felt as though he was being driven through an alien land where forces beyond his, or any, control held sway.

He did not believe in purgatory but, had he done so, this place and this time and this walk would have been it. His sins – and he had to accept that he had sinned 'through our own grievous fault' – were of little significance in the whole scale of things. His sins were more like 'weaknesses' (the word came easily into his mind) and yet they had led, slowly but surely, to the sleeping death of his wife and the supernatural abduction of his daughter. His sins – mere peccadilloes, in the totality of things – had paved the way for the awful predicament in which they were all consumed. Corvin knew in his heart that he had not turned his face against the idea of the vampire because the idea was preposterous; he had turned his face against it because he did not wish to face the abuse or ridicule involved in its acceptance. In this he had failed his 'flock' (who said that?); whoever it was had conjured a 'good and true' image.

He walked on passed the pumping station whose engines fought an eternal and useless battle against the waters, and came, eventually, to a boat moored against the river bank. It was unlit and quiet. There seemed to be no one aboard. 'Who pays the ferryman?' (Who said that?). Was this his passage across the river?

Across the dykes there was light – just a glimmering of light, but it was real. Was it the lights of a farmhouse, or the lights of Hell? Corvin laughed. He realised he was indulging his fantasies, but he was frightened. It had become very, very quiet since he had crossed the line and found the river. In that one half-mile he had walked out of the world.

The struggle within him was monstrous. He was, at one and the same time, trying to confront and deny his predicament. Was the boat really there, or was it a temptation? Cross the river and go away, far away. Once the river was crossed, there would be no return – no chance of a return. Beyond the marshes it broadened out and took its passengers far away. Dunburgh – and he was walking away from Dunburgh – would become a spattering of lights on the rear horizon. Lights that would grow fainter the further he travelled. Far away, safely out of reach, into the belly of 'Mother-church'. (Who said that?).

He walked on. Ahead, outlined against the night sky, were the giant forms of trees. They were dark and foreboding, but they were a relief from the never-ending stretches of cold water. To his left, the marshes stretched south and, beyond them, the occasional flurry of lights passed through the night. He looked at his watch. It was after six in the morning. He must have covered another three or four miles – mustn't he? Where was he? Corvin was wet, and the cold was getting to him. He felt it soaking through his socks and into his shoes. It would warm-up, but at the moment it slopped uncomfortably in his shoes – muddy and wet and cold. It chilled him.

The bend of the river took him south for a while and, suddenly, the vista of marshes opened up again. He could smell the stagnant water in the dykes and feel the earth slipping away under his feet. The trees were fewer here and stunted, as though someone with a grievance objected to their flourishing and had attacked them with a chain saw. If a tree could be unhappy, then these trees were unhappy. He stumbled again, this time over a mooring rope, and fell on his face in the mud. He struggled up, stumbled forward and before him was nothing but road and the occasional, sudden flash of lights.

Corvin looked around him. He recognised the road. He had driven it many times on his way to the cathedral. He had walked all night. He had walked into the dawn and could not have come more than nine or ten miles: at least, twenty more must lie before him.

It was Christmas morning: no wonder it was so quiet. Children would be awake by now, desperate to unwrap presents. Their own Christmas mornings had been special; if only they had been able to have one more child, even more so. He had always felt sorry for Rebecca on Christmas morning – alone, with just two adults to share her joy. It always started with breakfast and always on her plate was the Christingle she had saved from the day. The candle was always lit as she came into breakfast. They would say grace and eat, and then it would be time to clear the table and go into the lounge and enjoy the presents. The little wait always seemed to increase the anticipation, and hence the pleasure: or was that just the way his adult mind saw it?

Christmas morning! At least it was quiet, but he wanted to get off the road. A few yards along he found a muddy track which took him to the north bank of the Waveney. He passed an old boathouse, and was then obliged to take a road to his left. His heart sank. How far need he go on that hard ground? At least the sun was making an appearance: to his right, and sometimes, on his back, Corvin began to feel the warmth. Corvin yawned. He was tired and fat and unused to walking. 'It's good to strive?' (Who said that?) The sun was a blessed gift. Some truths are self-evident (and must, therefore, be stated ad nauseam?). It was his task to state the truths of life for others to share and remember. One's general philosophy could be expressed in simple truths.

The next six or seven miles were a hard walk. Several times, Corvin was tempted to cross fields for what appeared to be short cuts, but he resisted the temptation. His feet now ached, cruelly, and he could not face the thought of his shoes being caked in the freshly turned earth of the fields. Having to lift additional weight, while fighting the pain, was more than he could bear. He was aware that his progress was now slower – or appeared to be – and he was conscious that he was withdrawing into himself. 'Retreating from the world; cutting off all contact by closing down my senses. I do not want to feel the pain, so I eliminate touch.' The pain in his feet and ankles was matched by the numbness in his hands. Despite the woollen gloves, his fingers were cold – cold with that creeping dampness that seems to seep into your very bones. He sniffed, and the mucous was cold and his nose was red with the chill of the early morning. 'We are at our weakest in the hour before dawn.' (Who said that – and why?)

He passed farmyards – some silent, some alive with the clatter of early morning feeding – and wished he could crawl into a straw-filled barn and lie there and fade into oblivion. His sense of touch was gone. He could no longer feel the pain or the cold. He was hungry – not having eaten since just after the Crib Service on Christmas Eve; his mouth was foul and clammy – not having cleaned his teeth because he hadn't gone to bed. He would suck away the unpleasant taste, pick out the bits between his teeth with straw, and forget the smell of bacon frying on the kitchen stove. He would taste no more and smell no more. All that was left to him now was sight and hearing.

The walk bore him on, remorselessly. He could not be still, and he could not turn back – forward was his only choice. Corvin dropped his head and his vision was restricted to walking feet – two feet and the swinging of a dirty cassock. Black and brown were the colours he saw until they blurred into a general muddiness that resembled 'mother-earth'. He became more and more focussed, like the proverbial mystic contemplating his navel. Twice, he walked in front of tractors taking feed to the animals in the fields, but he barely heard the shouts of the farmers.

His way was lit by the slow rise of the sun which streaked red and azure across the sky. 'Red sky in the morning, shepherd's warning.' (Who said that, and was it true?) It was true – one of the simple truths by which we live: a heavy red sky seen beneath a layer of cloud is often the sign of stormy weather to come. It also had biblical authority. 'The Pharisees ... came and, tempting, desired him that he would show them a sign from heaven. He answered and said unto them, "When it is evening, you say 'It will be fair weather for the sky is red'. In the morning 'It will be foul weather today for the sky is red and lowering'. Matthew said that! 'We should not desire the signs of our senses, but become one with the truth of God.' I said that – Corvin Unwood, priest of the parish of St George's in Suffolk.

By back roads and side roads and, eventually, by taking a small lane which gave him a view over the water meadows that he had now ceased to hate, Corvin came at last to Loddon. He had lost his way by then and it was divine guidance alone which turned him into the quiet lane, and so to the churchyard of Holy Trinity, rather than along the muddy bank of the Chet. He was now beyond any sensation of hunger or cold and wanted only to rest, and so he sat on the wooden bench-seat, which was just inside the graveyard, and closed his eyes on the world. Silence, blissful silence, surrounded him and he was happy.

How long he sat, Corvin had no idea. Maybe the church clock struck an hour and roused him, but he could not remember. He only knew that he was walking down the main street of the village and all was silent and still. Not a dog-walker passed him, not a car drove by; he was alone in a desolated world and it was Christmas morning. Just before he arrived at the staithe, he passed a shop called Another Kettle of Fish. He laughed at the connection the name made in his memory. Ducks swarmed around his feet as he paused at the water's edge. They were hungry, and people were the bringers of food, but he had none to offer and walked on as the world quacked. He knew where he was going, but did not know what to do after he had crossed the bridge by the water mill. A footpath was leading him off to the right, but this way was by the water's edge and Corvin could not face the idea of endless marshes again. He would do better to stride the 'steep and rugged pathway.' (Who said that: what fool said that – someone who had never walked further than his cloisters?). He took the road (not in preference, but in aversion to the alternative) and, when he reached The White Horse public house, followed the right fork which seemed to pass between old cottages, craftsmen's shops and a warehouse.

He would arrive looking like a wreck, but he was past caring. He was unaware of his filthy appearance as he walked. 'I care for nobody, no not I, if nobody cares for me.' (Who said that?). Corvin absorbed the pain and humiliation into himself, as he walked, until he lost all consciousness of whatever might have been around him. The road was long and he had no chance to leave it; the road was hard but his feet kept on walking. He passed plantations, clumps and groves. He passed country churches and once-fine old mansions. He stopped by a stream and scooped some water into his mouth – not so much because he was thirsty but more because he felt he should. He wended his way through hamlets full of merriment he could not hear; the world was closed to him. Around noon – it may have been early afternoon – Corvin came to a river again. This far north it had to be the Norr, and he decided to let it lead him into the heart of the city. For a while he followed the bank and then found his way blocked by a public house; here the footpath seemed to disappear but the pub was open. Corvin found this an unpleasant surprise; he had always thought the world closed down on Christmas day. He sat for a while on one of the benches outside. There seemed to be no one about, and then a young woman approached him from the pub.

"Would you like anything, sir?"

Corvin hadn't thought about it and stared blankly at the young woman; he wasn't one who frequented pubs and wasn't sure what to say.

"Can I bring you a drink? We're closing soon. We're just open for a couple of hours"

"That would be nice, thank you."

"What would you like?"

"A pint?"

"We have IPA, Adnams Old ..."

"That sounds fine. Thank you."

He paid the girl when she brought the pint and told her to keep the change. He drank the beer slowly, sipping it as one would drink wine, rather than in swigs. It was another world to him – sitting outside an English pub drinking a beer, and looking out across the river. The feelings aroused in him, as he sat quietly, were ones of seclusion; he was in another place now. Afterwards, as he walked on, Corvin was ashamed that he did not even remember what the girl looked like or what she had said: all he could remember was her kindness.

He was unused to ale, and he felt light-headed as he walked on – light-headed but elated, and the horrible cold wetness and the throbbing pain in his feet, that scrunched his toes against his shoes, seemed to bother him less, if at all. He wandered in what amounted to a daze, and came to a hamlet. He wasn't sure how he got there, but knew it was in the wrong direction. He felt the sun on his right instead of his left, even as the sky darkened and night began to creep in over the horizon. He came across the old entrance to what must have been a stately house. It was broken down. The gates had gone, and been replaced with a strand of barbed wire. 'I am Ozymandias, king of kings, look on my works, ye mighty, and despair.' Shelley's words, capturing the futility of man's endeavours and vain boastings, came to him as he watched the ruin.

He eventually arrived in a woodland area – after about three or four miles – and passed the time of day with a lady walking two West Highland terriers. She put him right and was kind enough to offer him a lift into the city.

"I can't put you out to that extent. Besides, I am a stranger to you."

"People have helped me out in my life and I like to return that. Most people you meet are normal and decent."

Had she helped him because he was a priest? He didn't think so. Corvin was just grateful. He sank back into the comfort of the passenger seat and answered her when she spoke, but made no attempt to initiate conversation. It was the most relaxed he had ever been in a car with a woman, and he sank into oblivion. When he woke they were parked in Cryptacre, and the lady (and she was a lady, he was sure of that) was watching him.

"We've arrived," she said, "I hope you find what you've come for."

He stood on the cobblestones watching her car drive off. The dogs were watching him from the back of the car, and he waved before turning to the West Gate. 'Sanctuary.' Seeing the cathedral gate, Corvin realized that, for the first time for as long as he could remember, he had given God no thought at all since ... since many hours ago. He went in through the gate – glancing back at the still, bright lights of the city. He could see them because it was dark; night had come again. Strangely, he felt at one with himself; it was as though he had communed with some awesome force beyond his understanding. Once inside the cathedral walls, he saw before him the outer courtyard of the former monastery and, somewhere beyond that, the house of Bishop Twiddle.

Corvin knocked on the bishop's door and it was answered by the bishop's housekeeper, Mrs Cushion. Corvin looked at her and she looked at him and, for the first time for many hours, he became aware of himself and the impression he might create.

"Reverend Unwood!"

"Mrs Cushion, may I come in?"

"Why of course. You surprised me, that's all, and look at you. Where on earth have you been?"

Corvin looked at himself; he was filthy. His cassock was covered completely in wet mud from the knees down, and mud was splattered all over his chest, arms and hands. Bits of reed still hung from him, and his shoes were sodden and twisted beyond repair.

"I fear for your carpet, Mrs Cushion."

"Who calls upon us at this hour, Mrs Cushion?" the bishop's voice called from one of the rooms off the hallway.

"It's the Reverend Unwood, sir. We'll be with you after a few repairs."

It was the best part of half-an-hour before Mrs Cushion allowed Corvin into the bishop's presence. By then, he had bathed and was dressed in trousers, shirt, a cardigan and slippers. "My husband's, sir, God rest his soul. He was big, like you." After she had fussed around, and moved the bishop aside to make room for Corvin in front of the roaring log fire, she said:

"Have you eaten, Reverend Unwood?"

"Not, I fear, since just after the Crib Service, yesterday."

"Then – before you gentleman start your discussions – let me get you a little supper."

Mrs Cushion's "little supper" was cold turkey with piping hot bubble-and-squeak (produced from the Christmas dinner leftovers), accompanied by her own cranberry, pineapple and date chutney. She set it before Corvin on a padded lap-tray, with a pint of porter, checked that the bishop's cheese and biscuits were within easy reach and that his glass of port was topped-up and left the room, closing the door quietly behind her.

During her administrations, the bishop had sat sipping port with his feet stretched out to the fire. Corvin had remained in a daze, still cut off from the world but comfortable and warm. He had been in the bishop's study before but never under such circumstances, and its blend of parsimonious décor and dark-wood panels, with the firelight bouncing from them, was snug. He ate ravenously, attempting to slow himself, but not succeeding. Occasionally Peter Twiddle glanced up at him and smiled. Behind the façade, there was sincere concern that Corvin had come to disturb his composure.

The food brought Corvin part-way back into the world – far enough so that, when he did explain his visit, his story came without apology or stumbling. As the full horror of it descended on the bishop, Peter Twiddle's face lost its eternal smugness, and he stopped sipping his port or reaching for another piece of cheese. This was a shame because Mrs Cushion had provided his particular favourite – white Stilton. When Corvin had finished, Bishop Twiddle turned to him and said, his face expressionless:

"Why have you come to me, Corvin?"

"I had no one else to whom I could turn. I am at my wits' end."

"One always has the Lord, Corvin."

"That is why I have come, Bishop Peter. I am too confused to reach Him, but you are not."

"The Lord knows when the tiniest sparrow falls."

"It is my unworthiness that stands between us. I am beside myself. Reach out for me, Bishop Peter."

"The Lord is open to us all, Corvin. We have only to offer our prayers in all humility."

"I have the humility, Bishop Peter – no man more so, believe me – but I cannot find the words."

"They will come, Corvin, as you kneel before your Maker."

"Help me find my daughter and cure my wife."

"We cannot circumscribe the workings of the Almighty through our prayers, Corvin...."

"Help me."

"We can only offer up our pleas in true humbleness and sincere contrition."

"Then shrive me and help me find the words."

The bishop's composure was at breaking point, and every sinew of his being wanted Corvin out of the room and on his way so that he could return to the quiet contemplation of Christmas Day evening in front of the fire. He went to a cabinet in the wall, above which burned a permanent candle, and produced what he needed for their communion.

When the little office was completed, Corvin remained kneeling and looked up at his bishop as an injured child will look to their mother or father, but it was clear that Peter Twiddle, also, was lost for words. He had not questioned Corvin's story because he felt it best to hurry it away. He had not suggested counselling because he was wily enough to see that Corvin was in no state to accept. He had been obliged to cope with mad priests before, and felt that it was (for the greater good of all) time for Corvin to pursue his vocation elsewhere.

"I feel we should each offer up our own prayers, silently, Corvin."

He knelt beside his priest, over whom he had the same duty of care as Corvin had over his parish, and clasped his hands together. He raised his chin and closed his eyes, directing them towards the ceiling.

"I would feel reassured, Bishop Peter, if I might hear your prayers on my wife's and daughter's behalf."

The bishop did not answer, but tightened his mouth and then pursed his lips in a gesture which he hoped would appear thoughtful. After a while, a long while it seemed to Corvin, the bishop rose and led him across to the fire-side glow.

"The Lord knows our innermost thoughts, Corvin, when we offer them in humble contrition. Rest assured he is – as they say – 'on your case'."

Peter Twiddle liked to veer into the vernacular, occasionally; he felt it kept him in touch with modern trends. Corvin watched his bishop sipping his port, obviously relieved that things were 'back to normal', and wondered whether his bishop had framed any thoughts at all when in communion with his God. 'They sat thus for a goodly time' (Corvin smiled at the archaic nature of his own thoughts), before the bishop said:

"I wish you well on your journey home, Corvin."

He rose and rang a small bell that rested on the mantelpiece among the candlesticks and Christmas cards. Mrs Cushion tapped at the door as she entered.

"The Reverend Unwood will be returning to his home now, Mrs Cushion."

"Returning? But he's exhausted – and his clothes are saturated."

"The Lord calls us all where we may serve him best, Mrs Cushion."

"I'm sure he does, your lordship, but – if you don't mind my saying so – I'm sure He wouldn't want the Reverend Unwood to turn out again tonight. He's walked over thirty miles to get here, sir. He's been walking since the early hours of the day. He's exhausted and will serve the Lord better after a good night's sleep."

She turned to Corvin.

"I don't know why you've come here, sir, and it's no business of mine, but I do know exhaustion when I see it. You'll be far better after a good's night's sleep and a decent breakfast to send you on your way. I'm sure Bishop Peter can arrange for a car to take you home tomorrow, and I can make up and warm the bed for you in one of the spare rooms. Look after yourself, sir, and you'll be better placed to look after others."

"Thank you, Mrs Cushion. You're very kind."

During Mrs Cushion's exposition, delivered quietly and without emphasis, the bishop's face had expressed a wide range of emotions ranging from anger (through annoyance, displeasure, disbelief, incredulity, disappointment and frustration) to regret. He was unused to such a gamut of emotions, and the facial muscles now ached beyond all imagining. He turned, with the final feeling of exasperation clearly (and unusually) visible, and said:

"Perhaps, Mrs Cushion, the Reverend Unwood feels the need to return to his parish?"

"That's as maybe, your lordship, but I am concerned for his well-being and common sense tells me he will do better to rest before he does."

Corvin was glad not to be involved in the exchange of friendly fire, but to have his fate decided by others. Mrs Cushion carried the day, and Corvin found himself sharing the bishop's port and white Stilton, while his bed for the night was 'made up and warmed'. When the bishop's housekeeper returned to tell him that "all was ready when he was", Corvin had fallen asleep in the chair, the reflection of the flames dancing all over him.

CHAPTER 2

Mistress of the house

Peter Vishnya stopped shouting less than fifteen minutes after Corvin slammed the door behind him. With his hands tied securely to the chair, Peter could not see his watch, but guessed it to be around one-thirty in the morning of Christmas Day. He had no idea what was in Corvin's mind, or whether the priest would have any mind left if he returned. He regretted giving Anton so readily to Tony Crewes – but only momentarily. He knew his only hope of being released rested in Esther waking from her deep and false sleep. He surmised, hopefully, that Brultzner would not harm Rebecca; she was a card he would wait to play. He struggled with his bonds for a while but it was useless, as he knew it would be. He relaxed, and tried to think.

It was several hours – during which there had been one phone call, and his bladder had reached bursting point – before Esther appeared in the doorway of the dining room. She looked much younger. Her hair seemed fuller and her face less wrinkled with age. She looked at Peter calmly, scrutinising him as though waiting for an account of how he came to be tied to a chair in her dining room, before coming across and looking down at him.

"Where's Corvin?"

"I'm not sure, Esther. Can you ...?"

"Where's Rebecca?"

"I don't know – as yet. If you would ..."

Esther turned and left the room quietly. The expression on her face wasn't blank, as though she were immersed in some form of madness, but the look she had given Peter had been suspicious, as though he might be the cause of all her troubles. Peter was glad that Esther did not have a knife in her hand at that moment.

When she returned, she did – a knife in one hand and a cup of tea in the other. Her arthritic fingers seemed nimbler than usual.

"Tell me what happened," she said, as she sat at the table and sipped her tea.

"Would you just release me, first? I need to, eh, use the bathroom."

"What happened?"

"I really would appreciate ..."

"What happened?"

Her voice was nearly expressionless and she never used his name nor showed any sympathy for his predicament. He struggled against his bladder opening; the whole tenor of his upbringing militated against this, but nature had its limits. Esther did not look at him but continued sipping her tea, waiting for an answer.

"If you would just ..."

"What happened?"

"Rebecca has been abducted. Corvin ran out of the house after she ... left. I do not know where either of them is at the moment."

He expected her to ask who had abducted Rebecca – and he feared this because he expected her disbelief and her anger – but she didn't.

"You do not know where they are?" she said, repeating his words.

"No."

She looked at him, and trembled all over. Her body shuddered in spasms of fear and loathing. The cup in her hand splashed onto the carpet, and there were tears in her eyes when she looked up.

"Where's my daughter, Peter?"

"I don't know, Esther, but keeping me tied here will not find her."

"No, of course not," she said, with a smile.

Mark Chambers was already in his pyjamas when he and Nin heard the clatter from their back garden. They had returned from the Midnight Service, had a last drink "for Christmas Eve" (as Mark put it) and were getting ready for bed.

"It must be the cat, Mark. I'll go."

When she stepped outside the back door, Nin realised what had caused the noise: the metal bird table had fallen, striking the dustbin.

"Freddy? Freddy?"

She picked up the bird table and shoved it back in the ground. There was a deep scar in the lawn. 'You wouldn't think a cat had the strength.'

"Freddy? Come on, it's cold out here."

Beyond the poolside border with its ferns and irises and primroses and sedges and cowslips (so lovely in any season but winter) something moved, or Nin thought it did. She walked out over the lawn, drawing her coat round her. She wished she'd beaten Mark into bed because then it would be him looking for the cat.

"Freddy?"

She didn't know why she was doing this; he'd only want to go out again (probably around 3.30!) even if she got him in. It just didn't seem right to leave him out. He was a rescue cat and they always worried about him.

"Freddy?"

Nin walked round the edge of the border, just to take a quick look behind the little shed where she kept her gardening tools. Mark had been quite right – it did look rather "nifty", half-hidden by the willow tree and covered in variegated ivy. Shadows slipped over the ivy, emphasising the multifarious nature of the greens.

"Freddy – I shan't call you again!"

He was always prowling round the shed, and peering out at her when she was in the garden. He could leap on the water-butt and then on to the roof where he would stare down with those green eyes. Once round the shed, and then she'd go in to bed. It was Christmas Day. In a few hours, they'd all be up unwrapping presents. She looked up. The sky was dark, but bright with stars. Nin drew her coat closer, and shivered.

She saw something move again, and this time she felt it, too. It was as though someone had nudged passed her. Nin looked quickly around, but all was still: still and dark, nearly as dark as the sky. 'Thank goodness for the security light by the back door.' It was never completely dark in their back garden. You always felt that it was safer if you could see, although quite why that was Nin couldn't be sure. If there was someone there, would you want to see them?

She was behind the shed now, in the darkness beyond the poolside border and shut off from the lights of the house. The drooping branches of the weeping willow brushed against her, caressing her neck and whispering. She raised a hand to brush them aside and stepped forward round the corner of the shed, into the light thrown from the back door. She had the feeling that she wasn't alone in her garden. Perhaps Freddy was watching her? Cats are like that – crafty creatures that tease. She remembered going into her bedroom once and suddenly knowing that she was being watched. When she'd looked up, the cat had been eyeing her from the top of the wardrobe. Nin laughed. That cat had given them all so much fun! But cats were spooky; it was as though they had learned to read the human mind. Their cat seemed to anticipate what you were about to do; sometimes she thought that it actually led them on. Mark always said that the animals ruled the house.

He hadn't got stuck in the shed, had he? Don't be silly. If it was him who knocked the bird table over, how could he be in the shed? Nevertheless, she'd have a look – well, you do, don't you? It's like losing a bunch of keys: you look everywhere, even the silly places. Nin grasped the Suffolk latch and clicked it up with a sharp snap. The door opened with a gentle squeak. If he was in there, he'd come rushing out between her feet. Sometimes, when she opened the back door in the morning to let him in, the cat was behind her before she knew it. There was no movement in the shed. She reached in and rattled the handles of the rakes and hoes around to scare him.

She turned. Someone was standing by the back door, watching her: someone in an expensive leather jacket which nipped in at the waist and ended just above the crotch, emphasising the hips and buttocks. The figure was wearing jeans – skin-tight jeans that had been shrunk, in the bath, to fit the figure. These slid into boots – boots with high heels. The figure stood with a self-confident strut, which Nin did not like at all. It looked like the Culman tart who had tried to take her husband away.

Nin didn't want to believe that, but she stepped out across the lawn, her eyes never leaving the figure, which stood under the glare of the security light. 'Never turn your back on the Devil.' She blinked. There was no one there, and Nin sighed with relief. It was the night – and that bloody cat! – playing tricks on her nerves. She realized how cold she was and would be glad to get indoors, tucked up in bed with Mark. She seemed to have been out here for hours. Why hadn't Mark come for her? She looked up at their bedroom window; the light was still on.

"Nin," said a voice, speaking her name, insidiously, like an unbidden thought.
"Freddy?"

"Nin," said the voice, again – laughing in the night.

It was teasing laughter. Something was playing games, but she would have
none of it. She'd done her best – tried to call him in case he was hungry, but she'd
had enough now. He could wait until morning. She reached out for the back door,
meaning to go in and lock it behind her. She could then breathe easily.

"Nin," said the voice, behind her now, and still very soft.

'Very soft, but wanting its own way. That kind of voice – pretending to
possess the gentleness it lacked.' Her whole life passed before her. Mark's looks
bowling her over, coming into the family as a young married woman, the children
when little, trying to keep herself looking young, Grise at her table for bridge, her
house where everything was straight from each season's glossy magazines, the day
Mark had gone pigeon shooting ... She snapped out of it. It was always that
picture which snapped her mind shut: the one she couldn't bear to embellish.

Grise was attractive: more than attractive, she exciting. Grise was looking at
Nin, from across the lawn, with that way she had of looking down and then up
under her lashes without lifting her head. When she smiled – and her smile lit up
her whole face and made those eyes seem bigger than ever – it felt that she was
smiling just at you, as though you were the only person in the world. For Grise, at
that moment, Nin was the only person in the world and Nin felt, as Mark had done,
that this woman radiated ... affection. She couldn't believe that word had framed
itself in her thoughts. 'Affection, love, devotion, tenderness, warmth?' Nin
couldn't see any of those in the eyes that stared. 'Passion, craving, lust, desire,
obsession!' She saw all those in Grise as they stared at each other across the lawn.

"What are you doing here? I thought ... I'd heard ..."

"I've come for Mark, Nin, I've ached for him so long and now I'm going to
have him."

"But this is Christmas morning. Where have you come from?"

"Oh, Nin – how naïve your world is! Why are you trembling?" said Grise,
with a laugh.

Nin knew that she was; her legs were shaking from the calf muscles upwards.
If she didn't sit down soon, she would fall. Her hands, too, began to twitch.

"Are you frightened?"

The voice was calm and quiet, but mocking. Nin couldn't think what was
wrong. She didn't understand why this was happening – now! Why now, on this
morning? Grise had vanished, someone said, and Owen had taken the children
away. What was this woman – this mistress – doing here now, laughing at her from
across her own lawn? She felt herself faint; she felt her legs give way, and then
Grise was beside her, supporting her, stopping her from falling. God – she could
feel the strength in her; no wonder Mark had enjoyed it in her arms! She must have
gripped him and held him and ... Nin went into spasm, shaking herself from side
to side in a frenzy of anger, disgust and bewilderment. The paroxysm lasted
seconds, but seemed an age as she shook Grise from her, violently shrugged her

filthy hands away and, finally, pushed her in the chest so that Grise staggered backwards. It took all Nin's poor strength; she was left weakened, and collapsed to the ground.

When she came round, Grise was still on the spot where she had fallen, but crouching, her fine denim-clad legs ready to spring. That was the image which came into Nin's mind; the woman was like a cat biding its time before leaping upon a mouse it had taunted about the room. The leather jacket added to the effect: like an animal, this woman had come upon her Mark and taken him – and intended to take him again. Nin did not know what to do; her instincts told her that she was involved in the unnatural. There was something about the woman who leaned towards her that was ... not human. No normal person would have come to her home in the early hours of Christmas morning and said what she had just said. Was she mad? Nin had heard of women being driven mad by lust.

Get inside: that was what she had to do – simply get inside and lock the door before this mad cat grabbed hold of her. She was on her feet quickly, glanced at Grise and still the woman did not move. Nin turned towards her back door, but decided against it and looked at Grise. To think, they had played cards together, worked-out together; they had enjoyed each other's company. Nin backed towards her own door, slowly, her eyes never leaving the face of her enemy. She didn't doubt that they were enemies; the tart's behaviour had gone too far for any conciliation.

As Nin backed away, Grise rose slightly. Her legs still held enough spring for her to make the leap in one, but she moved forward on her toes and thrust her neck forward. She smiled and Nin saw the long, curved canine teeth glisten. 'Nightmare – I'm dreaming. Wake me up, Mark! Snore, and wake me up!' Mark didn't. Was he sleeping so soundly as not to know what was happening in his own garden?

"Would you like to join us, Nin?"

"Join you – what are you talking about?"

"I'm taking Mark into another world. He'll come this time, believe me. He won't be able to resist. Can you feel the lure of it, too?"

She could, but only for an instant. Nin's feeling of revulsion was so high that it excluded any possibility she might be seduced by Grise.

"Leave us alone."

"It's not enough, Nin. Protestations are not enough. Mark won't protest – he'll want it. Ooh, he'll want it so badly it'll tie him in knots."

She laughed as she must have laughed behind Nin's back when she was Mark's mistress. Nin was still backing slowly towards her door, fooling herself into believing that Grise had not noticed. Without warning, Grise was gone and Nin stared into space, across her lawn, across her poolside border, through the silvery-yellow branches of the willow tree into the darkness of her garden beyond. Gone – but where? She turned. While the opportunity was with her, she turned and ran towards the door. Grise hands caught her as Nin ran into them. The vampire held her a second time to prevent her falling, and then lifted her from the ground.

"Let me warm myself with your blood before I go for him. Your ecstasy will be brief; his will last for all eternity."

Nin felt the sharp teeth sink into her neck and then heard the sucking sounds. She felt her own blood trickle down her neck. She wriggled in Grise's grip; she felt the long teeth rocking inside her with the motion. She knew she had only minutes before unconsciousness overcame her, before this woman had done with her and moved into the house with her husband. The thought of it was more than Nin could bear. She writhed in Grise's arms, and struggled to reach the floor. Grise braced her legs apart and tightened her grip, bringing Nin's body hard up against her breasts and all the while that horrible sucking sound continued.

A feeling of utter disgust filled Nin, knowing that this filthy being was gorging herself; she had experienced the same feeling of nausea when, waking one night to a tickling on her arm, she found some loathsome insect bloating itself on her blood. She lashed out, beating Grise round the head and face with her free arm until the vampire was forced to drop her. Nin shook herself and looked up. She felt she had never seen such a look of hate on a human face – but then, Grise was no longer human, was she? The mouth was drawn back into a dog-like snarl, wrinkling the nose and removing any semblance of beauty from the face. As the mouth opened wider, Nin could see her own blood dripping from the teeth and trickling down over the creature's lips and onto her chin. Watching her own blood on another's lips, Nin was very conscious of where the fear came from; that dribbling mouth held the certainty of death. More than that – it held the horror of something vile beyond death.

This creature could do with her what she wanted. Nin realised her helplessness. She had often woken at night, startled into consciousness by some nightmare of rape, and dreading to find herself in that situation – at the mercy of someone without conscience or pity. 'Are you frightened?' Yes, she was frightened: that was the awful thing. She was too frightened to move or protect herself in case the violence was worse than it might be, but Nin had to do something, so she screamed and Grise was on her, pressing her foul mouth down onto her throat. Nin felt the teeth go in a second time and again listened to that ghastly slurping sound as the vampire drank. The creature was astride her as she might have been astride a lover, and yanked her body upwards to her mouth. She heard the voices around her before she passed into unconsciousness, and there was some momentary relief. Were they the voices of angels?

When Mark dashed into the garden, alarmed by his wife's scream, he found her sprawled across the lawn with blood coming in spurts from her throat. His son, Mark Junior, was close on his heels. It had been the sound of the two voices which had alerted Grise, who was nowhere to be seen.

"What's going on, dad?"

"Call Dr Read – now!"

"It's Christmas morning!"

"Mark!"

While his son was phoning, Mark Chambers looked around the garden. He knew Grise was watching him. His lover's instinct told him that, but the apprehension held no sense. 'Why should she be, and who did this to Nin?'

Shadows stirred even in the quiet stillness of that morning; the feeling of intense grandeur pervaded the garden. All the Christmases he had ever known and the collective feelings of each of those times surrounded him as he knelt by his wife's side, his hand clamped to her throat in an attempt to staunch the flow of blood. Mark knew trepidation as he nursed his wife's body but he knew anger as well, and it was the anger onto which he held.

Nin had stopped twitching and the blood flowed less readily through his fingers by the time Alan Read arrived, which was within five minutes of the call. His face turned a dreadful shade of grey-white as he looked at Nin. He took a cloth from his medical bag, splashed it with what Mark thought smelled like iodine and dabbed the wound. Nin began to jerk about with the pain and Alan grunted.

"Good – she's alive, and she must stay that way, Mark. She needs blood – a transfusion. We must get her to hospital – now. If you and your son carry her into the back of my car, I'll take a quick look around."

He snapped shut his bag and then opened a holdall which Mark had not noticed. Alan took a cross from it, muttered a few words in a trembling voice and moved quickly into the darkness of the garden. By the time Nin was positioned on the back seat of the Volvo, Alan was standing by the car, his mobile phone clamped to his ear. Mark, nursing Nin carefully in his arms, knew he was calling the hospital.

"Do you know Nin's blood group?"

"O positive."

Alan spoke once more into the phone, and then turned to Mark's son.

"Can you drive, son?"

Mark Junior looked startled.

"I have things to do. You do drive?"

"Yes."

"Then drive like hell. Never mind the men in the little white vans and ignore the radar traps – if there are any about at this time on Christmas morning. Put your foot down. Your mother's soul – let alone her life – will depend on it."

The young man switched on the ignition, turned out onto the London Road and pushed the accelerator to the floor. The journey was intense. No one spoke, although Mark was bursting with questions. Alan made three calls on his phone, the first one being to Martin Billings:

"... and the woman or Close, or both, are on the loose, Martin, and one or the other might have seen me in the garden. Get to Pen – phone her now and tell her to be ready, just in case. Tell her to take all precautions. OK?"

His second call reached a voicemail:

"... Peter, I don't know where the hell you are, but we agreed to leave our phones on all the time – remember? Christmas it may be, but I'm more concerned with a Happy New Year. When you receive this, get in touch with Nadine; she will explain."

He snapped off the phone and then rang his third number. Mark was still no wiser as he listened, but Alan's face looked relieved. He was obviously speaking to

Nadine Palmester, and seemed reassured. The doctor sank back into the seat and looked out of the window. They were already driving out of Oulton Broad towards the Yarmouth Road.

"Easy here, son; you're doing well, but there might be the odd drunk about and we don't want to take them with us – not on the bonnet of the car."

Father and son smiled at the dark humour. It always seemed to help when you were tense. Alan then busied himself with ampoules and syringes, finally binding Nin's wound "to assist the clotting of the blood and avoid unnecessary questions." He took from his pocket a gold cross and chain, which he placed around Nin's neck. Mark recognised it as his wife's.

"I took the liberty of bringing it from her dressing table. I'll explain later."

When they reached the open road, Alan tapped the young man's shoulder and indicated that he was to "go for it" again. He had expected the police to be pursuing them by now but the night was unnaturally quiet. The Christmas revellers had apparently been "put to bed", as he said to Mark, tapping his shoulder with a comforting smile. They turned into the hospital and Alan directed the car to the Accident and Emergency unit. As they pulled up, two paramedics came out with a stretcher and Alan thanked them profusely. Mark could see that he knew the couple – a man and a woman – who took Nin from the car and placed her carefully on the stretcher. Before Mark knew it, they were in a cubicle with the curtain drawn and Nin had life-giving tubes needled into her arm. As the tension subsided, Alan turned to the paramedics.

"Thanks."

The one word seemed to be enough because it was returned with beaming smiles.

"Busy night?"

"So, so – could have been worse."

"Ah, Dr Read, since you seem to have taken over the unit, perhaps you'd care to fill in the forms."

The voice came from a young woman who had brushed aside the curtain and stood watching them all around Nin's bed. Alan knew the type – stuffed with their own importance and using the 'procedures' to elevate that importance, with little regard for what the 'procedures' were intended to achieve – and he disliked them with all the intensity of his pragmatic nature. You met them everywhere nowadays: generated by an increasingly paper-active government they crawled through every walk of life from traffic wardens to consultants. 'And this one's on the way up!' He took the clip file from her before she could protest – he knew she really wanted to fill in the form herself, keeping him in the firing line of questions as she did so – and proceeded to complete the entry, checking odd things like 'date of birth' with Mark as he did so. When he'd finished, Alan handed the form back to the doctor and watched the expression on her face as she read it. Her eyebrows had been raised in a kind of affronted haughtiness, when she started; by the time she'd finished, they had flashed up and down her forehead, ending in a deep frown.

"You can't write this."

"You wanted to know why the patient was admitted for a blood transfusion. Now you know."

"Vampires?"

"That is my diagnosis."

The eyebrows of the paramedics, who had met them at the door, now shot up and down. They both knew Alan Read, as Mark had surmised, and supposed that it was a gag. They hid their amusement by staring fixedly at Nin on the bed.

"This isn't a joke, Dr Read. These forms provide a database by which we ascertain need and provision."

"You've met both targets tonight, doctor – congratulations."

"I can't possibly enter this on the system."

"No facility for entering 'vampire', then?"

"I'll have to consult …."

"No doctor – you decide, but I would suggest that you enter what I have written. The system is a bureaucratic device for cutting necessary finances to essential services, for generating unnecessary meetings where self-important people can pontificate and for giving the erroneous impression that those up there in government actually care and are doing something about our health service. All of us – you and I included – would be better employed using what time we have caring for the sick, which is exactly what these two professionals have done tonight. I'm the present, doctor, but you are the future and – unless you put your foot down, now – skilled people like yourself are going to wake up in a world where all the forms have been filled in correctly but where it is actually impossible to find time for nursing and doctoring."

He paused, realising he had vented his fear for that night and feeling a good deal of compassion for the young woman who had been obliged to listen to him.

"Enter it as written, doctor: let the bureaucrats worry about the details."

She left the cubicle and the two paramedics subsided into laughter.

"Trust you to fool around with forms Dr Read!"

"You don't believe me?"

"Vampires?"

"Whether you believe me or not, will you promise me one thing?"

"Go on – it was worth anything to see her face."

"Will you ensure that the gold cross is not taken from Nin Chamber's neck? I mean it. When you go off duty this morning, please tell whoever takes over from you – and God bless them, on Christmas Day – not to remove it. Don't write it down – ask them and stress the importance of it."

They were still laughing as the three men left, but they made their promises and Alan evidently trusted both people. The expressions on the faces of Mark and his son, however, were far from amused. Alan touched each on the shoulder and led them to the car.

"I'll explain when I get you home and, for your own safety and Nin's soul, you'll need to believe me."

Alan left them in the Chambers's kitchen just before dawn and made his way home. Penny was waiting for him, cross in hand. He looked at her and smiled. Penny smiled back. Penny cuddled into his arms and they both felt safer.

"I'm just glad you're safe. I had to go."

"I know that, Alan. Martin phoned, but I told him to stay with Amy. There was no point in closing down one weak spot in our defences by opening up another. We have to face the reality that *all* of us must be on our guard *all* of the time ... Do you want me to ..."

"... fill me in with the details? Yes, please. Are the children up yet?"

"No, but it will be light soon. Do you want a drink?"

"A coffee would be nice."

Alan sat down in the kitchen and huddled himself over the table, while Penny brewed their coffee. Alan always drank his black, but she dribbled some cream into hers and brandy into both cups.

"Martin phoned, as I said, and soon after that Nadine came round ..."

"Alone?"

"No – Simon was with her. They had been to the rectory because Peter did not answer your call. It was shut, but there were lights on and, eventually, Peter answered the door. Brultzner had been there and abducted Rebecca, as a kind of hostage – Peter thinks – and Corvin has disappeared ..."

"Disappeared?"

"It's been a long night, Alan. Let me finish ... No one has any idea where he is, but Peter thinks it likely – although he did not say so in front of Esther – that he will be making his way to the cathedral."

"Yes, I can agree with that. We must phone ..."

"No – that would only spread alarm and rumour if it isn't true. We have agreed to wait, and Simon will take the morning service, for those who want it, in the Bethel, putting it out that Corvin is unwell."

"And Rebecca?"

"Peter is convinced that Brultzner will not harm her. He is using her as a 'bargaining ploy' – don't ask me to explain that although I did listen carefully. If any man is cool, Peter Vishnya is that man! He is convinced that Brultzner – and I use his phrase – will 'be in touch'!"

"And you agreed to that – to do nothing?"

"I had no choice – both Nadine and Simon agree. These religious people have a good deal of savoir-faire when it comes to matters of the soul."

"Let me get this straight – Rebecca has been abducted and we wait for the kidnapper to get in touch. Corvin has disappeared and we wait for news ... How long?"

"We couldn't agree but if you think carefully about it, Alan, you will see that there is little we can do."

"Oh, I think there is something we can do – and the sooner the better."

"We've all spoken about it, at length, Alan – Nadine, Simon, Martin, Tony, Peter, Esther and me. That's seven of us."

"Very well, until this afternoon ..."

"Until Boxing Day. Everyone is convinced that Corvin will turn up and Rebecca will be found. In the meantime, it was felt that we owe it to our children to give them a good, normal Christmas Day. Bring me up to date on Nin Chambers."

Alan did, and then phoned Peter Vishnya who offered to get in touch with the other two – Nadine and Martin. At the same time, he assured Peter that he and Esther would be the main focus of attention for Christmas Day and "not to worry, but enjoy it with your families." When he put down the telephone, Alan turned to Penny.

"Is there some truth in racial stereotyping – are all Russians phlegmatic?"

"Peter is Estonian – and worried to death, but sure that the enemy will make contact sooner than later. We can only be on our guard over Close and Grise. Remember, that Esther now knows about Grise and what Esther knows Brultzner will know. Once he realises that she is on the loose, he will hurry back and is more certain to find her than we are. It was agreed that we should use Esther."

"Yes – all right, until tomorrow, then. Now I'm going to try and take a cat nap. You'll do well to do the same."

"Cat nap? Alan, it's Christmas morning, there are four children in the house and I can hear at least one of them on the stairs! I'm going to get the turkey in the oven!"

CHAPTER 3

Ainsley Bint realises his assets

Christmas morning meant little – or nothing – to Ainsley Bint. They were going round his mother-in-law's for lunch so that freed him up from having to help his wife get anything ready, and he had better things to do than chat to Milly. They had woken early, but lounged in bed. He knew what his main Christmas present from Milly was because he'd bought it himself – in case she got the wrong one – and Ainsley thought it would do her good to wait for hers.

He hadn't been altogether heartless, though, because he'd fancied a little bit, and decided to give it to her before they got up. He knew Milly hadn't enjoyed it much (she was too keen to find out what he had bought her), but that didn't matter because he had. It was a while since he'd done it with her, and she needed to remember that he cared.

Life was looking good. Like any good son, he'd taken his mother's advice – "You're a prick if you let that little girl go". She couldn't have said it plainer than that, could she? As always, mum was right. His mother-in-law's money was still proving useful – and he still had his thirty-something on the side. She'd certainly proved a good investment: coming to him for financial advice had done them both a favour. She couldn't get enough, and he never grew tired of giving it, but then – as his mum always said – he was a "very giving boy". She was married, which would make it easier if anything went wrong, and she had money to invest which always gave them a reason for meeting. Mind you, her husband must have been thick – or perhaps he had something on the side, too, and Ainsley was doing him a favour. But then, he was the kind of son who would "do anybody a good turn".

When they'd got up, at last – he'd allowed Milly to persuade him by bringing him breakfast in bed – she was just speechless about her present. It was a fur coat, and they were just coming back into fashion. Some celebrity tart had boasted on the television that she wouldn't hesitate to kill any animal for its fur, and that had opened the floodgates, so to speak. It was "all right" and "cool". Of course, for the likes of you and me, they weren't easy to come across – not your genuine fur coat. It was only those loaded with dosh, like the celebrity tart, who could lay their hands on one – unless your name happened to be Ainsley Bint! The brownie points would stack up rapidly for any likely lad who could get his little darling inside one of those – and Ainsley was your very likely lad. He had the contacts, didn't he – know what I mean? Milly's delight aside, he quite fancied taking her out in a real fur just to show off the coat to his mates and the lads on the block. It would do him a bit of good. While the rest of the slags were in fake fur, his little bit of all right would be wearing the genuine article. Not that Ainsley had actually bought the coat: his mother-in-law had done that, although she didn't know it. Thinking that he was making another shrewd investment on her behalf, she had given him the deposit. He had spent this on a weekend away with his thirty-something bit on the side, but not before ascertaining that a mate of his could find him such a coat for a favour. Ainsley had got Milly to walk round the lounge in it, naked underneath the fur, and that had got him going again so he'd given her another dose "to be going on with because he had to go out on business".

"On Christmas morning, Ainsley?"

"The wheels of industry never stop turning, girl. Anyway, I want to try out that SatNav you bought me."

That was true. It always paid to stick to the truth – or, at least, to make sure there was some truth in what you said because that helped to back-up the ... well, not to put too fine a point upon it, the not-quite-truths. It was true that he wanted to try out the SatNav. He had a very special reason for that – what one might call a "very desirable post code". He always felt that he'd make a good estate agent if his financial consultancy failed – which it might. Who knows which way the wind blows? Not that he had much time for estate agents. They were a bunch of crooks in his experience – although that had come in handy this time round. Without their special quality of dishonesty, he would never have got his hands on the Gobley house, which was where his SatNav was going to take him this Christmas morning. Not that he needed the SatNav to find the Gobley house, but it added a bit of class to the journey.

So Ainsley was whistling a merry tune as he fitted the device. It was a very merry tune because there was just a chance he might get to spend a little time with his bit-of-thirty-something-on-the-side, if she could convince her husband that she'd forgotten the stuffing. Ainsley could see to that nicely, thanks very much.

He drove slowly towards Dunburgh, feeling rather proud that he had managed to locate that lay-by on the A12 by postcode! The woman's voice told him to "turn right in 0.7 miles", and he had been happy to do so because he liked to oblige. When she said he'd "arrived at his destination" he knew she hadn't lied because there was his thirty-something's car parked ready and waiting.

It was all done in a bit of a rush with his eye over his shoulder, but then you couldn't have everything, could you? They'd both come all this way – she to borrow some stuffing from her friend Doreen, and he to cast an eye over his prospects, so they couldn't grumble really. After all, it isn't every day you get the icing on the cake, let alone having your cake and eating it. And on Christmas morning, too! That'd make one to tell the lads in a year or two, when he'd moved to pastures new. And there was something exciting about doing it in a lay-by – not much class, admitted, but nice, with your trousers round your ankles and your arse in the air! He didn't suppose they were there more than ten minutes, but it was worth it – and clever, because anyone can explain away ten minutes.

Ainsley was feeling like the cat that got the cream, as he waved her goodbye and drove back into the village. Getting his hands on the Gobley house had been a real achievement – a work of art, if you wanted to get lyrical about it. A lot of wheeler-dealing and greasing of palms and "knowing the right people" (a favourite phrase of his mum's, that one) because it involved mixing with the undesirables – councillors and estate agents – but you can't have everything if you want to get on in life. Sometimes you have to make sacrifices.

Ainsley turned into the dilapidated driveway of the Gobley house and pulled on the handbrake. For the first time, he felt himself a man of property. He looked around, but was undaunted. It took more than peeling paint and rotten wood covered in green and black mould to worry Ainsley. It wouldn't be him clearing it – he'd simply stroll off with the profits. He had to admit, however, that the place did look gloomy and forsaken. If ever a shroud hung over a building, it hung over this one.

He got out of his car and walked round to the back. The animal pens and cages were still there, but empty and forlorn. The soul had gone from the place. After all, he had a soul himself – he wasn't what you'd call insensitive. How had they lived with that smell? He liked animals well enough – the occasional cat or small dog, he found tolerable. Milly had wanted one, and he hadn't objected so long as she looked after it and didn't bother him. But there was no way he could live with a smell like this.

The council had done a good job with boarding-up the abandoned house. There was no sign of any vandalism or attempts at breaking in. Quite right, too – he didn't pay his council tax for nothing. Well, he didn't actually pay any council tax, of course – that would have been silly. Officially, he still lived with his mum and Milly lived with hers. The house they lived in was, officially, empty. It saved more to invest for the future. But he was pleased that the council had looked after his new property. They might even offer to clear it up. After all, it was their responsibility until yesterday, and the garden had got into its present state while in their care so they owed it to him, really.

He found himself approaching the front door with the same feeling of trepidation as Crafty all those months before. Perhaps it was the memory of what had happened to Crafty which made him feel like that. The Gobley woman had a way with animals – she may have set the wolves on him. You never knew what people might do. He turned the key in the lock and opened the door. The stench hit him straight up the nose. It had been bad enough when the Gobleys lived here, but at least they opened the door regularly. The place had been shut tight now for months. It had fermented. That foul combination of stale air, cats' urine, rancid food, faeces and English breakfast tea had stewed in its own juices. Like Crafty before him, Ainsley gagged and turned his head to catch a breath of fresh air. Returning quickly to the car, he pocketed a handful of Milly's wet-wipes and walked in through the front door.

Ainsley was a fastidious person. He liked everything in his own home to be just-so, especially the bathroom, and Milly (bless her heart) was very good at keeping it like that. He'd returned on many an evening to find her wiping the bottles in the bathroom and polishing the taps. He'd only had to pick her up once and that was about the lime-scale on the top of the shower hose, which she couldn't reach. Being the kind of guy he was, Ainsley had done that for her and she'd been grateful. She liked to keep things the way Ainsley liked them. His horror, then, at his first sight of the Gobley's sitting room can easily be imagined. The crow was no longer on the television set, but the pile of excrement still adorned the table beneath. On the bright side, the piles of old newspapers and magazines, calendars, the Marconi, the hard-backed books, the jumble of copper saucepans, the cobblers last, the standard lamp, the pile of 78s, the wrought-iron candlestick and the gramophone brought two words to his mind in a single conjunction – 'antiques-money.'

The white rats, the multitude of cats, the jackdaw with the splintered wing and the two hedgehogs had gone. He thought he saw something move as his eyes grew accustomed to the half-light, but took it to be a common rat. In a place like this, there had to be rats. Whatever it was, it scampered beneath one of the many sofas or chairs, which still littered the room. Pale light slanted in from a doorway somewhere across the room, and a rope hung in the corner. Ainsley, holding one of the wet-wipes to his nose, made his way through the tumble of chairs to the kitchen. He noticed a key in the back door and turned it, pulling the door open with a harsh, grating sound. The foul air of the kitchen was relieved by the stale air from the garden as it wafted in over Bert's compost heap and decaying vegetable beds.

Ainsley left the door open and turned back into the room, expecting to see someone behind him. He suddenly had the sensation that he was not alone in the house. He tried not to let it disturb him – because the important thing was the pile of dosh that the sale of this house was going to bring – but he couldn't help it. He didn't believe in ghosts, but he decided, there and then, that he wouldn't want to spend the night alone in the Gobley house. Two people had died here – horribly. One had been found hanging from the rafters, his face puffy and blue with his swollen tongue sticking out and his arms twitching. They'd laughed about that at the time – the image of old Bert ("the randy sod") hanging from his own rafters, but it didn't seem so funny now. Then there was her – the battleaxe. She'd been found, half-eaten by her cats, at the bottom of the stairs, all twisted and with her neck broken. "Perhaps they couldn't reach him. She can't have been very tasty". How they'd laughed!

Ainsley's knees began to tremble. Perhaps the buyers would feel like this when they looked round? No – there's always a sucker somewhere. He sighed with relief at the thought. 'Once it's cleaned up it won't feel like this.' Stop thinking, stop imagining. Neither activity did anyone any good. Just get on with it. Ainsley moved to the narrow door, squeezing between the two wartime chairs, and opened it onto the spiral staircase. He looked up, along the length of the rope, reached out his hand to pull it and then changed his mind. It might have been a bit of fun, but it didn't seem such a good idea, after all. It might pay him not to make too much noise in this house. 'You might wake the dead.' Ainsley shuddered and wanted to swear, just so he felt better, but stopped himself. Something told him that Clara

Gobley wouldn't have approved of swearing and he didn't want to upset her. He'd leave the turret room for the moment. He didn't fancy going up there. He'd take a look – a quick look – upstairs, instead. 'Why?' The ideas didn't seem to be coming from him anymore. 'I'm being taken over. I'm being fucked about.'

Ainsley didn't like 'sombre'. Such moods were not his style. He rushed across the kitchen and out into the garden, gulping down great lungfuls of the stale, vegetated air. Sweat was springing from every pore. He wanted to go and sit in the car for a while, just to listen to the radio, but stopped himself in time. He knew that once he did that, the car would be revved-up and he would be off up the road, never to return – and he had money invested in this place. OK – someone else had provided the deposit, but he had the mortgage round his neck. He was planning a slapdash make-over and a quick sale. He couldn't fuck-up now. He said the obscenity over and over again, quietly to himself, and it seemed to give him courage. Anyway, it got him back into the house and he was at the foot of the stairs before he knew it.

Here was where they had found her body – on the small landing at the foot of the stairs. She had come crashing down, blundering from stair to stair, from wall to banister until she smashed into the wall at the bottom, and lay there like last year's scarecrow dumped in the corner of a barn. Ainsley had no idea where the images came from. They seemed to tumble through his brain as he stood on the spot. He looked upwards. The ladder was still there, heading into the loft. It must have been painful. She must have suffered as she fell. The body must have been bruised and broken when she hit the bottom of the stairs. 'Was she conscious? Did she know what happened to her? Was she helpless? Couldn't she get up? Did she die instantly?' His brain was racing off again. He'd had enough: there was no mileage in this.

She must have seen her bloke hanging there and stumbled backwards. Ainsley made his way up the stairs. He paused before opening the door to the room and then pushed it open, violently. The body had gone but the rope was still there. Why hadn't they removed the rope? They'd just cut him down, the bastards, without any kind of … any kind of … concern. Yeah, that was the word – concern. For a time, Ainsley could see Bert's body swinging there, backwards and forwards, to and fro.

Daylight filtered in through the open ceiling and tendrils of ivy hung down into the room. Bloody hell, he didn't know that half the bleeding roof had gone. That was going to cost a pretty penny. They'd done him – sold him a pig in a poke. 'Sold as seen'! The bastards! The floor was covered with shit and newspaper. Ainsley stood gazing into the roof space, watching a few birds fluttering about. He'd startled them. They'd been on the perches round the walls, but with a flurry of feathers they'd gone. He was going to complain about this – too true! He'd be a laughing stock if this got out. He hadn't expected paradise, but this! 'Gutted – I felt gutted, and it ain't fair!'

Ainsley turned away, slammed the door shut behind him in his disappointment and tumbled down the stairs. Standing on the spot where they had found Clara, he looked across the room. Give him his due – he wasn't the sort of bloke who was down for long. There was always an angle, and it was the smart blokes, the ones who got on in life, who found it – and he would find it. Ainsley felt in his pocket for the packet of cigarettes. He wasn't a smoker – it made him wheezy – but he needed one now. He lit his 'life-saver' and drew the smoke down into his lungs, releasing it in great puffs as he stood gazing out across the room. After a few drags, he began to cough and splutter. He wasn't used to it, and suddenly he was coughing his lungs up. The tears streamed from his eyes and he jerked and twisted where the body had fallen. Then he stubbed the fag out on the banister and tossed the dog-end on the floor. 'Burn the place down – that was it – and claim the insurance.'

Ainsley, calm now, stepped down into the sitting room. He laughed as the words entered his thoughts: there was nowhere to sit! He looked around and saw another door leading off the room. Of course, people kept calling it a 'house' but it was a bungalow. The door would lead to the bedrooms. He didn't fancy having a look in Clara's bedroom, but he might as well. You never know. He might strike lucky.

The door opened easily. He stepped into the room and saw the coffin. His first thought was that Clara and her bloke had slept in coffins for some bizarre reason. 'Fancy having a shag in a coffin!' There wasn't much light! He looked across at the window and remembered – it was boarded up. The only light that entered the house filtered through the gaps in the boards. He could see the coffin clearly, though. His eyes must be getting used to the half-light. The coffin was actually resting on the bed – a double bed. This must have been where Clara and Bert slept. It was richly furnished – dirty, but richly. Perhaps they'd got the stuff from a sale in a stately home. The thick embossed curtains must have been worth a bob or two at one time, and the wardrobe was oak. He knew that all right. He couldn't resist looking in the coffin. He had to open it. What a story this would make! The lid slid off, easily and plumped onto the bed. 'Sidney Close! But he's dead and buried!' Ainsley ran to the corner of the room backwards (he daren't take his eyes off the coffin) and wretched. The sweat poured from him again, and he trembled all over. It wasn't just fear (although he was afraid). It was the enormity of what he had seen. He had to get his head round it.

Nothing came to him. It was as though his brain was struggling against an enormous wall – as though he was beating and pummelling against it, and getting nothing in return. He was unaware of anything that could explain this, and he wouldn't be able to tell anybody because nobody would believe him. Even if he got out of the house alive, he wouldn't be able to talk about it. He wouldn't be able to … to get rid of it from his head.

He daren't walk back to the coffin. He found himself sliding down the wall, his back pressed desperately against the musty wallpaper, and watching his own pile of vomit. Nothing stirred. There was no movement from the coffin. It was daylight – well, not in here but outside. He'd smash away the boards and … Was that a hand on the edge of the coffin? He didn't want Close between him and the door. Ainsley stood and stepped forward. He meant to run, but found, once more, that he was approaching the body in the coffin.

Sidney Close stared up at him, his eyes wide open, with that smug grin on his face and, instantly, Ainsley understood – not by any process of thought, but intuitively. He'd seen the films, although he had better things to do than read the books, and he knew what was what. He was looking at a vampire. Never mind the whys and wherefores. He, Ainsley Bint, was looking at a vampire, and the vampire was looking at him but couldn't do anything. He didn't like to touch the corpse, but he knew he was going to. Bloody hell, he'd bought a house, and now it was more like a crypt. He felt appalled as he reached into the coffin. Why was he doing this? His hand touched the smiling face, and the cheeks were as cold as ... as cold as charity, and there was no ... no charity here.

Apart from the horrible coldness, which reminded Ainsley of the time he had picked up a dead fish, Sidney Close looked younger than ever. His hair, combed forward in that Roman style, was darker than Ainsley remembered, and the muscles of the face were firm. The lips, twisted in that perpetual and self-righteous sneer, were full of life – red with life. He'd had his fill the night before. Some young girl had filled his veins – satisfied his needs. How many women in the village had he sucked dry? The shoulders, under the leather jacket, were powerful. Once he had a grip on you, nothing would budge him. Yet he looked so clean – there wasn't a blemish on his skin, which was free of wrinkles or sagging. It was hard to believe that he was dead, but it had been months now since they'd buried him. The eyes, which seemed to be watching him as though anticipating his every move, were bright with amusement and desire. Looking into them, Ainsley understood, for the first time, what the word 'charisma' meant – that special magnetic appeal. Sidney Close had charm – the power to fascinate and delight others: a quality he'd lacked in life. This was more than simple sex-appeal and his allure transcended force or violence. It held the victims quietly and drew them in, wishing – demanding – their own fate, their own fulfilment. Watching the corpse, and wanting with all the craving he had ever known for it to wake, Ainsley was filled with revulsion. Dragging his eyes from the face, he looked wildly about the room for something to drive into the corpse, to wipe that conceited smirk from the world forever. There was a candlestick (what the hell did the Gobley's need a candlestick for?) but what could he do with that – smash away at the smiling face? He ran from the room, slamming the door behind him.

Thank God the back door was open – that let a bit more light in. Ainsley rushed through to the kitchen and stood in the doorway, leaning against the door-jamb. The sweat was leaping from his pores again, pumping out in fearful spurts. Why didn't he go? Why the ... why didn't he go? This was his house, sod it! He was paying for it! What the ... was Close doing here? He'd burn it down. He'd already thought of that when he saw the state the roof was in. Burn it down, and burn Close with it. You could burn vampires. He was sure of that. But there'd be bodies, wouldn't there? The police would find 'charred remains', and what would happen then? You had to calculate the odds. No good ending up charged with murder.

Ainsley suddenly realised he had no one to turn to. There was no one in his whole world who he could go to and say "I found a vampire in my house. What the fuck shall I do?" His mates would laugh, his wife would scream and his mum would tell him to "get rid of it". Not much help there, then! He looked up at the sky for reassurance. It was still daylight – Christmas morning – and the buggers didn't move in daylight, did they? Where had he come from? Where do vampires begin? You're not born a bleeding vampire, are you? What had happened to Sidney Close? He used to run the electrical shop in the village, for heavens sake. For almost the first time in his life, Ainsley wanted to cry. Here was something out of the ordinary, and he couldn't make a bob or two on the side. There were no percentages here.

He turned and looked over his shoulder. There was nothing there – again! His own house was beginning to give him the jitters! He turned back into the kitchen and wandered – yes, wandered (as casual as that) – back into the cluttered sitting room. He was getting used to the place now. That gut-wrenching fear he'd felt earlier was passing; that trembling all along his legs was fading. He came again to the narrow doorway that led up into the turret room. He'd go there, out of the way. They had a sense of humour – the Gobleys. Who else would have built a turret room on the corner of their bungalow? It did make the place look special – almost (what was the word – Gothic?). Yeah, that was it – Gothic. The staircase wound upwards to another narrow door at the top. There was light peeping from under the door and from between the shutters. The turret room, which was quite small and circular, was almost bare. There was the telescope, a few sloping ledges (on which were placed notebooks and pencils) attached to the walls and – across the centre, like some huge compass needle – a second coffin.

This coffin was lidded, but he removed this carefully and placed it against the wall. Grise Culman smiled up at him. When he was a young teenager, at the mercy of his hormones, she had fed his fantasies night after night. He'd imagined himself at her beck and call, eager to satisfy her. She could have done anything with him. Looking down at her in the coffin, he knew that the passing good looks of some celebrity were nothing compared to Grise Culman's charms. He felt a frenzy of desire for her. He reached down into the coffin and lifted her up, meaning to wake her from this sleep of the dead and let her have her will with him. She was soft, but cold to his touch. 'Wait – only wait and all will be yours.' He knew it to be true. He eased her back into the coffin, and the smile on her face seemed to express gratitude. She spoke to him through his desires. He ran his fingers over her face. The coldness didn't bother him – he could soon warm her up. Just leave it to Ainsley. He fancied himself as her consort. Vampires do not grow old. There was money here somewhere. If only … there was madness in him now, he realised that, but it was a madness which would lead to a fortune, if only ….. .

Penny Read eased herself back into the armchair and enjoyed the warmth of the flames from the log fire as their reflection played over her body. She looked tenderly across at her husband who, likewise, had closed his eyes, but was intensely aware of all around him. They were giving their children a decent Christmas Day, despite everything. Penny wondered how that could be, but was so pleased. She and Alan had agreed that not a word would pass between them of the terrible catastrophe which hung over them. Outside it was cold, but inside their home it was warm. Christmas lunch was over, the children were playing with their presents and she and Alan were dozing by the fire. Later, as the afternoon wore on, they would wake.

She had often marvelled how people in extreme circumstances managed to carry on with some kind of life. Refugees on the road, prisoners in camps, relatives close to a loved one dying: always, there was something which lifted the human spirit. It offered reassurance that, at such times, love was only just beyond one's grasp. She had once read a newspaper report of a mother who, returning from the midnight service on Christmas Eve, was raped at knife point in the churchyard. When her ordeal was over, the lady had gone on home and given her family the Christmas she wanted for them. She had said nothing about the assault until the festivities were over. Penny hadn't understood, at the time, how this could be: now, she did.

CHAPTER 4

Rebecca wakes

When she opened her eyes, Rebecca could see nothing. Her final conscious memories flitted briefly through her mind – Brultzner lifting her from the floor, her struggles in his arms, his looking down at her, Peter's pitiful scream, her father's despairing cry and the sound of the car as it moved off – and then she squeezed her eyes shut and snapped them open; the darkness was total. 'Stay calm.' Her mind told her all that Peter Vishnya had already told the others. Brultzner was an undoubted menace. He would (if angered) act in retaliation (even spite), but he offered her no immediate threat. Had he intended her present harm, she would already have been one of his kind and her conscience told her that this was not so.

Rebecca was unsure how closely she was imprisoned. She was aware that she could not move her fingers or wiggle her toes. There was no apprehension, however, that walls were pressing in upon her. She closed her eyes again and breathed deeply. She wanted to drift into herself without actually sleeping. There was strength in quiescence and she was determined to find it. The most dangerous thing she could do would be to panic. Attempt to move, however, she did – the instinct was so natural that she could not avoid it. It was then Rebecca realized that she could not turn her head – let alone reach out with a hand. 'Panic – don't panic. Focus. Go into meditation mode.'

'At the centre is Brultzner; think of Brultzner and move to Sarah; do not think about Sarah, return to Brultzner and move to Esther; do not think of Esther but return to Brultzner and move to vampire; do not think of vampire but return to Brultzner and move to plague ... wait and search, do not force the mind, concentrate and focus the image ... create a mood of returning to the centre.' The multiplicity of images slipped gently into Rebecca's mind until Brultzner was surrounded by every memory and experience she had ever had of him.

She let them rest there, unimpaired by force or tension. How much time had passed was now beyond her concern. With infinite casualness she selected the first word upon which she was to meditate – plague – and ran back along the line of her concentration to Brultzner, seeking patiently the connections between the two. Brultzner – plague, Brultzner – fire, Brultzner – tomb, Brultzner – soul, Brultzner – sardines, Brultzner – roots ... always Brultzner.

She came out of herself as she meditated and slipped easily into contemplation. Somewhere in there was truth and the truth would help to ... reclaim him. Somewhere in there, in the webs of her contemplation (so clear to her now) was an intuition, a knowing beyond thought, which would illuminate their endeavours. She felt it as one might feel the kindly touch of an old friend. It was another mood: almost, perhaps certainly, another place.

She put herself out of mind and followed her route as she might have followed the pathways on a map, never confusing them but holding them singly with ease, and journeying from one to the other in unconscious search of her 'truth' – her 'salient fact'. She sought those things that were not visible to the senses. She sought the qualities within them that would enlighten the journey for her and her friends. Confinement conferred this benefit upon her, and she roamed effortlessly through the range of sensations held by each – the sounds of the plague, the smell of the fire, the touch of the tomb, the taste of the soul, the sight of Sardinia ... She reached out for the subtleness of the reality that surrounded him, and found herself in sympathy with him. His nature was there, deeper than the others realised, and within it were the seeds of his ... his redemption.

How long the light had been on was a mystery to Rebecca, but when her eyes opened – for she did not, consciously, open them of her own volition – she saw her prison for the first time. She did not move at first, not out of fear but in the wonder of her calmness. She was relaxed in unconscious thought, and had no wish to disturb insights that would come unbidden into her mind.

When she did move and look around her she saw that there was, apparently, no door to her cell – no door, no window and no hatch. No means of access or egress. Yet she knew he must have brought her here – and sealed her in? No, that was not his intention. Somewhere, air must be able to enter.

She was lying on a wooden bench upon which had been placed a thin but adequate mattress and a sleeping bag. To her left was the wall of the prison, and to her right a space of perhaps twenty feet. Rebecca sat up and looked around. The prison was up to thirty feet long, she guessed, and unfurnished except by wooden benches that ran along the sides for most of their length. The floor consisted of stone slabs and, although they were clean, there was the smell of earth around her as one might find in a cellar.

She listened, but no sounds came to her ears. She knew, however, that she was underground and that above her there was a building. She was sure of that although the ceiling of her cell was unmarked by any trapdoor. So, they must have entered from the side or the ends.

The light came from four fissures in the side walls and two at each end. There was no sign of a switch, and she concluded that the lights had been switched on from outside the room. She looked at her watch, which was still on her wrist. So there was no deliberate attempt to disorientate her: just a wish to keep her imprisoned. It was ten o'clock on Christmas morning. She had no idea how long they had travelled or how long she had slept, but knew they must have left Dunburgh sometime after one o'clock in the morning. That would be nine hours ago. What was her family wondering? How was Peter? Had her mum awoken from that dreadful sleep? Her dad had raced, pointlessly, to the car. What would he be doing now? Pacing up and down?

She left such thoughts for a moment – her mind was still in contemplative state, and she did not want to muddle her pathways – and stood. At the far end of the bench on the opposite wall she noticed something. Rebecca was surprised, in such a sparsely furnished space, that it had taken so long. It was a tray of food and drink. Rebecca walked over to it and looked. There was a portion of cold ham with ginger and cumin seed chutney, two slices of lightly-buttered bread, a glass of orange juice and what she took to be tea, in a flask. The cup for the tea had been placed upside down on the saucer and the small jug of milk was covered with a lace doily. Despite herself and her circumstances, she laughed. Propped against the flask was a note, written in an unnaturally fussy hand.

Dear Miss Unwood,

First of all, may I ask you to forgive me for importuning you, in such an unseemly manner, on your Christmas Day? Please believe that I had no choice in the matter; the forces against me were aligned in formidable opposition and, had I delayed for even one more day, would have crushed and removed me from the face of our so wonderful world. I could not allow this to happen, as I am sure you will understand.

Secondly, I beg you to be assured that I mean you no personal harm. It is only because you are so loved that I chose you as my means of negotiation. I shall hope over the next forty-eight – and certainly no more than seventy-two – hours to have concluded my treaty with your friends and colleagues.

I must also ask you to excuse my not attending on you this morning; you will appreciate the particular difficulties this might afford me as the day is particularly bright.

I trust, in my absence, that I have been able to provide you with an acceptable breakfast. Believe me, I anguished over this problem, but your mother's assurance that cold ham was the traditional breakfast for your family on Christmas morning came as a relief. I understand the custom sprang from her side of the family, and that you – despite your propensity towards vegetarianism – have always obliged the family sensibilities. I took the liberty of providing ginger-based chutney which I always feel complements ham so elegantly.

I am painfully aware that boredom will be a sore trial for you over the next few days and I have taken what steps I can to alleviate this: please to find a copy of Mrs Radcliffe's Mysteries of Udolpho by the breakfast tray. I know from our previous conversations that Miss Austen is a favourite of yours, and I happen to know that she herself was a great admirer of Ann Radcliffe's historical romances.

I have also taken the liberty of ensuring that you sleep at regular intervals: tiredness will overcome you and you will retire to your 'bed' at set times. After you are comfortable, the lights will fade so that your eyes are completely rested. Waking refreshed will enable you to enjoy the novel more readily and without the fatigue attendant upon reading for long periods. When you wake each time, a meal should be waiting for you.

I intend returning to our beautiful Dunburgh-on-sea late tonight, but shall hope to join you over the course of the evening when I anticipate we might indulge in another delightful tete-a-tete.

Believe me, Miss Unwood, to be your friend and protector,

Horst Brultzner

Rebecca picked up the volume to which Brutzner had referred in his letter and smiled to herself before she folded the note, which was written on fine vellum, and slipped it inside the book. The novel itself must have come from his library; it was leather bound and finely tooled in gilt with an embossed spine. 'Modern books are designed to be slipped into one's pocket; this actual volume is a work of art in itself.' Rebecca turned it in her hands; it was a pleasure to hold and she knew that the pages, smooth as silk, would slip easily and sensuously through her fingers. 'Those things which divide us, Lord, are of less importance than those which bind us together.' She felt infinitely sad. 'I shouldn't. He is an evil and wilful man ... Thing. I cannot feel sad for the longings of a corpse.'

She set the book down on the bench, picked up the silver tray and placed it on her lap. She was a vegetarian – he had remembered that – but always capitulated to the family will on Christmas Day. How awful that Brultzner had discovered that from her mother! It was Suffolk ham, cut in thick to-be-relished slices and he was right – the ginger chutney was perfect! Sad – how wicked to be sad! She poured and sipped the tea; it was English breakfast tea made with leaves from ... somewhere in Africa, she fancied. The butter was real, and the loaf fresh and thinly sliced. The orange juice had been freshly-squeezed. Rebecca felt spoilt – but then, her parents had always 'spoiled' her. She was used to such treatment.

'I once loved Sardinia and was loved there – during the time of the Empire, you understand? And then, when that fell and we were all called back home my little island was overrun by the scum of the earth .... .' As she sat enjoying her Christmas morning breakfast, the power of her contemplation had led her back; the pathway was clear. Rebecca remembered their conversation when she thought his mind had been wandering like the mind of any old man. It wasn't that, however, was it? He had actually been there. 'When did the Romans leave Britain? Around the year 400AD, wasn't it? Then he must be ... he must be ... he must be the best part of sixteen centuries old!'

Rebecca re-placed the tray on the bench. The idea had not panicked her, but the saliva had dried in her mouth and chewing was uncomfortable. 'Sixteen centuries!' The pathways opened up, routes appeared and journeys were taken within her consciousness.

She knew something of the Romans; she had once studied their art – particularly their religious art. '... to the left of the central aisle stood a short statue, holding a carved torch downwards towards darkness and twilight; to the right, a similar statue holding his torch upwards to light and the dawn ...' She heard Tony's description of the temple. His voice ran quickly along one of the pathways in her mind and returned to ... Brultzner. He was a Roman. He had been a Roman soldier in Roman Britain, and the temple on the Wangford estate had been, and was, his place of worship. '...On the carvings he is seen plunging his knife into the shoulder of a huge, white bull. In each temple there was some representation of this central event – the slaying of the white bull.'

The memory of her reading and the picture of the relief were vivid. Released through her meditation, they flowed back in line with Tony's story, but even Tony had not supposed he was Roman. 'The young man was leading an assault on his kind and he had him flogged to death on a trumped-up charge of drunkenness.' How many times in all those centuries had he returned to Dunburgh? And would again, and know their great-great-great grandchildren. So was that when he became nosferatu? But how? '... didn't see the black Bentley at first. It had been driven in and turned, ready to leave.' It was Wangford's Bentley, of course! Was that where she was – so near to home, on the Wangford estate?

Rebecca finished her tea and stood up. She walked thoughtfully along the walls of her cell: there must be a doorway. She paced and scrutinised for an hour or more, running her fingers in the gaps between the stone. They were all identical – nothing indicated that a doorway existed. She looked at the roof, and she examined the floor. Had she been brought in through a trapdoor?

She would wait. He would come and then she would know. Rebecca looked at her watch: it was noon on Christmas Day. What were her parents doing? What plans were Peter and the others making to rescue her? 'A cat nap!' She felt drowsy. It had been a long and exhausting two hours and she'd had a long night. She would take a cat nap before lunch. She didn't have to help her mother with the meal this year because ... she didn't have to help her mother with the meal this year ... because ... because ... It was warm in the sleeping bag and the pillows, stuffed with the down of the Eider duck, were the best in the world, and soon she would be asleep ... deep, deep sleep ... sinking into a deep, deep sleep. From the six fissures in the walls, the light faded until there was dusk and then darkness, and then nothing.

When she woke, Rebecca's realisation of what had happened was followed rapidly by anger. He had taken her by surprise; it wouldn't happen again! '*I have also taken the liberty of ensuring that you sleep at regular intervals: tiredness will overcome you and you will retire to your 'bed' at set times.*' She shook the sleeping bag from her and scrambled out of it. Post-hypnotic suggestion they called it, didn't they? It wouldn't happen again – not to her! Rebecca was revolted at the idea that someone had ... manipulated her – that he had willed her to sleep, and that she had slept. Just like that!

As she swung herself from the bench, Rebecca half-expected to find Christmas dinner waiting, but there was no 'turkey and all the trimmings'. It was nice to know that Brultzner didn't have everything his own way. Outside, it must still be bright and sunny so he was confined, too.

She went back to her exploration of the walls and this time she tapped them with the heel of her shoe – something she had not wanted to do previously for fear of ... waking the dead. Rebecca laughed quietly to herself: waking the dead – that was rich! Eventually, after going round many times, she found what she was looking for – a hollowness of sound. It was only faintly so – almost imperceptibly so. How thick were the walls? Here must be a door, but she could find no sign of it. Rebecca was reminded of those secret panels in the walls of old houses. No one knew they were there except the owner. So cunningly contrived were they, so cleverly constructed, that they were invisible. Did it open outwards or inwards? There was no telling and yet – and yet, it could make all the difference.

Rebecca walked back to her bench. Her bench! Had she already accepted this place as her prison? Was she already staking a claim to her space within it? How many others had been confined here, and what had happened to them? Her release depended upon her family and friends agreeing to terms that would be unacceptable to any decent person. The terror of being dropped into a dark, sealed space and left forever had tormented her ever since a childhood visit to a castle dungeon.

For when had he programmed her next sleep? She looked at her watch. It was three o'clock on Christmas afternoon. Time for the Queen's speech! Rebecca pictured the three of them sitting in front of the television watching it. Throughout her childhood years, the pattern had been the same. Always the Christmas dinner had been ready in time to be rounded off before the Queen made her speech to the country. Had her mother come out of that dreadful sleep? Were they watching the Queen's speech now, and waiting for Brultzner to return? His note had said he would not return to Dunburgh until 'late tonight'. Was that just to confuse her? Rebecca felt sure that they were somewhere on the Wangford estate. It made sense for him not to travel too far, and it would amuse him, wouldn't it, to have her incarcerated a stone's throw from home.

She was hungry. It was five hours since she had eaten. Brultzner would not have kept her waiting out of spite. It would appeal to his sense of propriety to be on time with her Christmas dinner. He must have encountered a problem. Why was she worrying about Brultzner's problems? She had been 'here' before; she was thinking round in circles, letting her mind be absorbed by trivia. Stop it! Stop it! She would read. He had provided her with one of the great narrative books. She would enjoy Mrs Radcliffe's prose, and wait for his suggestions that she might 'like to take a cat nap' and fight them. She must stay awake.

Rebecca read quietly, enjoying the delicate prose which meandered with antique leisureliness. She kept her mind on what the writer was describing so minutely and with such clarity that the pictures lived in her mind to the exclusion of all else. She allowed her mind to drift only within the context of the writing. She found visualisation easy and so the images became a place in which she was able to wander. She needed to escape from the dungeon and Mrs Radcliffe had shown her a way out. When the suggestion came – that she might be feeling sleepy, very sleepy, and might want to lie down, snuggled into the soft feathers of the pillow, wrapped in the warmth of the sleeping bag, going further down into a deep sleep, a warm and deep sleep, cuddled deeply and warmly, breathing deeply in and out, into a deep sleep, a deep sleep – Rebecca was ready for it.

She paused for a moment in the lanes of Mrs Radcliffe's imagining and listened. She was listening to a voice which came from elsewhere and was talking to someone else, elsewhere. She sensed the approached of the talker, and bundled the sleeping bag into a heaped shape with one of the pillows. She walked over to where the door might be with Mrs Radcliffe's volume in her hand, and Rebecca waited. The lights began to dim, the stone panel in the wall opened inwards and a figure stepped into the prison. It was taller than her, but surprise and an antique volume would make up for lack of height. Rebecca moved out from behind the door and brought the book crashing down onto the back of her gaoler's head. The figure, like some springing shadow in the half-light, bolted forward and the tray it was carrying crashed to the stone floor with the violent sound of smashing crockery, clattering cutlery and shattering glass. Such was her upbringing that Rebecca almost apologised, but fear got the better of her and she rushed from the cell, slamming the door behind her and feeling for the key.

There was one! 'Such a relief.' She turned, not knowing where she was going and half-wondering whether it had been Brultzner who had brought the tray. She found herself at the bottom of a long flight of steps – in fact, a double flight. Looking up, she saw the sky and guessed that the steps must lead to street level. It was a long way, as though she had been imprisoned in a cellar below a basement. There was no sound behind her, but she knew what little time she had – a door would not hold Brultzner. Once he had recovered from the surprise and negligible concussion, the vampire would be on her trail, enjoying the chase, his wolfish sense of smell guiding him. When she came out at the stop of the steps, Rebecca found herself in an alleyway. To her left seemed to be a graveyard and to her right, the street. Under her feet were cobbles! So she was wrong: this couldn't be the Wangford estate. Never mind – she was free, for the time-being. Beyond the alley way were more cobblestones and then a road. There were cafes and old book shops opening on to a square. Trees sprung from the ground – limes and sycamores, she thought. There was no one about. Should she turn back to the graveyard? Was there a church there? Surely her God would protect her? Turn right, go up into the town – find people!

Rebecca ran along the pavement – to her right was an old pub and ahead were more cobbles. A side street led away into the darkness. Houses leaned over into the street – here was a narrow place. She could hide here, knock on a door and ask for sanctuary! Offices, more restaurants, a chapel closed against her: who would leave a chapel door unlocked in a modern city on Christmas Day? Three, or was it now four, o'clock and the city was deserted: the English didn't stray far from their firesides on Christmas Day. She dare not return back the way she had come, and hurried on through a cut along the side of the chapel. Estate agents, estate agents! There were no homes in the middle of cities anymore: only offices and more offices – empty for the festive season. Those who worked there would all be at home now, basking in the warmth of their living rooms, full of turkey and Christmas pudding.

She looked about her for a telephone box. There were none. With the coming of the mobile, street phone boxes were disappearing. Besides, who could she summon? Who was there who could help her now? All around her were old walls and archways – Petergate, Swinegate, Stonegate, Feastgate. Churches and markets certainly went arm in arm! The Mansion House, the post office, the river – she could at least reach the river.

Now she was alone, late on Christmas afternoon, in a strange city, and night was closing in. To her left a hill ran down – perhaps towards the river. She followed the hill. There was another church to her right, and old buildings everywhere. There was a public house in front of her – closed and in blackness. Where were the sounds of human voices when you needed them? Goodramgate! Another wretched gate extolling the virtues of food, and another city wall! '....without a city wall, where our dear Lord was crucified who died to save us all.' One of the huge doorways led into what appeared to be a college. Rebecca went and banged upon it, thudding her fists against the huge doors until her hands ached and the bones of her wrist were sore and the flesh bloody. Then she saw the bell-pull and tugged on it again and again. Surely, somewhere in those great halls there was someone who would answer her call? She waited and waited, but no one came to the sound. Rebecca sat upon the doorstep, her knees pulled up to her chin. She would pray. Where was her upbringing now? The words came easily and, when she opened her eyes, the world around her – though lonely and forlorn – seemed a better place. She would go back, calmer now, and seek her escape. If Brultzner found her, then so be it. For a while, in the eagerness to escape her tormentor she had forgotten to place her trust in Him who can always be trusted.

Rebecca made her way into a square in the centre of which was a huge statue of some past notable riding a horse. 'A horse, a horse: my kingdom for a horse!' She laughed to herself as she saw the road sign to the left of it. 'Railway Station' – oh yes! Rebecca was exhilarated. She was fit, and running well. As she turned into what she saw to her delight was Station Road, Rebecca had not even broken sweat. How long had it been? Was Brultzner unconscious? He could not be: the blow would not have concussed a child for long. She reached the bridge and saw the station ahead. The bridge was the only way to cross the river. She could not throw him off the scent. She would have to run faster.

When she arrived at the station, in all its Victorian grandeur, Rebecca heaved a sigh of relief and looked around. There appeared to be no one about, but there must be – this was a railway station.

"What are you looking for, Miss?"

The speaker was a young man who lay curled up in his sleeping bag just inside the station entrance. He was resting on a flattened cardboard box and had a bottle of something to hand. Beside him, also curled in against the cold, was his dog. The man's face was grubby and his clothes filthy. The sleeping bag, covered in the grime of the pavements, looked as though it had never been washed. His few possessions were placed tidily to one side, wrapped in an old canvas holdall. Everything about the young man and his possessions was besmirched, soiled by the hardship of his way of life. Only the dog looked clean and well-groomed; its coat shone and had been brushed and combed.

"I need to get away from here."

"You might find a taxi in the rank – it's just round the corner – but I doubt it, and it'll cost you tonight."

"Cost me?"

"It's Christmas Day. You don't get anything for nothing on Christmas Day."

Money – she had no money! It hadn't occurred to Rebecca, but without money she was going nowhere. She could phone. They would take a reverse charge call and then her parents or Peter could pay over the phone on their cards. What was she talking about? There were no trains! The station was deserted – the ticket office closed. Christmas Day! If there were any trains running at all, the last one had gone. 'Why, why does the world come to a standstill on Christmas Day?' She looked at the young man.

"I'm sorry. I've no money on me."

"Don't worry, Miss. The dog and I have both eaten today. The hostels were open for Christmas dinner."

"Why aren't you there now?"

"I don't like being shut in. There's nothing worse than that."

She smiled and left him. The taxi driver – if he existed – would take her home. They could pay when she arrived. The driver would surely agree to that, wouldn't he? It seemed straightforward, now – if there was still a taxi on the rank. There was – in the shadows of the station a car waited, tucked back against the wall under the sign which read Taxi Rank, just beyond the lights thrown from the street lamps. Rebecca ran over to it and tapped on the driver's window. There was no one in the driving seat, and no sound of a movement behind her, but a hand closed over her mouth and held her tight. A body pressed her up against the car door until there was no breath left in her, and Rebecca passed out.

The telephone rang and Peter rushed through to Corvin's study. It was late on Christmas afternoon and he and Esther had waited all day. It was Mrs Cushion on the phone. Corvin had arrived at the bishop's house in the early evening, and Mrs Cushion had seen to it that he had a good meal – the poor man was starving. He was asleep now in front of the bishop's fire, but she'd soon have him tucked up in their guest room. It seemed the best thing to do; she hoped they wouldn't mind him staying the night. He was so tired, poor man. As far as Mrs Cushion was concerned, she couldn't see him waking until late in the morning, but he needed the rest, and it was wicked to wake someone from their sleep without good reason. She was sure Mrs Unwood would understand and, to rest assured, Reverend Unwood was in good hands. Anyway, she hoped she had put their minds at rest. He was safe and sound.

"I am disappointed in you, Miss Unwood. I had expected better," said Horst Brultzner, when Rebecca regained consciousness.

Rebecca, bitterly disappointed and shocked with the reversal of her fortunes, just stared at the vampire; it seemed pointless to say anything. She was back in her prison cell and her captor sat on the bench opposite watching her closely.

"I have done all that is humanly ..."

He paused at the word, and smiled,

"... possible to accommodate you and treat you with the respect, and how am I rewarded? I am served with treachery, violence and deceit!"

She stared at him, but remained silent. The means of her defeat was clear. He had anticipated her attempting to reach the railway station, and simply driven there to meet her, while she ran, aimlessly, round ... round where? Rebecca had no idea in which town or city she was incarcerated.

"I am doing all I can to preserve your world as you know it, Miss Unwood. I am attempting to negotiate an understanding between our two sides. It would be far simpler for me to have your rectory burned to the ground and destroy all within it. Tell me why I should not do just that? Your fiancé has betrayed me – his disloyalty is the act of a blackguard – and yet I try to spare him, for you. Tell me how I could have behaved more honourably, or with greater courtesy?"

Rebecca found herself unable, more than unwilling, to speak. Here was an evil ... creature justifying his actions with eloquence, while they were exhibited as the malefactors. Eventually words came from her, but she was unsure whether they were intended or thoughtful; they seemed only to sum up her feelings at that moment.

"You cannot live as you do in our world."

"My kind is small in number. Our needs are circumscribed. We do not plunder the earth as you do, nor are we two-faced. Your species, priding itself upon its magnanimity in saving threatened species from extinction, are – at the same time – destroying the very environments these species need to survive. You watch yourselves driving your own planet to destruction, yet your gluttonous desire for an evermore materialistic style of living precludes you doing anything to halt the damage. You sit, trapped in a web of meaningless dialogues, and deny me the right to exist."

"Your soul, Horst, is in a state of purgatory. Your evil is concomitant upon what you are and the way you live."

"My soul is my concern, Miss Unwood – not yours. I do not subscribe to your god or his view of this world. That does not deny me the right to survive. The 'harm' I do – and I use that word loosely – is no greater than that which you inflict upon your fellow beings and the other creatures with whom you share this planet. To condemn as evil something with which you are uncomfortable is typical – if I might say so – of the religious viewpoint, which sees nothing but its own point of view and condemns, in one way or another, all others ... All I wanted, Miss Unwood, was to live peaceably in my Victorian rectory for a while. Was that too much to ask?"

He spoke quietly but without hesitation, and with a clear and – to Rebecca – deadly vision of purpose. He was as angry as she had ever seen another being; even her mother's ireful outbursts were mild compared to the rage of Brultzner. She did not hear it in his voice, but she saw it in the coiled spring of his body; she felt it in the imprint of his hand across her mouth and she smelt it in the enclosed menace of the prison cell. Rebecca tasted fear such she had never known. She had heard how captives were reluctant to leave their confinement lest it angered their tormentors and made matters worse. She now regretted her futile attempt to escape because she was aware that Brultzner had been driven into a corner. What he had in store for her she dare not think about. She could only pray that it would not happen, while knowing that it was inevitable. She saw Brultzner as having no choice. He was determined to have his will and nothing would stop him. She remembered the recording Nadine had played to them, only four days ago, of Sarah's story in her own words. 'He told me that all creatures had to eat and then he took me in his arms, stroking my hair and paying me compliments and kissing me gently on the mouth. Then he opened his shirt, slit his chest and brought my mouth to the blood. I felt revolted for a moment, but as I sucked his warm blood I remembered Matthew at my breast and I felt his blood warming me and I sank my teeth into his chest, and he sighed like a man does in love.' That was Rebecca's great fear and the torment of her soul – that she would enjoy it and become like him, damned to wander for all eternity along the paths of a joyless existence, cut-off forever from the peace and tranquillity of her God, never to be at one with her parents again, and never to know Peter's love.

Brultzner seemed to know what she was thinking for he watched her face with the same intensity a weasel might watch a rabbit whose blood it was about to drink. Like the rabbit, Rebecca could only tremble and revert to a state of quivering terror as he stood and approached her.

"If I cannot appeal to your mind then I must bind you to me through the allegiances of your body. Your race does not repudiate what it desires, however vile that desire might be."

He lifted her from the bench by the nape of her neck, and brought Rebecca's face close to him. She felt his lips on hers and the sharp stab of his teeth as he kissed her. He pulled open his coat, yanked his shirt aside, slit his chest and brought her mouth down onto it. The blood spurted into her mouth and Rebecca gulped, breathless and in panic. She pulled back to scream, but his grip was inexorable and she could only hear her thoughts crying 'No, not this, spare me this for the sake of my immortal soul' as she wolfed down his blood, feeling it run over her chin and drip along her neck onto her breast.

Ainsley Bint was beside himself with joy. He had arrived late for Christmas dinner at his mother-in-law's because he had been chasing the details of his get-rich-quick-and-stay-rich-for-all-eternity scheme. He wouldn't have to do a thing to the Gobley House – even the name sounded just perfect, now! He could turn it into a tourist attraction – the Gobley House of Horror. He'd make a fortune. All he'd have to do was make sure the vampires couldn't get out. He'd seal them in with crosses and garlic, and stuff like that. He could fix the windows and replace the doors with glass, and charge people to come and see them. It would be like the House of Sheer Terror on Yarmouth seafront – only real. He'd have to dump some of the furniture just so that people could get round, but that wouldn't be too much trouble.

They could come in through the front door (where they could stump up the readies) and make their way up the stairs to the loft where Bert had hung himself. They would pass her body at the bottom of the stairs. He could have a couple of life-like dummies made for Bert and Clara. Then, they could peek into the bedroom at Close. He might even be able to arrange for them to go up to the coffin because Close could be confined. Then they could come back down the stairs and up to the turret room – he could just imagine them all shitting themselves as they made their way up those winding stairs – and see Grise Culman in her coffin.

He might have a bit of trouble getting the entertainment licence, but palms could be greased. The punters might not even believe it – people don't believe in vampires, do they? But they love to think they do, and that's where the perspicacious (he wasn't quite sure where he'd heard that word, but he knew it meant clever) man can make a little of what makes the world go round. It would out-ghost any Ghost Walk, out-rip any Ripper Trail and make your London Dungeon and its 'instruments of torture' look like a vicar's tea party – if you know what I mean! People loved that sort of thing – horror, terror. They couldn't get enough of it.

It was a shame it was Christmas Day because every bloody thing was closed! He'd need proper crosses, but he could get those blessed all right – the Reverend Unwood would oblige because he had always liked his mum. Well, who didn't? But sodding garlic flowers! Where the hell do you get garlic flowers? He'd spent an hour on the web and found nothing. Never mind – someone would know for a little consideration.

CHAPTER 5

Her heart's desire

Mark Chambers phoned Alan Read when he returned from hospital with Nin on Christmas afternoon. She felt much better and had insisted on discharging herself. Besides, she was terrified and wanted to be with Mark and her son. When she arrived home, everything Alan Read had recommended for her protection was in place. A young, 'Christian' vampire like Grise would have no chance of entering the house. Nin turned up her nose at the smell of garlic which pervaded her home, and straightened several of the crosses with which her husband and son had sealed the doors. Otherwise, she was satisfied and just hugged them both.

"She won't come again, will she?"

"I think it likely, Nin, but you leave it to me. The boy and I have talked about this. No more harm will come to you. Rest assured."

Nin opened her mouth to question him, but the expression on his face silenced her; they had been married a long time and in certain moods he was not approachable.

Alan Read put the phone down. He had contacted the key three but his head was in a whirl. 'Corvin safe ... we still wait for news of Rebecca ... Brultzner now at large ... Close and Grise on the rampage ... Nin safe ... Owen and family safe ... we must trace Brultzner ... we must find Close ... Grise will come to us ...'

"Ludo, Alan. We're waiting for you," said Penny, catching his eye.

They were – his wife and four children sat round the table with their counters at the ready. They always played Ludo at Christmas – at least once. Alan's father had been in the navy where the game was called 'huckers'. He had been obsessive about Ludo, and it was now a family tradition.

Nin had walked in to the smell of beef cooking. Mark hadn't known what else to do, and so had put it in the oven. It wasn't exactly Christmas dinner – not without turkey, at six o'clock in the afternoon and with none of Nin's usual trimmings – but it was a meal to share, and the day was special. She had steamed the usual vegetables, roasted the potatoes, "popped" the Yorkshire puddings in the oven (Nin always cooked these as individual puddings in the Suffolk way), and made the gravy in the meat juices. They were alone, of course. Mark had phoned round and apologised to the rest of his family. "Nin has been taken ill. Yes, she's in hospital. No, don't visit – not today. I'll let you know how she is."

"No one was really put out, Nin – don't worry. We're a big family – the other women will pull together. We were going to the farm, anyway."

Nin was satisfied with that; they had taken Mark's mother there on Christmas Eve ready for the big day, and so she was settled. It was quiet without the others, and Nin ate even less than usual. Her colour was unnaturally high – florid would be the word – and Mark found his eyes wandering to the marks on her throat. Four puncture wounds where his ex-mistress had sunk in her teeth and sucked away his wife's blood. He couldn't go on like this – not living in fear. The woman would strike again, and she had to be settled, one way or the other. One of his teachers had read a story in which some natives staked out a goat to attract a tiger that was terrorising the neighbourhood. Mark knew he was the goat.

Afternoon became evening and they watched television. He had told Alan Read not to interfere – that he would deal with it in his way. He didn't want Nin further upset. He and his son had spoken, and both agreed that Nin should know nothing of what they intended; and that Mark Junior should stay with his mother.

The evening wound into Christmas night and Nin became drowsy with the food and wine and loss of blood. Mark kept the fire stoked high and the central heating up: he wanted her to sleep and recover. At last, her head having nodded forward more than once, he persuaded her to go to bed. She leaned on him as far as the bedroom. If he could remove this curse from her, then that would go some way – surely – to make amends, wouldn't it? Not that it had ever been acknowledged between them, but he knew of his betrayal and he sought some peace, at last.

"You do love me, don't you Mark?"

"You know I do."

"But you do, don't you?"

"Yes, I love you Nin."

"And you always will?"

"Yes, I always will."

She seemed satisfied by that and snuggled her head down into the pillows as women will. He had always liked to see her warm and comfortable and safe – well, nearly always. Mark Chambers waited until his wife was snuffling, and then snoring lightly. He saw her asleep and secure before he went downstairs to where his son waited in front of the fire.

"All right, boy, you know what we agreed. Stay with her all the time. Never leave the bedroom. You promise me, don't you?"

"You know I do, dad."

"And don't fall asleep ... If she should come here, don't look at her. I mean it, Mark – don't be tempted in any way. You understand me, don't you? Because you will want to do as she asks, and your mother won't take another assault."

"I understand, dad. My crucifix won't leave my hand. You be careful."

"I'm not sure how my scheme will work out, but you must be patient and stick to our agreement."

"Don't worry, dad, I know what I'm doing!"

"Do you, son? I wish I did."

Mark squeezed his son on the shoulder and they both went into the kitchen where Mark's wax coat hung on the back of the door. He looked at it, ruefully, and put it on, stepped into his boots and then took his shotgun from the cabinet on the wall. He stuffed some cartridges into his pockets, hugged his son, pulled open the door and stepped outside. He heard the key click in the lock as his son closed the door behind him, as arranged. 'Vampires don't knock on the door – no, but it felt safer that way.'

He didn't know exactly what he was going to do, but then he didn't know too much about vampires. Alan had told him the usual stuff, as he and his son had listened with what would have been incredulity had they not seen Nin's plight. It didn't mean too much, though – not really: stakes, decapitation, burning, iron, earth ... you couldn't expect a normal person to get their heads round such things.

He knew that he would become aware of her if she was in the garden, but he didn't want to challenge her at home. He didn't want to foul his own nest. Should it turn out all right, they would hope to live on there afterwards. He had talked it over with his son because he thought someone should know – if only for Nin's sake, later – what he had in mind. That was when the idea of the fox occurred to Mark Junior. His family had been troubled by a fox after the chickens up on the farm. It would be natural to wander up there, just for a few minutes, even on Christmas night, just to take a look at the run. He had brought the Land Rover up to the house earlier in the day (and paid a fleeting but vital visit to the farm) after their discussion and before they went to fetch Nin from the hospital. Everything was ready, if she should come.

Mark looked up at the night sky. He enjoyed life, and staring at a starlit sky was one of its joys. 'Twinkle, twinkle, little star, how I wonder what you are ...' There were mysteries that could not be explained. A teacher had told him once that some of the stars we saw each night no longer existed. They had burned out long, long ago and yet their light continued travelling to Earth. If you could get your head round that, death lost its fear.

"Mark?!"

It was a question and an exclamation. She hadn't expected to see him, and there was elation in her voice. He hadn't heard her arrive; there had been no sound on the gravel of his driveway. So much for PC Billing's recommendations! He didn't turn. He had the feeling that she might be able to see through him, to know – by looking into his eyes – what was going on in his mind, and that he didn't want. It would be all right when the desire came: lust always drove out thought.

"Hello, Grise. I was hoping you'd come."

"You were expecting me?"

"Yes."

"You know ..."

"Yes."

"It's another world, Mark. You know what happened?"

"I know something of it – not all."

He didn't want her to know too much – didn't want her to think that he was in league with Alan Read and the others. For his half-formed plan to work, he had to be just Mark – her Mark – Mark of remembered and sought-after pleasures. He shuddered.

"Are you cold, Mark?"

"A bit," he lied, thinking it might take her thoughts in the right direction.

"It's not cold in my world, Mark. Where I am, you'll never be cold ... You've got your wax coat on. That's when it all started, wasn't it – you and me in your wax coat. Do you remember that?"

"Yes – very well."

"I've never forgotten that moment, Mark."

'It was the way she fitted so easily inside my wax coat that got me, and her arms round my neck, curling round my neck.' He still stood facing out towards the road, no longer looking at the sky and tensed with waiting.

"Aren't you going to look at me Mark?"

He turned and it was as he'd feared. Despite everything she had done to him, the attraction was still alive. Even the memory of Nin's mangled neck did nothing to alleviate his desire. He still felt the excitement – the dark eyes, the black hair, the way she had of looking down and then up under her lashes without lifting her head, the smile, the affection she radiated and that irresistible energy all overwhelmed him. He wanted her; her physical presence dominated his driveway. Somehow her attractions were now enhanced. Alan Read had warned him about that, and he'd warned his son again and again, but it made no difference. Their affair had begun in winter and blossomed throughout that season. Now, it was another winter and another beginning.

"Where were you going – with the shotgun?"

"Up to the farm. We've had a spot of bother with a fox in the chicken run."

He looked at her, and the next moment his left arm was round her waist, and he was lifting her to him. Grise reached up and clutched his mouth with hers.

"Not here, Mark. Let's go up to the farm."

His groin had that awful ache in it again. 'She was warm and inviting. I felt my juices flow into her and it was glorious – to be wanted like that.' Mark Chambers closed his eyes. He couldn't believe how easily it all came back to him, and not with distaste but with anticipation. He released her and felt for his car keys. When she saw them, Grise laughed in that way of hers and shook her head.

"No, let's do it as we did before – in my Range Rover."

They stood outside her back door. She'd been back several times to inure herself against the loss of her family and to fetch clothes which she would need: no one had thought to watch her home. Grise smiled at Mark and handed him the keys.

"You'll need to open doors for a while. Oh, Mark, take a shower with me! It's all right. I took precautions – I'm warm to the touch."

He had no idea what she meant, and a few minutes later their clothes were in a heap on the bathroom floor and they were under a warm shower and she was soaping him all over. Her eyes glistened with lust; he felt himself harden and reached down.

"Not here, Mark – wait until we reach the barn."

Later, he dressed with relief, realizing how close he had come to satisfying his desire for her; she smelled wonderful and the sight of the water coursing down over her body had brought back memories of the pleasures they had shared. She was luxury and beauty and satisfaction beyond dreaming.

When he came into her bedroom, Grise had on her wax coat and the jeans she had worn for their first tryst. Her hair glistened in the light of the stars shining through the window. Her desire for him was tangible. He didn't want to lose the moment, but he didn't want to share her thoughts. She leaned into him, under his arm, in that way she had when she wanted to indicate submission. He walked with her behind the bungalow at Beachlands, and helped Grise into her Range Rover.

"I drove last time," she said.

"It would be good if you drove again."

"Yes," replied Grise, scrambling over onto the driver's seat.

The drive to the farm was all he remembered – her scarves loosely about her, that boyish cap on her head pushed slightly back over the mop of hair, being driven by a woman …

"You're not used to being driven by a woman, are you Mark?"

"You …"

"… said that last time. I remember, Mark. I remember every word we ever spoke, every muscle on your body."

She still seemed strangely manly at the wheel, but this only excited him more. When she caught his eye looking at her as only a lover can look, dull and bemused with longing, his heart sighed. The tracks were muddy and rocky and, once again, they were thrown together and, once again, they laughed with affection.

When the vehicle pulled up by the barn, he jumped down and went round to help her out 'just like the first time.' Grise slipped down and slid inside his coat, looked up and laughed. The heavy coat no longer held her arms down but she shrugged it off anyway. Her nostrils flared, and he noticed how her mouth curled as she eased back from their kiss to look at him. There was triumph in the half-smile, the gloating satisfaction of a woman who had got her way. He carried her to the barn, and went in among the bales of straw stacked ready for the sheep. He had been warned that vampires were quick, 'so fast, so animated, you'll not see her until it's too late.' His mind was so focussed now, so intent on what he had to do that he felt his concentration to be brutal.

He didn't know how to kill, and had no instinct for it. Vermin, certainly, he had shot, but he had never killed as he must kill now – with a barbarous weapon, and in cold blood. Was it 'cold blood'? What the hell did that mean – there was nothing cold about the way he felt! Still holding her tightly against his chest with his left hand, he lifted her chin with his right as he had so often done. There were tears in his eyes. She saw them and wondered, and mistook them for gratitude. Grise stroked his cheek with her right hand, sliding it down along the edge of his nose and on to his neck. She unbuttoned his shirt and twiddled the hairs on his chest between her fingers. Her lips brushed gently against his; here was her heart's desire – the man she had wanted for such a long time. With her other hand she loosened the belt of his jeans and slid her hand across his hip. 'Once you've known a woman in that way, a woman who has given herself to you, freely, there is always a bond between the two of you.'

He took charge. He had no choice – another moment's delay, and he and his family were lost forever. Mark ran his arms along the sides of her body, allowing the fingers to brush against her breasts and slide to her waist. They nestled there, fleetingly, and then he turned away from her and let his coat drop to the floor of the barn. Grise saw his shoulders flex and a gasp of anticipation rose from her throat.

The next instant he reached down into the straw and turned with the pitch-fork in his hand. As fast as she was, Grise was weighed down with surprise and expectation. Mark lunged at her with all the savagery he could muster, bringing the pitch-fork up and under her rib cage. He heard the fragile bones crack and crush with the force of his blow and then he rammed the weapon home, shoving her backwards against one of the upright supports of the barn. His muscles tightened as he felt the weight of the flesh on the prongs of the fork and then he stepped forward remorselessly, and drove the fork through her and into the wood. It held her there, transfixed against the barn, one of the prongs having pierced her heart. For a moment he relaxed to re-gather his strength.

Grise looked down at him, her face expressing a mixture of betrayed love and unutterable sadness. Blood sprang from the gaping wound in her chest and spurted from her mouth. A harrowing cry accompanied the blood, splashing it in frenzied droplets over his face and neck and soaking the straw under his feet. Grise's red lips champed down on themselves as though attempting to stem the flow of life from her body, and then the mouth pulled back in a rictus of pain and anguish. Again, that tormented cry wrenched itself from her throat as she struggled against the pitch-fork. All the vitality of her newly-discovered power willed her to fight this killer, and live. Her hands and arms flailed in the air, her feet kicked backwards and she dropped to the floor, the pitch-fork hanging from her body.

'Transfixed to the earth with iron.' Alan Read's words came to Mark as he stared into the eyes of his former lover whose hands were reaching for the tool with which he had attempted to destroy her. He grasped the shaft again and lifted her skywards, bringing his body in under the weight. She dangled there, between him and the stars, until Mark brought her down to earth, changed his grip on the pitch-fork handle and rammed it hard into the earth of the barn floor. Grise writhed and twisted, as once she had in the ecstasy of love, and then her body trembled and was still. 'We've got all morning – and most of the afternoon, too, if we like.' Her words came to Mark as he collapsed onto the floor beside the women he had, however temporarily and however wrongly, loved. 'Well, are you going to get undressed or not? I can't do much on my own.' The tears, latent in his eyes until then, welled up and over his cheeks. Great sobs of misery came from him. Whatever the need for what he had done, his sense of disloyalty to the woman he had once loved abided.

He knelt beside her for a long, long time until the blood began to dry on the corpse, and became sticky on his face and hands. He tried to rub it off onto his trousers but the gore stuck to him, refusing to be moved. He did not look at her body, but saw only the memory of it in his mind's eye – the beauty that had once given him such enjoyment and which she had bestowed upon him. He may have been driven by physical need, but his feelings for Grise during their time as lovers had been ones of affection and love. He shuddered – not with cold, but with remorse.

Still averting his eyes from the corpse, he reached for his coat and fumbled inside the pocket. He needed to assure himself first, and he needed help. He couldn't do the rest of this alone. He thumbed-in the number and waited. His son answered.

"It's done. Take a look at your mother."

The silence that followed his request was broken only by his own breathing, which now broke from his chest in slow sobs. Then, Mark Junior was on the phone.

"They've gone, dad. Mum's neck is clear."

"Stay with her, son. Attend her when she needs it … but I expect she'll sleep, now. I'm sure she'll be all right, but there's still Close. We've to settle him yet."

There was anger in Mark Chambers now, and it was a relief to be able to vent anger against the perpetrator – the instigator of all this trouble. He didn't stop to think that it was pointless, or even untrue. It just felt good to be angry. Anger justifies. Anger is the hallmark of the self-righteous. He fumbled with his phone. Now was the time to end it all, and he wanted someone else to be responsible. He heard the phone ringing, and Alan Read's voice answering.

"Busy Christmas night, Mark," said Alan.

The grim humour appealed to both men, but Mark continued to look away from Grise's body. The very thought of what he might see was enough. Alan's medical bag, as well as his holdall, was by his side. He had offered Mark a sedative, but the builder declined. They were waiting for Martin Billings to arrive. Alan was determined that the night should bring 'closure' for Mark Chambers, and closure for all who had ever loved Grise.

He had found Mark numbed with guilt and grief and had approached Mark's family in the farm-house to assure them that "there was nothing to worry about. No – don't come out. This is nothing to do with the farm. Yes – Constable Billings is dealing with it". No – he couldn't say more: he would come round in the morning.

He had asked Martin to rouse the undertaker, but not to involve them yet. "Just pull rank, Martin, and come with a coffin". There had been a reluctance to oblige in Martin's voice. It was the fear of taking responsibility. Being a maverick in spirit was one thing: being a maverick in action is quite another. Alan sighed. They had to stick together now – had to help and support each other. Coping with the bereavement of Owen's family would be difficult enough without Corvin's help.

If they could just deal with Grise's body and have it placed in the coffin – that would be something. When the policeman's car pulled into the farm-yard, Alan heaved a sigh of relief.

"You have the coffin?"

"No."

"No? You know what we have to do, Martin. We must have somewhere to place her. It's not only decent – it's absolutely necessary."

"I'm not convinced that we should go this alone. Let the officer class get involved, let them earn their stripes, let them explain this one away. They were warned – Corvin rang Junket while we were in France. They were told this would happen – and did nothing. Call Junket! Call the bishop! Let the boys on the gravy train take the rap for this one, Alan. You and I are way down the rankings. This will get out! Things always do – you know that! Let them face it now."

"You're not thinking straight, Martin. Cast your mind back to the meeting at my house. We took an oath – 'Give us strength, Lord, to strive and conquer for we shall know fear and seek safety in retreat'. Remember? This is no time to retreat, Martin. Mark has accomplished this first cleansing for us. We face – here, now, in this village – at least another four. Stiffen our sinews, Lord, strengthen our backbone!"

"It just seems to me that it is us who take all the risks – the upper ranks should be involved."

"We can't do that, Constable Billlings," said Mark, "Gossip gets out. We need to keep the lid on this for all our sakes. Not least of all Owen and his family, and Nin. No-one need know the details – not even Nin and Owen. If we involve officialdom, they'll drown us in paperwork, and someone will have the press in on it."

"Mark's right – we can't take refuge by pushing this up the 'chain of command'. We have a policeman, a doctor and – when Corvin returns – a priest."

"All right, Alan," said Martin, feeling ashamed that he should be thought the weakest link in the chain, "I'll go and see Old Strowger. He'll be discreet."

"Tomorrow will have to do now, Martin. We have wasted enough time," said Alan, "is there anything here we can put the body in, Mark?"

"There's an old tool chest in the loft of the barn. I'll empty it."

The disrespect they felt showed as all three men looked at the corpse of Grise Culman, who had been 'dead' only a few days, and was now truly dead. The beauty which had flushed the imaginations of the men in the village was still there. Only the animal intensity had gone. Alive she had been an ardent woman; as a vampire she had found her desires unleashed in animalistic fashion. Dead, only the beauty remained.

"You can drive her Range Rover back, Mark. Martin and I can manage."

"I'll see it through, Alan."

"Very well – as you wish."

Knowing what had to be done was one thing: carrying it out quite another. They had heard it described in Sarah's testimony, and read about it in books and seen it enacted in films – but then the camera always moved away at the critical moment. The only consolation was that there was no blood in her now; Grise had screamed and bled her last when Mark's pitchfork shoved its way through her heart.

After they had yanked out the pitchfork, Mark and Martin lifted her body into the loft of the barn and laid it as respectfully as they could onto the boards of the floor. She was surrounded by straw and Mark saw her again in better times when she and he made love, but he shrugged that thought from him now as they prepared her for some kind of burial.

It was Alan, as the doctor, who did most of what was needed. He cut into her neck as a butcher might have cut into meat. As the head flopped back, Mark was actually reminded of Totto Briggs preparing a joint. He had expected the neck to give problems but Alan's knife seemed to work between the vertebrae neatly and quickly, and then the head was severed completely from the body. In Mark's eyes, the life seemed to go from her at that moment. She ceased to be the Grise he had known – the human animation was now lost. He couldn't shake that idea from him – not as they did their gruesome work, nor in the long years that lay before him.

At a nod from Alan, he took the hammer from the holdall, banged the wooden stake through her heart and cut it off short so that it did not protrude from the body. Martin then ferreted around in the holdall and found the garlic with which he stuffed the mouth. Finally, they lifted the headless corpse into the tool-chest and dressed it before replacing the head in position and drawing the wax jacket about to conceal the neck. Mark locked the toolbox and, at a nod from Alan, handed the key to Martin.

Mark sobbed when it was all over. He sat down on the floor of the hay loft and sobbed until his cries rent the air and wracked his body. He sat, his knees pulled up against his chest and his legs hugged in by his arms, and cried until no more tears would come, and he was dry and empty.

"Do you believe in the soul, Alan?"

"Corvin says that we inhabit eternity in our spiritual body, and that our spiritual body grows out of our earthly life as a plant grows from a seed. Our spiritual body expresses the personality we have developed in our earthly bodies, and lives in a state of consciousness with God."

"And is Grise there, now?"

"I can't answer that, Mark. If it brings you any comfort, I can say that many – including my wife – believe that is what happens."

"Yes."

It never failed to amaze Alan Read how much hope and despair could be contained in that single and simple word.

Late into the night of Christmas Day, Martin Billings made his several calls. Alan had insisted that it was he who made them, and Martin knew why. Alan was shrewd enough to realise that to keep people on-side you had to make sure that they were involved – committed to the cause.

Mrs Cushion said that she "would speak to the Reverend Unwood" but that "the poor man was exhausted and needed rest, so please bear that in mind, Constable Billings". Martin sighed and replaced the receiver.

Nadine offered Simon's comfort for Owen Culman's family, but Martin declined (on Alan's advice) "because Simon's brand of comfort might just be a little too stark for Owen and the children". Nadine smiled to herself at the hesitancy in the policeman's voice, but she understood and – privately – agreed. She and Simon had spent a quiet Christmas Day with her sister, where Matthew Brown was kept in safety, but now they were "back home in the village and waiting".

"Alan Read suggests that we wait no longer," said Martin, "if Rebecca or Brultzner have not contacted us by tomorrow morning – Boxing Day – he feels that we must act, and swiftly."

"What does he suggest?"

"He wouldn't say, but wants a meeting at his house – all of us except Esther and Tony. If we don't agree to his proposals, I have a feeling he will go it alone."

"He called the group together, Martin. Alan isn't going to break it now."

"Whatever – you will be there?"

"Yes. Do you want any help with what you have to do tomorrow?"

"Thank you – that would be appreciated. We'll arrange a time at the meeting. I'm giving Old Strowger a ring in a moment," replied Martin, after a moment's pause.

Peter and Esther had spent the day "prayerfully". Martin smiled at one of Corvin's words. The phone call, in the afternoon, from Mrs Cushion had "put their minds at rest over Corvin and now God must answer their prayers for Rebecca".

"Are you content to wait, Peter? Isn't "prayerfully" just what Brultzner wants?"

"I will listen to what Alan has to say. Certainly, I am anxious."

Martin replaced the receiver, but remained leaning on the telephone. After a while, he dialled a number, slowly. Few people knew that number, and even fewer had dialled it, but Martin needed a little taste of revenge. Even so, the wait was breathless, especially on Christmas night when the world stood still. He got the voicemail, and dialled again ... and again. He forgot how many times, but each one added to his pleasure. Eventually, the voice he hungered for answered.

"Superintendent Junket – may I help you?"

Who better to advise the lonesome copper than Superintendent Junket?

"It's Billings, sir."

"Billings?" repeated a slurred voice.

Superintendent Junket had obviously been enjoying his Christmas night – until now.

"From Dunburgh police house, sir."

"Dunburgh?"

"It's a small village, sir – just south of Lowestoft."

Martin could scarcely believe his luck. Junket was clearly drunk, and would be unable to consolidate any response. Martin had never felt so much in control.

"I have a slight problem, sir."

"It's Christmas night ... eh ..."

"Billings, sir."

"Billings?"

Junket usually uttered the name with weary disdain – but not tonight.

"Yes, sir."

Martin imagined Junket dragged away from his fireside to answer a nuisance call.

"Billings?"

"Yes, sir."

They might still be holding this conversation on Boxing Day morning.

"Billings?"

He daren't say "Yes, sir" again – dare he? Nothing, except heavy breathing, came from the other end of the phone. He thought he heard a voice in the background – probably Mrs Junket, wondering what was detaining her husband. Let her wonder.

"Yes, sir."

With how much contempt could you invest the word "sir"?

"Yes, sir?"

"Yes, sir – it's Billings, sir."

"Ah, Billings!"

"Yes, sir."

If only Tony was here! Moments like this ought to be shared. In the background, Martin heard the voice again. Junket was under fire from two quarters. Perhaps he could fire the fatal shot in one delicate pull of the trigger?

"It's about vampires, sir."

"Vampires?"

This was too good to be true. How many variations could they play on the four key words of Junket's life at that moment – "yes", "sir", "Billings" and "vampires"?

"Yes, sir."

"Vampires?"

"Yes, sir."

"You have a problem with vampires on Christmas night, Billings?"

Martin had the vague idea that Mrs Junket might be listening in the background: such was the summarising tone of the superintendent's reply.

"Yes, sir."

There was another pause which Martin decided to exploit.

"The Reverend Unwood phoned you about the matter when I was abroad, sir."

"Did he?"

"Yes, sir – he has a vivid recollection of having done so."

"I don't have a clear idea of where this conversation is going, Billings."

"No, sir?"

"Billings – why have you phoned me, and where did you get this number?"

"Most of the lads have your number, sir. It gives us a sense of well-being."

"Vampires?" said Junket after a further pause to consider the two key phrases.

"Yes, sir," replied Martin, just to enjoy the sound of the phrase, "Have you forgotten, sir? ... You told him that 'the force takes all such matters seriously' and that 'these things are best handled properly – by experts, by those trained for the job'."

"Quite right, Billings – call in the experts. Pass ..."

"... the buck, sir? Only I don't want to make the same mistake I made when Clive Brown was murdered. What were your words, sir – 'Do it by the Book'."

"Quite right, Billings."

"So have you got the Book, sir?"

"The Book?"

"Yes, sir. The Book that tells us what procedures and policies to follow when dealing with vampires. So that I get it right this time."

"Are you drunk, Billings?"

"No, sir – never touch a drop on duty, sir."

"It's Christmas Day, Martin."

"The village copper is always on duty, sir – 24/365."

"Perhaps you should phone HQ in the morning, Martin."

"I thought I'd better go to the top, sir – straight to the oracle, so to speak."

"It sounds to me more of an ecclesiastical matter, Martin. Is Corvin Unwood not available?"

"No, sir. His daughter has been abducted by a vampire – that's why I'm turning to you for policy help and procedural advice."

"Is this your idea of a festive joke, Martin? You've not been pulling Christmas crackers, have you?"

It was the nearest Junket had ever got to humour, as far as Martin could remember and, for a brief moment, he enjoyed it. Then, he played his line again.

"I just needed to 'run this one by you', sir. I was looking for a 'window in your week'. What is your advice?"

"I don't think the book's been written on this one, Martin."

"You mean we're in the vanguard, sir?"

"More the Van Helsing, Martin."

Martin laughed. The old man did have a sense of humour, then?

"You're not suggesting we should go around driving stakes through hearts and cutting off heads, are you, sir?"

"That seems to be the 'order of the day', Martin."

"If you say so, sir, that's good enough for me. Us humble coppers on the beat want to get it right, sir? Well, thanks for your help – we'll see what we can do."

He put the phone down, quickly, but waited. After a few seconds, it rang.

"Martin?"

"Yes, sir?"

"I think we need a talk, Billings. Make an appointment to see me when the holiday season is over."

"Yes, sir – I'll bring a copy of the CD with me."

"CD?"

"Yes, sir. The phone may be Victorian, sir, but the technology's not. I record all conversations that take place in this station, sir – or over this phone. It covers your back, doesn't it, sir? We don't want to lose our pensions, do we? Merry Christmas, sir, and a Happy New Year!"

"You want to do what, Ainsley?" shrieked Sandra Bint at her son, "You're going to put him on display? You can't display a vampire!"

"We've been all through that, mum. As soon as I've got the right stuff, we'll have him – and her – where we want them."

"But tonight he's on the loose in this village!"

"Not for long – just as soon as you make those calls to Dr Read about where I can get bleedin' garlic flowers, we'll have him."

"Don't swear, Ainsley – you know I don't like it."

"Sorry, ma."

"And don't call me 'ma'."

"No, mum … Don't get upset, Ma – mum, there have always been freaks. Look at the Elephant Man and that bloke who had a circus of freaks. People love it."

"I'm going to phone Alan Read, all right, but not for garlic flowers. He didn't know where Sidney Close was, but he will now."

"No, you're not, mum."

Sandra walked across to her sideboard to pick up the phone, but Ainsley's hand rested on the receiver.

"Come along, Ainsley – don't be silly."

"I'm not being silly, mum. The Gobley House is a little goldmine and you're not going to spoil it for me."

"Take your hand off the receiver, Ainsley."

"Certainly, mum."

He did so, and then stopped and pulled the telephone wire from its socket.

"Ainsley!"

"Mum?"

While she stood, gazing at him in disbelief, he lifted her hand from the receiver, took the phone from the sideboard and proceeded to wrap the wire around it.

"You need time to think, mum. You need a period of calm."

"Give me the phone. You don't understand what that Thing did to me."

"You give me your mobile, mum."

"You'll leave me here without a phone?"

"You need time to think, mum. Ainsley – contacts: financiers, dummy-makers, priests. Where's the vicar? Get him to bless a few crosses. Get some holy water and some garlic flowers. Where's your mobile?"

"If you want it, you'll have to find it."

"OK."

He tipped her bag out onto the floor and picked up the mobile from the debris.

"Give it back, Ainsley. You can't leave me here without a phone – not after what happened."

He walked to the door that led into Sandra's kitchen and turned to face his mother.

"Don't go out tonight, mum, and keep your door locked – ooh, and your crosses in place. We don't want anything to happen to you, do we?"

CHAPTER 6

Corvin at the cathedral

It was late on the morning of Boxing Day when Corvin awoke, unsure where he was but completely rested. Mrs Cushion had persuaded him away from the fire after the bishop had become restless with his snoring, but Corvin had no memory of how he came to be in this particular bed. In those first wonderful minutes of waking it did not matter in the least. He could not recall a morning for many years that had been so trouble-free. There was nothing to do, and no one to remind him of what he hadn't done, or might have done, or could be expected to have done. He was free. His soul was lighter, and there was a 'quiet certainty' in his heart. He couldn't have explained that phrase – 'quiet certainty' – but he knew it was true when it drifted into his mind.

It was, in part, a reaction to the total exhaustion that had overwhelmed him. He had arrived unable to walk any more. Had Mrs Cushion not welcomed him into the house, he would have collapsed and slept on the doorstep. There is something about utter physical exhaustion that becomes exhilarating as it passes away. Once you have gone beyond the point of 'utter' and the body has moved into a deep, natural and untroubled sleep, the way ahead is a gentle slope of consciousness. Corvin was moving along that slope now as he opened his eyes, slowly, and surveyed the room.

It was large, and so old and comfortable. There was plenty of space to move, without banging into furniture. There were wooden sills and leaded windows and oak floorboards, which had lasted hundreds of years and, more pertinently, would last hundreds more, long beyond the time when he was troubled by earthly concerns. All time was here – time that had been and time that was to be – and he was balanced delicately between the two. He would never return to the one, and there was nothing to hurry him into the other – not while Mrs Cushion guarded the telephone. Somehow, Corvin knew that she was doing just that; her concern for him was motherly. The sheets – yes, sheets! – were crisp and clean, starch-white clean, and folded over the heavy blankets that rested solidly on his torso He peeped out over the counterpane and smiled; it was a personal smile, one for himself that he need not explain.

His 'quiet certainty' owed, he knew, to Bishop Twiddle's rejection. He had come to the cathedral seeking his God in another man, and 'had found him wanting'. In that knowledge, there was a reassurance. To know that another person cannot be our salvation – or even lead us, unequivocally, towards it – brings peace of mind. Corvin realised that he was free, free to be himself, to be his 'own person'; he was free intellectually and spiritually. If one who vaunts himself as a spiritual leader is unable to lead spiritually, then you owe him no more than the common courtesies. Corvin felt himself to be 'his own man'; free of the petty restrictions another's intellect may wish to impose. He no longer felt he owed the bishop any allegiance; the man would no longer be in his thoughts as he planned 'his chartered course'. Moreover, he actually owed it to himself, both as a man and as a priest, to find the courage to chart that course.

As he stirred on that morning, Corvin did not think through any of this; it was, simply, a 'quiet certainty' in his mind. He slipped out of bed, put on the thickly-embossed dressing gown Mrs Cushion had laid ready for him, and knelt to pray. He prayed for a long time, without framing the thoughts as exact words. There was a purity about his prayers that language would have diminished; he had never felt so near to, or at one with, his God. His prayers touched on his wife and his daughter. He knew they were in safe hands, and all would be well. He understood clearly, for the first time, his soon-to-be son-in-law's calmness.

There was no sound coming from anywhere in the bishop's house, and yet Corvin knew there was the bustle of domesticity. He wandered into the bathroom and ran the steaming water. Corvin loved a bath but a good bath required time; it was not something one could enjoy with demanding voices in the background. He shaved while the water was running, enjoying the way in which it steamed-up his mirror. The razor was an old one: one of those on which a knurled ring raised and lowered the plates which gripped a double-edged blade. There was a shaving brush and bowl and the lather was thick and rich on his face.

It was when he came back into the bedroom that Corvin noticed his priest's garments hanging on the back of the door – washed and pressed and waiting for him. As he ran his fingers over the cassock, he realised that it was still warm from the iron; he felt grateful and complete. It wouldn't have mattered to him, on that morning, whether he went down in his own clothes or those he had borrowed on Christmas night – either way, he would still have been Corvin Unwood – but it seemed polite to wear his own. It showed consideration for the care which Mrs Cushion had bestowed upon them. It did no harm to please; gratitude was a virtue. When he arrived at the foot of the stairs, Corvin could smell breakfast cooking.

"You go to the breakfast room, Reverend Unwood. I won't be a moment."

She wasn't, but there was no hurry, anyway. The table was already laden with a range of cereals and fruit juice (orange or grapefruit), warm toast, soft butter in a flowered dish and white napkins. Corvin sat down and spread himself some toast, just as Mrs Cushion arrived with a steaming pot of tea.

"You do prefer tea, don't you?"

"Yes – thank you."

"I knew. I took the liberty of telephoning your wife this morning, when I heard you rise. You're to enjoy your breakfast, at your leisure, before you set off home. There's nothing to worry about."

"I know. Thank you for the tea, Mrs Cushion, and this fine spread," he said, extending his arms in a gesture that indicated he was beholden to her.

"It's good to feed a man who likes his food, again. The bishop tucks in – sometimes I wonder where he puts it, for such a slim man – but he knows what he likes, if you know what I mean. It gets a little samey – not that I'm complaining." She poured his first cup of tea, scalding and red, from the pot. "Your breakfast won't be a moment."

When it came – sufficiently far behind his plate of cereals to allow him to wipe the milk from his lips – it was all he had anticipated: two grilled pork sausages, two smoked back bacon rashers, two eggs fried in the bacon fat, a round of fried bread, one large tomato halved and grilled with the sausages, and fresh mushrooms also fried in the bacon fat – all arranged on a warmed plate. Corvin tucked in, watched by Mrs Cushion whose beaming smile only added to the enjoyment of the meal she had so lovingly prepared.

"I'll do you some warm toast, now – there's nothing like warm toast and marmalade to polish off a breakfast – and I'll freshen the pot."

She did, and it was a good hour before Corvin, full and pleasantly replenished but not bursting at the seams, moved from the table. As he wiped his mouth for the umpteenth time, it occurred to him that he had not asked after the bishop. It was Mrs Cushion who mentioned that he had gone for a walk in the cathedral grounds.

"There's no need for you to hurry after him, Reverend Unwood. He enjoys being alone. It gives him time to ponder. You will be staying for lunch?"

"I think I ought to be making my way home, thank you, Mrs Cushion."

"Mrs Unwood has her son-in-law with her. I am sure that she is quite content … You're a good man, Reverend Unwood."

"Thank you, Mrs Cushion …," he replied, and knew it to be true.

The cathedral grounds had always held an awesome attraction for Corvin. It was a bright, clear day; the sun was golden and unlikely to be interrupted by scudding clouds, and he walked across the green towards the river. To his left lay the beautifully-rendered flint walls of the Deanery, and he crossed by the old gas-lamp post, walking through the shadows of the beech tree. He looked up along the line of the long, smooth, silver-grey trunk with its high, broad crown and knew he stood in beauty. He loved the way the leaves hung in such a relaxed manner – suggesting an ease drawn from confidence. The tree might be at man's mercy but was, at the same time, beyond him. The leaves had blown away now, of course, but he remembered their golden-bronze of the autumn and the polished red-brown nuts dropping to the ground where they would be found and eaten by animals. It was a slow-growing tree but, over the years, its oval and pendulous leaves enriched the soil around it and – when its time came – the wood of the beech lived forever in furniture, floors and the sleepers that supported the rush of trains through the night.

He noted the herb garden to his right, and thought of Mrs Cushion. The Close covered many acres and contained a mixture of properties and he had often dreamed of ending his days here, but that attraction troubled him no more. With the acceptance of oneself came a release from the worries of the future. He headed for Hook's Ferry – the former water gate for the cathedral. He wanted to stand under its arch and look out over the river. He looked at the statue of Mother Catherine and understood her better after his own journey which, he now understood, had begun long ago – long before the vampire had taken his child. He had no desire to be 'in mystical union' with his God; it was enough to be 'at one' with Him, and at peace with himself.

Peter Twiddle would, no doubt, be around the cathedral and Corvin decided to find him. He headed back towards the West Door, his mind disregarding the bishop's unwelcoming words. Rather, he dwelt on the beauty of the building before him. Perhaps, Peter Twiddle had helped him – in his own, self-centred way – but Corvin accepted now that the journey had been his own. Corvin smiled to himself as he crossed the green of the Close, and then recognised two figures approaching the cathedral from the West Gate of the old wall. They were Miss Mealey and Mrs Teale. Corvin raised his right hand in a broad salute and crossed to them. Corvin's heart had often sunk when these two ladies approached him because he found himself having to make decisions about the colour of the tablecloths on the raffle table at the summer fete, or the position of the table, or the arrangement of the raffle prizes … or any other number of trivial matters. Now, a smile rose to his face.

"Ladies, how good to see you on such a pleasant day!" he said, knowing they were wondering what he was doing in Norbridge – alone.

"Lovely to see you, rector," they chorused.

"Have you come for the Boxing Day sales, ladies?"

"Gracious no, rector," replied Miss Mealey, laughing, "We don't go in for that sort of thing. We always go out somewhere on Boxing Day – don't we, Mrs Teale? This year we decided to come to Norbridge. We are having tea later at that little café near the art college. They are very nice there."

"I'm sure they are ladies. It does one good to get out into the world. So much of one's life is bound up with the indoors."

"Just what I was saying only the other day, wasn't it, Mrs Teale?"

"You haven't come to the sales, have you rector?" asked Mrs Teale.

"More in Mrs Unwood's line than mine, ladies."

"Mrs Unwood is with you then?" said Mrs Teale, smiling as he walked into her trap

"No, ladies," replied Corvin, without explanation.

"No?"

"No."

"I must confess, rector – we were wondering."

"Wondering, ladies?"

"Wondering about Mrs Unwood, rector."

"Mrs Unwood?"

"Where she was, rector."

"Where she was, ladies?"

"Oh, you're teasing us!"

He was, and enjoying it – no longer feeling that he had to explain and justify himself, no longer concerned that these ladies might walk away with the wrong impression. Their impression was their business; his life, and purpose, was his own. Was that what enlightenment boiled down to – a detachment from the trivia of life?

"You are wondering why I am here, ladies?" Corvin asked, comfortably.

"Ooh, rector, nothing of the sort!" they replied, embarrassed and blushing.

"I am here to see the bishop."

"The Bishop!" retorted Mrs Teale, using the capital 'b'.

"I am on my way to see him now."

"Oh," said Miss Mealey.

"Then you'd best be on your way, rector," said Mrs Teale.

"We mustn't keep the bishop waiting," said Corvin, with a laugh he felt most appropriate.

Peter Twiddle had been avoiding Corvin all morning – ever since his rural dean had been late up for breakfast. This tardiness had been to the bishop's relief because he preferred to dine alone, and, on this morning in particular, had been desperate to dine without Corvin. He just wanted Corvin to go. That wasn't too much to ask, was it? Peter Twiddle may, or may not, have known that he had let his priest down. Whatever the truth, he was never going to admit it either to himself or any other living soul. Only Mrs Cushion, in that side-swiping way of hers, might stand a small chance of penetrating the armour of his ... self-satisfaction.

He saw Corvin approaching him down the nave, and he was startled. Nave came from the Latin *navis*, meaning ship, and here was Corvin bearing down on him like a ship in the night, carrying his unseemly cargo. Drake had sent fire-ships in among the Spaniards, and look at the damage he had caused! Was Corvin a fire-ship?

"Ah, Peter – good to have found you at last."

'Peter?' Did he encourage such familiarity? 'Go away – let me exorcise you from my presence!' Was Corvin possessed? Did he need casting out? *Exorcism is usually performed by a person with special religious authority*. Had he, Peter Twiddle, got that authority? He hoped not: it was the last thing he needed. The Bible, of course, contained several references to it. Jesus was a 'dab-hand' – to use the vernacular – at that sort of thing, but Peter Twiddle doubted whether he had such command of the power. The Roman Catholics had been very sensible about the whole thing: special permission was needed (and, hopefully, not easy to obtain) and their guidance stated quite clearly that it was best to 'seek advice from experts in medical and psychiatric science'. Very sensible! Call in the medics! Was Corvin mad?

"I heard you were here, Peter. I hope I am not intruding."

He didn't sound as if he minded whether he was or not; indeed, his whole tone was one of indifference.

"You have come to say goodbye, Rural Dean?"

"Not yet, Peter – Mrs Cushion has invited me to lunch."

Corvin had invited himself to lunch on Boxing Day! Was further proof needed?

"I'm pleased to hear it, Corvin," replied the bishop, with his 'patient' smile ... "You will remember to be careful ... Corvin. Rash actions often spring from incomplete thought," said Peter Twiddle, feeling his own phrase to be empty.

"I wouldn't wish to confuse 'rash' with 'decisive', Peter, and the time for the latter has arrived – here – now – on our doorstep."

Corvin was pleased with "here", "now" and "on our doorstep". He thought he saw the bishop shudder as the words went home. Corvin found himself waiting patiently for the bishop's next inanity. It came, quite readily.

"Horst Brultzner is an esteemed member of ... our community. The actions of foreign ... of ethnic groups cannot always be explained within the framework ..."

Corvin allowed the bishop's voice to dwindle into nothing, and smiled.

"... of our conceptual apprehensions, Peter? Is that the phrase you seek?"

Sarcasm was so alien to the bishop's nature that he did not even begin to detect it in the tone of his rural dean. Corvin smiled at the bishop again. It was a smile that the recipient found unsettling. He had no wish for his ... his priest to ... to move beyond him – to be outside his reach.

"One must not over-reach oneself ..." began the bishop, not knowing where the phrase had come from.

"Before I go, Peter, I wish to make a full confession."

"Was not our communion ..."

"I have found the words, now, and there is more than just my daughter's soul at stake in all of this. I tried to explain on the telephone once – you will remember?"

"I feel, perhaps a more appropriate moment could be chosen ..."

"There will not be a more appropriate moment, bishop – there may, indeed, never be another moment. Last night, neither of us could find the words. Now, I can – and it is now I wish to make my confession, and it is now I wish you to hear it."

"It is not something that we see ..."

"... in the same light as 'other members of the Christian community'? No, but I wish you to hear it. I wish you to hear it, now."

Such an incisive little word – "now": rather like a child demanding ... Corvin did not stop looking at him. The rural dean's gaze was relentless. It would be most unsettling over lunch.

"Perhaps ..." he began.

"There is more to the cathedral than meets the eye, is there not Bishop Peter? There is, within it, a space for me? ... Where we can be alone, and you can listen."

It was not often – indeed, he could not recall it ever having happened before – that Peter Twiddle, Bishop of Norbridge, looked into the soul of another man, but he did that Boxing morning, as Corvin unwound to him 'all his manifold sins and wickedness'. His indecisions at every step of the way – indecisions that he put down to cowardice – plagued him. His mind had, on the long walk, had plenty of time to rove back over the eight months since Brultzner had arrived in Dunburgh. He had tried to latch on to the moment he had felt the first qualms of unease.

He had perceived Brultzner as 'gentry': that had been his first mistake. He saw himself walking submissively towards the King Vampire. What a fool! The only true gentry are the gentry of Jesus. He owed Brultzner no more deference than he owed everyone, and he had confused deference with humility. Esther had been "embarrassed for him" and "disliked Brultzner on sight". She had true religious instincts – not always right, but always unsullied by social niceties. He recalled his horror when Clara and Bert had been found dead, and tracked his failings back to the root of his weakness – the fear of confrontation. When he had hidden – yes, hidden – in his garden and study that night, he had been concerned for the repose of their souls – but had he been concerned enough? 'Did their souls reside in His safe arms?'

"The soul is not an aspect of the person, but the whole person as a living being," he said, breaking his confession and looking into the prelate's eyes.

'Where did Clara and Bert fit into God's scheme of things?' His failings with those two quarrelsome people had their source further back. They sprang from the same well of ineptitude as his lack of support for Penny Read when she stood up for the children in church. "Stop sitting on the fence, dad! Strap on your armour, pick up the sword of your faith and get out there into the battleground!"

He had now, but along the way he had failed so many. When he came across Sidney in the churchyard, Sidney had sought refuge and found none 'The ravings of a drunk?' He dragged his thoughts into his confession.

"Sins of omission, Bishop Peter – the failure to do what one knows is right. Sidney wanted to talk about his spiritual abyss, so deep was his shame. Nothing stood between him and God, except me. We knelt before Him, and I knew where my duty lay and yet – weak in my humanity – I drew back ... but we pray for him now ... in sure and certain hope of the resurrection to eternal life ... Somehow, Bishop Peter, that must come to be true."

He remembered screwing up his seventh attempt at a letter to Bishop Twiddle. He saw Necker's body under the shadow of the west porch. He saw Luke Turrel *'waiting for them, somewhere very near, just round the corner.'* And where was Sarah Brown, now? Why had she not come to him in the first place, and in the second? A young woman in turmoil had fled first to the sea and then into the open countryside. She had not turned to the church in Dunburgh, had she?

He had been accused of "watering down his religion", of "confusion and weakness – the people without leadership, the clergy without faith" by the very being who lurked at the centre of all their misery. This Thing had challenged him and, like the wolf he was, played havoc with Corvin's flock. "I can recall times, rector, when men died for their faith and, indeed, killed for it". At the memory of his reply, Corvin writhed in shame.

Bishop Twiddle felt rather proud of Corvin at that moment – as his priest's eyes rolled and he, the bishop, squirmed from foot to foot – but it was apparent that Corvin did not share his pride. He took his absolution and received the sacrament and, as he walked from the cathedral, his heart was lighter, his soul was eased and Corvin felt ready for whatever he was to face.

"Lunch, Peter," he said, "One must not neglect the stomach."

Even Bishop Twiddle did not miss the irony in that comment, as they made their way back Mrs Cushion's table.

"I'll not beat about the bush," said Alan Read, when the six members of their party were gathered at the White House, "I do not agree that we sit and wait. This hands the initiative entirely to Brultzner. Hostage-takers always dictate the terms unless one has the courage to tackle them. Brultzner wants our quiescence on this, and the price of that is Rebecca's freedom. What exactly he has in mind, we cannot be sure, but we will be obliged to agree to it unless we outwit him first. We need to find him, and we need to find him quickly."

He paused as though expecting opposition, but none of the others spoke. Nadine sat next to her father and noticed that Simon's eyes betrayed the faintest suggestion of pleasure, as though the prospect of strapping on his armour, picking up the sword of faith and getting out onto the battleground appealed to him. Penny, whose trust in her husband's judgement was absolute, looked at Peter, who had been the greatest advocate of calm at their previous meeting. His face betrayed no emotion.

"How are we to do that?" asked Martin.

"By following up Tony's lead. Charles Wangford may not be implicated in vampirism or in this abduction, but he has – to steal a Biblical term – given 'succour' to the enemy. This brotherhood of his probably brought Brultzner here, and has certainly shielded him. I think he will know where Brultzner might have taken Rebecca. It could be to some sort of safe house where he has a housekeeper along the lines of Eva Schulz or Katerina Schnell – in which case, perhaps Brultzner has kept such knowledge from his lordship – but it might be to another of these temples. In this case, Charles Wangford is certain to know."

"If we approach him," said Peter, "there is a chance he will inform Brultzner. There is nothing to be gained by antagonising him, and the lives of several people – including Rebecca and the boy, David Stokes – may be put at risk."

"He might inform Brultzner if we approached him – indeed, he would have to because it would be quite clear that someone had stumbled on their secret – but he would not dare inform Brultzner once he has betrayed him."

"And what makes you think he will do that, Alan?" said Martin.

"We must leave him no choice."

"Have you any experience of these societies, Alan?" asked Peter.

"No more than the average person. I only know what I read in the papers."

"Their oaths are binding. We're not talking about masonry here, where dissident members seem to spill the beans to every journalist who shows an interest. We're talking about organisations whose activities border – if necessary – on the criminal. Wangford would not dare to betray Brultzner; it would be a death sentence."

"So once he had betrayed him, Charles Wangford's life would be in our hands? We would be duty bound to succeed not only for our sakes but for his?"

"Why should Wangford turn traitor, or place his trust in us?"

"Again, I can only say that we must leave him no choice."

"How do you propose to put that kind of pressure on Wangford?"

"To be frank, I have not made up my mind how to deal with Charles Wangford, as yet. I would rather leave that to my instincts when talking to him, but there are several possibilities, not least of all the fact that he can neither be proud nor pleased about how Brultzner is using him. Whatever interests their society has, vampirism is unlikely to be one of them ..."

"You're not suggesting that he would co-operate?" said Martin.

"That would be my first tack – yes."

"Alan, you're in cloud-cuckoo land. These secret societies have wiped out whole families to protect themselves – fathers, mothers, children, grandparents: the lot! You can't negotiate with them!"

"As I started by saying – I do not think we have a choice. We cannot allow Brultzner to retain the initiative."

"You think," said Peter, "that Wangford might take our side in this, if he could be sure that we would defeat Brultzner?"

"It is a possibility. Whatever appearances might suggest to the contrary, Charles Wangford is a decent man. This village and its people have been an integral part of his life, and the lives of his ancestors. If he could help us rid the world of this creature, he might be tempted."

"If he is so 'decent' – as you put it," queried Nadine, "why has he allied himself with Brultzner for so long?"

"What the eye doesn't see ... Nadine? This is probably the first time they have actually met. How many times in one generation does Brultzner come here? Why should Charles Wangford incur the wrath of his society by opposing a man who has, until now, been no threat to him or those he loves?"

"He's right, Naddy. Wangford is a man of expedience – not principle."

"You agree with me, Simon?" asked Alan, seeking an ally.

"Only on the point of Wangford's duplicity – you have some distance to cover before I see eye to eye with you on seeking his aid."

"Hear! Hear!" said Martin.

"I can see your reasoning on this, Alan, and I agree that the temptation to outwit Brultzner is a strong one, but I do not share your faith in our ability to 'turn' Wangford and, if we fail, our position would be considerably weaker," said Peter.

"I can see that," replied Alan, "but if we succeed – and move fast – it will be immeasurably stronger. I would entreat you to consider this proposal seriously. Once Brultzner is back in the village – and he may return tonight – we have no option but to agree to his proposals. We must rescue Rebecca to have any chance of beating him."

"What do you think his proposals might be?" asked Nadine.

"That's not an issue, Naddy!"

"It is, dad. It would help to know what we would be agreeing to."

"He would attempt to bind us with oaths of faith and blood," said Simon, "and there are no circumstances under which I would agree to such an unholy treaty."

"You would have no choice," said Peter, "Rebecca's soul would be at stake."

"Rebecca is in the hands of the Lord, son. He will provide for her; it is Brultzner we have to deal with."

"Are you saying that if he returns, you will have nothing to do with his demands, anyway?"

"Exactly."

"Then what are your objections to us approaching Wangford," said Alan.

"It would open us up to reprisals from his accursed society."

"But it may give us a better chance of finding Rebecca – as I have explained."

"I have no fears for Rebecca, Alan. My mission in all this is to destroy this demon. If I thought approaching Wangford might increase our chances of doing that, I would not hesitate to back your proposal – but you have yet to convince me that that is so."

"Dad is coming at this from a different angle to the rest of us," said Nadine.

"My 'angle' on this is as plain as a pikestaff, Naddy."

"Not quite, Simon," said Penny, speaking for the first time, "Alan is arguing a case for finding Rebecca quickly. If you are not concerned with finding her at all then he is arguing against a brick wall – if you don't mind my saying so."

It was said with her usual quietness, but the anger behind the comment was not missed on Nadine.

"I don't think dad meant that he would throw Rebecca to the wolves, Penny – merely that Brultzner is his first priority."

"As I see it," said Penny, "we have no choice but to challenge Wangford, and find Rebecca. When this meeting started I had a completely open mind. I was no more likely to agree with Alan than any of you, but Simon's attitude has changed all that. It is quite clear he has no intention of agreeing to anything Brultzner might suggest – in which case Rebecca is doomed. While there was a chance we could negotiate, I felt approaching Charles was an unnecessary risk. That is no longer the case."

"I agree," said Peter, "and, if you don't mind my saying so, Simon – indeed, whether you mind or not – I find your attitude intolerable."

"That's as maybe, son – you've a right to your views as I have to mine. As far as I am concerned, Brultzner will be handed over to the Lord if he ever dares to rest his head in Dunburgh again. As far as approaching Wangford is concerned, I would caution you against it. Alan has said nothing to convince us that he can turn our local aristocrat, and such men – allied to such societies – are dangerous."

"Nadine?" said Penny.

"I respect dad's views and share them – to an extent – but I would rather have Rebecca back here as a friend than hand her over to the Lord, quite yet."

"Thanks," said Alan, "I would point out that if we oppose Brultzner, while Rebecca is in his hands, there is no certainty she will end up in the arms of her God."

Simon, hurt by Nadine siding with his opponents, took out his anger on Alan: "Rebecca – whatever the state of her soul – is always free to deliver herself unto salvation, Dr Read. None of these creatures need wallow in the swamp of their iniquity. The Lord has given us free choice. It is up to each of us to use it. I do not share your liberalised views about demons. Let them surrender to the Lord. If Rebecca is among them, she can look forward to paradise when her soul is free."

"Dad!"

"Naddy – are you my child?" Simon said, looking away.

Nadine did not answer, and Penny fancied she saw tears in both their eyes.

"Martin?" she asked.

"I share Simon's view about antagonising this secret society. I vote we wait."

"Four votes against two," said Alan, "I will ring Charles now. Excuse me."

When he returned from his study, the others knew by the grim smile on his face that Alan Read had secured his appointment.

"He will see us, now."

"Now?" queried Peter.

"There's no time to waste, Peter. We must act in daylight."

"How did you persuade him to see us so soon?"

"I mentioned the name of his god."

"You're playing a dangerous game, Dr Read. You are consorting with devilry, but I admire your courage. The vote went against me, but I will stand by the decision and come with you."

"No, Simon. I would rather you remained in the village – especially with Corvin away. Penny, you stay here with the children. Nadine, Martin – you have a gruesome task ahead and, anyway, Nadine must guard Matthew. Peter – you stay in touch with Esther. She is our only link with Brultzner – however tenuous."

"You can't go alone, Alan."

"I don't think Charles Wangford is an immediate threat to my well-being," he laughed, "Any reprisals from him will come later – if at all."

The six friends did not move, but stood or sat and looked at each other. Eventually Simon stood, shook his hand and left without a word. Nadine and Martin exchanged glances and followed.

"Are you sure, Alan?" asked Peter, "I am more than willing to come."

"It is far better for you to remain a free agent, Peter. Brultzner could return at any time and someone needs to be in the rectory. If I really need you, I'll be in touch."

"Are you as confident as you sound?" said Penny, when Peter had left.

"Yes, Pen. We're splashing around in uncertain waters, but I think that this is the right course to take. My only immediate worry is you and the children. Do you fancy taking them to your mother's?"

"No – not today. I've too much on my mind. We'll probably go for a long walk with Leo and then come back here. I feel as safe here as anywhere."

"Well as long as you don't leave them at all – under any circumstances – and do not let them out of your sight."

He took her in his arms and hugged her, feeling the warmth of her body against him and the softness of her breasts on his chest. He nuzzled her hair.

"I love you. Just keep your wits about you."

"I love you, too. Take care."

Martin and Nadine manoeuvred the coffin into the loft of the barn without attracting undue attention. They placed it beside the tool-chest and looked at each other. Martin took the key from his pocket. There was no point in wasting time. They both knew that, and Nadine set about unscrewing the lid of the coffin while Martin unlocked the chest. He didn't look at Grise's body, as he lifted the lid. He kept his eyes on Nadine as she loosened and removed the screws. He was fascinated by the way she placed them neatly in a small glass jar they found on a beam in the loft. Her movements were precise and controlled, with no wasted motion. Martin thought her feelings would be much the same.

Grise's soul was at rest now. Once the burial was over, there would be nothing more they could do for the woman with whom they had once shared food. Corvin would go to the family, once he was back, counsel their grief and lead them into the time of the funeral. It would be in the New Year now, surely, wouldn't it? Christmas, of course, would never be the same for any of them ever again, and for Owen Culman's family would always be a time of intense grief.

Where the hell was Sidney Close? 'None of these creatures need wallow in the swamp of their iniquity. The Lord has given us free choice; it is up to each of us to use it. Let them surrender to the Lord, and look forward to paradise.' Simon's words came back to Martin as he watched Nadine. The policeman was no more religious than the average man-in-the-street, and he had never looked at it like that before. To him, Sidney Close was something which had to be destroyed; to Simon, Sidney Close was someone whose salvation lay in his own hands.

"I'm ready, now, Martin. Shall we move her?"

Now that she was truly dead, Grise's corpse had stiffened over the hours which had elapsed since they had driven the stake through her. She was cold – dead-cold as distinct from vampire-cold – to the touch. He knew that rigor mortis – the stiffening of the skeletal muscles – set in anything between five to ten hours after death, and would disappear within three to four days. By the New Year, her corpse would be softer to the touch. It was unpleasant work, used as Martin was to handling corpses: corpses from car crashes, corpses from rivers, corpses of suicides, corpses from fires, corpses alone in their homes, corpses of those without homes, corpses ... it was at times like those that he wanted to throw in the job. He never had because someone had to do it; and who better than someone you knew – someone who might care.

Nadine did not share her father's beliefs. Her views were more informed, more in tune with current thinking, but she had lost, through listening to her father, any fear of the state of death. To her, Grise's body was a corpse; the soul had gone. Unlike her father, she was not sure where Grise was now, but she did not inhabit the body they lifted from the tool-chest.

They had discussed how she should be dressed, and decided that a small raid on Grise's wardrobes in the Beachlands bungalow was in order. There, Nadine had found a Chinese-style dress which Grise had bought for a New Year's party. It had the typical high neck, and was made from the finest shantung. Nadine thought, with a wry smile, that Grise would have approved of their choice.

They placed her, reverently, into the coffin – the body first, and then the severed head. They secured this as well as they could to the collar of the silk dress, tightening the neck so that the head did not come loose and wobble from the body. Old Strowger had supplied them with a good coffin, and the silken cloth on which she lay was well-padded to keep the corpse in position. By the time they had finished, Grise's body looked normal for a corpse. Martin had agreed with Old Strowger that the body would not be tampered with; the old man had asked no questions, trusting the village bobby implicitly. A few minor adjustments by the old man himself and Grise would be ready to be viewed by Owen and her children.

She did look beautiful, even in death and with her dark eyes closed. Looking at her, however, Nadine thought to herself that Grise Un-dead was not so dissimilar from Grise alive and well. The same animal passions and disregard for others had ruled her in both 'lives'. Perhaps Brultzner was no more than a catalyst, releasing Un-dead those passions which had ruled – or, at least, tormented – us in life. Grise wasn't someone for whom Nadine had much time, but she was the mother of children and that alone was too sad for words.

"It would be nice," said Martin, "to think she was at peace now."

"I do not share father's views, as you may have gathered. It seems to me that what peace we do not find in this world, we shall not find in the next."

"How would he see Grise?"

"Salvation is by the grace of God, through faith alone."

"So ... where is she now – her soul, I mean."

"With her maker, or cast into the outer darkness."

"Not in Purgatory?"

"That's a Catholic idea. Dad's kind of Christian sees salvation through faith."

"But she had no time to confess."

"She wouldn't need to, in dad's mind."

"He called Brultzner a demon. Did he think of Grise in the same way?"

"Yes. The stake through her heart would have driven the demon from her."

"Returning her to her true self?"

"Yes ... you're really troubled by all this, aren't you Martin?"

"Aren't you?"

"No – not so far as her soul's sojourn in eternity is concerned. We reap the rewards of the life we live."

"You didn't like Grise?"

"She wasn't my kind of person, I suppose. I found her self-centred. I'm rather with Corvin on this – our spiritual body expresses our earthly body, don't you think?" Martin turned away and reached for the jar of screws. He had seen so many bodies, and wondered. Most of them had died suddenly – without warning, with no time to 'make their peace with God'. The idea that Grise, who he had known and liked, might be out there in the ether somewhere, floating around for all eternity, scared him. Nobody deserved that. Well, perhaps some did – yes, there were some he had known who deserved just that for their fate, but Grise was not one of them.

Handling the coffin down from the loft was difficult, but he stood at the bottom and took the weight as Nadine slid it from the loft floor. Straw spattered all around him and he spat it out, but eventually the coffin was loaded into the back of his car and they drove off towards the undertakers with so many questions unanswered.

Sidney Close had returned to his coffin alone and in fresh agony from the disease he had picked up from Sandra Bint. His testicles had felt as though they were the size of melons and his tubes throbbed. He knew the disease was already in his bloodstream. His joints had stiffened and his heart and veins and arteries were on fire. To cap it all she had left him – she, the Culman bitch, had left him. Told him she had other furrows to plough. She had taken to their new life so readily, and Sidney knew that he would never hold her; his dreams of walking with her through the streets of Europe had already faded. She had left him to take her own path on Christmas Eve and, when he woke on Christmas Day, she had already gone from the Gobley house. He knew where, of course, but hadn't followed her. It didn't seem fair, but then life wasn't fair – not to the likes of Sidney Close. Life wasn't fair and neither was … this.

He had hunted: being wicked on Christmas Day of all days had given him some thrill, but not much. The zest for the new life was going from him. Grise had been his first conquest, and he had been all-powerful until she became like him with his powers. He had thought to posses all women, not realising that once they were released from their earthly lives, he held no power over them. Like him, they became vicious and dominating. His power lay in their fear or their desire for him. Why did that desire fade? He could teach her a lesson, of course. He could return for the daughter – the ripening blonde – but would she too then turn her back on him? He needed to hold them once they had been … turned. He needed to retain that power over them. He needed to perfect the art of … seduction. Perhaps he should hold many in thrall, draining them slowly until they came to know and want only him?

First, however, he must rid himself of this accursed infection. He dare not bleed himself white; he was unsure whether or not he could recover from such a drastic measure. The bad blood had to be purged, or cleansed. As he climbed into his coffin on Boxing Day morning, Sidney Close knew that, and determined that he would set out that same night to find a cure. His only hope was in Alan Read, the doctor. He would force him to serve his purpose. He'd have to go to him, bloodsucker or not. Read would not resist – but, if the doctor opposed him, then the wife would get it. He'd give Penny Read a dose of something she'd never forget.

CHAPTER 7

Loyalties

Alan Read drove out to Wangford Park with little more than a notion of how he was going to approach the aristocrat. Tony Crewes's revelations were really of little help; knowing the details of how this particular brotherhood had come into existence was not going to provide a lever. Alan knew that he was going to have to be persuasive; the exact nature of the oaths that bound Wangford was of less importance than his lordship's personal inclinations.

What he knew of secret societies would, as they say, 'have filled a postcard'. He had heard of the Mafia, of course: who hadn't? As far as he remembered, they had been formed to protect their families and later became criminal organisations dealing in drugs and prostitution. There were the Carbonari who were a political grouping of the middle classes and who fermented revolution in the name of constitutional government. There were the Nihilists, but they were confined to Russia and made up of young intellectuals who claimed that nothing was of value and the old had to be destroyed before any new order could be established. There was the Rosicrucian Order, which mingled science with mysticism. He knew of the Ku Klux Klan: again, who didn't? The Japanese had a group with the illustrious title of the Black Dragon Society; this had been a military organisation, he remembered, but with links to businessmen and political leaders. All displayed enormous self-interest, putting the needs of their members before anything else, but they had codes of behaviour to which members were expected to adhere.

His arrival was no less welcoming than Brultzner's had been in March. The gates were already open, and Alan barely had time to note the white bulls on the pillars of Cotswold stone hoofing the ground before he was absorbed in the typically English parkland through which he drove. The carefully spaced oak and chestnut trees that had so impressed the creature who was now his enemy, moved Alan, also. There was certainly an air of informality about Wangford Park and a lack of security that suggested all was well with the world. He found himself being drawn into Brultzner's conviction that all creatures had a right to live, provided their needs did not destroy those who shared the planet. Had Sidney Close not fallen that night in summer and broken his skull on the weights, would any of them now have been the wiser? Would any of their lives now be at mortal risk? Would their souls be in jeopardy? It was more likely, he thought, that they might all be looking forward to a New Year Party at the Old Vicarage. If only people would co-operate with him, and see things his way, all would be for the best in the best of all possible worlds. Instead of which, Alan was now on his way to a confrontation whose outcome would be vital to their task, but which was unpredictable and dangerous.

His car pulled up in the walled forecourt of Wangford Hall and Charles Wangford stood, waiting for him, under the three-storey porch. He smiled as Alan got out of his car, and walked towards him with his hand extended.

"Dr Read – welcome."

"Good morning, Charles."

"Indeed it is, and I should be out with my guests on the shoot. I do hope that we can settle this matter quickly, and to everyone's satisfaction. Come in."

Alan was led through the entrance lobby and into the library. He knew little of architecture or interior décor but he could see from his memory of costume dramas that this was in the Regency style. He noted the mahogany desk and the secretaire chiffonier and, like Brultzner before him, could not resist running his fingers along the reeding on the pilasters.

"Whisky? It is Boxing Day morning!"

"I'd love one."

Charles Wangford poured each of them a generous measure; they clinked glasses, and smiled at each other. The aristocrat's smile did not fade, but Alan became increasingly uneasy as he watched the baronet's gangling and immobile figure and the old eyes staring into him. He realized that he was in this man's power; however detailed the group's scheming (and it hadn't been!), however noble their purpose (and he knew it was) this old man in his tweeds and with his drooping moustache held sway over them all. At the end of their conversation, which the baronet would conclude when he was ready, Charles Wangford would make all the decisions.

"I did not expect you to come alone, Alan."

"It seemed the most sensible course of action."

"Oh, I agree. I simply didn't expect it."

"I think it only right to assure you that whatever is said in this room will not be discussed outside these walls."

"I am sure of that."

Wangford's tone implied that it was his actions, rather than Alan's word of honour, which would ensure the secrecy of their discussion. Alan decided to 'take the bull by the horns' (and the aptness of the phrase was not lost upon him).

"You have some notion of why I am here?"

"The reason you are here, on this particular morning of all mornings, is the name you mentioned over the telephone."

"Yes."

Outside in the grounds of Wangford Park there was the spasmodic sound of shotgun fire. Alan realized that Charles Wangford would normally have been out with the shoot, killing game. He instantly felt far from home, very far from home, and wondered what Penny was doing at that moment. Their life seemed made up of moments, recently: each one destined to support the next.

"You have done your research well, Alan, but you have yet to enlighten me as to why."

"I take no credit for the research."

"I thought not: so who has shown an interest?"

'First move to the old man.' Alan was surprised at his own naivety – to have slipped so easily into being wrong-footed, by a false appeal to his modesty, made him angry with himself.

"I think it might serve our ends best not to include others in this conversation."

"But others are involved? Many?"

'Second move to the old man.' The old man, suddenly, did not look so old, but remarkably sharp and alert to any threat. It was a second's comfort to Alan as he realized that Charles Wangford also had something to protect; but he couldn't shake the thought that the baronet was close to his desk, and the belief that in one of the drawers of that desk was a revolver, which he would not hesitate to use. From the grounds came another burst of shotgun fire.

"Many?"

He had to take control of the conversation. Alan realised that but, instinctively, he held back. He wanted to encourage Charles Wangford to talk himself round to what he must have already guessed. It was always best to listen to patients because given time they told the doctor what he wanted to know.

"There are ten of us."

The baronet's eyebrows flickered slightly; Alan could see that, despite himself, Charles Wangford was surprised.

"So many?" he replied.

"Do you know what has been happening, Charles?"

He insisted on using Wangford's Christian name. They had always been familiar: it seemed artificial, and menacing, to revert to a formal mode of address.

"The day to day life of the village seems to tick by quite peacefully."

"There are undercurrents of vulnerability, which render it an unsafe place."

The baronet smiled and took a long sip on his whisky.

"Are you personally involved in that 'vulnerability', Alan?"

It was a deliberately direct question. The old man had a soft spot for Penny Read, and Alan knew it would concern him to think that she was threatened.

"No, but the threat is always present."

"So you come on behalf of others?"

"I come on behalf of certain others, but also the village as a community."

Alan watched the baronet's eyes as he spoke. He wanted to set the old man back on his heels, but not too obviously. It struck him that Charles Wangford would not appreciate anyone trying to manipulate him.

"Is the knowledge of these 'others' as extensive as yours?"

"Yes."

"I see."

So now he knew that his secret society was exposed – at least within a group of ten people. There was no expression on the baronet's face as he faced this knowledge. The secret had remained within his family since the time of the

Norman Conquest – perhaps centuries before – and now it was covert no longer, unless he took action to ensure that it remained so.

"How did you come by this knowledge?"

Was he was looking for a traitor, or merely trying to ascertain the extent of the damage? From what Tony had said, the herdsman knew at least something. What about the other workers on the estate? Did they simply know enough to do their job, but not enough to ask questions? Did they fear enough not to gossip?

The two men looked at each other; both were sufficiently shrewd to know what was going through their opponent's mind. They were 'opponents' in as much as they both had something to protect and that 'something' might divide their interests. 'Something to protect.' That phrase had come to him twice already that morning. He had 'something to protect': his wife, his children and his way of life.

"I remember you coming to this village, Alan."

"I love this village. I think it a way of life worth preserving."

"I know. I recall speaking to your senior partner, Jim Maxwell, when you arrived on the scene. We were both impressed with your lack of ambition."

Wangford smiled. He enjoyed seeing things the way the world did not see them. It let him know that he was aware of older values – those values and codes of conduct the world was prepared to lose for a moment's excitement or gain.

"He admired the way you saw general practice as the pinnacle of the profession. We need to keep the community intact, Alan. We do not need the waters muddied."

Was it a warning, a plea or a moment of indecision before he arrived at the coup d'etat? He repeated his earlier question.

"How did you come by this knowledge?"

"One of our number has an interest in history."

"Not this kind of history, Alan. Where did the need to know spring from?"

Wangford knew that his society had been betrayed, but could not believe one of his people was the traitor. Alan knew that the boy's identity must remain a secret.

"You were not betrayed, Charles; it was a matter of disillusionment. We did – and do – have a need to know," Alan persisted.

"Another?" asked the baronet, with no trace of familiarity in his tone. His own glass was drained and he nodded at Alan's.

"I am driving."

"Not for a while; and I dislike drinking alone."

He took the whisky glass from Alan's hand and turned to the drinks cabinet. When both glasses were replenished he handed Alan's drink to him, but from over the desk and then sat down on the desk. Alan found this unsettling and moved to the french window: not that there would be any chance of escaping through them. It was merely that he felt safer the further he was away from Charles Wangford.

"So," said the baronet, "you will not tell me?"

"I think it better to keep names out of our conversation. We did agree."

"We agreed nothing of the sort. It was a suggestion on your part."

"But I think a sensible one."

"Sensible from whose point of view?"

"This is a matter of an issue, rather than one of personalities or proclivities."

"You're hiding behind words again, Dr Read. Who is to decide what is, or is not, reprehensible?"

"The threat to our community is reprehensible."

"We keep returning to 'our community', do we not? Do you consider that my weak point?"

"No – I consider it one of your strong points."

"You are a wily man, Alan," laughed Charles Wangford, "It is unfortunate that you were not wily enough to steer clear of this issue."

"How could I? I was drawn into it as a doctor, and as a man – just as you are."

"You have drawn me into it, Alan. Some things are best left alone. You should have been wily enough to realise that."

"Now you are playing with words."

"No ... I am stalling for time, while I think."

"Take your time. We have until darkness falls, at least."

Charles Wangford gave him a hard look, and Alan detected the asperity that had come bubbling to the surface at their meeting in his conservatory after the funeral of Luke Turrell. They had drunk coffee then, and Alan had felt somewhat less light-headed; he was not used to whisky in the morning. Charles Wangford took his glass and poured him another.

"I am driving, Charles."

"Don't worry about it, Alan. One of my men will see to you."

He brought the whisky over to Alan, and stood by him looking out of the french windows. The sounds of the shoot still reverberated across the parkland.

"I am lucky to be here, Alan. I know that. I am one of the privileged elite."

"None of us can be held responsible for our birth, Charles."

"No," laughed the baronet, and their conversation seemed, once more, to have reached the equilibrium they both desired.

"I warned you before about groping in the dark, didn't I, Alan? If only you had listened."

"Events have pushed us beyond connivance, Charles. From what I told you then, you must realise that ... After the funeral, I was unsure. Now, I know."

The baronet was silent and Alan thought he saw his eyes glisten, damply.

"You haven't actually asked me what it is I want of you," he said.

"No," said Charles Wangford.

"Or what has brought me here today with such urgency."

"You will tell me in time. There will be time."

'Charles – how well do you now Horst Brultzner?' The words of their first encounter came back to him, but such directness would not serve him now. Charles Wangford needed time to come round. Alan sipped his whisky and waited. Given time, patients always told the doctor what he wanted to know.

"What does loyalty mean to you, Alan?"

"Not betraying a friend; having an allegiance to someone or something."

"You believe that loyalty imposes a duty on one?"

"Yes."

"You will understand, then, that I would find disloyalty repugnant?"

"Yes, I can see that, Charles."

"It would be a dereliction of one's duty to one's ties or allegiances. Have you ever been disloyal, Alan."

"I hope – I think not."

"Yet I feel you are here to ask such faithlessness of me."

"I know, Charles ..."

"No, you do not know – excuse my interrupting you, but you can only imagine. The two things are not the same, not the same at all."

The baronet seemed tired again, and walked away from the window. When he reached his desk, he paused before opening the top drawer. Alan sensed, rather than noticed, that Charles Wangford had unlocked the drawer before pulling it out.

"This gun has always remained here – ever since my father shot himself. It is a reminder to us of that time and the fealty we owe the Brotherhood."

It was the first time he had used the word. It was a kind of acknowledgment, and Alan felt the crisis approaching.

"I said earlier that I admired your lack of ambition, but I do not admire your parochialism. You are very English, Alan – too English for the imbroglio in which you and your friends now find yourselves. The societies of which you talk are endemic to every country of the world. Some are scurrilous organisations – self-seeking and insular, yearning only for their own advancement in wealth, possessions or power – but many spring from the highest motives. They are based on principles outside your understanding and exist for the good – not to the detriment – of the societies which gave them birth. I say 'outside your understanding' because, like all of us in this country, you take your freedom for granted. There is no other country in the world that has such a long history of the simple democratic right to go about one's business unmolested – provided one inflicts no harm on others!"

He paused, still speaking to Alan's back and still holding the gun in his hand. Alan remained quite still, not wanting to concede the advantage he thought his ignorance might hold.

"Societies such as the one about which you think you have some knowledge exist for the destruction of evil in all its form. They oppose tyranny. They assert the rights of the individual in countries where such rights are not guaranteed by government, and where people are threatened by groups who would either dominate or despoil their lives. Cast your mind back over the news items of the past few months. What can you remember? Everywhere – or nearly everywhere – in the world there is persecution, often by small groups upon their own communities. Where there is no law and order, there is oppression. How many times recently have you seen foreign powers turn a blind eye to the activities of mercenary groups within their countries? How many times recently have corrupt politicians and warlords created mayhem amongst their own peoples, for their own ends? Need I go on?"

Alan had to turn; it was a direct question and he could not avoid it. He looked Charles Wangford in the eye, deliberately keeping his gaze from the revolver. Alan did not speak, but merely nodded his head.

"It was from such venality that these principled societies grew. Yet they are but men, and subject to the same temptations as other men. Such groups can be vulnerable – their leaders know that – and that is why initiations are undergone, allegiances sworn and unbreakable oaths solemnly declared. No one in the Brotherhood has ever broken the code of its origins or ever betrayed another of his brothers, and lived. Loyalty is paramount and secrecy a cardinal virtue. Once their existence is known, once their supposed purpose – always perceived by the ignorant as being lawlessness and disorder but in reality always the opposite of these vices – is 'known' they become impotent – open to manipulation and criminal activity."

The baronet paused again and looked closely at Alan, who felt he was reluctant to say more and yet impelled to continue. He had spoken in generalisations. Apart from the passion latent in his voice, his tone was that of a university lecturer. Alan had learned no more than he already knew of the Brotherhood. He saw that Wangford's discourse was an appeal, but beneath the address lurked a threat.

"You wonder how it is that a society pledged to oppose evil can support a brother who – by your lights – represents just that quality. For all of us, all the time, there is a question of balance. Have you asked yourself what harm has been done? ... I can see, by your face, that you have, and that your answer is the same as mine – none. All creatures have the right to life, have they not? Has the man you clearly view as your enemy ever taken another's life? Think carefully, Alan. I do not know why you are here – not exactly – so think carefully before you involve me further. Is another life at risk? It seems to me that – barring an accident, which was no fault of his – the one of which we speak has trodden a cautious, one might say circumspect, course. I am pledged to protect a brother. The circumstances under which I would break that pledge are unimaginable, and the consequences for me terminal."

Alan knew the time had come to state his request. No more whisky was poured. Charles Wangford had not moved from the desk to which he had gone before speaking. The baronet had tried to warn him off; he had attempted – through a quiet explanation of the origins of his society, and a hint at how it fulfilled its current role – to steer him away from action. He was as near death at that moment as he had ever been. Moreover, he was the only one in the group who had felt impelled to push the matter forward with some urgency. It would be easy to thank Charles for his hospitality, and leave. Alan knew that was what the aristocrat wanted. What had been said was known only between the two of them, and Alan would swear his friends to secrecy.

"Let nature take its course," said Charles Wangford.

The idea was seductive. Trust Brultzner to state his terms, abide by his proven quiescence and leave the village in peace. Even Peter Vishnya believed that Rebecca would be returned unharmed. What was to be gained from action? 'He can neither be proud nor pleased about how Brultzner is using him.' How wrong was he to think like that? Charles Wangford did not see it in those terms at all. Had Brultzner stood on the side of democracy and freedom in the countries he frequented? Was it him, and men like him, who removed the corrupt from power in quiet coups whose very nature did not make headlines? Clearly, Charles Wangford believed that to be so.

Quietly, and with great deliberation, he told Lord Wangford what had brought him there on that Boxing Day morning. He spoke of Brultzner as a plague, and expressed his fears not only for Rebecca's life but for her soul.

"We have still not waded in too deeply, Dr Read – not quite. I repeat, let nature take its course. If harm has been done, we are in no position to undo it. If it hasn't, action on our part can only exacerbate the situation."

"We are talking, almost flippantly, about a young woman's soul, Charles."

"You are talking flippantly, Dr Read, and with irreverence. Let us leave souls to the clergy. You go back to your medicine, and let me return to my farming."

It was almost Charles Wangford's final plea. It was Alan Read's final chance to shake hands and withdraw, but he advanced further.

"I need your help, Charles. I need to know where he might be."

"Even if I knew, I would not tell you ... The easiest way for both of us now is for me to shoot you, and then hand myself over to the police ... A whole way of life is at stake here, Alan. I have no desire to threaten you, but I must ask whether you are aware of what will happen should the Brotherhood be disturbed? You have thought of Penny and your four children?"

"Another whisky?" asked Alan.

The relief on Charles Wangford's face was a 'joy to behold'. Alan laughed at the familiar phrase, and future harvest festivals and Christmases – happier times to come – passed between them. The baronet offered his hand. Alan turned his shoulder slightly, as though loosening a stiff joint and then brought his fist forward in a long curving sweep which caught Charles Wangford under the jaw with all the weight of Alan's thirteen stone. As the aristocrat tottered backwards, Alan caught him and sat him gently in the desk chair.

When he came round, the chiffonier had been opened and the keys placed carefully on the table amongst a litter of books, papers and maps. Charles Wangford was taped to the chair with parcel tape from his own drawer and gagged with his own handkerchief, which was also taped round his mouth. Alan Read was crouched over the table, shuffling through the papers and holding a map in his left hand. Charles Wangford realised that the secrets of his Brotherhood were now in the hands of the enemy.

"Sorry I had to hit you, Charles. It's not really my style, but you left me no choice. I heard you unlock the desk drawer when you went for the gun, and guessed the key to unlock your secrets was somewhere on the ring. Where else would you keep such knowledge but in your study? I shall make a written record of what has passed here and what I know of the Brotherhood, for my own protection and that of my family. I shall include these papers with the letter. Everything will be placed where you have no hope of finding it. Should any harm come to me or my family, a second letter – also placed safely – will lead the authorities to your files. Do I make myself clear? Your continued existence as a Brotherhood depends upon my family's continued welfare. Brultzner will not arrive here until after dark. By then, I anticipate that Rebecca Unwood will be back among the living. I shall phone the house once I am away, just to make sure that you're not tied up all morning – forgive the office humour – and I presume you'll be able to explain things away. Should Brultzner contact you when he arrives back, I suggest that you keep all this from him. There's no point in stirring up muddy waters, is there? Once I return – hopefully, overnight – we can settle this once and for all. As you put it – "let nature take its course".

Alan gave the baronet a friendly smile, which was not returned by the grey eyes and walked out of the study, glancing briefly along the hall of the stately home as he did. He hadn't expected to have to hit Wangford and was still in a state of shock, but he did have the information he needed. He would phone the three, write his letter and hand everything over to Martin for safe-keeping and post another letter to a solicitor friend: this latter to be in a separate envelope marked 'Open only on my death' with a third, covering letter. There were two other temples of the Brotherhood, within a few hours driving from Dunburgh, marked on the map. Peter would drive south and he would take the northern run. Hopefully, Brultzner would be hiding Rebecca in one or other of the two. If not, he did not know where to turn and they would, yet again, be at the mercy of Brultzner and his allies. Alan Read had no time to be frightened as he drove out of Wangford Park and, therefore, no time for doubt. That was good; doubt in oneself was just another enemy.

Sandra Bint waited until first light and then left her house in search of help. She had spent a desperate night, more full of anguish than any night she could remember: none of her divorces had given her so much grief as Ainsley's betrayal. She found that she was making her way to the rectory, first. Somehow, talking to Corvin would help and Rebecca was so kind. She arrived to find them both missing, and it was Esther who answered the door.

"Sandra, can I help you, dear?" she said in a vacant manner.

"Are you all right, Esther?"

"Yes, dear, I think so … I feel so lost. I don't know where anyone is, anymore. I don't know where I am!"

"Let me make you a coffee," said Sandra.

She stayed longer than she had intended and got nowhere. Esther hadn't seemed to know anything, other than that Corvin would be coming home later. Peter had "gone for a walk" and she didn't know when he and Rebecca would be back. When Sandra left, the old lady was staring at the kitchen wall as though she was watching a film – an old film in black and white.

Sandra hurried on: she would find Alan Read quickly and leave everything in his hands. Sidney Close would be dealt with by lunchtime, but what about Grise? Ainsley hadn't been lying – he didn't have the imagination for that – and Sandra knew her friend had fallen foul of Close, and was with him now in that awful house.

Sandra suddenly felt very alone. Once she had seen Dr Read, he would take over and where would that leave her? Grise was ... whatever. Sandra had never cried, but she felt like doing so now: perhaps Alan and Penny Read would take pity on her? The White House was silent: not even their dog, Leo, barked. The family must have gone for a walk. It was, after all, Boxing Day. She must keep reminding herself about that: this was Christmas and everyone was on holiday.

CHAPTER 8

The house across the marsh

Rollie was as good as his word. He was waiting for Tony by the churchyard steps when he arrived with Anton. Rollie looked suspiciously at the wolf, which eyed him with reserve. They were natural antagonists and Tony smiled as he watched them.

"Don't worry, son, he won't hurt you – unless you piss me off."

He swore deliberately. He wasn't in the mood for any of Rollie's 'knows' this morning. Getting out of the house had been difficult enough. Beth had been up early and tried to stop him. When it became clear he had every intention of going, she'd said "at least take the children with you, Tony" in order to make his actions look less than fatherly. He did feel as though he was deserting them on a morning when they usually went for a long walk and a pub lunch.

Rollie chortled, rocking his body backwards and forwards until it looked as though his head would fall from his shoulders. Anton growled and the youth's laughter subsided into a steady, rhythmic shaking of his back.

They made their way along the lane by the church. Podd's Field had been freshly ploughed and a gaggle of rooks were picking worms from the upturned soil. They were always such quarrelsome birds, thought Tony – big, vicious, bloody things with their off-white, stabbing beaks. Overhead a flock of black-headed gulls circled; they were about to descend on the field, but were eyeing the rooks, and Tony saw the uncertainty in their flight. The cries of the gulls were harsh, but it was a sound he loved.

"You see that hare?" yelled Rollie, "I seen them dance. You've got to pick the right time of year. My granddad told me. It's their mating dance."

He lingered over the word "mating" and Tony could have sworn he heard the licking of lips. It didn't seem feasible that one day this youth would 'mate' and produce more like himself.

"They love to dance," continued Rollie, "They dash around all over the place, doubling back and jumping on each other. I've watched them. They keep circling back to the same place and then do that dancing on their back legs. My granddad calls it March madness."

"Something to look forward to, son?"

"I should say!"

Along the path, the ivy was in flower. Rollie reached out, and shook it; insects fell buzzing to the ground. A few green berries, which would feed the birds in spring, were forming. The youth leaned over, stuck his nose into the flowers and sniffed.

6 3 5

"Have a smell," he said, "it takes your head off."

The nectar the ivy flowers provided was honey to the insects that survived the winter. Tony felt annoyed that the youth had shaken them so casually: he had a townsman's view of the countryside. The ditches were full of dead bracken. The air was still, and there was no sign of a wind as they arrived on the edge of the marsh.

"She's there."

Tony looked at where Rollie's finger was pointing. It was towards the house across the marsh: the one that had been uninhabited forever. The copse of trees still straggled along the edge of the slope. The branches were bare as far as he could see, although a few dead and withered leaves would no doubt still cling to them with almost human desperation. He felt so miserable that he lost his temper with Rollie, grabbed him by the throat and yanked him from his feet.

"Look, son, I haven't come here to be messed about. It's Boxing Day and I should be with my family ... You know there's no way across the marsh, and that house is unreachable from anywhere, so why are you fucking me about?"

"I know it, I know the way. I can take you there. Let me go!"

His temper passed as quickly as it had been roused and Tony felt guilty for the second or third time that morning. He'd had no right to swear at the youth and no right to assault him.

"I'm sorry, son. My temper's a bit short at the moment. It gets like that sometimes. I'm sorry."

Rollie cracked up at that and, once again, Tony and Anton watched while the youth rocked to and fro in paroxysms of laughter; it only abated when the wolf growled. Rollie cast the animal a sideways glance.

"I've seen her. I go over the marsh sometimes ... I was in Ticker Tyler's scout group – we all were – your son as well, and Ticker showed us the way. You forget after a while because you can't see the path, but it's there and I loike ter go. There are strange things out on those marshes at noit – loits and dancin' things. I reckon oim the only one who still remembers, but I dew, and I can take yew there. She was there, walkin' around in that deserted gardun. It was a dark noit. The moon was only in its first quarter, but I saw her by the loit of the stars. It was cold. I loike being there in the cold – the animals are out, hungry for food. You see stoats prowlin' about lookin' for anything they cun kill – rabbits, the grebes you sometimes foind on the doikes. I've sin rabbits sucked dry out there. They hypnotoise them, you know – make the rabbits stay still and then jest bite them on the neck. Jest loike her. She was callin' somethun' to come to her – I couldn't see what, but she would bend down now and then, and pick somethun' from the ground. Maybe it was a rabbit or a rat: oi don't know, but she was feedin'. She never saw me, thank goodness. She jest stood there in front of the howse with the loit of the small moon and the stars around her. She was loike a ghost. Why are you going there?"

"Someone has to. We can't leave her there alone," said Tony, taken off-guard.

"Whoi?"

"You know."

"Can I see in your bag?"

"Perhaps, later," replied Tony, not wanting Rollie drooling over the holdall.

"Grown-ups always say that when they mean 'no'."

Tony opened the hold-all and Rollie leaned over to look at the contents.

"Can I come with you?"

"You're leading the way, aren't you?"

"No, I mean when we get there. Can I come with you into the house?"

There was no-way that was going to happen: no way on the face of the earth or under the sun that this ... this horror-inveigled youth was going to accompany him to Sarah. Tony Crewes wasn't even sure what he was going to do – let alone have this time with her interrupted by Rollie.

"Let's just go," he said.

"Can I? You can't stop me!"

"Are you going to lead me across this marsh, or are you not?"

Rollie scowled: he didn't like being denied. For a moment he was tempted to push this man into the marsh as he had once pushed his mother into a holly bush, but he placated himself with a smile. It was the smile of one who had power, the quiet laughter of one who had his hands on the jugular vein of life. Rollie liked his metaphor, and chuckled.

"How did she get there?"

"I don't know," muttered Rollie, "but they have no weight when it suits them: they can float and glide. She wouldn't sink into the marsh."

Rollie climbed the gate and made his way across the beckoning field where, in the spring, Tony and his family had seen the lambs jumping in that peculiar jerky style they had as all four feet left the ground together and, in the summer, the whole flock grazed. That time of year seemed inaccessibly ahead – as he followed Rollie over the gate.

Tony hated the marsh – ditches full of cold, brown water and thick stems of coarse, stagnant grasses sprouting from the soggy soil – and he shuddered. 'At least it's daylight. I wouldn't fancy being out here with this kid at night.' At the edge of the marsh were bulrushes, dry as bones despite the winter damp, their big seed-heads catching the breeze, their stalks making a rustling sound as they brushed against the yellowy-brown leaves. 'Somewhere down there, beneath all this decay, lies next spring.' In the branches of a tree above the reeds, a flock of birds was feeding from the crevices of the bark, occasionally fluttering down to the seed-heads.

"They're redpolls," said Rollie, "you don't see them much, no more. They come south in winter. They don't loike the cold."

The world over, thought Tony, creatures seek food and a place to rest. His thoughts strayed from the birds to Sarah Brown, alone in what he imagined was an awful house, living off rats and rabbits. The marsh stretched before them in a seemingly endless panorama of wet reeds, dank water and dying vegetation. Rollie seemed to know the way almost intuitively – no, absolutely intuitively. It looked the same to Tony, whichever way he peered.

"Once you get clear of these alder trees, you can't afford to make a mistake," said Rollie.

"Then let us trust you don't, son," replied Tony.

Where the ground beneath their feet was relatively dry it was also spongy so that they moved with a bounce as the grass gave way and then sprung back again. Tony had the impression that the tightly-matted blades of grass might give way at any moment and that his feet might disappear. Where the ground was wet, along the side of the many dykes, he found himself jumping from tussock to tussock, and slipping sideways. Anton brought up the rear with an uncomfortable lope. This wasn't his kind of country at all, and the wolf's eyes suggested he was far from pleased. Nevertheless, Tony was glad to have his company.

Rollie's excitement grew, the further they travelled into the marshland. He seemed to Tony like a creature from another time, at home in an outlandish environment, anticipating the weird creatures that lived here. He could imagine the youth becoming more and more eccentric the older he got until, finally, a kind of madness set in and he tripped one night and his body was swept out to sea, or lodged forever in the thick, clinging reeds.

It was difficult to balance on the undulating ground, and Tony slithered and fell many times. His hands would reach out and grab at a bulrush or tuft of grass. He would then pull himself up, eye Rollie's feet and stagger forward. The gulls they had seen earlier were circling and cawing above them now, 'like vultures. Am I going to die out here?'

"They're after the insects that drown in the doikes," said Rollie, reading Tony's gaze. "There're bodies everywhere, if you look."

He was right. The bodies of flies and worms were adrift on the black water. The gulls would swoop in twos and threes to scoop them up. 'Hungry: the poor bastards must be hungry to eat that crap.' After what seemed ages, they came to a stretch of dyke, which seemed impassable to Tony. He clutched the holdall and waited. Rollie's eyes were glistening; he was in control, and knew it. Tony could neither go on nor return without his help.

"I did her," he said.

For a moment, Tony's heart sank. Had this nutty youth already been to the house? Not wanting to go through another round of "Who? – Her – Who's her? – Her", he remained silent and waited. Rollie was watching, waiting for the battery of questions which had dogged his life, but Tony Crewes just stared into the dyke.

"I did her," repeated Rollie.

"Go on."

"Her."

Tony held on to his temper and continued looking down into the water, rubbing his hand in the mane of the wolf which sat beside him.

"Necker."

"Thank God it wasn't Sarah.' Having heard Sarah's testimony, they had wondered about Necker. She had been pencilled-in as a future concern; perhaps the youth had saved them the trouble.

"Of course, you went off in the hearse, didn't you?"

"It was before then."

He just had to tell someone and this was his chance, sitting on the edge of the black water with a man whose life depended on him. Only he knew the way across the marsh; only he knew how Necker's life had ended.

"Go on," said Tony, quietly.

Rollie told his gruesome tale, while Tony listened with a kind of prescient foreboding. As the youth came to the end of his tale he concluded "and when I started, I didn't stop. I hit and hit and hit. She didn't half squeal, I can tell yer. She looked up at me with her eyes poppin'. He hands reached for me but I kept hitting that stake ... There was blood and this sticky, white fluid everywhere. She squirmed, but I was doing right – I knew that ..." He looked at Tony. In his eyes, mixed with the joy of the memory, there were tears. Tony Crewes reached over and squeezed his arm. Nutty he may be, but he was only a boy when all was said and done.

"Let's get going, son. Lead on Macduff."

Rollie laughed and stood.

"Once we're over this doike, it aint so bad."

"How are we going to get over here?"

"Jump – it's not as difficult as it looks."

"I thought you said you knew the way!"

"This is the way."

"Your scoutmaster had you jumping dykes?"

"Yes – sometimes: it was part of the wide game. Watch me."

The bank on which they crouched was one of the few places in the marsh where it was possible to run and, therefore, build up some speed for a jump. There was a patch of dry ground stretching back into a tangle of tussocks but, provided one did not trip on these, a jump was feasible, although Tony did not like the idea. The distance across the dyke was no more than five feet, but the bank sloped so that the actual jump would be more. Rollie lolloped in among the tussocks, turned and ran, hell-for-leather, straight at the edge of the bank. His body, as it sped over the bumpy ground, was a bunched knot of muscle. At the very edge, just as he was about to totter down the slope into the brackish water, he leapt up and forward. His trajectory was perfect, the curve of his leap reaching its highest point over the centre of the dyke and he landed on the top of the far bank.

"Throw your bag. You can't jump with that," he called.

Tony had been edgy ever since they met. He didn't trust the youth, and could not shake off the feeling that he was up to something, but there was nothing for it, he would have to follow. He looked at Anton and nodded. The wolf scowled. He wasn't built for long jumps and padded around quite helplessly on the side of the dyke before lowering himself into the water – with a hard, sideways glance at Tony – and swimming to the other side. Rollie was beside himself, leaping up and down in a bouncing movement, as the wolf emerged, sodden-wet. It shook itself over the youth and eyed him. With a long swing, Tony threw his holdall over and Anton loped towards it, snarling at Rollie who recoiled, angrily.

Tony's run-up was hampered by his age and the fact that he loathed gymnasiums. Lacking Rollie's youthful energy and any semblance of fitness, his speed was well down when he jumped. He flailed about in the air for a time, further reducing any forward momentum, and then crashed to the ground, grasping at the wet reeds which lined the banks. They stopped him slithering back completely, but his feet still ended up in the black water and his shoes filled with scum. He said nothing, although the fall added further to his misery. Rollie chortled with delight, as he must have done in the past whenever his comrades had landed in the dyke, but Tony restrained himself from throttling the youth.

When he had squeezed his socks as dry as possible and shaken the dirty water from his shoes, he picked up the holdall and nodded that he was ready. He could smell the marsh now: perhaps it was because he was soaked through with it up to his knees. The odour, which he had initially described to himself as faintly miasmic, was now decidedly fetid. The vegetation on this side of the dyke was rotting, and the air was putrid. A distinct unwholesomeness pervaded the atmosphere. It slipped into his nostrils with deftness, and made him want to gag.

They struggled for what remained of their trek. Even Rollie found the going hard, and Tony saw him stumble many times as they made for the sycamore trees on the far bank. The sycamore was one tree Tony hated above all others. Its floppy leaves dripped wet everywhere in the rains of spring and, although next season's leaves were now curled tightly into their bracts, the trees still looked uninviting. Around them, and stretching towards the travellers as they clambered forward through the wet ground, were long stems of sedge, which poked out from the water. Being surrounded by so much wetness made Tony realise how cold he was; he hoped to God it wasn't cold enough for snow.

By the time they crawled out on the other side, the best part of two hours had passed, but the ground was now firm and there were several hours of daylight left, even if the sky was grey with lowering clouds.

"What's your phone number, son?" he asked abruptly, "Your phone number!"

"I'm not going back. I'm staying to help you."

"Give me your number and get off home."

"I'm not going backwards and forwards across that marsh all day!"

"I wouldn't expect you to. I'm not returning today. Now, please give me your phone number ... It's cold standing around."

"Are you staying in that house all night?"

"Yes."

"Why?"

"You wouldn't understand. I'm not sure that I do. You must go now."

"What if I don't come back?"

"Anton!"

The wolf's name was snapped at Rollie, loudly, and Anton – who had been licking himself clean on a patch of dryer ground – rose and loped over. Rollie misread the call, as Tony had intended, and scooted off to the marsh. He didn't leave his phone number, but Tony was not bothered. A slight, cold wind had sprung up as they left the marsh and he wanted to get inside. Having the youth's phone number was academic, anyway; he might never need it. He waited until he saw the black, curly hair disappearing across the marsh and then turned towards the house.

Sandra Bint found only Amy at the police house – an Amy who knew where her husband was, but kept it to herself. She left Amy her mobile number, and hurried off down School Road, hoping that someone had returned to the White House, but she found it empty. Sandra's natural cheerfulness left her. She just wanted to sleep, but first she just had to get rid of this burden. She turned through the new housing estate that offered a short-cut to Shore Lane. She was going round in circles: Sandra knew that but didn't care. She just wanted the weight off her shoulders, and onto somebody else's so that she could sleep. Her tiredness really was overwhelming.

The vicar, the doctor and the policeman were all out on other business: the only person she could think of now was Simon Palmester. Not that she could talk to him, anymore than she could to Esther, but Nadine would be there, hopefully, and she would listen and tell her father. When Simon answered the door and told her that Nadine was out, Sandra almost turned away, but he placed a hand on her shoulder and turned her gently to face him.

"What is wrong, child?"

She'd never been spoken to like that before. She didn't hold back; she told him everything in graphic detail. The longer she spoke, the easier her story flowed from her and the more comprehensive it became: Sandra even stopped wondering what Simon was thinking as he listened. She wasn't used to speaking, uninterrupted. Her social circle didn't operate like that: someone would always butt-in, and the conversations never failed to veer off on unexpected tangents until the original comment and purpose was lost in a welter of unconnected detail and trivia. This man, however, listened, and the more he heard the graver his face became: by the time she finished, Sandra knew she was free of worry.

"I want you to come with me," he said, "there is no one else I can call on at present – not if Mr Vishnya is out – and I need you to collect a holdall from the police house. It's too far for me to walk in a hurry. Once we get to the Gobley house, the Lord will give me strength. I'll phone Mrs Billings and then she'll let you have it. This is a grim business."

He paused and looked at Sandra. His eyes were thoughtful, but not compassionate. TLC was not something Simon Palmester spread around too freely. The only refuge he saw was the Lord.

"I know you're a wretched woman, Mrs Bint, and that you and your friend lived loosely – a priest picks up much gossip – but neither of you deserved what has happened. All I can hope is that you – it's too late for your friend, of course – have learned something from all this. Come here and we will pray. Then I'll leave a note for Nadine, and we'll get on our way."

He made her kneel before him and grasped her head in his hands with such force that Sandra squealed for a moment, but his hands did not falter as the prayers, asking God to forgive and protect her, fell from his mouth. He seemed to see himself as an instrument through which his God might pour redemption into Sandra Bint and cleanse her physically, morally and spiritually. When he had finished his first round of prayers, Simon released her head, knelt beside her and clutched her hands as he intoned a second battery of prayers for God's help "in the ordeal that lay before us".

Tony stood looking at the house for a long time, once he had assured himself that Rollie had gone and once he had reached the gravel driveway. It was a huge, old place: there were three stories above ground – perhaps twenty rooms in all. It was completely boarded-up, but had once been grand and imposing. Where was she going to be? He didn't fancy searching the whole house. It had been empty a long time; by now all kinds of creatures would have made it their home. There was a porch running along the front of the house: a porch that would once have overlooked the garden with its lawn stretching down to the marsh. Dilapidated – that was the word, the only word, to describe the house and his feelings. No wonder it had never been vandalised: it was miles from anywhere, and the neglected garden was ghostly. Tony was sensitive to houses, and already he sensed a presence pervading this one – nothing sinister: just decay, disintegration and downfall.

He didn't want to go in for a moment. Going in would involve him finding her – actually seeing her, and he didn't know how to react. He fancied the beauty would be gone, and that he would find an old woman rotting away in the cellar. Insisting that he was to be the one to find Sarah had been foolish – "Nadine will understand". Is that what he'd said? He had simply blurted it out; why was he so keen on finding Sarah?

Tony wasn't frightened in the usual sense of the word. He felt no need to reach into the holdall and clutch the holy cross he knew was there for his protection. His over-riding concern was not for himself, but for the young woman in the house. He could not shake from himself the memory of how happy she had been when they met on the cliff path that day during the summer. Having rid herself of that awful husband, she had been looking forward to a new life. Tony felt impelled to help her – to turn the tide of her misfortunes. There were other women, so much more fortunate than Sarah Brown, who spent so much time bemoaning their lot. He hated spoilt women who spent their time moaning, and Sarah's plight had honed his anger.

He wandered round to the back of the house looking for an entrance, but it had been boarded tightly. There was no way in unless he broke something, and he wanted to avoid making a noise. A noise might ... wake the dead! He laughed. Black humour was a special favourite of his – not a day would pass that he didn't see his life in that way for at least a moment. Perhaps if he just sat on the porch until nightfall, Sarah would open the door to him? He laughed again: it was a callous sound, but at least he was laughing at himself.

Sod it – he'd have to break in: there was nothing else for it. He had expected to: he had brought a crowbar for just that reason. Old Doc Read hadn't thought to include one of those in the holdall, had he? Tony walked down the cellar steps and, with his crowbar, prised the boarding away from the cellar door. He then smashed the glass, making sure he cleared the shards from the woodwork (he didn't want to castrate himself quite yet) and then squeezed in through where the broken pane had been. Once Anton had leapt through the gap after him, Tony pulled the boarding back into place. He wasn't sure why he did that, but he liked things rounded off neatly: loose ends were not his style.

It was dark in the cellar, but he picked his way through the scattered debris with the help of his torch, which he'd also put in the holdall. The basement rooms stank: he supposed that the faeces of innumerable animals were scattered around – the crapping of rats, the urine of mice – among the endless bodies of dead insects. He heard the broken remains of old pots crack under his feet; the sound was like that of turkey bones being snapped for the soup pot after Christmas. The steps led up from the cellar into the hall and there the smell of decay was replaced with mustiness: dusty floorboards, hanging wallpaper, damp skirting, bare flexes and flaking plaster – the list was endless. In the dust on the floor he saw footprints. 'So vampires do leave footprints.' He laughed to himself again; the sound was hollow in the empty hall. She had walked to the front door and passed out into the night: that would have been at feeding time. He followed the trail to a closed door and pushed it gently

Inside the room, which must have been the front parlour when the house was alive, her body was huddled into a corner. She was wrapped in silk sheets, sleeping like a baby. What must be going through her mind during the waking hours of night Tony could not imagine, but the loss of her son must be high on the list. Was this her way of committing suicide – or trying to? Vampires are immortal: one good feed and she would glow again and spring fresh into the world. Could he tempt her back?

Brultzner might be right, after all – moderation in all things, and we can live together in this world. Why should Sarah Brown simply cease to exist? Why should he be the one to drive home the 'mercy-bearing stake'? Where the hell had he come across a phrase like that: during a youth spent reading unfettered rubbish? The boy deserved a mother; the mother deserved her son. It wasn't difficult to see, and it wasn't impossible to achieve – was it?

As he watched her sleeping – not wanting and, in truth, not daring to go nearer – Tony was overcome with tiredness. Had it really been only five days since they all assembled in the White House? He needed to sit down, and slumped on the floor propped up against the wall didn't appeal to him. 'Get it over: do it now and go home.' He couldn't do that, and so he wandered through the house and eventually found an old armchair that he hauled into the parlour. He also found a table – a pasting table – and set up the little camping stove he had dropped into the holdall. He'd make a coffee and doze for a while; Tony had come prepared. 'I packed a night bag.' He laughed again; your own company was always best.

As the coffee brewed, he wondered why he was delaying what had to be done. What was his fascination for this young woman and her tragic plight? He had been over it so many times. "One of your lame ducks" Beth had said about the other woman. Was that one of those instances of purposeful feminine insight, or simply a moment of desperation and spite? The attraction certainly wasn't sexual. Even before he had realised what she was, Tony had never desired Sarah Brown in that way. He'd wanted to put his arms round her and tell her that everything would be all right. He'd wanted to wash that husband out of her life to give her a chance. That was all, wasn't it? Had there been more to it than that? Had he seen in her a fresh start for himself – the chance to try once more, just once more, to achieve an harmonious relationship?

He looked around him, as he set a bowl of water for Anton and poured the coffee into his enamel camping mug. Was this the culmination of humanity: two ill-assorted people – a woman all-but dead and a failed romantic – together in a decrepit house? What would Samuel Beckett have made of that, if the idea had occurred to him first? 'Hard luck, Sam: it's my idea, not yours and, anyway, you're passed doing anything about it now, aren't you?' he laughed. The coffee tasted good, and he could feel himself dozing off into one of his cat naps. If only he could sleep until she awoke and roused him!

He woke after noon, hungry, and warmed himself a tin of soup he had brought. He ate it with a piece of soft bread Beth had baked for Christmas, together with some hard Cheddar cheese. He offered Anton the raw steak he had brought wrapped in tinfoil. The wolf looked gratefully at him, and gulped it down in one.

It was cold. He couldn't go all night without a fire, but didn't dare light one before dark for fear that someone would see the smoke. In the meantime, he would gather some wood. There would be plenty about an old house, even if it meant breaking off skirting boards and shelving to keep warm. His search for wood occupied some little while, but he ended up with a good pile in the corner by the fireplace and it was still light when he'd finished.

Sarah remained asleep, of course, but on Boxing Day the dark comes early and he would not have long to wait. As he watched her, Tony couldn't help wondering. He still feared what he might see, but a full belly had given him a false sense of well-being and he walked over to her and drew back the sheets of golden silk, carefully. Her days of living off vermin had taken their toll. Although the blue light still shone within her (illuminating her skin with that unearthly iridescence) the flesh was dry, pale and wasted. It was drawn tightly over her bones, giving the face a near-skeletal appearance – not old, but primitive and worn-out like the priestess of an ancient religion. Such a woman could not but yearn for the return of her youth. If Sarah had come here to die, she was willing it against all the odds, but she seemed to be succeeding. One blow from him would take her across the river. He stroked her face, gently; it was cold like a corpse.

A little walk might do him good. It might help his lunch to go down. Tony peeped through the boarded window. It was snowing: soft flakes were falling. No wonder it had struck him cold when he woke! The ground was already covered with a light dusting of snow. He glanced briefly at Sarah and made for the front door; it was locked. He turned, and went down into the cellar, crow-barred off the boarding for a second time and stepped out through the door pane. He loved the snow. It was more than childish delight. He felt it surrounded and protected. It closed one in, and shut the rest of the world out. Homes became stranded – cut off from the outside world. A good covering of snow brought the country to a standstill. It drifted and blocked roads; it drove everyone to the fireside. He looked up. The bright sky was leaden with clouds now – heavy snow clouds that pressed in upon them. He knew he should phone home, but could see no point. What would be served by having her screaming down the end of the phone? This was a chosen moment in his life; let happen what might, and let it happen peacefully.

Tony Crewes wandered, with the wolf at his heels, in the garden, watching his footprints being quickly covered, even as they were made. These flakes were those big, light, fluffy ones that swirled and danced like fairies. He licked them from his nose, and wafted his arms among them. The snow lay lightly on his shoulders, and covered him until he looked like a walking snowman. He danced to the porch verandah, and stood looking out at this magically-charged world. He leaned on the thin, snow-covered banister, scooped a snowball into shape and tossed it out into the garden. The marsh was now invisible to him, but he knew enough time had passed for Rollie to make it safely home, and Tony was content. The vague track he had noticed leading off into a wilderness of shrubs and trees had also vanished as the snow twisted and turned the plants into obscurity. Nothing could get in and nothing could get out! The edginess he had felt earlier had gone from him; the snow was protective and inside the house, Sarah would be waking.

Not surprisingly, it was the first time he had watched a vampire wake. Not for them the slow meanderings from the realms of slumber, but a quick kindling into the world. Her eyes opened with a suddenness that startled him, and she was sitting up, her eyes on him, a bemused look around her mouth. Her eyes took in the room and, before he realised what was happening, she was behind him, her hand entangled in his hair, pulling his neck to full length. She looked down into his eyes with an expression of the deepest gratitude but, before she could batten onto his throat, the wolf was upon her. Anton knocked Sarah to the ground and worried at her throat, 'alive and waiting, fierce exultation in its gaze, drooling with anticipation.' She expected to feel its teeth rip into her body and tear great chunks of her flesh, but she heard Tony's voice yelling at the beast, and Anton slunk back into the warmth of the fire. She saw Tony standing over her with his hand outstretched, and she took it gratefully.

Sarah was breathing heavily and fearfully as he raised her from the ground, and her eyes never left the wolf whose presence she had not detected when she woke.

"What are you doing here?"

"I came to find you."

"How did you?"

"The boy Rollie saw you in the garden one night and brought me across the marsh. I think he's the only one who knows the way ... he's gone, and will say nothing."

He added the last comment to reassure her; he was surprised at his own perceptiveness. She looked at him, out of the depths of her ugliness and shame.

"Will you order that … thing into the hallway, please? I hate wolves."

Tony hesitated, but only for a moment. When Anton had been consigned to the hall, he shut the door, firmly. Her eyes were upon him again, with the same exultation he had seen when she woke. For a second he regretted sending Anton from the room, but the relief he saw in Sarah's face seemed to reassure him.

"It's snowing," he said, not quite understanding why he wanted her to know.

"Will you walk with me in the snow?" she asked.

Outside they drifted with the snowflakes along the pathways that once bordered the house, and which were found by the snow as it sought to rest. Sarah held him tightly, as though she feared he might become lost in this new country. They walked in silence, fears and anxieties strangely quiet, with no desire to talk.

"How attracted are you to me, now?" she asked, eventually.

She drew back the hood she had used to hide herself and made him look at her dead face – the face of the grave. Sarah then stroked his face and drew him to her, battened on his throat and drank deeply. The sound of her feasting was a gurgle in his ears. Tony felt himself unable to resist. Fainter and fainter he became, as his head whirled with the flurrying snow, until he fell into her arms.

When he woke, the fire was lit and he was slumped in the armchair before it. Sarah was standing with her back to him, looking out of the window at the falling snow. Tony realized that she had smashed off the boarding to give them a clear view of the old garden covered in its winter coat. She was aware of him stirring and turned to look at him.

"Is that what you wanted – to become like me?"

He felt his throat and realized what had happened.

"I'm not ….?"

"No."

She turned and looked at him. The face was more set now: no longer was she the delightful young woman, but a mature one ridden by experience. Nevertheless, that fragility of hers was still intact and he wondered again at the 'breathtaking beauty'. How many times had he used that stale phrase when thinking of her?

"You're taken by my beauty, aren't you Tony?"

She had hardened: there was something steely, almost callous, in the question that was really a challenge. She had read his thoughts and, in her isolation, wondered.

"The honey-coloured hair spilling over my shoulders, the pale yet lightly-tanned skin filled with that inner-radiance, the flawless complexion, the red lips slightly parted as though inviting a kiss, that dreamy look about the eyes ……….Do I encapsulate the attraction?"

"Yes, but don't sound so … so disillusioned with your own beauty, Sarah."

"It's your blood which has made the change. You fell for an illusion, Tony. Destroy it, before it destroys you."

"Is that what you want?"

"Yes."

"I cannot believe there is not another way."

"But you have brought your holdall?" she said.

He shrugged in order to ignore the question.

"I can still remember the first time we spoke," he said.

"In the churchyard when I was talking to mum and dad."

"Yes."

"It was the second time – we had already met in the Jolly Sailors – but that was the important meeting."

"Important?"

"You listened to me as no stranger had listened to me before. You treated me like an intelligent woman."

"You are – and there lies the waste."

"You're a romantic, Tony – a man who refuses to face the ordinary realities of life ... and death. That first time we met all you wanted to do was put your arms round me, and tell me that everything would be all right – yes?"

"Yes."

"Yet my father was lying dead on the beach? ... When we met a few days later, on the cliff-top – what were your thoughts then? ... You wanted to turn my life round. Undo all the mistakes I had made and set me off on the right path, and you would be at every corner along the way to help me – yes?"

"Is that so bad?"

"No – our meeting was a turning point for me in many ways. I began to think of what I might achieve, given the chance, but reality hemmed us in – and still does. It's that you will not accept."

"Someone once said that we ..."

"... can have too much reality. I know, but that doesn't mean we can run away to the sun and hide. Matthew is my reality, and I have made my decision for him."

"What are you going to do?"

"I have lingered too long. I should have walked out into the sun days ago."

"What stopped you?"

"Hope ..."

"... of salvation?"

"... and the desire to hold on just a day or two longer. My salvation – if salvation is there for me – lies beyond this world."

"Why did you take my blood?" he asked, just to turn the conversation for the moment, until he had time to think and come back with something persuasive.

"Vanity – I wanted to look beautiful for you for the last time. I wanted you to remember me the way I was."

He laughed and Sarah joined him. Weakly, he struggled out of the armchair, tossed some more wood on the fire and walked over to the window. He put his arms round her and they both looked out at the falling snow.

"This wasn't forecast," he said.

"You remind me of my dad," she said, laughing.

"Is that a factor in your decision?"

"Yes."

"And you believe your salvation lies ... elsewhere?"

"Yes ... mum was either right or wrong, and I choose to have faith in her."

"Oh, Sarah, it's a hard road."

"You hold on because that is nature's way, but there comes a time to let go, Tony, and I have reached that time."

"Just ..."

"... another day, or two, or three. Perhaps another month, or two, or three? Where does it end?"

"If there was a chance of reclaiming you for this world ..."

"Would I take it?"

"Would you?"

"Tempter."

"Would you?"

"You shouldn't do this, Tony. It's not fair. I have made up my mind. I have struggled with these questions. I am ready."

"None of us know what lies beyond the grave, Sarah. Don't be in a hurry to get there."

"Tony – I do know. I am there!" she laughed.

"Not ... finally."

"Yes – finally."

"You can't go – not in the state you're in."

"I cannot pray, Tony – don't you understand? I cannot pray for forgiveness. What I have become denies me that gift."

"The gift of prayer?"

"Yes. As I am, I stand outside the reach of Him. I can only trust that He knows what is in my true heart. Also, I cannot be brought closer to him through the normal ways. I cannot take part in communion. I cannot receive the sacrament. Absolution will come to me only in the ways you already know – through fire (God forbid), through the light of His sun, or by the hand of a friend. Will you be that friend, Tony? Will you do one more thing to help me on my path?"

He looked at her in answer, but didn't speak.

"It will not be easy, and I will fight you – you understand that? There is a part of me that will not submit. At this moment, I am touched by your kindness in coming here, but do not sleep tonight. Do not trust me."

He could think of nothing to say and Sarah became quiet, nestling softly into the crook of his arm, her head resting on his shoulder. Outside the snow dropped softly, but incessantly. Its cold beauty altered the appearance of everything. When it settled, when the flurry of flakes was over, the world would be changed. It would be a different place, an unreal place, and they would be the only people in it.

"Will you walk with me again?"

Outside, once more, in the falling snow they walked like lovers on a winter holiday, enjoying the snow before returning to the warmth of the fire. His thoughts were on keeping her there, while hers were on enjoying it for the last time; but they walked in harmony, and the falling flakes of ice covered their tracks. She had lured him out the first time, but he felt sure that her purpose now was different. They wandered to the very limits of the garden, and looked out over the, now transformed, marsh. As they stood, staring into space, Tony realized that Sarah was watching the lights of the village. Conceivably she could see, or imagine, where her own cottage stood in Beach Road, and where she had once been happy.

"A world worth struggling for?" he asked.

"Incurable romantic," she said.

"One must dream, Sarah. You cannot be forever shackled to the demands of this world."

"Oh, Tony, if only I could be."

"Could you have considered a life beyond Shane?"

"You know I could. But he was Matthew's father and we would, in some way, have been always tied to each other with the promises we made."

"And you can forgive him – now – for what he did to your father?"

"No! Shane's temper ended the life of a lovely man, and I cannot forgive him. But Matthew was conceived in love, and he is Shane's son."

Tony sighed – a sigh so deep that Sarah looked up at him.

"What's wrong?" she asked

"There's an Old Italian proverb – 'Love is everything to a woman: to a man, only a part of his life'."

"It is love which drives the better part of me now," she said.

"I had thought the same," he said, "but now I wonder."

They walked together, quietly, along the edge of the marsh, now transformed by winter. The whiteness of the snow lightened the night and they could see it clearly as it clung to the bare branches of the alder trees and the stems of the scrub grasses along their path. It was still falling, fleecily, and obscuring their tracks as they walked arm in arm. Sarah led him out from the old wood behind the house, pointed to a track which disappeared into the whirl of bushes and snow, and then they turned and walked back to the house. His head was hung low but she walked, once again, with her particular lightness of step; the suppleness in her shoulders when she leaned to catch his words and the way her legs swung loosely from the hips contrasted sharply with his hunched shoulders and stiff gait, but the ease with which they walked together and their wrapt expressions – as they leaned into the slight, but cold, easterly wind – showed the closeness of their affections.

CHAPTER 9

Peter heads south-west

As Peter Vishnya drove south and south-west on the afternoon of Boxing Day, it was Rebecca and what she would make of what was happening that occupied his thoughts. If only he were in the habit of writing things down, clearly, as she did!

When Alan returned from Wangford Hall, Peter had listened intently to all he said, and then – with only a brief word to Esther, which told her nothing – he set out for the cathedral town of Bath, using Corvin's car. According to the computer route-finder, it was the best part of two hundred and fifty miles and would take him about four hours. He estimated nearer five, and assumed it would be nearly six o'clock before he reached the city. If Alan was right, the coast would by then be clear: Brultzner would have left for Dunburgh-on-sea.

He did not share Alan's belief that seeking for Brultzner was the answer, but he went along with the group's decision. Simon Palmester's attitude had been the turning point in the argument for him. Simon would have left them no room to manoeuvre. To Peter, Simon's bigotry was unbelievable in the modern world. He had no time for the shilly-shally of modern religious thinking, but he found Simon's absolute conviction of always being right to be intolerable.

Brultzner's type of aristocrat was not uncommon in the land of Peter's birth, and he knew what was in the vampire's mind. Brultzner saw them as 'gentry', albeit 'lower gentry'. Once he had bound them with oaths and promises, he would feel safe in Dunburgh, at least for a time. It would not occur to him that any of them would break their word to leave him unmolested; and, indeed, none would have done so.

So he set out with his share of the maps and notes from Wangford's study on the seat beside him. It was, for the most part, a tedious journey, but quiet. The roads were largely motorways and trunk roads, but there was little traffic to hold him back. The A12 took him south. He had respect for the A12: it meandered with quiet contentment amongst the rolling East Anglian countryside, and along much of its route one saw trees and hedges that had been there for decades, farm buildings that had lasted centuries, cows and sheep grazing in the fields even at this time of year, tractors – pursued by crying gulls – ploughing, heath-land that sheltered an infinity of birdlife, the odd fox or deer for which cars would slow down, and rabbits feeding along the wayside. Here was the raggle-taggle of rural Britain, which reminded him so much of his homeland, just as the journey reminded him of his first wife. However, it was the slowest part of his journey.

Once he reached the M25 and the M4, he made up much time and reached Bath just before six o'clock. The London Road became The Paragon, and he was guided to a car park near Pulteney Bridge where he pulled on the handbrake with great relief. He wasted no time, and walked south passed the Victorian Art Gallery and the Guildhall until he came to the abbey churchyard in the heart of Bath.

He knew something of its history. Peter had looked up the history of Roman Britain after their December 21st meeting and Tony's disclosures. Foreigners always seem to know more than the local people. Peter was proud of that, and the information was so good that he would have no reason for remaining ignorant. 'Bath was founded by Bladud, the son of Lud. The boy had been exiled because he suffered from leprosy, and earned his living as a pig farmer. One day he saw his pigs rolling in the hot mud and noticed that it cured their scurvy. He copied them, to find that his illness was also gone. When he returned to court and, later, became king he had a temple built on the site of the hot spring. Here the Celts worshipped, guarding their sacred site with no less than five hill forts. In a druid's grove by the hot spring, the goddess Sul was worshipped. Ironically, she was the guardian of the gateway to the underworld! It was through her that the deities and the ancestors could be approached. The Romans, with all their flair for adopting local deities, transformed Sul into Sulis Minerva and built their temple where the druid's grove had stood. They revered the site and, by the third century, it attracted pilgrims from throughout the Roman world. Shrouded in steam, the pilgrims would have approached the sacred spring believing it to be the home of Minerva and believing that here they could not only cure the illnesses which plagued them but actually communicate with the underworld. Here, at its centre, was the sacrificial altar where animals would be slaughtered in an attempt to foretell the future. Here, too, were found the 'curses': written on thin sheets of pewter and placed in the hot spring, they offered up appeals to the goddess that their enemies, or those who had wronged them, should meet some foul end'.

He was grateful to the website, and he wondered. Had Brultzner really been here, all those centuries ago? He knew Brultzner went back a long way. He had no doubt that it was he who had ordered the flogging to death of the young man who was buried in the churchyard at St George's, but could he have been involved with the Brotherhood at its very birth in the Roman empire?

His more immediate concern, however, was to find that other temple detailed in the papers Alan had discovered in Wangford's study. Minerva was not the only Roman deity to have been worshipped in the ancient city of Bath. He knew that the Roman baths could be entered from either Stall Street or Abbey Church Yard, but could find neither on the map. He turned left out of the churchyard and made his way along Cheap Street. Just west of there, among the courts and old buildings, he found the doorway for which he was looking. It was set back into the wall, as the notes had described – dark, moody and unmistakeable. If Wangford's papers were reliable, this would take him below ground. Standing on the pavement, looking at the door and the grating to the side of it, his heart jumped. Rebecca could be within a few feet of him!

The street was deserted. The night was chill but clear: the stars actually brightened the rather dull glow of the street lamps. He tried the handle, rather foolishly, but the door was as solid as a rock. Behind the building he thought there must be a yard of some sort, and that he might find a back window that could be broken to gain entry. He walked down the street to the side of the building and found a wall about nine feet high, but easily scaleable if he could reach the top. A wheelie-bin gave him all the additional height he needed, and he was over the wall in seconds, looking up at an old window, covered with enough dust to suggest that it had not been opened for decades. The panes, however, were small and his heart sank. Then, at his feet, Peter saw a grating like the one on the street and, beneath it, another window. If he could shift the grating, perhaps the house would be his! It was as easily done as thought. The grating was wedged hard by years of dirt and grime, but his penknife scraped this away and he was in the well looking at the window. It was of the sash type, and so his penknife slid easily into the gap and slid the latch. He was inside.

It was unused and decrepit, but perhaps that was the idea. He didn't like the sensation of someone (or something) being behind him, and so Peter decided to check the upper rooms first. The building must have covered a goodly length of the street because there were, apparently, scores of them. All were fusty, with faded strips of paper hanging from the walls. There was barely any furniture, and this confirmed the feeling that the buildings were never used. The few items spread about were mouldy and torn. He didn't think he had ever been in a more depressing building or felt so out-of-this-world. The rooms did not make sense. They opened into each other in a casual and meaningless way and sometimes into small ante-chambers, big enough to hold a person but with barely room for them to move: yet they were not cupboards. There were lecterns in several of the rooms, and Peter imagined ghostly Victorian figures standing at them, addressing a scattering of frightened clerks.

It was with relief that he arrived back in the front hallway, down a flight of stairs which he hadn't noticed when he arrived. The front door was ahead of him and Peter knew he had to descend into the basement and cellars of this house. At Alan's suggestion, he had brought a few practical items such as the penknife, a torch and a crowbar. He gripped this latter as he descended into the cellar. Wangford's maps had indicated a temple of the Brotherhood underneath this building.

The smell was atrocious and he could not reconcile this with the pride Brultzner took in his secret society, but perhaps that was the point. Any burglar or hooligan would have turned tail, by now. There was obviously going to be nothing here except dead rats and insects, the odd spider trying to eke out a cannibalistic living, mould, damp and dust. At the bottom of the second flight of stairs, he discovered a small but heavy door and got to work with his crowbar. For well over fifteen minutes Peter struggled with the door, convinced that somewhere beyond it he would find Rebecca, supine and helpless, or banging and screaming on the other side but unable to make herself heard. His efforts were all in vain and he became desperate. By now, he was sweating liberally and covered in the dust of the place. He had rarely felt so helpless or hapless: why had he agreed to come?

Weak from his exertions, Peter clambered to the top of the stairs and collapsed into the hall. How long he lay there, he could not remember, but he was aware that his exhaustion was emotional as much as physical. To have come so far, against his better judgement, and to have put so much at risk for nothing went against his practical intelligence. Why? Why had he agreed when he knew it to be wrong? Simon Palmester: he had reacted against Simon Palmester – that was all!

He had more to go on, though, than a mere address. He had a telephone number and an e-mail address against the one word – Father. Peter could not see himself telephoning the 'Father' of the temple, but what choice did he have? The man would be shocked, and suppose that Peter was an important figure in the Brotherhood. He would offer him all assistance – if his acting was good enough. While he measured this alternative against descending once more into the darkness and finding another access to the cellars, Peter became aware that he was being watched. A man was standing in the hallway, his legs astride, watching him as he lay there on the floorboards.

"Evening, sir, may I be of any assistance?"

The tone was that of a music hall-style policeman. Peter took him to be a security guard – someone the premises had not appeared to warrant.

"Possibly. May I see your identification?"

The man smiled as though the humour was right up his street.

"Very amusing, sir, I'm sure. Perhaps I could see yours?"

"Certainly."

Peter handed him his passport (which he always carried as the habit of a lifetime) and the man read it carefully before handing it back.

"I'm pleased to meet you, Mr Vishnya. May I ask what you're doing on these premises at this time of night?"

There was a silence, thoughtful and amusing, as the two men looked at each other. Peter guessed that whoever this man was he must have come in through the front door, and wondered whether it might be worth making a run for it.

"I'm still waiting, sir – if you don't mind answering my question."

"I'm still waiting, too … eh, officer? I asked to see your identification."

"Of course, sir."

Peter hadn't noticed that the man wore a raincoat, but he now removed this to reveal a policeman's uniform beneath.

"Ah, so you are a police officer?"

"Very good, sir, but you still haven't answered my question."

"I wouldn't know quite where to begin … eh, Superintendent – is it?"

"Go on, sir; why not start at the beginning?"

"I have reason to suspect that a young woman may be held against her will on these premises."

"What makes you think that, sir?"

"She was abducted in the early hours of Christmas morning. We have traced her to several possible locations and this is one of them."

"Has this matter been reported to the appropriate authorities, sir?"

"No – we … eh didn't consider that appropriate."

"Yes: very amusing, sir. You're quite a quiet wit in your own way, aren't you, sir – if you don't mind my saying so? May I ask why it would be inappropriate?"

"It's a delicate matter. The young lady in question – who happens to be my fiancé – is the daughter of a vicar."

"Really, sir? This is not, if I may ask, an ... amorous abduction?"

"No – far from it. She was snatched from her home after the midnight service. Her mother and father are both distraught with worry."

"Rather naturally, sir. And who would they be, sir?"

Peter gave the policeman Corvin and Esther's details, which he noted down in a slow and deliberate manner.

"May I ask how you came across this address, sir?"

"A local doctor – a friend of mine – obtained it from a mutual friend."

"A mutual friend of ...?"

"The doctor and the person who has abducted the young woman."

"Would you care to furnish me with any names, sir? We have doctors, abductors and a mutual friend, but we are a little short on names, sir."

Again, Peter "furnished" the officer with the names and addresses he required.

"Now, we might be getting somewhere, sir. I take it these people would have no objection to answering a few questions?"

"I imagine not, but I do have another number – a local one – which it might be better to ring first."

"Who would that be, sir?"

Peter handed over the notebook and map, which contained the details of the temple and the local 'Father'.

"Have you anything else appertaining to this matter, sir?"

"No. Would you make those calls, officer, so that we can have these premises searched?"

"You can rely on me, sir. You certainly seem to have a battalion of notables allied with you, sir. It would be foolish of a mere policeman to fly in the face of such an entourage."

"May I have the notebook and map back, please? We would wish to return them once we have sorted this out."

"Naturally, sir – who wouldn't? But, if you don't mind, I'll hang on to them until we get to the station. They are what we call 'corroborative evidence' as far as your story is concerned."

"Station?"

"Oh, yes sir. We have some serious allegations here and they demand a thorough investigation. We can't do that standing in a draughty hallway, sir."

"No, of course."

Peter felt reassured, if annoyed, by the delay. It was clear that he had struck oil, as they say. The policeman had taken him seriously, and elicited his whole story in the space of minutes. In his country, when he was a boy not so long ago, the police were the last ones you would have gone to for help. In Britain, it had always been different. He thought one more appeal might hurry things on. If Rebecca was trapped in that cellar, she should be released as soon as possible.

"Officer – is there no chance we can get the man referred to as 'Father' here now? There is no suggestion he is involved in this. The young woman is likely – if she is here at all – to have been brought here without his knowledge."

"I understand your anxiety, sir, but it will only be a matter of minutes before we settle this issue. I'll have an officer on the door, sir. No one will enter or leave this building during the brief time we are at the station. I think we might pay this 'Father' of yours a visit, sir – you know, the personal touch. You can't beat the 'personal touch', sir. It's what policing was about in my day."

Peter smiled. He could imagine Martin Billings being overjoyed to meet his colleague in Bath.

"If you could just help me on with my coat, sir – it's a little chilly outside. I understand they've had snow on the other side of the country."

"Really?"

"Oh, yes sir. It wasn't snowing, I take it, when you left?"

"No."

"There you go, sir: there's no telling with the weather in this country – almost a white Christmas, but not quite."

The policeman locked the door to the old buildings behind them as they left, and shook the lock to check its secureness. They walked side by side through the dark streets until they reached the North Parade Bridge, and then paused to look down into the river.

"The Avon," said Peter, with a touch of wonder in his voice.

"Yes, sir, the very one: a tad down from the Bard's birthplace, of course, but that's your Avon. A river where history was made, you might say."

"Indeed."

Peter never felt the first blow, which took him in the solar plexus and removed the wind from him. While he was doubled-up in agony, he felt himself lifted from the ground and something struck him on the back of the neck: he collapsed, sick with agony and apparently unconscious. A second blow landed on the side of his skull. The pain was dull, but the blood flowed down his cheek and onto his collar, as he was lifted again and tossed over the balustrade of the bridge. He had heard that a person's life flashed before their eyes at such a moment, but his flight through the air before he hit the river was more realisation than vision. 'How had the officer known he was in the building? Why did he have a key? What was a police Superintendent doing on the beat?' Then he crashed into the cold, dark waters and sank without trace.

CHAPTER 10

Bludheath

Rebecca was 'of his kind' now; she knew that, and the knowledge stalked her mind, as a restless spirit stalks the places of its past. He had brought her breakfast, but her appetite for human food was passing, and she ate little of the scrambled eggs on toast and drunk little of the orange juice and coffee. He was solicitous, and sat with her while she looked at the food. After the violence, his manner had become calm. He was the old Brultzner, desiring only that he be left in peace to enjoy his way of life.

He assured her that she would not remain long imprisoned, that he would force a treaty with her people and release her once more into the village, but that she must be patient. He would return to Dunburgh tonight – Boxing Day night – and she must wait for him. Rebecca accepted his word more readily now. He was there, as a light in the darkness. Her great fear – the torment of her soul – was assuaged. She was cut off from her parents and would never know Peter's love, but the damnation did not seem quite so joyless. She had been agitated during the night, and sleep had been denied her until he came and she drifted off into a manipulated slumber. 'I was loved in Sardinia': the phrase kept creeping into her consciousness through the hours of the night and she determined to ask him about it ... about his ... about their ... origins. 'I must know. Was that when you became nosferatu?'

She denied what she did not wish to remember – the blood spurting into her mouth and his implacable grip, and her own thoughts crying. He sat watching her as she refused her breakfast.

"Tell me about it," she said, "I have to know where it was you were ... re-born as the ... Being you are."

He looked at her: his expression was one of amazement and relief. He did not desire to subjugate humans; he was fascinated by their objective curiosity. No vampire ever expressed an interest in another's history or circumstances: they lived only to survive and satiate their lust.

"It was so long ago," he said, "but I remember the time as though it were yesterday. The Empire – the great Roman Empire – was coming to an end, but we did not know that at the time. Your village was a great port in those days. We were charged with guarding the south-east coast from the scum of the continent – the Saxons, the Angles and the Jutes as they came to be known. It was the Angles with whom we fought on that fateful day at Blud Heath, but to understand all this you need to know just a little more about my faith."

It seemed strange to hear him use the word, but Rebecca was silent. He was recalling events that had shaped his life – events which had occurred about sixteen hundred years before.

"I was a Roman soldier and our God was a young God, born on a rock at the time of the winter solstice and armed with a sword and a torch. He led us in the fight against evil. He was, for us who believed in Him and followed His ways, the epitome of physical and moral courage. None of us came to Him, to serve Him, without first proving our courage by the ordeals of heat and cold. He was the God of Light and of Truth and we, His soldiers, once admitted to His presence, joined Him in the constant struggle for good. He was the Lord of Wide Pastures, our Saviour from Death, the Guardian of Creation, the giver of Happiness and Life. Ever wakeful, endowed with glory, un-deceivable, the speaker of truth He protected our homes and our farms, our social order and our spiritual life. His faith spread throughout the army, the Emperor Aurelian built a great temple built for Him in Rome, and the Emperor Commodius was a follower. By what you now call the third century virtually the whole Roman army had adopted Him as their Lord.

It was a triumphant time. Everywhere, there was peace and order and prosperity. Trade was established across the world, luxuries flowed into the houses of your country, markets sprang up, your warring tribes came under our command, roads were built, communities flourished, local government was established and able men were enabled to rise to positions of power and influence ..."

"But it was not to last. Barbarians were, as you say, 'knocking on the door' and your faith arrived to weaken our resolve. As late as the years you now call AD 380 the Roman Empire ruled the world but within thirty years your country was in ruins, civilised government had collapsed and trade flowed no longer. We were persecuted by the christians, our temples were desecrated, our religious carvings smashed to fragments and our statues beheaded. By the time of which I speak, Emperor Constantine had issued the Edict of Milan, your bishops were attending the Council of Arles, and Emperor Theodosius had banned all faiths except christianity.

It was against this background of viciousness and persecution that we faced the invaders from what you now call Europe. I was at the Dunburgh garrison. Our temple had been driven below ground, and those of us who still avowed the faith worshipped in secret. It was then that the Angles came to the hill of Blud Heath. We had a fortress there for which Dunburgh was the harbour. Their ships came into the estuary – tentatively, at first, but they became bolder when they realised many of our soldiers had been recalled to defend Rome. Instead of raiding parties, they came in greater numbers, sensing our weakness. They were pirates – nothing more. They did no work, produced nothing of value but came to take what they wanted – to steal, to pillage and to ravage our people, and yours.

I remember that day well. Their ships had arrived both in the harbour at Dunburgh and further south at Frostenham. We had been to pray the previous night when the first of them arrived, and I remember the houses burning and the women and children screaming as these savages came ashore. We bided our time. We thought our strategy secure – they would come to us and fight on our terms. Their greater numbers were of no concern; we were better organised, if no longer inspired. Our weakness, apparent to only a few, was that we were no longer bound as brothers, as servants of the one true God. The christian priest was there, before the battle, blessing our struggles against the heathen, commending our bodies to his god's care and our souls to his god's mercy; but he was not there when the fighting started and neither was his god. Both were conspicuous by their absence from the battlefield. Our Lord of Light had been deposed and we were to pay the price.

We must have been outnumbered by about ten to one. We had faced greater odds before, but He was no longer with us and we knew it. We formed our famous wall outside the fortress and waited. It is difficult to comprehend the chaos of their onslaught. Let us just say it was full-blooded in every sense. They came at us on all sides, and for a while the shields held. We were, after all, highly trained. Even in that melee, there was no fear, no waste of energy, no drifting away from the iron discipline of what today you would call the professional soldier. Surge upon surge of them broke against our shield-line and our swords – those wonderfully short swords, which stabbed their way to what might have been a victory. If you can imagine being attacked by pack after pack of wolves, intent on devouring you, then you have some idea of the scene that day on Blud Heath. They actually howled as they came, and were dressed in the skins of wolves and bears. Some carried severed heads on the end of their spears, while others decorated their weapons and hair with feathers splashed with the blood of old enemies. Their priests came with them, wearing deer antlers on their heads, raising their arms to their heathen gods and crying for the spirits of the dead to come to their aid. They slashed themselves with knives and carried flaming brands, which they tossed into our midst to accompany the showers of arrows.

None of this, you understand, was new to us. We had met it all before when we marched north against the Picts, but He was with us then. We had not turned our backs on Him – our masters had not forbidden us to worship the one true God. One of the shield walls broke – as had happened many times, as was bound to happen in battle; but his time, the place of the dying man was not taken by another. Not quickly enough did brother replace brother in the front line, and they swarmed through like ants upon a carcass. Try as we might, we could not reform, and then it was every man for himself. You should never think of yourself in battle, but only of your brother – if you want to survive and conquer.

They erupted among us. Flame and blood and the cries of the dying were everywhere. I heard our officers calling commands, and some of us re-grouped at times but were torn apart by the weight of their numbers. The smell of them and the tramp of their feet and the crunching of bone as their axes and spears jabbed into us, I remember to this day. Killing for us had always been a matter of duty – skilfully and expertly done – but they enjoyed the slaughter. They mutilated us, hanged dying men, crucified and impaled the wounded with stakes. I was mortally stricken, and left to bleed slowly to death, waiting only for the coming of the crows and nightfall when the rats would be upon us and we would be too weak to resist. The smell and silence of a battlefield when the fighting has stopped are truly terrifying. I say silence because even the moans of the dying seem far, far away and, as one of them, you are truly in a world of your own. The scavengers stayed among us for what they could loot after the main party had passed on, leaving the fortress burning; but soon they too left us and there were only the piles of burning bodies, the crying, the flapping of ragged wings, the snuffling of the rodents and the smell of putrescence. I was conscious among all this; I had lain, my life-blood seeping from me, waiting. I knew I would find movement a struggle, but I was determined not to die there on that battlefield with a heathen spear in my guts. If I was to die, and I had no doubt that I would do so, then it would be in the Roman way, on my own sword.

First, however, I had something to do, and that meant I had to crawl from among the dying and away from the scene of our defeat. I partly-snapped, partly-cut the shaft of the spear from me, leaving the blade to help staunch the flow of blood from my wound, and then began crawling through the dead. It was a slow business, as you will imagine, but I made it to the edge of Blud Heath and then down the slope to the forest of trees which shielded the farmland from the sea. Their shrine was there in a grove among the trees. I had been to look, out of curiosity. The priest was there, now the battle was over, on his knees, in front of the altar of their god. Beyond the altar was the emblem of their religion – the cross. It was fashioned from a tree, shaven of its leaves and branches, and the crossbar was the spar of a ship. It was where their god had been crucified. I knew that, but had no sympathy. I had seen too much death to be inspired by the death of one man. Besides, his followers had desecrated the temples of my god and attempted to wipe us from the face of the earth. Now, defeated and dying, I would avenge that wrong and punish his priest for betraying us to our enemies.

He saw me coming – a mortally wounded soldier, too weak to drag his body across the ground, let alone lift his sword – and he was terrified. His god left him in a breath, but the Lord of Light was with me – Him whom I had served so loyally and so long did not desert me in my hour of need. I took the priest by the throat as a terrier will take a rat, slit him open and knifed his entrails to the tree – his tree, the tree of his god. I whipped him round it with the flat of my blade until he could run no more and then hung him from it, upside down, and slit his throat. His blood spurted out over me as I collapsed, exhausted, to my knees. Whether I drank of it, I cannot say, but I may have done. His life left him quickly, like that of a hung pig, and I crawled away, away from that accursed grove to die nobly, somewhere quiet, on my own sword.

When I came to such a peaceful place, deep within the forest, I drove in my sword, disembowelled myself and dropped quietly to earth. Once you have made that decision, to carry it out is a moment of great joy and fulfilment. This was no act of cowardice, you understand – no fleeing from the world. I was dying anyway and better, in the end, by my sword than the spear of some half-crazed pagan.

Sounds and sights left me. I could no longer smell the grass, or taste the earth in my mouth. I became cold, very cold, and, although I still clutched my sword, I could no longer feel it in my hand. I passed from the world that night with great tranquillity, and never expected to return. If my God was pleased with me, he would take me into his arms and give me welcome: but it was not to be. How long I lay there I cannot tell you, but experience since suggests that it would have been three days and nights.

I woke then, re-born into a new kind of life. I looked at myself and found that I was intact – scarred, of course, but complete. I stood and gazed in wonder at my own body. How could this be? It had nothing to do with my faith, you understand? My God was not part of what had happened. He does not reclaim the dead to life. Those who die in His cause – the eternal fight with the forces of Evil to save mankind – do so gladly, not expecting a resurrection. Yet there was no doubt that I was alive. I felt strange – stronger and purer and more beautiful than I had ever felt; but I understood nothing at that moment, and I was frightened – not least of all because I seemed to be outside His love and guidance. I was yet to discover just how far. I was yet to learn what your generation knows from its reading. What a wonder are books and the knowledge they spread! You will know that the vampire is created in many ways. The victim of a vampire either dies or becomes one, a child born under the curse of its family, a black cat crossing the path of a coffin robs the body of its right to die, those practising witchcraft live on unnaturally, those drinking the blood of enemies they have slain – and suicides. I was twice damned, but of that I was ignorant!

I wandered back to where the fortress had stood on Blud Heath. Their main band of marauders had moved on, but the scavengers were there among the ruins of our burning fortress. They were looting and torturing the prisoners to death, and a gang of them saw me coming up the slope of the hill. I felt invulnerable, and knew no fear. Many of my kind – the kind I am now and have been for so long – have also spoken of that first exhilaration. Not that I cared. I had such contempt for them that dying as I fought would have been a pleasure. Yet, somehow, I knew I would not die – could not die. It was dark, but I saw their faces in the light of the funeral fires and they were gloating. Here was another Roman they could kill. I drew my sword and waited, meaning to circle them slowly, when they were within reach, so that the slope gave me a slight advantage. I was as surprised as they by the speed of my movement. They did not see me, and I had two dying at my feet before I realised what had happened. Their death groans brought others, and restored their confidence. There must have been ten of them, and I was surrounded. It made no difference: their spears, axes and swords simply passed through me, harmlessly. Within two minutes all were at my feet, crying their way into death.

The other scavengers had watched the fight in the light of the fires and they fled, so I moved into the remains of the fortress – a fortification we should have to rebuild if we were to hold the shore. Our women and children were there – staked, crucified, burning ... and worse. I put them out of their misery, and left that place to the flames and the crows and the rats.

My plan was to follow them inland and destroy all I found. I felt so powerful that defeat did not enter my mind. I knew they wouldn't go far. They would be expecting one of our legions to hurry from the north, and would not want to face a Roman foe intent on their destruction. I came across farmsteads they had burned on their way and, in one, a woman, hiding. Her family was dead around her, and she was relieved to see me and ran to me, and threw her arms around me. Her eyes were full of tears and she wanted comfort. It was my first contact with a human since what I now know was my re-birth, and I found her irresistible. I had always liked women. As a Roman soldier, of course, I was forbidden to marry until my twenty five years service was completed, and so my associations had always been spasmodic, but satisfying nonetheless. She came into my arms and, before I knew it, I had sunk my teeth into her neck and I was drinking her life-blood. She gave herself, readily, and I felt her jolt with pleasure in my grip. We lay together, and she slept in my arms for many hours.

When she woke, she prepared me a meal in the ruins of her home. I could not eat it, try as I might, but it was a gesture of gratitude and kindness which has stayed in my memory ever since. It was the first meal she had eaten for days. She had been frightened to light a fire, and was now relieved to be satiating her hunger. She knew I was not human – I could see that in her manner – and asked if I was one of the gods, and whether I lived off blood and honey. I laughed and said I did not know, but that I didn't think so. When she had eaten, we buried her dead and she thanked me for my help. I could see her fortitude was returning. These British women were tough and we, as their protectors, had always enjoyed their trust. I advised her to stay alert and hide out in the fields if the Angles returned. Then I left her, but I did not follow the invaders. Already, I had learned that I could not be killed, that I moved with inhuman speed, that I could not eat food and had a taste for blood, that my injured body would restore itself and I now felt the desire to 'return to earth' (that is the best way I can describe the sensation) and wanted to find somewhere safe. You will understand, better than I did then, the natural instincts that were guiding me: the body knows when it is thirsty, when it wants to sleep … and so on. By the time dawn rose on my first day in my new state, I had returned to Blud Heath and found a shielded ditch in which to sleep."

Rebecca stared at him. Why had any one of them ever thought that they stood any chance of challenging, let alone defeating, this creature? He smiled a smile that meant her no harm, and contained within it the wisdom of ages.

David Stokes wandered into the village on Boxing Day morning, quite deliberately. He had left his Christmas presents scattered around his bedroom, and got up to walk the dog. His dad would be out with his Lordship's shoot and that had never appealed to David so he avoided his father, rather than risk being invited. He knew that one day it would be expected. His mother was busy tidying-up after Christmas Day, and getting ready for the afternoon when various relatives were coming round for the traditional games and Boxing Day supper. David would be home for that: cold meat and pickles were a great favourite of his. In the meantime, he was free to walk the dog and decided to take the black Labrador along the beach and into the village where he hoped to find the man who promised to keep in touch, but from whom he had not heard since December 9th, almost three weeks ago – Tony Crewes.

He had never quite trusted Tony Crewes. Adults had the habit of saying things to get what they wanted, and then forgetting that what they'd said amounted to a promise. Still, he had taken him into the temple and the key was still under that stone, so he hadn't moved it afterwards; and they had shared that experience together – without saying anything. They had gazed down along the curve of the hillside, across the meadows to the River Cassyn, watching the herd of white cattle grazing, and feeling the chill, east wind as it gusted up the slope. As he stood with Tony Crewes, he had come to understand his home in quite a different way. He had become aware of the Presence. On that hillside he had felt dread, veneration and wonder.

He would find Tony Crewes and see what was going on. He knew where he lived – he had dropped that note through the door. When he arrived at the house, David heard the children inside, but he didn't know them and didn't like to knock, so he hung around for a while, hoping that Tony would come out. The boy kicked his heels, scattering pebbles, and then strolled on, intending to come back later

School-friends of his were about. Freed from Christmas day, they were playing with their presents and he joined them while the dog lolloped alongside. They roamed only a little way from home, but far enough, and challenged each other on the 'wreck' off Shore Lane. It was a good morning, if a muddy one, but when the others went in for dinner, David was left alone. He hadn't come expecting to stay and had brought nothing to eat. He forgot Tony Crewes and wandered into the churchyard; it was on the way home. Alone, sitting on one of the commemorative benches, was an old lady, white-haired and stooped. He recognised her, but couldn't remember who she was until he came up to the bench on which she was sitting and looked into her eyes. It was the rector's wife, Mrs Unwood. She looked at him, also without recognition, and smiled. Old ladies always smiled at him: he was that sort of boy – his mother had told him so.

"Hello," she said, "what are you doing here?"

"Playing," he replied.

"Where are your friends?"

"They've gone home for dinner," he answered.

"Where's your dinner?" she asked.

"I didn't bring any," David replied.

"I'm afraid I haven't any to give you, and it's too far to walk."

"I'm not in a hurry," said David.

"I'm tired," said Esther, "and I feel ... safer, here."

"Safer?"

"I don't want to go home, yet – not until Corvin's back. Here's the key. Go and make yourself a sandwich. They'll be something in the fridge. There's some soft cheese, too, if you'd like to make me one."

David Stokes looked at the old woman as though she were loopy but, then, old people were like that; it was always easier to agree with his granny, when she was pushing food at him, than not. When he returned, with two sets of sandwiches wrapped in foil and a drink for each of them, Esther thanked him.

"You're a very capable little boy. I could see that."

"Mum taught me to make sandwiches. I make them for my dad and me sometimes – when we're going out together all day."

"Where do you go?"

"Lots of places, but sometimes it's with the herd when the cows are calving."

"You like helping your dad?"

"Yes. He is Lord Wangford's herdsman."

"The white bull? ... I remember Mr Crewes talking about the white bull."

"Mr Crewes told you?"

"He told all of us. It's coming back now – you're David!"

"What did Tony say?"

Esther told him, in a vague and disjointed manner, about the meeting at Dr Read's house. For a while, as she spoke, David thought Tony had betrayed him and then he remembered what he had said 'David ... I'm not sure what is going on – and neither is anyone else.' This old lady was one of the 'anyone else' people, then!

"Do you now where Tony is?" he asked.

"No dear. I don't seem to know much anymore, but I will when Corvin gets back .....Just a moment – I've just remembered something.   Tony said that he would find Sarah Brown – that was his 'over-riding task'. He must be looking for her."

David looked at the white-haired old lady and felt sorry for her. His mum had said that old people's memories sometimes "came and went". Why should Tony be looking for someone called Sarah Brown?

"Do you remember anything else about the white bull?" he asked.

"No, dear, I don't think so," said Esther, looking at the boy, and then she started and asked, suddenly, "Do you know about the temple?"

David looked at her again; this time he did not feel sorry for her. She looked like a witch, asking a child where their "mummy and daddy" were. He sat silently, munching the remains of a ham sandwich.

"Do you know about the temple?" she repeated.

The old lady didn't speak like that; someone else was asking the questions. He was angry. Grown-ups always pushed you when they wanted something. It was him asking the questions, David knew instinctively. He was there – the slayer of the bull.

"Yes," he said.

"Have you seen it?"

"Yes," he said, quite deliberately, "It's a special place."

"Not evil?"

"It has the spirit of the place. I'd expected to be frightened, but I came out understanding the mystery. It was like the feeling you get standing in a church."

"Don't say anymore," said Esther, suddenly.

"What?" he asked, surprised at her change of tone.

"I said be quiet."

"Tony felt the same. I could tell."

"I said be quiet!"

"Time was suspended in there," the boy persisted, "You could feel the men who made it; they fought against the forces of darkness."

He didn't know what he was saying and, more especially, he didn't know why he was saying it – well, not quite, but almost.

"We hid the key under the mossy stone."

Esther sat bolt upright on the seat, sweat springing from her forehead, despite the crispness of the air.

"I was in touch with centuries past."

"Stop it," she shouted.

"I felt at peace in there," he said.

"Go on," said Esther, her voice quiet again.

She was opening her handbag; why did old women always carry handbags with them? She was taking out some slip of paper: it was a scrap – nothing more. She was writing on it. David looked at the lines, scrawled through the pain of her arthritis. They read 'The sun will destroy him.' There was an appeal in her eyes; the appeal said 'Do not speak these words; do not let me even think the words I have written.'

David reached for her handbag and removed another scrap of paper. He looked up at Esther, who was not watching him. Her eyes were gazing at the horizon. He wrote on the paper, and then folded it and sealed it from her sight. On the outside of the slip, he wrote 'Open at noon, tomorrow; read and remember.' He slipped it inside her handbag and looked at the old lady: she knew and he was glad.

When Esther returned to the rectory, Corvin was waiting for her; the bishop's car, under the direction of Mrs Cushion, had dropped him off at two-thirty and he was home again. Esther went quietly into his arms and held him close.

"Oh, Corvin, I am so glad to have you home."

"I have spoken with Nadine and Simon. I know what is happening."

"I wish I did, Corvin."

She did not mention the boy. She did not want to think about the boy, nor have a picture of him in her thoughts. Corvin could see the battle that Esther was fighting – alone and out of the reach of her friends and family. She knew, and he knew, that it was a battle of instinct – a battle in which she dare not frame a thought for too long. In her handbag was a slip of paper with lines written by the boy. She was the only one in the whole world who could use it, and she was not sure what the boy had written.

"We must go and see Owen and his family," said Corvin.

"Not for a moment, Corvin. Just give us a little time on our own."

They walked into their sitting room, his arm around her shoulder and sank back onto the settee where they always sat together – when they did sit together.

"Do you know what is happening with Rebecca? Where is my daughter?"

"We do not know."

"I need to know about her ... Have you been happy with me, Corvin?"

"I am happy with you, my love. It has always been so."

"I am so tired, Corvin. Sometimes, now, I feel I am ready to pass on."

"Once Rebecca is back with us, you will feel quite differently."

"Yes, I expect so ... Kiss me, Corvin."

He brought his lips down onto her forehead, and kissed her gently.

"On my lips."

She looked up at him as a young woman might look up at her lover, and he took her lips onto his and kissed them gently, feeling the silky softness that was still there, despite her age.

"Will things be all right, Corvin?"

"You know I can't answer that, Esther."

"I do love you, Corvin."

"I know, Esther, and have never doubted it. Rebecca was conceived in love."

"Do you remember that?"

"I am never likely to forget, Esther."

She was quiet then, and he was glad of it and they sat together, his right arm around her shoulders, her right hand stroking his left, her head snuggled into the space between his shoulder and chest. It was Boxing Day afternoon and, but for the despair and danger around them, they might have slept into the evening.

CHAPTER 11

Alan travels north

Alan had set out at more or less the same time as Peter Vishnya, and then they had lost touch. His journey was shorter, some two hundred miles, and he expected to arrive between four and five o'clock in the evening. He would then find a place to eat, giving Brultzner time to leave the city (if he was there) and himself time to prepare for what might lay ahead. Alan felt none of Peter's urgency: once things were on the move and they were committed to the task, Alan found that he was able to focus more easily.

However, his was a tedious journey, starting across the fenlands of north Norfolk and Lincolnshire. It wasn't just the flatness which drove him quietly nuts: it was also the expectation that it would rain. Sure enough, as he crossed Sutton Bridge it began to sleet. Alan began to suspect some kind of conspiracy of the elements.

Somehow, he had become the leader of their little party. He had brought them together and pushed their venture forward, and felt he had to keep alert to what was happening. They now seemed so spread out in their hunt for Brultzner: it was almost as though the creature had divided them to make them easier to conquer.

Hopefully, Nadine and Martin would have completed their task before nightfall and Grise's body would be waiting the return of Corvin, and burial. Corvin would tend Owen and his family (Alan had no doubt of that) once he returned.

Tony had contacted nobody since Christmas Day, but Alan had was sure he had set out on his mission. If Rollie was to be trusted in the matter, Tony had by now found and 'released' Sarah. He would contact Martin, who would arrange for the necessary body-bag to be supplied, and Old Strowger to accept a second corpse.   Nadine, Simon and Martin would be on the look-out for Sidney Close: they simply had to find him quickly. Close was more dangerous than either of the other vampires which they knew about: he was the one likely to continue the infliction of damage – the spread of this accursed plague.

Penny just had to look after the children until he returned. She had supported his call for action: hers had been the decisive voice at their Boxing morning meeting. There was nothing more she could do for the time being except stay alert.

What of the future? Alan hardly dare think about that, but he did. He had to come to terms with what they would need to accomplish. It wasn't so much the 'what' as the 'how'. They were breaking the law in their own country: no court would believe anything they might have to say in their own defence. All of them would be imprisoned and, probably, certified. What chance would they stand in another country? They could hardly travel across Europe staking vampires with impunity. Sooner or later someone was likely to ask what they were doing!

But first – think back home! Necker Utting had been cremated, but there was Shane Marjoram actually in the graveyard at St George's staring up at his own coffin lid. He should be easy, however – buried as he was in hallowed ground and awaiting only his final release. He would be easy because ... because Corvin would oblige. Would he – would the priest find his courage? Doubt weakened: Alan knew that and tried to shake it off – he had quite enough to do without worrying about future plans.

When he reached Newark and turned north, the sleet soon became snow. Cold winds were driving it down from the north or north-east. It would cover East Anglia by the end of the night. He had covered one hundred and fifty of his two hundred miles, and the end of the journey could not be more than an hour or so away. He had been driving for nearly three hours: it was nearly four o'clock in the afternoon. The snow whirled into his headlights in what he imagined to be a vortex of spite.

He was tired now, after the long and monotonous drive across the fens: the snow demanded such concentration. Alan peered into the snow, which rushed headlong onto his windscreen, and he wondered how this might be challenging the others. He pictured Penny and the children in the house with the world outside turning white and the fire lit and the logs spitting, and all of them closed in and warm and together. Should anything happen to them, it would be an anguish he could not bear.

Corvin and Esther had driven out to see Owen and the children at Owen's mother's house before the snow began to fall at Dunburgh-on-sea. Corvin was good with people, and Esther knew this strength of his well enough to follow his lead. They were all in that first state of shock when belief refuses to assert itself and the status quo must be maintained. The boy was curled by the fire, on the carpet with his granddad, and the teenage girl was in another room, with her Walkman plugged into her ear, oblivious to the world that screamed for her attention.

"What have you told them," asked Corvin, taking Owen aside.

"That Grise has gone away to think about things."

"Yes, that must be best for now. We have taken her into our care, Owen."

"Then ... she is dead? ... So I will need to talk to the children?"

"In time – we have time."

"Things have happened so quickly ... Dr Read told me a strange truth, and he said 'knowledge is the best protection you have'."

"He spoke the truth, however strange it may have seemed."

"My daughter is all right?"

"If Dr Read said so, then she is."

"What do I do now, Reverend Unwood?"

"We commit Grise's body to mercy of the Lord ... Perhaps the children will understand better than we do ... You might wait until after their mother's funeral, but you should tell them the truth sooner or later. There is no point in skirting round it. One day they will know, and how much better that they should be told by you. There is no shame in what happened to their mother; the shame belongs to another."

"Have you caught him?"

"No, but we will. It is only a matter of time. Do not frighten your children: tell them, simply. The evil here lies with those of us who knew and chose, for whatever reason, to do nothing – not with the innocent victims of this plague."

Owen was silent; he looked at Corvin, seeking advice but not asking.

"Do not be frightened, Owen. They will ask when they are ready to hear – you will not have to decide the moment," said the priest, with a smile, "Also, be concerned for yourself: you, too, need comfort ... Apart from me, and Alan and Penny Read, there is Nadine Palmester. She will understand, and listen ... Can I do more for you, now?"

"No, Reverend Unwood. Just telling me what has happened is enough for the moment. Let me take it in slowly and then I will be ready."

"Go home after Christmas, Owen. You will face the truth better, there."

"What happened, Corvin?"

"On my journey, I learned to have faith in myself and to stop blaming others for my lack of it."

"You mean people like Peter Twiddle?"

"People like Peter Twiddle, and people like you, Esther."

"Corvin!"

"There is no point in raising your voice to me, Esther – I am way beyond your style of verbal abuse."

"Corvin!"

"It becomes a habit, doesn't it?"

"Corvin!"

"I shied away from personal conflict, Esther, and ended up being caught between those people – like yourself and Clara Gobley – who used it as a weapon. I thought that it was enough to serve my God faithfully and tend my flock dutifully. I was so wrong. I failed to realise that I could do neither until I had put my own house in order ..."

"Don't hide behind clichés, Corvin."

"Very well – I failed to realise that I could do neither until I had sorted you out – you and the Bishop Twiddles and Clara Gobleys and Penny Reads of this world. I could offer no leadership until I was my own person – not someone who could be pushed about by the opinions of others, always seeking to placate those who would try to change their worlds through me," he said, without raising his voice, and in a matter-of-fact tone. He was finding himself.

"I thought you loved me, Corvin!"

"You're doing it now, Esther."

"Doing what!?"

"Attempting to bully me into feeling shame. I love you, and you know it. What I am talking about has nothing to do with our personal relationship, which you have used to influence change in the church – or no change, according to what you wanted at the time. You are not the priest of this parish, any more than Bishop Twiddle or Clara Gobley or Penny Read: that is my responsibility and mine alone. No one can take that duty of care from me, and I neglected it by not facing up to the divisive issues."

"And our daughter?!"

"You're doing it again. Rebecca has nothing to do with this discussion. You are simply trying to deflect the points I have made, which you cannot accept but with which you cannot disagree. I am as concerned about Rebecca as you – and, I am doing at least as much about it."

"So what are you doing?"

"What are you doing?"

"Corvin!!!"

"You are wasting your time, Esther – and your exclamation marks. Neither of us can do anything to help Rebecca, directly – except through prayer. On your knees."

Esther Unwood laughed. She loved Corvin, and knew her own faults. He was not challenging her, but his own incompetence; she loved him for it. Such feelings were beyond the comprehension of her present 'master'; if he was picking them up now, they could only serve to confuse. For the moment, anyway, she could pray again and Esther knelt beside her husband. Together they shared, as they had shared so many times before, Compline – the last service of the day.

Alan Read drove on into the snow that seemed to be trying to coerce him into retreat. It battered like shafts against his windscreen, but they were spent arrows as far as he was concerned. He was determined that nothing – not even a change in the weather – was going to deter him. The road slithered under his wheels so that the car was constantly sliding from side to side across the lanes of the motorway. At times, it seemed as though the front wheels were pulling him into the path of oncoming vehicles; at others, the back wheels shot sideways and he struggled to keep the car on a steady course. He hated it, but there was no turning back and no temptation to rest for a while in the next lay-by. The sweat poured from him, despite the cold, and his grip on the steering wheel shuddered, but he knew that all he had to do was to hold on and keep going.

His was not the only car on the road by any means, and often he caught up with tailbacks of traffic as cars and lorries waited for each other to peak a steep rise in the road. It was arduous, and slow beyond anything he could have thought possible. He smiled to himself as he slipped across lanes in order to overtake traffic. Penny never allowed him to do that on icy roads – ever! She and the children seemed to recede further, the nearer he got to York. Alan Read could not stop himself fearing that he might never see any of them again, or ever know what happened to them.

There were several accidents on the way and he pulled over to see if his help might be needed. There were no injuries, but only frustrated drivers waiting for the emergency services to arrive. Every time he stopped, the single-mindedness within him flickered for a while, and he wondered whether he was driving into nothing: there was no guarantee that he would find Rebecca in York. Each time he returned to his car, Alan phoned Peter but there was no reply and he pressed onward. Each time his sense of urgency increased, the travelling seemed to become slower.

The weather appeared to be drawing him into another world from where he felt there would be no escape. The blurring of the landscape around him, so that trees and buildings took on strange forms that beckoned, and the spinning tunnel of the snow, which drew him in, suggested alien places where he would be a stranger and alone. He had never been alone. Always there had been someone – his parents and brothers and sister, and then Penny and his own children. Suddenly, loneliness overwhelmed him and he wanted to cry. It was an irrational feeling, and Alan laughed at himself. He was on a prosaically English road and it just happened to be snowing! He could have phoned Pen, but didn't want the sound of her voice so far away and unreachable.

The worry of an accident was heavily upon him, and yet he felt obliged to take risks to push on as fast as he could, while knowing that one slip would mean hours of delay. The lights of the other vehicles were no help. They simply danced in the snow, red like the eyes of wolves or blindingly white, probing the road ahead like giant fingers as they sought for a way through. His feet were wet by now from where he had stopped to offer help, and they were cold, despite the heater. He had laughed off Pen's concern, saying that he would be sitting in a pub within a few hours, supping a pint and full of steak and kidney pudding.

Alan's relief was enormous when he finally saw the sign for which he had been looking, and he turned onto the A64 and headed for York. It was now after half-past five, but at least he had only ten miles to drive. He would be in the city by half-past six to seven o'clock. He soon realised, however, that he was heading north-east straight into the driving snow. He thought of home and how cold it would be in East Anglia with the snow coming in on an easterly wind. Snow and cold would favour the enemy, but at least it must slow even Brultzner down if he was travelling south.

He did not fear that Brultzner would retaliate should he discover, before the morning, what had happened. The man had too much sangfroid. He would wait and confront them all as he had confronted Corvin on his return from the midnight service. Nevertheless, Alan's plan to check the York temple after dark and be home with or without Rebecca "before the ten o'clock news" seemed unlikely. He would phone Pen and get her to leave the village.

The driving over the last ten miles was even worse than it had been on the A1, and he was now bewildered by the conflicting thoughts that passed through his head. One moment he knew that he did not want to hang about in York, and the next he realised that the choice was no longer his to make.

When he eventually arrived in the city, however, the lights cheered him up. The warmth melted the snow as it fell, and he was slopping through slush. Alan parked the car by the river and made his way into the centre, looking for the side street marked on Wangford's map. He would find that first and then compose himself; he needed a clear head for what he was to face, and the journey had fragmented the clarity of his thoughts. He was tired and jaded. His body ached from sitting in one position, crouched over the wheel, and his mind was exhausted by concentrating so intensely on the road for so many hours.

When he found the street, he saw the graveyard beyond and under his feet he felt cobblestones. Around him, stretching into the wet darkness, were bookshops and cafes. This didn't seem an evil place but, of course, it wasn't. Tony Crewes had commented on the sense of peace that pervaded him when he left the temple on the Wangford estate.

There was a pub close by, and he entered like an animal seeking warmth from the night. Here, among his own kind, he would find a moment's respite and contentment. He ordered a pint and then asked the landlord, a burly and cheerful man, whether he was "able to order food, yet".

"'Yet', sir? That depends on what you mean by 'yet'. If 'yet' should mean this time tomorrer, then the answer is an emphatic 'yes'. If – on the uvver hand – 'yet' means 'in the next hour or so', then the answer would be an equally emphatic 'no'."

Alan stared at the man who was smiling broadly. Alan was in no humour for a comedian, or for the sound of the London twang with which he had spoken.

"The notice says that you serve food all day."

"Not today, sir. In case you were not aware of the occasion …", he said, emphasising the word 'occasion' as though it was a foreign phrase with which Alan might not be familiar, "If you were not aware of the occasion," he repeated, for the benefit of the locals who had pricked up their ears, "it is Christmas."

There was general laughter at Alan's expense, good-natured, but not – at that moment – to his taste. He was shocked to find that he was about to punch the man.

"You must have a kitchen," he said, "and I have travelled a long way, through this awful weather, without food. It wouldn't be beyond the wit of man to toss something in the convection oven and slide it onto a plate, would it?"

"You seem an educated sort of man, sir, and so you must be aware of the hygiene regulations. It would be more than my licence is wurf to enter the kitchen and prepare food wivart the necessary cer-cificates and, as I have tried to explain, the establishment is not equipped to provide sustenance of the culinary variety, today – the chef being, as you might say, off-duty."

"I thought Yorkshire had a reputation for hospitality. 'Hello, John, come on in – take a seat at our table'."

"I'm not from Yorkshire, sir – you may have noticed."

"Do you know, you can travel anywhere in the world, and always there is the 'honoured meal of the stranger' – anywhere, that is, except in your own country. What is wrong with us? On Christmas Day, in foreign towns and cities, people are out on the streets in the evening, meeting friends and enjoying themselves. Cafés and restaurants are open – there is food and drink and bonhomie."

"Perhaps you should have gone abroad for Christmas then, sir."

There was more laughter from his cronies, and so Alan smiled and sat in the corner with his pint. His disappointment hung heavily upon him. It wasn't just the hunger – he could have ignored that, easily. It was simply that food would have brought him back into the real world, and away from the frozen void through which he had driven.

After a while, the landlord appeared at his elbow, and said "The wife overheard our conversation, sir, and gave me an earful. She was wondering whether you might find this acceptable."

He placed a plate of food in front of Alan. It was a huge portion, and the plate bulged with it – cold turkey, a ham and egg pie, pickled red cabbage, cranberry chutney, four roast potatoes which had been warmed through, a large knob of butter and a wedge of bread.

"There is a tian of root vegetables, should you still feel peckish when you've finished that lot, sir, but the wife wasn't sure that they would heat up nicely ... Ooh, and some Christmas pudding and custard ... The wife's from Yorkshire, sir. She might appreciate a word of thanks before you go."

"Yes, of course. I'm very grateful. Thank you."

The landlady did appreciate Alan's words of thanks and refused any payment. It was part of their own Boxing Day food, she said – not what they served in the pub – and he was very welcome. He glowed when he left, with a stomach at bursting point but ready for whatever the night might hold. There was something special about women – somehow, he had always known that, and no longer felt alone.

He found the steps that led down to the doorway through which Rebecca had made her fruitless escape only the previous night. As he examined the lock and the hinges (Martin had given him a few tips on hinges as a weak point on old doors), Alan became aware that he was being watched; and yet he had been so careful to survey the street thoroughly before descending. Turning, he saw a man at the top of the steps.

"Can I help you, sir?"

"Possibly – are you a police officer?"

"No, sir, I just happened to be passing and heard you struggling with the lock. I thought, perhaps, you'd dropped your keys. I have a torch, you see."

The torch was of the very old-fashioned sort. Alan had not seen any like it since he was a boy. His uncle had had one, and it always impressed Alan when he was young. It was a silver, metal tube about two feet long: the sort you might want in your hand if you had to go downstairs during the night because you thought you'd heard burglars. The man did not move, but stood very quietly. Alan shrugged his shoulders and began to ascend the steps towards him. As he reached the top, the man stepped aside to let him pass and Alan turned to look at him.

"Thanks for your help," he said, "I think I'll have to phone the owner."

"In that case, I'll be getting home. It's late to be out on Boxing night."

"Yes, good night."

He flicked through the papers he had stuffed into his pocket and found the telephone number he was after: it was by the side of the word 'Father'. The voice that answered was a woman's so he asked if he might speak to "the man of the house". It sounded ridiculously old-fashioned but he had no idea whether the man he was after was husband, partner, brother, uncle, lover or any of the other titles that might apply. The woman muttered something and then a man came onto the line.

"Would you answer to the title 'Father'?" Alan asked.

The man did not speak, but Alan sensed the feeling of panic in his silence. He repeated his question, but before he had reached the key word, the man snapped:

"I heard you. Give me your number and I'll call you back from my study."

At last he was getting somewhere. Alan heard the phone replaced and waited. He waited for a long time. There were still a few people about and from somewhere round the corner of the alleyway he heard the ring of a mobile phone. Still he waited, and then his mobile rang.

"Dr Read?"

"Yes."

"If you would care to wait a moment, I will join you. It will be much easier if we speak face to face."

The man who finally appeared from the direction of the graveyard, which Alan could just glimpse through the old archway, was slightly built and tremulous in his demeanour. Clearly ill at ease with Alan, he ushered him off the street and followed him down the steps. He took a ring of keys from his pocket and unlocked the heavy door; it was only later that Alan remembered he had not re-locked it. They entered a dark corridor or tunnel and the tremulous man turned on a dull, yellow light. He led Alan along the side of the basement of the building and into a small room, immaculately kept, with no window. There was a desk in the room and the little man sat behind it; he was obviously very nervous as he ushered Alan into the chair on the other side of the desk. Alan shut the door through which they'd come and sat down. He'd always disliked having open doors behind him.

"What can I do for you, Dr Read?"

"May I just ask how you know my name?"

"You know the answer to that question. I really do not want to waste time, doctor. Just tell me how I can help you."

"Very simply, someone connected with your temple has abducted a young woman and I think he may have hidden her here."

"I don't understand what you're talking about, doctor."

"You know my name, and you have turned out on a foul night to meet me and you have brought me into some kind of office that must be sited very close to your temple in this city. Please let us not play around … eh, Father. I have nothing against your or your Brotherhood. I just want your help to search your temple and any rooms attached to it to put my mind at rest."

"You must appreciate that what you are saying makes no sense to me."

"Then why have you come here tonight to meet a perfect stranger?"

The man was sweating. Great globs of perspiration broke out all over his forehead and around his mouth. Alan noticed that he was rubbing his hands together, and then he began to wipe the sweat from his face with the back of his hand.   "Why are you nervous?" he asked, in his best bedside manner.

"I don't understand," said the man.

"You keep saying that."

"That's because I don't."

"In that case, it might be best if I do not try to explain everything," said Alan, "unless you want me to. My story is not for anyone of a nervous disposition. I would be quite happy if you would just show me round."

He laughed in an attempt to reassure the man. He had dealt with hysterical patients many times and knew that it was best not to alarm them and to keep them relaxed.

"Explain everything – who are you to explain everything?"

"I was simply making the offer. It was very kind of you to turn out tonight."

"Kind?"

"Kind of you to show me round – if you would."

"You have no idea what you are up against, have you doctor? No idea at all."

"Tell me."

The tremulous man looked at him and there was cunning as well as fear in his eyes. Suddenly, an idea came to Alan – from nowhere but the regions of apprehension.

"Are you the man I phoned tonight – are you the one they call 'Father'?"

"You use that word a lot, doctor."

"Are you the man I phoned tonight?"

"No idea, have you?"

Now, it was Alan's turn to feel frightened. It seemed to him that the man may not have been so 'tremulous' after all. He was smirking and it was not the smirk of the weak, but the powerful. He did not move from the desk, however, but just sat and watched Alan as realisation began to dawn and both he and the man knew it was too late. Alan turned as the door behind him opened, only to see the torch come crashing down on his head. He felt his face open and blood pour into his collar and then the torch crashed down again, and all was black and the world, together with his wife and children, was forgotten.

Horst Brultzner had a far better journey home to Dunburgh-on-sea than Alan had leaving it because he was driving away from the oncoming snow. He set out soon after dark and was back at the Old Vicarage by early evening. His scheme was, as far as he knew, going according to plan; the mother and daughter were now his, and he was set to use them as necessary. He was fatigued after his journey and wanted to sit quietly for a while in his study, once he had taken some light refreshment. A woman he sometimes visited on Shoemaker's Lane provided this with her usual constrained eagerness (so English!), and he was soon back home with a book open before him.

He had wandered round the village (his village!) after the visit and was pleasantly excited to see the festive lights twinkling in every house and the festive sounds coming from them. It was a special time for these people, just as it was special across the whole of Europe. Never mind the religious bombast behind it. A much older festival had, after all, only been stolen by the Christians, in the same way they appropriated so many other folk traditions across the world. It was the spirit of the time which mattered. He knew the conspirators through his union with Esther, and his wanderings took him to each of their houses in turn. The doctor's house was alive with laughter as was that of the policeman and the one who had pledged to find Sarah. The rectory, as he expected, was subdued and the preacher and his wife seemed to be away. Throughout the village, he saw no one, but listened to the sounds of merriment. It was good to be home.

Wangford was probably staging an evening occasion, following a successful day's hunting, and he would leave him until the evening of the 28th since he needed the Bentley again to bring Rebecca home.

The intrusion into his home of Esther Unwood would have to be regarded as 'good fortune' (he didn't like the word 'luck' because it suggested reliance on factors one could not control), but his subsequent use of her was due entirely to his own cunning and entirely to his credit. It was through her that he had learned of the conspiracy against him and with her that he had been able to construct a counter-attack which would enable him to retain his life in the village with a satisfactory degree of safety. He would surround himself with sufficient malignant memories to 'make assurance double sure' (how he loved that phrase) but he was old-fashioned enough to believe that the English – especially the type with whom he was negotiating – had the quaint notion that 'their word was their bond' and once given, to protect their beloved Rebecca, they would not break their oath. If any of them refused – and he felt that the Bethel preacher might (he had met such men before) – then other arrangements would have to be made for them.

It was a shame that Rebecca had behaved as she did; he had treated her with all the courtesy possible, and had expected more from such a woman. She would hover now between the two worlds and he would need to be careful. Indeed, he may need to curtail any idea of visiting her on a regular basis. He had hoped that when she and Vishnya moved to Estonia after their wedding that ... but never mind; one could not expect everything to be perfect in either world.

He had known of Corvin's return from Esther and phoned him soon after taking his refreshment. The priest had seemed more assured than usual. Perhaps the visit to the cathedral had 're-energised his spiritual batteries'. That was the phrase they used, wasn't it? He had readily agreed to a meeting at the rectory before dawn on the 27th and said that he would contact the others. Esther seemed to know little, but Corvin Unwood sounded confident.

He still had the problems of Close and Sarah. If the one called Tony failed to find her then he would have to; it would add to his 'credibility' if he led them to 'restore her soul'. What a phrase that was, bred of an insatiable need to preserve the status quo! For such a humble people, they had such arrogance. How could they, or anyone else, 'restore a soul'? Souls were not theirs to restore and, besides, what conceit that they should suppose that he wanted to be 'restored'.

He knew Sarah's people: after the child, she had been honest with him and he had kept an eye on her to be sure that she took only what she needed. Anyway, she was sensible and circumspect and had the lovely boy Matthew; it was a shame that she had deserted him. He had enjoyed her company and her challenge, but betrayal could not be tolerated. Close was another matter; he had remained hidden, and how much damage he might have done was unknown. Once found, he would need to be questioned before the 'restorers' were allowed near him.

When Alan regained consciousness, it was very slowly. His first thought was of voices whispering in his ear and it was a while before he realised they were memories. They were the voices of the two men: the one who had sat trembling on the other side of the desk and the one with the torch who must have hit him. He could feel the blood, which was sticky on his face and under his collar. It no longer seemed to be trickling down his chin. When he opened his eyes, he saw that he was lying on a wooden bench. Something soft had been placed under his head and he was curled into the foetal position. The floor, which he could see through one eye, was made of stone slabs and there was the smell of earth. Alan knew he was in a cellar. The light came from a fissure in the wall. He stirred and groaned as he tried to swing his legs round and sit up. It was then he heard another voice, and this one was real. It was that of Rebecca Unwood. She was crouching by the side of the bench on which he lay, looking at him intently.

"Take it steadily, Dr Read. Don't try to do too much at first."

"Do I get the impression that things are not going too well, Nurse Unwood?"

Once he was sitting up with his feet on the ground, she sat beside him and offered him a drink. It was water, and he gulped it down greedily. The beer and food at the pub had made him thirsty.

"Are you all right, Rebecca – unharmed, I mean."

"Yes."

As soon as she spoke he knew it was a lie, but he left his questions until another time. He had found her, albeit not quite in the way he had expected but it was one tiny step forward. At least she was no longer alone, and the two of them might stand a chance of getting out.

"Did you see the men who brought me here?" he asked.

"No – at least, not their faces. It was dark, and they kept them turned away. One wore a hat, which shadowed his face."

"I thought not. They were not bothered about me seeing them, but they kept their faces out of your sight. What does that suggest to you?" he said.

"That it didn't matter in your case, but it did in mine?"

"Precisely. I don't think I am meant to be alive, Rebecca. They must have lost their nerve and dumped me."

"I don't follow your reasoning, Alan."

"Let me just get these clothes off and I'll explain."

Alan gradually removed his bloodstained clothes and laid them on the bench. While he did so, he explained to Rebecca what Brultzner might have discovered on his return.

"So you think Brultzner knows nothing about you being here, and that these men were sent by the Brotherhood on Wangford's orders?"

"Yes. What will happen when Brultzner finds out, I cannot imagine. Now tell me your story."

Rebecca did, making no mention of what had happened to her after her escape but including the full story of Brultzner's origins.

"The whole dynamic of this has changed, Rebecca. He could decide to support Wangford's action, or draw a discreet winding sheet over it. His decision could depend upon what has happened to Peter."

"Peter?"

"Yes – he has gone to Bath to look for you there."

"You think they might have …?"

"Yes. I must confess I had not expected this of Charles Wangford."

"He must be terrified, Alan, if the only way he could see of dealing with this was to silence you and Peter."

"He had the option to forestall us; there was no need for a killing. We could have been waylaid and imprisoned, until Brultzner considered the matter."

"Alan – does their reasoning matter? We're guessing! Stop guessing and let's do something! We know nothing – Wangford may have consulted Brultzner."

"There would be no point in him leaving you here if that was the case."

Suddenly, Rebecca looked at Alan as though he were not there and, picking up the sleeping bag that she had given him as a pillow, walked over to her own bench, climbed into the bag and settled down to sleep on the thin mattress. As she did so, the lights faded. It was dusk, and then darkness in the cellar.

Corvin and Esther, despite everything, were having a few minutes together. She was frightened and fretful, and Corvin's arm around her was reassuring. She didn't want to think, and she didn't dare think. All Esther wanted was to hold a picture of her child in her mind, and pray that they would soon be together again. Whatever Brultzner might require them to promise was irrelevant to Esther: she would swear any oath to get her child back.

Corvin was not fearful of the meeting that was due very early the next morning, but he, unlike Esther, thought that Brultzner was ignorant of the campaign against him. Corvin was hoping that Alan and Peter would return in time.

He had seen Owen Culman, but he must also have a word with Simon and Nadine. It was essential that Simon stay on side, if only for Rebecca's sake. Penny was alone: he would go and visit her soon, once Esther was settled.

Alan watched Rebecca as she reclined into sleep. 'This must be the post-hypnotic suggestion she spoke of. Is this when they deliver the food? They cannot leave her hungry until Brultzner returns. Please God – give her supper!'

He looked at her in sleep and ran his fingers over her face, lifting the lips aside so that he could see her teeth. He had known she was lying. She had shared Brultzner's blood, supped from his veins and was now part of him. He had wondered at her lack of concern over her fiancé. There had been no emotional outpourings – just a calm acceptance. Rebecca was drifting into the world of the vampire.

Alan sat by her bed for a long time. He wondered what kind of fate Peter Vishnya had met. He pondered on the hopeless position he found himself in with Rebecca – there seemed no chance of escape unless they could overpower the men, should they return with food. He reached in his pocket for his phone: it was gone.

How long it was before the sound at the door disturbed him, he couldn't remember, but Alan moved quickly to where he had been dumped by the two would-be killers. He curled into the foetal position and waited. He assumed that they would move cautiously, expecting him to be awake by now and ready to subdue him. With Rebecca alert, Alan thought the two of them might have stood some chance, but he did not see how he could tackle the men alone, without a weapon of any kind. The wall lights came up slightly as the door opened.

He kept very still, his eyes focussed on the ground and he saw someone enter and walk quite boldly into the room. Whoever it was wore brown suede boots over which flapped a thick, heavily-embroidered skirt. He heard a gasp and then silence. There was the rattle of plates and cutlery, and he heard the tray placed down on a wooden bench. Alan dare not move. Rebecca did not seem to stir, and he wondered whether the woman was going to wake her. He heard a sharp intake of breath, and the boots moved towards him. He knew who, or what, the woman was: she simply had to be one of Brultzner's housekeepers. Her sudden gasp must have been one of surprise. So, she wasn't expecting him to be there!

She stood over him for some time, sniffing the air. The blood had dried upon him. The scent would be alluring to her. Alan dare not move, but kept his eyes just open, fixed on the boots and skirt. Suddenly the woman knelt beside him and peered into his face. She was blonde like his wife, but far more beautiful. 'What a thought, that I should consider anyone more beautiful than Pen!' The blonde hair fell in waves from under the hood of her coat, spilling out over the fleecy brown of the breast; the combination of the two colours – the honey-gold of the hair and the dark brown of the coat – radiated warmth. Her face was without blemish or the marks of time and glowed with fresh health.

Still, Alan did not move or open his eyes further, but he knew the woman was aware that he was awake. She smiled a smile that turned her mouth neatly upwards at the corners – rather a mocking smile, but one he found enticing. Her lips were red but underpinned by a dash of gold – the same as the colour in her blonde hair and the shade which glowed under the skin of her cheeks. The teeth were the teeth of the vampire – pure, lustrous white and sharp.

"Who are you and what are you doing here?"

The question was unexpected. She spoke with a child-like curiosity and in a voice of caressing warmth. Alan opened his eyes and sat up.

"Who I am is simple to answer – my name is Alan Read and I am a doctor. What I am doing here, less so. I was attacked outside, as you can see, and woke up in here. I can only assume that the two men who assaulted me brought me in."

"Two men? What did they look like?"

"I only saw the face of one. He was a sweaty, weasel-faced little man."

She laughed at Alan's description, and the sound tingled through the hairs on his arms and along his backbone. It was a glorious sound, like Christmas bells shaken by the harness of a reindeer. Her face was thoughtful. Alan smiled up at the woman; there was both pleading and fear in the smile.

"If you wait, Dr Read, I will fetch some water and clean you up."

She left the room, leaving the door open, and he heard her moving along the corridor. He looked at Rebecca. She was still asleep. He was glad of that – otherwise, she might have suggested they made their escape. Alan didn't want that: he wanted to wait for this woman to return and bath him. She came with a white enamel bowl swilling with warm, soapy water and placed in on the bench beside him. She then removed his coat and shirt and washed him carefully in long, soothing strokes, working downwards from his forehead, along the bones of his face and over the muscles of his chest. No woman other than Penny had ever bathed him before, and he found it intoxicating. When she had cleared away the congealed blood, the woman tapped him dry with a soft hand-towel.

"You need a clean shirt, Dr Read. I'll find you one. I'll also have your coat cleaned for you – it's covered in blood. In the meantime, slip this on," she said, removing her coat and dropping it over his shoulders, so that he was encased in the warmth of it. He made as if to protest but she only smiled and said:

"It's all right. I don't feel the cold."

The softness of her brown-and-gold-striped, silk blouse (which billowed on her arms and across her breasts) was warm against his bare chest. He felt her arms slide up along the muscles of his back and pull him closer to her. She was a tall woman, and her lips were on a level with his throat which she began to caress softly, first with her breath, then with her lips and finally with the long, sharp, canine teeth. They hovered there for a while and then she slid down his body, her mouth following the silk of the blouse, until she knelt at his feet and ran her lips along the line of his belt, nuzzling his abdomen softly. He felt his stomach muscles stiffen with desire.

She was kneeling at his feet, but she was mistress of all that was happening. She looked up at him – her lips parted – and a heartless, calculated laugh pealed from her throat. It was the laugh of the coquette who held the man enthralled.

She wound herself up over his chest again, never missing a stroke or the chance to run her soft, tickling breath over him. He sensed her hesitation; she was unsure whether or not he was Brultzner's property and, therefore, untouchable. She wanted him, having awakened her own desires in rousing his, and he could feel her little, nibbling bites along the muscles of his chest and abdomen.

He, too, wanted her and he slid his hands along the curve of her back and pulled her to him so that her breasts rested on his chest and her open mouth was raised to his own. He could see the sharp teeth and his tongue flickered over them as their lips met. Here was a woman who wanted to be desired and was ready to give herself: nothing could be more exhilarating.

"My name is Maxine – Maxine Fox," she said, just before their lips met in the urgency of her own desire.

The woman was lost in him now, about to be taken and to take; but even as he heard her voice, Alan became aware of a movement from across the dungeon. If anger and loathing had a shape, it was in Rebecca as she launched herself across the stone-flagged prison. Maxine was so adrift in her own craving that she neither heard nor sensed Rebecca until she was grabbed by the neck and pulled backwards. Rebecca wrapped her arms round the woman, locked her fingers and gripped tight. Maxine shrank within the grip and slithered downwards. Rebecca dropped to her knees as the vampire attempted to slip from her grasp, and both women fell to the floor.

There could only be one outcome – fit as Rebecca was, she could not hope to match the other woman's strength or agility. The sight of Maxine's fury was terrifying. The golden eyes sparkled with hate, the red lips snarled like a wolf denied its prey, and the teeth gnashed together, while the vampire's mouth spat in rage at being denied her pleasure and her feast. As she struggled in Rebecca's weakening grip, Maxine's whole shape seemed to shift. The hands scratched at Rebecca's arms like claws, and she reared up from the floor as the leader of the pack might as he leapt for the kill. Rebecca looked at Alan, her eyes pleading for help.

He had already anticipated the desperateness of the struggle, and crouched to swing his fist up and under the vampire's foaming jaws, knowing it was the one way to render her unconscious – if only for a short time. His fist crashed into her. As Maxine fell, Alan lifted her by the blouse and punched her in the side of the head. Her skull rocked backwards and forwards. He released her, and she dropped to the floor

Alan turned away and vomited on the flagstones beside the bench on which he had been dumped. It was the second time he had thumped somebody in one day, and one of those people had been a woman. Alan had never struck a woman in his life before – ever. It was something a man never did, not if he wanted to be thought of as a man. When he turned back, Rebecca was rifling through the pockets of the coat, which had dropped from his shoulders. She stood, smiling, with the key in her hand.

"Oh, Alan, are things turning at last? ... What's wrong? ... Alan – you mustn't blame yourself: she wasn't a woman – she wasn't ... human."

"She was once," he said, quietly, and Rebecca noticed the tears in his eyes.

The next moment he looked up and grinned as though keeping the shame for himself. He grabbed his shirt and coat, took Rebecca's hand and led her from the prison. In the passageway, she turned and locked the door. When they reached the top of the steps, she said:

"I think we have time. She may not be insensible for long, but she'll need to return to where she rests to recover. Oh, Alan: how long before we are home?"

He looked up. Snow was still falling, but lightly and it was not lying on the streets. If it had not frozen on the roads, and the cloud cover suggested it was not cold enough for that, they might make it back to Dunburgh by the early hours of the 27th: He put on the blood-stained shirt and his coat. It was still cold, wet-cold and miserable, but they would soon be in his car with the heater on and, hopefully for the time being, a final journey before them.

CHAPTER 12

Atonement

Sitting on an old crate Bert had dropped in the driveway, Simon waited anxiously for Sandra to return with the holdall. The short walk from his bungalow in Shore Lane had been an agony for him, and he was leaning forward because that was the easiest way to breathe. The damage inflicted on him by Sidney Close, during his vigil, had never really healed: "old bones" would have been his mother's words. That moment came back to him as he sat waiting. He had been that creature's prey, but the Lord hadn't forsaken him. There was right and there was wrong, there was good and there was evil, and he was on the side of the Lord God of Israel. If the Lord would just give him enough strength to destroy the foul thing that was in the Gobley house, then he could go to his Maker a happy man.

"I've been sent by Simon," said Sandra, when she found Amy again.

"Yes, I know, Simon phoned. Where is he?" asked Amy.

"At the Gobley house. Please – just give me the holdall."

Amy had nothing against Sandra Bint, but she just didn't trust her and was reluctant to hand over the holdall. Simon had offered the briefest of explanations on the phone, and she could see that the woman was unusually desperate.

"I'll come with you," she said.

"Please yourself, but hurry."

The rudeness convinced Amy that she was right to go: rudeness was not one of Sandra Bint's social traits. If anything, she was always meltingly polite at parties.

"Do you know what's in the bag?" asked Amy.

"I can guess but, to be honest, I don't care anymore. Once Simon has the holdall, he can ... take over."

"He's an old man, stricken with his injuries. He'll need help."

"Do you know about this?"

"Martin told me some of it, as much as I 'needed to know'. Martin is a great one for 'knowing on a need to know basis'. He thinks too much information simply confuses people."

"But you believe all this?"

"I do now. I wouldn't have, five days ago."

"Were you ...?"

"Yes, I believe I was – last March, when he first came to the village – but I didn't believe it then."

"It wasn't like that for me. Close was brutal."

"I can imagine – wishing to be brutal in life, able to be brutal in death."

Sandra wanted to cry as she had not been able to with Simon, but there was no time for that; perhaps afterwards, when it was all over, she could talk to Amy Billings over a cup of tea? It didn't take long to regain your humanity. You just needed another human being to share it. The two women moved closer together, clutching the holdall between them, as they walked down School Road.

Simon looked up as the car pulled into the driveway. He hadn't expected Ainsley Bint to arrive.

"What are you doing, old man?"

"I've come to save your soul, son."

"You can leave my soul alone – thanks, all the same."

"I can, son, but the Lord has an interest in it and that concerns me."

Ainsley hadn't expected the potty priest from the Bethel. He'd gone round to his mum's to see if she was all right. When he'd found her gone, he thought she might be up to something and decided to have a little look-see for his own protection. Ainsley rushed at the door, but it was still locked and as secure as he had left it. For a moment he'd thought the game was up and they were going to spoil things for him.

"Where's mum?"

"On her way, and with the Lord."

"Don't ..."

He almost said "fuck me about", but the years in the village deterred him. The priest was here alone and his mother was "on the way". Never mind the 'Lord': he didn't have time to worry about him – he had enough on his plate. They were going to do Sidney Close in: he could tell. The old priest was just waiting for his mum to ... to come back with the gear. There was a shovel round the back, stuck up against the shed by the old vegetable patch. Ainsley rushed round and returned with it clutched in his hand like a weapon. The old man's face was as cool as a cucumber.

"Get into the car," Ainsley said, not quite knowing what he was doing, but knowing he had to get the priest out of the way.

"You've picked the wrong man to threaten with a shovel, Ainsley. When a man has given himself to the Lord, a shovel holds no fears for him."

The shovel caught Simon round the side of the head, gashing open his skull and dropping him to the ground like a sack of potatoes, splitting and falling in several directions at once. Ainsley was screaming within himself by now. He hadn't wanted to hit the old man – just get him out of the way.

Martin and Nadine looked at each other and sighed with relief. Handing the key back to Old Strowger was at least a step in the right direction.

"With the jobs we do – you and I – anyone would think we might have got used to death in one way or another, yet I don't think I could go through the last few hours again if I was promoted to superintendent."

"It was awful, wasn't it? I don't think I shall ever be able to put the sight of Grise out of my mind as long as I live."

The stiffened corpse so cold to the touch, and the way they had been forced to place the severed head into the neck of the dress sickened them. Both of them had looked at Old Strowger, hoping that he was a magician who could perform feats of cosmetic surgery so that everything would be, or at least look, all right. Now, both of them wanted to get back to normal – whatever that might be. Nadine took out her mobile phone and rang her father but there was no answer.

"I must get back to him," she said.

"I'll drop you off. Amy will be at home."

Martin rang Amy: he just wanted to hear her voice, but there was no answer.

Amy and Sandra turned into the driveway of the Gobley house, and saw Ainsley dragging Simon along the rough driveway. The old man was unconscious. Ainsley said the first thing that came into his head.

"I found Mr Palmester here. He was injured."

"What do you mean – injured?" said Amy, seeing the smear of blood and the tuft of iron-grey hair on the blade of the shovel.

"Someone hit him with a shovel," said Ainsley, knowing his scheme had almost fallen apart, but hoping he might just pull it together again.

"Who?" asked his mother.

"He didn't say," replied Ainsley, watching Amy Billings pick up the shovel.

Penny Read drew the curtains, shutting out the world which was now beginning to turn dark. There were snow clouds in the sky, driving down from the north-east and she wanted the children warm and cosy in front of the log fire. She hadn't heard from Alan. Leo moved over to the fire, frowning in the way Labradors do whenever a log spat.

The children had enjoyed the walk and were now spread around the house. Amos and Helen (always close together) were trying to outwit each other on a new computer game, George (the loner) was ensconced in his room, as usual, re-working the rules of a board game and Anna-Maria (mummy's girl) was in the kitchen preparing a snack for the two of them before they curled up together for a chat. People had laughed at their choice of names, but Penny was glad they had chosen old-fashioned, family names: it gave a sense of continuity. They hadn't said much all day, but she knew they missed Alan as much as she did. It had occurred to Penny, many times, that if anything happened to him she would not want to go on living.

She wandered round the house drawing all the curtains, and turning on her beloved lamps. She loved the sense of warmth and comfort given by subdued lighting. Seasonally, Christmas lights twinkled in discreet corners, on stairways and from unexpected niches. By the fireside, Anna-Maria was waiting and hitched herself up on the sofa to make room for her mother.

When Martin Billings and Nadine Palmester drew into the driveway of the Gobley house, snow was already falling lightly but definitely. Ainsley looked up anxiously at the sky. It was darker than it should have been for mid-afternoon, but then it was full of snow clouds. It seemed to Ainsley that the whole world was closing in on him. Both Amy and Sandra sighed with relief.

Martin took the shovel from his wife and held it loosely in his hand.

"This shovel seems to have fresh signs of blood and hair on the blade, Ainsley," said Martin, with a smile. He enjoyed smiling under such circumstances. It really got under his skin that smart-asses like Ainsley Bint took the police force for fools. "I wonder if it's got your fingerprints on it."

"I don't know what you mean, PC Billings," he said.

Martin noticed that he been honoured with the 'PC'.

"You can do better than that, Ainsley. They all say that. I'm surprised at you," replied Martin, his smile deepening.

"I'm wondering if the blood and hair on the shovel belongs to Simon Palmester ... and I'm wondering why you're dragging him along the pathway. I've got a little note in my pocket you see, Ainsley. Miss Palmester and I found it on her kitchen table. Her father had left it there to guide us here. He was a man of few words, Ainsley – unless they were religious words, of course – and we are wondering what brought him here ... Now, it seems to me that you're just the lad to fit all the pieces of our jigsaw together – and put us out of our misery, so to speak. No one likes a mystery, do they Ainsley? – a copper least of all ... Cheer up, sonny, you look like the cat who lost the cream."

Sidney Close had woken as Ainsley's car pulled into the driveway. He heard it vaguely as he was roused from his vampire sleep. It was early – too early to wake. He knew that, but the sun was obliterated by the black storm clouds, the snow was beginning to fall heavily and the pain in his penis was beyond endurance. It was time to find the doctor. The bad blood had to be ... expurgated – yes, that was the word: 'complete and unexpurgated' – cut out the bad bits. He couldn't move at first: the coffin seemed to hold him in place, as though the dead were not ready to yield him up to the living. He'd go to the White House before he took any refreshment, before he sampled any festive cheer.

When he eventually managed to manoeuvre himself out of the coffin, he walked over to the window and peeped through the boarding. It was still daylight outside, but only just; the world would soon be his for the taking. He could hear voices in the driveway, but they didn't bother him too much. He would slip by them like a shadow when the time came. They couldn't know he was there in the house, could they? No!

He looked around. His sense of cleanliness was offended and his sense of propriety was outraged. He deserved better than this – dusty beds and musty wallpaper – and he would have better. He would get away from the village and return at his leisure. When he returned, it would be as a wealthy man. He must have money, but first he had to rid himself of this burning in his testicles and there was only one way to do that: he must visit the doctor! Once Alan Read had given him the drugs he needed, he would ... he would what? Could he leave him alive? Could he leave any of the family alive? Sidney shook himself: thinking did not come easily in his new body.

The snow was falling quite heavily, when he left along the pathway cleared by Clara and Bert into the grounds of the Old Vicarage. He could still hear the voices from the driveway. They couldn't see him, but he did leave footprints in the snow – although they would soon be covered. He looked at St George's as he passed; memories flooded through him and past longings surged in his chest. He saw himself as rector's warden, with the tall silver cross on the black pole clutched firmly in his grasp as he led them all down the aisle to the sound of the organ. His wife smiled demurely at him from one of the pews; his daughters' eyes sparkled. He tried to quell the images; he tried to convince himself that they were the photographs of another person, but he knew that it was a deceit.

He turned, and dodging from shadow to shadow like the vampire he was, hurried along Beach Road to his house, to the place that had once been his home. He could see them through the window: Mavis, Wendy and Angela – all of whom he had once loved so dearly. They seemed to be enjoying themselves and, as he lurked in what had once been his own passageway, Sidney heard other voices. He recognised that of his father and mother, and he recognised Mavis's mother. They were all there, past enmities forgotten; they had come to comfort his family because he was ... no longer with them.

Sidney turned away, tears in his eyes, and walked slowly back along Beach Road. When he reached the corner of Shore Lane he looked back at his own house. It was the last point, before turning up Church Hill, from which he would be able to see it. The falling snow had covered his tracks, and his footprints were obliterated. When he saw that, Sidney turned away and walked quickly to find the doctor.

He knew the White House; he had been there once or twice, when he was rector's warden, for little gatherings hosted by Penny Read. He felt calm and purposeful as he stood in their garden, listening. The house was very quiet. He hadn't expected that: he'd anticipated the sounds of Christmas to emanate from their home. Lights barely managed to sneak through the drawn curtains, so thick was the material, so perfectly were they made and fitted. The house reeked perfection, like the Reads themselves, standing there in its own grounds surrounded by the trees and shrubs of ages. The snow only added to the sense of purity that the house permeated; being white, it was almost ghostly in the swirl of falling snow.

He wanted his knock upon the door or his ringing of the bell to summon the doctor. He wanted to arrive announced: not like a thief in the night. It was a bell-pull he found and, as Sidney drew it towards him he heard the bell ringing deep within the house. He heard the shouts of children and the thudding of bodies on the stairs, tumbling and running. "Daddy" was the shout he heard, four times over and then again. A small boy, blonde like his mother, opened the door. It was

George, the player of board games, and his face was alight with excitement – until he saw Sidney, and then he recoiled. Within the house the other children wondered. He saw two of them transfixed on the stairs and then he said:

"May I come in? I need to see Dr Read."

"Yes," said the child, "yes, of course, come in."

He had been brought up that way – the way of courtesy and good manners and politeness to strangers.

"I mean you no harm," said Sidney Close, as he stepped across the threshold.

By that time, Penny was at the door. Although her children knew that Mr Close was dead, it was something which had not registered with them. Why should they spend much time thinking about the death of a local shopkeeper? She – the mother – was the only one who took in the enormity of what had happened when he stepped into their lives. Something inhuman had crossed the threshold into their home, something unfettered by the concerns of conscience, something governed only by its own needs and desires. Here was something whose, once human, desires had become obsessive, something which saw them not merely in terms of needs but in terms of dominance, anger, frustration, capriciousness ... Name any frailty in human emotions, and that was what had walked into their home.

"Why have you come here?" said Penny, knowing that his visit went beyond the mere need for blood.

"I need to see the doctor."

"Go to your rooms," said Penny because it seemed safer for them that they should be out of the way, behind closed doors.

"I think we should stay, mummy," said Anna-Maria, "We want to be here with you."

Penny calmed down as her child spoke. The girl's voice accentuated the danger they faced and made the mother think. She had been so terrified when he stepped into the room that she could only think of getting her children out of the way. Now, she realized that they had weapons.

"My husband is not in," she said, "We are expecting him back at any time."

"Then I will wait. My need is great. I am in more pain than I can tell you."

"I think it would be better if you came back ... later, Mr Close."

She had nearly said "in the morning" but did not want to emphasise the differences between them; it seemed important to Penny that she treated what was happening as 'normal'. She knew he was dead, he knew he was dead and her children would soon realize he was dead. Yet, maintaining up this pretence seemed the only way to keep the awfulness of what was happening at bay. The tension, in the few minutes he had stood in their home, had mounted unbearably. Penny wondered whether she could hold on to her sanity long enough to cope with the situation. Women like her (mothers like her) were expected to cope.

As she and her children faced Sidney Close, Leo barked and broke the tension. The Labrador had, in fact, bounded over to the door – expecting Alan to be there behind George. The dog stood, disappointed and panting, by the boy. The dog sensed the nervousness more acutely than the rest of the family and, ridden with anxiety, barked. The bark became angry, and the dog curled back its lips. A deep bay came from its chest, and then it snarled. Leo and his kind had originally been bred to work, but now were more usually bred for companionship. There was no belligerence in him. Once only had he shown any aggression, and that was when an old man had put his arms round Penny in the local pub, meaning to kiss her goodnight. The old man had ended up on the floor with Leo snarling at his throat, and the regulars laughing. Everyone understood the dog's instincts to protect his mistress.

It was the same now. Leo apprehended the threat pose by Sidney Close and leapt at Sidney, landing on the vampire's chest and knocking him backwards to the ground. His claws dug into Sidney's shoulders, and he sunk his teeth into his throat. Sidney screamed like a wounded animal. He screamed in pain and in anger as Leo shook him to and fro. He pushed upwards at the dog, trying desperately to dislodge it from his body. As they rolled back into the driveway, Leo jumped clear. When Sidney tried to clamber to his feet, the dog struck in again at the stranger's face, snarling and growling as he did so. Crouching on the ground, poised himself like an animal, Sidney took the full force of the Labrador's second attack in the head. This time, however, he was braced for the assault and twisted sideways so that the dog sprung over him and crashed into one of the flower pots in the driveway.

Sidney, his neck knocked sideways by the power of the dog's onslaught, followed Leo and grabbed at his muzzle. Leo bit into the vampires fingers, shredding them to the bone and Sidney screamed again. Leo's front claws tore into his victim's chest and blood welled out, splashing over the snow, but Sidney closed with the dog and brought his right arm round its neck. Then he stood and, although Leo's back legs continued to slash away at the vampire's legs, the dog lost its purchase on the ground. He hung there clawing wildly for a few moments while the vampire's arms tightened around him and then, with a vice-like grip on the Labrador's muscular neck, Sidney wrenched the dogs head round and snapped its neck. He flung Leo's lifeless body to the ground.

The struggle had seemed like a battle of Titan's while it was waged, but could not have lasted more than a few minutes. The shock of their dog's death, following his instinctive attempt to fight for them, sapped the courage of the family. They shrank back into the house, backing from Sidney as he slammed the door behind him.

"Get them to their rooms."

"Go on," said Penny, "Do as he says. Go quietly to your rooms."

Amos looked at his mother briefly to see if she meant what she said, and then took his younger sister's hand and led her slowly backwards up the stairs. It was too early for tears. The shock of seeing their beloved dog's lifeless body slung down on the snow had yet to sink in. The eldest boy kept his dry eyes on Sidney Close who was in a state of near-collapse in their hall, leaning against the door and panting strenuously. Anna-Maria crossed quickly passed her mother and took

George's hand. George had not moved: of all the children, he'd had the closest affinity with Leo. The tears were springing from his eyes and the anger was burning in his heart. Like a dog himself, he rushed at Sidney and beat him with clenched fists, all the time muttering "Beast, beast!" The vampire took him by the shirt-front, lifted him from the ground and tossed the boy across onto the stairs. He landed heavily, snapping his right wrist on the stairs and knocking his head against the wall. His sister rushed to him and tried to help the boy to his feet, but he seemed to be unconscious. His brother and sisters crowded round him and, without a moment's thought, Penny crossed the hall, shaking Sidney's hand away as he tried to stop her. The shock of the dog's death was replaced by her anxiety for her child. Her fear had gone and was replaced by anger.

"Leave me alone. I will see to my son."

George stirred when his mother touched him, his eyes flashed open and he rose, as though about to stand, but Penny hushed him and placed a finger on her lips. There was a smile on her face that she did not feel in her heart, and the boy was quiet.

"Help George to his room, Nell," she said (Anna –Maria was always known as 'Nell' in the family), "and I will come up in a moment."

"Shall I strap his wrist, mummy?"

"Yes dear."

Penny watched until the last of her children had disappeared from the top of the stairs, heaved a silent sigh of relief and turned to face Sidney Close. In her heart, she was hoping that each of the children would understand what was happening and protect themselves. The expression on the vampire's face was sullen.

"I came here for help," he said, "not to cause you or your family harm."

"You are harm, Mr Close. You are a plague, and will spread your disease wherever you go."

It was an unfortunate choice of words that only exacerbated her predicament. The fire was still burning in his penis and testicles. Sidney grabbed her with his shredded fingers, pinning her arms to her side and drew Penny up to him. He'd always wanted to crack her composure when he saw her at church.

"The English rose – that's what they call you, isn't it? You've always been so elegant, haven't you – so calm, so cool, so composed. Do you feel composed now?" The blood from his facial wounds dripped onto her shoulders, trickling across her skin and under the neck of her dress. "They all admired you – even the women. Somehow you inspired their respect. How did you manage that – eh? Flawless beauty, impeccable mother – how does it feel to be perfect, spotless, the envy of all? ... well?"

He shook her when she did not answer and pressed her closer to him so that the blood from his chest wounds soaked through her dress. Penny knew he wanted to be provoked, wanted an excuse to do what he was going to do anyway. She was no physical match for him, and the weapons she needed were beyond her reach. He had breached their house through the natural courtesy of her youngest son, and she could see that they were all at his mercy.

"The qualities you speak of are nothing more than accidents of birth – you know that, Mr Close. They are things over which we can neither claim credit nor receive blame. It is our destinies which are of our own choosing."

"You think I chose to be like this?"

"No, but it is within your power to choose what to do about it."

There are watershed moments in everyone's life and this was one of Sidney's. The woman he grasped in his bloody clutches could be his victim – one of many who might swell his future – or be the instrument of his redemption. The choice was his.

"You know nothing of me – not me, Sidney Close. You have no right to stand in judgement."

"It is you who must make the judgement."

"Do you know what has happened to me – really happened?"

"Yes."

"I don't think you do, Mrs Read. Where is your husband? He's a doctor. I want medicines."

For a moment, hope sprang in Penny's breast but, even as it surged within her, she feared it was false – unless … unless she could appeal to the man Sidney Close had once been. 'We inhabit eternity in our spiritual body.' Corvin's words came to her, but Sidney Close was not inhabiting eternity; he was here, trapped forever in the world. Yet the Being that Sidney had become reflected only part of the man he once was – the side of his personality which had been suppressed, given no release, hemmed in by upbringing and marriage. There was a horrible, innate sadness about life. Tears welled from Penny's eyes as the thought invaded. 'The soul is not an aspect of the person but the whole person as a living being.' There was nothing 'whole' about the creature Sidney had become; somewhere in the transformation from man to vampire he had shed the 'better part of him'.

"Medicine cannot help you, Sidney. It's a palliative and you are beyond all that. In shedding what you were, you have become something even you hate. You cannot live in part; you must find what once was whole."

"That is your answer – to drive me from the world, so that you can all return to your smug, contented lives?"

"Our lives will never be the same again, Sidney. Irrespective of what happens here tonight – and is happening elsewhere – none of us will ever be the same again."

They stood in a unison that was unearthly – the man whose soul was shattered, and the woman whose only defence was her words, both covered in his unholy blood. Penny felt revulsion and fear, but mingled with this, deep within her own soul, was sorrow and pity. She felt pity for Sidney Close, a pity that transcended their enmity and reached – as far as any human being is capable of such a reach – into his very soul. Yet she was aware, despite all she believed and all she wanted to believe, that he needed to survive. It was the call of every creature – the call of the wild, the over-reigning need to eat, to satisfy one's hunger. Covered in his blood (blood scratched from him by her own dog) Penny looked up into the vampire's eyes. She wished, but she gave up hope. As a mother, her only desire was that he should feed and go, and leave her children alone. If she were to be the sacrifice, then so be it – if she could ensure the safety of her children.

"Leave my children alone. I will give you what you want. Alan will give you what you want, but leave our children alone."

As they stood, poised, both became aware of a presence in the room. It surrounded them and waited. Penny's eyes were torn first from their mutual gaze, and she saw her children, each bearing a cross, each holding it at arm's length towards Sidney Close. The four held them in a circle, one at each point of the compass. They may not have understood, but they knew their mother was in the arms of a dead man. Sidney followed her gaze, and eyed each of the children in turn. The crosses blinded him, but they were held in the hands of uncertainty. He understood, however fleetingly, how he might outwit them – how he might defy the Lord God Almighty.

"Tell them to go," he said, "I beg you – tell them to go."

It was his last chance and he was pleading for it, pleading to be allowed the moment that was slipping from them, the moment when he might have accepted his plight, the moment when he might have taken his destiny into his own hands.

"Go to your rooms," she said, as though she were speaking to strangers.

None of her children moved. They did not recognise their mother in the arms of the stranger, covered in his blood. They saw him subjugating her to his will – not, as she did, on the edge of redemption.

"We are conscious of God – and of each other – through all eternity! But we only come to the Father through the Son and, in accepting Him as our Saviour our sins are taken from us. It is no sleep of death, but of everlasting life."

"Amen," said Sidney Close.

"Go to your rooms," said Penny.

The children did not move and the crosses they held – her golden one on the necklace which had belonged to her mother and which Nell must have found in her room, the metal one she had found in the old soldier's cash-box and which they all assumed had been with her grandfather in the trenches, one of the palm crosses given to them on Palm Sunday at St George's and the large crucifix which had belonged to an old Roman Catholic aunt of Alan's and which he kept on one of the bookshelves in his study – surrounded both her and Sidney Close in a silent ring of power. Sidney's eyes never strayed from her face, but he twisted an arm up her back, until Penny bit her lips with the pain, and then shifted his other hand across her throat.

"Throw those things in the fire and go to your rooms as your mother said, or I'll tear her throat open and drain every drop of blood from her."

The children hesitated. Sidney tightened his grip on Penny's arms until the tears sprung from her eyes with the pain.

"You saw what happened to the dog. Do you want me to twist your mother's head off?"

"He won't do that," said Penny, her lips barely able to speak the words so severe was the pain in her arm, "I am all he has to bargain with. Once I am no longer a hostage, he has no power and you can hold him here until your father returns."

It was true, but it was a truth the children could not bear to watch. The agony in their mother's face defeated them.

"Very well," said Anna-Maria, "Loosen your grip on mummy's arm and we'll do as you say. Only promise that you will not hurt her."

"No, Nell – that's what he wants," cried Penny.

"Nell's right, mum – we can't watch him doing this to you. Make your promise, Mr Close, and our crosses are yours."

Sidney loosened his grip. The relief was unbelievable, and Penny breathed in gasps. George walked to the fireplace and tossed the palm cross into the flames; it was consumed to ash in seconds. Helen tossed the crucifix after it and the wood charred and burned leaving the image of Christ to grow hot and melt in the flames. Amos threw in the metal soldier's cross; it snagged on the top of a log and rested there, waiting for the flames to find it. Lastly, Anna-Maria laid her mother's necklace on a branch and watched the flames dance up and around it.

"Now – go to your rooms!" shouted Sidney, sensing their last movements.

When the last door clicked to, Sidney forced Penny down into a chair and she collapsed forward onto her knees, her left arm hanging uselessly across them. Sidney moved behind her and she heard the standard lamp, which lit the niche by the fireplace, crash to the ground. There was an electric flash as he ripped the wire from the plug and the lights flickered on the landing. Penny turned her head in time to see him tearing the other end of the long flex from the base of the lamp and then he was on her, looping the flex around her neck and yanking it backwards until it tore into her throat. He tied it to the back of the chair and, with the remaining flex, lashed her arms and feet to the seat and legs. She could barely move her head, let alone struggle to be free.

"You promised…"

"I said nothing. I came here for help and your family has subjected me to abuse. I'll fix them."

Before she could say more or scream a warning, he had pulled a handkerchief from his pocket and stuffed it in her mouth. He tied it in place, tightly, with the end of the flex and then went up the stairs to the children's bedrooms.

When he came back downstairs, Penny had struggled herself into a state of collapse on the floor. The chair was tipped forward and she was under it, her head pressed into the carpet and bearing the whole weight of her body. Sidney straightened her up, removed the handkerchief and untied her. Penny felt grateful and was ashamed.

"What have you …?"

"When do you expect Dr Read to return?"

"I don't know. He has not been in touch. What have you done …?"

"You expect me to believe …."

"What have you done …?"

He slapped her across the face – hard. No one in her whole life had ever struck her before, and the shock took her breath away.

"Where is Dr Read?"

"He went to York."

He was covered in dried blood, his face and fingers were shredded by the teeth of the dog, his bared chest was scored in deep gashes by its claws and his manhood was being eaten away by venereal disease. Now, in anger that plunged into wrath, his eyes burned red. In the only way he knew how to retaliate he slapped her again and again across the face, first with the palm and then with the back of his hand on the return stroke, until Penny's face was a bruised and bloody mess.

"I'll ask you just once again where your husband is and if I don't get a straight answer I'll bring your children down here, and drain you dry in front of them."

Relief that her children were alive flooded through Penny with as much joy as she had ever felt. She looked up at her tormentor and smiled.

"I have told you the truth," she said, through torn lips, "He has gone to York. If I began to tell you why, it would make a very long might of it, indeed."

Sidney Close believed her. She spoke with such quiet conviction, and he knew that her children were her only concern.

"I have VD," he said, "contracted from the Bint whore and I want it treated – now! Where are his medicines?"

"In the surgery."

"Then you will call his partner, Jim Maxwell, and get him here and we will go to the surgery together. I must start my treatment tonight. I may have eternity in which to live, but I cannot bear this pain any longer. Do you understand? You will be my hostage until I am clean again."

"I understand."

It was a relief, in a way, to be moving forward. Once he had untied her, and with her torn and beaten body aching all over, Penny struggled to the telephone. If Jim were involved, then at least there would be an intelligent adult who could think calmly, and help Alan and the children through the ordeal when he returned. As long as Alan and the children were safe she could cope with Close wherever, and however, he intended to keep her prisoner while his treatment lasted. It was madness, or the very edge of it, but the only course of action was to move on. As she picked up the telephone, wondering what she was going to say to get Jim out on Boxing Night, the doorbell rang. She and Sidney looked at each other; in both their eyes there was huge relief. She looked at Close, trying to keep any sign of hope from her eyes.

"Remember the children," he whispered, and nodded towards the door.

Her heart sank twice as she opened the door: in the driveway, stood Corvin.

"Penny, what is happening? Your face … the blood! Your dog …?"

Before she could answer, Sidney was at the door, had grabbed Corvin by the collar and flung him into the room. The priest collapsed over the chair to which Penny had been tied. Sidney reached for the strap from which Corvin's crucifix always hung about his neck. He tore it from him, and heaved it into the fire with the others. He then turned Corvin on his back and smiled.

"Get up, priest."

Corvin did and glanced about the room. He ignored Sidney and crossed to Penny, placing his right arm about her shoulders.

"Come, my child, and sit down. I do not know all, but I can guess some of what has happened here this evening. Where are your children?"

"Upstairs," she whispered, "I believe they are safe."

He sat beside her on the sofa, his right arm dropping to her back, and took her left hand in his, stroking gently the scars left by the flex.

"Alan is not yet back?"

"No – we thought …"

"I am sorry to have dashed your hopes."

Penny smiled at Corvin, trying to give him the assurance she did not feel. 'Oh, any one of them but Corvin (lovely man though he is) and we might have stood a chance.' At this moment in her life, Penny needed a companion who was stalwart – who could face the awfulness of what they had to do without a backward glance. Penny stroked his hand gently, while Sidney Close watched and wondered.

"Sit on the chair, priest. Mrs Read and I have things to do and I cannot have you on the loose."

"I think not. I think our moment has come, Sidney. I think it is time we settled our differences," said Corvin, very quietly, as he rose from the sofa, walked to the fireplace and saw the ashes of his cross in the red hot embers.

"You were too feeble to face me alive, Corvin Unwood: what makes you think you are up to it now?"

"I am not the man I once was, and I am a better priest for it."

The quiet certainty in Corvin's voice caught the attention of both Penny and Sidney. A smile flickered suddenly across her torn lips and a frown creased the bloody forehead of Close.

"I am free from doubt about myself, as I have never been before."

"Free?"

"Of earthly concerns. I am balanced in time between this world and the next."

"My world?"

"No – not your world, but the world you may yet inhabit," said Corvin with a calmness in his face that Penny had never expected to see there. He was guiding this vampire to the moment when he might take his destiny into his own hands.

"You are talking of eternal life?"

"Yes. I am living it now and, for me, it will continue into eternity. After death, I shall have a spiritual body," replied Corvin.

"Such as I do not?"

"Yes."

"I will live forever – is that not immortality enough?" yelled Sidney Close.

"No – you are trapped forever as the creature you are. Imagine that – for all eternity," insisted the priest.

"You have something better to offer, Corvin Unwood?"

"My eternity is timeless. Imagine that, Sidney – being with God for all time and consciously aware of his presence ... Kneel, and free yourself ... remember, we can only come to the Father through the Son and, in accepting Him as our Saviour, our sins are taken from us."

Corvin reached out towards Sidney as he might have reached out to a child he wished to comfort. The vampire dropped to his knees and Corvin brought both their hands together in a gesture of supplication. For a second or so Sidney seemed to yield as he looked Heavenwards and his mouth dropped in prayer, and then a terrible cry came from his lips – a lamentation more deep and fearful than Penny or Corvin had ever heard in their lives. If all the heartache the village had ever known could have been drawn into one wailing, that would have been the cry that came from Sidney Close. He rose sharply to his feet, turned his back on them and sobbed into his hands.

Corvin glanced at Penny and walked over to the fireplace. He smiled at her. He was free and that brought such a peace of mind. He was free intellectually and spiritually. He was free to lead where he should. He had a sense of purity about him as he stood in front of the fire – such a consciousness as he had never felt. Corvin turned to Penny and smiled again.

"Forgive me," he said, "and save your children."

Corvin reached into the fire and brought out a flaming log. It was as wide as his chest and burning brightly – a true yule log. "Catch," he said, and tossed the log at Sidney Close. As he did so, the small metal soldier's cross dropped at his feet, burning a hole in the carpet. It was an inspired moment, a moment elevated by his faith. Corvin knew only that the vampire must be removed and redeemed. He was the only one who could do that, and realised fire was his only means. It was for him, also, atonement. 'Sin breaks the relationship between a man and God. God wants the relationship restored.' He, as the village priest had committed 'sins of omission'. He saw the heroes of his faith – he who had thrust his right hand into the fire, exclaiming "This hath offended" and then had died in the flames with 'extraordinary fortitude ... courageous in his timidity, and timid in his courage'.

The vampire turned as the log swept towards him and caught it, holding it unwillingly against his chest for seconds before throwing it from him across the room. The burning log crashed into the curtains which caught alight immediately, the flames rushing along them to the wooden poles and the ceiling. It was three old cottages knocked into one large house – lathe and plaster would burn ferociously and quickly. A ceiling would rapidly ignite the floors above, and the children were spread out across the second floor. Stairs and doorways opened everywhere, rooms ran into rooms. "I don't like to feel trapped, Pen – I like to meander a bit".

Now, the flames would be doing just that – meandering quickly and mortally throughout the whole building with a speed that Penny feared she could not match. As she rushed passed the burning Close to the stairs, he was too shocked to grab her and she reached the banisters without hindrance. Penny look back at Corvin, only partly understanding what was in his mind. The priest had snatched the red-hot cross from the floor and, as it seared the flesh on his fingers, he held it out towards Close. The vampire recoiled and Corvin closed with him, first slamming the cross onto his chest and then gripping him round the waist, pinning his arms to his sides and holding him tight. The priest's hands locked, his fingers entwined and he held fast to the vampire, gripping him in a ring of iron.

The sitting room was ablaze by now from end to end. The sofa on which Penny had sat with Nell was burning fiercely, with flames snaking their way through and across the arms and legs. The niches she had so adored were part of the fireplace, a gathering of burning shelves and treasures which were gone forever. Penny rushed to the top of the stairs and burst into Amos's room. He was trussed up on his bed with tape and gagged, also with tape. Penny looked around wildly: surely a boy had a knife – somewhere? Amos nodded frantically. Smoke was already curling up the stairs and winding its way along the landing. She followed his nodding head and pulled his pen-knife from the drawer. It took her seconds to cut him free.

"Free Helen," she said, very quietly and with considered calmness, "and get her out and away from the house. Do not stop for anything."

He was off along the landing in a flash, passing into what had been the third cottage. He knew why his mother had sent him for Helen: she would be terrified and he was the one to whom she always came. The fire was roaring now: it seemed to be shouting at them as it devoured their home like some ravenous beast. He hadn't realized that flames could roar but they did with an almost musical swelling of sound. The cacophony raged as he pushed into Helen's room, lifted his little sister over his shoulder and ran down through the conservatory and out of the house. The street was deserted and he crossed to the other side, standing away from the heat in the shadow of the Methodist chapel, and began to remove her bonds.

The trees around their home were on fire. Sparks splashed into the air and dropped onto the foliage, hissing as they spattered on the freshly-fallen snow and then crawling, insidiously, along the branches, warming and then burning. Now there were shouts along the street: people had come to watch or help, according to their natures. Mobile phones were flashed; emergency numbers were dialled.

Penny simply trusted her oldest son to do exactly as he was told; two of her children must be safe. She ran along the landing towards the next bedroom and found George. She did not need to wonder where his knife might be: it was stabbed into the rafter above his bed and she had cut him free in no time.

"Get out, George – now. Don't argue and don't hang around to find anything. Just go! You'll find Amos and Helen outside – I hope."

She knew George. He was 'one on his own' (as they say) – trustworthy but wilful and, therefore, not to be relied upon to do exactly as he was told!

"I'm going for Nell."

'Nell, Nell – my lovely Nell. I didn't leave you until last by choice. Let me be in time.' The flames had reached the first of the cottages where Nell had her bedroom, zigzagging their way through the dining room and coiling up the banisters of the second staircase. Smoke accompanied the flames, no longer aimless but drifting in thick clouds that choked and blinded. It was coarse in her throat and it stung her eyes as Penny found the door and burst in; already the floor was hot – she could feel it through the soles of her shoes. Close had strung her eldest daughter up to one of the beams that passed down through the centre of the room, but Penny had George's knife in her hand and, once she cut through the ropes which bound the girl's feet and ankles, Nell was able to run. As they left, the floor began to disintegrate and collapse into the room below.

By the time Penny, with Nell, joined Amos and Helen in the shelter of the Methodist chapel their home was an inferno of flame and black, curling smoke. People in the street were dodging the falling debris and brushing cinders from their clothes; the heat was intolerable. Perhaps fifteen minutes had passed – no more; in the distance Penny heard the sound of fire-bells.

The fire was tearing at their home, dragging it down to the earth and leaving it smouldering in heaps of randomly-scattered ash. There was fear everywhere as the flames drove inwards and then thrust skyward. It was relentless; there was no mercy. Beams they had loved bounced and scattered across the garden in which they had played; smouldering tiles crashed from the roof, shattering on the earth and sending searing ceramic shrapnel into the air. Doors and windows were bursting with tongues of flame that licked around the seals and jambs. Walls cracked in the heat and then exploded outwards, sending showers of abrasive plaster into the crowd that was gathering on the street. The fire shrieked, reminding those who watched of bonfire night when fireworks exploded. The thickening smoke blackened the sky and settled like some angel of death on the pure-white, snow-white trees and ground. As the roof collapsed, the exultant flames dashed and twisted, drifted and strayed but ever upwards, reaching for the heavens. Still Penny waited, her eyes fixed on the driveway: it was the only way from which her youngest son could run from the wreckage of their home.

George had run straight from the house as his mother had told him, without "hanging around to find anything", but he had gone down the second flight of stairs, through the sitting room and out through the front door. The stairs were afire as he leapt down them, two at a time, and he saw Corvin and Sidney Close struggling together in the fury of the conflagration; so fierce were the flames around them that they seemed like silhouettes against a lava flow and George was reminded of a picture he had seen of Daniel in the fiery furnace. Corvin's grip on Sidney had never faltered; the vampire might as well have been bound by iron. He was stronger than Corvin and capable of shifting his shape within the clergyman's grip but he never succeeded in slithering from his grasp. The flames took their clothes and then scourged their bodies and, while the vampire screamed both in agony and remorse, the priest was steadfast, lifting his head up to his Heaven. "Lord Jesus," George heard him say, "Receive my spirit that I might live in consciousness with my God."

George burst out through the fragmented front door. He ran towards what he had come for: lifting Leo's dead body from the ground, with a strength he could not possibly have possessed, Penny's youngest son ran with his pet across the road to the shelter and safety of the chapel.

"Thank God you're here, George. We'd begun to worry."

"I didn't hang about, mum, but I couldn't leave Leo there."

"No, of course you couldn't."

"The Reverend Unwood is dead, mum. I saw him in the flames."

Penny put her arm round the head of her child.

"It was his way of upholding his faith, his way of being true."

"He was a brave man, wasn't he?"

"Yes, George, and he was a good one."

"It's like burying someone, isn't it mummy?" said Anna-Maria, suddenly.

"Yes," she said, wondering at the girl's perception, "I suppose it is."

"Saying goodbye."

"Yes – you're right."

"But somehow knowing you'll see them again."

Penny smiled in the darkness that was reddened by the fury of the flames; 'sharing those moments of understanding with a child is one of the most beautiful things.' She recalled her words to Alan after the Harvest Supper. 'The giving of a life, that others may live ... beyond understanding ... a glimpse beyond the grave – an apprehension ... a conception of what might be ... the continuity of life and death.'

CHAPTER 13

No greater love

Tony Crewes insisted, once they were back in the house, that Anton be allowed in with them by the fire. The wolf, a naturally gregarious creature, had kept up a low whine ever since Tony had ordered him from the room. There had been more than distress in the wolf's cry: there had been concern. The whine had about it an element of keening and Tony Crewes, taken quietly aback by Sarah's sucking of his blood, realized that he was at the vampire's mercy. The presence of Anton, stretched out before the fire and taking no apparent interest in proceedings, was reassuring.

Once the wolf slept, Sarah seemed almost relieved that he was there. '....do not sleep tonight, do not trust me.' They had been her words, after all. Tony had dragged another old chair into the room, and they both sat by the fire like a married couple, speaking only when a thought occurred, out of desire rather than necessity.

"You do not believe in Heaven, Tony?"

"No – I've tried, but the idea seems ludicrous to me."

"That is what frightens you, isn't it – that you will simply destroy me rather than send me to salvation? ... So where do you think we go after we are dead?"

"I don't know. The nearest I got to understanding it was when Corvin described Heaven as 'the state of being with God. It is when we are with God all the time and consciously aware of his presence' – and that just scares the life out of me!"

"I don't understand that, either. To me Heaven is a place. Do you remember dad's funeral? ... The Reverend Unwood talked about dad as a ship, passing away from us 'over the horizon'. He said it was 'time to let him pass' and that mum would be there and it was her who would cry out 'Here she comes!' That's how I see Heaven, Tony – as a far shore where mum is waiting."

"Yes, I can understand that, too."

It wasn't meant to be condescending; he simply recoiled from plaguing this young and vulnerable woman with what he saw as the endless, pointless chattering of abstract theology.

"There's no need to talk down to me, Tony. I know that it was an image, but it's an image that helps me understand. Do you see?"

"Yes, yes, Sarah – I do."

"I am still at sea, stuck between this shore and the next. I died in the sea, but could not find the farther shore because his mark was upon me and I was – and am – loathsome to God. Do you understand?"

"Yes."

"Help me."

There was a long silence. She wanted, but did not expect, an answer. He could not accept that his would be the hand which drove her finally from this world. Tony Crewes grappled with his conscience, and sought contentment in the crackling of the fire. Sarah lit his stove and warmed some more soup for him. She placed it in his hand with another piece of the soft bread his wife had baked and some more cheese. He wanted to talk her back.

"I can't shake off the memory of how happy you were last summer when we met on the cliff path. You were looking forward to a new life."

'Over and over, time and again, we keep saying the same things, holding on to the one reality we know and of which we can be sure – this world, now!'

"We can live together – your kind and mine – in this world. Brultzner has, for God knows how long."

"I don't want to live like Horst! If I was to stay, I would want to be human! This is Christmas, Tony. What do people do at Christmas? Families come together, friends visit, we share a celebration that links us all to each other – there's life everywhere, but it has no meaning for me now. This so very special time is meaningless – do you understand?"

"The 'soul' – how loosely we use that word! – has gone out of it?"

"Yes."

"But it needn't – give it a chance, Sarah. This is your first Christmas as … as you are. Time and experience will change things for you … and for Matthew."

"Don't – don't dare use my son to give your arguments force. Persuade me on the basis that Horst has led … an acceptable life, but don't use my son!"

Tony had always been excited when challenged to justify his views and he turned on Sarah with an argument that was intended to bully her into agreement.

"Horst has done no lasting damage in this village …"

"No damage?"

"No – the damage has been done by you and vampires like you – inexperienced vampires whose lust took them over. It does you no credit to run away. We have all done things we regret. Human or not, we have to learn to live with them and face up to them. You cannot undo what you have done and running away from it – leaving others to clear up the mess – is cowardly and unseemly."

It was a calculated assault on her better nature. He knew the kind of world in which she had been brought up – the world of the village church, which taught you to be in touch with your conscience and put others first. He was questioning her motives in seeking to destroy herself.

"The nature of the vampire is unstable – fragile, unpredictable," she replied, "You could not wish me to remain here, not knowing what I might do."

"You are not likely to repeat what you did to Luke Turrel, Sidney Close, Necker Utting and your husband."

"You do not know that, and it is arrogant of you to suppose that you do."

"No, I do not know that, but I do know that Horst has conducted himself with great abstemiousness, and so can you. You have a duty to remain here, Sarah."

"Are you suggesting that I should live as Horst has done – like some parasite on the people of this village?"

"Things have gone too far for you to remain here in Dunburgh – I can see that – but it is conceivable you could start afresh somewhere else. What harm do Eva Schulz and Katerina Schnell do in Prague and Leipzig? They take what they need, no doubt, as we all do. Yes, even humans take what they need, and leave half of it on their plates to be thrown away as waste! Think positively, Sarah! How many of us even considered Horst Brultzner a threat? We loved him – admired him! We all agreed what an admirable contribution he was making to village life. Brultzner's crime – if you can call it that – was to act as a catalyst."

"He released the worst in others."

"He released what was simmering under the surface – that was hardly his crime – and you are not Horst Brultzner. You are a far, far better person who could do much good by living on, rather than running away."

"You want me to live off the blood of your children?"

"I wasn't thinking quite so specifically. We all turn a blind eye to what we do not wish to see. Which of us would eat meat if we saw a stunned pig hanging by its back feet having its throat cut, or a calf in the killing pen, or a little lamb tossed on a pile of his brothers and sisters in the slaughter-house? We know these things go on, but we choose to ignore them. It's inconvenient to think about something dying so that we might live when, in fact, we could live quite as well – and far more cheaply – in other ways … We all ignore what we do not wish to think about. Those of us who knew – and there would only be a few – could, I am sure, turn a blind eye to how you sustained yourself."

"Get thee behind me, Satan."

"Beth has called me a few things, but never that," he laughed.

"You're not happily married, are you, Tony?"

It was something he had never talked about. Following the affair (a glamorous word for a time in his life that was, at the end of the day, simply dirty), the whole business had been hushed-up and he and Beth had tried to get on with their life. He loved her, but the process of day-to-day living had been, and was (and, as far as he could see, would be forever) extremely difficult.

"No, I suppose, I'm not," he said, "but that's not what we are talking about."

"But it is relevant to your line of argument. In 'saving' me, you are out to 'save' yourself. I'm not saying that your motives are essentially selfish, but my salvation would also be yours … wouldn't it?"

He was filled with sadness, overwhelming sadness, again. Here was this girl, this young woman, who was so intelligent, so perceptive and so good-natured, who could give so much to the community in which she chose to live, who was talking him round to taking her life. 'One of your lame ducks' was Beth's contemptuous phrase, spoken in that cheese-cutter voice of hers, which came back to him as he looked at Sarah. They were saying the same thing, weren't they, these two women in his life? He had left his family on Boxing Day to seek his own salvation. He wanted to do something good to prove to himself that he was not a failure. He wanted to 'be there' for someone and actually matter. He looked at Sarah, who watched him quietly.

"Yes, I want to see you on your way for my own satisfaction. I want to know that there is a woman in this world for whom I have been important – and successful. I want to get out of the rut of being constantly conscious of what I haven't done, and to be able to delight in those things which I have done. OK? Is that so bad? I am not after anything (how shall I put it?) material for myself. I am not wishing that we might run away and set up home together. I just want to know that you and Matthew will be all right, and that I have played my part in that success story."

Sarah came over to him and knelt at his feet. She ran her hands over his thighs, took his hands and looked up at him. There was nothing coquettish in the gesture; she did it as a daughter might to a father who she saw in distress.

"Tony, you're a nice man. Stop torturing yourself. It's not for me to say, but it does seem to me that you've been emotionally hurt – and that may not be down purely to your wife, you know – but it is something you must work out for yourself and for her. It has no place here."

He stood and walked over to the door.

"I won't be a moment," he said, "Don't follow me."

She knew why he had gone, and went over to the window. Sarah watched him walk down to the edge of the marsh and look out over the village. By morning, if God gave this man the strength he would need, her ordeal would be over; his, unless he took the bull by the horns (or, more exactly, the wife) would go on forever. He would grow more and more embittered, and it would spill over into everyone he knew and everything he did. She'd seen those old men following their wives around, their eyes red with inexplicable anger. Perhaps, in some ways, Tony was right: perhaps, if she stayed …? Sarah smiled quietly. He was alone, and she was alone: each needed the other so much.

When he returned his eyes were red but not with anger, and he smiled at her:

"Thanks," he said, "I deserved, and needed, that …"

"I didn't …"

"You spoke from the heart. I couldn't ask you to be fairer. I am a dreamer – a 'romantic' my wife calls me, as though the word was inherently contemptible – and I ought to sort myself out for everyone's sake, and I will. You are right! I have this image of a perfect and harmonious relationship with a woman, free of imposition by either, without rancour and run through with joy unimaginable. Only I can imagine it, and for me it is real: hence, my dilemma!"

"Tony …"

"It's all right. Once in a while someone is honest enough to speak openly, and we all need that: just leave me to absorb the thought – that's all I ask. But – aside from that and just so I can say I played every shot I knew – please let me try one, last persuasion – please?"

"Matthew?"

"Matthew: how can you bear to leave him?"

"You …" She would have said "bastard", but had not been brought up to think, let alone speak, that way, "…don't pull any punches or take any prisoners, do you Tony? … I cannot bear to leave him. You must understand that, mustn't you? But I cannot offer him a life. I will sleep when he is awake – OK, there are ways around that, but not ways that are satisfactory. You must realise that – yes? How would we ever share a summer holiday? How would I ever be able to go to a school concert – if it wasn't held on a dark, winter's night? Would he be able to invite his friends round to play, while mummy provided a picnic?"

Sarah rushed out the thoughts that had plagued her and which, until now, she had been able to express only to herself.

"Don't think that I am not tempted, Tony. I have imagined myself in some other place, living quietly as Horst lives here and coming back at times – just occasionally – to watch how he is doing, how Nadine is bringing him up. Of course I have – what woman wouldn't?"

She paused and looked at him, at Tony Crewes, this man, this tempter, and suddenly it did all seem possible. She had provided for Matthew: there was the cottage, Nadine would be a good mother and he would soon come to love her, and the boy's almost mystic rapport with animals ensured his future. She would drift in and out of his life, unbeknown to him, like a kindly aunt.

"We shall destroy Brultzner," said Tony, as though reading her thoughts, "He is not of a forgiving nature."

"No," she said, "and over the centuries I should become like him: someone with no real friends and whose family died around them. Far, far better that one day (when Nadine knows it to be time) that he should understand his mother was once a woman who – frail though she was and a prey to forces over which she had no control – did, at last, show she knew right from wrong and did the decent thing."

There seemed nothing more to say. Outside, the night was cold with fallen snow which had, somehow, lost its earlier beauty; inside, the fire roared a welcome. It was her last night on earth; tomorrow she would be released from her purgatory, if the courage of the man was strong enough. She walked over to him and sat on his lap, her legs outstretched across the arm of the old, decaying armchair. Anton stirred by the fire, and growled; it was a warning and his eye never left her face.

It was comfortable like that; she had often sat with her dad in the same way. 'Sitting in the quiet, after a hard day's work' he would say, and then light a cigar – his only vice. How she had taken his love for granted; and his need of her! She recalled the night they had dug her mother's grave, when Corvin had tried to console them, but when all her dad wanted had been her company. He hadn't hesitated to ask her; he had simply assumed that she would be there, as family, to share the sadness and the anticipation of what was to come. March! Less than a year ago! In the end she had helped him through her mother's death; it had been a great burden, but she had done her best. Now, she would see them again, and soon, so soon; she could hear her mother's voice, excited, almost exultant – 'Here she comes!'

Her mother's body had looked so old in the coffin, but she would be younger now – as she remembered her as a child: her spiritual body. 'Our spiritual body expresses the personality we have developed in our earthly bodies'; how wonderful her mum would look when they met! She was repentant. She hoped she would meet little Luke Turrell: she couldn't bear not to meet him, of all people. How horrible her vampire nature had been, but she had asked for forgiveness: not directly, of course, but quietly – to herself – without being able to mouth His name. Her dad hadn't expected to see her mum again. She knew that, although he had said nothing; but he was wrong. The wisdom of women is far greater than that of men; they are in touch with the old and everlasting truths. She had sobbed her heart out and then got on with what she had to do; her Dad had never got over it, and never would have done.

She looked at Tony Crewes. He was dozing, worn out with worry and the anticipation of the ordeal to come. She stroked his face. It was a kind face, and he was a good man. She was beholden to him. She knew that, and she knew that what he had to do for her would be done in love. 'Greater love hath no man but that he lay down his life for a friend.' Someone said something like that – she wasn't sure who or when. He wasn't 'laying down his life', of course, but what he was to do would haunt him forever. He was an atheist and saw her 'reconciliation' as 'death'. There was no comfort for him in what he had to undertake: it was an ending, nothing more. Had he looked upon her as evil, then it would have been easier for him. It would simply be the removal of a plague from the face of the earth, but he could draw no comfort from such a belief.

He was asleep: yes, he was asleep. One more taste of his warm blood, to help her on her way, to take her across to the other side? She saw the marks on his neck: soon they would be gone. She reached over and touched the scars with her finger tips and Anton growled, eying her with malevolence. Sarah slid from Tony's lap and strolled over to the window. Across the marsh, somewhere in the village, she could see a great fire burning. That was what they once did to her kind – dug them up, cut off their heads and tossed them onto the fire, or simply burnt them alive. At least she'd been spared that suffering, spared the flames. 'I have lingered too long already. I should have walked out into the sun days ago.' 'What stopped you?' 'Hope …' 'What hope?' 'You fell for an illusion, Tony. Destroy it, before it destroys you.'

Morning came and Alan Read walked with his wife and children to the ruins of their house. The whole lawn was blackened and the hedge, which had bordered the house on the road side, was nothing more than a few fragmented, sooty spears. The front door frame, through which Leo had launched himself at Close, still (amazingly) stood, but it was all that was left of their home. All else had collapsed into heaps – the washed-out, charred and ashy remains of their lifetime and that of their ancestors whose photographs, dating back to the 1840s, had perished in the blaze. Yet they were together, and the sense of dispiritedness, which should have hung over the devastation, was absent. Here, amidst the wreck of their lives and the death of their friend, there was hope.

Martin had taken control on the previous evening and what remained of the bodies were now in the morgue with Old Strowger holding the key. "It's a rum un, Constable Billings. If it weren't yew, I'd think there was sumthun fishy goin' on. Three bodies in one day is goin' sumthun even fer Dunburgh." Martin had laughed, made a phone call to Junket, "scared the shit out of him" and taken charge. It had been a fire, a terrible accident; the only body was that of the Reverend Unwood, who had died in the flames while helping to rescue the children. "Yes, everyone else had got out safely. Yes, it was a miracle. The family were staying with Dr Maxwell overnight. Yes, he was the Senior Partner (capital letters always impress)."

Having found Sidney's coffin empty, Martin and Nadine had taken a battered Simon, and a shaken Amy, to A&E, under protest. He'd been bandaged and x-rayed: there were no signs of any underlying damage. He had then taken him and Nadine to their bungalow on Shore Lane, and taken Amy and Sandra to the Police House. "No – you will stay the night with us. Amy will see to you. I'll just drop Ainsley off home and then get back. We've still to hear from Peter, Alan and Tony. Let's pull this together."

Before dropping Ainsley off, Martin had 'ushered' him into a concealed lay-by (funnily enough the one where Ainsley had spent a little time with his bit-of-thirty-something-on-the-side, putting the icing on his Christmas cake, so to speak). There, he had given him the kind of talking-to which has gone out of fashion in the modern police force and thereby ensured that Ainsley did not leave his house "even temporary like" till he (PC Billings) had decided that everyone had come to their senses. Needless to say, Ainsley remained housebound until after the New Year which quite surprised Milly and tickled her pink; but then, you can't keep a good man down, can you?

It was as Martin finally slumped into his Windsor chair with a glass of Medoc that Alan Read rang: he had found Rebecca and they were well on their way home. Had Peter phoned? No? There had been consternation in the voice. Martin told him that a lot has happened, and to come straight to the Police House when he arrived. "Do not go home. You understand? No – your family are fine, but everyone here is exhausted. We'll all talk together when you get here." Martin had then made his phone calls to Nadine and Penny: "Yes. They would be there." He collapsed and sipped the wine: 'deep mahogany body, complex but easy on the nose.'

With the exception of Esther, they now all stood looking at the blackened ruins of the White House. They were all up-to-date, having spent the early hours at the Police House, and all were too shattered to think clearly – Nadine and Simon, Martin with Amy, Penny and Alan, Rebecca without Peter. Alan and Penny's children were with them; she had brought them round after the meeting at Martin's.

"Where will we live, daddy/" asked Helen.

"We'll find somewhere in the village until our house is re-built."

"We shall live in the White House again?" said Amos.

"What do you think, Pen?" asked Alan.

"I think that it would be a lovely idea."

"Then we can bury Leo in the garden?" said George.

"Yes," said Alan, "we'll do that later this morning. I'm sad about Leo, as sad as you – he was a lovely dog and a good, brave friend."

Looking at the burnt mess, it didn't seem possible that it would, once more, be a house again. Everything had gone, of course – every single thing they had ever owned, every single possession they had ever treasured. It would be a long hill to climb, but they would reach the top, gathering shared memories along the way.

"I must see mum, now," said Rebecca, "if you'll excuse me."

She let go of Anna-Maria's hand, not remembering who had grasped who, and stepped back.

"I'll come with you," said Penny, who had been told by Alan of Rebecca's "critical state" and didn't want to leave mother and daughter alone together at what they all now saw as a decisive moment.

"Are you sure?"

"Yes, it will be easier that way."

Esther listened in utter silence. Not for her the uncertainties that plagued Tony Crewes or the unshakeable convictions that put the steel into Simon Palmester's spine. Her Corvin's death was not God's will, but the outcome of acts of the Devil. She absorbed all that Rebecca and Penny told her – absorbed it and screamed it within her skull. He would hear: he would need to hear, but not yet. The old beliefs were rampant within Esther: an eye for an eye, a tooth for a tooth but none of this anger entered her thoughts. She saw only Corvin alight in the flames. Her white knight had gone and she was alone with her daughter, conceived in love and who they had reared in love together. She held on to that thought and she let it grow.

"Dad sacrificed himself, mum, but he knew what he was doing, and he knew why."

"Yes – your father had his faults, but a lack of faith wasn't one of them. He was worth ten (a hundred!) of your Bishop Twiddles. Few have ever gone willingly to death for their faith: nowadays, none but your father. I do not doubt that he died in the sure and certain knowledge of his faith, but I do not forgive his death. He came late into my life and has left too soon. He was a young priest, you know, in my father's parish when we met, and it was love at first sight. We married quickly. We had to. I was past forty and we wanted ... you," said Esther, as she reached out and took her daughter's hand. She squeezed it gently, but with a relentlessness that was typical of her way in life.

"And you cannot begin to imagine the joy you brought – not even when you have children of your own will you quite understand what your arrival meant to me and Corvin. He deserved better than giving his life to rid us of that diseased man. He deserved an old age in peace and tranquillity. I was possessive of him, I know. I plagued him at times but he loved me, despite all that. There is no life for me outside him ..."

Rebecca's hand flinched and Esther looked, searchingly, at her daughter.

"Oh no, I do not mean that! Would I, would I, Rebecca, while I still have you? No, no. But Corvin and I meant so much to each other, and now he is gone. I can state it baldly, but I cannot begin to describe the complete devastation that I feel."

She was silent, then, for a long time. Neither Rebecca nor Penny liked to disturb her reverie. Eventually, it was Penny, perturbed by Esther's attitude, who spoke.

"Esther, would you like Alan to prescribe a sedative?"

The look Esther gave Penny with her cold, grey eyes said everything about her unforgiving, relentless nature.

"No, my dear," she said, "I need to stay awake ..." and then added, as though talking to some distant abstraction, "....but I don't know why."

Some hours before dawn, Sarah woke Tony. She did not want to be alone at the end, not for her last few hours. She was glad he had come, so unexpectedly, to her aid. The idea of walking out into the sun had horrified Sarah. Her leaving of this world had to be at the hands of a friend and, preferably, a friend whose feelings for her were ones of love. She did not doubt that Tony loved her, deny it as he might. No one leaves their family at Christmas without the deepest of reasons.

She woke him and he was ashamed that he had slept, ashamed that his fatigue overcame him, and that he could not stay awake for her this night of all nights.

"You won't leave me here, not in this house, alone, when it is done?"

"No. You need have no fear of that, Sarah."

"I want to rest ..."

"...with your mum and dad?"

"Yes – oh, yes, please Tony."

"I promise you ..."

"How ...?"

"Corvin will see to it – believe me."

Their talk was unreal – part of their being together rather than thoughts spoken or promises made, but they gave Sarah the reassurance she needed.

They walked down to the edge of the marsh again and discussed the garden of the old house as though they were going to build a life there together. They watched the fire in the village flickering into embers, and they wondered. They walked through the shrubs and trees, which shielded the track that Sarah had followed to the old house. Sarah was concerned that Tony understood that he could return that way. The snow had stopped falling and their tracks remained imprinted where their steps had passed. They were like lovers at a railway station about to say goodbye, yet filling in the time with aimless chatter.

They talked of journeys they may have taken together – could take together were she to ... live. The night could be turned around so easily. She had only to drain him dry of his blood and then wait, and tend him for ... three days (was that the time it took to realise a new life?) and he, too, would be unleashed upon the world and they could leave together, forever. A new life awaited them. All it took was the courage to make it happen. Sarah curled lovingly into his side, cosseted under his arm, pulled in against his coat.

She could feel it coming: that change of mood, that change of state. Now that she was ready, now that she had accepted what must be done – for Matthew's sake, for her parent's sake, for her sake – she must be steadfast. It was, after all, like taking a journey and the pain – the pain of the stake – would only be for a moment. Beyond that, if God was merciful, there would be an eternity of peace. She saw again her mother's park bench and the green grass and the trees, and the fear went from her.

"One more walk?"

"You'll walk me off my feet," he laughed.

Outside, the day was grey. Snow clouds still hung in the sky, obscuring any chance of sun. She led him once more to the edge of the marsh and then to the track upon which he could return.

"How will you destroy Horst?"

"I have no idea. It may be the others."

"I don't want him near Matthew. You will see to that, won't you, Tony?"

"I'll keep a fatherly eye on him."

"Nadine will look after him well, won't she?"

"You know she will."

"And the little cottage that is his?"

"We'll look after it."

The talking, about things which they had discussed over and over again since she had woken the previous evening, was beginning to irritate them both. They knew what lay before them, had decided that it must be so, and there really was nothing more to say. If the dawn was much longer in coming, he would again try persuading her that there was an alternative way, yet both of them knew her mind and did not want to weary one another.

Even had they been young lovers, they could not have lost themselves in kisses or a long time-defying embrace. It was not part of their relationship, not part of what, in so short a time, they had become, one to the other. So they walked in silence, none the less entwined for that, she tucked in under his arm, he with his cheek resting on that mane of honey-coloured hair.

The dark was lifting, not in bands of brilliant colour as it might have done but unobtrusively, as the sun struggled to pierce the gloom of the winter's day. The dawn was little more than the lightening of the clouds where they touched the horizon. The light filtered through slowly, turning pale the very edge of the sea and taking that bruised plum colour from the lower clouds. They looked at each other, both surprised to see tears in each pair of eyes. Now, even now, it was not too late. There was still time. There is always still time to change one's mind, and seek another way. 'You cannot undo what you have done and running away from it – leaving others to clear up the mess – is cowardly and unseemly.' He had said that to her, not in spite but in anger and fear. He kissed her gently on the forehead, and they walked back into the house for the last time.

She was asleep in his arms when they arrived back into that derelict old room, and Tony placed her gently down onto the sheets she had brought. It seemed so comfortless, so awful – her body lying there separated from the dusty floorboards only by a sheet. Yet, it was best for what he had to do – a firm surface was best. He had rehearsed it in his mind so many times during the night, during those moments when she thought he was asleep and when he had reclined in the chair, hoping to feel her teeth in his neck so that he would sink into oblivion and be at one with Sarah.

He opened the holdall and placed everything carefully on the ground within hands reach. He didn't trust himself to move once he had begun. He had seen it all – the wooden stake over her heart, the sudden awakening with her dreamy eyes wide in fear, her hands reaching up to him in one last (now futile) appeal, the shaking of the body as it went into spasm and her blood splashing up and around and over him. He just hoped, so much hoped, that there would be a look of gratitude in her eyes in that final moment; something that would let him know he had done the right thing, had sent her on that journey to her parents. 'And just at the moment when someone at my side says, 'There, she is gone!' there are other eyes watching her coming, and other voices ready to take up the glad shout 'Here she comes!"

Tony Crewes, kneeling as though in prayer, placed the point of the stake carefully, raised the coal hammer and brought it down in one bone-crunching blow with as much force and passion as he could muster. 'And that is dying'.

CHAPTER 14

Requital

David Stokes rose early on the morning of December 27th and clambered quietly out of his bed. He had a lot of work to do before noon and wasn't sure whether he would have all the time he needed. He couldn't explain to his mum and dad why he had to go off by himself "yet again" (he could hear his mother asking it!), so it was best to go quietly. He'd leave a note, just saying that he was walking the dog. He dressed silently and then crept downstairs. The black Labrador looked up from her basket by the stove in the kitchen, but she didn't move: she wasn't expecting this – it wasn't part of the routine. David signalled her to be quiet and then rummaged through the cupboard for the cornflake packet. He didn't like cornflakes particularly, but it was always the packet nearest to the front and he would make less noise finding it. He poured out a bowlful, added milk and sugar and munched away, watched by the dog. She'd be good company, anyway, for what he had to do: he was on his own now and frightened. He measured out the dog's food, and she wolfed it down in the way Labradors do. David put on his coat, gloves and a scarf, turned the key in the kitchen door and slipped out.

Tony had let him down, but he wasn't too surprised. He had waited long enough for the man to come back, and now he must go it alone. He did have the old woman's help. He'd left her the note. He must trust that she would read it at the right time. Mrs Unwood had unnerved him a bit, but somehow he thought she was reliable. He remembered her sitting alone in the churchyard, stooped on one of the benches, and how she had sat bolt upright when he said "We hid the key under the mossy stone". But it wasn't just her who had been listening to him; it wasn't her who had sat up so quickly. It was Him. So where had He been yesterday morning? He wasn't around the estate. David knew that because he would have seen Him. It just had to be hoped that He wouldn't turn up this morning – at least not before noon, and then He would be very welcome. It was the old lady who had given him the idea, scribbling 'The sun will destroy him' on that piece of paper. They'd been talking about Him when they all had the meeting – Him, the one who had killed the bull. "Do you know about the temple?" The old lady didn't speak like that: it was Him who had asked the question, and David could only trust that he had tricked Him.

David made his way to the wood, the one that ran up from the Ness, the one from which Tony Crewes had emerged less than three weeks before. He'd brought his dad's axe and bow-saw with him in case he needed them, but he didn't want to make too much noise and the sound of chopping would echo all over the estate on such a quiet morning. He also slung a coil of rope around his shoulders. Everything else was up there; he knew that because he had seen to it when he got back on Boxing Day. He wasn't sure how much wood he might need, but it could be a lot and he would have to haul it all himself – and without being discovered.

The sweat that poured from David Stokes as he gathered the wood was not merely the sweat of labour: it was the sweat of fear. He had thought about it all night. He had hardly slept for thinking about it, and as he worked he realized that he too – just like Mrs Unwood – was terrified. He hardly knew why he was there, working away gathering wood, but he was convinced, in the still morning air, that he didn't want to be. He wanted to be back at home with his mum and dad. It wasn't the apprehension that He might suddenly be there, behind him in the wood. Mrs Unwood had said 'The sun will destroy him', so he couldn't come in daylight, could he? That was part of the plan – to force Him out of his bolt-hole into the sunlight. If only the sun would shine! Breathing deeply was calming; all the heroes did it before going into battle. He must just concentrate and carry out his plan, step by step, moment by moment. He had until noon – when the old lady should open the note.

The snow had nearly gone; it hadn't been a real storm, anyway. It was what his dad called "a mild flurry": not like the real snowstorms, which drifted as high as barns and blocked roads for weeks, that they had years ago. It still hung around in the woods though, but not thickly enough to deter the rabbits who popped in and out of the brambles nibbling at the grass. Bess and the rabbits just ignored each other: his dad called it "familiarity breeding contempt". David smiled to himself as he made his way among them. In the disappearing snow there was the distinctive trail of a running fox, two footmarks, then a gap, then two more. He wasn't around now; he must have passed through in the night.

David's father, John, and the other workers on the estate didn't like rabbits: in a cold winter, unable to find grass and plants, they would gnaw at the bark of trees. David did like them, although he saw no harm in the fox taking one or two whenever it needed to eat: that was nature's way. Here, among the animals, he felt safer – part of the way of things, part of the never-ending cycle of life and death. His teacher had used that phrase and he'd been the only one in the class who could say what it meant. It wasn't that he'd heard it before: he just seemed to know, instinctively.

He worked solidly for two hours and built up a large pile of old, seasoned wood – mainly branches and small logs and the odd piece of discarded fencing, steeped in creosote, that would burn well. There had been no sounds anywhere: it was a Friday and Lord Wangford had told the men to take the week off, as there was no point going back to work on a Friday after the Christmas break. His lordship was a good man and David's dad liked him. The sun was up: you could feel it, even if you couldn't see it behind the thick layer of cloud. David wasn't looking forward to the next part of his task: it would be hard work. More than that, he could have explained why he was out collecting wood, but not why he was dragging it towards the temple. The most difficult part would be getting it up the slope in the open, without anyone stopping him. David had no idea what he would say if his dad appeared. There was no way that he could begin to explain what he was doing or why he was doing it. If only Tony Crewes had kept his word and got in touch! An adult could explain, but then he did not know what Tony had in mind. He, too, might have objected to David's plan – yes, he would certainly have objected.

Out on the open hillside, a barn owl circled. They often hunted in daylight and David watched in fascination as the bird looked for mice in the grass. He had once seen a large owl pick up a small rabbit, but that had been later in the year, of course. The owl flew off down the slope and settled on one of the posts that fenced off the herd of white cattle. They didn't have to worry about finding their own food: they were well fed with extra hay supplied by his dad.

David began the long haul, backwards and forwards, time and again. He had roped the wood, and dragged it in bundles to the top of the short flight of steps that led down to the doorway of the temple. When it was all in place, he heaved a sigh of relief. Another hour had passed. He was exhausted, and would have loved just to go home for breakfast. It was half-past nine; they would be getting up at home. They would read the note, but they wouldn't worry about him – not when he was with Bess. She had walked backwards and forwards with him, up and down the slope, in rhythm with his work and the hillside. The fear had gone now, partly because his work was almost completed but also because he was exhausted. Once he had put his hand to the tiller, there was no turning back.

Suddenly, looking at the pile of wood, David realised that more than the temple was going up in flames this morning. His whole future would be going with it – and his dad's present? He couldn't worry, much as he loved his dad. Perhaps someone else would explain? He found the key under the mossy stone and unlocked the temple. He pushed open the oak door on its dark and silent hinges. He took one of the torches from the wall in the antechamber and lit it. The torch spluttered, flared and then burned steadily, lighting his way into the inner sanctuary. David felt it as soon as he stepped inside – the Presence; there was no evil here. Perhaps he was the evil one. The old lady had been good, hadn't she? She'd seemed to approve – hadn't she?

To the left and right of the central aisle stood the two statues with their torches held down to the darkness and up to light. Both wore their short Roman cloaks and the bright red Phrygian cap, and beyond them, at the far end, stood the three altars. The curtains were drawn but, should they move back, the eyes of the god would be upon him. David ran his finger along the benches and looked up at the beamed ceiling. They were solid wood, dry as bones and would burn so fiercely. It would be a crime to destroy them: how much trouble would he be in with his parents and everybody. It wasn't really fair, was it – that he should have to do this alone?

He would run back and tell his dad; his dad loved and trusted him – but he wouldn't understand. The old lady would – if she was still on his side! He thought of Tony Crewes again, and how they had stood on the hillside not speaking but knowing what the other was thinking. He thought of the voice he had heard 'The many times I have stood here never diminish my feelings towards this place', and realised now that it had been His, the slayer of the bull. He had come to understand his home in quite a different way, after that experience. He had become aware of the Presence. On that hillside he had felt dread, veneration and wonder. He was part of something he didn't understand. Perhaps the killing of the bull had been necessary – like the fox taking a rabbit or the owl a mouse?

No – no, no, no: it had been a ritual killing. None of the thirty-one had needed to eat the bull as the owl needs to eat the mouse or the fox the rabbit. He did not know why they had killed it, but it was not out of need. Besides, it had not been a fair fight: the bull had stood no chance against Him. He had moved like ... like the Shadow of Death. When the bull had gored him, the horns had passed straight through; it was unnatural. After the slaying, they had moved forward, closing their circle around the dying bull. The way they closed in, filling their cups and gorging, had been horrible.

David ran out onto the hillside, the torch in his hand. No one was there. He was not there. David went back inside, shoved the torch into the bracket and began to heave the wood into the temple. It took him an hour but, by half-past ten to eleven o'clock, he was ready. Out on the hillside, he uncovered the can of petrol he had placed there on the previous day; it was the one his dad used for the lawn-mower. It was secreted under an outcrop of bracken because that had seemed safer than hiding it in the temple itself. Over David's world hung the shadow of Him and what He might discover. David splashed the petrol everywhere and then placed the can back carefully in the bracken. The torch would burn for an hour, wouldn't it? Anyhow, there was another. He would keep that with him – that and the matches. There was just one more thing then – just one more thing to do, and then he would wait for Him to come. David walked back into the temple. What he needed was there, waiting for Him.

So tangled were Rebecca Unwood's emotions that she found it impossible to bring herself to a state of calm. None of her old, well-worn, up-to-the-minute, stylish strategies for self-assurance worked. Her father was dead (of that there was no doubt) and the shock was yet to drive home. Peter was missing (and the faces of her friends told her to fear the worst) and she and her mother were under His influence. She thought of Him with a capital 'H' because he was now her God. She would spell that with a capital 'G' when she wrote of Him in her journal.

Peter seemed a distant memory, and Rebecca felt no regret. He might be dead or he might be alive – it really made no significant difference. Their walks down Marsh Lane and the promises they had made were things of the past. 'At the lych-gate we said goodnight, without a kiss, but with enough shared understanding to fill both our hearts.' She remembered writing that in her journal, but it was a long time ago, about a man she had once loved. When you loved the One God, the One True God, there was no room for anyone else – not even your family.

Her father had chosen his fate, pitted himself haplessly against the greatest, and lost. She had tried to dissuade him, tried to reassure him but to no avail. 'Oh dad, stop torturing yourself. You're a good man and a good priest.' She remembered saying that to him, the night he had come to her, distraught and overwhelmed by guilt. He had been a good village priest serving his turn as his god demanded – nothing more, and he had died trying to prove otherwise.

Only her mother perturbed her. Lurking in the old woman was a disloyalty to their Lord. Rebecca could not get at her thoughts. The old lady was closed off, staring at the wall, afraid to think. Her mother had always irritated her. They had never got on, and now Rebecca felt that she was betraying Him, but could not understand how.

She had remained silent on the journey home, kept her own council and told Alan Read nothing he could not see for himself. It seemed better that he did not know. Standing by the ruins of Alan's house, watching the dying embers with his family, Rebecca had wanted only to get home and be done with it all.

They were all frightened now – all at a loss about what to do. Once before, they had tried to invade His house and ran from it, terrified, their tails between their legs. He was more than a match for all of them. What a story He had to tell! She had told Alan Read that, and enjoyed the look of dread upon his face as it unfolded.

They had all gone home after looking at the Reads' burned-out house. All of them had been tired, dead-beat, with nothing left in them, dried-out husks of their former selves. They had arranged to meet for coffee at the Police House; they were running out of houses! Rebecca laughed. The rectory was no good because they all suspected her mother of being in league with Him, and now the White House was a shell – a burnt-out shell. She liked that phrase; it summed them all up, but it said nothing about her.

"It's all right," she'd said, "meet here – it's closer." "I don't think …" Alan Read had begun, but she had interrupted him "Meet here – please! There are many rooms." It had been a crafty "please". She didn't want them plotting against Him – not behind her back.

Her mother hadn't slept, but just sat staring at the wall. Rebecca had left her, gone upstairs and stretched out on her bed. As she lay there, Rebecca remembered the first night He had come. She hadn't realised it then but the *room had darkened* as she massaged herself and other hands had taken over, filling the room with *a strange intense silence* and her dreams took her *into wild mountains* and she saw *the shadows of the men who lived there. Somewhere an animal called in the night.* Her eyes opened and around her was the 'soft urgent movement of flesh'. She hadn't written that in her journal, but she remembered thinking it at the time. She could 'do nothing but wait the moment of satisfaction' and 'her arms reached up and held him. The room was filled with the sound of her moaning – soft, low, contented moaning.' *The pale room was full of shadows that gathered about my bed and leaned towards me; a gentle touch flickered across my lips and passed to my throat; the sensitive skin of my neck fluttered.* It had been Him.

Ten-thirty came and they all arrived on time and met in the dining room. Alan and Penny Read, Martin Billings with Amy, Nadine and Simon – and Tony

Crewes. He was like the walking dead. She had never seen a face so white or a frame so ravaged. He had rung Martin early in the morning and the policeman had driven round through the back roads of Eastwold to an old house where Tony had been with the young woman, Sarah Brown. Tony told his story in a few words, only. As he finished, he said "I hoped, just hoped, that there would be a look of gratitude in her eyes in that final moment; something that would let me know I had done the right thing, had sent her on that journey to her parents." "And was there?" asked Penny Read. "Yes, oh thank God – yes." And then he had collapsed and sobbed as Rebecca had never seen any man sob, except perhaps her father when life overwhelmed him.

Esther came into the room as he cried, stared for a while as though cancelling her thoughts and then said:

"Rebecca, have you seen my handbag?"

"Handbag? Why do you want your handbag?"

"Is it here? Will you pass it?"

The handbag was on the table where Esther had dropped it on returning from the churchyard on Boxing Day afternoon. She reached for it, but Rebecca forestalled her and opened the bag.

"It's my bag, Rebecca, pass it here."

"Why do you want your bag?"

She knew there was something amiss. The old witch was up to something. Esther grabbed at the bag and they struggled frantically, watched in amazement by the others. Alan Read stepped between them, and took the bag, easing the women apart.

"Here you are, Esther."

She reached into the handbag and removed a scrap of paper, folded in two. All their eyes were on her, but she was not watching them. Her eyes were far away, gazing out through the french windows. On the outside of the slip, was written 'Open at noon, tomorrow; read and remember.' She knew and was glad; they could all see it in her face.

"What does it say?"

Her face was afire with delight. The struggle was over. All could be revealed.

"The temple is ablaze. I have fired the sanctuary of the Order of the White Bull," Esther almost shouted aloud, and the words roared in her mind.

Horst Brultzner sat upright in his coffin, shaken by the words which stormed into him from Esther Unwood. He had tried to renew his union with her upon his return but the old woman's mind was a blank; he saw nothing but bare walls and the face of the village priest – her husband. She was no doubt asleep, thinking of the foolish and weak Corvin. But he was awake now! 'The temple is ablaze. I have fired the sanctuary of the Order of the White Bull.' He should not have slept. The game was not yet over. Who had fired the temple?

He struggled from his coffin. Far better that he should have stayed awake as he had done many times before; now he was weakened even more. A vampire's daytime state was always fragile – always vulnerable. He could not transform himself, nor move with the same speed. His strength, though formidable, lacked the power and sinew it acquired after dark. Yet he must make his way to Wangford Park!

The sky was still thick with cloud as he emerged from his front door, and he was grateful. One of those beautiful, crisp winter days – so beloved of the English – was not what he wanted. He was dressed in his favourite night attire – slim, black trousers, and the little jacket with the Chinese-inspired collar over a white shirt. So sleek was he, that Brultzner resembled one of his wolves as he ran. The sight of him, long-legged and ravenous for revenge, was awe-inspiring. He knew that battles were usually won by those who looked and acted the part. He had cowed many a more skilful opponent simply by dressing appropriately for the occasion and believing in himself: 'I am vengeance and will smite my enemies from the face of the earth.'

Across country he sped, following the route he had taken with Crafty Catchpole, the night he had fed him to the wolves – off the beaten track, somewhere down beside the church and then along Dovehouse Close beside Cassyn's River. The lanes became tracks and the tracks disappeared. He kept to the east of the river and followed its course towards the north-west and so to the Wildlife Park where he paused for a moment to look up into the sky above Wangford Park. A great column of thick, black smoke was rising towards the heavy winter clouds and flames flickered beyond the line of trees. He remembered his words to Charles Wangford. He did not know who had fired his temple, but Brultzner swore that the culprit would suffer a long and painful death. He crossed the river and made his way by hawthorn hedges and willow trees to Blacksands Ness and so to the estate. He covered the distance, some two or three miles, in less than ten minutes.

"It must be the boy," said Tony, "What have you done, you old witch?"

"The boy asked me! I have sent him on his way. He will preserve the temple."

"Brultzner will kill the boy."

"No," screeched Esther, "no, that cannot be. I do not believe that! The boy knew what he was doing. I have faith in the boy."

"Cars – get cars," screamed Tony, weak with fatigue, desperate with a sense of failure over his use of David Stokes.

None of them had driven to the rectory – the distance was too short and the walk "would do them good". They set off towards their own vehicles, hell-for-leather. Only Esther and her daughter hung back, and then clambered into Rebecca's car.

"We'll come with you," said Simon, who was waiting at the gate with Nadine, "and may God have mercy on your soul, woman."

Brultzner sped out of the marsh to the north of the park, and so across the informal, relaxed parkland he loved so much. The roof of the temple was crumbling as the mess of smouldering turfs dropped into the inner sanctuary, and the earth baked beneath them. Inside, the wooden benches and roof beams were burning fiercely. Brultzner could not believe what he was seeing; he felt defiled. Who had a grievance so great against the temple of the Brotherhood? Who knew of its existence? Wangford was a safe pair of hands: what did he know of this atrocity? Fifteen hundred years of history and faith was becoming a blackened ruin as he watched. At first he wanted to rush in and tear from the flames what was left of his temple, but he knew the effort would be futile. Everything would be corrupted. Brultzner felt besmirched.

The ancient vampire turned and looked about him, expecting to see Wangford and his men rushing towards the degradation. He could not imagine who might be responsible for this contamination of his faith – this tainting of his God. On the slope, the Wangford herd grazed, oblivious to the turmoil about them. Among the cattle, Brultzner saw a figure. It was a child – a boy – and he stood watching Brultzner. It was the boy he had seen with his father, the herdsman. Stokes! His very quietude told Brultzner all he needed to know. The boy's stillness was a challenge, but the vampire still did not understand. He could not accept that this boy had fired his temple.

He walked down the slope towards the boy. He was such a slight figure, as he stood watching Brultzner approach – a trivial thing of no consequence in the great scale of things. Something glittered in the boy's hand, but he did not stir. Fair-haired and tousled he stood, waiting. Brultzner knew how to cast fear into his opponents – a look, a gesture, a certain movement of the shoulders – but the boy did not so much as blink. When he was younger, the vampire had seen his victims so transfixed with fear that they dare not move. The boy was not like that – his composure was that of a warrior who had thrown his spear and was waiting to see where it would land, not doubting his aim. Brultzner closed his eyes to shut out the vision: blink and the boy, an illusion, would disappear – vanish in the mists of winter.

When he opened them again the boy had not so much as shrugged his shoulders. A voice whispered in his ear, but Brultzner shook it off, and away. Behind him, the temple of his God crackled and roared as the oak benches fired and seared the stones which the legions had shipped from the north, and which had weathered in the soil of Suffolk. Inside the temple the stones were burnished with care and use. No more: this boy had destroyed them forever. He had wiped out generations of love and solicitude in one single act of vandalism.

Brultzner reached the fence and paused, but only for seconds, before placing his hand on a post and leaping into the pasture from a standing jump. The boy's eyes widened. Brultzner did not move once he was inside the fence, but stood and peered into the boy. They were very steady eyes and the mind behind them was used to looking straight into his enemies and turning their thoughts over as they struggled to find the words to speak.

"Did you fire my temple, David Stokes – or is the question fatuous?"
"I did."

"What is the most fearful death you can imagine?"

The boy looked back at the master vampire, but he did not answer. He had no protection against this Creature's retribution, should it come to that, and he was committed to the fight. Suddenly, without a hint as to why, Brultzner laughed.

"Do you see yourself as the Biblical David?" he asked.

"No."

The hushed response would have been chilling had Horst Brultzner been a man of normal emotions: as it was, he took it as a warning – underestimating his opponents had never been a fault. The vampire had not moved since leaping the fence, and he was too curious to wish to fluster the boy. He waited with the fence at his back, and – as he thought – intimidated David Stokes. He was not a merciful man to those who betrayed or even opposed him, but the killing here would be too easy for a soldier to take pride in its accomplishment. He wondered about the boy: he wondered how he should kill him with suitable cruelty to make a fitting punishment. More than that he wondered why the boy had carried out this abomination. He would talk very quickly once Brultzner laid hands on him, but one could always enjoy more detail when the victim talked willingly.

It was as he watched the boy ready to make his move, which would be so sudden the child would be in his grasp before he could blink, that Brultzner noticed, for the second time, something glitter in the boy's right hand. It was flat against the boy's legs and the vampire, sharp though his eyes were, could not make out what it was the boy held. Asking would have been a sign of weakness and beneath Brultzner's dignity. Here he was, a seasoned soldier of Rome, being gulled by a child. However, the game had gone far enough: others would be on the move by now, drawn by the fire that howled and spluttered, growled and rumbled behind him, ripping the heart from his faith. 'Armed with a sword and a torch at birth, he fought to deliver the world from evil.' In his left hand the boy held a torch – one taken from the temple – and it was pointing downwards to darkness and twilight; he had not noticed that before, so still had the child stood. In his right hand, whatever it was the boy held glittered and Brultzner knew with absolute and deadly certainty that it was his sword, the one with which he had slain the white bull and which he had placed on the altar as a gift to his God.

Brultzner took a step forward and, immediately, the boy raised his right arm. It was the sword. Could he be proposing to do battle? The boy's arm swept forward in one beautifully long stroke; the sword flew from his hand, perfectly balanced, and landed in the grass about half-way between the two of them.

"This time," said David Stokes, "the duel will be a fair one."

It was then that Brultzner realized the young bull – the animal who had taken the place of the one slain – had been lying in the grass by the feet of the boy. Until that moment, the creature had simply been part of the herd. Before the animal was on its feet, Brultzner had reached the sword and stood holding it in his right hand.

"Within minutes, boy, I'll have your head on one of these fence posts."

Still the boy did not speak, but he moved aside and ran his fingers through the mane of the bull. The animal pawed the ground, the nostrils snorted and the head shook. David ran his fingers along the white back and slapped under the chest and belly. There was love in his strokes; his fingers probed every inch of the bull's body.

"Viros servasti eternali sanguini fuso," he said, very quietly.

You can only die horribly once, and David Stokes realized that he now had nothing to lose. The man who was to kill him could do no more harm than he already intended. Brultzner accepted the lines at their face value – "You have saved men by the spilling of the eternal blood", but wondered what the boy meant. The young bull, which was used to the boy, sensed the vampire's antagonism. It pawed the ground, snorted and then charged. David's heart gladdened, and he felt hope spring within him. He had reared the animal, with his father, since it arrived. He loved and knew it and, like a dog, it felt the comradeship.

Brultzner was taken aback by the suddenness of the onslaught and stepped swiftly aside, but not before one of the bull's horns tore through his body. The vampire gasped, buckled at the knees and fell to the ground, clutching his abdomen. Blood seeped through his fingers, and trickled onto the grass. The look of bafflement on his face was an expression David had never expected to see rest there. Brultzner stood, still grasping his guts, and turned to face the young bull which, delighted with its success, charged again. This time, weakened though he was, Brultzner stepped aside and slashed viciously across the back of the beast's neck as it passed. David hadn't expected that; he'd sought a fair fight, one where the bull stood a chance. He had expected – expected what, a clean kill one way or the other? What he had not expected was ... was for the young bull to rush by him, its neck flowing red.

Behind Brultzner, the temple still burned brightly, flames leaping and diving – blood-red flames that danced a dance of death in the crisp air of the winter's morning. The vampire was silhouetted by the flames and David remembered his father's words. "That's not for us to ask." But David had asked, and the answer was being fought out in front of him. "Long before your god there was another, who brought salvation to the world – but not by slaying his dearly beloved son. It was the blood of a bull which brought life to the Earth." Brultzner had said that and now he was fighting for his own salvation. A third time the bull stopped and turned. It pawed the ground furiously and ran at Brultzner. The vampire wheeled round. He was fighting with one hand now but the spirit did not leave him. He seemed invigorated as though here, at last, he had met a worthy opponent. The field thundered under the hooves of the bull. Despite himself, David was excited – no longer daunted by the sights and sounds of the fight as he had been on that first night.

Brultzner held his position, conserving all his energy. If he could defeat the bull – and he had slain many in his time, not always at night or in his Un-dead state – then his guts would have time to heal, as they had so many centuries before. He had only to control his own jeopardy, hold on to his own precariousness and bring the ritual full circle. Time and again, the movement brought them close together until bull and vampire were both covered in their own blood and the blood of each other, as the bull charged and Brultzner slashed. He was skilful soldier, and he knew that, in the end – provided he held himself together – that he must prevail. Already the young bull's neck was a mangled mess of gore and flesh. The creature must eventually weaken, and then he would drive home the blade and finish the ordeal.

When the moment came, David had to admire them both – bull and man; the combat was intense and fought with verve. Brultzner and the bull really were "one being", oblivious to all around them. At last, the bull passed so close that the horns tore through Brultzner for a second time, digging deep in under his ribs and lifting him from the ground. He grabbed its left horn with his left hand and tried to swing onto the beast's back, but the young white bull had the better of the conflict and with a brutal toss of its horns threw Brultzner up and over, so that he crashed down at David's feet, stretched and exposed. David saw Brultzner open his eyes and look up at him with a sneer on his face. He was immortal and could not be destroyed – he knew that and, ignoring the pain which racked through him, he smiled at the boy.

"Well," he murmured, "what now, David Stokes?"

The boy saw the sword and wrenched it from the vampire's feeble grip. He raised it with both hands over the rib cage, gripping it so tightly that his knuckles turned white. He brought it down once over the vampire's heart, and faltered. He brought it down twice, and met the gloating eyes.

"It is not easy to kill, is it David Stokes – to rule out a life forever? Have you the courage? I think not."

At that moment, as the tears flowed from the boy's eyes in frustration and acknowledgement, a hand touched his shoulder. It was a kindly hand, reassuring and bringing with it comfort: it was his father's. He had come running from their home when he saw the flames. John Stokes – not knowing what was happening, but thinking only of his son and trusting in his goodness – took the short sword from his boy and brought it down for the third time. It sheered into Brultzner's chest, cutting through his ribs, opening up his heart and transfixing the vampire to the earth beneath him. Brultzner turned a look on them both – a questioning look of bewilderment and anger, his eyes not believing what he had seen or what had happened, a look full of the realisation of what he had lost – and then the corpse crumpled and became as autumn leaves that drifted away in the chill east wind which gusted up the slope from the old harbour.

CHAPTER 15

The social scene – New Year's Eve

John Stokes took his son in his arms and hugged him. They stood together for a long time, although he knew full well that a crowd had gathered while the conflict raged. No one disturbed them, and to all intents and purposes they were the only people on the hillside. David felt the trust in his father's hands and it eased his anguish; he had behaved instinctively, not foreseeing the outcome of his actions. He dare not look up, but held on to the hope in his heart. How long they stood there he could never remember, but the stillness was finally shattered by the sound of the shot. His father held on to him then and would not let him go, but held his face close to his jacket so that he smelt the herd in the fabric; then, he heard his father's voice.

"I don't know what's been going on here, your lordship, and I don't say my boy has behaved as he might have done, but I think the greater fault lies with you. I think it's time we all had an explanation."

"We can leave it now, John, until a better time. There will be a time – when your son is able to speak for himself. As for now, just let me say that no one lays any blame at his door."

"I agree with Mr Stokes," said a third voice, which David recognised as Dr Read, "I think the matter needs settling now for all our sakes. Look around you, Charles Wangford, and acknowledge your responsibility for what you see – as we all must."

"There is no need for the boy to be involved any further in this, Dr Read."

"There is every need – at least so that he knows enough to placate his heart. I think your study might be a more suitable place than this hillside," replied the doctor.

His father lifted David and carried him down the slope. He looked back over his father's shoulder. Where Brultzner had been there was nothing but a dark stain on the grass and, beyond, David saw the young white bull around which some of Lord Wangford's men (drawn there by the smoke and flames) were already gathered.

Once in the study, David looked about him. The first person he saw was Mrs Unwood who sat, white as death, but with a smile on her face as she met his eyes. Her daughter sat by her, looking only at the old lady and hugging her. She too was pale, but David thought he saw relief in her face, as though she had walked a long way and had finally dropped her rucksack from her back. Dr Read's wife was also

721

sitting on the leather sofa, her face torn and bruised. She was being hugged by her husband, whose face bore a long scar from the top of his cheekbone to the corner of his mouth. The scar had been stitched, but it gave him a rather sinister appearance. He then saw Tony (so he had come, if late in the day!) who walked over to him.

"I'm sorry you were left to face this alone, David. Believe me, you were not only brave but right to do what you did," he whispered.

He sat down on the floor at David's feet, stretched his long legs in front of him and looked up rather sheepishly at David's father.

PC Billings and his wife stood by the window; she looked upset and he looked stern and purposeful. On the big leather chair sat the old priest from the Bethel with his daughter who was perched on the arm of the chair. David could not make out what her expression said, but she was looking straight at Lord Wangford, who stood by his desk, alone and friendless.

The first to speak was the old priest whose loud voice echoed round the study.

"You did what the Lord would have you do, son. There may be dark nights ahead for you, while the sight of your friend remains in your memory, but you were doing the Lord's work – that others should have done, and spared you the pain."

He paused after he said this, and looked around. His face bore the kind of expression that David's mother would have called "meaningful".

"But you have everything to be proud of, and you've brought honour on your house. He's a brave lad, Mr Stokes, and a righteous one," continued the old priest.

"I'm pleased to hear you say that, sir," replied John Stokes.

"If David tells us his story first," said PC Billings, quietly, "that would give us a starting point."

David did, helped by the policeman who seemed to know how to coax his story from him. He told them everything – most of which all of them (except Lord Wangford) seemed to know. When he'd finished, his father said:

"My son's interests were only in fair play. He had seen the old bull killed by Lord Wangford's Brotherhood. It was a sight that would have sickened any of you here in this room, believe me. We may not have done as my son did, but he is a child and his sense of justice is simpler than ours. I apologise for the destruction of your temple, your lordship. Any one of us has the right to worship our god freely. I don't dispute that, but you harboured that Thing in our midst and you had no right to do so. I'm with Simon Palmester on this one – my son has done us all a service."

"I should apologise, Mr Stokes, to both you and David," said Tony Crewes, standing as he spoke, "None of this was very clear to any of us, and I wanted the key to the temple."

"As you say, you would have done better not to have involved a child."

"Mr Stokes," said Esther Unwood, rising unsteadily and making her way towards David, "there were times when none of us knew what we were doing. I might say," she added, with a laugh, "most of us did not know what we were doing most of the time. We were all taken up with our own little lives. When David and I met in the churchyard at St George's – only yesterday morning, but it seems an age ago – it was his instincts that were right. They were the instincts of a child. I did not know what I was saying most of the time. All I knew was that … Brultzner should not know. It was David who so cleverly turned Brultzner's power over me against the Devil himself. He had to burn the temple because it was the only thing that would have drawn Brultzner from his grave. Only then could he be destroyed. My dear little boy," she continued, turning to David, "do not blame yourself for the death of your bull. We had both hoped for the sun, but it was not to be and you had no way of knowing the outcome of the fight. As it is, you and your friend have rid the world of an evil that should never have walked here."

She turned to face Charles Wangford, and pointed her finger towards his face.

"I lay that squarely at your door. I agree with John Stokes – you have every right to practise your faith as you see fit, but if you choose to harbour evil in your midst, then you lose that right. You knew what Brultzner was and you might have surmised what he would unleash within our village. If you choose to ride with the Devil then you take the consequences. Your Brotherhood may have had nothing to do with what Brultzner was, but you shielded him and gave him succour."

Esther Unwood looked around her and then back at Charles Wangford, who had not moved and whose face gave no indication of his feelings.

"I can see now that the rest of our little band kept things from me – once they realized that I had spoken with him – and I do not know what has happened in the last few days, but I would be right in thinking, would I not, that the faces of Alan and Penny owe much to Brultzner's influence? I also see that Peter is not with us. Would that be down to him, as well? If so, Charles Wangford, it is also down to you. I shall not expect John Stokes or his son to suffer at your hands. I shall expect you to do the right thing."

She turned again to the boy and placed her hand on his shoulder.

"Are you feeling a little better about what happened now, David? I know you have lost your friend, but he died in a good cause and it was not your fault. Lord Wangford's man put him out of his misery very quickly, while your dad held you and we will see that he is buried properly in a place where you can visit him every day. It is like losing a loved one – do you understand? – and it is important that we continue to talk with them."

David nodded; the tears were running freely, now. His mother was kind, but he didn't think she would understand (they were country people and a bull was just another animal), but this old lady did – at least, a little.

"Yes," he said, "but I don't want him anywhere else. I want him here, with me."

Quietness descended on the room at the boy's words and his father shifted uncomfortably, while continuing to stroke his son and run his fingers through his hair. He seemed about to speak, but could not, and then Charles Wangford spoke for the first time.

"If you were thinking that you might resign from my service, John Stokes — there is no need for that. Whatever its future, the herd needs you and your son."

"I don't feel able to carry on working for you, your lordship — not after what's happened."

"I don't think that need trouble you, John."

"May I suggest that you take David home now, Mr Stokes? There are matters we have to discuss with Lord Wangford, and they do not concern your boy. If you wish to stay, of course, please do," said Alan Read.

"No, I think you're right, Dr Read. I'll take David home now. He needs his breakfast."

Smiles floated about the study as David and his father left the room. Martin Billings held open the door for them.

"I'll see to the young bull, son. I'll be in touch in the next few days," he said.

Once the door was closed behind them, Alan Read turned to Charles Wangford and said, simply:

"Well?"

The baronet's tone changed immediately and he replied:

"I have nothing to say to you — any of you. I would suggest that you all leave now."

"No, Charles. We have all known you a long time and need to hear your side of things."

Charles Wangford did not reply, but struck a bell push on his desk. After a few minutes of intense silence, a servant entered.

"Please show these people out, Hewitt."

"Yes, sir."

Nobody moved. Hewitt looked at his master, and at the nine people in the study. He raised his eyebrows and said:

"Shall I return in a moment, sir?"

"PC Billings, I am requesting that you assist my butler in removing these people, who are not welcome here, from my house."

"It's too late for that, Lord Wangford, and you are in no position to make a phone call to my superiors."

"I would find your continued presence quite intolerable."

Still no one moved, but the only tension in the room was within Wangford himself and between him and his butler. Eventually, he turned and said:

"Thank you, Hewitt."

"Thank you, your lordship. I will remain at hand."

"You're beaten, Wangford. You've sinned and the time for repentance is at hand. Start by giving us an explanation."

"I have no intention of saying anything further. You are wasting your time."

"I was attacked, in or near your York temple, by two men I could, and will, identify quite easily. I have no doubt they were members of your Brotherhood," said Alan Read, "Rebecca was imprisoned there and both of us are very willing to find Maxine Fox ..."

"I do not know a Maxine Fox."

"Possibly not, but Brultzner did. Maxine Fox has a key to your temple, or a cellar beneath it. Peter Vishnya has been missing since yesterday afternoon. He was investigating your temple in Bath. It would seem a fair conclusion to draw that someone has attempted – perhaps successfully – to silence him as well. The link between each of these events and people is you, Charles. We have all your papers and I am prepared to hand these over to the authorities."

"I have nothing to say."

"Charles, you owe us an explanation."

"I owe you nothing."

"Do you know where my fiancé is?" said Rebecca.

"No, Miss Unwood, I do not."

"But you could find out for me, couldn't you?"

Charles Wangford looked at her, and there was a second's hesitation before he spoke.

"No, Miss Unwood, I could not."

"We are wasting our time here," said Nadine, "I'll drive down to Bath now, with Martin. We have all the information we need in those papers."

"I would strongly advise against that, Miss Palmester," said Charles Wangford.

"I'm sure you would, Lord Wangford. Never apologise, never explain: the catechism of the English aristocracy. The 'little people' are not only beneath contempt, but quite outside any finer feelings. The fact that one of our number is missing, possibly worse, and that you are clearly implicated in this, as you have been implicated in harbouring a plague in our midst, does not even begin to touch your conscience, does it? We have offered you an olive branch today, Charles Wangford, and you have tossed it to the ground."

Simon Palmester looked at his daughter as she spoke: whatever her religious views, she spoke the language of the Lord.

"Please Charles," cut in Penny Read, "A phone call from you would spare us all hours of anguish. Is it too much to ask an old friend?"

"I really do have nothing to say, Penny."

Without another word, all nine stood and left. When they had gone, Charles Wangford reached for the telephone.

Martin Billings did not hesitate. Once he reached the village, he cordoned off the churchyard at St George's and (together with Alan, Tony and Simon) began to remove Shane Marjoram's coffin from the earth. It was still only early afternoon and they had several hours of daylight left. It was too good an opportunity to miss: before nightfall, they would remove the last known vampire from the soil of Dunburgh-on-sea. It was a cathartic moment. Only a week had passed since they met at the White House, but for all of them it had been time in a purgatory they could never have imagined. Simon sat quietly and watched while the younger men dug. Alan and Tony worked quietly, neither having any stomach for the task, but

Martin was exhilarated: for him it was a "big buzz" moment. Psyching himself up was the only way he could cope with what lay ahead.

The soil had not impacted heavily and the digging was easy. Within half-an-hour they had Shane's coffin raised beside the open grave. The wood had already begun to rot and gave off the musty smell one finds in the attics of old houses. Only Mary Brown's crucifix, which Sarah had had fixed to the coffin lid, seemed unscathed. Martin unscrewed the lid and slipped a crow bar between it and the body of the coffin. They knew from her testimony that Sarah's revenge had been carefully planned – the coffin's inner shell was metal – and Martin had brought his blow torch. This, however, proved unnecessary because the metal lining of the lid was not connected to that of the actual coffin. As soon as the screws were removed, and they raised the lid, the stench of the vampire assailed them. He had taken no blood and was as dry as autumn leaves, but the slough of his re-birth filled the coffin. The white pus had turned a greenish-brown with decay, and the unmistakeable smell of old ditches surrounded the corpse.

There was a smirk on his face; the same kind of swagger that had been contained in his walk when alive now invaded his countenance. Only Sarah had ever loved him. Others were intimidated, nauseated, charmed for a while, "taken in" then dumped, angered, disappointed – according to their inclination. Shane Marjoram had no lasting affect on anybody: now, he awaited his Maker. The task fell to Martin who was the only one of the younger men who had not faced the ordeal of the staking. Truth to tell, despite having had to handle Grise's restored body, he was looking forward to the job. Marjoram had been a blot on his patch – a festering sore: had he lived, the lout would have been a curse on the village all his life. Martin had no doubt that one day he would have hit Sarah (just to test how much she loved him), and then hit her again, only harder the second time – and so on. There would have been drunken brawls in the pubs and village streets, silly young girls carrying his spawn, others who walked in fear of his temper and Matthew growing ever more like him. It really was "good riddance to bad rubbish" and, for Martin, driving home the stake was simply putting the last nail in the coffin.

They left the corpse where it was; Martin placed the stake over the heart and banged it home with three massive strokes. Shane Marjoram, so used in life to protesting loudly when things did not go his way, so full of the righteous indignation of the truly vile, had no time to protest. If he regained any kind of consciousness at all as the stake was driven in, it was only to hear Simon intoning the prayer for the dead. He had barely opened his mouth to yell, and opened his eyes in feigned disbelief that it was happening to him, before his now-dead body collapsed in on itself and the odour of his putrescence filled the air. Alan took his surgical knives and removed the head. Tony Crewes stuffed the mouth with garlic and rubbed the edges of the coffin with the flowers. Martin screwed back the lid; each screw he turned one extra measure, just to make sure. They lowered the coffin back into the grave and re-filled the pit. There was no memorial (Sarah had not wanted that) and it seemed a fitting end that the mound above him should grass over once and for all.

Martin heaved a sigh of relief and looked at the others.

"You can leave the rest to me," he said, "I'll see Old Strowger tomorrow and arrange for Sarah, Grise and the remains of Corvin and Sidney Close to be decently interred. I take it we can leave the religious side of things to you, Simon? You will have no objection to conducting the services for the families – Owen and his children, and Rebecca and Esther?"

"Yes," said Simon, looking the policeman up and down with some distaste at the very question, "you can leave that side of things to me. I will see the families."

"Good. Then by New Year we can have settled this business as far as we are concerned here in Dunburgh."

"Yes," said Alan, slowly and carefully, "as far as Dunburgh is concerned. What about David Stokes?"

"I said I would see to that," said Martin, "I promised the boy. I can't wait to take a digger onto Wangford Park. I think we can all envisage a very suitable burial ground for the white bull."

"I would like to help," said Tony Crewes.

"I thought you might. We'll have to think of a fitting memorial, too – won't we? I'm sure you'll come up with something that will satisfy the boy."

He paused and looked around at the others; a grin crossed his face.

"There's always a buzz somewhere, isn't there?" he said, "In addition to all the grimness, I have a report to write for my superiors."

"I wish I could share your sense of satisfaction, Martin. There are so many missing pieces yet to be placed and the most urgent is Peter Vishnya," replied Alan.

When Rebecca and Esther returned to the rectory there was a message on their voicemail: it was the voice of Peter Vishnya. 'He was sorry he hadn't phoned before, but there had been problems. He was all right, but had lost his car keys. Someone was sorting that out for him. It had taken longer than expected. He would explain when he returned. Don't worry. He was all right.' Rebecca did not really think that she could take too much more. The relief did little to assuage the anxiety because, somehow, in the back of her mind, she felt that someone was playing a very cruel joke.

Esther simply stared. She had been trying, so desperately, to contain everything. She needed to grieve for Corvin, she needed to love her daughter and she needed to cherish the child. How could one so old be expected to accomplish so much under circumstances so trying? The boy, at least, was safe and, for the moment, Corvin must wait. She could not, anyway, actually believe that he was dead: not in the sense that she would never see him again. They sat in the kitchen over a cup of tea. It had seemed the only thing to do. They could give each other no comfort. Their friends had left them. Penny and Amy and Nadine had gone to their respective homes.

At least He – yes, He – had gone from them forever. On that, at least, both mother and daughter were agreed. As those dry leaves had disintegrated and gusted up the slope, they had felt the weight drop from their shoulders. They had felt His grip on their minds broken forever. Rebecca's tongue slid over her canine teeth; already they were less sharp, less ... incisive? She laughed. She could laugh again. A lightness of heart had returned to their lives – for the moment. It was preparing them for the shock when the realisation of what had happened to Corvin struck home. What had happened to Corvin? Was it something so inexpressibly horrible that they could not begin to conceive what it might be – not yet, not until their sanity had a chance of holding on to itself?

Rebecca walked over to her mother where she sat, as Esther had so often sat with her husband for their last drink at night before they began Compline, and put her arms round her shoulders. They only had each other now. Even if Peter returned, there was a sense in which they only had each other – two women who had been together so long, with the distraction of only one man who was now dead. They sobbed. It was the easiest thing to do, and expressed so accurately and so elegantly the depth and extent of their feelings. Had Corvin, or any man, walked in on them he would not have begun to understand. Women could not compartmentalise their lives, taking each piece in turn as it suited. They had to embrace it as it occurred, in one huge, overlapping lump of awfulness. One could not settle things bit by bit, but only by the consideration of the whole.

As they clung to each other, Rebecca and Esther heard Corvin's car in the driveway. Both rushed to the door, and on the threshold stood Peter Vishnya. Rebecca was so angry with him. How could he do this to her? Did he realise what she had been through? What had happened to him? Why hadn't he got in touch before? She and Peter clung to each other, and then drew Esther into their embrace. There was much to discuss, much to sort out, many differences to be reconciled, but at least they were now together. In a shattered world they were, at least, together. 'At least' – what did that mean? Were they to be forever satisfied with 'at least'? Why 'least'? Why not 'most' – the most that life could give?

Two things had saved Peter Vishnya – the thick coat that he was wearing, which had trapped a layer of air against his body, and the cold as he hit the water. He recalled hitting the freezing waters of the Avon, and then floating to the surface. At that moment he had been warm, but it had been the cold on his face which shook him into consciousness. Somehow (somehow – how often that word had played its part in their little drama!) he had struggled to the towpath. He must have passed out then because he could recall no more until he woke the following morning in hospital. A man, giving his dog a last walk at night, had found him and called an ambulance. It sounded so old-fashioned, but the man's action had saved Peter's life

"We must phone the others," said Rebecca.

"I already have," replied her fiancé.

Those few days between December 27th and New Year's Eve were the busiest, and in their own way the most fulfilling, that Martin Billings could ever remember. He bludgeoned every necessity through without a backward glance or a retrospective thought. Old Strowger proved his worth in every respect: his support of Martin was unstinting and unquestioning. In order to keep the circumstances as close as possible, he undertook all the necessary preparations himself. It was years since he had touched a corpse, and "it was good to be back in the front line – hands on, like the old days".

Martin executed the practical details with military precision, leaving the emotional and religious side to others more suited to the task. The funerals were all quickly arranged at a time of the year not conducive to the purpose. Old Strowger worked on the bodies over the weekend and the remains of Sidney Close were re-interred quietly on the Sunday evening. The funerals of Grise and Sarah took place on the Monday, one in the morning and the other in the afternoon: both were buried in St George's churchyard – Grise in a new plot and Sarah with her parents. Nadine Palmester, who wrote a thoughtful and careful newspaper report for each, brought Matthew. The little boy stood by his mother's coffin not knowing what was happening. Within the last year, he had lost his grandma, granddad and dad, and now his mummy; and "Granddad Horst" had gone away. No, no one was sure where, but they didn't think he would be coming back. He held his Auntie Nadine's hand. At that time, it seemed to be all he had left in the world, except the animals. "Yes, Auntie Nadine would take him round to look after them later."

Corvin was buried on the last day of the year – New Year's Eve – and the church was packed. He had died in the fire trying, successfully, to save one of the doctor's children. It had been an heroic death – "fitting for a man who had dedicated his life to serving God. He had been a good priest, always ready to stop and listen." He was secure now – not in his study, but in a better place. He had not aspired to greatness, but had made his mark at last and, when he reached his journey's end, there would be Someone to pat him on the back and say "Well done, Corvin, my good and faithful servant." Perhaps even Martin Luther might smile at him. "Everything that is done in the world is done by hope." He had not compromised, not in the end, and he had brought hope. Perhaps, like Mary, he would find his Master in the garden and walk with Him there where his spiritual body would express the personality he had developed in his earthly body.

Sitting in the police station that evening, Martin thought back over the events of the past ten months and, in particular, the past eleven days, and composed his report to Superintendent Junket. He intended to leave nothing out. It was, after all, witnessed by the most reputable people – two priests and one's wife and daughter, a doctor and his wife, a policeman and his wife and an aristocrat. Even if you discounted the likes of farm-workers, an insurance statistician, a journalist and an Estonian immigrant, these were rankings with which to conjure.

He sent it directly to Junket's private e-mail address (it was the only way he could guarantee spoiling his New Year) and phoned him to make sure he read it that evening. "It's very important, sir, and rather out of the ordinary. There could be repercussions." He loved that last phrase – 'repercussions': it was said with relish. It was some while later that Junket phoned back.

"I think this joke has gone too far, Billings. Enough's enough – if you know what I mean."

"We followed the Book, sir. The one you recommended – the one that told us how to deal with vampires."

"The Book I recommended?"

"Yes, sir. You said that 'Driving stakes through hearts and cutting off heads seemed to be the order of the day', sir."

"Look, Billings, I don't expect you to ..."

"... lay this one on you, sir?"

"I don't like your tone, Billings."

"I'm quite serious, sir. Everything I wrote in my report can be verified. We have Brultzner's papers, and Lord Wangford is hardly likely to lie, is he sir? Why don't you give him a ring?"

The silence at the other end of the phone was, to put it mildly, deathly.

"Ooh, and sir, we also have eye-witness accounts of the various assaults ....ooh, and a sworn and taped testimony."

"I'll need to think about this one, Billings."

"There'll be remnants of the temple left after the fire, sir. There's always something for the forensic boys and girls to get their teeth into."

"I think this is outside their normal range of enquiry, Martin. Martin, I would want you to leave this in my hands. No stray phone calls. You say Nadine Palmester was involved? Would you speak with her?"

"Perhaps you'd better, sir. It might carry more clout coming from someone important – or perhaps you could get the press officer to handle it, sir – someone who is used to talking to the newspapers."

"I don't think this need to get into the papers, Martin. What did Lord Wangford have to say/"

"Very little, sir: we were rather disappointed."

"I think you need to take care with the tone of your voice, Billings. Lord Wangford is a personal friend of the Chief Constable."

"Really, sir? Perhaps that will help to expedite matters."

"Expedite, Martin?"

"You know, sir – get things moving, hurry them along."

"I think this is a matter of fools not rushing in, Martin."

"You mean we'd do well to leave it to the wise men, sir – or even the angels?"

Again, that deathly silence: Martin pictured Junket's face. Here was a man whose whole future was crumbling before him and there was no procedure, policy or mission statement to help him out. He was a high-ranking, modern police officer and he had to think for himself – as Martin had done every day of his working life on the beat. It was unheard of – no policeman should have to do that, let alone one who was making his way in the force.

"Good night, sir," he said, "Happy New Year."

He put the phone down. It rang again immediately, but Martin ignored it and there was a broad smile on his face as he sipped his glass of Crozes-Hermitage.

New Year celebrations in the village of Dunburgh-on-sea were in full swing. As always, the decision of where to go had been a difficult one. It was so important not to become set in one's ways. Lianne Snooks was tired of going to Pliny and Boller's – year in, year out – and Pliny wouldn't move because of her mother who didn't want to leave the house when the nights were dark. Well, you couldn't blame her, could you: she was over eighty? Barry Snooks didn't want to go anywhere, particularly. A nice bottle of wine or two and a steak would do him, and the television was usually good on New Year's Eve – not as good as when Andy Stewart used to do it, but good enough. Ideas had been tossed about and hinted at since the harvest but no one had come to any decision except Pliny, who wasn't going to leave her mother at home alone. Boller didn't mind: he was happy to go anywhere (or stay anywhere) as long as there was plenty to drink. There'd be no backsides to grab this year – well, none worth grabbing. They'd just buried Grise, and Sandra Bint wasn't going anywhere for the New Year. Ample didn't mind where she went (perhaps somewhere out of the village would be nice?), but Billy Bassett had "put his foot down". He wasn't going anywhere out of the village because that meant he'd have to drive and he wouldn't be able to drink, and he couldn't see the point of celebrating the New Year unless you had a drink. Joney and Ben Chine were abroad (no one knew where) and so it was no good asking them. Mavis wouldn't be coming this year, of course – not so soon after Sid's funeral: it didn't seem decent, somehow. Beth Crewes might come, but rumour had it (on the grape vine) that Tony had walked out on her on Boxing Day. Christmas was always a difficult time for everybody, but if he had walked out then she wouldn't feel like coming either.

Late in the day (but not too late) Ample heard that Plumptious and Benny Walters were putting on a special night at the Jolly Sailors – "special night at the Jolly Sailors," repeated Billy, who now saw a way out of his predicament. They were booking up fast, but were sure they could make room for a group of old friends – "group of old friends," repeated Billy, to emphasise the favour being bestowed upon them. More than that, Plumptious was going to bring in a Scottish piper – "Scottish piper," repeated Billy. No, Pliny's mum didn't mind going to the Jolly Sailors, as long as someone drove her: Boller Skeat declined to be the driver at first, but then thought of getting a grip on Plumptious's backside and bring those big, firm breasts up against his chest when they sang Auld Lang Syne, and he agreed. Not that he had any intention of not drinking, or driving the old girl back, but they'd worry about that when the time came – someone would sort it out. Barry Snooks blanched at the thought of the Scottish piper but "anything for a quiet life," he said with what he thought was a nice touch of irony. Martin and Amy Billings had said they'd come, but suddenly pulled out just after Christmas. Something funny was going on with them, but Ample hadn't been able to find out what – yet! They'd been in and out of the rectory a lot recently: Amy wasn't becoming religious, was she?

The evening "went like wildfire" – and the fire at the doctor's house was one of the many topics of conversation that were aired during the night. It was finally agreed that hooligans had been responsible: there were lots of them in the village these days. No sooner had they got rid of Shane Marjoram (God rest his soul) than the next generation arrived to make everybody's life a misery. Plumptious (in the kitchen until nine) and Benny (at the bar all night) did everyone proud. It was a carvery, whether you liked it or not, but what a carvery – the kind of home-cooked meal that no longer graced all Sunday dinner tables! It was quintessentially English – prime roast beef, crisply-coated roast potatoes with a melt-in-the-mouth centre, light-as-air Yorkshire puddings served with richly-flavoured gravy and freshly-cooked vegetables. When Plumptious came out of the kitchen, was she hot and did she steam! The bar-side banter was lustier than usual: indeed Lianne Snooks found it a bit too raucous, but enjoyed herself anyway. It was "nice to see everybody again", people circulated and there were ready smiles and pleasantness everywhere. The log fire burned brightly all night and Plumptious and Benny had decorated the pub so that it looked very festive, with a Christmas tree brightening-up the rather tatty children's area. Pliny had told Boller to remove their log fire because it made a mess, but she really appreciated this one and might tell Boller to put theirs back in again.

The locals trickled through from their back room (indeed, the normally closed door had remained open all night) and mingled. They were full of what Martin Billings might have called "high-grade intelligence": their ears being close to the ground they didn't miss too much and what they missed was augmented by a muddle of village imagination. The rector, who had been a good man, was in some way involved with the fire at the White House. No, they didn't think the teenagers had done it – in fact they knew they hadn't; there was more to it than met the eye. Lots of bodies had been in and out of the undertaker's over the weekend and Old Strowger, who could usually be relied upon to appear in the Fishermen's Hut at least once during that time, had not appeared at all. A surfeit of corpses was not in the usual run of things and there was "something fishy afoot". One of the bodies had come from Eastwold. Butch Strowger had seen his Uncle – Old Strowger – take it in: the policeman had brought it. And there'd been "funny goings on up at Mark Chambers's family's farm", and a bull had run amok on Lord Wangford's estate and he'd had to step in and "calm things down". Sam Cleat knew about that, and he knew the person responsible – the foreigner who had bought the old rectory. 'Since that bloke – whatever his name is – came here, yew think how many people hev gone ter their Maker.' The alcohol flowed and fuelled the self-righteousness.

Midnight came and the television told everyone across the nation that it was almost the New Year (capital letters, please!). An interweaving and spasmodic circle was formed: this strung itself throughout the pub and drunken voices held their breath while the piper played. People kissed people they had never seen before and they all broke into song. Auld Lang Syne took them round the pub and down Beach Road in a never-ending conga until they reached the Old Vicarage. Their blood was up and they rushed into the grounds. The house watched them, alert to all harm. "Let's burn her down!" It was a challenge, a dare – 'He who dares, wins': they'd all heard that somewhere before. They lit straw and tossed it at the house; the straw spluttered and died. Someone picked up a stone and threw it at the morning room window: there was a shattering of glass. More stones flew from drunken hands: more windows were shattered. Someone managed to light a straw bale that was used for the animals. While it was still burning, two of the men from the Fishermen's Hut picked it up and got ready to toss it through the window. A voice bellowed at them. They recoiled in terror, but the voice didn't come from the house. Martin Billings stood in the driveway: he usually did a nightly walk around the village, especially on New Year's Eve. He wondered what they were up to: he expected Harry Bailey to put things right in the morning. Harry expected to also. The night quietened down; revellers drifted home to their beds. Life returned to normal.

New Year's Day was always a favourite with walkers. On that particular day, the early birds came across a body at Blacksands Ness. Charles Wangford was spread-eagled on the beach with half his skull blown away. The shotgun (his own) was placed awkwardly by the body, as though it had jerked from his hands at the moment of death.

CHAPTER 16

Epilogue

It was Easter Sunday of the following year before the group met together again in the garden of the new White House; during that period their lives had crossed so many times they were more like a large family than a group of friends. The gentle warmth of spring came early and they were able to sit in Alan and Penny's new garden and share their thoughts. They shared a need to move forward from the horror.

The rectory had passed to a new incumbent and so Rebecca and Peter, who had married the previous Easter in St George's, stayed with Alan and Penny. Esther came with them and would sit in the newly-planted orchard, joggling her first grandchild on her knee and watching Alan and Penny's children running round the garden.

The wedding had run smoothly enough except for the initial recalcitrance of Bishop Twiddle in agreeing to allow Simon Palmester to take the service. St George's was going through an Interregnum at the time and they had not wished some nameless priest to officiate. Besides, Simon was one of their little band and they wanted him to conduct the marriage. When the bishop suggested, over the telephone, that he might take the ceremony himself Esther wouldn't hear of it, and went to the cathedral to confront him. On his evening constitutional, Peter Twiddle found himself faced not only by Esther Unwood but also by the Dean and Mrs Cushion. The three musketeers came to mind, and he glanced uneasily over his shoulder to see if Mother Catherine was to become their D'Artagnan: he could well do without a mystical nun. Esther had rallied her forces shrewdly and this made him realise how fortunate he was to have remained a bachelor. Mrs Cushion expatiated yet again on what a good man the Reverend Unwood was and the Dean took the opportunity to hold forth on such ideas as "all brothers under God" and (Heaven forbid) "gathering the forces of good to re-energise the faith". He even had the temerity to use one of the bishop's favourite phrases – "patient forbearance". Besides, they caught him smoking a furtive cigar: Easter was close and he had succumbed rather early that year.

Peter and Rebecca's first child was born in the New Year – not on the day Rebecca's dad died as they had wanted, but in January. However, they christened the boy Corvin (and hoped that he wouldn't hold that against them).

Penny reclaimed her English-rose looks. The beating Close gave her left no scars, except perhaps a slight darkness about the left eye. Alan, on the other hand, still bore the scar from cheek to jaw that he received when the man with the torch failed to strike him dead. They had only just moved to their new home. While the new White House was being built, they rented a house in the village. Penny said it was because she didn't want to "inflict the children" on Jim Maxwell who had invited them to stay with him and his wife, but Rebecca thought it was just a manifestation of her independent spirit.

They had all needed that over the past year. They had taken it in turns, working in pairs, to do what had to be done across Europe. Tony and Martin had worked together and Alan and Peter: none of the women had been involved in what they all referred to as "the restoration". Eva Schulz, Katerina Schnell and Maxine Fox (among many others associated with Horst Brultzner) had all found their final rest. The men didn't talk about it much, but it was grisly, dangerous work: the authorities were on their backs all the time, but having access to all Horst's papers had been a great help.

As they lounged in the garden, enjoying the tea that Penny provided, it might have been supposed that the terror had passed from them, but the tranquillity of the scene belied the truth. There was the long table, covered with a white cloth, conjuring images that took them back decades. Penny's rather English cucumber sandwiches, cheese muffins, leek and onion tartlets, lemon curd tart, almond cream puffs and marbled brownies were all gathered around her centrepiece which was an angel cake. She poured tea for the adults and the children had lemonade – real lemonade made with lemons.

Rebecca and Esther had escaped the spell cast by Horst Brultzner as soon as his corpse crumpled and became as autumn leaves that drifted away in the chill east wind. They had hugged each other with the joy of their freedom, but then the shock of Corvin's terrible death had overwhelmed them both and few days passed without Peter finding them crying together. Each in their own way had supported Corvin, each had given their love and they knew in their hearts that he realised that. They also knew that they had driven him along the path of their own desires, and that he had been unable to cope. His final release owed nothing to either of the women in his life.

Tony Crewes stretched his long legs before him, and sipped from the bone china cup which Penny placed into his hands. He had a particularly sweet tooth, but it was part of his pretension to deny himself and eat only the "savoury morsels", which he did with relish, consuming more than his share of cucumber sandwiches and cheese muffins. Penny had grown fond of Tony – a fondness brought on by what he had done for Sarah Brown. Scarcely a day must pass without him seeing the face of the young woman. He and Martin Billings, however, had been a good team, taking on the lion's share of the work. Both of them, through a humour black enough to detach them from the abhorrent 'killings', had taken much of the load from her husband and Peter Vishnya.

Martin had forced his superiors so far into the corner of truth that they had no choice but to try to dismiss him from the force. It was not possible to acknowledge the authenticity of what he said, and so he was deemed "in need of a rest". Medical retirement loomed, but Martin did not want that at any cost. He loved his job and even two lump sums were no temptation to leave it. Instead he 'obliged' them to re-consider their intention to close his village police station. Moreover, he offered them the chance to off-set some of the costs by selling the house to him. He did not delude himself. Eventually, they would overcome, but not in his lifetime and, after that, it was up to those who followed to protect what they might.

Peter Vishnya lifted his second child from Esther's lap and carried him over to the table, teasing his mother and grand-mother by pretending to offer the baby a cucumber sandwich. Then he dashed around the house, Corvin in his arms, and handed the baby over to Anna-Maria who, one day, was going to make a fine mother. He winked at Rebecca and helped himself to a large slice of lemon curd tart. From the first day of his marriage, he had taken no nonsense from Esther. He recognised her for the strong woman that she was, and believed that strong women drove men into themselves. He respected her and he loved her, but he was not having her decide anything regarding his children, even if they were her grandchildren. Rebecca appealed, but it was only a gesture. She, too, knew her mother had to be tamed for the good of them all.

Horst Brultzner's propensity for undisturbed tranquillity provided Peter Vishnya with a moral problem and a pragmatic solution. He took over the vampire's affairs – not for any financial or material gain (he continued to pay himself what Brultzner had agreed) but for the benefit of all, particularly in Estonia where he pursued those endeavours which Brultzner had initiated. The vampire's influence continued to spread across the New Europe, and his patronage was appreciated by all who benefited. "It was a shame that Herr Brultzner is so disinclined to appear in public these days – the world owes him so much." Peter smiled, and "carried on the good work". Meanwhile, his commercial interests, that supported his philanthropic enterprises, flourished under the Estonian's hand.

In Dunburgh itself, the Old Vicarage posed a particular problem. It was sold twice within the year, but neither buyer lived in it long. The first family left after a day and the second, more stubborn by nature, persevered for most of a week. Finally, the wife left with her children but the husband stood firm, only to be discovered on the Saturday morning sprawled on the Italianate terrace, his hair white and his reason gone. Only Matthew Brown seemed at peace there, as though the vicarage welcomed him, and he tended his wounded animals in the grounds. Eventually, on the recommendation of Marshall and Willox, the house was handed over to the National Trust as a superb example of Victorian building and décor, but it never became a tourist attraction. It filled those who visited with unease. It was as though the house awaited the return of its Master, and would not be at peace until he once again stepped through the front door.

Matthew had become a child again once the baleful influence passed, and he was among the children who played in the new grounds of the White House on Easter Sunday. The affinity he had with animals did not diminish and his knowledge increased at a rate that was astounding, but he spoke now like a child, albeit a child whose wisdom exceeded that of his teachers. He ran easily with the others, and no one was more relieved than Nadine, whose introduction to parenthood had been sudden and frightening.

As she sat talking to Tony and watching the boy, her sense of gratitude overwhelmed her; she had never forgotten the trust placed in her by Sarah. Each night she would go to his room and watch him sleep, and wonder that such a thing could be; each morning she would walk him to school, and then leave for her work which, ironically she felt, had become so much more important to her now that she had a child for which she cared. Tony would laugh and whisper "biological" and she would kick him gently. Their friendship was centred round the boy and the memory of his mother, which they both valued. Each week she walked with Matthew to his mother's grave and refreshed the flowers, and they spoke with her as Sarah had spoken with her own mother and father. Often, Nadine would look at the boy and wonder how she would introduce him to his mother's tape, but then she would hear Sarah's voice and know that everything was going to be all right. Living in a village as part of a small community may have been stifling at times but it made one aware of the continuity of life and the inconsequential nature of death.

Through the boy she also came to understand her father better: how, on the one hand, he could take a religious view that was so uncompromising and, on the other, how his tenderness towards her had never been in question even when she was a young girl. She saw it all in his attitude to Matthew as he led the child to understand that his mother had so loved him that she had "dared to risk Hell for his sake". He would hold the boy's hand and look down at her grave and say "no greater love, son: no greater love".

The old man sat now with Esther Unwood telling her for the umpteenth time that Corvin's relationship with the God of his faith was the dead priest's own concern, that no one could hold others responsible for their lack of conviction and that Corvin had found the pathway to his God in his own way. "It was a slippery track he took, Esther, and he may have lost his way at times in the Marsh of Compromise and the Fog of Deceit but he saw Him at the end, through the fire and the pain. He knew his God was waiting, and smiling down upon him. I had my tussles with Corvin's soul but never doubted he was a good man: a coward at times, maybe, but with his faith well placed."

Rebecca ran with the children. Her marriage had been a release from her maidenhood, and a relief of unimagined dimensions. It wasn't simply that she was happy; in her own way, she had always found joy in her work. It was that she had discovered such fulfilment in the art of motherhood. Already she was expecting her second child, although only she and Peter knew that – well, she and Peter and Penny Read to whom she had formed a deep attachment. She had given up her work; it was quite enough to be looking after her husband, Yevgeny (who she now thought if as her own), her child and her home. She sometimes joked that she would propose a degree course in the 'Art and Science of Parenthood and Housekeeping'. She missed her father, of course: she missed him, bitterly. It wasn't simply the pain of his dying that still appalled her – "at least he is over that now". It was more that he was no longer able to share with her the joy of being father and daughter. No longer could they look out across the garden and hear the birds sing and watch the flowers grow – "little things, but more important than we understand".

Penny Read's compassion had brought Rebecca a new wisdom, and as the bond between them grew so did the delight in each other's children. Penny had always put her home and family first. Once she was committed to marriage with Alan, she had given up any idea of her own career. She saw, with that uncluttered insight of hers, that the two things were not compatible; there was "no such thing as a part-time housewife and mother. I could see Alan's vocation was strong: I had no choice." She floated around now, that white dress with the blue polka-dots flapping gently in the light breeze. Not that they saw much of each other, but when they did the two women made the most of it.

Rebecca spent much of her time abroad in Europe (often in Estonia where they had a house), which was where Brultzner's interests and Peter's work lay. Now that Brultzner had given him the chance, Peter was determined that Yevgeny would come to love his native country and he couldn't do that living in England. Anton travelled with them – Anton, Peter's great friend and ally: the wolf that guaranteed the safety of his family, the wolf that Rebecca had taken a while getting used to, the wolf that still worried Esther (who would have had him caged, given the chance), the wolf that now ran around the garden with the children picking up the scraps from their table. George loved Anton and would take him to see Leo's grave; Anton would listen to anyone!

On that particular Easter Sunday, another child had joined them with his father. He was not one of the original company, but one who their little band had brought close to death and who had, through a simple sense of fair-play, brought about the requital. He, too, was a child again, and the adults who cared about him were grateful that children were so able to return to normal. They watched him in the spring garden, Bess at his heels, playing with the Read children, and were glad.

The death of the white bull had haunted David Stokes, and his own part in the death of the young one had intensified his grief. In assuaging that, Martin and Tony had played their part. Within twenty-four hours, regardless of Charles Wangford's sudden death, they had invaded the park with a digger and created a grave where the temple had been buried in the hillside. The remaining stones were reformed to create a tomb and the young bull was lowered gently between them; the charred remains of the oak benches formed a roof over the bull's resting place. By spring of that year, the first green shoots of grass were showing.

John Stokes, who had continued as herdsman, stood in the garden of the White House (he didn't think it right to sit!), talking to Alan Read, balancing a plate of angel cake and a cup of tea in one hand. He was talking with pride about his son as he watched him run with the other seven about the garden. Amos was climbing an old tree on the edge of their land with Helen. Anna-Maria was playing with young Corvin on the grass. George, Yevgeny and David were playing tag. Matthew was chasing Bess. The two men exchanged glances and smiled.

It was the two of them, with Peter Vishnya, who had spoken with Charles Wangford's son. Henry Wangford had opened the envelope on his father's death and picked up the phone to the doctor. Like his father before him, Henry Wangford knew nothing of the Brotherhood until he opened the letter. On New Year's Day, Alan and Peter had come to see him, bringing John Stokes with them. Henry Wangford was the spitting image of his father: he had the same chinless face and tall, stooped figure. His expression was the same mixture of eccentricity and guile. He was direct with Alan Read, asking simply for the return of his father's papers which, he understood, the doctor had stolen. Alan Read wondered if Henry Wangford had learned anything from the death of his father. He would return the papers, but would make a copy of everything and place it somewhere it would never be found – unless he or any of his friends were threatened. One of their group – a journalist – had written a full account of their ordeals, and this would be concealed with the papers. Henry Wangford was not satisfied: he would seek advice. Alan thought not: this was his secret – it was not something he could share with the Brotherhood.

The following day, Easter Monday, they all met where the temple had been in Wangford Park – the spot that was now the tomb of the white bull. Tony had arranged the carving of the gravestone, which was a huge slab of granite from beyond the Roman wall. It was lowered in place on the hillside, in an opening dug that morning by Alan and Nadine. The group, now twenty strong, stood and watched. Tony caught David's eye. It was still here – the Presence – stronger than ever. There was no evil in this place except the evil brought by men and women. They stood, over-whelmed by their spiritual journey, the same journey that men and women had made down the ages; men had striven here against what they perceived as the forces of darkness. A smile passed around the group, a smile shared by Henry Wangford, who stood with them. A chill, east wind gusted up the slope. 'The many times I have stood here never diminish my feelings towards this place.' This was home and they had come to understand it better through their struggles. On the slab the words chosen by David Stokes were carved – *You have saved men by the spilling of the eternal blood.* For each of them it held a quite different truth.

Kessingland, Suffolk   1990 – 1997
Loddon, Norfolk   2007 – 2009

Lightning Source UK Ltd.
Milton Keynes UK
UKOW050628290911

179495UK00001B/7/P